LIBRARY OF
CLASSIC
WOMEN'S
LITERATURE

LIBRARY OF CLASSIC WOMEN'S LITERATURE

AN IMPRINT OF
RUNNING PRESS
PHILADELPHIA • LONDON

© 2000 by Running Press
All rights reserved under the Pan-American and International
Copyright Conventions
Printed in U.S.A.

9 8 7 6 5 4 3 2 1
Digit on the right indicates the number of this printing

Library of Congress Cataloging-in-Publication Number 00-131940

ISBN 0-7624-0837-1

Cover design by Bill Jones

This book may be ordered by mail from the publisher.
Please add $2.50 for postage and handling.
But try your bookstore first!

Published by Courage Books, an imprint of
Running Press Book Publishers
125 South Twenty-second Street
Philadelphia, Pennsylvania 19103-4399

Visit us on the web!
www.runningpress.com

Contents

Pride and Prejudice

by
Jane Austen

VOLUME I

CHAPTER 1

It is a truth universally acknowledged, that a single man in possession of a good fortune, must be in want of a wife.

However little known the feelings or views of such a man may be on his first entering a neighbourhood, this truth is so well fixed in the minds of the surrounding families, that he is considered as the rightful property of some one or other of their daughters.

"My dear Mr. Bennet," said his lady to him one day, "have you heard that Netherfield Park is let at last?"

Mr. Bennet replied that he had not.

"But it is," returned she; "for Mrs. Long has just been here, and she told me all about it."

Mr. Bennet made no answer.

"Do not you want to know who has taken it?" cried his wife impatiently.

"*You* want to tell me, and I have no objection to hearing it."

This was invitation enough.

"Why, my dear, you must know, Mrs. Long says that Netherfield is taken by a young man of large fortune from the north of England; that he came down on Monday in a chaise and four to see the place, and was so much delighted with it that he agreed with Mr. Morris immediately; that he is to take possession before Michaelmas, and some of his servants are to be in the house by the end of next week."

"What is his name?"

"Bingley."

"Is he married or single?"

"Oh! single, my dear, to be sure! A single man of large fortune; four or five thousand a year. What a fine thing for our girls!"

"How so? how can it affect them?"

"My dear Mr. Bennet," replied his wife, "how can you be so tiresome! You must know that I am thinking of his marrying one of them."

"Is that his design in settling here?"

"Design! nonsense, how can you talk so! But it is very likely that he *may* fall in love with one of them, and therefore you must visit him as soon as he comes."

"I see no occasion for that. You and the girls may go, or you may send them by themselves, which perhaps will be still better, for as you are as handsome as any of them, Mr. Bingley might like you the best of the party."

"My dear, you flatter me. I certainly *have* had my share of beauty, but I do not pretend to be any thing extraordinary now. When a woman has five grown up daughters, she ought to give over thinking of her own beauty."

"In such cases, a woman has not often much beauty to think of."

"But, my dear, you must indeed go and see Mr. Bingley when he comes into the neighbourhood."

"It is more than I engage for, I assure you."

"But consider your daughters. Only think what an establishment it would be for one of them. Sir William and Lady Lucas are determined to go, merely on that account, for in general you know they visit no new comers. Indeed you must go, for it will be impossible for *us* to visit him, if you do not."

"You are over scrupulous surely. I dare say Mr. Bingley will be very glad to see you; and I will send a few lines by you to assure him of my hearty consent to his marrying which ever he chuses of the girls; though I must throw in a good word for my little Lizzy."

"I desire you will do no such thing. Lizzy is not a bit better than the others; and I am sure she is not half so handsome as Jane, nor half so good humoured as Lydia. But you are always giving *her* the preference."

"They have none of them much to recommend them," replied

he; "they are all silly and ignorant like other girls; but Lizzy has something more of quickness than her sisters."

"Mr. Bennet, how can you abuse your own children in such a way? You take delight in vexing me. You have no compassion on my poor nerves."

"You mistake me, my dear. I have a high respect for your nerves. They are my old friends. I have heard you mention them with consideration these twenty years at least."

"Ah! you do not know what I suffer."

"But I hope you will get over it, and live to see many young men of four thousand a year come into the neighbourhood."

"It will be no use to us, if twenty such should come since you will not visit them."

"Depend upon it, my dear, that when there are twenty, I will visit them all."

Mr. Bennet was so odd a mixture of quick parts, sarcastic humour, reserve, and caprice, that the experience of three and twenty years had been insufficient to make his wife understand his character. *Her* mind was less difficult to develope. She was a woman of mean understanding, little information, and uncertain temper. When she was discontented she fancied herself nervous. The business of her life was to get her daughters married; its solace was visiting and news.

CHAPTER 2

Mr. Bennet was among the earliest of those who waited on Mr. Bingley. He had always intended to visit him, though to the last always assuring his wife that he should not go; and till the evening after the visit was paid, she had no knowledge of it. It was then disclosed in the following manner. Observing his second daughter employed in trimming a hat, he suddenly addressed her with,

"I hope Mr. Bingley will like it Lizzy."

"We are not in a way to know *what* Mr. Bingley likes," said her mother resentfully, "since we are not to visit."

"But you forget, mama," said Elizabeth, "that we shall meet him at the assemblies, and that Mrs. Long has promised to introduce him."

"I do not believe Mrs. Long will do any such thing. She has two neices of her own. She is a selfish, hypocritical woman, and I have no opinion of her."

"No more have I," said Mr. Bennet; "and I am glad to find that you do not depend on her serving you."

Mrs. Bennet deigned not to make any reply; but unable to contain herself, began scolding one of her daughters.

"Don't keep coughing so, Kitty, for heaven's sake! Have a little compassion on my nerves. You tear them to pieces."

"Kitty has no discretion in her coughs," said her father; "she times them ill."

"I do not cough for my own amusement," replied Kitty fretfully. "When is your next ball to be, Lizzy?"

"To-morrow fortnight."

"Aye, so it is," cried her mother, "and Mrs. Long does not come back till the day before; so, it will be impossible for her to introduce him, for she will not know him herself."

"Then, my dear, you may have the advantage of your friend, and introduce Mr. Bingley to *her*."

"Impossible, Mr. Bennet, impossible, when I am not acquainted with him myself; how can you be so teazing?"

"I honour your circumspection. A fortnight's acquaintance is certainly very little. One cannot know what a man really is by the end of a fortnight. But if *we* do not venture, somebody else will; and after all, Mrs. Long and her neices must stand their chance; and therefore, as she will think it an act of kindness, if you decline the office, I will take it on myself."

The girls stared at their father. Mrs. Bennet said only, "Nonsense, nonsense!"

"What can be the meaning of that emphatic exclamation?" cried
he. "Do you consider the forms of introduction, and the stress
that is laid on them, as nonsense? I cannot quite agree with you
there. What say you, Mary? for you are a young lady of deep reflection I know, and read great books, and make extracts."

Mary wished to say something very sensible, but knew not how.

"While Mary is adjusting her ideas," he continued, "let us return
to Mr. Bingley."

"I am sick of Mr. Bingley." cried his wife.

"I am sorry to hear *that;* but why did not you tell me so before? If I had known as much this morning, I certainly would not
have called on him. It is very unlucky; but as I have actually paid
the visit, we cannot escape the acquaintance now."

The astonishment of the ladies was just what he wished; that
of Mrs. Bennet perhaps surpassing the rest; though when the first
tumult of joy was over, she began to declare that it was what she
had expected all the while.

"How good it was in you, my dear Mr. Bennet? But I knew I
should persuade you at last. I was sure you loved your girls too
well to neglect such an acquaintance. Well, how pleased I am!
and it is such a good joke, too, that you should have gone this
morning, and never said a word about it till now."

"Now, Kitty, you may cough as much as you chuse," said Mr.
Bennet; and, as he spoke, he left the room, fatigued with the raptures of his wife.

"What an excellent father you have, girls," said she, when the
door was shut. "I do not know how you will ever make him amends
for his kindness; or me either, for that matter. At our time of life,
it is not so pleasant I can tell you, to be making new acquaintance every day; but for your sakes, we would do any thing. Lydia,
my love, though you *are* the youngest, I dare say Mr. Bingley will
dance with you at the next ball."

"Oh!" said Lydia stoutly, "I am not afraid; for though I *am* the
youngest, I'm the tallest."

The rest of the evening was spent in conjecturing how soon

he would return Mr. Bennet's visit, and determining when they should ask him to dinner.

CHAPTER 3

Not all that Mrs. Bennet, however, with the assistance of her five daughters, could ask on the subject was sufficient to draw from her husband any satisfactory description of Mr. Bingley. They attacked him in various ways; with barefaced questions, ingenious suppositions, and distant surmises; but he eluded the skill of them all; and they were at last obliged to accept the second-hand intelligence of their neighbour Lady Lucas. Her report was highly favourable. Sir William had been delighted with him. He was quite young, wonderfully handsome, extremely agreeable, and to crown the whole, he meant to be at the next assembly with a large party. Nothing could be more delightful! To be fond of dancing was a certain step towards falling in love; and very lively hopes of Mr. Bingley's heart were entertained.

"If I can but see one of my daughters happily settled at Netherfield," said Mrs. Bennet to her husband, "and all the others equally well married, I shall have nothing to wish for."

In a few days Mr. Bingley returned Mr. Bennet's visit, and sat about ten minutes with him in his library. He had entertained hopes of being admitted to a sight of the young ladies, of whose beauty he had heard much; but he saw only the father. The ladies were somewhat more fortunate, for they had the advantage of ascertaining from an upper window, that he wore a blue coat and rode a black horse.

An invitation to dinner was soon afterwards dispatched; and already had Mrs. Bennet planned the courses that were to do credit to her housekeeping, when an answer arrived which deferred it all. Mr. Bingley was obliged to be in town the following day, and consequently unable to accept the honour of their invitation, &c.

Mrs. Bennet was quite disconcerted. She could not imagine what business he could have in town so soon after his arrival in Hertfordshire; and she began to fear that he might be always flying about from one place to another, and never settled at Netherfield as he ought to be. Lady Lucas quieted her fears a little by starting the idea of his being gone to London only to get a large party for the ball; and a report soon followed that Mr. Bingley was to bring twelve ladies and seven gentlemen with him to the assembly. The girls grieved over such a number of ladies; but were comforted the day before the ball by hearing, that instead of twelve, he had brought only six with him from London, his five sisters and a cousin. And when the party entered the assembly room, it consisted of only five altogether; Mr. Bingley, his two sisters, the husband of the eldest, and another young man.

Mr. Bingley was good looking and gentlemanlike; he had a pleasant countenance, and easy, unaffected manners. His sisters were fine women, with an air of decided fashion. His brother-in-law, Mr. Hurst, merely looked the gentleman; but his friend Mr. Darcy soon drew the attention of the room by his fine, tall person, handsome features, noble mein; and the report which was in general circulation within five minutes after his entrance, of his having ten thousand a year. The gentlemen pronounced him to be a fine figure of a man, the ladies declared he was much handsomer than Mr. Bingley, and he was looked at with great admiration for about half the evening, till his manners gave a disgust which turned the tide of his popularity; for he was discovered to be proud, to be above his company, and above being pleased; and not all his large estate in Derbyshire could then save him from having a most forbidding, disagreeable countenance, and being unworthy to be compared with his friend.

Mr. Bingley had soon made himself acquainted with all the principal people in the room; he was lively and unreserved, danced every dance, was angry that the ball closed so early, and talked of giving one himself at Netherfield. Such amiable qualities must speak for themselves. What a contrast between him and his friend!

Mr. Darcy danced only once with Mrs. Hurst and once with Miss Bingley, declined being introduced to any other lady, and spent the rest of the evening in walking about the room, speaking occasionally to one of his own party. His character was decided. He was the proudest, most disagreeable man in the world, and every body hoped that he would never come there again. Amongst the most violent against him was Mrs. Bennet, whose dislike of his general behaviour, was sharpened into particular resentment, by his having slighted one of her daughters.

Elizabeth Bennet had been obliged, by the scarcity of gentlemen, to sit down for two dances; and during part of that time, Mr. Darcy had been standing near enough for her to overhear a conversation between him and Mr. Bingley, who came from the dance for a few minutes, to press his friend to join it.

"Come, Darcy," said he, "I must have you dance. I hate to see you standing about by yourself in this stupid manner. You had much better dance."

"I certainly shall not. You know how I detest it, unless I am particularly acquainted with my partner. At such an assembly as this, it would be insupportable. Your sisters are engaged, and there is not another woman in the room, whom it would not be a punishment to me to stand up with."

"I would not be so fastidious as you are," cried Bingley, "for a kingdom! Upon my honour, I never met with so many pleasant girls in my life, as I have this evening; and there are several of them you see uncommonly pretty."

"*You* are dancing with the only handsome girl in the room," said Mr. Darcy, looking at the eldest Miss Bennet.

"Oh! she is the most beautiful creature I ever beheld! But there is one of her sisters sitting down just behind you, who is very pretty, and I dare say, very agreeable. Do let me ask my partner to introduce you."

"Which do you mean?" and turning round, he looked for a moment at Elizabeth, till catching her eye, he withdrew his own and coldly said, "She is tolerable; but not handsome enough to tempt *me;* and I am in no humour at present to give consequence to young ladies who are slighted by other men. You had better return to your partner and enjoy her smiles, for you are wasting your mite with me."

Mr. Bingley followed his advice. Mr. Darcy walked off; and Elizabeth remained with no very cordial feelings towards him. She told the story however with great spirit among her friends; for she had a lively, playful disposition, which delighted in any thing ridiculous.

The evening altogether passed off pleasantly to the whole family. Mrs. Bennet had seen her eldest daughter much admired by the Netherfield party. Mr. Bingley had danced with her twice, and she had been distinguished by his sisters. Jane was as much gratified by this, as her mother could be, though in a quieter way. Elizabeth felt Jane's pleasure. Mary had heard herself mentioned to Miss Bingley as the most accomplished girl in the neighbourhood; and Catherine and Lydia had been fortunate enough to be never without partners, which was all that they had yet learnt to care for at a ball. They returned therefore in good spirits to Longbourn, the village where they lived, and of which they were the principal inhabitants. They found Mr. Bennet still up. With a book he was regardless of time; and on the present occasion he had a good deal of curiosity as to the event of an evening which had raised such splendid expectations. He had rather hoped that all his wife's views on the stranger would be disappointed; but he soon found that he had a very different story to hear.

"Oh! my dear Mr. Bennet," as she entered the room, "we have had a most delightful evening, a most excellent ball. I wish you had been there. Jane was so admired, nothing could be like it. Every body said how well she looked; and Mr. Bingley thought her quite beautiful, and danced with her twice. Only think of *that* my dear; he actually danced with her twice; and she was the only creature in the room that he asked a second time. First of all, he asked Miss Lucas. I was so vexed to see him stand up with her; but, however, he did not admire her at all: indeed, nobody can, you know; and he seemed quite struck with Jane as she was going down the dance. So, he enquired who she was, and got introduced, and asked her for the two next. Then, the two third he danced with Miss King, and the two fourth with Maria Lucas, and the two fifth with Jane again, and the two sixth with Lizzy, and the Boulanger."

"If he had had any compassion for *me*," cried her husband impatiently, "he would not have danced half so much! For God's sake, say no more of his partners. Oh! that he had sprained his ancle in the first dance!"

"Oh! my dear," continued Mrs. Bennet, "I am quite delighted with him. He is so excessively handsome! and his sisters are charming women. I never in my life saw any thing more elegant than their dresses. I dare say the lace upon Mrs. Hurst's gown—"

Here she was interrupted again. Mr. Bennet protested against any description of finery. She was therefore obliged to seek another branch of the subject, and related, with much bitterness of spirit and some exaggeration, the shocking rudeness of Mr. Darcy.

"But I can assure you," she added, "that Lizzy does not lose much by not suiting *his* fancy; for he is a most disagreeable, horrid man, not at all worth pleasing. So high and so conceited that there was no enduring him! He walked here, and he walked there, fancying himself so very great! Not handsome enough to dance with! I wish you had been there, my dear, to have given him one of your set downs. I quite detest the man."

CHAPTER 4

When Jane and Elizabeth were alone, the former, who had been cautious in her praise of Mr. Bingley before, expressed to her sister how very much she admired him.

"He is just what a young man ought to be," said she, "sensible, good humoured, lively; and I never saw such happy manners! – so much ease, with such perfect good breeding!"

"He is also handsome," replied Elizabeth, "which a young man ought likewise to be, if he possibly can. His character is thereby complete."

"I was very much flattered by his asking me to dance a second time. I did not expect such a compliment."

"Did not you? *I* did for you. But that is one great difference between us. Compliments always take *you* by surprise, and *me* never. What could be more natural than his asking you again? He could not help seeing that you were about five times as pretty as every other woman in the room. No thanks to his gallantry for that. Well, he certainly is very agreeable, and I give you leave to like him. You have liked many a stupider person."

"Dear Lizzy!"

"Oh! you are a great deal too apt you know, to like people in general. You never see a fault in any body. All the world are good and agreeable in your eyes. I never heard you speak ill of a human being in my life."

"I would wish not to be hasty in censuring any one; but I always speak what I think."

"I know you do; and it is *that* which makes the wonder. With *your* good sense, to be so honestly blind to the follies and nonsense of others! Affectation of candour is common enough; – one meets it every where. But to be candid without ostentation or design – to take the good of every body's character and make it still better, and say nothing of the bad – belongs to you alone. And so, you like this man's sisters too, do you? Their manners are not equal to his."

"Certainly not; at first. But they are very pleasing women when you converse with them. Miss Bingley is to live with her brother and keep his house; and I am much mistaken if we shall not find a very charming neighbour in her."

Elizabeth listened in silence, but was not convinced; their behaviour at the assembly had not been calculated to please in general; and with more quickness of observation and less pliancy of temper than her sister, and with a judgment too unassailed by any attention to herself, she was very little disposed to approve them. They were in fact very fine ladies; not deficient in good humour when they were pleased, nor in the power of being agreeable where they chose it; but proud and conceited. They were rather handsome, had been educated in one of the first private seminaries in town, had a fortune of twenty thousand pounds, were in the habit of spending more than they ought, and of associating with people of rank; and were therefore in every respect entitled to think well of themselves, and meanly of others. They were of a respectable family in the north of England; a circumstance more deeply impressed on their memories than that their brother's fortune and their own had been acquired by trade.

Mr. Bingley inherited property to the amount of nearly an hundred thousand pounds from his father, who had intended to purchase an estate, but did not live to do it.—Mr. Bingley intended it likewise, and sometimes made choice of his county; but as he was now provided with a good house and the liberty of a manor, it was doubtful to many of those who best knew the easiness of his temper, whether he might not spend the remainder of his days at Netherfield, and leave the next generation to purchase.

His sisters were very anxious for his having an estate of his own; but though he was now established only as a tenant, Miss Bingley was by no means unwilling to preside at his table, nor was Mrs. Hurst, who had married a man of more fashion than fortune, less disposed to consider his house as her home when it suited her. Mr. Bingley had not been of age two years, when he was tempted by an accidental recommendation to look at Netherfield House. He did look at it and into it for half an hour, was pleased with the situation and the principal rooms, satisfied with what the owner said in its praise, and took it immediately.

Between him and Darcy there was a very steady friendship, in spite of a great opposition of character.—Bingley was endeared to Darcy by the easiness, openness, ductility of his temper, though no disposition could offer a greater contrast to his own, and though with his own he never appeared dissatisfied. On the strength of Darcy's regard Bingley had the firmest reliance, and of his judgment the highest opinion. In understanding Darcy was the superior. Bingley was by no means deficient, but Darcy was clever. He was at the same time haughty, reserved, and fastidious, and his manners, though well bred, were not inviting. In that respect his friend had greatly the advantage. Bingley was sure of being liked wherever he appeared, Darcy was continually giving offence.

The manner in which they spoke of the Meryton assembly was sufficiently characteristic. Bingley had never met with pleasanter people or prettier girls in his life; every body had been most kind and attentive to him, there had been no formality, no stiffness, he had soon felt acquainted with all the room; and as to Miss Bennet, he could not conceive an angel more beautiful. Darcy, on the contrary, had seen a collection of people in whom there was little beauty and no fashion, for none of whom he had felt the smallest interest, and from none received either attention or pleasure. Miss Bennet he acknowledged to be pretty, but she smiled too much.

Mrs. Hurst and her sister allowed it to be so—but still they admired her and liked her, and pronounced her to be a sweet girl, and one whom they should not object to know more of. Miss Bennet was therefore established as a sweet girl, and their brother felt authorised by such commendation to think of her as he chose.

CHAPTER 5

Within a short walk of Longbourn lived a family with whom the Bennets were particularly intimate. Sir William Lucas had been formerly in trade in Meryton, where he had made a tolerable fortune and risen to the honour of knighthood by an address to the King, during his mayoralty. The distinction had perhaps been felt too strongly. It had given him a disgust to his business and to his residence in a small market town; and quitting them both, he had removed with his family to a house about a mile from Meryton, denominated from that period Lucas Lodge, where he could think with pleasure of his own importance, and unshackled by business, occupy himself solely in being civil to all the world. For though elated by his rank, it did not render him supercilious; on the contrary, he was all attention to every body. By nature inoffensive, friendly and obliging, his presentation at St. James's had made him courteous.

Lady Lucas was a very good kind of woman, not too clever to be a valuable neighbour to Mrs. Bennet.–They had several children. The eldest of them a sensible, intelligent young woman, about twenty-seven, was Elizabeth's intimate friend.

That the Miss Lucases and the Miss Bennets should meet to talk over a ball was absolutely necessary; and the morning after the assembly brought the former to Longbourn to hear and to communicate.

"*You* began the evening well, Charlotte," said Mrs. Bennet with civil self-command to Miss Lucas. "*You* were Mr. Bingley's first choice."

"Yes;–but he seemed to like his second better."

"Oh!–you mean Jane, I suppose–because he danced with her twice. To be sure that *did* seem as if he admired her–indeed I rather believe he *did*–I heard something about it–but I hardly know what–something about Mr. Robinson."

"Perhaps you mean what I overheard between him and Mr. Robinson; did not I mention it to you? Mr. Robinson's asking him how he liked our Meryton assemblies, and whether he did not think there were a great many pretty women in the room, and *which* he thought the prettiest? and his answering immediately to the last question–Oh! the eldest Miss Bennet beyond a doubt, there cannot be two opinions on that point."

"Upon my word!–Well, that was very decided indeed–that does seem as if–but however, it may all come to nothing you know."

"*My* overhearings were more to the purpose than *yours*, Eliza," said Charlotte. "Mr. Darcy is not so well worth listening to as his friend, is he?–Poor Eliza!–to be only just *tolerable*."

"I beg you would not put it into Lizzy's head to be vexed by his ill-treatment; for he is such a disagreeable man that it would be quite a misfortune to be liked by him. Mrs. Long told me last night that he sat close to her for half an hour without once opening his lips."

"Are you quite sure, Ma'am?–is not there a little mistake?" said Jane.–"I certainly saw Mr. Darcy speaking to her."

"Aye–because she asked him at last how he liked Netherfield, and he could not help answering her;–but she said he seemed very angry at being spoke to."

"Miss Bingley told me," said Jane, "that he never speaks much unless among his intimate acquaintance. With *them* he is remarkably agreeable."

"I do not believe a word of it, my dear. If he had been so very agreeable he would have talked to Mrs. Long. But I can guess how it was; every body says that he is ate up with pride, and I dare say he had heard somehow that Mrs. Long does not keep a carriage, and had come to the ball in a hack chaise."

"I do not mind his not talking to Mrs. Long," said Miss Lucas, "but I wish he had danced with Eliza."

"Another time, Lizzy," said her mother, "I would not dance with *him*, if I were you."

"I believe, Ma'am, I may safely promise you *never* to dance with him."

"His pride," said Miss Lucas, "does not offend *me* so much as pride often does, because there is an excuse for it. One cannot wonder that so very fine a young man, with family, fortune, every thing in his favour, should think highly of himself. If I may so express it, he has a *right* to be proud."

"That is very true," replied Elizabeth, "and I could easily forgive *his* pride, if he had not mortified *mine*."

"Pride," observed Mary, who piqued herself upon the solidity

of her reflections, "is a very common failing I believe. By all that
I have ever read, I am convinced that it is very common indeed,
that human nature is particularly prone to it, and that there are
very few of us who do not cherish a feeling of self-complacency
on the score of some quality or other, real or imaginary. Vanity
and pride are different things, though the words are often used
synonimously. A person may be proud without being vain. Pride
relates more to our opinion of ourselves, vanity to what we would
have others think of us."

"If I were as rich as Mr. Darcy," cried a young Lucas who came
with his sisters, "I should not care how proud I was. I would keep
a pack of foxhounds, and drink a bottle of wine every day."

"Then you would drink a great deal more than you ought,"
said Mrs. Bennet; "and if I were to see you at it I should take away
your bottle directly."

The boy protested that she should not; she continued to declare
that she would, and the argument ended only with the visit.

CHAPTER 6

The ladies of Longbourn soon waited on those of Netherfield. The
visit was returned in due form. Miss Bennet's pleasing manners
grew on the good will of Mrs. Hurst and Miss Bingley; and though
the mother was found to be intolerable and the younger sisters
not worth speaking to, a wish of being better acquainted with *them,*
was expressed towards the two eldest. By Jane this attention was
received with the greatest pleasure; but Elizabeth still saw super-
ciliousness in their treatment of every body, hardly excepting even
her sister, and could not like them; though their kindness to Jane,
such as it was, had a value as arising in all probability from the
influence of their brother's admiration. It was generally evident
whenever they met, that he *did* admire her; and to *her* it was equally evident that Jane was yielding to the preference which she had

begun to entertain for him from the first, and was in a way to be very much in love; but she considered with pleasure that it was not likely to be discovered by the world in general, since Jane united with great strength of feeling, a composure of temper and a uniform cheerfulness of manner, which would guard her from the suspicions of the impertinent. She mentioned this to her friend Miss Lucas.

"It may perhaps be pleasant," replied Charlotte, "to be able to impose on the public in such a case; but it is sometimes a disadvantage to be so very guarded. If a woman conceals her affection with the same skill from the object of it, she may lose the opportunity of fixing him; and it will then be but poor consolation to believe the world equally in the dark. There is so much of gratitude or vanity in almost every attachment, that it is not safe to leave any to itself. We can all *begin* freely – a slight preference is natural enough; but there are very few of us who have heart enough to be really in love without encouragement. In nine cases out of ten, a woman had better shew *more* affection than she feels. Bingley likes your sister undoubtedly; but he may never do more than like her, if she does not help him on."

"But she does help him on, as much as her nature will allow. If *I* can perceive her regard for him, he must be a simpleton indeed not to discover it too."

"Remember, Eliza, that he does not know Jane's disposition as you do."

"But if a woman is partial to a man, and does not endeavour to conceal it, he must find it out."

"Perhaps he must, if he sees enough of her. But though Bingley and Jane meet tolerably often, it is never for many hours together; and as they always see each other in large mixed parties, it is impossible that every moment should be employed in conversing together. Jane should therefore make the most of every half hour in which she can command his attention. When she is secure of him, there will be leisure for falling in love as much as she chuses."

"Your plan is a good one," replied Elizabeth, "where nothing is in question but the desire of being well married; and if I were determined to get a rich husband, or any husband, I dare say I should adopt it. But these are not Jane's feelings; she is not acting by design. As yet, she cannot even be certain of the degree of her own regard, nor of its reasonableness. She has known him only a fortnight. She danced four dances with him at Meryton; she saw him one morning at his own house, and has since dined in company with him four times. This is not quite enough to make her understand his character."

"Not as you represent it. Had she merely *dined* with him, she might only have discovered whether he had a good appetite; but you must remember that four evenings have been also spent together—and four evenings may do a great deal."

"Yes; these four evenings have enabled them to ascertain that they both like Vingt-un better than Commerce; but with respect to any other leading characteristic, I do not imagine that much has been unfolded."

"Well," said Charlotte, "I wish Jane success with all my heart; and if she were married to him to-morrow, I should think she had as good a chance of happiness, as if she were to be studying his character for a twelvemonth. Happiness in marriage is entirely a matter of chance. If the dispositions of the parties are ever so well known to each other, or ever so similar before-hand, it does not advance their felicity in the least. They always continue to grow sufficiently unlike afterwards to have their share of vexation; and it is better to know as little as possible of the defects of the person with whom you are to pass your life."

"You make me laugh, Charlotte; but it is not sound. You know it is not sound, and that you would never act in this way yourself."

Occupied in observing Mr. Bingley's attentions to her sister, Elizabeth was far from suspecting that she was herself becoming an object of some interest in the eyes of his friend. Mr. Darcy had at first scarcely allowed her to be pretty; he had looked at her without admiration at the ball; and when they next met, he looked at her only to criticise. But no sooner had he made it clear to himself and his friends that she had hardly a good feature in her face, than he began to find it was rendered uncommonly intelligent by the beautiful expression of her dark eyes. To this discovery succeeded some others equally mortifying. Though he had detected with a critical eye more than one failure of perfect symmetry in her form, he was forced to acknowledge her figure to be light and pleasing; and in spite of his asserting that her manners were not those of the fashionable world, he was caught by their easy playfulness. Of this she was perfectly unaware; – to her he was only the man who made himself agreeable no where, and who had not thought her handsome enough to dance with.

He began to wish to know more of her, and as a step towards conversing with her himself, attended to her conversation with others. His doing so drew her notice. It was at Sir William Lucas's, where a large party were assembled.

"What does Mr. Darcy mean," said she to Charlotte, "by listening to my conversation with Colonel Forster?"

"That is a question which Mr. Darcy only can answer."

"But if he does it any more I shall certainly let him know that I see what he is about. He has a very satirical eye, and if I do not begin by being impertinent myself, I shall soon grow afraid of him."

On his approaching them soon afterwards, though without seeming to have any intention of speaking, Miss Lucas defied her friend to mention such a subject to him, which immediately provoking Elizabeth to do it, she turned to him and said,

"Did not you think, Mr. Darcy, that I expressed myself uncommonly well just now, when I was teazing Colonel Forster to give us a ball at Meryton?"

"With great energy; – but it is a subject which always makes a lady energetic."

"You are severe on us."

"It will be *her* turn soon to be teazed," said Miss Lucas. "I am going to open the instrument, Eliza, and you know what follows."

"You are a very strange creature by way of a friend! – always wanting me to play and sing before any body and every body! – If my vanity had taken a musical turn, you would have been invaluable, but as it is, I would really rather not sit down before those who must be in the habit of hearing the very best performers." On Miss Lucas's persevering, however, she added, "Very well; if it must be so, it must." And gravely glancing at Mr. Darcy, "There is a fine old saying, which every body here is of course familiar with –'Keep your breath to cool your porridge,' – and I shall keep mine to swell my song."

Her performance was pleasing, though by no means capital. After a song or two, and before she could reply to the entreaties of several that she would sing again, she was eagerly succeeded at the instrument by her sister Mary, who having, in consequence of being the only plain one in the family, worked hard for knowledge and accomplishments, was always impatient for display.

Mary had neither genius nor taste; and though vanity had given her application, it had given her likewise a pedantic air and conceited manner, which would have injured a higher degree of excellence than she had reached. Elizabeth, easy and unaffected, had been listened to with much more pleasure, though not playing half so well; and Mary, at the end of a long concerto, was glad to purchase praise and gratitude by Scotch and Irish airs, at the request of her younger sisters, who with some of the Lucases and two or three officers joined eagerly in dancing at one end of the room.

Mr. Darcy stood near them in silent indignation at such a mode of passing the evening, to the exclusion of all conversation, and was too much engrossed by his own thoughts to perceive that Sir William Lucas was his neighbour, till Sir William thus began.

"What a charming amusement for young people this is, Mr. Darcy! – There is nothing like dancing after all. – I consider it as one of the first refinements of polished societies."

"Certainly, Sir; – and it has the advantage also of being in vogue amongst the less polished societies of the world. – Every savage can dance."

Sir William only smiled. "Your friend performs delightfully;" he continued after a pause, on seeing Bingley join the group;— "and I doubt not that you are an adept in the science yourself, Mr. Darcy."

"You saw me dance at Meryton, I believe, Sir."

"Yes, indeed, and received no inconsiderable pleasure from the sight. Do you often dance at St. James's?"

"Never, Sir."

"Do you not think it would be a proper compliment to the place?"

"It is a compliment which I never pay to any place if I can avoid it."

"You have a house in town, I conclude."

Mr. Darcy bowed.

"I had once some thoughts of fixing in town myself—for I am fond of superior society; but I did not feel quite certain that the air of London would agree with Lady Lucas."

He paused in hopes of an answer; but his companion was not disposed to make any; and Elizabeth at that instant moving towards them, he was struck with the notion of doing a very gallant thing, and called out to her,

"My dear Miss Eliza, why are not you dancing?—Mr. Darcy, you must allow me to present this young lady to you as a very desirable partner.—You cannot refuse to dance, I am sure, when so much beauty is before you." And taking her hand, he would have given it to Mr. Darcy, who, though extremely surprised, was not unwilling to receive it, when she instantly drew back, and said with some discomposure to Sir William,

"Indeed, Sir, I have not the least intention of dancing.—I entreat you not to suppose that I moved this way in order to beg for a partner."

Mr. Darcy with grave propriety requested to be allowed the honour of her hand; but in vain. Elizabeth was determined; nor did Sir William at all shake her purpose by his attempt at persuasion.

"You excel so much in the dance, Miss Eliza, that it is cruel to deny me the happiness of seeing you; and though this gentleman dislikes the amusement in general, he can have no objection, I am sure, to oblige us for one half hour."

"Mr. Darcy is all politeness," said Elizabeth, smiling.

"He is indeed—but considering the inducement, my dear Miss Eliza, we cannot wonder at his complaisance; for who would object to such a partner?"

Elizabeth looked archly, and turned away. Her resistance had not injured her with the gentleman, and he was thinking of her with some complacency, when thus accosted by Miss Bingley,

"I can guess the subject of your reverie."

"I should imagine not."

"You are considering how insupportable it would be to pass many evenings in this manner—in such society; and indeed I am quite of your opinion. I was never more annoyed! The insipidity and yet the noise; the nothingness and yet the self-importance of all these people!—What would I give to hear your strictures on them!"

"Your conjecture is totally wrong, I assure you. My mind was more agreeably engaged. I have been meditating on the very great pleasure which a pair of fine eyes in the face of a pretty woman can bestow."

Miss Bingley immediately fixed her eyes on his face, and desired he would tell her what lady had the credit of inspiring such reflections. Mr. Darcy replied with great intrepidity,

"Miss Elizabeth Bennet."

"Miss Elizabeth Bennet!" repeated Miss Bingley. "I am all astonishment. How long has she been such a favourite?—and pray when am I to wish you joy?"

"That is exactly the question which I expected you to ask. A lady's imagination is very rapid; it jumps from admiration to love, from love to matrimony in a moment. I knew you would be wishing me joy."

"Nay, if you are so serious about it, I shall consider the matter absolutely settled. You will have a charming mother-in-law, indeed, and of course she will be always at Pemberley with you."

He listened to her with perfect indifference, while she chose to entertain herself in this manner, and as his composure convinced her that all was safe, her wit flowed long.

CHAPTER 7

Mr. Bennet's property consisted almost entirely in an estate of two thousand a year, which, unfortunately for his daughters, was entailed in default of heirs male, on a distant relation; and their mother's fortune, though ample for her situation in life, could but ill supply the deficiency of his. Her father had been an attorney in Meryton, and had left her four thousand pounds.

She had a sister married to a Mr. Phillips, who had been a clerk to their father, and succeeded him in the business, and a brother settled in London in a respectable line of trade.

The village of Longbourn was only one mile from Meryton; a most convenient distance for the young ladies, who were usually tempted thither three or four times a week, to pay their duty to their aunt and to a milliner's shop just over the way. The two youngest of the family, Catherine and Lydia, were particularly frequent in these attentions; their minds were more vacant than their sisters', and when nothing better offered, a walk to Meryton was necessary to amuse their morning hours and furnish conversation for the evening; and however bare of news the country in general might be, they always contrived to learn some from their aunt. At present, indeed, they were well supplied both with news and happiness by the recent arrival of a militia regiment in the neighbourhood; it was to remain the whole winter, and Meryton was the head quarters.

Their visits to Mrs. Philips were now productive of the most interesting intelligence. Every day added something to their knowledge of the officers' names and connections. Their lodgings were not long a secret, and at length they began to know the officers themselves. Mr. Philips visited them all, and this opened to his nieces a source of felicity unknown before. They could talk of nothing but officers; and Mr. Bingley's large fortune, the mention of which gave animation to their mother, was worthless in their eyes when opposed to the regimentals of an ensign.

After listening one morning to their effusions on this subject, Mr. Bennet coolly observed,

"From all that I can collect by your manner of talking, you must be two of the silliest girls in the country. I have suspected it some time, but I am now convinced."

Catherine was disconcerted, and made no answer; but Lydia, with perfect indifference, continued to express her admiration of Captain Carter, and her hope of seeing him in the course of the day, as he was going the next morning to London.

"I am astonished, my dear," said Mrs. Bennet, "that you should be so ready to think your own children silly. If I wished to think slightingly of any body's children, it should not be my own however."

"If my children are silly I must hope to be always sensible of it."

"Yes—but as it happens, they are all of them very clever."

"This is the only point, I flatter myself, on which we do not agree. I had hoped that our sentiments coincided in every particular, but I must so far differ from you as to think our two youngest daughters uncommonly foolish."

"My dear Mr. Bennet, you must not expect such girls to have the sense of their father and mother.—When they get to our age I dare say they will not think about officers any more than we do. I remember the time when I liked a red-coat myself very well—and indeed so I do still at my heart; and if a smart young colonel, with five or six thousand a year, should want one of my girls, I shall not say nay to him; and I thought Colonel Forster looked very becoming the other night at Sir William's in his regimentals."

"Mama," cried Lydia, "my aunt says that Colonel Forster and

Captain Carter do not go so often to Miss Watson's as they did when they first came; she sees them now very often standing in Clarke's library."

Mrs. Bennet was prevented replying by the entrance of the footman with a note for Miss Bennet; it came from Netherfield, and the servant waited for an answer. Mrs. Bennet's eyes sparkled with pleasure, and she was eagerly calling out, while her daughter read,

"Well, Jane, who is it from? what is it about? what does he say? well, Jane, make haste and tell us; make haste, my love."

"It is from Miss Bingley." said Jane, and then read it aloud.

> My dear Friend,
>
> If you are not so compassionate as to dine to-day with Louisa and me, we shall be in danger of hating each other for the rest of our lives, for a whole day's tête-à-tête between two women can never end without a quarrel. Come as soon as you can on the receipt of this. My brother and the gentlemen are to dine with the officers. Yours ever,
>
> Caroline Bingley.

"With the officers!" cried Lydia. "I wonder my aunt did not tell us of *that*."

"Dining out," said Mrs. Bennet, "that is very unlucky."

"Can I have the carriage," said Jane.

"No, my dear, you had better go on horseback, because it seems likely to rain; and then you must stay all night."

"That would be a good scheme," said Elizabeth, "if you were sure that they would not offer to send her home."

"Oh! but the gentlemen will have Mr. Bingley's chaise to go to Meryton; and the Hursts have no horses to theirs."

"I had much rather go in the coach."

"But, my dear, your father cannot spare the horses, I am sure. They are wanted in the farm, Mr. Bennet, are not they?"

"They are wanted in the farm much oftener than I can get them."

"But if you have got them to day," said Elizabeth, "my mother's purpose will be answered."

She did at last extort from her father an acknowledgment that

the horses were engaged, Jane was therefore obliged to go on horseback, and her mother attended her to the door with many cheerful prognostics of a bad day. Her hopes were answered; Jane had
not been gone long before it rained hard. Her sisters were uneasy
for her, but her mother was delighted. The rain continued the
whole evening without intermission; Jane certainly could not
come back.

"This was a lucky idea of mine, indeed!" said Mrs. Bennet, more
than once, as if the credit of making it rain were all her own.
Till the next morning, however, she was not aware of all the felicity of her contrivance. Breakfast was scarcely over when a servant from Netherfield brought the following note for Elizabeth:

> My dearest Lizzy,
>   I find myself very unwell this morning, which, I suppose, is
> to be imputed to my getting wet through yesterday. My kind
> friends will not hear of my returning home till I am better. They
> insist also on my seeing Mr. Jones – therefore do not be alarmed
> if you should hear of his having been to me – and excepting a
> sore-throat and head-ache there is not much the matter with me.
>   Yours, &c.

"Well, my dear," said Mr. Bennet, when Elizabeth had read the
note aloud, "if your daughter should have a dangerous fit of illness, if she should die, it would be a comfort to know that it was
all in pursuit of Mr. Bingley, and under your orders."

"Oh! I am not at all afraid of her dying. People do not die of
little trifling colds. She will be taken good care of. As long as she
stays there, it is all very well. I would go and see her, if I could
have the carriage."

Elizabeth, feeling really anxious, was determined to go to her,
though the carriage was not to be had; and as she was no horse-
woman, walking was her only alternative. She declared her resolution.

"How can you be so silly," cried her mother, "as to think of
such a thing, in all this dirt! You will not be fit to be seen when
you get there."

"I shall be very fit to see Jane—which is all I want."

"Is this a hint to me, Lizzy," said her father, "to send for the horses?"

"No, indeed. I do not wish to avoid the walk. The distance is nothing, when one has a motive; only three miles. I shall be back by dinner."

"I admire the activity of your benevolence," observed Mary, "but every impulse of feeling should be guided by reason; and, in my opinion, exertion should always be in proportion to what is required."

"We will go as far as Meryton with you," said Catherine and Lydia.—Elizabeth accepted their company, and the three young ladies set off together.

"If we make haste," said Lydia, as they walked along, "perhaps we may see something of Captain Carter before he goes."

In Meryton they parted; the two youngest repaired to the lodgings of one of the officers' wives, and Elizabeth continued her walk alone, crossing field after field at a quick pace, jumping over stiles and springing over puddles with impatient activity, and finding herself at last within view of the house, with weary ancles, dirty stockings, and a face glowing with the warmth of exercise.

She was shewn into the breakfast-parlour, where all but Jane were assembled, and where her appearance created a great deal of surprise.—That she should have walked three miles so early in the day, in such dirty weather, and by herself, was almost incredible to Mrs. Hurst and Miss Bingley; and Elizabeth was convinced that they held her in contempt for it. She was received, however, very politely by them; and in their brother's manners there was something better than politeness; there was good humour and kindness.—Mr. Darcy said very little, and Mr. Hurst nothing at all. The former was divided between admiration of the brilliancy which exercise had given to her complexion, and doubt as to the occasion's justifying her coming so far alone. The latter was thinking only of his breakfast.

Her enquiries after her sister were not very favourably answered. Miss Bennet had slept ill, and though up, was very feverish and not well enough to leave her room. Elizabeth was glad to be taken to her immediately; and Jane, who had only been withheld by fear of giving alarm or inconvenience, from expressing in her note how much she longed for such a visit, was delighted at her entrance. She was not equal, however, to much conversation, and when Miss Bingley left them together, could attempt little beside expressions of gratitude for the extraordinary kindness she was treated with. Elizabeth silently attended her.

When breakfast was over, they were joined by the sisters; and Elizabeth began to like them herself, when she saw how much affection and solicitude they shewed for Jane. The apothecary came, and having examined his patient, said, as might be supposed, that she had caught a violent cold, and that they must endeavour to get the better of it; advised her to return to bed, and promised her some draughts. The advice was followed readily, for the feverish symptoms increased, and her head ached acutely. Elizabeth did not quit her room for a moment, nor were the other ladies often absent; the gentlemen being out, they had in fact nothing to do elsewhere.

When the clock struck three, Elizabeth felt that she must go; and very unwillingly said so. Miss Bingley offered her the carriage, and she only wanted a little pressing to accept it, when Jane testified such concern in parting with her, that Miss Bingley was obliged to convert the offer of the chaise into an invitation to remain at Netherfield for the present. Elizabeth most thankfully consented, and a servant was dispatched to Longbourn to acquaint the family with her stay, and bring back a supply of clothes.

CHAPTER 8

At five o'clock the two ladies retired to dress, and at half past six Elizabeth was summoned to dinner. To the civil enquiries which then poured in, and amongst which she had the pleasure of distinguishing the much superior solicitude of Mr. Bingley's, she could not make a very favourable answer. Jane was by no means better. The sisters, on hearing this, repeated three or four times how much they were grieved, how shocking it was to have a bad cold, and how excessively they disliked being ill themselves; and then thought no more of the matter: and their indifference towards Jane when not immediately before them, restored Elizabeth to the enjoyment of all her original dislike.

Their brother, indeed, was the only one of the party whom she could regard with any complacency. His anxiety for Jane was evident, and his attentions to herself most pleasing, and they prevented her feeling herself so much an intruder as she believed she was considered by the others. She had very little notice from any but him. Miss Bingley was engrossed by Mr. Darcy, her sister scarcely less so; and as for Mr. Hurst, by whom Elizabeth sat, he was an indolent man, who lived only to eat, drink, and play at cards, who when he found her prefer a plain dish to a ragout, had nothing to say to her.

When dinner was over, she returned directly to Jane, and Miss Bingley began abusing her as soon as she was out of the room. Her manners were pronounced to be very bad indeed, a mixture of pride and impertinence; she had no conversation, no stile, no taste, no beauty. Mrs. Hurst thought the same, and added,

"She has nothing, in short, to recommend her, but being an excellent walker. I shall never forget her appearance this morning. She really looked almost wild."

"She did indeed, Louisa. I could hardly keep my countenance. Very nonsensical to come at all! Why must *she* be scampering about the country, because her sister had a cold? Her hair so untidy, so blowsy!"

"Yes, and her petticoat; I hope you saw her petticoat, six inches deep in mud, I am absolutely certain; and the gown which had been let down to hide it, not doing its office."

"Your picture may be very exact, Louisa," said Bingley; "but this was all lost upon me. I thought Miss Elizabeth Bennet looked remarkably well, when she came into the room this morning. Her dirty petticoat quite escaped my notice."

"*You* observed it, Mr. Darcy, I am sure," said Miss Bingley; "and I am inclined to think that you would not wish to see *your sister* make such an exhibition."

"Certainly not."

"To walk three miles, or four miles, or five miles, or whatever it is, above her ancles in dirt, and alone, quite alone! what could she mean by it? It seems to me to shew an abominable sort of conceited independence, a most country town indifference to decorum."

"It shews an affection for her sister that is very pleasing," said Bingley.

"I am afraid, Mr. Darcy," observed Miss Bingley, in a half whisper, "that this adventure has rather affected your admiration of her fine eyes."

"Not at all," he replied; "they were brightened by the exercise."–A short pause followed this speech, and Mrs. Hurst began again.

"I have an excessive regard for Jane Bennet, she is really a very sweet girl, and I wish with all my heart she were well settled. But with such a father and mother, and such low connections, I am afraid there is no chance of it."

"I think I have heard you say, that their uncle is an attorney in Meryton."

"Yes; and they have another, who lives somewhere near Cheapside."

"That is capital," added her sister, and they both laughed heartily.

"If they had uncles enough to fill *all* Cheapside," cried Bingley, "it would not make them one jot less agreeable."

"But it must very materially lessen their chance of marrying men of any consideration in the world," replied Darcy.

To this speech Bingley made no answer; but his sisters gave it their hearty assent, and indulged their mirth for some time at the expense of their dear friend's vulgar relations.

With a renewal of tenderness, however, they repaired to her room on leaving the dining-parlour, and sat with her till summoned to coffee. She was still very poorly, and Elizabeth would not quit her at all, till late in the evening, when she had the comfort of seeing her asleep, and when it appeared to her rather right than pleasant that she should go down stairs herself. On entering the drawing-room she found the whole party at loo, and was immediately invited to join them; but suspecting them to be playing high she declined it, and making her sister the excuse, said she would amuse herself for the short time she could stay below with a book. Mr. Hurst looked at her with astonishment.

"Do you prefer reading to cards?" said he; "that is rather singular."

"Miss Eliza Bennet," said Miss Bingley, "despises cards. She is a great reader and has no pleasure in any thing else."

"I deserve neither such praise nor such censure," cried Elizabeth; "I am *not* a great reader, and I have pleasure in many things."

"In nursing your sister I am sure you have pleasure," said Bingley; "and I hope it will soon be increased by seeing her quite well."

Elizabeth thanked him from her heart, and then walked towards a table where a few books were lying. He immediately offered to fetch her others; all that his library afforded.

"And I wish my collection were larger for your benefit and my own credit; but I am an idle fellow, and though I have not many, I have more than I ever look into."

Elizabeth assured him that she could suit herself perfectly with those in the room.

"I am astonished," said Miss Bingley, "that my father should have left so small a collection of books.–What a delightful library you have at Pemberley, Mr. Darcy!"

"It ought to be good," he replied, "it has been the work of many generations."

"And then you have added so much to it yourself, you are always buying books."

"I cannot comprehend the neglect of a family library in such days as these."

"Neglect! I am sure you neglect nothing that can add to the beauties of that noble place. Charles, when you build *your* house, I wish it may be half as delightful as Pemberley."

"I wish it may."

"But I would really advise you to make your purchase in that neighbourhood, and take Pemberley for a kind of model. There is not a finer county in England than Derbyshire."

"With all my heart; I will buy Pemberley itself if Darcy will sell it."

"I am talking of possibilities, Charles."

"Upon my word, Caroline, I should think it more possible to get Pemberley by purchase than by imitation."

Elizabeth was so much caught by what passed, as to leave her very little attention for her book; and soon laying it wholly aside, she drew near the card-table, and stationed herself between Mr. Bingley and his eldest sister, to observe the game.

"Is Miss Darcy much grown since the spring?" said Miss Bingley; "will she be as tall as I am?"

"I think she will. She is now about Miss Elizabeth Bennet's height, or rather taller."

"How I long to see her again! I never met with anybody who delighted me so much. Such a countenance, such manners! – and so extremely accomplished for her age! Her performance on the piano-forte is exquisite."

"It is amazing to me," said Bingley, "how young ladies can have patience to be so very accomplished, as they all are."

"All young ladies accomplished! My dear Charles, what do you mean?"

"Yes, all of them, I think. They all paint tables, cover skreens and net purses. I scarcely know any one who cannot do all this, and I am sure I never heard a young lady spoken of for the first time, without being informed that she was very accomplished."

"Your list of the common extent of accomplishments," said

Darcy, "has too much truth. The word is applied to many a woman who deserves it no otherwise than by netting a purse, or covering a skreen. But I am very far from agreeing with you in your estimation of ladies in general. I cannot boast of knowing more than half a dozen, in the whole range of my acquaintance, that are really accomplished."

"Nor I, I am sure," said Miss Bingley.

"Then," observed Elizabeth, "you must comprehend a great deal in your idea of an accomplished woman."

"Yes; I do comprehend a great deal in it."

"Oh! certainly," cried his faithful assistant, "no one can be really esteemed accomplished, who does not greatly surpass what is usually met with. A woman must have a thorough knowledge of music, singing, drawing, dancing, and the modern languages, to deserve the word; and besides all this, she must possess a certain something in her air and manner of walking, the tone of her voice, her address and expressions, or the word will be but half deserved."

"All this she must possess," added Darcy, "and to all this she must yet add something more substantial, in the improvement of her mind by extensive reading."

"I am no longer surprised at your knowing *only* six accomplished women. I rather wonder now at your knowing *any.*"

"Are you so severe upon your own sex, as to doubt the possibility of all this?"

"*I* never saw such a woman. *I* never saw such capacity, and taste, and application, and elegance, as you describe, united."

Mrs. Hurst and Miss Bingley both cried out against the injustice of her implied doubt, and were both protesting that they knew many women who answered this description, when Mr. Hurst called them to order, with bitter complaints of their inattention to what was going forward. As all conversation was thereby at an end, Elizabeth soon afterwards left the room.

"Eliza Bennet," said Miss Bingley, when the door was closed on her, "is one of those young ladies who seek to recommend themselves to the other sex, by undervaluing their own; and with many men, I dare say, it succeeds. But, in my opinion, it is a paltry device, a very mean art."

"Undoubtedly," replied Darcy, to whom this remark was chiefly addressed, "there is meanness in *all* the arts which ladies sometimes condescend to employ for captivation. Whatever bears affinity to cunning is despicable."

Miss Bingley was not so entirely satisfied with this reply as to continue the subject.

Elizabeth joined them again only to say that her sister was worse, and that she could not leave her. Bingley urged Mr. Jones's being sent for immediately; while his sisters, convinced that no country advice could be of any service, recommended an express to town for one of the most eminent physicians. This, she would not hear of; but she was not so unwilling to comply with their brother's proposal; and it was settled that Mr. Jones should be sent for early in the morning, if Miss Bennet were not decidedly better. Bingley was quite uncomfortable; his sisters declared that they were miserable. They solaced their wretchedness, however, by duets after supper, while he could find no better relief to his feelings than by giving his housekeeper directions that every possible attention might be paid to the sick lady and her sister.

CHAPTER 9

Elizabeth passed the chief of the night in her sister's room, and in the morning had the pleasure of being able to send a tolerable answer to the enquiries which she very early received from Mr. Bingley by a housemaid, and some time afterwards from the two elegant ladies who waited on his sisters. In spite of this amendment, however, she requested to have a note sent to Longbourn, desiring her mother to visit Jane, and form her own judgment of her situation. The note was immediately dispatched, and its contents as quickly complied with. Mrs. Bennet, accompanied by her two youngest girls, reached Netherfield soon after the family breakfast.

Had she found Jane in any apparent danger, Mrs. Bennet would have been very miserable; but being satisfied on seeing her that her illness was not alarming, she had no wish of her recovering immediately, as her restoration to health would probably remove her from Netherfield. She would not listen therefore to her daughter's proposal of being carried home; neither did the apothecary, who arrived about the same time, think it at all advisable. After sitting a little while with Jane, on Miss Bingley's appearance and invitation, the mother and three daughters all attended her into the breakfast parlour. Bingley met them with hopes that Mrs. Bennet had not found Miss Bennet worse than she expected.

"Indeed I have, Sir," was her answer. "She is a great deal too ill to be moved. Mr. Jones says we must not think of moving her. We must trespass a little longer on your kindness."

"Removed!" cried Bingley. "It must not be thought of. My sister, I am sure, will not hear of her removal."

"You may depend upon it, Madam," said Miss Bingley, with cold civility, "that Miss Bennet shall receive every possible attention while she remains with us."

Mrs. Bennet was profuse in her acknowledgments.

"I am sure," she added, "if it was not for such good friends I do not know what would become of her, for she is very ill indeed, and suffers a vast deal, though with the greatest patience in the world, which is always the way with her, for she has, without exception, the sweetest temper I ever met with. I often tell my other girls they are nothing to *her*. You have a sweet room here, Mr. Bingley, and a charming prospect over that gravel walk. I do not know a place in the country that is equal to Netherfield. You will not think of quitting it in a hurry I hope, though you have but a short lease."

"Whatever I do is done in a hurry," replied he; "and therefore if I should resolve to quit Netherfield, I should probably be off in five minutes. At present, however, I consider myself as quite fixed here."

"That is exactly what I should have supposed of you," said Elizabeth.

"You begin to comprehend me, do you?" cried he, turning towards her.

"Oh! yes—I understand you perfectly."

"I wish I might take this for a compliment; but to be so easily seen through I am afraid is pitiful."

"That is as it happens. It does not necessarily follow that a deep, intricate character is more or less estimable than such a one as yours."

"Lizzy," cried her mother, "remember where you are, and do not run on in the wild manner that you are suffered to do at home."

"I did not know before," continued Bingley immediately, "that you were a studier of character. It must be an amusing study."

"Yes; but intricate characters are the *most* amusing. They have at least that advantage."

"The country," said Darcy, "can in general supply but few subjects for such a study. In a country neighbourhood you move in a very confined and unvarying society."

"But people themselves alter so much, that there is something new to be observed in them for ever."

"Yes, indeed," cried Mrs. Bennet, offended by his manner of mentioning a country neighbourhood. "I assure you there is quite as much of *that* going on in the country as in town."

Every body was surprised; and Darcy, after looking at her for a moment, turned silently away. Mrs. Bennet, who fancied she had gained a complete victory over him, continued her triumph.

"I cannot see that London has any great advantage over the country for my part, except the shops and public places. The country is a vast deal pleasanter, is not it, Mr. Bingley?"

"When I am in the country," he replied, "I never wish to leave it; and when I am in town it is pretty much the same. They have each their advantages, and I can be equally happy in either."

"Aye—that is because you have the right disposition. But that

gentleman," looking at Darcy, "seemed to think the country was
nothing at all."

"Indeed, Mama, you are mistaken," said Elizabeth, blushing for
her mother. "You quite mistook Mr. Darcy. He only meant that
there were not such a variety of people to be met with in the country as in town, which you must acknowledge to be true."

"Certainly, my dear, nobody said there were; but as to not meeting with many people in this neighbourhood, I believe there are
few neighbourhoods larger. I know we dine with four and twenty
families."

Nothing but concern for Elizabeth could enable Bingley to keep
his countenance. His sister was less delicate, and directed her eye
towards Mr. Darcy with a very expressive smile. Elizabeth, for the
sake of saying something that might turn her mother's thoughts,
now asked her if Charlotte Lucas had been at Longbourn since
her coming away.

"Yes, she called yesterday with her father. What an agreeable
man Sir William is, Mr. Bingley – is not he? so much the man of
fashion! so genteel and so easy! – He has always something to say
to every body. – *That* is my idea of good breeding; and those persons who fancy themselves very important and never open their
mouths, quite mistake the matter."

"Did Charlotte dine with you?"

"No, she would go home. I fancy she was wanted about the
mince pies. For my part, Mr. Bingley, *I* always keep servants that
can do their own work; *my* daughters are brought up differently.
But every body is to judge for themselves, and the Lucases are
very good sort of girls, I assure you. It is a pity they are not handsome! Not that *I* think Charlotte so *very* plain – but then she is
our particular friend."

"She seems a very pleasant young woman," said Bingley.

"Oh! dear, yes; – but you must own she is very plain. Lady Lucas
herself has often said so, and envied me Jane's beauty. I do not
like to boast of my own child, but to be sure, Jane – one does not
often see any body better looking. It is what everybody says. I

do not trust my own partiality. When she was only fifteen, there was a gentleman at my brother Gardiner's in town, so much in love with her, that my sister-in-law was sure he would make her an offer before we came away. But however he did not. Perhaps he thought her too young. However, he wrote some verses on her, and very pretty they were."

"And so ended his affection," said Elizabeth impatiently. "There has been many a one, I fancy, overcome in the same way. I wonder who first discovered the efficacy of poetry in driving away love!"

"I have been used to consider poetry as the *food* of love," said Darcy.

"Of a fine, stout, healthy love it may. Every thing nourishes what is strong already. But if it be only a slight, thin sort of inclination, I am convinced that one good sonnet will starve it entirely away."

Darcy only smiled; and the general pause which ensued made Elizabeth tremble lest her mother should be exposing herself again. She longed to speak, but could think of nothing to say; and after a short silence Mrs. Bennet began repeating her thanks to Mr. Bingley for his kindness to Jane, with an apology for troubling him also with Lizzy. Mr. Bingley was unaffectedly civil in his answer, and forced his younger sister to be civil also, and say what the occasion required. She performed her part indeed without much graciousness, but Mrs. Bennet was satisfied, and soon afterwards ordered her carriage. Upon this signal, the youngest of her daughters put herself forward. The two girls had been whispering to each other during the whole visit, and the result of it was, that the youngest should tax Mr. Bingley with having promised on his first coming into the country to give a ball at Netherfield.

Lydia was a stout, well-grown girl of fifteen, with a fine complexion and good-humoured countenance; a favourite with her mother, whose affection had brought her into public at an early age. She had high animal spirits, and a sort of natural self-consequence, which the attentions of the officers, to whom her uncle's good dinners and her own easy manners recommended

her, had increased into assurance. She was very equal therefore
to address Mr. Bingley on the subject of the ball, and abruptly
reminded him of his promise; adding, that it would be the most
shameful thing in the world if he did not keep it. His answer to
this sudden attack was delightful to their mother's ear.

"I am perfectly ready, I assure you, to keep my engagement;
and when your sister is recovered, you shall if you please name
the very day of the ball. But you would not wish to be dancing
while she is ill."

Lydia declared herself satisfied. "Oh! yes—it would be much
better to wait till Jane was well, and by that time most likely Captain Carter would be at Meryton again. And when you have given
your ball," she added, "I shall insist on their giving one also. I shall
tell Colonel Forster it will be quite a shame if he does not."

Mrs. Bennet and her daughter then departed, and Elizabeth
returned instantly to Jane, leaving her own and her relations' behaviour to the remarks of the two ladies and Mr. Darcy; the latter
of whom, however, could not be prevailed on to join in their
censure of *her,* in spite of all Miss Bingley's witticisms on *fine eyes.*

CHAPTER 10

The day passed much as the day before had done. Mrs. Hurst and
Miss Bingley had spent some hours of the morning with the invalid, who continued, though slowly, to mend; and in the evening Elizabeth joined their party in the drawing-room. The loo
table, however, did not appear. Mr. Darcy was writing, and Miss
Bingley, seated near him, was watching the progress of his letter,
and repeatedly calling off his attention by messages to his sister.
Mr. Hurst and Mr. Bingley were at piquet, and Mrs. Hurst was observing their game.

Elizabeth took up some needlework, and was sufficiently
amused in attending to what passed between Darcy and his com-

panion. The perpetual commendations of the lady either on his hand-writing, or on the evenness of his lines, or on the length of his letter, with the perfect unconcern with which her praises were received, formed a curious dialogue, and was exactly in unison with her opinion of each.

"How delighted Miss Darcy will be to receive such a letter!"

He made no answer.

"You write uncommonly fast."

"You are mistaken. I write rather slowly."

"How many letters you must have occasion to write in the course of the year! Letters of business too! How odious I should think them!"

It is fortunate, then, that they fall to my lot instead of to yours."

"Pray tell your sister that I long to see her."

"I have already told her so once, by your desire."

"I am afraid you do not like your pen. Let me mend it for you. I mend pens remarkably well."

"Thank you—but I always mend my own."

"How can you contrive to write so even?"

He was silent.

"Tell your sister I am delighted to hear of her improvement on the harp, and pray let her know that I am quite in raptures with her beautiful little design for a table, and I think it infinitely superior to Miss Grantley's."

"Will you give me leave to defer your raptures till I write again?—At present I have not room to do them justice."

"Oh! it is of no consequence. I shall see her in January. But do you always write such charming long letters to her, Mr. Darcy?"

"They are generally long; but whether always charming, it is not for me to determine."

"It is a rule with me, that a person who can write a long letter, with ease, cannot write ill."

"That will not do for a compliment to Darcy, Caroline," cried her brother—"because he does *not* write with ease. He studies too much for words of four syllables.—Do not you, Darcy?"

"My stile of writing is very different from yours."

"Oh!" cried Miss Bingley, "Charles writes in the most careless way imaginable. He leaves out half his words, and blots the rest."

"My ideas flow so rapidly that I have not time to express them – by which means my letters sometimes convey no ideas at all to my correspondents."

"Your humility, Mr. Bingley." said Elizabeth, "must disarm reproof."

"Nothing is more deceitful," said Darcy, "than the appearance of humility. It is often only carelessness of opinion, and sometimes an indirect boast."

"And which of the two do you call *my* little recent piece of modesty?"

"The indirect boast; – for you are really proud of your defects in writing, because you consider them as proceeding from a rapidity of thought and carelessness of execution, which if not estimable, you think at least highly interesting. The power of doing any thing with quickness is always much prized by the possessor, and often without any attention to the imperfection of the performance. When you told Mrs. Bennet this morning that if you ever resolved on quitting Netherfield you should be gone in five minutes, you meant it to be a sort of panegyric, of compliment to yourself – and yet what is there so very laudable in a precipitance which must leave very necessary business undone, and can be of no real advantage to yourself or any one else?"

"Nay," cried Bingley "this is too much, to remember at night all the foolish things that were said in the morning. And yet, upon my honour, I believed what I said of myself to be true, and I believe it at this moment. At least, therefore, I did not assume the character of needless precipitance merely to shew off before the ladies."

"I dare say you believed it; but I am by no means convinced that you would be gone with such celerity. Your conduct would be quite as dependant on chance as that of any man I know; and if, as you were mounting your horse, a friend were to say, 'Bingley, you had better stay till next week,' you would probably do it, you would probably not go – and, at another word, might stay a month."

"You have only proved by this," cried Elizabeth, "that Mr. Bingley did not do justice to his own disposition. You have shewn him off now much more than he did himself."

"I am exceedingly gratified," said Bingley, "by your converting what my friend says into a compliment on the sweetness of my temper. But I am afraid you are giving it a turn which that gentleman did by no means intend; for he would certainly think the better of me, if under such a circumstance I were to give a flat denial, and ride off as fast as I could."

"Would Mr. Darcy then consider the rashness of your original intention as atoned for by your obstinacy in adhering to it?"

"Upon my word I cannot exactly explain the matter, Darcy must speak for himself."

"You expect me to account for opinions which you chuse to call mine, but which I have never acknowledged. Allowing the case, however, to stand according to your representation, you must remember, Miss Bennet, that the friend who is supposed to desire his return to the house, and the delay of his plan, has merely desired it, asked it without offering one argument in favour of its propriety."

"To yield readily – easily – to the *persuasion* of a friend is no merit with you."

"To yield without conviction is no compliment to the understanding of either."

"You appear to me, Mr. Darcy, to allow nothing for the influence of friendship and affection. A regard for the requester would often make one readily yield to a request, without waiting for arguments to reason one into it. I am not particularly speaking of such a case as you have supposed about Mr. Bingley. We may as well wait, perhaps, till the circumstance occurs, before we discuss the discretion of his behaviour thereupon. But in general and ordinary cases between friend and friend, where one of them is desired by the other to change a resolution of no very great moment, should you think ill of that person for complying with the desire, without waiting to be argued into it?"

"Will it not be advisable, before we proceed on this subject, to arrange with rather more precision the degree of importance which is to appertain to this request, as well as the degree of intimacy subsisting between the parties?"

"By all means," cried Bingley; "let us hear all the particulars, not forgetting their comparative height and size; for that will have more weight in the argument, Miss Bennet, than you may be aware of. I assure you that if Darcy were not such a great tall fellow, in comparison with myself, I should not pay him half so much deference. I declare I do not know a more aweful object than Darcy, on particular occasions, and in particular places; at his own house especially, and of a Sunday evening when he has nothing to do."

Mr. Darcy smiled; but Elizabeth thought she could perceive that he was rather offended; and therefore checked her laugh. Miss Bingley warmly resented the indignity he had received, in an expostulation with her brother for talking such nonsense.

"I see your design, Bingley." said his friend.—"You dislike an argument, and want to silence this."

"Perhaps I do. Arguments are too much like disputes. If you and Miss Bennet will defer yours till I am out of the room, I shall be very thankful; and then you may say whatever you like of me."

"What you ask," said Elizabeth, "is no sacrifice on my side; and Mr. Darcy had much better finish his letter."

Mr. Darcy took her advice, and did finish his letter.

When that business was over, he applied to Miss Bingley and Elizabeth for the indulgence of some music. Miss Bingley moved with alacrity to the piano-forte, and after a polite request that Elizabeth would lead the way, which the other as politely and more earnestly negatived, she seated herself.

Mrs. Hurst sang with her sister, and while they were thus employed Elizabeth could not help observing as she turned over some music books that lay on the instrument, how frequently Mr. Darcy's eyes were fixed on her. She hardly knew how to suppose that she could be an object of admiration to such a great man; and yet that he should look at her because he disliked her, was still more strange. She could only imagine however at last, that she drew his notice because there was something about her more wrong and reprehensible, according to his ideas of right, than in any other person present. The supposition did not pain her. She liked him too little to care for his approbation.

After playing some Italian songs, Miss Bingley varied the charm by a lively Scotch air; and soon afterwards Mr. Darcy, drawing near Elizabeth, said to her—

"Do not you feel a great inclination, Miss Bennet, to seize such an opportunity of dancing a reel?"

She smiled, but made no answer. He repeated the question, with some surprise at her silence.

"Oh!" said she, "I heard you before; but I could not immediately determine what to say in reply. You wanted me, I know, to say 'Yes,' that you might have the pleasure of despising my taste; but I always delight in overthrowing those kind of schemes, and cheating a person of their premeditated contempt. I have therefore made up my mind to tell you, that I do not want to dance a reel at all—and now despise me if you dare."

"Indeed I do not dare."

Elizabeth, having rather expected to affront him, was amazed at his gallantry; but there was a mixture of sweetness and archness in her manner which made it difficult for her to affront anybody; and Darcy had never been so bewitched by any woman as he was by her. He really believed, that were it not for the inferiority of her connections, he should be in some danger.

Miss Bingley saw, or suspected enough to be jealous; and her great anxiety for the recovery of her dear friend Jane, received some assistance from her desire of getting rid of Elizabeth.

She often tried to provoke Darcy into disliking her guest, by talking of their supposed marriage, and planning his happiness in such an alliance.

"I hope," said she, as they were walking together in the shrub-bery the next day, "you will give your mother-in-law a few hints, when this desirable event takes place, as to the advantage of holding her tongue; and if you can compass it, do cure the younger girls of running after the officers.—And, if I may mention so delicate a subject, endeavour to check that little something, bordering on conceit and impertinence, which your lady possesses."

"Have you any thing else to propose for my domestic felicity?"

"Oh! yes.—Do let the portraits of your uncle and aunt Philips be placed in the gallery at Pemberley. Put them next to your great uncle the judge. They are in the same profession, you know; only in different lines. As for your Elizabeth's picture, you must not attempt to have it taken, for what painter could do justice to those beautiful eyes?"

"It would not be easy, indeed, to catch their expression, but their colour and shape, and the eye-lashes, so remarkably fine, might be copied."

At that moment they were met from another walk, by Mrs. Hurst and Elizabeth herself.

"I did not know that you intended to walk," said Miss Bingley, in some confusion, lest they had been overheard.

"You used us abominably ill," answered Mrs. Hurst, "in running away without telling us that you were coming out."

Then taking the disengaged arm of Mr. Darcy, she left Elizabeth to walk by herself. The path just admitted three. Mr. Darcy felt their rudeness and immediately said,—

"This walk is not wide enough for our party. We had better go into the avenue."

But Elizabeth who had not the least inclination to remain with them, laughingly answered,

"No, no; stay where you are.—You are charmingly group'd, and appear to uncommon advantage. The picturesque would be spoilt by admitting a fourth. Good bye."

She then ran gaily off, rejoicing as she rambled about, in the

hope of being at home again in a day or two. Jane was already
so much recovered as to intend leaving her room for a couple
of hours that evening.

CHAPTER 11

When the ladies removed after dinner, Elizabeth ran up to her
sister, and seeing her well guarded from cold, attended her into
the drawing-room; where she was welcomed by her two friends
with many professions of pleasure; and Elizabeth had never seen
them so agreeable as they were during the hour which passed
before the gentlemen appeared. Their powers of conversation were
considerable. They could describe an entertainment with accuracy,
relate an anecdote with humour, and laugh at their acquaintance
with spirit.

But when the gentlemen entered, Jane was no longer the first
object. Miss Bingley's eyes were instantly turned towards Darcy,
and she had something to say to him before he had advanced
many steps. He addressed himself directly to Miss Bennet, with
a polite congratulation; Mr. Hurst also made her a slight bow, and
said he was "very glad;" but diffuseness and warmth remained
for Bingley's salutation. He was full of joy and attention. The first
half hour was spent in piling up the fire, lest she should suffer
from the change of room; and she removed at his desire to the
other side of the fire-place, that she might be farther from the
door. He then sat down by her, and talked scarcely to any one
else. Elizabeth, at work in the opposite corner, saw it all with great
delight.

When tea was over, Mr. Hurst reminded his sister-in-law of
the card-table – but in vain. She had obtained private intelligence
that Mr. Darcy did not wish for cards; and Mr. Hurst soon found
even his open petition rejected. She assured him that no one intended to play, and the silence of the whole party on the subject,

seemed to justify her. Mr. Hurst had therefore nothing to do, but to stretch himself on one of the sophas and go to sleep. Darcy took up a book; Miss Bingley did the same; and Mrs. Hurst, principally occupied in playing with her bracelets and rings, joined now and then in her brother's conversation with Miss Bennet.

Miss Bingley's attention was quite as much engaged in watching Mr. Darcy's progress through *his* book, as in reading her own; and she was perpetually either making some inquiry, or looking at his page. She could not win him, however, to any conversation; he merely answered her question, and read on. At length, quite exhausted by the attempt to be amused with her own book, which she had only chosen because it was the second volume of his, she gave a great yawn and said, "How pleasant it is to spend an evening in this way! I declare after all there is no enjoyment like reading! How much sooner one tires of anything than of a book!—When I have a house of my own, I shall be miserable if I have not an excellent library."

No one made any reply. She then yawned again, threw aside her book, and cast her eyes round the room in quest of some amusement; when hearing her brother mentioning a ball to Miss Bennet, she turned suddenly towards him and said,

"By the bye, Charles, are you really serious in meditating a dance at Netherfield?—I would advise you, before you determine on it, to consult the wishes of the present party; I am much mistaken if there are not some among us to whom a ball would be rather a punishment than a pleasure."

"If you mean Darcy," cried her brother, "he may go to bed, if he chuses, before it begins—but as for the ball, it is quite a settled thing; and as soon as Nicholls has made white soup enough I shall send round my cards."

"I should like balls infinitely better," she replied, "if they were carried on in a different manner; but there is something insufferably tedious in the usual process of such a meeting. It would surely be much more rational if conversation instead of dancing made the order of the day."

"Much more rational, my dear Caroline, I dare say, but it would not be near so much like a ball."

Miss Bingley made no answer; and soon afterwards got up and walked about the room. Her figure was elegant, and she walked well;–but Darcy, at whom it was all aimed, was still inflexibly studious. In the desperation of her feelings she resolved on one effort more; and, turning to Elizabeth, said,

"Miss Eliza Bennet, let me persuade you to follow my example, and take a turn about the room.–I assure you it is very refreshing after sitting so long in one attitude."

Elizabeth was surprised, but agreed to it immediately. Miss Bingley succeeded no less in the real object of her civility; Mr. Darcy looked up. He was as much awake to the novelty of attention in that quarter as Elizabeth herself could be, and unconsciously closed his book. He was directly invited to join their party, but he declined it, observing, that he could imagine but two motives for their chusing to walk up and down the room together, with either of which motives his joining them would interfere. "What could he mean? she was dying to know what could be his meaning"–and asked Elizabeth whether she could at all understand him?

"Not at all," was her answer; "but depend upon it, he means to be severe on us, and our surest way of disappointing him, will be to ask nothing about it."

Miss Bingley, however, was incapable of disappointing Mr. Darcy in any thing, and persevered therefore in requiring an explanation of his two motives.

"I have not the smallest objection to explaining them," said he, as soon as she allowed him to speak. "You either chuse this method of passing the evening because you are in each other's confidence and have secret affairs to discuss, or because you are conscious that your figures appear to the greatest advantage in walking;–if the first, I should be completely in your way;–and if the second, I can admire you much better as I sit by the fire."

"Oh! shocking!" cried Miss Bingley. "I never heard any thing so abominable. How shall we punish him for such a speech?"

"Nothing so easy, if you have but the inclination," said Elizabeth. "We can all plague and punish one another. Teaze him—laugh at him.—Intimate as you are, you must know how it is to be done."

"But upon my honour I do *not*. I do assure you that my intimacy has not yet taught me *that*. Teaze calmness of temper and presence of mind! No, no—I feel he may defy us there. And as to laughter, we will not expose ourselves, if you please, by attempting to laugh without a subject. Mr. Darcy may hug himself."

"Mr. Darcy is not to be laughed at!" cried Elizabeth. "That is an uncommon advantage, and uncommon I hope it will continue, for it would be a great loss to *me* to have many such acquaintance. I dearly love a laugh."

"Miss Bingley," said he, "has given me credit for more than can be. The wisest and the best of men, nay, the wisest and best of their actions, may be rendered ridiculous by a person whose first object in life is a joke."

"Certainly," replied Elizabeth—"there are such people, but I hope I am not one of *them*. I hope I never ridicule what is wise or good. Follies and nonsense, whims and inconsistencies *do* divert me, I own, and I laugh at them whenever I can.—But these, I suppose, are precisely what you are without."

"Perhaps that is not possible for any one. But it has been the study of my life to avoid those weaknesses which often expose a strong understanding to ridicule."

"Such as vanity and pride."

"Yes, vanity is a weakness indeed. But pride—where there is a real superiority of mind, pride will be always under good regulation."

Elizabeth turned away to hide a smile.

"Your examination of Mr. Darcy is over, I presume," said Miss Bingley;—"and pray what is the result?"

"I am perfectly convinced by it that Mr. Darcy has no defect. He owns it himself without disguise."

"No"—said Darcy, "I have made no such pretension. I have faults enough, but they are not, I hope, of understanding. My temper

I dare not vouch for.–It is I believe too little yielding–certainly too little for the convenience of the world. I cannot forget the follies and vices of others so soon as I ought, nor their offences against myself. My feelings are not puffed about with every attempt to move them. My temper would perhaps be called resentful.–My good opinion once lost is lost for ever."

That is a failing indeed!"–cried Elizabeth. "Implacable resentment *is* a shade in a character. But you have chosen your fault well.–I really cannot *laugh* at it. You are safe from me."

"There is, I believe, in every disposition a tendency to some particular evil, a natural defect, which not even the best education can overcome."

"And *your* defect is a propensity to hate every body."

"And yours," he replied with a smile, "is wilfully to misunderstand them."

"Do let us have a little music,"–cried Miss Bingley, tired of a conversation in which she had no share.–"Louisa, you will not mind my waking Mr. Hurst."

Her sister made not the smallest objection, and the piano forte was opened, and Darcy, after a few moments recollection, was not sorry for it. He began to feel the danger of paying Elizabeth too much attention.

CHAPTER 12

In consequence of an agreement between the sisters, Elizabeth wrote the next morning to her mother, to beg that the carriage might be sent for them in the course of the day. But Mrs. Bennet, who had calculated on her daughters remaining at Netherfield till the following Tuesday, which would exactly finish Jane's week, could not bring herself to receive them with pleasure before. Her answer, therefore, was not propitious, at least not to Elizabeth's wishes, for she was impatient to get home. Mrs. Bennet sent them word that they could not possibly have the carriage before Tuesday; and in her postscript it was added, that if Mr. Bingley and his sister pressed them to stay longer, she could spare them very well.–Against staying longer, however, Elizabeth was positively resolved–nor did she much expect it would be asked; and fearful, on the contrary, as being considered as intruding themselves needlessly long, she urged Jane to borrow Mr. Bingley's carriage immediately, and at length it was settled that their original design of leaving Netherfield that morning should be mentioned, and the request made.

The communication excited many professions of concern; and enough was said of wishing them to stay at least till the following day to work on Jane; and till the morrow, their going was deferred. Miss Bingley was then sorry that she had proposed the delay, for her jealousy and dislike of one sister much exceeded her affection for the other.

The master of the house heard with real sorrow that they were to go so soon, and repeatedly tried to persuade Miss Bennet that it would not be safe for her–that she was not enough recovered; but Jane was firm where she felt herself to be right.

To Mr. Darcy it was welcome intelligence–Elizabeth had been at Netherfield long enough. She attracted him more than he liked–and Miss Bingley was uncivil to *her*, and more teazing than usual to himself. He wisely resolved to be particularly careful that no sign of admiration should *now* escape him, nothing that could elevate her with the hope of influencing his felicity; sensible that if such an idea had been suggested, his behaviour during the last day must have material weight in confirming or crushing it. Steady to his purpose, he scarcely spoke ten words to her through the whole of Saturday, and though they were at one time left by themselves for half an hour, he adhered most conscientiously to his book, and would not even look at her.

On Sunday, after morning service, the separation, so agreeable to almost all, took place. Miss Bingley's civility to Elizabeth increased at last very rapidly, as well as her affection for Jane;

and when they parted, after assuring the latter of the pleasure it would always give her to see her either at Longbourn or Netherfield, and embracing her most tenderly, she even shook hands with the former.—Elizabeth took leave of the whole party in the liveliest spirits.

They were not welcomed home very cordially by their mother. Mrs. Bennet wondered at their coming, and thought them very wrong to give so much trouble, and was sure Jane would have caught cold again.—But their father, though very laconic in his expressions of pleasure, was really glad to see them; he had felt their importance in the family circle. The evening conversation, when they were all assembled, had lost much of its animation, and almost all its sense, by the absence of Jane and Elizabeth.

They found Mary, as usual, deep in the study of thorough bass and human nature; and had some new extracts to admire, and some new observations of thread-bare morality to listen to. Catherine and Lydia had information for them of a different sort. Much had been done, and much had been said in the regiment since the preceding Wednesday; several of the officers had dined lately with their uncle, a private had been flogged, and it had actually been hinted that Colonel Forster was going to be married.

CHAPTER 13

"I hope, my dear," said Mr. Bennet to his wife, as they were at breakfast the next morning, "that you have ordered a good dinner to-day, because I have reason to expect an addition to our family party."

"Who do you mean, my dear? I know of nobody that is coming I am sure, unless Charlotte Lucas should happen to call in, and I hope *my* dinners are good enough for her. I do not believe she often sees such at home."

"The person of whom I speak, is a gentleman and a stranger."

Mrs. Bennet's eyes sparkled.–"A gentleman and a stranger! It is Mr. Bingley I am sure. Why Jane–you never dropt a word of this; you sly thing! Well, I am sure I shall be extremely glad to see Mr. Bingley.–But–good lord! how unlucky! there is not a bit of fish to be got to-day. Lydia, my love, ring the bell. I must speak to Hill, this moment."

"It is *not* Mr. Bingley." said her husband; "it is a person whom I never saw in the whole course of my life."

This roused a general astonishment; and he had the pleasure of being eagerly questioned by his wife and five daughters at once.

After amusing himself some time with their curiosity, he thus explained. "About a month ago I received this letter, and about a fortnight ago I answered it, for I thought it a case of some delicacy, and requiring early attention. It is from my cousin, Mr. Collins, who, when I am dead, may turn you all out of this house as soon as he pleases."

"Oh! my dear," cried his wife, "I cannot bear to hear that mentioned. Pray do not talk of that odious man. I do think it is the hardest thing in the world, that your estate should be entailed away from your own children; and I am sure if I had been you, I should have tried long ago to do something or other about it."

Jane and Elizabeth attempted to explain to her the nature of an entail. They had often attempted it before, but it was a subject on which Mrs. Bennet was beyond the reach of reason; and she continued to rail bitterly against the cruelty of settling an estate away from a family of five daughters, in favour of a man whom nobody cared anything about.

"It certainly is a most iniquitous affair," said Mr. Bennet, "and nothing can clear Mr. Collins from the guilt of inheriting Longbourn. But if you will listen to his letter, you may perhaps be a little softened by his manner of expressing himself."

"No, that I am sure I shall not; and I think it was very impertinent of him to write to you at all, and very hypocritical. I hate such false friends. Why could not he keep on quarrelling with you, as his father did before him?"

"Why, indeed, he does seem to have had some filial scruples on that head, as you will hear."

Hunsford, near Westerham, Kent,
15th October.

Dear Sir,

The disagreement subsisting between yourself and my late honoured father, always gave me much uneasiness, and since I have had the misfortune to lose him, I have frequently wished to heal the breach but for some time I was kept back by my own doubts, fearing lest it might seem disrespectful to his memory for me to be on good terms with any one, with whom it had always pleased him to be at variance.-"There, Mrs. Bennet."- My mind however is now made up on the subject, for having received ordination at Easter, I have been so fortunate as to be distinguished by the patronage of the Right Honourable Lady Catherine de Bourgh, widow of Sir Lewis de Bourgh, whose bounty and beneficence has preferred me to the valuable rectory of this parish, where it shall be my earnest endeavour to demean myself with grateful respect towards her Ladyship, and be ever ready to perform those rites and ceremonies which are instituted by the Church of England. As a clergyman, moreover, I feel it my duty to promote and establish the blessing of peace in all families within the reach of my influence; and on these grounds I flatter myself that my present overtures of good-will are highly commendable, and that the circumstance of my being next in the entail of Longbourn estate, will be kindly overlooked on your side, and not lead you to reject the offered olive branch. I cannot be otherwise than concerned at being the means of injuring your amiable daughters, and beg leave to apologise for it, as well as to assure you of my readiness to make them every possible amends,-but of this hereafter. If you should have no objection to receive me into your house, I propose myself the satisfaction of waiting on you and your family, Monday, November 18th, by four o'clock, and shall probably trespass on your hospitality till the Saturday se'night following, which I can do without any inconvenience, as Lady Catherine is far from objecting to my occasional absence on a Sunday, provided that some other clergyman is engaged to do the duty of the day. I remain, dear sir, with respectful compliments to your lady and daughters, your well-wisher and friend,

William Collins.

"At four o'clock, therefore, we may expect this peace-making gentleman," said Mr. Bennet, as he folded up the letter. "He seems to be a most conscientious and polite young man, upon my word; and I doubt not will prove a valuable acquaintance, especially if Lady Catherine should be so indulgent as to let him come to us again."

"There is some sense in what he says about the girls however; and if he is disposed to make them any amends, I shall not be the person to discourage him."

"Though it is difficult," said Jane, "to guess in what way he can mean to make us the atonement he thinks our due, the wish is certainly to his credit."

Elizabeth was chiefly struck with his extraordinary deference for Lady Catherine, and his kind intention of christening, marrying, and burying his parishioners whenever it were required.

"He must be an oddity, I think," said she. "I cannot make him out.—There is something very pompous in his stile.—And what can he mean by apologizing for being next in the entail?—We cannot suppose he would help it, if he could.—Can he be a sensible man, sir?"

"No, my dear; I think not. I have great hopes of finding him quite the reverse. There is a mixture of servility and self-importance in his letter, which promises well. I am impatient to see him."

"In point of composition," said Mary, "his letter does not seem defective. The idea of the olive branch perhaps is not wholly new, yet I think it is well expressed."

To Catherine and Lydia, neither the letter nor its writer were in any degree interesting. It was next to impossible that their cousin should come in a scarlet coat, and it was now some weeks since they had received pleasure from the society of a man in any other colour. As for their mother, Mr. Collins's letter had done away much of her ill-will, and she was preparing to see him with a degree of composure, which astonished her husband and daughters.

Mr. Collins was punctual to his time, and was received with great politeness by the whole family. Mr. Bennet indeed said little; but the ladies were ready enough to talk, and Mr. Collins seemed neither in need of encouragement, nor inclined to be silent himself. He was a tall, heavy looking young man of five and twenty. His air was grave and stately, and his manners were very formal. He had not been long seated before he complimented Mrs. Bennet on having so fine a family of daughters, said he had heard much of their beauty, but that, in this instance, fame had fallen short of the truth; and added, that he did not doubt her seeing them all in due time well disposed of in marriage. This gallantry was not much to the taste of some of his hearers, but Mrs. Bennet, who quarrelled with no compliments, answered most readily,

"You are very kind, sir, I am sure; and I wish with all my heart it may prove so; for else they will be destitute enough. Things are settled so oddly."

"You allude perhaps to the entail of this estate."

"Ah! sir, I do indeed. It is a grievous affair to my poor girls, you must confess. Not that I mean to find fault with *you,* for such things I know are all chance in this world. There is no knowing how estates will go when once they come to be entailed."

"I am very sensible, madam, of the hardship to my fair cousins,—and could say much on the subject, but that I am cautious of appearing forward and precipitate. But I can assure the young ladies that I come prepared to admire them. At present I will not say more, but perhaps when we are better acquainted—"

He was interrupted by a summons to dinner; and the girls smiled on each other. They were not the only objects of Mr. Collins's admiration. The hall, the dining-room, and all its furniture were examined and praised; and his commendation of every thing would have touched Mrs. Bennet's heart, but for the mortifying supposition of his viewing it all as his own future property. The dinner too in its turn was highly admired; and he begged to know to which of his fair cousins, the excellence of its cookery was owing. But here he was set right by Mrs. Bennet, who assured him with some asperity that they were very well able to keep a good cook, and that her daughters had nothing to do in the kitchen. He begged pardon for having displeased her. In a softened tone she declared herself not at all offended; but he continued to apologise for about a quarter of an hour.

CHAPTER 14

During dinner, Mr. Bennet scarcely spoke at all; but when the servants were withdrawn, he thought it time to have some conversation with his guest, and therefore started a subject in which he expected him to shine, by observing that he seemed very fortunate in his patroness. Lady Catherine de Bourgh's attention to his wishes, and consideration for his comfort, appeared very remarkable. Mr. Bennet could not have chosen better. Mr. Collins was eloquent in her praise. The subject elevated him to more than usual solemnity of manner, and with a most important aspect he protested that he had never in his life witnessed such behaviour in a person of rank – such affability and condescension, as he had himself experienced from Lady Catherine. She had been graciously pleased to approve of both the discourses, which he had already had the honour of preaching before her. She had also asked him twice to dine at Rosings, and had sent for him only the Saturday before, to make up her pool of quadrille in the evening. Lady Catherine was reckoned proud by many people he knew, but *he* had never seen any thing but affability in her. She had always spoken to him as she would to any other gentleman; she made not the smallest objection to his joining in the society of the neighbourhood, nor to his leaving his parish occasionally for a week or two, to visit his relations. She had even condescended to advise him to marry as soon as he could, provided he chose with discretion; and had once paid him a visit in his humble parsonage; where she had perfectly approved all the alterations he had been making, and had even vouchsafed to suggest some herself,–some shelves in the closets up stairs."

"That is all very proper and civil, I am sure," said Mrs. Bennet, "and I dare say she is a very agreeable woman. It is a pity that great ladies in general are not more like her. Does she live near you, sir?"

"The garden in which stands by humble abode, is separated only by a lane from Rosings Park, her ladyship's residence."

"I think you said she was a widow, sir? has she any family?"

"She has one only daughter, the heiress of Rosings, and of very extensive property."

"Ah!" cried Mrs. Bennet, shaking her head, then she is better off than many girls. And what sort of young lady is she? is she handsome?"

"She is a most charming young lady indeed. Lady Catherine herself says that in point of true beauty, Miss De Bourgh is far superior to the handsomest of her sex; because there is that in her features which marks the young woman of distinguished birth. She is unfortunately of a sickly constitution, which has prevented her making that progress in many accomplishments, which she could not otherwise have failed of; as I am informed by the lady who superintended her education, and who still resides with them. But she is perfectly amiable, and often condescends to drive by my humble abode in her little phaeton and ponies."

"Has she been presented? I do not remember her name among the ladies at court."

"Her indifferent state of health unhappily prevents her being in town; and by that means, as I told Lady Catherine myself one day, has deprived the British court of its brightest ornament. Her ladyship seemed pleased with the idea, and you may imagine that I am happy on every occasion to offer those little delicate compliments which are always acceptable to ladies. I have more than once observed to Lady Catherine, that her charming daughter seemed born to be a duchess, and that the most elevated rank, instead of giving her consequence, would be adorned by her.–

These are the kind of little things which please her ladyship, and it is a sort of attention which I conceive myself peculiarly bound to pay."

"You judge very properly," said Mr. Bennet, "and it is happy for you that you possess the talent of flattering with delicacy. May I ask whether these pleasing attentions proceed from the impulse of the moment, or are the result of previous study?"

"They arise chiefly from what is passing at the time, and though I sometimes amuse myself with suggesting and arranging such little elegant compliments as may be adapted to ordinary occasions, I always wish to give them as unstudied an air as possible."

Mr. Bennet's expectations were fully answered. His cousin was as absurd as he had hoped, and he listened to him with the keenest enjoyment, maintaining at the same time the most resolute composure of countenance, and except in an occasional glance at Elizabeth, requiring no partner in his pleasure.

By tea-time however the dose had been enough, and Mr. Bennet was glad to take his guest into the drawing-room again, and when tea was over, glad to invite him to read aloud to the ladies. Mr. Collins readily assented, and a book was produced; but on beholding it, (for every thing announced it to be from a circulating library,) he started back, and begging pardon, protested that he never read novels.—Kitty stared at him, and Lydia exclaimed.— Other books were produced, and after some deliberation he chose Fordyce's Sermons. Lydia gaped as he opened the volume, and before he had, with very monotonous solemnity, read three pages, she interrupted him with,

"Do you know, mama, that my uncle Philips talks of turning away Richard, and if he does, Colonel Forster will hire him. My aunt told me so herself on Saturday. I shall walk to Meryton tomorrow to hear more about it, and to ask when Mr. Denny comes back from town."

Lydia was bid by her two eldest sisters to hold her tongue; but Mr. Collins, much offended, laid aside his book, and said,

"I have often observed how little young ladies are interested

by books of a serious stamp, though written solely for their benefit. It amazes me, I confess; – for certainly, there can be nothing
so advantageous to them as instruction. But I will no longer importune my young cousin."

Then turning to Mr. Bennet, he offered himself as his antagonist
at backgammon. Mr. Bennet accepted the challenge, observing
that he acted very wisely in leaving the girls to their own trifling
amusements. Mrs. Bennet and her daughters apologised most civilly for Lydia's interruption, and promised that it should not occur
again, if he would resume his book; but Mr. Collins, after assuring them that he bore his young cousin no ill will, and should
never resent her behaviour as any affront, seated himself at another
table with Mr. Bennet, and prepared for backgammon.

CHAPTER 15

Mr. Collins was not a sensible man, and the deficiency of nature
had been but little assisted by education or society; the greatest
part of his life having been spent under the guidance of an il-
literate and miserly father; and though he belonged to one of the
universities, he had merely kept the necessary terms, without forming at it any useful acquaintance. The subjection in which his
father had brought him up, had given him originally great humility of manner, but it was now a good deal counteracted by
the self-conceit of a weak head, living in retirement, and the con-
sequential feelings of early and unexpected prosperity. A fortunate
chance had recommended him to Lady Catherine de Bourgh when
the living of Hunsford was vacant; and the respect which he felt
for her high rank, and his veneration for her as his patroness,
mingling with a very good opinion of himself, of his authority
as a clergyman, and his rights as a rector, made him altogether
a mixture of pride and obsequiousness, self-importance and
humility.

Having now a good house and very sufficient income, he intended to marry; and in seeking a reconciliation with the Longbourn family he had a wife in view, as he meant to chuse one of the daughters, if he found them as handsome and amiable as they were represented by common report. This was his plan of amends – of atonement – for inheriting their father's estate; and he thought it an excellent one, full of eligibility and suitableness, and excessively generous and disinterested on his own part.

His plan did not vary on seeing them. – Miss Bennet's lovely face confirmed his views, and established all his strictest notions of what was due to seniority; and for the first evening *she* was his settled choice. The next morning, however, made an alteration; for in a quarter of an hour's tête-à-tête with Mrs. Bennet before breakfast, a conversation beginning with his parsonage-house, and leading naturally to the avowal of his hopes, that a mistress for it might be found at Longbourn, produced from her, amid very complaisant smiles and general encouragement, a caution against the very Jane he had fixed on. – "As to her *younger* daughters she could not take upon her to say – she could not positively answer – but she did not *know* of any prepossession; – her *eldest* daughter, she must just mention – she felt it incumbent on her to hint, was likely to be very soon engaged."

Mr. Collins had only to change from Jane to Elizabeth – and it was soon done – done while Mrs. Bennet was stirring the fire. Elizabeth, equally next to Jane in birth and beauty, succeeded her of course.

Mrs. Bennet treasured up the hint, and trusted that she might soon have two daughters married; and the man whom she could not bear to speak of the day before, was now high in her good graces.

Lydia's intention of walking to Meryton was not forgotten; every sister except Mary agreed to go with her; and Mr. Collins was to attend them, at the request of Mr. Bennet, who was most anxious to get rid of him, and have his library to himself; for thither Mr. Collins had followed him after breakfast, and there he would con-

tinue, nominally engaged with one of the largest folios in the collection, but really talking to Mr. Bennet, with little cessation, of
his house and garden at Hunsford. Such doings discomposed Mr.
Bennet exceedingly. In his library he had been always sure of leisure
and tranquillity; and though prepared, as he told Elizabeth, to
meet with folly and conceit in every other room in the house,
he was used to be free from them there: his civility, therefore,
was most prompt in inviting Mr. Collins to join his daughters in
their walk; and Mr. Collins, being in fact much better fitted for
a walker than a reader, was extremely well pleased to close his
large book, and go.

In pompous nothings on his side, and civil assents on that
of his cousins, their time passed till they entered Meryton. The
attention of the younger ones was then no longer to be gained
by *him*. Their eyes were immediately wandering up in the street
in quest of the officers, and nothing less than a very smart bonnet indeed, or a really new muslin in a shop window, could recal
them.

But the attention of every lady was soon caught by a young
man, whom they had never seen before, of most gentlemanlike
appearance, walking with an officer on the other side of the way.
The officer was the very Mr. Denny, concerning whose return from
London Lydia came to inquire, and he bowed as they passed. All
were struck with the stranger's air, all wondered who he could
be, and Kitty and Lydia, determined if possible to find out, led
the way across the street, under pretence of wanting something
in an opposite shop, and fortunately had just gained the pavement when the two gentlemen turning back had reached the same
spot. Mr. Denny addressed them directly, and entreated permission to introduce his friend, Mr. Wickham, who had returned with
him the day before from town, and he was happy to say had accepted a commission in their corps. This was exactly as it should
be; for the young man wanted only regimentals to make him completely charming. His appearance was greatly in his favour; he
had all the best part of beauty, a fine countenance, a good figure,

and very pleasing address. The introduction was followed up on his side by a happy readiness of conversation – a readiness at the same time perfectly correct and unassuming; and the whole party were still standing and talking together very agreeably, when the sound of horses drew their notice, and Darcy and Bingley were seen riding down the street. On distinguishing the ladies of the group, the two gentlemen came directly towards them, and began the usual civilities. Bingley was the principal spokesman, and Miss Bennet the principal object. He was then, he said, on his way to Longbourn on purpose to inquire after her. Mr. Darcy corroborated it with a bow, and was beginning to determine not to fix his eyes on Elizabeth, when they were suddenly arrested by the sight of the stranger, and Elizabeth happening to see the countenance of both as they looked at each other, was all astonishment at the effect of the meeting. Both changed colour, one looked white, the other red. Mr. Wickham, after a few moments, touched his hat – a salutation which Mr. Darcy just deigned to return. What could be the meaning if it? – It was impossible to imagine; it was impossible not to long to know.

In another minute Mr. Bingley, but without seeming to have noticed what passed, took leave and rode on with his friend.

Mr. Denny and Mr. Wickham walked with the young ladies to the door of Mr. Philips's house, and then made their bows, in spite of Miss Lydia's pressing entreaties that they would come in, and even in spite of Mrs. Philips's throwing up the parlour window, and loudly seconding the invitation.

Mrs. Philips was always glad to see her nieces, and the two eldest, from their recent absence, were particularly welcome, and she was eagerly expressing her surprise at their sudden return home, which, as their own carriage had not fetched them, she should have known nothing about, if she had not happened to see Mr. Jones's shop boy in the street, who had told her that they were not to send any more draughts to Netherfield because the Miss Bennets were come away, when her civility was claimed towards Mr. Collins by Jane's introduction of him. She received him with her very best politeness, which he returned with as much more, apologising for his intrusion, without any previous acquaintance with her, which he could not help flattering himself however might be justified by his relationship to the young ladies who introduced him to her notice. Mrs. Philips was quite awed by such an excess of good breeding; but her contemplation of one stranger was soon put an end to by exclamations and inquiries about the other, of whom, however, she could only tell her nieces what they already knew, that Mr. Denny had brought him from London, and that he was to have a lieutenant's commission in the ——shire. She had been watching him the last hour, she said, as he walked up and down the street, and had Mr. Wickham appeared Kitty and Lydia would certainly have continued the occupation, but unluckily no one passed the windows now except a few of the officers, who in comparison with the stranger, were become "stupid, disagreeable fellows." Some of them were to dine with the Philipses the next day, and their aunt promised to make her husband call on Mr. Wickham, and give him an invitation also, if the family from Longbourn would come in the evening. This was agreed to, and Mrs. Philips protested that they would have a nice comfortable noisy game of lottery tickets, and a little bit of hot supper afterwards. The prospect of such delights was very cheering, and they parted in mutual good spirits. Mr. Collins repeated his apologies in quitting the room, and was assured with unwearying civility that they were perfectly needless.

As they walked home, Elizabeth related to Jane what she had seen pass between the two gentlemen; but though Jane would have defended either or both, had they appeared to be wrong, she could no more explain such behaviour than her sister.

Mr. Collins on his return highly gratified Mrs. Bennet by admiring Mrs. Philips's manners and politeness. He protested that except Lady Catherine and her daughter, he had never seen a more elegant woman; for she had not only received him with the utmost civility, but had even pointedly included him in her invitation for the next evening, although utterly unknown to her before.

Something he supposed might be attributed to his connection with them, but yet he had never met with so much attention in the whole course of his life.

CHAPTER 16

As no objection was made to the young people's engagement with their aunt, and all Mr. Collins's scruples of leaving Mr. and Mrs. Bennet for a single evening during his visit were most steadily resisted, the coach conveyed him and his five cousins at a suitable hour to Meryton; and the girls had the pleasure of hearing, as they entered the drawing-room, that Mr. Wickham had accepted their uncle's invitation, and was then in the house.

When this information was given, and they had all taken their seats, Mr. Collins was at leisure to look around him and admire, and he was so much struck with the size and furniture of the apartment, that he declared he might almost have supposed himself in the small summer breakfast parlour at Rosings; a comparison that did not at first convey much gratification; but when Mrs. Philips understood from him what Rosings was, and who was its proprietor, when she had listened to the description of only one of Lady Catherine's drawing-rooms, and found that the chimney-piece alone had cost eight hundred pounds, she felt all the force of the compliment, and would hardly have resented a comparison with the housekeeper's room.

In describing to her all the grandeur of Lady Catherine and her mansion, with occasional digressions in praise of his own humble abode, and the improvements it was receiving, he was happily employed until the gentlemen joined them; and he found in Mrs. Philips a very attentive listener, whose opinion of his consequence increased with what she heard, and who was resolving to retail it all among her neighbours as soon as she could. To the girls, who could not listen to their cousin, and who had nothing to do but to wish for an instrument, and examine their own indifferent imitations of china on the mantlepiece, the interval of waiting appeared very long. It was over at last however. The gentlemen did approach; and when Mr. Wickham walked into the room, Elizabeth felt that she had neither been seeing him before, nor thinking of him since, with the smallest degree of unreasonable admiration. The officers of the ——shire were in general a very creditable, gentlemanlike set, and the best of them were of the present party; but Mr. Wickham was as far beyond them all in person, countenance, air, and walk, as *they* were superior to the broad-faced stuffy uncle Philips, breathing port wine, who followed them into the room.

Mr. Wickham was the happy man towards whom almost every female eye was turned, and Elizabeth was the happy woman by whom he finally seated himself; and the agreeable manner in which he immediately fell into conversation, though it was only on its being a wet night, and on the probability of a rainy season, made her feel that the commonest, dullest, most threadbare topic might be rendered interesting by the skill of the speaker.

With such rivals for the notice of the fair, as Mr. Wickham and the officers, Mr. Collins seemed likely to sink into insignificance; to the young ladies he certainly was nothing; but he had still at intervals a kind listener in Mrs. Philips, and was, by her watchfulness, most abundantly supplied with coffee and muffin.

When the card tables were placed, he had an opportunity of obliging her in return, by sitting down to whist.

"I know little of the game, at present," said he, "but I shall be glad to improve myself, for in my situation of life"–Mrs. Philips was very thankful for his compliance, but could not wait for his reason.

Mr. Wickham did not play at whist, and with ready delight was he received at the other table between Elizabeth and Lydia. At first there seemed danger of Lydia's engrossing him entirely, for she was a most determined talker; but being likewise extremely fond of lottery tickets, she soon grew too much interested in the game, too eager in making bets and exclaiming after prizes, to have attention for any one in particular. Allowing for the common demands of the game, Mr. Wickham was therefore at leisure to talk to Elizabeth, and she was very willing to hear him, though what she chiefly wished to hear she could not hope to be told, the history of his acquaintance with Mr. Darcy. She dared not even mention that gentleman. Her curiosity however was unexpectedly relieved. Mr. Wickham began the subject himself. He inquired how far Netherfield was from Meryton; and after receiving her answer, asked in an hesitating manner how long Mr. Darcy had been staying there.

"About a month," said Elizabeth; and then, unwilling to let the subject drop, added, "he is a man of very large property in Derbyshire, I understand."

"Yes," replied Wickham;—"his estate there is a noble one. A clear ten thousand per annum. You could not have met with a person more capable of giving you certain information on that head than myself—for I have been connected with his family in a particular manner from my infancy."

Elizabeth could not but look surprised.

"You may well by surprised, Miss Bennet, at such an assertion, after seeing, as you probably might, the very cold manner of our meeting yesterday.—Are you much acquainted with Mr. Darcy?"

"As much as I ever wish to be," cried Elizabeth warmly,—"I have spent four days in the same house with him, and I think him very disagreeable."

"I have no right to give *my* opinion," said Wickham, "as to his being agreeable or otherwise. I am not qualified to form one. I have known him too long and too well to be a fair judge. It is impossible for *me* to be impartial. But I believe your opinion of him would in general astonish—and perhaps you would not express it quite so strongly any where else.—Here you are in your own family."

"Upon my word I say no more *here* than I might say in any house in the neighbourhood, except Netherfield. He is not at all liked in Hertfordshire. Every body is disgusted with his pride. You will not find him more favourably spoken of by any one."

"I cannot pretend to be sorry," said Wickham, after a short interruption, "that he or that any man should not be estimated beyond their deserts; but with *him* I believe it does not often happen. The world is blinded by his fortune and consequence, or frightened by his high and imposing manners, and sees him only as he chuses to be seen."

"I should take him, even on *my* slight acquaintance, to be an ill-tempered man." Wickham only shook his head.

"I wonder," said he, at the next opportunity of speaking, "whether he is likely to be in this country much longer."

"I do not at all know; but I *heard* nothing of his going away when I was at Netherfield. I hope your plans in favour of the ——shire will not be affected by his being in the neighbourhood."

"Oh! no—it is not for *me* to be driven away by Mr. Darcy. If *he* wishes to avoid seeing *me,* he must go. We are not on friendly terms, and it always gives me pain to meet him, but I have no reason for avoiding *him* but what I might proclaim to all the world; a sense of very great ill usage, and most painful regrets at his being what he is. His father, Miss Bennet, the late Mr. Darcy, was one of the best men that ever breathed, and the truest friend I ever had; and I can never be in company with this Mr. Darcy without being grieved to the soul by a thousand tender recollections. His behaviour to myself has been scandalous; but I verily believe I could forgive him any thing and every thing, rather than his disappointing the hopes and disgracing the memory of his father."

Elizabeth found the interest of the subject increase, and listened with all her heart; but the delicacy of it prevented farther inquiry.

Mr. Wickham began to speak on more general topics, Meryton, the neighbourhood, the society, appearing highly pleased with all that he had yet seen, and speaking of the latter especially, with gentle but very intelligible gallantry.

"It was the prospect of constant society, and good society," he added, "which was my chief inducement to enter the ——shire. I knew it to be a most respectable, agreeable corps, and my friend Denny tempted me farther by his account of their present quarters, and the very great attentions and excellent acquaintance Meryton had procured them. Society, I own, is necessary to me. I have been a disappointed man, and my spirits will not bear solitude. I *must* have employment and society. A military life is not what I was intended for, but circumstances have now made it eligible. The church *ought* to have been my profession—I was brought up for the church, and I should at this time have been in possession of a most valuable living, had it pleased the gentleman we were speaking of just now."

"Indeed!"

"Yes—the late Mr. Darcy bequeathed me the next presentation of the best living in his gift. He was my godfather, and excessively attached to me. I cannot do justice to his kindness. He meant to provide for me amply, and thought he had done it; but when the living fell, it was given elsewhere."

"Good heavens!" cried Elizabeth; "but how could *that* be?—How could his will be disregarded?—Why did not you seek legal redress?"

"There was just such an informality in the terms of the bequest as to give me no hope from law. A man of honour could not have doubted the intention, but Mr. Darcy chose to doubt it—or to treat it as a merely conditional recommendation, and to assert that I had forfeited all claim to it by extravagance, imprudence, in short anything or nothing. Certain it is, that the living became vacant two years ago, exactly as I was of an age to hold it, and that it was given to another man; and no less certain is it, that I cannot accuse myself of having really done any thing to deserve to lose it. I have a warm, unguarded temper, and I may perhaps have sometimes spoken my opinion *of* him, and *to* him, too freely. I can recal nothing worse. But the fact is, that we are very different sort of men, and that he hates me."

"This is quite shocking!—He deserves to be publicly disgraced."

"Some time or other he *will* be—but it shall not be by *me*. Till I can forget his father, I can never defy or expose *him*.

Elizabeth honoured him for such feelings, and thought him handsomer than ever as he expressed them.

"But what," said she, after a pause, "can have been his motive?— what can have induced him to behave so cruelly?"

"A thorough, determined dislike of me—a dislike which I cannot but attribute in some measure to jealousy. Had the late Mr. Darcy liked me less, his son might have borne with me better; but his father's uncommon attachment to me, irritated him I believe very early in life. He had not a temper to bear the sort of competition in which we stood—the sort of preference which was often given me."

"I had not thought Mr. Darcy so bad as this—though I have never liked him, I had not thought so very ill of him—I had supposed him to be despising his fellow-creatures in general, but did not suspect him of descending to such malicious revenge, such injustice, such inhumanity as this!"

After a few minutes reflection, however, she continued, "I *do* remember his boasting one day, at Netherfield, of the implacability of his resentments, of his having an unforgiving temper. His disposition must be dreadful."

"I will not trust myself on the subject," replied Wickham, "*I* can hardly be just to him."

Elizabeth was again deep in thought, and after a time exclaimed, "To treat in such a manner, the godson, the friend, the favourite of his father!"—She could have added, "A young man too, like *you*, whose very countenance may vouch for your being amiable"— but she contented herself with "And one, too, who had probably been his own companion from childhood, connected together, as I think you said, in the closest manner!"

"We were born in the same parish, within the same park, the greatest part of our youth was passed together; inmates of the same house, sharing the same amusements, objects of the same parental care. My father began life in the profession which your uncle, Mr. Philips, appears to do so much credit to – but he gave up every thing to be of use to the late Mr. Darcy, and devoted all his time to the care of the Pemberley property. He was most highly esteemed by Mr. Darcy, a most intimate, confidential friend. Mr. Darcy often acknowledged himself to be under the greatest obligations to my father's active superintendance, and when immediately before my father's death, Mr. Darcy gave him a voluntary promise of providing for me, I am convinced that he felt it to be as much a debt of gratitude to *him,* as of affection to myself."

"How strange!" cried Elizabeth. "How abominable! – I wonder that the very pride of this Mr. Darcy has not made him just to you! – If from no better motive, that he should not have been too proud to be dishonest, – for dishonesty I must call it."

"It *is* wonderful," – replied Wickham, – "for almost all his actions may be traced to pride; – and pride has often been his best friend. It has connected him nearer with virtue than any other feeling. But we are none of us consistent; and in his behaviour to me, there were stronger impulses even than pride."

"Can such abominable pride as his have ever done him good?"

"Yes. It has often led him to be liberal and generous, – to give his money freely, to display hospitality, to assist his tenants, and relieve the poor. Family pride, and *filial* pride, for he is very proud of what his father was, have done this. Not to appear to disgrace his family, to degenerate from the popular qualities, or lose the influence of the Pemberley House, is a powerful motive. He has also *brotherly* pride, which with *some* brotherly affection, makes him a very kind and careful guardian of his sister; and you will hear him generally cried up as the most attentive and best of brothers."

"What sort of a girl is Miss Darcy?"

He shook his head. – "I wish I could call her amiable. It gives me pain to speak ill of a Darcy. But she is too much like her brother, – very, very proud. – As a child, she was affectionate and pleasing, and extremely fond of me; and I have devoted hours and hours to her amusement. But she is nothing to me now. She is a handsome girl, about fifteen or sixteen, and I understand highly accomplished. Since her father's death, her home has been London, where a lady lives with her, and superintends her education."

After many pauses and many trials of other subjects, Elizabeth could not help reverting once more to the first, and saying,

"I am astonished at his intimacy with Mr. Bingley! How can Mr. Bingley, who seems good humour itself, and is, I really believe, truly amiable, be in friendship with such a man? How can they suit each other?—Do you know Mr. Bingley?"

"Not at all."

"He is a sweet tempered, amiable, charming man. He cannot know what Mr. Darcy is."

"Probably not;—but Mr. Darcy can please where he chuses. He does not want abilities. He can be a conversible companion if he thinks it worth his while. Among those who are at all his equals in consequence, he is a very different man from what he is to the less prosperous. His pride never deserts him; but with the rich, he is liberal-minded, just, sincere, rational, honourable, and perhaps agreeable,—allowing something for fortune and figure."

The whist party soon afterwards breaking up, the players gathered round the other table, and Mr. Collins took his station between his cousin Elizabeth and Mrs. Philips.—The usual inquiries as to his success were made by the latter. It had not been very great; he had lost every point; but when Mrs. Philips began to express her concern thereupon, he assured her with much earnest gravity that it was not of the least importance, that he considered the money as a mere trifle, and begged she would not make herself uneasy.

"I know very well, madam," said he, "that when persons sit down to a card table, they must take their chance of these things,—and happily I am not in such circumstances as to make five shillings any object. There are undoubtedly many who could not say the same, but thanks to Lady Catherine de Bourgh, I am removed far beyond the necessity of regarding little matters."

Mr. Wickham's attention was caught; and after observing Mr. Collins for a few moments, he asked Elizabeth in a low voice whether her relation were very intimately acquainted with the family of de Bourgh.

"Lady Catherine de Bourgh," she replied, "has very lately given him a living. I hardly know how Mr. Collins was first introduced to her notice, but he certainly has not known her long."

"You know of course that Lady Catherine de Bourgh and Lady Anne Darcy were sisters; consequently that she is aunt to the present Mr. Darcy."

"No, indeed, I did not.—I knew nothing at all of Lady Catherine's connections. I never heard of her existence till the day before yesterday."

"Her daughter, Miss de Bourgh, will have a very large fortune, and it is believed that she and her cousin will unite the two estates."

This information made Elizabeth smile, as she thought of poor Miss Bingley. Vain indeed must be all her attentions, vain and useless her affection for his sister and her praise of himself, if he were already self-destined to another.

"Mr. Collins," said she, "speaks highly both of Lady Catherine and her daughter; but from some particulars that he has related of her ladyship, I suspect his gratitude misleads him, and that in spite of her being his patroness, she is an arrogant, conceited woman."

"I believe her to be both in a great degree," replied Wickham; "I have not seen her for many years, but I very well remember that I never liked her, and that her manners were dictatorial and insolent. She has the reputation of being remarkably sensible and clever; but I rather believe she derives part of her abilities from her rank and fortune, part from her authoritative manner, and the rest from the pride of her nephew, who chuses that every one connected with him should have an understanding of the first class."

Elizabeth allowed that he had given a very rational account of it, and they continued talking together with mutual satisfaction till supper put an end to cards; and gave the rest of the ladies their share of Mr. Wickham's attentions. There could be no conversation in the noise of Mrs. Philips's supper party, but his manners recommended him to every body. Whatever he said, was said well; and whatever he did, done gracefully. Elizabeth went away with her head full of him. She could think of nothing but of Mr. Wickham, and of what he had told her, all the way home; but there was not time for her even to mention his name as they went, for neither Lydia nor Mr. Collins were once silent. Lydia talked incessantly of lottery tickets, of the fish she had lost and the fish she had won, and Mr. Collins, in describing the civility of Mr. and Mrs. Philips, protesting that he did not in the least regard his losses at whist, enumerating all the dishes at supper, and repeatedly fearing that he crouded his cousins, had more to say than he could well manage before the carriage stopped at Longbourn House.

CHAPTER 17

Elizabeth related to Jane the next day, what had passed between Mr. Wickham and herself. Jane listened with astonishment and concern;—she knew not how to believe that Mr. Darcy could be so unworthy of Mr. Bingley's regard; and yet, it was not in her nature to question the veracity of a young man of such amiable appearance as Wickham.—The possibility of his having really endured such unkindness, was enough to interest all her tender feelings; and nothing therefore remained to be done, but to think well of them both, to defend the conduct of each, and throw into the account of accident or mistake, whatever could not be otherwise explained.

"They have both," said she, "been deceived, I dare say, in some way or other, of which we can form no idea. Interested people have perhaps misrepresented each to the other. It is, in short, impossible for us to conjecture the causes or circumstances which may have alienated them, without actual blame on either side."

"Very true, indeed;—and now, my dear Jane, what have you got to say in behalf of the interested people who have probably been concerned in the business?—Do clear *them* too, or we shall be obliged to think ill of somebody."

"Laugh as much as you chuse, but you will not laugh me out of my opinion. My dearest Lizzy, do but consider in what a disgraceful light it places Mr. Darcy, to be treating his father's favourite in such a manner,—one, whom his father had promised to provide for.—It is impossible. No man of common humanity, no man who had any value for his character, could be capable of it. Can his most intimate friends be so excessively deceived in him? oh! no."

"I can much more easily believe Mr. Bingley's being imposed on, than that Mr. Wickham should invent such a history of himself as he gave me last night; names, facts, every thing mentioned without ceremony.—If it be not so, let Mr. Darcy contradict it. Besides, there was truth in his looks."

"It is difficult indeed—it is distressing.—One does not know what to think."

"I beg your pardon;—one knows exactly what to think."

But Jane could think with certainty on only one point,—that Mr. Bingley, if he *had been* imposed on, would have much to suffer when the affair became public.

The two young ladies were summoned from the shrubbery where this conversation passed, by the arrival of some of the very persons of whom they had been speaking; Mr. Bingley and his sisters came to give their personal invitation for the long expected ball at Netherfield, which was fixed for the following Tuesday. The two ladies were delighted to see their dear friend again, called it an age since they had met, and repeatedly asked what she had been doing with herself since their separation. To the rest of the family they paid little attention; avoiding Mrs. Bennet as much as possible, saying not much to Elizabeth, and nothing at all to the others. They were soon gone again, rising from their seats with an activity which took their brother by surprise, and hurrying off as if eager to escape from Mrs. Bennet's civilities.

The prospect of the Netherfield ball was extremely agreeable to every female of the family. Mrs. Bennet chose to consider it as given in compliment to her eldest daughter, and was particularly flattered by receiving the invitation from Mr. Bingley himself, instead of a ceremonious card. Jane pictured to herself a happy evening in the society of her two friends, and the attentions of their brother; and Elizabeth thought with pleasure of dancing a great deal with Mr. Wickham, and of seeing a confirmation of every thing in Mr. Darcy's looks and behaviour. The happiness anticipated by Catherine and Lydia, depended less on any single event, or any particular person, for though they each, like Elizabeth, meant to dance half the evening with Mr. Wickham, he was by no means the only partner who could satisfy them, and a ball was at any rate, a ball. And even Mary could assure her family that she had no disinclination for it.

"While I can have my mornings to myself," said she, "it is enough.—I think it no sacrifice to join occasionally in evening engagements. Society had claims on us all; and I profess myself one of those who consider intervals of recreation and amusement as desirable for every body."

Elizabeth's spirits were so high on the occasion, that though she did not often speak unnecessarily to Mr. Collins, she could not help asking him whether he intended to accept Mr. Bingley's invitation, and if he did, whether he would think it proper to join in the evening's amusement; and she was rather surprised to find that he entertained no scruple whatever on that head, and was very far from dreading a rebuke either from the Archbishop, or Lady Catherine de Bourgh, by venturing to dance.

"I am by no means of opinion, I assure you," said he, "that a ball of this kind, given by a young man of character, to respectable people, can have any evil tendency; and I am so far from objecting to dancing myself that I shall hope to be honoured with

the hands of all my fair cousins in the course of the evening, and
I take this opportunity of soliciting yours, Miss Elizabeth, for the
two first dances especially,—a preference which I trust my cousin
Jane will attribute to the right cause, and not to any disrespect
for her."

Elizabeth felt herself completely taken in. She had fully proposed being engaged by Wickham for those very dances:—and
to have Mr. Collins instead!—her liveliness had been never worse
timed. There was no help for it however. Mr. Wickham's happiness and her own was per force delayed a little longer, and Mr.
Collins's proposal accepted with as good a grace as she could.
She was not the better pleased with his gallantry, from the idea
it suggested of something more.—It now first struck her, that *she*
was selected from among her sisters as worthy of being the mistress of Hunsford Parsonage, and of assisting to form a quadrille
table at Rosings, in the absence of more eligible visitors. The idea
soon reached to conviction, as she observed his increasing civilities towards herself, and heard his frequent attempt at a compliment on her wit and vivacity; and though more astonished than
gratified herself, by this effect of her charms, it was not long before her mother gave her to understand that the probability of
their marriage was exceedingly agreeable to *her.* Elizabeth however
did not chuse to take the hint, being well aware that a serious
dispute must be the consequence of any reply. Mr. Collins might
never make the offer, and till he did, it was useless to quarrel
about him.

If there had not been a Netherfield ball to prepare for and talk
of, the younger Miss Bennets would have been in a pitiable state
at this time, for from the day of the invitation, to the day of the
ball, there was such a succession of rain as prevented their walking to Meryton once. No aunt, no officers, no news could be sought
after;—the very shoe-roses for Netherfield were got by proxy. Even
Elizabeth might have found some trial of her patience in weather,
which totally suspended the improvement of her acquaintance
with Mr. Wickham; and nothing less than a dance on Tuesday,

could have made such a Friday, Saturday, Sunday and Monday, endurable to Kitty and Lydia.

CHAPTER 18

Till Elizabeth entered the drawing-room at Netherfield and looked in vain for Mr. Wickham among the cluster of red coats there assembled, a doubt of his being present had never occurred to her. The certainty of meeting him had not been checked by any of those recollections that might not unreasonably have alarmed her. She had dressed with more than usual care, and prepared in the highest spirits for the conquest of all that remained un-subdued of his heart, trusting that it was not more than might be won in the course of the evening. But an instant arose the dreadful suspicion of his being purposely omitted for Mr. Darcy's pleasure in the Bingley's invitation to the officers; and though this was not exactly the case, the absolute fact of his absence was pronounced by his friend Mr. Denny, to whom Lydia eagerly ap-plied, and who told them that Wickham had been obliged to go to town on business the day before, and was not yet returned; adding, with a significant smile,

"I do not imagine his business would have called him away just now, if he had not wished to avoid a certain gentleman here."

This part of his intelligence, though unheard by Lydia, was caught by Elizabeth, and as it assured her that Darcy was not less answerable for Wickham's absence than if her first surmise had been just, every feeling of displeasure against the former was so sharpened by immediate disappointment, that she could hardly reply with tolerable civility to the polite inquiries which he directly afterwards approached to make.—Attention, forbearance, patience with Darcy was injury to Wickham. She was resolved against any sort of conversation with him, and turned away with a degree of ill humour, which she could not wholly surmount even in speaking to Mr. Bingley, whose blind partiality provoked her.

But Elizabeth was not formed for ill-humour; and though every prospect of her own was destroyed for the evening, it could not dwell long on her spirits; and having told all her griefs to Charlotte Lucas, whom she had not seen for a week, she was soon able to make a voluntary transition to the oddities of her cousin, and to point him out to her particular notice. The two first dances, however, brought a return of distress; they were dances of mortification. Mr. Collins, awkward and solemn, apologising instead of attending, and often moving wrong without being aware of it, gave her all the shame and misery which a disagreeable partner for a couple of dances can give. The moment of her release from him was exstacy.

She danced next with an officer, and had the refreshment of talking of Wickham, and of hearing that he was universally liked. When those dances were over she returned to Charlotte Lucas, and was in conversation with her, when she found herself suddenly addressed by Mr. Darcy, who took her so much by surprise in his application for her hand, that, without knowing what she did, she accepted him. He walked away again immediately, and she was left to fret over her own want of presence of mind; Charlotte tried to console her.

"I dare say you will find him very agreeable."

"Heaven forbid! – *That* would be the greatest misfortune of all! – To find a man agreeable whom one is determined to hate! – Do not wish me such an evil."

When the dancing recommenced, however, and Darcy approached to claim her hand, Charlotte could not help cautioning her in a whisper not to be a simpleton and allow her fancy for Wickham to make her appear unpleasant in the eyes of a man of ten times his consequence. Elizabeth made no answer, and took her place in the set, amazed at the dignity to which she was arrived in being allowed to stand opposite to Mr. Darcy, and reading in her neighbours' looks their equal amazement in beholding it. They stood for some time without speaking a word; and she began to imagine that their silence was to last through the two dances, and at first was resolved not to break it; till suddenly fancying that it would be the greater punishment to her partner to oblige him to talk, she made some slight observation on the dance. He replied, and was silent again. After a pause of some minutes she addressed him a second time with

"It is *your* turn to say something now, Mr. Darcy.–I talked about the dance, and *you* ought to make some kind of remark on the size of the room, or the number of couples."

He smiled, and assured her that whatever she wished him to say should be said.

"Very well.–That reply will do for the present.–Perhaps by and bye I may observe that private balls are much pleasanter than public ones.–But *now* we may be silent."

"Do you talk by rule then, while you are dancing?"

"Sometimes. One must speak a little, you know. It would look odd to be entirely silent for half an hour together, and yet for the advantage of *some,* conversation ought to be so arranged as that they may have the trouble of saying as little as possible."

"Are you consulting your own feelings in the present case, or do you imagine that you are gratifying mine?"

"Both," replied Elizabeth archly; "for I have always seen a great similarity in the turn of our minds.–We are each of an unsocial, taciturn disposition, unwilling to speak, unless we expect to say something that will amaze the whole room, and be handed down to posterity with all the eclat of a proverb."

"This is no very striking resemblance of your own character, I am sure," said he. "How near it may be to *mine,* I cannot pretend to say.–*You* think it a faithful portrait undoubtedly."

"I must not decide on my own performance."

He made no answer, and they were silent till they had gone down the dance, when he asked her if she and her sisters did not very often walk to Meryton. She answered in the affirmative, and, unable to resist the temptation, added, "When you met us there the other day, we had just been forming a new acquaintance."

The effect was immediate. A deeper shade of hauteur over-spread his features, but he said not a word, and Elizabeth, though blaming herself for her own weakness, could not go on. At length Darcy spoke, and in a constrained manner said,

"Mr. Wickham is blessed with such happy manners as may ensure his *making* friends—whether he may be equally capable of *retaining* them, is less certain."

"He has been so unlucky as to lose *your* friendship," replied Elizabeth with emphasis, "and in a manner which he is likely to suffer from all his life."

Darcy made no answer, and seemed desirous of changing the subject. At that moment Sir William Lucas appeared close to them, meaning to pass through the set to the other side of the room; but on perceiving Mr. Darcy he stopt with a bow of superior cour-tesy to compliment him on his dancing and his partner.

"I have been most highly gratified indeed, my dear Sir. Such very superior dancing is not often seen. It is evident that you be-long to the first circles. Allow me to say, however, that your fair partner does not disgrace you, and that I must hope to have this pleasure often repeated, especially when a certain desirable event, my dear Miss Eliza, (glancing at her sister and Bingley,) shall take place. What congratulations will then flow in! I appeal to Mr. Darcy:—but let me not interrupt you, Sir.— You will not thank me for detaining you from the bewitching converse of that young lady, whose bright eyes are also upbraiding me."

The latter part of this address was scarcely heard by Darcy; but Sir William's allusion to his friend seemed to strike him forcibly, and his eyes were directed with a very serious expres-sion towards Bingley and Jane, who were dancing together. Recovering himself, however, shortly, he turned to his partner, and said,

"Sir William's interruption has made me forget what we were talking of."

"I do not think we were speaking at all. Sir William could not have interrupted any two people in the room who had less to say for themselves.—We have tried two or three subjects already without success, and what we are to talk of next I cannot imagine."

"What think you of books?" said he, smiling.

"Books—Oh! no.—I am sure we never read the same, or not with the same feelings."

"I am sorry you think so; but if that be the case, there can at least be no want of subject.—We may compare our different opinions."

"No—I cannot talk of books in a ball-room; my head is always full of something else."

"The *present* always occupies you in such scenes—does it?" said he, with a look of doubt.

"Yes, always," she replied, without knowing what she said, for her thoughts had wandered far from the subject, as soon afterwards appeared by her suddenly exclaiming, "I remember hearing you once say, Mr. Darcy, that you hardly ever forgave, that your resentment once created was unappeasable. You are very cautious, I suppose, as to its *being created*."

"I am," said he, with a firm voice.

"And never allow yourself to be blinded by prejudice?"

"I hope not."

"It is particularly incumbent on those who never change their opinion, to be secure of judging properly at first."

"May I ask to what these questions tend?"

"Merely to the illustration of *your* character," said she, endeavouring to shake off her gravity. "I am trying to make it out."

"And what is your success?"

She shook her head. "I do not get on at all. I hear such different accounts of you as puzzle me exceedingly."

"I can readily believe," answered he gravely, "that report may vary greatly with respect to me; and I could wish, Miss Bennet, that you were not to sketch my character at the present moment, as there is reason to fear that the performance would reflect no credit on either."

"But if I do not take your likeness now, I may never have another opportunity."

"I would by no means suspend any pleasure of yours," he coldly replied. She said no more, and they went down the other dance and parted in silence; on each side dissatisfied, though not to an equal degree, for in Darcy's breast there was a tolerable powerful feeling towards her, which soon procured her pardon, and directed all his anger against another.

They had not long separated when Miss Bingley came towards her, and with an expression of civil disdain thus accosted her,

"So, Miss Eliza, I hear you are quite delighted with George Wickham!—Your sister has been talking to me about him, and asking me a thousand questions; and I find that the young man forgot to tell you among his other communications, that he was the son of old Wickham, the late Mr. Darcy's steward. Let me recommend you, however, as a friend, not to give implicit confidence to all his assertions; for as to Mr. Darcy's using him ill, it is perfectly false; for, on the contrary, he has been always remarkably kind to him, though George Wickham has treated Mr. Darcy in a most infamous manner. I do not know the particulars, but I know very well that Mr. Darcy is not in the least to blame, that he cannot bear to hear George Wickham mentioned, and that though my brother thought he could not well avoid including him in his invitation to the officers, he was excessively glad to find that he had taken himself out of the way. His coming into the country at all, is a most insolent thing indeed, and I wonder how he could presume to do it. I pity you, Miss Eliza, for this discovery of your favourite's guilt; but really considering his descent, one could not expect much better."

"His guilt and his descent appear by your account to be the same," said Elizabeth angrily; "for I have heard you accuse him of nothing worse than of being the son of Mr. Darcy's steward, and of *that,* I can assure you, he informed me himself."

"I beg your pardon," replied Miss Bingley, turning away with a sneer. "Excuse my interference.—It was kindly meant."

"Insolent girl!" said Elizabeth to herself.—"You are much mistaken if you expect to influence me by such a paltry attack as this. I see nothing in it but your own wilful ignorance and the malice of Mr. Darcy." She then sought her eldest sister, who had undertaken to make inquiries on the same subject of Bingley. Jane met her with a smile of such sweet complacency, a glow of such happy expression, as sufficiently marked how well she was satisfied with the occurrences of the evening.—Elizabeth instantly read her feelings, and at that moment solicitude for Wickham, resentment against his enemies, and every thing else gave way before the hope of Jane's being in the fairest way for happiness.

"I want to know," said she, with a countenance no less smiling that her sister's, "what you have learnt about Mr. Wickham. But perhaps you have been too pleasantly engaged to think of any third person; in which case you may be sure of my pardon."

"No," replied Jane, "I have not forgotten him; but I have nothing satisfactory to tell you. Mr. Bingley does not know the whole of his history, and is quite ignorant of the circumstances which have principally offended Mr. Darcy; but he will vouch for the good conduct, the probity and honour of his friend, and is perfectly convinced that Mr. Wickham has deserved much less attention from Mr. Darcy than he has received; and I am sorry to say that by his account as well as his sister's, Mr. Wickham is by no means a respectable young man. I am afraid he has been very imprudent, and has deserved to lose Mr. Darcy's regard."

"Mr. Bingley does not know Mr. Wickham himself?"

"No; he never saw him till the other morning at Meryton."

"This account then is what he has received from Mr. Darcy. I am perfectly satisfied. But what does he say of the living?"

"He does not exactly recollect the circumstances, though he has heard them from Mr. Darcy more than once, but he believes that it was left to him *conditionally* only."

"I have not a doubt of Mr. Bingley's sincerity," said Elizabeth warmly; "but you must excuse my not being convinced by assurances only. Mr. Bingley's defence if his friend was a very able one I dare say, but since he is unacquainted with several parts of the story, and has learnt the rest from that friend himself, I shall venture still to think of both gentlemen as I did before."

She then changed the discourse to one more gratifying to each, and on which there could be no difference of sentiment. Elizabeth listened with delight to the happy, though modest hopes which Jane entertained of Bingley's regard, and said all in her power to heighten her confidence in it. On their being joined by Mr. Bingley himself, Elizabeth withdrew to Miss Lucas; to whose inquiry after the pleasantness of her last partner she had scarcely replied, before Mr. Collins came up to them and told her with great exultation that he had just been so fortunate as to make a most important discovery.

"I have found out," said he, "by a singular accident, that there is now in the room a near relation of my patroness. I happened to overhear the gentleman himself mentioning to the young lady who does the honours of this house the names of his cousin Miss de Bourgh, and of her mother Lady Catherine. How wonderfully these sort of things occur! Who would have thought of my meeting with – perhaps – a nephew of Lady Catherine de Bourgh in this assembly! – I am most thankful that the discovery is made in time for me to pay my respects to him, which I am now going to do, and trust he will excuse my not having done it before. My total ignorance of the connection must plead my apology."

"You are not going to introduce yourself to Mr. Darcy?"

"Indeed I am. I shall intreat his pardon for not having done it earlier. I believe him to be Lady Catherine's *nephew*. It will be in my power to assure him that her ladyship was quite well yesterday se'nnight."

Elizabeth tried hard to dissuade him from such a scheme; assuring him that Mr. Darcy would consider his addressing him without introduction as an impertinent freedom, rather than a compliment to his aunt; that it was not in the least necessary there should be any notice on either side, and that if it were, it must belong to Mr. Darcy, the superior in consequence, to begin the acquaintance.—Mr. Collins listened to her with the determined air of following his own inclination, and when she ceased speaking, replied thus,

"My dear Miss Elizabeth, I have the highest opinion in the world of your excellent judgment in all matters within the scope of your understanding, but permit me to say that there must be a wide difference between the established forms of ceremony amongst the laity, and those which regulate the clergy; for give me leave to observe that I consider the clerical office as equal in point of dignity with the highest rank in the kingdom – provided that a proper humility of behaviour is at the same time maintained. You must therefore allow me to follow the dictates of my conscience on this occasion, which leads me to perform what I look on as a point of duty. Pardon me for neglecting to profit by your advice, which on every other subject shall be my constant guide, though in the case before us I consider myself more fitted by education and habitual study to decide on what is right than a young lady like yourself." And with a low bow he left her to attack Mr. Darcy, whose reception of his advances she eagerly watched, and whose astonishment at being so addressed was very evident. Her cousin prefaced his speech with a solemn bow, and though she could not hear a word of it, she felt as if hearing it all, and saw in the motion of his lips the words "apology," "Hunsford," and "Lady Catherine de Bourgh." – It vexed her to see him expose himself to such a man. Mr. Darcy was eyeing him with unrestrained wonder, and when at last Mr. Collins allowed him time to speak, replied with an air of distant civility. Mr. Collins, however, was not discouraged from speaking again, and Mr. Darcy's contempt seemed abundantly increasing with the length of his second speech, and at the end of it he only made him a slight bow, and moved another way. Mr. Collins then returned to Elizabeth.

"I have no reason, I assure you," said he, "to be dissatisfied with my reception. Mr. Darcy seemed much pleased with the attention. He answered me with the utmost civility, and even paid me the compliment of saying, that he was so well convinced of Lady Catherine's discernment as to be certain she could never bestow a favour unworthily. It was really a very handsome thought. Upon the whole, I am much pleased with him."

As Elizabeth had no longer any interest of her own to pursue, she turned her attention almost entirely on her sister and Mr. Bingley, and the train of agreeable reflections which her observations gave birth to, made her perhaps almost as happy as Jane. She saw her in idea settled in that very house in all the felicity which a marriage of true affection could bestow; and she felt capable under such circumstances, of endeavouring even to like Bingley's two sisters. Her mother's thoughts she plainly saw were bent the same way, and she determined not to venture near her, lest she might hear too much. When they sat down to supper, therefore, she considered it a most unlucky perverseness which placed them within one of each other; and deeply was she vexed to find that her mother was talking to that one person (Lady Lucas) freely, openly, and of nothing else but of her expectation that Jane would be soon married to Mr. Bingley.–It was an animating subject, and Mrs. Bennet seemed incapable of fatigue while enumerating the advantages of the match. His being such a charming young man, and so rich, and living but three miles from them, were the first points of self-gratulation; and then it was such a comfort to think how fond the two sisters were of Jane, and to be certain that they must desire the connection as much as she could do. It was, moreover, such a promising thing for her younger daughters, as Jane's marrying so greatly must throw them in the way of other rich men; and lastly, it was so pleasant at her time of life to be able to consign her single daughters to the care of their sister, that she might not be obliged to go into company more than she liked. It was necessary to make this circumstance a matter of pleasure, because on such occasions it is the etiquette; but no one was less likely than Mrs. Bennet to find comfort in staying at home at any period of her life. She concluded with many good wishes that Lady Lucas might soon be equally fortunate, though evidently and triumphantly believing there was not chance of it.

In vain did Elizabeth endeavour to check the rapidity of her mother's words, or persuade her to describe her felicity in a less audible whisper; for to her inexpressible vexation, she could perceive that the chief of it was overheard by Mr. Darcy, who sat opposite to them. Her mother only scolded her for being nonsensical.

"What is Mr. Darcy to me, pray, that I should be afraid of him? I am sure we owe him no such particular civility as to be obliged to say nothing *he* may not like to hear."

"For heaven's sake, madam, speak lower.—What advantage can it be to you to offend Mr. Darcy?—You will never recommend yourself to his friend by so doing."

Nothing that she could say, however, had any influence. Her mother would talk of her views in the same intelligible tone. Elizabeth blushed and blushed again with shame and vexation. She could not help frequently glancing her eye at Mr. Darcy, though every glance convinced her of what she dreaded; for though he was not always looking at her mother, she was convinced that his attention was invariably fixed by her. The expression of his face changed gradually from indignant contempt to a composed and steady gravity.

At length however Mrs. Bennet had no more to say; and Lady Lucas, who had been long yawning at the repetition of delights which she saw no likelihood of sharing, was left to the comforts of cold ham and chicken. Elizabeth now began to revive. But not long was the interval of tranquillity; for when supper was over, singing was talked of, and she had the mortification of seeing Mary, after very little entreaty, preparing to oblige the company. By many significant looks and silent entreaties, did she endeavour to prevent such a proof of complaisance,—but in vain; Mary would not understand them; such an opportunity of exhibiting was delightful to her, and she began her song. Elizabeth's eyes were fixed on her with most painful sensations; and she watched her progress through the several stanzas with an impatience which was very ill rewarded at their close; for Mary, on receiving amongst the thanks of the table, the hint of a hope that she might be prevailed on to favour them again, after the pause of half a minute began another. Mary's powers were by no means fitted for such a display; her voice was weak, and her manner affected.—Elizabeth was in agonies. She looked at Jane, to see how she bore it; but Jane was very composedly talking to Bingley. She looked at his two sisters, and saw them making signs of derision at each other, and at Darcy, who continued however impenetrably grave. She looked at her father to entreat his interference, lest Mary should be singing all night. He took the hint, and when Mary finished her second song, said aloud,

"That will do extremely well, child. You have delighted us long enough. Let the other young ladies have time to exhibit."

Mary, though pretending not to hear, was somewhat disconcerted; and Elizabeth sorry for her, and sorry for her father's speech, was afraid her anxiety had done no good.—Others of the party were now applied to.

"If I," said Mr. Collins, "were so fortunate as to be able to sing, I should have great pleasure, I am sure, in obliging the company with an air; for I consider music as a very innocent diversion, and perfectly compatible with the profession of a clergyman.—I do not mean however to assert that we can be justified in devoting too much of our time to music, for there are certainly other things to be attended to. The rector of a parish has much to do.—In the first place, he must make such an agreement for tythes as may be beneficial to himself and not offensive to his patron. He must write his own sermons; and the time that remains will not be too much for his parish duties, and the care and improvement of his dwelling, which he cannot be excused from making as comfortable as possible. And I do not think it of light importance that he should have attentive and conciliatory manners towards every body, especially towards those to whom he owes his preferment. I cannot acquit him of that duty; nor could I think well of the man who should omit an occasion of testifying his respect towards any body connected with the family." And with a bow to Mr. Darcy, he concluded his speech, which had been spoken so loud as to be heard by half the room.—Many stared.—Many smiled; but no one looked more amused than Mr. Bennet himself, while his wife seriously commended Mr. Collins for having spoken so sensibly, and observed in a half-whisper to Lady Lucas, that he was a remarkably clever, good kind of young man.

To Elizabeth it appeared, that had her family made an agreement to expose themselves as much as they could during the evening, it would have been impossible for them to play their parts with more spirit, or finer success; and happy did she think it for Bingley and her sister that some of the exhibition had escaped his notice, and that his feelings were not of a sort to be much distressed by the folly which he must have witnessed. That his two sisters and Mr. Darcy, however, should have such an opportunity of ridiculing her relations was bad enough, and she could not determine whether the silent contempt of the gentleman, or the insolent smiles of the ladies, were more intolerable.

The rest of the evening brought her little amusement. She was teazed by Mr. Collins, who continued most perseveringly by her side, and though he could not prevail with her to dance with him again, put it out of her power to dance with others. In vain did she entreat him to stand up with somebody else, and offer to introduce him to any young lady in the room. He assured her that as to dancing, he was perfectly indifferent to it; that his chief object was by delicate attentions to recommend himself to her, and that he should therefore make a point of remaining close to her the whole evening. There was no arguing upon such a project. She owed her greatest relief to her friend Miss Lucas, who often joined them, and goodnaturedly engaged Mr. Collins's conversation to herself.

She was at least free from the offence of Mr. Darcy's farther notice; though often standing within a very short distance of her, quite disengaged, he never came near enough to speak. She felt it to be the probable consequence of her allusions to Mr. Wickham, and rejoiced in it.

The Longbourn party were the last of all the company to depart; and by a manœuvre of Mrs. Bennet had to wait for their carriages a quarter of an hour after every body else was gone, which gave them time to see how heartily they were wished away by some of the family. Mrs. Hurst and her sister scarcely opened their mouths except to complain of fatigue, and were evidently impatient to have the house to themselves. They repulsed every attempt of Mrs. Bennet at conversation, and by so doing, threw a languor over the whole party, which was very little relieved by the long speeches of Mr. Collins, who was complimenting Mr. Bingley and his sisters of the elegance of their entertainment, and the hospitality and politeness which had marked their behaviour to their guests. Darcy said nothing at all. Mr. Bennet, in equal silence, was enjoying the scene. Mr. Bingley and Jane were standing together, a little detached from the rest, and talked only to each other. Elizabeth preserved as steady a silence as either Mrs. Hurst or Miss Bingley; and even Lydia was too much fatigued to utter more than the occasional exclamation of "Lord, how tired I am!" accompanied by a violent yawn.

When at length they arose to take leave, Mrs. Bennet was most pressingly civil in her hope of seeing the whole family soon at Longbourn; and addressed herself particularly to Mr. Bingley, to assure him how happy he would make them, by eating a family dinner with them at any time, without the ceremony of a formal invitation. Bingley was all grateful pleasure, and he readily engaged for taking the earliest opportunity of waiting on her, after his return from London, whither he was obliged to go the next day for a short time.

Mrs. Bennet was perfectly satisfied; and quitted the house under the delightful persuasion that, allowing for the necessary preparations of settlements, new carriages and wedding clothes, she should undoubtedly see her daughter settled at Netherfield, in the course of three or four months. Of having another daughter married to Mr. Collins, she thought with equal certainty, and with considerable, though not equal, pleasure. Elizabeth was the least dear to her of all her children; and though the man and the match were quite good enough for *her*, the worth of each was eclipsed by Mr. Bingley and Netherfield.

CHAPTER 19

The next day opened a new scene at Longbourn. Mr. Collins made his declaration in form. Having resolved to do it without loss of time, as his leave of absence extended only to the following Saturday, and having no feelings of diffidence to make it distressing to himself even at the moment, he set about it in a very orderly manner, with all the observances which he supposed a regular part of the business. On finding Mrs. Bennet, Elizabeth, and one of the younger girls together, soon after breakfast, he addressed the mother in these words,

"May I hope, Madam, for your interest with your fair daughter Elizabeth, when I solicit for the honour of a private audience with her in the course of this morning?"

Before Elizabeth had time for any thing but a blush of surprise, Mrs. Bennet instantly answered,

"Oh dear!—Yes—certainly.—I am sure Lizzy will be very happy—I am sure she can have no objection,—Come, Kitty, I want you up stairs." And gathering her work together, she was hastening away, when Elizabeth called out,

"Dear Ma'am, do not go.—I beg you will not go.—Mr. Collins must excuse me.—He can have nothing to say to me that any body need not hear. I am going away myself."

"No, no, nonsense, Lizzy.—I desire you will stay where you are."—And upon Elizabeth's seeming really, with vexed and embarrassed looks, about to escape, she added, "Lizzy, I *insist* upon your staying and hearing Mr. Collins."

Elizabeth would not oppose such an injunction—and a moment's consideration making her also sensible that it would be wisest to get it over as soon and as quietly as possible, she sat down again, and tried to conceal by incessant employment the feelings which were divided between distress and diversion. Mrs. Bennet and Kitty walked off, and as soon as they were gone Mr. Collins began.

"Believe me, my dear Miss Elizabeth, that your modesty, so

far from doing you any disservice, rather adds to your other perfections. You would have been less amiable in my eyes had there
not been this little unwillingness; but allow me to assure you that
I have your respected mother's permission for this address. You
can hardly doubt the purport of my discourse, however your natural delicacy may lead you to dissemble; my attentions have been
too marked to be mistaken. Almost as soon as I entered the house
I singled you out as the companion of my future life. But before
I am run away with by my feelings on this subject, perhaps it will
be advisable for me to state my reasons for marrying—and
moreover for coming into Hertfordshire with the design of selecting a wife, as I certainly did."

The idea of Mr. Collins, with all his solemn composure, being run away with by his feelings, made Elizabeth so near laughing that she could not use the short pause he allowed in any
attempt to stop him farther, and he continued:

"My reasons for marrying are, first, that I think it a right thing
for every clergyman in easy circumstances (like myself) to set the
example of matrimony in his parish. Secondly, that I am convinced
it well add very greatly to my happiness; and thirdly—which
perhaps I ought to have mentioned earlier, that it is the particular advice and recommendation of the very noble lady whom I
have the honour of calling patroness. Twice has she condescended to give me her opinion (unasked too!) on this subject; and
it was but the very Saturday night before I left Hunsford—between
our pools at quadrille, while Mrs. Jenkinson was arranging Miss
deBourgh's foot-stool, that she said, 'Mr. Collins, you must marry. A clergyman like you must marry.—Chuse properly, chuse a
gentlewoman for *my* sake; and for your *own,* let her be an active,
useful sort of person, not brought up high, but able to make a
small income go a good way. This is my advice. Find such a woman
as soon as you can, bring her to Hunsford, and I will visit her.'
Allow me, by the way, to observe, my fair cousin, that I do not
reckon the notice and kindness of Lady Catherine de Bourgh as
among the least of the advantages in my power to offer. You will

find her manners beyond any thing I can describe; and your wit and vivacity I think must be acceptable to her, especially when tempered with the silence and respect which her rank will inevitably excite. Thus much for my general intention in favour of matrimony; it remains to be told why my views were directed to Longbourn instead of my own neighbourhood, where I assure you there are many amiable young women. But the fact is, that being, as I am, to inherit this estate after the death of your honoured father, (who, however, may live many years longer,) I could not satisfy myself without resolving to chuse a wife from among his daughters, that the loss to them might be as little as possible, when the melancholy event takes place – which, however, as I have already said, may not be for several years. This has been my motive, my fair cousin, and I flatter myself it will not sink me in your esteem. And now nothing remains for me but to assure you in the most animated language of the violence of my affection. To fortune I am perfectly indifferent, and shall make no demand of that nature on your father, since I am well aware that it could not be complied with; and that one thousand pounds in the 4 per cents. which will not be yours till after your mother's decease, is all that you may ever be entitled to. On that head, therefore, I shall be uniformly silent; and you may assure yourself that no ungenerous reproach shall ever pass my lips when we are married."

It was absolutely necessary to interrupt him now.

"You are too hasty, Sir," she cried. "You forget that I have made no answer. Let me do it without farther loss of time. Accept my thanks for the compliment you are paying me. I am very sensible of the honour of your proposals, but it is impossible for me to do otherwise than decline them."

"I am not now to learn," replied Mr. Collins, with a formal wave of the hand, "that it is usual with young ladies to reject the addresses of the man whom they secretly mean to accept, when he first applies for their favour; and that sometimes the refusal is repeated a second or even a third time. I am therefore by no means discouraged by what you have just said, and shall hope to lead you to the altar ere long."

"Upon my word, Sir," cried Elizabeth, "your hope is rather an extraordinary one after my declaration. I do assure you that I am not one of those young ladies (if such young ladies there are) who are so daring as to risk their happiness on the chance of being asked a second time. I am perfectly serious in my refusal.—You could not make *me* happy, and I am convinced that I am the last woman in the world who would make *you* so.—Nay, were your friend Lady Catherine to know me, I am persuaded she would find me in every respect ill qualified for the situation."

"Were it certain that Lady Catherine would think so," said Mr. Collins very gravely—"but I cannot imagine that her ladyship would at all disapprove of you. And you may be certain that when I have the honour of seeing her again I shall speak in the highest terms of your modesty, economy, and other amiable qualifications."

"Indeed, Mr. Collins, all praise of me will be unnecessary. You must give me leave to judge for myself, and pay me the compliment of believing what I say. I wish you very happy and very rich, and by refusing your hand, do all in my power to prevent your being otherwise. In making me the offer, you must have satisfied the delicacy of your feelings with regard to my family, and may take possession of Longbourn estate whenever it falls, without any self-reproach. This matter may be considered, therefore, as finally settled." And rising as she thus spoke, she would have quitted the room, had not Mr. Collins thus addressed her,

"When I do myself the honour of speaking to you next on this subject I shall hope to receive a more favourable answer than you have now given me; though I am far from accusing you of cruelty at present, because I know it to be the established custom of your sex to reject a man on the first application, and perhaps you have even now said as much to encourage my suit as would be consistent with the true delicacy of the female character."

"Really, Mr. Collins," cried Elizabeth with some warmth, "you puzzle me exceedingly. If what I have hitherto said can appear to you in the form of encouragement, I know not how to express my refusal in such a way as may convince you of its being one."

"You must give me leave to flatter myself, my dear cousin, that your refusal of my addresses are merely words of course. My reasons for believing it are briefly these: — It does not appear to me that my hand is unworthy your acceptance, or that the establishment I can offer would be any other than highly desirable. My situation in life, my connections with the family of De Bourgh, and my relationship to your own, are circumstances highly in my favour; and you should take it into farther consideration that in spite of your manifold attractions, it is by no means certain that another offer of marriage may ever be made you. Your portion is unhappily so small that it will in all likelihood undo the effects of your loveliness and amiable qualifications. As I must therefore conclude that you are not serious in your rejection of me, I shall chuse to attribute it to your wish of increasing my love by suspense, according to the usual practice of elegant females."

"I do assure you, Sir, that I have no pretension whatever to that kind of elegance which consists in tormenting a respectable man. I would rather be paid the compliment of being believed sincere. I thank you again and again for the honour you have done me in your proposals, but to accept them is absolutely impossible. My feelings in every respect forbid it. Can I speak plainer? Do not consider me now as an elegant female intending to plague you, but as a rational creature speaking the truth from her heart."

"You are uniformly charming!" cried he, with an air of awkward gallantry; "and I am persuaded that when sanctioned by the express authority of both your excellent parents, my proposals will not fail of being acceptable."

To such perseverance in wilful self-deception Elizabeth would make no reply, and immediately and in silence withdrew; determined, that if he persisted in considering her repeated refusals as flattering encouragement, to apply to her father, whose negative might be uttered in such a manner as must be decisive, and whose behaviour at least could not be mistaken for the affectation and coquetry of an elegant female.

CHAPTER 20

Mr. Collins was not left long to the silent contemplation of his successful love; for Mrs. Bennet, having dawdled about in the vestibule to watch for the end of the conference, no sooner saw Elizabeth open the door and with quick step pass her towards the staircase, than she entered the breakfast-room, and congratulated both him and herself in warm terms on the happy prospect of their nearer connection. Mr. Collins received and returned these felicitations with equal pleasure, and then proceeded to relate the particulars of their interview, with the result of which he trusted he had every reason to be satisfied, since the refusal which his cousin had stedfastly given him would naturally flow from her bashful modesty and the genuine delicacy of her character.

This information, however, startled Mrs. Bennet;—she would have been glad to be equally satisfied that her daughter had meant to encourage him by protesting against his proposals, but she dared not to believe it, and could not help saying so.

"But depend upon it, Mr. Collins," she added, "that Lizzy shall be brought to reason. I will speak to her about it myself directly. She is a very headstrong foolish girl, and does not know her own interest; but I will *make* her know it."

"Pardon me for interrupting you, Madam," cried Mr. Collins; "but if she is really headstrong and foolish, I know not whether she would altogether be a very desirable wife to a man in my situation, who naturally looks for happiness in the marriage state. If therefore she actually persists in rejecting my suit, perhaps it were better not to force her into accepting me, because if liable to such defects of temper, she could not contribute much to my felicity."

"Sir, you quite misunderstand me," said Mrs. Bennet, alarmed. "Lizzy is only headstrong in such matters as these. In every thing else she is as good natured a girl as ever lived. I will go directly to Mr. Bennet, and we shall very soon settle it with her, I am sure."

She would not give him time to reply, but hurrying instantly to her husband, called out as she entered the library,

"Oh! Mr. Bennet, you are wanted immediately; we are all in an uproar. You must come and make Lizzy marry Mr. Collins, for she vows she will not have him, and if you do not make haste he will change his mind and not have *her*."

Mr. Bennet raised his eyes from his book as she entered, and fixed them on her face with a calm unconcern which was not in the least altered by her communication.

"I have not the pleasure of understanding you," said he, when she had finished her speech. "Of what are you talking?"

"Of Mr. Collins and Lizzy. Lizzy declares she will not have Mr. Collins, and Mr. Collins begins to say that he will not have Lizzy."

"And what am I to do on the occasion?—It seems an hopeless business."

"Speak to Lizzy about it yourself. Tell her that you insist upon her marrying him."

"Let her be called down. She shall hear my opinion."

Mrs. Bennet rang the bell, and Miss Elizabeth was summoned to the library.

"Come here, child," cried her father as she appeared. "I have sent for you on an affair of importance. I understand that Mr. Collins has made you an offer of marriage. Is it true?" Elizabeth replied that it was. "Very well—and this offer of marriage you have refused?"

"I have, Sir."

"Very well. We now come to the point. Your mother insists upon your accepting it. Is not it so, Mrs. Bennet?"

"Yes, or I will never see her again."

"An unhappy alternative is before you, Elizabeth. From this day you must be a stranger to one of your parents.—Your mother

will never see you again if you do *not* marry Mr. Collins, and I
will never see you again if you *do*."

Elizabeth could not but smile at such a conclusion of such
a beginning; but Mrs. Bennet, who had persuaded herself that her
husband regarded the affair as she wished, was excessively disappointed.

"What do you mean, Mr. Bennet, by talking in this way? You
promised me to *insist* upon her marrying him."

"My dear," replied her husband, "I have two small favours to
request. First, that you will allow me the free use of my understanding on the present occasion; and secondly, of my room. I
shall be glad to have the library to myself as soon as may be."

Not yet, however, in spite of her disappointment in her husband, did Mrs. Bennet give up the point. She talked to Elizabeth
again and again; coaxed and threatened her by turns. She endeavoured to secure Jane in her interest, but Jane with all possible mildness declined interfering; – and Elizabeth sometimes with
real earnestness and sometimes with playful gaiety replied to her
attacks. Though her manner varied however, her determination
never did.

Mr. Collins, meanwhile, was meditating in solitude on what
had passed. He thought too well of himself to comprehend on
what motive his cousin could refuse him; and though his pride
was hurt, he suffered in no other way. His regard for her was quite
imaginary; and the possibility of her deserving her mother's
reproach prevented his feeling any regret.

While the family were in this confusion, Charlotte Lucas came
to spend the day with them. She was met in the vestibule by Lydia,
who, flying to her, cried in half whisper, "I am glad you are come,
for there is such fun here! –What do you think has happened this
morning? –Mr. Collins has made an offer to Lizzy, and she will
not have him."

Charlotte had hardly time to answer, before they were joined
by Kitty, who came to tell the same news, and no sooner had they
entered the breakfast-room, where Mrs. Bennet was alone, than

she likewise began on the subject, calling on Miss Lucas for her compassion, and entreating her to persuade her friend Lizzy to comply with the wishes of all her family. "Pray do, my dear Miss Lucas," she added in a melancholy tone, "for nobody is on my side, nobody takes part with me, I am cruelly used, nobody feels for my poor nerves."

Charlotte's reply was spared by the entrance of Jane and Elizabeth.

"Aye, there she comes," continued Mrs. Bennet, "looking as unconcerned as may be, and caring no more for us than if we were at York, provided she can have her own way.—But I tell you what, Miss Lizzy, if you take it into your head to go on refusing every offer of marriage in this way, you will never get a husband at all—and I am sure I do not know who is to maintain you when your father is dead.—I shall not be able to keep you—and so I warn you.—I have done with you from this very day.—I told you in the library, you know, that I should never speak to you again, and you will find me as good as my word. I have no pleasure in talking to undutiful children.—Not that I have much pleasure indeed in talking to any body. People who suffer as I do from nervous complaints can have no great inclination for talking. Nobody can tell what I suffer!—But it is always so. Those who do not complain are never pitied."

Her daughters listened in silence to this effusion, sensible that any attempt to reason with or sooth her would only increase the irritation. She talked on, therefore, without interruption from any of them till they were joined by Mr. Collins, who entered with an air more stately than usual, and on perceiving whom, she said to the girls,

"Now, I do insist upon it, that you, all of you, hold your tongues, and let Mr. Collins and me have a little conversation together."

Elizabeth passed quietly out of the room, Jane and Kitty followed, but Lydia stood her ground, determined to hear all she could; and Charlotte, detained first by the civility of Mr. Collins, whose inquiries after herself and all her family were very minute, and then by a little curiosity, satisfied herself with walking to the window and pretending not to hear. In a doleful voice Mrs. Bennet thus began the projected conversation.—"Oh! Mr. Collins!"—

"My dear Madam," replied he, "let us be forever silent on this point. Far be it from me," he presently continued in a voice that marked his displeasure, "to resent the behaviour of your daughter. Resignation to inevitable evils is the duty of us all; the peculiar duty of a young man who has been so fortunate as I have been in early preferment; and I trust I am resigned. Perhaps not the less so from feeling a doubt of my positive happiness had my fair cousin honoured me with her hand; for I have often observed that resignation is never so perfect as when the blessing denied begins to lose somewhat of its value in our estimation. You will not, I hope, consider me as shewing any disrespect to your family, my dear Madam, by thus withdrawing my pretensions to your daughter's favour, without having paid yourself and Mr. Bennet the compliment of requesting you to interpose your authority in my behalf. My conduct may I fear be objectionable in having accepted my dismission from your daughter's lips instead of your own. But we are all liable to error. I have certainly meant well through the whole affair. My object has been to secure an amiable companion for myself, with due consideration for the advantage of all your family, and if my *manner* has been at all reprehensible, I here beg leave to apologise."

CHAPTER 21

The discussion of Mr. Collins's offer was now nearly at an end, and Elizabeth had only to suffer from the uncomfortable feelings necessarily attending it, and occasionally from some peevish allusion of her mother. As for the gentleman himself, *his* feelings were chiefly expressed, not by embarrassment or dejection, or by trying to avoid her, but by stiffness of manner and resentful

silence. He scarcely ever spoke to her, and the assiduous attentions which he had been so sensible of himself, were transferred
for the rest of the day to Miss Lucas, whose civility in listening
to him, was a seasonable relief to them all, and especially to her
friend.

The morrow produced no abatement of Mrs. Bennet's ill humour or ill health. Mr. Collins was also in the same state of angry pride. Elizabeth had hoped that his resentment might shorten
his visit, but his plan did not appear in the least affected by it.
He was always to have gone on Saturday, and to Saturday he still
meant to stay.

After breakfast, the girls walked to Meryton to inquire if Mr.
Wickham were returned, and to lament over his absence from
the Netherfield ball. He joined them on their entering the town
and attended them to their aunt's, where his regret and vexation,
and the concern of every body was well talked over.–To Elizabeth,
however, he voluntarily acknowledged that the necessity of his
absence *had* been self imposed.

"I found," said he, "as the time drew near, that I had better not
meet Mr. Darcy;–that to be in the same room, the same party
with him for so many hours together, might be more than I could
bear, and that scenes might arise unpleasant to more than myself."

She highly approved his forbearance, and they had leisure for
a full discussion of it, and for all the commendation which they
civilly bestowed on each other, as Wickham and another officer
walked back with them to Longbourn, and during the walk, he
particularly attended to her. His accompanying them was a double advantage; she felt all the compliment it offered to herself,
and it was most acceptable as an occasion of introducing him
to her father and mother.

Soon after their return, a letter was delivered to Miss Bennet;
it came from Netherfield, and was opened immediately. The envelope contained a sheet of elegant, little, hot pressed paper, well
covered with a lady's fair, flowing hand; and Elizabeth saw her
sister's countenance change as she read it, and saw her dwelling

intently on some particular passages. Jane recollected herself soon, and putting the letter away, tried to join with her usual cheerfulness in the general conversation; but Elizabeth felt an anxiety on the subject which drew off her attention even from Wickham; and no sooner had he and his companion taken leave, than a glance from Jane invited her to follow her upstairs. When they had gained their own room, Jane taking out the letter, said,

"This is from Caroline Bingley; what it contains, has surprised me a good deal. The whole party have left Netherfield by this time, and are on their way to town; and without any intention of coming back again. You shall hear what she says."

She then read the first sentence aloud, which comprised the information of their having just resolved to follow their brother to town directly, and of their meaning to dine that day in Grosvenor street, where Mr. Hurst had a house. The next was in these words. "I do not pretend to regret any thing I shall leave in Hertfordshire, except your society, my dearest friend; but we will hope at some future period, to enjoy many returns of the delightful intercourse we have known, and in the mean while may lessen the pain of separation by a very frequent and most unreserved correspondence. I depend on you for that." To these high flown expressions, Elizabeth listened with all the insensibility of distrust; and though the suddenness of their removal surprised her, she saw nothing in it really to lament; it was not to be supposed that their absence from Netherfield would prevent Mr. Bingley's being there; and as to the loss of their society, she was persuaded that Jane must soon cease to regard it, in the enjoyment of his.

"It is unlucky," said she, after a short pause, "that you should not be able to see your friends before they leave the country. But may we not hope that the period of future happiness to which Miss Bingley looks forward, may arrive earlier than she is aware, and that the delightful intercourse you have known as friends, will be renewed with yet greater satisfaction as sisters? – Mr. Bingley will not be detained in London by them."

"Caroline decidedly says that none of the party will return into Hertfordshire this winter. I will read it to you—

"When my brother left us yesterday, he imagined that the business which took him to London, might be concluded in three or four days, but as we are certain it cannot be so, and at the same time convinced that when Charles gets to town, he will be in no hurry to leave it again, we have determined on following him thither, that he may not be obliged to spend his vacant hours in a comfortless hotel. Many of my acquaintance are already there for the winter; I wish I could hear that you, my dearest friend, had any intention of making one in the croud, but of that I despair. I sincerely hope your Christmas in Hertfordshire may abound in the gaieties which that season generally brings, and that your beaux will be so numerous as to prevent your feeling the loss of the three, of whom we shall deprive you."

"It is evident by this," added Jane, "that he comes back no more this winter."

"It is only evident that Miss Bingley does not mean he *should*."

"Why will you think so? It must be his own doing.—He is his own master. But you do not know *all*. I *will* read you the passage which particularly hurts me. I will have no reserves from *you*."

"Mr. Darcy is impatient to see his sister, and to confess the truth, *we* are scarcely less eager to meet her again. I really do not think Georgiana Darcy has her equal for beauty, elegance, and accomplishments; and the affection she inspires in Louisa and myself, is heightened into something still more interesting, from the hope we dare to entertain of her being hereafter our sister. I do not know whether I ever before mentioned to you my feelings on this subject, but I will not leave the country without confiding them, and I trust you will not esteem them unreasonable. My brother admires her greatly already, he will have frequent opportunity now of seeing her on the most intimate footing, her relations all wish the connection as much as his own, and a sister's partiality is not misleading me, I think, when I call Charles most capable of engaging any woman's heart. With all these circumstances to favour an attachment and nothing to prevent it, am I wrong, my dearest Jane, in indulging the hope of an event which will secure the happiness of so many?" "What think you of *this* sentence, my dear Lizzy?"–said Jane as she finished it. "Is it not clear enough?– Does it not expressly declare that Caroline neither expects nor wishes me to be her sister; that she is perfectly convinced of her brother's indifference, and that if she suspects the nature of my feelings for him, she means (most kindly!) to put me on my guard? Can there be any other opinion on the subject?"

"Yes, there can; for mine is totally different.–Will you hear it?"

"Most willingly."

"You shall have it in few words. Miss Bingley sees that her brother is in love with you, and wants him to marry Miss Darcy. She follows him to town in the hope of keeping him there, and tries to persuade you that he does not care about you."

Jane shook her head.

"Indeed, Jane, you ought to believe me.–No one who has ever seen you together, can doubt his affection. Miss Bingley I am sure cannot. She is not such a simpleton. Could she have seen half as much love in Mr. Darcy for herself, she would have ordered her wedding clothes. But the case is this. We are not rich enough, or grand enough for them; and she is the more anxious to get Miss Darcy for her brother, from the notion that when there has been *one* intermarriage, she may have less trouble in achieving a second; in which there is certainly some ingenuity, and I dare say it would succeed, if Miss de Bourgh were out of the way. But, my dearest Jane, you cannot seriously imagine that because Miss Bingley tells you her brother greatly admires Miss Darcy, he is in the smallest degree less sensible of *your* merit than when he took leave of you on Tuesday, or that it will be in her power to persuade him that instead of being in love with you, he is very much in love with her friend."

"If we thought alike of Miss Bingley." replied Jane, "your representation of all this, might make me quite easy. But I know the foundation is unjust. Caroline is incapable of wilfully deceiving any one; and all that I can hope in this case is, that she is deceived herself."

"That is right.—You could not have started a more happy idea, since you will not take comfort in mine. Believe her to be deceived by all means. You have now done your duty by her, and must fret no longer."

"But, my dear sister, can I be happy, even supposing the best, in accepting a man whose sisters and friends are all wishing him to marry elsewhere?"

"You must decide for yourself," said Elizabeth, "and if upon mature deliberation, you find that the misery of disobliging his two sisters is more than equivalent to the happiness of being his wife, I advise you by all means to refuse him."

"How can you talk so?"—said Jane faintly smiling,—"you must know that though I should be exceedingly grieved at their disapprobation, I could not hesitate."

"I did not think you would;—and that being the case, I cannot consider your situation with much compassion."

"But if he returns no more this winter, my choice will never be required. A thousand things may arise in six months!"

The idea of his returning no more Elizabeth treated with the utmost contempt. It appeared to her merely the suggestion of Caroline's interested wishes, and she could not for a moment suppose that those wishes, however openly or artfully spoken, could influence a young man so totally independent of every one.

She represented to her sister as forcibly as possible what she felt on the subject, and had soon the pleasure of seeing its happy effect. Jane's temper was not desponding, and she was gradually led to hope, though the diffidence of affection sometimes overcame the hope, that Bingley would return to Netherfield and answer every wish of her heart.

They agreed that Mrs. Bennet should only hear of the departure of the family, without being alarmed on the score of the gentleman's conduct; but even this partial communication gave her a great deal of concern, and she bewailed it as exceedingly unlucky

that the ladies should happen to go away, just as they were all
getting so intimate together. After lamenting it however at some
length, she had the consolation of thinking that Mr. Bingley would
be soon down again and soon dining at Longbourn, and the conclusion of all was the comfortable declaration that, though he had
been invited only to a family dinner, she would take care to have
two full courses.

CHAPTER 22

The Bennets were engaged to dine with the Lucases, and again
during the chief of the day, was Miss Lucas so kind as to listen
to Mr. Collins. Elizabeth took an opportunity of thanking her. "It
keeps him in good humour," said she, "and I am more obliged
to you than I can express." Charlotte assured her friend of her
satisfaction in being useful, and that it amply repaid her for the
little sacrifice of her time. This was very amiable, but Charlotte's
kindness extended farther than Elizabeth had any conception of;—
its object was nothing less, than to secure her from any return
of Mr. Collins's addresses, by engaging them towards herself. Such
was Miss Lucas's scheme; and appearances were so favourable that
when they parted at night, she would have felt almost sure of success if he had not been to leave Hertfordshire so very soon. But
here, she did injustice to the fire and independence of his character, for it led him to escape out of Longbourn House the next morning with admirable slyness, and hasten to Lucas Lodge to throw
himself at her feet. He was anxious to avoid the notice of his cousins, from a conviction that if they saw him depart, they could not
fail to conjecture his design, and he was not willing to have the
attempt known till its success could be known likewise; for though
feeling almost secure, and with reason, for Charlotte had been
tolerably encouraging, he was comparatively diffident since the
adventure of Wednesday. His reception however was of the most

flattering kind. Miss Lucas perceived him from an upper window as he walked towards the house, and instantly set out to meet him accidentally in the lane. But little had she dared to hope that so much love and eloquence awaited her there.

In as short a time as Mr. Collins's long speeches would allow, every thing was settled between them to the satisfaction of both; and as they entered the house, he earnestly entreated her to name the day that was to make him the happiest of men; and though such a solicitation must be waved for the present, the lady felt no inclination to trifle with his happiness. The stupidity with which he was favoured by nature, must guard his courtship from any charm that could make a woman wish for its continuance; and Miss Lucas, who accepted him solely from the pure and disinterested desire of an establishment, cared not how soon that establishment were gained.

Sir William and Lady Lucas were speedily applied to for their consent; and it was bestowed with a most joyful alacrity. Mr. Collins's present circumstances made it a most eligible match for their daughter, to whom they could give little fortune; and his prospects of future wealth were exceedingly fair. Lady Lucas began directly to calculate with more interest than the matter had ever excited before, how many years longer Mr. Bennet was likely to live; and Sir William gave it as his decided opinion, that whenever Mr. Collins should be in possession of the Longbourn estate, it would be highly expedient that both he and his wife should make their appearance at St. James's. The whole family in short were properly overjoyed on the occasion. The younger girls formed hopes of *coming out* a year or two sooner than they might otherwise have done; and the boys were relieved from their apprehension of Charlotte's dying an old maid. Charlotte herself was tolerably composed. She had gained her point, and had time to consider of it. Her reflections were in general satisfactory. Mr. Collins to be sure was neither sensible nor agreeable; his society was irksome, and his attachment to her must be imaginary. But still he would be her husband.–Without thinking highly either of men or of matrimony, marriage had always been her object; it was the only honourable provision for well-educated young women of small fortune, and however uncertain of giving happiness, must be their pleasantest preservative from want. This preservative she had now obtained; and at the age of twenty-seven, without having ever been handsome, she felt all the good luck of it. The least agreeable circumstance in the business, was the surprise it must occasion to Elizabeth Bennet, whose friendship she valued beyond that of any other person. Elizabeth would wonder, and probably would blame her; and though her resolution was not to be shaken, her feelings must be hurt by such disapprobation. She resolved to give her the information herself, and therefore charged Mr. Collins when he returned to Longbourn to dinner, to drop no hint of what had passed before any of the family. A promise of secrecy was of course very dutifully given, but it could not be kept without difficulty; for the curiosity excited by his long absence, burst forth in such very direct questions on his return, as required some ingenuity to evade, and he was at the same time exercising great self-denial, for he was longing to publish his prosperous love.

As he was to begin his journey too early on the morrow to see any of the family, the ceremony of leave-taking was performed when the ladies moved for the night; and Mrs. Bennet with great politeness and cordiality said how happy they should be to see him at Longbourn again, whenever his other engagements might allow him to visit them.

"My dear Madam," he replied, "this invitation is particularly gratifying, because it is what I have been hoping to receive; and you may be very certain that I shall avail myself of it as soon as possible."

They were all astonished; and Mr. Bennet, who could by no means wish for so speedy a return, immediately said,

"But is there not danger of Lady Catherine's disapprobation here, my good sir?—You had better neglect your relations, than run the risk of offending your patroness."

"My dear sir," replied Mr. Collins, "I am particularly obliged to you for this friendly caution, and you may depend upon my not taking so material a step without her ladyship's concurrence."

"You cannot be too much on your guard. Risk any thing rather than her displeasure; and if you find it likely to be raised by your coming to us again, which I should think exceedingly probable, stay quietly at home, and be satisfied that *we* shall take no offence."

"Believe me, my dear sir, my gratitude is warmly excited by such affectionate attention; and depend upon it, you will speedily receive from me a letter of thanks for this, as well as for every other mark of your regard during my stay in Hertfordshire. As for my fair cousins, though my absence may not be long enough to render it necessary, I shall now take the liberty of wishing them health and happiness, not excepting my cousin Elizabeth."

With proper civilities the ladies then withdrew; all of them equally surprised to find that he meditated a quick return. Mrs. Bennet wished to understand by it that he thought of paying his addresses to one of her younger girls, and Mary might have been prevailed on to accept him. She rated his abilities much higher than any of the others; there was a solidity in his reflections which often struck her, and though by no means so clever as herself, she thought that if encouraged to read and improve himself by such an example as her's, he might become a very agreeable companion. But on the following morning, every hope of this kind was done away. Miss Lucas called soon after breakfast, and in a private conference with Elizabeth related the event of the day before.

The possibility of Mr. Collins's fancying himself in love with her friend had once occurred to Elizabeth within the last day or two; but that Charlotte could encourage him, seemed almost as far from possibility as that she could encourage him herself, and her astonishment was consequently so great as to overcome at first the bounds of decorum, and she could not help crying out,

"Engaged to Mr. Collins! my dear Charlotte,—impossible!"

The steady countenance which Miss Lucas had commanded in telling her story, gave way to a momentary confusion here on receiving so direct a reproach; though, as it was no more than she expected, she soon regained her composure, and calmly replied,

"Why should you be surprised, my dear Eliza?—Do you think it incredible that Mr. Collins should be able to procure any woman's good opinion, because he was not so happy as to succeed with you?"

But Elizabeth had not recollected herself, and making a strong effort for it, was able to assure her with tolerable firmness that the prospect of their relationship was highly grateful to her and that she wished her all imaginable happiness.

"I see what you are feeling," replied Charlotte,—"you must be surprised, very much surprised,—so lately as Mr. Collins was wishing to marry you. But when you have had time to think it all over, I hope you will be satisfied with what I have done. I am not romantic you know. I never was. I ask only a comfortable home; and considering Mr. Collins's character, connections, and situation in life, I am convinced that my chance of happiness with him is as fair, as most people can boast on entering the marriage state."

Elizabeth quietly answered "Undoubtedly;"—and after an awkward pause, they returned to the rest of the family. Charlotte did not stay much longer, and Elizabeth was then left to reflect on what she had heard. It was a long time before she became at all reconciled to the idea of so unsuitable a match. The strangeness of Mr. Collins's making two offers of marriage within three days, was nothing in comparison of his being now accepted. She had always felt that Charlotte's opinion of matrimony was not exactly like her own, but she could not have supposed it possible that when called into action, she would have sacrificed every better feeling to worldly advantage. Charlotte the wife of Mr. Collins, was a most humiliating picture!—And to the pang of a friend disgracing herself and sunk in her esteem, was added the distressing conviction that it was impossible for that friend to be tolerably happy in the lot she had chosen.

CHAPTER 23

Elizabeth was sitting with her mother and sisters, reflecting on what she had heard, and doubting whether she were authorised to mention it, when Sir William Lucas himself appeared, sent by his daughter to announce her engagement to the family. With many compliments to them, and much self-gratulation on the prospect of a connection between the houses, he unfolded the matter,–to an audience not merely wondering, but incredulous; for Mrs. Bennet, with more perseverance than politeness, protested he must be entirely mistaken, and Lydia, always unguarded and often uncivil, boisterously exclaimed,

"Good Lord! Sir William, how can you tell such a story?–Do not you know that Mr. Collins wants to marry Lizzy?"

Nothing less than the complaisance of a courtier could have borne without anger such treatment; but Sir William's good breeding carried him through it all; and though he begged leave to be positive as to the truth of his information, he listened to all their impertinence with the most forbearing courtesy.

Elizabeth, feeling it incumbent on her to relieve him from so unpleasant a situation, now put herself forward to confirm his account, by mentioning her prior knowledge of it from Charlotte herself; and endeavoured to put a stop to the exclamations of her mother and sisters, by the earnestness of her congratulations to Sir William, in which she was readily joined by Jane, and by making a variety of remarks on the happiness that might be expected from the match, the excellent character of Mr. Collins, and the convenient distance of Hunsford from London.

Mrs. Bennet was in fact too much overpowered to say a great deal while Sir William remained; but no sooner had he left them than her feelings found a rapid vent. In the first place, she persisted in disbelieving the whole of the matter; secondly, she was very sure that Mr. Collins had been taken in; thirdly, she trusted that they would never be happy together; and fourthly, that the match might be broken off. Two inferences, however, were plainly deduced from the whole; one, that Elizabeth was the real cause of all the mischief; and the other, that she herself had been barbarously used by them all; and on these two points she principally dwelt during the rest of the day. Nothing could console and nothing appease her.–Nor did that day wear out her resentment. A week elapsed before she could see Elizabeth without scolding her, a month passed away before she could speak to Sir William or Lady Lucas without being rude, and many months were gone before she could at all forgive their daughter.

Mr. Bennet's emotions were much more tranquil on the occasion, and such as he did experience he pronounced to be of a most agreeable sort; for it gratified him, he said, to discover that Charlotte Lucas, whom he had been used to think tolerably sensible, was as foolish as his wife, and more foolish than his daughter!

Jane confessed herself a little surprised at the match; but she said less of her astonishment than of her earnest desire for their happiness; nor could Elizabeth persuade her to consider it as improbable. Kitty and Lydia were far from envying Miss Lucas, for Mr. Collins was only a clergyman; and it affected them in no other way than as a piece of news to spread at Meryton.

Lady Lucas could not be insensible of triumph on being able to retort on Mrs. Bennet the comfort of having a daughter well married; and she called at Longbourn rather oftener than usual to say how happy she was, though Mrs. Bennet's sour looks and ill-natured remarks might have been enough to drive happiness away.

Between Elizabeth and Charlotte there was a restraint which kept them mutually silent on the subject; and Elizabeth felt persuaded that no real confidence could ever subsist between them again. Her disappointment in Charlotte made her turn with fonder regard to her sister, of whose rectitude and delicacy she was sure her opinion could never be shaken, and for whose happiness she grew daily more anxious, as Bingley had now been gone a week, and nothing was heard of his return.

Jane had sent Caroline an early answer to her letter, and was counting the days till she might reasonably hope to hear again. The promised letter of thanks from Mr. Collins arrived on Tuesday, addressed to their father, and written with all the solemnity of gratitude which a twelve-month's abode in the family might have prompted. After discharging his conscience on that head, he proceeds to inform them, with many rapturous expressions, of his happiness in having obtained the affection of their amiable neighbour, Miss Lucas, and then explained that it was merely with the view of enjoying her society that he had been so ready to close with their kind wish of seeing him again at Longbourn, whither he hoped to be able to return on Monday fortnight; for Lady Catherine, he added, so heartily approved his marriage, that she wished it to take place as soon as possible, which he trusted would be an unanswerable argument with his amiable Charlotte to name an early day for making him the happiest of men.

Mr. Collins's return into Hertfordshire was no longer a matter of pleasure to Mrs. Bennet. On the contrary she was as much disposed to complain of it as her husband.—It was very strange that he should come to Longbourn instead of to Lucas Lodge; it was also very inconvenient and exceedingly troublesome.—She hated having visitors in the house while her health was so indifferent, and lovers were of all people the most disagreeable. Such were the gentle murmurs of Mrs. Bennet, and they gave way only to the greater distress of Mr. Bingley's continued absence.

Neither Jane nor Elizabeth were comfortable on this subject. Day after day passed away without bringing any other tidings of him than the report which shortly prevailed in Meryton of his coming no more to Netherfield the whole winter; a report which highly incensed Mrs. Bennet, and which she never failed to contradict as a most scandalous falsehood.

Even Elizabeth began to fear—not that Bingley was indifferent—but that his sisters would be successful in keeping him away. Unwilling as she was to admit an idea so destructive of Jane's happiness, and so dishonourable to the stability of her lover, she could not prevent its frequently recurring. The united efforts of his two unfeeling sisters and of his overpowering friend, assisted by the attractions of Miss Darcy and the amusements of London, might be too much, she feared, for the strength of his attachment.

As for Jane, *her* anxiety under this suspense was, of course, more painful than Elizabeth's; but whatever she felt she was desirous of concealing; and between herself and Elizabeth, therefore, the subject was never alluded to. But as no such delicacy restrained her mother, an hour seldom passed in which she did not talk of Bingley, express her impatience for his arrival, or even require Jane to confess that if he did not come back, she would think herself very ill used. It needed all Jane's steady mildness to bear these attacks with tolerable tranquillity.

Mr. Collins returned most punctually on the Monday fortnight, but his reception at Longbourn was not quite so gracious as it had been on his first introduction. He was too happy, however, to need much attention; and luckily for the others, the business of love-making relieved them from a great deal of his company. The chief of every day was spent by him at Lucas Lodge, and he sometimes returned to Longbourn only in time to make an apology for his absence before the family went to bed.

Mrs. Bennet was really in a most pitiable state. The very mention of any thing concerning the match threw her into an agony of ill humour, and wherever she went she was sure of hearing it talked of. The sight of Miss Lucas was odious to her. As her successor in that house, she regarded her with jealous abhorrence. Whenever Charlotte came to see them she concluded her to be anticipating the hour of possession; and whenever she spoke in a low voice to Mr. Collins, was convinced that they were talking of the Longbourn estate, and resolving to turn herself and her daughters out of the house, as soon as Mr. Bennet were dead. She complained bitterly of all this to her husband.

"Indeed, Mr. Bennet," said she, "it is very hard to think that Charlotte Lucas should ever be mistress of this house, that *I* should be forced to make way for *her,* and live to see her take my place in it!"

"My dear, do not give way to such gloomy thoughts. Let us hope for better things. Let us flatter ourselves that *I* may be the survivor."

This was not very consoling to Mrs. Bennet, and, therefore, instead of making any answer, she went on as before,

"I cannot bear to think that they should have all this estate. If it was not for the entail I should not mind it."

"What should not you mind?"

"I should not mind any thing at all."

"Let us be thankful that you are preserved from a state of such insensibility."

"I never can be thankful, Mr. Bennet, for any thing about the entail. How any one could have the conscience to entail away an estate from one's own daughters I cannot understand; and all for the sake of Mr. Collins too!—Why should *he* have it more than anybody else?"

"I leave it to yourself to determine," said Mr. Bennet.

Volume II

CHAPTER 1

Miss Bingley's letter arrived, and put an end to doubt. The very first sentence conveyed the assurance of their being all settled in London for the winter, and concluded with her brother's regret at not having had time to pay his respects to his friends in Hertfordshire before he left the country.

Hope was over, entirely over; and when Jane could attend to the rest of the letter, she found little, except the professed affection of the writer, that could give her any comfort. Miss Darcy's praise occupied the chief of it. Her many attractions were again dwelt on, and Caroline boasted joyfully of their increasing intimacy, and ventured to predict the accomplishment of the wishes which had been unfolded in her former letter. She wrote also with great pleasure of her brother's being an inmate of Mr. Darcy's house, and mentioned with raptures, some plans of the latter with regard to new furniture.

Elizabeth, to whom Jane very soon communicated the chief of all this, heard it in silent indignation. Her heart was divided between concern for her sister, and resentment against all the others. To Caroline's assertion of her brother's being partial to Miss Darcy she paid no credit. That he was really fond of Jane, she doubted no more than she had ever done; and much as she had always been disposed to like him, she could not think without anger, hardly without contempt, on that easiness of temper, that want of proper resolution which now made him the slave of his designing friends, and led him to sacrifice his own happiness to the caprice of their inclinations. Had his own happiness, however, been the only sacrifice, he might have been allowed to sport with it in what ever manner he thought best; but her sister's was involved in it, as she thought he must be sensible himself. It was a subject, in short, on which reflection would be long indulged, and must be unavailing. She could think of nothing else, and yet whether Bingley's regard had really died away, or were suppressed by his friends' interference; whether he had been aware of Jane's attachment, or whether it had escaped his observation; whichever were the case, though her opinion of him must be materially affected by the difference, her sister's situation remained the same, her peace equally wounded.

A day or two passed before Jane had courage to speak of her feelings to Elizabeth; but at last on Mrs. Bennet's leaving them together, after a longer irritation than usual about Netherfield and its master, she could not help saying,

"Oh! that my dear mother had more command over herself; she can have no idea of the pain she gives me by her continual reflections on him. But I will not repine. It cannot last long. He well be forgot, and we shall all be as we were before."

Elizabeth looked at her sister with incredulous solicitude, but said nothing.

"You doubt me," cried Jane slightly colouring; "indeed you have no reason. He may live in my memory as the most amiable man of my acquaintance, but that is all. I have nothing either to hope or fear, and nothing to reproach him with. Thank God! I have not *that* pain. A little time therefore.—I shall certainly try to get the better."

With a stronger voice she soon added, "I have this comfort immediately, that it has not been more than an error of fancy on my side, and that it has done no harm to any one but myself."

"My dear Jane!" exclaimed Elizabeth, "you are too good. Your sweetness and disinterestedness are really angelic; I do not know what to say to you. I feel as if I had never done you justice, or loved you as you deserve."

Miss Bennet eagerly disclaimed all extraordinary merit, and threw back the praise on her sister's warm affection.

"Nay," said Elizabeth, "this is not fair. *You* wish to think all the world respectable, and are hurt if I speak ill of any body. *I* only want to think *you* perfect, and you set yourself against it. Do not be afraid of my running into any excess, of my encroaching on your privilege of universal good will. You need not. There are few people whom I really love, and still fewer of whom I think well. The more I see of the world, the more am I dissatisfied with it; and every day confirms my belief of the inconsistency of all human characters, and of the little dependence that can be placed on the appearance of either merit or sense. I have met with two instances lately; one I will not mention; the other is Charlotte's marriage. It is unaccountable! in every view it is unaccountable!"

"My dear Lizzy, do not give way to such feelings as these. They will ruin your happiness. You do not make allowance enough for difference of situation and temper. Consider Mr. Collins's respectability, and Charlotte's prudent, steady character. Remember that she is one of a large family; that as to fortune, it is a most eligible match; and be ready to believe, for every body's sake, that she may feel something like regard and esteem for our cousin."

"To oblige you, I would try to believe almost any thing, but no one else could be benefited by such a belief as this; for were I persuaded that Charlotte had any regard for him, I should only think worse of her understanding, than I now do of her heart. My dear Jane, Mr. Collins is a conceited, pompous, narrow-minded, silly man; you know he is, as well as I do; and you must feel, as well as I do, that the woman who marries him, cannot have a proper way of thinking. You shall not defend her, though it is Charlotte Lucas. You shall not, for the sake of one individual, change the meaning of principle and integrity, nor endeavour to persuade yourself or me, that selfishness is prudence, and insensibility of danger, security for happiness."

"I must think your language too strong in speaking of both," replied Jane, "and I hope you will be convinced of it, by seeing them happy together. But enough of this. You alluded to something else. You mentioned *two* instances. I cannot misunderstand you, but I intreat you, dear Lizzy, not to pain me by thinking *that person* to blame, and saying your opinion of him is sunk. We must not be so ready to fancy ourselves intentionally injured. We must not expect a lively young man to be always so guarded and circumspect. It is very often nothing but our own vanity that deceives us. Women fancy admiration means more than it does."

"And men take care that they should."

"If it is designedly done, they cannot be justified; but I have no idea of there being so much design in the world as some persons imagine."

"I am far from attributing any part of Mr. Bingley's conduct to design," said Elizabeth; "but without scheming to do wrong, or to make others unhappy, there may be error, and there may be misery. Thoughtlessness, want of attention to other people's feelings, and want of resolution, will do the business."

"And do you impute it to either of those?"

"Yes; to the last. But if I go on, I shall displease you by saying what I think of persons you esteem. Stop me whilst you can."

"You persist, then, in supposing his sisters influence him."

"Yes, in conjunction with his friend."

"I cannot believe it. Why should they try to influence him? They can only wish his happiness, and if he is attached to me, no other woman can secure it."

"Your first position is false. They may wish many things besides his happiness; they may wish his increase of wealth and consequence; they may wish him to marry a girl who has all the importance of money, great connections, and pride."

"Beyond a doubt, they *do* wish him to chuse Miss Darcy," replied Jane; "but this may be from better feelings than you are supposing. They have known her much longer than they have known me; no wonder if they love her better. But, whatever may be their own wishes, it is very unlikely they should have opposed their brother's. What sister would think herself at liberty to do it, unless there were something very objectionable? If they believed him attached to me, they would not try to part us; if he were so, they could not succeed. By supposing such an affection, you make every body acting unnaturally and wrong, and me most unhappy. Do not distress me by the idea. I am not ashamed of having been mistaken—or, at least, it is slight, it is nothing in comparison of what I should feel in thinking ill of him or his sisters. Let me take it in the best light, in the light in which it may be understood."

Elizabeth could not oppose such a wish; and from this time Mr. Bingley's name was scarcely ever mentioned between them.

Mrs. Bennet still continued to wonder and repine at his returning no more, and though a day seldom passed in which Elizabeth did not account for it clearly, there seemed little chance of her ever considering it with less perplexity. Her daughter endeavoured to convince her of what she did not believe herself, that his attentions to Jane had been merely the effect of a common and transient liking, which ceased when he saw her no more; but though the probability of the statement was admitted at the time, she had the same story to repeat every day. Mrs. Bennet's best comfort was, that Mr. Bingley must be down again in the summer.

Mr. Bennet treated the matter differently. "So, Lizzy," said he one day, "your sister is crossed in love I find. I congratulate her. Next to being married, a girl likes to be crossed in love a little now and then. It is something to think of, and gives her a sort of distinction among her companions. When is your turn to come? You will hardly bear to be long outdone by Jane. Now is your time. Here are officers enough at Meryton to disappoint all the young ladies in the country. Let Wickham be *your* man. He is a pleasant fellow, and would jilt you creditably."

"Thank you, Sir, but a less agreeable man would satisfy me. We must not all expect Jane's good fortune."

"True," said Mr. Bennet, "but it is a comfort to think that, whatever of that kind may befal you, you have an affectionate mother who will always make the most of it."

Mr. Wickham's society was of material service in dispelling the gloom, which the late perverse occurrences had thrown on many of the Longbourn family. They saw him often, and to his other recommendations was now added that of general unreserve.

The whole of what Elizabeth had already heard, his claims on Mr. Darcy, and all that he had suffered from him, was now openly acknowledged and publicly canvassed; and every body was pleased to think how much they had always disliked Mr. Darcy before they had known any thing of the matter.

Miss Bennet was the only creature who could suppose there might be any extenuating circumstances in the case, unknown to the society of Hertfordshire; her mild and steady candour always pleaded for allowances, and urged the possibility of mistakes—but by every body else Mr. Darcy was condemned as the worst of men.

CHAPTER 2

After a week spent in professions of love and schemes of felicity, Mr. Collins was called from his amiable Charlotte by the arrival of Saturday. The pain of separation, however, might be alleviated on his side, by preparations for the reception of his bride, as he had reason to hope, that shortly after his next return into Hertfordshire, the day would be fixed that was to make him the happiest of men. He took leave of his relations at Longbourn with as much solemnity as before; wished his fair cousins health and happiness again, and promised their father another letter of thanks.

On the following Monday, Mrs. Bennet had the pleasure of receiving her brother and his wife, who came as usual to spend the Christmas at Longbourn. Mr. Gardiner was a sensible, gentlemanlike man, greatly superior to his sister as well by nature as education. The Netherfield ladies would have had difficulty in believing that a man who lived by trade, and within view of his own warehouses, could have been so well bred and agreeable. Mrs. Gardiner, who was several years younger than Mrs. Bennet and Mrs. Philips, was an amiable, intelligent, elegant woman, and a great favourite with all her Longbourn nieces. Between the two eldest and herself especially, there subsisted a very particular regard. They had frequently been staying with her in town.

The first part of Mrs. Gardiner's business on her arrival, was to distribute her presents and describe the newest fashions. When this was done, she had a less active part to play. It became her turn to listen. Mrs. Bennet had many grievances to relate, and much to complain of. They had all been very ill-used since she last saw her sister. Two of her girls had been on the point of marriage, and after all there was nothing in it.

"I do not blame Jane," she continued, "for Jane would have got Mr. Bingley, if she could. But, Lizzy! Oh, sister! it is very hard to think that she might have been Mr. Collins's wife by this time, had not it been for her own perverseness. He made her an offer in this very room, and she refused him. The consequence of it is, that Lady Lucas will have a daughter married before I have, and that Longbourn estate is just as much entailed as ever. The Lucases are very artful people indeed, sister. They are all for what they can get. I am sorry to say it of them, but so it is. It makes me very nervous and poorly, to be thwarted so in my own family, and to have neighbours who think of themselves before anybody else. However, your coming just at this time is the greatest of comforts, and I am very glad to hear what you tell us, of long sleeves."

Mrs. Gardiner, to whom the chief of this news had been given before, in the course of Jane and Elizabeth's correspondence with her, made her sister a slight answer, and in compassion to her nieces turned the conversation.

When alone with Elizabeth afterwards, she spoke more on the subject. "It seems likely to have been a desirable match for Jane," said she. "I am sorry it went off. But these things happen so often! A young man, such as you describe Mr. Bingley, so easily falls in love with a pretty girl for a few weeks, and when accident separates them, so easily forgets her, that these sort of inconstancies are very frequent."

"An excellent consolation in its way," said Elizabeth, "but it will not do for *us*. We do not suffer by *accident*. It does not often happen that the interference of friends will persuade a young man of independent fortune to think no more of a girl, whom he was violently in love with only a few days before."

"But that expression of 'violently in love' is so hackneyed, so doubtful, so indefinite, that it gives me very little idea. It is as often applied to feelings which arise only from an half-hour's acquaintance, as to a real, strong attachment. Pray, how *violent was* Mr. Bingley's love?"

"I never saw a more promising inclination. He was growing quite inattentive to other people, and wholly engrossed by her. Every time they met, it was more decided and remarkable. At his own ball he offended two or three young ladies, by not asking them to dance, and I spoke to him twice myself, without receiving an answer. Could there be finer symptoms? Is not general incivility the very essence of love?"

"Oh, yes! – of that kind of love which I suppose him to have felt. Poor Jane! I am sorry for her, because, with her disposition, she may not get over it immediately. It had better have happened to *you*, Lizzy; you would have laughed yourself out of it sooner. But do you think she would be prevailed on to go back with us? Change of scene might be of service – and perhaps a little relief from home, may be as useful as anything."

Elizabeth was exceedingly pleased with this proposal, and felt persuaded of her sister's ready acquiescence.

"I hope," added Mrs. Gardiner, that no consideration with regard to this young man will influence her. We live in so different a part of town, all our connections are so different, and, as you well know, we go out so little, that it is very improbable they should meet at all, unless he really comes to see her."

"And *that* is quite impossible; for he is now in the custody of his friend, and Mr. Darcy would no more suffer him to call on Jane in such a part of London! My dear aunt, how could you think of it? Mr. Darcy may perhaps have *heard* of such a place as Grace Church Street, but he would hardly think a month's ablution enough to cleanse him from its impurities, were he once to enter it; and depend upon it, Mr. Bingley never stirs without him."

"So much the better. I hope they will not meet at all. But does not Jane correspond with the sister? *She* will not be able to help calling."

"She will drop the acquaintance entirely."

But in spite of the certainty in which Elizabeth affected to place this point, as well as the still more interesting one of Bingley's being withheld from seeing Jane, she felt a solicitude on the subject which convinced her, on examination, that she did not consider it entirely hopeless. It was possible, and sometimes she thought it probable, that his affection might be re-animated, and the influence of his friends successfully combated by the more natural influence of Jane's attractions.

Miss Bennet accepted her aunt's invitation with pleasure; and the Bingleys were no otherwise in her thoughts at the time, than as she hoped that, by Caroline's not living in the same house with her brother, she might occasionally spend a morning with her, without any danger of seeing him.

The Gardiners staid a week at Longbourn; and what with the Philipses, the Lucases, and the officers there was not a day without its engagement. Mrs. Bennet had so carefully provided for the entertainment of her brother and sister, that they did not once sit down to a family dinner. When the engagement was for home, some of the officers always made part of it, of which officers Mr. Wickham was sure to be one; and on these occasions, Mrs. Gardiner, rendered suspicious by Elizabeth's warm commendation of him, narrowly observed them both. Without supposing them, from what she saw, to be very seriously in love, their preference of each other was plain enough to make her a little uneasy; and she resolved to speak to Elizabeth on the subject before she left Hertfordshire, and represent to her the imprudence of encouraging such an attachment.

To Mrs. Gardiner, Wickham had one means of affording pleasure, unconnected with his general powers. About ten or a dozen years ago, before her marriage, she had spent a considerable time in that very part of Derbyshire, to which he belonged. They had, therefore, many acquaintance in common; and, though Wickham had been little there since the death of Darcy's father, five years before, it was yet in his power to give her fresher intelligence of her former friends, than she had been in the way of procuring.

Mrs. Gardiner had seen Pemberley, and known the late Mr. Darcy by character perfectly well. Here consequently was an inexhaustible subject of discourse. In comparing her recollection of Pemberley, with the minute description which Wickham could give, and in bestowing her tribute of praise on the character of its late possessor, she was delighting both him and herself. On being made acquainted with the present Mr. Darcy's treatment of him, she tried to remember something of that gentleman's reputed disposition when quite a lad, which might agree with it, and was confident at last, that she recollected having heard Mr. Fitzwilliam Darcy formerly spoken of as a very proud, ill-natured boy.

CHAPTER 3

Mrs. Gardiner's caution to Elizabeth was punctually and kindly given on the first favourable opportunity of speaking to her alone; after honestly telling her what she thought, she thus went on:

"You are too sensible a girl, Lizzy, to fall in love merely because you are warned against it; and, therefore, I am not afraid of speaking openly. Seriously, I would have you be on your guard. Do not involve yourself, or endeavour to involve him in an affection which the want of fortune would make so very imprudent. I have nothing to say against *him;* he is a most interesting young man; and if he had the fortune he ought to have, I should think you could not do better. But as it is—you must not let your fancy run away with you. You have sense, and we all expect you to use

it. Your father would depend on *your* resolution and good conduct, I am sure. You must not disappoint your father."

"My dear aunt, this is being serious indeed."

"Yes, and I hope to engage you to be serious likewise."

"Well, then, you need not be under any alarm. I will take care
of myself, and of Mr. Wickham too. He shall not be in love with
me, if I can prevent it."

"Elizabeth, you are not serious now."

"I beg your pardon. I will try again. At present I am not in
love with Mr. Wickham; no, I certainly am not. But he is, beyond
all comparison, the most agreeable man I ever saw—and if he becomes really attached to me—I believe it will be better that he
should not. I see the imprudence of it.—Oh! *that* abominable Mr.
Darcy!—My father's opinion of me does me the greatest honor;
and I should be miserable to forfeit it. My father, however, is partial to Mr. Wickham. In short, my dear aunt, I should be very
sorry to be the means of making any of you unhappy; but since
we see every day that where there is affection, young people are
seldom withheld by immediate want of fortune, from entering
into engagements with each other, how can I promise to be wiser
than so many of my fellow-creatures if I am tempted, or how am
I even to know that it would be wisdom to resist? All that I can
promise you, therefore, is not to be in a hurry. I will not be in
a hurry to believe myself his first object. When I am in company
with him, I will not be wishing. In short, I will do my best."

"Perhaps it will be as well, if you discourage his coming here
so very often. At least, you should not *remind* your Mother of inviting him."

"As I did the other day," said Elizabeth, with a conscious smile;
"very true, it will be wise in me to refrain from *that*. But do not
imagine that he is always here so often. It is on your account that
he has been so frequently invited this week. You know my mother's
ideas as to the necessity of constant company for her friends. But
really, and upon my honour, I will try to do what I think to be
wisest; and now, I hope you are satisfied."

Her aunt assured her that she was; and Elizabeth having thanked her for the kindness of her hints, they parted; a wonderful instance of advice being given on such a point, without being resented.

Mr. Collins returned into Hertfordshire soon after it had been quitted by the Gardiners and Jane; but as he took up his abode with the Lucases, his arrival was no great inconvenience to Mrs. Bennet. His marriage was now fast approaching, and she was at length so far resigned as to think it inevitable, and even repeatedly to say in an ill-natured tone that she "*wished* they might be happy." Thursday was to be the wedding day, and on Wednesday Miss Lucas paid her farewell visit; and when she rose to take leave, Elizabeth, ashamed of her mother's ungracious and reluctant good wishes, and sincerely affected herself, accompanied her out of the room. As they went down stairs together, Charlotte said,

"I shall depend on hearing from you very often, Eliza."

"*That* you certainly shall."

"And I have another favour to ask. Will you come and see me?"

"We shall often meet, I hope, in Hertfordshire."

"I am not likely to leave Kent for some time. Promise me, therefore, to come to Hunsford."

Elizabeth could not refuse, though she foresaw little pleasure in the visit.

"My father and Maria are to come to me in March," added Charlotte, "and I hope you will consent to be of the party. Indeed, Eliza, you will be as welcome to me as either of them."

The wedding took place; the bride and bridegroom set off for Kent from the church door, and every body had as much to say or to hear on the subject as usual. Elizabeth soon heard from her friend; and their correspondence was as regular and frequent as it had ever been; that it should be equally unreserved was impossible. Elizabeth could never address her without feeling that all the comfort of intimacy was over, and, though determined not to slacken as a correspondent, it was for the sake of what had been, rather than what was. Charlotte's first letters were received with a good deal of eagerness; there could not but be curiosity to know how she would speak of her new home, how she would like Lady Catherine, and how happy she would dare pronounce herself to be; though, when the letters were read, Elizabeth felt that Charlotte expressed herself on every point exactly as she might have foreseen. She wrote cheerfully, seemed surrounded with comforts, and mentioned nothing which she could not praise. The house, furniture, neighbourhood, and roads, were all to her taste, and Lady Catherine's behaviour was most friendly and obliging. It was Mr. Collins's picture of Hunsford and Rosings rationally softened; and Elizabeth perceived that she must wait for her own visit there, to know the rest.

Jane had already written a few lines to her sister to announce their safe arrival in London; and when she wrote again, Elizabeth hoped it would be in her power to say something of the Bingleys.

Her impatience for this second letter was as well rewarded as impatience generally is. Jane had been a week in town, without either seeing or hearing from Caroline. She accounted for it, however, by supposing that her last letter to her friend from Longbourn, had by some accident been lost.

"My aunt," she continued, "is going to-morrow into that part of the town, and I shall take the opportunity of calling in Grosvenor street."

She wrote again when the visit was paid, and she had seen Miss Bingley. "I did not think Caroline in spirits," were her words, "but she was very glad to see me, and reproached me for giving her no notice of my coming to London. I was right, therefore; my last letter had never reached her. I enquired after their brother, of course. He was well, but so much engaged with Mr. Darcy, that they scarcely ever saw him. I found that Miss Darcy was expected to dinner. I wish I could see her. My visit was not long, as Caroline and Mrs. Hurst were going out. I dare say I shall soon see them here."

Elizabeth shook her head over this letter. It convinced her, that accident only could discover to Mr. Bingley her sister's being in town.

Four weeks passed away, and Jane saw nothing of him. She endeavoured to persuade herself that she did not regret it; but she could no longer be blind to Miss Bingley's inattention. After waiting at home every morning for a fortnight, and inventing every evening a fresh excuse for her, the visitor did at last appear; but the shortness of her stay, and yet more, the alteration of her manner would allow Jane to deceive herself no longer. The letter which she wrote on this occasion to her sister, will prove what she felt.

My dearest Lizzy will, I am sure, be incapable of triumphing in her better judgment, at my expense, when I confess myself to have been entirely deceived in Miss Bingley's regard for me. But, my dear sister, though the event has proved you right, do not think me obstinate if I still assert, that, considering what her behaviour was, my confidence was as natural as your suspicion. I do not at all comprehend her reason for wishing to be intimate with me, but if the same circumstances were to happen again, I am sure I should be deceived again. Caroline did not return my visit till yesterday; and not a note, not a line, did I receive in the mean time. When she did come, it was very evident that she had no pleasure in it; she made a slight, formal, apology, for not calling before, said not a word of wishing to see me again, and was in every respect so altered a creature, that when she went away, I was perfectly resolved to continue the acquaintance no longer. I pity, though I cannot help blaming her. She was very wrong in singling me out as she did; I can safely say, that every advance to intimacy began on her side. But I pity her, because she must feel that she has been acting wrong, and because I am very sure that anxiety for her brother is the cause of it. I need not explain myself farther; and though *we* know this anxiety to be quite needless, yet if she feels it, it will easily account for her behaviour to me; and so deservedly dear as he is to his sister, whatever anxiety she may feel on his behalf, is natural and amiable. I cannot but wonder, however, at her having any such fears now, because, if he had at all cared about me, we must have met long, long ago. He knows of my being in town, I am certain, from something she said herself; and yet it should seem by her manner of talking, as if she wanted to persuade herself that he is really partial to Miss Darcy. I cannot understand it. If I were not afraid of judging harshly, I should be almost tempted to say, that there is a strong appearance of duplicity in all this. But I will endeavour to banish every painful thought, and think only of what will make me happy, your affection, and the invariable kindness of my dear uncle and aunt. Let me hear from you very soon. Miss Bingley said something of his never returning to Netherfield again, of giving up the house, but not with any certainty. We had better not mention it. I am extremely glad that you have such pleasant accounts from our friends at Hunsford. Pray go see them, with Sir William and Maria. I am sure you will be very comfortable there.

Your's, &c.

This letter gave Elizabeth some pain; but her spirits returned as she considered that Jane would no longer be duped, but the sister at least. All expectation from the brother was now absolutely over. She would not even wish for any renewal of his attentions. His character sunk on every review of it; and as a punishment for him, as well as a possible advantage to Jane, she seriously hoped he might really soon marry Mr. Darcy's sister, as, by Wickham's account, she would make him abundantly regret what he had thrown away.

Mrs. Gardiner about this time reminded Elizabeth of her promise concerning that gentleman, and required information; and Elizabeth had such to send as might rather give contentment to her aunt than to herself. His apparent partiality had subsided, his attentions were over, he was the admirer of some one else. Elizabeth was watchful enough to see it all, but she could see it and write of it without material pain. Her heart had been but slightly touched, and her vanity was satisfied with believing that *she* would have been his only choice, had fortune permitted it. The sudden acquisition of ten thousand pounds was the most remarkable charm of the young lady, to whom he was now rendering himself agreeable; but Elizabeth, less clear sighted perhaps in his case than in Charlotte's did not quarrel with him for his wish of independence. Nothing, on the contrary, could be more natural; and while able to suppose that it cost him a few struggles to relinquish her, she was ready to allow it a wise and desirable measure for both, and could very sincerely wish him happy.

All this was acknowledged to Mrs. Gardiner; and after relating the circumstances, she thus went on:—"I am now convinced, my dear aunt, that I have never been much in love; for had I really experienced that pure and elevating passion, I should at present detest his very name, and wish him all manner of evil. But my feelings are not only cordial towards *him;* they are even impartial towards Miss King. I cannot find out that I hate her at all, or that I am in the least unwilling to think her a very good sort of girl. There can be no love in all this. My watchfulness has been effectual; and though I should certainly be a more interesting object to all my acquaintance, were I distractedly in love with him, I cannot say that I regret my comparative insignificance. Importance may sometimes be purchased too dearly. Kitty and Lydia take his defection much more to heart than I do. They are young in the ways of the world, and not yet open to the mortifying conviction that handsome young men must have something to live on, as well as the plain."

CHAPTER 4

With no greater events than these in the Longbourn family, and otherwise diversified by little beyond the walks to Meryton, sometimes dirty and sometimes cold, did January and February pass away. March was to take Elizabeth to Hunsford. She had not at first thought very seriously of going thither; but Charlotte, she soon found, was depending on the plan, and she gradually learned to consider it herself with greater pleasure and well as greater certainty. Absence had increased her desire of seeing Charlotte again, and weakened her disgust of Mr. Collins. There was novelty in the scheme, and as, with such a mother and such uncompanionable sisters, home could not be faultless, a little change was not unwelcome for its own sake. The journey would moreover give her a peep at Jane; and, in short, as the time drew near, she would have been very sorry for any delay. Every thing, however, went on smoothly, and was finally settled according to Charlotte's first sketch. She was to accompany Sir William and his second daughter. The improvement of spending a night in London was added in time, and the plan became perfect as plan could be.

The only pain was in leaving her father, who would certainly miss her, and who, when it came to the point, so little liked her going, that he told her to write to him, and almost promised to answer her letter.

The farewell between herself and Mr. Wickham was perfectly friendly; on his side even more. His present pursuit could not make him forget that Elizabeth had been the first to excite and to deserve his attention, the first to listen and to pity, the first to be admired; and in his manner of bidding her adieu, wishing her every enjoyment, reminding her of what she was to expect in Lady Catherine de Bourgh, and trusting their opinion of her — their opinion of everybody — would always coincide, there was a solicitude, an interest which she felt must ever attach her to him with a most sincere regard; and she parted from him convinced, that whether married or single, he must always be her model of the amiable and pleasing.

Her fellow travellers the next day, were not of a kind to make her think him less agreeable. Sir William Lucas, and his daughter Maria, a good humoured girl, but as empty-headed as himself, had nothing to say that could be worth hearing, and were listened to with about as much delight as the rattle of the chaise. Elizabeth loved absurdities, but she had known Sir William's too long. He could tell her nothing new of the wonders of his presentation and knighthood; and his civilities were worn out like his information.

It was a journey of only twenty-four miles, and they began it so early as to be in Gracechurch Street by noon. As they drove to Mr. Gardiner's door, Jane was at a drawing-room window watching their arrival; when they entered the passage she was there to welcome them, and Elizabeth, looking earnestly in her face, was pleased to see it healthful and lovely as ever. On the stairs were a troop of little boys and girls, whose eagerness for their cousin's appearance would not allow them to wait in the drawing-room, and whose shyness, as they had not seen her for a twelve-month, prevented their coming lower. All was joy and kindness. The day passed most pleasantly away; the morning in bustle and shopping, and the evening at one of the theatres.

Elizabeth then contrived to sit by her aunt. Their first subject was her sister; and she was more grieved than astonished to hear, in reply to her minute enquiries, that though Jane always struggled to support her spirits, there were periods of dejection. It was reasonable, however, to hope, that they would not continue long. Mrs. Gardiner gave her the particulars also of Miss Bingley's visit in Grace Church Street, and repeated conversations occurring at different times between Jane and herself, which proved that the former had, from her heart, given up the acquaintance.

Mrs. Gardiner then rallied her niece on Wickham's desertion, and complimented her on bearing it so well.

"But, my dear Elizabeth," she added, "what sort of girl is Miss King? I should be sorry to think our friend mercenary."

"Pray, my dear aunt, what is the difference in matrimonial affairs, between the mercenary and the prudent motive? Where does discretion end, and avarice begin? Last Christmas you were afraid of his marrying me, because it would be imprudent; and now, because he is trying to get a girl with only ten thousand pounds, you want to find out that he is mercenary."

"If you will only tell me what sort of girl Miss King is, I shall know what to think."

"She is a very good kind of girl, I believe. I know no harm of her."

"But he paid her not the smallest attention, till her grandfather's death made her mistress of this fortune."

"No — why should he? If it was not allowable for him to gain *my* affections, because I had no money, what occasion could there be for making love to a girl whom he did not care about, and who was equally poor?"

"But there seems indelicacy in directing his attentions towards her, so soon after this event."

"A man in distressed circumstances has not time for all those elegant decorums which other people may observe. If *she* does not object to it, why should *we?*"

"*Her* not objecting, does not justify *him*. It only shews her being deficient in something herself—sense or feeling."

"Well," cried Elizabeth, "have it as you choose. He shall be mercenary, and *she* shall be foolish."

"No, Lizzy, that is what I do *not* choose. I should be sorry, you know, to think ill of a young man who has lived so long in Derbyshire."

"Oh! if that is all, I have a very poor opinion of young men who live in Derbyshire; and their intimate friends who live in Hertfordshire are not much better. I am sick of them all. Thank Heaven! I am going to-morrow where I shall find a man who has not one agreeable quality, who has neither manner nor sense to recommend him. Stupid men are the only ones worth knowing, after all."

"Take care, Lizzy; that speech savours strongly of disappointment."

Before they were separated by the conclusion of the play, she had the unexpected happiness of an invitation to accompany her uncle and aunt in a tour of pleasure which they proposed taking in the summer.

"We have not quite determined how far it shall carry us," said Mrs. Gardiner, "but perhaps to the Lakes."

No scheme could have been more agreeable to Elizabeth, and her acceptance of the invitation was most ready and grateful. "My dear, dear aunt," she rapturously cried, "what delight! what felicity! You give me fresh life and vigour. Adieu to disappointment and spleen. What are men to rocks and mountains? Oh! what hours of transport we shall spend! And when we *do* return, it shall not be like other travellers, without being able to give one accurate idea of any thing. We *will* know where we have gone – we will recollect what we have seen. Lakes, mountains, and rivers, shall not be jumbled together in our imaginations; nor, when we attempt to describe any particular scene, will we begin quarrelling about its relative situation. Let *our* first effusions be less insupportable than those of the generality of travellers."

CHAPTER 5

Every object in the next day's journey was new and interesting to Elizabeth; and her spirits were in a state for enjoyment; for she had seen her sister looking so well as to banish all fear for her health, and the prospect of her northern tour was a constant source of delight.

When they left the high road for the lane to Hunsford, every eye was in search of the Parsonage, and every turning expected to bring it in view. The paling of Rosings park was their boundary on one side. Elizabeth smiled at the recollection of all that she had heard of its inhabitants.

At length the Parsonage was discernible. The garden sloping to the road, the house standing in it, the green pales and the laurel hedge, every thing declared they were arriving. Mr. Collins and Charlotte appeared at the door, and the carriage stopped at the small gate, which led by a short gravel walk to the house, amidst the nods and smiles of the whole party. In a moment they were all out of the chaise, rejoicing at the sight of each other. Mrs. Collins welcomed her friend with the liveliest pleasure, and Elizabeth was more and more satisfied with coming, when she found herself so affectionately received. She saw instantly that her cousin's manners were not altered by his marriage; his formal civility was just what it had been, and he detained her some minutes at the gate to hear and satisfy his enquiries after all her family. They were then, with no other delay than his pointing out the neatness of the entrance, taken into the house; and as soon as they were in the parlour, he welcomed them a second time with ostentatious formality to his humble abode, and punctually repeated all his wife's offers of refreshment.

Elizabeth was prepared to see him in his glory; and she could not help fancying that in displaying the good proportion of the room, its aspect and its furniture, he addressed himself particularly to her, as if wishing to make her feel what she had lost in refusing him. But though every thing seemed neat and comfortable, she was not able to gratify him by any sigh of repentance; and rather looked with wonder at her friend that she could have so cheerful an air, with such a companion. When Mr. Collins said any thing of which his wife might reasonably be ashamed, which certainly was not unseldom, she involuntarily turned her eye on Charlotte. Once or twice she could discern a faint blush; but in general Charlotte wisely did not hear. After sitting long enough to admire every article of furniture in the room, from the sideboard to the fender, to give an account of their journey and of all that had happened in London, Mr. Collins invited them to take a stroll in the garden, which was large and well laid out, and to the cultivation of which he attended himself. To work in his garden was one of his most respectable pleasures; and Elizabeth admired the command of countenance with which Charlotte talked of the healthfulness of the exercise, and owned she encouraged it as much as possible. Here, leading the way through every walk and cross walk, and scarcely allowing them an interval to utter the praises he asked for, every view was pointed out with a minuteness which left beauty entirely behind. He could number the fields in every direction, and could tell how many trees there were in the most distant clump. But of all the views which his garden, or which the county, or the kingdom could boast, none were to be compared with the prospect of Rosings, afforded by an opening in the trees that bordered the park nearly opposite the front of his house. It was a handsome modern building, well situated on rising ground.

From his garden, Mr. Collins would have led them round his two meadows, but the ladies not having shoes to encounter the remains of a white frost, turned back; and while Sir William accompanied him, Charlotte took her sister and friend over the house, extremely well pleased, probably, to have the opportunity of shewing it without her husband's help. It was rather small, but well built and convenient; and every thing was fitted up and arranged with a neatness and consistency of which Elizabeth gave Charlotte all the credit. When Mr. Collins could be forgotten, there was really a great air of comfort throughout, and by Charlotte's evident enjoyment of it, Elizabeth supposed he must be often forgotten.

She had already learnt that Lady Catherine was still in the country. It was spoken of again while they were at dinner, when Mr. Collins joining in, observed,

"Yes, Miss Elizabeth, you will have the honour of seeing Lady Catherine de Bourgh on the ensuing Sunday at church, and I need not say you will be delighted with her. She is all affability and condescension, and I doubt not but you will be honoured with some portion of her notice when service is over. I have scarcely any hesitation in saying that she will include you and my sister Maria in every invitation with which she honours us during your stay here. Her behaviour to my dear Charlotte is charming. We dine at Rosings twice every week, and are never allowed to walk home. Her ladyship's carriage is regularly ordered for us. I *should* say, one of her ladyship's carriages, for she has several."

"Lady Catherine is a very respectable, sensible woman indeed," added Charlotte, "and a most attentive neighbour."

"Very true, my dear, that is exactly what I say. She is the sort of woman whom one cannot regard with too much deference."

The evening was spent chiefly in talking over Hertfordshire news, and telling again what had been already written; and when it closed, Elizabeth in the solitude of her chamber had to meditate upon Charlotte's degree of contentment, to understand her address in guiding, and composure in bearing with her husband, and to acknowledge that it was all done very well. She had also to anticipate how her visit would pass, the quiet tenor of their usual employments, the vexatious interruptions of Mr. Collins, and the gaieties of their intercourse with Rosings. A lively imagination soon settled it all.

About the middle of the next day, as she was in her room getting ready for a walk, a sudden noise below seemed to speak the whole house in confusion; and after listening a moment, she heard somebody running up stairs in a violent hurry, and calling loudly after her. She opened the door, and met Maria in the landing place, who, breathless with agitation, cried out,

"Oh, my dear Eliza! pray make haste and come into the dining-room, for there is such a sight to be seen! I will not tell you what it is. Make haste, and come down this moment."

Elizabeth asked questions in vain; Maria would tell her nothing more, and down they ran into the dining-room, which fronted the lane, in quest of this wonder; it was two ladies stopping in a low phaeton at the garden gate.

"And is this all?" cried Elizabeth. "I expected at least that the pigs were got into the garden, and here is nothing but Lady Catherine and her daughter!"

"La! my dear," said Maria quite shocked at the mistake, "it is not Lady Catherine. The old lady is Mrs. Jenkinson, who lives with them. The other is Miss De Bourgh. Only look at her. She is quite a little creature. Who would have thought she could be so thin and small!"

"She is abominably rude to keep Charlotte out of doors in all this wind. Why does she not come in?"

"Oh! Charlotte says, she hardly ever does. It is the greatest of favours when Miss De Bourgh comes in."

"I like her appearance," said Elizabeth, struck with other ideas. "She looks sickly and cross.–Yes, she will do for him very well. She will make him a very proper wife."

Mr. Collins and Charlotte were both standing at the gate in conversation with the ladies; and Sir William, to Elizabeth's high diversion, was stationed in the door-way, in earnest contemplation of the greatness before him, and constantly bowing whenever Miss De Bourgh looked that way.

At length there was nothing more to be said; the ladies drove on, and the others returned into the house. Mr. Collins no sooner saw the two girls than he began to congratulate them on their good fortune, which Charlotte explained by letting them know that the whole party was asked to dine at Rosings the next day.

CHAPTER 6

Mr. Collins's triumph in consequence of this invitation was complete. The power of displaying the grandeur of his patroness to his wondering visitors, and of letting them see her civility towards himself and his wife, was exactly what he had wished for; and that an opportunity of doing it should be given so soon, was such an instance of Lady Catherine's condescension as he knew not how to admire enough.

"I confess," said he, "that I should not have been at all surprised by her Ladyship's asking us on Sunday to drink tea and spend the evening at Rosings. I rather expected, from my knowledge of her affability, that it would happen. But who could have foreseen such an attention as this? Who could have imagined that we should receive an invitation to dine there (an invitation moreover including the whole party) so immediately after your arrival!" "I am the less surprised at what has happened," replied Sir William, "from that knowledge of what the manners of the great really are, which my situation in life has allowed me to acquire. About the Court, such instances of elegant breeding are not uncommon."

Scarcely any thing was talked of the whole day or next morning, but their visit to Rosings. Mr. Collins was carefully instructing them in what they were to expect, that the sight of such rooms, so many servants, and so splendid a dinner might not wholly overpower them.

When the ladies were separating for the toilette, he said to Elizabeth,

"Do not make yourself uneasy, my dear cousin, about your apparel. Lady Catherine is far from requiring that elegance of dress in us, which becomes herself and daughter. I would advise you merely to put on whatever of your clothes is superior to the rest, there is no occasion for any thing more. Lady Catherine will not think the worse of you for being simply dressed. She likes to have the distinction of rank preserved."

While they were dressing, he came two or three times to their different doors, to recommend their being quick, as Lady Catherine very much objected to be kept waiting for her dinner.—Such formidable accounts of her Ladyship, and her manner of living, quite frightened Maria Lucas, who had been little used to company, and she looked forward to her introduction at Rosings, with as much apprehension, as her father had done to his presentation at St. James's.

As the weather was fine, they had a pleasant walk of about half a mile across the park.—Every park has its beauty and its prospects; and Elizabeth saw much to be pleased with, though she could not be in such raptures as Mr. Collins expected the scene to inspire, and was but slightly affected by his enumeration of the windows in front of the house, and his relation of what the glazing altogether had originally cost Sir Lewis De Bourgh.

When they ascended the steps to the hall, Maria's alarm was every moment increasing, and even Sir William did not look perfectly calm.—Elizabeth's courage did not fail her. She had heard nothing of Lady Catherine that spoke her awful from any extraordinary talents or miraculous virtue, and the mere stateliness of money and rank, she thought she could witness without trepidation.

From the entrance hall, of which Mr. Collins pointed out, with a rapturous air, the fine proportion and finished ornaments, they followed the servants through an antichamber, to the room where Lady Catherine, her daughter, and Mrs. Jenkinson were sitting.– Her Ladyship, with great condescension, arose to receive them; and as Mrs. Collins had settled it with her husband that the office of introduction should be her's, it was performed in a proper manner, without any of those apologies and thanks which he would have thought necessary.

In spite of having been at St. James's, Sir William was so completely awed, by the grandeur surrounding him, that he had but just courage enough to make a very low bow, and take his seat without saying a word; and his daughter, frightened almost out of her senses, sat on the edge of her chair, not knowing which way to look. Elizabeth found herself quite equal to the scene, and could observe the three ladies before her composedly.– Lady Catherine was a tall, large woman, with strongly-marked features, which might once have been handsome. Her air was not conciliating, nor was her manner of receiving them, such as to make her visitors forget their inferior rank. She was not rendered formidable by silence; but whatever she said, was spoken in so authoritative a tone, as marked her self-importance, and brought Mr. Wickham immediately to Elizabeth's mind; and from the observation of the day altogether, she believed Lady Catherine to be exactly what he had represented.

When, after examining the mother, in whose countenance and deportment she soon found some resemblance of Mr. Darcy, she turned her eyes on the daughter, she could almost have joined in Maria's astonishment, at her being so thin, and so small. There was neither in figure nor face, any likeness between the ladies. Miss De Bourgh was pale and sickly; her features, though not plain, were insignificant; and she spoke very little, except in a low voice, to Mrs. Jenkinson, in whose appearance there was nothing remarkable, and who was entirely engaged in listening to what she said, and placing a screen in the proper direction before her eyes.

After sitting a few minutes, they were all sent to one of the windows, to admire the view, Mr. Collins attending them to point out its beauties, and Lady Catherine kindly informing them that it was much better worth looking at in the summer.

The dinner was exceedingly handsome, and there were all the servants, and all the articles of plate which Mr. Collins had promised; and, as he had likewise foretold, he took his seat at the bottom of the table, by her ladyship's desire, and looked as if he felt that life could furnish nothing greater.—He carved, and ate, and praised with delighted alacrity; and every dish was commended, first by him, and then by Sir William, who was now enough recovered to echo whatever his son in law said, in a manner which Elizabeth wondered Lady Catherine could bear. But Lady Catherine seemed gratified by their excessive admiration, and gave most gracious smiles, especially when any dish on the table proved a novelty to them. The party did not supply much conversation. Elizabeth was ready to speak whenever there was an opening, but she was seated between Charlotte and Miss De Bourgh—the former of whom was engaged in listening to Lady Catherine, and the latter said not a word to her all dinner time. Mrs. Jenkinson was chiefly employed in watching how little Miss De Bourgh ate, pressing her to try some other dish, and fearing she were indisposed. Maria thought speaking out of the question, and the gentlemen did nothing but eat and admire.

When the ladies returned to the drawing room, there was little to be done but to hear Lady Catherine talk, which she did without any intermission till coffee came in, delivering her opinion on every subject in so decisive a manner as proved that she was not used to have her judgment controverted. She enquired into Charlotte's domestic concerns familiarly and minutely, and gave her a great deal of advice, as to the management of them all; told her how every thing ought to be regulated in so small a family as her's, and instructed her as to the care of her cows and her poultry. Elizabeth found that nothing was beneath this great Lady's attention, which could furnish her with an occasion of dictating to others. In the intervals of her discourse with Mrs. Collins, she addressed a variety of questions to Maria and Elizabeth, but especially to the latter, of whose connections she knew the least, and who she observed to Mrs. Collins, was a very genteel, pretty kind of girl. She asked her at different times, how many sisters she had, whether they were older or younger than herself, whether any of them were likely to be married, whether they were handsome, where they had been educated, what carriage her father kept, and what had been her mother's maiden name?—Elizabeth felt all the impertinence of her questions, but answered them very composedly.—Lady Catherine then observed,

"Your father's estate is entailed on Mr. Collins, I think. For your sake," turning to Charlotte, "I am glad of it; but otherwise I see no occasion for entailing estates from the female line.—It was not thought necessary in Sir Lewis de Bourgh's family.—Do you play and sing, Miss Bennet?"

"A little."

"Oh! then—some time or other we shall be happy to hear you. Our instrument is a capital one, probably superior to—You shall try it some day.—Do your sisters play and sing?"

"One of them does."

"Why did not you all learn?—You ought all to have learned. The Miss Webbs all play, and their father has not so good an income as your's.—Do you draw?"

"No, not at all."

"What, none of you?"

"Not one."

"That is very strange. But I suppose you had no opportunity. Your mother should have taken you to town every spring for the benefit of masters."

"My mother would have had no objection, but my father hates London."

"Has your governess left you?"

"We never had any governess."

"No governess! How was that possible? Five daughters brought up at home without a governess!—I never heard of such a thing.

Your mother must have been quite a slave to your education."

Elizabeth could hardly help smiling, as she assured her that had not been the case.

"Then, who taught you? who attended to you?—Without a governess you must have been neglected."

"Compared with some families, I believe we were; but such of us as wished to learn, never wanted the means. We were always encouraged to read, and had all the masters that were necessary. Those who chose to be idle, certainly might."

"Aye, no doubt; but that is what a governess will prevent, and if I had known your mother, I should have advised her most strenuously to engage one. I always say that nothing is to be done in education without steady and regular instruction, and nobody but a governess can give it. It is wonderful how many families I have been the means of supplying in that way. I am always glad to get a young person well placed out. Four nieces of Mrs. Jenkinson are most delightfully situated through my means; and it was but the other day, that I recommended another young person, who was merely accidentally mentioned to me, and the family are quite delighted with her. Mrs. Collins, did I tell you of Lady Metcalfe's calling yesterday to thank me? She finds Miss Pope a treasure. 'Lady Catherine,' said she, 'you have given me a treasure.' Are any of your younger sisters out, Miss Bennet?"

"Yes, Ma'am, all."

"All!—What, all five out at once? Very odd!—And you only the second.—The younger ones out before the elder are married!—Your younger sisters must be very young?"

"Yes, my youngest is not sixteen. Perhaps *she* is full young to be much in company. But really, Ma'am, I think it would be very hard upon younger sisters, that they should not have their share of society and amusement because the elder may not have the means or inclination to marry early.—The last born has as good a right to the pleasures of youth, as the first.—And to be kept back on *such* a motive!—I think it would not be very likely to promote sisterly affection or delicacy of mind."

"Upon my word," said her Ladyship, "you give your opinion very decidedly for so young a person.–Pray, what is your age?"

"With three younger sisters grown up," replied Elizabeth smiling, "your Ladyship can hardly expect me to own it."

Lady Catherine seemed quite astonished at not receiving a direct answer; and Elizabeth suspected herself to be the first creature who had ever dared to trifle with so much dignified impertinence?

"You cannot be more than twenty, I am sure,–therefore you need not conceal your age."

"I am not one and twenty."

When the gentlemen had joined them, and tea was over, the card tables were placed. Lady Catherine, Sir William, and Mr. and Mrs. Collins sat down to quadrille; and as Miss De Bourgh chose to play at cassino, the two girls had the honour of assisting Mrs. Jenkinson to make up her party. Their table was superlatively stupid. Scarcely a syllable was uttered that did not relate to the game, except when Mrs. Jenkinson expressed her fears of Miss De Bourgh's being too hot or too cold, or having too much or too little light. A great deal more passed at the other table. Lady Catherine was generally speaking–stating the mistakes of the three others, or relating some anecdote of herself. Mr. Collins was employed in agreeing to every thing her Ladyship said, thanking her for every fish he won, and apologising if he thought he won too many. Sir William did not say much. He was storing his memory with anecdotes and noble names.

When Lady Catherine and her daughter had played as long as they chose, the tables were broke up, the carriage was offered to Mrs. Collins, gratefully accepted, and immediately ordered. The party then gathered round the fire to hear Lady Catherine determine what weather they were to have on the morrow. From these instructions they were summoned by the arrival of the coach, and with many speeches of thankfulness on Mr. Collins's side, and as many bows on Sir William's, they departed. As soon as they had driven from the door, Elizabeth was called on by her cousin,

to give her opinion of all that she had seen at Rosings, which,
for Charlotte's sake, she made more favourable than it really was.
But her commendation, though costing her some trouble, could
by no means satisfy Mr. Collins, and he was very soon obliged
to take her Ladyship's praise into his own hands.

CHAPTER 7

Sir William staid only a week at Hunsford; but his visit was long
enough to convince him of his daughter's being most comfortably settled, and of her possessing such a husband and such a
neighbour as were not often met with. While Sir William was
with them, Mr. Collins devoted his mornings to driving him out
in his gig, and shewing him the country; but when he went away,
the whole family returned to their usual employments, and
Elizabeth was thankful to find that they did not see more of her
cousin by the alteration, for the chief of the time between breakfast and dinner was now passed by him either at work in the
garden, or in reading and writing, and looking out of window in
his own book room, which fronted the road. The room in which
the ladies sat was backwards. Elizabeth at first had rather wondered that Charlotte should not prefer the dining parlour for common use; it was a better sized room, and had a pleasanter aspect;
but she soon saw that her friend had an excellent reason for what
she did, for Mr. Collins would undoubtedly have been much less
in his own apartment, had they sat in one equally lively; and she
gave Charlotte credit for the arrangement.

From the drawing room they could distinguish nothing in the
lane, and were indebted to Mr. Collins for the knowledge of what
carriages went along, and how often especially Miss De Bourgh
drove by in her phaeton, which he never failed coming to inform
them of, though it happened almost every day. She not unfrequently stopped at the Parsonage, and had a few minutes'

conversation with Charlotte, but was scarcely ever prevailed on to get out.

Very few days passed in which Mr. Collins did not walk to Rosings, and not many in which his wife did not think it necessary to go likewise; and till Elizabeth recollected that there might be other family livings to be disposed of, she could not understand the sacrifice of so many hours. Now and then, they were honoured with a call from her Ladyship, and nothing escaped her observation that was passing in the room during these visits. She examined into their employments, looked at their work, and advised them to do it differently; found fault with the arrangement of the furniture, or detected the housemaid in negligence; and if she accepted any refreshment, seemed to do it only for the sake of finding out that Mrs. Collins's joints of meat were too large for her family.

Elizabeth soon perceived that though this great lady was not in the commission of the peace for the county, she was a most active magistrate in her own parish, the minutest concerns of which were carried to her by Mr. Collins; and whenever any of the cottagers were disposed to be quarrelsome, discontented or too poor, she sallied forth into the village to settle their differences, silence their complaints, and scold them into harmony and plenty.

The entertainment of dining at Rosings was repeated about twice a week; and, allowing for the loss of Sir William, and there being only one card table in the evening, every such entertainment was the counterpart of the first. Their other engagements were few; as the style of living of the neighbourhood in general, was beyond the Collinses' reach. This however was no evil to Elizabeth, and upon the whole she spent her time comfortably enough; there were half hours of pleasant conversation with Charlotte, and the weather was so fine for the time of year, that she had often great enjoyment out of doors. Her favourite walk, and where she frequently went while the others were calling on Lady Catherine, was along the open grove which edged that side of the park, where there was a nice sheltered path, which no one seemed to value but herself, and where she felt beyond the reach of Lady Catherine's curiosity.

In this quiet way, the first fortnight of her visit soon passed away. Easter was approaching, and the week preceding it, was to bring an addition to the family at Rosings, which in so small a circle must be important. Elizabeth had heard soon after her arrival, that Mr. Darcy was expected there in the course of a few weeks, and though there were not many of her acquaintance whom she did not prefer, his coming would furnish one comparatively new to look at in their Rosings parties, and she might be amused in seeing how hopeless Miss Bingley's designs on him were, by his behaviour to his cousin, for whom he was evidently destined by Lady Catherine; who talked of his coming with the greatest satisfaction, spoke of him in terms of the highest admiration, and seemed almost angry to find that he had already been frequently seen by Miss Lucas and herself.

His arrival was soon known at the Parsonage, for Mr. Collins was walking the whole morning within view of the lodges opening into Hunsford Lane, in order to have the earliest assurance of it; and after making his bow as the carriage turned into the Park, hurried home with the great intelligence. On the following morning he hastened to Rosings to pay his respects. There were two nephews of Lady Catherine to require them, for Mr. Darcy had brought with him a Colonel Fitzwilliam, the younger son of his uncle, Lord —— and to the great surprise of all the party, when Mr. Collins returned the gentlemen accompanied him. Charlotte had seen them from her husband's room, crossing the road, and immediately running into the other, told the girls what an honour they might expect, adding,

"I may thank you, Eliza, for this piece of civility. Mr. Darcy would never have come so soon to wait upon me."

Elizabeth had scarcely time to disclaim all right to the compliment, before their approach was announced by the door-bell, and shortly afterwards the three gentlemen entered the room.

Colonel Fitzwilliam, who led the way, was about thirty, not hand-some, but in person and address most truly the gentleman. Mr. Darcy looked just as he has been used to look in Hertfordshire, paid his compliments, with his usual reserve, to Mrs. Collins; and whatever might be his feelings towards her friend, met her with every appearance of composure. Elizabeth merely curtseyed to him, without saying a word.

Colonel Fitzwilliam entered into conversation directly with the readiness and ease of a well-bred man, and talked very pleasantly; but his cousin, after having addressed a slight obser-vation on the house and garden to Mrs. Collins, sat for some time without speaking to any body. At length, however, his civility was so far awakened as to enquire of Elizabeth after the health of her family. She answered him in the usual way, and after a moment's pause, added,

"My eldest sister has been in town these three months. Have you never happened to see her there?"

She was perfectly sensible that he never had; but she wished to see whether he would betray any consciousness of what had passed between the Bingleys and Jane; and she thought he looked a little confused as he answered that he had never been so fortu-nate as to meet Miss Bennet. The subject was pursued no farther, and the gentlemen soon afterwards went away.

CHAPTER 8

Colonel Fitzwilliam's manners were very much admired at the parsonage, and the ladies all felt that he must add considerably to the pleasure of their engagements at Rosings. It was some days, however, before they received any invitation thither, for while there were visitors in the house, they could not be necessary; and it was not till Easter-day, almost a week after the gentlemen's ar-rival, that they were honoured by such an attention, and then they were merely asked on leaving church to come there in the evening. For the last week they had seen very little of either Lady Catherine or her daughter. Colonel Fitzwilliam had called at the parsonage more than once during the time, but Mr. Darcy they had only seen at church.

The invitation was accepted of course, and at a proper hour they joined the party in Lady Catherine's drawing room. Her ladyship received them civilly, but it was plain that their company was by no means so acceptable as when she could get nobody else; and she was, in fact, almost engrossed by her nephews, speaking to them, especially to Darcy, much more than to any other person in the room.

Colonel Fitzwilliam seemed really glad to see them; any thing was a welcome relief to him at Rosings; and Mrs. Collins's pretty friend had moreover caught his fancy very much. He now seated himself by her, and talked so agreeably of Kent and Hertfordshire, of travelling and staying at home, of new books and music, that Elizabeth had never been half so well entertained in that room before; and they conversed with so much spirit and flow, as to draw the attention of Lady Catherine herself, as well as of Mr. Darcy. *His* eyes had been soon and repeatedly turned towards them with a look of curiosity; and that her ladyship after a while shared the feeling, was more openly acknowledged, for she did not scruple to call out,

"What is that you are saying, Fitzwilliam? What is it you are talking of? What are you telling Miss Bennet? Let me hear what it is."

"We are speaking of music, Madam," said he, when no longer able to avoid a reply.

"Of music! Then pray speak aloud. It is of all subjects my delight. I must have my share in the conversation, if you are speaking of music. There are few people in England, I suppose, who have more true enjoyment of music than myself, or a better natural taste. If I had ever learnt, I should have been a great proficient. And so would Anne, if her health had allowed her to apply. I am confident that she would have performed delightfully. How does Georgiana get on, Darcy?"

Mr. Darcy spoke with affectionate praise of his sister's proficiency.

"I am very glad to hear such a good account of her," said Lady Catherine; "and pray tell her from me, that she cannot expect to excel, if she does not practise a great deal."

"I assure you, Madam," he replied, "that she does not need such advice. She practises very constantly."

"So much the better. It cannot be done too much; and when I next write to her, I shall charge her not to neglect it on any account. I often tell young ladies, that no excellence in music is to be acquired, without constant practice. I have told Miss Bennet several times, that she will never play really well, unless she practises more; and though Mrs. Collins has no instrument, she is very welcome, as I have often told her, to come to Rosings every day, and play on the piano forte in Mrs. Jenkinson's room. She would be in nobody's way, you know, in that part of the house."

Mr. Darcy looked a little ashamed of his aunt's ill breeding, and made no answer.

When coffee was over, Colonel Fitzwilliam reminded Elizabeth of having promised to play to him; and she sat down directly to the instrument. He drew a chair near her. Lady Catherine listened to half a song, and then talked, as before, to her other nephew; till the latter walked away from her, and moving with his usual deliberation towards the piano forte, stationed himself so as to command a full view of the fair performer's countenance. Elizabeth saw what he was doing, and at the first convenient pause, turned to him with an arch smile and said,

"You mean to frighten me, Mr. Darcy, by coming in all this state to hear me? But I will not be alarmed though your sister *does* play so well. There is a stubbornness about me that never can bear to be frightened at the will of others. My courage always rises with every attempt to intimidate me."

"I shall not say that you are mistaken," he replied, "because you could not really believe me to entertain any design of alarming you; and I have had the pleasure of your acquaintance long enough to know, that you find great enjoyment in occasionally professing opinions which in fact are not your own."

Elizabeth laughed heartily at this picture of herself, and said to Colonel Fitzwilliam, "Your cousin will give you a very pretty notion of me, and teach you not to believe a word I say. I am particularly unlucky in meeting with a person so well able to expose my real character, in a part of the world, where I had hoped to pass myself off with some degree of credit. Indeed, Mr. Darcy, it is very ungenerous in you to mention that you knew to my disadvantage in Hertfordshire—and, give me leave to say, very impolitic too—for it is provoking me to retaliate, and such things may come out, as will shock your relations to hear."

"I am not afraid of you," said he, smilingly.

"Pray let me hear what you have to accuse him of," cried Colonel Fitzwilliam, "I should like to know how he behaves among strangers."

"You shall hear then—but prepare for something very dreadful. The first time of my ever seeing him in Hertfordshire, you must know, was at a ball—and at this ball, what do you think he did? He danced only four dances! I am sorry to pain you—but so it was. He danced only four dances, though gentlemen were scarce; and, to my certain knowledge, more than one young lady was sitting down in want of a partner. Mr. Darcy, you cannot deny the fact."

"I had not at that time the honour of knowing any lady in the assembly beyond my own party."

"True; and nobody can ever be introduced in a ball-room. Well, Colonel Fitzwilliam, what do I play next? My fingers wait your orders."

"Perhaps," said Darcy, "I should have judged better, had I sought an introduction, but I am ill qualified to recommend myself to strangers."

"Shall we ask your cousin the reason of this?" said Elizabeth, still addressing Colonel Fitzwilliam. "Shall we ask him why a man of sense and education, and who has lived in the world, is ill-qualified to recommend himself to strangers?"

"I can answer your question," said Fitzwilliam, "without applying to him. It is because he will not give himself the trouble."

"I certainly have not the talent which some people possess," said Darcy, "of conversing easily with those I have never seen before. I cannot catch their tone of conversation, or appear interested in their concerns, as I often see done."

"My fingers," said Elizabeth, "do not move over this instrument in the masterly manner which I see so many women's do. They have not the same force or rapidity, and do not produce the same expression. But then I have always supposed it to be my own fault—because I would not take the trouble of practising. It is not that I do not believe *my* fingers as capable as any other woman's of superior execution."

Darcy smiled and said, "You are perfectly right, You have employed your time much better. No one admitted to the privilege of hearing you, can think any thing wanting. We neither of us perform to strangers."

Here they were interrupted by Lady Catherine, who called out to know what they were talking of. Elizabeth immediately began playing again. Lady Catherine approached, and, after listening for a few minutes, said to Darcy,

"Miss Bennet would not play at all amiss, if she practised more, and could have the advantage of a London master. She has a very good notion of fingering, though her taste is not equal to Anne's. Anne would have been a delightful performer, had her health allowed her to learn."

Elizabeth looked at Darcy to see how cordially he assented to his cousin's praise; but neither at that moment nor at any other could she discern any symptom of love; and from the whole of his behaviour to Miss De Bourgh she derived this comfort for Miss Bingley, that, he might have been just as likely to marry *her,* had she been his relation.

Lady Catherine continued her remarks on Elizabeth's performance, mixing with them many instructions on execution and taste. Elizabeth received them with all the forbearance of civility; and at the request of the gentlemen remained at the instrument till her Ladyship's carriage was ready to take them all home.

CHAPTER 9

Elizabeth was sitting by herself the next morning, and writing to Jane, while Mrs. Collins and Maria were gone on business into the village, when she was startled by a ring at the door, the certain signal of a visitor. As she had heard no carriage, she thought it not unlikely to be Lady Catherine, and under that apprehension was putting away her half-finished letter that she might escape all impertinent questions, when the door opened, and to her very great surprise, Mr. Darcy, and Mr. Darcy only, entered the room.

He seemed astonished too on finding her alone, and apologised for his intrusion, by letting her know that he had understood all the ladies to be within.

They then sat down, and when her enquiries after Rosings were made, seemed in danger of sinking into total silence. It was absolutely necessary, therefore, to think of something, and in this emergence recollecting *when* she had seen him last in Hertfordshire, and feeling curious to know what he would say on the subject of their hasty departure, she observed,

"How very suddenly you all quitted Netherfield last November, Mr. Darcy! It must have been a most agreeable surprise to Mr. Bingley to see you all after him say so soon; for, if I recollect right, he went but the day before. He and his sisters were well, I hope, when you left London."

"Perfectly so—I thank you."

She found that she was to receive no other answer—and, after a short pause, added,

"I think I have understood that Mr. Bingley has not much idea of ever returning to Netherfield again?"

"I have never heard him say so; but it is probable that he may spend very little of his time there in future. He has many friends, and he is at a time of life when friends and engagements are continually increasing."

"If he means to be but little at Netherfield, it would be better for the neighbourhood that he should give up the place entirely, for then we might possibly get a settled family there. But perhaps Mr. Bingley did not take the house so much for the convenience of the neighbourhood as for his own, and we must expect him to keep or quit it on the same principle."

"I should not be surprised," said Darcy, "if he were to give it up, as soon as any eligible purchase offers."

Elizabeth made no answer. She was afraid of talking longer of his friend; and, having nothing else to say, was now determined to leave the trouble of finding a subject to him.

He took the hint, and soon began with, "This seems a very comfortable house. Lady Catherine, I believe, did a great deal to it when Mr. Collins first came to Hunsford."

"I believe she did – and I am sure she could not have bestowed her kindness on a more grateful object."

"Mr. Collins appears very fortunate in his choice of a wife."

"Yes, indeed; his friends may well rejoice in his having met with one of the very few sensible women who would have accepted him, or have made him happy if they had. My friend has an excellent understanding – though I am not certain that I consider her marrying Mr. Collins as the wisest thing she ever did. She seems perfectly happy, however, and in a prudential light, it is certainly a very good match for her."

"It must be very agreeable to her to be settled within so easy a distance of her own family and friends."

"An easy distance do you call it? It is nearly fifty miles."

"And what is fifty miles of good road? Little more than half a day's journey. Yes, I call it a *very easy* distance."

"I should never have considered the distance as one of the *advantages* of the match," cried Elizabeth. "I should never have said Mrs. Collins was settled *near* her family."

"It is a proof of your own attachment to Hertfordshire. Any thing beyond the very neighbourhood of Longbourn, I suppose, would appear far."

As he spoke there was a sort of smile, which Elizabeth fancied she understood; he must be supposing her to be thinking of Jane and Netherfield, and she blushed as she answered,

"I do not mean to say that a woman may not be settled too near her family. The far and the near must be relative, and depend on many varying circumstances. Where there is fortune to make the expence of travelling unimportant, distance becomes no evil. But that is not the case *here*. Mr. and Mrs. Collins have a comfortable income, but not such a one as will allow of frequent journeys—and I am persuaded my friend would not call herself *near* her family under less than *half* the present distance."

Mr. Darcy drew his chair a little towards her, and said, "*You* cannot have a right to such very strong local attachment. *You* cannot have been always at Longbourn."

Elizabeth looked surprised. The gentleman experienced some change of feeling; he drew back his chair, took a newspaper from the table, and, glancing over it, said, in a colder voice,

"Are you pleased with Kent?"

A short dialogue on the subject of the country ensued, on either side calm and concise—and soon put an end to by the entrance of Charlotte and her sister, just returned from their walk. The tête a tête surprised them. Mr. Darcy related the mistake which had occasioned his intruding on Miss Bennet, and after sitting a few minutes longer without saying much to any body, went away.

"What can be the meaning of this!" said Charlotte, as soon as he was gone. "My dear Eliza he must be in love with you, or he would never have called on us in this familiar way."

But when Elizabeth told of his silence, it did not seem very likely, even to Charlotte's wishes, to be the case; and after vari-

ous conjectures, they could at last only suppose his visit to proceed from the difficulty of finding any thing to do, which was
the more probable from the time of year. All field sports were
over. Within doors there was Lady Catherine, books, and a billiard table, but gentlemen cannot be always within doors; and
in the nearness of the Parsonage, or the pleasantness of the walk
to it, or of the people who lived in it, the two cousins found a
temptation from this period of walking thither almost every day.
They called at various times of the morning, sometimes separately,
sometimes together, and now and then accompanied by their aunt.
It was plain to them all that Colonel Fitzwilliam came because
he had pleasure in their society, a persuasion which of course
recommended him still more; and Elizabeth was reminded by her
own satisfaction in being with him, as well as by his evident admiration of her, of her former favourite George Wickham; and
though, in comparing them, she saw there was less captivating
softness in Colonel Fitzwilliam's manners, she believed he might
have the best informed mind.

But why Mr. Darcy came so often to the Parsonage, it was more
difficult to understand. It could not be for society, as he frequently
sat there ten minutes together without opening his lips; and when
he did speak, it seemed the effect of necessity rather than of
choice—a sacrifice to propriety, not a pleasure to himself. He seldom appeared really animated. Mrs. Collins knew not what to
make of him. Colonel Fitzwilliam's occasionally laughing at his
stupidity, proved that he was generally different, which her own
knowledge of him could not have told her; and as she would have
liked to believe this change the effect of love, and the object of
that love, her friend Eliza, she sat herself seriously to work to find
it out—She watched him whenever they were at Rosings, and
whenever he came to Hunsford; but without much success. He
certainly looked at her friend a great deal, but the expression of
that look was disputable. It was an earnest, stedfast gaze, but she
often doubted whether there were much admiration in it, and
sometimes it seemed nothing but absence of mind.

She had once or twice suggested to Elizabeth the possibility of his being partial to her, but Elizabeth always laughed at the idea; and Mrs. Collins did not think it right to press the subject, from the danger of raising expectations which might only end in disappointment; for in her opinion it admitted not of a doubt, that all her friend's dislike would vanish, if she could suppose him to be in her power.

In her kind schemes for Elizabeth, she sometimes planned her marrying Colonel Fitzwilliam. He was beyond comparison the pleasantest man; he certainly admired her, and his situation in life was most eligible; but, to counter-balance these advantages, Mr. Darcy had considerable patronage in the church, and his cousin could have none at all.

CHAPTER 10

More than once did Elizabeth in her ramble within the Park, un-expectedly meet Mr. Darcy.—She felt all the perverseness of the mischance that should bring him where no one else was brought; and to prevent its ever happening again, took care to inform him at first, that it was a favourite haunt of hers.—How it could occur a second time therefore was very odd!—Yet it did, and even a third. It seemed like the wilful ill-nature, or a voluntary penance, for on these occasions it was not merely a few formal enquiries and an awkward pause and then away, but he actually thought it neces-sary to turn back and walk with her. He never said a great deal, nor did she give herself the trouble of talking or of listening much; but it struck her in the course of their third rencontre that he was asking some odd unconnected questions—about her pleas-ure in being at Hunsford, her love of solitary walks, and her opin-ion of Mr. and Mrs. Collins's happiness; and that in speaking of Rosings and her not perfectly understanding the house, he seemed to expect that whenever she came into Kent again she would be staying *there* too. His words seemed to imply it. Could he have Colonel Fitzwilliam in his thoughts? She supposed, if he meant any thing, he must mean an allusion to what might arise in that quarter. It distressed her a little, and she was quite glad to find herself at the gate in the pales opposite the Parsonage.

She was engaged one day as she walked, in re-perusing Jane's last letter, and dwelling on some passages which proved that Jane had not written in spirits, when, instead of being again surprised by Mr. Darcy, she saw on looking up that Colonel Fitzwilliam was meeting her. Putting away the letter immediately and forcing a smile, she said,

"I did not know before that you ever walked this way."

"I have been making the tour of the Park," he replied, "as I generally do every year, and intended to close it with a call at the Parsonage. Are you going much farther?"

"No, I should have turned in a moment."

And accordingly she did turn, and they walked towards the Parsonage together.

"Do you certainly leave Kent on Saturday?" said she.

"Yes—if Darcy does not put it off again. But I am at his disposal. He arranges the business just as he pleases."

"And if not able to please himself in the arrangement, he has at least great pleasure in the power of choice. I do not know any body who seems more to enjoy the power of doing what he likes than Mr. Darcy."

"He likes to have his own way very well," replied Colonel Fitzwilliam. "But so we all do. It is only that he has better means of having it than many others, because he is rich, and many others are poor. I speak feelingly. A younger son, you know, must be inured to self-denial and dependence."

"In my opinion, the younger son of an Earl can know very little of either. Now, seriously, what have you ever known of self-denial and dependence? When have you been prevented by want of money from going wherever you chose, or procuring any thing you had a fancy for?"

"These are home questions—and perhaps I cannot say that I have experienced many hardships of that nature. But in matters of greater weight, I may suffer from the want of money. Younger sons cannot marry where they like."

"Unless where they like women of fortune, which I think they very often do."

"Our habits of expense make us too dependant, and there are not many in my rank of life who can afford to marry without some attention to money."

"Is this," thought Elizabeth, "meant for me?" and she coloured at the idea; but, recovering herself, said in a lively tone, "and pray, what is the usual price of an Earl's younger son? Unles the elder brother is very sickly, I suppose you would not ask above fifty thousand pounds."

He answered her in the same style, and the subject dropped. To interrupt a silence which might make him fancy her affected with what had passed, she soon afterwards said,

"I imagine your cousin brought you down with him chiefly for the sake of having somebody at his disposal. I wonder he does not marry, to secure a lasting convenience of that kind. But, perhaps his sister does as well for the present, and, as she is under his sole care, he may do what he likes with her."

"No," said Colonel Fitzwilliam, "that is an advantage which he must divide with me. I am joined with him in the guardianship of Miss Darcy."

"Are you, indeed? And pray what sort of guardians do you make? Does your charge give you much trouble? Young ladies of her age, are sometimes a little difficult to manage, and if she has the true Darcy spirit, she may like to have her own way."

As she spoke, she observed him looking at her earnestly, and the manner in which he immediately asked her why she supposed Miss Darcy likely to give them any uneasiness, convinced her that she had somehow or other got pretty near the truth. She directly replied,

"You need not be frightened. I never heard any harm of her; and I dare say she is one of the most tractable creatures in the world. She is a very great favourite with some ladies of my acquaintance, Mrs. Hurst and Miss Bingley. I think I have heard you say that you know them."

"I know them a little. Their brother is a pleasant gentleman-like man—he is a great friend of Darcy's."

"Oh! yes," said Elizabeth drily—"Mr. Darcy is uncommonly kind to Mr. Bingley, and takes a prodigious deal of care of him."

"Care of him!—Yes, I really believe Darcy *does* take care of him in those points where he most wants care. From something that he told me in our journey hither, I have reason to think Bingley very much indebted to him. But I ought to beg his pardon, for I have no right to suppose that Bingley was the person meant. That was all conjecture."

"What is it you mean?"

"It is a circumstance which Darcy of course would not wish to be generally known, because if it were to get round to the lady's family, it would be an unpleasant thing."

"You may depend upon my not mentioning it."

"And remember that I have not much reason for supposing it to be Bingley. What he told me was merely this; that he congratulated himself on having lately saved a friend from the inconveniences of a most imprudent marriage, but without mentioning names or any other particulars, and I only suspected it to be Bingley from believing him the kind of young man to get into a scrape of that sort, and from knowing them to have been together the whole of last summer."

"Did Mr. Darcy give you his reasons for this interference?"

"I understood that there were some very strong objections against the lady."

"And what arts did he use to separate them?"

"He did not talk to me of his own arts," said Fitzwilliam smiling. "He only told me, what I have now told you."

Elizabeth made no answer, and walked on, her heart swelling with indignation. After watching her a little, Fitzwilliam asked her why she was so thoughtful.

"I am thinking of what you have been telling me," said she. "Your cousin's conduct does not suit my feelings. Why was he to be the judge?"

"You are rather disposed to call his interference officious?"

"I do not see what right Mr. Darcy had to decide on the propriety of his friend's inclination, or why, upon his own judgment alone, he was to determine and direct in what manner that friend was to be happy." "But," she continued, recollecting herself, "as we know none of the particulars, it is not fair to condemn him. It is not to be supposed that there was much affection in the case."

"That is not an unnatural surmise," said Fitzwilliam, "but it is lessening the honour of my cousin's triumph very sadly."

This was spoken jestingly, but it appeared to her so just a picture of Mr. Darcy, that she would not trust herself with an answer; and, therefore, abruptly changing the conversation, talked on indifferent matters till they reached the parsonage. There, shut into her own room, as soon as their visitor left them; she could think without interruption of all that she had heard. It was not to be supposed that any other people could be meant than those with whom she was connected. There could not exist in the world *two* men, over whom Mr. Darcy could have such boundless influence. That he had been concerned in the measures taken to separate Mr. Bingley and Jane, she had never doubted; but she had always attributed to Miss Bingley the principal design and arrangement of them. If his own vanity, however, did not mislead him, *he* was the cause, his pride and caprice were the cause of all that Jane had suffered, and still continued to suffer. He had ruined for a while every hope of happiness for the most affectionate, generous heart in the world; and no one could say how lasting an evil he might have inflicted.

"There were some very strong objections against the lady," were Colonel Fitzwilliam's words, and these strong objections probably were, her having one uncle who was a country attorney, and another who was in business in London. "To Jane herself," she exclaimed, "there could be no possibility of objection. All loveliness and goodness as she is! Her understanding excellent, her mind improved, and her manners captivating. Neither could any thing be urged against my father, who, though with some peculiarities, has abilities which Mr. Darcy himself need not disdain, and respectability which he will probably never reach." When she thought of her mother indeed, her confidence gave way a little, but she would not allow that any objections *there* had material weight with Mr. Darcy, whose pride, she was convinced, would receive a deeper wound from the want of importance in his friend's connections, than from their want of sense; and she was quite decided at last, that he had been partly governed by this worst kind of pride, and partly by the wish of retaining Mr. Bingley for his sister.

The agitation and tears which the subject occasioned, brought on a headach; and it grew so much worse towards the evening that, added to her unwillingness to see Mr. Darcy, it determined her not to attend her cousins to Rosings, where they were engaged to drink tea. Mrs. Collins, seeing that she was really unwell, did not press her to go, and as much as possible prevented her husband from pressing her, but Mr. Collins could not conceal his apprehension of Lady Catherine's being rather displeased by her staying at home.

CHAPTER 11

When they were gone, Elizabeth, as if intending to exasperate herself as much as possible against Mr. Darcy, chose for her employment the examination of all the letters which Jane had written to her since her being in Kent. They contained no actual complaint, nor was there any revival of past occurrences, or any communication of present suffering. But in all, and in almost every line of each, there was a want of that cheerfulness which had been used to characterize her style, and which, proceeding from the serenity of a mind at ease with itself, and kindly disposed towards every one, and been scarcely ever clouded. Elizabeth noticed every sentence conveying the idea of uneasiness, with an attention which it had hardly received on the first perusal. Mr. Darcy's shameful boast of what misery he had been able to inflict, gave her a keener sense of her sister's sufferings. It was some consolation to think that his visit to Rosings was to end on the day after the next, and a still greater, that in less than a fortnight she should herself be with Jane again, and enabled to contribute to the recovery of her spirits, by all that affection could do.

She could not think of Darcy's leaving Kent, without remembering that his cousin was to go with him; but Colonel Fitzwilliam had made it clear that he had no intentions at all, and agreeable as he was, she did not mean to be unhappy about him.

While settling this point, she was suddenly roused by the sound of the door bell, and her spirits were a little fluttered by the idea of its being Colonel Fitzwilliam himself, who had once before called late in the evening, and might now come to enquire particularly after her. But this idea was soon banished, and her spirits were very differently affected, when, to her utter amazement, she saw Mr. Darcy walk into the room. In an hurried manner he immediately began an enquiry after her health, imputing his visit to a wish of hearing that she were better. She answered him with cold civility. He sat down for a few moments, and then getting up walked about the room. Elizabeth was surprised, but said not a word. After a silence of several minutes he came towards her in an agitated manner, and thus began,

"In vain have I struggled. It will not do. My feelings will not be repressed. You must allow me to tell you how ardently I admire and love you."

Elizabeth's astonishment was beyond expression. She stared, coloured, doubted, and was silent. This he considered sufficient encouragement, and the avowal of all that he felt and had long felt for her, immediately followed. He spoke well, but there were feelings besides those of the heart to be detailed, and he was not more eloquent on the subject of tenderness than of pride. His sense of her inferiority—of its being a degradation—of the family obstacles which judgment had always opposed to inclination, were dwelt on with a warmth which seemed due to the consequence he was wounding, but was very unlikely to recommend his suit.

In spite of her deeply-rooted dislike she could not be insensible to the compliment of such a man's affection, and though her intentions did not vary for an instant, she was at first sorry for the pain he was to receive; till, roused to resentment by his subsequent language she lost all compassion in anger. She tried, however, to compose herself to answer him with patience, when he should have done. He concluded with representing to her the strength of that attachment which, in spite of all his endeavours, he had found impossible to conquer; and with expressing his hope that it would now be rewarded by her acceptance of his hand. As he said this, she could easily see that he had no doubt of a favourable answer. He *spoke* of apprehension and anxiety, but his countenance expressed real security. Such a circumstance could only exasperate farther, and when he ceased, the colour rose into her cheeks, and she said,

"In such cases as this, it is, I believe, the established mode to express a sense of obligation for the sentiments avowed, however unequally they may be returned. It is natural that obligation should be felt, and if I could *feel* gratitude, I would now thank you. But I cannot—I have never desired your good opinion, and you have certainly bestowed it most unwillingly. I am sorry to have occasioned pain to any one. It has been most unconsciously done, however, and I hope will be of short duration. The feelings which, you tell me, have long prevented the acknowledgment of your regard, can have little difficulty in overcoming it after this explanation."

Mr. Darcy, who was leaning against the mantle-piece with his eyes fixed on her face, seemed to catch her words with no less resentment than surprise. His complexion became pale with anger, and the disturbance of his mind was visible in every feature. He was struggling for the appearance of composure, and would not open his lips, till he believed himself to have attained it. The pause was to Elizabeth's feelings dreadful. At length, in a voice of forced calmness, he said,

"And this is all the reply which I am to have the honour of expecting! I might, perhaps, wish to be informed why, with so little *endeavour* at civility, I am thus rejected. But it is of small importance."

"I might as well enquire," replied she, "why with so evident a design of offending and insulting me, you chose to tell me that you liked me against your will, against your reason, and even against your character? Was not this some excuse for incivility, if I *was* uncivil? But I have other provocations. You know I have. Had not my own feelings decided against you, had they been in-different, or had they even been favourable, do you think that any consideration would tempt me to accept the man, who has been the means of ruining, perhaps for ever, the happiness of a most beloved sister?"

As she pronounced these words, Mr. Darcy changed colour; but the emotion was short, and he listened without attempting to interrupt her while she continued.

"I have every reason in the world to think ill of you. No motive can excuse the unjust and ungenerous part you acted *there*. You dare not, you cannot deny that you have been the principal, if not the only means of dividing them from each other, of expos-ing one to the censure of the world for caprice and instability, the other to its derision for disappointed hopes, and involving them both in misery of the acutest kind."

She paused, and saw with no slight indignation that he was listening with an air which proved him wholly unmoved by any feeling of remorse. He even looked at her with a smile of affected incredulity.

"Can you deny that you have done it?" she repeated.

With assumed tranquillity he then replied, "I have no wish of denying that I did every thing in my power to separate my friend from your sister, or that I rejoice in my success. Towards *him* I have been kinder than towards myself."

Elizabeth disdained the appearance of noticing this civil reflection, but its meaning did not escape, nor was it likely to conciliate her.

"But it is not merely this affair," she continued, "on which my dislike is founded. Long before it had taken place, my opinion of you was decided. Your character was unfolded in the recital which I received many months ago from Mr. Wickham. On this subject, what can you have to say? In what imaginary act of friendship can you here defend yourself? or under what misrepresentation, can you here impose upon others?"

"You take an eager interest in that gentleman's concerns," said Darcy in a less tranquil tone, and with a heightened colour.

"Who that knows what his misfortunes have been, can help feeling an interest in him?"

"His misfortunes!" repeated Darcy contemptuously; "yes, his misfortunes have been great indeed."

"And of your infliction," cried Elizabeth with energy. "You have reduced him to his present state of poverty, comparative poverty. You have withheld the advantages, which you must know to have been designed for him. You have deprived the best years of his life, of that independence which was no less his due than his desert. You have done all this! and yet you can treat the mention of his misfortunes with contempt and ridicule."

"And this," cried Darcy, as he walked with quick steps across the room, "is your opinion of me! This is the estimation in which you hold me! I thank you for explaining it so fully. My faults, according to this calculation, are heavy indeed! But perhaps," added he, stopping in his walk, and turning towards her, "these offences might have been overlooked, had not your pride been hurt by my honest confession of the scruples that had long prevented my forming any serious design. These bitter accusations might have been suppressed, had I with greater policy concealed my struggles, and flattered you into the belief of my being impelled by unqualified, unalloyed inclination; by reason, by reflection, by every thing. But disguise of every sort is my abhorrence. Nor am I ashamed of the feelings I related. They were natural and just. Could you expect me to rejoice in the inferiority of your connections? To congratulate myself on the hope of relations, whose condition in life is so decidedly beneath my own?"

Elizabeth felt herself growing more angry every moment; yet she tried to the utmost to speak with composure when she said,

"You are mistaken, Mr. Darcy, if you suppose that the mode of your declaration affected me in any other way, than as it spared me the concern which I might have felt in refusing you, had you behaved in a more gentleman-like manner."

She saw him start at this, but he said nothing, and she continued,

"You could not have made me the offer of your hand in any possible way that would have tempted me to accept it."

Again his astonishment was obvious; and he looked at her with an expression of mingled incredulity and mortification. She went on.

"From the very beginning, from the first moment I may almost say, of my acquaintance with you, your manners impressing me with the fullest belief of your arrogance, your conceit, and your selfish disdain of the feelings of others, were such as to form that ground-work of disapprobation, on which succeeding events have built so immovable a dislike; and I had not known you a month before I felt that you were the last man in the world whom I could ever be prevailed on to marry."

"You have said quite enough, madam. I perfectly comprehend your feelings, and have now only to be ashamed of what my own have been. Forgive me for having taken up so much of your time, and accept my best wishes for your health and happiness."

And with these words he hastily left the room, and Elizabeth heard him the next moment open the front door and quit the house.

The tumult of her mind was now painfully great. She knew

not how to support herself, and from actual weakness sat down and cried for half an hour. Her astonishment, as she reflected on what had passed, was increased by every review of it. That she should receive an offer of marriage from Mr. Darcy! that he should have been in love with her for so many months! so much in love as to wish to marry her in spite of all the objections which had made him prevent his friend's marrying her sister, and which must appear at least with equal force in his own case, was almost incredible! it was gratifying to have inspired unconsciously so strong an affection. But his pride, his abominable pride, his shameless avowal of what he had done with respect to Jane, his unpardonable assurance in acknowledging, though he could not justify it, and the unfeeling manner in which he had mentioned Mr. Wickham, his cruelty towards whom he had not attempted to deny, soon overcame the pity which the consideration of his attachment had for a moment excited.

She continued in very agitating reflections till the sound of Lady Catherine's carriage made her feel how unequal she was to encounter Charlotte's observation, and hurried her away to her room.

CHAPTER 12

Elizabeth awoke the next morning to the same thoughts and meditations which had at length closed her eyes. She could not yet recover from the surprise of what had happened; it was impossible to think of any thing else, and totally indisposed for employment, she resolved soon after breakfast to indulge herself in air and exercise. She was proceeding directly to her favourite walk, when the recollection of Mr. Darcy's sometimes coming there stopped her, and instead of entering the park, she turned up the lane, which led her farther from the turnpike road. The park paling was still the boundary on one side, and she soon passed one of the gates into the ground.

After walking two or three times along that part of the lane,
she was tempted, but the pleasantness of the morning, to stop
at the gates and look into the park. The five weeks which she
had now passed in Kent, had made a great difference in the country, and every day was adding to the verdure of the early trees.
She was on the point of continuing her walk, when she caught
a glimpse of a gentleman within the sort of grove which edged
the park; he was moving that way; and fearful of its being Mr.
Darcy, she was directly retreating. But the person who advanced,
was now near enough to see her, and stepping forward with eagerness, pronounced her name. She had turned away, but on hearing herself called, though in a voice which proved it to be Mr.
Darcy, she moved again towards the gate. He had by that time
reached it also, and holding out a letter, which she instinctively
took, said with a look of haughty composure, "I have been walking in the grove some time in the hope of meeting you. Will you
do me the honour of reading that letter?"–And then, with a slight
bow, turned again into the plantation, and was soon out of sight.

With no expectation of pleasure, but with the strongest curiosity, Elizabeth opened the letter, and to her still increasing wonder,
perceived an envelope containing two sheets of letter paper, written
quite through, in a very close hand.–The envelope itself was likewise full.–Pursuing her way along the lane, she then began it.
It was dated from Rosings, at eight o'clock in the morning, and
was as follows:–

Be not alarmed, Madam, on receiving this letter, by the apprehension of its containing any repetition of those sentiments,
or renewal of those offers, which were last night so disgusting
to you. I write without any intention of paining you, or humbling myself, by dwelling on wishes, which, for the happiness
of both, cannot be too soon forgotten; and the effort which
the formation, and the perusal of this letter must occasion,
should have been spared, had not my character required it to
be written and read. You must, therefore, pardon the freedom
with which I demand your attention; your feelings, I know, will
bestow it unwillingly, but I demand it of your justice.

Two offences of a very different nature, and by no means of equal magnitude, you last night laid to my charge. The first mentioned was, that, regardless of the sentiments of either, I had detached Mr. Bingley from your sister,—and the other, that I had, in defiance of various claims, in defiance of honour and humanity, ruined the immediate prosperity, and blasted the prospects of Mr. Wickham.—Wilfully and wantonly to have thrown off the companion of my youth, the acknowledged favourite of my father, a young man who had scarcely any other dependence than on our patronage, and who had been brought up to expect its exertion, would be a depravity, to which the separation of two young persons, whose affection could be the growth of only a few weeks, could bear no comparison.—But from the severity of that blame which was last night so liberally bestowed, respecting each circumstance, I shall hope to be in future secured, when the following account of my actions and their motives has been read.—If, in the explanation of them which is due to myself, I am under the necessity of relating feelings which may be offensive to your's, I can only say that I am sorry.—The necessity must be obeyed—and farther apology would be absurd. I had not been long in Hertfordshire, before I saw, in common with others, that Bingley preferred your eldest sister, to any other young woman in the country.—But it was not till the evening of the dance at Netherfield that I had any apprehension of his feeling a serious attachment.—I had often seen him in love before.—At that ball, while I had the honour of dancing with you, I was first made acquainted, by Sir William Lucas's accidental information, that Bingley's attentions to your sister had given rise to a general expectation of their marriage. He spoke of it as a certain event, of which the time alone could be undecided. From that moment I observed my friend's behaviour attentively; and I could then perceive that his partiality for Miss Bennet was beyond what I had ever witnessed in him. Your sister I also watched.—Her look and manners were open, cheerful and engaging as ever, but without any symptom of peculiar regard, and I remained convinced from the evening's scrutiny, that though she received his attentions with pleasure, she did not invite them by any participation of sentiment.—If *you* have not been mistaken here, I must have been in an error. Your superior knowledge of your sister must make the latter probable.—If it be so, if I have been

misled by such error, to inflict pain on her, your resentment
has not been unreasonable. But I shall not scruple to assert,
that the serenity of your sister's countenance and air was such,
as might have given the most acute observer, a conviction that,
however amiable her temper, her heart was not likely to be easily
touched.–That I was desirous of believing her indifferent is certain,–but I will venture to say that my investigations and decisions are not usually influenced by my hopes or fears.–I did
not believe her to be indifferent because I wished it;–I believed
it on impartial conviction, as truly as I wished it in reason.–
My objections to the marriage were not merely those, which
I last night acknowledged to have required the utmost force
of passion to put aside, in my own case; the want of connection could not be so great an evil to my friend as to me.–But
there were other causes of repugnance;–causes which, though
still existing, and existing to an equal degree in both instances,
I had myself endeavoured to forget, because they were not immediately before me.–These causes must be stated, though
briefly.–The situation of your mother's family, though objectionable, was nothing in comparison of that total want of propriety so frequently, so almost uniformly betrayed by herself, by
your three younger sisters, and occasionally even by your
father.–Pardon me.–It pains me to offend you. But amidst your
concern for the defects of your nearest relations, and your displeasure at this representation of them, let it give you consolation to consider that, to have conducted yourselves so as to
avoid any share of the like censure, is praise no less generally
bestowed on you and your eldest sister, than it is honourable
to the sense and disposition of both.–I will only say farther,
that from what passed that evening, my opinion of all parties
was confirmed, and every inducement heightened, which could
have led me before, to preserve my friend from what I esteemed
a most unhappy connection.–He left Netherfield for London,
on the day following, as you, I am certain, remember, with the
design of soon returning.–The part which I acted, is now to
be explained,–His sisters' uneasiness had been equally excited with my own; our coincidence of feeling was soon discovered; and alike sensible that no time was to be lost in
detaching their brother, we shortly resolved on joining him
directly in London.–We accordingly went–and there I readily
engaged in the office of pointing out to my friend, the certain

evils of such a choice.–I described, and enforced them earnestly.–But, however this remonstrance might have staggered or
delayed his determination, I do not suppose that it would ulti-
mately have prevented the marriage, had it not been seconded
by the assurance which I hesitated not in giving, of your sister's indifference. He had before believed her to return his affection with sincere, if not with equal regard.–But Bingley has
great natural modesty, with a stronger dependence on my judgment than on his own.–To convince him, therefore, that he had
deceived himself, was no very difficult point. To persuade him
against returning into Hertfordshire, when that conviction had
been given, was scarcely the work of a moment.–I cannot blame
myself for having done thus much. There is but one part of
my conduct in the whole affair, on which I do not reflect with
satisfaction; it is that I condescended to adopt the measures
of art so far as to conceal from him your sister's being in town.
I knew it myself, as it was known to Miss Bingley, but her brother
is even yet ignorant of it.–That they might have met without
ill consequence, is perhaps probable;–but his regard did not
appear to me enough extinguished for him to see her without
some danger.–Perhaps this concealment, this disguise, was
beneath me.–It is done, however, and it was done for the best.–
On this subject I have nothing more to say, no other apology
to offer. If I have wounded your sister's feelings, it was unknow-
ingly done; and though the motives which governed me may
to you very naturally appear insufficient, I have not yet learnt
to condemn them.–With respect to that other, more weighty
accusation, of having injured Mr. Wickham, I can only refute
it by laying before you the whole of his connection with my
family. Of what he has *particularly* accused me I am ignorant;
but of the truth of what I shall relate, I can summon more than
one witness of undoubted veracity. Mr. Wickham is the son
of a very respectable man, who had for many years the management of all the Pemberley estates; and whose good conduct
in the discharge of his trust, naturally inclined my father to
be of service to him, and on George Wickham, who was his
god-son, his kindness was therefore liberally bestowed. My
father supported him at school, and afterwards at Cambridge;–
most important assistance, as his own father, always poor from
the extravagance of his wife, would have been unable to give
him a gentleman's education. My father was not only fond of

this young man's society, whose manners were always engaging; he had also the highest opinion of him, and hoping the church would be his profession, intended to provide for him in it. As for myself, it is many, many years since I first began to think of him in a very different manner. The vicious propensities—the want of principle which he was careful to guard from the knowledge of his best friend, could not escape the observation of a young man of nearly the same age with himself, and who had opportunities of seeing him in unguarded moments, which Mr. Darcy could not have. Here again I shall give you pain—to what degree you only can tell. But whatever may be the sentiments which Mr. Wickham has created, a suspicion of their nature shall not prevent me from unfolding his real character. It adds even another motive. My excellent father died about five years ago; and his attachment to Mr. Wickham was to the last so steady, that in his will he particularly recommended it to me, to promote his advancement in the best manner that his profession might allow, and if he took orders, desired that a valuable family living might be his as soon as it became vacant. There was also a legacy of one thousand pounds. His own father did not long survive mine, and within half a year from these events, Mr. Wickham wrote to inform me that, having finally resolved against taking orders, he hoped I should not think it unreasonable for him to expect some more immediate pecuniary advantage, in lieu of the preferment, by which he could not be benefited. He had some intention, he added, of studying the law, and I must be aware that the interest of one thousand pounds would be a very insufficient support therein. I rather wished, than believed him to be sincere; but at any rate, was perfectly ready to accede to his proposal. I knew that Mr. Wickham ought not to be a clergyman. The business was therefore soon settled. He resigned all claim to assistance in the church, were it possible that he could ever be in a situation to receive it, and accepted in return three thousand pounds. All connection between us seemed now dissolved. I thought too ill of him, to invite him to Pemberley, or admit his society in town. In town I believe he chiefly loved, but his studying the law was a mere pretence, and being now free from all restraint, his life was a life of idleness and dissipation. For about three years I heard little of him; but on the decease of the incumbent of the living which had been designed for him, he applied to me again by letter for the presentation. His circumstances, he assured me, and I had no difficulty in believing it, were exceedingly bad. He had found the law a most unprofitable study, and was now absolutely resolved on being ordained, if I would present him to the living in question – of which he trusted there could be little doubt, as he was well assured that I had no other person to provide for, and I could not have forgotten my revered father's intentions. You will hardly blame me for refusing to comply with this entreaty, or for resisting every repetition of it. His resentment was in proportion to the distress of his circumstances – and he was doubtless as violent in his abuse of me to others, as in his reproaches to myself. After this period, every appearance of acquaintance was dropt. How he lived I know not. But last summer he was again most painfully obtruded on my notice. I must now mention a circumstance which I would wish to forget myself, and which no obligation less than the present should induce me to unfold to any human being. Having said thus much, I feel no doubt of your secrecy. My sister, who is more than ten years my junior, was left to the guardianship of my mother's nephew, Colonel Fitzwilliam, and myself. About a year ago, she was taken from school, and an establishment formed for her in London; and last summer she went with the lady who presided over it, to Ramsgate; and thither also went Mr. Wickham, undoubtedly by design; for there proved to have been a prior acquaintance between him and Mrs. Younge, in whose character we were most unhappily deceived; and by her connivance and aid, he so far recommended himself to Georgiana, whose affectionate heart retained a strong impression of his kindness to her as a child, that she was persuaded to believe herself in love, and to consent to an elopement. She was then but fifteen, which must be her excuse; and after stating her imprudence, I am happy to add, that I owed the knowledge of it to herself. I joined them unexpectedly a day or two before the intended elopement, and then Georgiana, unable to support the idea of grieving and offending a brother whom she almost looked up to as a father, acknowledged the whole to me. You may imagine what I felt and how I acted. Regard for my sister's credit and feelings prevented any public exposure, but I wrote to Mr. Wickham, who left the place immediately, and Mrs. Younge was of course removed from her charge. Mr. Wickham's chief object was

unquestionably my sister's fortune, which is thirty thousand
pounds; but I cannot help supposing that the hope of revenging himself on me, was a strong inducement. His revenge would
have been complete indeed. This, madam, is a faithful narrative of every event in which we have been concerned together;
and if you do not absolutely reject it as false, you will, I hope,
acquit me henceforth of cruelty towards Mr. Wickham. I know
not in what manner, under what form of falsehood he has imposed on you; but his success is not perhaps to be wondered
at, ignorant as you previously were of every thing concerning
either. Detection could not be in your power, and suspicion
certainly not in your inclination. You may possibly wonder why
all this was not told you last night. But I was not then master
enough of myself to know what could or ought to be revealed.
For the truth of every thing here related, I can appeal more
particularly to the testimony of Colonel Fitzwilliam, who from
our near relationship and constant intimacy, and still more as
one of the executors of my father's will, has been unavoidably
acquainted with every particular of these transactions. If your
abhorrence of *me* should make *my* assertions valueless, you cannot be prevented by the same cause from confiding in my cousin; and that there may be the possibility of consulting him,
I shall endeavour to find some opportunity of putting this letter in your hands in the course of the morning. I will only add,
God bless you.

Fitzwilliam Darcy.

CHAPTER 13

If Elizabeth, when Mr. Darcy gave her the letter, did not expect
it to contain a renewal of his offers, she had formed no expectation at all of its contents. But such as they were, it may be well
supposed how eagerly she went through them, and what a contrariety of emotion they excited. Her feelings as she read were
scarcely to be defined. With amazement did she first understand
that he believed any apology to be in his power; and stedfastly
was she persuaded that he could have no explanation to give,

which a just sense of shame would not conceal. With a strong prejudice against every thing he might say, she began his account of what had happened at Netherfield. She read, with an eagerness which hardly left her power of comprehension, and from impatience of knowing what the next sentence might bring, was incapable of attending to the sense of the one before her eyes. His belief of her sister's insensibility, she instantly resolved to be false, and his account of the real, the worst objections to the match, made her too angry to have any wish of doing him justice. He expressed no regret for what he had done which satisfied her; his style was not penitent, but haughty. It was all pride and insolence.

But when this subject was succeeded by his account of Mr. Wickham, when she read with somewhat clearer attention, a relation of events, which, if true, must overthrow every cherished opinion of his worth, and which bore so alarming an affinity to his own history of himself, her feelings were yet more acutely painful and more difficult of definition. Astonishment, apprehension, and even horror, oppressed her. She wished to discredit it entirely, repeatedly exclaiming, "This must be false! This cannot be! This must be the grossest falsehood!"—and when she had gone through the whole letter, though scarcely knowing any thing of the last page or two, put it hastily away, protesting that she would not regard it, that she would never look in it again.

In this perturbed state of mind, with thoughts that could rest on nothing, she walked on; but it would not do; in half a minute the letter was unfolded again, and collecting herself as well as she could, she again began the mortifying perusal of all that related to Wickham, and commanded herself so far as to examine the meaning of every sentence. The account of his connection with the Pemberley family, was exactly what he had related himself; and the kindness of the late Mr. Darcy, though she had not before known its extent, agreed equally well with his own words. So far each recital confirmed the other: but when she came to the will, the difference was great. What Wickham had said of the living was fresh in her memory, and as she recalled his very words, it was impossible not to feel that there was gross duplicity on one side or the other; and, for a few moments, she flattered herself that her wishes did not err. But when she read, and re-read with the closest attention, the particulars immediately following of Wickham's resigning all pretensions to the living, of his receiving in lieu, so considerable a sum as three thousand pounds, again was she forced to hesitate. She put down the letter, weighed every circumstance with what she meant to be impartiality – deliberated on the probability of each statement – but with little success. On both sides it was only assertion. Again she read on. But every line proved more clearly that the affair, which she had believed it impossible that any contrivance could so represent, as to render Mr. Darcy's conduct in it less than infamous, was capable of a turn which must make him entirely blameless throughout the whole.

The extravagance and general profligacy which he scrupled not to lay to Mr. Wickham's charge, exceedingly shocked her; the more so, as she could bring no proof of its injustice. She had never heard of him before his entrance into the ——shire Militia, in which he had engaged at the persuasion of the young man, who, on meeting him accidentally in town, had there renewed a slight acquaintance. Of his former way of life, nothing had been known in Hertfordshire but what he told himself. As to his real character, had information been in her power, she had never felt a wish of enquiring. His countenance, voice, and manner, had established him at once in the possession of every virtue. She tried to recollect some instance of goodness, some distinguished trait of integrity or benevolence, that might rescue him from the attacks of Mr. Darcy; or at least, by the predominance of virtue, atone for those casual errors, under which she would endeavour to class, what Mr. Darcy had described as the idleness and vice of many years continuance. But no such recollection befriended her. She could see him instantly before her, in every charm of air and address; but she could remember no more substantial good than the general approbation of the neighbourhood, and the regard which his social powers had gained him in the mess. After pausing on this point a considerable while, she once more continued to read. But, alas! the story which followed of his designs on Miss Darcy, received some confirmation from what had passed between Colonel Fitzwilliam and herself only the morning before; and at last she was referred for the truth of every particular to Colonel Fitzwilliam himself—from whom she had previously received the information of his near concern in all his cousin's affairs, and whose character she had no reason to question. At one time she had almost resolved on applying to him, but the idea was checked by the awkwardness of the application, and at length wholly banished by the conviction that Mr. Darcy would never have hazarded such a proposal, if he had not been well assured of his cousin's corroboration.

She perfectly remembered every thing that had passed in conversation between Wickham and herself, in their first evening at Mr. Philips's. Many of his expressions were still fresh in her memory. She was *now* struck with the impropriety of such communications to a stranger, and wondered it had escaped her before. She saw the indelicacy of putting himself forward as he had done, and the inconsistency of his professions with his conduct. She remembered that he had boasted of having no fear of seeing Mr. Darcy—that Mr. Darcy might leave the country, but that *he* should stand his ground; yet he had avoided the Netherfield ball the very next week. She remembered also, that till the Netherfield family had quitted the country, he had told his story to no one but herself; but that after their removal, it had been every where discussed; that he had then no reserves, no scruples in sinking Mr. Darcy's character, though he had assured her that respect for the father, would always prevent his exposing the son.

How differently did every thing now appear in which he was concerned! His attentions to Miss King were now the consequence of views solely and hatefully mercenary; and the mediocrity of her fortune proved no longer the moderation of his wishes, but his eagerness to grasp at any thing. His behaviour to herself could

now have had no tolerable motive; he had either been deceived
with regard to her fortune, or had been gratifying his vanity by
encouraging the preference which she believed she had most incautiously shewn. Every lingering struggle in his favour grew fainter
and fainter; and in farther justification of Mr. Darcy, she could
not but allow that Mr. Bingley, when questioned by Jane, had long
ago asserted his blamelessness in the affair; that proud and repulsive as were his manners, she had never, in the whole course of
their acquaintance, an acquaintance which had latterly brought
them much together, and given her a sort of intimacy with his
ways, seen any thing that betrayed him to be unprincipled or
unjust – any thing that spoke him of irreligious or immoral habits.
That among his own connections he was esteemed and valued –
that even Wickham had allowed him merit as a brother, and that
she had often heard him speak so affectionately of his sister as
to prove him capable of *some* amiable feeling. That had his actions
been what Wickham represented them, so gross a violation of
every thing right could hardly have been concealed from the world;
and that friendship between a person capable of it, and such an
amiable man as Mr. Bingley, was incomprehensible.

She grew absolutely ashamed of herself. – Of neither Darcy nor
Wickham could she think, without feeling that she had been blind,
partial, prejudiced, absurd.

"How despicably have I acted!" she cried. – "I, who have prid-
ed myself on my discernment! – I, who have valued myself on my
abilities! who have often disdained the generous candour of my
sister, and gratified my vanity, in useless or blameable distrust. –
How humiliating is this discovery! – Yet, how just a humiliation! –
Had I been in love, I could not have been more wretchedly blind.
But vanity, not love, has been my folly. – Pleased with the preference of one, and offended by the neglect of the other, on the very
beginning of our acquaintance, I have courted prepossession and
ignorance, and driven reason away, where either were concerned.
Till this moment, I never knew myself."

From herself to Jane – from Jane to Bingley, her thoughts were

in a line which soon brought to her recollection that Mr. Darcy's
explanation *there,* had appeared very insufficient; and she read
it again. Widely different was the effect of a second perusal.–
How could she deny that credit to his assertions, in one instance,
which she had been obliged to give in the other?–He declared
himself to have been totally unsuspicious of her sister's attachment;–and she could not help remembering what Charlotte's
opinion had always been.–Neither could she deny the justice of
his description of Jane.–She felt that Jane's feelings, though fervent, were little displayed, and that there was a constant complacency in her air and manner, not often united with great
sensibility.

When she came to that part of the letter, in which her family
were mentioned, in terms of such mortifying, yet merited reproach,
her sense of shame was severe. The justice of the charge struck
her too forcibly for denial, and the circumstances to which he
particularly alluded, as having passed at the Netherfield ball, and
as confirming all his first disapprobation, could not have made
a stronger impression on his mind than on hers.

The compliment to herself and her sister, was not unfelt. It
soothed, but it could not console her for the contempt which
had been thus self-attracted by the rest of her family;–and as she
considered that Jane's disappointment had in fact been the work
of her nearest relations, and reflected how materially the credit
of both must be hurt by such impropriety of conduct, she felt
depressed beyond any thing she had ever known before.

After wandering along the lane for two hours, giving way to
every variety of thought; re-considering events, determining prob-
abilities, and reconciling herself as well as she could, to a change
so sudden and so important, fatigue, and a recollection of her
long absence, made her at length return home; and she entered
the house with the wish of appearing cheerful as usual, and the
resolution of repressing such reflections as must make her unfit
for conversation.

She was immediately told, that the two gentlemen from Rosings

had each called during her absence; Mr. Darcy, only for a few
minutes to take leave, but that Colonel Fitzwilliam had been sitting with them at least an hour, hoping for her return, and almost
resolving to walk after her till she could be found.—Elizabeth could
but just *affect* concern in missing him; she really rejoiced at it.
Colonel Fitzwilliam was no longer an object. She could think only
of her letter.

CHAPTER 14

The two gentlemen left Rosings the next morning; and Mr. Collins having been in waiting near the lodges, to make them his
parting obeisance, was able to bring home the pleasing intelligence, of their appearing in very good health, and in as tolerable
spirits as could be expected, after the melancholy scene so lately
gone through at Rosings. To Rosings he then hastened to console
Lady Catherine, and her daughter; and on his return, brought back,
with great satisfaction, a message from her Ladyship, importing
that she felt herself so dull as to make her very desirous of having them all to dine with her.

Elizabeth could not see Lady Catherine without recollecting,
that had she chosen it, she might by this time have been presented to her, as her future niece; nor could she think, without a smile,
of what her ladyship's indignation would have been. "What would
she have said?—how would she have behaved?" were questions
with which she amused herself.

Their first subject was the diminution of the Rosings party.—"I
assure you, I feel it exceedingly," said Lady Catherine; "I believe
nobody feels the loss of friends so much as I do. But I am particularly attached to these young men; and know them to be so
much attached to me!—They were excessively sorry to go! But
so they always are. The dear colonel rallied his spirits tolerably
till just at last; but Darcy seemed to feel it most acutely, more

I think than last year. His attachment to Rosings, certainly increases."

Mr. Collins had a compliment, and an allusion to throw in here, which were kindly smiled on by the mother and daughter.

Lady Catherine observed, after dinner, that Miss Bennet seemed out of spirits, and immediately accounting for it herself, by supposing that she did not like to go home again so soon, she added,

"But if that is the case, you must write to your mother to beg that you may stay a little longer. Mrs. Collins will be very glad of your company, I am sure."

"I am much obliged to your ladyship for your kind invitation," replied Elizabeth, "but it is not in my power to accept it.—I must be in town next Saturday."

"Why, at that rate, you will have been here only six weeks. I expected you to stay two months. I told Mrs. Collins so before you came. There can be no occasion for your going so soon. Mrs. Bennet could certainly spare you for another fortnight."

"But my father cannot.—He wrote last week to hurry my return."

"Oh! your father of course may spare you, if your mother can.— Daughters are never of so much consequence to a father. And if you will stay another *month* complete, it will be in my power to take one of you as far as London, for I am going there early in June, for a week; and as Dawson does not object to the Barouche box, there will be very good room for one of you—and indeed, if the weather should happen to be cool, I should not object to taking you both, as you are neither of you large."

"You are all kindness, Madam; but I believe we must abide by our original plan."

Lady Catherine seemed resigned.—"Mrs. Collins, you must send a servant with them. You know I always speak my mind, and I cannot bear the idea of two young women travelling post by themselves. It is highly improper. You must contrive to send somebody. I have the greatest dislike in the world to that sort of thing.—Young women should always be properly guarded and attended, according to their situation in life. When my niece

Georgiana went to Ramsgate last summer, I made a point of having two men servants go with her.—Miss Darcy, the daughter of
Mr. Darcy, of Pemberley, and Lady Anne, could not have appeared
with propriety in a different manner.—I am excessively attentive
to all those things. You must send John with the young ladies,
Mrs. Collins. I am glad it occurred to me to mention it; for it would
really be discreditable to *you* to let them go alone."

"My uncle is to send a servant for us."

"Oh!—Your uncle!—He keeps a man-servant, does he?—I am
very glad you have somebody who thinks of those things. Where
shall you change horses?—Oh! Bromley, of course.—If you mention my name at the Bell, you will be attended to."

Lady Catherine had many other questions to ask respecting
their journey, and as she did not answer them all herself, attention was necessary, which Elizabeth believed to be lucky for her;
or, with a mind so occupied, she might have forgotten where she
was. Reflection must be reserved for solitary hours; whenever she
was alone, she gave way to it as the greatest relief; and not a day
went by without a solitary walk, in which she might indulge in
all the delight of unpleasant recollections.

Mr. Darcy's letter, she was in a fair way of soon knowing by
heart. She studied every sentence: and her feelings towards its
writer were at times widely different. When she remembered the
style of his address, she was still full of indignation; but when
she considered how unjustly she had condemned and upbraided him, her anger was turned against herself; and his disappointed feelings became the object of compassion. His attachment
excited gratitude, his general character respect; but she could not
approve him; nor could she for a moment repent her refusal, or
feel the slightest inclination ever to see him again. In her own
past behaviour, there was a constant source of vexation and regret;
and in the unhappy defects of her family a subject of yet heavier
chagrin. They were hopeless of remedy. Her father, contented with
laughing at them, would never exert himself to restrain the wild
giddiness of his youngest daughters; and her mother, with manners

so far from right herself, was entirely insensible of the evil. Elizabeth had frequently united with Jane in an endeavour to check the imprudence of Catherine and Lydia; but while they were supported by their mother's indulgence, what chance could there be of improvement? Catherine, weak-spirited, irritable, and completely under Lydia's guidance, had been always affronted by their advice; and Lydia, self-willed and careless, would scarcely give them a hearing. They were ignorant, idle, and vain. While there was an officer in Meryton, they would flirt with him; and while Meryton was within a walk of Longbourn, they would be going there for ever.

Anxiety on Jane's behalf, was another prevailing concern, and Mr. Darcy's explanation, by restoring Bingley to all her former good opinion, heightened the sense of what Jane had lost. His affection was proved to have been sincere, and his conduct cleared of all blame, unless any could attach to the implicitness of his confidence in his friend. How grievous then was the thought that, of a situation so desirable in every respect, so replete with advantage, so promising for happiness, Jane had been deprived, by the folly and indecorum of her own family!

When to these recollections was added the developement of Wickham's character, it may be easily believed that the happy spirits which had seldom been depressed before, were now so much affected as to make it almost impossible for her to appear tolerably cheerful.

Their engagements at Rosings were as frequent during the last week of her stay, as they had been at first. The very last evening was spent there; and her Ladyship again enquired minutely into the particulars of their journey, gave them directions as to the best method of packing, and was so urgent on the necessity of placing gowns in the only right way, that Maria thought herself obliged, on her return, to undo all the work of the morning, and pack her trunk afresh.

When they parted, Lady Catherine, with great condescension, wished them a good journey, and invited them to come to

Hunsford again next year; and Miss De Bourgh exerted herself so far as to curtsey and hold out her hand to both.

CHAPTER 15

On Saturday morning Elizabeth and Mr. Collins met for breakfast a few minutes before the others appeared; and he took the opportunity of paying the parting civilities which he deemed indispensably necessary.

"I know not, Miss Elizabeth," said he, "whether Mrs. Collins has yet expressed her sense of your kindness in coming to us, but I am very certain you will not leave the house without receiving her thanks for it. The favour of your company has been much felt, I assure you. We know how little there is to tempt any one to our humble abode. Our plain manner of living, our small rooms, and few domestics, and the little we see of the world, must make Hunsford extremely dull to a young lady like yourself; but I hope you will believe us grateful for the condescension, and that we have done every thing in our power to prevent your spending your time unpleasantly."

Elizabeth was eager with her thanks and assurances of happiness. She had spent six weeks with great enjoyment; and the pleasure of being with Charlotte, and the kind attentions she had received, must make *her* feel the obliged. Mr. Collins was gratified; and with a more smiling solemnity replied,

"It gives me the greatest pleasure to hear that you have passed your time not disagreeably. We have certainly done our best; and most fortunately having it in our power to introduce you to very superior society, and from our connection with Rosings, the frequent means of varying the humble home scene, I think we may flatter ourselves that your Hunsford visit cannot have been entirely irksome. Our situation with regard to Lady Catherine's family is indeed the sort of extraordinary advantage and blessing which few can boast. You see on what a footing we are. You see how continually we are engaged there. In truth I must acknowledge that, with all the disadvantages of this humble parsonage, I should not think any one abiding in it an object of compassion, while they are sharers of our intimacy at Rosings."

Words were insufficient for the elevation of his feelings; and he was obliged to walk about the room, while Elizabeth tried to unite civility and truth in a few short sentences.

"You may, in fact, carry a very favourable report of us into Hertfordshire, my dear cousin. I flatter myself at least that you will be able to do so. Lady Catherine's great attentions to Mrs. Collins you have been a daily witness of; and altogether I trust it does not appear that your friend has drawn an unfortunate—but on this point it will be as well to be silent. Only let me assure you, my dear Miss Elizabeth, that I can from my heart most cordially wish you equal felicity in marriage. My dear Charlotte and I have but one mind and one way of thinking. There is in every thing a most remarkable resemblance of character and ideas between us. We seem to have been designed for each other."

Elizabeth could safely say that it was a great happiness where that was the case, and with equal sincerity could add that she firmly believed and rejoiced in his domestic comforts. She was not sorry, however, to have the recital of them interrupted by the entrance of the lady from whom they sprung. Poor Charlotte!—it was melancholy to leave her to such society!—But she had chosen it with her eyes open; and though evidently regretting that her visitors were to go, she did not seem to ask for compassion. Her home and her housekeeping, her parish and her poultry, and all their dependent concerns, had not yet lost their charms.

At length the chaise arrived, the trunks were fastened on, the parcels placed within, and it was pronounced to be ready. After an affectionate parting between the friends, Elizabeth was attended to the carriage by Mr. Collins, and as they walked down the garden, he was commissioning her with his best respects to all her family, not forgetting his thanks for the kindness he had received at

Longbourn in the winter, and his compliments to Mr. and Mrs. Gardiner, though unknown. He then handed her in, Maria followed, and the door was on the point of being closed, when he suddenly reminded them, with some consternation, that they had hitherto forgotten to leave any message for the ladies of Rosings.

"But," he added, "you will of course wish to have your humble respects delivered to them, with your grateful thanks for their kindness to you while you have been here."

Elizabeth made no objection; – the door was then allowed to be shut, and the carriage drove off.

"Good gracious!" cried Maria, after a few minutes silence, "it seems but a day or two since we first came! – and yet how many things have happened!"

"A great many indeed," said her companion, with a sigh. "We have dined nine times at Rosings, besides drinking tea there twice! – How much I shall have to tell!"

Elizabeth privately added, "and how much I shall have to conceal."

Their journey was performed without much conversation, or any alarm; and within four hours of their leaving Hunsford, they reached Mr. Gardiner's house, where they were to remain a few days.

Jane looked well, and Elizabeth had little opportunity of studying her spirits, amidst the various engagements which the kindness of her aunt had reserved for them. But Jane was to go home with her, and at Longbourn there would be leisure enough for observation.

It was not without an effort meanwhile that she could wait even for Longbourn, before she told her sister of Mr. Darcy's proposals. To know that she had the power of revealing what would so exceedingly astonish Jane, and must, at the same time, so highly gratify whatever of her own vanity she had not yet been able to reason away, was such a temptation to openness as nothing could have conquered, but the state of indecision in which she remained, as to the extent of what she should communicate; and her fear, if she once entered on the subject, of being hurried into repeating something of Bingley, which might only grieve her sister farther.

CHAPTER 16

It was the second week in May, in which the three young ladies set out together from Grace Church Street, for the town of —— in Hertfordshire; and as they drew near the appointed inn where Mr. Bennet's carriage was to meet them, they quickly perceived, in token of the coachman's punctuality, both Kitty and Lydia looking out of a dining room up stairs. These two girls had been above an hour in the place, happily employed in visiting an opposite milliner, watching the sentinel on guard, and dressing a sallad and cucumber.

After welcoming their sisters, they triumphantly displayed a table set out with such cold meat as an inn larder usually affords, exclaiming, "Is not this nice? is not this an agreeable surprise?"

"And we mean to treat you all," added Lydia; "but you must lend us the money, for we have just spent ours at the shop out there." Then shewing her purchases: "Look here, I have bought this bonnet. I do not think it is very pretty; but I thought I might as well buy it as not. I shall pull it to pieces as soon as I get home, and see if I can make it up any better."

And when her sisters abused it as ugly, she added, with perfect unconcern, "Oh! but there were two or three much uglier in the shop; and when I have bought some prettier-coloured satin to trim it with fresh, I think it will be very tolerable. Besides, it will not much signify what one wears this summer, after the ——shire have left Meryton, and they are going in a fortnight."

"Are they indeed?" cried Elizabeth, with the greatest satisfaction.

"They are going to be encamped near Brighton; and I do so want papa to take us all there for the summer! It would be such a delicious scheme, and I dare say would hardly cost any thing at all. Mamma would like to go too of all things! Only think what a miserable summer else we shall have!"

"Yes," thought Elizabeth; " *that* would be a delightful scheme, indeed, and completely do for us at once. Good Heaven! Brighton, and a whole campful of soldiers, to us, who have been overset already by one poor regiment of militia, and the monthly balls of Meryton."

"Now I have got some news for you," said Lydia, as they sat down to table. "What do you think? It is excellent news, capital news, and about a certain person that we all like."

Jane and Elizabeth looked at each other, and the waiter was told that he need not stay. Lydia laughed, and said,

"Aye, that is just like your formality and discretion. You thought the waiter must not hear, as if he cared! I dare say he often hears worse things said than I am going to say. But he is an ugly fellow! I am glad he is gone. I never saw such a long chin in my life. Well, but now for my news: it is about dear Wickham; too good for the waiter, is not it? There is no danger of Wickham's marrying Mary King. There's for you! She is gone down to her uncle at Liverpool; gone to stay. Wickham is safe."

"And Mary King is safe!" added Elizabeth; "safe from a connection imprudent as to fortune."

"She is a great fool for going away, if she liked him."

"But I hope there is no strong attachment on either side," said Jane.

"I am sure there is not on *his*. I will answer for it he never cared three straws about her. Who *could* about such a nasty little freckled thing?"

Elizabeth was shocked to think that, however incapable of such coarseness of *expression* herself, the coarseness of the *sentiment* was little other than her own breast had formerly harboured and fancied liberal!

As soon as all had ate, and the elder ones paid, the carriage was ordered; and after some contrivance, the whole party, with all their boxes, workbags, and parcels, and the unwelcome addition of Kitty's and Lydia's purchases, were seated in it.

"How nicely we are crammed in!" cried Lydia. "I am glad I bought my bonnet, if it is only for the fun of having another bandbox! Well, now let us be quite comfortable and snug, and talk and laugh all the way home. And in the first place, let us hear what has happened to you all, since you went away. Have you seen any pleasant men? Have you had any flirting? I was in great hopes that one of you would have got a husband before you came back. Jane will be quite an old maid soon, I declare. She is almost three and twenty! Lord, how ashamed I should be of not being married before three and twenty! My aunt Philips wants you so to get husbands, you can't think. She says Lizzy had better have taken Mr. Collins; but *I* do not think there would have been any fun in it. Lord! how I should like to be married before any of you; and then I would chaperon you about to all the balls. Dear me! we had such a good piece of fun the other day at Colonel Forster's! Kitty and me were to spend the day there, and Mrs. Forster promised to have a little dance in the evening; (by the bye, Mrs. Forster and me are *such* friends!) and so she asked the two Harringtons to come, but Harriet was ill, and so Pen was forced to come by herself; and then, what do you think we did? We dressed up Chamberlay in woman's clothes, on purpose to pass for a lady—only think what fun! Not a soul knew it, but Colonel and Mrs. Forster, and Kitty and me, except my aunt, for we were forced to borrow one of her gowns; and you cannot imagine how well he looked! When Denny, and Wickham, and Pratt, and two or three more of the men came in, they did not know him in the least. Lord! how I laughed! and so did Mrs. Forster. I thought I should have died. And that made the men suspect something, and then they soon found out what was the matter."

With such kind of histories of their parties and good jokes, did Lydia, assisted by Kitty's hints and additions, endeavour to amuse her companions all the way to Longbourn. Elizabeth listened as little as she could, but there was no escaping the frequent mention of Wickham's name.

Their reception at home was most kind. Mrs. Bennet rejoiced to see Jane in undiminished beauty; and more than once during dinner did Mr. Bennet say voluntarily to Elizabeth,

"I am glad you are come back, Lizzy."

Their party in the dining-room was large, for almost all the Lucases came to meet Maria and hear the news: and various were the subjects which occupied them; Lady Lucas was enquiring of Maria across the table, after the welfare and poultry of her eldest daughter; Mrs. Bennet was doubly engaged, on one hand collecting an account of the present fashions from Jane, who sat some way below her, and on the other, retailing them all to the younger Miss Lucases; and Lydia, in a voice rather louder than any other person's, was enumerating the various pleasures of the morning to any body who would hear her.

"Oh! Mary," said she, "I wish you had gone with us, for we had such fun! As we went along, Kitty and me drew up all the blinds, and pretended there was nobody in the coach; and I should have gone so all the way, if Kitty had not been sick; and when we got to the George, I do think we behaved very handsomely, for we treated the other three with the nicest cold luncheon in the world, and if you would have gone, we would have treated you too. And then when we came away it was such fun! I thought we never should have got into the coach. I was ready to die of laughter. And then we were so merry all the way home! We talked and laughed so loud that any body might have heard us ten miles off!"

To this, Mary very gravely replied,

"Far be it from me, my dear sister, to depreciate such pleasures. They would doubtless be congenial with the generality of female minds. But I confess they would have no charms for *me*. I should infinitely prefer a book."

But of this answer Lydia heard not a word. She seldom listened to any body for more than half a minute, and never attended to Mary at all.

In the afternoon Lydia was urgent with the rest of the girls to walk to Meryton and see how every body went on; but Elizabeth steadily opposed the scheme. It should not be said, that the Miss Bennets could not be at home half a day before they were in pursuit of the officers. There was another reason too for her opposition. She dreaded seeing Wickham again, and was resolved to avoid it as long as possible. The comfort to *her,* of the regiment's approaching removal, was indeed beyond expression. In a fortnight they were to go, and once gone, she hoped there could be nothing more to plague her on his account.

She had not been many hours at home, before she found that the Brighton scheme, of which Lydia had given them a hint at the inn, was under frequent discussion between her parents. Elizabeth saw directly that her father had not the smallest intentions of yielding; but his answers were at the same time so vague and equivocal, that her mother, though often disheartened, had never yet despaired of succeeding at last.

CHAPTER 17

Elizabeth's impatience to acquaint Jane with what had happened could no longer be overcome; and at length resolving to suppress every particular in which her sister was concerned, and preparing her to be surprised, she related to her the next morning the chief of the scene between Mr. Darcy and herself.

Miss Bennet's astonishment was soon lessened by the strong sisterly partiality which made any admiration of Elizabeth appear perfectly natural; and all surprise was shortly lost in other feelings. She was sorry that Mr. Darcy should have delivered his sentiments in a manner so little suited to recommend them; but still more was she grieved for the unhappiness which her sister's refusal must have given him.

"His being so sure of succeeding, was wrong," said she; "and certainly ought not to have appeared; but consider how much it must increase his disappointment."

"Indeed," replied Elizabeth, "I am heartily sorry for him: but he has other feelings which will probably soon drive away his regard for me. You do not blame me, however, for refusing him?"

"Blame you! Oh, no."

"But you blame me for having spoken so warmly of Wickham."

"No—I do not know that you were wrong in saying what you did."

"But you *will* know it, when I have told you what happened the very next day."

She then spoke of the letter, repeating the whole of its contents as far as they concerned George Wickham. What a stroke was this for poor Jane! who would willingly have gone through the world without believing that so much wickedness existed in the whole race of mankind, as was here collected in one individual. Nor was Darcy's vindication, though grateful to her feelings, capable of consoling her for such discovery. Most earnestly did she labour to prove the probability of error, and seek to clear one, without involving the other.

"This will not do," said Elizabeth. "You never will be able to make both of them good for any thing. Take your choice, but you must be satisfied with only one. There is but such a quantity of merit between them; just enough to make one good sort of man; and of late it has been shifting about pretty much. For my part, I am inclined to believe it all Mr. Darcy's, but you shall do as you chuse."

It was some time, however, before a smile could be extorted from Jane.

"I do not know when I have been more shocked," said she. "Wickham so very bad! It is almost past belief. And poor Mr. Darcy! dear Lizzy, only consider what he must have suffered. Such a disappointment! and with the knowledge of your ill opinion too! and having to relate such a thing of his sister! It is really too distressing. I am sure you must feel it so."

"Oh! no, my regret and compassion are all done away by seeing you so full of both. I know you will do him such ample justice, that I am growing every moment more unconcerned and indifferent. Your profusion makes me saving; and if you lament over him much longer, my heart will be as light as a feather."

"Poor Wickham; there is such an expression of goodness in his countenance! such an openness and gentleness in his manner."

"There certainly was some great mismanagement in the education of those two young men. One has got all the goodness, and the other all the appearance of it."

"I never thought Mr. Darcy so deficient in the *appearance* of it as you used to do."

"And yet I meant to be uncommonly clever in taking so decided a dislike to him, without any reason. It is such a spur to one's genius, such an opening for wit to have a dislike of that kind. One may be continually abusive without saying any thing just; but one cannot be always laughing at a man without now and then stumbling on something witty."

"Lizzy, when you first read that letter, I am sure you could not treat the matter as you do now."

"Indeed I could not. I was uncomfortable enough. I was very uncomfortable, I may say unhappy. And with no one to speak to, of what I felt, no Jane to comfort me and say that I had not been so very weak and vain and nonsensical as I knew I had! Oh! how I wanted you!"

"How unfortunate that you should have used such very strong expressions in speaking of Wickham to Mr. Darcy, for now they *do* appear wholly undeserved."

"Certainly. But the misfortune of speaking with bitterness, is a most natural consequence of the prejudices I had been encouraging. There is one point, on which I want your advice. I want to be told whether I ought, or ought not to make our acquaintance in general understand Wickham's character."

Miss Bennet paused a little and then replied, "Surely there can be no occasion for exposing him so dreadfully. What is your own opinion?"

"That it ought not to be attempted. Mr. Darcy has not authorised me to make his communication public. On the contrary every particular relative to his sister, was meant to be kept as much as possible to myself; and if I endeavour to undeceive people as to the rest of his conduct, who will believe me? The general prejudice against Mr. Darcy is so violent, that it would be the death of half the good people in Meryton, to attempt to place him in an amiable light. I am not equal to it. Wickham will soon be gone; and therefore it will not signify to any body here, what he really is. Sometime hence it will be all found out, and then we may laugh at their stupidity in not knowing it before. At present I will say nothing about it."

"You are quite right. To have his errors made public might ruin him for ever. He is now perhaps sorry for what he has done, and anxious to re-establish a character. We must not make him desperate."

The tumult of Elizabeth's mind was allayed by this conversation. She had got rid of two of the secrets which had weighed on her for a fortnight, and was certain of a willing listener in Jane, whenever she might wish to talk again of either. But there was still something lurking behind, of which prudence forbad the disclosure. She dared not relate the other half of Mr. Darcy's letter, nor explain to her sister how sincerely she had been valued by his friend. Here was knowledge in which no one could partake; and she was sensible that nothing less than a perfect understanding between the parties could justify her in throwing off this last incumbrance of mystery. "And then," said she, "if that very improbable event should ever take place, I shall merely be able to tell what Bingley may tell in a much more agreeable manner himself. The liberty of communication cannot be mine till it has lost all its value!"

She was now, on being settled at home, at leisure to observe the real state of her sister's spirits. Jane was not happy. She still cherished a very tender affection for Bingley. Having never even fancied herself in love before, her regard had all the warmth of first attachment, and from her age and disposition, greater steadiness than first attachments often boast; and so fervently did she value his remembrance, and prefer him to every other man, that all her good sense, and all her attention to the feelings of her friends, were requisite to check the indulgence of those regrets, which must have been injurious to her own health and their tranquillity.

"Well, Lizzy," said Mrs. Bennet one day, "what is your opinion *now* of this sad business of Jane's? For my part, I am determined never to speak of it again to anybody. I told my sister Philips so the other day. But I cannot find out that Jane saw any thing of him in London. Well, he is a very undeserving young man – and I do not suppose there is the least chance in the world of her ever getting him now. There is no talk of his coming to Netherfield again in the summer; and I have enquired of every body too, who is likely to know."

"I do not believe that he will ever live at Netherfield any more."

"Oh, well! it is just as he chooses. Nobody wants him to come. Though I shall always say that he used my daughter extremely ill; and if I was her, I would not have put up with it. Well, my comfort is, I am sure Jane will die of a broken heart, and then he will be sorry for what he has done."

But as Elizabeth could not receive comfort from any such expectation, she made no answer.

"Well, Lizzy," continued her mother soon afterwards, "and so the Collinses live very comfortable, do they? Well, well, I only hope it will last. And what sort of table do they keep? Charlotte is an excellent manager, I dare say. If she is half as sharp as her mother, she is saving enough. There is nothing extravagant in *their* housekeeping, I dare say."

"No, nothing at all."

"A great deal of good management depend upon it. Yes, yes. *They* will take care not to outrun their income. *They* will never be distressed for money. Well, much good may it do them! And so, I suppose, they often talk of having Longbourn when your father is dead. They look upon it quite as their own, I dare say, whenever that happens."

"It was a subject which they could not mention before me."

"No. It would have been strange if they had. But I make no doubt, they often talk of it between themselves. Well, if they can be easy with an estate that is not lawfully their own, so much the better. *I* should be ashamed of having one that was only entailed on me."

CHAPTER 18

The first week of their return was soon gone. The second began. It was the last of the regiment's stay in Meryton, and all the young ladies in the neighbourhood were drooping apace. The dejection was almost universal. The elder Miss Bennets alone were still able to eat, drink, and sleep, and pursue the usual course of their employments. Very frequently were they reproached for this insensibility by Kitty and Lydia, whose own misery was extreme, and who could not comprehend such hard-heartedness in any of the family.

"Good Heaven! What is to become of us! What are we to do!" Would they often exclaim in the bitterness of woe. "How can you be smiling so, Lizzy?" Their affectionate mother shared all their grief; she remembered what she had herself endured on a similar occasion, five and twenty years ago.

"I am sure," said she, "I cried for two days together when Colonel Millar's regiment went away. I thought I should have broke my heart."

"I am sure I shall break *mine*," said Lydia.

"If one could but go to Brighton!" observed Mrs. Bennet.

"Oh, yes! – if one could but go to Brighton! But papa is so disagreeable."

"A little sea-bathing would set me up for ever."

"And my aunt Philips is sure it would do *me* a great deal of good," added Kitty.

Such were the kind of lamentations resounding perpetually through Longbourn-house. Elizabeth tried to be diverted by them; but all sense of pleasure was lost in shame. She felt anew the justice of Mr. Darcy's objections; and never had she before been so much disposed to pardon his interference in the views of his friend.

But the gloom of Lydia's prospect was shortly cleared away; for she received an invitation from Mrs. Forster, the wife of the Colonel of the regiment, to accompany her to Brighton. This invaluable friend was a very young woman, and very lately married. A resemblance in good humour and good spirits had recommended her and Lydia to each other, and out of their *three* months' acquaintance they had been intimate *two*.

The rapture of Lydia on this occasion, her adoration of Mrs. Forster, the delight of Mrs. Bennet, and the mortification of Kitty, are scarcely to be described. Wholly inattentive to her sister's feelings, Lydia flew about the house in restless ecstacy, calling for every one's congratulations, and laughing and talking with more violence than ever; whilst the luckless Kitty continued in the parlour repining at her fate in terms as unreasonable as her accent was peevish.

"I cannot see why Mrs. Forster should not ask *me* as well as Lydia," said she, "though I am *not* her particular friend. I have just as much right to be asked as she has, and more too, for I am two years older."

In vain did Elizabeth attempt to make her reasonable, and Jane to make her resigned. As for Elizabeth herself, this invitation was so far from exciting in her the same feelings as in her mother and Lydia, that she considered it as the death warrant of all possibility of common sense for the latter; and detestable as such a step must make her were it known, she could not help secretly advising her father not to let her go. She represented to him all the improprieties of Lydia's general behaviour, the little advantage she could derive from the friendship of such a woman as

Mrs. Forster, and the probability of her being yet more imprudent with such a companion at Brighton, where the temptations
must be greater than at home. He heard her attentively, and then
said,

"Lydia will never be easy till she has exposed herself in some
public place or other, and we can never expect her to do it with
so little expense or inconvenience to her family as under the
present circumstances."

"If you were aware," said Elizabeth, "of the very great disadvantage to us all, which must arise from the public notice of Lydia's
unguarded and imprudent manner; nay, which has already aris-
en from it, I am sure you would judge differently in the affair."

"Already arisen!" repeated Mr. Bennet. "What, has she frightened away some of your lovers? Poor little Lizzy! But do not be
cast down. Such squeamish youths as cannot bear to be connected
with a little absurdity, are not worth a regret. Come, let me see
the list of the pitiful fellows who have been kept aloof by Lydia's
folly."

"Indeed you are mistaken. I have no such injuries to resent.
It is not of peculiar, but of general evils, which I am now complaining. Our importance, our respectability in the world, must
be affected by the wild volatility, the assurance and disdain of
all restraint which mark Lydia's character. Excuse me – for I must
speak plainly. If you, my dear father, will not take the trouble of
checking her exuberant spirits, and of teaching her that her present
pursuits are not to be the business of her life, she will soon be
beyond the reach of amendment. Her character will be fixed, and
she will, at sixteen, be the most determined flirt that ever made
herself and her family ridiculous. A flirt too, in the worst and
meanest degree of flirtation; without any attraction beyond youth
and a tolerable person; and from the ignorance and emptiness
of her mind, wholly unable to ward off any portion of that universal contempt which her rage for admiration will excite. In this
danger Kitty is also comprehended. She will follow wherever Lydia
leads. Vain, ignorant, idle, and absolutely uncontrouled! Oh! my

dear father, can you suppose it possible that they will not be censured and despised wherever they are known, and that their sisters will not be often involved in the disgrace?"

Mr. Bennet saw that her whole heart was in the subject; and affectionately taking her hand, said in reply,

"Do not make yourself uneasy, my love. Whenever you and Jane are known, you must be respected and valued; and you will not appear to less advantage for having a couple of–or I may say, three very silly sisters. We shall have no peace at Longbourn if Lydia does not go to Brighton. Let her go then. Colonel Forster is a sensible man, and will keep her out of any real mischief; and she is luckily too poor to be an object of prey to any body. At Brighton she will be of less importance even as a common flirt than she has been here. The officers will find women better worth their notice. Let us hope, therefore, that her being there may teach her her own insignificance. At any rate, she cannot grow many degrees worse, without authorizing us to lock her up for the rest of her life."

With this answer Elizabeth was forced to be content; but her own opinion continued the same, and she left him disappointed and sorry. It was not in her nature, however, to increase her vexations, by dwelling on them. She was confident of having performed her duty, and to fret over unavoidable evils, or augment them by anxiety, was no part of her disposition.

Had Lydia and her mother known the substance of her conference with her father, their indignation would hardly have found expression in their united volubility. In Lydia's imagination, a visit to Brighton comprised every possibility of earthly happiness. She saw with the creative eye of fancy, the streets of that gay bathing place covered with officers. She saw herself the object of attention, to tens and to scores of them at present unknown. She saw all the glories of the camp; its tents stretched forth in beauteous uniformity of lines, crowded with the young and the gay, and dazzling with scarlet; and to complete the view, she saw herself seated beneath a tent, tenderly flirting with at least six officers at once.

Had she known that her sister sought to tear her from such prospects and such realities as these, what would have been her sensations? They could have been understood only by her mother, who might have felt nearly the same. Lydia's going to Brighton was all that consoled her for the melancholy conviction of her husband's never intending to go there himself.

But they were entirely ignorant of what had passed; and their raptures continued with little intermission to the very day of Lydia's leaving home.

Elizabeth was now to see Mr. Wickham for the last time. Having been frequently in company with him since her return, agitation was pretty well over; the agitations of former partiality entirely so. She had even learnt to detect, in the very gentleness which had first delighted her, an affectation and a sameness to disgust and weary. In his present behaviour to herself, moreover, she had a fresh source of displeasure, for the inclination he soon testified of renewing those attentions which had marked the early part of their acquaintance, could only serve, after what had since passed, to provoke her. She lost all concern for him in finding herself thus selected as the object of such idle and frivolous gallantry; and while she steadily repressed it, could not but feel the reproof contained in his believing, that however long, and for whatever cause, his attentions had been withdrawn, her vanity would be gratified and her preference secured at any time by their renewal.

On the very last day of the regiment's remaining in Meryton, he dined with others of the officers at Longbourn; and so little was Elizabeth disposed to part from him in good humour, that on his making some enquiry as to the manner in which her time had passed at Hunsford, she mentioned Colonel Fitzwilliam's and Mr. Darcy's having both spent three weeks at Rosings, and asked him if he were acquainted with the former.

He looked surprised, displeased, alarmed; but with a moment's recollection and a returning smile, replied, that he had formerly seen him often; and after observing that he was a very gentlemanlike man, asked her how she had liked him. Her answer was warmly in his favour. With an air of indifference he soon afterwards added, "How long did you say that he was at Rosings?"

"Nearly three weeks."

"And you saw him frequently?"

"Yes, almost every day."

"His manners are very different from his cousin's."

"Yes, very different. But I think Mr. Darcy improves on acquaintance."

"Indeed!" cried Wickham with a look which did not escape her. "And pray may I ask?" but checking himself, he added in a gayer tone. "Is it in address that he improves? Has he deigned to add ought of civility to his ordinary style? for I dare not hope," he continued in a lower and more serious tone, "that he is improved in essentials."

"Oh, no!" said Elizabeth. "In essentials, I believe, he is very much what he ever was."

While she spoke, Wickham looked as if scarcely knowing whether to rejoice over her words, or to distrust their meaning. There was a something in her countenance which made him listen with an apprehensive and anxious attention, while she added,

"When I said that he improved on acquaintance, I did not mean that either his mind or manners were in a state of improvement, but that from knowing him better, his disposition was better understood."

Wickham's alarm now appeared in a heightened complexion and agitated look; for a few minutes he was silent; till, shaking off his embarrassment, he turned to her again, and said in the gentlest of accents,

"You, who so well know my feelings towards Mr. Darcy, will readily comprehend how sincerely I must rejoice that he is wise enough to assume even the *appearance* of what is right. His pride, in that direction, may be of service, if not to himself, to many others, for it must deter him from such foul misconduct as I have suffered by. I only fear that the sort of cautiousness, to which you,

I imagine, have been alluding, is merely adopted on his visits to his aunt, of whose good opinion and judgment he stands much in awe. His fear of her, has always operated, I know, when they were together; and a good deal is to be imputed to his wish of forwarding the match with Miss De Bourgh, which I am certain he has very much at heart."

Elizabeth could not repress a smile at this, but she answered only by a slight inclination of the head. She saw that he wanted to engage her on the old subject of his grievances, and she was in no humour to indulge him. The rest of the evening passed with the *appearance,* on her side, of usual cheerfulness, but with no farther attempt to distinguish Elizabeth; and they parted at last with mutual civility, and possibly a mutual desire of never meeting again.

When the party broke up, Lydia returned with Mrs. Forster to Meryton, from whence they were to set out early the next morning. The separation between her and her family was rather noisy than pathetic. Kitty was the only one who shed tears; but she did weep from vexation and envy. Mrs. Bennet was diffuse in her good wishes for the felicity of her daughter, and impressive in her injunctions that she would not miss the opportunity of enjoying herself as much as possible; advice, which there was every reason to believe would be attended to; and in the clamorous happiness of Lydia herself in bidding farewell, the more gentle adieus of her sisters were uttered without being heard.

CHAPTER 19

Had Elizabeth's opinion been all drawn from her own family, she could not have formed a very pleasing picture of conjugal felicity or domestic comfort. Her father captivated by youth and beauty, and that appearance of good humour, which youth and beauty generally give, had married a woman whose weak understanding and illiberal mind, had very early in their marriage put an end to all real affection for her. Respect, esteem, and confidence, had vanished for ever; and all his views of domestic happiness were overthrown. But Mr. Bennet was not of a disposition to seek comfort for the disappointment which his own imprudence had brought on, in any of those pleasures which too often console the unfortunate for their folly or their vice. He was fond of the country and of books; and from these tastes had arisen his principal enjoyments. To his wife he was very little otherwise indebted, than as her ignorance and folly had contributed to his amusement. This is not the sort of happiness which a man would in general wish to owe to his wife; but where other powers of entertainment are wanting, the true philosopher will derive benefit from such as are given.

Elizabeth, however, had never been blind to the impropriety of her father's behaviour as a husband. She had always seen it with pain; but respecting his abilities, and grateful for his affectionate treatment of herself, she endeavoured to forget what she could not overlook, and to banish from her thoughts that continual breach of conjugal obligation and decorum which, in exposing his wife to the contempt of her own children, was so highly reprehensible. But she had never felt so strongly as now, the disadvantages which must attend the children of so unsuitable a marriage, nor ever been so fully aware of the evils arising from so ill-judged a direction of talents; talents which rightly used, might at least have preserved the respectability of his daughters, even if incapable of enlarging the mind of his wife.

When Elizabeth had rejoiced over Wickham's departure, she found little other cause for satisfaction in the loss of the regiment. Their parties abroad were less varied than before; and at home she had a mother and sister whose constant repinings at the dulness of every thing around them, threw a real gloom over their domestic circle; and, though Kitty might in time regain her natural degree of sense, since the disturbers of her brain were removed, her other sister, from whose disposition greater evil might be apprehended, was likely to be hardened in all her folly and assurance, by a situation of such double danger as a watering place and a camp. Upon the whole, therefore, she found, what has been sometimes found before, that an event to which she had looked forward with impatient desire, did not in taking place, bring all the satisfaction she had promised herself. It was consequently necessary to name some other period for the commencement of actual felicity; to have some other point on which her wishes and hopes might be fixed, and by again enjoying the pleasure of anticipation, console herself for the present, and prepare for another disappointment. Her tour to the Lakes was now the object of her happiest thoughts; it was her best consolation for all the uncomfortable hours, which the discontentedness of her mother and Kitty made inevitable; and could she have included Jane in the scheme, every part of it would have been perfect.

"But it is fortunate," thought she "that I have something to wish for. Were the whole arrangement complete, my disappointment would be certain. But here, my carrying with me one ceaseless source of regret in my sister's absence, I may reasonably hope to have all my expectations of pleasure realized. A scheme of which every part promises delight, can never be successful; and general disappointment is only warded off by the defence of some little peculiar vexation."

When Lydia went away, she promised to write very often and very minutely to her mother and Kitty; but her letters were always long expected, and always very short. Those to her mother, contained little else, than that they were just returned from the library, where such and such officers had attended them, and where she had seen such beautiful ornaments as made her quite wild; that she had a new gown, or a new parasol, which she would have described more fully, but was obliged to leave off in a violent hurry, as Mrs. Forster called her, and they were going to the camp;—and from her correspondence with her sister, there was still less to be learnt—for her letters to Kitty, though rather longer, were much too full of lines under the words to be made public.

After the first fortnight or three weeks of her absence, health, good humour and cheerfulness began to re-appear at Longbourn. Every thing wore a happier aspect. The families who had been in town for the winter came back again, and summer finery and summer engagements arose. Mrs. Bennet was restored to her usual querulous serenity, and by the middle of June Kitty was so much recovered as to be able to enter Meryton without tears; an event of such happy promise as to make Elizabeth hope, that by the following Christmas, she might be so tolerably reasonable as not to mention an officer above once a day, unless by some cruel and malicious arrangement at the war-office, another regiment should be quartered in Meryton.

The time fixed for the beginning of their Northern tour was now fast approaching; and a fortnight only was wanting of it, when a letter arrived from Mrs. Gardiner, which at once delayed its commencement and curtailed its extent. Mr. Gardiner would be prevented by business from setting out till a fortnight later in July, and must be in London again within a month; and as that left too short a period for them to go far, and see so much as they had proposed, or at least to see it with the leisure and comfort they had built on, they were obliged to give up the Lakes, and substitute a more contracted tour; and, according to the present plan, were to go no farther northward than Derbyshire. In that county, there was enough to be seen, to occupy the chief of their three weeks; and to Mrs. Gardiner it had a peculiarly strong attraction. The town where she had formerly passed some years of her life, and where they were now to spend a few days, was probably as great an object of her curiosity, as all the celebrated beauties of Matlock, Chatsworth, Dovedale, or the Peak.

Elizabeth was excessively disappointed; she had set her heart on seeing the Lakes; and still thought there might have been time enough. But it was her business to be satisfied – and certainly her temper to be happy; and all was soon right again.

With the mention of Derbyshire, there were many ideas connected. It was impossible for her to see the word without thinking of Pemberley and its owner. "But surely," said she, "I may enter his county with impunity, and rob it of a few petrified spars without his perceiving me."

The period of expectation was now doubled. Four weeks were to pass away before her uncle and aunt's arrival. But they did pass away, and Mr. and Mrs. Gardiner, with their four children, did at length appear at Longbourn. The children, two girls of six and eight years old, and two younger boys, were to be left under the particular care of their cousin Jane, who was the general favourite, and whose steady sense and sweetness of temper exactly adapted her for attending to them in every way–teaching them, playing with them, and loving them.

The Gardiners staid only one night at Longbourn, and set off the next morning with Elizabeth in pursuit of novelty and amusement. One enjoyment was certain–that suitableness as companions; a suitableness which comprehended health and temper to bear inconveniences–cheerfulness to enhance every pleasure–and affection and intelligence, which might supply it among themselves if there were disappointments abroad.

It is not the object of this work to give a description of Derbyshire, nor of any of the remarkable places through which their route thither lay; Oxford, Blenheim, Warwick, Kenelworth, Birmingham, &c. are sufficiently known. A small part of Derbyshire is all the present concern. To the little town of Lambton, the scene of Mrs. Gardiner's former residence, and where she had lately learned that some acquaintance still remained, they bent their steps, after having seen all the principal wonders of the country; and within five miles of Lambton, Elizabeth found from her aunt, that Pemberley was situated. It was not in their direct road, nor more than a mile or two out of it. In talking over their route the evening before, Mrs. Gardiner expressed an inclination to see the place again. Mr. Gardiner declared his willingness, and Elizabeth was applied to for her approbation.

"My love, should not you like to see a place of which you have heard so much?" said her aunt. "A place too, with which so many of your acquaintance are connected. Wickham passed all his youth there, you know."

Elizabeth was distressed. She felt that she had no business at Pemberley, and was obliged to assume a disinclination for seeing it. She must own that she was tired of great houses; after going over so many, she really had no pleasure in fine carpets or satin curtains."

Mrs. Gardiner abused her stupidity. "If it were merely a fine house richly furnished," said she, "I should not care about it myself; but the grounds are delightful. They have some of the finest woods in the country."

Elizabeth said no more – but her mind could not acquiesce. The possibility of meeting Mr. Darcy, while viewing the place, instantly occurred. It would be dreadful! She blushed at the very idea; and thought it would be better to speak openly to her aunt, than to run such a risk. But against this, there were objections; and she finally resolved that it could be the last resource, if her private enquiries as to the absence of the family, were unfavourably answered.

Accordingly, when she retired at night, she asked the chambermaid whether Pemberley were not a very fine place, what was the name of its proprietor, and with no little alarm, whether the family were down for the summer. A most welcome negative followed the last question – and her alarms being now removed, she was at leisure to feel a great deal of curiosity to see the house herself; and when the subject was revived the next morning, and she was again applied to, could readily answer, and with a proper air of indifference, that she had not really any dislike to the scheme.

To Pemberley, therefore, they were to go.

222

VOLUME III

CHAPTER 1

Elizabeth, as they drove along, watched for the first appearance of Pemberley Woods with some perturbation; and when at length they turned in at the lodge, her spirits were in a high flutter.

The park was very large, and contained great variety of ground. They entered it in one of its lowest points, and drove for some time through a beautiful wood, stretching over a wide extent.

Elizabeth's mind was too full for conversation, but she saw and admired every remarkable spot and point of view. They gradually ascended for half a mile, and then found themselves at the top of a considerable eminence, where the wood ceased, and the eye was instantly caught by Pemberley House, situated on the opposite side of a valley, into which the road with some abruptness wound. It was a large, handsome, stone building, standing well on rising ground, and backed by a ridge of high woody hills; – and in front, a stream of some natural importance was swelled into greater, but without any artificial appearance. Its banks were neither formal, nor falsely adorned. Elizabeth was delighted. She had never seen a place for which nature had done more, or where natural beauty had been so little counteracted by an awkward taste. They were all of them warm in their admiration; and at that moment she felt, that to be mistress of Pemberley might be something!

They descended the hill, crossed the bridge, and drove to the door; and, while examining the nearer aspect of the house, all her apprehensions of meeting its owner returned. She dreaded lest the chambermaid had been mistaken. On applying to see the place, they were admitted into the hall; and Elizabeth, as they waited for the housekeeper, had leisure to wonder at her being where she was.

The housekeeper came; a respectable-looking, elderly woman, much less fine, and more civil, than she had any notion of finding her. They followed her into the dining-parlour. It was a large, well-proportioned room, handsomely fitted up. Elizabeth, after slightly surveying it, went to a window to enjoy its prospect. The hill, crowned with wood, from which they had descended, receiving increased abruptness from the distance, was a beautiful object. Every disposition of the ground was good; and she looked on the whole scene, the river, the trees scattered on its banks, and the winding of the valley, as far as she could trace it, with delight. As they passed into other rooms, these objects were taking different positions; but from every window there were beauties to be seen. The rooms were lofty and handsome, and their furniture suitable to the fortune of their proprietor; but Elizabeth saw, with admiration of his taste, that it was neither gaudy nor uselessly fine; with less of splendor, and more real elegance, than the furniture of Rosings.

"And of this place," thought she, "I might have been mistress! With these rooms I might now have been familiarly acquainted! Instead of viewing them as a stranger, I might have rejoiced in them as my own, and welcomed to them as visitors my uncle and aunt.—But no,"— recollecting herself,—that could never be: my uncle and aunt would have been lost to me: I should not have been allowed to invite them."

This was a lucky recollection—it saved her from something like regret.

She longed to enquire of the housekeeper, whether her master were really absent, but had not courage for it. At length, however, the question was asked by her uncle; and she turned away with alarm, while Mrs. Reynolds replied, that he was, adding, "but we expect him to morrow, with a large party of friends." How rejoiced was Elizabeth that their own journey had not by any circumstance been delayed a day!

Her aunt now called her to look at a picture. She approached, and saw the likeness of Mr. Wickham suspended, amongst several other miniatures, over the mantle-piece. Her aunt asked her, smilingly, how she liked it. The housekeeper came forward, and told them it was the picture of a young gentleman, the son of her late master's steward, who had been brought up by him at his own expence.–"He is now gone into the army," she added, "but I am afraid he has turned out very wild."

Mrs. Gardiner looked at her niece with a smile, but Elizabeth could not return it.

"And that," said Mrs. Reynolds, pointing to another of the miniatures, "is my master–and very like him. It was drawn at the same time as the other–about eight years ago."

"I have heard much of your master's fine person," said Mrs. Gardiner, looking at the picture; "it is a handsome face. But, Lizzy, you can tell us whether it is like or not."

Mrs. Reynolds's respect for Elizabeth seemed to increase on this intimation of her knowing her master.

"Does that young lady know Mr. Darcy?"

Elizabeth coloured, and said–"A little."

"And do not you think him a very handsome gentleman, Ma'am?"

"Yes, very handsome."

"I am sure I know none so handsome; but in the gallery up stairs you will see a finer, larger picture of him than this. This room was my late master's favourite room, and these miniatures are just as they used to be then. He was very fond of them."

This accounted to Elizabeth for Mr. Wickham's being among them.

Mrs. Reynolds then directed their attention to one of Miss Darcy, drawn when she was only eight years old.

"And is Miss Darcy as handsome as her brother?" said Mr. Gardiner.

"Oh! yes–the handsomest young lady that ever was seen; and so accomplished!–She plays and sings all day long. In the next room is a new instrument just come down for her–a present from my master; she comes here tomorrow with him."

Mr. Gardiner, whose manners were easy and pleasant, encouraged her communicativeness by his questions and remarks; Mrs. Reynolds, either from pride or attachment, had evidently great pleasure in talking of her master and his sister.

"Is your master much at Pemberley in the course of the year?"

"Not so much as I could wish, Sir; but I dare say he may spend half his time here; and Miss Darcy is always down for the summer months."

"Except," thought Elizabeth, "when she goes to Ramsgate." "If your master would marry, you might see more of him."

"Yes, Sir; but I do not know when *that* will be. I do not know who is good enough for him."

Mr. and Mrs. Gardiner smiled. Elizabeth could not help saying, "It is very much to his credit, I am sure, that you should think so."

"I say no more than the truth, and what every body will say that knows him," replied the other. Elizabeth thought this was going pretty far; and she listened with increasing astonishment as the housekeeper added, "I have never had a cross word from him in my life, and I have known him ever since he was four years old."

This was praise, of all others most extraordinary, most opposite to her ideas. That he was not a good-tempered man, had been her firmest opinion. Her keenest attention was awakened; she longed to hear more, and was grateful to her uncle for saying,

"There are very few people of whom so much can be said. You are lucky in having such a master."

"Yes, Sir, I know I am. If I was to go through the world, I could not meet with a better. But I have always observed that they who are good-natured when children, are good-natured when they grow up; and he was always the sweetest-tempered, most generous-hearted, boy in the world."

Elizabeth almost stared at her.–"Can this be Mr. Darcy!" thought she.

"His father was an excellent man," said Mrs. Gardiner.

Yes, Ma'am, that he was indeed; and his son will be just like him–just as affable to the poor."

Elizabeth listened, wondered, doubted, and was impatient for more. Mrs. Reynolds could interest her on no other point. She related the subject of the pictures, the dimensions of the rooms, and the price of the furniture, in vain. Mr. Gardiner, highly amused by the kind of family prejudice, to which he attributed her excessive commendation of her master, soon led again to the subject; and she dwelt with energy on his many merits, as they proceeded together up the great staircase.

"He is the best landlord, and the best master," said she, "that ever lived. Not like the wild young men now-a-days, who think of nothing but themselves. There is not one of his tenants or servants but what will give him a good name. Some people call him proud; but I am sure I never saw any thing of it. To my fancy, it is only because he does not rattle away like other young men."

"In what an amiable light does this place him!" thought Elizabeth.

"This fine account of him," whispered her aunt, as they walked away, is not quite consistent with his behaviour to our poor friend."

"Perhaps we might be deceived."

"That is not very likely; our authority was too good."

"On reaching the spacious lobby above, they were shewn into a very pretty sitting-room, lately fitted up with greater elegance and lightness than the apartments below; and were informed that it was but just done, to give pleasure to Miss Darcy, who had taken a liking to the room, when last at Pemberley.

"He is certainly a good brother," said Elizabeth, as she walked towards one of the windows.

Mrs. Reynolds anticipated Miss Darcy's delight, when she should enter the room. "And this is always the way with him," she added.—"Whatever can give his sister any pleasure, is sure to be done in a moment. There is nothing he would not do for her."

The picture-gallery, and two or three of the principal bed-rooms, were all that remained to be shewn. In the former were many good paintings; but Elizabeth knew nothing of the art; and from such as had been already visible below, she had willingly turned to look at some drawings of Miss Darcy's, in crayons, whose subjects were usually more interesting, and also more intelligible.

In the gallery there were many family portraits, but they could have little to fix the attention of a stranger. Elizabeth walked on in quest of the only face whose features would be known to her. At last it arrested her – and she beheld a striking resemblance of Mr. Darcy, with such a smile over the face, as she remembered to have sometimes seen, when he looked at her. She stood several minutes before the picture in earnest contemplation, and returned to it again before they quitted the gallery. Mrs. Reynolds informed them, that it had been taken in his father's life time.

There was certainly at this moment, in Elizabeth's mind, a more gentle sensation towards the original, than she had ever felt in the height of their acquaintance. The commendation bestowed on him by Mrs. Reynolds was of no trifling nature. What praise is more valuable than the praise of an intelligent servant? As a brother, a landlord, a master, she considered how many people's happiness were in his guardianship! – How much of pleasure or pain it was in his power to bestow! – How much of good or evil must be done by him! Every idea that had been brought forward by the housekeeper was favourable to his character, and as she stood before the canvas, on which he was represented, and fixed his eyes upon herself, she thought of his regard with a deeper sentiment of gratitude than it had ever raised before; she remembered its warmth and softened its impropriety of expression.

When all of the house that was open to general inspection had been seen, they returned down stairs, and taking leave of the housekeeper, were consigned over to the gardener, who met them at the hall door.

As they walked across the lawn towards the river, Elizabeth turned back to look again; her uncle and aunt stopped also, and while the former was conjecturing as to the date of the building, the owner of it himself suddenly came forward from the road, which led behind it to the stables.

They were within twenty yards of each other, and so abrupt

was his appearance, that it was impossible to avoid his sight. Their eyes instantly met, and the cheeks of each were overspread with the deepest blush. He absolutely started, and for a moment seemed immoveable from surprise; but shortly recovering himself, advanced towards the party, and spoke to Elizabeth, if not in terms of perfect composure, at least of perfect civility.

She had instinctively turned away; but, stopping on his approach, received his compliments with an embarrassment impossible to be overcome. Had his first appearance, or his resemblance to the picture they had just been examining, been insufficient to assure the other two that they now saw Mr. Darcy, the gardener's expression of surprise, on beholding his master, must immediately have told it. They stood a little aloof while he was talking to their niece, who, astonished and confused, scarcely dared lift her eyes to his face, and knew not what answer she returned to his civil enquiries after her family. Amazed at the alteration in his manner since they last parted, every sentence that he uttered was increasing her embarrassment; and every idea of the impropriety of her being found there, recurring to her mind, the few minutes in which they continued together, were some of the most uncomfortable of her life. Nor did he seem much more at ease; when he spoke, his accent had none of its usual sedateness; and he repeated his enquiries as to the time of her having left Longbourn, and of her stay in Derbyshire, so often, and in so hurried a way, as plainly spoke the distraction of his thoughts.

At length, every idea seemed to fail him; and, after standing a few moments without saying a word, he suddenly recollected himself, and took leave.

The others then joined her, and expressed their admiration of his figure; but Elizabeth heard not a word, and wholly engrossed by her own feelings followed them in silence. She was overpowered by shame and vexation. Her coming there was the most unfortunate, the most ill-judged thing in the world! How strange must it appear to him! In what a disgraceful light might it not strike so vain a man! It might seem as if she had purposely thrown herself in his way again! Oh! why did she come? or, why did he thus come a day before he was expected? Had they been only ten minutes sooner, they should have been beyond the reach of his discrimination, for it was plain that he was that moment arrived, that moment alighted from his horse or his carriage. She blushed again and again over the perverseness of the meeting. And his behaviour, so strikingly altered,—what could it mean? That he should even speak to her was amazing!—but to speak with such civility, to enquire after her family! Never in her life had she seen his manners so little dignified, never had he spoken with such gentleness as on this unexpected meeting. What a contrast did it offer to his last address in Rosing's Park, when he put his letter into her hand! She knew not what to think, nor how to account for it.

They had now entered a beautiful walk by the side of the water, and every step was bringing forward a nobler fall of ground, or a finer reach of the woods to which they were approaching: but it was some time before Elizabeth was sensible of any of it; and, though she answered mechanically to the repeated appeals of her uncle and aunt, and seemed to direct her eyes to such objects as they pointed out, she distinguished no part of the scene. Her thoughts were all fixed on that one spot of Pemberley House, whichever it might be, where Mr. Darcy then was. She longed to know what at that moment was passing in his mind; in what manner he thought of her, and whether, in defiance of every thing, she was still dear to him. Perhaps he had been civil, only because he felt himself at ease; yet there had been *that* in his voice, which was not like ease. Whether he had felt more of pain or of pleasure in seeing her, she could not tell, but he certainly had not seen her with composure.

At length, however, the remarks of her companions on her absence of mind roused her, and she felt the necessity of appearing more like herself.

They entered the woods, and bidding adieu to the river for a while, ascended some of the higher grounds; whence, in spots

where the opening of the trees gave the eye power to wander, were
many charming views of the valley, the opposite hills, with the
long range of woods overspreading many, and occasionally part
of the stream. Mr. Gardiner expressed a wish of going round the
whole Park, but feared it might be beyond a walk. With a triumphant smile, they were told, that it was ten miles round. It settled
the matter; and they pursued the accustomed circuit; which
brought them again, after some time, in a descent among hanging woods, to the edge of the water, in one of its narrowest parts.
They crossed it by a simple bridge, in character with the general
air of the scene; it was a spot less adorned than any they had
yet visited; and the valley, here contracted into a glen, allowed
room only for the stream, and a narrow walk amidst the rough
coppice-wood which bordered it. Elizabeth longed to explore its
windings; but when they had crossed the bridge, and perceived
their distance from the house, Mrs. Gardiner, who was not a great
walker, could go no farther, and thought only of returning to the
carriage as quickly as possible. Her niece was, therefore, obliged
to submit, and they took their way towards the house on the opposite side of the river, in the nearest direction; but their progress
was slow, for Mr. Gardiner, though seldom able to indulge the
taste, was very fond of fishing, and was so much engaged in watching the occasional appearance of some trout in the water, and
talking to the man about them, that he advanced but little. Whilst
wandering on in this slow manner, they were again surprised, and
Elizabeth's astonishment was quite equal to what it had been at
first, by the sight of Mr. Darcy approaching them, and at no great
distance. The walk being here less sheltered than on the other
side, allowed them to see him before they met. Elizabeth, however
astonished, was at least more prepared for an interview than before, and resolved to appear and to speak with calmness, if he
really intended to meet them. For a few moments, indeed, she
felt that he would probably strike into some other path. This idea
lasted while a turning in the walk concealed him from their view;
the turning past, he was immediately before them. With a glance

she saw, that he had lost none of his recent civility; and, to imitate his politeness, she began, as they met, to admire the beauty of the place; but she had not got beyond the words "delightful," and "charming," when some unlucky recollections obtruded, and she fancied that praise of Pemberley from her, might be mischievously construed. Her colour changed, and she said no more.

Mrs. Gardiner was standing a little behind; and on her pausing, he asked her, if she would do him the honour of introducing him to her friends. This was a stroke of civility for which she was quite unprepared; and she could hardly suppress a smile, at his being now seeking the acquaintance of some of those very people, against whom his pride had revolted, in his offer to herself. "What will be his surprise," thought she, "when he knows who they are! He takes them now for people of fashion."

The introduction, however, was immediately made; and as she named her relationship to herself, she stole a sly look at him, to see how he bore it; and was not without the expectation of his decamping as fast as he could from such disgraceful companions. That he was *surprised* by the connexion was evident; he sustained it however with fortitude, and so far from going away, turned back with them, and entered into conversation with Mr. Gardiner. Elizabeth could not but be pleased, could not but triumph. It was consoling, that he should know she had some relations for whom there was no need to blush. She listened most attentively to all that passed between them, and gloried in every expression, every sentence of her uncle, which marked his intelligence, his taste, or his good manners.

The conversation soon turned upon fishing, and she heard Mr. Darcy invite him, with the greatest civility to fish there as often as he chose, while he continued in the neighbourhood, offering at the same time to supply him with fishing tackle, and pointing out those parts of the stream where there was usually most sport. Mrs. Gardiner, who was walking arm in arm with Elizabeth, gave her a look expressive of her wonder. Elizabeth said nothing, but it gratified her exceedingly; the compliment must be all for herself. Her astonishment, however, was extreme; and continually was she repeating, "Why is he so altered? From what can it proceed? It cannot be for *me*, it cannot be for *my* sake that his manners are thus softened. My reproofs at Hunsford could not work such a change as this. It is impossible that he should still love me."

After walking some time in this way, the two ladies in front, the two gentlemen behind, on resuming their places, after descending to the brink of the river for the better inspection of some curious water-plant, there chanced to be a little alteration. It originated in Mrs. Gardiner, who, fatigued by the exercise of the morning, found Elizabeth's arm inadequate to her support, and consequently preferred her husband's. Mr. Darcy took her place by her niece, and they walked on together. After a short silence, the lady first spoke. She wished him to know that she had been assured of his absence before she came to the place, and accordingly began by observing, that his arrival had been very unexpected—"for your housekeeper," she added, "informed us that you would certainly not be here till to morrow; and indeed, before we left Bakewell, we understood that you were not immediately expected in the country." He acknowledged the truth of it all; and said that business with his steward had occasioned his coming forward a few hours before the rest of the party with whom he had been travelling. "They will join me early to morrow," he continued, "and among them are some who will claim an acquaintance with you,— Mr. Bingley and his sisters."

Elizabeth answered only by a slight bow. Her thoughts were instantly driven back to the time when Mr. Bingley's name had been last mentioned between them; and if she might judge from his complexion, *his* mind was not very differently engaged.

"There is also one other person in the party," he continued after a pause, "who more particularly wishes to be known to you,— Will you allow me, or do I ask too much, to introduce my sister to your acquaintance during your stay at Lambton?"

The surprise of such an application was great indeed; it was too great for her to know in what manner she acceded to it. She immediately felt that whatever desire Miss Darcy might have of being acquainted with her, must be the work of her brother, and without looking farther, it was satisfactory; it was gratifying to know that his resentment had not made him think really ill of her.

They now walked on in silence; each of them deep in thought. Elizabeth was not comfortable; that was impossible; but she was flattered and pleased. His wish of introducing his sister to her, was a compliment of the highest kind. They soon outstripped the others, and when they had reached the carriage, Mr. and Mrs. Gardiner were half a quarter of a mile behind.

He then asked her to walk into the house—but she declared herself not tired, and they stood together on the lawn. At such a time, much might have been said, and silence was very awkward. She wanted to talk, but there seemed an embargo on every subject. At last she recollected that she had been travelling, and they talked of Matlock and Dove Dale with great perseverance. Yet time and her aunt moved slowly—and her patience and her ideas were nearly worn out before the tete-a-tete was over. On Mr. and Mrs. Gardiner's coming up, they were all pressed to go into the house and take some refreshment; but this was declined, and they parted on each side with the utmost politeness. Mr. Darcy handed the ladies into the carriage, and when it drove off, Elizabeth saw him walking slowly towards the house.

The observations of her uncle and aunt now began; and each of them pronounced him to be infinitely superior to any thing they had expected. "He is perfectly well behaved, polite, and unassuming," said her uncle.

"There is something a little stately in him to be sure," replied her aunt, "but it is confined to his air, and is not unbecoming. I can now say with the housekeeper, that though some people may call him proud, I have seen nothing of it."

"I was never more surprised than by his behaviour to us. It was more than civil; it was really attentive; and there was no necessity for such attention. His acquaintance with Elizabeth was very trifling."

"To be sure, Lizzy," said her aunt, "he is not so handsome as Wickham; or rather he has not Wickham's countenance, for his features are perfectly good. But how came you to tell us that he was so disagreeable?"

Elizabeth excused herself as well as she could; said that she had liked him better when they met in Kent than before, and that she had never seen him so pleasant as this morning.

"But perhaps he may be a little whimsical in his civilities," replied her uncle. "Your great men often are; and therefore I shall not take him at his word about fishing, as he might change his mind another day, and warn me off his grounds."

Elizabeth felt that they had entirely mistaken his character, but said nothing.

"From what we have seen of him," continued Mrs. Gardiner, "I really should not have thought that he could have behaved in so cruel a way by any body, as he has done by poor Wickham. He has not an ill-natured look. On the contrary, there is something pleasing about his mouth when he speaks. And there is something of dignity in his countenance, that would not give one an unfavourable idea of his heart. But to be sure, the good lady who shewed us the house, did give him a most flaming character! I could hardly help laughing aloud sometimes. But he is a liberal master, I suppose, and *that* in the eye of a servant comprehends every virtue."

Elizabeth here felt herself called on to say something in vindication of his behaviour to Wickham; and therefore gave them to understand, in as guarded a manner as she could, that by what she had heard from his relations in Kent, his actions were capable of a very different construction; and that his character was by no means so faulty, nor Wickham's so amiable, as they had been considered in Hertfordshire. In confirmation of this, she related the particulars of all the pecuniary transactions in which they had been connected, without actually naming her authority, but stating it to be such as might be relied on.

Mrs. Gardiner was surprised and concerned; but as they were

now approaching the scene of her former pleasures, every idea gave way to the charm of recollection; and she was too much engaged in pointing out to her husband all the interesting spots in its environs, to think of any thing else. Fatigued as she had been by the morning's walk, they had no sooner dined than she set off again in quest of her former acquaintance, and the evening was spent in the satisfactions of an intercourse renewed after many years discontinuance.

The occurrences of the day were too full of interest to leave Elizabeth much attention for any of these new friends; and she could do nothing but think, and think with wonder, of Mr. Darcy's civility, and above all, of his wishing her to be acquainted with his sister.

CHAPTER 2

Elizabeth had settled it that Mr. Darcy would bring his sister to visit her, the very day after her reaching Pemberlay; and was consequently resolved not to be out of sight of the inn the whole of that morning. But her conclusion was false; for on the very morning after their own arrival at Lambton, these visitors came. They had been walking about the place with some of their new friends, and were just returned to the inn to dress themselves for dining with the same family, when the sound of a carriage drew them to a window, and they saw a gentleman and lady in a curricle, driving up the street. Elizabeth immediately recognising the livery, guessed what it meant, and imparted no small degree of surprise to her relations, by acquainting them with the honour which she expected. Her uncle and aunt were all amazement; and the embarrassment of her manner as she spoke, joined to the circumstance itself, and many of the circumstances of the preceding day, opened to them a new idea on the business. Nothing had ever suggested it before, but they now felt that there was no other

way of accounting for such attentions from such a quarter, than
by supposing a partiality for their niece. While these newly-born
notions were passing in their heads, the perturbation of Elizabeth's
feelings was every moment increasing. She was quite amazed at
her own discomposure; but amongst other causes of disquiet, she
dreaded lest the partiality of the brother should have said too
much in her favour; and more than commonly anxious to please,
she naturally suspected that every power of pleasing would fail her.

She retreated from the window, fearful of being seen; and as
she walked up and down the room, endeavouring to compose
herself, saw such looks of enquiring surprise in her uncle and
aunt, as made every thing worse.

Miss Darcy and her brother appeared, and this formidable introduction took place. With astonishment did Elizabeth see, that
her new acquaintance was at least as much embarrassed as herself. Since her being at Lambton, she had heard that Miss Darcy
was exceedingly proud; but the observation of a very few minutes
convinced her, that she was only exceedingly shy. She found it
difficult to obtain even a word from her beyond a monosyllable.

Miss Darcy was tall, and on a larger scale than Elizabeth; and,
though little more than sixteen, her figure was formed, and her
appearance womanly and graceful. She was less handsome than
her brother, but there was sense and good humour in her face,
and her manners were perfectly unassuming and gentle. Elizabeth,
who had expected to find in her as acute and unembarrassed an
observer as ever Mr. Darcy had been, was much relieved by discerning such different feelings.

They had not been long together, before Darcy told her that
Bingley was also coming to wait on her; and she had barely time
to express her satisfaction, and prepare for such a visitor, when
Bingley's quick step was heard on the stairs, and in a moment
he entered the room. All Elizabeth's anger against him had been
long done away; but, had she still felt any, it could hardly have
stood its ground against the unaffected cordiality with which he
expressed himself, on seeing her again. He enquired in a friend-

ly, though general way, after her family, and looked and spoke with the same good-humoured ease that he had ever done.

To Mr. and Mrs. Gardiner he was scarcely a less interesting personage than to herself. They had long wished to see him. The whole party before them, indeed, excited a lively attention. The suspicions which had just arisen of Mr. Darcy and their niece, directed their observation towards each with an earnest, though guarded, enquiry; and they soon drew from those enquiries the full conviction that one of them at least knew what it was to love. Of the lady's sensations they remained a little in doubt; but that the gentleman was overflowing with admiration was evident enough.

Elizabeth, on her side, had much to do. She wanted to ascertain the feelings of each of her visitors, she wanted to compose her own, and to make herself agreeable to all; and in the latter object, where she feared most to fail, she was most sure of success, for those to whom she endeavoured to give pleasure were prepossessed in her favour. Bingley was ready, Georgiana was eager, and Darcy determined, to be pleased.

In seeing Bingley, her thoughts naturally flew to her sister; and oh! how ardently did she long to know, whether any of his were directed in a like manner. Sometimes she could fancy, that he talked less than on former occasions, and once or twice pleased herself with the notion that as he looked at her, he was trying to trace a resemblance. But, though this might be imaginary, she could not be deceived as to his behaviour to Miss Darcy, who had been set up as a rival of Jane. No look appeared on either side that spoke particular regard. Nothing occurred between them that could justify the hopes of his sister. On this point she was soon satisfied; and two or three little circumstances occurred ere they parted, which, in her anxious interpretation, denoted a recollection of Jane, not untinctured by tenderness, and a wish of saying more that might lead to the mention of her, had he dared. He observed to her, at a moment when the others were talking together, and in a tone which had something of real regret, that it "was a very long time since he had had the pleasure of seeing her;" and, before she could reply, he added, "It is above eight months. We have not met since the 26th of November, when we were all dancing together at Netherfield."

Elizabeth was pleased to find his memory so exact; and he afterwards took occasion to ask her, when unattended to by any of the rest, whether *all* her sisters were at Longbourn. There was not much in the question, nor in the preceding remark, but there was a look and a manner which gave them meaning.

It was not often that she could turn her eyes on Mr. Darcy himself; but whenever she did catch a glimpse, she saw an expression of general complaisance, and in all that he said, she heard an accent so far removed from hauteur or disdain of his companions, as convinced her that the improvement of manners which she had yesterday witnessed, however temporary its existence might prove, had at least outlived one day. When she saw him thus seeking the acquaintance, and courting the good opinion of people, with whom any intercourse a few months ago would have been a disgrace; when she saw him thus civil, not only to herself, but to the very relations whom he had openly disdained, and recollected their last lively scene in the Hunsford Parsonage, the difference, the change was so great, and struck so forcibly on her mind, that she could hardly restrain her astonishment from being visible. Never, even in the company of his dear friends at Netherfield, or his dignified relations at Rosings, had she seen him so desirous to please, so free from self-consequence, or unbending reserve as now, when no importance could result from the success of his endeavours, and when even the acquaintance of those to whom his attentions were addressed, would draw down the ridicule and censure of the ladies both of Netherfield and Rosings.

Their visitors staid with them above half an hour, and when they arose to depart, Mr. Darcy called on his sister to join him in expressing their wish of seeing Mr. and Mrs. Gardiner, and Miss Bennet, to dinner at Pemberley, before they left the country. Miss

Darcy, though with a diffidence which marked her little in the habit of giving invitations, readily obeyed. Mrs. Gardiner looked at her niece, desirous of knowing how *she,* whom the invitation most concerned, felt disposed as to its acceptance, but Elizabeth had turned away her head. Presuming, however, that this studied avoidance spoke rather a momentary embarrassment, than any dislike of the proposal, and seeing in her husband, who was fond of society, a perfect willingness to accept it, she ventured to engage for her attendance, and the day after the next was fixed on.

Bingley expressed great pleasure in the certainty of seeing Elizabeth again, having still a great deal to say to her, and many enquiries to make after all their Hertfordshire friends. Elizabeth construing all this into a wish of hearing her speak of her sister, was pleased; and on this account, as well as some others, found herself, when their visitors left them, capable of considering the last half hour with some satisfaction, though while it was passing, the enjoyment of it had been little. Eager to be alone, and fearful of enquiries or hints from her uncle and aunt, she staid with them only long enough to hear their favourable opinion of Bingley, and then hurried away to dress.

But she had no reason to fear Mr. and Mrs. Gardiner's curiosity; it was not their wish to force her communication. It was evident that she was much better acquainted with Mr. Darcy than they had before any idea of; it was evident that he was very much in love with her. They saw much to interest, but nothing to justify enquiry.

Of Mr. Darcy it was now a matter of anxiety to think well; and, as far as there acquaintance reached, there was no fault to find. They could not be untouched by his politeness, and had they drawn his character from their own feelings, and his servant's report, without any reference to any other account, the circle in Hertfordshire to which he was known, would not have recognised it for Mr. Darcy. There was now an interest, however, in believing the housekeeper; and they soon became sensible, that the authority of a servant who had known him since he was four years old,

and whose own manners indicated respectability, was not to be
hastily rejected. Neither had any thing occurred in the intelligence
of their Lambton friends, that could materially lessen its weight.
They had nothing to accuse him of but pride; pride he probably
had, and if not, it would certainly be imputed by the inhabitants
of a small market-town, where the family did not visit. It was acknowledged, however, that he was a liberal man, and did much
good among the poor.

With respect to Wickham, the travellers soon found that he
was not held there in much estimation; for though the chief of
his concerns, with the son of his patron, were imperfectly understood, it was yet a well known fact that, on his quitting Derbyshire, he had left many debts behind him, which Mr. Darcy
afterwards discharged.

"As for Elizabeth, her thoughts were at Pemberley this evening
more than the last; and the evening, though as it passed it seemed
long, was not long enough to determine her feelings towards *one*
in that mansion; and she lay awake two whole hours, endeavouring
to make them out. She certainly did not hate him. No; hatred
had vanished long ago, and she had almost as long been ashamed
of ever feeling a dislike against him, that could be so called. The
respect created by the conviction of his valuable qualities, though
at first unwillingly admitted, had for some time ceased to be repug-
nant to her feelings; and it was now heightened into somewhat
of a friendlier nature, by the testimony so highly in his favour,
and bringing forward his disposition in so amiable a light, which
yesterday had produced. But above all, above respect and esteem,
there was a motive within her of good will which could not be
overlooked. It was gratitude.–Gratitude, not merely for having
once loved her, but for loving her still well enough, to forgive all
the petulance and acrimony of her manner in rejecting him, and
all the unjust accusations accompanying her rejection. He who,
she had been persuaded, would avoid her as his greatest enemy,
seemed, on this accidental meeting, most eager to preserve the
acquaintance, and without any indelicate display of regard, or any

peculiarity of manner, where their two selves only were concerned, was soliciting the good opinion of her friends, and bent on making her known to his sister. Such a change in a man of so much pride, excited not only astonishment but gratitude – for to love, ardent love, it must be attributed; and as such its impression of her was of a sort to be encouraged, as by no means unpleasing, though it could not be exactly defined. She respected, she esteemed, she was grateful to him, she felt a real interest in his welfare; and she only wanted to know how far she wished that welfare to depend upon herself, and how far it would be for the happiness of both that she should employ the power, which her fancy told her she still possessed, of bringing on the renewal of his addresses.

It had been settled in the evening, between the aunt and niece, that such a striking civility as Miss Darcy's, in coming to them on the very day of her arrival at Pemberley, for she had reached it only to a late breakfast, ought to be imitated, though it could not be equalled, by some exertion of politeness on their side; and, consequently, that it would be highly expedient to wait on her at Pemberley the following morning. They were, therefore, to go. – Elizabeth was pleased, though, when she asked herself the reason, she had very little to say in reply.

Mr. Gardiner left them soon after breakfast. The fishing scheme had been renewed the day before, and a positive engagement made of his meeting some of the gentlemen at Pemberley by noon.

CHAPTER 3

Convinced as Elizabeth now was that Miss Bingley's dislike of her had originated in jealousy, she could not help feeling how very unwelcome her appearance at Pemberley must be to her, and was curious to know with how much civility on that lady's side, the acquaintance would now be renewed.

On reaching the house, they were shewn through the hall into the saloon, whose northern aspect rendered it delightful for summer. Its windows opening to the ground, admitted a most refreshing view of the high woody hills behind the house, and of the beautiful oaks and Spanish chesnuts which were scattered over the intermediate lawn.

In this room they were received by Miss Darcy, who was sitting there with Mrs. Hurst and Miss Bingley, and the lady with whom she lived in London. Georgiana's reception of them was very civil; but attended with all that embarrassment which, though proceeding from shyness and the fear of doing wrong, would easily give to those who felt themselves inferior, the belief of her being proud and reserved. Mrs. Gardiner and her niece, however, did her justice, and pitied her.

By Mrs. Hurst and Miss Bingley, they were noticed only by a curtsey; and on their being seated, a pause, awkward as such pauses must always be, succeeded for a few moments. It was first broken by Mrs. Annesley, a genteel, agreeable-looking woman, whose endeavour to introduce some kind of discourse, proved her to be more truly well bred than either of the others; and between her and Mrs. Gardiner, with occasional help from Elizabeth, the conversation was carried on. Miss Darcy looked as if she wished for courage enough to join in it; and sometimes did venture a short sentence, when there was least danger of its being heard.

Elizabeth soon saw that she was herself closely watched by Miss Bingley, and that she could not speak a word, especially to Miss Darcy, without calling her attention. This observation would not have prevented her from trying to talk to the latter, had they not been seated at an inconvenient distance; but she was not sorry to be spared the necessity of saying much. Her own thoughts were employing her. She expected every moment that some of the gentlemen would enter the room. She wished, she feared that the master of the house might be amongst them; and whether she wished or feared it most, she could scarcely determine. After sitting in this manner a quarter of an hour, without hearing Miss Bingley's voice, Elizabeth was roused by receiving from her a cold enquiry after the health of her family. She answered with equal indifference and brevity, and the other said no more.

The next variation which their visit afforded was produced by the entrance of servants with cold meat, cake, and a variety of all the finest fruits in season; but this did not take place till after many a significant look and smile from Mrs. Annesley to Miss Darcy had been given, to remind her of her post. There was now employment for the whole party; for though they could not all talk, they could all eat; and the beautiful pyramids of grapes, nectarines, and peaches, soon collected them round the table.

While thus engaged, Elizabeth had a fair opportunity of deciding whether she most feared or wished for the appearance of Mr. Darcy, by the feelings which prevailed on his entering the room; and then, though but a moment before she had believed her wishes to predominate, she began to regret that he came.

He had been some time with Mr. Gardiner, who, with two or three other gentlemen from the house, was engaged by the river, and had left him only on learning that the ladies of the family intended a visit to Georgiana that morning. No sooner did he appear, than Elizabeth wisely resolved to be perfectly easy and unembarrassed;–a resolution the more necessary to be made, but perhaps not the more easily kept, because she saw that the suspicions of the whole party were awakened against them, and that there was scarcely an eye which did not watch his behaviour when he first came into the room. In no countenance was attentive curiosity so strongly marked as in Miss Bingley's in spite of the smiles which overspread her face whenever she spoke to one of its objects; for jealousy had not yet made her desperate, and her attentions to Mr. Darcy were by no means over. Miss Darcy, on her brother's entrance, exerted herself much more to talk; and Elizabeth saw that he was anxious for his sister and herself to get acquainted, and forwarded, as much as possible, every attempt at conversation on either side. Miss Bingley saw all this likewise;

and, in the imprudence of anger, took the first opportunity of saying with sneering civility,

"Pray, Miss Eliza, are not the ——shire militia removed from Meryton? They must be a great loss to *your* family."

In Darcy's presence she dared not mention Wickham's name; but Elizabeth instantly comprehended that he was uppermost in her thoughts; and the various recollections connected with him gave her a moment's distress; but, exerting herself vigorously to repel the ill-natured attack, she presently answered the question in a tolerably disengaged tone. While she spoke, an involuntary glance shewed her Darcy with an heightened complexion, earnestly looking at her, and his sister overcome with confusion, and unable to lift up her eyes. Had Miss Bingley known what pain she was then giving her beloved friend, she undoubtedly would have refrained from the hint; but she had merely intended to discompose Elizabeth, by bringing forward the idea of a man to whom she believed her partial, to make her betray a sensibility which might injure her in Darcy's opinion, and perhaps to remind the latter of all the follies and absurdities, by which some part of her family were connected with that corps. Not a syllable had ever reached her of Miss Darcy's meditated elopement. To no creature had it been revealed, where secresy was possible, except to Elizabeth; and from all Bingley's connections her brother was particularly anxious to conceal it, from that very wish which Elizabeth had long ago attributed to him, of their becoming hereafter her own. He had certainly formed such a plan, and without meaning that it should affect his endeavour to separate him from Miss Bennet, it is probable that it might add something to his lively concern for the welfare of his friend.

Elizabeth's collected behaviour, however, soon quieted his emotion; and as Miss Bingley, vexed and disappointed, dared not approach nearer to Wickham, Georgiana also recovered in time, though not enough to be able to speak any more. Her brother, whose eye she feared to meet, scarcely recollected her interest in the affair, and the very circumstance which had been designed to turn his thoughts from Elizabeth, seemed to have fixed them on her more, and more cheerfully.

Their visit did not continue long after the question and answer above-mentioned; and while Mr. Darcy was attending them to their carriage, Miss Bingley was venting her feelings in criticisms on Elizabeth's person, behaviour, and dress. But Georgiana would not join her. Her brother's recommendation was enough to ensure her favour; his judgment could not err, and he had spoken in such terms of Elizabeth, as to leave Georgiana without the power of finding her otherwise than lovely and amiable. When Darcy returned to the saloon, Miss Bingley could not help repeating to him some part of what she had been saying to his sister.

"How very ill Eliza Bennet looks this morning, Mr. Darcy," she cried; "I never in my life saw any one so much altered as she is since the winter. She is grown so brown and coarse! Louisa and I were agreeing that we should not have known her again."

However little Mr. Darcy might have liked such an address, he contented himself with coolly replying, that he perceived no other alteration than her being rather tanned,—no miraculous consequence of travelling in the summer.

"For my own part," she rejoined, "I must confess that I never could see any beauty in her. Her face is too thin; her complexion has no brilliancy; and her features are not at all handsome. Her nose wants character; there is nothing marked in its lines. Her teeth are tolerable, but not out of the common way; and as for her eyes, which have sometimes been called so fine, I never could perceive any thing extraordinary in them. They have a sharp, shrewish look, which I do not like at all; and in her air altogether, there is a self-sufficiency without fashion, which is intolerable."

Persuaded as Miss Bingley was that Darcy admired Elizabeth, this was not the best method of recommending herself; but angry people are not always wise; and in seeing him at last look somewhat nettled, she had all the success she expected. He was resolutely silent however; and, from a determination of making him speak, she continued,

"I remember, when we first knew her in Hertfordshire, how amazed we all were to find that she was a reputed beauty; and I particularly recollect your saying one night, after they had been dining at Netherfield, '*She* a beauty!—I should as soon call her mother a wit.' But afterwards she seemed to improve on you, and I believe you thought her rather pretty at one time."

"Yes," replied Darcy, who could contain himself no longer, "but *that* was only when I first knew her, for it is many months since I have considered her as one of the handsomest women of my acquaintance."

He then went away, and Miss Bingley was left to all the satisfaction of having forced him to say what gave no one any pain but herself.

Mrs. Gardiner and Elizabeth talked of all that had occurred, during their visit, as they returned, except what had particularly interested them both. The looks and behaviour of every body they had seen were discussed, except of the person who had mostly engaged their attention. They talked of his sister, his friends, his house, his fruit, of every thing but himself; yet Elizabeth was longing to know what Mrs. Gardiner thought of him, and Mrs. Gardiner would have been highly gratified by her niece's beginning the subject.

CHAPTER 4

Elizabeth had been a good deal disappointed in not finding a letter from Jane, on their first arrival at Lambton; and this disappointment had been renewed on each of the mornings that had now been spent there; but on the third, her repining was over, and her sister justified by the receipt of two letters from her at once, on one of which was marked that it had been missent elsewhere. Elizabeth was not surprised at it, as Jane had written the direction remarkably ill.

They had just been preparing to walk as the letters came in;

and her uncle and aunt, leaving her to enjoy them in quiet, set off by themselves. The one missent must be first attended to; it had been written five days ago. The beginning contained an account of all their little parties and engagements, with such news as the country afforded; but the latter half, which was dated a day later, and written in evident agitation, gave more important intelligence. It was to this effect:

> Since writing the above, dearest Lizzy, something has occurred of a most unexpected and serious nature; but I am afraid of alarming you—be assured that we are all well. What I have to say relates to poor Lydia. An express came at twelve last night, just as we were all gone to bed, from Colonel Forster, to inform us that she was gone off to Scotland with one of his officers; to own the truth, with Wickham!—Imagine our surprise. To Kitty, however, it does not seem so wholly unexpected. I am very, very sorry. So imprudent a match on both sides!—But I am willing to hope the best, and that his character has been misunderstood. Thoughtless and indiscreet I can easily believe him, but this step (and let us rejoice over it) marks nothing bad at heart. His choice is disinterested at least, for he must know my father can give her nothing. Our poor mother is sadly grieved. My father bears it better. How thankful am I, that we never let them know what has been said against him; we must forget it ourselves. They were off Saturday night about twelve, as is conjectured, but were not missed till yesterday morning at eight. The express was sent off directly. My dear Lizzy, they must have passed within ten miles of us. Colonel Forster gives us reason to expect him here soon. Lydia left a few lines for his wife, informing her of their intention. I must conclude, for I cannot be long from my poor mother. I am afraid you will not be able to make it out, but I hardly know what I have written.

Without allowing herself time for consideration, and scarcely knowing what she felt, Elizabeth on finishing this letter, instantly seized the other, and opening it with the utmost impatience, read as follows: it had been written a day later than the conclusion of the first.

By this time, my dearest sister, you have received my hurried letter; I wish this may be more intelligible, but though not confined for time, my head is so bewildered that I cannot answer for being coherent. Dearest Lizzy, I hardly know what I would write, but I have bad news for you and it cannot be delayed. Imprudent as a marriage between Mr. Wickham and our poor Lydia would be, we are now anxious to be assured it has taken place, for there is but too much reason to fear they are not gone to Scotland. Colonel Forster came yesterday, having left Brighton the day before, not many hours after the express. Though Lydia's short letter to Mrs. F. gave them to understand that they were going to Gretna Green, something was dropped by Denny expressing his belief that W. never intended to go there, or to marry Lydia at all, which was repeated to Colonel F. who instantly taking the alarm, set off from B. intending to trace their route. He did trace them easily to Clapham, but no farther; for on entering that place they removed into a hackney-coach and dismissed the chaise that brought them from Epsom. All that is known after this is, that they were seen to continue the London road. I know not what to think. After making every possible enquiry of that side London, Colonel F. came on into Hertfordshire, anxiously renewing them at all the turnpikes, and at the inns in Barnet and Hatfield, but without any success, no such people had been seen to pass through. With the kindest concern he came on to Longbourn, and broke his apprehensions to us in a manner most creditable to his heart. I am sincerely grieved for him and Mrs. F. but no one can throw any blame on them. Our distress, my dear Lizzy, is very great. My father and mother believe the worst, but I cannot think so ill of him. Many circumstances might make it more eligible for them to be married privately in town than to pursue their first plan; and even if *he* could form such a design against a young woman of Lydia's connections, which is not likely, can I suppose her so lost to every thing?—Impossible. I grieve to find, however, that Colonel F. is not disposed to depend upon their marriage; he shook his head when I expressed my hopes, and said he feared W. was not a man to be trusted. My poor mother is really ill and keeps her room. Could she exert herself it would be better, but this is not to be expected; and as to my father, I never in my life saw him so affected. Poor Kitty has anger for having concealed their attachment; but as it was a matter of confidence one cannot wonder. I am truly glad, dearest Lizzy, that you have been spared something of these distressing scenes; but now as the first shock is over, shall I own that I long for your return? I am not so selfish, however, as to press for it, if inconvenient. Adieu. I take up my pen again to do, what I have just told you I would not, but circumstances are such, that I cannot help earnestly begging you all to come here, as soon as possible. I know my dear uncle and aunt so well, that I am not afraid of requesting it, though I have still something more to ask of the former. My father is going to London with Colonel Forster instantly, to try to discover her. What he means to do, I am sure I know not; but his excessive distress will not allow him to pursue any measure in the best and safest way, and Colonel Forster is obliged to be at Brighton again to-morrow evening. In such an exigence my uncle's advice and assistance would be every thing in the world; he will immediately comprehend what I must feel, and I rely upon his goodness.

"Oh! where, where is my uncle?" cried Elizabeth, darting from her seat as she finished the letter, in eagerness to follow him, without losing a moment of the time so precious; but as she reached the door, it was opened by a servant, and Mr. Darcy appeared. Her pale face and impetuous manner made him start, and before he could recover himself enough to speak, she, in whose mind every idea was superseded by Lydia's situation hastily exclaimed, "I beg your pardon but I must leave you. I must find Mr. Gardiner this moment, on business that cannot be delayed; I have not an instant to lose."

"Good God! what is the matter?" cried he, with more feeling than politeness; then recollecting himself, "I will not detain you a minute, but let me, or let the servant, go after Mr. and Mrs. Gardiner. You are not well enough;–you cannot go yourself."

Elizabeth hesitated, but her knees trembled under her, and she felt how little would be gained by her attempting to pursue them. Calling back the servant, therefore, she commissioned him, though in so breathless an accent as made her almost unintelligible, to fetch his master and mistress home, instantly.

On his quitting the room, she sat down, unable to support herself, and looking so miserably ill, that it was impossible for Darcy to leave her, or to refrain from saying, in a tone of gentleness and commiseration, "Let me call your maid. Is there nothing you could take, to give you present relief?—A glass of wine;—shall I get you one?—You are very ill."

"No, I thank you;" she replied, endeavouring to recover herself. "There is nothing the matter with me. I am quite well. I am only distressed by some dreadful news which I have just received from Longbourn."

She burst into tears as she alluded to it, and for a few minutes could not speak another word. Darcy, in wretched suspense, could only say something indistinctly of his concern, and observe her in compassionate silence. At length, she spoke again. "I have just had a letter from Jane, with such dreadful news. It cannot be concealed from any one. My youngest sister has left all her friends—has eloped;—has thrown herself into the power of—of Mr. Wickham. They are gone off together from Brighton. *You* know him too well to doubt the rest. She has no money, no connections, nothing that can tempt him to—she is lost for ever."

Darcy was fixed in astonishment. "When I consider," she added, in a yet more agitated voice, "that *I* might have prevented it!—*I* who knew what he was. Had I but explained some part of it only—some part of what I learnt, to my own family! Had his character been known, this could not have happened. But it is all, all too late now."

"I am grieved, indeed," cried Darcy; "grieved—shocked. But is it certain, absolutely certain?"

"Oh, yes!—They left Brighton together on Sunday night, and were traced almost to London, but not beyond; they are certainly not gone to Scotland."

"And what has been done, what has been attempted, to recover her?"

"My father is gone to London, and Jane has written to beg my uncle's immediate assistance, and we shall be off, I hope in half an hour. But nothing can be done; I know very well that nothing can be done. How is such a man to be worked on? How are they even to be discovered? I have not the smallest hope. It is every way horrible!"

Darcy shook his head in silent acquiescence.

"When *my* eyes were opened to his real character.—Oh! had I known what I ought, what I dared, to do! But I knew not—I was afraid of doing too much. Wretched, wretched, mistake!"

Darcy made no answer. He seemed scarcely to hear her, and was walking up and down the room in earnest meditation; his brow contracted, his air gloomy. Elizabeth soon observed, and instantly understood it. Her power was sinking; every thing *must* sink under such a proof of family weakness, such an assurance of the deepest disgrace. She could neither wonder nor condemn, but the belief of his self-conquest brought nothing consolatory to her bosom, afforded no palliation of her distress. It was, on the contrary, exactly calculated to make her understand her own wishes; and never had she so honestly felt that she could have loved him, as now, when all love must be in vain.

But self, though it would intrude, could not engross her. Lydia—the humiliation, the misery, she was bringing on them all, soon swallowed up every private care; and covering her face with her handkerchief, Elizabeth was soon lost to every thing else; and, after a pause of several minutes, was only recalled to a sense of her situation by the voice of her companion, who, in a manner, which though it spoke compassion, spoke likewise restraint, said, "I am afraid you have been long desiring my absence, nor have I any thing to plead in excuse of my stay, but real, though un-availing concern. Would to heaven, that any thing could be either said or done on my part, that might offer consolation to such distress.—But I will not torment you with vain wishes, which may seem purposely to ask for your thanks. This unfortunate affair will, I fear, prevent my sister's having the pleasure of seeing you at Pemberley to day."

"Oh, yes. Be so kind as to apologize for us to Miss Darcy. Say

that urgent business calls us home immediately. Conceal the unhappy truth as long as it is possible.—I know it cannot be long."

He readily assured her of his secrecy—again expressed his sorrow for her distress, wished it a happier conclusion than there
was at present reason to hope, and leaving his compliments for
her relations, with only one serious, parting look, went away.

As he quitted the room, Elizabeth felt how improbable it was
that they should ever see each other again on such terms of cordiality as had marked their several meetings in Derbyshire; and
as she threw a retrospective glance over the whole of their acquaintance, so full of contradictions and varieties, sighed at the
perverseness of those feelings which would now have promoted
its continuance, and would formerly have rejoiced in its termination.

If gratitude and esteem are good foundations of affection,
Elizabeth's change of sentiment will be neither improbable nor
faulty. But if otherwise, if the regard springing from such sources
is unreasonable or unnatural, in comparison of what is so often
described as arising on a first interview with its object, and even
before two words have been exchanged, nothing can be said in
her defence, except that she had given somewhat of a trial to the
latter method, in her partiality for Wickham, and that its ill success might perhaps authorise her to seek the other less interesting mode of attachment. Be that as it may, she saw him go with
regret; and in this early example of what Lydia's infamy must
produce, found additional anguish as she reflected on that
wretched business. Never, since reading Jane's second letter, had
she entertained a hope of Wickham's meaning to marry her. No
one but Jane, she thought, could flatter herself with such an expectation. Surprise was the least of her feelings on this developement. While the contents of the first letter remained on her mind,
she was all surprise—all astonishment that Wickham should marry
a girl, whom it was impossible he could marry for money; and
how Lydia could ever have attached him, had appeared incomprehensible. But now it was all to natural. For such an attach-

ment as this, she might have sufficient charms; and though she did not suppose Lydia to be deliberately engaging in an elopement, without the intention of marriage, she had no difficulty in believing that neither her virtue nor her understanding would preserve her from falling an easy prey.

She had never perceived, while the regiment was in Hertfordshire, that Lydia had any partiality for him, but she was convinced that Lydia had wanted only encouragement to attach herself to any body. Sometimes one officer, sometimes another had been her favourite, as their attentions raised them in her opinion. Her affections had been continually fluctuating, but never without an object. The mischief of neglect and mistaken indulgence towards such a girl.—Oh! how acutely did she now feel it.

She was wild to be at home—to hear, to see, to be upon the spot, to share with Jane in the cares that must now fall who'ly upon her, in a family so deranged; a father absent, a mother incapable of exertion, and requiring constant attendance; and though almost persuaded that nothing could be done for Lydia, her uncle's interference seemed of the utmost importance, and till he entered the room, the misery of her impatience was severe. Mr. and Mrs. Gardiner had hurried back in alarm, supposing, by the servant's account, that their niece was taken suddenly ill;—but satisfying them instantly on that head, she eagerly communicated the cause of their summons, reading the two letters aloud, and dwelling on the postscript of the last, with trembling energy.—Though Lydia had never been a favourite with them, Mr. and Mrs. Gardiner could not but be deeply affected. Not Lydia only, but all were concerned in it; and after the first exclamations of surprise and horror, Mr. Gardiner readily promised every assistance in his power.—Elizabeth, though expecting no less, thanked him with tears of gratitude; and all three being actuated by one spirit, every thing relating to their journey was speedily settled. They were to be off as soon as possible. "But what is to be done about Pemberley?" cried Mrs. Gardiner. "John told us Mr. Darcy was here when you sent for us;—was it so?"

"Yes; and I told him we should not be able to keep our engagement. *That* is all settled."

"That is all settled;" repeated the other, as she ran into her room to prepare. And are they upon such terms as for her to disclose the real truth! Oh, that I knew how it was!"

But wishes were vain; or at best could serve only to amuse her in the hurry and confusion of the following hour. Had Elizabeth been at leisure to be idle, she would have remained certain that all employment was impossible to one so wretched as herself; but she had her share of business as well as her aunt, and amongst the rest there were notes to be written to all their friends in Lambton, with false excuses for their sudden departure. An hour, however, saw the whole completed; and Mr. Gardiner meanwhile having settled his account at the inn, nothing remained to be done but to go; and Elizabeth, after all the misery of the morning, found herself, in a shorter space of time than she could have supposed, seated in the carriage, and on the road to Longbourn.

CHAPTER 5

"I have been thinking it over again, Elizabeth," said her uncle, as they drove from the town; "and really, upon serious consideration, I am much more inclined than I was to judge as your eldest sister does of the matter. It appears to me so very unlikely, that any young man should form such a design against a girl who is by no means unprotected or friendless, and who was actually staying in his colonel's family, that I am strongly inclined to hope the best. Could he expect that her friends would not step forward? Could he expect to be noticed again by the regiment, after such an affront to Colonel Forster? His temptation is not adequate to the risk?"

"Do you really think so?" cried Elizabeth, brightening up for a moment.

"Upon my word," said Mrs. Gardiner, "I begin to be of your uncle's opinion. It is really too great a violation of decency, honour, and interest, for him to be guilty of it. I cannot think so very ill of Wickham. Can you, yourself, Lizzy, so wholly give him up as to believe him capable of it?"

"Not perhaps of neglecting his own interest. But of every other neglect I can believe him capable. If, indeed, it should be so! But I dare not hope it. Why should they not go on Scotland, if that had been the case?"

"In the first place," replied Mr. Gardiner, "there is no absolute proof that they are not gone to Scotland."

"Oh! but their removing from the chaise into an hackney coach is such a presumption! And, besides, no traces of them were to be found on the Barnet road."

"Well, then—supposing them to be in London. They may be there, though for the purpose of concealment, for no more exceptionable purpose. It is not likely that money should be very abundant on either side; and it might strike them that they could be more economically, though less expeditiously, married in London, than in Scotland."

"But why all this secrecy? Why any fear of detection? Why must their marriage be private? Oh! no, no, this is not likely. His most particular friend, you see by Jane's account, was persuaded of his never intending to marry her. Wickham will never marry a woman without some money. He cannot afford it. And what claims has Lydia, what attractions has she beyond youth, health, and good humour, that could make him for her sake, forego every chance of benefiting himself by marrying well. As to what restraint the apprehension of disgrace in the corps might throw on a dishonourable elopement with her, I am not able to judge; for I know nothing of the effects that such a step might produce. But as to your other objection, I am afraid it will hardly hold good. Lydia has no brothers to step forward; and he might imagine, from my father's behaviour, from his indolence and the little attention he has ever seemed to give to what was going forward in his family, that *he* would do as little, and think as little about it, as any father could do, in such a matter."

"But can you think that Lydia is so lost to every thing but love of him, as to consent to live with him on any other terms than marriage?"

"It does seem, and it is most shocking indeed," replied Elizabeth, with tears in her eyes, "that a sister's sense of decency and virtue in such a point should admit of doubt. But, really, I know not what to say. Perhaps I am not doing her justice. But she is very young; she has never been taught to think on serious subjects; and for the last half year, nay, for a twelvemonth, she has been given up to nothing but amusement and vanity. She has been allowed to dispose of her time in the most idle and frivolous manner, and to adopt any opinions that came in her way. Since the ——shire were first quartered in Meryton, nothing but love, flirtation, and officers, have been in her head. She has been doing every thing in her power by thinking and talking on the subject, to give greater–what shall I call it? susceptibility to her feelings; which are naturally lively enough. And we all know that Wickham has every charm of person and address that can captivate a woman."

"But you see that Jane," said her aunt, "does not think so ill of Wickham, as to believe him capable of the attempt."

"Of whom does Jane ever think ill? And who is there, whatever might be their former conduct, that she would believe capable of such an attempt, till it were proved against them? But Jane knows, as well as I do, what Wickham really is. We both know that he has been profligate in every sense of the word. That he has neither integrity nor honour. That he is as false and deceitful, as he is insinuating."

"And do you really know all this?" cried Mrs. Gardiner, whose curiosity as to the mode of her intelligence was all alive.

"I do, indeed," replied Elizabeth, colouring. "I told you the other day, of his infamous behaviour to Mr. Darcy; and you, yourself, when last at Longbourn, heard in what manner he spoke of the man, who had behaved with such forbearance and liberality towards him. And there are other circumstances which I am not at liberty--which it is not worth while to relate; but his lies about the whole Pemberley family are endless. From what he said of Miss Darcy, I was thoroughly prepared to see a proud, reserved, disagreeable girl. Yet he knew of the contrary himself. He must know that she was as amiable and unpretending as we have found her."

"But does Lydia know nothing of this? Can she be ignorant of what you and Jane seem so well to understand?"

"Oh, yes!--that, that is the worst of all. Till I was in Kent, and saw so much both of Mr. Darcy and his relation, Colonel Fitzwilliam, I was ignorant of the truth myself. And when I returned home, the ——shire was to leave Meryton in a week or fortnight's time. As that was the case, neither Jane, to whom I related the whole, nor I, thought it necessary to make our knowledge public; for what use could it apparently be to any one, that the good opinion which all the neighbourhood had of him, should then be overthrown? And even when it was settled that Lydia should go with Mrs. Forster, the necessity of opening her eyes to his character never occurred to me. That *she* could be in any danger from the deception never entered my head. That such a consequence as *this* should ensue, you may easily believe was far enough from my thoughts."

"When they all removed to Brighton, therefore, you had no reason, I suppose, to believe them fond of each other."

"Not the slightest. I can remember no symptom of affection on either side; and had any thing of the kind been perceptible, you must be aware that ours is not a family, on which it could be thrown away. When first he entered the corps, she was ready enough to admire him; but so we all were. Every girl in, or near Meryton, was out of her senses about him for the first two months; but he never distinguished *her* by any particular attention, and, consequently, after a moderate period of extravagant and wild admiration, her fancy for him gave way, and others of the regiment, who treated her with more distinction, again became her favourites."

It may be easily believed, that however little of novelty could be added to their fears, hopes, and conjectures, on this interesting subject, by its repeated discussion, no other could detain them from it long, during the whole of the journey. From Elizabeth's thoughts it was never absent. Fixed there by the keenest of all anguish, self reproach, she could find no interval of ease or forgetfulness.

They travelled as expeditiously as possible; and sleeping one night on the road, reached Longbourn by dinner-time the next day. It was a comfort to Elizabeth to consider that Jane could not have been wearied by long expectations.

The little Gardiners, attracted by the sight of a chaise, were standing on the steps of the house, as they entered the paddock; and when the carriage drove up to the door, the joyful surprise that lighted up their faces, and displayed itself over their whole bodies, in a variety of capers and frisks, was the first pleasing earnest of their welcome.

Elizabeth jumped out; and, after giving each of them an hasty kiss, hurried into the vestibule, where Jane, who came running down stairs from her mother's apartment, immediately met her.

Elizabeth, as she affectionately embraced her, whilst tears filled the eyes of both, lost not a moment in asking whether any thing had been heard of the fugitives.

"Not yet," replied Jane. "But now that my dear uncle is come, I hope every thing will be well."

"Is my father in town?"

"Yes, he went on Tuesday as I wrote you word."

"And have you heard from him often?"

"We have heard only once. He wrote me a few lines on Wednesday, to say that he had arrived in safety, and to give me his directions, which I particularly begged him to do. He merely added, that he should not write again, till he had something of importance to mention."

"And my mother—How is she? How are you all?"

"My mother is tolerably well, I trust; though her spirits are greatly shaken. She is up stairs, and will have great satisfaction in seeing you all. She does not yet leave her dressing-room. Mary and Kitty, thank Heaven! are quite well."

"But you—How are you?" cried Elizabeth. "You look pale. How much you must have gone through!"

Her sister, however, assured her, of her being perfectly well; and their conversation, which had been passing while Mr. and Mrs. Gardiner were engaged with their children, was now put an end to, by the approach of the whole party. Jane ran to her uncle and aunt, and welcomed and thanked them both, with alternate smiles and tears.

When they were all in the drawing room, the questions which Elizabeth had already asked, were of course repeated by the others, and they soon found that Jane had no intelligence to give. The sanguine hope of good, however, which the benevolence of her heart suggested, had not yet deserted her; she still expected that it would all end well, and that every morning would bring some letter, either from Lydia or her father, to explain their proceedings, and perhaps to announce the marriage.

Mrs. Bennet, to whose apartment they all repaired, after a few minutes conversation together, received them exactly as might be expected; with tears and lamentations of regret, invectives against the villanous conduct of Wickham, and complaints of her own sufferings and ill usage. Blaming every body but the person to whose ill judging indulgence the errors of her daughter must be principally owing.

"If I had been able," said she, "to carry my point of going to Brighton, with all my family *this* would not have happened; but poor dear Lydia had nobody to take care of her. Why did the Forsters ever let her go out of their sight? I am sure there was some great neglect or other on their side, for she is not the kind of girl to do such a thing, if she had been well looked after. I always thought they were very unfit to have the charge of her; but I was overruled, as I always am. Poor dear child! And now here's Mr. Bennet gone away, and I know he will fight Wickham, wherever he meets him, and then he will be killed, and what is to become of us all? The Collinses will turn us out, before he is cold in his grave; and if you are not kind to us, brother, I do not know what we shall do."

They all exclaimed against such terrific ideas; and Mr. Gardiner, after general assurances of his affection for her and all her family, told her that he meant to be in London the very next day, and would assist Mr. Bennet in every endeavour for recovering Lydia.

"Do not give way to useless alarm," added he, "though it is right to be prepared for the worst, there is no occasion to look on it as certain. It is not quite a week since they left Brighton. In a few days more, we may gain some news of them, and till we know that they are not married, and have no design of marrying, do not let us give the matter over as lost. As soon as I get to town, I shall go to my brother, and make him come home with me to Grace Church Street, and then we may consult together as to what is to be done."

"Oh! my dear brother," replied Mrs. Bennet, "that is exactly what I could most wish for. And now do, when you get to town, find them out, wherever they may be; and if they are not married already, *make* them marry. And as for wedding clothes, do not let them wait for that, but tell Lydia she shall have as much money as she chuses, to buy them, after they are married. And, above all things, keep Mr. Bennet from fighting. Tell him what a dreadful state I am in,–that I am frightened out of my wits; and have such tremblings, such flutterings, all over me, such spasms in my side, and pains in my head, and such beatings at heart, that I can get no rest by night nor by day. And tell my dear Lydia, not to give any directions about her clothes, till she has seen me, for she does not know which are the best warehouses. Oh, brother, how kind you are! I know you will contrive it all.

But Mr. Gardiner, though he assured her again of his earnest endeavours in the cause, could not avoid recommending moderation to her, as well in her hopes as her fears; and, after talking with her in this manner till dinner was on table, they left her to vent all her feelings on the housekeeper, who attended, in the absence of her daughters.

Though her brother and sister were persuaded that there was no real occasion for such a seclusion from the family, they did not attempt to oppose it, for they knew that she had not prudence enough to hold her tongue before the servants, while they waited at table, and judged it better that *one* only of the household, and the one whom they could most trust, should comprehend all her fears and solicitude on the subject.

In the dining-room they were soon joined by Mary and Kitty, who had been too busily engaged in their separate apartments, to make their appearance before. One came from her books, and the other from her toilette. The faces of both, however, were tolerably calm; and no change was visible in either, except that the loss of her favourite sister, or the anger which she had herself incurred in the business, had given something more of fretfulness than usual, to the accents of Kitty. As for Mary, she was mistress enough of herself to whisper to Elizabeth with a countenance of grave reflection, soon after they were seated at table,

"This is a most unfortunate affair; and will probably be much talked of. But we must stem the tide of malice, and pour into the wounded bosoms of each other, the balm of sisterly consolation."

Then, perceiving in Elizabeth no inclination of replying, she added, "Unhappy as the event must be for Lydia, we may draw from it this useful lesson; that loss of virtue in a female is irretrievable–that one false step involves her in endless ruin–that her reputation is no less brittle than it is beautiful,–and that she cannot be too much guarded in her behaviour towards the undeserving of the other sex."

Elizabeth lifted up her eyes in amazement, but was too much oppressed to make any reply. Mary, however, continued to console herself with such kind of moral extractions from the evil before them.

In the afternoon, the two elder Miss Bennets were able to be for half an hour by themselves; and Elizabeth instantly availed herself of the opportunity of making many enquiries, which Jane was equally eager to satisfy. After joining in general lamentations over the dreadful sequel of this event, which Elizabeth considered as all but certain, and Miss Bennet could not assert to be wholly impossible; the former continued the subject, by saying, "But tell me all and every thing about it, which I have not already heard. Give me farther particulars. What did Colonel Forster say? Had they no apprehension of any thing before the elopement took place? They must have seen them together for ever."

"Colonel Forster did own that he had often suspected some partiality, especially on Lydia's side, but nothing to give him any alarm. I am so grieved for him. His behaviour was attentive and kind to the utmost. He *was* coming to us, in order to assure us of his concern, before he had any idea of their not being gone to Scotland: when that apprehension first got abroad, it hastened his journey."

"And was Denny convinced that Wickham would not marry? Did he know of their intending to go off? Had Colonel Forster seen Denny himself?"

"Yes; but when questioned by *him* Denny denied knowing any thing of their plan, and would not give his real opinion about it. He did not repeat his persuasion of their not marrying—and from *that,* I am inclined to hope, he might have been misunderstood before."

"And till Colonel Forster came himself, not one of you entertained a doubt, I suppose, of their being really married?"

"How was it possible that such an idea should enter our brains! I felt a little uneasy—a little fearful of my sister's happiness with him in marriage, because I knew that his conduct had not been always quite right. My father and mother knew nothing of that, they only felt how imprudent a match it must be. Kitty then owned, with a very natural triumph on knowing more than the rest of us, that in Lydia's last letter, she had prepared her for such a step. She had known, it seems, of their being in love with each other, many weeks."

"But not before they went to Brighton?"

"No, I believe not."

"And did Colonel Forster appear to think ill of Wickham himself? Does he know his real character?"

"I must confess that he did not speak so well of Wickham as he formerly did. He believed him to be imprudent and extravagant. And since this sad affair has taken place, it is said, that he left Meryton greatly in debt; but I hope this may be false."

"Oh, Jane, had we been less secret, had we told what we knew of him, this could not have happened!"

"Perhaps it would have better;" replied her sister. "But to expose the former faults of any person, without knowing what their present feelings were, seemed unjustifiable. We acted with the best intentions."

"Could Colonel Forster repeat the particulars of Lydia's note to his wife?"

"He brought it with him for us to see."

Jane then took it from her pocket-book, and gave it to Elizabeth. These were the contents:

> My dear Harriet,
>
> You will laugh when you know where I am gone, and I cannot help laughing myself at your surprise to-morrow morning, as soon as I am missed. I am going to Gretna Green, and if you cannot guess with who, I shall think you a simpleton, for there is but one man in the world I love, and he is an angel. I should never be happy without him, so think it no harm to be off. You need not send them word at Longbourn of my going, if you do not like it, for it will make the surprise the greater, when I write to them, and sign my name Lydia Wickham. What a good joke it will be! I can hardly write for laughing. Pray make my excuses to Pratt, for not keeping my engagement, and dancing with him to night. Tell him I hope he will excuse me when he knows all, and tell him I will dance with him at the next ball we meet, with great pleasure. I shall send for my clothes when I get to Longbourn; but I wish you would tell Sally to mend a great slit in my worked muslin gown, before they are packed up. Good bye. Give my love to Colonel Forster, I hope you will drink to our good journey.
>
>   Your affectionate friend,
>
>   Lydia Bennet.

"Oh! thoughtless, thoughtless Lydia!" cried Elizabeth when she had finished it. "What a letter is this, to be written at such a moment. But at least it shews, that *she* was serious in the object of her journey. Whatever he might afterwards persuade her to, it was not on her side a *scheme* of infamy. My poor father! how he must have felt it!"

"I never saw any one so shocked. He could not speak a word for full ten minutes. My mother was taken ill immediately, and the whole house in such confusion!"

"Oh! Jane," cried Elizabeth, "was there a servant belonging to it, who did not know the whole story before the end of the day?"

"I do not know.—I hope there was.—But to be guarded at such a time, is very difficult. My mother was in hysterics, and though I endeavoured to give her every assistance in my power, I am afraid I did not do so much as I might have done! but the horror of what might possibly happen, almost took from me my faculties."

"Your attendance upon her, has been too much for you. You do not look well. Oh! that I had been with you, you have had every care and anxiety upon yourself alone."

"Mary and Kitty have been very kind, and would have shared in every fatigue, I am sure, but I did not think it right for either of them. Kitty is slight and delicate, and Mary studies so much, that her hours of repose should not be broken in on. My aunt Philips came to Longbourn on Tuesday, after my father went away; and was so good as to stay till Thursday with me. She was of great use and comfort to us all, and lady Lucas has been very kind; she walked here on Wednesday morning to condole with us, and offered her services, or any of her Daughters, if they could be of use to us."

"She had better have stayed at home," cried Elizabeth; "perhaps she *meant* well, but, under such a misfortune as this, one cannot see too little of one's neighbours. Assistance is impossible; condolence, insufferable. Let them triumph over us at a distance, and be satisfied.

She then proceeded to enquire into the measures which her

father had intended to pursue, while in town, for the recovery of his daughter.

"He meant, I believe," replied Jane, to go to Epsom, the place where they last changed horses, see the postilions, and try if any thing could be made out from them. His principal object must be, to discover the number of the hackney coach which took them from Clapham. It had come with a fare from London; and as he thought the circumstance of a gentleman and lady's removing from one carriage into another, might be remarked, he meant to make enquiries at Clapham. If he could any how discover at what house the coachman had before set down his fare, he determined to make enquiries there, and hoped it might not be impossible to find out the stand and number of the coach. I do not know of any other designs that he had formed: but he was in such a hurry to be gone, and his spirits so greatly discomposed, that I had difficulty in finding out even so much as this."

CHAPTER 6

The whole party were in hopes of a letter from Mr. Bennet the next morning, but the post came in without bringing a single line from him. His family knew him to be on all common occasions, a most negligent and dilatory correspondent, but at such a time, they had hoped for exertion. They were forced to conclude, that he had no pleasing intelligence to send, but even of *that* they would have been glad to be certain. Mr. Gardiner had waited only for the letters before he set off.

When he was gone, they were certain at least of receiving constant information of what was going on, and their uncle promised, at parting, to prevail on Mr. Bennet to return to Longbourn, as soon as he could, to the great consolation of his sister, who considered it as the only security for her husband's not being killed in a duel.

Mrs. Gardiner and the children were to remain in Hertford-shire a few days longer, as the former thought her presence might be serviceable to her nieces. She shared in their attendance on Mrs. Bennet, and was a great comfort to them, in their hours of freedom. Their other aunt also visited them frequently, and always, as she said, with the design of cheering and heartening them up, though as she never came without reporting some fresh instance of Wickham's extravagance or irregularity, she seldom went away without leaving them more dispirited than she found them.

All Meryton seemed striving to blacken the man, who, but three months before, had been almost an angel of light. He was declared to be in debt to every tradesman in the place, and his intrigues, all honoured with the title of seduction, had been extended into every tradesman's family. Every body declared that he was the wick-edest young man in the world; and every body began to find out, that they had always distrusted the appearance of his goodness. Elizabeth, though she did not credit above half of what was said, believed enough to make her former assurance of her sister's ruin still more certain; and even Jane, who believed still less of it, be-came almost hopeless, more especially as the time was now come, when if they had gone to Scotland, which she had never before entirely despaired of, they must in all probability have gained some news of them.

Mr. Gardiner left Longbourn on Sunday; on Tuesday, his wife received a letter from him; it told them, that on his arrival, he had immediately found out his brother, and persuaded him to come to Grace Church Street. That Mr. Bennet had been to Ep-som and Clapham, before his arrival, but without gaining any satis-factory information; and that he was now determined to enquire at all the principal hotels in town, as Mr. Bennet thought it pos-sible they might have gone to one of them, on their first coming to London, before they procured lodgings. Mr. Gardiner himself did not expect any success from this measure, but as his brother was eager in it, he meant to assist him in pursuing it. He added, that Mr. Bennet seemed wholly disinclined at present, to leave

London, and promised to write again very soon. There was also a postscript to this effect.

"I have written to Colonel Forster to desire him to find out, if possible, from some of the young man's intimates in the regiment, whether Wickham has any relations or connections, who would be likely to know in what part of the town he has now concealed himself. If there were any one, that one could apply to, with a probability of gaining such a clue as that, it might be of essential consequence. At present we have nothing to guide us. Colonel Forster will, I dare say, do every thing in his power to satisfy us on this head. But, on second thoughts, perhaps Lizzy could tell us, what relations he has now living, better than any other person."

Elizabeth was at no loss to understand from whence this deference for her authority proceeded; but it was not in her power to give any information of so satisfactory a nature, as the compliment deserved.

She had never heard of his having had any relations, except a father and mother, both of whom had been dead many years. It was possible, however, that some of his companions in the ——shire, might be able to give more information; and, though she was not very sanguine in expecting it, the application was a something to look forward to.

Every day at Longbourn was now a day of anxiety; but the most anxious part of each was when the post was expected. The arrival of letters was the first grand object of every morning's impatience. Through letters, whatever of good or bad was to be told, would be communicated, and every succeeding day was expected to bring some news of importance.

But before they heard again from Mr. Gardiner, a letter arrived for their father, from a different quarter, from Mr. Collins; which, as Jane had received directions to open all that came for him in his absence, she accordingly read; and Elizabeth, who knew what curiosities his letters always were, looked over her, and read it likewise. It was as follows:

My dear Sir,

I feel myself called upon, by our relationship, and my situation in life, to condole with you on the grievous affliction you are now suffering under, of which we were yesterday informed by a letter from Hertfordshire. Be assured, my dear Sir, that Mrs. Collins and myself sincerely sympathise with you, and all your respectable family, in your present distress, which must be of the bitterest kind, because proceeding from a cause which no time can remove. No arguments shall be wanting on my part, that can alleviate so severe a misfortune; or that may comfort you, under a circumstance that must be of all others most afflicting to a parent's mind. The death of your daughter would have been a blessing in comparison of this. And it is the more to be lamented, because there is reason to suppose, as my dear Charlotte informs me, that this licentiousness of behaviour in your daughter, has proceeded from a faulty degree of indulgence, though, at the same time, for the consolation of yourself and Mrs. Bennet, I am inclined to think that her own disposition must be naturally bad, or she could not be guilty of such an enormity at so early an age. Howsoever that may be, you are grievously to be pitied, in which opinion I am not only joined by Mrs. Collins, but likewise by lady Catherine and her daughter, to whom I have related the affair. They agree with me in apprehending that this false step in one daughter, will be injurious to the fortunes of all the others, for who, as lady Catherine herself condescendingly says, will connect themselves with such a family. And this consideration leads me moreover to reflect with augmented satisfaction on a certain event of last November, for had it been otherwise, I must have been involved in all your sorrow and disgrace. Let me advise you then, my dear Sir, to console yourself as much as possible, to throw off your unworthy child from your affection for ever, and leave her to reap the fruits of her own heinous offence.

I am, dear Sir, &c. &c.

Mr. Gardiner did not write again till he had received an answer from Colonel Forster; and then he had nothing of a pleasant nature to send. It was not known that Wickham had a single relation, with whom he kept up any connection, and it was certain that he had no near one living. His former acquaintance had been numerous; but since he had been in the militia, it did not appear that he was on terms of particular friendship with any of them. There was no one therefore who could be pointed out, as likely to give any news of him. And in the wretched state of his own finances, there was a very powerful motive for secrecy, in addition to his fear of discovery by Lydia's relations, for it had just transpired that he had left gaming debts behind him, to a very considerable amount. Colonel Forster believed that more than a thousand pounds would be necessary to clear his expenses at Brighton. He owed a good deal in the town, but his debts of honour were still more formidable. Mr. Gardiner did not attempt to conceal these particulars from the Longbourn family, Jane heard them with horror. "A gamester!" she cried. "This is wholly unexpected. I had not an idea of it."

Mr. Gardiner added in his letter, that they might expect to see their father at home on the following day, which was Saturday. Rendered spiritless by the ill-success of their endeavours, he had yielded to his brother-in-law's intreaty that he would return to his family, and leave it to him to do, whatever occasion might suggest to be advisable for continuing their pursuit. When Mrs. Bennet was told of this, she did not express so much satisfaction as her children expected, considering what her anxiety for his life had been before.

"What, is he coming home, and without poor Lydia!" she cried. "Sure he will not leave London before he has found them. Who is to fight Wickham, and make him marry her, if he comes away?"

As Mrs. Gardiner began to wish to be at home, it was settled that she and her children should go to London, at the same time that Mr. Bennet came from it. The coach, therefore, took them the first stage of their journey, and brought its master back to Longbourn.

Mrs. Gardiner went away in all the perplexity about Elizabeth and her Derbyshire friend, that had attended her from that part of the world. His name had never been voluntarily mentioned before them by her niece; and the kind of half-expectation which Mrs. Gardiner had formed, of their being followed by a letter from him, had ended in nothing. Elizabeth had received none since her return from Pemberley.

The present unhappy state of the family, rendered any other excuse for the slowness of her spirits unnecessary; nothing, therefore, could be fairly conjectured from *that,* though Elizabeth, who was by this time tolerably well acquainted with her own feelings, was perfectly aware, that, had she known nothing of Darcy, she could have borne the dread of Lydia's infamy somewhat better. It would have spared her, she thought, one sleepless night out of two.

When Mr. Bennet arrived, he had all the appearance of his usual philosophic composure. He said as little as he had ever been in the habit of saying; made no mention of the business that had taken him away, and it was some time before his daughters had courage to speak of it.

It was not till the afternoon, when he joined them at tea, that Elizabeth ventured to introduce the subject; and then, on her briefly expressing her sorrow for what he must have endured, he replied, "Say nothing of that. Who should suffer but myself? It has been my own doing, and I ought to feel it."

"You must not be too severe upon yourself," replied Elizabeth.

"You may well warn me against such an evil. Human nature is so prone to fall into it! No, Lizzy, let me once in my life feel how much I have been to blame. I am not afraid of being over-powered by the impression. It will pass away soon enough."

"Do you suppose them to be in London?"

"Yes; where else can they be so well concealed?"

"And Lydia used to want to go to London," added Kitty.

"She is happy, then," said her father, drily; "and her residence there will probably be of some duration."

Then, after a short silence, he continued, "Lizzy, I bear you no ill-will for being justified in your advice to me last May, which, considering the event, shews some greatness of mind."

They were interrupted by Miss Bennet, who came to fetch her mother's tea.

"This is a parade," cried he, "which does one good; it gives such an elegance to misfortune! Another day I will do the same; I will sit in my library, in my night cap and powdering gown, and give as much trouble as I can,–or, perhaps, I may defer it, till Kitty runs away."

"I am not going to run away, Papa," said Kitty, fretfully; "if *I* should ever go to Brighton, I would behave better than Lydia."

"*You* go to Brighton!–I would not trust you so near it as East Bourne, for fifty pounds! No, Kitty, I have at last learnt to be cautious, and you will feel the effects of it. No officer is ever to enter my house again, nor even to pass through the village. Balls will be absolutely prohibited, unless you stand up with one of your sisters. And you are never to stir out of doors, till you can prove, that you have spent ten minutes of every day in a rational manner."

Kitty, who took all these threats in a serious light, began to cry.

"Well, well," said he, "do not make yourself unhappy. If you are a good girl for the next ten years, I will take you to a review at the end of them."

CHAPTER 7

Two days after Mr. Bennet's return, as Jane and Elizabeth were walking together in the shrubbery behind the house, they saw the housekeeper coming towards them, and, concluding that she came to call them to their mother, went forward to meet her; but, instead of the expected summons, when they approached her, she said to Miss Bennet, "I beg your pardon, madam, for interrupting you, but I was in hopes you might have some good news from town, so I took the liberty of coming to ask."

"What do you mean, Hill? We have heard nothing from town."

"Dear madam," cried Mrs. Hill, in great astonishment, "don't you know there is an express come for master from Mr. Gardiner? He has been here this half hour, and master has had a letter."

Away ran the girls, too eager to get in to have time for speech.

They ran through the vestibule into the breakfast room; from thence to the library;–their father was in neither; and they were on the point of seeking him up stairs with their mother, when they were met by the butler, who said,

"If you are looking for my master, ma'am, he is walking towards the little copse."

Upon this information, they instantly passed through the hall once more, and ran across the lawn after their father, who was deliberately pursuing his way towards a small wood on one side of the paddock.

Jane, who was not so light, nor so much in the habit of running as Elizabeth, soon lagged behind, while her sister, panting for breath, came up with him, and eagerly cried out,

"Oh, Papa, what news? what news? have you heard from my uncle?"

"Yes, I have had a letter from him by express."

"Well, and what news does it bring? good or bad?"

"What is there of good to be expected?" said he, taking the letter from his pocket; "but perhaps you would like to read it."

Elizabeth impatiently caught it from his hand. Jane now came up.

"Read it aloud," said their father, "for I hardly know myself what it is about."

> Grace Church Street, Monday,
> August 2.

My dear Brother,

At last I am able to send you some tidings of my niece, and such as, upon the whole, I hope will give you satisfaction. Soon after you left me on Saturday, I was fortunate enough to find out in what part of London they were. The particulars, I reserve till we meet. It is enough to know they are discovered, I have seen them both—

Then it is as I always hoped," cried Jane; "they are married!" Elizabeth read on;

I have seen them both. They are not married, nor can I find

there was any intention of being so; but if you are willing to perform the engagements which I have ventured to make on your side, I hope it will not be long before they are. All that is required of you is, to assure your daughter, by settlement, her equal share of the five thousand pounds, secured among your children after the decease of yourself and my sister; and, moreover, to enter into an engagement of allowing her, during your life, one hundred pounds per annum. These are conditions, which, considering every thing, I had no hesitation in complying with, as far as I thought myself privileged, for you. I shall send this by express, that no time may be lost in bringing me your answer. You will easily comprehend, from these particulars, that Mr. Wickham's circumstances are not so hopeless as they are generally believed to be. The world has been deceived in that respect; and I am happy to say, there will be some little money, even when all his debts are discharged, to settle on my niece, in addition to her own fortune. If, as I conclude will be the case, you send me full powers to act in your name, throughout the whole of this business, I will immediately give directions to Haggerston for preparing a proper settlement. There will not be the smallest occasion for your coming to town again; therefore, stay quietly at Longbourn, and depend on my diligence and care. Send back your answer as soon as you can, and be careful to write explicitly. We have judged it best, that my niece should be married from this house, of which I hope you will approve. She comes to us to-day. I shall write again as soon as any thing is determined on. Your's &c.

Edw. Gardiner.

"Is it possible!" cried Elizabeth, when she had finished. "Can it be possible that he will marry her?"

"Wickham is not so undeserving, then, as we have thought him;" said her sister. "My dear father, I congratulate you."

"And have you answered the letter?" said Elizabeth.

"No; but it must be done soon."

Most earnestly did she then intreat him to lose no more time before he wrote.

"Oh! my dear father," she cried, "come back, and write immediately. Consider how important every moment is, in such a case."

"Let me write for you," said Jane, "if you dislike the trouble yourself."

"I dislike it very much," he replied; "but it must be done."

And so saying, he turned back with them, and walked towards the house.

"And may I ask?" said Elizabeth, "but the terms, I suppose, must be complied with."

"Complied with! I am only ashamed of his asking so little."

"And they *must* marry! Yet he is *such* a man."

"Yes, yes, they must marry. There is nothing else to be done. But there are two things that I want very much to know:—one is, how much money your uncle has laid down, to bring it about; and the other, how I am ever to pay him."

"Money! my uncle!" cried Jane, "what do you mean, Sir?"

"I mean, that no man in his senses would marry Lydia on so slight a temptation as one hundred a-year during my life, and fifty after I am gone."

"That is very true," said Elizabeth; "though it had not occurred to me before. His debts to be discharged, and something still to remain! Oh! it must be my uncle's doings! Generous, good man, I am afraid he has distressed himself. A small sum could not do all this."

"No," said her father, "Wickham's a fool, if he takes her with a farthing less than ten thousand pounds. I should be sorry to think so ill of him, in the very beginning of our relationship."

"Ten thousand pounds! Heaven forbid! How is half such a sum to be repaid?"

Mr. Bennet made no answer, and each of them deep in thought, continued silent till they reached the house. Their father then went to the library to write, and the girls walked into the breakfast room.

"And they are really to be married!" cried Elizabeth, as soon as they were by themselves, "How strange this is! And for *this* we are to be thankful. That they should marry, small as is their chance of happiness, and wretched as is his character, we are forced to rejoice! Oh, Lydia!"

"I comfort myself with thinking," replied Jane, "that he certainly would not marry Lydia, if he had not a real regard for her. Though our kind uncle has done something towards clearing him, I cannot believe that ten thousand pounds, or any thing like it, has been advanced. He has children of his own, and may have more. How could he spare half ten thousand pounds?"

"If we are ever able to learn what Wickham's debts have been," said Elizabeth, "and how much is settled on his side on our sister, we shall exactly know what Mr. Gardiner has done for them, because Wickham has not sixpence of his own. The kindness of my uncle and aunt can never be requited. Their taking her home, and affording her their personal protection and countenance, is such a sacrifice to her advantage, as years of gratitude cannot enough acknowledge. By this time she is actually with them! If such goodness does not make her miserable now, she will never deserve to be happy! What a meeting for her, when she first sees my aunt!"

"We must endeavour to forget all that has passed on either side," said Jane: "I hope and trust they will yet be happy. His consenting to marry her is a proof, I will believe, that he is come to a right way of thinking. Their mutual affection will steady them; and I flatter myself they will settle so quietly, and live in so rational a manner, as may in time make their past imprudence forgotten."

"Their conduct has been such," replied Elizabeth, "as neither you, nor I, nor any body, can ever forget. It is useless to talk of it."

It now occurred to the girls that their mother was in all likelihood perfectly ignorant of what had happened. They went to the library; therefore, and asked their father, whether he would not wish them to make it known to her. He was writing, and, without raising his head, coolly replied,

"Just as you please."

"May we take my uncle's letter to read to her?"

"Take whatever you like, and get away."

Elizabeth took the letter from his writing table, and they went up stairs together. Mary and Kitty were both with Mrs. Bennet:

one communication would, therefore, do for all. After a slight preparation for good news, the letter was read aloud. Mrs. Bennet could hardly contain herself. As soon as Jane had read Mr. Gardiner's hope of Lydia's being soon married, her joy burst forth, and every following sentence added to its exuberance. She was now in an irritation as violent from delight, as she had ever been fidgetty from alarm and vexation. To know that her daughter would be married was enough. She was disturbed by no fear for her felicity, nor humbled by any remembrance of her misconduct.

"My dear, dear Lydia!" she cried: "This is delightful indeed!—She will be married!—I shall see her again!—She will be married at sixteen!—My good, kind brother!—I knew how it would be—I knew he would manage every thing. How I long to see her! and to see dear Wickham too! But the clothes, the wedding clothes! I will write to my sister Gardiner about them directly. Lizzy, my dear, run down to your father, and ask him how much he will give her. Stay, stay, I will go myself. Ring the bell, Kitty, for Hill. I will put on my things in a moment. My dear, dear Lydia!—How merry we shall be together when we meet!"

Her eldest daughter endeavoured to give some relief to the violence of these transports, by leading her thoughts to the obligations which Mr. Gardiner's behaviour laid them all under.

"For we must attribute this happy conclusion," she added, "in a great measure, to his kindness. We are persuaded that he has pledged himself to assist Mr. Wickham with money."

"Well," cried her mother, "it is all very right; who should do it but her own uncle? If he had not had a family of his own, I and my children must have had all his money you know, and it is the first time we have ever had any thing from him, except a few presents. Well, I am so happy. In a short time, I shall have a daughter married. Mrs. Wickham! How well it sounds. And she was only sixteen last June. My dear Jane, I am in such a flutter, that I am sure I can't write; so I will dictate, and you will write for me. We will settle with your father about the money afterwards; but the things should be ordered immediately."

She was then proceeding to all the particulars of calico, muslin, and cambric, and would shortly have dictated some very plentiful orders, had not Jane, though with some difficulty, persuaded her to wait, till her father was at leisure to be consulted. One day's delay she observed, would be of small importance; and her mother was too happy, to be quite so obstinate as usual. Other schemes too came into her head.

"I will go to Meryton," said she, "as soon as I am dressed, and tell the good, good news to my sister Phillips. And as I come back, I can call on Lady Lucas and Mrs. Long. Kitty, run down and order the carriage. An airing would do me a great deal of good, I am sure. Girls, can I do any thing for you in Meryton? Oh! here comes Hill. My dear Hill, have you heard the good news? Miss Lydia is going to be married; and you shall all have a bowl of punch, to make merry at her wedding."

Mrs. Hill began instantly to express her joy. Elizabeth received her congratulations amongst the rest, and then, sick of this folly, took refuge in her own room, that she might think with freedom.

Poor Lydia's situation must, at best be bad enough; but that it was not worse, she had need to be thankful. She felt it so; and though, in looking forward, neither rational happiness nor worldly prosperity, could be justly expected for her sister; in looking back to what they had feared, only two hours ago, she felt all the advantages of what they had gained.

CHAPTER 8

Mr. Bennet had very often wished, before this period of his life, that, instead of spending his whole income, he had laid by an annual sum, for the better provision of his children, and of his wife, if she survived him. He now wished it more than ever. Had he done his duty in that respect, Lydia need not have been indebted to her uncle, for whatever of honour or credit could now be purchased for her. The satisfaction of prevailing on one of the most worthless young men in Great Britain to be her husband, might then have rested in its proper place.

He was seriously concerned, that a cause of so little advantage to any one, should be forwarded at the sole expense of his brother-in-law, and he was determined, if possible, to find out the extent of his assistance, and to discharge the obligation as soon as he could.

When first Mr. Bennet had married, economy was held to be perfectly useless; for, of course, they were to have a son. This son was to join in cutting off the entail, as soon as he should be of age, and the widow and younger children would by that means be provided for. Five daughters successively entered the world, but yet the son was to come; and Mrs. Bennet, for many years after Lydia's birth, had been certain that he would. This event had at last been despaired of, but it was then too late to be saving. Mrs. Bennet had no turn for economy, and her husband's love of independence had alone prevented their exceeding their income.

Five thousand pounds was settled by marriage articles on Mrs. Bennet and the children. But in what proportions it should be divided amongst the latter, depended on the will of the parents. This was one point, with regard to Lydia at least, which was now to be settled, and Mr. Bennet could have no hesitation in acceding to the proposal before him. In terms of grateful acknowledgment for the kindness of his brother, though expressed most concisely, he then delivered on paper his perfect approbation of all that was done, and his willingness to fulfil the engagements that had been made for him. He had never before supposed that, could Wickham be prevailed on to marry his daughter, it would be done with so little inconvenience to himself, as by the present arrangement. He would scarcely be ten pounds a-year the loser, by the hundred that was to be paid them; for, what with her board and pocket allowance, and the continual presents in money, which passed to her, through her mother's hands, Lydia's expenses had been very little within that sum.

That it would be done with such trifling exertion on his side, too, was another very welcome surprise; for his chief wish at present, was to have as little trouble in the business as possible. When the first transports of rage which had produced his activity in seeking her were over, he naturally returned to all his former indolence. His letter was soon dispatched; for though dilatory in undertaking business, he was quick in its execution. He begged to know farther particulars of what he was indebted to his brother; but was too angry with Lydia, to send any message to her.

The good news quickly spread through the house; and with proportionate speed through the neighbourhood. It was borne in the latter with decent philosophy. To be sure it would have been more for the advantage of conversation, had Miss Lydia Bennet come upon the town; or, as the happiest alternative, been secluded from the world, in some distant farm house. But there was much to be talked of, in marrying her; and the good-natured wishes for her well-doing, which had proceeded before, from all the spiteful old ladies in Meryton, lost but little of their spirit in this change of circumstances, because with such an husband, her misery was considered certain.

It was a fortnight since Mrs. Bennet had been down stairs, but on this happy day, she again took her seat at the head of her table, and in spirits oppressively high. No sentiment of shame gave a damp to her triumph. The marriage of a daughter, which had been the first object of her wishes, since Jane was sixteen, was now on the point of accomplishment, and her thoughts and her words ran wholly on those attendants of elegant nuptials, fine muslins, new carriages, and servants. She was busily searching through the neighbourhood for a proper situation for her daughter, and, without knowing or considering what their income might be, rejected many as deficient in size and importance.

"Haye-Park might do," said she, "if the Gouldings would quit it, or the great house at Stoke, if the drawing-room were larger; but Ashworth is too far off! I could not bear to have her ten miles from me; and as for Purvis Lodge, the attics are dreadful."

Her husband allowed her to talk on without interruption, while the servants remained. But when they had withdrawn, he said to her, "Mrs. Bennet, before you take any, or all of these houses, for your son and daughter, let us come to a right understanding. Into *one* house in this neighbourhood, they shall never have admittance. I will not encourage the impudence of either, by receiving them at Longbourn."

A long dispute followed this declaration; but Mr. Bennet was firm: it soon led to another; and Mrs. Bennet found, with amazement and horror, that her husband would not advance a guinea to buy clothes for his daughter. He protested that she should receive from him no mark of affection whatever, on the occasion. Mrs. Bennet could hardly comprehend it. That his anger could be carried to such a point of inconceivable resentment, as to refuse his daughter a privilege, without which her marriage would scarcely seem valid, exceeded all that she could believe possible. She was more alive to the disgrace, which the want of new clothes must reflect on her daughter's nuptials, than to any sense of shame at her eloping and living with Wickham, a fortnight before they took place.

Elizabeth was now most heartily sorry that she had, from the distress of the moment, been led to make Mr. Darcy acquainted with their fears for her sister since her marriage would so shortly give the proper termination to the elopement, they might hope to conceal its unfavourable beginning, from all those who were not immediately on the spot.

She had no fear of its spreading farther, through his means. There were few people on whose secrecy she would have more confidently depended; but at the same time, there was no one, whose knowledge of a sister's frailty would have mortified her so much. Not, however from any fear of disadvantage from it, individually to herself; for at any rate there seemed a gulf impossible between them. Had Lydia's marriage been concluded on the most honourable terms, it was not to be supposed that Mr. Darcy would connect himself with a family where to every other objection would now be added, an alliance and relationship of the nearest kind with the man whom he so justly scorned.

From such a connection she could not wonder that he should shrink. The wish of procuring her regard, which she had assured herself of his feeling in Derbyshire, could not in rational expectation survive such a blow as this. She was humbled, she was grieved; she repented, though she hardly knew of what. She became jealous of his esteem, when she could no longer hope to be benefited by it. She wanted to hear of him, when there seemed the least chance of gaining intelligence. She was convinced that she could have been happy with him; when it was no longer likely they should meet.

What a triumph for him, as she often thought, could he know that the proposals which she had proudly spurned only four months ago, would now have been gladly and gratefully received! He was as generous, she doubted not, as the most generous of his sex. But while he was mortal, there must be a triumph.

She began now to comprehend that he was exactly the man, who, in disposition and talents, would most suit her. His understanding and temper, though unlike her own, would have answered all her wishes. It was an union that must have been to the advantage of both; by her ease and liveliness, his mind might have been softened, his manners improved, and from his judgment, information, and knowledge of the world, she must have received benefit of greater importance.

But no such happy marriage could now teach the admiring multitude what connubial felicity really was. An union of a different tendency, and precluding the possibility of the other, was soon to be formed in their family.

How Wickham and Lydia were to be supported in tolerable independence, she could not imagine. But how little of permanent happiness could belong to a couple who were only brought together because their passions were stronger than their virtue, she could easily conjecture.

Mr. Gardiner soon wrote again to his brother. To Mr. Bennet's acknowledgments he briefly replied, with assurances of his eagerness to promote the welfare of any of his family; and concluded with entreaties that the subject might never be mentioned to him again. The principal purport of his letter was to inform them, that Mr. Wickham had resolved on quitting the Militia.

"It was greatly my wish that he should do so," he added, "as soon as his marriage was fixed on. And I think you will agree with me, in considering a removal from that corps as highly advisable, both on his account and my niece's. It is Mr. Wickham's intention to go into the regulars; and, among his former friends, there are still some who are able and willing to assist him in the army. He has the promise of an ensigncy in General ——'s regiment, now quartered in the North. It is an advantage to have it so far from this part of the kingdom. He promises fairly, and I hope among different people, where they may each have a character to preserve, they will both be more prudent. I have written to Colonel Forster, to inform him of our present arrangements, and to request that he will satisfy the various creditors of Mr. Wickham in and near Brighton, with assurances of speedy payment, for which I have pledged myself. And will you give yourself the trouble of carrying similar assurances to his creditors in Meryton, of whom I shall subjoin a list, according to his information. He has given in all his debts; I hope at least he has not deceived us. Haggerston has our directions, and all will be completed in a week. They will then join his regiment, unless they are first invited to Longbourn; and I understand from Mrs. Gardiner, that my niece is very desirous of seeing you all, before she leaves the South. She is well, and begs to be dutifully remembered to you and her mother.—Your's, &c.

E. GARDINER.

Mr. Bennet and his daughters saw all the advantages of Wickham's removal from the —— shire, as clearly as Mr. Gardiner could do. But Mrs. Bennet, was not so well pleased with it. Lydia's being settled in the North, just when she had expected most pleasure and pride in her company, for she had by no means given up her plan of their residing in Hertfordshire, was a severe disappointment; and besides, it was such a pity that Lydia should be taken from a regiment where she was acquainted with everybody, and had so many favourites.

"She is so fond of Mrs. Forster," said she, "it will be quite shocking to send her away! And there are several of the young men, too, that she likes very much. The officers may not be so pleasant in General ——'s regiment."

His daughter's request, for such it might be considered, of being admitted into her family again, before she set off for the North, received at first an absolute negative. But Jane and Elizabeth, who agreed in wishing, for the sake of their sister's feelings and consequence, that she should be noticed on her marriage by her parents, urged him so earnestly, yet so rationally and so mildly, to receive her and her husband at Longbourn, as soon as they were married, that he was prevailed on to think as they thought, and act as they wished. And their mother had the satisfaction of knowing, that she should be able to shew her married daughter in the neighbourhood, before she was banished to the North. When Mr. Bennet wrote again to his brother, therefore, he sent his permission for them to come; and it was settled, that as soon as the ceremony was over, they should proceed to Longbourn. Elizabeth was surprised, however, that Wickham should consent to such a scheme, and had she consulted only her own inclination, any meeting with him would have been the last object of her wishes.

CHAPTER 9

Their sister's wedding day arrived; and Jane and Elizabeth felt for her probably more than she felt for herself. The carriage was sent to meet them at ——, and they were to return in it, by dinnertime. Their arrival was dreaded by the elder Miss Bennets; and

Jane more especially, who gave Lydia the feelings which would have attended herself, had *she* been the culprit, was wretched in the thought of what her sister must endure.

They came. The family were assembled in the breakfast room, to receive them. Smiles decked the face of Mrs. Bennet, as the carriage drove up to the door; her husband looked impenetrably grave; her daughters, alarmed, anxious, uneasy.

Lydia's voice was heard in the vestibule; the door was thrown open, and she ran into the room. Her mother stepped forwards, embraced her, and welcomed her with rapture; gave her hand with an affectionate smile to Wickham, who followed his lady, and wished them both joy, with an alacrity which shewed no doubt of their happiness.

Their reception from Mr. Bennet, to whom they then turned, was not quite so cordial. His countenance rather gained in austerity; and he scarcely opened his lips. The easy assurance of the young couple, indeed, was enough to provoke him. Elizabeth was disgusted, and even Miss Bennet was shocked. Lydia was Lydia still; untamed, unabashed, wild, noisy, and fearless. She turned from sister to sister, demanding their congratulations, and when at length they all sat down, looked eagerly round the room, took notice of some little alteration in it, and observed, with a laugh, that it was a great while since she had been there.

Wickham was not at all more distressed than herself, but his manners were always so pleasing, that had his character and his marriage been exactly what they ought, his smiles and his easy address, while he claimed their relationship, would have delighted them all. Elizabeth had not before believed him quite equal to such assurance; but she sat down, resolving within herself, to draw no limits in future to the impudence of an impudent man. *She* blushed, and Jane blushed; but the cheeks of the two who caused their confusion, suffered no variation of colour.

There was no want of discourse. The bride and her mother could neither of them talk fast enough; and Wickham, who happened to sit near Elizabeth, began enquiring after his acquaintance in that neighbourhood, with a good humoured ease, which she felt very unable to equal in her replies. They seemed each of them to have the happiest memories in the world. Nothing of the past was recollected with pain; and Lydia led voluntarily to subjects, which her sisters would not have alluded to for the world.

"Only think of its being three months," she cried, "since I went away; it seems but a fortnight I declare; and yet there have been things enough happened in the time. Good gracious! when I went away, I am sure I had no more idea of being married till I came back again! though I thought it would be very good fun if I was."

Her father lifted up his eyes. Jane was distressed. Elizabeth looked expressively at Lydia; but she, who never heard nor saw any thing of which she chose to be insensible, gaily continued, "Oh! mamma, do the people here abouts know I am married to day? I was afraid they might not; and we overtook William Goulding in his curricle, so I was determined he should know it, and so I let down the side glass next to him, and took off my glove, and let my hand just rest upon the window frame, so that he might see the ring, and them I bowed and smiled like any thing."

Elizabeth could bear it no longer. She got up, and ran out of the room; and returned no more, till she heard them passing through the hall to the dining parlour. She then joined them soon enough to see Lydia, with anxious parade, walk up to her mother's right hand, and hear her say to her eldest sister, "Ah! Jane, I take your place now, and you must go lower, because I am a married woman."

It was not to be supposed that time would give Lydia that embarrassment, from which she had been so wholly free at first. Her ease and good spirits increased. She longed to see Mrs. Phillips, the Lucasses, and all their other neighbours, and to hear herself called "Mrs. Wickham," by each of them; and in the mean time, she went after dinner to shew her ring and boast of being married, to Mrs. Hill and the two housemaids.

"Well, mamma," said she, when they were all returned to the breakfast room, "and what do you think of my husband? Is not he a charming man? I am sure my sisters must all envy me. I only hope they may have half my good luck. They must all go to Brighton. That is the place to get husbands. What a pity it is, mamma, we did not all go."

"Very true; and if I had my will, we should. But my dear Lydia, I don't at all like your going such a way off. Must it be so,"

"Oh, lord! yes;–there is nothing in that. I shall like it of all things. You and papa, and my sisters, must come down and see us. We shall be at Newcastle all the winter, and I dare say there will be some balls, and I will take care to get good partners for them all."

"I should like it beyond any thing!" said her mother.

"And then when you go away! you may leave one or two of my sisters behind you; and I dare say I shall get husbands for them before the winter is over."

"I thank you for my share of the favour," said Elizabeth; "but I do not particularly like your way of getting husbands."

Their visitors were not to remain above ten days with them. Mr. Wickham had received his commission before he left London, and he was to join his regiment at the end of a fortnight.

No one but Mrs. Bennet, regretted that their stay would be so short; and she made the most of the time, by visiting about with her daughter, and having very frequent parties at home. These parties were acceptable to all, to avoid a family circle was even more desirable to such as did think, than such as did not.

Wickham's affection for Lydia, was just what Elizabeth had expected to find it; not equal to Lydia's for him. She had scarcely needed her present observation to be satisfied, from the reason of things, that their elopement had been brought on by the strength of her love, rather than by his; and she would have wondered why, without violently caring for her, he chose to elope with her at all had she not felt certain that his flight was rendered necessary by distress of circumstances; and if that were the case, he was not the young man to resist an opportunity of having a companion.

Lydia was exceedingly fond of him. He was her dear Wickham on every occasion; no one was to be put in competition with him. He did every thing best in the world; and she was sure he would kill more birds on the first of September, than any body else in the country.

One morning, soon after their arrival, as she was sitting with her two elder sisters, she said to Elizabeth,

"Lizzy, I never gave *you* an account of my wedding, I believe. You were not by, when I told mamma, and the others, all about it. Are not you curious to hear how it was managed?"

"No really," replied Elizabeth; "I think there cannot be too little said on the subject."

"La! You are so strange! But I must tell you how it went off. We were married, you know, at St. Clement's because Wickham's lodgings were in that parish. And it was settled that we should all be there by eleven o'clock. My uncle and aunt and I were to go together; and the others were to meet us at the church. Well, Monday morning came, and I was in such a fuss! I was so afraid you know that something would happen to put it off, and then I should have gone quite distracted. And there was my aunt, all the time I was dressing, preaching and talking away just as if she was reading a sermon. However, I did not hear above one word in ten, for I was thinking, you may suppose, of my dear Wickham. I longed to know whether he would be married in his blue coat.

Well, and so we breakfasted at ten as usual; I thought it would never be over; for, by the bye, you are to understand, that my uncle and aunt were horrid unpleasant all the time I was with them. If you'll believe me, I did not once put my foot out of doors, though I was there a fortnight. Not one party, or scheme, or any thing. To be sure London was rather thin, but however the little Theatre was open. Well, and so just as the carriage came to the door, my uncle was called away upon business to that horrid man Mr. Stone. And then, you know, when once they get together, there is no end of it. Well, I was so frightened I did not know what to do, for my uncle was to give me away; and if we were beyond an hour, we could not be married all day. But, luckily, he came back again in ten minutes time, and then we all set out. However, I recollected afterwards, that if he *had* been prevented going, the wedding need not be put off, for Mr. Darcy might have done as well."

"Mr. Darcy!" repeated Elizabeth, in utter amazement.

"Oh, yes! – he was to come here with Wickham, you know. But gracious me! I quite forgot! I ought not to have said a word about it. I promised them so faithfully! What will Wickham say? It was to be such a secret!"

"If it was to be secret," said Jane, "say not another word on the subject. You may depend upon my seeking no further."

"Oh! certainly," said Elizabeth, though burning with curiosity; "we will ask you no questions."

"Thank you," said Lydia, "for if you did, I should certainly tell you all, and then Wickham would be angry."

On such encouragement to ask, Elizabeth was forced to put it out of her power, by running away.

But to live in ignorance on such a point was impossible; or at least it was impossible not to try for information. Mr. Darcy had been at her sister's wedding. It was exactly a scene, and exactly among people, where he had apparently least to do, and least temptation to go. Conjectures as to the meaning of it, rapid and wild, hurried into her brain; but she was satisfied with none. Those that best pleased her, as placing his conduct in the noblest light, seemed most improbable. She could not bear such suspense; and hastily seizing a sheet of paper, wrote a short letter to her aunt, to request an explanation of what Lydia had dropt, if it were compatible with the secrecy which had been intended.

"You may readily comprehend," she added, "what my curiosity must be to know how a person unconnected with any of us, and (comparatively speaking) a stranger to our family, should have been amongst you at such a time. Pray write instantly, and let me understand it – unless it is, for very cogent reasons, to remain

in the secrecy which Lydia seems to think necessary; and then
I must endeavour to be satisfied with ignorance."

"Not that I *shall* though," she added to herself, as she finished
the letter; "and my dear aunt, if you do not tell me in an honourable manner, I shall certainly be reduced to tricks and stratagems
to find out."

Jane's delicate sense of honour would not allow her to speak
to Elizabeth privately of what Lydia had let fall; Elizabeth was
glad of it; – till it appeared whether her inquiries would receive
any satisfaction, she had rather be without a confidante.

CHAPTER 10

Elizabeth had the satisfaction of receiving an answer to her letter,
as soon as she possibly could. She was no sooner in possession
of it, than hurrying into the little copse, where she was least likely to be interrupted, she sat down on one of the benches, and
prepared to be happy; for the length of the letter convinced her,
that it did not contain a denial.

Grace Church Street, Sept. 6.

My dear Niece,

 I have just received your letter, and shall devote this whole
morning to answering it, as I foresee that a *little* writing will
not comprise what I have to tell you. I must confess myself
surprised by your application; I did not expect it from *you*. Don't
think me angry, however, for I only mean to let you know, that
I had not imagined such enquiries to be necessary on *your* side.
If you do not choose to understand me, forgive my impertinence. Your uncle is as much surprised as I am – and nothing
but the belief of your being a party concerned, would have allowed him to act as he has done. But if you are really innocent
and ignorant, I must be more explicit. On the very day of my
coming home from Longbourn, your uncle had a most unexpected visitor. Mr. Darcy called, and was shut up with him several hours. It was all over before I arrived; so my curiosity was

not so dreadfully racked as *your's* seems to have been. He came
to tell Mr. Gardiner that he had found out where your sister
and Mr. Wickham were, and that he had seen and talked with
them both, Wickham repeatedly, Lydia once. From what I can
collect, he left Derbyshire only one day after ourselves, and
came to town with the resolution of hunting for them. The motive professed, was his conviction of its being owing to himself
that Wickham's worthlessness had not been so well known,
as to make it impossible for any young woman of character,
to love or confide in him. He generously imputed the whole
to his mistaken pride, and confessed that he had before thought
it beneath him, to lay his private actions open to the world.
His character was to speak for itself. He called it, therefore, his
duty to step forward, and endeavour to remedy an evil, which
had been brought on by himself. If he *had another* motive, I
am sure it would never disgrace him. He had been some days
in town, before he was able to discover them; but he had something to direct his search, which was more than *we* had; and
the consciousness of this, was another reason for his resolving
to follow us. There is a lady, it seems, a Mrs. Younge, who was
some time ago governess to Miss Darcy, and was dismissed from
her charge on some cause of disapprobation, though he did
not say what. She then took a large house in Edward-street,
and has since maintained herself by letting lodgings. This Mrs.
Younge was, he knew, intimately acquainted with Wickham;
and he went to her for intelligence of him, as soon as he got
to town. But it was two or three days before he could get from
her what he wanted. She would not betray her trust, I suppose,
without bribery and corruption, for she really did know where
her friend was to be found. Wickham indeed had gone to her,
on their first arrival in London, and had she been able to receive
them into her house, they would have taken up their abode
with her. At length, however, our kind friend procured the
wished-for direction. They were in —— street. He saw Wickham, and afterwards insisted on seeing Lydia. His first object
with her, he acknowledged, had been to persuade her to quit
her present disgraceful situation, and return to her friends as
soon as they could be prevailed on to receive her, offering his
assistance, as far as it would go. But he found Lydia absolutely
resolved on remaining where she was. She cared for none of
her friends, she wanted no help of his, she would not hear of

leaving Wickham. She was sure they should be married some time or other, and it did not much signify when. Since such were her feelings, it only remained, he thought, to secure and expedite a marriage, which, in his very first conversation with Wickham, he easily learnt, had never been *his* design. He confessed himself obliged to leave the regiment, on account of some debts of honour, which were very pressing; and scrupled not to lay all the ill-consequences of Lydia's flight, on her own folly alone. He meant to resign his commission immediately; and as to his future situation, he could conjecture very little about it. He must go somewhere, but he did not know where, and he knew he should have nothing to live on. Mr. Darcy asked him why he had not married your sister at once. Though Mr. Bennet was not imagined to be very rich, he would have been able to do something for him, and his situation must have been benefited by marriage. But he found, in reply to this question, that Wickham still cherished the hope of more effectually making his fortune by marriage, in some other country. Under such circumstances, however, he was not likely to be proof against the temptation of immediate relief. They met several times, for there was much to be discussed. Wickham of course wanted more than he could get; but at length was reduced to be reasonable. Every thing being settled between *them,* Mr. Darcy's next step was to make your uncle acquainted with it, and he first called in Grace Church Street the evening before I came home. But Mr. Gardiner could not be seen, and Mr. Darcy found, on farther enquiry, that your father was still with him, but would quit town the next morning. He did not judge your father to be a person whom he could so properly consult as your uncle, and therefore readily postponed seeing him, till after the departure of the former. He did not leave his name, and till the next day, it was only known that a gentleman had called on business. On Saturday he came again. Your father was gone, your uncle at home, and, as I said before, they had a great deal of talk together. They met again on Sunday, and then *I* saw him too. It was not all settled before Monday: as soon as it was, the express was sent off to Longbourn. But our visitor was very obstinate. I fancy, Lizzy, that obstinacy is the real defect of his character after all. He has been accused of many faults at different times; but *this* is the true one. Nothing was to be done that he did not do himself; though I am sure (and I do not speak it to be thanked, therefore say nothing about it,) your uncle would most readily have settled the whole. They battled it together for a long time, which was more than either the gentleman or lady concerned in it deserved. But at last your uncle was forced to yield, and instead of being allowed to be of use to his niece, was forced to put up with only having probable credit of it, which went sorely against the grain; and I really believe your letter this morning gave him great pleasure, because it required an explanation that would rob him of his borrowed feathers, and give the praise where it was due. But, Lizzy, this must go no farther than yourself, or Jane at most. You know pretty well, I suppose, what has been done for the young people. His debts are to be paid, amounting, I believe, to considerably more than a thousand pounds, another thousand in addition to her own settled upon *her*, and his commission purchased. The reason why all this was to be done by him alone, was such as I have given above. It was owing to him, to his reserve, and want of proper consideration, that Wickham's character had been so misunderstood, and consequently that he had been received and noticed as he was. Perhaps there was some truth in *this*; though I doubt whether *his* reserve, or *anybody's* reserve, can be answerable for the event. But in spite of all this fine talking, my dear Lizzy, you may rest perfectly assured, that your uncle would never have yielded, if we had not given him credit for *another interest* in the affair. When all this was resolved on, he returned again to his friends, who were still staying at Pemberley; but it was agreed that he should be in London once more when the wedding took place, and all money matters were then to receive the last finish. I believe I have now told you every thing. It is a relation which you tell me is to give you great surprise; I hope at least it will not afford you any displeasure. Lydia came to us; and Wickham had constant admission to the house. *He* was exactly what he had been, when I knew him in Hertfordshire; but I would not tell you how little I was satisfied with *her* behaviour while she staid with us, if I had not perceived, by Jane's letter last Wednesday, that her conduct on coming home was exactly a piece with it, and therefore what I now tell you, can give you no fresh pain. I talked to her repeatedly in the most serious manner, representing to her all the wickedness of what she had done, and all the unhappiness she had brought on her family. If she heard me, it was by good luck, for I am sure she did not listen. I was sometimes quite provoked, but then I recollected my dear Elizabeth and Jane, and for their sakes had patience with her. Mr. Darcy was punctual in his return, and as Lydia informed you, attended the wedding. He dined with us the next day, and was to leave town again on Wednesday or Thursday. Will you be very angry with me, my dear Lizzy, if I take this opportunity of saying (what I was never bold enough to say before) how much I like him. His behaviour to us has, in every respect, been as pleasing as when we were in Derbyshire. His understanding and opinions all please me; he wants nothing but a little more liveliness, and *that,* if he marry *prudently,* his wife may teach him. I thought him very sly;—he hardly ever mentioned your name. But slyness seems the fashion. Pray forgive me, if I have been very presuming or at least do not punish me so far, as to exclude me from P. I shall never be quite happy till I have been all round the park. A low phæton, with a nice little pair of ponies, would be the very thing. But I must write no more. The children have been wanting me this half hour. Yours, very sincerely,

M. Gardiner.

The contents of this letter threw Elizabeth into a flutter of spirits, in which it was difficult to determine whether pleasure or pain bore the greatest share. The vague and unsettled suspicions which uncertainty had produced of what Mr. Darcy might have been doing to forward her sister's match, which she had feared to encourage, as an exertion of goodness too great to be probable, and at the same time dreaded to be just, from the pain of obligation, were proved beyond their greatest extent to be true! He had followed them purposely to town, he had taken on himself all the trouble and mortification attendant on such a research; in which supplication had been necessary to a woman whom he must abominate and despise, and where he was reduced to meet, frequently meet, reason with, persuade, and finally bribe, the man whom he always most wished to avoid, and whose very name it was punishment to him to pronounce. He had done all this for a girl whom he could neither regard nor esteem. Her heart did whisper, that he had done it for her. But it was a hope shortly checked by other considerations, and she soon felt that even her vanity was insufficient, when required to depend on his affection for her, for a woman who had already refused him, as able to overcome a sentiment so natural as abhorrence against relationship with Wickham. Brother in law of Wickham! Every kind of pride must revolt from the connection. He had to be sure done much. She was ashamed to think how much. But he had given a reason for his interference, which asked no extraordinary stretch of belief. It was reasonable that he should feel he had been wrong; he had liberality, and he had the means of exercising it; and though she would not place herself as his principal inducement, she could, perhaps, believe, that remaining partiality for her, might assist his endeavours in a cause where her peace of mind must be materially concerned. It was painful, exceedingly painful, to know that they were under obligations to a person who could never receive a return. They owed the restoration of Lydia, her character, every thing to him. Oh! how heartily did she grieve over every ungracious sensation she had ever encouraged, every saucy speech she had ever directed towards him. For herself she was humbled; but she was proud of him. Proud that in a cause of compassion and honour, he had been able to get the better of himself. She read over her aunt's commendation of him again and again. It was hardly enough; but it pleased her. She was even sensible of some pleasure, though mixed with regret, on finding how stedfastly both she and her uncle had been persuaded that affection and confidence subsisted between Mr. Darcy and herself.

She was roused from her seat, and her reflections, by some one's approach; and before she could strike into another path, she was overtaken by Wickham.

"I am afraid I interrupt your solitary ramble, my dear sister?" said he, as he joined her.

"You certainly do," she replied with a smile; "but it does not follow that the interruption must be unwelcome."

"I should be sorry indeed, if it were. We were always good friends; and now we are better."

"True. Are the others coming out?"

"I do not know. Mrs. Bennet and Lydia are going in the carriage to Meryton. And so, my dear sister, I find from our uncle and aunt, that you have actually seen Pemberley."

She replied in the affirmative.

"I almost envy you the pleasure, and yet I believe it would be too much for me, or else I could take it in my way to Newcastle. And you saw the old housekeeper, I suppose? Poor Reynolds, she was always very fond of me. But of course she did not mention my name to you."

"Yes, she did."

"And what did she say?"

"That you were gone into the army, and she was afraid had—not turned out well. At such a distance as *that,* you know, things are strangely misrepresented."

"Certainly," he replied, biting his lips. Elizabeth hoped she had silenced him; but he soon afterwards said,

"I was surprised to see Darcy in town last month. We passed each other several times. I wonder what he can be doing there."

"Perhaps preparing for his marriage with Miss de Bourgh," said Elizabeth. It must be something particular, to take him there at this time of year."

"Undoubtedly. Did you see him while you were at Lambton? I thought I understood from the Gardiners that you had."

"Yes; he introduced us to his sister."

"And do you like her?"

"Very much."

"I have heard, indeed, that she is uncommonly improved within this year or two. When I last saw her, she was not very promising. I am very glad you liked her. I hope she will turn out well."

"I dare say she will; she has got over the most trying age."

"Did you go by the village of Kympton?"

"I do not recollect that we did."

"I mention it, because it is the living which I ought to have had. A most delightful place! Excellent Parsonage House! It would have suited me in every respect."

"How should you have liked making sermons?"

"Exceedingly well. I should have considered it as part of my duty, and the exertion would soon have been nothing. One ought not to repine;—but, to be sure, it would have been such a thing for me! The quiet, the retirement of such a life, would have answered all my ideas of happiness! But it was not to be. Did you ever hear Darcy mention the circumstance, when you were in Kent?"

"I *have* heard from authority, which I thought *as good,* that it was left you conditionally only, and at the will of the present patron."

You have. Yes, there was something in *that;* I told you so from the first, you may remember."

"I *did* hear, too, that there was a time, when sermon-making was not so palatable to you, as it seems to be at present; that you actually declared your resolution of never taking orders, and that the business had been compromised accordingly."

You did! and it was not wholly without foundation. You may remember what I told you on that point, when first we talked of it."

They were now almost at the door of the house, for she had walked fast to get rid of him; and unwilling, for her sister's sake, to provoke him, she only said in reply, with a good-humoured smile,

"Come, Mr. Wickham, we are brother and sister, you know. Do not let us quarrel about the past. In future, I hope we shall be always of one mind."

She held out her hand; he kissed it with affectionate gallantry, though he hardly knew how to look, and they entered the house.

CHAPTER 11

Mr. Wickham was so perfectly satisfied with this conversation, that he never again distressed himself, or provoked his dear sister

Elizabeth, by introducing the subject of it; and she was pleased to find that she had said enough to keep him quiet.

The day of his and Lydia's departure soon came, and Mrs. Bennet was forced to submit to a separation, which, as her husband by no means entered into her scheme of their all going to Newcastle, was likely to continue at least a twelve-month.

"Oh! my dear Lydia," she cried, "when shall we meet again?"

"Oh, lord! I don't know. Not these two or three years perhaps."

"Write to me very often, my dear."

"As often as I can. But you know married women have never much time for writing. My sisters may write to *me*. They will have nothing else to do."

Mr. Wickham's adieus were much more affectionate than his wife's. He smiled, looked handsome, and said many pretty things.

"He is as fine a fellow," said Mr. Bennet, as soon as they were out of the house, "as ever I saw. He simpers, and smirks, and makes love to us all. I am prodigiously proud of him. I defy even Sir William Lucas himself, to produce a more valuable son-in-law."

The loss of her daughter made Mrs. Bennet very dull for several days.

"I often think," said she "that there is nothing so bad as parting with one's friends. One seems so forlorn without them."

"This is the consequence you see, Madam. of marrying a daughter," said Elizabeth. "It must make you better satisfied that your other four are single."

"It is no such thing. Lydia does not leave me because she is married; but only because her husband's regiment happens to be so far off. If that had been nearer, she would not have gone so soon."

But the spiritless condition which this event threw her into, was shortly relieved, and her mind opened again to the agitation of hope, by an article of news, which then began to be in circulation. The housekeeper at Netherfield had received orders to prepare for the arrival of her master, who was coming down in a day or two, to shoot there for several weeks. Mrs. Bennet was quite in the fidgets. She looked at Jane, and smiled, and shook her head by turns.

"Well, well, and so Mr. Bingley is coming down, sister," (for Mrs. Phillips first brought her the news.) "Well, so much the better. Not that I care about it, though. He is nothing to us, you know, and I am sure I never want to see him again. But, however, he is very welcome to come to Netherfield, if he likes it. And who knows what *may* happen? But that is nothing to us. You know, sister, we agreed long ago never to mention a word about it. And so, is it quite certain he is coming?"

"You may depend on it," replied the other, "for Mrs. Nicholls was in Meryton last night; I saw her passing by, and went out myself on purpose to know the truth of it; and she told me that it was certain true. He comes down on Thursday at the latest, very likely on Wednesday. She was going to the butcher's, she told me, on purpose to order in some more meat on Wednesday, and she has got three couple of ducks, just fit to be killed."

Miss Bennet had not been able to hear of his coming, without changing colour. It was many months since she had mentioned his name to Elizabeth; but now, as soon as they were alone together, she said,

"I saw you look at me to day, Lizzy, when my aunt told us of the present report; and I know I appeared distressed. But don't imagine it was from any silly cause. I was only confused for the moment, because I felt that I *should* be looked at. I do assure you, that the news does not affect me either with pleasure or pain. I am glad of one thing, that he comes alone; because we shall see the less of him. Not that I am afraid of *myself*, but I dread other people's remarks."

Elizabeth did not know what to make of it. Had she not seen him in Derbyshire, she might have supposed him capable of coming there, with no other view than what was acknowledged; but she still thought him partial to Jane, and she wavered as to the greater probability of his coming there *with* his friend's permission, or being bold enough to come without it.

"Yet it is hard," she sometimes thought, "that this poor man cannot come to a house, which he has legally hired, without raising all this speculation! I *will* leave him to himself."

In spite of what her sister declared, and really believed to be her feelings, in the expectation of his arrival, Elizabeth could easily perceive that her spirits were affected by it. They were more disturbed, more unequal, than she had often seen them.

The subject which had been so warmly canvassed between their parents, about a twelvemonth ago, was now brought forward again.

"As soon as ever Mr. Bingley comes, my dear," said Mrs. Bennet, "you will wait on him of course."

"No, no. You forced me into visiting him last year, and promised if I went to see him, he should marry one of my daughters. But it ended in nothing, and I will not be sent on a fool's errand again."

His wife represented to him how absolutely necessary such an attention would be from all the neighbouring gentlemen, on his returning to Netherfield.

"'Tis an etiquette I despise," said he. If he wants our society, let him seek it. He knows where we live. I will not spend *my* hours in running after my neighbours every time they go away, and come back again."

"Well, all I know is, that it will be abominably rude if you do not wait on him. But, however, that shan't prevent my asking him to dine here, I am determined. We must have Mrs. Long and the Gouldings soon. That will make thirteen with ourselves, so there will be just room at table for him."

Consoled by this resolution, she was the better able to bear her husband's incivility; though it was very mortifying to know that her neighbours might all see Mr. Bingley in consequence of it, before *they* did. As the day of his arrival drew near,

"I begin to be sorry that he comes at all," said Jane to her sister. "It would be nothing; I could see him with perfect indifference, but I can hardly bear to hear it thus perpetually talked of. My mother means well; but she does not know, no one can know

how much I suffer from what she says. Happy shall I be, when
his stay at Netherfield is over!"

"I wish I could say any thing to comfort you," replied Elizabeth;
"but it is wholly out of my power. You must feel it; and the usual
satisfaction of preaching patience to a sufferer is denied me, because you have always so much."

Mr. Bingley arrived. Mrs. Bennet, through the assistance of servants, contrived to have the earliest tidings of it, that the period
of anxiety and fretfulness on her side, might be as long as it could.
She counted the days that must intervene before their invitation
could be sent; hopeless of seeing him before. But on the third
morning after his arrival in Hertfordshire, she saw him from her
dressing-room window, enter the paddock, and ride towards the
house.

Her daughters were eagerly called to partake of her joy. Jane
resolutely kept her place at the table; but Elizabeth, to satisfy her
mother, went to the window–she looked,–she saw Mr. Darcy with
him, and sat down again by her sister.

"There is a gentleman with him, mamma," said Kitty; "who
can it be?"

"Some acquaintance or other, my dear, I suppose; I am sure
I do not know."

"La! replied Kitty, "it looks just like that man that used to be
with him before. Mr. what's his name. That tall, proud man."

"Good gracious! Mr. Darcy!–and so it does I vow. Well, any
friend of Mr. Bingley's will always be welcome here to be sure;
but else I must say that I hate the very sight of him."

Jane looked at Elizabeth with surprise and concern. She knew
but little of their meeting in Derbyshire, and therefore felt for the
awkwardness which must attend her sister, in seeing him almost
for the first time after receiving his explanatory letter. Both sisters were uncomfortable enough. Each felt for the other, and of
course for themselves; and their mother talked on, of her dislike
of Mr. Darcy, and her resolution to be civil to him only as Mr.
Bingley's friend, without being heard by either of them. But

Elizabeth had sources of uneasiness which could not be suspect-ed by Jane, to whom she had never yet had courage to shew Mrs. Gardiner's letter, or to relate her own change of sentiment towards him. To Jane, he could be only a man whose proposals she had refused, and whose merit she had undervalued; but to her own more extensive information, he was the person, to whom the whole family were indebted for the first of benefits, and whom she regard-ed herself with an interest, if not quite so tender, at least as reasona-ble and just, as what Jane felt for Bingley. Her astonishment at his coming—at his coming to Netherfield, to Longbourn, and voluntarily seeking her again, was almost equal to what she had known on first witnessing his altered behaviour in Derbyshire.

The colour which had been driven from her face, returned for half a minute with an additional glow, and a smile of delight added lustre to her eyes, as she thought for that space of time, that his affection and wishes must still be unshaken. But she would not be secure.

"Let me first see how he behaves," said she; "it will then be early enough for expectation."

She sat intently at work, striving to be composed, and without daring to lift up her eyes, till anxious curiosity carried them to the face of her sister, as the servant was approaching the door. Jane looked a little paler than usual, but more sedate than Elizabeth had expected. On the gentlemen's appearing, her colour increased; yet she received them with tolerable ease, and with a propriety of behaviour equally free from any symptom of resentment, or any unnecessary complaisance.

Elizabeth said as little to either as civility would allow, and sat down again to her work, with an eagerness which it did not often command. She had ventured only one glance at Darcy. He looked serious as usual; and she thought, more as he had been used to look in Hertfordshire, than as she had seen him at Pem-berley. But, perhaps he could not in her mother's presence be what he was before her uncle and aunt. It was a painful, but not an improbable, conjecture.

Bingley, she had likewise seen for an instant, and in that short period saw him looking both pleased and embarrassed. He was received by Mrs. Bennet with a degree of civility, which made her two daughters ashamed, especially when contrasted with the cold and ceremonious politeness of her curtsey and address to his friend.

Elizabeth particularly, who knew that her mother owed to the latter the preservation of her favourite daughter from immediable infamy, was hurt and distressed to a most painful degree by a distinction so ill applied.

Darcy, after enquiring of her how Mr. and Mrs. Gardiner did, a question which she could not answer without confusion, said scarcely any thing. He was not seated by her; perhaps that was the reason of his silence; but it had not been so in Derbyshire. There he had talked to her friends, when he could not to herself. But now several minutes elapsed, without bringing the sound of his voice; and when occasionally, unable to resist the impulse of curiosity, she raised her eyes to his face, she as often found him looking at Jane, as at herself, and frequently on no object but the ground. More thoughtfulness, and less anxiety to please than when they last met, were plainly expressed. She was disappointed, and angry with herself for being so.

"Could I expect it to be otherwise!" said she. "Yet why did he come?"

She was in no humour for conversation with any one but himself; and to him she had hardly courage to speak.

She enquired after his sister, but could do no more.

"It is a long time, Mr. Bingley, since you went away," said Mrs. Bennet.

He readily agreed to it.

"I began to be afraid you would never come back again. People *did* say, you meant to quit the place entirely at Michaelmas; but, however, I hope it is not true. A great many changes have happened in the neighbourhood since you went away. Miss Lucas is married and settled. And one of my own daughters. I suppose you have heard of it; indeed, you must have seen it in the papers. It was in the Times and the Courier, I know; though it was not put in as it ought to be. It was only said, 'Lately, George Wickham, Esq. to Miss Lydia Bennet,' without there being a syllable said of her father, or the place where she lived, or any thing. It was my brother Gardiner's drawing up too, and I wonder how he came to make such an awkward business of it. Did you see it?"

Bingley replied that he did, and made his congratulations. Elizabeth dared not lift up her eyes. How Mr. Darcy looked, therefore, she could not tell.

"It is a delightful thing, to be sure, to have a daughter well married," continued her mother; "but at the same time, Mr. Bingley, it is very hard to have her taken such a way from me. They are gone down to Newcastle, a place quite northward, it seems, and there they are to stay, I do not know how long. His regiment is there; for I suppose you have heard of his leaving the —— shire, and of his being gone into the regulars. Thank Heaven! he has *some* friends, though perhaps not so many as he deserves."

Elizabeth, who knew this to be levelled at Mr. Darcy, was in such misery of shame, that she could hardly keep her seat. It drew from her, however, the exertion of speaking, which nothing else had so effectually done before; and she asked Bingley, whether he meant to make any stay in the country at present. A few weeks, he believed.

"When you have killed all your own birds, Mr. Bingley," said her mother, "I beg you will come here, and shoot as many as you please, on Mr. Bennet's manor. I am sure he will be vastly happy to oblige you, and will save all the best of the covies for you."

Elizabeth's misery increased, at such unnecessary, such officious attention! Were the same fair prospect to arise at present, as had flattered them a year ago, every thing, she was persuaded, would be hastening to the same vexatious conclusion. At that instant she felt, that years of happiness could not make Jane or herself amends, for moments of such painful confusion.

"The first wish of my heart," said she to herself, "is never more to be in company with either of them. Their society can afford no pleasure, that will atone for such wretchedness as this! Let me never see either one or the other again!"

Yet the misery, for which years of happiness were to offer no compensation, received soon afterwards material relief, from observing how much the beauty of her sister re-kindled the admiration of her former lover. When first he came in, he had spoken to her but little; but every five minutes seemed to be giving her more of his attention. He found her as handsome as she had been last year; as good natured, and as unaffected, though not quite so chatty. Jane was anxious that no difference should be perceived in her at all, and was really persuaded that she talked as much as ever. But her mind was so busily engaged, that she did not always know when she was silent.

When the gentlemen rose to go away, Mrs. Bennet was mindful of her intended civility, and they were invited and engaged to dine at Longbourn in a few days time.

"You are quite a visit in by debt, Mr. Bingley." she added, "for when you went to town last winter, you promised to take a family dinner with us, as soon as you returned. I have not forgot, you see; and I assure you, I was very much disappointed that you did not come back and keep your engagement."

Bingley looked a little silly at this reflection, and said something of his concern, at having been prevented by business. They then went away.

Mrs. Bennet had been strongly inclined to ask them to stay and dine there, that day; but, though she always kept a very good table, she did not think any thing less than two courses, could be good enough for a man, on whom she had such anxious designs, or satisfy the appetite and pride of one who had ten thousand a-year.

CHAPTER 12

As soon as they were gone, Elizabeth walked out to recover her spirits; or in other words, to dwell without interruption on those subjects that must deaden them more. Mr. Darcy's behaviour astonished and vexed her.

"Why, if he came only to be silent, grave, and indifferent," said she, "did he come at all?"

She could settle it in no way that gave her pleasure.

"He could be still amiable, still pleasing, to my uncle and aunt, when he was in town; and why not to me? If he fears me, why come hither? If he no longer cares for me, why silent? Teazing, teazing, man! I will think no more about him."

Her resolution was for a short time involuntarily kept by the approach of her sister, who joined her with a cheerful look, which shewed her better satisfied with their visitors, than Elizabeth.

"Now," said she, "that this first meeting is over, I feel perfectly easy. I know my own strength, and I shall never be embarrassed again by his coming. I am glad he dines here on Tuesday. It will then be publicly seen, that on both sides, we meet only as common and indifferent acquaintance."

"Yes, very indifferent indeed," said Elizabeth, laughingly. "Oh, Jane, take care."

"My dear Lizzy, you cannot think me so weak, as to be in danger now."

"I think you are in very great danger of making him as much in love with you as ever."

——

They did not see the gentlemen again till Tuesday; and Mrs. Bennet, in the meanwhile, was giving way to all the happy schemes, which the good humour, and common politeness of Bingley, in half an hour's visit, had revived.

On Tuesday there was a large party assembled at Longbourn; and the two, who were most anxiously expected, to the credit of their punctuality as sportsmen, were in very good time. When

they repaired to the dining-room, Elizabeth eagerly watched to
see whether Bingley would take the place, which, in all their former
parties, had belonged to him, by her sister. Her prudent mother,
occupied by the same ideas, forbore to invite him to sit by herself. On entering the room, he seemed to hesitate; but Jane happened to look round, and happened to smile: it was decided. He
placed himself by her.

Elizabeth, with a triumphant sensation, looked towards his
friend. He bore it with noble indifference, and she would have
imagined that Bingley had received his sanction to be happy, had
she not seen his eyes likewise turned towards Mr. Darcy, with an
expression of half-laughing alarm.

His behaviour to her sister was such, during dinner time, as
shewed an admiration of her, which, though more guarded than
formerly, persuaded Elizabeth, that if left wholly to himself, Jane's
happiness, and his own, would be speedily secured. Though she
dared not depend upon the consequence, she yet received pleasure from observing his behaviour. It gave her all the animation
that her spirits could boast; for she was in no cheerful humour.
Mr. Darcy was almost as far from her, as the table could divide
them. He was on one side of her mother. She knew how little
such a situation would give pleasure to either, or make either appear to advantage. She was not near enough to hear any of their
discourse, but she could see how seldom they spoke to each other,
and how formal and cold was their manner, whenever they did.
Her mother's ungraciousness, made the sense of what they owed
him more painful to Elizabeth's mind; and she would, at times,
have given any thing to be privileged to tell him, that his kindness was neither unknown nor unfelt by the whole of the family.

She was in hopes that the evening would afford some opportunity of bringing them together; that the whole of the visit would
not pass away without enabling them to enter into something more
of conversation, than the mere ceremonious salutation attending his entrance. Anxious and uneasy, the period which passed
in the drawing-room, before the gentlemen came, was wearisome

and dull to a degree, that almost made her uncivil. She looked forward to their entrance, as the point of which all her chance of pleasure for the evening must depend.

"If he does not come to me, *then*," said she, "I shall give him up for ever."

The gentlemen came; and she thought he looked as if he would have answered her hopes; but, alas! the ladies had crowded round the table, where Miss Bennet was making tea, and Elizabeth pouring out the coffee, in so close a confederacy, that there was not a single vacancy near her, which would admit of a chair. And on the gentlemen's approaching, one of the girls moved closer to her than ever, and said, in a whisper,

"The men shan't come and part us, I am determined. We want none of them; do we?"

Darcy had walked away to another part of the room. She followed him with her eyes, envied every one to whom he spoke, had scarcely patience enough to help anybody to coffee; and then was enraged against herself for being so silly!

"A man who has once been refused! How could I ever be foolish enough to expect a renewal of his love? Is there one among the sex, who would not protest against such a weakness as a second proposal to the same woman? There is no indignity so abhorrent to their feelings!"

She was a little revived, however, by his bringing back his coffee cup himself; and she seized the opportunity of saying,

"Is your sister at Pemberley still?"

"Yes, she will remain there till Christmas."

"And quite alone? Have all her friends left her?"

"Mrs. Annesley is with her. The others have been gone on to Scarborough, these three weeks."

She could think of nothing more to say; but if he wished to converse with her, he might have better success. He stood by her, however, for some minutes, in silence; and, at last, on the young lady's whispering to Elizabeth again, he walked away.

When the tea-things were removed, and the card tables placed, the ladies all rose, and Elizabeth was then hoping to be soon joined by him, when all her views were overthrown, by seeing him fall a victim to her mother's rapacity for whist players, and in a few moments after seated with the rest of the party. She now lost every expectation of pleasure. They were confined for the evening at different tables, and she had nothing to hope, but that his eyes were so often turned towards her side of the room, as to make him play as unsuccessfully as herself.

Mrs. Bennet had designed to keep the two Netherfield gentlemen to supper; but their carriage was unluckily ordered before any of the others, and she had no opportunity of detaining them.

"Well girls," said she, as soon as they were left to themselves, "What say you to the day? I think every thing has passed off uncommonly well, I assure you. The dinner was as well dressed as any I ever saw. The venison was roasted to a turn – and everybody said, they never saw so fat a haunch. The soup was fifty times better than what we had at the Lucas's last week; and even Mr. Darcy acknowledged, that the partridges were remarkably well done; and I suppose he has two or three French cooks at least. And, my dear Jane, I never saw you look in greater beauty. Mrs. Long said so too, for I asked her whether you did not. And what do you think she said besides? 'Ah! Mrs. Bennet, we shall have her at Netherfield at last.' She did indeed. I do think Mrs. Long is as good a creature as ever lived – and her nieces are very pretty behaved girls, and not at all handsome: I like them prodigiously."

Mrs. Bennet, in short, was in very great spirits; she had seen enough of Bingley's behaviour to Jane, to be convinced that she would get him at last; and her expectations of advantage to her family, when in a happy humour, were so far beyond reason, that she was quite disappointed at not seeing him there again the next day, to make his proposals.

"It has been a very agreeable day." said Miss Bennet to Elizabeth. "The party seemed so well selected, so suitable one with the other. I hope we may often meet again."

Elizabeth smiled.

"Lizzy, you must not do so. You must not suspect me. It mortifies me. I assure you that I have now learnt to enjoy his conversation as an agreeable and sensible young man, without having a wish beyond it. I am perfectly satisfied from what his manners now are, that he never had any design of engaging my affection. It is only that he is blessed with greater sweetness of address, and a stronger desire of generally pleasing than any other man."

"You are very cruel," said her sister, "you will not let me smile, and are provoking me to it every moment."

"How hard it is in some cases to be believed! And how impossible in others!"

"But why should you wish to persuade me that I feel more than I acknowledge?"

"That is a question which I hardly know how to answer. We all love to instruct, though we can teach only what is not worth knowing. Forgive me; and if you persist in indifference, so not make *me* your confidante."

CHAPTER 13

A few days after this visit, Mr. Bingley called again, and alone. His friend had left him that morning for London, but was to return home in ten days time. He sat with them above an hour, and was in remarkably good spirits. Mrs. Bennet invited him to dine with them; but, with many expressions of concern, he confessed himself engaged elsewhere.

"Next time you call," said she, "I hope we shall be more lucky."

He should be particularly happy at any time, &c. &c.; and if she would give him leave, would take an early opportunity of waiting on them.

"Can you come to-morrow?"

Yes, he had no engagement at all for to-morrow; and her invitation was accepted with alacrity.

He came, and in such very good time, that the ladies were none of them dressed. In ran Mrs. Bennet to her daughter's room, in her dressing gown, and with her hair half finished, crying out,

"My dear Jane, make haste and hurry down. He is come—Mr. Bingley is come.—He is,indeed. Make haste, make haste. Here, Sarah, come to Miss Bennet this moment, and help her on with her gown. Never mind Miss Lizzy's hair."

"We will be down as soon as we can," said Jane; "but I dare say Kitty is forwarder than either of us, for she went up stairs half an our ago."

"Oh! hang Kitty! what has she to do with it? Come be quick, be quick! where is your sash my dear?"

But when her mother was gone, Jane would not be prevailed on to go down without one of her sisters.

The same anxiety to get them by themselves, was visible again in the evening. After tea, Mr. Bennet retired to the library, as was his custom, and Mary went up stairs to her instrument. Two obstacles of the five being thus removed, Mrs. Bennet say looking and winking at Elizabeth and Catherine for a considerable time, without making any impression on them. Elizabeth would not observe her; and when at last Kitty did, she very innocently said, "What is the matter mamma. What do you keep winking at me for? What am I to do?"

"Nothing child, nothing. I did not wink at you." She then sat still five minutes longer; but unable to waste such a precious occasion, she suddenly got up, and saying to Kitty,

"Come here, my love, I want to speak to you," took her out of the room. Jane instantly gave a look at Elizabeth, which spoke her distress at such premeditation, and her entreaty that *she* would not give into it. In a few minutes, Mrs. Bennet half opened the door and called out,

"Lizzy, my dear, I want to speak with you."

Elizabeth was forced to go.

"We may as well leave them by themselves you know;" said

her mother as soon as she was in the hall. Kitty and I are going up stairs to sit in my dressing room."

Elizabeth made no attempt to reason with her mother, but remained quietly in the hall, till she and Kitty were out of sight, then returned into the drawing room."

Mrs. Bennet's schemes for this day were ineffectual. Bingley was every thing that was charming, except the professed lover of her daughter. His ease and cheerfulness rendered him a most agreeable addition to their evening party; and he bore with the ill-judged officiousness of the mother, and heard all her silly remarks with a forbearance and command of countenance, particularly grateful to the daughter.

He scarcely needed an invitation to stay supper; and before he went away, an engagement was formed, chiefly through his own and Mrs. Bennet's means, for his coming next morning to shoot with her husband.

After this day, Jane said no more of her indifference. Not a word passed between the sisters concerning Bingley; but Elizabeth went to bed in the happy belief that all must speedily be concluded, unless Mr. Darcy returned within the stated time. Seriously, however, she felt tolerably persuaded that all this must have taken place with that gentleman's concurrence.

Bingley was punctual to his appointment; and he and Mr. Bennet spent the morning together, as had been agreed on. The latter was much more agreeable than his companion expected. There was nothing of presumption or folly in Bingley, that could provoke his ridicule, or disgust him into silence; and he was more communicative, and less eccentric than the other had ever seen him. Bingley of course returned with him to dinner; and in the evening Mrs. Bennet's invention was again at work to get every body away from him and her daughter. Elizabeth, who had a letter to write, went into the breakfast room for that purpose soon after tea; for as the others were all going to sit down to cards, she could not be wanted to counteract her mother's schemes.

But on returning to the drawing room, when her letter was

finished, she saw, to her infinite surprise, there was reason to fear that her mother had been too ingenious for her. On opening the door, she perceived her sister and Bingley standing together over the hearth, as if engaged in earnest conversation; and had this led to no suspicion, the faces of both as they hastily turned round, and moved away from each other, would have told it all; *Their* situation was awkward enough; but *her's* she thought was still worse. Not a syllable was uttered by either; and Elizabeth was on the point of going away again, when Bingley, who as well as the others had sat down, suddenly rose; and whispering a few words to her sister, ran out of the room.

Jane could have no reserves from Elizabeth, where confidence would give pleasure; and instantly embracing her, acknowledged, with the liveliest emotion, that she was the happiest creature in the world.

"'Tis too much!" she added, "by far too much. I do not deserve it. Oh! why is not every body as happy."

Elizabeth's congratulations were given with a sincerity, a warmth, a delight, which words could but poorly express. Every sentence of kindness was a fresh source of happiness to Jane. But she would not allow herself to stay with her sister, or say half that remained to be said, for the present.

"I must go instantly to my mother;" she cried. "I would not on any account trifle with her affectionate solicitude; or allow her to hear it from any one but myself. He is gone to my father already. Oh! Lizzy, to know that what I have to relate will give such pleasure to all my dear family! how shall I bear so much happiness!"

She then hastened away to her mother, who had purposely broken up the card party, and was sitting up stairs with Kitty.

Elizabeth, who was left by herself, now smiled at the rapidity and ease with which an affair was finally settled, that had given them so many previous months of suspense and vexation.

"And this," said she, "is the end of all his friend's anxious circumspection! of all his sister's falsehood and contrivance! the happiest, wisest, most reasonable end!"

In a few minutes she was joined by Bingley, whose conference with her father had been short and to the purpose.

"Where is your sister?" said he hastily, as he opened the door.

"With my mother up stairs. She will be down in a moment I dare say."

He then shut the door, and coming up to her, claimed the good wishes and affection of a sister. Elizabeth honestly and heartily expressed her delight in the prospect of their relationship. They shook hands with great cordiality; and then till her sister came down, she had to listen to all he had to say, of his own happiness, and of Jane's perfections; and in spite of his being a lover, Elizabeth really believed all his expectations of felicity, to be rationally founded, because they had for basis the excellent understanding, and super-excellent disposition of Jane, and a general similarity of feeling and taste between her and himself.

It was an evening of no common delight to them all; the satisfaction of Miss Bennet's mind gave a glow of such sweet animation to her face, as made her look handsomer than ever. Kitty simpered and smiled, and hoped her turn was coming soon. Mrs. Bennet could not give her consent, or speak her approbation in terms warm enough to satisfy her feelings, though she talked to Bingley of nothing else, for half an hour; and when Mr. Bennet joined them at supper, his voice and manner plainly shewed how really happy he was.

Not a word, however, passed his lips in allusion to it, till their visitor took his leave for the night; but as soon as he was gone, he turned to his daughter and said,

"Jane, I congratulate you. You will be a very happy woman."

Jane went to him instantly, kissed him, and thanked him for his goodness.

"You are a good girl;" he replied, "and I have great pleasure in thinking you will be so happily settled. I have not a doubt of your doing very well together. Your tempers are by no means unlike. You are each of you so complying, that nothing will ever be resolved on; so easy, that every servant will cheat you; and so generous, that you will always exceed your income."

"I hope not so. Imprudence or thoughtlessness in money matters, would be unpardonable in *me*."

"Exceed their income! My dear Mr. Bennet," cried his wife, "what are you talking of? Why, he has four or five thousand a-year, and very likely more." Then addressing her daughter, "Oh! my dear, dear Jane, I am so happy! I am sure I sha'nt get a wink of sleep all night. I knew how it would be. I always said it must be so, at last. I was sure you could not be so beautiful for nothing! I remember, as soon as ever I saw him, when he first came into Hertfordshire last year, I thought how likely it was that you should come together. Oh! he is the handsomest young man that ever was seen!"

Wickham, Lydia, were all forgotten. Jane was beyond competition her favourite child. At that moment, she cared for no other. Her youngest sisters soon began to make interest with her for objects of happiness which she might in future be able to dispense.

Mary petitioned for the use of the library at Netherfield; and Kitty begged very hard for a few balls there every winter.

Bingley, from this time, was of course a daily visitor at Longbourn; coming frequently before breakfast, and always remaining till after supper; unless when some barbarous neighbour, who could not be enough detested, had given him an invitation to dinner, which he thought himself obliged to accept.

Elizabeth had now but little time for conversation with her sister; for while he was present, Jane had no attention to bestow on any one else; but she found herself considerably useful to both of them, in those hours of separation that must sometimes occur. In the absence of Jane, he always attached himself to Elizabeth, for the pleasure of talking of her; and when Bingley was gone, Jane constantly sought the same means of relief.

"He has made me so happy," said she, one evening, "by telling me, that he was totally ignorant of my being in town last spring! I had not believed it possible."

"I suspected as much," replied Elizabeth. "But how did he account for it?"

"It must have been his sister's doing. They were certainly no friends to his acquaintance with me, which I cannot wonder at, since he might have chosen so much more advantageously in many respects. But when they see, as I trust they will, that their brother is happy with me, they will learn to be contented, and we shall be on good terms again; though we can never be what we once were to each other."

"That is the most unforgiving speech," said Elizabeth, "that I ever heard you utter. Good girl! It would vex me, indeed, to see you again the dupe of Miss Bingley's pretended regard."

"Would you believe it, Lizzy, that when he went to town last November he really loved me, and nothing but persuasion of *my* being indifferent, would have prevented his coming down again."

"He made a little mistake to be sure; but it is to the credit of his modesty."

This naturally introduced a panegyric from Jane on his diffidence, and the little value he put on his own good qualities.

Elizabeth was pleased to find, that he had not betrayed the interference of his friends, for, though Jane had the most generous and forgiving heart in the world, she knew it was a circumstance which must prejudice her against him.

"I am certainly the most fortunate creature that ever existed!" cried Jane. "Oh! Lizzy, why am I thus singled from my family, and blessed above them all! If I could but see *you* as happy! If there *were* but such another man for you!"

"If you were to give me forty such men, I never could be so happy as you. Till I have your disposition, your goodness, I never can have your happiness. No, no, let me shift for myself; and, perhaps, if I have very good luck, I may meet with another Mr. Collins in time."

The situation of affairs in the Longbourn family could not be long a secret. Mrs. Bennet was privileged to whisper it to Mrs.

Phillips, and *she* ventured, without any permission, to do the same by all her neighbours in Meryton.

The Bennets were speedily pronounced to be the luckiest family in the world, though only a few weeks before, when Lydia had first run away, they had been generally proved to be marked out for misfortune.

CHAPTER 14

One morning, about a week after Bingley's engagement with Jane had been formed, as he and the females of the family were sitting together in the dining room, their attention was suddenly drawn to the window, by the sound of a carriage; and they perceived a chaise and four driving up the lawn. It was too early in the morning for visitors, and besides, the equipage did not answer to that of any of their neighbours. The horses were post; and neither the carriage, nor the livery of the servant who preceded it, were familiar to them. As it was certain, however, that somebody was coming, Bingley instantly prevailed on Miss Bennet to avoid the confinement of such an intrusion, and walk away with him into the shrubbery. They both set off, and the conjectures of the remaining three continued, though with little satisfaction, till the door was thrown open, and their visitor entered. It was lady Catherine de Bourgh.

They were of course all intending to be surprised; but their astonishment was beyond their expectation; and on the part of Mrs. Bennet and Kitty, though she was perfectly unknown to them, even inferior to what Elizabeth felt.

She entered the room with an air more than usually ungracious, made no other reply to Elizabeth's salutation, than a slight inclination of the head, and sat down without saying a word. Elizabeth had mentioned her name to her mother, on her ladyship's entrance, though no request of introduction had been made.

Mrs. Bennet all amazement, though flattered by having a guest of such high importance, received her with the utmost politeness. After sitting for a moment in silence, she said very stiffly to Elizabeth,

"I hope you are well, Miss Bennet. That lady I suppose is your mother."

Elizabeth replied very concisely that she was.

"And *that* I suppose is one of your sisters."

"Yes, madam," said Mrs. Bennet, delighted to speak to a lady Catherine. She is my youngest girl but one. My youngest of all, is lately married, and my eldest is some-where about the grounds, walking with a young man, who I believe will soon become a part of the family.

"You have a very small park here," returned lady Catherine after a short silence.

"It is nothing in comparison of Rosings, my lady, I dare say; but I assure you it is much larger than Sir William Lucas's."

"This must be a most inconvenient sitting room for the evening, in summer; the windows are full west."

Mrs. Bennet assured her that they never sat there after dinner; and then added,

"May I take the liberty of asking your ladyship whether you left Mr. and Mrs. Collins well."

"Yes, very well. I saw them the night before last."

Elizabeth now expected that she would produce a letter for her from Charlotte, as it seemed the only probable motive for her calling. But no letter appeared, and she was completely puzzled.

Mrs. Bennet, with great civility, begged her ladyship to take some refreshment; but Lady Catherine very resolutely, and not very politely, declined eating any thing; and then rising up, said to Elizabeth,

"Miss Bennet, there seemed to be a prettyish kind of a little wilderness on one side of your lawn. I should be glad to take a turn in it, if you will favour me with your company."

"Go, my dear," cried her mother, "and shew her ladyship about the different walks. I think she will be pleased with the hermitage."

Elizabeth obeyed, and running into her own room for her parasol, attended her noble guest down stairs. As they passed through the hall, Lady Catherine opened the doors into the dining-parlour and drawing room, and pronouncing them, after a short survey, to be decent looking rooms, walked on.

Her carriage remained at the door, and Elizabeth saw that her waiting-woman was in it. They proceeded in silence along the gravel walk that led to the copse; Elizabeth was determined to make no effort for conversation with a woman, who was now more than usually insolent and disagreeable.

"How could I ever think her like her nephew?" said she, as she looked in her face.

As soon as they entered the copse, Lady Catherine began in the following manner:—

"You can be at no loss, Miss Bennet, to understand the reason of my journey hither. Your own heart, your own conscience, must tell you why I come."

Elizabeth looked with unaffected astonishment.

"Indeed, you are mistaken, Madam. I have not been at all able to account for the honour of seeing you here."

"Miss Bennet," replied her ladyship, in an angry tone, "you ought to know, that I am not to be trifled with. But however insincere *you* may choose to be, you shall not find *me* so. My character has ever been celebrated for its sincerity and frankness, and in a cause of such moment as this, I shall certainly not depart from it. A report of a most alarming nature, reached me two days ago. I was told, that not only your sister was on the point of being most advanta-geously married, but that *you,* that Miss Elizabeth Bennet, would, in all likelihood, be soon afterwards united to my nephew, my own nephew, Mr. Darcy. Though I *know* it must be a scandalous false-hood; though I would not injure him so much as to suppose the truth of it possible, I instantly resolved on setting off for this place, that I might make my sentiments known to you."

"If you believed it impossible to be true," said Elizabeth, colouring with astonishment and disdain, "I wonder you took the trouble of coming so far. What could your ladyship propose by it?"

"At once to insist upon having such a report universally contradicted."

"Your coming to Longbourn, to see me and my family," said Elizabeth, coolly, "will be rather a confirmation of it; if, indeed, such a report is in existence."

"If! do you then pretend to be ignorant of it? Has it not been industriously circulated by yourselves? Do you not know that such a report is spread abroad?"

"I never heard that it was."

"And can you likewise declare, that there is no *foundation* for it?"

"I do not pretend to possess equal frankness with your ladyship. *You* may ask questions, which I shall not choose to answer."

"This is not to be borne. Miss Bennet, I insist on being satisfied. Has he, has my nephew, made you an offer of marriage?"

"Your ladyship has declared it to be impossible."

"It ought to be so; it must be so, while he retains the use of his reason. But *your* arts and allurements may, in a moment of infatuation, have made him forget what he owes to himself and to all his family. You may have drawn him in."

"If I have, I shall be the last person to confess it."

"Miss Bennet, do you know who I am? I have not been accustomed to such language as this. I am almost the nearest relation he has in the world, and am entitled to know all his dearest concerns."

"But you are not entitled to know *mine;* nor will such behaviour as this, ever induce me to be explicit."

"Let me be rightly understood. This match, to which you have the presumption to aspire, can never take place. No, never. Mr. Darcy is engaged to *my daughter.* Now what have you to say?"

"Only this; that if he is so, you can have no reason to suppose he will make an offer to me."

Lady Catherine hesitated for a moment, and then replied,

"The engagement between them is of a peculiar kind. From their infancy, they have been intended for each other. It was the favourite wish of *his* mother, as well as her's. While in their cradles, we planned the union: and now, at the moment when the wishes of both sisters would be accomplished, in their marriage, to be prevented by a young woman of inferior birth, of no importance in the world, and wholly unallied to the family? Do you pay no regard to the wishes of his friends? To his tacit engagement with Miss De Bourgh? Are you lost to every feeling of propriety and delicacy? Have you not heard me say, that from his earliest hours he was destined for his cousin?"

"Yes, and I had heard it before. But what is that to me? If there is no other objection to my marrying your nephew, I shall certainly not be kept from it, by knowing that his mother and aunt wished him to marry Miss De Bourgh. You both did as much as you could, in planning the marriage. Its completion depended on others. If Mr. Darcy is neither by honour nor inclination confined to his cousin, why is not he to make another choice? And if I am that choice, why may not I accept him?"

"Because honour, decorum, prudence, nay, interest, forbid it. Yes, Miss Bennet, interest; for do not expect to be noticed by his family or friends, if you wilfully act against the inclinations of all. You will be censured, slighted, and despised, by every one connected with him. Your alliance will be a disgrace; your name will never even be mentioned by any of us."

"These are heavy misfortunes," replied Elizabeth. "But the wife of Mr. Darcy must have such extraordinary sources of happiness necessarily attached to her situation, that she could, upon the whole, have no cause to repine."

"Obstinate, headstrong girl! I am ashamed of you! Is this your gratitude for my attentions to you last spring? Is nothing due to me on that score?

"Let us sit down. You are to understand, Miss Bennet, that I came here with the determined resolution of carrying my purpose; nor will I be dissuaded from it. I have not been used to submit to any person's whims. I have not been in the habit of brooking disappointment."

"*That* will make your ladyship's situation at present more pitiable; but it will have no effect on *me*."

"I will not be interrupted. Hear me in silence. My daughter and my nephew are formed for each other. They are descended on the maternal side, from the same noble line; and, on the father's, from respectable, honourable, and ancient, though untitled families. Their fortune on both sides is splendid. They are destined for each other by the voice of every member of their respective houses; and what is to divide them? The upstart pretensions of a young woman without family, connections, or fortune. Is this to be endured! But it must not, shall not be. If you were sensible of your own good, you would not wish to quit the sphere, in which you have been brought up."

"In marrying your nephew, I should not consider myself as quitting that sphere. He is a gentleman; I am a gentleman's daughter; so far we are equal."

"True. You *are* a gentleman's daughter. But who was your mother? Who are your uncles and aunts? Do not imagine me ignorant of their condition."

"Whatever my connections may be," said Elizabeth, "if your nephew does not object to them, they can be nothing to *you*."

"Tell me once for all, are you engaged to him?"

Though Elizabeth would not, for the mere purpose of obliging Lady Catherine, have answered this question; she could not but say, after a moment's deliberation,

"I am not."

Lady Catherine seemed pleased.

"And will you promise me, never to enter into such an engagement?"

"I will make no promise of the kind."

"Miss Bennet, I am shocked and astonished. I expected to find a more reasonable young woman. But do not deceive yourself into a belief that I will ever recede. I shall not go away, till you have given me the assurance I require."

"And I certainly *never* shall give it. I am not to be intimidated into anything so wholly unreasonable. Your ladyship wants Mr. Darcy to marry your daughter; but would my giving you the wished-for promise, make *their* marriage at all more probable? Supposing him to be attached to me, would *my* refusing to accept his hand, make him wish to bestow it on his cousin? Allow me to say, Lady Catherine, that the arguments with which you have supported this extraordinary application, have been as frivolous as the application was ill-judged. You have widely mistaken my character, if you think I can be worked on by such persuasions as these. How far your nephew might approve of your interference in *his* affairs, I cannot tell; but you have certainly no right to concern yourself in mine. I must beg, therefore, to be importuned no farther on the subject."

"Not so hasty, if you please. I have by no means done. To all the objections I have already urged, I have still another to add. I am no stranger to the particulars of your youngest sister's infamous elopement. I know it all; that the young man's marrying her, was a patched-up business, at the expence of your father and uncles. And is *such* a girl to be my nephew's sister? Is *her* husband, is the son of his late father's steward, to be his brother? Heaven and earth!—of what are you thinking? Are the shades of Pemberley to be thus polluted?"

"You can *now* have nothing farther to say," she resentfully answered. "You have insulted me, in every possible method. I must beg to return to the house."

And she rose as she spoke. Lady Catherine rose also, and they turned back. Her ladyship was highly incensed.

"You have no regard, then, for the honour and credit of my nephew! Unfeeling, selfish girl! Do you not consider that a connection with you, must disgrace him in the eyes of everybody."

"Lady Catherine, I have nothing farther to say. You know my sentiments."

"You are then resolved to have him?"

"I have said no such thing. I am only resolved to act in that manner, which will, in my own opinion, constitute my happiness, without reference to *you,* or to any person so wholly unconnected with me."

"It is well. You refuse, then, to oblige me. You refuse to obey the claims of duty, honour, and gratitude. You are determined to ruin him in the opinion of all his friends, and make him the contempt of the world.

"Neither duty, nor honour, nor gratitude," replied Elizabeth, "have any possible claim on me, in the present instance. No principle of either, would be violated by my marriage with Mr. Darcy. And with regard to the resentment of his family, or the indignation of the world, if the former *were* excited by his marrying me, it would not give me one moment's concern—and the world in general would have too much sense to join in the scorn."

"And this is your real opinion! This is your final resolve! Very well. I shall now know how to act. Do not imagine, Miss Bennet, that your ambition will ever be gratified. I came to try you. I hoped to find you reasonable; but depend upon it I will carry my point."

In this manner Lady Catherine talked on, till they were at the door of the carriage, when turning hastily round, she added,

"I take no leave of you, Miss Bennet. I send no compliments to your mother. You deserve no such attention. I am most seriously displeased."

Elizabeth made no answer; and without attempting to persuade her ladyship to return into the house, walked quietly into it herself. She heard the carriage drive away as she proceeded up stairs. Her mother impatiently met her at the door of the dressing room, to ask why Lady Catherine would not come in again and rest herself.

"She did not choose it," said her daughter, "she would go."

"She is a very fine-looking woman! and her calling here was prodigiously civil! for she only came, I suppose, to tell us the Collinses were well. She is on her road somewhere, I dare say, and so passing through Meryton, thought she might as well call on you. I suppose she had nothing particular to say to you, Lizzy?"

whose behaviour at least could not be mistaken for the affectation and coquetry of an elegant female.

CHAPTER 15

The discomposure of spirits, which this extraordinary visit threw
Elizabeth into, could not be easily overcome; nor could she for
many hours, learn to think of it less than incessantly. Lady Catherine it appeared, had actually taken the trouble of this journey from
Rosings, for the sole purpose of breaking off her supposed engagement with Mr. Darcy. It was a rational scheme to be sure! but
from what the report of their engagement could originate, Elizabeth
was at a loss to imagine; till she recollected that *his* being the
intimate friend of Bingley, and *her* being the sister of Jane, was
enough, at a time when the expectation of one wedding, made
every body eager for another, to supply the idea. She had not herself forgotten to feel that the marriage of her sister must bring
them more frequently together. And her neighbours at Lucas lodge,
therefore, (for through their communication with the Collinses,
the report she concluded had reached lady Catherine) had only
set *that* down, as almost certain and immediate, which *she* had
looked forward to as possible, at some future time.

In revolving lady Catherine's expressions, however, she could
not help feeling some uneasiness as to the possible consequence
of her persisting in this interference. From what she had said of
her resolution to prevent their marriage, it occurred to Elizabeth
that she must meditate an application to her nephew; and how
he might take a similar representation of the evils attached to a
connection with her, she dared not pronounce. She knew not the
exact degree of his affection for his aunt, or his dependence on
her judgment, but it was natural to suppose that he thought much
higher of her ladyship than *she* could do; and it was certain, that
in enumerating the miseries of a marriage with *one,* whose im-

mediate connections were so unequal to his own, his aunt would address him on his weakest side. With his notions of dignity, he would probably feel that the arguments, which to Elizabeth had appeared weak and ridiculous, contained much good sense and solid reasoning.

If he had been wavering before, as to what he should do, which had often seemed likely, the advice and intreaty of so near a relation might settle every doubt, and determine him at once to be as happy, as dignity unblemished could make him. In that case he would return no more. Lady Catherine might see him in her way through town; and his engagement to Bingley of coming again to Netherfield must give way.

"If, therefore, an excuse for not keeping his promise, should come to his friend within a few days," she added, "I shall know how to understand it. I shall then give over every expectation, every wish of his constancy. If he is satisfied with only regretting me, when he might have obtained my affections and hand, I shall soon cease to regret him at all."

———

The surprise of the rest of the family, on hearing who their visitor had been, was very great; but they obligingly satisfied it, with the same kind of supposition, which had appeased Mrs. Bennet's curiosity; and Elizabeth was spared from much teazing on the subject.

The next morning, as she was going down stairs, she was met by her father, who came out of his library with a letter in his hand.

"Lizzy," said he, "I was going to look for you; come into my room."

She followed him thither; and her curiosity to know what he had to tell her, was heightened by the supposition of its being in some manner connected with the letter he held. It suddenly struck her that it might be from lady Catherine; and she anticipated with dismay all the consequent explanations.

She followed her father to the fire place, and they both sat down. He then said,

"I have received a letter this morning that has astonished me exceedingly. As it principally concerns yourself, you ought to know its contents. I did not know before, that I had *two* daughters on the brink of matrimony. Let me congratulate you, on a very important conquest."

The colour now rushed into Elizabeth's cheeks in the instantaneous conviction of its being a letter from the nephew, instead of the aunt; and she was undetermined whether most to be pleased that he explained himself at all, or offended that his letter was not rather addressed to herself; when her father continued,

"You look conscious. Young ladies have great penetration in such matters as these; but I think I may defy even *your* sagacity, to discover the name of your admirer. This letter is from Mr. Collins."

"From Mr. Collins! and what can *he* have to say?"

"Something very much to the purpose of course. He begins with congratulations on the approaching nuptials of my eldest daughter, of which it seems he has been told, by some of the good-natured, gossiping Lucases. I shall not sport with your impatience, by reading what he says on that point. What relates to yourself, is as follows. 'Having thus offered you the sincere congratulations of Mrs. Collins and myself on this happy event, let me now add a short hint on the subject of another; of which we have been advertised by the same authority. Your daughter Elizabeth, it is presumed, will not long bear the name of Bennet, after her elder sister had resigned, and the chosen partner of her fate, may be reasonably looked up to, as one of the most illustrious personages in this land.'

"Can you possibly guess, Lizzy, who is meant by this?" "This young gentleman is blessed in a peculiar way, with every thing the heart of mortal can most desire,–splendid property, noble kindred, and extensive patronage. Yet in spite of all these temptations, let me warn my cousin Elizabeth, and yourself, of what evils you may incur, by a precipitate closure with this gentleman's proposals, which, of course, you will be inclined to take immediate advantage of."

"Have you any idea, Lizzy, who this gentleman is? But now it comes out."

"My motive for cautioning you, is as follows. We have reason to imagine that his aunt, lady Catherine de Bourgh, does not look on the match with a friendly eye."

"*Mr. Darcy*, you see, is the man! Now, Lizzy, I think I *have* surprised you. Could he, or the Lucases, have pitched on any man, within the circle of our acquaintance, whose name would have given the lie more effectually to what they related? Mr. Darcy, who never looks at any woman but to see a blemish, and who probably never looked at *you* in his life! It is admirable!"

Elizabeth tried to join in her father's pleasantry, but could only force one most reluctant smile. Never had his wit been directed in a manner so little agreeable to her.

"Are you not diverted?"

"Oh! yes. Pray read on!"

"After mentioning the likelihood of this marriage to her ladyship last night, she immediately, with her usual condescension, expressed what she felt on the occasion; when it became apparent, that on the score of some family objections on the part of my cousin, she would never give her consent to what she termed so disgraceful a match. I thought it my duty to give the speediest intelligence of this to my cousin, that she and her noble admirer may be aware of what they are about, and not run hastily into a marriage which has not been properly sanctioned." "Mr. Collins moreover adds," "I am truly rejoiced that my cousin Lydia's sad business has been so well hushed up, and am only concerned that their living together before the marriage took place, should be so generally known. I must not, however, neglect the duties of my station, or refrain from declaring my amazement, at hearing that you received the young couple into your house as soon as they were married. It was an encouragement of vice; and had I been the rector of Longbourn, I should very strenuously have opposed it. You ought certainly to forgive them as a christian, but never to admit them in your sight, or allow their names to be mentioned in your hearing." "*That* is his notion of christian forgiveness! The rest of his letter is only about his dear Charlotte's situation, and his expectation of a young olive branch. But, Lizzy, you look as if you did not enjoy it. You are not going to be *Missish,* I hope, and pretend to be affronted at an idle report. For what do we live, but to make sport for our neighbours, and laugh at them in our turn?"

"Oh!" cried Elizabeth, "I am excessively diverted. But it is so strange!"

"Yes – *that* is what makes it amusing. Had they fixed on any other man it would have been nothing; but *his* perfect indifference, and *your* pointed dislike, make it so delightfully absurd! Much as I abominate writing, I would not give up Mr. Collins's correspondence for any consideration. Nay, when I read a letter of his, I cannot help giving him the preference even over Wickham, much as I value the impudence and hypocrisy of my son-in-law. And pray, Lizzy, what said Lady Catherine about this report? Did she call to refuse her consent?"

To this question his daughter replied only with a laugh; and as it had been asked without the least suspicion, she was not distressed by his repeating it. Elizabeth had never been more at a loss to make her feelings appear what they were not. It was necessary to laugh, when she would rather have cried. Her father had most cruelly mortified her, by what he said of Mr. Darcy's indifference, and she could do nothing but wonder at such a want of penetration, or fear that perhaps, instead of his seeing too *little,* she might have fancied too *much.*

CHAPTER 16

Instead of receiving any such letter of excuse from his friend, as Elizabeth half expected Mr. Bingley to do, he was able to bring Darcy with him to Longbourn before many days had passed after

Lady Catherine's visit. The gentlemen arrived early; and, before Mrs. Bennet had time to tell him of their having seen his aunt, of which her daughter sat in momentary dread, Bingley, who wanted to be alone with Jane, proposed their all walking out. It was agreed to. Mrs. Bennet was not in the habit of walking, Mary could never spare time, but the remaining five set off together. Bingley and Jane, however, soon allowed the others to outstrip them. They lagged behind, while Elizabeth, Kitty, and Darcy, were to entertain each other. Very little was said by either; Kitty was too much afraid of him to talk; Elizabeth was secretly forming a desperate resolution; and perhaps he might be doing the same.

They walked towards the Lucases, because Kitty wished to call upon Maria; and as Elizabeth saw no occasion for making it a general concern, when Kitty left them, she went boldly on with him alone. Now was the moment for her resolution to be executed, and, while her courage was high, she immediately said,

"Mr. Darcy, I am a very selfish creature; and, for the sake of giving relief to my own feelings, care not how much I may be wounding your's. I can no longer help thanking you for your unexampled kindness to my poor sister. Ever since I have known it, I have been most anxious to acknowledge to you how gratefully I feel it. Were it known to the rest of my family, I should not have merely my own gratitude to express."

"I am sorry, exceedingly sorry," replied Darcy, in a tone of surprise and emotion, "that you have ever been informed of what may, in a mistaken light, have given you uneasiness. I did not think Mrs. Gardiner was so little to be trusted."

"You must not blame my aunt. Lydia's thoughtlessness first betrayed to me that you had been concerned in the matter; and, of course, I could not rest till I knew the particulars. Let me thank you again and again, in the name of all my family, for that generous compassion which induced you to take so much trouble, and bear so many mortifications, for the sake of discovering them."

"If you *will* thank me," he replied, "let it be for yourself alone. That the wish of giving happiness to you, might add force to the other inducements which led me on, I shall not attempt to deny. But your *family* owe me nothing. Much as I respect them, I believe, I thought only of *you*."

Elizabeth was too much embarrassed to say a word. After a short pause, her companion added, "You are too generous to trifle with me. If your feelings are still what they were last April, tell me so at once. My affections and wishes are unchanged, but one word from you will silence me on this subject for ever."

Elizabeth feeling all the more than common awkwardness and anxiety of his situation, now forced herself to speak; and immediately, though not very fluently, gave him to understand, that her sentiments had undergone so material a change, since the period to which he alluded, as to make her receive with gratitude and pleasure, his present assurances. The happiness which this reply produced, was such as he had probably never felt before; and he expressed himself on the occasion as sensibly and as warmly as a man violently in love can be supposed to do. Had Elizabeth been able to encounter his eye, she might have seen how well the expression of heartfelt delight, diffused over his face, became him; but, though she could not look, she could listen, and he told her of feelings, which, in proving of what importance she was to him, made his affection every moment more valuable.

They walked on, without knowing in what direction. There was too much to be thought and felt, and said, for attention to any other objects. She soon learnt that they were indebted for their present good understanding to the efforts of his aunt, who *did* call on him in her return through London, and there relate her journey to Longbourn, its motive, and the substance of her conversation with Elizabeth; dwelling emphatically on every expression of the latter, which, in her ladyship's apprehension, peculiarly denoted her perverseness and assurance, in the belief that such a relation must assist her endeavours to obtain that promise from her nephew, which *she* had refused to give. But, unluckily for her ladyship, its effect had been exactly contrariwise.

"It taught me to hope," said he, "as I had scarcely ever allowed myself to hope before. I knew enough of your disposition to be certain, that, had you been absolutely, irrevocably decided against me, you would have acknowledged it to Lady Catherine, frankly and openly."

Elizabeth coloured and laughed as she replied, "Yes, you know enough of my *frankness* to believe me capable of *that*. After abusing you so abominably to your face, I could have no scruple in abusing you to all your relations."

"What did you say of me, that I did not deserve? For, though your accusations were ill-founded, formed on mistaken premises, my behaviour to you at the time, had merited the severest reproof. It was unpardonable. I cannot think of it without abhorrence."

"We will not quarrel for the greater share of blame annexed to that evening." said Elizabeth. "The conduct of neither, if strictly examined, will be irreproachable; but since then, we have both, I hope, improved in civility."

"I cannot be so easily reconciled to myself. The recollection of what I then said, of my conduct, my manners, my expressions during the whole of it, is now, and has been many months, inexpressibly painful to me. Your reproof, so well applied, I shall never forget: 'had you behaved in a more gentlemanlike manner.' Those were your words. You know not, you can scarcely conceive, how they have tortured me; – though it was some time, I confess, before I was reasonable enough to allow their justice.

"I was certainly very far from expecting them to make so strong an impression. I had not the smallest idea of their being ever felt in such a way."

"I can easily believe it. You thought me then devoid of every proper feeling, I am sure you did. The turn of your countenance I shall never forget, as you said that I could not have addressed you in any possible way, that would induce you to accept me."

"Oh! do not repeat what I then said. These recollections will not do at all. I assure you, that I have long been most heartily ashamed of it."

Darcy mentioned his letter. "Did it," said he, "did it *soon* make

you think better of me? Did you, on reading it, give any credit
to its contents?"

She explained what its effect on her had been, and how gradually all her former prejudices had been removed.

"I knew," said he, "that what I wrote must give you pain, but
it was necessary. I hope you have destroyed the letter. There was
one part especially, the opening of it, which I should dread your
having the power of reading again. I can remember some expressions which might justly make you hate me."

"The letter shall certainly be burnt, if you believe it essential
to the preservation of my regard; but, though we have both reason to think my opinions not entirely unalterable, they are not,
I hope, quite so easily changed as that implies."

"When I wrote that letter," replied Darcy, "I believed myself
perfectly calm and cool, but I am since convinced that it was written in a dreadful bitterness of spirit."

"The letter, perhaps, began in bitterness, but it did not end
so. The adieu is charity itself. But think no more of the letter. The
feelings of the person who wrote, and the person who received
it, are now so widely different from what they were then, that
every unpleasant circumstance attending it, ought to be forgotten. You must learn some of my philosophy. Think only of the
past as its remembrances gives you pleasure."

"I cannot give you credit for any philosophy of the kind. *Your*
retrospection must be so totally void of reproach, that the contentment arising from them, is not of philosophy, but what is much
better, of ignorance. But with *me,* it is not so. Painful recollections will intrude, which cannot, which ought not to be repelled.
I have been a selfish being all my life, in practice, though not
in principle. As a child I was taught what was *right,* but I was
not taught to correct my temper. I was given good principles, but
left to follow them in pride and conceit. Unfortunately an only
son, (for many years an only *child*) I was spoilt by my parents,
who though good themselves, (my father particularly, all that was
benevolent and amiable,) allowed, encouraged, almost taught me

to be selfish and overbearing, to care for none beyond my own family circle, to think meanly of all the rest of the world, to *wish* at least to think meanly of their sense and worth compared with my own. Such I was, from eight to eight and twenty; and such I might still have been but for you, dearest, loveliest Elizabeth! What do I not owe you! You taught me a lesson, hard indeed at first, but most advantageous. By you, I was properly humbled. I came to you without a doubt of my reception. You shewed me how insufficient were all my pretensions to please a woman worthy of being pleased."

"Had you then persuaded yourself that I should?"

"Indeed I had. What will you think of my vanity? I believed you to be wishing, expecting my addresses."

"My manners must have been in fault, but not intentionally I assure you. I never meant to deceive you, but my spirits might often lead me wrong. How you must have hated me after *that* evening?"

"Hate you! I was angry perhaps at first, but my anger soon began to take a proper direction."

"I am almost afraid of asking what you thought of me; when we met at Pemberley. You blamed me for coming?"

"No indeed; I felt nothing but surprise."

"Your surprise could not be greater than *mine* in being noticed by you. My conscience told me that I deserved no extraordinary politeness, and I confess that I did not expect to receive *more* than my due."

"My object *then*," replied Darcy, "was to shew you, by every civility in my power, that I was not so mean as to resent the past; and I hoped to obtain your forgiveness, to lessen your ill opinion, by letting you see that your reproofs had been attended to. How soon any other wishes introduced themselves I can hardly tell, but I believe in about half an hour after I had seen you."

He then told her of Georgiana's delight in her acquaintance, and of her disappointment at its sudden interruption; which naturally leading to the cause of that interruption, she soon learnt that his resolution of following her from Derbyshire in quest of her sister, had been formed before he quitted the inn, and that his gravity and thoughtfulness there, had arisen from no other struggles that what such a purpose must comprehend.

She expressed her gratitude again, but it was too painful a subject to each, to be dwelt on farther.

After walking several miles in a leisurely manner, and too busy to know any thing about it, they found at last, on examining their watches, that it was time to be at home.

"What could become of Mr. Bingley and Jane!" was a wonder which introduced the discussion of *their* affairs. Darcy was delighted with their engagement; his friend had given the earliest information of it.

"I must ask whether you were surprised?" said Elizabeth.

"Not at all. When I went away, I felt that it would soon happen."

"That is to say, you had given your permission. I guessed as much." And though he exclaimed at the term, she found that it had been pretty much the case.

"On the evening before my going to London," said he, "I made a confession to him, which I believe I ought to have made long ago. I told him of all that had occurred to make my former interference in his affairs, absurd and impertinent. His surprise was great. He had never had the slightest suspicion. I told him, moreover, that I believed myself mistaken in supposing, as I had done, that your sister was indifferent to him; and as I could easily perceive that his attachment to her was unabated, I felt no doubt of their happiness together."

Elizabeth could not help smiling at his easy manner of directing his friend.

"Did you speak from your own observation," said she, "when you told him that my sister loved him, or merely from my information last spring?"

"From the former. I had narrowly observed her during the two visits which I had lately made her here; and I was convinced of her affection."

"And your assurance of it, I suppose, carried immediate conviction to him."

"It did. Bingley is most unaffectedly modest. His diffidence had prevented his depending on his own judgment in so anxious a case, but his reliance in mine, made every thing easy. I was obliged to confess one thing, which for a time, and not unjustly, offended him. I could not allow myself to conceal that your sister had been in town three months last winter, that I had known it, and purposely kept it from him. He was angry. But his anger, I am persuaded, lasted no longer than he remained in any doubt of your sister's sentiments. He has heartily forgiven me now."

Elizabeth longed to observe that Mr. Bingley had been a most delightful friend; so easily guided that his worth was invaluable; but she checked herself. She remembered that he had yet to learn to be laught at, and it was rather too early to begin. In anticipating the happiness of Bingley, which of course was to be inferior only to his own, he continued the conversation till they reached the house. In the hall they parted.

CHAPTER 17

"My dear Lizzy, where can you have been walking to?" was a question which Elizabeth received from Jane as soon as she entered the room, and from all the others when they sat down to table. She had only to say in reply, that they had wandered about, till she was beyond her own knowledge. She coloured as she spoke; but neither that, nor any thing else, awakened a suspicion of the truth.

The evening passed quietly, unmarked by any thing extraordinary. The acknowledged lovers talked and laughed, the unacknowledged were silent. Darcy was not of a disposition in which happiness overflows in mirth; and Elizabeth, agitated and confused, rather *knew* that she was happy, then *felt* herself to be so; for, besides the immediate embarrassment, there were other evils before her. She anticipated what would be felt in the family when her situation become known; she was aware that no one liked him but Jane; and even feared that with the others it was a *dislike* which not all his fortune and consequence might do away.

At night she opened her heart to Jane. Though suspicion was very far from Miss Bennet's general habits, she was absolutely incredulous here.

"You are joking, Lizzy. This cannot be!—engaged to Mr. Darcy! No, no, you shall not deceive me. I know it to be impossible."

"This is a wretched beginning indeed! My sole dependence was on you; and I am sure nobody else will believe me, if you do not. Yet, indeed, I am in earnest. I speak nothing but the truth. He still loves me, and we are engaged."

Jane looked at her doubtingly. "Oh, Lizzy! it cannot be. I know how much you dislike him."

"You know nothing of the matter. *That* is all to be forgot. Perhaps I did not always love him so well as I do now. But in some cases as these, a good memory in unpardonable. This is the last time I shall ever remember it myself."

Miss Bennet still looked all amazement. Elizabeth again, and more seriously assured her of its truth.

Good Heaven! can it be really so! Yet now I must believe you," cried Jane. "My dear, dear Lizzy, I would—I do congratulate you—but are you certain? forgive the question—but are you quite certain that you can be happy with him?"

"There can be no doubt of that. It is settled between us already, that we are to be the happiest couple in the world. But are you pleased, Jane? Shall you like to have such a brother?"

"Very, very much. Nothing could give either Bingley or myself more delight. But we considered it, we talked of it as impossible. And do you really love him quite well enough? Oh, Lizzy! do any thing rather than marry without affection. Are you quite sure that you feel what you ought to do?"

"Oh, yes! You will only think I feel *more* than I ought to do, when I tell you all."

"What do you mean?"

"Why, I must confess, that I love him better than I do Bingley. I am afraid you will be angry."

"My dearest sister, now *be* serious. I want to talk very seriously. Let me know every thing that I am to know, without delay. Will you tell me how long you have loved him?"

"It has been coming on so gradually, that I hardly know when it began. But I believe I must date it from my first seeing his beautiful grounds at Pemberley."

Another intreaty that she would be serious, however, produced the desired effect; and she soon satisfied Jane by her solemn assurances of attachment. When convinced on that article, Miss Bennet had nothing farther to wish.

"Now I am quite happy," said she, "for you will be as happy as myself. I always had a value for him. Were it for nothing but his love of you, I must always have esteemed him; but now, as Bingley's friend and your husband, there can be only Bingley and yourself more dear to me. But Lizzy, you have been very sly, very reserved with me. How little did you tell me of what passed at Pemberley and Lambton! I owe all that I know of it, to another, not to you."

Elizabeth told her the motives of her secrecy. She had been unwilling to mention Bingley; and the unsettled state of her own feelings had made her equally avoid the name of his friend. But now she would no longer conceal from her, his share in Lydia's marriage. All was acknowledged, and half the night spent in conversation.

———

"Good gracious!" cried Mrs. Bennet, as she stood at a window the next morning, "if that disagreeable Mr. Darcy is not coming here again with our dear Bingley! What can he mean by being so tiresome as to be always coming here? I had no notion but he would go a shooting, or something or other, and not disturb us with his company. What shall we do with him? Lizzy, you must walk out with him again, that he may not be in Bingley's way."

Elizabeth could hardly help laughing at so convenient a proposal; yet was really vexed that her mother should be always giving him such an epithet.

As soon as they entered, Bingley looked at her so expressively, and shook hands with such warmth, as left no doubt of his good information; and he soon afterwards said aloud, "Mr. Bennet, have you no more lanes hereabouts in which Lizzy may lose her way again to-day."

"I advise Mr. Darcy, and Lizzy, and Kitty," said Mrs. Bennet, "to walk to Oakham Mount this morning. It is a nice long walk, and Mr. Darcy has never seen the view."

"It may do very well for the others," replied Mr. Bingley; "but I am sure it will be too much for Kitty. Wont it, Kitty?"

Kitty owned that she had rather stay at home. Darcy professed a great curiosity to see the view from the Mount, and Elizabeth silently consented. As she went up stairs to get ready, Mrs. Bennet followed her, saying,

"I am quite sorry, Lizzy, that you should be forced to have that disagreeable man all to yourself. But I hope you will not mind it: it is all for Jane's sake, you know; and there is no occasion for talking to him, except just now and then. So, do not put yourself to inconvenience."

During their walk, it was resolved that Mr. Bennet's consent should be asked in the course of the evening. Elizabeth reserved to herself the application for her mother's. She could not determine how her mother would take it; sometimes doubting whether all his wealth and grandeur would be enough to overcome her abhorrence of the man. But whether she were violently set against the match, or violently delighted with it, it was certain that her manner would be equally ill adapted to do credit to her sense; and she could no more bear that Mr. Darcy should hear the first raptures of her joy, than the first vehemence of her disapprobation.

In the evening, soon after Mr. Bennet withdrew to the library, she saw Mr. Darcy rise also and follow him, and her agitation on seeing it was extreme. She did not fear her father's opposition, but he was going to be made unhappy, and that it should be through her means, that *she,* his favourite child, should be distressing him by her choice, should be filling him with fears and regrets in disposing of her, was a wretched reflection, and she sat in misery till Mr. Darcy appeared again, when, looking at him, she was a little relieved by his smile. In a few minutes he approached the table where she was sitting with Kitty; and, while pretending to admire her work, said in a whisper, "Go to your father, he wants you in the library." She was gone directly.

Her father was walking about the room, looking grave and anxious. "Lizzy," said he, "what are you doing? Are you out of your senses, to be accepting this man? Have not you always hated him?"

How earnestly did she then wish that her former opinions had been more reasonable, her expressions more moderate! It would have spared her from explanations and professions which it was exceedingly awkward to give; but they were now necessary, and she assured him with some confusion, of her attachment to Mr. Darcy.

"Or in other words, you are determined to have him. He is rich, to be sure, and you may have more fine clothes and fine carriages than Jane. But will they make you happy?"

"Have you any other objection," said Elizabeth, "than your belief of my indifference?"

"None at all. We all know him to be a proud, unpleasant sort of man; but this would be nothing if you really liked him."

"I do, I do like him," she replied, with tears in her eyes, "I love him. Indeed he has no improper pride. He is perfectly amiable. You do not know what he really is; then pray do not pain me by speaking of him in such terms."

"Lizzy," said her father, "I have given him my consent. He is the kind of man, indeed, to whom I should never dare refuse any thing, which he condescended to ask. I now give it to *you,* if you are resolved on having him. But let me advise you to think better of it. I know your disposition, Lizzy. I know that you could be neither happy nor respectable, unless you truly esteemed your husband; unless you looked up to him as a superior. Your lively talents would place you in the greatest danger in an unequal marriage. You could scarcely escape discredit and misery. My child, let me not have the grief of seeing *you* unable to respect your partner in life. You know not what you are about."

"Elizabeth, still more affected, was earnest and solemn in her reply; and at length by repeated assurances that Mr. Darcy was really the object of her choice, by explaining the gradual change which her estimation of him had undergone, relating her absolute certainty that his affection was not the work of a day, but had stood the test of many months suspense, and enumerating with energy all his good qualities, she did conquer her father's incredulity, and reconcile him to the match.

"Well, my dear," said he, when she ceased speaking, "I have no more to say. If this be the case, he deserves you. I could not have parted with you, my Lizzy, to any one less worthy."

To complete the favourable impression, she then told him what Mr. Darcy had voluntarily done for Lydia. He heard her with astonishment.

"This is an evening of wonders, indeed! And so, Darcy did every thing; made up the match, gave the money, paid the fellow's debts, and got him his commission! So much the better. It will save me a world of trouble and economy. Had it been your uncle's doing, I must and *would* have paid him; but these violent young lovers carry every thing their own way. I shall offer to pay him to-morrow; he will rant and storm about his love for you, and there will be an end of the matter."

He then recollected her embarrassment a few days before, on his reading Mr. Collins's letter; and after laughing at her some time, allowed her at last to go—saying, as she quitted the room, "If any young men come for Mary or Kitty, send them in, for I am quite at leisure."

Elizabeth's mind was now relieved from a very heavy weight; and, after half an hour's quiet reflection in her own room, she was able to join the others with tolerable composure. Every thing was too recent for gaiety, but the evening passed tranquilly away; there was no longer any thing material to be dreaded, and the comfort of ease and familiarity would come in time.

When her mother went up to her dressing-room at night, she followed her, and made the important communication. Its effect was most extraordinary; for on first hearing it, Mrs. Bennet sat quite still, and unable to utter a syllable. Nor was it under many, many minutes, that she could comprehend what she heard; though not in general backward to credit what was for the advantage of her family, or that came in the shape of a lover to any of them. She began at length to recover, to fidget about in her chair, get up, sit down again, wonder, and bless herself.

"Good gracious! Lord bless me! only think! dear me! Mr. Darcy! Who would have thought it! And is it really true? Oh! my sweetest Lizzy! how rich and how great you will be! What pin-money, what jewels, what carriages you will have! Jane's is nothing to it—nothing at all. I am so pleased—so happy. Such a charming man!—so handsome! so tall!—Oh, my dear Lizzy! pray apologise for my having disliked him so much before. I hope he will overlook it. Dear, dear Lizzy. A house in town! Every thing that is charming! Three daughters married! Ten thousand a year! Oh, Lord! What will become of me. I shall go distracted."

This was enough to prove that her approbation need not be doubted: and Elizabeth, rejoicing that such an effusion was heard only by herself, soon went away. But before she had been three minutes in her own room, her mother followed her.

"My dearest child," she cried, "I can think of nothing else! Ten thousand a year, and very likely more! 'Tis as good as a Lord! And a special licence. You must and shall be married by a special licence. But my dearest love, tell me what dish Mr. Darcy is particularly fond of, that I may have it tomorrow."

This was a sad omen of what her mother's behaviour to the gentleman himself might be; and Elizabeth found, that though in the certain possession of his warmest affection, and secure of her relations' consent, there was still something to be wished for. But the morrow passed off much better than she expected; for Mrs. Bennet luckily stood in such awe of her intended son-in-law, that she ventured not to speak to him, unless it was in her power to offer him any attention, or mark her deference for his opinion.

Elizabeth had the satisfaction of seeing her father taking pains to get acquainted with him; and Mr. Bennet soon assured her that he was rising every hour in his esteem.

"I admire all my three sons-in-law highly," said he. "Wickham, perhaps, is my favourite; but I think I shall like *your* husband quite as well as Jane's."

CHAPTER 18

Elizabeth's spirits soon rising to playfulness again, she wanted Mr. Darcy to account for his having ever fallen in love with her. "How could you begin?" said she. "I can comprehend your going on charmingly, when you had once made a beginning; but what could set you off in the first place?"

"I cannot fix on the hour, or the spot, or the look, or the words, which laid the foundation. It is too long ago. I was in the middle before I knew that I *had* begun."

"My beauty you had early withstood, and as for my manners— my behaviour to *you* was at least always bordering on the uncivil, and I never spoke to you without rather wishing to give you pain than not. Now be sincere; did you admire me for my impertinence?"

"For the liveliness of your mind, I did."

"You may as well call it impertinence at once. It was very little less. The fact is, that you were sick of civility, of deference, of officious attention. You were disgusted with the women who were always speaking and looking, and think for *your* approbation alone. I roused, and interested you, because I was so unlike *them*. Had you not been really amiable you would have hated me for it; but in spite of the pains you took to disguise yourself, your feelings were noble and just; and in your heart, you thoroughly despised the persons who so assiduously courted you. There—I have saved you the trouble of accounting for it; and really, all things considered, I begin to think it perfectly reasonable. To be sure, you know no actual good of me—but nobody thinks of *that* when they fall in love."

"Was there no good in your affectionate behaviour to Jane, while she was ill at Netherfield?"

"Dearest Jane! who could have done less for her? But make a virtue of it by all means. My good qualities are under your protection, and you are to exaggerate them as much as possible; and, in return, it belongs to me to find occasions for teazing and quarrelling with you as often as may be; and I shall begin directly by asking you what made you so unwilling to come to the point at last. What made you so shy of me, when you first called, and afterwards dined here? Why, especially, when you called, did you look as if you did not care about me?"

"Because you were grave and silent, and gave me no encouragement."

"But I was embarrassed."

"And so was I."

"You might have talked to me more when you came to dinner."

"A man who had felt less, might."

"How unlucky that you should have a reasonable answer to give, and that I should be so reasonable as to admit it! But I wonder how long you *would* have gone on, if you had been left to yourself. I wonder when you *would* have spoken, if I had not asked you! My resolution of thanking you for your kindness to Lydia had certainly great effect. *Too much,* I am afraid; for what becomes of the moral, if our comfort springs from a breach of promise, for I ought not to have mentioned the subject? This will never do."

"You need not distress yourself. The moral will be perfectly fair. Lady Catherine's unjustifiable endeavours to separate us, were the means of removing all my doubts. I am not indebted for my

present happiness to your eager desire of expressing your gratitude. I was not in a humour to wait for any opening of your's.
My aunt's intelligence had given me hope, and I was determined
at once to know every thing."

"Lady Catherine has been of infinite use, which ought to make
her happy, for she loves to be of use. But tell me, what did you
come down to Netherfield for? Was it merely to ride to Longbourn and be embarrassed? or had you intended any more serious consequence?"

"My real purpose was to see *you,* and to judge, if I could,
whether I might ever hope to make you love me. My avowed one,
or what I avowed to myself, was to see whether your sister were
still partial to Bingley, and if she were, to make the confession
to him which I have since made."

"Shall you ever have courage to announce to Lady Catherine,
what is to befall her?

"I am more likely to want time than courage, Elizabeth. But
it ought to be done, and if you will give me a sheet of paper, it
shall be done directly."

"And if I had not a letter to write myself, I might sit by you, and
admire the evenness of your writing, as another young lady once
did. But I have an aunt, too, who must not be longer neglected."

From an unwillingness to confess how much her intimacy with
Mr. Darcy had been over-rated, Elizabeth had never yet answered
Mrs. Gardiner's long letter, but now, having *that* to communicate
which she knew would be most welcome, she was almost ashamed
to find, that her uncle and aunt had already lost three days of
happiness, and immediately wrote as follows:

"I would have thanked you before, my dear aunt, as I ought
to have done, for your long, kind, satisfactory, detail of particulars; but to say the truth, I was too cross to write. You supposed
more than really existed. But *now* suppose as much as you chuse;
give a loose to your fancy, indulge your imagination in every possible flight which the subject will afford, and unless you believe
me actually married, you cannot greatly err. You must write again

very soon, and praise him a great deal more than you did in your last. I thank you, again and again, for not going to the Lakes. How could I be so silly as to wish it! Your idea of the ponies is delightful. We will go round the Park every day. I am the happiest creature in the world. Perhaps other people have said so before, but not one with such justice. I am happier even than Jane; she only smiles, I laugh. Mr. Darcy sends you all the love in the world, that he can spare from me. You are all to come to Pemberley at Christmas. Your's, &c."

Mr. Darcy's letter to Lady Catherine, was in a different style; and still different from either, was what Mr. Bennet sent to Mr. Collins, in reply to his last.

> Dear Sir,
>
> I must trouble you once more for congratulations. Elizabeth will soon be the wife of Mr. Darcy. Console Lady Catherine as well as you can. But, if I were you, I would stand by the nephew. He has more to give.
>
> Your's sincerely, &c.

Miss Bingley's congratulations to her brother, on his approaching marriage, were all that was affectionate and insincere. She wrote even to Jane on the occasion, to express her delight, and repeat all her former professions of regard. Jane was not deceived, but she was affected; and though feeling no reliance on her, could not help writing her a much kinder answer than she knew was deserved.

The joy which Miss Darcy expressed on receiving similar information, was as sincere as her brother's in sending it. Four sides of paper were insufficient to contain all her delight, and all her earnest desire of being loved by her sister.

Before any answer could arrive from Mr. Collins, or any congratulations to Elizabeth, from his wife, the Longbourn family heard that the Collinses were come themselves to Lucas lodge. The reason of this sudden removal was soon evident. Lady Catherine had been rendered so exceedingly angry by the contents of her nephew's letter, that Charlotte, really rejoicing in the match, was anxious to get away till the storm was blown over. At such a moment, the arrival of her friend was a sincere pleasure to Elizabeth, though in the course of their meetings she must sometimes think the pleasure dearly bought, when she saw Mr. Darcy exposed to all the parading and obsequious civility of her husband. He bore it however with admirable calmness. He could even listen to Sir William Lucas, when he complimented him on carrying away the brightest jewel of the country, and expressed his hopes of their all meeting frequently at St. James's, with very decent composure. If he did shrug his shoulders, it was not till Sir William was out of sight.

Mrs. Philips's vulgarity was another, and perhaps a greater tax on his forbearance; and though Mrs. Philips, as well her sister, stood in too much awe of him to speak with the familiarity which Bingley's good humour encouraged, yet, whenever she *did* speak, she must be vulgar. Nor was her respect for him, though it made her more quiet, at all likely to make her more elegant. Elizabeth did all she could, to shield him from the frequent notice of either, and was ever anxious to keep him to herself, and to those of her family with whom he might converse without mortification; and though the uncomfortable feelings arising from all this took from the season of courtship much of its pleasure, it added to the hope of the future; and she looked forward with delight to the time when they should be removed from society so little pleasing to either, to all the comfort and elegance of their family party at Pemberley.

CHAPTER 19

Happy for all her maternal feelings was the day on which Mrs. Bennet got rid of her two most deserving daughters. With what delighted pride she afterwards visited Mrs. Bingley and talked of Mrs. Darcy may be guessed. I wish I could say, for the sake of her family, that the accomplishment of her earnest desire in the establishment of

so many of her children, produced so happy an effect as to make
her a sensible, amiable, well-informed woman for the rest of her
life; though perhaps it was lucky for her husband, who might not
have relished domestic felicity in so unusual a form, that she still
was occasionally nervous and invariably silly.

Mr. Bennet missed his second daughter exceedingly; his affection for her drew him oftener from home than any thing else could
do. He delighted in going to Pemberley, especially when he was
least expected.

Mr. Bingley and Jane remained at Netherfield only a twelve-
month. So near a vicinity to her mother and Meryton relations
was not desirable even to *his* easy temper, or *her* affectionate heart.
The darling wish of his sisters was then gratified; he bought an
estate in a neighbouring county to Derbyshire, and Jane and
Elizabeth, in addition to every other source of happiness, were
within thirty miles of each other.

Kitty, to her very material advantage, spent the chief of her
time with her two elder sisters. In society so superior to what
she had generally known, her improvement was great. She was
not of so ungovernable a temper as Lydia, and, removed from the
influence of Lydia's example, she became, by proper attention and
management, less irritable, less ignorant, and less insipid. From
the farther disadvantage of Lydia's society she was of course carefully kept, and though Mrs. Wickham frequently invited her to
come and stay with her, with the promise of balls and young men,
her father would never consent to her going.

Mary was the only daughter who remained at home; and she
was necessarily drawn from the pursuit of accomplishments by
Mrs. Bennet's being quite unable to sit alone. Mary was obliged
to mix more with the world, but she could still moralize over every
morning visit; and as she was no longer mortified by compari-
sons between her sisters' beauty and her own, it was suspected
by her father that she submitted to the change without much
reluctance.

As for Wickham and Lydia, their characters suffered no revolution from the marriage of her sisters. He bore with philosophy the conviction that Elizabeth must now become acquainted with whatever of his ingratitude and falsehood had before been unknown to her; and in spite of every thing, was not wholly without hope that Darcy might yet be prevailed on to make his fortune. The congratulatory letter which Elizabeth received from Lydia on her marriage, explained to her that, by his wife at least, if not by himself, such a hope was cherished. The letter was to this effect:

My dear Lizzy,

I wish you joy. If you love Mr. Darcy half as well as I do my dear Wickham, you must be very happy. It is a great comfort to have you so rich, and when you have nothing else to do, I hope you will think of us. I am sure Wickham would like a place at court very much, and I do not think we shall have quite money enough to live upon without some help. Any place would do, of about three or four hundred a year; but, however, do not speak to Mr. Darcy about it, if you had rather not.

Your's, &c.

As it happened that Elizabeth had *much* rather not; she endeavoured in her answer to put an end to every intreaty and expectation of the kind. Such relief, however, as it was in her power to afford, by the practice of what might be called economy in her own private expences, she frequently sent them. It had always been evident to her that such an income as theirs, under the direction of two persons so extravagant in their wants, and heedless of the future, must be very insufficient to their support; and whenever they changed their quarters, either Jane or herself were sure of being applied to, for some little assistance towards discharging their bills. Their manner of living, even when the restoration of peace dismissed them to a home, was unsettled in the extreme. They were always moving from place to place in quest of a cheap situation, and always spending more than they ought. His affection for her soon sunk into indifference; her's lasted a little longer; and in spite of her youth and her manners, she retained all the claims to reputation which her marriage had given her.

Though Darcy could never receive *him* at Pemberley, yet, for Elizabeth's sake, he assisted him farther in his profession. Lydia was occasionally a visitor there, when her husband was gone to enjoy himself in London or Bath; and with the Bingleys they both of them frequently staid so long, that even Bingley's good humour was overcome, and he proceeded so far as to *talk* of giving them a hint to be gone.

Miss Bingley was very deeply mortified by Darcy's marriage; but as she thought it advisable to retain the right of visiting at Pemberley, she dropt all her resentment; was fonder than ever of Georgiana, almost as attentive to Darcy as heretofore, and paid off every arrear of civility to Elizabeth.

Pemberley was now Georgiana's home; and the attachment of the sisters was exactly what Darcy had hoped to see. They were able to love each other, even as well as they intended. Georgiana had the highest opinion in the world of Elizabeth; though at first she often listened with an astonishment bordering on alarm, at her lively, sportive, manner of talking to her brother. He, who had always inspired in herself a respect which almost overcame her affection, she now saw the object of open pleasantry. Her mind received knowledge which had never before fallen in her way. By Elizabeth's instructions she began to comprehend that a woman may take liberties with her husband, which a brother will not always allow in a sister more than ten years younger than himself.

Lady Catherine was extremely indignant on the marriage of her nephew; and as she gave way to all the genuine frankness of her character, in her reply to the letter which announced its arrangement, she sent him language so very abusive, especially of Elizabeth, that for some time all intercourse was at an end. But at length, by Elizabeth's persuasion, he was prevailed on to overlook the offence, and seek a reconciliation; and, after a little farther resistance on the part of his aunt, her resentment gave way, either to her affection for him, or her curiosity to see how his wife conducted herself; and she condescended to wait on them at Pemberley, in spite of that pollution which its woods had received, not merely from the presence of such a mistress, but the visits of her uncle and aunt from the city.

With the Gardiners, they were always on the most intimate terms. Darcy, as well as Elizabeth, really loved them; and they were both ever sensible of the warmest gratitude towards the persons who, by bringing her into Derbyshire, had been the means of uniting them.

Jane Eyre

by
Charlotte Brontë

·······

Chapter 1

There was no possibility of taking a walk that day. We had been wandering, indeed, in the leafless shrubbery an hour in the morning; but since dinner (Mrs. Reed, when there was no company, dined early) the cold winter wind had brought with it clouds so sombre, and a rain so penetrating, that further outdoor exercise was now out of the question.

I was glad of it; I never liked long walks, especially on chilly afternoons: dreadful to me was the coming home in the raw twilight, with nipped fingers and toes, and a heart saddened by the chidings of Bessie, the nurse, and humbled by the consciousness of my physical inferiority to Eliza, John, and Georgiana Reed.

The said Eliza, John and Georgiana were now clustered round their mama in the drawing-room: she lay reclined on a sofa by the fireside, and with her darlings about her (for the time neither quarrelling nor crying) looked perfectly happy. Me, she had dispensed from joining the group; saying, "She regretted to be under the necessity of keeping me at a distance; but that until she heard from Bessie, and could discover by her own observation that I was endeavouring in good earnest to acquire a more sociable and childlike disposition, a more attractive and sprightly manner,—something lighter, franker, more natural as it were—she really must exclude me from privileges intended only for contented, happy, little children."

"What does Bessie say I have done?" I asked.

"Jane, I don't like cavillers or questioners: besides, there is something truly forbidding in a child taking up her elders in that manner. Be seated somewhere; and until you can speak pleasantly, remain silent."

A small breakfast-room adjoined the drawing-room. I slipped in there. It contained a book-case: I soon possessed myself of a volume, taking care that it should be one stored with pictures. I mounted into the window-seat: gathering up my feet, I sat cross-legged, like a Turk; and, having drawn the red moreen curtain nearly close, I was shrined in double retirement.

Folds of scarlet drapery shut in my view to the right hand; to the left were the clear panes of glass, protecting, but not separating me from the drear November day. At intervals, while turning over the leaves of my book, I studied the aspect of that winter afternoon. Afar it offered a pale blank of mist and cloud; near, a scene of wet lawn and storm-beat shrub, with ceaseless rain sweeping away wildly before a long and lamentable blast.

I returned to my book—Bewick's History of British Birds: the letter-press thereof I cared little for, generally speaking; and yet there were certain introductory pages that, child as I was, I could not pass quite as a blank. They were those which treat of the haunts of sea-fowl; of "the solitary rocks and promontories" by them only inhabited; of the coast of Norway, studded with isles from its southern extremity, the Lindeness, or Naze, to the North Cape—

> "Where the Northern Ocean, in vast whirls
> Boils round the naked, melancholy isles
> Of farthest Thule; and the Atlantic surge
> Pours in among the stormy Hebrides."

Nor could I pass unnoticed the suggestion of the bleak shores of Lapland, Siberia, Spitzbergen, Nova Zembla, Iceland, Greenland, with "the vast sweep of the Arctic Zone, and those forlorn regions of dreary space—that reservoir of frost and snow, where firm fields of ice, the accumulation of centuries of winters, glazed in Alpine heights above heights, surround the pole, and concentre the multiplied rigors of extreme cold." Of these death-white realms I formed an idea of my own; shadowy, like all the half-comprehended notions that float dim through children's brains, but strangely impressive. The words in these introductory pages connected themselves with the succeeding vignettes, and gave significance to the rock standing up alone in a sea of billow and spray; to the broken boat stranded on a desolate coast; to the cold and ghastly moon glancing through bars of cloud at a wreck just sinking.

I cannot tell what sentiment haunted the quite solitary churchyard with its inscribed headstone; its gate, its two trees, its low horizon, girdled by a broken wall, and its newly-risen crescent, attesting the hour of even-tide.

The two ships becalmed on a torpid sea, I believed to be marine phantoms.

The fiend pinning down the thief's pack behind him, I passed over quickly: it was an object of terror.

So was the black, horned thing seated aloof on a rock, surveying a distant crowd surrounding a gallows.

Each picture told a story; mysterious often to my undeveloped understanding and imperfect feelings, yet ever profoundly interesting; as interesting as the tales Bessie sometimes narrated on winter evenings, when she chanced to be in good humour; and when, having brought her ironing-table to the nursery-hearth, she allowed us to sit about it, and while she got up Mrs. Reed's lace frills, and crimped her night-cap borders, fed our eager attention with passages of love and adventure taken from old fairy tales and older ballads; or (as at a later period I discovered) from the pages of Pamela, and Henry, Earl of Moreland.

With Bewick on my knee, I was then happy; happy at least in my way. I feared nothing but interruption, and that came too soon. The breakfast-room door opened.

"Boh! Madam Mope!" cried the voice of John Reed; then he paused: he found the room apparently empty.

"Where the dickens is she?" he continued. "Lizzy! Georgy!" (calling to his sisters) "Joan is not here: tell mama she is run out into the rain—bad animal!"

"It is well I drew the curtain," thought I; and I wished fervently he might not discover my hiding-place: nor would John Reed have found it out himself; he was not quick either of vision or conception: but Eliza just put her head in at the door and said at once:—

"She is in the window-seat, to be sure, Jack."

And I came out immediately; for I trembled at the idea of being dragged forth by the said Jack.

"What do you want?" I asked, with awkward diffidence.

"Say, 'what do you want, Master Reed;' " was the answer. "I want you to come here," and seating himself in an arm-chair, he intimated by a gesture that I was to approach and stand before him.

John Reed was a schoolboy of fourteen years old; four years older than I, for I was but ten; large and stout for his age, with a dingy and unwholesome skin; thick lineaments in a spacious visage, heavy limbs and large extremities. He gorged himself habitually at table, which made him bilious, and gave him a dim and bleared eye and flabby cheeks. He ought now to have been at school; but his mama had taken him home for a month or two, "on account of his delicate health." Mr. Miles, the master, affirmed that he would do very well if he had fewer cakes and sweetmeats sent him from home; but the mother's heart turned from an opinion so harsh, and inclined rather to the more refined idea that John's sallowness was owing to over-application and, perhaps, to pining after home.

John had not much affection for his mother and sisters, and an antipathy to me. He bullied and punished me; not two or three times in the week, nor once or twice in the day, but continually: every nerve I had feared him, and every morsel of flesh on my bones shrank when he came near. There were moments when I was bewildered by the terror he inspired; because I had no appeal whatever against either his menaces or his inflictions; the servants did not like to offend their young master by taking my part against him, and Mrs. Reed was blind and deaf on the subject: she never saw him strike or heard him abuse me; though he did both now and then in her very presence: more frequently, however, behind her back.

Habitually obedient to John, I came up to his chair: he spent some three minutes in thrusting out his tongue at me as far as he could without damaging the roots: I knew he would soon strike, and while dreading the blow, I mused on the disgusting and ugly appearance of him who would presently deal it. I wonder if he read that notion in my face; for, all at once, without speaking, he struck suddenly and strongly. I tottered, and on regaining my equilibrium retired back a step or two from his chair.

"That is for your impudence in answering mama a while since," said he, "and for your sneaking way of getting behind curtains, and for the look you had in your eyes two minutes since, you rat!"

Accustomed to John Reed's abuse, I never had an idea of replying to it; my care was how to endure the blow which would certainly follow the insult.

"What were you doing behind the curtain?" he asked.

"I was reading."

"Show the book."

I returned to the window and fetched it thence.

"You have no business to take our books; you are a dependant, mama says; you have no money; your father left you none; you ought to beg, and not to live here with gentlemen's children like us, and eat the same meals we do, and wear clothes at our mama's expense. Now, I'll teach you to rummage my book-shelves: for they *are* mine; all the house belongs to me or will do in a few years. Go and stand by the door, out of the way of the mirror and the windows."

I did so, not at first aware what was his intention; but when I saw him lift and poise the book and stand in act to hurl it, I instinctively started aside with a cry of alarm: not soon enough, however; the volume was flung, it hit me, and I fell, striking my head against the door and cutting it. The cut bled, the pain was sharp: my terror had passed its climax; other feelings succeeded.

"Wicked and cruel boy!" I said. "You are like a murderer—you are like a slavedriver—you are like the Roman emperors!"

I had read Goldsmith's History of Rome, and had formed my opinion of Nero, Caligula, etc. Also I had drawn parallels in silence, which I never thought thus to have declared aloud.

"What! What!" he cried. "Did she say that to me? Did you hear her, Eliza and Georgiana? Won't I tell mama? but first"—

He ran headlong at me; I felt him grasp my hair and my shoulder; he had closed with a desperate thing. I really saw in him a tyrant: a murderer. I felt a drop or two of blood from my head trickle down my neck, and was sensible of somewhat pungent suffering: these sensations for the time predominated over fear, and I received him in frantic sort. I don't very well know what I did with my hands, but he called me "Rat! rat!" and bellowed out aloud. Aid was near him: Eliza and Georgiana had run for Mrs. Reed, who was gone up stairs; she now came upon the scene, followed by Bessie and her maid Abbot. We were parted: I heard the words:—

"Dear! dear! What a fury to fly at Master John!"

"Did ever anybody see such a picture of passion!"

Then Mrs. Reed subjoined:—

"Take her away to the red-room, and lock her in there." Four hands were immediately laid upon me, and I was borne up stairs.

· · · · · · ·

Chapter 2

I resisted all the way: a new thing for me, and a circumstance which greatly strengthened the bad opinion Bessie and Miss Abbot were disposed to entertain of me. The fact is, I was a trifle beside myself; or rather *out* of myself, as the French would say: I was conscious that a moment's mutiny had already rendered me liable to strange penalties, and like any other rebel slave, I felt resolved, in my desperation, to go all lengths.

"Hold her arms, Miss Abbot; she's like a mad cat."

"For shame! for shame!" cried the lady's-maid. "What shocking conduct, Miss Eyre, to strike a young gentleman, your benefactress's son! Your young master!"

"Master! How is he my master? Am I a servant?"

"No; you are less than a servant, for you do nothing for your keep. There, sit down, and think over your wickedness."

They had got me by this time into the apartment indicated by Mrs. Reed, and had thrust me upon a stool: my impulse was to rise from it like a spring; their two pairs of hands arrested me instantly.

"If you don't sit still, you must be tied down," said Bessie. "Miss Abbot, lend me your garters; she would break mine directly."

Miss Abbot turned to divest a stout leg of the necessary ligature. This preparation for bonds, and the additional ignominy it inferred, took a little of the excitement out of me.

"Don't take them off," I cried; "I will not stir."

In guarantee whereof, I attached myself to my seat by my hands.

"Mind you don't," said Bessie; and when she had ascertained that I was really subsiding, she loosened her hold of me; then she and Miss Abbot stood with folded arms, looking darkly and doubtfully on my face, as incredulous of my sanity.

"She never did so before," at last said Bessie, turning to the Abigail.

"But it was always in her," was the reply. "I've told Missis often my opinion about the child, and Missis agreed with me. She's an underhand little thing: I never saw a girl of her age with so much cover."

Bessie answered not; but ere long, addressing me, she said:

"You ought to be aware, Miss, that you are under obligations to Mrs. Reed: she keeps you; if she were to turn you off, you would have to go to the poor-house."

, I had nothing to say to these words: they were not new to me: my very first recollections of existence included hints of the same kind. This reproach of my dependence had become a vague sing-song in my ear; very painful and crushing, but only half intelligible. Miss Abbot joined in:—

"And you ought not to think yourself on an equality with the Misses Reed and Master Reed, because Missis kindly allows you to be brought up with them. They will have a great deal of money, and you will have none: it is your place to be humble, and to try to make yourself agreeable to them."

"What we tell you, is for your good," added Bessie, in no harsh voice: "you should try to be useful and pleasant, then perhaps you would have a home here; but if you become passionate and rude, Missis will send you away, I am sure."

"Besides," said Miss Abbot, "God will punish her: he might strike her dead in the midst of her tantrums, and then where would she go? Come, Bessie, we will leave her: I wouldn't have her heart for anything. Say your prayers, Miss Eyre, when you are by yourself; for if you don't repent, something bad might be permitted to come down the chimney, and fetch you away."

They went, shutting the door, and locking it behind them.

The red-room was a spare chamber, very seldom slept in; I might say never, indeed; unless when a chance influx of visitors at Gateshead Hall rendered it necessary to turn to account all the accommodation it contained; yet it was one of the largest and stateliest chambers in the mansion. A bed supported on massive pillars of mahogany, hung with curtains of deep red damask, stood out like a tabernacle in the centre; the two large windows, with their blinds always drawn down, were half-shrouded in festoons and falls of similar drapery; the carpet was red; the table at the foot of the bed was covered with a crimson cloth; the walls were a soft fawn colour, with a blush of pink in it; the wardrobe, the toilet-table, the chairs were of darkly polished old mahogany. Out of these deep surrounding shades rose high, and glared white, the piled-up mattresses and pillows of the bed, spread with a snowy Marseilles counterpane. Scarcely less prominent was an ample, cushioned easy-chair near the head of the bed, also white, with a footstool before it; and looking, as I thought, like a pale throne.

This room was chill, because it seldom had a fire; it was silent, because remote from the nursery and kitchens; solemn, because it was known to be so seldom entered. The housemaid alone came here on Saturdays, to wipe from the mirrors and the furniture a week's quiet dust; and Mrs. Reed herself, at far intervals, visited it to review the contents of a certain secret drawer in the wardrobe, where were stored divers parchments, her jewel-casket, and a miniature of her deceased husband; and in those last words lies the secret of the red-room; the spell which kept it so lonely in spite of its grandeur.

Mr. Reed had been dead nine years: it was in this chamber he breathed his last; here he lay in state; hence his coffin was borne by the under-taker's men; and, since that day, a sense of dreary consecration had guarded it from frequent intrusion.

My seat, to which Bessie and the bitter Miss Abbot had left me riv-eted, was a low ottoman near the marble chimney-piece: the bed rose before me; to my right hand there was the high, dark wardrobe, with sub-dued, broken reflections varying the gloss of its panels; to my left were the muffled windows: a great looking-glass between them repeated the vacant majesty of the bed and room. I was not quite sure whether they had locked the door; and, when I dared move, I got up, and went to see. Alas! yes: no jail was ever more secure. Returning, I had to cross before the looking-glass; my fascinated glance involuntarily explored the depth it revealed. All looked colder and darker in that visionary hollow than in reality: and the strange little figure there gazing at me, with a white face and arms specking the gloom, and glittering eyes of fear moving where all else was still, had the effect of a real spirit: I thought it like one of the tiny phantoms, half fairy, half imp, Bessie's evening stories rep-resented as coming up out of lone, ferny dells in moors, and appearing before the eyes of belated travellers. I returned to my stool.

Superstition was with me at that moment; but it was not yet her hour for complete victory: my blood was still warm; the mood of the revolted slave was still bracing me with its bitter vigour; I had to stem a rapid rush of retrospective thought before I quailed to the dismal present.

All John Reed's violent tyrannies, all his sisters' proud indifference, all his mother's aversion, all the servants' partiality, turned up in my disturbed mind like a dark deposit in a turbid well. Why was I always suffering, always brow-beaten, always accused, for ever condemned? Why could I never please? Why was it useless to try to win any one's favour? Eliza, who was headstrong and selfish, was respected. Georgiana, who had a spoiled temper, a very acrid spite, a captious and insolent carriage, was universally indulged. Her beauty, her pink cheeks and golden curls, seemed to give delight to all who looked at her, and to purchase indem-nity for every fault. John, no one thwarted, much less punished; though he twisted the necks of the pigeons, killed the little pea-chicks, set the dogs at the sheep, stripped the hothouse vines of their fruit, and broke the buds off the choicest plants in the conservatory: he called his mother "old girl," too; sometimes reviled her for her dark skin, similar to his own; bluntly disregarded her wishes; not unfrequently tore and spoiled her silk attire; and he was still "her own darling." I dared commit no fault; I strove to fulfil every duty; and I was termed naughty and tiresome, sullen and sneaking, from morning to noon, and from noon to night.

My head still ached and bled with the blow and fall I had received: no one had reproved John for wantonly striking me; and because I had turned against him to avert farther irrational violence, I was loaded with general opprobrium.

"Unjust!—unjust!" said my reason, forced by the agonizing stimulus into precocious though transitory power; and Resolve, equally wrought up, instigated some strange expedient to achieve escape from insupportable oppression—as running away, or, if that could not be effected, never eating or drinking more, and letting myself die.

What a consternation of soul was mine that dreary afternoon! How all my brain was in tumult, and all my heart in insurrection! Yet in what darkness, what dense ignorance, was the mental battle fought! I could not answer the ceaseless inward question—*why* I thus suffered; now, at the distance of—I will not say how many years, I see it clearly.

I was a discord in Gateshead Hall; I was like nobody there; I had nothing in harmony with Mrs. Reed or her children, or her chosen vassalage. If they did not love me, in fact, as little did I love them. They were not bound to regard with affection a thing that could not sympathize with one amongst them; a heterogeneous thing, opposed to them in temperament, in capacity, in propensities; a useless thing, incapable of serving their interest, or adding to their pleasure; a noxious thing, cherishing the germs of indignation at their treatment, of contempt of their judgment, I know, that had I been a sanguine, brilliant, careless, exacting, handsome, romping child—though equally dependent and friendless—Mrs. Reed would have endured my presence more complacently; her children would have entertained for me more of the cordiality of fellow-feeling; the servants would have been less prone to make me the scape-goat of the nursery.

Daylight began to forsake the red-room; it was past four o'clock, and the beclouded afternoon was tending to drear twilight. I heard the rain still beating continuously on the staircase window, and the wind howling in the grove behind the hall; I grew by degrees cold as a stone, and then my courage sank. My habitual mode of humiliation, self-doubt, forlorn depression, fell damp on the embers of my decaying ire. All said I was wicked, and perhaps I might be so: what thought had I been but just conceiving of starving myself to death? That certainly was a crime; and was I fit to die? Or was the vault under the chancel of Gateshead church an inviting bourne! In such vault I had been told did Mr. Reed lie buried; and led by this thought to recall his idea, I dwelt on it with gathering dread. I could not remember him; but I knew that he was my own uncle—my mother's brother—that he had taken me when a parentless infant to his house; and that in his last moments he had required a promise of Mrs. Reed that she would rear and maintain me as one of her own children. Mrs. Reed probably considered she had kept this promise; and so she had I dare say, as well as her nature would permit her; but how could she really like an interloper not of her race, and unconnected with her, after her husband's death, by any tie? It must have been most irksome to find herself bound by a hard-wrung pledge to stand in the stead of a parent to a strange child she could not love, and to see an uncongenial alien permanently intruded on her own family group.

A singular notion dawned upon me. I doubted not—never doubted—that if Mr. Reed had been alive he would have treated me kindly; and now, as I sat looking at the white bed and overshadowed walls—occasionally also turning a fascinated eye towards the dimly gleaming mirror—I began to recall what I had heard of dead men, troubled in their graves by the violation of their last wishes, revisiting the earth to punish the perjured and avenge the oppressed; and I thought Mr. Reed's spirit, harassed by the wrongs of his sister's child, might quit its abode—whether in the church vault or in the unknown world of the departed—and rise before me in this chamber. I wiped my tears and hushed my sobs; fearful lest any sign of violent grief might waken a preternatural voice to comfort me, or elicit from the gloom some haloed face, bending over me with strange pity. This idea, consolatory in theory, I felt would be terrible if realized: with all my might I endeavoured to stifle it—I endeavoured to be firm. Shaking my hair from my eyes, I lifted my head and tried to look boldly round the dark room: at this moment a light gleamed on the wall. Was it, I asked myself, a ray from the moon penetrating some aperture in the blind? No; moonlight was still, and this stirred; while I gazed, it glided up to the ceiling and quivered over my head. I can now conjecture readily that this streak of light was, in all likelihood, a gleam from a lantern, carried by some one across the lawn: but then, prepared as my mind was for horror, shaken as my nerves were by agitation, I thought the swift-darting beam was a herald of some coming vision from another world. My heart beat thick, my head grew hot; a sound filled my ears, which I deemed the rushing of wings: something seemed near me; I was oppressed, suffocated: endurance broke down; I rushed to the door and shook the lock in desperate effort. Steps came running along the outer passage; the key turned; Bessie and Abbot entered.

"Miss Eyre, are you ill?" said Bessie.

"What a dreadful noise! it went quite through me!" exclaimed Abbot.

"Take me out! Let me go into the nursery!" was my cry.

"What for? Are you hurt? Have you seen something?" again demanded Bessie.

"Oh! I saw a light, and I thought a ghost would come." I had now got hold of Bessie's hand, and she did not snatch it from me.

"She has screamed out on purpose," declared Abbot, in some disgust. "And what a scream! If she had been in great pain one would have excused it, but she only wanted to bring us all here: I know her naughty tricks."

"What is all this?" demanded another voice peremptorily; and Mrs. Reed came along the corridor, her cap flying wide, her gown rustling stormily. "Abbot and Bessie, I believe I gave orders that Jane Eyre should be left in the red-room till I came to her myself."

"Miss Jane screamed so loud, ma'am," pleaded Bessie.

"Let her go;" was the only answer. "Loose Bessie's hand, child: you cannot succeed in getting out by these means, be assured. I abhor artifice, particularly in children; it is my duty to show you that tricks will not answer: you will now stay here an hour longer, and it is only on condition of perfect submission and stillness that I shall liberate you then."

"Oh aunt, have pity! Forgive me! I cannot endure it—let me be punished some other way! I shall be killed if——"

"Silence! This violence is all most repulsive:" and so, no doubt, she felt it. I was a precocious actress in her eyes: she sincerely looked on me as a compound of virulent passions, mean spirit, and dangerous duplicity.

Bessie and Abbot having retreated, Mrs. Reed, impatient of my now frantic anguish and wild sobs, abruptly thrust me back and locked me in, without farther parley. I heard her sweeping away; and soon after she was gone, I suppose I had a species of fit: unconsciousness closed the scene.

. . . .

Chapter 3

The next thing I remember is, waking up with a feeling as if I had had a frightful nightmare, and seeing before me a terrible red glare, crossed with thick black bars. I heard voices, too, speaking with a hollow sound, and as if muffled by a rush of wind or water: agitation, uncertainty, and an all-predominating sense of terror confused my faculties. Ere long, I became aware that some one was handling me; lifting me up and supporting me in a sitting posture: and that more tenderly than I had ever been raised or upheld before. I rested my head against a pillow or an arm, and felt easy.

In five minutes more, the cloud of bewilderment dissolved: I knew quite well that I was in my own bed, and that the red glare was the nursery fire. It was night: a candle burnt on the table; Bessie stood at the bed-foot with a basin in her hand, and a gentleman sat in a chair near my pillow, leaning over me.

I felt an inexpressible relief, a soothing conviction of protection and security, when I knew that there was a stranger in the room; an individual not belonging to Gateshead, and not related to Mrs. Reed. Turning from Bessie (though her presence was far less obnoxious to me than that of Abbot, for instance, would have been), I scrutinized the face of the gentleman: I knew him; it was Mr. Lloyd, an apothecary, sometimes called in by Mrs. Reed when the servants were ailing: for herself and the children she employed a physician.

"Well, who am I?" he asked.

I pronounced his name, offering him at the same time my hand: he took it, smiling and saying, "We shall do very well by-and-by." Then he laid me down, and addressing Bessie, charged her to be very careful that I was not disturbed during the night. Having given some further directions, and intimated that he should call again the next day, he departed; to my grief: I felt so sheltered and befriended while he sat in the chair near my pillow; and as he closed the door after him, all the room darkened and my heart again sank: inexpressible sadness weighed it down.

"Do you feel as if you should sleep, Miss?" asked Bessie, rather softly.

Scarcely dared I answer her; for I feared the next sentence might be rough. "I will try."

"Would you like to drink, or could you eat anything?"

"No, thank you, Bessie."

"Then I think I shall go to bed, for it is past twelve o'clock; but you may call me if you want anything in the night."

Wonderful civility this! It emboldened me to ask a question.

"Bessie, what is the matter with me? Am I ill?"

"You fell sick, I suppose, in the red-room with crying; you'll be better soon, no doubt."

Bessie went into the housemaid's apartment which was near. I heard her say:—

"Sarah, come and sleep with me in the nursery; I daren't for my life be alone with that poor child to-night; she might die: it's such a strange thing she should have that fit: I wonder if she saw anything. Missis was rather too hard."

Sarah came back with her; they both went to bed; they were whispering together for half an hour before they fell asleep. I caught scraps of their conversation, from which I was able only too distinctly to infer the main subject discussed.

"Something passed her, all dressed in white, and vanished"—"A great black dog behind him"—"Three loud raps on the chamber door"—"A light in the church-yard just over his grave"—etc., etc.

At last both slept; the fire and the candle went out. For me, the watches of that long night passed in ghastly wakefulness; ear, eye, and mind were alike strained by dread: such dread as children only can feel.

No severe or prolonged bodily illness followed this incident of the red-room: it only gave my nerves a shock; of which I feel the reverberation to this day. Yes, Mrs. Reed, to you I owe some fearful pangs of mental suffering. But I ought to forgive you, for you knew not what you did: while rending my heart-strings, you thought you were only up-rooting my bad propensities.

Next day, by noon, I was up and dressed, and sat wrapped in a shawl by the nursery hearth, I felt physically weak and broken down: but my worst ailment was an unutterable wretchedness of mind: a wretchedness which kept drawing from me silent tears; no sooner had I wiped one salt drop from my cheek than another followed. Yet I thought, I ought to have been happy, for none of the Reeds were there; they were all gone out in the carriage with their mama: Abbot, too, was sewing in another room, and Bessie, as she moved hither and thither, putting away toys and arranging drawers, addressed to me every now and then a word of unwonted kindness. This state of things should have been to me a paradise of peace, accustomed as I was to a life of ceaseless reprimand and thankless fagging; but, in fact, my racked nerves were now in such a state that no calm could soothe, and no pleasure excite them agreeably.

Bessie had been down into the kitchen, and she brought up with her a tart on a certain brightly painted china plate, whose bird of paradise, nestling in a wreath of convolvuli and rosebuds, had been wont to stir in me a most enthusiastic sense of admiration; and which plate I had often petitioned to be allowed to take in my hand in order to examine it more closely, but had always hitherto been deemed unworthy of such a privilege. This precious vessel was now placed on my knee, and I was cordially invited to eat the circlet of delicate pastry upon it. Vain favour! coming, like most other favours long deferred and often wished for, too late! I could not eat the tart; and the plumage of the bird, the tints of the flowers, seemed strangely faded: I put both plate and tart away. Bessie asked if I would have a book: the word *book* acted as a transient stimulus, and I begged her to fetch Gulliver's Travels from the library. This book I had again and again perused with delight; I considered it a narrative of facts, and discovered in it a vein of interest deeper than what I found in fairy tales: for as to the elves, having sought them in vain among foxglove leaves and bells, under mushrooms and beneath the ground-ivy mantling old wall-nooks, I had at length made up my mind to the sad truth that they were all gone out of England to some savage country, where the woods were wilder and thicker, and the population more scant; whereas, Lilliput and Brobdignag being, in my creed, solid parts of the earth's surface, I doubted not that I might one day, by taking a long voyage, see with my own eyes the little fields, houses, and trees, the diminutive people, the tiny cows, sheep, and birds of the one realm, and the corn-fields forest-high, the mighty mastiffs, the monster cats, the tower-like men and women, of the other. Yet, when this cherished volume was now placed in my hand—when I turned over its leaves, and sought in its marvellous pictures the charm I had, till now, never failed to find—all was eerie and dreary; the giants were gaunt goblins, the pigmies malevolent and fearful imps, Gulliver a most desolate wanderer in most dread and dangerous regions. I closed the book, which I dared no longer peruse, and put it on the table, beside the untasted tart.

Bessie had now finished dusting and tidying the room, and having washed her hands, she opened a certain little drawer, full of splendid shreds of silk and satin, and began making a new bonnet for Georgiana's doll. Meantime she sang: her song was—

> "In the days when we went gipsying,
>   A long time ago."

I had often heard the song before, and always with lively delight; for Bessie had a sweet voice,—at least, I thought so. But now, though her voice was still sweet, I found in its melody an indescribable sadness. Sometimes, pre-occupied with her work, she sang the refrain very low, very lingeringly; "A long time ago" came out like the saddest cadence of a funeral hymn. She passed into another ballad, this time a really doleful one.

> "My feet they are sore, and my limbs they are weary;
>   Long is the way, and the mountains are wild;
> Soon will the twilight close moonless and dreary
>   Over the path of the poor orphan child.
>
> "Why did they send me so far and so lonely,
>   Up where the moors spread and grey rocks are piled?
> Men are hard-hearted, and kind angels only
>   Watch o'er the steps of a poor orphan child.
>
> "Yet distant and soft the night-breeze is blowing,
>   Clouds there are none, and clear stars beam mild;
> God, in His mercy, protection is showing,
>   Comfort and hope to the poor orphan child.
>
> "Ev'n should I fall o'er the broken bridge passing,
>   Or stray in the marshes, by false lights beguiled,
> Still will my Father, with promise and blessing,
>   Take to His bosom the poor orphan child.

> "There is a thought that for strength should avail me,
>   Though both of shelter and kindred despoiled;
> Heaven is a home, and a rest will not fail me;
>   God is a friend to the poor orphan child."

"Come, Miss Jane, don't cry," said Bessie, as she finished. She might as well have said to the fire "don't burn!" but how could she divine the morbid suffering to which I was a prey? In the course of the morning Mr. Lloyd came again.

"What, already up!" said he, as he entered the nursery. "Well, nurse, how is she?"

Bessie answered that I was doing very well.

"Then she ought to look more cheerful. Come here, Miss Jane: your name is Jane, is it not?"

"Yes, sir, Jane Eyre."

"Well, you have been crying, Miss Jane Eyre, can you tell me what about? Have you any pain?"

"No, sir."

"Oh! I daresay she is crying because she could not go out with Missis in the carriage," interposed Bessie.

"Surely not! why, she is too old for such pettishness."

I thought so too; and my self-esteem being wounded by the false charge, I answered promptly, "I never cried for such a thing in my life: I hate going out in the carriage. I cry because I am miserable."

"Oh fie, Miss!" said Bessie.

The good apothecary appeared a little puzzled. I was standing before him; he fixed his eyes on me very steadily: his eyes were small and grey; not very bright, but I daresay I should think them shrewd now: he had a hard-featured yet good-natured looking face. Having considered me at leisure, he said—

"What made you ill yesterday?"

"She had a fall," said Bessie, again putting in her word.

"Fall! why that is like a baby again! Can't she manage to walk at her age? She must be eight or nine years old."

"I was knocked down," was the blunt explanation jerked out of me by another pang of mortified pride: "but that did not make me ill," I added; while Mr. Lloyd helped himself to a pinch of snuff.

As he was returning the box to his waist-coat pocket, a loud bell rang for the servants' dinner; he knew what it was. "That's for you, nurse," said he; "you can go down; I'll give Miss Jane a lecture till you come back."

Bessie would rather have stayed; but she was obliged to go, because punctuality at meals was rigidly enforced at Gateshead Hall.

"The fall did not make you ill; what did, then?" pursued Mr. Lloyd, when Bessie was gone.

"I was shut up in a room where there is a ghost, till after dark."

I saw Mr. Lloyd smile and frown at the same time: "Ghost! What, you are a baby after all! You are afraid of ghosts?"

"Of Mr. Reed's ghost I am: he died in that room, and was laid out there. Neither Bessie nor any one else will go into it at night, if they can help it; and it was cruel to shut me up alone without a candle,—so cruel that I think I shall never forget it."

"Nonsense! And is it that makes you so miserable? Are you afraid now in daylight?"

"No; but night will come again before long: and besides, I am unhappy,—very unhappy, for other things."

"What other things? Can you tell me some of them?"

How much I wished to reply fully to this question! How difficult it was to frame any answer! Children can feel, but they cannot analyze their feelings; and if the analysis is partially effected in thought, they know not how to express the result of the process in words. Fearful, however, of losing this first and only opportunity of relieving my grief by imparting it, I, after a disturbed pause, contrived to frame a meagre, though as far as it went, true response.

"For one thing, I have no father or mother, brothers or sisters."

"You have a kind aunt and cousins."

Again I paused; then bunglingly enounced:

"But John Reed knocked me down, and my aunt shut me up in the red-room."

Mr. Lloyd a second time produced his snuff box.

"Don't you think Gateshead Hall a very beautiful house?" asked he. "Are you not very thankful to have such a fine place to live at?"

"It is not my house, sir; and Abbot says I have less right to be here than a servant."

"Pooh! you can't be silly enough to wish to leave such a splendid place?"

"If I had anywhere else to go, I should be glad to leave it; but I can never get away from Gateshead till I am a woman."

"Perhaps you may—who knows? Have you any relations besides Mrs. Reed?"

"I think not, sir."

"None belonging to your father?"

"I don't know: I asked Aunt Reed once, and she said possibly I might have some poor, low relations called Eyre, but she knew nothing about them."

"If you had such, would you like to go to them?"

I reflected. Poverty looks grim to grown people; still more so to children: they have not much idea of industrious, working, respectable poverty; they think of the word only as connected with ragged clothes, scanty food, fireless grates, rude manners, and debasing vices: poverty for me was synonymous with degradation.

"No; I should not like to belong to poor people," was my reply.

"Not even if they were kind to you?"

I shook my head: I could not see how poor people had the means of being kind; and then to learn to speak like them, to adopt their manners, to be uneducated, to grow up like one of the poor women I saw sometimes nursing their children or washing their clothes at the cottage doors of the village of Gateshead: no, I was not heroic enough to purchase liberty at the price of caste.

"But are your relatives so very poor? Are they working people?"

"I cannot tell; Aunt Reed says if I have any, they must be a beggarly set: I should not like to go a-begging."

"Would you like to go to school?"

Again I reflected: I scarcely knew what school was; Bessie sometimes spoke of it as a place where young ladies sat in the stocks, wore backboards, and were expected to be exceedingly genteel and precise; John Reed hated his school, and abused his master: but John Reed's tastes were no rule for mine, and if Bessie's accounts of school-discipline (gathered from the young ladies of a family where she had lived before coming to Gateshead) were somewhat appalling, her details of certain accomplishments attained by these same young ladies were, I thought, equally attractive. She boasted of beautiful paintings of landscapes and flowers by them executed; of songs they could sing and pieces they could play, of purses they could net, of French books they could translate; till my spirit was moved to emulation as I listened. Besides, school would be a complete change: it implied a long journey, an entire separation from Gateshead, an entrance into a new life.

"I should indeed like to go to school," was the audible conclusion of my musings.

"Well, well; who knows what may happen?" said Mr. Lloyd, as he got up: "The child ought to have change of air and scene," he added, speaking to himself, "nerves not in a good state."

Bessie now returned; at the same moment the carriage was heard rolling up the gravel-walk.

"Is that your mistress, nurse?" asked Mr. Lloyd: "I should like to speak to her before I go."

Bessie invited him to walk into the breakfast-room, and led the way out. In the interview which followed between him and Mrs. Reed, I presume, from after-occurrences, that the apothecary ventured to recommend my being sent to school; and the recommendation was no doubt readily enough adopted; for as Abbot said, in discussing the subject with Bessie when both sat sewing in the nursery one night, after I was in bed, and, as they thought, asleep, "Missis was, she dared say, glad enough to get rid of such a tiresome, ill-conditioned child, who always looked as if she were watching everybody, and scheming plots underhand." Abbot, I think, gave me credit for being a sort of infantine Guy Fawkes.

On that same occasion I learned, for the first time, from Miss Abbot's communications to Bessie, that my father had been a poor clergy-man; that my mother had married him against the wishes of her friends, who considered the match beneath her; that my grandfather Reed was so irritated at her disobedience, he cut her off without a shilling; that after my mother and father had been married a year, the latter caught the typhus fever while visiting among the poor of a large manufacturing town where his curacy was situated, and where that disease was then prevalent; that my mother took the infection from him, and both died within a month of each other.

Bessie, when she heard this narrative, sighed and said, "Poor Miss Jane is to be pitied, too, Abbot."

"Yes," responded Abbot, "if she were a nice, pretty child, one might compassionate her forlornness, but one really cannot care for such a little toad as that."

"Not a great deal, to be sure," agreed Bessie: "at any rate a beauty like Miss Georgiana would be more moving in the same condition."

"Yes, I dote on Miss Georgiana!" cried the fervent Abbot. "Little darling!—with her long curls and her blue eyes, and such a sweet colour as she has; just as if she were painted! Bessie, I could fancy a Welsh rabbit for supper."

"So could I—with a roast onion. Come, we'll go down." They went.

· · · · · · ·

Chapter 4

From my discourse with Mr. Lloyd, and from the above reported conference between Bessie and Abbot, I gathered enough of hope to suffice as a motive for wishing to get well: a change seemed near,—I desired and waited it in silence. It tarried, however; days and weeks passed: I had regained my normal state of health, but no new allusion was made to the subject over which I brooded. Mrs. Reed surveyed me at times with a severe eye, but seldom addressed me: since my illness, she had drawn a more marked line of separation than ever between me and her own children; appointing me a small closet to sleep in by myself, condemning me to take my meals alone, and pass all my time in the nursery while my cousins were constantly in the drawing-room. Not a hint, however, did she drop about sending me to school: still I felt an instinctive certainty that she would not long endure me under the same roof with her; for her glance, now more than ever, when turned on me, expressed an insuperable and rooted aversion.

Eliza and Georgiana, evidently acting according to orders, spoke to me as little as possible: John thrust his tongue in his cheek whenever he saw me, and once attempted chastisement; but as I instantly turned against him, roused by the same sentiment of deep ire and desperate revolt which had stirred my corruption before, he thought it better to desist, and ran from me uttering execrations, and vowing I had burst his nose. I had indeed levelled at that prominent feature as hard a blow as my knuckles could inflict; and when I saw that either that or my look daunted him, I had the greatest inclination to follow up my advantage to purpose; but he was already with his mama. I heard him in a blubbering tone commence the tale of how "that nasty Jane Eyre" had flown at him like a mad cat: he was stopped rather harshly—

"Don't talk to me about her, John: I told you not to go near her; she is not worthy of notice: I do not choose that either you or your sisters should associate with her."

Here, leaning over the bannister, I cried out suddenly, and without at all deliberating on my words,—

"They are not fit to associate with me."

Mrs. Reed was rather a stout woman; but, on hearing this strange and audacious declaration, she ran nimbly up the stair, swept me like a whirlwind into the nursery, and crushing me down on the edge of my crib, dared me in an emphatic voice to rise from that place, or utter one syllable during the remainder of the day.

"What would uncle Reed say to you, if he were alive?" was my scarcely voluntary demand. I say scarcely voluntary, for it seemed as if my tongue pronounced words without my will consenting to their utterance: something spoke out of me over which I had no control.

"What?" said Mrs. Reed under her breath: her usually cold, composed grey eye became troubled with a look like fear, she took her hand from my arm, and gazed at me as if she really did not know whether I were child or fiend. I was now in for it.

"My uncle Reed is in heaven, and can see all you do and think; and so can papa and mama: they know how you shut me up all day long, and how you wish me dead."

Mrs. Reed soon rallied her spirits: she shook me most soundly, she boxed both my ears, and then left me without a word. Bessie supplied the hiatus by a homily of an hour's length, in which she proved beyond a doubt that I was the most wicked and abandoned child ever reared under a roof. I half believed her; for I felt indeed only bad feelings surging in my breast.

November, December, and half of January passed away. Christmas and the New Year had been celebrated at Gateshead with the usual festive cheer; presents had been interchanged, dinners and evening parties given. From every enjoyment I was, of course, excluded: my share of the gaiety consisted in witnessing the daily apparelling of Eliza and Georgiana, and seeing them descend to the drawing-room, dressed out in thin muslin frocks and scarlet sashes, with hair elaborately ringleted; and afterwards, in listening to the sound of the piano or the harp played below, to the passing to and fro of the butler and footmen, to the jingling of glass and china as refreshments were handed, to the broken hum of conversation as the drawing-room doors opened and closed. When tired of this occupation, I would retire from the stair-head to the solitary and silent nursery: there, though somewhat sad, I was not miserable. To speak truth, I had not the least wish to go into company, for in company I was very rarely noticed; and if Bessie had but been kind and companionable, I should have deemed it a treat to spend the evenings quietly with her, instead of passing them under the formidable eye of Mrs. Reed, in a room full of ladies and gentlemen. But Bessie, as soon as she had dressed her young ladies, used to take herself off to the lively regions of the kitchen and housekeeper's room, generally bearing the candle along with her. I then sat with my doll on my knee, till the fire got low, glancing round occasionally, to make sure that nothing worse than myself haunted the shadowy room; and when the embers sank to a dull red, I undressed hastily, tugging at knots and strings as I best might, and sought shelter from cold and darkness in my crib. To this crib I always took my doll: human beings must love something, and, in the dearth of worthier objects of affection, I contrived to find a pleasure in loving and cherishing a faded graven image, shabby as a miniature scarecrow. It puzzles me now to remember with what absurd sincerity I doted on this little toy; half-fancying it alive and capable of sensation. I could not sleep unless it was folded in my night-gown; and when it lay there safe and warm, I was comparatively happy, believing it to be happy likewise.

Long did the hours seem while I waited the departure of the company, and listened for the sound of Bessie's step on the stairs: sometimes she would come up in the interval to seek her thimble or her scissors, or perhaps to bring me something by way of supper—a bun or a cheese-cake; then she would sit on the bed while I ate it, and when I had finished, she would tuck the clothes round me, and twice she kissed me, and said, "Good-night, Miss Jane." When thus gentle, Bessie seemed to me the best, prettiest, kindest being in the world; and I wished most intensely that she would always be so pleasant and amiable, and never push me about, or scold, or task me unreasonably, as she was too often wont to do. Bessie Lee must, I think, have been a girl of good natural capacity; for she was smart in all she did, and had a remarkable knack of narrative: so, at least, I judge from the impression made on me by her nursery tales. She was pretty, too, if my recollections of her face and person are correct. I remember her as a slim young woman, with black hair, dark eyes, very nice features, and good, clear complexion; but she had a capricious and hasty temper, and indifferent ideas of principle or justice: still, such as she was, I preferred her to any one else at Gateshead Hall.

It was the fifteenth of January, about nine o'clock in the morning: Bessie was gone down to breakfast; my cousins had not yet been summoned to their mama; Eliza was putting on her bonnet and warm garden-coat to go and feed her poultry, an occupation of which she was fond: and not less so of selling the eggs to the housekeeper and hoarding up the money she thus obtained. She had a turn for traffic, and a marked propensity for saving; shown not only in the vending of eggs and chickens, but also in driving hard bargains with the gardener about flower-roots, seeds, and slips of plants; that functionary having orders from Mrs. Reed to buy of his young lady all the products of her parterre she wished to sell: and Eliza would have sold the hair off her head if she could have made a handsome profit thereby. As to her money, she first secreted it in odd corners, wrapped in a rag or an old curl-paper; but some of these hoards having been discovered by the housemaid, Eliza, fearful of one day losing her valued treasure, consented to entrust it to her mother, at a usurious rate of interest—fifty or sixty per cent: which interest she exacted every quarter, keeping her accounts in a little book with anxious accuracy.

Georgiana sat on a high stool, dressing her hair at the glass and interweaving her curls with artificial flowers and faded feathers, of which she had found a store in a drawer in the attic. I was making my bed; having received strict orders from Bessie to get it arranged before she returned (for Bessie now frequently employed me as a sort of under nursery-maid, to tidy the room, dust the chairs, etc.). Having spread the quilt and folded my night-dress, I went to the window-seat to put in order some picture-books and doll's house furniture scattered there; an abrupt command from Georgiana to let her playthings alone (for the tiny chairs and mirrors, the fairy plates and cups were her property) stopped my proceedings; and then, for lack of other occupation, I fell to breathing on the frost-flowers with which the window was fretted, and thus clearing a space in the glass through which I might look out on the grounds, where all was still and petrified under the influence of a hard frost.

From this window were visible the porter's lodge and the carriage-road, and just as I had dissolved so much of the silver-white foliage veiling the panes, as left room to look out, I saw the gates thrown open and a car-

riage roll through. I watched it ascending the drive with indifference: carriages often came to Gateshead, but none ever brought visitors in whom
I was interested; it stopped in front of the house, the door-bell rang loudly, the new comer was admitted. All this being nothing to me, my vacant
attention soon found livelier attraction in the spectacle of a little hungry
robin, which came and chirruped on the twigs of the leafless cherry-tree
nailed against the wall near the casement. The remains of my breakfast
of bread and milk stood on the table, and having crumbled a morsel of
roll, I was tugging at the sash to put out the crumbs on the window-sill,
when Bessie came running upstairs into the nursery.

"Miss Jane, take off your pinafore: what are you doing there? Have you
washed your hands and face this morning?" I gave another tug before I
answered, for I wanted the bird to be secure of its bread: the sash yielded; I scattered the crumbs, some on the stone sill, some on the cherry-
tree bough, then closing the window, I replied:—

"No, Bessie; I have only just finished dusting."

"Troublesome, careless child! and what are you doing now? You look
quite red as if you had been about some mischief: what were you opening the window for?"

I was spared the trouble of answering, for Bessie seemed in too great
a hurry to listen to explanations; she hauled me to the wash-stand, inflicted
a merciless, but happily brief, scrub on my face and hands with soap,
water, and a coarse towel; disciplined my head with a bristly brush, denud-
ed me of my pinafore, and then hurrying me to the top of the stairs, bid
me go down directly, as I was wanted in the breakfast-room.

I would have asked who wanted me: I would have demanded if Mrs.
Reed was there; but Bessie was already gone, and had closed the nursery-
door upon me: I slowly descended. For nearly three months, I had never
been called to Mrs. Reed's presence: restricted so long to the nursery,
the breakfast, dining, and drawing rooms were become for me awful
regions, on which it dismayed me to intrude.

I now stood in the empty hall; before me was the breakfast-room door,
and I stopped, intimidated and trembling. What a miserable little poltroon
had fear, engendered of unjust punishment, made of me in those days!
I feared to return to the nursery; I feared to go forward to the parlour;
ten minutes I stood in agitated hesitation: the vehement ringing of the
breakfast-room bell decided me; I *must* enter.

"Who could want me?" I asked inwardly, as with both hands I turned
the stiff door-handle which, for a second or two, resisted my efforts.
"What should I see besides aunt Reed in the apartment?—a man or a
woman?" The handle turned, the door unclosed, and passing through and
curtesying low, I looked up at—a black pillar!—such, at least, appeared
to me, at first sight, the straight, narrow, sable-clad shape standing erect
on the rug: the grim face at the top was like a carved mask, placed above
the shaft by way of capital.

Mrs. Reed occupied her usual seat by the fireside: she made a signal
for me to approach: I did so, and she introduced me to the stony stranger
with the words: "This is the little girl respecting whom I applied to you."

He, for it was a man, turned his head slowly towards where I stood,
and having examined me with the two inquisitive-looking grey eyes which
twinkled under a pair of bushy brows, said solemnly, and in a bass voice:
"Her size is small: what is her age?"

"Ten years."

"So much?" was the doubtful answer; and he prolonged his scrutiny for some minutes. Presently he addressed me:—

"Your name, little girl?"

"Jane Eyre, sir."

In uttering these words, I looked up: he seemed to me a tall gentleman; but then I was very little; his features were large, and they and all the lines of his frame were equally harsh and prim.

"Well, Jane Eyre, and are you a good child?"

Impossible to reply to this in the affirmative: my little world held a contrary opinion: I was silent. Mrs. Reed answered for me by an expressive shake of the head, adding soon, "Perhaps the less said on that subject the better, Mr. Brocklehurst."

"Sorry indeed to hear it! she and I must have some talk;" and bending from the perpendicular, he installed his person in the arm-chair, opposite Mrs. Reed's. "Come here," he said.

I stepped across the rug; he placed me square and straight before him. What a face he had, now that it was almost on a level with mine! what a great nose! and what a mouth! and what large prominent teeth!

"No sight so sad as that of a naughty child," he began, "especially a naughty little girl. Do you know where the wicked go after death?"

"They go to hell," was my ready and orthodox answer.

"And what is hell? Can you tell me that?"

"A pit full of fire."

"And should you like to fall into that pit, and to be burning there for ever?"

"No, sir."

"What must you do to avoid it?"

I deliberated a moment; my answer, when it did come, was objectionable: "I must keep in good health, and not die."

"How can you keep in good health? Children younger than you die daily. I buried a little child of five years old only a day or two since,—a good little child, whose soul is now in heaven. It is to be feared the same could not be said of you, were you to be called hence."

Not being in a condition to remove his doubt, I only cast my eyes down on the two large feet planted on the rug, and sighed; wishing myself far enough away.

"I hope that sigh is from the heart, and that you repent of ever having been the occasion of discomfort to your excellent benefactress."

"Benefactress! benefactress!" said I, inwardly: "they all call Mrs. Reed my benefactress; if so, a benefactress is a disagreeable thing."

"Do you say your prayers night and morning?" continued my interrogator.

"Yes, sir."

"Do you read your bible?"

"Sometimes."

"With pleasure? Are you fond of it?"

"I like Revelations, and the book of Daniel, and Genesis and Samuel, and a little bit of Exodus, and some parts of Kings and Chronicles, and Job and Jonah."

"And the Psalms? I hope you like them."

"No, sir"

"No? oh, shocking! I have a little boy, younger than you, who knows six Psalms by heart; and when you ask him which he would rather have, a ginger bread-nut to eat, or a verse of a Psalm to learn, he says: 'Oh! the verse of a Psalm! angels sing Psalms;' says he, 'I wish to be a little angel here below;' he then gets two nuts in recompense for his infant piety."

"Psalms are not interesting," I remarked.

"That proves you have a wicked heart; and you must pray to God to change it: to give you a new and a clean one: to take away your heart of stone and give you a heart of flesh."

I was about to propound a question, touching the manner in which that operation of changing my heart was to be performed, when Mrs. Reed interposed, telling me to sit down; she then proceeded to carry on the conversation herself.

"Mr. Brocklehurst, I believe I intimated in the letter which I wrote to you three weeks ago, that this little girl has not quite the character and disposition I could wish: should you admit her into Lowood school, I should be glad if the superintendent and teachers were requested to keep a strict eye on her, and, above all, to guard against her worst fault, a tendency to deceit. I mention this in your hearing, Jane, that you may not attempt to impose on Mr. Brocklehurst."

Well might I dread, well might I dislike Mrs. Reed; for it was her nature to wound me cruelly: never was I happy in her presence: however carefully I obeyed, however strenuously I strove to please her, my efforts were still repulsed and repaid by such sentences as the above. Now, uttered before a stranger, the accusation cut me to the heart: I dimly perceived that she was already obliterating hope from the new phase of existence which she destined me to enter; I felt, though I could not have expressed the feeling, that she was sowing aversion and unkindness along my future path; I saw myself transformed under Mr. Brocklehurst's eye into an artful, noxious child, and what could I do to remedy the injury?"

"Nothing, indeed;" thought I, as I struggled to repress a sob, and hastily wiped away some tears, the impotent evidences of my anguish.

"Deceit is, indeed, a sad fault in a child," said Mr. Brocklehurst; "it is akin to falsehood, and all liars will have their portion in the lake burning with fire and brimstone: she shall, however, be watched, Mrs. Reed; I will speak to Miss Temple and the teachers."

"I should wish her to be brought up in a manner suiting her prospects," continued my benefactress; "to be made useful, to be kept humble: as for the vacations, she will, with your permission, spend them always at Lowood."

"Your decisions are perfectly judicious, madam," returned Mr. Brocklehurst. "Humility is a Christian grace, and one peculiarly appropriate to the pupils of Lowood; I, therefore, direct that especial care shall be bestowed on its cultivation amongst them. I have studied how best to mortify in them the worldly sentiment of pride; and only the other day, I had a pleasing proof of my success. My second daughter, Augusta, went with her mama to visit the school, and on her return she exclaimed: 'Oh, dear papa, how quiet and plain all the girls at Lowood look! with their hair combed behind their ears, and their long pinafores, and those little holland pockets outside their frocks—they are almost like poor people's children! and,' said she, 'they looked at my dress and mama's, as if they had never seen a silk gown before.' "

"This is the state of things I quite approve," returned Mrs. Reed; "had I sought all England over, I could scarcely have found a system more exactly fitting a child like Jane Eyre. Consistency, my dear Mr. Brocklehurst; I advocate consistency in all things."

"Consistency, madam, is the first of Christian duties; and it has been observed in every arrangement connected with the establishment of Lowood: plain fare, simple attire, unsophisticated accommodations, hardy and active habits; such is the order of the day in the house and its inhabitants."

"Quite right, sir. I may then depend upon this child being received as a pupil at Lowood, and there being trained in conformity to her position and prospects?"

"Madam, you may: she shall be placed in that nursery of chosen plants—and I trust she will show herself grateful for the inestimable privilege of her election."

"I will send her, then, as soon as possible, Mr. Brocklehurst; for, I assure you, I feel anxious to be relieved of a responsibility that was becoming too irksome."

"No doubt, no doubt, madam: and now I wish you good-morning. I shall return to Brocklehurst Hall in the course of a week or two: my good friend, the Archdeacon, will not permit me to leave him sooner. I shall send Miss Temple notice that she is to expect a new girl, so that there will be no difficulty about receiving her. Good-bye."

"Good-bye, Mr. Brocklehurst; remember me to Mrs. and Miss Brocklehurst, and to Augusta and Theodore, and Master Broughton Brocklehurst."

"I will, madam. Little girl, here is a book entitled the 'Child's Guide;' read it with prayer, especially that part containing 'an account of the awfully sudden death of Martha G——, a naughty child addicted to falsehood and deceit.' "

With these words Mr. Brocklehurst put into my hand a thin pamphlet sewn in a cover; and having rung for his carriage, he departed.

Mrs. Reed and I were left alone: some minutes passed in silence; she was sewing, I was watching her. Mrs. Reed might be at that time some six or seven-and-thirty; she was a woman of robust frame, square shouldered and strong-limbed, not tall, and though stout not obese; she had a somewhat large face, the under-jaw being much developed and very solid; her brow was low, her chin large and prominent, mouth and nose sufficiently regular; under her light eye-brows glimmered an eye devoid of ruth; her skin was dark and opaque, her hair nearly flaxen; her constitution was sound as a bell—illness never came near her; she was an exact, clever manager, her household and tenantry were thoroughly under her control; her children, only, at times defied her authority, and laughed it to scorn; she dressed well, and had a presence and port calculated to set off handsome attire.

Sitting on a low stool, a few yards from her arm-chair, I examined her figure; I perused her features. In my hand I held the tract, containing the sudden death of the Liar: to which narrative my attention had been pointed as to an appropriate warning. What had just passed; what Mrs. Reed had said concerning me to Mr. Brocklehurst; the whole tenor of their conversation, was recent, raw, and stinging in my mind: I had felt every word as acutely, as I had heard it plainly; and a passion of resentment fomented now within me.

Mrs. Reed looked up from her work; her eye settled on mine, her fingers at the same time suspended their nimble movements.

"Go out of the room: return to the nursery," was her mandate. My look or something else must have struck her as offensive, for she spoke with extreme, though suppressed irritation. I got up, I went to the door: I came back again: I walked to the window, across the room, then close up to her.

Speak I must: I had been trodden on severely, and *must* turn: but how? What strength had I to dart retaliation at my antagonist? I gathered my energies and launched them in this blunt sentence:—

"I am not deceitful: if I were, I should say I loved *you*; but I declare I do not love you: I dislike you the worst of anybody in the world except John Reed; and this book about the liar, you may give to your girl, Georgiana, for it is she who tells lies, and not I."

Mrs. Reed's hands still lay on her work inactive: her eye of ice continued to dwell freezingly on mine:—

"What more have you to say?" she asked, rather in the tone in which a person might address an opponent of adult age than such as is ordinarily used to a child.

That eye of hers, that voice stirred every antipathy I had. Shaking from head to foot, thrilled with ungovernable excitement, I continued:—

"I am glad you are no relation of mine: I will never call you aunt again as long as I live. I will never come to see you when I am grown up; and if any one asks me how I liked you, and how you treated me, I will say the very thought of you makes me sick, and that you treated me with miserable cruelty."

"How dare you affirm that, Jane Eyre?"

"How dare I, Mrs. Reed? How dare I? Because it is the *truth*. You think I have no feelings, and that I can do without one bit of love or kindness; but I cannot live so: and you have no pity. I shall remember how you thrust me back—roughly and violently thrust me back—into the red-room, and locked me up there, to my dying day; though I was in agony; though I cried out, while suffocating with distress, 'Have mercy! Have mercy, aunt Reed!' And that punishment you made me suffer because your wicked boy struck me—knocked me down for nothing. I will tell anybody who asks me questions, this exact tale. People think you a good woman, but you are bad; hard-hearted. *You* are deceitful!"

Ere I had finished this reply, my soul began to expand, to exult, with the strangest sense of freedom, of triumph, I ever felt. It seemed as if an invisible bond had burst, and that I had struggled out into unhoped-for liberty. Not without cause was this sentiment: Mrs. Reed looked frightened; her work had slipped from her knee; she was lifting up her hands, rocking herself to and fro, and even twisting her face as if she would cry.

"Jane, you are under a mistake: what is the matter with you? Why do you tremble so violently? Would you like to drink some water?"

"No, Mrs. Reed."

"Is there anything else you wish for, Jane? I assure you, I desire to be your friend."

"Not you. You told Mr. Brocklehurst I had a bad character, a deceitful disposition; and I'll let everybody at Lowood know what you are, and what you have done."

"Jane, you don't understand these things: children must be corrected for their faults."

"Deceit is not my fault!" I cried out in a savage, high voice.

"But you are passionate, Jane, that you must allow: and now return to the nursery—there's a dear—and lie down a little."

"I am not your dear; I cannot lie down: send me to school soon, Mrs. Reed, for I hate to live here."

"I will indeed send her to school soon," murmured Mrs. Reed, *sotto voce*; and gathering up her work, she abruptly quitted the apartment.

I was left there alone—winner of the field. It was the hardest battle I had fought, and the first victory I had gained: I stood awhile on the rug, where Mr. Brocklehurst had stood, and I enjoyed my conqueror's solitude. First, I smiled to myself and felt elated; but this fierce pleasure subsided in me as fast as did the accelerated throb of my pulses. A child cannot quarrel with its elders, as I had done; cannot give its furious feelings uncontrolled play, as I had given mine; without experiencing afterwards the pang of remorse and the chill of reaction. A ridge of lighted heath, alive, glancing, devouring, would have been a meet emblem of my mind when I accused and menaced Mrs. Reed: the same ridge, black and blasted after the flames are dead, would have represented as meetly my subsequent condition, when half an hour's silence and reflection had shown me the madness of my conduct, and the dreariness of my hated and hating position.

Something of vengeance I had tasted for the first time; as aromatic wine it seemed, on swallowing, warm and racy: its after-flavour, metallic and corroding, gave me a sensation as if I had been poisoned. Willingly would I now have gone and asked Mrs. Reed's pardon; but I knew, partly from experience and partly from instinct, that was the way to make her repulse me with double scorn, thereby re-exciting every turbulent impulse of my nature.

I would fain exercise some better faculty than that of fierce speaking; fain find nourishment for some less fiendish feeling that that of sombre indignation. I took a book—some Arabian tales; I sat down and endeavoured to read. I could make no sense of the subject; my own thoughts swam always between me and the page I had usually found fascinating. I opened the glass-door in the breakfast-room: the shrubbery was quite still; the black frost reigned, unbroken by sun or breeze, through the grounds. I covered my head and arms with the skirt of my frock, and went out to walk in a part of the plantation which was quite sequestered: but I found no pleasure in the silent trees, the fallen fir-cones, the congealed relics of autumn, russet leaves, swept by past winds in heaps, and now stiffened together. I leaned against a gate, and looked into an empty field where no sheep were feeding, where the short grass was nipped and blanched. It was a very gray day; a most opaque sky, "onding on snaw," canopied all; thence flakes fell at intervals, which settled on the hard path and on the hoary lea without melting. I stood, a wretched child enough, whispering to myself over and over again, "What shall I do?—what shall I do?"

All at once I heard a clear voice call, "Miss Jane! where are you? Come to lunch!"

It was Bessie, I knew well enough; but I did not stir; her light step came tripping down the path.

"You naughty little thing!" she said. "Why don't you come when you are called?"

Bessie's presence, compared with the thoughts over which I had been brooding, seemed cheerful; even though, as usual, she was somewhat cross. The fact is, after my conflict with, and victory over Mrs. Reed, I was not disposed to care much for the nursemaid's transitory anger; and I *was* disposed to bask in her youthful lightness of heart. I just put my two arms round her, and said, "Come, Bessie! don't scold."

The action was more frank and fearless than any I was habituated to indulge in: somehow it pleased her.

"You are a strange child, Miss Jane," she said, as she looked down at me: "a little roving, solitary thing: and you are going to school, I suppose?"

I nodded.

"And won't you be sorry to leave poor Bessie?"

"What does Bessie care for me? She is always scolding me."

"Because you're such a queer, frightened, shy little thing. You should be bolder."

"What! to get more knocks?"

"Nonsense! But you are rather put upon, that's certain. My mother said, when she came to see me last week, that she would not like a little one of her own to be in your place.—Now, come in, and I've some good news for you."

"I don't think you have, Bessie."

"Child! what do you mean? What sorrowful eyes you fix on me! Well! but Missis and the young ladies and Master John are going out to tea this afternoon, and you shall have tea with me. I'll ask cook to bake you a little cake, and then you shall help me to look over your drawers; for I am soon to pack your trunk. Missis intends you to leave Gateshead in a day or two, and you shall choose what toys you like to take with you."

"Bessie, you must promise not to scold me any more till I go."

"Well, I will: but mind, you are a very good girl, and don't be afraid of me. Don't start when I chance to speak rather sharply: it's so provoking."

"I don't think I shall ever be afraid of you again, Bessie, because I have got used to you; and I shall soon have another set of people to dread."

"If you dread them, they'll dislike you."

"As you do, Bessie?"

"I don't dislike you, Miss; I believe I am fonder of you than of all the others."

"You don't show it."

"You little sharp thing! you've got quite a new way of talking. What makes you so venturesome and hardy?

"Why, I shall soon be away from you, and besides——" I was going to say something about what had passed between me and Mrs. Reed; but on second thoughts I considered it better to remain silent on that head.

"And so you're glad to leave me?"

"Not at all, Bessie; indeed, just now I am rather sorry."

"Just now! and rather! How coolly my little lady says it! I daresay now if I were to ask you for a kiss you wouldn't give it me: you'd say you would *rather* not."

"I'll kiss you and welcome: bend your head down." Bessie stooped; we mutually embraced, and I followed her into the house quite comforted. That afternoon lapsed in peace and harmony; and in the evening Bessie told me some of her most enchaining stories, and sang me some of her sweetest songs. Even for me life had its gleams of sunshine.

·······

Chapter 5

Five o'clock had hardly struck on the morning of the 19th of January, when Bessie brought a candle into my closet and found me already up and nearly dressed. I had risen half an hour before her entrance, and had washed my face, and put on my clothes by the light of a half-moon just setting, whose ray streamed through the narrow window near my crib. I was to leave Gateshead that day by a coach which passed the lodge gates at six A.M. Bessie was the only person yet risen; she had lit a fire in the nursery, where she now proceeded to make my breakfast. Few children can eat when excited with the thoughts of a journey; nor could I. Bessie, having pressed me in vain to take a few spoonfuls of the boiled milk and bread she had prepared for me, wrapped up some biscuits in a paper and put them into my bag; then she helped me on with my pelisse and bonnet, and wrapping herself in a shawl, she and I left the nursery. As we passed Mrs. Reed's bed-room, she said, "Will you go in and bid Missis good-bye?"

"No, Bessie: she came to my crib last night when you were gone down to supper, and said I need not disturb her in the morning, or my cousins either; and she told me to remember that she had always been my best friend, and to speak of her and be grateful to her accordingly."

"What did you say, Miss?"

"Nothing: I covered my face with the bed-clothes, and turned from her to the wall."

That was wrong, Miss Jane."

"It was quite right, Bessie: your Missis has not been my friend; she has been my foe."

"Oh, Miss Jane! don't say so!"

"Good-bye to Gateshead!" cried I, as we passed through the hall and went out at the front door.

The moon was set, and it was very dark; Bessie carried a lantern, whose light glanced on wet steps and gravel road sodden by a recent thaw. Raw and chill was the winter morning; my teeth chattered as I hastened down the drive. There was a light in the porter's lodge; when we reached it we found the porter's wife just kindling her fire: my trunk, which had been carried down the evening before, stood corded at the door. It wanted but a few minutes of six, and shortly after that hour had struck, the distant

roll of wheels announced the coming coach; I went to the door and
watched its lamps approach rapidly through the gloom.

"Is she going by herself?" asked the porter's wife.

"Yes."

"And how far is it?"

"Fifty miles."

"What a long way! I wonder Mrs. Reed is not afraid to trust her so far
alone."

The coach drew up; there it was at the gates with its four horses and
its top laden with passengers: the guard and coachman loudly urged haste;
my trunk was hoisted up; I was taken from Bessie's neck, to which I clung
with kisses.

"Be sure and take good care of her," cried she to the guard, as he lifted
me into the inside.

"Ay, ay!" was the answer: the door was clapped to, a voice exclaimed
"All right," and on we drove. Thus was I severed from Bessie and Gateshead: thus whirled away to unknown, and, as I then deemed, remote and
mysterious regions.

I remember but little of the journey: I only know that the day seemed
to me of a preternatural length, and that we appeared to travel over hundreds of miles of road. We passed through several towns, and in one, a
very large one, the coach stopped; the horses were taken out, and the
passengers alighted to dine. I was carried into an inn, where the guard
wanted me to have some dinner; but, as I had no appetite, he left me in
an immense room with a fire-place at each end, a chandelier pendent from
the ceiling, and a little red gallery high up against the wall filled with
musical instruments. Here I walked about for a long time, feeling very
strange, and mortally apprehensive of some one coming in and kidnapp-
ing me: for I believed in kidnappers; their exploits have frequently figured
in Bessie's fire-side chronicles. At last the guard returned; once more I
was stowed away in the coach, my protector mounted his own seat, sounded his hollow horn, and away we rattled over the "stony street" of L——.

The afternoon came on wet and somewhat misty; as it waned into dusk,
I began to feel that we were getting very far indeed from Gateshead: we
ceased to pass through towns; the country changed; great gray hills heaved
up round the horizon: as twilight deepened, we descended a valley, dark
with wood, and long after night had overclouded the prospect, I heard
a wild wind rushing amongst trees.

Lulled by the sound, I at last dropped asleep: I had not long slumbered
when the sudden cessation of motion awoke me; the coach-door was open,
and a person like a servant was standing at it: I saw her face and dress
by the light of the lamps.

"Is there a little girl called Jane Eyre here?" she asked. I answered
"Yes," and was then lifted out; my trunk was handed down, and the coach
instantly drove away.

I was stiff with long sitting, and bewildered with the noise and motion
of the coach: gathering my faculties, I looked about me. Rain, wind, and
darkness filled the air; nevertheless, I dimly discerned a wall before me
and a door open in it; through this door I passed with my new guide: she
shut and locked it behind her. There was now visible a house or houses—
for the building spread far—with many windows; and lights burning in
some; we went up a broad pebbly path, splashing wet, and were admit-

ted at a door; then the servant led me through a passage into a room with a fire, where she left me alone.

I stood and warmed my numbed fingers over the blaze, then I looked round; there was no candle, but the uncertain light from the hearth showed by intervals, papered walls, carpet, curtains, shining mahogany furniture: it was a parlour, not so spacious or splendid as the drawing-room at Gateshead, but comfortable enough. I was puzzling to make out the subject of a picture on the wall, when the door opened, and an individual carrying a light entered; another followed close behind.

The first was a tall lady with dark hair, dark eyes, and a pale and large forehead; her figure was partly enveloped in a shawl, her countenance was grave, her bearing erect.

"The child is very young to be sent alone;" said she, putting her candle down on the table. She considered me attentively for a minute or two, then further added:—

"She had better be put to bed soon; she looks tired: are you tired?" she asked, placing her hand on my shoulder.

"A little, ma'am."

"And hungry, too, no doubt: let her have some supper before she goes to bed, Miss Miller. Is this the first time you have left your parents to come to school, my little girl?"

I explained to her that I had no parents. She inquired how long they had been dead; then how old I was, what was my name, whether I could read, write, and sew a little: then she touched my cheek gently with her forefinger, and saying, "She hoped I should be a good child," dismissed me along with Miss Miller.

The lady I had left might be about twenty-nine; the one who went with me appeared some years younger: the first impressed me by her voice, look, and air. Miss Miller was more ordinary; ruddy in complexion, though of a careworn countenance; hurried in gait and action, like one who had always a multiplicity of tasks on hand: she looked, indeed, what I afterwards found she really was, an under-teacher. Led by her, I passed from compartment to compartment, from passage to passage, of a large and irregular building; till, emerging from the total and somewhat dreary silence pervading that portion of the house we had traversed, we came upon the hum of many voices, and presently entered a wide, long room, with great deal tables, two at each end, on each of which burnt a pair of candles, and seated all round on benches, a congregation of girls of every age, from nine or ten to twenty. Seen by the dim light of the dips, their number to me appeared countless, though not in reality exceeding eighty; they were uniformly dressed in brown stuff frocks of quaint fashion, and long holland pinafores. It was the hour of study; they were engaged in conning over their to-morrow's task, and the hum I had heard was the combined result of their whispered repetitions.

Miss Miller signed to me to sit on a bench near the door, then walking up to the top of the long room, she cried out:—

"Monitors, collect the lesson-books and put them away!"

Four tall girls arose from different tables, and going round, gathered the books and removed them. Miss Miller again gave the word of command:—

"Monitors, fetch the supper-trays!"

The tall girls went out and returned presently, each bearing a tray, with

portions of something, I knew not what, arranged thereon, and a pitcher of
water and mug in the middle of each tray. The portions were handed round;
those who liked took a draught of the water, the mug being common to all.
When it came to my turn, I drank, for I was thirsty, but did not touch the food;
excitement and fatigue rendering me incapable of eating: I now saw, however,
that it was a thin oaten cake, shared into fragments.

The meal over, prayers were read by Miss Miller, and the classes filed
off—two and two, up stairs. Overpowered by this time with weariness, I
scarcely noticed what sort of a place the bed-room was; except that, like the
school-room, I saw it was very long. To-night I was to be Miss Miller's bed-
fellow; she helped me to undress: when laid down I glanced at the long rows
of beds, each of which was quickly filled with two occupants; in ten minutes
the single light was extinguished; amidst silence and complete darkness, I
fell asleep.

The night passed rapidly: I was too tired even to dream; I only once awoke
to hear the wind rave in furious gusts, and the rain fall in torrents, and to be
sensible that Miss Miller had taken her place by my side. When I again
unclosed my eyes, a loud bell was ringing: the girls were up and dressing;
day had not yet begun to dawn, and a rushlight or two burnt in the room. I
too rose reluctantly; it was bitter cold, and I dressed as well as I could for
shivering, and washed when there was a basin at liberty: which did not occur soon, as there was but one basin to six girls, on the stands down the middle of the room. Again the bell rang: all formed in file, two and two, and in
that order descended the stairs and entered the cold and dimly-lit school-
room: here prayers were read by Miss Miller; afterwards she called out:—

"Form classes!"

A great tumult succeeded for some minutes, during which Miss Miller
repeatedly exclaimed, "Silence!" and "Order!" When it subsided, I saw
them all drawn up in four semicircles, before four chairs, placed at the
four tables; all held books in their hands, and a great book, like a bible,
lay on each table, before the vacant seat. A pause of some seconds succeeded, filled up by the low, vague hum of numbers: Miss Miller walked
from class to class, hushing this indefinite sound.

A distant bell tinkled: immediately three ladies entered the room, each
walked to a table and took her seat; Miss Miller assumed the fourth vacant chair, which was that nearest the door, and around which the smallest
of the children were assembled: to this inferior class I was called, and
placed at the bottom of it.

Business now began: the day's Collect was repeated, then certain texts
of scripture were said, and to these succeeded a protracted reading of chapters in the Bible, which lasted an hour. By the time that exercise was terminated, day had fully dawned. The indefatigable bell now sounded for the
fourth time: the classes were marshalled and marched into another room
to breakfast: how glad I was to behold a prospect of getting something
to eat! I was now nearly sick from inanition, having taken so little the
day before.

The refectory was a great, low-ceiled gloomy room; on two long tables
smoked basins of something hot, which, however, to my dismay, sent forth
an odour far from inviting. I saw a universal manifestation of discontent
when the fumes of the repast met the nostrils of those destined to swallow
it: from the van of the procession, the tall girls of the first class, rose the
whispered words:—

"Disgusting! The porridge is burnt again!"

"Silence!" ejaculated a voice; not that of Miss Miller, but of one of the upper teachers, a little and dark personage, smartly dressed, but of somewhat morose aspect, who installed herself at the top of one table, while a more buxom lady presided at the other. I looked in vain for her I had first seen the night before; she was not visible: Miss Miller occupied the foot of the table where I sat, and a strange foreign-looking, elderly lady, the French teacher, as I afterwards found, took the corresponding seat at the other board. A long grace was said and a hymn sung; then a servant brought in some tea for the teachers and the meal began.

Ravenous, and now very faint, I devoured a spoonful or two of my portion without thinking of its taste; but the first edge of hunger blunted, I perceived I had got in hand a nauseous mess: burnt porridge is almost as bad as rotten potatoes; famine itself soon sickens over it. The spoons were moved slowly: I saw each girl taste her food and try to swallow it; but in most cases the effort was soon relinquished. Breakfast was over, and none had breakfasted. Thanks being returned for what we had not got, and a second hymn chanted, the refectory was evacuated for the school-room. I was one of the last to go out, and in passing the tables, I saw one teacher take a basin of the porridge and taste it; she looked at the others; all their countenances expressed displeasure, and one of them, the stout one, whispered:—

"Abominable stuff! How shameful!"

A quarter of an hour passed before lessons again began, during which the school-room was in a glorious tumult; for that space of time, it seemed to be permitted to talk loud and more freely, and they used their privilege. The whole conversation ran on the breakfast, which one and all abused roundly. Poor things! it was the sole consolation they had. Miss Miller was now the only teacher in the room: a group of great girls standing about her, spoke with serious and sullen gestures. I heard the name of Mr. Brocklehurst pronounced by some lips; at which Miss Miller shook her head disapprovingly; but she made no great effort to check the general wrath: doubtless she shared in it.

A clock in the school-room struck nine; Miss Miller left her circle, and standing in the middle of the room, cried:—

"Silence! To your seats!

Discipline prevailed: in five minutes the confused throng was resolved into order, and comparative silence quelled the Babel clamour of tongues. The upper teachers now punctually resumed their posts; but still, all seemed to wait. Ranged on benches down the sides of the room, the eighty girls sat motionless and erect: a quaint assemblage they appeared, all with plain locks combed from their faces, not a curl visible; in brown dresses, made high and surrounded by a narrow tucker about the throat; with little pockets of holland (shaped something like a Highlander's purse) tied in front of their frocks, and destined to serve the purpose of a work-bag: all too wearing woollen stockings and country-made shoes, fastened with brass buckles. Above twenty of those clad in this costume were full-grown girls; or rather young women: it suited them ill, and gave an air of oddity even to the prettiest.

I was still looking at them, and also at intervals examining the teachers—none of whom precisely pleased me; for the stout one was a little coarse, the dark one not a little fierce, the foreigner harsh and grotesque, and

Miss Miller, poor thing! looked purple, weather-beaten, and over-worked
—when, as my eye wandered from face to face, the whole school rose
simultaneously, as if moved by a common spring.

What was the matter? I had heard no order given: I was puzzled. Ere
I had gathered my wits, the classes were again seated: but as all eyes were
now turned to one point, mine followed the general direction, and encountered the personage who had received me last night. She stood at the
bottom of the long room, on the hearth; for there was a fire at each end:
she surveyed the two rows of girls silently and gravely. Miss Miller approaching, seemed to ask her a question, and having received her answer,
went back to her place, and said aloud,—

"Monitor of the first class, fetch the globes!"

While the direction was being executed, the lady consulted moved slowly up the room. I suppose I have a considerable organ of veneration, for
I retain yet the sense of admiring awe with which my eyes tracked her
steps. Seen now, in broad daylight, she looked tall, fair, and shapely;
brown eyes, with a benignant light in their irids, and a fine pencilling of
long lashes round, relieved the whiteness of her large front; on each of
her temples her hair, of a very dark brown, was clustered in round curls,
according to the fashion of those times, when neither smooth bands nor
long ringlets were in vogue; her dress, also in the mode of the day, was
of purple cloth, relieved by a sort of Spanish trimming of black velvet;
a gold watch (watches were not so common then as now) shown at her
girdle. Let the reader add, to complete the picture, refined features; a complexion, if pale, clear; and a stately air and carriage, and he will have,
at least as clearly as words can give it, a correct idea of the exterior of
Miss Temple,—Maria Temple, as I afterwards saw the name written in
a prayer-book entrusted to me to carry to church.

The superintendent of Lowood (for such was this lady) having taken
her seat before a pair of globes placed on one of the tables, summoned
the first class round her, and commenced giving a lesson in geography;
the lower classes were called by the teachers: repetitions in history, grammar, etc. went on for an hour; writing and arithmetic succeeded, and
music lessons were given by Miss Temple to some of the elder girls. The
duration of each lesson was measured by the clock, which at last struck
twelve. The superintendent rose:—

"I have a word to address to the pupils," said she.

The tumult of cessation from lessons was already breaking forth, but
it sank at her voice. She went on:—

"You had this morning a breakfast which you could not eat; you must
be hungry:—I have ordered that a lunch of bread and cheese shall be
served to all."

The teachers looked at her with a sort of surprise.

"It is to be done on my responsibility," she added, in an explanatory
tone to them, and immediately afterwards left the room.

The bread and cheese was presently brought in and distributed, to the
high delight and refreshment of the whole school. The order was now
given "To the garden!" Each put on a coarse straw bonnet, with strings
of coloured calico, and a cloak of grey frieze. I was similarly equipped,
and, following the stream, I made my way into the open air.

The garden was a wide enclosure, surrounded with walls so high as to
exclude every glimpse of prospect; a covered veranda ran down one side,

and broad walks bordered a middle space divided into scores of little beds: these beds were assigned as gardens for the pupils to cultivate, and each bed had an owner. When full of flowers they would, doubtless, look pretty; but now, at the latter end of January, all was wintry blight and brown decay. I shuddered as I stood and looked round me: it was an inclement day for out-door exercise; not positively rainy, but darkened by a drizzling yellow fog; all underfoot was still soaking wet with the floods of yesterday. The stronger among the girls ran about and engaged in active games, but sundry pale and thin ones herded together for shelter and warmth in the veranda; and amongst these as the dense mist penetrated to their shivering frames, I heard frequently the sound of a hollow cough.

As yet I had spoken to no one, nor did anybody seem to take notice of me; I stood lonely enough: but to that feeling of isolation I was accustomed; it did not oppress me much. I leant against a pillar of the veranda, drew my gray mantle close about me, and trying to forget the cold which nipped me without, and the unsatisfied hunger which gnawed me within, delivered myself up to the employment of watching and thinking. My reflections were too undefined and fragmentary to merit record: I hardly yet knew where I was; Gateshead and my past life seemed floated away to an immeasurable distance; the present was vague and strange, and of the future I could form no conjecture. I looked round the convent-like garden, and then up at the house; a large building, half of which seemed gray and old, the other half quite new. The new part, containing the school-room and dormitory, was lit by mullioned and latticed windows, which gave it a church-like aspect; a stone tablet over the door, bore this inscription:—

"Lowood Institution—This portion was rebuilt A.D.——, by Naomi Brocklehurst, of Brocklehurst Hall, in this country." "Let your light so shine before men that they may see your good works, and glorify your Father which is in heaven."—St. Matt. v. 16.

I read these words over and over again: I felt that an explanation belonged to them, and was unable fully to penetrate their import. I was still pondering the signification of "Institution," and endeavouring to make out a connection between the first words and the verse of scripture, when the sound of a cough close behind me, made me turn my head. I saw a girl sitting on a stone bench near; she was bent over a book, on the perusal of which she seemed intent: from where I stood I could see the title—it was "Rasselas"; a name that struck me as strange, and consequently attractive. In turning a leaf she happened to look up, and I said to her directly:—

"Is your book interesting?" I had already formed the intention of asking her to lend it to me some day.

"I like it," she answered, after a pause of a second or two, during which she examined me.

"What is it about?" I continued. I hardly know where I found the hardihood thus to open a conversation with a stranger; the step was contrary to my nature and habits: but I think her occupation touched a cord of sympathy somewhere; for I too liked reading, though of a frivolous and childish kind; I could not digest or comprehend the serious or substantial.

"You may look at it," replied the girl, offering me the book.

I did so; a brief examination convinced me that the contents were less taking than the title: "Rasselas" looked dull to my trifling taste; I saw nothing about fairies, nothing about genii; no bright variety seemed spread over the closely-printed pages. I returned it to her; she received it quickly, and without saying anything she was about to relapse into her former studious mood: again I ventured to disturb her:—

"Can you tell me what the writing on the stone over the door means? What is Lowood Institution?"

"This house where you are come to live."

"And why do they call it Institution? Is it in any way different from other schools?"

"It is partly a charity-school: you and I, and all the rest of us, are charity-children. I suppose you are an orphan: are not either your father or your mother dead?"

"Both died before I can remember."

"Well, all the girls here have lost either one or both parents, and this is called an institution for educating orphans."

"Do we pay no money? Do they keep us for nothing?"

"We pay, or our friends pay, fifteen pounds a year for each."

"Then why do they call us charity-children?"

"Because fifteen pounds is not enough for board and teaching, and the deficiency is supplied by subscription."

"Who subscribes?"

"Different benevolent-minded ladies and gentlemen in this neighbourhood and in London."

"Who was Naomi Brocklehurst?"

"The lady who built the new part of this house as that tablet records, and whose son overlooks and directs everything here."

"Why?"

"Because he is treasurer and manager of the establishment."

"Then this house does not belong to that tall lady who wears a watch, and who said we were to have some bread and cheese?"

"To Miss Temple? Oh, no! I wish it did: she has to answer to Mr. Brocklehurst for all she does. Mr. Brocklehurst buys all our food and all our clothes."

"Does he live here?"

"No—two miles off, at a large hall."

"Is he a good man?"

"He is a clergyman, and is said to do a great deal of good."

"Did you say that tall lady was called Miss Temple?"

"Yes."

"And what are the other teachers called?"

"The one with red cheeks is called Miss Smith; she attends to the work, and cuts out—for we make our own clothes, our frocks, and pelisses, and everything; the little one with black hair is Miss Scatcherd; she teaches history and grammar, and hears the second class repetitions; and the one who wears a shawl, and has a pocket-handkerchief tied to her side with a yellow riband, is Madame Pierrot: she comes from Lisle, in France, and teaches French."

"Do you like the teachers?

"Well enough."

"Do you like the little black one, and the Madame ——? I cannot pronounce her name as you do."

"Miss Scatcherd is hasty—you must take care not to offend her;

Madame Pierrot is not a bad sort of person."

"But Miss Temple is the best—isn't she?"

"Miss Temple is very good, and very clever; she is above the rest, because she knows far more than they do."

"Have you been long here?"

"Two years."

"Are you an orphan?"

"My mother is dead."

"Are you happy here?"

"You ask rather too many questions. I have given you answers enough for the present: now I want to read."

But at that moment the summons sounded for dinner: all re-entered the house. The odour which now filled the refectory was scarcely more appetizing than that which had regaled our nostrils at breakfast: the dinner was served in two huge tin-plated vessels, whence rose a strong steam redolent of rancid fat. I found the mess to consist of indifferent potatoes and strange shreds of rusty meat, mixed and cooked together. Of this preparation a tolerably abundant plateful was apportioned to each pupil. I ate what I could, and wondered within myself whether every day's fare would be like this.

After dinner, we immediately adjourned to the school-room: lessons recommenced, and were continued till five o'clock.

The only marked event of the afternoon was, that I saw the girl with whom I had conversed in the veranda, dismissed in disgrace, by Miss Scatcherd, from a history class, and sent to stand in the middle of the large school-room. The punishment seemed to me in a high degree ignominious, especially for so great a girl—she looked thirteen or upwards. I expected she would show signs of great distress and shame; but to my surprise she neither wept nor blushed: composed, though grave, she stood, the central mark of all eyes. "How can she bear it so quietly—so firmly?" I asked of myself. "Were I in her place, it seems to me I should wish the earth to open and swallow me up. She looks as if she were thinking of something beyond her punishment—beyond her situation: of something not round her nor before her. I have heard of day-dreams—is she in a day-dream now? Her eyes are fixed on the floor, but I am sure they do not see it—her sight seems turned in, gone down into her heart: she is looking at what she can remember, I believe; not at what is really present. I wonder what sort of a girl she is—whether good or naughty."

Soon after five P.M. we had another meal, consisting of a small mug of coffee, and half a slice of brown bread. I devoured my bread and drank my coffee with relish; but I should have been glad of as much more—I was still hungry. Half an hour's recreation succeeded, then study; then the glass of water and the piece of oat-cake, prayers, and bed. Such was my first day at Lowood.

. . . .

Chapter 6

The next day commenced as before, getting up and dressing by rushlight; but this morning we were obliged to dispense with the ceremony of washing: the water in the pitchers was frozen. A change had taken place

in the weather the preceding evening, and a keen north-east wind, whist-
ling through the crevices of our bed-room windows all night long, had
made us shiver in our beds, and turned the contents of the ewers to ice.

Before the long hour and a half of prayers and Bible reading was over,
I felt ready to perish with cold. Breakfast-time came at last, and this morning the porridge was not burnt; the quality was eatable, the quantity small:
how small my portion seemed! I wished it had been doubled.

In the course of the day I was enrolled a member of the fourth class,
and regular tasks and occupations were assigned me: hitherto, I had only been a spectator of the proceedings at Lowood, I was now to become
an actor therein. At first, being little accustomed to learn by heart, the
lessons appeared to me both long and difficult; the frequent change from
task to task, too, bewildered me; and I was glad, when, about three o'clock
in the afternoon, Miss Smith put into my hands a border of muslin two
yards long, together with needle, thimble, etc., and sent me to sit in a quiet
corner of the school-room, with directions to hem the same. At that hour
most of the others were sewing likewise; but one class still stood round
Miss Scatcherd's chair reading, and as all was quiet, the subject of their
lessons could be heard, together with the manner in which each girl acquitted herself, and the animadversions or commendations of Miss Scatcherd on the performance. It was English history: among the readers, I
observed my acquaintance of the veranda; at the commencement of the
lesson, her place had been at the top of the class, but for some error of
pronunciation or some inattention to stops, she was suddenly sent to the
very bottom. Even in that obscure position, Miss Scatcherd continued to
make her an object of constant notice: she was continually addressing to
her such phrases as the following:—

"Burns, (such it seems was her name: the girls here, were all called
by their surnames, as boys are elsewhere); Burns, you are standing on
the side of your shoe, turn your toes out immediately." "Burns, you poke
your chin most unpleasantly, draw it in." "Burns, I insist on your holding
your head up: I will not have you before me in that attitude," etc., etc.

A chapter having been read through twice, the books were closed and
the girls examined. The lesson had comprised part of the reign of Charles
I, and there were sundry questions about tonnage and poundage, and ship-
money, which most of them appeared unable to answer; still, every little
difficulty was solved instantly when it reached Burns: her memory seemed
to have retained the substance of the whole lesson, and she was ready with
answers on every point. I kept expecting that Miss Scatcherd would praise
her attention; but, instead of that, she suddenly cried out:—

"You dirty, disagreeable girl! you have never cleaned your nails this
morning!"

Burns made no answer: I wondered at her silence.

"Why," thought I, "does she not explain that she could neither clean
her nails nor wash her face, as the water was frozen?"

My attention was now called off by Miss Smith, desiring me to hold
a skein of thread: while she was winding it, she talked to me from time
to time, asking, whether I had ever been at school before, whether I could
mark, stitch, knit, etc.; till she dismissed me, I could not pursue my observations on Miss Scatcherd's movements. When I returned to my seat, that
lady was just delivering an order, of which I did not catch the import; but
Burns immediately left the class, and, going into the small inner room

where the books were kept, returned in half a minute, carrying in her hand a bundle of twigs tied together at one end. This ominous tool she presented to Miss Scatcherd with a respectful courtesy; then she quietly, and without being told, unloosed her pinafore, and the teacher instantly and sharply inflicted on her neck a dozen strokes with the bunch of twigs. Not a tear rose to Burns's eye; and, while I paused from my sewing, because my fingers quivered at this spectacle with a sentiment of unavailing and impotent anger, not a feature of her pensive face altered its ordinary expression.

"Hardened girl!" exclaimed Miss Scatcherd, "nothing can correct you of your slatternly habits: carry the rod away."

Burns obeyed: I looked at her narrowly as she emerged from the book-closet; she was just putting back her handkerchief into her pocket, and the trace of a tear glistened on her thin cheek.

The play-hour in the evening I thought the pleasantest fraction of the day at Lowood: the bit of bread, the draught of coffee swallowed at five o'clock had revived vitality, if it had not satisfied hunger; the long restraint of the day was slackened; the school-room felt warmer than in the morning: its fires being allowed to burn a little more brightly to supply, in some measure, the place of candles, not yet introduced; the ruddy gloaming, the licensed uproar, the confusion of many voices gave one a welcome sense of liberty.

On the evening of the day on which I had seen Miss Scatcherd flog her pupil, Burns, I wandered as usual among the forms and tables and laughing groups without a companion, yet not feeling lonely: when I passed the windows, I now and then lifted a blind and looked out; it snowed fast, a drift was already forming against the lower panes; putting my ear close to the window, I could distinguish from the gleeful tumult within, the disconsolate moan of the wind outside.

Probably, if I had lately left a good home and kind parents, this would have been the hour when I should most keenly have regretted the separation: that wind would then have saddened my heart; this obscure chaos would have disturbed my peace: as it was I derived from both a strange excitement, and reckless and feverish, I wished the wind to howl more wildly, the gloom to deepen to darkness, and the confusion to rise to clamour.

Jumping over forms, and creeping under tables, I made my way to one of the fire-places: there, kneeling by the high wire fender, I found Burns, absorbed, silent, abstracted from all round her by the companionship of a book, which she read by the dim glare of the embers.

"Is it still Rasselas?" I asked, coming behind her.

"Yes," she said, "and I have just finished it."

And in five minutes more she shut it up. I was glad of this.

"Now," thought I, "I can perhaps get her to talk." I sat down by her on the floor.

"What is your name besides Burns?"

"Helen."

"Do you come a long way from here?"

"I come from a place further north; quite on the borders of Scotland."

"Will you ever go back?"

"I hope so; but nobody can be sure of the future."

"You must wish to leave Lowood?"

"No: why should I? I was sent to Lowood to get an education; and it would be of no use going away until I have attained that object."

"But that teacher, Miss Scatcherd, is so cruel to you?"

"Cruel? Not at all! She is severe: she dislikes my faults."

"And if I were in your place I should dislike her: I should resist her; if she struck me with that rod, I should get it from her hand; I should break it under her nose."

"Probably you would do nothing of the sort: but if you did, Mr. Brocklehurst would expel you from the school; that would be a great grief to your relations. It is far better to endure patiently a smart which nobody feels but yourself, than to commit a hasty action whose evil consequences will extend to all connected with you—and, besides, the Bible bids us return good for evil."

"But then it seems disgraceful to be flogged, and to be sent to stand in the middle of a room full of people; and you are such a great girl: I am far younger than you, and I could not bear it."

"Yet it would be your duty to bear it, if you could not avoid it: it is weak and silly to say you *cannot bear* what it is your fate to be required to bear."

I heard her with wonder: I could not comprehend this doctrine of endurance; and still less could I understand or sympathize with the forbearance she expressed for her chastiser. Still I felt that Helen Burns considered things by a light invisible to my eyes. I suspected she might be right and I wrong; but I would not ponder the matter deeply: like Felix, I put it off to a more convenient season.

"You say you have faults, Helen: what are they? To me you seem very good."

"Then learn from me, not to judge by appearances: I am, as Miss Scatcherd said, slatternly; I seldom put, and never keep, things in order; I am careless; I forget rules; I read when I should learn my lessons; I have no method; and sometimes I say, like you, I cannot *bear* to be subjected to systematic arrangements. This is all very provoking to Miss Scatcherd, who is naturally neat, punctual, and particular."

"And cross and cruel," I added; but Helen Burns would not admit my addition: she kept silence.

"Is Miss Temple as severe to you as Miss Scatcherd?"

At the utterance of Miss Temple's name, a soft smile flitted over her grave face.

"Miss Temple is full of goodness; it pains her to be severe to any one, even the worst in the school: she sees my errors, and tells me of them gently; and, if I do anything worthy of praise, she gives me my meed liberally. One strong proof of my wretchedly defective nature is, that even her expostulations, so mild, so rational, have not influence to cure me of my faults; and even her praise, though I value it most highly, cannot stimulate me to continued care and foresight."

"That is curious," said I: "it is so easy to be careful."

"For *you* I have no doubt it is. I observed you in your class this morning, and saw you were closely attentive: your thoughts never seemed to wander while Miss Miller explained the lesson and questioned you. Now, mine continually rove away: when I should be listening to Miss Scatcherd, and collecting all she says with assiduity, often I lose the very sound of her voice; I fall into a sort of dream. Sometimes I think I am in Northumberland, and that the noises I hear round me are the bubbling of a little brook which runs through Deepden, near our house;—then, when it comes to my turn to reply, I have to be wakened; and, having heard nothing of what was read for listening to the visionary brook, I have no answer ready."

"Yet how well you replied this afternoon!"

"It was mere chance: the subject on which we had been reading had interested me. This afternoon, instead of dreaming of Deepden, I was wondering how a man who wished to do right could act so unjustly and unwisely as Charles the First sometimes did; and I thought what a pity it was that, with his integrity and conscientiousness, he could see no farther than the prerogatives of the crown. If he had but been able to look to a distance, and see how what they call the spirit of the age was tending! Still, I like Charles—I respect him—I pity him, poor murdered king! Yes, his enemies were the worst: they shed blood they had no right to shed. How dared they kill him!"

Helen was talking to herself now: she had forgotten I could not very well understand her—that I was ignorant, or nearly so, of the subject she discussed. I recalled her to my level.

"And when Miss Temple teaches you, do your thoughts wander then?"

"No, certainly, not often; because Miss Temple has generally something to say which is newer than my own reflections: her language is singularly agreeable to me, and the information she communicates is often just what I wished to gain."

"Well, then, with Miss Temple you are good?"

"Yes, in a passive way: I make no effort; I follow as inclination guides me. There is no merit in such goodness."

"A great deal: you are good to those who are good to you. It is all I ever desire to be. If people were always kind and obedient to those who are cruel and unjust, the wicked people would have it all their own way: they would never feel afraid, and so they would never alter, but would grow worse and worse. When we are struck at without a reason, we should strike back again very hard; I am sure we should—so hard as to teach the person who struck us never to do it again."

"You will change your mind, I hope, when you grow older: as yet you are but a little untaught girl."

"But I feel this, Helen: I must dislike those who, whatever I do to please them, persist in disliking me; I must resist those who punish me unjustly. It is as natural as that I should love those who show me affection, or submit to punishment when I feel it is deserved."

"Heathens and savage tribes hold that doctrine; but Christians and civilized nations disown it."

"How? I don't understand."

"It is not violence that best overcomes hate—nor vengeance that most certainly heals injury."

"What then?"

"Read the New Testament, and observe what Christ says, and how he acts—make his word your rule, and his conduct your example."

"What does he say?"

"Love your enemies; bless them that curse you; do good to them that hate you and despitefully use you."

"Then I should love Mrs. Reed, which I cannot do; I should bless her son John, which is impossible."

In her turn, Helen Burns asked me to explain; and I proceeded forthwith to pour out, in my own way, the tale of my sufferings and resentments. Bitter and truculent when excited; I spoke as I felt, without reserve or softening.

Helen heard me patiently to the end: I expected she would then make a remark, but she said nothing.

"Well," I asked impatiently, "is not Mrs. Reed a hard-hearted, bad woman?"

"She has been unkind to you, no doubt; because, you see, she dislikes your cast of character, as Miss Scatcherd does mine: but how minutely you remember all she has done and said to you! What a singularly deep impression her injustice seems to have made on your heart! No ill usage so brands its record on my feelings. Would you not be happier if you tried to forget her severity, together with the passionate emotions it excited? Life appears to me too short to be spent in nursing animosity, or registering wrongs. We are, and must be, one and all, burdened with faults in this world: but the time will soon come when, I trust, we shall put them off in putting off our corruptible bodies; when debasement and sin will fall from us with this cumbrous frame of flesh, and only the spark of the spirit will remain,—the impalpable principle of life and thought, pure as when it left the Creator to inspire the creature: whence it came it will return; perhaps again to be communicated to some being higher than man— perhaps to pass through gradations of glory, from the pale human soul to brighten to the seraph! Surely it will never, on the contrary, be suffered to degenerate from man to fiend? No; I cannot believe that: I hold another creed; which no one ever taught me, and which I seldom mention; but in which I delight, and to which I cling; for it extends hope to all: it makes Eternity a rest—a mighty home, not a terror and an abyss. Besides, with this creed, I can so clearly distinguish between the criminal and his crime; I can so sincerely forgive the first while I abhor the last: with this creed revenge never worries my heart, degradation never too deeply disgusts me, injustice never crushes me too low: I live in calm, looking to the end."

Helen's head, always drooping, sank a little lower as she finished this sentence. I saw by her look she wished no longer to talk to me, but rather to converse with her own thoughts. She was not allowed much time for meditation: a monitor, a great rough girl, presently came up, exclaiming in a strong Cumberland accent:—

"Helen Burns, if you don't go and put your drawer in order, and fold up your work this minute, I'll tell Miss Scatcherd to come and look at it!"

Helen sighed as her reverie fled, and getting up, obeyed the monitor without reply as without delay.

• • • • • • •

Chapter 7

My first quarter at Lowood seemed an age; and not the golden age either: it comprised an irksome struggle with difficulties in habituating myself to new rules and unwonted tasks. The fear of failure in these points

harassed me worse than the physical hardships of my lot; though these
were no trifles.

During January, February, and part of March, the deep snows, and after
their melting, the almost impassable roads prevented our stirring beyond
the garden walls, except to go to church; but within these limits we had
to pass an hour every day in the open air. Our clothing was insufficient
to protect us from the severe cold: we had no boots, the snow got into
our shoes and melted there; our ungloved hands became numbed and
covered with chilblains, as were our feet: I remember well the distract-
ing irritation I endured from this cause, every evening when my feet inflamed; and the torture of thrusting the swelled, raw, and stiff toes into
my shoes in the morning. Then the scanty supply of food was distressing: with the keen appetites of growing children, we had scarcely sufficient to keep alive a delicate invalid. From this deficiency of nourishment
resulted an abuse, which pressed hardly on the younger pupils: whenever
the famished great girls had an opportunity, they would coax or menace
the little ones out of their portion. Many a time I have shared between
two claimants the precious morsel of brown bread distributed at tea-time;
and after relinquishing to a third, half the contents of my mug of coffee,
I have swallowed the remainder with an accompaniment of secret tears,
forced from me by the exigency of hunger.

Sundays were dreary days in that wintry season. We had to walk two
miles to Brocklebridge church, where our patron officiated. We set out
cold, we arrived at church colder: during the morning service we became
almost paralyzed. It was too far to return to dinner, and an allowance of
cold meat and bread, in the same penurious proportion observed in our
ordinary meals, was served round between the services.

At the close of the afternoon service we returned by an exposed and
hilly road, where the bitter winter wind, blowing over a range of snowy
summits to the north, almost flayed the skin from our faces.

I can remember Miss Temple walking lightly and rapidly along our
drooping line, her plaid cloak, which the frosty wind fluttered, gathered
close about her, and encouraging us, by precept and example, to keep up
our spirits, and march forward, as she said, "like stalwart soldiers." The
other teachers, poor things, were generally themselves too much dejected
to attempt the task of cheering others.

How we longed for the light and heat of a blazing fire when we got back!
But, to the little ones at least, this was denied: each hearth in the school-
room was immediately surrounded by a double row of great girls, and
behind them the younger children crouched in groups, wrapping their
starved arms in their pinafores.

A little solace came at tea time, in the shape of a double ration of bread
—a whole, instead of a half-slice—with the delicious addition of a thin
scrape of butter: it was the hebdomadal treat to which we all looked forward from Sabbath to Sabbath. I generally contrived to reserve a moiety
of this bounteous repast for myself; but the remainder I was invariably
obliged to part with.

The Sunday evening was spent in repeating, by heart, the Church
Catechism, and the fifth, sixth, and seventh chapters of St. Matthew; and
in listening to a long sermon, read by Miss Miller, whose irrepressible
yawns attested her weariness. A frequent interlude of these performances

girls; who, overpowered with sleep, would fall down, if not out of the third loft, yet off the fourth form, and be taken up half dead. The remedy was, to thrust them forward into the centre of the school-room, and oblige them to stand there till the sermon was finished. Sometimes their feet failed them, and they sank together in a heap; they were then propped up with the monitor's high stools.

I have not yet alluded to the visits of Mr. Brocklehurst; and indeed that gentleman was from home during the greater part of the first month after my arrival; perhaps prolonging his stay with his friend the archdeacon: his absence was a relief to me. I need not say that I had my own reasons for dreading his coming: but come he did at last.

One afternoon (I had then been three weeks at Lowood), as I was sitting with a slate in my hand, puzzling over a sum in long division, my eyes, raised in abstraction to the window, caught sight of a figure just passing: I recognised almost instinctively that gaunt outline; and when, two minutes after, all the school, teachers included, rose *en masse*, it was not necessary for me to look up in order to ascertain whose entrance they thus greeted. A long stride measured the school-room, and presently beside Miss Temple, who herself had risen, stood the same black column which had frowned on me so ominously from the hearth-rug of Gateshead. I now glanced sideways at this piece of architecture. Yes, I was right: it was Mr. Brocklehurst, buttoned up in a surtout, and looking longer, narrower, and more rigid than ever.

I had my own reasons for being dismayed at this apparition: too well I remembered the perfidious hints given by Mrs. Reed about my disposition, etc.; the promise pledged by Mr. Brocklehurst to apprise Miss Temple and the teachers of my vicious nature. All along I had been dreading the fulfilment of this promise,—I had been looking out daily for the "Coming Man," whose information respecting my past life and conversation was to brand me as a bad child for ever: now there he was. He stood at Miss Temple's side; he was speaking low in her ear: I did not doubt he was making disclosures of my villany; and I watched her eye with painful anxiety, expecting every moment to see its dark orb turn on me a glance of repugnance and contempt. I listened too; and as I happened to be seated quite at the top of the room, I caught most of what he said: its import relieved me from immediate apprehension.

"I suppose, Miss Temple, the thread I bought at Lowton will do; it struck me that it would be just of the quality for the calico chemises, and I sorted the needles to match. You may tell Miss Smith that I forgot to make a memorandum of the darning needles, but she shall have some papers sent in next week; and she is not, on any account, to give out more than one at a time to each pupil: if they have more, they are apt to be careless and lose them. And, oh, ma'am! I wish the woollen stockings were better looked to!—when I was here last, I went into the kitchen-garden and examined the clothes drying on the line; there was a quantity of black hose in a very bad state of repair: from the size of the holes in them I was sure they had not been well mended from time to time."

He paused.

"Your directions shall be attended to, sir," said Miss Temple.

"And, ma'am," he continued, "the laundress tells me some of the girls have two clean tuckers in the week; it is too much: the rules limit them to one."

"I think I can explain that circumstance, sir. Agnes and Catherine Johnstone were invited to take tea with some friends at Lowton last Thursday, and I gave them leave to put on clean tuckers for the occasion."

Mr. Brocklehurst nodded.

"Well, for once it may pass; but please not to let the circumstance occur too often. And there is another thing which surprised me: I find, in settling accounts with the housekeeper, that a lunch, consisting of bread and cheese, has twice been served out to the girls during the past fortnight. How is this? I look over the regulations, and I find no such meal as lunch mentioned. Who introduced this innovation? and by what authority?"

"I must be responsible for the circumstance, sir," replied Miss Temple: "the breakfast was so ill prepared that the pupils could not possibly eat it; and I dared not allow them to remain fasting till dinner time."

"Madam, allow me an instant.—You are aware that my plan in bringing up these girls is, not to accustom them to habits of luxury and indulgence, but to render them hardy, patient, self-denying. Should any little accidental disappointment of the appetite occur, such as the spoiling of a meal, the under or the over dressing of a dish, the incident ought not to be neutralized by replacing with something more delicate the comfort lost, thus pampering the body and obviating the aim of this institution; it ought to be improved to the spiritual edification of the pupils, by encouraging them to evince fortitude under the temporary privation. A brief address on those occasions would not be mistimed, wherein a judicious instructor would take the opportunity of referring to the sufferings of the primitive Christians; to the torments of martyrs; to the exhortations of our blessed Lord himself, calling upon his disciples to take up their cross and follow him; to his warnings that man shall not live by bread alone, but by every word that proceedeth out of the mouth of God; to his divine consolations, 'if ye suffer hunger or thirst for my sake, happy are ye.' Oh, madam, when you put bread and cheese, instead of burnt porridge into these children's mouths, you may indeed feed their vile bodies, but you little think how you starve their immortal souls!"

Mr. Brocklehurst again paused—perhaps overcome by his feelings. Miss Temple had looked down when he first began to speak to her; but she now gazed straight before her, and her face, naturally pale as marble, appeared to be assuming also the coldness and fixity of that material; especially her mouth closed as if it would have required a sculptor's chisel to open it, and her brow settled gradually into petrified severity.

Meantime, Mr. Brocklehurst, standing on the hearth with his hands behind his back, majestically surveyed the whole school. Suddenly his eye gave a blink, as if it had met something that either dazzled or shocked its pupil; turning, he said in more rapid accents than he had hitherto used:—

"Miss Temple, Miss Temple, what—*what* is that girl with curled hair? Red hair, ma'am, curled—curled all over?" And extending his cane he pointed to the awful object, his hand shaking as he did so.

"It is Julia Severn," replied Miss Temple, very quietly.

"Julia Severn, ma'am! And why has she, or any other, curled hair? Why, in defiance of every precept and principle of this house, does she conform to the world so openly—here in an evangelical, charitable establishment—as to wear her hair one mass of curls?"

"Julia's hair curls naturally," returned Miss Temple, still more quietly.

"Naturally! Yes, but we are not to conform to nature: I wish these girls to be the children of Grace: and why that abundance? I have again and again intimated that I desire the hair to be arranged closely, modestly, plainly. Miss Temple, that girl's hair must be cut off entirely; I will send a barber tomorrow: and I see others who have far too much of the excrescence—that tall girl, tell her to turn round. Tell all the first form to rise up and direct their faces to the wall."

Miss Temple passed her handkerchief over her lips, as if to smooth away the involuntary smile that curled them; she gave the order, however, and when the first class could take in what was required of them, they obeyed. Leaning a little back on my bench, I could see the looks and grimaces with which they commented on this manœuvre: it was a pity Mr. Brocklehurst could not see them too; he would perhaps have felt that, whatever he might do with the outside of the cup and platter, the inside was further beyond his interference than he imagined.

He scrutinized the reverse of these living medals some five minutes, then pronounced sentence. These words fell like the knell of doom:—

"All those top-knots must be cut off."

Miss Temple seemed to remonstrate.

"Madam," he pursued, "I have a Master to serve whose kingdom is not of this world: my mission is to mortify in these girls the lusts of the flesh; to teach them to clothe themselves with shame-facedness and sobriety, not with braided hair and costly apparel; and each of the young persons before us has a string of hair twisted in plaits which vanity itself might have woven: these, I repeat, must be cut off; think of the time wasted, of —"

Mr. Brocklehurst was here interrupted: three other visitors, ladies, now entered the room. They ought to have come a little sooner to have heard his lecture on dress, for they were splendidly attired in velvet, silk, and furs. The two younger of the trio (fine girls of sixteen and seventeen) had gray beaver hats, then in fashion, shaded with ostrich plumes, and from under the brim of this graceful head-dress fell a profusion of light tresses, elaborately curled; the elder lady was enveloped in a costly velvet shawl, trimmed with ermine, and she wore a false front of French curls.

These ladies were deferentially received by Miss Temple, as Mrs. and the Misses Brocklehurst, and conducted to seats of honour at the top of the room. It seems they had come in the carriage with their reverend relative, and had been conducting a rummaging scrutiny of the rooms up stairs, while he transacted business with the housekeeper, questioned the laundress, and lectured the superintendent. They now proceeded to address divers remarks and reproofs to Miss Smith, who was charged with the care of the linen and the inspection of the dormitories: but I had no time to listen to what they said; other matters called off and enchained my attention.

Hitherto, while gathering up the discourse of Mr. Brocklehurst and Miss Temple, I had not, at the same time, neglected precautions to secure my personal safety; which I thought would be effected, if I could only elude observation. To this end, I had sat well back on the form, and while seeming to be busy with my sum, had held my slate in such a manner as to conceal my face: I might have escaped notice, had not my treacherous slate somehow happened to slip from my hand, and falling with an obtrusive crash, directly drawn every eye upon me; I knew it was all over now, and, as I stooped to pick up the two fragments of slate, I rallied my forces for the worst. It came.

"A careless girl!" said Mr. Brocklehurst, and immediately after—"It is the new pupil, I perceive." And before I could draw breath, "I must not forget I have a word to say respecting her." Then aloud: how loud it seemed to me! "Let the child who broke her slate, come forward!"

Of my own accord, I could not have stirred; I was paralyzed: but the two great girls who sat on each side of me, set me on my legs and pushed me towards the dread judge, and then Miss Temple gently assisted me to his very feet, and I caught her whispered counsel.

"Don't be afraid, Jane, I saw it was an accident; you shall not be punished."

The kind whisper went to my heart like a dagger.

"Another minute, and she will despise me for a hypocrite," thought I; and an impulse of fury against Reed, Brocklehurst, and Co., bounded in my pulses at the conviction. I was no Helen Burns.

"Fetch that stool," said Mr. Brocklehurst, pointing to a very high one from which a monitor had just risen: it was brought.

"Place the child upon it."

And I was placed there, by whom I don't know: I was in no condition to note particulars; I was only aware that they had hoisted me up to the height of Mr. Brocklehurst's nose, that he was within a yard of me, and that a spread of shot orange and purple silk pelisses, and a cloud of silvery plumage extended and waved below me.

Mr. Brocklehurst hemmed.

"Ladies," said he, turning to his family; "Miss Temple, teachers, and children, you all see this girl?"

Of course they did; for I felt their eyes directed like burning-glasses against my scorched skin.

"You see she is yet young; you observe she possesses the ordinary form of childhood; God has graciously given her the shape that He has given to all of us; no signal deformity points her out as a marked character. Who would think that the Evil One had already found a servant and agent in her? Yet such—I grieve to say, is the case."

A pause—in which I began to steady the palsy of my nerves, and to feel that the Rubicon was passed; and that the trial, no longer to be shirked, must be firmly sustained.

"My dear children," pursued the black marble clergyman, with pathos, "this is a sad, a melancholy occasion; for it becomes my duty to warn you, that this girl, who might be one of God's own lambs, is a little castaway: not a member of the true flock, but evidently an interloper and an alien. You must be on your guard against her; you must shun her example: if necessary, avoid her company, exclude her from your sports, and shut her out from your converse. Teachers, you must watch her: keep your eyes on her movements, weigh well her words, scrutinize her actions, punish her body to save her soul; if, indeed, such salvation be possible, for (my tongue falters while I tell it) this girl, this child, the native of a Christian land, worse than many a little heathen who says its prayers to Brahma and kneels before Juggernaut—this girl is—a liar!"

Now came a pause of ten minutes; during which I, by this time in perfect possession of my wits, observed all the female Brocklehursts produce their pocket-handkerchiefs and apply them to their optics, while the elderly lady swayed herself to and fro, and the two younger ones whispered, "How shocking!"

Mr. Brocklehurst resumed.

"This I learned from her benefactress; from the pious and charitable lady who adopted her in her orphan state, reared her as her own daughter, and whose kindness, whose generosity, the unhappy girl repaid by an ingratitude so bad, so dreadful, that at last her excellent patroness was obliged to separate her from her own young ones, fearful lest her vicious example should contaminate their purity: she has sent her here to be healed, even as the Jews of old sent their diseased to the troubled pool of Bethesda; and, teachers, superintendent, I beg of you not to allow the waters to stagnate round her."

With this sublime conclusion, Mr. Brocklehurst adjusted the top button of his surtout, muttered something to his family, who rose, bowed to Miss Temple, and then all the great people sailed in state from the room. Turning at the door, my judge said:—

"Let her stand half an hour longer on that stool, and let no one speak to her during the remainder of the day."

There I was, then, mounted aloft: I, who had said I could not bear the shame of standing on my natural feet in the middle of the room, was now exposed to general view on a pedestal of infamy. What my sensations were, no language can describe; but just as they all rose, stifling my breath and constricting my throat, a girl came up and passed me: in passing, she lifted her eyes. What a strange light inspired them! What an extraordinary sensation that ray sent through me! How the new feeling bore me up! It was as if a martyr, a hero, had passed a slave or victim, and imparted strength in the transit. I mastered the rising hysteria, lifted up my head, and took a firm stand on the stool. Helen Burns asked some slight question about her work of Miss Smith, was chidden for the triviality of the inquiry, returned to her place, and smiled at me as she again went by. What a smile! I remember it now, and I know that it was the effluence of fine intellect, of true courage; it lit up her marked lineaments, her thin face, her sunken gray eye, like a reflection from the aspect of an angel. Yet at that moment Helen Burns wore on her arm "the untidy badge;" scarcely an hour ago I had heard her condemned by Miss Scatcherd to a dinner of bread and water on the morrow, because she had blotted an exercise in copying it out. Such is the imperfect nature of man! such spots are there on the disc of the clearest planet; and eyes like Miss Scatcherd's can only see those minute defects, and are blind to the full brightness of the orb.

·······

Chapter 8

Ere the half-hour ended, five o'clock struck; school was dismissed, and all were gone into the refectory to tea. I now ventured to descend: it was deep dusk: I retired into a corner and sat down on the floor. The spell by which I had been so far supported began to dissolve; reaction took place, and soon, so overwhelming was the grief that seized me, I sank prostrate with my face to the ground. Now I wept: Helen Burns was not here; nothing sustained me: left to myself I abandoned myself, and my tears watered the boards. I had meant to be so good, and to do so much at Lowood; to make so many friends, to earn respect, and win affection. Already I had made visible progress: that very morning I had reached the head of my class; Miss Miller had praised me warmly; Miss Temple had smiled approbation; she had promised to teach me drawing, and to let me learn French, if I continued to make similar improvement two months longer: and then I was well received by my fellow-pupils; treated as an equal by those of my own age, and not molested by any: now, here I lay again crushed and trodden on; and could I ever rise more.

"Never," I thought; and ardently I wished to die. While sobbing out this wish in broken accents, some one approached: I started up—again Helen Burns was near me; the fading fires just showed her coming up the long, vacant room; she brought my coffee and bread.

"Come, eat something," she said; but I put both away from me, feeling as if a drop or a crumb would have choked me in my present condition. Helen regarded me, probably with surprise: I could not now abate my agitation, though I tried hard; I continued to weep aloud. She sat down on the ground near me, embraced her knees with her arms, and rested her head upon them; in that attitude she remained silent as an Indian. I was the first who spoke:—

"Helen, why do you stay with a girl whom everybody believes to be a liar?"

"Everybody, Jane? Why, there are only eighty people who have heard you called so, and the world contains hundreds of millions."

"But what have I to do with millions? The eighty I know despise me."

"Jane, you are mistaken: probably not one in the school either despises or dislikes you: many, I am sure, pity you much."

"How can they pity me after what Mr. Brocklehurst said?"

"Mr. Brocklehurst is not a god; nor is he even a great and admired man: he is little liked here; he never took steps to make himself liked. Had he treated you as an especial favourite, you would have found enemies, declared or covert, all around you; as it is, the greater number would offer you sympathy if they dared. Teachers and pupils may look coldly on you for a day or two, but friendly feelings are concealed in their hearts; and if you persevere in doing well, these feelings will ere long appear so much the more evidently for their temporary suppression. Besides, Jane,"——she paused.

"Well, Helen?" said I, putting my hand into hers: she chafed my fingers gently to warm them, and went on:—

"If all the world hated you, and believed you wicked, while your own conscience approved you, and absolved you from guilt, you would not be without friends."

"No; I know I should think well of myself; but that is not enough: if others don't love me, I would rather die than live—I cannot bear to be solitary and hated, Helen. Look here; to gain some real affection from you, or Miss Temple, or any other whom I truly love, I would willingly submit to have the bone of my arm broken, or to let a bull toss me, or to stand behind a kicking horse, and let it dash its hoof at my chest,——"

"Hush, Jane! you think too much of the love of human beings; you are too impulsive, too vehement: the sovereign hand that created your frame, and put life into it, has provided you with other resources than your feeble self, or than creatures feeble as you. Besides this earth, and besides the race of men, there is an invisible world and a kingdom of spirits: that world is round us, for it is everywhere; and those spirits watch us, for they are commissioned to guard us; and if we were dying in pain and shame, if scorn smote us on all sides, and hatred crushed us, angels see our tortures, recognise our innocence (if innocent we be: as I know you are of this charge which Mr. Brocklehurst has weakly and pompously repeated at second hand from Mrs. Reed; for I read a sincere nature in your ardent eyes and on your clear front), and God waits only the separation of spirit from flesh to crown us with a full reward. Why, then, should we ever sink overwhelmed with distress, when life is so soon over, and death is so certain an entrance to happiness: to glory?"

I was silent; Helen had calmed me; but in the tranquility she imparted there was an alloy of inexpressible sadness. I felt the impression of woe as she spoke, but I could not tell whence it came; and when, having done speaking, she breathed a little fast and coughed a short cough, I momentarily forgot my own sorrows to yield to a vague concern for her.

Resting my head on Helen's shoulder, I put my arms round her waist; she drew me to her, and we reposed in silence. We had not sat long thus, when another person came in. Some heavy clouds, swept from the sky by a rising wind, had left the moon bare; and her light, streaming in through a window near, shone full both on us and on the approaching figure, which we at once recognised as Miss Temple.

"I came on purpose to find you, Jane Eyre," said she; "I want you in my room; and as Helen Burns is with you, she may come too."

We went; following the superintendent's guidance, we had to thread some intricate passages, and mount a staircase before we reached her apartment; it contained a good fire, and looked cheerful. Miss Temple told Helen Burns to be seated in a low arm- chair on one side of the hearth, and herself taking another, she called me to her side.

"Is it all over?" she asked, looking down at my face. "Have you cried your grief away?"

"I am afraid I never shall do that."

"Why?"

"Because I have been wrongly accused; and you, ma'am, and everybody else will now think me wicked."

"We shall think you what you prove yourself to be, my child. Continue to act as a good girl, and you will satisfy me."

"Shall I, Miss Temple?"

"You will," said she passing her arm round me. "And now tell me who is the lady whom Mr. Brocklehurst called your benefactress?"

"Mrs. Reed, my uncle's wife. My uncle is dead, and he left me to her care."

"Did she not, then, adopt you of her own accord?"

"No, ma'am; she was sorry to have to do it: but my uncle, as I have often heard the servants say, got her to promise, before he died, that she would always keep me."

"Well now, Jane, you know, or at least I will tell you, that when a criminal is accused, he is always allowed to speak in his own defence. You have been charged with falsehood: defend yourself to me as well as you can. Say whatever your memory suggests as true; but add nothing and exaggerate nothing."

I resolved in the depth of my heart that I would be most moderate:

most correct; and, having reflected a few minutes in order to arrange coherently what I had to say, I told her all the story of my sad childhood. Exhausted by emotion, my language was more subdued than it generally was when it developed that sad theme; and mindful of Helen's warnings against the indulgence of resentment, I infused into the narrative far less of gall and wormwood than ordinary. Thus restrained and simplified, it sounded more credible: I felt as I went on that Miss Temple fully believed me.

In the course of the tale I had mentioned Mr. Lloyd as having come to see me after the fit: for I never forgot the, to me, frightful episode of the red room; in detailing which, my excitement was sure, in some degree, to break bounds; for nothing could soften in my recollection the spasm of agony which clutched my heart when Mrs. Reed spurned my wild supplication for pardon, and locked me a second time in the dark and haunted chamber.

I had finished: Miss Temple regarded me a few minutes in silence; she then said:—

"I know something of Mr. Lloyd; I shall write to him; if his reply agrees with your statement, you shall be publicly cleared from every imputation: to me, Jane, you are clear now."

She kissed me, and still keeping me at her side (where I was well contented to stand, for I derived a child's pleasure from the contemplation of her face, her dress, her one or two ornaments, her white forehead, her clustered and shining curls, and beaming dark eyes), she proceeded to address Helen Burns.

"How are you to-night, Helen? Have you coughed much to-day?"

"Not quite so much I think, ma'am."

"And the pain in your chest?"

"It is a little better."

Miss Temple got up, took her hand and examined her pulse; then she returned to her own seat: as she resumed it, I heard her sigh low. She was pensive a few minutes, then rousing herself, she said cheerfully:—

"But you two are my visitors to-night; I must treat you as such." She rang her bell.

"Barbara," she said to the servant who answered it, "I have not yet had tea; bring the tray, and place cups for these two young ladies."

And a tray was soon brought. How pretty to my eyes, did the china cups and bright teapot look, placed on the little round table near the fire! How fragrant was the steam of the beverage, and the scent of the toast! of which, however, I, to my dismay (for I was beginning to be hungry), discerned only a very small portion: Miss Temple discerned it too:—

"Barbara," said she, "can you not bring a little more bread and butter? There is not enough for three."

Barbara went out: she returned soon:—

"Madam, Mrs. Harden says she has sent up the usual quantity."

Mrs. Harden, be it observed, was the house-keeper; a woman after Mr. Brocklehurst's own heart, made up of equal parts whalebone and iron.

"Oh, very well!" returned Miss Temple; "we must make it do, Barbara, I suppose." And as the girl withdrew, she added, smiling, "Fortunately, I have it in my power to supply deficiencies for this once."

Having invited Helen and me to approach the table, and placed before each of us a cup of tea with one delicious but thin morsel of toast, she got up, unlocked a drawer, and taking from it a parcel wrapped in paper, disclosed presently to our eyes a good-sized seed-cake.

"I meant to give each of you some of this to take with you," said she; "but as there is so little toast you must have it now," and she proceeded to cut slices with a generous hand.

We feasted that evening as on nectar and ambrosia; and not the least delight of the entertainment was the smile of gratification with which our hostess regarded us, as we satisfied our famished appetites on the delicate fare she liberally supplied. Tea over and the tray removed, she again summoned us to the fire; we sat one on each side of her, and now a conversation followed between her and Helen, which it was indeed a privilege to be admitted to hear.

Miss Temple had always something of serenity in her air, of state in her mien, of refined propriety in her language, which precluded deviation into the ardent, the excited, the eager: something which chastened the pleasure of those who looked on her and listened to her, by a controlling sense of awe; and such was my feeling now: but as to Helen Burns, I was struck with wonder.

The refreshing meal, the brilliant fire, the presence and kindness of her beloved instructress, or, perhaps more than all these, something in her own unique mind, had roused her powers within her. They woke, they kindled: first, they glowed in the bright tint of her cheek, which till this hour I had never seen but pale and bloodless; then they shone in the liquid lustre of her eyes, which had suddenly acquired a beauty more singular than that of Miss Temple's—a beauty neither of fine colour nor long eyelash, nor pencilled brow, but of meaning, of movement, of radiance. Then her soul sat on her lips, and language flowed, from what source I cannot tell: has a girl of fourteen a heart large enough, vigorous enough to hold the swelling spring of pure, full, fervid eloquence? Such was the characteristic of Helen's discourse on that, to me, memorable evening; her spirit seemed hastening to live within a very brief span as much as many live during a protracted existence.

They conversed of things I had never heard of; of nations and times past; of countries far away: of secrets of nature discovered or guessed at: they spoke of books: how many they had read! What stores of knowledge they possessed! Then they seemed so familiar with French names and French authors: but my amazement reached its climax when Miss Temple asked Helen if she sometimes snatched a moment to recall the Latin her father had taught her, and taking a book from a shelf, bade her read and construe a page of "Virgil"; and Helen obeyed, my organ of Veneration expanding at every sounding line. She had scarcely finished ere the bell announced bed-time: no delay could be admitted; Miss Temple embraced us both, saying, as she drew us to her heart:—

"God bless you, my children!"

Helen she held a little longer than me: she let her go more reluctantly; it was Helen her eye followed to the door; it was for her she a second time breathed a sad sigh; for her she wiped a tear from her cheek.

On reaching the bed-room, we heard the voice of Miss Scatcherd: she was examining drawers; she had just pulled out Helen Burns's, and when we entered Helen was greeted with a sharp reprimand, and told that tomorrow she should have half a dozen of untidily folded articles pinned to her shoulder.

"My things were indeed in shameful disorder," murmured Helen to me, in a low voice, "I intended to have arranged them, but I forgot."

Next morning, Miss Scatcherd wrote in conspicuous characters on a piece of pasteboard the word "Slattern," and bound it like a phylactery round Helen's large, mild, intelligent, and benign-looking forehead. She wore it till evening, patient, unresentful, regarding it as a deserved punishment. The moment Miss Scatcherd withdrew after afternoon-school, I ran to Helen, tore it off, and thrust it into the fire: the fury of which she was incapable had been burning in my soul all day, and tears, hot and large, had continually been scalding my cheek; for the spectacle of her sad resignation gave me an intolerable pain at the heart.

About a week subsequently to the incidents above narrated, Miss Temple, who had written to Mr. Lloyd, received his answer: it appeared that what he said went to corroborate my account. Miss Temple, having assembled the whole school, announced that inquiry had been made into the charges alleged against Jane Eyre, and that she was most happy to be able to pronounce her completely cleared from every imputation. The teachers then shook hands with me and kissed me, and a murmur of pleasure ran through the ranks of my companions.

Thus relieved of a grievous load, I from that hour set to work afresh, resolved to pioneer my way through every difficulty: I toiled hard, and my success was proportionate to my efforts; my memory, not naturally tenacious, improved with practice; exercise sharpened my wits; in a few weeks I was promoted to a higher class; in less than two months I was allowed to commence French and drawing. I learned the first two tenses of the verb *Etre*, and sketched my first cottage (whose walls, by-the-by, outrivalled in slope those of the leaning tower of Pisa), on the same day. That night, on going to bed, I forgot to prepare in imagination the Barmecide supper of hot roast potatoes, or white bread and new milk, with which I was wont to amuse my inward cravings: I feasted instead on the spectacle of ideal drawings, which I saw in the dark; all the work of my own hands: freely pencilled houses and trees, picturesque rocks and ruins, Cuyp-like groups of cattle, sweet paintings of butterflies hovering over unblown roses, of birds picking at ripe cherries, of wrens' nests enclosing pearl-like eggs, wreathed about with young ivy sprays. I examined, too, in thought, the possibility of my ever being able to translate currently a certain little French story-book which Madam Pierrot had that day shown me; nor was that problem solved to my satisfaction ere I fell sweetly asleep.

Well has Solomon said—"Better is a dinner of herbs where love is, than a stalled ox and hatred therewith."

I would not now have exchanged Lowood with all its privations, for Gateshead and its daily luxuries.

·······

Chapter 9

But the privations, or rather the hardships, of Lowood lessened. Spring drew on: she was indeed already come; the frosts of winter had ceased; its snows were melted; its cutting winds ameliorated. My wretched feet,

flayed and swollen to lameness by the sharp air of January, began to heal
and subside under the gentler breathings of April; the nights and mornings no longer by their Canadian temperature froze the very blood in our
veins; we could now endure the play-hour passed in the garden: sometimes
on a sunny day it began even to be pleasant and genial, and a greenness
grew over those brown beds which, freshening daily, suggested the thought
that Hope traversed them at night, and left each morning brighter traces
of her steps. Flowers peeped out amongst the leaves; snow-drops,
crocuses, purple auriculas, and golden-eyed pansies. On Thursday afternoons (half holidays) we now took walks, and found still sweeter flowers
opening by the way-side, under the hedges.

I discovered, too, that a great pleasure, an enjoyment which the horizon
only bounded, lay all outside the high and spike-guarded walls of our
garden: this pleasure consisted in a prospect of noble summits girdling
a great hill-hollow, rich in verdure and shadow; in a bright beck, full of
dark stones and sparkling eddies. How different had this scene looked
when I viewed it laid out beneath the iron sky of winter, stiffened in frost,
shrouded with snow! When mists as chill as death wandered to the impulse of east winds along those purple peaks, and rolled down 'ing' and
holm till they blended with the frozen fog of the beck! That beck itself
was then a torrent, turbid and curbless: it tore asunder the wood, and sent
a raving sound through the air, often thickened with wild rain or whirling sleet; and for the forest on its banks, *that* showed only ranks of
skeletons.

April advanced to May: a bright, serene May it was; days of blue sky,
placid sunshine, and soft western or southern gales filled up its duration.
And now vegetation matured with vigour; Lowood shook loose its tresses;
it became all green, all flowery; its great elm, ash, and oak skeletons were
restored to majestic life; woodland plants sprang up profusely in its
recesses; unnumbered varieties of moss filled its hollows, and it made a
strange ground-sunshine out of the wealth of its wild primrose plants: I
have seen their pale gold gleam in overshadowed spots like scatterings
of the sweetest lustre. All this I enjoyed often and fully, free, unwatched,
and almost alone: for this unwonted liberty and pleasure, there was a
cause, to which it now becomes my task to advert.

Have I not described a pleasant site for a dwelling, when I speak of it
as bosomed in hill and wood, and rising from the verge of a stream?
Assuredly, pleasant enough: but whether healthy or not is another
question.

That forest-dell, where Lowood lay, was the cradle of fog and fog-bred
pestilence; which, quickening with the quickening spring, crept into the
Orphan Asylum, breathed typhus through its crowded school-room and
dormitory, and, ere May arrived, transformed the seminary into an
hospital.

Semi-starvation and neglected colds had predisposed most of the pupils
to receive infection: forty-five out of the eighty girls lay ill at one time.
Classes were broken up, rules relaxed. The few who continued well were
allowed almost unlimited license; because the medical attendant insisted
on the necessity of frequent exercise to keep them in health: and had it
been otherwise, no one had leisure to watch or restrain them. Miss Temple's whole attention was absorbed by the patients: she lived in the sick-
room; never quitting it except to snatch a few hours' rest at night. The

teachers were fully occupied with packing up and making other necessary preparations for the departure of those girls who were fortunate enough to have friends and relations able and willing to remove them from the seat of contagion. Many, already smitten, went home only to die: some died at the school, and were buried quietly and quickly; the nature of the malady forbidding delay.

While disease had thus become an inhabitant of Lowood, and death its frequent visitor; while there was gloom and fear within its walls; while its rooms and passages steamed with hospital smells: the drug and the pastille striving vainly to overcome the effluvia of mortality; that bright May shone unclouded over the bold hills and beautiful woodland out of doors. Its garden, too, glowed with flowers: hollyhocks had sprung up tall as trees, lilies had opened, dahlias and roses were in bloom; the borders of the little beds were gay with pink thrift and crimson double-daisies; the sweet-briars gave out, morning and evening, their scent of spice and apples; and these fragrant treasures were all useless for most of the inmates of Lowood: except to furnish now and then a handful of herbs and blossoms to put in a coffin.

But I, and the rest who continued well, enjoyed fully the beauties of the scene and season: they let us ramble in the wood, like gipsies, from morning till night; we did what we liked, went where we liked: we lived better too. Mr. Brocklehurst and his family never came near Lowood now: household matters were not scrutinized into; the cross housekeeper was gone, driven away by the fear of infection; her successor, who had been matron at the Lowton Dispensary, unused to the ways of her new abode, provided with comparative liberality. Besides, there were fewer to feed: the sick could eat little; our breakfast-basins were better filled: when there was no time to prepare a regular dinner, which often happened, she would give us a large piece of cold pie, or a thick slice of bread and cheese, and this we carried away with us to the wood, where we each chose the spot we liked best, and dined sumptuously.

My favourite seat was a smooth and broad stone, rising white and dry from the very middle of the beck, and only to be got at by wading through the water; a feat I accomplished barefoot. The stone was just broad enough to accommodate, comfortably, another girl and me, at that time my chosen comrade—one Mary Ann Wilson; a shrewd observant personage, whose society I took pleasure in, partly because she was witty and original, and partly because she had a manner which set me at my ease. Some years older than I, she knew more of the world, and could tell me many things I liked to hear: with her my curiosity found gratification: to my faults also she gave ample indulgence; never imposing curb or rein on anything I said. She had a turn for narrative, I for analysis; she liked to inform, I to question; so we got on swimmingly together, deriving much entertainment, if not much improvement, from our mutual intercourse.

And where, meantime, was Helen Burns? Why did I not spend these sweet days of liberty with her? Had I forgotten her; or was I so worthless as to have grown tired of her pure society? Surely the Mary Ann Wilson I have mentioned was inferior to my first acquaintance: she could only tell me amusing stories, and reciprocate any racy and pungent gossip I chose to indulge in; while, if I have spoken truth of Helen, she was qualified to give those who enjoyed the privilege of her converse, a taste of far higher things.

True, reader; and I knew and felt this: and though I am a defective be-ing, with many faults and few redeeming points, yet I never tired of Helen Burns; nor ever ceased to cherish for her a sentiment of attachment, as strong, tender, and respectful as any that ever animated my heart. How could it be otherwise, when Helen, at all times and under all cir-cumstances, evinced for me a quiet and faithful friendship, which ill-humour never soured nor irritation ever troubled? But Helen was ill at present: for some weeks she had been removed from my sight to I knew not what room up stairs. She was not, I was told, in the hospital portion of the house with the fever patients; for her complaint was consumption, not typhus: and by consumption I, in my ignorance, understood something mild, which time and care would be sure to alleviate.

I was confirmed in this idea by the fact of her once or twice coming down stairs on very warm sunny afternoons, and being taken by Miss Tem-ple into the garden: but, on these occasions, I was not allowed to go and speak to her; I only saw her from the school-room window, and then not distinctly; for she was much wrapped up, and sat at a distance under the veranda.

One evening in the beginning of June, I had stayed out very late with Mary Ann in the wood; we had, as usual, separated ourselves from the others, and had wandered far: so far that we lost our way, and had to ask it at a lonely cottage, where a man and woman lived, who looked after a herd of half-wild swine that fed on the mast in the wood. When we got back, it was after moon-rise: a pony, which we knew to be the surgeon's, was standing at the garden door. Mary Ann remarked that she supposed some one must be very ill, as Mr. Bates had been sent for at that time of the evening. She went into the house; I stayed behind a few minutes to plant in my garden a handful of roots I had dug up in the forest, and which I feared would wither if I left them till morning. This done, I lingered yet a little longer: the flowers smelt so sweet as the dew fell; it was such a pleasant evening, so serene, so warm; the still glowing west promised so fairly another fine day on the morrow; the moon rose with such majesty in the grave east. I was noting these things and enjoying them as a child might when it entered my mind as it had never done before:—

"How sad to be lying now on a sickbed, and to be in danger of dying! This world is pleasant—it would be dreary to be called from it, and to have to go who knows where?"

And then my mind made its first earnest effort to comprehend what had been infused into it concerning heaven and hell: and for the first time it recoiled, baffled; and for the first time glancing behind, on each side, and before it, it saw all round an unfathomed gulf: it felt the one point where it stood—the present; all the rest was formless cloud and vacant depth: and it shuddered at the thought of tottering, and plunging amid that chaos. While pondering this new idea, I heard the front door open; Mr. Bates came out, and with him was a nurse. After she had seen him mount his horse and depart, she was about to close the door, but I ran up to her.

"How is Helen Burns?"

"Very poorly," was the answer.

"Is it her Mr. Bates has been to see?"

"Yes."

"And what does he say about her?"

"He says she'll not be here long."

This phrase uttered in my hearing yesterday, would have only conveyed the notion that she was about to be removed to Northumberland, to her own home. I should not have suspected that it meant she was dying; but I knew instantly now: it opened clear on my comprehension that Helen Burns was numbering her last days in this world, and that she was going to be taken to the region of spirits, if such region there were. I experienced a shock of horror, then a strong thrill of grief, then a desire—a necessity to see her; and I asked in what room she lay.

"She is in Miss Temple's room," said the nurse.

"May I go up and speak to her?"

"Oh, no, child! It is not likely; and now it is time for you to come in; you'll catch the fever if you stop out when the dew is falling."

The nurse closed the front door; I went in by the side entrance which led to the school-room: I was just in time; it was nine o'clock, and Miss Miller was calling the pupils to go to bed.

It might be two hours later, probably near eleven, when I—not having been able to fall asleep, and deeming, from the perfect silence of the dormitory, that my companions were all wrapt in profound repose—rose softly, put on my frock over my night-dress, and, without shoes, crept from the apartment, and set off in quest of Miss Temple's room. It was quite at the other end of the house; but I knew my way; and the light of the unclouded summer moon, entering here and there at passage windows, enabled me to find it without difficulty. An odour of camphor and burnt vinegar warned me when I came near the fever room; and I passed its door quickly, fearful lest the nurse who sat up all night should hear me. I dreaded being discovered and sent back; for I *must* see Helen,—I must embrace her before she died,—I must give her one last kiss, exchange with her one last word.

Having descended a staircase, traversed a portion of the house below, and succeeded in opening and shutting, without noise, two doors, I reached another flight of steps; these I mounted, and then just opposite to me was Miss Temple's room. A light shone through the key-hole, and from under the door: a profound stillness pervaded the vicinity. Coming near, I found the door slightly ajar; probably to admit some fresh air into the close abode of sickness. Indisposed to hesitate, and full of impatient impulses— soul and senses quivering with keen throes—I put it back and looked in. My eye sought Helen, and feared to find death.

Close by Miss Temple's bed, and half covered with its white curtains, there stood a little crib. I saw the outline of a form under the clothes, but the face was hid by the hangings: the nurse I had spoken to in the garden sat in an easy chair, asleep; an unsnuffed candle burnt dimly on the table. Miss Temple was not to be seen: I knew afterwards that she had been called to a delirious patient in the fever-room. I advanced; then paused by the crib side: my hand was on the curtain, but I preferred speaking before I withdrew it. I still recoiled at the dread of seeing a corpse.

"Helen!" I whispered softly; "are you awake?"

She stirred, herself put back the curtain, and I saw her face, pale, wasted, but quite composed: she looked so little changed that my fear was instantly dissipated.

"Can it be you, Jane?" she asked in her own gentle voice.

"Oh!" I thought, "she is not going to die; they are mistaken: she could not speak and look so calmly if she were."

I got on to her crib and kissed her: her forehead was cold, and her cheek both cold and thin, and so were her hand and wrist; but she smiled as of old.

"Why are you come here, Jane? It is past eleven o'clock: I heard it strike some minutes since."

"I came to see you, Helen: I heard you were very ill, and I could not sleep till I had spoken to you."

"You came to bid me good-bye, then: you are just in time probably."

"Are you going somewhere, Helen? Are you going home?"

"Yes; to my long home—my last home."

"No, no, Helen!" I stopped, distressed. While I tried to devour my tears, a fit of coughing seized Helen; it did not, however, wake the nurse; when it was over, she lay some minutes exhausted; then she whispered:—

"Jane, your little feet are bare; lie down and cover yourself with my quilt."

I did so: she put her arm over me, and I nestled close to her. After a long silence, she resumed; still whispering:—

"I am very happy, Jane; and when you hear that I am dead you must be sure and not grieve: there is nothing to grieve about. We all must die one day, and the illness which is removing me is not painful; it is gentle and gradual: my mind is at rest. I leave no one to regret me much: I have only a father; and he is lately married, and will not miss me. By dying young I shall escape great sufferings. I had not qualities or talents to make my way very well in the world: I should have been continually at fault."

"But where are you going to, Helen? Can you see? Do you know?"

"I believe; I have faith: I am going to God."

"Where is God? What is God?"

"My Maker and yours; who will never destroy what he created. I rely implicitly on his power, and confide wholly in his goodness: I count the hours till that eventful one arrives which shall restore me to him, reveal him to me."

"You are sure, then, Helen, that there is such a place as heaven; and that our souls can get to it when we die?"

"I am sure there is a future state; I believe God is good: I can resign my immortal part to him without any misgiving. God is my father; God is my friend: I love him; I believe he loves me."

"And shall I see you again, Helen, when I die?"

"You will come to the same region of happiness: be received by the same mighty, universal Parent, no doubt, dear Jane."

Again I questioned; but this time only in thought. "Where is that region? Does it exist?" And I clasped my arms closer round Helen: she seemed dearer to me than ever; I felt as if I could not let her go; I lay with my face hidden on her neck. Presently she said in the sweetest tone:—

"How comfortable I am! That last fit of coughing has tired me a little; I feel as if I could sleep: but don't leave me, Jane; I like to have you near me."

"I'll stay with you, dear Helen: no one shall take me away."

"Are you warm, darling?"

"Yes."

"Good-night, Jane."

"Good-night, Helen."

She kissed me, and I her; and we both soon slumbered.

When I awoke it was day: an unusual movement roused me; I looked up; I was in somebody's arms; the nurse held me; she was carrying me through the passage back to the dormitory. I was not reprimanded for leaving my bed; people had something else to think about: no explanation was afforded then to my many questions; but a day or two afterwards I learned that Miss Temple, on returning to her own room at dawn, had found me laid in a little crib; my face against Helen Burn's shoulder, my arms around her neck. I was asleep, and Helen was—dead.

Her grave is in Brocklebridge churchyard: for fifteen years after her death it was only covered by a grassy mound; but now a gray marble tablet marks the spot, inscribed with her name, and the word "*Resurgam*."

• • • • • • •

Chapter 10

Hitherto I have recorded in detail the events of my insignificant existence: to the first ten years of my life, I have given almost as many chapters. But this is not to be a regular autobiography: I am only bound to invoke memory where I know her responses will possess some degree of interest; therefore I now pass a space of eight years almost in silence: a few lines only are necessary to keep up the links of connection.

When the typhus fever had fulfilled its mission of devastation at Lowood, it gradually disappeared from thence; but not till its virulence and the number of its victims had drawn public attention on the school. Inquiry was made into the origin of the scourge, and by degrees various facts came out which excited public indignation in a high degree. The unhealthy nature of the site; the quantity and quality of the children's food; the brackish, fetid water used in its preparation; the pupils' wretched clothing and accommodations: all these things were discovered; and the discovery produced a result mortifying to Mr. Brocklehurst, but beneficial to the institution.

Several wealthy and benevolent individuals in the county subscribed largely for the erection of a more convenient building in a better situation; new regulations were made; improvements in diet and clothing introduced; the funds of the school were entrusted to the management of a committee. Mr. Brocklehurst, who, from his wealth and family connections, could not be overlooked, still retained the post of treasurer; but he was aided in the discharge of his duties by gentlemen of rather more enlarged and sympathizing minds: his office of inspector, too, was shared by those who knew how to combine reason with strictness, comfort with economy, compassion with uprightness. The school, thus improved, became in time a truly useful and noble institution. I remained an inmate of its walls, after its regeneration, for eight years: six as pupil, and two as teacher; and in both capacities I bear my testimony to its value and importance.

During these eight years my life was uniform: but not unhappy, because it was not inactive. I had the means of an excellent education placed within my reach; a fondness for some of my studies, and a desire to excel in all, together with a great delight in pleasing my teachers, especially such as I loved, urged me on: I availed myself fully of the advantages offered me.

In time I rose to be the first girl of the first class; then I was invested with the office of teacher; which I discharged with zeal for two years: but at the end of that time I altered.

Miss Temple, through all changes, had thus far continued superintendent of the seminary: to her instruction I owed the best part of my acquirements; her friendship and society had been my continual solace; she had stood me in the stead of mother, governess, and latterly, companion. At this period she married, removed with her husband (a clergyman, an excellent man, almost worthy of such a wife) to a distant county, and consequently was lost to me.

From the day she left I was no longer the same: with her was gone every settled feeling, every association that had made Lowood in some degree a home to me. I had imbibed from her something of her nature and much of her habits: more harmonious thoughts; what seemed better regulated feelings had become the inmates of my mind. I had given in allegiance to duty and order; I was quiet; I believed I was content: to the eyes of others, usually even to my own, I appeared a disciplined and subdued character.

But destiny, in the shape of the Rev. Mr. Nasmyth, came between me and Miss Temple: I saw her in her travelling dress step into a post-chaise, shortly after the marriage ceremony, I watched the chaise mount the hill and disappear beyond its brow; and then retired to my own room; and there spent in solitude the greatest part of the half-holiday granted in honour of the occasion.

I walked about the chamber most of the time. I imagined myself only to be regretting my loss and thinking how to repair it; but when my reflections were concluded, and I looked up and found that the afternoon was gone, and evening far advanced, another discovery dawned on me: namely, that in the interval I had undergone a transforming process; that my mind had put off all it had borrowed of Miss Temple—or rather that she had taken with her the serene atmosphere I had been breathing in her vicinity—and that now I was left in my natural element; and beginning to feel the stirring of old emotions. It did not seem as if a prop were withdrawn, but rather as if a motive were gone: it was not the power to be tranquil which had failed me, but the reason for tranquillity was no more. My world had for some years been in Lowood: my experience had been of its rules and systems; now I remembered that the real world was wide, and that a varied field of hopes and fears, of sensations and excitements, awaited those who had courage to go forth into its expanse to seek real knowledge of life amidst its perils.

I went to my window, opened it, and looked out. There were the two wings of the building; there was the garden; there were the skirts of Lowood; there was the hilly horizon. My eye passed all other objects to rest on those most remote, the blue peaks: it was those I longed to surmount; all within their boundary of rock and heath seemed prison-ground, exile limits. I traced the white road winding round the base of one mountain, and vanishing in a gorge between two: how I longed to follow it further! I recalled the time when I had travelled that very road in a coach; I remembered descending that hill at twilight: an age seemed to have elapsed since the day which brought me first to Lowood; and I had never quitted it since. My vacations had all been spent at school: Mrs. Reed had never sent for me to Gateshead; neither she nor any of her family had ever been to visit me. I had had no communication by letter or message with the outer world: school-rules, school-duties, school-habits and notions, and voices, and faces, and phrases, and costumes, and preferences, and antipathies: such was what I knew of existence. And now I felt that it was not enough: I tired of the routine of eight years in one afternoon. I desired liberty; for liberty I gasped; for liberty I uttered a prayer; it seemed scattered on the wind then faintly blowing. I abandoned it, and framed a humbler supplication; for change, stimulus: that petition, too, seemed swept off into vague space; "Then," I cried, half desperate, "Grant me at least a new servitude!"

Here, a bell, ringing the hour of supper, called me down stairs.

I was not free to resume the interrupted chain of my reflections till bed-time: even then a teacher who occupied the same room with me kept me from the subject to which I longed to recur, by a prolonged effusion of small talk. How I wished sleep would silence her! It seemed as if, could I but go back to the idea which had last entered my mind as I stood at the window, some inventive suggestion would rise for my relief.

Miss Gryce snored at last: she was a heavy Welshwoman, and till now her habitual nasal strains had never been regarded by me in any other light than as a nuisance: to-night I hailed the first deep notes with satisfaction; I was debarrassed of interruption; my half-effaced thought instantly revived.

"A new servitude! There is something in that," I soliloquized (mentally, be it understood; I did not talk aloud). "I know there is, because it does not sound too sweet; it is not like such words as Liberty, Excitement, Enjoyment: delightful sounds truly; but no more than sounds for me; and so hollow and fleeting that it is mere waste of time to listen to them. But Servitude! That must be matter of fact. Any one may serve: I have served here eight years; now all I want is to serve elsewhere. Can I not get so much of my own will? Is not the thing feasible? Yes—yes—the end is not so difficult; if I had only a brain active enough to ferret out the means of attaining it."

I sat up in bed by way of arousing this said brain: it was a chilly night; I covered my shoulders with a shawl, and then I proceeded *to think* again with all my might.

"What do I want? A new place, in a new house, amongst new faces, under new circumstances: I want this because it is of no use wanting anything better. How do people do to get a new place? They apply to friends, I suppose: I have no friends. There are many others who have no friends, who must look about for themselves and be their own helpers; and what is their resource?"

I could not tell: nothing answered me; I then ordered my brain to find a response, and quickly. It worked and worked faster: I felt the pulses throb in my head and temples; but for nearly an hour it worked in chaos, and no result came of its efforts. Feverish with vain labour, I got up and took a turn in the room; undrew the curtain, noted a star or two, shivered with cold, and again crept to bed.

A kind fairy, in my absence, had surely dropped the required suggestion on my pillow; for as I lay down it came quietly and naturally to my mind:—"Those who want situations advertise; you must advertise in the ——*shire Herald*."

"How? I know nothing about advertising."

Replies rose smooth and prompt now:—

"You must inclose the advertisement and the money to pay for it under a cover directed to the Editor of the Herald; you must put it, the first opportunity you have, into the post at Lowton; answers must be addressed to J.E. at the post-office there: you can go and inquire in about a week after you send your letter, if any are come, and act accordingly."

This scheme I went over twice, thrice; it was then digested in my mind: I had it in a clear practical form; I felt satisfied, and fell asleep.

With earliest day, I was up: I had my advertisement written, enclosed, and directed before the bell rang to rouse the school; it ran thus:—

"A young lady accustomed to tuition (had I not been a teacher two years?) is desirous of meeting with a situation in a private family where the children are under fourteen (I thought that as I was barely eighteen, it would not do to undertake the guidance of pupils nearer my own age). She is qualified to teach the usual branches of a good English education, together with French, Drawing, and Music (in those days, reader, this now narrow catalogue of accomplishments, would have been held tolerably comprehensive). Address J.E., Post-office, Lowton, ——shire."

This document remained locked in my drawer all day: after tea, I asked leave of the new Superintendent to go to Lowton, in order to perform some small commissions for myself and one or two of my fellow-teachers; permission was readily granted; I went. It was a walk of two miles, and the evening was wet, but the days were still long; I visited a shop or two, slipped the letter into the post-office, and came back through heavy rain, with streaming garments, but with a relieved heart.

The succeeding week seemed long: it came to an end at last, however, like all sublunary things, and once more, towards the close of a pleasant autumn day, I found myself afoot on the road to Lowton. A picturesque track it was, by the way; lying along the side of the beck and through the sweetest curves of the dale: but that day I thought more of the letters, that might or might not be awaiting me at the little burgh whither I was bound, than of the charms of lea and water.

My ostensible errand on this occasion was to get measured for a pair of shoes; so I discharged that business first, and when it was done, I stepped across the clean and quiet little street from the shoemaker's to the post-office: it was kept by an old dame, who wore horn spectacles on her nose, and black mittens on her hands.

"Are there any letters for J.E.?" I asked.

She peered at me over her spectacles, and then she opened a drawer and fumbled among its contents for a long time; so long that my hopes began to falter. At last, having held a document before her glasses for nearly five minutes, she presented it across the counter; accompanying the act by another inquisitive and mistrustful glance—it was for J.E.

"Is there only one?" I demanded.

"There are no more," said she; and I put it in my pocket and turned my face homeward: I could not open it then; rules obliged me to be back by eight, and it was already half-past seven.

Various duties awaited me on my arrival: I had to sit with the girls during their hour of study; then it was my turn to read prayers; to see them to bed: afterwards I supped with the other teachers. Even when we finally retired for the night, the inevitable Miss Gryce was still my companion: we had only a short end of candle in our candlestick, and I dreaded lest

she should talk till it was all burnt out; fortunately, however, the heavy
supper she had eaten produced a soporific effect: she was already snor-
ing, before I had finished undressing. There still remained an inch of candle: I now took out my letter; the seal was an initial F.; I broke it; the
contents were brief.

"If J.E., who advertised in the ——*shire Herald* of last Thursday,
possesses the acquirements mentioned; and if she is in a position to give
satisfactory references as to character and competency; a situation can be
offered her where there is but one pupil, a little girl, under ten years of
age; and where the salary is thirty pounds per annum. J.E. is requested
to send references, name, address, and all particulars to the direction:—

"Mrs. Fairfax, Thornfield, near Millcote, ——shire."

I examined the document long: the writing was old fashioned and rather
uncertain, like that of an elderly lady. This circumstance was satisfactory:
a private fear had haunted me, that in thus acting for myself, and by my
own guidance, I ran the risk of getting into some scrape; and above all
things, I wished the result of my endeavours to be respectable, proper, *en
règle*. I now felt that an elderly lady was no bad ingredient in the business
I had on hands. Mrs. Fairfax! I saw her in a black gown and widow's cap;
frigid, perhaps, but not uncivil: a model of elderly English respectability. Thornfield! that, doubtless was the name of her house: a neat, orderly spot, I was sure; though I failed in my efforts to conceive a correct plan
of the premises. Millcote, ——shire: I brushed up my recollections of the
map of England; yes, I saw it; both the shire and the town. ——shire was
seventy miles nearer London than the remote county where I now resided: that was a recommendation to me. I longed to go where there was
life and movement: Millcote was a large manufacturing town on the banks
of the A——; a busy place enough, doubtless: so much the better, it would
be a complete change at least. Not that my fancy was much captivated
by the idea of long chimneys and clouds of smoke—"but," I argued,
"Thornfield will, probably, be a good way from the town."

Here the socket of the candle dropped, and the wick went out.

Next day new steps were to be taken: my plans could no longer be confined to my own breast; I must impart them in order to achieve their success. Having sought and obtained an audience of the Superintendent, during the noontide recreation, I told her I had a prospect of getting a new
situation where the salary would be double what I now received (for, at
Lowood, I only got £15 per annum); and requested she would break the
matter for me to Mr. Brocklehurst or some of the committee, and ascertain whether they would permit me to mention them as references. She
obligingly consented to act as mediatrix in the matter. The next day she
laid the affair before Mr. Brocklehurst; who said that Mrs. Reed must
be written to, as she was my natural guardian. A note was accordingly
addressed to that lady, who returned for answer, that "I might do as I
pleased; she had long relinquished all interference in my affairs." This
note went the round of the committee, and at last, after what appeared
to me most tedious delay, formal leave was given me to better my condition if I could; and an assurance added, that as I had always conducted
myself well, both as teacher and pupil, at Lowood, a testimonial of character and capacity signed by the inspectors of that institution, should forthwith be furnished me.

This testimonial I accordingly received in about a week; forwarded a copy of it to Mrs. Fairfax, and got that lady's reply, stating that she was satisfied, and fixing that day fortnight as the period for my assuming the post of governess in her house.

I now busied myself in preparations: the fortnight passed rapidly. I had not a very large wardrobe, though it was adequate to my wants; and the last day sufficed to pack my trunk,—the same I had brought with me eight years ago from Gateshead.

The box was corded, the card nailed on. In half an hour the carrier was to call for it to take it to Lowton; whither I myself was to repair at an early hour the next morning to meet the coach. I had brushed my black stuff travelling dress, prepared my bonnet, gloves, and muff; sought in all my drawers to see that no article was left behind; and now, having nothing more to do, I sat down and tried to rest. I could not; though I had been on foot all day, and could not now repose an instant; I was too much excited. A phase of my life was closing to-night, a new one opening to-morrow: impossible to slumber in the interval; I must watch feverishly while the change was being accomplished.

"Miss," said a servant who met me in the lobby, where I was wandering like a troubled spirit, "a person below wishes to see you."

"The carrier, no doubt," I thought, and ran down stairs without inquiry. I was passing the back parlour, or teachers' sitting-room, the door of which was half open, to go to the kitchen, when some one ran out:—

"It's her, I am sure!—I could have told her anywhere!" cried the individual who stopped my progress and took my hand.

I looked: I saw a woman attired like a well-dressed servant, matronly, yet still young; very good looking, with black hair and eyes, and lively complexion.

"Well, who is it?" she asked in a voice and with a smile I half recognised; "you've not quite forgotten me, I think, Miss Jane?"

In another second I was embracing and kissing her rapturously: "Bessie! Bessie! Bessie!" that was all I said; whereat she half laughed, half cried, and we both went into the parlour. By the fire stood a little fellow of three years old, in plaid frock and trousers.

"That is my little boy," said Bessie, directly.

"Then you are married, Bessie?"

"Yes: nearly five years since, to Robert Leaven, the coachman; and I've a little girl besides Bobby there, that I've christened Jane."

"And you don't live at Gateshead?"

"I live at the Lodge: the old porter has left."

"Well, and how do they all get on? Tell me everything about them, Bessie: but sit down first; and, Bobby, come and sit on my knee, will you?" but Bobby preferred sidling over to his mother.

"You're not grown so very tall, Miss Jane, nor so very stout," continued Mrs. Leaven. "I dare say they've not kept you too well at school: Miss Reed is the head and shoulders taller than you are; and Miss Georgiana would make two of you in breadth."

"Georgiana is handsome, I suppose, Bessie?"

"Very. She went up to London last winter with her mama, and there everybody admired her, and a young lord fell in love with her: but his relations were against the match; and—what do you think?—he and Miss Georgiana made it up to run away: but they were found out and stopped. It was Miss Reed that found them out: I believe she was envious; and now she and her sister lead a cat and dog life together; they are always quarrelling."

"Well, and what of John Reed?"

"Oh, he is not doing so well as his mama could wish. He went to college, and he got—plucked, I think they call it: and then his uncles wanted him to be a barrister, and study the law: but he is such a dissipated young man, they will never make much of him, I think."

"What does he look like?"

"He is very tall: some people call him a fine looking young man; but he has such thick lips."

"And Mrs. Reed?"

"Missis looks stout and well enough in the face, but I think she's not quite easy in her mind: Mr. John's conduct does not please her—he spends a deal of money."

"Did she send you here, Bessie?"

"No, indeed: but I have long wanted to see you, and when I heard that there had been a letter from you, and that you were going to another part of the country, I thought I'd just set off, and get a look at you before you were quite out of my reach."

"I am afraid you are disappointed in me, Bessie." I said this laughing: I perceived that Bessie's glance, though it expressed regard, did in no shape denote admiration.

"No, Miss Jane, not exactly: you are genteel enough; you look like a lady, and it is as much as ever I expected of you: you were no beauty as a child."

I smiled at Bessie's frank answer: I felt that it was correct, but I confess I was not quite indifferent to its import: at eighteen most people wish to please, and the conviction that they have not an exterior likely to second that desire brings anything but gratification."

"I daresay you are clever, though," continued Bessie, by way of solace. "What can you do? Can you play on the piano?"

"A little."

There was one in the room; Bessie went and opened it, and then asked me to sit down and give her a tune: I played a waltz or two and she was charmed.

"The Miss Reeds could not play as well!" said she exultingly. "I always said you would surpass them in learning: and can you draw?"

"That is one of my paintings over the chimney-piece." It was a landscape in water colours, of which I had made a present to the Superintendent in acknowledgment of her obliging mediation with the committee on my behalf; and which she had framed and glazed.

"Well, that is beautiful, Miss Jane! It is as fine a picture as any Miss Reed's drawing-master could paint, let alone the young ladies themselves; who could not come near it: and have you learnt French?"

"Yes, Bessie, I can both read it and speak it."

"And you can work on muslin and canvass?"

"I can."

"Oh, you are quite a lady, Miss Jane! I knew you would be: you will get on whether your relations notice you or not. There was something I wanted to ask you.—Have you ever heard anything from your father's kinsfolk, the Eyres?"

"Never in my life."

"Well, you know Missis always said they were poor and quite despicable: and they may be poor; but I believe they are as much gentry as the Reeds are; for one day, nearly seven years ago, a Mr. Eyre came to Gateshead and wanted to see you; Missis said you were at school fifty miles off; he seemed so much disappointed, for he could not stay: he was going on a voyage to a foreign country, and the ship was to sail from London in a day or two. He looked quite a gentleman, and I believe he was your father's brother."

"What foreign country was he going to, Bessie?"

"An island thousands of miles off, where they make wine—the butler did tell me——"

"Madeira?" I suggested.

"Yes, that is it—that is the very word."

"So he went?"

"Yes; he did not stay many minutes in the house: Missis was very high with him; she called him afterwards a 'sneaking tradesman.' My Robert believes he was a wine-merchant."

"Very likely," I returned; "or perhaps clerk or agent to a wine-merchant."

Bessie and I conversed about old times an hour longer, and then she was obliged to leave me: I saw her again for a few minutes the next morning at Lowton, while I was waiting for the coach. We parted finally at the door of the Brocklehurst Arms there: each went her separate way; she set off for the brow of Lowood Fell to meet the conveyance which was to take her back to Gateshead, I mounted the vehicle which was to bear me to new duties and a new life in the unknown environs of Millcote.

········

Chapter 11

A new chapter in a novel is something like a new scene in a play; and when I draw up the curtain this time, reader, you must fancy you see a room in the George Inn at Millcote, with such large figured papering on the walls as inn rooms have; such a carpet, such furniture, such ornaments on the mantel-piece, such prints; including a portrait of George the Third, and another of the Prince of Wales, and a representation of the death of Wolfe. All this is visible to you by the light of an oil-lamp hanging from the ceiling, and by that of an excellent fire, near which I sit in my cloak and bonnet; my muff and umbrella lie on the table, and I am warming away the numbness and chill contracted by sixteen hours' exposure to the rawness of an October day: I left Lowton at four o'clock A.M. and the Millcote town clock is now just striking eight.

Reader, though I look comfortably accommodated, I am not very tranquil in my mind. I thought when the coach stopped here there would be some one to meet me; I looked anxiously round as I descended the wooden steps the "boots" placed for my convenience, expecting to hear my name pronounced, and to see some description of carriage waiting to convey me to Thornfield. Nothing of the sort was visible; and when I asked a waiter if any one had been to inquire after a Miss Eyre, I was answered in the negative; so I had no resource but to request to be shown into a private room: and here I am waiting, while all sorts of doubts and fears are troubling my thoughts.

It is a very strange sensation to inexperienced youth to feel itself quite alone in the world: cut adrift from every connection; uncertain whether the port to which it is bound can be reached, and prevented by many impediments from returning to that it has quitted. The charm of adventure sweetens that sensation, the glow of pride warms it; but then the throb of fear disturbs it; and fear with me became predominant, when half an hour elapsed and still I was alone. I bethought myself to ring the bell.

"Is there a place in this neighbourhood called Thornfield?" I asked of the waiter who answered the summons.

"Thornfield? I don't know, ma'am; I'll inquire at the bar." He vanished, but reappeared instantly:—

"Is your name Eyre, Miss?"

"Yes."

"Person here waiting for you."

I jumped up, took my muff and umbrella, and hastened into the inn-passage: a man was standing by the open door, and in the lamp-lit street, I dimly saw a one-horse conveyance.

"This will be your luggage, I suppose?" said the man rather abruptly when he saw me, pointing to my trunk in the passage.

"Yes." He hoisted it on to the vehicle, which was a sort of car, and then I got in: before he shut me up, I asked him how far it was to Thornfield.

"A matter of six miles."

"How long shall we be before we get there?"

"Happen an hour and a half."

He fastened the car door, climbed to his own seat outside, and we set off. Our progress was leisurely, and gave me ample time to reflect: I was content to be at length so near the end of my journey; and as I leaned back in the comfortable though not elegant conveyance, I meditated much at my ease.

"I suppose," thought I, "judging from the plainness of the servant and carriage, Mrs. Fairfax is not a very dashing person: so much the better; I never lived amongst fine people but once, and I was very miserable with them. I wonder if she lives alone except this little girl; if so, and if she is in any degree amiable, I shall surely be able to get on with her; I will do my best: it is a pity that doing one's best does not always answer. At Lowood, indeed, I took that resolution, kept it, and succeeded in pleasing; but with Mrs. Reed, I remember my best was always spurned with scorn. I pray God Mrs. Fairfax may not turn out a second Mrs. Reed; but if she does, I am not bound to stay with her! let the worst come to the worst, I can advertise again. How far are we on our road now, I wonder?"

I let down the window and looked out: Millcote was behind us; judging by the number of its lights, it seemed a place of considerable magnitude, much larger than Lowton. We were now, as far as I could see, on a sort of common; but there were houses scattered all over the district; I felt we were in a different region to Lowood, more populous, less picturesque; more stirring, less romantic.

The roads were heavy, the night misty; my conductor let his horse walk all the way, and the hour and a half extended, I verily believe, to two hours; at last he turned in his seat and said:—

"You're noan so far fro' Thornfield now."

Again I looked out: we were passing a church: I saw its low broad tower against the sky, and its bell was tolling a quarter; I saw a narrow galaxy of lights too, on a hill-side, marking a village or hamlet. About ten minutes after, the driver got down and opened a pair of gates: we passed through, and they clashed to behind us. We now slowly ascended a drive, and came upon the long front of a house: candle-light gleamed from one curtained bow-window; all the rest were dark. The car stopped at the front door; it was opened by a maid-servant; I alighted and went in.

"Will you walk this way, ma'am," said the girl; and I followed her across a square hall with high doors all round: she ushered me into a room whose double illumination of fire and candle at first dazzled me, contrasting as it did with the darkness to which my eyes had been for two hours inured; when I could see, however, a cozy and agreeable picture presented itself to my view.

A snug, small room; a round table by a cheerful fire; an arm-chair high-backed and old-fashioned, wherein sat the neatest imaginable little elderly lady, in widow's cap, black silk gown and snowy muslin apron: exactly like what I had fancied Mrs. Fairfax, only less stately and milder looking. She was occupied in knitting; a large cat sat demurely at her feet; nothing in short was wanting to complete the beau-ideal of domestic comfort. A more reassuring introduction for a new governess could scarcely be conceived: there was no grandeur to overwhelm, no stateliness to embarrass; and then, as I entered, the old lady got up, and promptly and kindly came forward to meet me.

"How do you do, my dear? I am afraid you have had a tedious ride; John drives so slowly: you must be cold, come to the fire."

"Mrs. Fairfax, I suppose?" said I.

"Yes, you are right: do sit down."

She conducted me to her own chair, and then began to remove my shawl and untie my bonnet-strings: I begged she would not give herself so much trouble.

"Oh, it is no trouble; I dare say your own hands are almost numbed with cold. Leah, make a little hot negus and cut a sandwich or two: here are the keys of the store-room."

And she produced from her pocket a most housewifely bunch of keys, and delivered them to the servant.

"Now, then, draw nearer to the fire;" she continued. "You've brought your luggage with you, haven't you, my dear?"

"Yes, ma'am."

"I'll see it carried into your room," she said, and bustled out.

"She treats me like a visitor," thought I. "I little expected such a reception; I anticipated only coldness and stiffness: this is not like what I have heard of the treatment of governesses; but I must not exult too soon."

She returned; with her own hands cleared her knitting apparatus and a book or two from the table, to make room for the tray which Leah now brought, and then herself handed me the refreshments. I felt rather confused at being the object of more attention than I had ever before received, and that, too, shown by my employer and superior; but as she did not herself seem to consider she was doing anything out of her place, I thought it better to take her civilities quietly.

"Shall I have the pleasure of seeing Miss Fairfax to-night?" I asked, when I had partaken of what she offered me.

"What did you say, my dear? I am a little deaf," returned the good lady, approaching her ear to my mouth.

I repeated the question more distinctly.

"Miss Fairfax? Oh, you mean Miss Varens! Varens is the name of your future pupil."

"Indeed! Then she is not your daughter?"

"No,—I have no family."

I should have followed up my first inquiry, by asking in what way Miss Varens was connected with her; but I recollected it was not polite to ask too many questions: besides, I was sure to hear in time.

"I am so glad—" she continued, as she sat down opposite to me, and took the cat on her knee: "I am so glad you are come; it will be quite pleasant living here now with a companion. To be sure it is pleasant at any time; for Thornfield is a fine old hall, rather neglected of late years, perhaps, but still it is a respectable place; yet you know in winter time, one feels dreary quite alone, in the best quarters. I say alone—Leah is a nice girl to be sure, and John and his wife are very decent people; but then you see they are only servants, and one can't converse with them on terms of equality: one must keep them at due distance, for fear of losing one's authority. I'm sure last winter (it was a very severe one, if you recollect, and when it did not snow, it rained and blew), not a creature but the butcher and postman came to the house, from November till February; and I really got quite melancholy with sitting night after night alone; I had Leah in to read to me sometimes; but I don't think the poor girl liked the task much: she felt it confining. In spring and summer one got on better: sunshine and long days make such a difference; and then just at the commencement of this autumn, little Adela Varens came and her nurse: a child makes a house alive all at once; and now you are here I shall be quite gay."

My heart really warmed to the worthy lady as I heard her talk; and I drew my chair a little nearer to her, and expressed my sincere wish that she might find my company as agreeable as she anticipated.

"But I'll not keep you sitting up late to-night," she said; "it is on the stroke of twelve now, and you have been travelling all day: you must feel tired. If you have got your feet well warmed, I'll show you your bed-room. I've had the room next to mine prepared for you; it is only a small apartment, but I thought you would like it better than one of the large front chambers: to be sure they have finer furniture, but they are so dreary and solitary, I never sleep in them myself."

I thanked her for her considerate choice, and as I really felt fatigued with my long journey, expressed my readiness to retire. She took her candle, and I followed her from the room. First she went to see if the hall-door was fastened; having taken the key from the lock, she led the way up stairs. The steps and banisters were of oak; the staircase window was high and latticed: both it and the long gallery into which the bed-room doors opened, looked as if they belonged to a church rather than a house. A very chill and vault-like air pervaded the stairs and gallery, suggesting cheerless ideas of space and solitude; and I was glad when finally ushered into my chamber, to find it of small dimensions and furnished in ordinary modern style.

When Mrs. Fairfax had bidden me a kind good-night, and I had fastened my door, gazed leisurely round, and in some measure effaced the eerie impression made by that wide hall, that dark and spacious staircase, and that long, cold gallery, by the livelier aspect of my little room, I remembered that after a day of bodily fatigue and mental anxiety, I was now at last in safe haven. The impulse of gratitude swelled my heart, and I knelt down at the bed-side and offered up thanks where thanks were due; not forgetting, ere I rose, to implore aid on my further path, and the power of meriting the kindness which seemed so frankly offered me before it was earned. My couch had no thorns in it that night; my solitary room no fears. At once weary and content, I slept soon and soundly: when I awoke it was broad day.

The chamber looked such a bright little place to me as the sun shone in between the gay blue chintz window curtains, showing papered walls and a carpeted floor, so unlike the bare planks and stained plaster of Lowood, that my spirits rose at the view. Externals have a great effect on the young: I thought that a fairer era of life was beginning for me, one that was to have its flowers and pleasures, as well as its thorns and toils. My faculties, roused by the change of scene, the new field offered to hope, seemed all astir. I cannot precisely define what they expected, but it was something pleasant: not perhaps that day or that month, but at an indefinite future period.

I rose; I dressed myself with care: obliged to be plain—for I had no article of attire that was not made with extreme simplicity—I was still by nature solicitous to be neat. It was not my habit to be disregardful of appearance, or careless of the impression I made: on the contrary, I ever wished to look as well as I could, and to please as much as my want of beauty would permit. I sometimes regretted that I was not handsomer: I sometimes wished to have rosy cheeks, a straight nose, and small cherry mouth; I desired to be tall, stately, and finely developed in figure; I felt it a misfortune that I was so little, so pale, and had features so irregular and so marked. And why had I these aspirations and these regrets? It would be difficult to say: I could not then distinctly say it to myself; yet I had a reason, and a logical, natural reason too. However, when I had brushed my hair very smooth, and put on my black frock—which, Quaker-like as it was, at least had the merit of fitting to a nicety—and adjusted my clean white tucker, I thought I should do respectably enough to appear before Mrs. Fairfax; and that my new pupil would not at least recoil from me with antipathy. Having opened my chamber window, and seen that I left all things straight and neat on the toilet table, I ventured forth.

Traversing the long and matted gallery, I descended the slippery steps of oak; then I gained the hall: I halted there a minute; I looked at some pictures on the walls (one I remember represented a grim man in a cuirass, and one a lady with powdered hair and a pearl necklace), at a bronze lamp pendent from the ceiling, at a great clock whose case was of oak curiously carved, and ebon black with time and rubbing. Everything appeared very stately and imposing to me: but then I was so little accustomed to grandeur. The hall-door, which was half of glass, stood open; I stepped over the threshold. It was a fine autumn morning; the early sun shone serenely on embrowned groves and still green fields: advancing on to the lawn, I looked up and surveyed the front of the mansion. It was three stories high, of proportions not vast, though considerable; a gentleman's manor-

house, not a nobleman's seat: battlements round the top gave it a picturesque look. Its gray front stood out well from the back ground of a
rookery, whose cawing tenants were now on the wing: they flew over the
lawn and grounds to alight in a great meadow, from which these were
separated by a sunk fence, and where an array of mighty old thorn trees,
strong, knotty, and broad as oaks, at once explained the etymology of the
mansion's designation. Farther off were hills: not so lofty as those round
Lowood, nor so craggy, nor so like barriers of separation from the living
world; but yet quiet and lonely hills enough, and seeming to embrace
Thornfield with a seclusion I had not expected to find existent so near
the stirring locality of Millcote. A little hamlet, whose roofs were blent
with trees, straggled up the side of one of these hills; the church of the
district stood nearer Thornfield: its old tower-top looked over a knoll between the house and gates.

I was yet enjoying the calm prospect and pleasant fresh air, yet listening with delight to the cawing of the rooks, yet surveying the wide, hoary
front of the hall, and thinking what a great place it was for one lonely
little dame like Mrs. Fairfax to inhabit, when that lady appeared at the
door.

"What! out already?" said she. "I see you are an early riser." I went
up to her, and was received with an affable kiss and shake of the hand.

"How do you like Thornfield?" she asked. I told her I liked it very
much.

"Yes," she said, "it is a pretty place; but I fear it will be getting out
of order, unless Mr. Rochester should take it into his head to come and
reside here permanently; or, at least, visit it rather oftener: great houses
and fine grounds require the presence of the proprietor."

"Mr. Rochester!" I exclaimed. "Who is he?"

"The owner of Thornfield," she responded quietly. "Did you not know
he was called Rochester?"

Of course I did not—I had never heard of him before; but the old lady
seemed to regard his existence as a universally understood fact, with which
everybody must be acquainted by instinct.

"I thought," I continued, "Thornfield belonged to you."

"To me? Bless you child; what an idea! To me? I am only the housekeeper—the manager. To be sure I am distantly related to the Rochesters
by the mother's side; or, at least, my husband was: he was a clergyman,
incumbent of Hay—that little village yonder on the hill— and that church
near the gates was his. The present Mr. Rochester's mother was a Fairfax, and second cousin to my husband; but I never presume on the connection—in fact, it is nothing to me; I consider myself quite in the light
of an ordinary housekeeper: my employer is always civil, and I expect
nothing more."

"And the little girl—my pupil?"

"She is Mr. Rochester's ward; he commissioned me to find a governess
for her. He intends to have her brought up in ——shire, I believe. Here
she comes, with her '*bonne*,' as she calls her nurse." The enigma then
was explained: this affable and kind little widow was no great dame, but
a dependant like myself. I did not like her the worse for that; on the contrary, I felt better pleased than ever. The equality between her and me
was real; not the mere result of condescension on her part: so much the
better—my position was all the freer.

As I was meditating on this discovery, a little girl, followed by her attendant, came running up the lawn. I looked at my pupil, who did not at first appear to notice me: she was quite a child, perhaps seven or eight years old, slightly built, with a pale small-featured face, and a redundancy of hair falling in curls to her waist.

"Good-morning, Miss Adela," said Mrs. Fairfax. "Come and speak to the lady who is to teach you, and to make you a clever woman some day." She approached.

"*C'est là ma gouvernante?*" said she, pointing to me, and addressing her nurse; who answered:

"*Mais oui, certainement.*"

"Are they foreigners?" I inquired, amazed at hearing the French language.

"The nurse is a foreigner, and Adela was born on the continent; and, I believe, never left it till within six months ago. When she first came here she could speak no English; now she can make shift to talk it a little: I don't understand her, she mixes it so with French; but you will make out her meaning very well, I daresay."

Fortunately I had had the advantage of being taught French by a French lady; and as I had always made a point of conversing with Madame Pierrot, as often as I could, and had, besides, during the last seven years, learnt a portion of French by heart daily—applying myself to take pains with my accent, and imitating as closely as possible the pronunciation of my teacher—I had acquired a certain degree of readiness and correctness in the language, and was not likely to be much at a loss with Mademoiselle Adela. She came and shook hands with me when she heard that I was her governess; and as I led her into breakfast, I addressed some phrases to her in her own tongue; she replied briefly at first, but after we were seated at the table, and she had examined me some ten minutes with her large hazel eyes, she suddenly commenced chattering fluently.

"Ah!" cried she, in French, "you speak my language as well as Mr. Rochester does: I can talk to you as I can to him, and so can Sophie. She will be glad: nobody here understands her: Madame Fairfax is all English. Sophie is my nurse; she came with me over the sea in a great ship with a chimney that smoked—how it did smoke!—and I was sick, and so was Sophie, and so was Mr. Rochester. Mr. Rochester lay down on a sofa in a pretty room called the salon, and Sophie and I had little beds in another place. I nearly fell out of mine; it was like a shelf. And, Mademoiselle—— what is your name?"

"Eyre—Jane Eyre."

"Aire? Bah! I cannot say it. Well: our ship stopped in the morning, before it was quite daylight, at a great city—a huge city, with very dark houses and all smoky; not at all like the pretty clean town I came from; and Mr. Rochester carried me in his arms over a plank to the land, and Sophie came after, and we all got into a coach, which took us to a beautiful large house, larger than this and finer, called an hotel. We stayed there nearly a week: I and Sophie used to walk every day in a great green place full of trees, called the Park; and there were many children there besides me, and a pond with beautiful birds in it, that I fed with crumbs."

"Can you understand her when she runs on so fast?" asked Mrs. Fairfax.

I understood her very well, for I had been accustomed to the fluent tongue of Madame Pierrot.

"I wish," continued the good lady, "you would ask her a question or two about her parents: I wonder if she remembers them?"

"Adèle," I inquired, "with whom did you live when you were in that pretty clean town you spoke of?"

"I lived long ago with mama; but she is gone to the Holy Virgin. Mama used to teach me to dance and sing, and to say verses. A great many gentlemen and ladies came to see mama, and I used to dance before them, or to sit on their knees and sing to them: I liked it. Shall I let you hear me sing now?"

She had finished her breakfast, so I permitted her to give a specimen of her accomplishments. Descending from her chair, she came and placed herself on my knee; then, folding her little hands demurely before her, shaking back her curls and lifting her eyes to the ceiling, she commenced singing a song from some opera. It was the strain of a forsaken lady, who, after bewailing the perfidy of her lover, calls pride to her aid; desires her attendant to deck her in her brightest jewels and richest robes, and resolves to meet the false one that night at a ball, and prove to him by the gaiety of her demeanor how little his desertion has affected her.

The subject seemed strangely chosen for an infant singer; but I suppose the point of the exhibition lay in hearing the notes of love and jealousy warbled with the lisp of childhood; and in very bad taste that point was: at least I thought so.

Adèle sang the canzonette tunefully enough, and with the naïveté of her age. This achieved, she jumped from her knee and said, "Now, mademoiselle, I will repeat you some poetry."

Assuming an attitude, she began "*La Ligue des Rats; fable de La Fontaine*." She then declaimed the little piece with an attention to punctuation and emphasis, a flexibility of voice and an appropriateness of gesture, very unusual indeed at her age; and which proved she had been carefully trained.

"Was it your mama who taught you that piece?" I asked.

"Yes, and she just used to say it in this way: '*Qu'avez vous donc? lui dit un de ces rats; parlez!*' She made me lift my hand—so—to remind me to raise my voice at the question. Now shall I dance for you?"

"No, that will do: but after your mama went to the Holy Virgin, as you say, with whom did you live then?"

"With Madame Frédéric and her husband: she took care of me, but she is nothing related to me. I think she is poor, for she had not so fine a house as mama. I was not long there; Mr. Rochester asked me if I would like to go and live with him in England, and I said yes; for I knew Mr. Rochester before I knew Madame Frédéric, and he was always kind to me and gave me pretty dresses and toys: but you see he has not kept his word, for he has brought me to England, and now he is gone back again himself, and I never see him."

After breakfast, Adele and I withdrew to the library; which room, it appears, Mr. Rochester had directed should be used as the school-room. Most of the books were locked up behind glass doors; but there was one book-case left open containing everything that could be needed in the way of elementary works, and several volumes of light literature, poetry, biography, travels; a few romances, etc. I suppose he had considered that these were all the governess would require for her private perusal; and, indeed, they contented me amply for the present; compared with the scanty pickings I had now and then been able to glean at Lowood, they seemed to offer an abundant harvest of entertainment and information. In this room, too, there was a cabinet piano, quite new and of superior tone; also an easel for painting, and a pair of globes.

I found my pupil sufficiently docile, though disinclined to apply: she had not been used to regular occupation of any kind. I felt it would be injudicious to confine her too much at first; so, when I had talked to her a great deal, and got her to learn a little, and when the morning had advanced to noon, I allowed her to return to her nurse. I then proposed to occupy myself till dinner-time in drawing some little sketches for her use.

As I was going up stairs to fetch my portfolio and pencils, Mrs. Fairfax called to me: "Your morning school-hours are over now, I suppose," said she. She was in a room the folding-doors of which stood open: I went in when she addressed me. It was a large, stately apartment, with purple chairs and curtains, a Turkey carpet, walnut-panelled walls, one vast window rich in stained glass, and a lofty ceiling, nobly moulded. Mrs. Fairfax was dusting some vases of fine purple spar, which stood on a side-board.

"What a beautiful room!" I exclaimed, as I looked round: for I had never before seen any half so imposing.

"Yes; this is the dining-room. I have just opened the window, to let in a little air and sunshine; for everything gets so damp in apartments that are seldom inhabited: the drawing-room yonder feels like a vault."

She pointed to a wide arch corresponding to the window, and hung like it with a Tyrian-dyed curtain, now looped up. Mounting to it by two broad steps and looking through, I thought I caught a glimpse of a fairy place: so bright to my novice-eyes appeared the view beyond. Yet it was merely a very pretty drawing-room, and within it a boudoir, both spread with white carpets, on which seemed laid brilliant garlands of flowers; both ceiled and snowy mouldings of white grapes and vine-leaves, beneath which glowed in rich contrast crimson couches and ottomans; while the ornaments on the pale Parian mantle-piece were of sparkling Bohemian glass, ruby red; and between the windows large mirrors repeated the general blending of snow and fire.

"In what order you keep these rooms, Mrs. Fairfax!" said I. "No dust, no canvas coverings: except that the air feels chilly, one would think they were inhabited daily."

"Why, Miss Eyre, though Mr. Rochester's visits here are rare, they are always sudden and unexpected; and as I observed that it put him out to find everything swathed up, and to have a bustle of arrangement on his arrival, I thought it best to keep the rooms in readiness."

"Is Mr. Rochester an exacting, fastidious sort of man?"

"Not particularly so; but he has a gentleman's tastes and habits, and he expects to have things managed in conformity to them."

"Do you like him? Is he generally liked?"

"Oh, yes; the family have always been respected here. Almost all the land in this neighbourhood, as far as you can see, has belonged to the Rochesters time out of mind."

"Well, but, leaving his land out of the question, do you like him? Is he liked for himself?"

"I have no cause to do otherwise than like him; and I believe he is considered a just and liberal landlord by his tenants: but he has never lived much amongst them."

"But has he no peculiarities? What, in short, is his character?"

"Oh! his character is unimpeachable, I suppose. He is rather peculiar, perhaps: he has travelled a great deal, and seen a great deal of the world, I should think. I dare say he is clever: but I never had much conversation with him."

"In what way is he peculiar?"

"I don't know—it is not easy to describe—nothing striking, but you feel it when he speaks to you: you cannot be always sure whether he is in jest or earnest, whether he is pleased or the contrary; you don't thoroughly understand him, in short—at least, I don't: but it is of no consequence, he is a very good master."

This was all the account I got from Mrs. Fairfax, of her employer and mine. There are people who seem to have no notion of sketching a character, or observing and describing salient points, either in persons or things: the good lady evidently belonged to this class; my queries puzzled, but did not draw her out. Mr. Rochester was Mr. Rochester in her eyes; a gentleman, a landed proprietor—nothing more: she inquired and searched no further, and evidently wondered at my wish to gain a more definite notion of his identity.

When we left the dining-room, she proposed to show me over the rest of the house; and I followed her up stairs and down stairs, admiring as I went: for all was well arranged and handsome. The large front chambers I thought especially grand; and some of the third story rooms, though dark and low, were interesting from their air of antiquity. The furniture once appropriated to the lower apartments had from time to time been removed here, as fashions changed; and the imperfect light entering by their narrow casements showed bedsteads of a hundred years old; chests in oak or walnut, looking, with their strange carvings of palm branches and cherubs' heads, like types of the Hebrew ark; rows of venerable chairs, high-backed and narrow; stools still more antiquated, on whose cushioned tops were yet apparent traces of half-effaced embroideries, wrought by fingers that for two generations had been coffin-dust. All these relics gave to the third story of Thornfield Hall the aspect of a home of the past: a shrine of memory. I liked the hush, the gloom, the quaintness of these retreats in the day; but I by no means coveted a night's repose on one of those wide and heavy beds: shut in, some of them with doors of oak; shaded, others with wrought old English hangings crusted with thick work, portraying effigies of strange flowers, and stranger birds, and strangest human beings,—all which would have looked strange, indeed, by the pallid gleam of moonlight.

"Do the servants sleep in these rooms?" I asked.

"No; they occupy a range of smaller apartments to the back; no one ever sleeps here: one would almost say that, if there were a ghost at Thornfield Hall, this would be its haunt."

"So I think: you have no ghost then?"

"None that I ever heard of," returned Mrs. Fairfax, smiling.

"Nor any traditions of one? no legends or ghost stories?"

"I believe not. And yet it is said, the Rochesters have been rather a violent than a quiet race in their time: perhaps, though, that is the reason they rest tranquilly in their graves now."

"Yes—'after life's fitful fever they sleep well,' " I muttered. "Where are you going now, Mrs. Fairfax?" for she was moving away.

"On to the leads; will you come and see the view from thence?" I followed still, up a very narrow staircase to the attics, and thence by a ladder and through a trap-door to the roof of the hall. I was now on a level with the crow-colony, and could see into their nests. Leaning over the battlements and looking far down, I surveyed the grounds laid out like a map: the bright and velvet lawn closely girdling the gray base of the mansion; the field, wide as a park, dotted with its ancient timber; the wood, dun and sere, divided by a path visibly overgrown, greener with moss than the trees were with foliage; the church at the gates, the road, the tranquil hills all reposing in the autumn day's sun; the horizon bounded by a propitious sky, azure, marbled with pearly white. No feature in the scene was extraordinary, but all was pleasing. When I turned from it and repassed the trap-door, I could scarcely see my way down the ladder; the attic seemed black as a vault compared with that arch of blue air to which I had been looking up, and to that sunlit scene of grove, pasture and green hill of which the hall was the centre, and over which I had been gazing with delight.

Mrs. Fairfax stayed behind a moment to fasten the trap-door; I, by dint of groping, found the outlet from the attic, and proceeded to descend the narrow garret staircase. I lingered in the long passage to which this led, separating the front and back rooms of the third story: narrow, low, and dim, with only one little window at the far end, and looking, with its two rows of small black doors all shut, like a corridor in some Bluebeard's castle.

While I paced softly on, the last sound I expected to hear in so still a region, a laugh, struck my ear. It was a curious laugh; distinct, formal, mirthless. I stopped: the sound ceased, only for an instant; it began again, louder: for at first, though distinct, it was very low. It passed off in a clamorous peal that seemed to wake an echo in every lonely chamber; though it originated but in one, and I could have pointed out the door whence the accents issued.

"Mrs. Fairfax!" I called out: for I now heard her descending the great stairs. "Did you hear that loud laugh? Who is it?"

"Some of the servants very likely," she answered: "perhaps Grace Poole."

"Did you hear it?" I again inquired.

"Yes, plainly: I often hear her; she sews in one of these rooms. Sometimes Leah is with her: they are frequently noisy together."

The laugh was repeated in its low, syllabic tone, and terminated in an odd murmur.

"Grace!" exclaimed Mrs. Fairfax.

I really did not expect any Grace to answer; for the laugh was as tragic, as preternatural a laugh as any I ever heard; and, but that it was high noon, and that no circumstance of ghostliness accompanied the curious cachination; but that neither scene nor season favoured fear, I should have been superstitiously afraid. However, the event showed me I was a fool for entertaining a sense even of surprise.

The door nearest me opened, and a servant came out,—a woman of between thirty and forty; a set, square-made figure, red-haired, and with a hard, plain face: any apparition less romantic or less ghostly could scarcely be conceived.

"Too much noise, Grace," said Mrs. Fairfax. "Remember directions!" Grace curtseyed silently and went in.

"She is a person we have to sew and assist Leah in her housemaid's work," continued the widow; "not altogether unobjectionable in some points, but she does well enough. By-the-by, how have you got on with your new pupil this morning?"

The conversation, thus turned on Adèle, continued till we reached the light and cheerful region below. Adèle came running to meet us in the hall, exclaiming:—

"Mesdames, vous êtes servies!" adding *"J'ai bien faim, moi!"*

We found dinner ready, and waiting for us in Mrs. Fairfax's room.

·······

Chapter 12

The promise of a smooth career, which my first calm introduction to Thornfield Hall seemed to pledge, was not belied on a longer acquaintance with the place and its inmates. Mrs. Fairfax turned out to be what she appeared, a placid-tempered, kind-natured woman, of competent education and average intelligence. My pupil was a lively child, who had been spoilt and indulged, and therefore was sometimes wayward; but as she was committed entirely to my care, and no injudicious interference from any quarter ever thwarted my plans for her improvement, she soon forgot her little freaks, and became obedient and teachable. She had no great talents, no marked traits of character, no peculiar development of feeling or taste which raised her one inch above the ordinary level of childhood; but neither had she any deficiency or vice which sunk her below it. She made reasonable progress, entertained for me a vivacious, though perhaps not very profound affection, and by her simplicity, gay prattle, and efforts to please, inspired me, in return, with a degree of attachment sufficient to make us both content in each other's society.

This *par parenthèse,* will be thought cool language by persons who entertain solemn doctrines about the angelic nature of children, and the duty of those charged with their education to conceive for them an idolatrous devotion: but I am not writing to flatter parental egotism, to echo cant, or prop up humbug; I am merely telling the truth. I felt a conscientious solicitude for Adèle's welfare and progress, and a quiet liking to her little self; just as I cherished towards Mrs. Fairfax a thankfulness for her kindness, and a pleasure in her society proportionate to the tranquil regard she had for me, and the moderation of her mind and character.

Anybody may blame me who likes, when I add further, that, now and then, when I took a walk by myself in the grounds; when I went down to the gates and looked through them along the road; or when, while Adèle played with her nurse, and Mrs. Fairfax made jellies in the store-room, I climbed the three stair-cases, raised the trap-door of the attic, and having reached the leads, looked out afar over sequestered field and hill, and along dim skyline: that then I longed for a power of vision which might overpass that limit; which might reach the busy world, towns, regions full of life I had heard of but never seen: that then I desired more of practical experience than I possessed; more of intercourse with my kind, of acquaintance with variety of character, than was here within my reach. I valued what was good in Mrs. Fairfax, and what was good in Adèle; but I believed in the existence of other and more vivid kinds of goodness, and what I believed in I wished to behold.

Who blames me? Many no doubt; and I shall be called discontented. I could not help it: the restlessness was in my nature; it agitated me to pain sometimes. Then my sole relief was to walk along the corridor of the third story, backwards and forwards, safe in the silence and solitude of the spot, and allow my mind's eye to dwell on whatever bright visions rose before it—and certainly they were many and glowing; to let my heart be heaved by the exultant movement which, while it swelled it in trouble, expanded it with life; and, best of all, to open my inward ear to a tale that was never ended—a tale my imagination created, and narrated continuously; quickened with all of incident, life, fire, feeling, that I desired and had not in my actual existence.

It is in vain to say human beings ought to be satisfied with tranquillity: they must have action; and they will make it if they cannot find it. Millions are condemned to a stiller doom than mine, and millions are in silent revolt against their lot. Nobody knows how many rebellions besides political rebellions ferment in the masses of life which people earth. Women are supposed to be very calm generally: but women feel just as men feel; they need exercise for their faculties, and a field for their efforts as much as their brothers do; they suffer from too rigid a restraint, too absolute a stagnation, precisely as men would suffer; and it is narrow-minded in their more privileged fellow-creatures to say that they ought to confine themselves to making puddings and knitting stockings, to playing on the piano and embroidering bags. It is thoughtless to condemn them, or laugh at them, if they seek to do more or learn more than custom has pronounced necessary for their sex.

When thus alone, I not unfrequently heard Grace Poole's laugh: the same peal, the same low, slow ha! ha! which, when first heard, had thrilled me: I heard, too, her eccentric murmurs; stranger than her laugh. There were days when she was quite silent; but there were others when I could not account for the sounds she made. Sometimes I saw her: she would come out of her room with a basin, or a plate, or a tray in her hand, go down to the kitchen and shortly return, generally (oh, romantic reader, forgive me for telling the plain truth!) bearing a pot of porter. Her appearance always acted as a damper to the curiosity raised by her oral oddities: hard-featured and staid, she had no point to which interest could attach. I made some attempts to draw her into conversation, but she seemed a person of few words: a monosyllabic reply usually cut short every effort of that sort.

The other members of the household, viz., John and his wife, Leah the housemaid, and Sophie the French nurse, were decent people; but in no respect remarkable: with Sophie I used to talk French, and sometimes I asked her questions about her native country; but she was not of a descriptive or narrative turn, and generally gave such vapid and confused answers as were calculated rather to check than encourage inquiry.

October, November, December passed away. One afternoon in January, Mrs. Fairfax had begged a holiday for Adèle, because she had a cold; and, as Adèle seconded the request with an ardour that reminded me how precious occasional holidays had been to me in my own childhood, I accorded it; deeming that I did well in showing pliability on the point. It was a fine, calm day, though very cold; I was tired of sitting still in the library through a whole long morning: Mrs. Fairfax had just written a letter which was waiting to be posted, so I put on my bonnet and cloak and volunteered to carry it to Hay; the distance, two miles, would be a pleasant winter afternoon walk. Having seen Adèle comfortably seated in her little chair by Mrs. Fairfax's parlour fireside, and given her her best wax doll (which I usually kept enveloped in silver paper in a drawer) to play with, and a story-book for change of amusement; and having replied to her "Revenez bientôt ma bonne amie, ma chère Mdlle. Jeannette," with a kiss, I set out.

The ground was hard, the air was still, my road was lonely; I walked fast till I got warm, and then I walked slowly to enjoy and analyze the species of pleasure brooding for me in the hour and situation. It was three o'clock; the church bell tolled as I passed under the belfry: the charm of the hour lay in its approaching dimness, in the low-gliding and pale-beaming sun. I was a mile from Thornfield, in a lane noted for wild roses in summer, for nuts and blackberries in autumn, and even now possessing a few coral treasures in hips and haws; but whose best winter delight lay in its utter solitude and leafless repose. If a breath of air stirred, it made no sound here; for there was not a holly, not an evergreen to rustle, and the stripped hawthorn and hazel bushes were as still as the white, worn stones which causewayed the middle of the path. Far and wide, on each side, there were only fields, where no cattle now browsed; and the little brown birds which stirred occasionally in the hedge, looked like single russet leaves that had forgotten to drop.

This lane inclined up-hill all the way to Hay: having reached the middle, I sat down on a stile which led thence into a field. Gathering my mantle about me, and sheltering my hands in my muff, I did not feel the cold, though it froze keenly; as was attested by a sheet of ice covering the causeway, where a little brooklet, now congealed, had overflowed after a rapid thaw some days since. From my seat I could look down on Thornfield: the gray and battlemented hall was the principal object in the vale below me; its woods and dark rookery rose against the west. I lingered till the sun went down amongst the trees, and sank crimson and clear behind them. I then turned eastward.

On the hill-top above me sat the rising moon; pale yet as a cloud, but brightening momently: she looked over Hay, which, half lost in trees, sent up a blue smoke from its few chimneys; it was yet a mile distant, but in the absolute hush I could hear plainly its thin murmurs of life. My ear too felt the flow of currents; in what dales and depths I could not tell: but there were many hills beyond Hay, and doubtless many becks threading their passes. That evening calm betrayed alike the tinkle of the nearest streams, the sough of the most remote.

A rude noise broke on these fine ripplings and whisperings, at once so far away and so clear: a positive tramp, tramp; a metallic clatter, which effaced the soft wave-wanderings; as, in a picture, the solid mass of a crag, or the rough boles of a great oak, drawn in dark and strong on the foreground, efface the aerial distance of azure hill, sunny horizon and blended clouds, where tint melts into tint.

The din was on the causeway: a horse was coming; the windings of the lane yet hid it, but it approached. I was just leaving the stile; yet as the path was narrow, I sat still to let it go by. In those days I was young, and all sorts of fancies bright and dark tenanted my mind: the memories of nursery stories were there amongst other rubbish; and when they recurred, maturing youth added to them a vigour and vividness beyond what childhood could give. As this horse approached, and as I watched for it to appear through the dusk, I remembered certain of Bessie's tales wherein figured a North-of-England spirit, called a "Gytrash"; which, in the form of horse, mule, or large dog, haunted solitary ways, and sometimes came upon belated travellers, as this horse was now coming upon me.

It was very near, but not yet in sight; when, in addition to the tramp, tramp, I heard a rush under the hedge, and close down by the hazel stems glided a great dog, whose black and white colour made him a distinct object against the trees. It was exactly one mask of Bessie's Gytrash,—a lion-like creature with long hair and a huge head: it passed me, however, quietly enough; not staying to look up, with strange pretercanine eyes, in my face, as I half expected it would. The horse followed,—a tall steed, and on its back a rider. The man, the human being, broke the spell at once. Nothing ever rode the Gytrash: it was always alone; and goblins, to my notions, though they might tenant the dumb carcasses of beasts, could scarce covet shelter in the common-place human form. No Gytrash was this,—only a traveller taking the short cut to Millcote. He passed, and I went on; a few steps, and I turned: a sliding sound and an explanation of "What the deuce is to do now?" and a clattering tumble, arrested my attention. Man and horse were down; they had slipped on the sheet of ice which glazed the causeway. The dog came bounding back, and seeing his master in a predicament, and hearing the horse groan, barked till the evening hills echoed the sound; which was deep in proportion to his magnitude. He snuffed round the prostrate group, and then he ran up to me; it was all he could do,—there was no other help at hand to summon. I obeyed him, and walked down to the traveller, by this time struggling himself free of his steed. His efforts were so vigorous, I thought he could not be much hurt; but I asked him the question:—

"Are you injured, sir?"

I think he was swearing, but am not certain; however, he was pronouncing some formula which prevented him from replying to me directly.

"Can I do anything?" I asked again.

"You must just stand on one side," he answered as he rose, first to his knees, and then to his feet. I did; whereupon began a heaving, stamping, clattering process, accompanied by a barking and baying which removed me effectually some yards distance: but I would not be driven quite away till I saw the event. This was finally fortunate; the horse was re-established, and the dog was silenced with a "Down, Pilot!" The traveller now, stooping, felt his foot and leg, as if trying whether they were sound; apparently something ailed them, for he halted to the stile whence I had just risen, and sat down.

I was in the mood for being useful, or at least officious, I think, for I now drew near him again.

"If you are hurt, and want help, sir, I can fetch some one, either from Thornfield Hall or from Hay."

"Thank you; I shall do: I have no broken bones,—only a sprain;" and again he stood up and tried his foot, but the result extorted an involuntary "Ugh!"

Something of daylight still lingered, and the moon was waxing bright: I could see him plainly. His figure was enveloped in a riding cloak, fur collared, and steel clasped; its details were not apparent, but I traced the general points of middle height, and considerable breadth of chest. He had a dark face, with stern features and a heavy brow; his eyes and gathered eyebrows looked ireful and thwarted just now; he was past youth, but had not reached middle age: perhaps he might be thirty-five. I felt no fear of him, and but little shyness. Had he been a handsome, heroic-looking young gentleman, I should not have dared to stand thus question-ing him against his will, and offering my services unasked. I had hardly ever seen a handsome youth: never in my life spoken to one. I had a theoretical reverence and homage for beauty, elegance, gallantry, fascina-tion; but had I met those qualities incarnate in masculine shape, I should have known instinctively that they neither had nor could have sympathy with anything in me, and should have shunned them as one would fire, lightning, or anything else that is bright but antipathetic.

If even this stranger had smiled and been good-humoured to me when I addressed him; if he had put off my offer of assistance gaily and with thanks, I should have gone on my way and not felt any vocation to renew inquiries: but the frown, the roughness of the traveller set me at my ease: I retained my station when he waved to me to go, and announced:—

"I cannot think of leaving you, sir, at so late an hour, in this solitary lane, till I see you are fit to mount your horse."

He looked at me when I said this: he had hardly turned his eyes in my direction before.

"I should think you ought to be at home yourself," said he, "if you have a home in this neighbourhood: where do you come from?"

"From just below; and I am not at all afraid of being out late when it is moonlight: I will run over to Hay for you with pleasure, if you wish it—indeed, I am going there to post a letter."

"You live just below—do you mean at that house with the battlements?" pointing to Thornfield Hall, on which the moon cast a hoary gleam, bring-ing it out distinct and pale from the woods, that, by contrast with the western sky, now seemed one mass of shadow.

"Yes, sir."

"Whose house is it?"

"Mr. Rochester's."

"Do you know Mr. Rochester?"

"No, I have never seen him."

"He is not resident then?"

"No."

"Can you tell me where he is?"

"I cannot."

"You are not a servant at the hall, of course. You are ——" He stopped, ran his eye over my dress, which, as usual, was quite simple: a black merino cloak, a black beaver bonnet; neither of them half fine enough for a lady's maid. He seemed puzzled to decide what I was: I helped him.

"I am the governess."

"Ah, the governess!" he repeated; "deuce take me, if I had not forgot-ten! The governess!" and again my raiment underwent scrutiny. In two minutes he rose from the stile: his face expressed pain when he tried to move.

"I cannot commission you to fetch help," he said; "but you may help me a little yourself, if you will be so kind."

"Yes, sir."

"You have not an umbrella that I can use as a stick?"

"No."

"Try to get hold of my horse's bridle and lead him to me: you are not afraid?"

I should have been afraid to touch a horse when alone, but when told to do it, I was disposed to obey. I put down my muff on the stile, and went up to the tall steed; I endeavoured to catch the bridle, but it was a spirited thing, and would not let me come near its head; I made effort on effort, though in vain: meantime, I was mortally afraid of its trampling forefeet. The traveller waited and watched for some time, and at last he laughed.

"I see," he said, "the mountain will never be brought to Mahomet, so all you can do is to aid Mahomet to go to the mountain; I must beg of you to come here."

I came. "Excuse me," he continued, "necessity compels me to make you useful." He laid a heavy hand on my shoulder, and leaning on me with some stress, limped to his horse. Having once caught the bridle, he mastered it directly and sprang to his saddle; grimacing grimly as he made the effort, for it wrenched his sprain.

"Now," said he, releasing his under lip from a hard bite, "just hand me my whip; it lies there under the hedge."

I sought it and found it.

"Thank you; now make haste with the letter to Hay, and return as fast as you can."

A touch of a spurred heel made his horse first start and rear, and then bound away; the dog rushed in his traces: all three vanished

> "Like heath that in the wilderness
> The wild wind whirls away."

I took up my muff and walked on. The incident had occurred and was gone for me: it *was* an incident of no moment, no romance, no interest in a sense; yet it marked with change one single hour of a monotonous life. My help had been needed and claimed; I had given it: I was pleased to have done something; trivial, transitory though the deed was, it was yet an active thing, and I was weary of an existence all passive. The new face, too, was like a new picture introduced to the gallery of memory; and it was dissimilar to all the others hanging there: firstly, because it was masculine; and secondly, because it was dark, strong, and stern. I had it still before me when I entered Hay, and slipped the letter into the post-office; I saw it as I walked fast down hill all the way home. When I came to the stile I stopped a minute, looked round and listened; with an idea that a horse's hoofs might ring on the causeway again, and that a rider in a cloak, and a Gytrash-like Newfoundland dog, might be again apparent: I saw only the hedge and a pollard willow before me, rising up still and straight to meet the moonbeams; I heard only the faintest waft of wind, roaming fitful among the trees round Thornfield, a mile distant; and when I glanced down in the direction of the murmur, my eye, traversing the hall-front, caught a light kindling in a window: it reminded me that I was late, and I hurried on.

I did not like re-entering Thornfield. To pass its threshold was to return to stagnation: to cross the silent hall, to ascend the darksome staircase, to seek my own lonely little room, and then to meet tranquil Mrs. Fairfax, and spend the long winter evening with her, and her only, was to quell wholly the faint excitement wakened by my walk,—to slip again over my faculties the viewless fetters of an uniform and too still existence; of an existence whose very privileges of security and ease I was becoming incapable of appreciating. What good it would have done me at that time to have been tossed in the storms of an uncertain struggling life, and to have been taught by rough and bitter experience to long for the calm amidst which I now repined! Yes, just as much good as it would do a man tired of sitting still in a "too easy chair" to take a long walk: and just as natural was the wish to stir, under my circumstances, as it would be under his.

I lingered at the gates; I lingered on the lawn; I paced backwards and forwards on the pavement: the shutters of the glass door were closed; I could not see into the interior; and both my eyes and spirit seemed drawn from the gloomy house—from the gray hollow filled with rayless cells, as it appeared to me—to that sky expanded before me,—a blue sea absolved from taint of cloud; the moon ascending it in solemn march; her orb seeming to look up as she left the hill tops, from behind which she had come, far and farther below her, and aspired to the zenith, midnight-dark in its fathomless depth and measureless distance: and for those trembling stars that followed her course, they made my heart tremble, my veins glow when I viewed them. Little things recall us to earth: the clock struck in the hall; that sufficed; I turned from moon and stars, opened a side-door and went in.

The hall was not dark, nor yet was it lit, only by the high-hung bronze lamp: a warm glow suffused both it and the lower steps of the oak staircase. This ruddy shine issued from the great dining-room, whose two-leaved door stood open and showed a genial fire in the grate, glancing on marble hearth and brass fire-irons, and revealing purple draperies and polished furniture in the most pleasant radiance. It revealed, too, a group near the mantelpiece: I had scarcely caught it, and scarcely become aware of a cheerful mingling of voices, amongst which I seemed to distinguish the tones of Adèle, when the door closed.

I hastened to Mrs. Fairfax's room: there was a fire there, too; but no candle, and no Mrs. Fairfax. Instead, all alone, sitting upright on the rug, and gazing with gravity at the blaze, I beheld a great black and white long-haired dog, just like the Gytrash of the lane. It was so like it that I went forward and said—

"Pilot," and the thing got up and came to me and snuffed me. I caressed him, and he wagged his great tail: but he looked an eerie creature to be alone with, and I could not tell whence he had come. I rang the bell, for I wanted a candle; and I wanted, too, to get an account of this visitant. Leah entered.

"What dog is this?"

"He came with master."

"With whom?"

"With master—Mr. Rochester—he is just arrived."

"Indeed! and is Mrs. Fairfax with him?"

"Yes, and Miss Adela; they are in the dining-room, and John is gone for a surgeon: for master has had an accident; his horse fell and his ankle is sprained."

"Did the horse fall in Hay Lane?"

"Yes, coming down hill; it slipped on some ice."

"Ah! Bring me a candle, will you, Leah?"

Leah brought it; she entered, followed by Mrs. Fairfax, who repeated the news; adding that Mr. Carter the surgeon was come and was now with Mr. Rochester: then she hurried out to give orders about tea, and I went up stairs to take off my things.

·······

Chapter 13

Mr. Rochester, it seems, by the surgeon's orders, went to bed early that night; nor did he rise soon next morning. When he did come down, it was to attend to business: his agent and some of his tenants were arrived, and waiting to speak with him.

Adèle and I had now to vacate the library: it would be in daily requisition as a reception-room for callers. A fire was lit in an apartment up stairs, and there I carried our books, and arranged it for the future school-room. I discerned in the course of the morning that Thornfield Hall was a changed place: no longer silent as a church, it echoed every hour or two to a knock at the door or a clang of the bell; steps, too, often traversed the hall, and new voices spoke in different keys below: a rill from the outer world was flowing through it; it had a master: for my part, I liked it better.

Adèle was not easy to teach that day; she could not apply: she kept running to the door and looking over the banisters to see if she could get a glimpse of Mr. Rochester; then she coined pretexts to go down stairs, in order, as I shrewdly suspected, to visit the library, where I knew she was not wanted; then, when I got a little angry, and made her sit still, she continued to talk incessantly of her *"ami, Monsieur Edouard Fairfax de Rochester,"* as she dubbed him (I had not before heard his prenomens), and to conjecture what presents he had brought her: for it appears he had intimated the night before that when his luggage came from Millcote, there would be found amongst it a little box in whose contents she had an interest.

"Et cela doit signifier," said she, *"qu'il y aura là dedans un cadeau pour moi, et peut-être pour vous aussi, mademoiselle. Monsieur a parlé de vous: il m'a demandé le nom de ma gouvernante, et si elle n'était pas une petite personne, assez mince et un peu pâle. J'ai dit qu'oui: car c'est vrai, n'est-ce pas, mademoiselle?"*

I and my pupil dined as usual in Mrs. Fairfax's parlour; the afternoon was wild and snowy, and we passed it in the school-room. At dark I allowed Adèle to put away books and work, and to run down stairs; for, from the comparative silence below, and from the cessation of appeals to the door-bell, I conjectured that Mr. Rochester was now at liberty. Left alone, I walked to the window; but nothing was to be seen thence: twilight and snow-flakes together thickened the air, and hid the very shrubs on the lawn. I let down the curtain and went back to the fireside.

In the clear embers I was tracing a view, not unlike a picture I remembered to have seen of the castle of Heidelberg, on the Rhine; when Mrs. Fairfax came in: breaking up by her entrance the fiery mosaic I had been piecing together, and scattering too some heavy, unwelcome thoughts that were beginning to throng on my solitude.

"Mr. Rochester would be glad if you and your pupil would take tea with him in the drawing-room this evening," said she: "he has been so much engaged all day that he could not ask to see you before."

"When is his tea-time?" I inquired.

"Oh, at six o'clock: he keeps early hours in the country. You had better change your frock now; I will go with you and fasten it. Here is a candle."

"Is it necessary to change my frock?"

"Yes, you had better: I always dress for the evening when Mr. Rochester is here."

This additional ceremony seemed somewhat stately: however, I repaired to my room, and, with Mrs. Fairfax's aid, replaced my black stuff dress by one of black silk; the best and the only additional one I had, except one of light gray, which, in my Lowood notions of the toilette, I thought too fine to be worn, except on first-rate occasions.

"You want a brooch," said Mrs. Fairfax. I had a single little pearl ornament which Miss Temple gave me as a parting keepsake: I put it on, and then we went down stairs. Unused as I was to strangers, it was rather a trail to appear thus formally summoned in Mr. Rochester's presence. I let Mrs. Fairfax precede me into the dining-room, and kept in her shade as we crossed that apartment; and, passing the arch, whose curtain was now dropped, entered the elegant recess beyond.

Two wax candles stood lighted on the table, and two on the mantelpiece; basking in the light and heat of a superb fire, lay Pilot—Adèle knelt near him. Half reclined on a couch appeared Mr. Rochester, his foot supported by the cushion; he was looking at Adèle and the dog: the fire shone full on his face. I knew my traveller with his broad and jetty eyebrows; his square forehead, made squarer by the horizontal sweep of his black hair. I recognised his decisive nose, more remarkable for character than beauty; his full nostrils, denoting, I thought, choler; his grim mouth, chin, and jaw—yes, all three were very grim, and no mistake. His shape, now divested of cloak, I perceived harmonized in squareness with his physiognomy: I suppose it was a good figure in the athletic sense of the term—broad chested and thin flanked; though neither tall nor graceful.

Mr. Rochester must have been aware of the entrance of Mrs. Fairfax and myself; but it appeared he was not in the mood to notice us, for he never lifted his head as we approached.

"Here is Miss Eyre, sir," said Mrs. Fairfax, in her quiet way. He bowed; still not taking his eyes from the group of the dog and child.

"Let Miss Eyre be seated," said he: and there was something in the forced stiff bow, in the impatient yet formal tone, which seemed further to express, "What the deuce is it to me whether Miss Eyre be there or not? At this moment I am not disposed to accost her."

I sat down quite disembarrassed. A reception of finished politeness would probably have confused me: I could not have returned or repaid it by answering grace and elegance on my part; but harsh caprice laid me under no obligation; on the contrary, a decent quiescence, under the freak of manner, gave me the advantage. Besides, the eccentricity of the proceeding was piquant: I felt interested to see how he would go on.

He went on as a statue would: that is, he neither spoke nor moved. Mrs. Fairfax seemed to think it necessary that some one should be amiable, and she began to talk. Kindly, as usual—and, as usual, rather trite—she condoled with him on the pressure of business he had had all day; on the annoyance it must have been to him with that painful sprain: then she commended his patience and perseverance in going through with it.

"Madam, I should like some tea," was the sole rejoinder she got. She hastened to ring the bell; and, when the tray came, she proceeded to arrange the cups, spoons, etc., with assiduous celerity. I and Adèle went to the table; but the master did not leave his couch.

"Will you hand Mr. Rochester's cup?" said Mrs. Fairfax to me; "Adèle might perhaps spill it."

I did as requested. As he took the cup from my hand, Adèle, thinking the moment propitious for making a request in my favour, cried out:—

"N'est-ce pas, Monsieur, qu'il y a un cadeau pour Mademoiselle Eyre, dans votre petit coffre?"

"Who talks of cadeaux?" said he gruffly: "Did you expect a present, Miss Eyre? Are you fond of presents?" and he searched my face with eyes that I saw were dark, irate, and piercing.

"I hardly know, sir; I have little experience of them: they are generally thought pleasant things."

"Generally thought? But what do you think?"

"I should be obliged to take time, sir, before I could give you an answer worthy of your acceptance: a present has many faces to it, has it not? and one should consider all, before pronouncing an opinion as to its nature."

"Miss Eyre, you are not so unsophisticated as Adèle: she demands a 'cadeau,' clamorously the moment she sees me; you beat about the bush."

"Because I have less confidence in my desserts than Adèle has: she can prefer the claim of old acquaintance, and the right too of custom; for she says you have always been in the habit of giving her playthings; but if I had to make out a case I should be puzzled, since I am a stranger and have done nothing to entitle me to an acknowledgment."

"Oh, don't fall back on over-modesty! I have examined Adèle, and find you have taken great pains with her: she is not bright, she has no talents; yet in a short time she has made much improvement."

"Sir, you have now given me my 'cadeau'; I am obliged to you: it is the meed teachers most covet; praise of their pupil's progress."

"Humph!" said Mr. Rochester, and he took his tea in silence.

"Come to the fire," said the master, when the tray was taken away and Mrs. Fairfax had settled into a corner with her knitting; while Adèle was leading me by the hand round the room, showing me the beautiful books and ornaments on the consoles and chiffonières. We obeyed, as in duty bound: Adèle wanted to take a seat on my knee, but she was ordered to amuse herself with Pilot.

"You have been resident in my house three months?"

"Yes, sir."

"And you came from —?"

"From Lowood school in ——shire."

"Ah! a charitable concern. How long were you there?"

"Eight years."

"Eight years! you must be tenacious of life. I thought half the time in such a place would have done up any constitution! No wonder you have rather the look of another world. I marvelled where you had got that sort of face. When you came on me in Hay Lane last night, I thought unaccountably of fairy tales, and had half a mind to demand whether you had bewitched my horse: I am not sure yet. Who are your parents?"

"I have none."

"Nor ever had, I suppose: do you remember them?"

"No."

"I thought not. And so you were waiting for your people when you sat on that stile?"

"For whom, sir?"

"For the men in green: it was a proper moonlight evening for them. Did I break through one of your rings, that you spread that damned ice on the causeway?"

I shook my head. "The men in green all forsook England a hundred years ago," said I, speaking as seriously as he had done. "And not even in Hay Lane or the fields about it could you find a trace of them. I don't think either summer or harvest, or winter moon, will ever shine on their revels more."

Mrs. Fairfax had dropped her knitting, and with raised eyebrows, seemed wondering what sort of talk this was.

"Well," resumed Mr. Rochester, "if you disown parents, you must have some sort of kinsfolk: uncles and aunts?"

"No; none that I ever saw."

"And your home?"

"I have none."

"Where do your brothers and sisters live?"

"I have no brothers or sisters."

"Who recommended you to come here?"

"I advertised, and Mrs. Fairfax answered my advertisement."

"Yes," said the good lady, who now knew what ground we were upon, "and I am daily thankful for the choice Providence led me to make. Miss Eyre has been an invaluable companion to me, and a kind and careful teacher to Adèle."

"Don't trouble yourself to give her a character," returned Mr. Rochester: "eulogiums will not bias me; I shall judge for myself. She began by felling my horse."

"Sir?" said Mrs. Fairfax.

"I have to thank her for this sprain."

The widow looked bewildered.

"Miss Eyre, have you ever lived in a town?"

"No, sir."

"Have you seen much society?"

"None but the pupils and teachers of Lowood; and now the inmates of Thornfield."

"Have you read much?"

"Only such books as came in my way; and they have not been numerous or very learned."

"You have lived the life of a nun: no doubt you are well drilled in religious forms;--Brocklehurst, who I understand directs Lowood, is a parson, is he not?"

"Yes, sir."

"And you girls probably worshipped him, as a convent full of religieuses would worship their director."

"Oh, no."

"You are very cool! No! What! a novice not worship her priest? That sounds blasphemous."

"I disliked Mr. Brocklehurst; and I was not alone in the feeling. He is a harsh man; at once pompous and meddling: he cut off our hair; and for economy's sake, bought us bad needles and thread, with which we could hardly sew."

"That was very false economy," remarked Mrs. Fairfax, who now again caught the drift of the dialogue.

"And was that the head and front of his offending?" demanded Mr. Rochester.

"He starved us when he had the sole superintendence of the provision department, before the committee was appointed; and he bored us with long lectures once a week, and with evening readings from books of his own inditing, about sudden deaths and judgments, which made us afraid to go to bed."

"What age were you when you went to Lowood?"

"About ten."

"And you stayed there eight years: you are now, then, eighteen?"

I assented.

"Arithmetic, you see, is useful: without its aid, I should hardly have been able to guess your age. It is a point difficult to fix where the features and countenance are so much at variance as in your case. And now, what did you learn at Lowood? Can you play?"

"A little."

"Of course: that is the established answer. Go into the library—I mean, if you please. (Excuse my tone of command; I am used to say 'Do this,' and it is done: I cannot alter my customary habits for one new inmate.)—Go, then, into the library; take a candle with you; leave the door open; sit down to the piano, and play a tune."

I departed, obeying his directions.

"Enough!" he called out in a few minutes. "You play *a little*, I see; like any other English school-girl: perhaps rather better than some, but not well."

I closed the piano, and returned. Mr. Rochester continued.

"Adèle showed me some sketches this morning, which she said were yours. I don't know whether they were entirely of your doing: probably a master aided you?"

"No, indeed!" I interjected.

"Ah! that pricks pride. Well, fetch me your portfolio, if you can vouch for its contents being original; but don't pass your word unless you are certain: I can recognise patchwork."

"Then I will say nothing, and you shall judge for yourself, sir."

I brought the portfolio from the library.

"Approach the table," said he; and I wheeled it to his couch. Adèle and Mrs. Fairfax drew near to see the pictures.

"No crowding," said Mr. Rochester: "take the drawings from my hand as I finish with them; but don't push your faces up to mine."

He deliberately scrutinized each sketch and painting. Three he laid aside; the others, when he had examined them, he swept from him.

"Take them off to the other table, Mrs. Fairfax," said he, "and look at them with Adèle;—you" (glancing at me) "resume your seat, and answer my questions. I perceive these pictures were done by one hand: was that hand yours?"

"Yes."

"And when did you find time to do them? They have taken much time, and some thought."

"I did them in the last two vacations I spent at Lowood, when I had no other occupation."

"Where did you get your copies?"

"Out of my head."

"That head I see now on your shoulders?"

"Yes, sir."

"Has it other furniture of the same kind within?"

"I should think it may have: I should hope—better."

He spread the pictures before him, and again surveyed them alternately.

While he is so occupied, I will tell you, reader, what they are: and first, I must premise that they are nothing wonderful. The subjects had indeed risen vividly on my mind. As I saw them with the spiritual eye, before I attempted to embody them, they were striking; but my hand would not second my fancy, and in each case it had wrought out but a pale portrait of the thing I had conceived.

These pictures were in water colours. The first represented clouds low and livid, rolling over a swollen sea: all the distance was in eclipse; so, too, was the foreground; or rather, the nearest billows, for there was no land. One gleam of light lifted into relief a half-submerged mast, on which sat a cormorant, dark and large, with wings flecked with foam; its beak held a gold bracelet, set with gems, that I had touched with as brilliant tints as my palette could yield, and as glittering distinctness as my pencil could impart. Sinking below the bird and mast, a drowned corpse glanced through the green water; a fair arm was the only limb clearly visible, whence the bracelet had been washed or torn.

The second picture contained for foreground only the dim peak of a hill, with grass and some leaves slanting as if by a breeze. Beyond and above spread an expanse of sky, dark blue as at twilight: rising into the sky, was a woman's shape to the bust, portrayed in tints as dusk and soft as I could combine. The dim forehead was crowned with a star; the lineaments below were seen as through the suffusion of vapour; the eyes shone dark and wild; the hair streamed shadowy, like a beamless cloud torn by storm or by electric travail. On the neck lay a pale reflection like moonlight; the same faint lustre touched the train of thin clouds from which rose and bowed this vision of the Evening Star.

The third showed the pinnacle of an iceberg piercing a polar winter sky: a muster of northern lights reared their dim lances, close serried, along the horizon. Throwing these into distance, rose, in the foreground, a head,—a colossal head, inclined towards the iceberg, and resting against it. Two thin hands, joined under the forehead, and supporting it, drew up before the lower features a sable veil; a brow quite bloodless, white as bone, and an eye hollow and fixed, blank of meaning but for the glassiness of despair, alone were visible. Above the temples, amidst wreathed turban folds of black drapery, vague in its character and consistency as cloud, gleamed a ring of white flame, gemmed with sparkles of a more lurid tinge. This pale crescent was "The likeness of a Kingly Crown"; what it diademed was "the shape which shape had none."

"Were you happy when you painted these pictures?" asked Mr. Rochester, presently.

"I was absorbed, sir: yes, and I was happy. To paint them, in short, was to enjoy one of the keenest pleasures I have ever known."

"That is not saying much. Your pleasures, by your own account, have been few; but I daresay you did exist in a kind of artist's dreamland while you blent and arranged these strange tints. Did you sit at them long each day?"

"I had nothing else to do, because it was the vacation, and I sat at them from morning till noon, and from noon till night: the length of the mid-summer days favoured my inclination to apply."

"And you felt self-satisfied with the result of your ardent labours?"

"Far from it. I was tormented by the contrast between my idea and my handiwork: in each case I had imagined something which I was quite powerless to realize."

"Not quite: you have secured the shadow of your thought; but no more, probably. You had not enough of the artist's skill and science to give it full being: yet the drawings are, for a school girl, peculiar. As to the thoughts, they are elfish. These eyes in the Evening Star you must have seen in a dream. How could you make them look so clear, and yet not at all brilliant? for the planet above quells their rays. And what meaning is that in their solemn depth? And who taught you to paint wind? There is a high gale in that sky, and on this hill-top. Where did you see Latmos? For that is Latmos. There,—put the drawings away!"

I had scarce tied the strings of the portfolio, when, looking at his watch, he said abruptly—

"It is nine o'clock: what are you about, Miss Eyre, to let Adèle sit up so long? Take her to bed."

Adèle went to kiss him before quitting the room: he endured the caress, but scarcely seemed to relish it more than Pilot would have done, nor so much.

"I wish you all good-night, now," said he, making a movement of the hand towards the door, in token that he was tired of our company, and wished to dismiss us. Mrs. Fairfax folded up her knitting: I took my port-folio: we curtseyed to him, received a frigid bow in return, and so withdrew.

"You said Mr. Rochester was not strikingly peculiar, Mrs. Fairfax," I observed, when I rejoined her in her room, after putting Adèle to bed.

"Well, is he?"

"I think so: he is very changeful and abrupt."

"True: no doubt he may appear so to a stranger, but I am so accustomed to his manner, I never think of it; and then, if he has peculiarities of temper, allowance should be made."

"Why?"

"Partly, because it is his nature—and we can none of us help our nature; and partly, he has painful thoughts, no doubt, to harass him, and make his spirits unequal."

"What about?"

"Family troubles, for one thing."

"But he has no family."

"Not now; but he has had—or, at least, relatives. He lost his elder brother a few years since."

"His *elder* brother?"

"Yes. The present Mr. Rochester has not been very long in possession of the property: only about nine years."

"Nine years is a tolerable time. Was he so very fond of his brother as to be still inconsolable for his loss?"

"Why, no—perhaps not. I believe there were some misunderstandings between them. Mr. Rowland Rochester was not quite just to Mr. Edward; and perhaps he prejudiced his father against him. The old gentleman was fond of money, and anxious to keep the family estate together. He did not like to diminish the property by division, and yet he was anxious that Mr. Edward should have wealth, too, to keep up the consequence of the name; and soon after he was of age, some steps were taken that were not quite fair, and made a great deal of mischief. Old Mr. Rochester and Mr. Rowland combined to bring Mr. Edward into what he considered a painful position, for the sake of making his fortune: what the precise nature of that position was I never clearly knew, but his spirit could not brook what he had to suffer in it. He is not very forgiving: he broke with his family, and now for many years he has led an unsettled kind of life. I don't think he has ever been resident at Thornfield for a fortnight together, since the death of his brother without a will, left him master of the estate: and, indeed, no wonder he shuns the old place."

"Why should he shun it?"

"Perhaps he thinks it gloomy."

The answer was evasive—I should have liked something clearer; but Mrs. Fairfax either could not, or would not, give me more explicit information of the origin and nature of Mr. Rochester's trials. She averred they were a mystery to herself, and that what she knew was chiefly from conjecture. It was evident, indeed, that she wished me to drop the subject; which I did accordingly.

·······

Chapter 14

For several subsequent days I saw little of Mr. Rochester. In the mornings he seemed much engaged with business, and in the afternoon, gentlemen from Millcote or the neighbourhood called, and sometimes stayed to dine with him. When his sprain was well enough to admit of horse exercise, he rode out a good deal; probably to return these visits, as he generally did not come back till late at night.

During this interval, even Adèle was seldom sent for to his presence, and all my acquaintance with him was confined to an occasional rencontre in the hall, on the stairs, or in the gallery; when he would sometimes pass me haughtily and coldly, just acknowledging my presence by a distant nod or a cool glance, and sometimes bow and smile with gentlemanlike affability. His changes of mood did not offend me, because I saw that I had nothing to do with their alteration, the ebb and flow depended on causes quite disconnected with me.

One day he had had company to dinner, and had sent for my portfolio; in order, doubtless, to exhibit its contents: the gentlemen went away early, to attend a public meeting at Millcote, as Mrs. Fairfax informed me; but the night being wet and inclement, Mr. Rochester did not accompany them. Soon after they were gone, he rang the bell: a message came that

I and Adèle were to go down stairs. I brushed Adèle's hair and made her neat, and having ascertained that I was myself in my usual Quaker trim, where there was nothing to retouch—all being too close and plain, braided locks included, to admit of disarrangement—we descended; Adèle wondering whether the *petit coffre* was at length come: for owing to some mistake, its arrival had hitherto been delayed. She was gratified: there it stood, a little carton, on the table when we entered the dining-room. She appeared to know it by instinct.

"*Ma boîte! ma boîte!*" exclaimed she, running towards it.

"Yes—there is your *'boîte'* at last: take it into a corner, you genuine daughter of Paris, and amuse yourself with disembowelling it," said the deep and rather sarcastic voice of Mr. Rochester, proceeding from the depths of an immense easy-chair at the fire-side. "And mind," he continued, "don't bother me with any details of the anatomical process, or any notice of the condition of the entrails: let your operation be conducted in silence—*tiens-toi tranquille, enfant; comprends-tu?*"

Adèle seemed scarcely to need the warning; she had already retired to a sofa with her treasure, and was busy untying the cord which secured the lid. Having removed this impediment, and lifted certain silvery envelopes of tissue paper, she merely exclaimed:—

"*Oh, Ciel! Que c'est beau!*" and then remained absorbed in ecstatic contemplation.

"Is Miss Eyre, there?" now demanded the master, half rising from his seat to look round to the door, near which I still stood.

"Ah! well; come forward: be seated here." He drew a chair near his own. "I am not fond of the prattle of children," he continued; "for, old bachelor as I am, I have no pleasant associations connected with their lisp. It would be intolerable to me to pass a whole evening *tête à tête* with a brat. Don't draw that chair further off, Miss Eyre; sit down exactly where I placed it—if you please, that is. Confound these civilities! I continually forget them. Nor do I particularly affect simple-minded old ladies. By-the-by, I must have in mine; it won't do to neglect her: she is a Fairfax, or wed to one; and blood is said to be thicker than water."

He rang and despatched an invitation to Mrs. Fairfax, who soon arrived, knitting-basket in hand.

"Good evening, madam; I sent to you for a charitable purpose: I have forbidden Adèle to talk to me about her presents, and she is bursting with repletion; have the goodness to serve her as auditress and interlocutrice: it will be one of the most benevolent acts you ever performed."

Adèle, indeed, no sooner saw Mrs. Fairfax, than she summoned her to her sofa, and there quickly filled her lap with the porcelain, the ivory, the waxen contents of her "boîte"; pouring out, meantime, explanations and raptures in such broken English as she was mistress of.

"Now I have performed the part of a good host," pursued Mr. Rochester; "put my guests into the way of amusing each other, I ought to be at liberty to attend to my own pleasure. Miss Eyre, draw your chair still a little further forward: you are yet too far back; I cannot see you without disturbing my position in this comfortable chair, which I have no mind to do."

I did as I was bid; though I would much rather have remained somewhat in the shade: but Mr. Rochester had such a direct way of giving orders, it seemed a matter of course to obey him promptly.

We were, as I have said, in the dining-room: the lustre, which had been lit for dinner, filled the room with a festal breadth of light; the large fire was all red and clear; the purple curtains hung rich and ample before the lofty window and loftier arch: everything was still, save the subdued chat of Adèle (she dared not speak loud), and, filling up each pause, the beating of winter rain against the panes.

Mr. Rochester, as he sat in his damask-covered chair, looked different to what I had seen him look before,—not quite so stern; much less gloomy. There was a smile on his lips, and his eyes sparkled, whether with wine or not, I am not sure; but I think it very probable. He was, in short, in his after-dinner-mood; more expanded and genial, and also more self-indulgent than the frigid and rigid temper of the morning: still, he looked preciously grim, cushioning his massive head against the swelling back of his chair, and receiving the light of the fire on his granite-hewn features, and in his great, dark eyes—for he had great, dark eyes, and very fine eyes, too: not without a certain change in their depths sometimes, which, if it was not softness, reminded you, at least, of that feeling.

He had been looking two minutes at the fire, and I had been looking the same length of time at him, when, turning suddenly, he caught my gaze fastened on his physiognomy.

"You examine me, Miss Eyre," said he: "do you think me handsome?"

I should, if I had deliberated, have replied to this question by something conventionally vague and polite; but the answer somehow slipped from my tongue before I was aware:—"No, sir."

"Ah! By my word! there is something singular about you," said he: "you have the air of a little nonnette; quaint, quiet, grave, and simple, as you sit with your hands before you, and your eyes generally bent on the carpet (except, by-the-by, when they are directed piercingly to my face; as just now, for instance); and when one asks you a question, or makes a remark to which you are obliged to reply, you rap out a round rejoinder, which, if not blunt, is at least brusque. What do you mean by it?"

"Sir, I was too plain: I beg your pardon. I ought to have replied that it was not easy to give an impromptu answer to a question about appearances; that tastes differ; that beauty is of little consequence, or something of that sort."

"You ought to have replied no such thing. Beauty of little consequence, indeed! And so, under pretence of softening the previous outrage, of stroking and soothing me into placidity, you stick a sly penknife under my ear! Go on: what fault do you find with me, pray? I suppose I have all my limbs and all my features like any other man?"

"Mr. Rochester, allow me to disown my first answer: I intended no pointed repartee: it was only a blunder."

"Just so: I think so: and you shall be answerable for it. Criticize me: does my forehead not please you?"

He lifted up the sable waves of hair which lay horizontally over his brow, and showed a solid enough mass of intellectual organs, but an abrupt deficiency where the suave sign of benevolence should have risen.

"Now, ma'am, am I a fool?"

"Far from it, sir. You would, perhaps, think me rude if I inquired in return whether you are a philanthropist?"

"There again! Another stick of the penknife, when she pretended to pat my head: and that is because I said I did not like the society of children and old women (low be it spoken!). No, young lady, I am not a general philanthropist; but I bear a conscience"; and he pointed to the prominences which are said to indicate that faculty—and which, fortunately for him, were sufficiently conspicuous; giving, indeed, a marked breadth to the upper part of his head: "and besides, I once had a kind of rude tenderness of heart. When I was as old as you, I was a feeling fellow enough; partial to the unfledged, unfostered, and unlucky; but fortune has knocked me about since: she has even kneaded me with her knuckles, and now I flatter myself I am hard and tough as an Indian-rubber ball; pervious, though, through a chink or two still, and with one sentient point in the middle of the lump. Yes: does that leave hope for me?"

"Hope of what, sir?"

"Of my final re-transformation from Indian-rubber back to flesh?"

"Decidedly he has had too much wine," I thought; and I did not know what answer to make to his queer question: how could I tell whether he was capable of being re-transformed?

"You look very much puzzled, Miss Eyre; and though you are not pretty any more than I am handsome, yet a puzzled air becomes you; besides, it is convenient, for it keeps those searching eyes of yours away from my physiognomy, and busies them with the worsted flowers of the rug; so puzzle on. Young lady, I am disposed to be gregarious and communicative to-night."

With this announcement he rose from his chair, and stood, leaning his arm on the marble mantel-piece: in that attitude his shape was seen plainly as well as his face; his unusual breadth of chest, disproportionate almost to his length of limb. I am sure most people would have thought him an ugly man; yet there was so much unconscious pride in his port; so much ease in his demeanor; such a look of complete indifference to his own external appearance; so haughty a reliance on the power of other qualities, intrinsic or adventitious, to atone for the lack of mere personal attractiveness, that in looking at him, one inevitably shared the indifference; and even in a blind, imperfect sense, put faith in the confidence.

"I am disposed to be gregarious and communicative to-night," he repeated; "and that is why I sent for you: the fire and the chandelier were not sufficient company for me; nor would Pilot have been, for none of these can talk. Adèle is a degree better, but still far below the mark; Mrs. Fairfax ditto; you, I am persuaded, can suit me if you will: you puzzled me the first evening I invited you down here. I have almost forgotten you since: other ideas have driven yours from my head; but to-night I am resolved to be at ease; to dismiss what importunes, and recall what pleases. It would please me now to draw you out: to learn more of you—therefore speak."

Instead of speaking, I smiled: and not a very complacent or submissive smile either.

"Speak," he urged.

"What about, sir?"

"Whatever you like. I leave both the choice of subject and the manner of treating it, entirely to yourself."

Accordingly I sat and said nothing: "If he expects me to talk for the mere sake of talking and showing off, he will find he has addressed himself to the wrong person," I thought.

"You are dumb, Miss Eyre."

I was dumb still. He bent his head a little towards me and with a single hasty glance seemed to dive into my eyes.

"Stubborn?" he said, "and annoyed. Ah, it is consistent. I put my request in an absurd, almost insolent form. Miss Eyre, I beg your pardon. The fact is, once for all, I don't wish to treat you like an inferior: that is (correcting himself), I claim only such superiority as must result from twenty years' difference in age and a century's advance in experience. This is legitimate, *et j'y tiens*, as Adèle would say; and it is by virtue of this superiority and this alone that I desire you to have the goodness to talk to me a little now, and divert my thoughts, which are galled with dwelling on one point: cankering as a rusty nail."

He had deigned an explanation; almost an apology: I did not feel insensible to his condescension, and would not seem so.

"I am willing to amuse you if I can, sir: quite willing; but I cannot introduce a topic, because how do I know what will interest you? Ask me questions, and I will do my best to answer them."

"Then, in the first place, do you agree with me that I have a right to be a little masterful, abrupt; perhaps exacting, sometimes, on the grounds I stated: namely, that I am old enough to be your father, and that I have battled through a varied experience with many men of many nations, and roamed over half the globe, while you have lived quietly with one set of people in one house?"

"Do as you please, sir."

"That is no answer; or rather it is a very irritating, because a very evasive one—reply clearly."

"I don't think, sir, you have a right to command me, merely because you are older than I, or because you have seen more of the world than I have—your claim to superiority depends on the use you have made of your time and experience."

"Humph! Promptly spoken. But I won't allow that, seeing that it would never suit my case; as I have made an indifferent, not to say a bad use of both advantages. Leaving superiority out of the question then, you must still agree to receive my orders now and then, without being piqued or hurt by the tone of command— will you?"

I smiled: I thought to myself Mr. Rochester *is* peculiar—he seems to forget that he pays me £30 per annum for receiving his orders.

"The smile is very well," said he, catching instantly the passing expression; "but speak too."

"I was thinking, sir, that very few masters would trouble themselves to inquire whether or not their paid subordinates were piqued and hurt by their orders."

"Paid subordinates! What, you are my paid subordinate, are you? Oh yes, I had forgotten the salary! Well then, on that mercenary ground, will you agree to let me hector a little?"

"No, sir, not on that ground: but, on the ground that you did forget it, and that you care whether or not a dependant is comfortable in his dependency, I agree heartily."

"And will you consent to dispense with a great many conventional forms and phrases, without thinking that the omission arises from insolence?"

"I am sure, sir, I should never mistake informality for insolence: one I rather like, the other nothing free-born would submit to, even for a salary."

"Humbug! Most things free-born will submit to anything for a salary; therefore, keep to yourself, and don't venture on generalities of which you are intensely ignorant. However, I mentally shake hands with you for your answer, despite its inaccuracy; and as much for the manner in which it was said, as for the substance of the speech: the manner was frank and sincere; one does not often see such a manner: no, on the contrary, affectation, or coldness, or stupid, coarse-minded misapprehension of one's meaning are the usual rewards of candour. Not three in three thousand raw school-girl-governesses would have answered me as you have just done. But I don't mean to flatter you: if you are cast in a different mould to the majority, it is no merit of yours: Nature did it. And then, after all, I go too fast in my conclusions: for what I yet know, you may be no better than the rest; you may have intolerable defects to counter-balance your few good points."

"And so may you," I thought. My eye met his as the idea crossed my mind: he seemed to read the glance, answering as if its import had been spoken as well as imagined.—

"Yes, yes, you are right," said he; "I have plenty of faults of my own: I know it, and I don't wish to palliate them, I assure you. God wot I need not be too severe about others; I have a past existence, a series of deeds, a colour of life to contemplate within my own breast, which might well call my sneers and censures from my neighbours to myself. I started, or rather (for like other defaulters, I like to lay half the blame on ill fortune and adverse circumstances) was thrust on to a wrong tack at the age of one and twenty, and have never recovered the right course since: but I might have been very different; I might have been as good as you,— wiser,—almost as stainless. I envy you your peace of mind, your clean conscience, your unpolluted memory. Little girl, a memory without blot or contamination must be an exquisite treasure,—an inexhaustible source of pure refreshment: is it not?"

"How was your memory when you were eighteen, sir?"

"All right then; limpid, salubrious: no gush of bilge water had turned it to fetid puddle. I was your equal at eighteen— quite your equal. Nature meant me to be, on the whole, a good man, Miss Eyre: one of the better end; and you see I am not so. You would say you don't see it: at least I flatter myself I read as much in your eye (beware, by-the-by, what you express with that organ, I am quick at interpreting its language). Then take my word for it,—I am not a villain: your are not to suppose that— not to attribute to me any such bad eminence; but, owing, I verily believe, rather to circumstances than to my natural bent, I am a trite commonplace sinner, hackneyed in all the poor petty dissipations with which the rich and worthless try to put on life. Do you wonder that I avow this to you? Know, that in the course of your future life you will often find yourself elected the involuntary confidant of your acquaintances' secrets: people will instinctively find out, as I have done, that it is not your forte to talk of yourself, but to listen while others talk of themselves; they will feel, too, that you listen with no malevolent scorn of their indiscretion, but with a kind of innate sympathy; not the less comforting and encouraging because it is very unobtrusive in its manifestations."

"How do you know?—how can you guess all this, sir?"

"I know it well; therefore I proceed almost as freely as if I were writing my thoughts in a diary. You would say, I should have been superior to circumstances: so I should—so I should; but you see I was not. When fate wronged me, I had not the wisdom to remain cool: I turned desperate;

then I degenerated. Now, when any vicious simpleton excites my disgust by his paltry ribaldry, I cannot flatter myself that I am better than he: I am forced to confess that he and I are on a level. I wish I had stood firm—God knows I do! Dread remorse when you are tempted to err, Miss Eyre: remorse is the poison of life."

"Repentance is said to be its cure, sir."

"It is not its cure. Reformation may be its cure; and I could reform—I have strength yet for that—if—but where is the use of thinking of it, hampered, burdened, cursed as I am? Besides, since happiness is irrevocably denied me, I have a right to get pleasure out of life: and I *will* get it, cost what it may."

"Then you will degenerate still more, sir."

"Possibly: yet why should I, if I can get sweet, fresh pleasure? And I may get it as sweet and fresh as the wild honey the bee gathers on the moor."

"It will sting—it will taste bitter, sir."

"How do you know? you never tried it. How very serious—how very solemn you look; and you are as ignorant of the matter as this cameo head (taking one from the mantel-piece)! You have no right to preach to me; you neophyte, that have not passed the porch of life, and are absolutely unacquainted with its mysteries."

"I only remind you of your own words, sir: you said error brought remorse, and you pronounced remorse the poison of existence."

"And who talks of error now? I scarcely think the notion that flittered across my brain was an error. I believe it was an inspiration rather than a temptation: it was very genial, very soothing,—I know that. Here it comes again! It is no devil, I assure you: or if it be, it has put on the robes of an angel of light. I think I must admit so fair a guest when it asks entrance to my heart."

"Distrust it, sir; it is not a true angel."

"Once more, how do you know? By what instinct do you pretend to distinguish between a fallen seraph of the abyss, and a messenger from the eternal throne—between a guide and a seducer?"

"I judged by your countenance, sir; which was troubled: when you said the suggestion had returned upon you. I feel sure it will work you more misery if you listen to it."

"Not at all—it bears the most gracious message in the world: for the rest, you are not my conscience-keeper, so don't make yourself uneasy. Here, come in, bonny wanderer!"

He said this as if he spoke to a vision, viewless to any eye but his own; then folding his arms, which he had half extended, on his chest, he seemed to enclose in their embrace the invisible being.

"Now," he continued, again addressing me, "I have received the pilgrim—a disguised deity, as I verily believe. Already it has done me good: my heart was a sort of charnel; it will now be a shrine."

"To speak truth, sir, I don't understand you at all: I cannot keep up the conversation, because it has got out of my depth. Only one thing I know: you said you were not as good as you should like to be, and that you regretted your own imperfection—one thing I can comprehend: you intimated that to have a sullied memory was a perpetual bane. It seems to me, that if you tried hard, you would in time find it possible to become what you yourself would approve; and that if from this day you began with resolution to correct your thoughts and actions, you would in a few years have laid up a new and stainless store of recollections, to which you might revert with pleasure."

"Justly thought; rightly said, Miss Eyre; and at this moment, I am paving hell with energy."

"Sir?"

"I am laying down good intentions, which I believe durable as flint. Certainly, my associates and pursuits shall be other than they have been."

"And better?"

"And better—so much better as pure ore is than foul dross. You seem to doubt me; I don't doubt myself: I know what my aim is, what my motives are; and at this moment I pass a law, unalterable as that of the Medes and Persians, that both are right."

"They cannot be, sir, if they require a new statute to legalize them."

"They are, Miss Eyre, though they absolutely require a new statute: unheard-of combinations of circumstances demand unheard-of rules."

"That sounds a dangerous maxim, sir; because one can see at once that it is liable to abuse."

"Sententious sage! so it is: but I swear by my household gods not to abuse it."

"You are human and fallible."

"I am: so are you—what then?"

"The human and fallible should not arrogate a power with which the divine and perfect alone can be safely entrusted."

"What power?"

"That of saying of any strange, unsanctioned line of action,—'Let it be right.' "

" 'Let it be right'—the very words: you have pronounced them."

"*May* it be right then," I said, as I rose; deeming it useless to continue a discourse which was all darkness to me; and, besides, sensible that the character of my interlocutor was beyond my penetration: at least, beyond its present reach; and feeling the uncertainty, the vague sense of insecurity, which accompanies a conviction of ignorance.

"Where are you going?"

"To put Adèle to bed: it is past her bedtime."

"You are afraid of me, because I talk like a Sphynx."

"Your language is enigmatical, sir: but though I am bewildered, I am certainly not afraid."

"You *are* afraid—your self-love dreads a blunder."

"In that sense I do feel apprehensive—I have no wish to talk nonsense."

"If you did, it would be in such a grave, quiet manner, I should mistake if for sense. Do you never laugh, Miss Eyre? Don't trouble yourself to answer—I see, you laugh rarely; but you can laugh very merrily: believe me, you are not naturally austere, any more than I am naturally vicious. The Lowood constraint still clings to you somewhat; controlling your features, muffling your voice, and restricting your limbs; and you fear in the presence of a man and a brother—or father, or master, or what you will— to smile too gaily, speak too freely, or move too quickly: but in time, I think you will learn to be natural with me, as I find it impossible to be conventional with you; and then your looks and movements will have more vivacity and variety than they dare offer now. I see, at intervals, the glance of a curious sort of bird through the close-set bars of a cage: a vivid, restless, resolute captive is there; were it but free, it would soar cloud-high. You are still bent on going?"

"It has struck nine, sir."

"Never mind,—wait a minute: Adèle is not ready to go to bed yet. My position, Miss Eyre, with my back to the fire, and my face to the room, favours observation. While talking to you, I have also occasionally watched Adèle; (I have my own reasons for thinking her a curious study,—reasons that I may, nay that I shall, impart to you some day;) she pulled out of her box, about ten minutes ago, a little pink silk frock; rapture lit her face as she unfolded it: coquetry runs in her blood, blends with her brains, and seasons the marrow of her bones. '*Il faut que je l'essaie!*' cried she; '*et à l'instant même!*' and she rushed out òf the room. She is now with Sophie, undergoing a robing process: in a few minutes she will re-enter; and I know what I shall see,—a miniature of Céline Varens, as she used to appear on the boards at the rising of ——: but never mind that. However, my tenderest feelings are about to receive a shock: such is my presentiment; stay now, to see whether it will be realized."

Ere long, Adèle's little foot was heard tripping across the hall. She entered, transformed as her guardian had predicted. A dress of rose-coloured satin, very short, and as full in the skirt as it could be gathered, replaced the brown frock she had previously worn; a wreath of rosebuds circled her forehead; her feet were dressed in silk stockings and small white satin sandals.

"*Est-ce que ma robe va bien?*" cried she, bounding forwards; "*et mes souliers? et mes bas? Tenez, je crois que je vais danser!*"

And spreading out her dress, she chasséed across the room; till having reached Mr. Rochester, she wheeled lightly round before him on tip-toe, then dropped on one knee at his feet, exclaiming:—

"*Monsieur, je vous remercie mille fois de votre bonté*;" then rising, she added, "*C'est comme cela que maman faisait, n'est-ce pas, Monsieur?*"

"Pre-cise-ly!" was the answer; and " '*comme cela,*' she charmed my English gold out of my British breeches' pocket. I have been green, too, Miss Eyre,—ay, grass green: not a more vernal tint freshens you now than once freshened me. My Spring is gone, however: but it has left me that French floweret on my hands; which, in some moods, I would fain be rid of. Not valuing now the root whence it sprang; having found that it was a sort which nothing but gold dust could manure, I have but half a liking to the blossom: especially when it looks so artificial, as just now. I keep it and rear it rather on the Roman Catholic principle of expiating numerous sins, great or small, by one good work. I'll explain all this some day. Good-night."

· · · · · · ·

Chapter 15

Mr. Rochester did, on a future occasion, explain it.

It was one afternoon, when he chanced to meet me and Adèle in the grounds; and while she played with Pilot and her shuttlecock, he asked me to walk up and down a long beech avenue within sight of her.

He then said that she was the daughter of a French opera dancer, Céline

Varens; towards whom he had once cherished what he called a "*grande passion*." This passion Céline had professed to return with even superior ardour. He thought himself her idol; ugly as he was: he believed, as he said, that she preferred his "*taille d'athl*ète" to the elegance of the Apollo Belvidere.

"And, Miss Eyre, so much was I flattered by this preference of the Gallic sylph for her British gnome, that I installed her in an hotel; gave her a complete establishment of servants, a carriage, cashmeres, diamonds, dentelles, etc. In short, I began the process of ruining myself in the received style; like any other spoonie. I had not, it seems, the originality to chalk out a new road to shame and destruction, but trode the old track with stupid exactness not to deviate an inch from the beaten centre. I had—and I deserved to have—the fate of all other spoonies. Happening to call one evening, when Céline did not expect me, I found her out; but it was a warm night, and I was tired with strolling through Paris, so I sat down in her boudoir; happy to breathe the air consecrated so lately by her presence. No,—I exaggerate; I never thought there was any consecrating virtue about her: it was rather a sort of pastile perfume she had left; a scent of musk and amber, than an odour of sanctity. I was just beginning to stifle with the fumes of conservatory flowers and sprinkled essences, when I bethought myself to open the window and step out to the balcony. It was moonlight, and gas-light besides, and very still and serene. The balcony was furnished with a chair or two; I sat down, took out a cigar,—I will take one now, if you will excuse me."

Here ensued a pause, filled by the producing and lighting of a cigar; having placed it to his lips and breathed a trail of Havannah incense on the freezing and sunless air, he went on:—

"I liked bonbons too, in those days, Miss Eyre, and I was *croquant*—(overlook the barbarism) *croquant* chocolate comfits, and smoking alternately, watching meantime the equipages that rolled along the fashionable streets towards the neighbouring opera-house, when in an elegant close carriage drawn by a beautiful pair of English horses, and distinctly seen in the brilliant city-night, I recognised the '*voiture*' I had given Céline. She was returning: of course my heart thumped with impatience against the iron rails I leant upon. The carriage stopped, as I had expected, at the hotel door; my flame (that is the very word for an opera inammorata) alighted: though muffled in a cloak—an unnecessary incumbrance, by-the-by, on so warm a June evening—I knew her instantly by her little foot, seen peeping from the skirt of her dress, as she skipped from the carriage-step. Bending over the balcony I was about to murmur, '*Mon ange*'—in a tone, of course, which should be audible to the ear of love alone—when a figure jumped from the carriage after her; cloaked also; but that was a spurred heel which had rung on the pavement, and that was a hatted head which now passed under the arched *porte cochère* of the hotel.

"You never felt jealousy, did you, Miss Eyre? Of course not: I need not ask you; because you have never felt love. You have both sentiments yet to experience: your soul sleeps; the shock is yet to be given which shall waken it. You think all existence lapses in as quiet a flow as that in which your youth has hitherto slid away. Floating on with closed eyes and muffled ears, you neither see the rocks bristling not far off in the bed of the flood, nor hear the breakers boil at their base. But I tell you—and you may mark my words—you will come some day to a craggy pass of the channel, where the whole of life's stream will be broken up into whirl and tumult, foam and noise: either you will be dashed to atoms on crag points, or lifted up and borne on by some master wave into a calmer current—as I am now.

"I like this day: I like that sky of steel; I like the sternness and stillness of the world under this frost. I like Thornfield; its antiquity; its retirement; its old crow-trees and thorn-trees; its gray façade, and lines of dark windows reflecting that metal welkin: and yet how long have I abhorred the very thought of it; shunned it like a great plague-house! How I do still abhor——"

He ground his teeth and was silent: he arrested his step and struck his boot against the hard ground. Some hated thought seemed to have him in its grip, and to hold him so tightly that he could not advance.

We were ascending the avenue when he thus paused; the hall was before us. Lifting his eye to its battlements, he cast over them a glare such as I never saw before or since. Pain, shame, ire—impatience, disgust, detestation—seemed momentarily to hold a quivering conflict in the large pupil dilating under his ebon eyebrow. Wild was the wrestle which should be paramount; but another feeling rose and triumphed: something hard and cynical; self-willed and resolute: it settled his passion and petrified his countenance: he went on:—

"During the moment I was silent, Miss Eyre, I was arranging a point with my destiny. She stood there, by that beech-trunk—a hag like one of those who appeared to Macbeth on the heath of Forres. 'You like Thornfield?' she said, lifting her finger; and then she wrote in the air a memento, which ran in lurid hieroglyphics all along the housefront, between the upper and lower row of windows. 'Like it if you can!' 'Like it if you dare!' "

" 'I will like it,' said I. 'I dare like it; and (he subjoined moodily) I will keep my word: I will break obstacles to happiness, to goodness—yes, goodness; I wish to be a better man than I have been; than I am—as Job's leviathan broke the spear the dart and the habergeon, hinderances which others count as iron and brass, I will esteem but straw and rotten wood."

Adèle here ran before him with her shuttlecock. "Away!" he cried harshly; "keep at a distance, child; or go in to Sophie!" Continuing then to pursue his walk in silence, I ventured to recall him to the point when he had abruptly diverged:—

"Did you leave the balcony, sir," I asked, "when Mdlle. Varens entered?"

I almost expected a rebuff for this hardly well-timed question: but, on the contrary, waking out of his scowling abstraction, he turned his eyes towards me, and the shade seemed to clear off his brow.

"Oh, I had forgotten Céline! Well, to resume. When I saw my charmer thus come in accompanied by a cavalier, I seemed to hear a hiss, and the green snake of jealousy, rising on undulating coils from the moonlit balcony, glided within my waistcoat and ate its way in two minutes to my heart's core. Strange!" he exclaimed, suddenly starting again from the point. "Strange that I should choose you for the confidant of all this, young lady: passing strange that you should listen to me quietly, as if it were the most usual thing in the world for a man like me to tell stories of his opera-mistresses to a quaint, inexperienced girl like you! But the last singularity explains the first, as I intimated once before: you, with your gravity, considerateness, and caution were made to be the recipient of secrets. Besides, I know what sort of a mind I have placed in communication with my own; I know it is one not liable to take infection: it is a peculiar mind; it is an unique one. Happily I do not mean to harm it: but if I did, it would not take harm from me. The more you and I converse, the better; for while I cannot blight you, you may refresh me." After this digression he proceeded:—

"I remained in the balcony. 'They will come to her boudoir no doubt,' thought I: 'let me prepare an ambush.' So putting my hand in through the open window, I drew the curtain over it, leaving only an opening through which I could take observations; then I closed the casement, all but a chink just wide enough to furnish an outlet to lovers' whispered vows: then I stole back to my chair; and as I resumed it the pair came in. My eye was quickly at the aperture. Céline's chamber-maid entered, lit a lamp, left it on the table and withdrew. The couple were thus revealed to me clearly: both removed their cloaks, and there was 'the Varens' shining in satin and jewels,—my gifts of course,—and there was her companion in an officer's uniform; and I knew him for a young roué of a vicomte—a brainless and vicious youth whom I had sometimes met in society, and had never thought of hating because I despised him so absolutely. On recognising him, the fang of the snake,—jealousy, was instantly broken; because at the same moment my love for Céline sank under an extinguisher. A woman who could betray me for such a rival was not worth contending for: she deserved only scorn; less, however, than I, who had been her dupe."

They began to talk; their conversation eased me completely; frivolous, mercenary, heartless, and senseless, it was rather calculated to weary than enrage a listener. A card of mine lay on the table; this being perceived brought my name under discussion. Neither of them possessed energy or wit to belabour me soundly; but they insulted me as coarsely as they could in their little way: especially Céline; who even waxed rather brilliant on my personal defects—deformities she termed them. Now it had been her custom to launch out into fervent admiration of what she called my 'beauté mâle': wherein she differed diametrically from you, who told me point blank at the second interview, that you did not think me handsome. The contrast struck me at the time, and—"

Adèle here came running up again.

"Monsieur, John has just been to say that your agent has called and wishes to see you."

"Ah! in that case I must abridge. Opening the window, I walked in upon them; liberated Céline from my protection; gave her notice to vacate her hotel; offered her a purse for immediate exigencies; disregarded screams, hysterics, prayers, protestations, convulsions; made an appointment with the vicomte for a meeting at the Bois de Boulogne. Next morning I had the pleasure of encountering him; left a bullet in one of his poor, etiolated arms, feeble as the wing of a chicken in the pip, and then thought I had done with the whole crew. But unluckily the Varens, six months before, had given me this fillette Adèle; who she affirmed was my daughter; and perhaps she may be; though I see no proofs of such grim paternity written in her countenance: Pilot is more like me than she. Some years after I had broken with the mother, she abandoned her child and ran away to Italy with a musician, or singer. I acknowledged no natural claim on Adèle's part to be supported by me; nor do I now acknowledge any, for I am not her father; but hearing that she was quite destitute, I e'en took the poor thing out of the slime and mud of Paris, and transplanted it here, to grow up clean in the wholesome soil of an English country garden. Mrs. Fairfax found you to train it; but now you know that it is the illegitimate offspring of a French opera-girl, you will perhaps think differently of your post and protégée: you will be coming to me some day with notice that you have found another place—that you beg me to look out for a new governess, etc.—eh?"

"No—Adèle is not answerable for either her mother's faults or yours: I have a regard for her, and now that I know she is, in a sense, parentless—forsaken by her mother and disowned by you, sir,—I shall cling closer to her than before. How could I possibly prefer the spoilt pet of a wealthy family, who would hate her governess as a nuisance, to a lonely little orphan, who leans towards her as a friend?"

"Oh, that is the light in which you view it! Well, I must go in now; and you too: it darkens."

But I stayed out a few minutes longer with Adèle and Pilot—ran a race with her, and played a game of battledore and shuttlecock. When we went in and I had removed her bonnet and coat, I took her on my knee; kept her there an hour, allowing her to prattle as she liked: not rebuking even some little freedoms and trivialities into which she was apt to stray when much noticed; and which betrayed in her a superficiality of character, inherited probably from her mother, hardly congenial to an English mind. Still she had her merits; and I was disposed to appreciate all that was good in her to the utmost. I sought in her countenance and features a likeness to Mr. Rochester, but found none: no trait, no turn of expression announced relationship. It was a pity: if she could but have been proved to resemble him, he would have thought more of her.

It was not till after I had withdrawn to my own chamber for the night, that I steadily reviewed the tale Mr. Rochester had told me. As he had said, there was probably nothing at all extraordinary in the substance of the narrative itself: a wealthy Englishman's passion for a French dancer, and her treachery to him, were every-day matters enough, no doubt, in society; but there was something decidedly strange in the paroxysm of emotion which had suddenly seized him, when he was in the act of expressing the present contentment of his mood, and his newly revived pleasure in the old Hall and its environs. I meditated wonderingly on this incident: but gradually quitting it, as I found it for the present inexplicable, I turned to the consideration of my master's manner to myself. The confidence he had thought fit to repose in me seemed a tribute to my discretion: I regarded and accepted it as such. His deportment had now for some weeks been more uniform towards me than at the first. I never seemed in his way; he did not take fits of chilling hauteur: when he met me unexpectedly, the encounter seemed welcome; he had always a word and sometimes a smile for me: when summoned by formal invitation to his presence, I was honoured by a cordiality of reception that made me feel I really possessed the power to amuse him, and that these evening conferences were sought as much for his pleasure as for my benefit.

I, indeed, talked comparatively little; but I heard him talk with relish. It was his nature to be communicative; he liked to open to a mind unacquainted with the world, glimpses of its scenes and ways (I do not mean its corrupt scenes and wicked ways, but such as derived their interest from the great scale on which they were acted, the strange novelty by which they were characterized); and I had a keen delight in receiving the new ideas he offered, in imagining the new pictures he portrayed, and following him in thought through the new regions he disclosed; never startled or troubled by one noxious allusion.

The ease of his manner freed me from painful restraint: the friendly frankness, as correct as cordial, with which he treated me, drew me to him. I felt at times, as if he were my relation, rather than my master: yet he was imperious sometimes still; but I did not mind that; I saw it was his way. So happy, so gratified did I become with this new interest added to life, that I ceased to pine after kindred: my thin crescent-destiny seemed to enlarge; the blanks of existence were filled up; my bodily health improved; I gathered flesh and strength.

And was Mr. Rochester now ugly in my eyes? No, reader: gratitude, and many associations, all pleasurable and genial, made his face the object I best liked to see; his presence in a room was more cheering than the brightest fire. Yet I had not forgotten his faults: indeed, I could not, for he brought them frequently before me. He was proud, sardonic, harsh to inferiority of every description: in my secret soul I knew that his great kindness to me was balanced by unjust severity to many others. He was moody, too; unaccountably so: I more than once, when sent for to read to him, found him sitting in his library alone, with his head bent on his folded arms; and, when he looked up, a morose, almost a malignant, scowl blackened his features. But I believed that his moodiness, his harshness, and his former faults of morality (I say *former*, for now he seemed corrected of them) had their source in some cruel cross of fate. I believed he was naturally a man of better tendencies, higher principles, and purer tastes than such as circumstances had developed, education instilled, or destiny encouraged. I thought there were excellent materials in him; though for the present they hung together somewhat spoiled and tangled. I cannot deny that I grieved for his grief, whatever that was, and would have given much to assuage it.

Though I had now extinguished my candle and was laid down in bed, I could not sleep, for thinking of his look when he paused in the avenue, and told how his destiny had risen up before him and dared him to be happy at Thornfield.

"Why not?" I asked myself: "what alienates him from the house? Will he leave it again soon? Mrs. Fairfax said he seldom stayed here longer than a fortnight at a time; and he has now been resident eight weeks. If he does go, the change will be doleful. Suppose he should be absent, spring, summer, and autumn: how joyless sunshine and fine days will seem!"

I hardly know whether I had slept or not after this musing; at any rate I started wide awake on hearing a vague murmur, peculiar and lugubrious, which sounded, I thought, just above me. I wished I had kept my candle burning: the night was drearily dark; my spirits were depressed. I rose and sat up in bed, listening. The sound was hushed.

I tried again to sleep; but my heart beat anxiously: my inward tranquillity was broken. The clock, far down in the hall, struck two. Just then it seemed my chamber-door was touched; as if fingers had swept the panels in groping a way along the dark gallery outside. I said, "Who is there?" Nothing answered. I was chilled with fear.

All at once I remembered that it might be Pilot; who, when the kitchen-door chanced to be left open, not unfrequently found his way up to the threshold of Mr. Rochester's chamber: I had seen him lying there myself, in the mornings. The idea calmed me somewhat: I lay down. Silence composes the nerves; and as an unbroken hush now reigned again through the whole house, I began to feel the return of slumber. But it was not fated that I should sleep that night. A dream had scarcely approached my ear, when it fled affrighted, scared by a marrow-freezing incident enough.

This was a demoniac laugh—low, suppressed, and deep—uttered, as it seemed, at the very key-hole of my chamber-door. The head of my bed was near the door, and I thought at first, the goblin-laugher stood at my bedside—or rather, crouched by my pillow: but I rose, looked round, and could see nothing; while, as I still gazed, the unnatural sound was reiterated: and I knew it came from behind the panels. My first impulse was to rise and fasten the bolt; my next, again to cry out, "Who is there?"

Something gurgled and moaned. Ere long, steps retreated up the gallery towards the third story staircase: a door had lately been made to shut in that staircase; I heard it open and close, and all was still.

"Was that Grace Poole? and is she possessed with a devil?" thought I. Impossible now to remain longer by myself: I must go to Mrs. Fairfax. I hurried on my frock and a shawl; I withdrew the bolt and opened the door with a trembling hand. There was a candle burning just outside, left on the matting in the gallery. I was surprised at this circumstance: but still more was I amazed to perceive the air quite dim, as if filled with smoke; and, while looking to the right hand and left, to find whence these blue wreaths issued, I became further aware of a strong smell of burning.

Something creaked: it was a door ajar; and that door was Mr. Rochester's, and the smoke rushed in a cloud from thence. I thought no more of Mrs. Fairfax; I thought no more of Grace Poole or the laugh; in an instant, I was within the chamber. Tongues of flame darted round the bed: the curtains were on fire. In the midst of blaze and vapour, Mr. Rochester lay stretched motionless, in deep sleep.

"Wake! Wake!" I cried—I shook him, but he only murmured and turned: the smoke had stupified him. Not a moment could be lost: the very sheets were kindling. I rushed to his basin and ewer; fortunately, one was wide and the other deep, and both were filled with water. I heaved them up, deluged the bed and its occupant, flew back to my own room, brought my own water-jug, baptized the couch afresh, and by God's aid, succeeded in extinguishing the flames which were devouring it.

The hiss of the quenched element, the breakage of a pitcher which I flung from my hand when I had emptied it, and above all, the splash of the shower-bath I had liberally bestowed, roused Mr. Rochester at last. Though it was now dark, I knew he was awake; because I heard him fulminating strange anathemas at finding himself lying in a pool of water.

"Is there a flood?" he cried.

"No, sir," I answered; "but there has been a fire: get up, do, you are quenched now; I will fetch you a candle."

"In the name of all the elves in Christendom, is that Jane Eyre?" he demanded. "What have you done with me, witch, sorceress? Who is in the room besides you? Have you plotted to drown me?"

"I will fetch you a candle, sir; and in Heaven's name, get up. Somebody has plotted something: you cannot too soon find out who and what it is."

"There—I am up now; but at your peril you fetch a candle yet: wait two minutes till I get into some dry garments, if any dry there be—yes, here is my dressing-gown, now run!"

I did run; I brought the candle which still remained in the gallery. He took it from my hand, held it up, and surveyed the bed, all blackened and scorched, the sheets drenched the carpet round swimming in water.

"What is it? and who did it?" he asked.

I briefly related to him what had transpired: the strange laugh I had heard in the gallery; the step ascending to the third story; the smoke,—the smell of fire which had conducted me to his room; in what state I had found matters there, and how I had deluged him with all the water I could lay hands on.

He listened very gravely; his face, as I went on, expressed more concern then astonishment: he did not immediately speak when I had concluded.

"Shall I call Mrs. Fairfax?" I asked.

"Mrs. Fairfax? No: what the deuce would you call her for? What can she do? Let her sleep unmolested."

"Then I will fetch Leah, and wake John and his wife."

"Not at all: just be still. You have a shawl on; if you are not warm enough, you may take my cloak yonder; wrap it about you, and sit down in the arm-chair: there,—I will put it on. Now place your feet on the stool, to keep them out of the wet. I am going to leave you a few minutes. I shall take the candle. Remain where you are till I return; be as still as a mouse. I must pay a visit to the second story. Don't move, remember, or call any one."

He went: I watched the light withdraw. He passed up the gallery very softly, unclosed the staircase door with as little noise as possible, shut it after him, and the last ray vanished. I was left in total darkness. I listened for some noise, but heard nothing. A very long time elapsed. I grew weary: it was cold, in spite of the cloak; and then I did not see the use of staying, as I was not to rouse the house. I was on the point of risking Mr. Rochester's displeasure, by disobeying his orders, when the light once more gleamed dimly on the gallery-wall, and I heard his unshod feet tread the matting. "I hope it is he," thought I, "and not something worse."

He re-entered, pale and very gloomy. "I have found it all out," said he, setting his candle down on the wash-stand; "it is as I thought."

"How, sir?"

He made no reply, but stood with his arms folded, looking on the ground. At the end of a few minutes, he inquired in rather a peculiar tone:—

"I forget whether you said you saw anything when you opened your chamber door."

"No, sir, only the candlestick on the ground."

"But you heard an odd laugh? You have heard that laugh before I should think, or something like it?"

"Yes, sir: there is a woman who sews here, called Grace Poole,—she laughs in that way. She is a singular person."

"Just so. Grace Poole—you have guessed it. She is, as you say, singular,—very. Well, I shall reflect on the subject. Meantime, I am glad that you are the only person, besides myself, acquainted with the precise details of to-night's incident. You are no talking fool: say nothing about it. I will account for this state of affairs (pointing to the bed): and now return to your own room. I shall do very well on the sofa in the library for the rest of the night. It is near four:—in two hours the servants will be up."

"Good-night, then, sir," said I departing.

He seemed surprised—very inconsistently so, as he had just told me to go.

"What!" he exclaimed, "are you quitting me already: and in that way?"

"You said I might go, sir."

"But not without taking leave; not without a word or two of acknowledgment and good will: not, in short, in that brief, dry fashion. Why, you have saved my life!—snatched me from a horrible and excruciating death!—and you walk past me as if we were mutual strangers! At least shake hands."

He held out his hand; I gave him mine: he took it first in one, then in both his own.

"You have saved my life: I have a pleasure in owing you so immense a debt. I cannot say more. Nothing else that has being would have been tolerable to me in the character of creditor for such an obligation: but you; it is different;—I feel your benefits no burden, Jane."

He paused; gazed at me: words almost visible trembled on his lips,—but his voice was checked.

"Good-night again, sir. There is no debt, benefit, burden, obligation, in the case."

"I knew," he continued, "you would do me good in some way, at some time;—I saw it in your eyes when I first beheld you: their expression and smile did not—(again he stopped)—did not (he proceeded hastily) strike delight to my very inmost heart so for nothing. People talk of natural sympathies; I have heard of good genii:—there are grains of truth in the wildest fable. My cherished preserver, good-night!"

Strange energy was in his voice; strange fire in his look.

"I am glad I happened to be awake," I said; and then I was going.

"What! you *will* go?"

"I am cold, sir."

"Cold? Yes,—and standing in a pool! Go, then, Jane; go!" But he still retained my hand, and I could not free it. I bethought myself of an expedient.

"I think I hear Mrs. Fairfax move, sir," said I.

"Well, leave me:" he relaxed his fingers, and I was gone.

I regained my couch, but never thought of sleep. Till morning dawned I was tossed on a buoyant but unquiet sea, where billows of trouble rolled under surges of joy. I thought sometimes I saw beyond its wild waters a shore, sweet as the hills of Beulah; and now and then a freshening gale wakened by hope, bore my spirit triumphantly towards the bourne: but I could not reach it, even in fancy,—a counteracting breeze blew off land, and continually drove me back. Sense would resist delirium: judgment would warn passion. Too feverish to rest, I rose as soon as day dawned.

Chapter 16

I both wished and feared to see Mr. Rochester on the day which followed this sleepless night: I wanted to hear his voice again, yet feared to meet his eye. During the early part of the morning, I momentarily expected his coming: he was not in the frequent habit of entering the school-room; but he did step in for a few minutes sometimes, and I had the impression that he was sure to visit it that day.

But the morning passed just as usual: nothing happened to interrupt the quiet course of Adele's studies; only, soon after breakfast, I heard some bustle in the neighbourhood of Mr. Rochester's chamber, Mrs. Fairfax's voice, and Leah's, and the cook's—that is, John's wife—and even John's own gruff tones. There were exclamations of "What a mercy master was not burnt in his bed!" "It is always dangerous to keep a candle lit at night." "How providential that he had presence of mind to think of the water-jug!" "I wonder he waked nobody!" "It is to be hoped he will not take cold with sleeping on the library sofa," etc.

To much confabulation succeeded a sound of scrubbing and setting to rights; and when I passed the room, in going down stairs to dinner, I saw through the open door that all was again restored to complete order: only the bed was stripped of its hangings. Leah stood up in the window seat, rubbing the panes of glass dimmed with smoke. I was about to address her; for I wished to know what account had been given of the affair: but, on advancing, I saw a second person in the chamber—a woman sitting on a chair by the bed-side, and sewing rings to new curtains. That woman was no other than Grace Poole.

There she sat, staid and taciturn-looking, as usual, in her brown stuff gown, her check apron, white handkerchief, and cap. She was intent on her work, in which her whole thoughts seemed absorbed: on her hard forehead, and in her common-place features, was nothing either of the paleness or desperation one would have expected to see marking the countenance of a woman who had attempted murder; and whose intended victim had followed her last night to her lair, and (as I believed) charged her with the crime she wished to perpetrate. I was amazed—confounded. She looked up while I still gazed at her: no start, no increase or failure of colour betrayed emotion, consciousness of guilt, or fear of detection. She said, "Good-morning, Miss," in her usual phlegmatic and brief manner; and taking up another ring and more tape went on with her sewing.

"I will put her to some test," thought I: "such absolute impenetrability is past comprehension."

"Good-morning, Grace," I said, "Has anything happened here? I thought I heard the servants all talking together a while ago."

"Only master had been reading in his bed last night; he fell asleep with his candle lit, and the curtains got on fire: but, fortunately, he awoke before the bed-clothes or the wood-work caught, and contrived to quench the flame with the water in the ewer."

"A strange affair!" I said, in a low voice: then, looking at her fixedly,— "Did Mr. Rochester wake nobody? Did no one hear him move?"

She again raised her eyes to me; and this time there was something of consciousness in their expression. She seemed to examine me warily; then she answered,—

"The servants sleep so far off, you know, Miss, they would not be likely to hear. Mrs. Fairfax's room and yours are the nearest to master's; but Mrs. Fairfax said she heard nothing: when people get elderly, they often sleep heavy." She paused, and then added, with a sort of assumed indifference, but still in a marked and significant tone, "But you are young,

Miss; and I should say a light sleeper: perhaps you may have heard a noise?"

"I did," said I, dropping my voice, so that Leah, who was still polishing the panes, could not hear me, "and at first I thought is was Pilot: but Pilot cannot laugh; and I am certain I heard a laugh, and a strange one."

She took a new needleful of thread, waxed it carefully, threaded her needle with a steady hand, and then observed, with perfect composure,—

"It is hardly likely master would laugh, I should think, Miss, when he was in such danger: you must have been dreaming."

"I was not dreaming," I said, with some warmth: for her brazen coolness provoked me. Again she looked at me; and with the same scrutinizing and conscious eye.

"Have you told master that you heard a laugh?" she inquired.

"I have not had the opportunity of speaking to him this morning."

"You did not think of opening your door and looking out into the gallery?" she further asked.

She appeared to be cross-questioning me; attempting to draw from me information unawares: the idea struck me that if she discovered I knew or suspected her guilt, she would be playing off some of her malignant pranks on me; I thought it advisable to be on my guard.

"On the contrary," said I, "I bolted my door."

"Then you are not in the habit of bolting your door every night before you get into bed?"

"Fiend! she wants to know my habits that she may lay her plans accordingly!" Indignation again prevailed over prudence; I replied sharply: "Hitherto I have often omitted to fasten the bolt: I did not think it necessary. I was not aware any danger or annoyance was to be dreaded at Thornfield Hall: but in future (and I laid marked stress on the words) I shall take good care to make all secure before I venture to lie down."

"It will be wise so to do," was her answer: "this neighbourhood is as quiet as any I know, and I never heard of the Hall being attempted by robbers since it was a house; though there are hundreds of pounds' worth of plate in the plate-closet, as is well known. And you see, for such a large house, there are very few servants, because master has never lived here much; and when he does come, being a bachelor, he needs little waiting on: but I always think it best to err on the safe side; a door is soon fastened, and it is as well to have a drawn bolt between one and any mischief that may be about. A deal of people, Miss, are for trusting all to Providence; but I say Providence will not dispense with the means, though he often blesses them when they are used discreetly." And here she closed her harangue: a long one for her, and uttered with the demureness of a Quakeress.

I still stood absolutely dumbfounded at what appeared to me her miraculous self-possession and most inscrutable hypocrisy; when the cook entered.

"Mrs. Poole," said she, addressing Grace, "the servants' dinner will soon be ready: will you come down?"

"No; just put my pint of porter and bit of pudding on a tray, and I'll carry it upstairs."

"You'll have some meat?"

"Just a morsel, and a taste of cheese, that's all."

"And the sago?"

"Never mind it, at present: I shall be coming down before tea time: I'll make it myself."

The cook here turned to me, saying that Mrs. Fairfax was waiting for me: so I departed.

I hardly heard Mrs. Fairfax's account of the curtain conflagration during dinner, so much was I occupied in puzzling my brains over the enigmatical character of Grace Poole:; and still more in pondering the problem of her position at Thornfield: in questioning why she had not been given into custody that morning; or at the very least dismissed from her master's service. He had almost as much as declared his conviction of her criminality last night: what mysterious cause withheld him from accusing her? Why had he enjoined me too to secrecy? It was strange: a bold, vindictive, and haughty gentleman seemed somehow in the power of one of the meanest of his dependants; so much in her power, that even when she lifted her hand against his life, he dared not openly charge her with the attempt, much less punish her for it.

Had Grace been young and handsome, I should have been tempted to think that tenderer feelings than prudence or fear influenced Mr. Rochester in her behalf; but hard-favoured and matronly as she was, the idea could not be admitted. "Yet," I reflected, "she has been young once; her youth would be contemporary with her master's: Mrs. Fairfax told me once, she had lived here many years. I don't think she can ever have been pretty; but for aught I know she may possess originality and strength of character to compensate for the want of personal advantages. Mr. Rochester is an amateur of the decided and eccentric: Grace is eccentric at least. What if a former caprice (a freak very possible to a nature so sudden and headstrong as his) has delivered him into her power, and she now exercises over his actions a secret influence, the result of his own indiscretion, which he cannot shake off and dare not disregard?" But, having reached this point of conjecture, Mrs. Poole's square, flat figure, and uncomely, dry, even coarse face, recurred so distinctly to my mind's eye, that I thought "No; impossible! my supposition cannot be correct. Yet," suggested the secret voice which talks to us in our own hearts, *"you* are not beautiful either, and perhaps Mr. Rochester approves you: at any rate you have often felt as if he did; and last night—remember his words; remember his look; remember his voice!"

I well remembered all: language, glance, and tone seemed at the moment vividly renewed. I was now in the school-room; Adèle was drawing; I bent over her and directed her pencil. She looked up with a sort of start.

"Qu'avez-vous, mademoiselle?" said she; *"Vos doigts tremblent comme la feuille, et vos joues sont rouges: mais, rouges comme des cerises!"*

"I am hot, Adèle, with stooping!" She went on sketching, I went on thinking.

I hastened to drive from my mind the hateful notion I had been conceiving respecting Grace Poole: it disgusted me. I compared myself with her, and found we were different. Bessie Leaven had said I was quite a lady; and she spoke truth: I was a lady. And now I looked much better than I did when Bessie saw me: I had more colour and more flesh; more life, more vivacity; because I had brighter hopes and keener enjoyments.

"Evening approaches," said I, as I looked towards the window. "I have never heard Mr. Rochester's voice or step in the house to-day; but surely I shall see him before night: I feared the meeting in the morning; now I desire it, because expectation has been so long baffled that it is grown impatient."

When dusk actually closed, and when Adèle left me to go and play in the nursery with Sophie, I did most keenly desire it. I listened for the bell to ring below; I listened for Leah coming up with a message; I fancied sometimes I heard Mr. Rochester's own tread, and I turned to the door, expecting it to open and admit him. The door remained shut: darkness only came in through the window. Still it was not late: he often sent for me at seven and eight o'clock, and it was yet but six. Surely I should not be wholly disappointed to-night, when I had so many things to say to him! I wanted again to introduce the subject of Grace Poole, and to hear what he would answer; I wanted to ask him plainly if he really believed it was she who had made last night's hideous attempt; and if so, why he kept her wickedness a secret. It little mattered whether my curiosity irritated him; I knew the pleasure of vexing and soothing him by turns; it was one I chiefly delighted in, and a sure instinct always prevented me from going too far: beyond the verge of provocation I never ventured; on the extreme brink I liked well to try my skill. Retaining every minute form of respect, every propriety of my station, I could still meet him in argument without fear or uneasy restraint: this suited both him and me.

A tread creaked on the stairs at last; Leah made her appearance: but it was only to intimate that tea was ready in Mrs. Fairfax's room. Thither I repaired, glad at least to go down stairs; for that brought me, I imagined, nearer to Mr. Rochester's presence.

"You must want your tea," said the good lady as I joined her; "you ate so little at dinner. I am afraid," she continued, "you are not well to-day: you look flushed and feverish."

"Oh, quite well! I never felt better."

"Then you must prove it by evincing a good appetite; will you fill the tea-pot while I knot off this needle?" Having completed her task, she rose to draw down the blind which she had hitherto kept up; by way, I suppose, of making the most of daylight: though dusk was now fast deepening into total obscurity.

"It is fair to-night," said she, as she looked through the panes, "though not starlight; Mr. Rochester has, on the whole, had a favourable day for his journey."

"Journey!—Is Mr. Rochester gone anywhere? I did not know he was out."

"Oh, he set off the moment he had breakfasted! He is gone to the Leas; Mr. Eshton's place, ten miles on the other side Millcote; I believe there is quite a party assembled there; Lord Ingram, Sir George Lynn, Colonel Dent, and others."

"Do you expect him back to-night?"

"No—nor to-morrow either; I should think he is very likely to stay a week or more: when these fine, fashionable people get together, they are so surrounded by elegance and gaiety; so well provided with all that can please and entertain, they are in no hurry to separate. Gentlemen, especially, are often in request on such occasions; and Mr. Rochester is so talented and so lively in society, that I believe he is a general favourite: the ladies are very fond of him; though you would not think his appearance calculated to recommend him particularly in their eyes: but I suppose his acquirements and abilities, perhaps his wealth and good blood, make amends for any little fault of look."

"Are there ladies at the Leas?"

"There are Mrs. Eshton and her three daughters—very elegant young ladies, indeed; and there are the honourable Blanche and Mary Ingram; most beautiful women, I suppose: indeed I have seen Blanche, six or seven years since, when she was a girl of eighteen. She came here to a Christmas ball and party Mr. Rochester gave. You should have seen the dining-room that day—how richly it was decorated, how brilliantly lit up! I should think there were fifty ladies and gentlemen present—all of the first county-families; and Miss Ingram was considered the belle of the evening."

"You saw her, you say, Mrs. Fairfax: what was she like?"

"Yes, I saw her. The dining-room doors were thrown open; and, as it was Christmas-time, the servants were allowed to assemble in the hall, to hear some of the ladies sing and play. Mr. Rochester would have me to come in, and I sat down in a quiet corner and watched them. I never saw a more splendid scene: the ladies were magnificently dressed; most of them—at least most of the younger ones—looked handsome; but Miss Ingram was certainly the queen."

"And what was she like?"

"Tall, fine bust, sloping shoulders; long, graceful neck: olive complexion, dark and clear; noble features; eyes rather like Mr. Rochester's: large and black, and as brilliant as her jewels. And then she had such a fine head of hair; raven-black, and so becomingly arranged: a crown of thick plaits behind, and in front the longest, the glossiest curls I ever saw. She was dressed in pure white; an amber-coloured scarf was passed over her shoulder and across her breast, tied at the side, and descending in long, fringed ends below her knee. She wore an amber-coloured flower, too, in her hair: it contrasted well with the jetty mass of her curls."

"She was greatly admired of course?"

"Yes, indeed: and not only for her beauty, but for her accomplishments. She was one of the ladies who sang: a gentleman accompanied her on the piano. She and Mr. Rochester sang a duet."

"Mr. Rochester? I was not aware he could sing."

"Oh! he has a fine bass voice, and an excellent taste for music."

"And Miss Ingram: what sort of a voice had she?"

"A very rich and powerful one: she sang delightfully; it was a treat to listen to her;—and she played afterwards. I am no judge of music, but Mr. Rochester is; and I heard him say her execution was remarkably good."

"And this beautiful and accomplished lady is not yet married?"

"It appears not: I fancy neither she nor her sister have very large fortunes. Old Lord Ingram's estates were chiefly entailed, and the eldest son came in for everything almost."

"But I wonder no wealthy nobleman or gentleman has taken a fancy to her: Mr. Rochester, for instance. He is rich, is he not?"

"Oh! yes. But you see there is a considerable difference in age: Mr. Rochester is near forty; she is but twenty-five."

"What of that? More unequal matches are made every day."

"True: yet I should scarcely fancy Mr. Rochester would entertain an idea of the sort. But you eat nothing: you have scarcely tasted since you began tea."

"No: I am too thirsty to eat. Will you let me have another cup?"

I was about again to revert to the probability of a union between Mr. Rochester and the beautiful Blanche: but Adèle came in, and the conversation was turned into another channel.

When once more alone, I reviewed the information I had got; looked into my heart, examined its thoughts and feelings, and endeavoured to bring back with a strict hand such as had been straying through imagination's boundless and trackless waste, into the safe fold of common sense.

Arraigned at my own bar, Memory having given her evidence of the hopes, wishes, sentiments I had been cherishing since last night—of the general state of mind in which I had indulged for nearly a fortnight past; Reason having come forward and told in her own quiet way, a plain, unvarnished tale, showing how I had rejected the real, and rabidly devoured the ideal;—I pronounced judgment to this effect:—

That a greater fool than Jane Eyre had never breathed the breath of life: that a more fantastic idiot had never surfeited herself on sweet lies, and swallowed poison as if it were nectar.

"You," I said, "a favourite with Mr. Rochester? *You* gifted with the power of pleasing him? *You* of importance to him in any way? Go! your folly sickens me. And you have derived pleasure from occasional tokens of preference—equivocal tokens, shown by a gentleman of family, and a man of the world, to a dependant and a novice. How dared you? Poor stupid dupe!—Could not even self-interest make you wiser? You repeated to yourself this morning the brief scene of last night?—Cover your face and be ashamed! He said something in praise of your eyes, did he? Blind puppy! Open their bleared lids and look on your own accursed senselessness! It does good to no woman to be flattered by her superior, who cannot possibly intend to marry her; and it is madness in all women to let a secret love kindle within them, which, if unreturned and unknown, must devour the life that feeds it: and, if discovered and responded to, must lead, *ignis-fatuus*-like, into miry wilds whence there is no extrication.

"Listen, then, Jane Eyre, to your sentence: to-morrow, place the glass before you, and draw in chalk your own picture, faithfully; without softening one defect: omit no harsh line, smooth away no displeasing irregularity; write under it, 'Portrait of a Governess, disconnected, poor and plain.'

"Afterwards, take a piece of smooth ivory—you have one prepared in your drawing-box: take your palette, mix your freshest, finest, clearest tints; choose your most delicate camel-hair pencils; delineate carefully the loveliest face you can imagine; paint it in your softest shades and sweetest hues, according to the description given by Mrs. Fairfax of Blanche Ingram: remember the raven ringlets, the oriental eye;—what! you revert to Mr. Rochester as a model! Order! No snivel!—no sentiment!—no regret! I will endure only sense and resolution. Recall the august yet harmonious lineaments, the Grecian neck and bust: let the round and dazzling arm be visible, and the delicate hand; omit neither diamond ring nor gold bracelet; portray faithfully the attire, aerial lace and glistening satin, graceful scarf and golden rose: call it 'Blanche, an accomplished lady of rank.'

"Whenever, in future, you should chance to fancy Mr. Rochester thinks well of you, take out these two pictures and compare them: say, 'Mr. Rochester might probably win that noble lady's love, if he chose to strive for it; is it likely he would waste a serious thought on this indigent and insignificant plebeian?' "

"I'll do it," I resolved: and having framed this determination, I grew calm, and fell asleep.

I kept my word. An hour or two sufficed to sketch my own portrait in crayons; and in less than a fortnight I had completed an ivory miniature of an imaginary Blanche Ingram. It looked a lovely face enough, and when compared with the real head in chalk, the contrast was as great as self-control could desire. I derived benefit from the task: it had kept my head and hands employed, and had given force and fixedness to the new impressions I wished to stamp indelibly on my heart.

Ere long, I had reason to congratulate myself on the course of wholesome discipline to which I had thus forced my feelings to submit: thanks to it, I was able to meet subsequent occurrences with a decent calm; which, had they found me unprepared, I should probably have been unequal to maintain, even externally.

· · · · · · ·

Chapter 17

A week passed, and no news arrived of Mr. Rochester: ten days; and still he did not come. Mrs. Fairfax said she should not be surprised if he were to go straight from the Leas to London, and thence to the continent, and not show his face again at Thornfield for a year to come: he had not unfrequently quitted it in a manner quite as abrupt and unexpected. When I heard this I was beginning to feel a strange chill and failing at the heart. I was actually permitting myself to experience a sickening sense of disappointment: but rallying my wits, and recollecting my principles, I at once called my sensations to order; and it was wonderful how I got over the temporary blunder—How I cleared up the mistake of supposing Mr. Rochester's movements a matter in which I had any cause to take a vital interest. Not that I humbled myself by a slavish notion of inferiority: on the contrary, I just said:—

"You have nothing to do with the master of Thornfield, further than to receive the salary he gives you for teaching his protégée, and to be grateful for such respectful and kind treatment as, if you do your duty, you have a right to expect at his hands. Be sure that is the only tie he seriously acknowledges between you and him: so don't make him the object of your fine feelings, your raptures, agonies, and so forth. He is not of your order: keep to your caste; and be too self-respecting to lavish the love of the whole heart, soul, and strength, where such a gift is not wanted and would be despised."

I went on with my day's business tranquilly; but ever and anon, vague suggestions kept wandering across my brain of reasons why I should quit Thornfield; and I kept involuntarily framing advertisements and pondering conjectures about new situations: these thoughts I did not think it necessary to check; they might germinate and bear fruit if they could.

Mr. Rochester had been absent upwards of a fortnight, when the post brought Mrs. Fairfax a letter.

"It is from the master," said she, as she looked at the direction. "Now

I suppose we shall know whether we are to expect his return or not."

And while she broke the seal and perused the document, I went on taking my coffee: (we were at breakfast) it was hot, and I attributed to that circumstance a fiery glow which suddenly rose to my face. Why my hand shook, and why I involuntarily spilt half the contents of my cup into my saucer, I did not choose to consider.

"Well—I sometimes think we are too quiet; but we run a chance of being busy enough: for a little while at least," said Mrs. Fairfax, still holding the note before her spectacles.

Ere I permitted myself to request an explanation, I tied the string of Adèle's pinafore which happened to be loose: having helped her also to another bun and refilled her mug with milk, I said nonchalantly:—

"Mr. Rochester is not likely to return soon, I suppose?"

"Indeed, he is—in three days, he says; that will be next Thursday; and not alone either. I don't know how many of the fine people at the Leas are coming with him: he sends directions for all the best bed-rooms to be prepared; and the library and drawing-rooms are to be cleaned out; and I am to get more kitchen hands from the George Inn, at Millcote, and from wherever else I can; and the ladies will bring their maids and the gentlemen their valets: so we shall have a full house of it." And Mrs. Fairfax swallowed her breakfast and hastened away to commence operations.

The three days were, as she had foretold, busy enough. I had thought all the rooms at Thornfield beautifully clean and well-arranged: but it appears I was mistaken. Three women were got to help; and such scrubbing, such brushing, such washing of paint and beating of carpets, such taking down and putting up of pictures, such polishing of mirrors and lustres, such lighting of fires in bedrooms, such airing of sheets and feather-beds on hearths, I never beheld, either before or since. Adèle ran quite wild in the midst of it: the preparations for company and the prospect of their arrival, seemed to throw her into ecstasies. She would have Sophie to look over all her "*toilettes*" as she called frocks; to furbish up any that were "*passées*," and to air and arrange the new. For herself, she did nothing but caper about in front chambers, jump on and off the bedsteads, and lie on the mattresses and piled-up bolsters and pillows before the enormous fires roaring in the chimneys. From school duties she was exonerated: and I was all day in the store-room, helping (or hindering) her and the cook; learning to make custards and cheesecakes and French pastry, to truss game and garnish dessert-dishes.

The party were expected to arrive on Thursday afternoon, in time for dinner at six. During the intervening period I had no time to nurse chimeras; and I believe I was as active and gay as anybody—Adèle excepted. Still, now and then, I received a damping check to my cheerfulness; and was, in spite of myself, thrown back on the region of doubts and portents, and dark conjectures. This was when I chanced to see the third story staircase door (which of late had always been kept locked) open slowly, and give passage to the form of Grace Poole, in prim cap, white apron, and handkerchief; when I watched her glide along the gallery, her quiet tread muffled in a list slipper; when I saw her look into the bustling, topsy-turvy bed-rooms,—just say a word, perhaps, to the charwoman about the proper way to polish a grate, or clean a marble mantel-piece, or take stains from papered walls, and then pass on. She would thus descend to the kitchen once a day, eat her dinner, smoke a moderate pipe on the hearth, and go back, carrying her pot of porter with her, for her private solace, in her own gloomy upper haunt. Only one hour in the twenty-four did she pass with her fellow-servants below; all the rest of her time was spent in some low-ceiled, oaken chamber of the second story: there she sat and sewed—and probably laughed drearily to herself,—as companionless as a prisoner in his dungeon.

The strangest thing of all was, that not a soul in the house, except me, noticed her habits, or seemed to marvel at them: no one discussed her position or employment; no one pitied her solitude or isolation. I once, indeed, overheard part of a dialogue between Leah and one of the char-women, of which Grace formed the subject. Leah had been saying something I had not caught, and the charwoman remarked:—

"She gets good wages, I guess?"

"Yes," said Leah; "I wish I had as good; not that mine are to complain of,—there's no stinginess at Thornfield; but they're not one-fifth of the sum Mrs. Poole receives. And she is laying by: she goes every quarter to the bank at Millcote. I should not wonder but she has saved enough to keep her independent if she liked to leave; but I suppose she's got used to the place; and then she's not forty yet, and strong and able for anything. It is too soon for her to give up business."

"She is a good hand, I daresay," said the charwoman.

"Ah!—she understands what she has to do,—nobody better," rejoined Leah, significantly; "and it is not every one could fill her shoes: not for all the money she gets."

"That it is not!" was the reply. "I wonder whether master—"

The charwoman was going on; but here Leah turned and perceived me, and she instantly gave her companion a nudge.

"Doesn't she know?" I heard the woman whisper.

Leah shook her head, and the conversation was of course dropped. All I had gathered from it amounted to this,—that there was a mystery at Thornfield; and that from participation in that mystery, I was purposely excluded.

Thursday came: all work had been completed the previous evening; carpets were laid down, bed-hangings festooned, radiant white counterpanes spread, toilet tables arranged, furniture rubbed, flowers piled in vases: both chambers and saloons looked as fresh and bright as hands could make them. The hall, too, was scoured; and the great carved clock, as well as the steps and banisters of the staircase, were polished to the brightness of glass: in the dining-room, the sideboard flashed resplendent with plate; in the drawing-room and boudoir, vases of exotics bloomed on all sides.

Afternoon arrived: Mrs. Fairfax assumed her best black satin gown, her gloves, and her gold watch; for it was her part to receive the company,—to conduct the ladies to their rooms, etc. Adèle, too, would be dressed: though I thought she had little chance of being introduced to the party that day at least. However, to please her, I allowed Sophie to apparel her in one of her short, full muslin frocks. For myself, I had no need to make any change; I should not be called upon to quit my sanctum of the school-room; for a sanctum it was now become to me,—"a very pleasant refuge in time of trouble."

It had been a mild, serene spring day: one of those days which towards the end of March or the beginning of April, rise shining over the earth as heralds of summer. It was drawing to an end now; but the evening was even warm, and I sat at work in the school-room with the window open.

"It gets late," said Mrs. Fairfax, entering in rustling state. "I am glad I ordered dinner an hour after the time Mr. Rochester mentioned; for it is past six now. I have sent John down to the gates to see if there is anything on the road: one can see a long way from thence in the direction of Millcote." She went to the window. "Here he is!" said she. "Well, John," (leaning out) "any news?"

"They're coming, ma'am," was the answer. "They'll be here in ten minutes."

Adèle flew to the window. I followed; taking care to stand on one side, so that, screened by the curtain, I could see without being seen.

The ten minutes John had given seemed very long, but at last wheels were heard; four equestrians galloped up the drive, and after them came two open carriages. Fluttering veils and waving plumes filled the vehicles; two of the cavaliers were young, dashing looking gentlemen; the third was Mr. Rochester on his black horse, Mesrour; Pilot bounding before him: at his side rode a lady, and he and she were the first of the party. Her purple riding-habit almost swept the ground, her veil streamed long on the breeze; mingling with its transparent folds, and gleaming through them, shone rich raven ringlets.

"Miss Ingram!" exclaimed Mrs. Fairfax, and away she hurried to her post below.

The cavalcade, following the sweep of the drive, quickly turned the angle of the house, and I lost sight of it. Adèle now petitioned to go down; but I took her on my knee and gave her to understand that she must not on any account think of venturing in sight of the ladies, either now or at any other time, unless expressly sent for: that Mr. Rochester would be very angry, etc. "Some natural tears she shed" on being told this; but as I began to look very grave, she consented at last to wipe them.

A joyous stir was now audible in the hall: gentlemen's deep tones, and ladies' silvery accents blent harmoniously together, and distinguishable above all, though not loud, was the sonorous voice of the master of Thornfield Hall, welcoming his fair and gallant guests under its roof. Then light steps ascended the stairs; and there was a tripping through the gallery, and soft, cheerful laughs, and opening and closing doors, and, for a time, a hush.

"Elles changent de toilettes," said Adèle; who, listening attentively, had followed every movement; and she sighed.

"Chez maman," said she, *"quand il y avait du monde, je les suivais partout, au salon et à leurs chambres; souvent je regardais les femmes de chambre coiffer et habiller les dames, et c'était si amusant: comme cela on apprend."*

"Don't you feel hungry, Adèle?"

"Mais oui, mademoiselle: voilà cinq ou six heures que nous n'avons pas mangé."

"Well now, while the ladies are in their rooms, I will venture down and get you something to eat."

And issuing from my asylum with precaution, I sought a back-stairs which conducted directly to the kitchen. All in that region was fire and commotion; the soup and fish were in the last stage of projection, and the cook hung over her crucibles in a frame of mind and body threatening spontaneous combustion. In the servants' hall two coachmen and three gentlemen's gentlemen stood or sat round the fire; the Abigails I suppose were up-stairs with their mistresses: the new servants that had been hired from Millcote were bustling about everywhere. Threading this chaos, I at last reached the larder; there I took possession of a cold chicken, a roll of bread, some tarts, a plate or two and a knife and fork: with this booty I made a hasty retreat. I had regained the gallery, and was just shutting the back-door behind me, when an accelerated hum warned me that the ladies were about to issue from their chambers. I could not proceed to the school-room without passing some of their doors, and running the risk of being surprised with my cargo of victualage; so I stood still at this end, which, being windowless, was dark: quite dark now, for the sun was set and twilight gathering.

Presently the chambers gave up their fair tenants one after another: each came out gaily and airily, with dress that gleamed lustrous through the dusk. For a moment they stood grouped together at the other extremity of the gallery, conversing in a key of sweet subdued vivacity: they then descended the staircase almost as noiselessly as a bright mist rolls down a hill. Their collective appearance had left on me an impression of high-born elegance, such as I had never before received.

I found Adèle peeping through the school-room door, which she held ajar. "What beautiful ladies!" cried she in English. "Oh, I wish I might go to them! Do you think Mr. Rochester will send for us by-and-by, after dinner?"

"No, indeed, I don't; Mr. Rochester has something else to think about. Never mind the ladies to-night; perhaps you will see them to-morrow: here is your dinner."

She was really hungry, so the chicken and tarts served to divert her attention for a time. It was well I secured this forage; or both she, I and Sophie, to whom I conveyed a share of our repast would have run a chance of getting no dinner at all: every one down stairs was too much engaged to think of us. The dessert was not carried out till after nine, and at ten, footmen were still running to and fro with trays and coffee-cups. I allowed Adèle to sit up much later than usual; for she declared she could not possibly go to sleep while the doors kept opening and shutting below, and people bustling about. Besides, she added, a message might possibly come from Mr. Rochester when she was undressed; *"et alors quel dommage!"*

I told her stories as long as she would listen to them; and then for a change I took her out into the gallery. The hall lamp was now lit, and it amused her to look over the balustrade and watch the servants passing backwards and forwards. When the evening was far advanced, a sound of music issued from the drawing-room, whither the piano had been removed; Adèle and I sat down on the top step of the stairs to listen. Presently a voice blent with the rich tones of the instrument; it was a lady who sang, and very sweet her notes were. The solo over, a duet followed, and then a glee: a joyous conversational murmur filled up the intervals. I listened long: suddenly I discovered that my ear was wholly intent on analyzing the mingled sounds, and trying to discriminate amidst the confusion of accents those of Mr. Rochester; and when it caught them, which it soon did, it found a further task in framing the tones, rendered by distance inarticulate, into words.

The clock struck eleven. I looked at Adèle, whose head leant against my shoulder; her eyes were waxing heavy, so I took her up in my arms and carried her off to bed. It was near one before the gentlemen and ladies sought their chambers.

The next day was as fine as its predecessor; it was devoted by the party to an excursion to some site in the neighbourhood. They set out early in the forenoon, some on horseback, the rest in carriages; I witnessed both the departure and the return. Miss Ingram, as before, was the only lady equestrian; and as before, Mr. Rochester galloped at her side; the two rode a little apart from the rest. I pointed out this circumstance to Mrs. Fairfax, who was standing at the window with me:—

"You said it was not likely they should think of being married," said I, "but you see Mr. Rochester evidently prefers her to any of the other ladies."

"Yes; I daresay: no doubt he admires her."

"And she him," I added; "look how she leans her head towards him as if she were conversing confidentially! I wish I could see her face; I have never had a glimpse of it yet."

"You will see her this evening," answered Mrs. Fairfax. "I happened to remark to Mr. Rochester how much Adèle wished to be introduced to the ladies, and he said: 'Oh! let her come into the drawing-room after dinner; and request Miss Eyre to accompany her.' "

"Yes—he said that from mere politeness: I need not go, I am sure," I answered.

"Well—I observed to him that as you were unused to company, I did not think you would like appearing before so gay a party—all strangers; and he replied, in his quick way: 'Nonsense! If she objects, tell her it is my particular wish; and if she resists, say I shall come and fetch her in case of contumacy.' "

"I will not give him that trouble;" I answered. "I will go, if no better may be: but I don't like it. Shall you be there, Mrs. Fairfax?"

"No; I pleaded off, and he admitted my plea. I'll tell you how to manage so as to avoid the embarrassment of making a formal entrance, which is the most disagreeable part of the business. You must go into the drawing-room while it is empty, before the ladies leave the dinner-table; choose your seat in any quiet nook you like; you need not stay long after the gentlemen come in, unless you please: just let Mr. Rochester see you are there and then slip away—nobody will notice you."

"Will these people remain long, do you think?"

"Perhaps two or three weeks; certainly not more. After the Easter recess, Sir George Lynn, who was lately elected member for Millcote, will have to go up to town and take his seat; I dare say Mr. Rochester will accompany him: it surprises me that he has already made so protracted a stay at Thornfield."

It was with some trepidation that I perceived the hour approach when I was to repair with my charge to the drawing-room. Adèle had been in a state of ecstasy all day, after hearing she was to be presented to the ladies in the evening; and it was not till Sophie commenced the operation of dressing her, that she sobered down. Then the importance of the process quickly steadied her; and by the time she had her curls arranged in well-smoothed, drooping clusters, her pink satin frock put on, her long sash tied, and her lace mittens adjusted, she looked as grave as any judge. No need to warn her not to disarrange her attire: when she was dressed, she

sat demurely down in her little chair, taking care previously to lift up the
satin skirt for fear she should crease it, and assured me she would not
stir thence till I was ready. This I quickly was: my best dress (the silver-
gray one, purchased for Miss Temple's wedding, and never worn since)
was soon put on; my hair was soon smoothed; my sole ornament, the pearl
brooch, soon assumed. We descended.

Fortunately there was another entrance to the drawing-room than that
through the saloon where they were all seated at dinner. We found the
apartment vacant; a large fire burning silently on the marble hearth, and
wax candles shining in bright solitude, amid the exquisite flowers with
which the tables were adorned. The crimson curtain hung before the arch:
slight as was the separation this drapery formed from the party in the
adjoining saloon, they spoke in so low a key that nothing of their conversation could be distinguished beyond a soothing murmur.

Adèle, who appeared to be still under the influence of a most solemnizing impression, sat down without a word on the footstool I pointed out
to her. I retired to a window seat, and taking a book from a table near,
endeavoured to read. Adèle brought her stool to my feet; ere long she
touched my knee.

"What is it, Adèle?"

*"Est-ce que je ne puis pas prendre une seule de ces fleurs magnifiques,
mademoiselle? Seulement pour completer ma toilette."*

"You think too much of your *'toilette,'* Adèle: but you may have a
flower." And I took a rose from a vase and fastened it in her sash. She
sighed a sigh of ineffable satisfaction, as if her cup of happiness were now
full. I turned my face away to conceal a smile I could not suppress: there
was something ludicrous as well as painful in the little Parisienne's earnest
and innate devotion to matters of dress.

A soft sound of rising now became audible; the curtain was swept back
from the arch; through it appeared the dining-room, with its lit lustre pouring down light on the silver and glass of a magnificent dessert-service
covering a long table; a band of ladies stood in the opening; they entered,
and the curtain fell behind them.

There were but eight; yet somehow as they flocked in, they gave the impression of a much larger number. Some of them were very tall; many were
dressed in white; and all had a sweeping amplitude of array that seemed to
magnify their persons as a mist magnifies the moor. I rose and curtseyed
to them: one or two bent their heads in return; the others only stared at me.

They dispersed about the room; reminding me, by the lightness and
buoyancy of their movements, of a flock of white plumy birds. Some of
them threw themselves in half-reclining positions on the sofas and ottomans; some bent over the tables and examined the flowers and books;
the rest gathered in a group round the fire: all talked in a low but clear
tone which seemed habitual to them. I knew their names afterwards, and
may as well mention them now.

First, there was Mrs. Eshton and two of her daughters. She had evidently
been a handsome woman, and was well preserved still. Of her daughters,
the eldest, Amy, was rather little; naïve, and child-like in face and manner, and piquant in form: her white muslin dress and blue sash became
her well. The second, Louisa, was taller and more elegant in figure; with
a very pretty face of that order the French term *"minois chiffoné":* both
sisters were fair as lilies.

Lady Lynn was a large and stout personage of about forty; very erect, very haughty-looking, richly dressed in a satin robe of changeful sheen: her dark hair shone glossily under the shade of an azure plume, and within the circlet of a band of gems.

Mrs. Colonel Dent was less showy; but, I thought, more lady-like. She had a slight figure, a pale, gentle face, and fair hair. Her black satin dress, her scarf of rich foreign lace, and her pearl ornaments, pleased me better than the rainbow radiance of the titled dame.

But the three most distinguished—partly perhaps, because the tallest figures of the band—were the Dowager Lady Ingram and her daughters, Blanche and Mary. They were all three of the loftiest stature of woman. The dowager might be between forty and fifty: her shape was still fine; her hair (by candle light at least) still black; her teeth, too, were still apparently perfect. Most people would have termed her a splendid woman of her age: and so she was, no doubt, physically speaking; but then there was an expression of almost insupportable haughtiness in her bearing and countenance. She had Roman features and a double chin, disappearing into a throat like a pillar: these features appeared to me not only inflated and darkened, but even furrowed with pride; and the chin was sustained by the same principle, in a position of almost preternatural erectness. She had, likewise, a fierce and a hard eye: it reminded me of Mrs. Reed's; she mouthed her words in speaking; her voice was deep, its inflections very pompous, very dogmatical,—very intolerable, in short. A crimson velvet robe, and a shawl turban of some gold-wrought Indian fabric, invested her (I suppose she thought) with a truly imperial dignity.

Blanche and Mary were of equal stature,—straight and tall as poplars. Mary was too slim for her height; but Blanche was moulded like a Diana. I regarded her, of course, with special interest. First, I wished to see whether her appearance accorded with Mrs. Fairfax's description; secondly, whether it at all resembled the fancy miniature I had painted of her; and thirdly—it will out!—whether it were such as I should fancy likely to suit Mr. Rochester's taste.

As far as person went, she answered point for point, both to my picture and Mrs. Fairfax's description. The noble bust, the sloping shoulders, the graceful neck, the dark eyes and black ringlets were all there;—but her face?—Her face was like her mother's; a youthful unfurrowed likeness: the same pride. It was not, however, so saturnine a pride: she laughed continually; her laugh was satirical, and so was the habitual expression of her arched and haughty lip.

Genius is said to be self-conscious: I cannot tell whether Miss Ingram was a genius, but she was self-conscious—remarkably self-conscious indeed. She entered into a discourse on botany with the gentle Mrs. Dent. It seems Mrs. Dent had not studied that science: though, as she said, she liked flowers, "especially wild ones"; Miss Ingram had, and she ran over its vocabulary with an air. I presently perceived she was (what is vernacularly termed) *trailing* Mrs. Dent; that is playing on her ignorance: her *trail* might be clever, but it was decidedly not good-natured. She played: her execution was brilliant; she sang: her voice was fine; she talked French apart to her mama; and she talked it well, with fluency and with a good accent.

Mary had a milder and more open countenance than Blanche; softer features too, and a skin some shades fairer (Miss Ingram was dark as a

Spaniard)—but Mary was deficient in life: her face lacked expression, her eye lustre; she had nothing to say, and having once taken her seat, remained fixed like a statue in its niche. The sisters were both attired in spotless white.

And did I now think Miss Ingram such a choice as Mr. Rochester would be likely to make? I could not tell—I did not know his taste in female beauty. If he liked the majestic, she was the very type of majesty: then she was accomplished, sprightly. Most gentlemen would admire her, I thought; and that he *did* admire her, I already seemed to have obtained proof: to remove the last shade of doubt, it remained but to see them together.

You are not to suppose, reader, that Adèle has all this time been sitting motionless on the stool at my feet: no; when the ladies entered, she rose, advanced to meet them, made a stately reverence, and said, with gravity,—

"Bon jour, mesdames."

And Miss Ingram had looked down at her with a mocking air, and exclaimed, "Oh, what a little puppet!"

Lady Lynn had remarked, "It is Mr. Rochester's ward, I suppose—the little French girl he was speaking of."

Mrs. Dent had kindly taken her hand, and given her a kiss. Amy and Louisa Eshton had cried out simultaneously,—

"What a love of a child!"

And then they had called her to a sofa, where she now sat, ensconced between them, chattering alternately in French and broken English; absorbing not only the young ladies' attention, but that of Mrs. Eshton and Lady Lynn, and getting spoilt to her heart's content.

At last coffee is brought in, and the gentlemen are summoned. I sit in the shade—if any shade there be in this brilliantly-lit apartment; the window-curtain half hides me. Again the arch yawns: they come. The collective appearance of the gentlemen, like that of the ladies, is very imposing: they are all costumed in black; most of them are tall, some young. Henry and Frederick Lynn are very dashing sparks, indeed; and Colonel Dent is a fine soldierly man. Mr. Eshton, the magistrate of the district, is gentleman-like: his hair is quite white, his eyebrows and whiskers still dark, which gives him something of the appearance of a *"père noble de théâtre."* Lord Ingram, like his sisters, is very tall; like them, also, he is handsome; but he shares Mary's apathetic and listless look: he seems to have more length than vivacity of blood or vigour of brain.

And where is Mr. Rochester?

He comes in last: I am not looking at the arch, yet I see him enter. I try to concentrate my attention on these netting-needles, on the meshes of the purse I am forming—I wish to think only of the work I have in my hands, to see only the silver beads and silk threads that lie in my lap; whereas, I distinctly behold his figure, and I inevitably recall the moment when I last saw it: just after I had rendered him, what he deemed, an essential service—and he, holding my hand, and looking down on my face, surveyed me with eyes that revealed a heart full and eager to overflow; in whose emotions I had a part. How near had I approached him at that moment! What had occurred since, calculated to change his and my relative positions? Yet now, how distant, how far estranged we were! So far estranged, that I did not expect him to come and speak to me. I did not wonder, when, without looking at me, he took a seat at the other side of the room, and began conversing with some of the ladies.

No sooner did I see that his attention was riveted on them, and that I might gaze without being observed, than my eyes were drawn involuntarily to his face: I could not keep their lids under control: they would rise, and the irids would fix on him. I looked, and had an acute pleasure in looking,—a precious, yet poignant pleasure; pure gold, with a steely point of agony: a pleasure like what the thirst-perishing man might feel who knows the well to which he has crept is poisoned, yet stoops and drinks divine draughts nevertheless.

Most true is it that "beauty is in the eye of the gazer." My master's colourless, olive face, square, massive brow, broad and jetty eyebrows, deep eyes, strong features, firm, grim mouth,—all energy, decision, will,—were not beautiful, according to rule; but they were more than beautiful to me: they were full of an interest, an influence that quite mastered me,—that took my feelings from my own power and fettered them in his. I had not intended to love him: the reader knows I had wrought hard to extirpate from my soul the germs of love there detected; and now, at the first renewed view of him, they spontaneously revived, green and strong! He made me love him without looking at me.

I compared him with his guests. What was the gallant grace of the Lynns, the languid elegance of Lord Ingram,—even the military distinction of Colonel Dent, contrasted with his look of native pith and genuine power? I had no sympathy in their appearance, their expression: yet I could imagine that most observers would call them attractive, handsome, imposing; while they would pronounce Mr. Rochester at once harsh-featured and melancholy-looking. I saw them smile, laugh—it was nothing: the light of the candles had as much soul in it as their smile; the tinkle of the bell as much significance as their laugh. I saw Mr. Rochester smile:—his stern features softened; his eye grew both brilliant and gentle, its ray both searching and sweet. He was talking, at the moment, to Louisa and Amy Eshton. I wondered to see them receive with calm that look which seemed to me so penetrating: I expected their eyes to fall, their colour to rise under it; yet I was glad when I found they were in no sense moved. "He is not to them what he is to me," I thought: "he is not of their kind. I believe he is of mine;—I am sure he is,—I feel akin to him,—I understand the language of his countenance and movements: though rank and wealth sever us widely, I have something in my brain and heart, in my blood and nerves, that assimilates me mentally to him. Did I say, a few days since, that I had nothing to do with him but to receive my salary at his hands? Did I forbid myself to think of him in any other light than as a paymaster? Blasphemy against nature! Every good, true, vigorous feeling I have, gathers impulsively round him. I know I must conceal my sentiments: I must smother hope; I must remember that he cannot care much for me. For when I say that I am of his kind, I do not mean that I have his force to influence, and his spell to attract: I mean only that I have certain tastes and feelings in common with him. I must, then, repeat continually that we are for ever sundered:—and yet, while I breathe and think, I must love him."

Coffee is handed. The ladies, since the gentlemen entered, have become lively as larks: conversation waxes brisk and merry. Colonel Dent and Mr. Eshton argue on politics; their wives listen. The two proud dowagers, Lady Lynn and Lady Ingram, confabulate together. Sir George—whom, by-the-by, I have forgotten to describe,—a very big, and very fresh-looking country gentleman, stands before their sofa, coffee-cup in hand, and occasionally puts in a word. Mr. Frederick Lynn has taken a seat beside Mary Ingram, and is showing her the engravings of a splendid volume: she looks, smiles now and then, but apparently says little. The tall and phlegmatic Lord Ingram leans with folded arms on the chair-back of the little and lively Amy Eshton; she glances up at him, and chatters like a wren: she likes him better than she does Mr. Rochester. Henry Lynn has taken possession of an ottoman at the feet of Louisa; Adèle shares it with him: he is trying to talk French with her, and Louisa laughs at his blunders. With whom will Blanche Ingram pair? She is standing alone at the table, bending gracefully over an album. She seems waiting to be sought; but she will not wait too long: she herself selects a mate.

Mr. Rochester, having quitted the Eshtons, stands on the hearth as solitary as she stands by the table; she confronts him, taking her station on the opposite side of the mantel-piece.

"Mr. Rochester, I thought you were not fond of children?"

"Nor am I."

"Then, what induced you to take charge of such a little doll as that? (pointing to Adèle). Where did you pick her up?"

"I did not pick her up, she was left on my hands."

"You should have sent her to school."

"I could not afford it: schools are so dear."

"Why, I suppose you have a governess for her: I saw a person with her just now—is she gone? Oh, no! there she is still behind the window-curtain. You pay her, of course; I should think it quite as expensive,—more so; for you have them both to keep in addition."

I feared—or should I say, hoped?—the allusion to me would make Mr. Rochester glance my way; and I involuntarily shrank further into the shade: but he never turned his eyes.

"I have not considered the subject," said he indifferently, looking straight before him.

"No—you men never do consider economy and common sense. You should hear mama on the chapter of governesses: Mary and I have had, I should think, a dozen at least in our day; half of them detestable and the rest ridiculous, and all incubi—were they not, mama?"

"Did you speak, my own?"

The young lady thus claimed as the dowager's special property, reiterated her question with an explanation.

"My dearest, don't mention governesses: the word makes me nervous. I have suffered a martyrdom from their incompetency and caprice: I thank Heaven I have now done with them!"

Mrs. Dent here bent over to the pious lady, and whispered something in her ear: I suppose from the answer elicited, it was a reminder that one of the anathematized race was present.

"*Tant pis!*" said her ladyship, "I hope it may do her good!" Then, in a lower tone, but still loud enough for me to hear. "I noticed her: I am a judge of physiognomy, and in hers I see all the faults of her class."

"What are they, madam?" inquired Mr. Rochester aloud.

"I will tell you in your private ear," replied she, wagging her turban three times with portentous significancy.

"But my curiosity will be past its appetite: it craves food now."

"Ask Blanche: she is nearer you than I."

"Oh, don't refer him to me, mama! I have one word to say of the whole tribe: they are a nuisance. Not that I ever suffered much from them: I took care to turn the tables. What tricks Theodore and I used to play on our Miss Wilsons, and Mrs. Greys, and Madame Jouberts! Mary was always too sleepy to join in a plot with spirit. The best fun was with Madame Joubert: Miss Wilson was a poor sickly thing, lachrymose and low-spirited: not worth the trouble of vanquishing, in short; and Mrs. Grey was coarse and insensible: no blow took effect on her. But poor Madame Joubert! I see her yet in her raging passions, when we had driven her to extremities—spilt our tea, crumbled our bread and butter, tossed our books up to the ceiling, and played a charivari with the ruler and desk, the fender and fire-irons. Theodore, do you remember those merry days?"

"Yaas, to be sure I do," drawled Lord Ingram: "and the poor old stick used to cry out 'Oh you villains childs!'—and then we sermonized her on the presumption of attempting to teach such clever blades as we were, when she was herself so ignorant."

"We did: and Tedo, you know, I helped you in prosecuting (or persecuting) your tutor, whey-faced Mr. Vining—the parson in the pip, as we used to call him. He and Miss Wilson took the liberty of falling in love with each other—at least Tedo and I thought so: we surprised sundry tender glances and sighs which we interpreted as tokens of '*la belle passion*,' and I promise you the public soon had the benefit of our discovery: we employed it as a sort of lever to hoist our dead-weights from the house. Dear mama there, as soon as she got an inkling of the business, found out that it was of an immoral tendency. Did you not, my lady-mother?"

"Certainly, my best. And I was quite right; depend on that: there are a thousand reasons why liaisons between governesses and tutors should never be tolerated a moment in any well-regulated house; firstly—"

"Oh gracious, mama! Spare us the enumeration! *Au reste,* we all know them: danger of bad example to innocence of childhood; distractions and consequent neglect of duty on the part of the attached mutual alliance and reliance; confidence thence resulting—insolence accompanying—mutiny and general blow-up. Am I right, Baroness Ingram of Ingram Park?"

"My lily-flower, you are right now, as always."

"Then no more need be said: change the subject."

Amy Eshton, not hearing or not heeding this dictum, joined in with her soft, infantine tone: "Louisa and I used to quiz our governess too; but she was such a good creature, she would bear anything: nothing put her out. She was never cross with us; was she, Louisa?"

"No, never: we might do what we pleased; ransack her desk and her workbox, and turn her drawers inside out; and she was so good-natured, she would give us anything we asked for."

"I suppose now," said Miss Ingram, curling her lip sarcastically, "we shall have an abstract of the memoirs of all the governesses extant: in order to avert such a visitation, I again move the introduction of a new topic. Mr. Rochester, do you second my motion?"

"Madam, I support you on this point as on every other."

"Then on me be the onus of bringing it forward. Signior Eduardo, are you in voice to-night?"

"Donna Bianca, if you command it, I will be."

"Then Signior, I lay on you my sovereign behest to furbish up your lungs and other vocal organs, as they will be wanted on my royal service."

"Who would not be the Rizzio of so divine a Mary?"

"A fig for Rizzio!" cried she, tossing her head with all its curls, as she moved to the piano. "It is my opinion the fiddler David must have been an insipid sort of fellow: I like black Bothwell better: to my mind a man is nothing without a spice of the devil in him; and history may say what it will of James Hepburn, but I have a notion, he was just the sort of wild, fierce, bandit-hero whom I could have consented to gift with my hand."

"Gentlemen, you hear! Now which of you most resembles Bothwell?" cried Mr. Rochester.

"I should say the preference lies with you," responded Colonel Dent.

"On my honour, I am much obliged to you," was the reply.

Miss Ingram, who had now seated herself with proud grace at the piano, spreading out her snowy robes in queenly amplitude, commenced a brilliant prelude; talking meantime. She appeared to be on her high horse to-night; both her words and her air seemed intended to excite not only the admiration, but the amazement of her auditors: she was evidently bent on striking them as something very dashing and daring indeed.

"Oh, I am so sick of the young men of the present day!" exclaimed she, rattling away at the instrument. "Poor, puny things not fit to stir a step beyond papa's park-gates: nor to go even so far without mama's permission and guardianship! Creatures so absorbed in care about their pretty faces and their white hands, and their small feet; as if a man had anything to do with beauty! As if loveliness were not the special prerogative of woman—her legitimate appanage and heritage! I grant an ugly *woman* is a blot on the fair face of creation; but as to the *gentlemen*, let them be solicitous to possess only strength and valour: let their motto be:— Hunt, shoot, and fight: the rest is not worth a fillip. Such should be my device, were I a man."

"Whenever I marry," she continued, after a pause which none interrupted, "I am resolved my husband shall not be a rival, but a foil to me. I will suffer no competitor near the throne; I shall exact an undivided homage: his devotions shall not be shared between me and the shape he sees in his mirror. Mr. Rochester, now sing, and I will play for you."

"I am all obedience," was the response.

"Here then is a Corsair-song. Know that I dote on Corsairs; and for that reason, sing it *'con spirito.'* "

"Commands from Miss Ingram's lips would put spirit into a mug of milk and water."

"Take care, then: if you don't please me, I will shame you by showing how such things *should* be done."

"That is offering a premium on incapacity: I shall now endeavour to fail."

"Gardez-vous en bien! If you err wilfully, I shall devise a proportionate punishment."

"Miss Ingram ought to be clement, for she has it in her power to inflict a chastisement beyond mortal endurance."

"Ha! explain!" commanded the lady.

"Pardon me, madam: no need of explanation; your own fine sense must inform you that one of your frowns would be a sufficient substitute for capital punishment."

"Sing!" said she, and again touching the piano, she commenced an accompaniment in spirited style.

"Now is my time to slip away," thought I: but the tones that then severed the air arrested me. Mrs. Fairfax had said Mr. Rochester possessed a fine voice: he did—a mellow, powerful bass, into which he threw his own feeling, his own force; finding a way through the ear to the heart, and there waking sensation strangely. I waited till the last deep and full vibration had expired—till the tide of talk, checked an instant, had resumed its flow; I then quitted my sheltered corner and made my exit by the side-door, which was fortunately near. Thence a narrow passage led into the hall: in crossing it, I perceived my sandal was loose; I stopped to tie it, kneeling down for that purpose on the mat at the foot of the staircase. I heard the dining-room door unclose; a gentleman came out; rising hastily, I stood face to face with him: it was Mr. Rochester.

"How do you do?" he asked.

"I am very well, sir."

"Why did you not come and speak to me in the room?"

I thought I might have retorted the question on him who put it: but I would not take that freedom. I answered:—

"I did not wish to disturb you, as you seemed engaged, sir."

"What have you been doing during my absence?"

"Nothing particular; teaching Adèle as usual."

"And getting a good deal paler than you were—as I saw at first sight. What is the matter?"

"Nothing at all, sir."

"Did you take any cold that night you half drowned me?"

"Not the least."

"Return to the drawing-room: you are deserting too early."

"I am tired, sir."

He looked at me for a minute.

"And a little depressed," he said. "What about? Tell me."

"Nothing—nothing, sir. I am not depressed."

"But I affirm that you are: so much depressed that a few more words would bring tears to your eyes—indeed, they are there now, shining and swimming; and a bead has slipped from the lash and fallen on to the flag. If I had time, and was not in mortal dread of some prating prig of a servant passing, I would know what all this means. Well, to-night I excuse you; but understand that so long as my visitors stay, I expect you to appear in the drawing-room every evening; it is my wish; don't neglect it. No go, and send Sophie for Adèle. Good-night my——" He stopped, bit his lip, and abruptly left me.

. . . .

Chapter 18

Merry days were these at Thornfield Hall; and busy days too: how different from the first three months of stillness, monotony, and solitude I had passed beneath its roof! All sad feelings seemed now driven from the house, all gloomy associations forgotten: there was life everywhere, movement all day long. You could not now traverse the gallery, once so hushed, nor enter the front chamber, once so tenantless, without encountering a smart lady's maid or a dandy valet.

The kitchen, the butler's pantry, the servant's hall, the entrance hall, were equally alive; and the saloons were only left void and still, when the blue sky and halcyon sunshine of the genial spring weather called their occupants out into the grounds. Even when that weather was broken, and continuous rain set in for some days, no damp seemed cast over enjoyment: in-door amusements only became more lively and varied, in consequence of the stop put to out-door gaiety.

I wondered what they were going to do the first evening a change of entertainment was proposed: they spoke of "playing charades," but in my ignorance I did not understand the term. The servants were called in, the dining-room tables wheeled away, the lights otherwise disposed, the chairs placed in a semicircle opposite the arch. While Mr. Rochester and the other gentlemen directed these alterations, the ladies were running up and down stairs ringing for their maids. Mrs. Fairfax was summoned to give information respecting the resources of the house in shawls, dresses, draperies of any kind; and certain wardrobes of the third story were ransacked, and their contents, in the shape of brocaded and hooped petticoats, satin sacques, black modes, lace lappets, etc., were brought down in armfuls by the Abigails; then a selection was made, and such things as were chosen were carried to the boudoir within the drawing-room.

Meantime, Mr. Rochester had again summoned the ladies round him, and was selecting certain of their number to be of his party.

"Miss Ingram is mine, of course," said he: afterwards he named the two Misses Eshton, and Mrs. Dent. He looked at me: I happened to be near him, as I had been fastening the clasp of Mrs. Dent's bracelet, which had got loose.

"Will you play?" he asked. I shook my head. He did not insist, which I rather feared he would have done: he allowed me to return quietly to my usual seat.

He and his aids now withdrew behind the curtain: the other party, which was headed by Colonel Dent, sat down on the crescent of chairs. One of the gentlemen, Mr. Eshton, observing me, seemed to propose that I should be asked to join them; but Lady Ingram instantly negatived the notion. "No," I heard her say: "she looks too stupid for any game of the sort."

Ere long, a bell tinkled, and the curtain drew up. Within the arch, the bulky figure of Sir George Lynn, whom Mr. Rochester had likewise chosen, was seen enveloped in a white sheet: before him, on a table, lay open a large book; and at his side stood Amy Eshton, draped in Mr. Rochester's cloak, and holding a book in her hand. Somebody, unseen, rung the bell merrily; then Adèle (who had insisted in being one of her guardian's party) bounded forward, scattering round her the contents of a basket of flowers she carried on her arm. Then appeared the magnificent figure of Miss Ingram, clad in white, a long veil on her head, and a wreath of roses round her brow: by her side walked Mr. Rochester, and together they drew near the table. They knelt; while Mrs. Dent and Louisa Eshton, dressed also in white, took up their stations behind them. A ceremony followed, in dumb show, in which it was easy to recognise the pantomime of a marriage. At its termination, Colonel Dent and his party consulted in whispers for two minutes, then the Colonel called,—

"Bride!" Mr. Rochester bowed, and the curtain fell.

A considerable interval elapsed before it again rose. Its second rising displayed a more elaborately prepared scene than the last. The drawing-room, as I have before observed, was raised two steps above the dining-room, and on the top of the upper step, placed a yard or two back within the room, appeared a large marble basin, which I recognised as an ornament of the conservatory—where it usually stood surrounded by exotics, and tenanted by gold fish—and whence it must have been transported with some trouble, on account of its size and weight.

Seated on the carpet, by the side of this basin, was seen Mr. Rochester, costumed in shawls, with a turban on his head. His dark eyes and swarth skin and Paynim features suited the costume exactly: he looked the very model of an eastern emir; an agent or a victim of the bowstring. Presently advanced into view Miss Ingram. She, too, was attired in oriental fashion: a crimson scarf tied sash-like round the waist; an embroidered handkerchief knotted about her temples; her beautifully-moulded arms bare, one of them up-raised in the act of supporting a pitcher, poised gracefully on her head. Both her cast of form and feature, her complexion and her general air, suggested the idea of some Israelitish princess of the patriarchal days; and such was doubtless the character she intended to represent.

She approached the basin, and bent over it as if to fill her pitcher; she again lifted it to her head. The personage on the well-brink now seemed to accost her; to make some request:—"She hasted, let down her pitcher on her hand and gave him to drink." From the bosom of his robe, he then produced a casket, opened it and showed magnificent bracelets and earrings; she acted astonishment and admiration; kneeling, he laid the treasure at her feet; incredulity and delight were expressed by her looks and gestures; the stranger fastened the bracelets on her arms, and the rings in her ears. It was Eliezer and Rebecca: the camels only were wanting.

The divining party again laid their heads together: apparently they could not agree about the word or syllable this scene illustrated. Colonel Dent, their spokesman, demanded "the tableau of the whole"; whereupon the curtain again descended.

On its third rising only a portion of the drawing-room was disclosed; the rest being concealed by a screen, hung with some sort of dark and coarse drapery. The marble basin was removed; in its place stood a deal table and a kitchen chair: these objects were visible by a very dim light prodeeding from a horn lantern, the wax candles being all extinguished.

Amidst this sordid scene, sat a man with his clenched hands resting on his knees, and his eyes bent on the ground. I knew Mr. Rochester; though the begrimed face, the disordered dress (his coat hanging loose from one arm, as if it had been almost torn from his back in a scuffle), the desperate and scowling countenance, the rough, bristling hair might well have disguised him. As he moved, a chain clanked: to his wrists were attached fetters.

"Bridewell!" exclaimed Colonel Dent, and the charade was solved.

A sufficient interval having elapsed for the performers to resume their ordinary costume, they re-entered the dining-room. Mr. Rochester led in Miss Ingram; she was complimenting him on his acting.

"Do you know," said she, "that, of the three characters, I liked you in the last best? Oh, had you but lived a few years earlier, what a gallant gentleman-highwayman you would have made!"

"Is all the soot washed from my face?" he asked, turning towards her.

"Alas! yes; the more's the pity! Nothing could be more becoming to your complexion than that ruffian's rouge."

"You would like a hero of the road then?"

"An English hero of the road would be the next best thing to an Italian bandit; and that could only be surpassed by a Levantine pirate."

"Well, whatever I am, remember you are my wife; we were married an hour since, in the presence of all these witnesses." She giggled, and her colour rose.

"Now, Dent," continued Mr. Rochester, "it is your turn." And as the other party withdrew, he and his band took the vacated seats. Miss Ingram placed herself at her leader's right hand; the other diviners filled the chairs on each side of him and her. I did not now watch the actors; I no longer waited with interest for the curtain to rise; my attention was absorbed by the spectators; my eyes, erewhile fixed on the arch, were now irresistibly attracted to the semicircle of chairs. What charade Colonel Dent and his party played, what word they chose, how they acquitted themselves, I no longer remember; but I still see the consultation which followed each scene: I see Mr. Rochester turn to Miss Ingram, and Miss Ingram to him; I see her incline her head towards him, till the jetty curls almost touch his shoulder and wave against his cheek; I hear their mutual whisperings; I recall their interchanged glances; and something even of the feeling roused by the spectacle returns in memory at this moment.

I have told you, reader, that I had learnt to love Mr. Rochester: I could not unlove him now, merely because I found that he had ceased to notice me—because I might pass hours in his presence, and he would never once turn his eyes in my direction—because I saw all his attentions appropriated by a great lady, who scorned to touch me with the hem of her robes as she passed; who, if ever her dark and imperious eye fell on me by chance, would withdraw it instantly as from an object too mean to merit observation. I could not unlove him, because I felt sure he would soon marry this very lady—because I read daily in her a proud security in his intentions respecting her—because I witnessed hourly in him a style of courtship which, if careless and choosing rather to be sought than to seek, was yet, in its very carelessness, captivating, and in its very pride, irresistible.

There was nothing to cool or banish love in these circumstances; though much to create despair. Much too, you will think, reader, to engender jealousy: if a woman, in my position, could presume to be jealous of a woman in Miss Ingram's. But I was not jealous: or very rarely;—the nature of the pain I suffered could not be explained by that word. Miss Ingram was a mark beneath jealousy: she was too inferior to excite the feeling. Pardon the seeming paradox: I mean what I say. She was very showy, but she was not genuine: she had a fine person, many brilliant attainments; but her mind was poor, her heart barren by nature: nothing bloomed spontaneously on that soil; no unforced natural fruit delighted by its freshness. She was not good; she was not original: she used to repeat sounding phrases from books: she never offered, nor had, an opinion of her own. She advocated a high tone of sentiment; but she did not know the sensations of sympathy and pity; tenderness and truth were not in her. Too often she betrayed this, by the undue vent she gave to a spiteful antipathy she had conceived against little Adèle: pushing her away with some contumelious epithet if she happened to approach her; sometimes ordering her from the room, and always treating her with coldness and acrimony. Other eyes besides mine watched these manifestations of character—watched them closely, keenly, shrewdly. Yes: the future bridegroom, Mr. Rochester himself, exercised over his intended a ceaseless surveillance: and it was from this sagacity—this guardedness of his—this perfect, clear consciousness of his fair one's defects—this obvious absence of passion in his sentiments towards her, that my ever-torturing pain arose.

I saw he was going to marry her, for family, perhaps political reasons; because her rank and connections suited him; I felt he had not given her his love, and that her qualifications were ill adapted to win from him that treasure. This was the point—this was where the nerve was touched and teased—this was where the fever was sustained and fed: *she could not charm him.*

If she had managed the victory at once, and he had yielded and sincerely laid his heart at her feet, I should have covered my face, turned to the wall, and (figuratively) have died to them. If Miss Ingram had been a good and noble woman, endowed with force, fervour, kindness, sense, I should have had one vital struggle with two tigers—jealousy and despair: then, my heart torn out and devoured, I should have admired her— acknowledged her excellence, and been quiet for the rest of my days: and the more absolute her superiority, the deeper would have been my admiration—the more truly tranquil my quiescence. But as matters really stood, to watch Miss Ingram's efforts at fascinating Mr. Rochester; to witness their repeated failure—herself unconscious that they did fail; vainly fancying that each shaft launched, hit the mark, and infatuatedly pluming herself on success, when her pride and self-complacency repelled further and further what she wished to allure—to witness *this,* was to be at once under ceaseless excitation and ruthless restraint.

Because, when she failed, I saw how she might have succeeded. Arrows that continually glanced off from Mr. Rochester's breast and fell harmless at his feet, might, I knew, if shot by a surer hand, have quivered keen in his proud heart—have called love into his stern eye, and softness into his sardonic face: or, better still, without weapons a silent conquest might have been won.

"Why can she not influence him more, when she is privileged to draw so near to him?" I asked myself. "Surely she cannot truly like him; or not like him with true affection! If she did, she need not coin her smiles so lavishly; flash her glances so unremittingly; manufacture airs so elaborate, graces so multitudinous. It seems to me, that she might, by merely sitting quietly at his side, saying little and looking less, get nigher his heart. I have seen in his face a far different expression from that which hardens it now while she is so vivaciously accosting him; but then it came of itself: it was not elicited by meretricious arts and calculated manœuvres; and one had but to accept it—to answer what he asked without pretension, to address him when needful without grimace—and it increased and grew kinder and more genial, and warmed one like a fostering sunbeam. How will she manage to please him when they are married? I do not think she will manage it: and yet it might be managed; and his wife might, I verily believe, be the very happiest woman the sun shines on."

I have not yet said anything condemnatory of Mr. Rochester's project of marrying for interest and connections. It surprised me when I first discovered that such was his intention: I had thought him a man unlikely to be influenced by motives so common-place in his choice of a wife; but the longer I considered the position, education, etc. of the parties, the less I felt justified in judging and blaming either him or Miss Ingram, for acting on conformity to ideas and principles instilled into them, doubtless, from their childhood. All their class held these principles: I supposed, then, they had reasons for holding them such as I could not fathom. it seemed to me that, were I a gentleman like him, I would take to my bosom only such a wife as I could love; but the very obviousness of the advantages to the husband's own happiness, offered by this plan, convinced me that there must be arguments against its general adoption of which I was quite ignorant: otherwise I felt sure all the world would act as I wished to act.

But in other points, as well as this, I was growing very lenient to my master: I was forgetting all his faults, for which I had once kept a sharp look-out. It had formerly been my endeavour to study all sides of his character: to take the bad with the good; and from the just weighing of both, to form an equitable judgment. Now I saw no bad. The sarcasm that had repelled, the harshness that had startled me once, were only like keen condiments in a choice dish: their presence was pungent, but their absence would be felt as comparatively insipid. And as for the vague something— was it a sinister or a sorrowful, a designing or a desponding expression?— that opened upon a careful observer, now and then, in his eye, and closed again before one could fathom the strange depth partially disclosed; that something which used to make me fear and shrink, as if I had been wandering amongst volcanic-looking hills, and had suddenly felt the ground quiver, and seen it gape: that something, I, at intervals, beheld still; and with throbbing heart, but not with palsied nerves. Instead of wishing to shun, I longed only to dare—to divine it; and I thought Miss Ingram happy, because one day she might look into the abyss at her leisure, explore its secrets and analyze their nature.

Meantime, while I thought only of my master and his future bride— saw only them, heard only their discourse, and considered only their movements of importance—the rest of the party were occupied with their own separate interests and pleasures. The ladies Lynn and Ingram continued to consort in solemn conferences; where they nodded their two turbans at each other, and held up their four hands in confronting gestures of surprise, or mystery, or horror, according to the theme on which their gossip ran, like a pair of magnified puppets. Mild Mrs. Dent talked with good-natured Mrs. Eshton; and the two sometimes bestowed a courteous word or smile on me. Sir George Lynn, Colonel Dent, and Mr. Eshton, discussed politics, or county affairs, or justice business. Lord Ingram flirted with Amy Eshton; Louisa played and sang to and with one of the Messrs. Lynn, and Mary Ingram listened languidly to the gallant speeches of the other. Sometimes all, as with one consent, suspended their by-play to observe and listen to the principal actors: for, after all, Mr. Rochester, and—because closely connected with him—Miss Ingram, were the life and soul of the party. If he was absent from the room an hour, a perceptible dullness seemed to steal over the spirits of his guests; and his reentrance was sure to give a fresh impulse to the vivacity of conversation.

The want of his animating influence appeared to be peculiarly felt one day that he had been summoned to Millcote on business, and was not likely to return till late. The afternoon was wet: a walk the party had proposed to take to see a gipsy camp, lately pitched on a common beyond Hay, was consequently deferred. Some of the gentlemen were gone to the stables: the younger ones, together with the younger ladies, were playing billiards in the billiard-room. The dowagers Ingram and Lynn sought solace in a quiet game at cards. Blanche Ingram, after having repelled, by supercilious taciturnity, some efforts of Mrs. Dent and Mrs. Eshton to draw her into conversation, had first murmured over some sentimental tunes and airs on the piano, and then, having fetched a novel from the library, had flung herself in haughty listlessness on a sofa, and prepared to beguile, by the spell of fiction, the tedious hours of absence. The room and house were silent: only now and then the merriment of the billiard players was heard from above.

It was verging on dusk, and the clock had already given warning of the hour to dress for dinner, when little Adèle, who knelt by me in the drawing-room window seat, exclaimed:—

"Voilà Monsieur Rochester, qui revient!"

I turned, and Miss Ingram darted forwards from her sofa: the others, too, looked up from their several occupations; for at the same time a crunching of wheels, and splashing tramp of horse-hoofs became audible on the wet gravel. A post-chaise was approaching.

"What can possess him to come home in that style?" said Miss Ingram. "He rode Mesrour (the black horse) did he not, when he went out? and Pilot was with him:—what has he done with the animals?"

As she said this, she approached her tall person and ample garments so near the window that I was obliged to bend back almost to the breaking of my spine: in her eagerness she did not observe me at first, but when she did, she curled her lip and moved to another casement. The post-chaise stopped; the driver rang the door-bell, and a gentleman alighted, attired in travelling garb; but it was not Mr. Rochester; it was a tall fashionable-looking man, a stranger.

"Provoking!" exclaimed Miss Ingram: "you tiresome monkey!" (apostrophizing Adèle) "who perched you up in the window to give false intelligence?" and she cast on me an angry glance, as if I were in fault.

Some parleying was audible in the hall, and soon the new comer entered. He bowed to Lady Ingram, as deeming her the eldest lady present.

"It appears I come at an inopportune time, madam," said he, "when my friend, Mr. Rochester, is from home; but I arrive from a very long journey, and I think I may presume so far on old and intimate acquaintance as to instal myself here till he returns."

His manner was polite; his accent, in speaking, struck me as being somewhat unusual,—not precisely foreign, but still not altogether English: his age might be about Mr. Rochester's,—between thirty and forty; his complexion was singularly sallow: otherwise he was a fine-looking man, at first sight especially. On closer examination, you detected something in his face that displeased: or rather, that failed to please. His features were regular, but too relaxed: his eye was large and well cut, but the life looking out of it was a tame, vacant life—at least so I thought.

The sound of the dressing-bell dispersed the party. It was not till after dinner that I saw him again: he then seemed quite at his ease. But I liked his physiognomy even less than before: it struck me as being, at the same time, unsettled and inanimate. His eye wandered, and had no meaning in its wandering: this gave him an odd look, such as I never remembered to have seen. For a handsome and not an unamiable-looking man, he repelled me exceedingly: there was no power in that smooth-skinned face of a full oval shape; no firmness in that aquiline nose, and small, cherry mouth; there was no thought on the low, even forehead; no command on that blank, brown eye.

As I sat in my usual nook, and looked at him with the light of the girandoles on the mantel-piece beaming full over him—for he occupied an armchair, drawn close to the fire, and kept shrinking still nearer, as if he were cold—I compared him with Mr. Rochester. I think (with deference be it spoken) the contrast could not be much greater between a sleek gander and a fierce falcon: between a meek sheep and the rough-coated keen-eyed dog, its guardian.

He had spoken of Mr. Rochester as an old friend. A curious friendship theirs must have been: a pointed illustration, indeed, of the old adage that "extremes meet."

Two or three of the gentlemen sat near him, and I caught at times scraps of their conversation across the room. At first I could not make much sense of what I heard; for the discourse of Louisa Eshton and Mary Ingram, who sat nearer to me, confused the fragmentary sentences that reached me at intervals. These last were discussing the stranger: they both called him "a beautiful man." Louisa said he was "a love of a creature," and she "adored him"; and Mary instanced his "pretty little mouth, and nice nose," as her ideal of the charming.

"And what a sweet-tempered forehead he has?" cried Louisa,—"so smooth—none of those frowning irregularities I dislike so much: and such a placid eye and smile!"

And then, to my great relief, Mr. Henry Lynn summoned them to the other side of the room, to settle some point about the deferred excursion to Hay Common.

I was now able to concentrate my attention on the group by the fire, and I presently gathered that the new comer was called Mr. Mason: then I learnt that he was but just arrived in England, and that he came from some hot country; which was the reason, doubtless, his face was so sallow, and that he sat so near the hearth, and wore a surtout in the house. Presently the words Jamaica, Kingston, Spanish Town, indicated the West Indies as his residence; and it was with no little surprise I gathered, ere long, that he had there first seen and become acquainted with Mr. Rochester. He spoke of his friend's dislike of the burning heats, the hurricanes, and rainy seasons of that region. I knew Mr. Rochester had been a traveller: Mrs. Fairfax had said so; but I thought the continent of Europe had bounded his wanderings: till now I had never heard a hint given to visits to more distant shores.

I was pondering these things, when an incident, and a somewhat unexpected one, broke the thread of my musings. Mr. Mason, shivering as some one chanced to open the door, asked for more coal to be put on the fire, which had burnt out its flame, though its mass of cinder still shone hot and red. The footman who brought the coal, in going out, stopped near Mr. Eshton's chair, and said something to him in a low voice, of which I heard only the words "old woman"—"quite troublesome."

"Tell her she shall be put in the stocks, if she does not take herself off," replied the magistrate.

"No—stop!" interrupted Colonel Dent. "Don't send her away, Eshton; we might turn the thing to account: better consult the ladies." And speaking aloud, he continued, "Ladies, you talked of going to Hay Common to visit the gipsy camp; Sam, here, says that one of the old Mother Bunches is in the servants' hall at this moment, and insists upon being brought in before 'the quality,' to tell them their fortunes. Would you like to see her?"

"Surely, Colonel," cried Lady Ingram, "you would not encourage such a low impostor? Dismiss her, by all means, at once!"

"But I cannot persuade her to go away, my lady," said the footman; "nor can any of the servants: Mrs. Fairfax is with her just now, entreating her to be gone; but she has taken a chair in the chimney-corner, and says nothing shall stir her from it till she gets leave to come in here."

"What does she want?" asked Mrs. Eshton.

" 'To tell the gentry their fortunes,' she says, ma'am: and she swears she must and will do it."

"What is she like?" inquired the Misses Eshton in a breath.

"A shockingly ugly old creature, Miss; almost as black as a crock."

"Why, she's a real sorceress!" cried Frederick Lynn. "Let us have her in, of course."

"To be sure," rejoined his brother; "it would be a thousand pities to throw away such a chance of fun."

"My dear boys, what are you thinking about?" exclaimed Lady Lynn.

"I cannot possibly countenance any such inconsistent proceeding," chimed in the Dowager Ingram.

"Indeed, mama, but you can—and will," pronounced the haunty voice of Blanche, as she turned round on the piano-stool; where till now she had sat silent, apparently examining sundry sheets of music. "I have a curiosity to hear my fortune told: therefore, Sam, order the beldame forwards."

"My darling Blanche! recollect—"

"I do—I recollect all you can suggest; and I must have my will—quick, Sam!"

"Yes—yes—yes!" cried all the juveniles, both ladies and gentlemen. "Let her come—it will be excellent sport!"

The footman still lingered. "She looks such a rough one," said he.

"Go!" ejaculated Miss Ingram, and the man went.

Excitement instantly seized the whole party: a running fire of raillery and jests was proceeding when Sam returned.

"She won't come now," said he. "She says its not her mission to appear before the 'vulgar herd' (them's her words). I must show her into a room by herself, and then those who wish to consult her must go to her one by one."

"You see now, my queenly Blanche," began Lady Ingram, "she encroaches. Be advised, my angel-girl—and—"

"Show her into the library, of course," cut in the "angel girl." "It is not my mission to listen to her before the vulgar herd either: I mean to have her all to myself. Is there a fire in the library?"

"Yes, ma'am—but she looks such a tinkler."

"Cease that chatter, blockhead! and do my bidding."

Again Sam vanished; and mystery, animation, expectation rose to full flow once more.

"She's ready now," said the footman, as he re-appeared. "She wishes to know who will be her first visitor."

"I think I had better just look in upon her before any of the ladies go," said Colonel Dent.

"Tell her, Sam, a gentleman is coming."

Sam went and returned.

"She says, sir, that she'll have no gentlemen; they need not trouble themselves to come near her: nor," he added, with difficulty suppressing a titter, "any ladies either, except the young and single."

"By Jove, she has taste!" exclaimed Henry Lynn.

Miss Ingram rose solemnly: "I go first," she said, in a tone which might have befitted the leader of a forlorn hope, mounting a breach in the van of his men.

"Oh, my best! oh, my dearest! pause—reflect!" was her mama's cry; but she swept past her in stately silence, passed through the door which Colonel Dent held open, and we heard her enter the library.

A comparative silence ensued. Lady Ingram thought it "*le cas*" to wring her hands: which she did accordingly. Miss Mary declared she felt, for her part, she never dared venture. Amy and Louisa Eshton tittered under their breath, and looked a little frightened.

The minutes passed very slowly: fifteen were counted before the library-door again opened. Miss Ingram returned to us through the arch.

Would she laugh? Would she take it as a joke? All eyes met her with a glance of eager curiosity, and she met all eyes with one of rebuff and coldness: she walked stiffly to her seat, and took it in silence.

"Well, Blanche?" said Lord Ingram.

"What did she say, sister?" asked Mary.

"What did you think? How do you feel? Is she a real fortune-teller?" demanded the Misses Eshton.

"Now, now, good people," returned Miss Ingram, "don't press upon me. Really your organs of wonder and credulity are easily excited: you seem by the importance you all—my good mama included—ascribe to this matter—absolutely to believe we have a genuine witch in the house, who is in close alliance with the old gentleman. I have seen a gipsy-vagabond; she has practised in hackneyed fashion the science of palmistry, and told me what such people usually tell. My whim is gratified; and now I think Mr. Eshton will do well to put the hag in the stocks to-morrow morning, as he threatened."

Miss Ingram took a book, leant back in her chair, and so declined further conversation. I watched her for nearly half an hour: during all that time she never turned a page, and her face grew momently darker, more dissatisfied, and more sourly expressive of disappointment. She had obviously not heard anything to her advantage; and it seemed to me, from her prolonged fit of gloom and taciturnity, that she herself, notwithstanding her professed indifference, attached undue importance to whatever revelations had been made her.

Meantime, Mary Ingram, Amy and Louisa Eshton, declared they dared not go alone; and yet they all wished to go. A negotiation was opened through the medium of the ambassador, Sam; and after much pacing to and fro, till, I think, the said Sam's calves must have ached with the exercise, permission was at last, with great difficulty, extorted from the rigorous Sybil, for the three to wait upon her in a body.

Their visit was not so still as Miss Ingram's had been: we heard hysterical giggling and little shrieks proceeding from the library; and at the end of about twenty minutes they burst the door open, and came running across the hall, as if they were half-scared out of their wits.

"I'm sure she is something not right!" they cried, one and all. "She told us such things! She knows all about us!" and they sank breathless into the various seats the gentlemen hastened to bring them.

Pressed for further explanation, they declared she had told them of things they had said and done when they were mere children; described books and ornaments they had in their boudoirs at home: keepsakes that different relations had presented to them. They affirmed that she had even divined their thoughts, and had whispered in the ear of each the name of the person she liked best in the world, and informed them of what they most wished for.

Here the gentlemen interposed with earnest petitions to be further enlightened on these two last-named points; but they got only blushes, ejaculations, tremors, and titters, in return for their importunity. The matrons, meantime, offered vinaigrettes and wielded fans; and again and again reiterated the expression of their concern that their warning had not been taken in time; and the elder gentlemen laughed, and the younger urged their services on the agitated fair ones.

In the midst of the tumult, and while my eyes and ears were fully engaged in the scene before me, I heard a hem close at my elbow: I turned, and saw Sam.

"If you please, Miss, the gipsy declares that there is another young single lady in the room who has not been to her yet, and she swears she will not go till she has seen all. I thought it must be you: there is no one else for it. What shall I tell her?"

"Oh, I will go by all means," I answered; and I was glad of the unexpected opportunity to gratify my much-excited curiosity. I slipped out of the room, unobserved by any eye—for the company were gathered in one mass about the trembling trio just returned—and I closed the door quietly behind me.

"If you like, Miss," said Sam, "I'll wait in the hall for you; and if she frightens you, just call and I'll come in."

"No, Sam, return to the kitchen: I am not in the least afraid." Nor was I; but I was a good deal interested and excited.

. . . .

Chapter 19

The library looked tranquil enough as I entered it, and the Sybil—if Sybil she were, was seated snugly enough in an easy chair at the chimney-corner. She had on a red cloak and a black bonnet: or rather, a broad-brimmed gipsy hat, tied down with a striped handkerchief under her chin. An extinguished candle stood on the table; she was bending over the fire, and seemed reading in a little black book, like a prayer-book, by the light of the blaze: she muttered the words to herself, as most old women do, while she read; she did not desist immediately on my entrance: it appeared she wished to finish a paragraph.

I stood on the rug and warmed my hands, which were rather cold with sitting at a distance from the drawing-room fire. I felt now as composed as ever I did in my life: there was nothing in the gipsy's appearance to trouble one's calm. She shut her book and slowly looked up; her hat-brim partially shaded her face, yet I could see, as she raised it, that it was a strange one. It looked all brown and black: elf-locks bristled out from beneath a white band which passed under her chin, and came half over her cheeks or rather jaws; her eye confronted me at once, with a bold and direct gaze.

"Well, and you want your fortune told?" she said in a voice as decided as her glance, as harsh as her features.

"I don't care about it, mother; you may please yourself: but I ought to warn you I have no faith."

"It's like your impudence to say so: I expected it of you; I heard it in your step as you crossed the threshold."

"Did you? You've a quick ear."

"I have; and a quick eye, and a quick brain."

"You need them all in your trade."

"I do; especially when I've customers like you to deal with. Why don't you tremble?"

"I'm not cold."

"Why don't you turn pale?"

"I am not sick."

"Why don't you consult my art?"

"I'm not silly."

The old crone "nichered" a laugh under her bonnet and bandage: she then drew out a short black pipe, and lighting it, began to smoke. Having indulged awhile in this sedative, she raised her bent body, took the pipe from her lips, and while gazing steadily at the fire, said 'very deliberately:—

"You are cold; you are sick; and you are silly."

"Prove it," I rejoined.

"I will; in few words. You are cold, because you are alone: no contact strikes the fire from you that is in you. You are sick; because the best of feelings, the highest and the sweetest given to man, keeps far away from you. You are silly, because, suffer as you may, you will not beckon it to approach; nor will you stir one step to meet it where it waits you."

She again put her short, black pipe to her lips and renewed her smoking with vigour.

"You might say all that to almost anyone who, you knew, lived as a solitary dependant in a great house."

"I might say it to almost any one; but would it be true of almost any one?"

"In my circumstances."

"Yes; just so, in *your* circumstances: but find me another precisely placed as you are."

"It would be easy to find you thousands."

"You could scarcely find me one. If you knew it, you are peculiarly situated: very near happiness; yes; within reach of it. The materials are all prepared; there only wants a movement to combine them. Chance laid them somewhat apart; let them be once approached and bliss results."

"I don't understand enigmas. I never could guess a riddle in my life."

"If you wish me to speak more plainly, show me your palm."

"And I must cross it with silver, I suppose?"

"To be sure."

I gave her a shilling; she put it into an old stocking-foot which she took out of her pocket, and having tied it round and returned it, she told me to hold out my hand. I did. She approached her face to the palm, and pored over it without touching it.

"It is too fine," said she. "I can make nothing of such a hand as that; almost without lines: besides, what is in a palm? Destiny is not written there."

"I believe you," said I.

"No," she continued, "it is in the face: on the forehead, about the eyes, in the eyes themselves, in the lines of the mouth. Kneel, and lift up your head."

"Ah! now you are coming to reality," I said as I obeyed her. "I shall begin to put some faith in you presently."

I knelt within half a yard of her. She stirred the fire, so that a ripple of light broke from the disturbed coal: the glare, however, as she sat, only threw her face into deeper shadow: mine, it illumined.

"I wonder with what feelings you came to me to-night," she said, when she had examined me a while. "I wonder what thoughts are busy in your heart during all the hours you sit in yonder room with the fine people flitting before you like shapes in a magic-lantern: just as little sympathetic communion passing between you and them, as if they were really mere shadows of human forms and not the actual substance."

"I feel tired often, sleepy sometimes; but seldom sad."

"Then you have some secret hope to buoy you up and please you with whispers of the future?"

"Not I. The utmost I hope is, to save money enough out of my earnings to set up a school some day in a little house rented by myself."

"A mean nutriment for the spirit to exist on: and sitting in that window-seat (you see I know your habits)——"

"You have learned them from the servants."

"Ah! you think yourself sharp. Well—perhaps I have: to speak truth, I have an acquaintance with one of them—Mrs. Poole——"

I started to my feet when I heard the name.

"You have—have you?" thought I; "there is diablerie in the business after all, then!"

"Don't be alarmed," continued the strange being; "she's a safe hand, is Mrs. Poole: close and quiet: any one may repose confidence in her. But, as I was saying: sitting in that window-seat, do you think of nothing but your future school? Have you no present interest in any of the company who occupy the sofas and chairs before you? Is there not one face you study? One figure whose movements you follow with, at least, curiosity?"

"I like to observe faces, and all the figures."

"But do you never single one from the rest—or it may be, two?"

"I do frequently; when the gestures or looks of a pair seem telling a tale: it amuses me to watch them."

"What tale do you like best to hear?"

"Oh, I have not much choice! They generally run on the same theme—courtship; and promise to end in the same catastrophe—marriage."

"And do you like that monotonous theme?"

"Positively, I don't care about it: it is nothing to me."

"Nothing to you? When a lady, young and full of life and health, charming with beauty and endowed with the gifts of rank and fortune, sits and smiles in the eyes of a gentleman you——"

"I what?"

"You know—and, perhaps, think well of."

"I don't know the gentlemen here. I have scarcely interchanged a syllable with one of them; and as to thinking well of them, I consider some respectable and stately, and middle-aged, and others young, dashing, handsome and lively: but certainly they are all at liberty to be the recipients of whose smiles they please, without my feeling disposed to consider the transaction of any moment to me."

"You don't know the gentlemen here? You have not exchanged a syllable with one of them? Will you say that of the master of the house?"

"He is not at home."

"A profound remark! A most ingenious quibble! He went to Millcote this morning, and will be back here to-night, or to-morrow: does that circumstance exclude him from the list of your acquaintance—blot him, as it were, out of existence?"

"No: but I can scarcely see what Mr. Rochester has to do with the theme you had introduced."

"I was talking of ladies smiling in the eyes of gentlemen; and of late so many smiles have been shed into Mr. Rochester's eyes that they overflow like two cups filled above the brim: have you never remarked that?"

"Mr. Rochester has a right to enjoy the society of his guests."

"No question about his right: but have you never observed that, of all the tales told here about matrimony, Mr. Rochester has been favoured with the most lively and the most continuous?"

"The eagerness of a listener quickens the tongue of a narrator." I said this rather to myself than to the gipsy; whose strange talk, voice, manner, had by this time wrapped me in a kind of dream. One unexpected sentence came from her lips after another, till I got involved in a web of mystification; and wondered what unseen spirit had been sitting for weeks by my heart watching its workings, and taking record of every pulse.

"Eagerness of a listener!" repeated she: "yes; Mr. Rochester has sat by the hour, his ear inclined to the fascinating lips that took such delight in their task of communicating; and Mr. Rochester was so willing to receive, and looked so grateful for this pastime given him: you have noticed this?"

"Grateful! I cannot remember detecting gratitude in his face."

"Detecting! You have analyzed, then. And what did you detect, if not gratitude?"

I said nothing.

"You have seen love: have you not?—and, looking forward, you have seen him married, and beheld his bride happy?"

"Humph! Not exactly. Your witch's skill is rather at fault sometimes."

"What the devil have you seen, then?"

"Never mind: I came here to inquire, not to confess. Is it known that Mr. Rochester is to be married?"

"Yes; and to the beautiful Miss Ingram."

"Shortly?"

"Appearances would warrant that conclusion; and, no doubt (though, with an audacity that wants chastising out of you, you seem to question it), they will be a superlatively happy pair. He must love such a handsome, noble, witty, accomplished lady; and probably she loves him: or, if not his person, at least his purse. I know she considers the Rochester estate eligible to the last degree; though (God pardon me!) I told her something on that point about an hour ago, which made her look wondrous grave: the corners of her mouth fell half an inch. I would advise her black-aviced suitor to look out: if another comes, with a longer or clearer rent-roll,—he's dished——"

"But, mother, I did not come to hear Mr. Rochester's fortune: I came to hear my own; and you have told me nothing of it."

"Your fortune is yet doubtful: when I examined your face, one trait contradicted another. Chance has meted you a measure of happiness: that I know. I knew it before I came here this evening. She has laid it carefully on one side for you. I saw her do it. It depends on yourself to stretch out your hand, and take it up: but whether you will do so, is the problem I study. Kneel again on the rug."

"Don't keep me long; the fire scorches me."

I knelt. She did not stoop towards me, but only gazed leaning back in her chair. She began muttering:

"The flame flickers in the eye; the eye shines like dew; it looks soft and full of feeling; it smiles at my jargon: it is susceptible; impression follows impression through its clear sphere; where it ceases to smile, it is sad; an unconscious lassitude weighs on the lid: that signifies melancholy resulting from loneliness. It turns from me; it will not suffer farther scrutiny; it seems to deny, by a mocking glance, the truth of the discoveries I have already made,—to disown the charge both of sensibility and chagrin: its pride and reserve only confirm me in my opinion. The eye is favourable.

"As to the mouth, it delights at times in laughter: it is disposed to impart all that the brain conceives; though I dare say it would be silent on much the heart experiences. Mobile and flexible, it was never intended to be compressed in the eternal silence of solitude: it is a mouth which should speak much and smile often, and have human affection for its interlocutor. That feature too is propitious.

"I see no enemy to a fortunate issue but in the brow; and that brow professes to say,—'I can live alone, if self-respect and circumstances require me so to do. I need not sell my soul to buy bliss. I have an inward treasure, born with me, which can keep me alive if all extraneous delights should be withheld; or offered only at a price I cannot afford to give.' The forehead declares, 'Reason sits firm and holds the reins, and she will not let the feelings burst sway and hurry her to wild chasms. The passions may rage furiously, like true heathens, as they are; and the desires may imagine all sorts of vain things: but judgment shall still have the last word in every argument, and the casting vote in every decision. Strong wind, earthquake-shock, and fire may pass by: I shall follow the guiding but of that still small voice which interprets the dictates of conscience.'

"Well said, forehead; your declaration shall be respected. I have formed my plans—right plans I deem them—and in them I have attended to the claims of conscience, the counsels of reason. I know how soon youth would fade and bloom perish, if, in the cup of bliss offered, but one dreg

of shame, or one flavour of remorse were detected; and I do not want sacrifice, sorrow, dissolution—such is not my taste. I wish to foster, not to
blight—to earn gratitude, not to wring tears of blood—no, nor of brine:
my harvest must be in smiles, in endearments, in sweet—That will do.
I think I rave in a kind of exquisite delirium. I should wish now to protract this moment *ad infinitum;* but I dare not. So far I have governed
myself thoroughly. I have acted as I inwardly swore I would act; but farther might try me beyond my strength. Rise, Miss Eyre: leave me; 'the
play is played out.' "

Where was I? Did I wake or sleep? Had I been dreaming? Did I dream
still? The old woman's voice had changed: her accent, her gesture, and
all were familiar to me as my own face in the glass—as the speech of my
own tongue. I got up, but did not go. I looked; I stirred the fire, and I
looked again: but she drew her bonnet and her bandage closer about her
face, and again beckoned me to depart. The flame illuminated her hand
stretched out: roused now, and on the alert for discoveries, I at once
noticed that hand. It was no more the withered limb of eld than my own:
it was a rounded supple member, with smooth fingers, symmetrically
turned; a broad ring flashed on the little finger, and stooping forward,
I looked at it, and saw a gem I had seen a hundred times before. Again
I looked at the face; which was no longer turned from me—on the contrary, the bonnet was doffed, the bandage displaced, the head advanced.

"Well, Jane, do you know me?" asked the familiar voice.

"Only take off the red cloak, sir, and then——"

"But the string is in a knot—help me."

"Break it, sir?"

"There, then—'Off, ye lendings!' " And Mr. Rochester stepped out of
his disguise.

"Now, sir, what a strange idea!"

"But well carried out, eh? Don't you think so?"

"With the ladies you must have managed well."

"But not with you?"

"You did not act the character of a gipsy with me."

"What character did I act? My own?"

"No; some unaccountable one. In short, I believe you have been trying to draw me out—or in: you have been talking nonsense to make me
talk nonsense. It is scarcely fair, sir."

"Do you forgive me, Jane?"

"I cannot tell till I have thought it all over. If, on reflection, I find I
have fallen into no great absurdity, I shall try to forgive you: but it was
not right."

"Oh! you have been very correct—very careful, very sensible."

I reflected, and thought, on the whole, I had. It was a comfort: but,
indeed, I had been on my guard almost from the beginning of the interview. Something of masquerade I suspected. I knew gipsies and fortune-
tellers did not express themselves as this seeming old woman had
expressed herself: besides, I had noted her feigned voice, her anxiety to
conceal her features. But my mind had been running on Grace Poole—
that living enigma, that mystery of mysteries, as I considered her: I had
never thought of Mr. Rochester.

"Well," said he, "what are you musing about? What does that grave
smile signify?"

"Wonder and self-congratulation, sir. I have your permission to retire now, I suppose?"

"No: stay a moment; and tell me what the people in the drawing-room yonder are doing."

"Discussing the gipsy, I daresay."

"Sit down!—Let he hear what they said about me."

"I had better not stay long, sir: it must be near eleven o'clock. Oh! are you aware, Mr. Rochester, that a stranger has arrived here since you left this morning?"

"A stranger!—no: who can it be? I expected no one: is he gone?"

"No: he said he had known you long, and that he could take the liberty of installing himself here till you returned."

"The devil he did! Did he give his name?"

"His name is Mason, sir; and he comes from the West Indies: from Spanish Town, in Jamaica, I think."

Mr. Rochester was standing near me: he had taken my hand, as if to lead me to a chair. As I spoke, he gave my wrist a convulsive grip; the smile on his lips froze: apparently a spasm caught his breath.

"Mason!—the West Indies!" he said, in the tone one might fancy a speaking automaton to enounce its single words; "Mason!—the West Indies!" he reiterated; and he went over the syllables three times, growing, in the intervals of speaking, whiter than ashes; he hardly seemed to know what he was doing.

"Do you feel ill, sir?" I inquired.

"Jane, I've got a blow;—I've got a blow, Jane!" he staggered.

"Oh!—lean on me, sir."

"Jane, you offered me your shoulder once before; let me have it now."

"Yes, sir, yes; and my arm."

He sat down, and made me sit beside him. Holding my hand in both his own, he chafed it; gazing on me, at the same time with the most troubled and dreary look.

"My little friend!" said he, "I wish I were in a quiet island with only you; and trouble, and danger, and hideous recollections removed from me."

"Can I help you, sir?—I'd give my life to serve you."

"Jane, if aid is wanted, I'll seek it at your hands: I promise you that."

"Thank you, sir: tell me what to do,—I'll try, at least, to do it."

"Fetch me now, Jane, a glass of wine from the dining-room: they will be at supper there; and tell me if Mason is with them, and what he is doing."

I went. I found all the party in the dining-room at supper, as Mr. Rochester had said; they were not seated at table,—the supper was arranged on the sideboard; each had taken what he chose, and they stood about here and there in groups, their plates and glasses in their hands. Every one seemed in high glee; laughter and conversation were general and animated. Mr. Mason stood near the fire, talking to Colonel and Mrs. Dent, and appeared as merry as any of them. I filled a wine-glass (I saw Miss Ingram watch me frowningly as I did so: she thought I was taking a liberty, I dare say), and returned to the library.

Mr. Rochester's extreme pallor had disappeared, and he looked once more firm and stern. He took the glass from my hand.

"Here is to your health, ministrant spirit!" he said: he swallowed the contents and returned it to me. "What are they doing, Jane?"

"Laughing and talking, sir."

"They don't look grave and mysterious, as if they had heard something strange?"

"Not at all:—they are full of jests and gaiety."

"And Mason?"

"He was laughing too."

"If all these people came in a body and spat at me, what would you do, Jane?"

"Turn them out of the room, sir, if I could."

He half smiled. "But if I were to go to them, and they only looked at me coldly, and whispered sneeringly amongst each other, and then dropt off and left me one by one, what then? Would you go with them?"

"I rather think not, sir: I should have more pleasure in staying with you."

"To comfort me?"

"Yes, sir, to comfort you, as well as I could."

"And if they laid you under a ban for adhering to me?"

"I, probably, should know nothing about their ban; and if I did, I should care nothing about it."

"Then, you could dare censure for my sake?"

"I could dare it for the sake of any friend who deserved my adherence; as you, I am sure do."

"Go back now into the room; step quietly up to Mason, and whisper in his ear that Mr. Rochester is come and wishes to see him: show him in here, and then leave me."

"Yes, sir."

I did his behest. The company all stared at me as I passed straight among them. I sought Mr. Mason, delivered the message, and preceded him from the room: I ushered him into the library, and then I went up stairs.

At a late hour, after I had been in bed some time, I heard the visitors repair to their chambers: I distinguished Mr. Rochester's voice, and heard him say, "This way, Mason; this is your room."

He spoke cheerfully: the gay tones set my heart at ease. I was soon asleep.

* * * * * * *

Chapter 20

I had forgotten to draw my curtain, which I usually did; and also to let down my window-blind. The consequence was, that when the moon, which was full and bright (for the night was fine) came in her course to that space in the sky opposite my casement, and looked in at me through the unveiled panes, her glorious gaze aroused me. Awaking in the dead of night, I opened my eyes on her disk—silver-white and crystal-clear. It was beautiful, but too solemn: I half rose, and stretched my arm to draw the curtain.

Good God! What a cry!

The night—its silence—its rest, was rent in twain by a savage, a sharp, a shrilly sound that ran from end to end of Thornfield Hall.

My pulse stopped: my heart stood still; my stretched arm was paralyzed.

The cry died, and was not renewed. Indeed, whatever being uttered that fearful shriek could not soon repeat it: not the widest-winged condor on the Andes could, twice in succession, send out such a yell from the cloud shrouding his eyrie. The thing delivering such utterance must rest ere it could repeat the effort.

It came out of the third story; for it passed overhead. And overhead—yes, in the room just above my chamber-ceiling—I now heard a struggle: a deadly one it seemed from the noise; and a half-smothered voice shouted—

"Help! help! help!" three times rapidly.

"Will no one come?" it cried; and then while the staggering and stamping went on wildly I distinguished through plank and plaster:—

"Rochester! Rochester! for God's sake, come!"

A chamber-door opened: some one ran, or rushed, along the gallery. Another step stamped on the flooring above, and something fell; and there was silence.

I had put on some clothes, though horror shook all my limbs: I issued from my apartment. The sleepers were all aroused: ejaculations, terrified murmurs sounded in every room; door after door unclosed; one looked out and another looked out; the gallery filled. Gentlemen and ladies alike had quitted their beds; and "Oh! what is it?"—"Who is hurt?"—"What has happened?"—"Fetch a light!"—"Is it fire?"—"Are there robbers?"—"Where shall we run?" was demanded confusedly on all hands. But for the moonlight they would have been in complete darkness. They ran to and fro; they crowded together: some sobbed, some stumbled: the confusion was inextricable.

"Where the devil is Rochester?" cried Colonel Dent. "I cannot find him in his bed."

"Here! here!" was shouted in return. "Be composed, all of you: I'm coming."

And the door at the end of the gallery opened, and Mr. Rochester advanced with a candle: he had just descended from the upper story. One of the ladies ran to him directly; she seized his arm: it was Miss Ingram.

"What awful event has taken place?" said she. "Speak! let us know the worst at once."

"But don't pull me down or strangle me," he replied: for the Misses Eshton were clinging about him now; and the two dowagers, in vast white wrappers, were bearing down on him like ships in full sail.

"All's right!—all's right!" he cried. "It's a mere rehearsal of Much Ado About Nothing. Ladies, keep off; or I shall wax dangerous."

And dangerous he looked: his black eyes darted sparks. Calming himself by an effort he added:—

"A servant has had the nightmare; that is all. She's an excitable, nervous person: she construed her dream into an apparition, or something of that sort, no doubt; and has taken a fit with fright. Now, then I must see you all back into your rooms; for, till the house is settled, she cannot be looked after. Gentlemen, have the goodness to set the ladies the example. Miss Ingram, I am sure you will not fail in evincing superiority to idle terrors. Amy and Louisa, return to your nests like a pair of doves, as you are. Mesdames," (to the dowagers) "you will take cold to a dead certainty, if you stay in this chill gallery any longer."

And so, by dint of alternate coaxing and commanding, he contrived to get them all once more enclosed in their separate dormitories. I did not wait to be ordered back to mine; but retreated unnoticed: as unnoticed I had left it.

Not, however, to go to bed: on the contrary, I began and dressed myself carefully. The sounds I had heard after the scream, and the words that had been uttered, had probably been heard only by me; for they had proceeded from the room above mine: but they assured me that it was not a servant's dream which had thus struck horror through the house; and that the explanation Mr. Rochester had given was merely an invention framed to pacify his guests. I dressed, then, to be ready for emergencies. When dressed, I sat a long time by the window, looking out over the silent grounds and silvered fields, and waiting for I knew not what. It seemed to me that some event must follow the strange cry, struggle, and call.

No: stillness returned: each murmur and movement ceased gradually, and in about an hour Thornfield Hall was again as hushed as a desert. It seemed that sleep and night had resumed their empire. Meantime the moon declined: she was about to set. Not liking to sit in the cold and darkness, I thought I would lie down on my bed, dressed as I was. I left the window, and moved with little noise across the carpet; as I stooped to take off my shoes, a cautious hand tapped low at the door.

"Am I wanted?" I asked.

"Are you up?" asked the voice I expected to hear, viz., my master's.

"Yes, sir."

"And dressed?"

"Yes."

"Come out, then, quietly."

I obeyed. Mr. Rochester stood in the gallery, holding a light.

"I want you," he said: "come this way: take your time, and make no noise."

My slippers were thin: I could walk the matted floor as softly as a cat. He glided up the gallery and up the stairs, and stopped in the dark, low corridor of the fateful third story: I had followed and stood at his side.

"Have you a sponge in your room?" he asked in a whisper.

"Yes, sir."

"Have you any salts—volatile salts?"

"Yes."

"Go back and fetch both."

I returned, sought the sponge on the wash-stand, the salts in my drawer, and once more retraced my steps. He still waited; he held a key in his hand: approaching one of the small, black doors, he put it in the lock; he paused and addressed me again.

"You don't turn sick at the sight of blood?"

"I think I shall not: I have never been tried yet."

I felt a thrill while I answered him; but no coldness, and no faintness.

"Just give me your hand," he said; "it will not do to risk a fainting fit."

I put my fingers into his. "Warm and steady," was his remark: he turned the key and opened the door.

I saw a room I remembered to have seen before; the day Mrs. Fairfax showed me over the house: it was hung with tapestry; but the tapestry was now looped up in one part, and there was a door apparent, which had then been concealed. This door was open; a light shone out of the room within: I heard thence a snarling, snatching sound, almost like a dog quarrelling. Mr. Rochester, putting down his candle, said to me, "wait a minute," and he went forward to the inner apartment. A shout of laughter greeted his entrance; noisy at first, and terminating in Grace Poole's own goblin ha! ha! *She* then was there. He made some sort of arrangement, without speaking: though I heard a low voice address him: he came out and closed the door behind him.

"Here, Jane!" he said; and I walked round to the other side of a large bed, which with its drawn curtains concealed a considerable portion of the chamber. An easy-chair was near the bed-head: a man sat in it, dressed with the exception of his coat; he was still; his head leant back; his eyes were closed. Mr. Rochester held the candle over him; I recognised in his pale and seemingly lifeless face—the stranger, Mason: I saw too that his linen on one side, and one arm, was almost soaked in blood.

"Hold the candle," said Mr. Rochester, and I took it; he fetched a basin of water from the wash-stand: "Hold that," said he. I obeyed. He took the sponge, dipped it in and moistened the corpse-like face: he asked for my smelling-bottle, and applied it to the nostrils. Mr. Mason shortly unclosed his eyes; he groaned. Mr. Rochester opened the shirt of the wounded man, whose arm and shoulder were bandaged: he sponged away blood, trickling fast down.

"Is there immediate danger?" murmured Mr. Mason.

"Pooh! No—a mere scratch. Don't be so overcome, man: bear up! I'll fetch a surgeon for you now, myself: you'll be able to be removed by morning, I hope. Jane—" he continued.

"Sir?"

"I shall have to leave you in this room with this gentleman, for an hour, or perhaps two hours; you will sponge the blood as I do when it returns: if he feels faint, you will put the glass of water on that stand to his lips and your salts to his nose. You will not speak to him on any pretext—and—Richard—it will be at the peril of your life if you speak to her: open your lips—agitate yourself—and I'll not answer for the consequences."

Again the poor man groaned: he looked as if he dared not move: fear, either of death or of something else, appeared almost to paralyze him. Mr. Rochester put the now bloody sponge into my hand, and I proceeded to use it as he had done. He watched me a second, then saying, "Remember!—No conversation," he left the room. I experienced a strange feeling as the key grated in the lock, and the sound of his retreating step ceased to be heard.

Here then I was in the third story, fastened into one of its mystic cells; night around me; a pale and bloody spectacle under my eyes and hands; a murderess hardly separated from me by a single door: yes—that was appalling—the rest I could bear; but I shuddered at the thought of Grace Poole bursting out upon me.

I must keep to my post, however. I must watch this ghastly countenance—these blue, still lips forbidden to unclose—these eyes now shut, now opening, now wandering through the room, now fixing on me, and ever glazed with the dullness of horror. I must dip my hand again and again in the basin of blood and water, and wipe away the trickling gore. I must see the light of the unsnuffed candle wane on my employment; the shadows darken on the wrought, antique tapestry round me, and grow black under the hangings of the vast old bed, and quiver strangely over the doors of a great cabinet opposite—whose front, divided into twelve panels, bore in grim design, the heads of the twelve apostles, each enclosed in its separate panel as in a frame; while above them at the top rose an ebon crucifix and a dying Christ.

According as the shifting obscurity and flickering gleam hovered here or glanced there, it was now the bearded physician, Luke, that bent his brow; now St. John's long hair that waved; and anon the devilish face of Judas, that grew out of the panel and seemed gathering life and threatening a revelation of the arch-traitor—of Satan himself—in his subordinate's form.

Amidst all this, I had to listen as well as watch: to listen for the movements of the wild beast or the fiend in yonder side den. But since Mr. Rochester's visit it seemed spellbound: all the night I heard but three sounds at three long intervals,—a step creak, a momentary renewal of the snarling, canine noise, and a deep human groan.

Then my own thoughts worried me. What crime was this, that lived incarnate in this sequestered mansion, and could neither be expelled or subdued by the owner?—What mystery, that broke out, now in fire and now in blood, at the deadest hours of night?—What creature was it, that, masked in an ordinary woman's face and shape, uttered the voice, now of a mocking demon, and anon of a carrion-seeking bird of prey?

And this man I bent over—this common-place, quiet stranger—how had he become involved in the web of horror? and why had the Fury flown at him? What made him seek this quarter of the house at an untimely season, when he should have been asleep in bed? I had heard Mr. Rochester assign him an apartment below—what brought him here? And why, now, was he so tame under the violence or treachery done him? Why did he so quietly submit to the concealment Mr. Rochester enforced? Why *did* Mr. Rochester enforce this concealment? His guest had been outraged, his own life on a former occasion had been hideously plotted against; and both attempts he smothered in secrecy and sank in oblivion! Lastly, I saw Mr. Mason was submissive to Mr. Rochester; that the impetuous will of the latter held complete sway over the inertness of the former: the few words which had passed between them assured me of this. It was evident that in their former intercourse the passive disposition of the one had been habitually influenced by the active energy of the other: whence then had arisen Mr. Rochester's dismay when he heard of Mr. Mason's arrival? Why had the mere name of this unresisting individual—whom his word now sufficed to control like a child—fallen on him, a few hours since, as a thunderbolt might fall on an oak?

Oh! I could not forget his look and his paleness when he whispered: "Jane, I have got a blow—I have got a blow, Jane." I could not forget how the arm had trembled which he rested on my shoulder: and it was no light matter which could thus bow the resolute spirit and thrill the vigorous frame of Fairfax Rochester.

"When will he come? When will he come?" I cried inwardly, as the night lingered and lingered—as my bleeding patient drooped, moaned, sickened: and neither day nor aid arrived. I had, again and again, held the water to Mason's white lips; again and again offered him the stimulating salts: my efforts seemed ineffectual: either bodily or mental suffering, or loss of blood, or all three combined, were fast prostrating his strength. He moaned so, and looked so weak, wild, and lost, I feared he was dying; and I might not even speak to him!

The candle, wasted at last, went out; as it expired, I perceived streaks of grey light edging the window curtains: dawn was then approaching. Presently I heard Pilot bark far below, out of his distant kennel in the courtyard: hope revived. Nor was it unwarranted: in five minutes more the grating key, the yielding lock, warned my my watch was relieved. It could not have lasted more than two hours: many a week has seemed shorter.

Mr. Rochester entered, and with him the surgeon he had been to fetch.

"Now, Carter, be on the alert," he said to this last: "I give you but half an hour for dressing the wound, fastening the bandages, getting the patient down stairs and all."

"But is he fit to move, sir?"

"No doubt of it; it is nothing serious: he is nervous, his spirits must be kept up. Come set to work."

Mr. Rochester drew back the thick curtain, drew up the holland blind, let in all the daylight he could; and I was surprised and cheered to see how far dawn was advanced: what rosy streaks were beginning to brighten the east. Then he approached Mason, whom the surgeon was already handling.

"Now, my good fellow, how are you?" he asked.

"She's done for me, I fear," was the faint reply.

"Not a whit!—courage! This day fortnight you'll hardly be a pin the worse of it: you've lost a little blood; that's all. Carter, assure him there's no danger."

"I can do that conscientiously," said Carter, who had now undone the bandages; "only I wish I could have got here sooner: he would not have bled so much—but how is this? The flesh on the shoulder is torn as well as cut. This wound was not done with a knife: there have been teeth here?"

"She bit me," he murmured. "She worried me like a tigress, when Rochester got the knife from her."

"You should not have yielded: you should have grappled with her at once," said Mr. Rochester.

"But under such circumstances, what could one do?" returned Mason. "Oh, it was frightful!" he added, shuddering. "And I did not expect it: she looked so quiet at first."

"I warned you," was his friend's answer; "I said—be on your guard when you go near her. Besides, you might have waited till to-morrow, and had me with you: it was mere folly to attempt the interview to-night, and alone."

"I thought I could have done some good."

"You thought! you thought! Yes; it makes me impatient to hear you: but, however, you have suffered, and are likely to suffer enough for not taking my advice; so I'll say no more. Carter—hurry!—hurry! The sun will soon rise, and I must have him off."

"Directly, sir; the shoulder is just bandaged. I must look to this other wound in the arm: she has had her teeth here too, I think."

"She sucked the blood: she said she'd drain my heart," said Mason.

I saw Mr. Rochester shudder: a singularly marked expression of disgust, horror, hatred warped his countenance almost to distortion; but he only said:—

"Come, be silent, Richard, and never mind her gibberish: don't repeat it."

"I wish I could forget it," was the answer.

"You will when you are out of the country: when you get back to Spanish Town, you may think of her as dead and buried—or rather you need not think of her at all."

"Impossible to forget this night!"

"It is not impossible: have some energy, man. You thought you were dead as a herring two hours since, and you are all alive and talking now. There!—Carter has done with you or nearly so; I'll make you decent in a trice. Jane," (he turned to me for the first time since his re-entrance) "take this key: go down into my bed-room, and walk straight forward into my dressing-room; open the top drawer of the wardrobe and take out a clean shirt and neck-handkerchief: bring them here; and be nimble."

I went; sought the repository he had mentioned, found the articles named, and returned with them.

"Now," said he, "go to the other side of the bed while I order his toilet; but don't leave the room: you may be wanted again."

I retired as directed.

"Was anybody stirring below when you went down, Jane?" inquired Mr. Rochester, presently.

"No, sir: all was very still."

"We shall get you off cannily, Dick: and it will be better for your sake, and for that of the poor creature in yonder. I have striven long to avoid exposure, and I should not like it to come at last. Here, Carter, help him on with his waistcoat. Where did you leave your furred cloak? You can't travel a mile without that, I know, in this cold climate. In your room?—Jane, run down to Mr. Mason's room,—the one next mine,—and fetch a cloak you will see there."

Again I ran, and again returned, bearing an immense mantle lined and edged with fur.

"Now I've another errand for you," said my untiring master; "you must away to my room again. What a mercy you are shod with velvet, Jane!—a clod-hopping messenger would never do at this juncture. You must open the middle drawer of my toilet-table and take out a little phial and a little glass you will find there,—quick!"

I flew thither and back, bringing the desired vessels.

"That's well! Now, doctor, I shall take the liberty of administering a dose myself; on my own responsibility. I got this cordial at Rome, of an Italian charlatan—a fellow you would have kicked, Carter. It is not a thing to be used indiscriminately, but it is good upon occasion: as now, for instance. Jane, a little water."

He held out the tiny glass, and I half filled it from the water bottle on the wash-stand.

"That will do:—now wet the lip of the phial."

I did so: he measured twelve drops of a crimson liquid, and presented it to Mason.

"Drink, Richard: it will give you the heart you lack, for an hour or so."

"But will it hurt me?—is it inflammatory?"

"Drink! drink! drink!"

Mr. Mason obeyed, because it was evidently useless to resist. He was dressed now: he still looked pale, but he was no longer gory and sullied. Mr. Rochester let him sit three minutes after he had swallowed the liquid; he then took his arm:—

"Now I am sure you can get on your feet," he said:—"try."

The patient rose.

"Carter, take him under the other shoulder. Be of good cheer, Richard; step out:—that's it!"

"I do feel better," remarked Mr. Mason.

"I am sure you do. Now, Jane, trip on before us away to the backstairs; unbolt the side passage door, and tell the driver of the post-chaise you will see in the yard—or just outside, for I told him not to drive his rattling wheels over the pavement—to be ready; we are coming: and Jane, if any one is about, come to the foot of the stairs and hem."

It was by this time half-past five, and the sun was on the point of rising; but I found the kitchen still dark and silent. The side-passage door was fastened; I opened it with as little noise as possible: all the yard was quiet; but the gates stood wide open, and there was a post-chaise, with horses ready harnessed, and driver seated on the box, stationed outside. I approached him, and said the gentlemen were coming; he nodded: then I looked carefully round and listened. The stillness of early morning slumbered everywhere; the curtains were yet drawn over the servants' chamber windows; little birds were just twittering in the blossom-blanched orchard trees, whose boughs drooped like white garlands over the wall enclosing one side of the yard; the carriage horses stamped from time to time in their closed stables: all else was still.

The gentlemen now appeared. Mason, supported by Mr. Rochester and the surgeon, seemed to walk with tolerable ease: they assisted him into the chaise; Carter followed.

"Take care of him," said Mr. Rochester to the latter, "and keep him at your house till he is quite well: I shall ride over in a day or two to see how he gets on. Richard, how is it with you?"

"The fresh air revives me, Fairfax."

"Leave the window open on his side, Carter; there is no wind—good-bye, Dick."

"Fairfax——"

"Well, what is it?"

"Let her be taken care of; let her be treated as tenderly as may be: let her——" he stopped and burst into tears.

"I do my best; and have done it, and will do it," was the answer: he shut up the chaise door, and the vehicle drove away.

"Yet would to God there was an end of all this!" added Mr. Rochester, as he closed and barred the heavy yard-gates. This done, he moved with slow step and abstracted air, towards a door in the wall bordering the orchard. I, supposing he had done with me, prepared to return to the house; again, however, I heard him call "Jane!" He had opened the portal and stood at it, waiting for me.

"Come where there is some freshness, for a few moments," he said; "that house is a mere dungeon: don't you feel it so?"

"It seems to me a splendid mansion, sir."

"The glamour of inexperience is over your eyes," he answered; "and you see it through a charmed medium: you cannot discern that the gilding is slime and the silk draperies cobwebs; that the marble is sordid slate, the polished woods mere refuse chips and scaly bark. Now *here* (he pointed to the leafy enclosure we had entered) all is real, sweet, and pure."

He strayed down a walk edged with box; with apple trees, pear trees, and cherry trees on one side, and a border on the other, full of all sorts

of old-fashioned flowers, stocks, sweet-williams, primroses, pansies, mingled with southernwood, sweet-briar, and various fragrant herbs. They
were fresh now as a succession of April showers and gleams, followed
by a lovely spring morning, could make them: the sun was just entering
the dappled east, and his light illumined the wreathed and dewy orchard
trees and shone down the quiet walks under them.

"Jane, will you have a flower?"

He gathered a half-blown rose, the first on the bush, and offered it to me.

"Thank you, sir."

"Do you like this sunrise, Jane? That sky with its high and light clouds
which are sure to melt away as the day waxes warm—this placid and balmy
atmosphere?"

"I do, very much."

"You have passed a strange night, Jane."

"Yes, sir."

"And it has made you look pale—were you afraid when I left you alone
with Mason?"

"I was afraid of some one coming out of the inner room."

"But I had fastened the door—I had the key in my pocket: I should have
been a careless shepherd if I had left a lamb—my pet lamb—so near a
wolf's den, unguarded: you were safe."

"Will Grace Poole live here still, sir?"

"Oh, yes! don't trouble your head about her—put the thing out of your
thoughts."

"Yet it seems to me your life is hardly secure while she stays."

"Never fear—I will take care of myself."

"Is the danger you apprehended last night gone by now, sir?"

"I cannot vouch for that till Mason is out of England: nor even then.
To live, for me, Jane, is to stand on a crater-crust which may crack and
spue fire any day."

"But Mr. Mason seems a man easily led. Your influence, sir, is evidently
potent with him: he will never set you at defiance, or willfully injure you."

"Oh, no! Mason will not defy me; nor knowing it, will he hurt me—
but, unintentionally, he might in a moment, by one careless word, deprive
me, if not of life, yet for ever happiness."

"Tell him to be cautious, sir: let him know what you fear, and show
him how to avert the danger."

He laughed sardonically, hastily took my hand, and as hastily threw
it from him.

"If I could do that, simpleton, where would the danger be? Annihilated
in a moment. Ever since I have known Mason, I have only had to say to
him 'Do that,' and the thing has been done. But I cannot say 'Beware of
harming me, Richard;' for it is imperative that I should keep him ignorant
that harm to me is possible. Now you look puzzled; and I will puzzle you
farther. You are my little friend, are you not?"

"I like to serve you, sir, and to obey you in all that is right."

"Precisely: I see you do. I see genuine contentment in your gait and
mien, your eye and face, when you are helping me and pleasing me—
working for me, and with me, in, as you characteristically say, 'all that
is right;' for if I bid you do what you thought wrong, there would be no
light-footed running, no neat-handed alacrity, no lively glance and
animated complexion. My friend would then turn to me, quiet and pale,

and would say, 'No, sir; that is impossible: I cannot do it, because it is wrong;' and would become immutable as a fixed star. Well, you too have power over me, and may injure me: yet I dare not show you where I am vulnerable, lest, faithful and friendly as you are, you should transfix me at once."

"If you have no more to fear from Mr. Mason than you have from me, sir, you are very safe."

"God grant it may be so! Here, Jane, is an arbour; sit down."

The arbour was an arch in the wall, lined with ivy; it contained a rustic seat. Mr. Rochester took it, leaving room, however, for me: but I stood before him.

"Sit," he said; "the bench is long enough for two. You don't hesitate to take a place at my side, do you? Is that wrong, Jane?"

I answered him by assuming it: to refuse would, I felt, have been unwise.

"Now, my little friend, while the sun drinks the dew—while all the flowers in this old garden awake and expand, and the birds fetch their young ones' breakfast out of the Thornfield, and the early bees do their first spell of work—I'll put a case to you; which you must endeavour to suppose your own: but first, look at me, and tell me you are at ease, and not fearing that I err in detaining you, or that you err in staying."

"No, sir; I am content."

"Well then, Jane, call to aid your fancy:—suppose you were no longer a girl well reared and disciplined, but a wild boy indulged from childhood upwards; imagine yourself in a remote foreign land; conceive that you there commit a capital error, no matter of what nature or from what motives, but one whose consequences must follow you through life and taint all your existence. Mind, I don't say a *crime;* I am not speaking of shedding of blood or any other guilty act, which might make the perpetrator amenable to the law: my word is *error.* The results of what you have done become in time to you utterly insupportable; you take measures to obtain relief: unusual measures, but neither unlawful nor culpable. Still you are miserable; for hope has quitted you on the very confines of life: your sun at noon darkens in an eclipse, which you feel will not leave it till the time of setting. Bitter and base associations have become the sole food of your memory: you wander here and there, seeking rest in exile: happiness in pleasure—I mean in heartless, sensual pleasure—such as dulls intellect and blights feeling. Heart-weary and soul-withered, you come home after years of voluntary banishment; you make a new acquaintance—how or where no matter: you find in this stranger much of the good and bright qualities which you have sought for twenty years, and never before encountered; and they are all fresh, healthy, without soil and without taint. Such society revives, regenerates: you feel better days come back—higher wishes, purer feelings; you desire to recommence your life, and to spend what remains to you of days in a way more worthy of an immortal being. To attain this end, are you justified in overleaping an obstacle of custom—a mere conventional impediment, which neither your conscience sanctifies nor your judgment approves?"

He paused for an answer: and what was I to say? Oh, for some good spirit to suggest a judicious and satisfactory response! Vain aspiration! The west wind whispered in the ivy round me; but no gentle Ariel borrowed its breath as a medium of speech: the birds sang in the tree-tops; but their song, however sweet, was inarticulate.

Again Mr. Rochester propounded his query:

"Is the wandering and sinful, but now rest-seeking and repentant man, justified in daring the world's opinion, in order to attach to him for ever, this gentle, gracious, genial stranger; thereby securing his own peace of mind and regeneration of life?"

"Sir," I answered, "a wanderer's repose or a sinner's reformation should never depend on a fellow-creature. Men and women die; philosophers falter in wisdom, and Christians in goodness: if any one you know has suffered and erred, let him look higher than his equals for strength to amend, and solace to heal."

"But the instrument—the instrument! God, who does the work, ordains the instrument. I have myself—I tell it you without parable—been a worldly, dissipated, restless man; and I believe I have found the instrument for my cure in——"

He paused: the birds went on carolling, the leaves lightly rustling. I almost wondered they did not check their songs and whispers to catch the suspended revelation: but they would have had to wait many minutes—so long was the silence protracted. At last I looked up at the tardy speaker: he was looking eagerly at me.

"Little friend," said he, in quite a changed tone—while his face changed too; losing all its softness and gravity, and becoming harsh and sarcastic,—"you have noticed my tender penchant for Miss Ingram: don't you think if I married her she would regenerate me with a vengeance!"

He got up instantly; went quite to the other end of the walk, and when he came back he was humming a tune.

"Jane, Jane," said he, stopping before me, "you are quite pale with your vigils: don't you curse me for disturbing your rest?"

"Curse you? No, sir."

"Shake hands in confirmation of the word. What cold fingers! They were warmer last night when I touched them at the door of the mysterious chamber. Jane, when will you watch with me again?"

"Whenever I can be useful, sir."

"For instance, the night before I am married? I am sure I shall not be able to sleep. Will you promise to sit up with me to bear me company? To you I can talk of my lovely one: for now you have seen her and know her."

"Yes, sir."

"She's a rare one, is she not, Jane?"

"Yes, sir."

"A strapper—a real strapper, Jane: big, brown, and buxom; with hair just such as the ladies of Carthage must have had. Bless me! there's Dent and Lynn in the stables! Go in by the shrubbery, through that wicket."

As I went one way, he went another, and I heard him in the yard, saying cheeringly:—

"Mason got the start of you all this morning; he was gone before sunrise: I rose at four to see him off."

·······

Chapter 21

Presentiments are strange things! and so are sympathies; and so are signs: and the three combined make one mystery to which humanity has not yet found the key. I never laughed at presentiments in my life; because I have had strange ones of my own. Sympathies, I believe, exist: (for instance, between far-distant, long-absent, wholly estranged relatives; asserting, notwithstanding their alienation, the unity of the source to which each traces his origin) whose workings baffle moral comprehension. And signs, for aught we know, may be but the sympathies of Nature with man.

When I was a little girl, only six years old, I, one night, heard Bessie Leaven say to Martha Abbott that she had been dreaming about a little child; and that to dream of children was a sure sign of trouble, either to one's self or one's kin. The saying might have worn out of my memory, had not a circumstance immediately followed which served indelibly to fix it there. The next day Bessie was sent for home to the deathbed of her little sister.

Of late I had often recalled this saying and this incident; for during the past week scarcely a night had gone over my couch that had not brought with it a dream of an infant: which I sometimes hushed in my arms, sometimes dandled on my knee, sometimes watched playing with daisies on a lawn; or again, dabbling its hands in running water. It was a wailing child this night, and a laughing one the next: now it nestled close to me, and now it ran from me; but whatever mood the apparition evinced, whatever aspect it wore, it failed not for seven successive nights to meet me the moment I entered the land of slumber.

I did not like this iteration of one idea—this strange recurrence of one image; and I grew nervous as bed-time approached, and the hour of the vision drew near. It was from companionship with this baby-phantom I had been roused on that moonlight night when I heard the cry; and it was on the afternoon of the day following I was summoned down stairs by a message that some one wanted me in Mrs. Fairfax's room. On repairing thither, I found a man waiting for me, having the appearance of a gentleman's servant: he was dressed in deep mourning, and the hat he held in his hand was surrounded with a crape band.

"I daresay you hardly remember me, Miss," he said, rising as I entered; "but my name is Leaven: I lived coachman with Mrs. Reed when you were at Gateshead eight or nine years since, and I live there still."

"Oh, Robert! how do you do? I remember you very well: you used to give me a ride sometimes on Miss Georgiana's bay pony. And how is Bessie? You are married to Bessie?"

"Yes, Miss: my wife is very hearty, thank you; she brought me another little one about two months since—we have three now—and both mother and child are thriving."

"And are the family well at the House, Robert?"

"I am sorry I can't give you better news of them, Miss: they are very badly at present—in great trouble."

"I hope no one is dead," I said, glancing at his black dress. He too looked down at the crape round his hat and replied:—

"Mr. John died yesterday was a week, at his chambers in London."

"Mr. John?"

"Yes."

"And how does his mother bear it?"

"Why you see, Miss Eyre, it is not a common mishap: his life has been very wild: these last three years he gave himself up to strange ways; and his death was shocking."

"I heard from Bessie he was not doing well."

"Doing well! He could not do worse: he ruined his health and his estate amongst the worst men and the worst women. He got into debt and into jail: his mother helped him out twice, but as soon as he was free he returned to his old companions and habits. His head was not strong: the knaves he lived amongst fooled him beyond anything I ever heard. He came down to Gateshead about three weeks ago and wanted Missis to give up all to him. Missis refused; her means have long been much reduced by his extravagance; so he went back again, and the next news was that he was dead. How he died, God knows!—they say he killed himself."

I was silent: the tidings were frightful. Robert Leaven resumed:—

"Missis had been out of health herself for some time: she had got very stout, but was not strong with it; and the loss of money and fear of poverty were quite breaking her down. The information about Mr. John's death and the manner of it came too suddenly: it brought on a stroke. She was three days without speaking; but last Tuesday she seemed rather better: she appeared as if she wanted to say something, and kept making signs to my wife and mumbling. It was only yesterday morning, however, that Bessie understood she was pronouncing your name; and at last she made out the words, 'Bring Jane—fetch Jane Eyre: I want to speak to her.' Bessie is not sure whether she is in her right mind, or means anything by the words; but she told Miss Reed and Miss Georgiana, and advised them to send for you. The young ladies put it off at first: but their mother grew so restless and said, 'Jane, Jane,' so many times, that at last they consented. I left Gateshead yesterday; and if you can get ready, Miss, I should like to take you back with me early to-morrow morning."

"Yes, Robert, I shall be ready: it seems to me that I ought to go."

"I think so too, Miss. Bessie said she was sure you would not refuse: but I suppose you will have to ask leave before you can get off?"

"Yes; and I will do it now;" and having directed him to the servants' hall, and recommended him to the care of John's wife, and the attentions of John himself, I went in search of Mr. Rochester.

He was not in any of the lower rooms; he was not in the yard, the stables, or the grounds. I asked Mrs. Fairfax if she had seen him;—yes: she believed he was playing billiards with Miss Ingram. To the billiard-room I hastened: the click of balls and the hum of voices resounded thence; Mr. Rochester, Miss Ingram, the two Misses Eshton, and their admirers, were all busied in the game. It required some courage to disturb so interesting a party; my er-rand, however, was one I could not defer, so I approached the master where he stood at Miss Ingram's side. She turned as I drew near, and looked at me haughtily: her eyes seemed to demand, "What can the creeping creature want now?" and when I said, in a low voice, "Mr. Rochester," she made a movement as if tempted to order me away. I remember her appearance at the moment,—it was very graceful and very striking: she wore a morning robe of sky-blue crape; a gauzy azure scarf was twisted in her hair. She had been all animation with the game, and irritated pride did not lower the expression of her haught lineaments.

"Does that person want you?" she inquired of Mr. Rochester; and Mr. Rochester turned to see who the "person" was. He made a curious gri-mace,—one of his strange and equivocal demonstrations—threw down his cue and followed me from the room.

"Well, Jane?" he said, as he rested his back against the school-room door, which he had shut.

"If you please, sir, I want leave of absence for a week or two."

"What to do?—Where to go?"

"To see a sick lady who has sent for me."

"What sick lady?—Where does she live?"

"At Gateshead, in ——shire."

"——shire? That is a hundred miles off! Who may she be that sends for people to see her that distance?"

"Her name is Reed, sir,—Mrs. Reed."

"Reed of Gateshead? There was a Reed of Gateshead, a magistrate."

"It is his widow, sir."

"And what have you to do with her? How do you know her?"

"Mr. Reed was my uncle,—my mother's brother."

"The deuce he was! You never told me that before: you always said you had no relations."

"None that would own me, sir. Mr. Reed is dead, and his wife cast me off."

"Why?"

"Because I was poor, and burdensome, and she disliked me."

"But Reed left children?— you must have cousins? Sir George Lynn was talking of a Reed of Gateshead, yesterday—who, he said, was one of the veriest rascals on town; and Ingram was mentioning a Georgiana Reed of the same place, who was much admired for her beauty, a season or two ago, in London."

"John Reed is dead, too, sir: he ruined himself and half-ruined his fami-ly, and is supposed to have committed suicide. The news so shocked his mother that it brought on an apoplectic attack."

"And what good can you do her? Nonsense, Jane! I would never think of running a hundred miles to see an old lady who will, perhaps, be dead before you reach her: besides you say she cast you off."

"Yes, sir, but that is long ago; and when her circumstances were very different: I could not be easy to neglect her wishes now."

"How long will you stay?"

"As short a time as possible, sir."

"Promise me only to stay a week——"

"I had better not pass my word: I might be obliged to break it."

"At all events you *will* come back: you will not be induced under any pretext to take up a permanent residence with her?"

"Oh, no! I shall certainly return if all be well."

"And who goes with you? You don't travel a hundred miles alone?"

"No, sir, she has sent her coachman."

"A person to be trusted?"

"Yes, sir, he has lived ten years in the family."

Mr. Rochester meditated. "When do you wish to go?"

"Early to-morrow morning, sir."

"Well, you must have some money; you can't travel without money, and I dare say you have not much: I have given you no salary yet. How much have you in the world, Jane?" he asked, smiling.

I drew out my purse; a meagre thing it was. "Five shillings, sir." He took the purse, poured the hoard into his palm and chuckled over it as if its scantiness pleased him. Soon he produced his pocket-book: "Here," said he, offering me a note: it was fifty pounds, and he owed me but fifteen, I told him I had no change.

"I don't want change: you know that. Take your wages."

I declined accepting more than was my due. He scowled at first; then, as if recollecting something, he said:—

"Right, right! Better not give you all now: you would, perhaps, stay away three months if you had fifty pounds. There are ten: is it not plenty?"

"Yes, sir, but now you owe me five."

"Come back for it then: I am your banker for forty pounds."

"Mr. Rochester, I may as well mention another matter of business to you while I have the opportunity."

"Matter of business? I'm curious to hear it."

"You have as good as informed me, sir, that you are going shortly to be married?"

"Yes: what then?"

"In that case, sir, Adèle ought to go to school: I am sure you will perceive the necessity of it."

"To get her out of my bride's way; who might otherwise walk over her rather too emphatically. There's sense in the suggestion; not a doubt of it: Adèle, as you say, must go to school; and you, of course, must march straight to—the devil?"

"I hope not, sir: but I must seek another situation somewhere."

"In course!" he exclaimed, with a twang of voice and a distortion of features equally fantastic and ludicrous. He looked at me some minutes.

"And old Madam Reed, or the Misses, her daughters, will be solicited by you to seek a place, I suppose?"

"No, sir; I am not on such terms with my relatives as would justify me in asking favours of them—but I shall advertise."

"You shall walk up the pyramids of Egypt!" he growled. "At your peril you advertise! I wish I had only offered you a sovereign instead of ten pounds. Give me back nine pounds, Jane; I've a use for it."

"And so have I, sir," I returned, putting my hands and my purse behind me. "I could not spare the money on any account."

"Little niggard!" said he, "refusing me a pecuniary request! Give me five pounds, Jane."

"Not five shillings, sir; nor five pence."

"Just let me look at the cash."

"No, sir; you are not to be trusted."

"Jane!"

"Sir?"

"Promise me one thing."

"I'll promise you anything, sir, that I think I am likely to perform."

"Not to advertise: and to trust this one quest of a situation to me. I'll find you one in time."

"I shall be glad so to do, sir, if you, in your turn, will promise that I and Adèle shall be both safe out of the house before your bride enters it."

"Very well! very well! I'll pledge my word on it. You go to-morrow, then?"

"Yes, sir; early."

"Shall you come down to the drawing-room after dinner?"

"No, sir, I must prepare for the journey."

"Then you and I must bid good-bye for a little while?"

"I suppose so, sir."

"And how do people perform that ceremony of parting, Jane? Teach me; I'm not quite up to it."

"They say, Farewell; or any other form they prefer."

"Then say it."

"Farewell, Mr. Rochester, for the present."

"What must I say?"

"The same, if you like, sir."

"Farewell, Miss Eyre, for the present: is that all?"

"Yes."

"It seems stingy, to my notions, and dry, and unfriendly. I should like something else: a little addition to the rite. If one shook hands, for instance; but no,—that would not content me either. So you'll do no more than say Farewell, Jane?"

"It is enough, sir: as much good-will may be conveyed in one hearty word as in many."

"Very likely; but it is blank and cool—'farewell.' "

"How long is he going to stand with his back against that door?" I asked myself; "I want to commence my packing." The dinner-bell rang, and suddenly away he bolted, without another syllable: I saw him no more during the day, and was off before he had risen in the morning.

I reached the lodge at Gateshead about five o'clock in the afternoon of the first of May: I stepped in there before going up to the hall. It was very clean and neat: the ornamental windows were hung with little white curtains; the floor was spotless; the grate and fire-irons were burnished bright, and the fire burnt clear. Bessie sat on the hearth, nursing her last-born, and Robert and his sister played quietly in a corner.

"Bless you!—I knew you would come!" exclaimed Mrs. Leaven, as I entered.

"Yes, Bessie," said I, after I had kissed her; "and I trust I am not too late. How is Mrs. Reed?—Alive still, I hope."

"Yes, she is alive; and more sensible and collected than she was. The doctor says she may linger a week or two yet; but he hardly thinks she will finally recover."

"Has she mentioned me lately?"

"She was talking of you only this morning, and wishing you would come: but she is sleeping now; or was ten minutes ago, when I was up at the house. She generally lies in a kind of lethargy all the afternoon, and wakes up about six or seven. Will you rest yourself here an hour, Miss, and then I will go up with you?"

Robert here entered, and Bessie laid her sleeping child in the cradle and went to welcome him: afterwards she insisted on my taking off my bonnet and having some tea; for she said I looked pale and tired. I was glad to accept her hospitality; and I submitted to be relieved of my travelling garb just as passively as I used to let her undress me when a child.

Old times crowded fast back on me as I watched her bustling about—setting out the tea-tray with her best china, cutting bread and butter, toasting a tea-cake, and, between whiles, giving little Robert or Jane an occasional tap or push, just as she used to give me in former days. Bessie had retained her quick temper as well as her light foot and good looks.

Tea ready, I was going to approach the table; but she desired me to sit still, quite in her old, peremptory tones. I must be served at the fire-side, she said; and she placed before me a little round stand with my cup and a plate of toast, absolutely as she used to accommodate me with some privately purloined dainty on a nursery chair: and I smiled and obeyed her as in bygone days.

She wanted to know if I was happy at Thornfield Hall, and what sort of a person the mistress was; and when I told her there was only a master, whether he was a nice gentleman, and if I liked him. I told her he was rather an ugly man, but quite a gentleman; and that he treated me kindly, and I was content. Then I went on to describe to her the gay company that had lately been staying at the house; and to these details Bessie listened with interest: they were precisely of the kind she relished.

In such conversation an hour was soon gone: Bessie restored to me my bonnet, etc., and, accompanied by her, I quitted the lodge for the hall. It was also accompanied by her that I had, nearly nine years ago, walked down the path I was now ascending. On a dark, misty, raw morning in January, I had left a hostile roof with a desperate and embittered heart—a sense of outlawry and almost of reprobation—to seek the chilly harbourage of Lowood: that bourne so far away and unexplored. The same hostile roof now again rose before me: my prospects were doubtful yet; and I had yet an aching heart. I still felt as a wanderer on the face of the earth; but I experienced firmer trust in myself and my own powers, and less withering dread of oppression. The gaping wound of my wrongs, too, was now quite healed; and the flame of resentment extinguished.

"You shall go into the breakfast-room first," said Bessie, as she preceded me through the hall; "the young ladies will be there."

In another moment I was within that apartment. There was every article of furniture looking just as it did on the morning I was first introduced to Mr. Brocklehurst: the very rug he had stood upon still covered the hearth. Glancing at the book-cases, I thought I could distinguish the two volumes of Bewick's British Birds occupying their old place on the third shelf, and Gulliver's Travels and the Arabian Nights ranged just above. The inanimate objects were not changed: but the living things had altered past recognition.

Two young ladies appeared before me; one very tall, almost as tall as

Miss Ingram,—very thin too, with a sallow face and severe mien. There was something ascetic in her look, which was augmented by the extreme plainness of a straight-skirted, black, stuff dress, a starched linen collar, hair combed away from the temples, and the nun-like ornament of a string of ebony beads and a crucifix. This I felt sure was Eliza, though I could trace little resemblance to her former self in that elongated and colourless visage.

The other was as certainly Georgiana: but not the Georgiana I remembered—the slim and fairy-like girl of eleven. This was a full-blown, very plump damsel, fair as wax-work; with handsome and regular features, languishing blue eyes, and ringleted yellow hair. The hue of her dress was black too; but its fashion was so different from her sister's—so much more flowing and becoming—it looked as stylish as the other's looked puritanical.

In each of the sisters there was one trait of the mother—and only one: the thin and pallid elder daughter had her parent's Cairngorm eye: the blooming and luxuriant younger girl had her contour of jaw and chin,— perhaps a little softened, but still imparting an indescribable hardness to the countenance, otherwise so voluptuous and buxom.

Both ladies, as I advanced, rose to welcome me, and both addressed me by the name of "Miss Eyre," Eliza's greeting was delivered in a short, abrupt voice, without a smile; and then she sat down again, fixed her eyes on the fire, and seemed to forget me. Georgiana added to her "How d'ye do?" several common-places about my journey, the weather and so on, uttered in rather a drawling tone; and accompanied by sundry side-glances that measured me from head to foot—now traversing the folds of my drab merino pelisse, and now lingering on the plain trimming of my cottage bonnet. Young ladies have a remarkable way of letting you know that they think you a "quiz," without actually saying the words. A certain super-ciliousness of look, coolness of manner, nonchalance of tone, express fully their sentiments on the point, without committing them by any positive rudeness in word or deed.

A sneer, however, whether covert or open, had now no longer that power over me it once possessed: as I sat between my cousins, I was surprised to find how easy I felt under the total neglect of the one and the semi-sarcastic attentions of the other—Eliza did not mortify, nor Georgiana ruf-fle me. The fact was, I had other things to think about; within the last few months feelings had been stirred in me so much more potent than any they could raise—pains and pleasures so much more acute and exqui-site had been excited, than any it was in their power to inflict or bestow— that their airs gave me no concern either for good or bad.

"How is Mrs. Reed?" I asked soon, looking calmly at Georgiana; who thought fit to bridle at the direct address, as if it were an unexpected liberty.

"Mrs. Reed? Ah! mama you mean; she is extremely poorly: I doubt if you can see her to-night."

"If," said I, "you would just step up stairs and tell her I am come, I should be much obliged to you."

Georgiana almost started, and she opened her blue eyes wild and wide. "I know she had a particular wish to see me," I added, "and I would not defer attending to her desire longer than is absolutely necessary."

"Mama dislikes being disturbed in an evening," remarked Eliza. I soon

rose, quietly took off my bonnet and gloves, uninvited, and said I would
just step out to Bessie—who was, I dared say, in the kitchen—and ask her
to ascertain whether Mrs. Reed was disposed to receive me or not to-night.
I went, and having found Bessie and despatched her on my errand, I proceeded to take further measures. It had heretofore been my habit always
to shrink from arrogance: received as I had been to-day, I should, a year
ago, have resolved to quit Gateshead the very next morning; now, it was
disclosed to me all at once, that that would be a foolish plan. I had taken
a journey of a hundred miles to see my aunt, and I must stay with her
till she was better—or dead: as to her daughters' pride or folly, I must
put it on one side: make myself independent of it. So I addressed the
housekeeper; asked her to show me a room, told her I should probably
be a visitor here for a week or two, had my trunk conveyed to my chamber, and followed it thither myself: I met Bessie on the landing.

. "Missis is awake," said she; "I have told her you are here: come and
let us see if she will know you."

I did not need to be guided to the well-known room: to which I had
so often been summoned for chastisement or reprimand in former days.
I hastened before Bessie, I softly opened the door: a shaded light stood
on the table, for it was now getting dark. There was the great four-post
bed with amber hangings as of old; there the toilet-table, the arm-chair,
and the footstool: at which I had a hundred times been sentenced to kneel,
to ask pardon for offences, by me, uncommitted. I looked into a certain
corner near, half-expecting to see the slim outline of a once-dreaded
switch; which used to lurk there, waiting to leap out imp-like and lace
my quivering palm or shrinking neck. I approached the bed; I opened
the curtains and leant over the high-piled pillows.

Well did I remember Mrs. Reed's face, and I eagerly sought the familiar image. It is a happy thing that time quells the longings of vengeance,
and hushes the promptings of rage and aversion: I had left this woman
in bitterness and hate, and I came back to her now with no other emotion than a sort of ruth for her great sufferings, and a strong yearning to
forget and forgive all injuries—to be reconciled, and clasp hands in amity.

The well-known face was there: stern, relentless as ever—there was that
peculiar eye which nothing could melt; and the somewhat raised, imperious, despotic eyebrow. How often had it lowered on me menace and
hate! and how the recollection of childhood's terrors and sorrows revived
as I traced its harsh line now! And yet I stooped down and kissed her:
she looked at me.

"Is this Jane Eyre?" she said.

"Yes, aunt Reed. How are you, dear aunt?"

I had once vowed that I would never call her aunt again: I thought it
no sin to forget and break that vow, now. My fingers had fastened on her
hand which lay outside the sheet: had she pressed mine kindly, I should
at that moment have experienced true pleasure. But unimpressionable natures are not so soon softened, nor are natural antipathies so readily
eradicated: Mrs Reed took her hand away, and turning her face rather from
me, she remarked that the night was warm. Again she regarded me, so
icily, I felt at once that her opinion of me—her feeling towards me—was
unchanged, and unchangeable. I knew by her stony eye—that she was
resolved to consider me bad to the last; because to believe me good, would
give her no generous pleasure: only a sense of mortification.

I felt pain and then I felt ire; and then I felt a determination to subdue her—to be her mistress in spite both of her nature and her will. My tears had risen, just as in childhood: I ordered them back to their source. I brought a chair to the bed-head: I sat down and leaned over the pillow.

"You sent for me," I said, "and I am here; and it is my intention to stay till I see how you get on."

"Oh, of course! You have seen my daughters?"

"Yes."

"Well, you may tell them I wish you to stay, till I can talk some things over with you I have on my mind: to-night is too late, and I have a difficulty in recalling them. But there was something I wished to say—let me see——"

The wandering look and changed utterance told what wreck had taken place in her once-vigourous frame. Turning restlessly, she drew the bed-clothes round her; my elbow, resting on a corner of the quilt, fixed it down: she was at once irritated.

"Sit up!" said she; "don't annoy me with holding the clothes fast—are you Jane Eyre?"

"I am Jane Eyre."

"I have had more trouble with that child than any one would believe. Such a burden to be left on my hands—and so much annoyance as she caused me, daily and hourly, with her incomprehensible disposition, and her sudden starts of temper, and her continual, unnatural watchings of one's movements! I declare she talked to me once like something mad, or like a fiend—no child ever spoke or looked as she did; I was glad to get her away from the house. What did they do with her at Lowood? The fever broke out there, and many of the pupils died. She, however, did not die: but I said she did—I wish she had died!"

"A strange wish, Mrs. Reed: why do you hate her so?"

"I had a dislike to her mother always; for she was my husband's only sister, and a great favourite with him: he opposed the family's disowning her when she made her low marriage; and when news came of her death, he wept like a simpleton. He would send for the baby; though I entreated him rather to put it out to nurse and pay for its maintenance. I hated it the first time I set my eyes on it—a sickly, whining, pining thing! It would wail in its cradle all night long—not screaming heartily like any other child, but whimpering and moaning. Reed pitied it; and he used to nurse it and notice it as if it had been his own: more, indeed, than he ever noticed his own at that age. He would try to make my children friendly to the little beggar: the darlings could not bear it, and he was angry with them when they showed their dislike. In his last illness, he had it brought continually to his bedside; and but an hour before he died, he bound me by vow to keep the creature. I would as soon have been charged with a pauper brat out of a work-house: but he was weak, naturally weak. John does not at all resemble his father, and I am glad of it: John is like me and like my brothers—he is quite a Gibson. Oh, I wish he would cease tormenting me with letters for money! I have no more money to give him: we are getting poor. I must send away half the servants and shut up part of the house; or let it off. I can never submit to do that—yet how are we to get on? Two-thirds of my income goes in paying the interest of mortgages. John gambles dreadfully, and always loses—poor boy! He is beset by sharpers: John is sunk and degraded—his look is frightful—I feel ashamed for him when I see him."

She was getting much excited. "I think I had better leave her now," said I to Bessie, who stood on the other side of the bed.

"Perhaps you had, Miss: but she often talks in this way towards night—in the morning she is calmer."

I rose. "Stop!" exclaimed Mrs. Reed, "There is another thing I wished to say. He threatens me—he continually threatens me with his own death, or mine: and I dream sometimes that I see him laid out with a great wound in his throat, or with a swollen and blackened face. I am come to a strange pass: I have heavy troubles. What is to be done? How is the money to be had?"

Bessie now endeavoured to persuade her to take a sedative draught: she succeeded with difficulty. Soon after, Mrs. Reed grew more composed, and sank into a dozing state. I then left her.

More than ten days elapsed before I had again any conversation with her. She continued either delirious or lethargic; and the doctor forbade everything which could painfully excite her. Meantime, I got on as well as I could with Georgiana and Eliza. They were very cold, indeed, at first. Eliza would sit half the day sewing, reading, or writing, and scarcely utter a word either to me or her sister. Georgiana would chatter nonsense to her canary bird by the hour, and take no notice of me. but I was determined not to seem at a loss for occupation or amusement: I had brought my drawing materials with me, and they served me for both.

Provided with a case of pencils, and some sheets of paper, I used to take a seat apart from them, near the window, and busy myself in sketching fancy vignettes, representing any scene that happened momentarily to shape itself in the ever-shifting kaleidoscope of imagination: a glimpse of sea between two rocks; the rising moon, and a ship crossing its disk; a group of reeds and water-flags, and a naiad's head, crowned with lotus-flowers, rising out of them; an elf sitting in a hedge-sparrow's nest, under a wreath of hawthorn-bloom.

One morning I fell to sketching a face: what sort of a face it was to be, I did not care or know. I took a soft black pencil, gave it a broad point, and worked away. Soon I had traced on the paper a broad and prominent forehead and a square lower outline of visage: that contour gave me pleasure; my fingers proceeded actively to fill it with features. Strongly-marked horizontal eyebrows must be traced under that brow; then followed, naturally, a well-defined nose, with a straight ridge and full nostrils; then a flexible-looking mouth, by no means narrow; then a firm chin, with a decided cleft down the middle of it: of course, some black whiskers were wanted, and some jetty hair, tufted on the temples, and waved above the forehead. Now for the eyes: I had left them to the last, because they required the most careful working. I drew them large; I shaped them well: the eye-lashes I traced long and sombre; the irids lustrous and large. "Good! but not quite the thing," I thought, as I surveyed the effect: "They want more force and spirit;" and I wrought the shades blacker, that the lights might flash more brilliantly—a happy touch or two secured success. There, I had a friend's face under my gaze; and what did it signify that those young ladies turned their backs on me? I looked at it; I smiled at the speaking likeness: I was absorbed and content.

"Is that a portrait of some one you know?" asked Eliza, who had approached me unnoticed. I responded that it was merely a fancy head, and hurried it beneath the other sheets. Of course, I lied: it was, in fact, a very faithful representation of Mr. Rochester. But what was that to her; or to any one but myself? Georgiana also advanced to look. The other drawings pleased her much, but she called that "an ugly man." They both seemed surprised at my skill. I offered to sketch their portraits; and each, in turn, sat for a pencil outline. Then Georgiana produced her album. I promised to contribute a water-colour drawing: this put her at once into good humour. She proposed a walk in the grounds. Before we had been out two hours, we were deep in a confidential conversation: she had favoured me with a description of the brilliant winter she had spent in London two seasons ago—of the admiration she had there excited—the attention she had received; and I even got hints of the titled conquest she had made. In the course of the afternoon and evening these hints were enlarged on: various soft conversations were reported, and sentimental scenes represented; and, in short, a volume of a novel of fashionable life was that day improvised by her for my benefit. The communications were renewed from day to day: they always ran on the same theme—herself, her loves, and woes. It was strange she never once adverted either to her mother's illness, or her brother's death, or the present gloomy state of the family prospects. Her mind seemed wholly taken up with reminiscences of past gaiety, and aspirations after dissipations to come. She passed about five minutes each day in her mother's sick-room, and no more.

Eliza still spoke little: she had evidently no time to talk. I never saw a busier person than she seemed to be; yet it was difficult to say what she did: or rather, to discover any result of her diligence. She had an alarum to call her up early. I know not how she occupied herself before breakfast, but after that meal she divided her time into regular portions; and each hour had its allotted task. Three times a day she studied a little book, which I found, on inspection, was a Common Prayer Book. I asked her once what was the great attraction of that volume, and she said "the Rubric." Three hours she gave to stitching, with gold thread, the border of a square crimson cloth, almost large enough for a carpet. In answer to my inquiries after the use of this article, she informed me it was a covering for the altar of a new church lately erected near Gateshead. Two hours she devoted to her diary; two to working by herself in the kitchen-garden; and one to the regulation of her accounts. She seemed to want no company; no conversation. I believe she was happy in her way: this routine sufficed to her; and nothing annoyed her so much as the occurrence of any incident which forced her to vary its clock-work regularity.

She told me one evening, when more disposed to be communicative than usual, that John's conduct, and the threatened ruin of the family, had been a source of profound affliction to her: but she had now, she said, settled her mind, and formed her resolution. Her own fortune she had taken care to secure; and when her mother died,—and it was wholly improbable, she tranquilly remarked, that she should either recover or linger long,—she would execute a long-cherished project: seek a retirement where punctual habits would be permanently secured from disturbance, and place safe barriers between herself and a frivolous world. I asked if Georgiana would accompany her.

"Of course not. Georgiana and she had nothing in common: they never had had. She would not be burdened with her society for any consideration. Georgiana should take her own course; and she, Eliza, would take hers."

Georgiana, when not unburdening her heart to me, spent most of her
time in lying on the sofa, fretting about the dullness of the house, and
wishing over and over again that her aunt Gibson would send her an invitation up to town. "It would be so much better," she said, "if she could
only get out of the way for a month or two, till all was over." I did not
ask what she meant by "all being over," but I suppose she referred to her
mother, and the gloomy sequel of funeral rites. Eliza generally took no
more notice of her sister's indolence and complaints than if no such murmuring, lounging object had been before her. One day, however, as she
put away her account-book, and unfolded her embroidery, she suddenly
took her up thus:—

"Georgiana, a more vain and absurd animal than you, was certainly
never allowed to cumber the earth. You had no right to be born; for you
make no use of life. Instead of living for, in, and with yourself, as a reasonable being ought, you seek only to fasten your feebleness on some other
person's strength: if no one can be found willing to burden her or himself with such a fat, weak, puffy, useless thing, you cry out that you are
ill-treated, neglected, miserable. Then, too, existence for you must be a
scene of continual change and excitement, or else the world is a dungeon:
you must be admired, you must be courted, you must be flattered—you
must have music, dancing, and society—or you languish, you die away.
Have you no sense to devise a system which will make you independent
of all efforts, and all wills, but your own? Take one day; share it into sections; to each section apportion its task: leave no stray unemployed quarters of an hour, ten minutes, five minutes, include all; do each piece of
business in its turn with rigid regularity. The day will close almost before
you are aware it has begun; and you are indebted to no one for helping
you to get rid of one vacant moment: you have had to seek no one's company, conversation, sympathy, forbearance: you have lived, in short, as
an independent being ought to do. Take this advice: the first and last I
shall offer you; then you will not want me or any one else, happen what
may. Neglect it—go on as heretofore, craving, whining, and idling—and
suffer the results of your idiocy: however bad and insufferable they may
be. I tell you this plainly; and listen: for though I shall no more repeat
what I am now about to say, I shall steadily act on it. After my mother's
death, I wash my hands of you: from the day her coffin is carried to the
vault in Gateshead church, you and I will be as separate as if we had never
known each other. You need not think that because we chanced to be born
of the same parents, I shall suffer you to fasten me down by even the
feeblest claim: I can tell you this—if the whole human race, ourselves
excepted, were swept away, and we two stood alone on the earth, I would
leave you in the old world, and betake myself to the new."

She closed her lips.

"You might have spared yourself the trouble of delivering that tirade,"
answered Georgiana. "Everybody knows you are the most selfish, heartless creature in existence; and I know your spiteful hatred towards me:
I have had a specimen of it before in the trick you played me about Lord
Edwin Vere: you could not bear me to be raised above you, to have a title,
to be received into circles where you dare not show your face, and so you
acted the spy and informer, and ruined my prospects for ever." Georgiana
took out her handkerchief and blew her nose for an hour afterwards; Eliza
sat cold, impassible, and assiduously industrious.

True, generous feeling is made small account of by some: but here were two natures rendered, the one intolerably acrid, the other despicably savourless for the want of it. Feeling without judgment is a washy draught indeed; but judgment untempered by feeling is too bitter and husky a morsel for human deglutition.

It was a wet and windy afternoon: Georgiana had fallen asleep on the sofa over the perusal of a novel; Eliza was gone to attend a saint's-day service at the new church—for in matters of religion she was a rigid formalist: no weather ever prevented the punctual discharge of what she considered her devotional duties; fair or foul, she went to church thrice every Sunday, and as often on week-days as there were prayers.

I bethought myself to go up stairs and see how the dying woman sped, who lay there almost unheeded: the very servants paid her but a remittent attention; the hired nurse, being little looked after, would slip out of the room whenever she could. Bessie was faithful; but she had her own family to mind, and could only come occasionally to the Hall. I found the sick-room unwatched, as I had expected: no nurse was there; the patient lay still, and seemingly lethargic; her livid face sunk in the pillows: the fire was dying in the grate. I renewed the fuel, re-arranged the bed-clothes, gazed awhile on her who could not now gaze on me, and then I moved away to the window.

The rain beat strongly against the panes, the wind blew tempestuously: "One lies there," I thought, "who will soon be beyond the war of earthly elements. Whither will that spirit—now struggling to quit its material tenement—flit when at length released?"

In pondering the great mystery, I thought of Helen Burns: recalled her dying words—her faith—her doctrine of the equality of disembodied souls. I was still listening in thought to her well-remembered tones—still picturing her pale and spiritual aspect, her wasted face and sublime gaze, as she lay on her placid deathbed, and whispered her longing to be restored to her divine Father's bosom—when a feeble voice murmured from the couch behind: "Who is that?"

I knew Mrs. Reed had not spoken for days: was she reviving? I went up to her.

"It is I, aunt Reed."

"Who—I?" was her answer. "Who are you? looking at me with surprise and a sort of alarm, but still not wildly. "You are quite a stranger to me—where is Bessie?"

"She is at the lodge, aunt."

"Aunt!" she repeated. "Who calls me Aunt? You are not one of the Gibsons; and yet I know you—that face, and the eyes and forehead are quite familiar to me: you are like—why, you are like Jane Eyre!"

I said nothing: I was afraid of occasioning some shock by declaring my identity.

"Yet," said she, "I am afraid it is a mistake: my thoughts deceive me. I wished to see Jane Eyre, and I fancy a likeness where none exists: besides, in eight years she must be so changed." I now gently assured her that I was the person she supposed and desired me to be: and seeing that I was understood, and that her senses were quite collected, I explained how Bessie had sent her husband to fetch me from Thornfield.

"I am very ill, I know," she said ere long. "I was trying to turn myself

a few minutes since, and find I cannot move a limb. It is well I should
ease my mind before I die: what we think little of in health, burdens us
at such an hour as the present is to me. Is the nurse here? or is there no
one in the room but you?"

I assured her we were alone.

"Well, I have twice done you a wrong which I regret now. One was in
breaking the promise which I gave my husband to bring you up as my
own child; the other——" she stopped. "After all,.it is of no great importance perhaps," she murmured to herself: "and then I may get better; and
to humble myself so to her is painful."

She made an effort to alter her position, but failed: her face changed;
she seemed to experience some inward sensation—the precursor, perhaps,
of the last pang.

"Well: I must get it over. Eternity is before me: I had better tell her.—
Go to my dressing-case, open it, and take out a letter you will see there."

I obeyed her directions. "Read the letter," she said.

It was short, and thus conceived:—

"MADAM,

"Will you have the goodness to send me the address of my niece, Jane
Eyre, and to tell me how she is: it is my intention to write shortly and desire
her to come to me at Madeira. Providence has blessed my endeavours to
secure a competency; and as I am unmarried and childless, I wish to adopt
her during my life, and bequeath her at my death whatever I may have to
leave.

"I am, Madam, etc., etc.
"JOHN EYRE, Madeira."

It was dated three years back.

"Why did I never hear of this?" I asked.

"Because I disliked you too fixedly and thoroughly ever to lend a hand
in lifting you to prosperity. I could not forget your conduct to me, Jane—
the fury with which you once turned on me; the tone in which you declared
you abhorred me the worst of anybody in the world; the unchildlike look
and voice with which you affirmed that the very thought of me made you
sick, and asserted that I had treated you with miserable cruelty. I could
not forget my own sensations when you thus started up and poured out
the venom of your mind: I felt fear, as if an animal that I had struck or
pushed had looked up at me with human eyes and cursed me in a man's
voice.—Bring me some water! Oh, make haste!"

"Dear Mrs. Reed," said I, as I offered her the draught she required,
"think no more of all this, let it pass away from your mind. Forgive me
for my passionate language: I was a child then; eight, nine years have
passed since that day."

She heeded nothing of what I said; but when she had tasted the water
and drawn breath, she went on thus:—

"I tell you I could not forget it; and I took my revenge: for you to be
adopted by your uncle, and placed in a state of ease and comfort was what
I could not endure. I wrote to him; I said I was sorry for his disappointment, but Jane Eyre was dead: she had died of typhus fever at Lowood.
Now act as you please: write and contradict my assertion—expose my
falsehood as soon as you like. You were born, I think, to be my torment:

my last hour is racked by the recollection of a deed, which but for you, I should never have been tempted to commit."

"If you could but be persuaded to think no more of it, aunt, and to regard me with kindness and forgiveness——"

"You have a very bad disposition," said she, "and one to this day I feel it is impossible to understand: how for nine years you could be patient and quiescent under any treatment, and in the tenth break out all fire and violence, I can never comprehend."

"My disposition is not so bad as you think: I am passionate, but not vindictive. Many a time, as a little child, I should have been glad to love you if you would have let me; and I long earnestly to be reconciled to you now: kiss me, aunt."

I approached my cheek to her lips: she would not touch it. She said I oppressed her by leaning over the bed; and again demanded water. As I laid her down—for I raised her and supported her on my arm while she drank—I covered her ice-cold and clammy hand with mine: the feeble fingers shrank from my touch—the glazing eyes shunned my gaze.

"Love me, then, or hate me, as you will," I said at last, "you have my full and free forgiveness: ask now for God's; and be at peace."

Poor, suffering woman! it was too late for her to make now the effort to change her habitual frame of mind: living, she had ever hated me— dying, she must hate me still.

The nurse now entered, and Bessie followed. I yet lingered half an hour longer, hoping to see some sign of amity: but she gave none. She was fast relapsing into stupor; nor did her mind again rally: at twelve o'clock that night she died. I was not present to close her eyes; nor were either of her daughters. They came to tell us the next morning that all was over. She was by that time laid out. Eliza and I went to look at her: Georgiana, who had burst out into loud weeping, said she dared not go. There was stretched Sarah Reed's once robust and active frame, rigid and still: her eye of flint was covered with its cold lid; her brow and strong traits wore yet the impress of her inexorable soul. A strange and solemn object was that corpse to me. I gazed on it with gloom and pain: nothing soft, nothing sweet, nothing pitying, or hopeful, or subduing, did it inspire; only a grating anguish for *her* woes—not *my* loss—and a sombre tearless dismay at the fearfulness of death in such a form.

Eliza surveyed her parent calmly. After a silence of some minutes she observed,—

"With her constitution she should have lived to a good old age: her life was shortened by trouble." And then a spasm constricted her mouth for an instant: as it passed away she turned and left the room, and so did I. Neither of us had dropt a tear.

． ． ． ． ． ． ．

Chapter 22

Mr. Rochester had given me but one week's leave of absence: yet a month elapsed before I quitted Gateshead. I wished to leave immediately after the funeral; but Georgiana entreated me to stay till she could get off to London: whither she was now at last invited by her uncle, Mr. Gibson; who had come down to direct his sister's interment, and settle the family affairs. Georgiana said she dreaded being left alone with Eliza; from her she got neither sympathy in her dejection, support in her fears, nor aid in her preparations; so I bore with her feeble-minded quailings, and selfish lamentations, as well as I could, and did my best in sewing for her and packing her dresses. it is true, that while I worked, she would idle; and I thought to myself, "If you and I were destined to live always together, cousin, we would commence matters on a different footing. I should not settle tamely down into being the forbearing party; I should assign you your share of labour, and compel you to accomplish it, or else it should be left undone: I should insist, also, on your keeping some of those drawling, half-insincere complaints hushed in your own breast. It is only because our connection happens to be very transitory, and comes at a peculiarly mournful season, that I consent thus to render it so patient and compliant on my part."

At last I saw Georgiana off; but now it was Eliza's turn to request me to stay another week. Her plans required all her time and attention, she said: she was about to depart for some unknown bourne; and all day long she stayed in her own room, her door bolted within, filling trunks, emptying drawers, burning papers, and holding no communication with any one. She wished me to look after the house, to see callers, and answer notes of condolence.

One morning, she told me I was at liberty. "And," she added, "I am obliged to you for your valuable services and discreet conduct. There is some difference between living with such a one as you, and with Georgiana: you perform your own part in life, and burden no one. Tomorrow," she continued, "I set out for the continent. I shall take up my abode in a religious house, near Lisle—a nunnery you would call it: there I shall be quiet and unmolested. I shall devote myself for a time to the examination of the Roman Catholic dogmas, and to a careful study of the workings of their system: if I find it to be, as I half suspect it is, the one best calculated to ensure the doing of all things decently and in order, I shall embrace the tenets of Rome and probably take the veil."

I neither expressed surprise at this resolution nor attempted to dissuade her from it. "The vocation will fit you to a hair," I thought: "much good may it do you!"

When we parted, she said: "Good-bye, cousin Jane Eyre; I wish you well: you have some sense."

I then returned: "You are not without sense, cousin Eliza; but what you have, I suppose in another year will be walled up alive in a French convent. However, it is not my business, and so it suits you—I don't much care."

"You are in the right," said she: and with these words we each went our separate way. As I shall not have occasion to refer either to her or her sister again, I may as well mention here, that Georgiana made an advantageous match with a wealthy worn-out man of fashion; and that Eliza actually took the veil, and is at this day superior of the convent where she passed the period of her novitiate: and which she endowed with her fortune.

How people feel when they are returning home from an absence, long or short, I did not know: I had never experienced the sensation. I had known what it was to come back to Gateshead when a child, after a long walk—to be scolded for looking cold or gloomy; and later, what it was to come back from church to Lowood—to long for a plenteous meal and a good fire, and to be unable to get either. Neither of these returnings were very pleasant or desirable: no magnet drew me to a given point, increasing in its strength of attraction the nearer I came. The return to Thornfield was yet to be tried.

My journey seemed tedious—very tedious: fifty miles one day, a night spent at an inn; fifty miles the next day. During the first twelve hours I thought of Mrs. Reed in her last moments: I saw her disfigured and discoloured face, and heard her strangely altered voice. I mused on the funeral day, the coffin, the hearse, the black train of tenants and servants—few was the number of relatives—the gaping vault, the silent church, the solemn service. Then I thought of Eliza and Georgiana: I beheld one the cynosure of a ball-room, the other the inmate of a convent cell; and I dwelt on and analyzed their separate peculiarities of person and character. The evening arrival at the great town of —— scattered these thoughts; night gave them quite another turn: laid down on my traveller's bed, I left reminiscence for anticipation.

I was going back to Thornfield: but how long was I to stay there? Not long; of that I was sure. I had heard from Mrs. Fairfax in the interim of my absence: the party at the hall was dispersed; Mr. Rochester had left for London three weeks ago, but he was then expected to return in a fortnight. Mrs. Fairfax surmised that he was gone to make arrangements for his wedding, as he had talked of purchasing a new carriage: she said the idea of his marrying Miss Ingram still seemed strange to her; but from what everybody said and from what she had herself seen, she could no longer doubt that the event would shortly take place. "You would be strangely incredulous if you did doubt it," was my mental comment. "I don't doubt it."

The question followed, "Where was I to go?" I dreamt of Miss Ingram all the night: in a vivid morning dream I saw her closing the gates of Thornfield against me and pointing me out another road; and Mr. Rochester looked on with his arms folded—smiling sardonically, as it seemed, at both her and me.

I had not notified to Mrs. Fairfax the exact day of my return; for I did not wish either car or carriage to meet me at Millcote. I proposed to walk the distance quietly by myself; and very quietly, after leaving my box in the ostler's care, did I slip away from the George Inn, about six o'clock of a June evening, and take the old road to Thornfield: a road which lay chiefly through fields, and was now little frequented.

It was not a bright or splendid summer evening, though fair and soft: the hay-makers were at work all along the road; and the sky, though far from cloudless, was such as promised well for the future: its blue—where blue was visible—was mild and settled, and its cloud strata high and thin. The west, too, was warm: no watery gleam chilled it—it seemed as if there was a fire lit, an altar burning behind its screen of marbled vapour, and out of apertures shone a golden redness.

I felt glad as the road shortened before me: so glad that I stopped once to ask myself what that joy meant: and to remind reason that it was not to my home I was going, or to a permanent resting-place, or to a place where fond friends looked out for me and waited my arrival. "Mrs. Fairfax will smile you a calm welcome, to be sure," said I; "and little Adèle will clap her hands and jump to see you: but you know very well you are thinking of another than they; and that he is not thinking of you."

But what is so headstrong as youth? What so blind as inexperience? These affirmed that it was pleasure enough to have the privilege of again looking on Mr. Rochester, whether he looked on me or not; and they added —"Hasten! hasten! be with him while you may: but a few more days or weeks, at most, and you are parted with him for ever!" And then I strangled a new-born agony—a deformed thing which I could not persuade myself to own and rear—and ran on.

They are making hay, too, in Thornfield meadows: or rather, the labourers are just quitting their work, and returning home with their rakes on their shoulders: now, at the hour I arrive. I have but a field or two to traverse, and then I shall cross the road and reach the gates. How full the hedges are of roses! But I have no time to gather any; I want to be at the house. I passed a tall briar, shooting leafy and flowery branches across the path; I see the narrow stile with stone steps; and I see—Mr. Rochester sitting there, a book and a pencil in his hand: he is writing.

Well, he is not a ghost; yet every nerve I have is unstrung: for a moment I am beyond my own mastery. What does it mean? I did not think I should tremble in this way when I saw him—or lose my voice or the power of motion in his presence. I will go back as soon as I can stir: I need not make an absolute fool of myself. I know another way to the house. It does not signify if I knew twenty ways; for he has seen me.

"Hello!" he cries; and he puts up his book and his pencil. "There you are! Come on, if you please."

I suppose I do come on; though in what fashion I know not: being scarcely cognizant of my movements, and solicitous only to appear calm; and, above all, to control the working muscles of my face—which I feel rebel insolently against my will, and struggle to express what I had resolved to conceal. But I have a veil—it is down: I may make shift yet to behave with decent composure.

"And this is Jane Eyre? Are you coming from Millcote, and on foot? Yes—just one of your tricks: not to send for a carriage, and come clattering over street and road like a common mortal, but to steal into the vicinage of your home along with twilight, just as if you were a dream or a shade. What the deuce have you done with yourself this last month?"

"I have been with my aunt, sir, who is dead."

"A true Janian reply! Good angels be my guard! She comes from the other world—from the abode of people who are dead; and tells me so when she meets me alone here in the gloaming! If I dared, I'd touch you, to see if you are substance or shadow, you elf!—but I'd as soon offer to take hold of a blue *ignis fatuus* light in a marsh. Truant! truant!" he added, when he had paused an instant. "Absent from me a whole month: and forgetting me quite, I'll be sworn!"

I knew there would be pleasure in meeting my master again; even though broken by the fear that he was so soon to cease to be my master, and by the knowledge that I was nothing to him: but there was ever in Mr. Rochester (so at least I thought) such a wealth of the power of communicating happiness, that to taste but of the crumbs he scattered to stray and stranger birds like me, was to feast genially. His last words were balm: they seemed to imply that it imported something to him whether I forgot him or not. And he had spoken of Thornfield as my home—would that it were my home!

He did not leave the stile, and I hardly liked to ask to go by. I inquired soon if he had not been to London.

"Yes: I suppose you found that out by second-sight."

"Mrs. Fairfax told me in a letter."

"And did she inform you what I went to do?"

"Oh, yes, sir! Everybody knew your errand."

"You must see the carriage, Jane, and tell me if you don't think it will suit Mrs. Rochester exactly; and whether she won't look like Queen Boadicea, leaning back against those purple cushions. I wish, Jane, I were a trifle better adapted to match with her externally. Tell me now, fairy as you are,—can't you give me a charm, or a philter, or something of that sort, to make me a handsome man?"

"It would be past the power of magic, sir;" and, in thought, I added, "A loving eye is all the charm needed: to such you are handsome enough; or rather, your sternness has a power beyond beauty."

Mr. Rochester had sometimes read my unspoken thoughts with an acumen to me incomprehensible: in the present instance he took no notice of my abrupt vocal response; but he smiled at me with a certain smile he had of his own, and which he used but on rare occasions. He seemed to think it too good for common purposes: it was the real sunshine of feeling—he shed it over me now.

"Pass, Janet," said he, making room for me to cross the stile: "go up home, and stay your weary little wandering feet at a friend's threshold."

All I had now to do was to obey him in silence: no need for me to colloquize further. I got over the stile without a word, and meant to leave him calmly. An impulse held me fast,—a force turned me round. I said—or something in me said for me, and in spite of me:—

"Thank you, Mr. Rochester, for your great kindness. I am strangely glad to get back again to you; and wherever you are is my home,—my only home."

I walked on so fast that even he could hardly have overtaken me had he tried. Little Adèle was half wild with delight when she saw me. Mrs. Fairfax received me with her usual plain friendliness. Leah smiled; and even Sophie bid me *"bon soir"* with glee. This was very pleasant: there is no happiness like that of being loved by your fellow-creatures, and feeling that your presence is an addition to their comfort.

I, that evening, shut my eyes resolutely against the future: I stopped my ears against the voice that kept warning me of near separation and coming grief. When tea was over, and Mrs. Fairfax had taken her knitting, and I had assumed a low seat near her, and Adèle, kneeling on the carpet, had nestled close up to me, and a sense of mutual affection seemed to surround us with a ring of golden peace, I uttered a silent prayer that we might not be parted far or soon; but when, as we thus sat, Mr. Rochester entered, unannounced, and looking at us, seemed to take pleasure in the spectacle of a group so amicable—when he said he supposed the old lady was all right now that she had got her adopted daughter back again, and added that he saw Adèle was *"prête à croquer sa petite maman Anglaise"*—I half ventured to hope that he would, even after his marriage, keep us together somewhere under the shelter of his protection, and not quite exiled from the sunshine of his presence.

A fortnight of dubious calm succeeded my return to Thornfield Hall. Nothing was said of the master's marriage, and I saw no preparation going

on for such an event. Almost every day I asked Mrs. Fairfax if she had
yet heard anything decided: her answer was always in the negative. Once,
she said, she had actually put the question to Mr. Rochester as to when
he was going to bring his bride home; but he had answered her only by
a joke, and one of his queer looks, and she could not tell what to make
of him.

One thing specially surprised me, and that was, there was no journey-
ings backward and forward, no visits to Ingram Park: to be sure it was
twenty miles off, on the borders of another county; but what was that distance to an ardent lover? To so practised and indefatigable a horseman
as Mr. Rochester, it would be but a morning's ride. I began to cherish
hopes I had no right to conceive: that the match was broken off; that
rumour had been mistaken; that one or both parties had changed their
minds. I used to look at my master's face to see if it were sad or fierce;
but I could not remember the time when it had been so uniformly clear
of clouds or evil feelings. If, in the moments I and my pupil spent with
him, I lacked spirits and sank into inevitable dejection, he became even
gay. Never had he called me more frequently to his presence; never been
kinder to me when there—and, alas! never had I loved him so well.

·······

Chapter 23

A splendid Midsummer shone over England: skies so pure, suns so
radiant as were then seen in long succession, seldom favour, even singly,
our wave-grit land. It was as if a band of Italian days had come from the
South, like a flock of glorious passenger birds, and lighted to rest them
on the cliffs of Albion. The hay was all got in; the fields round Thornfield were green and shorn; the roads white and baked; the trees were
in their dark prime: hedge and wood, full-leaved and deeply tinted, contrasted well with the sunny hue of the cleared meadows between.

On Midsummer-eve, Adèle, weary with gathering wild strawberries in
Hay Lane half the day, had gone to bed with the sun. I watched her drop
asleep, and when I left her I sought the garden.

It was now the sweetest hour of the twenty-four:—"Day its fervid fires
had wasted," and dew fell cool on panting plain and scorched summit.
Where the sun had gone down in simple state—pure of the pomp of
clouds—spread a solemn purple, burning with the light of red jewel and
furnace flame at one point, on one hill-peak, and extending high and wide,
soft and still softer, over half heaven. The east had its own charm of fine,
deep blue, and its own modest gem, a rising and solitary star: soon it
would boast the moon; but she was yet beneath the horizon.

I walked awhile on the pavement; but a subtle, well-known scent—that
of a cigar—stole from some window; I saw the library casement open a
handbreadth; I knew I might be watched thence; so I went apart into the
orchard. No nook in the grounds more sheltered and more Eden-like; it
was full of trees, it bloomed with flowers: a very high wall shut it out
from the court, on one side; on the other, a beech avenue screened it from
the lawn. At the bottom was a sunk fence; its sole separation from lonely
fields: a winding walk, bordered with laurels and terminating in a giant

horse-chestnut, circled at the base by a seat, led down to the fence. Here one could wander unseen. While such honey-dew fell, such silence reigned, such gloaming gathered, I felt as if I could haunt such shade for ever: but in threading the flower and fruit-parterres at the upper part of the enclosure, enticed there by the light the now-rising moon casts on this more open quarter, my step is stayed—not by sound, not by sight, but once more by a warning fragrance.

Sweet-briar and southernwood, jasmine, pink, and rose have long been yielding their evening sacrifice of incense: this new scent is neither of shrub nor flower; it is—I know it well—it is Mr. Rochester's cigar. I look round and I listen. I see trees laden with ripening fruit. I hear a nightingale warbling in a wood half a mile off; no moving form is visible, no coming step audible; but that perfume increases: I must flee. I make for the wicket leading to the shrubbery, and I see Mr. Rochester entering. I step aside into the ivy recess; he will not stay long: he will soon return whence he came, and if I sit still he will never see me.

But no—eventide is as pleasant to him as to me, and this antique garden as attractive; and he strolls on, now lifting the gooseberry-tree branches to look at the fruit, large as plums, with which they are laden; now taking a ripe cherry from the wall; now stooping towards a knot of flowers, either to inhale their fragrance or to admire the dew-beads on their petals. A great moth goes humming by me; it alights on a plant at Mr. Rochester's foot: he sees it, and bends to examine it.

"Now, he has his back towards me," thought I, "and he is occupied too; perhaps, if I walk softly, I can slip away unnoticed."

I trod on an edging of turf that the crackle of the pebbly gravel might not betray me: he was standing among the beds at a yard or two distant from where I had to pass; the moth apparently engaged him. "I shall get by very well," I meditated. As I crossed his shadow, thrown long over the garden by the moon, not yet risen high, he said quietly without turning:—

"Jane, come and look at this fellow."

I had made no noise: he had not eyes behind—could his shadow feel? I started at first, and then I approached him.

"Look at his wings," said he, "he reminds me rather of a West Indian insect; one does not often see so large and gay a night-rover in England: there! he is flown."

The moth roamed away; I was sheepishly retreating also: but Mr. Rochester followed me, and when we reached the wicket, he said:—

"Turn back: on so lovely a night it is a shame to sit in the house; and surely no one can wish to go to bed while sunset is thus at meeting with moonrise."

It is one of my faults, that though my tongue is sometimes prompt enough at an answer, there are times when it sadly fails me in framing an excuse; and always the lapse occurs at some crisis, when a facile word or plausible pretext is specially wanted to get me out of painful embarrassment. I did not like to walk at this hour alone with Mr. Rochester in the shadowy orchard; but I could not find a reason to allege for leaving him. I followed with lagging step, and thoughts busily bent on discovering a means of extrication; but he himself looked so composed and so grave also, I became ashamed of feeling any confusion: the evil—if evil existent or prospective there was—seemed to lie with me only; his mind was unconscious and quiet.

"Jane," he recommenced, as we entered the laurel-walk, and slowly strayed down in the direction of the sunk fence and the horse-chestnut, "Thornfield is a pleasant place in summer, is it not?"

"Yes, sir."

"You must have become in some degree attached to the house,—you, who have an eye for natural beauties, and a good deal of the organ of Adhesiveness?"

"I am attached to it, indeed."

"And, though I don't comprehend how it is, I perceive you have acquired a degree of regard for that foolish little child Adèle, too; and even for simple dame Fairfax?"

"Yes, sir; in different ways, I have an affection for both."

"And would be sorry to part with them?"

"Yes."

"Pity!" he said, and sighed and paused. "It is always the way of events in this life," he continued presently: "no sooner have you got settled in a pleasant resting-place, than a voice calls out to you to rise and move on, for the hour of repose is expired."

"Must I move on, sir?" I asked. "Must I leave Thornfield?"

"I believe you must, Jane. I am sorry, Janet, but I believe indeed you must."

This was a blow: but I did not let it prostrate me.

"Well, sir, I shall be ready when the order to march comes."

"It is come now—I must give it to-night."

"Then you are going to be married, sir?"

"Ex-act-ly—pre-cise-ly: with your usual acuteness, you have hit the nail straight on the head."

"Soon, sir?"

"Very soon, my —— that is, Miss Eyre: and you'll remember, Jane, the first time I, or Rumour, plainly intimated to you that it was my intention to put my old bachelor's neck into the sacred noose, to enter into the holy estate of matrimony—to take Miss Ingram to my bosom, in short, (she's an extensive armful: but that's not to the point—one can't have too much of such a very excellent thing as my beautiful Blanche): well, as I was saying—listen to me, Jane! You're not turning your head to look after more moths, are you? That was only a lady-clock, child, 'flying away home.' I wish to remind you that it was you who first said to me with that discretion, I respect in you—with that foresight, prudence, and humility which befit your responsible and dependent position—that in case I married Miss Ingram, both you and little Adèle had better trot forthwith. I pass over the sort of slur conveyed in this suggestion on the character of my beloved; indeed, when you are far away, Janet, I'll try to forget it: I shall notice only its wisdom; which is such that I have made it my law of action. Adèle must go to school; and you, Miss Eyre, must get a new situation."

"Yes, sir, I will advertise immediately: and meantime, I suppose ——" I was going to say, "I suppose I may stay here, till I find another shelter to betake myself to:" but I stopped, feeling it would not do to risk a long sentence, for my voice was not quite under command.

"In about a month I hope to be a bride groom," continued Mr. Rochester; "and in the interim, I shall myself look out for employment and an asylum for you."

"Thank you, sir; I am sorry to give ——"

"Oh, no need to apologize! I consider that when a dependent does her duty as well as you have done yours, she has a sort of claim upon her employer for any little assistance he can conveniently render her; indeed I have already, through my future mother-in-law, heard of a place that I think will suit: it is to undertake the education of the five daughters of Mrs. Dionysius O'Gall of Bitternutt Lodge, Connaught, Ireland. You'll like Ireland, I think: they're such warm-hearted people there, they say."

"It is a long way off, sir."

"No matter—a girl of your sense will not object to the voyage or the distance."

"Not the voyage, but the distance: and then the sea is a barrier——"

"From what, Jane?"

"From England and from Thornfield: and ——"

"Well?"

"From *you*, sir."

I said this almost involuntarily; and with as little sanction of free will, my tears gushed out. I did not cry so as to be heard, however; I avoided sobbing. The thought of Mrs. O'Gall and Bitternutt Lodge struck cold to my heart; and colder the thought of all the brine and foam, destined, as it seemed, to rush between me and the master at whose side I now walked; and coldest the remembrance of the wider ocean—wealth, caste, custom intervened between me and what I naturally and inevitably loved.

"It is a long way," I again said.

"It is to be sure; and when you get to Bitternutt Lodge, Connaught, Ireland, I shall never see you again, Jane: that's morally certain. I never go over to Ireland, not having myself much of a fancy for the country. We have been good friends, Jane; have we not?"

"Yes, sir."

"And when friends are on the eve of separation, they like to spend the little time that remains to them close to each other. Come—we'll talk over the voyage and the parting quietly, half an hour or so, while the stars enter into their shining life up in heaven yonder: here is the chestnut tree; here is the bench at its old roots. Come, we will sit there in peace to-night, though we should never more be destined to sit there together." He seated me and himself.

"It is a long way to Ireland, Janet, and I am sorry to send my little friend on such weary travels: but if I can't do better, how is it to be helped? Are you anything akin to me, do you think, Jane?"

I could risk no sort of answer by this time: my heart was full.

"Because," he said, "I sometimes have a queer feeling with regard to you—especially when you are near me, as now: it is as if I had a string somewhere under my left ribs, tightly and inextricably knotted to a similar string situated in the corresponding quarter of your little frame. And if that boisterous channel, and two hundred miles or so of land come broad between us, I am afraid that cord of communion will be snapt; and then I've a nervous notion I should take to bleeding inwardly. As for you—you'd forget me."

"That I *never* should, sir: you know ——" impossible to proceed.

"Jane, do you hear that nightingale singing in the wood?—Listen!"

In listening, I sobbed convulsively; for I could repress what I endured no longer; I was obliged to yield, and I was shaken from head to foot with acute distress. When I did speak, it was only to express an impetuous wish that I had never been born, or never come to Thornfield.

"Because you are sorry to leave it?"

The vehemence of emotion, stirred by grief and love within me, was claiming mastery, and struggling for full sway; and asserting a right to predominate: to overcome, to live, rise, and reign at last; yes,—and to speak.

"I grieve to leave Thornfield: I love Thornfield:—I love it, because I have lived in it a full and delightful life,—momentarily at least. I have not been trampled on. I have not been petrified. I have not been buried with inferior minds, and excluded from every glimpse of communion with what is bright, and energetic, and high. I have talked, face to face, with what I reverence; with what I delight in,—with an original, a vigorous, an expanded mind. I have known you, Mr. Rochester; and it strikes me with terror and anguish to feel I absolutely must be torn from you for ever. I see the necessity of departure; and it is looking on the necessity of death."

"Where do you see the necessity?" he asked, suddenly.

"Where? You, sir, have placed it before me."

"In what shape?"

"In the shape of Miss Ingram; a noble and beautiful woman,—your bride."

"My bride! What bride? I have no bride!"

"But you will have."

"Yes:—I will!—I will!" He set his teeth.

"Then I must go:—you have said it yourself."

"No: you must stay! I swear it—and the oath shall be kept."

"I tell you I must go!" I retorted, roused to something like passion. "Do you think I can stay to become nothing to you? Do you think I am an automaton?—a machine without feelings? and can bear to have my morsel of bread snatched from my lips, and my drop of living water dashed from my cup? Do you think, because I am poor, obscure, plain, and little, I am soulless and heartless?—You think wrong!—I have as much soul as you,—and full as much heart! And if God had gifted me with some beauty, and some wealth, I should have made it as hard for you to leave me, as it is now for me to leave you. I am not talking to you now through the medium of custom, conventionalities, nor even of mortal flesh:—it is my spirit that addresses your spirit; just as if both had passed through the grave, and we stood at God's feet, equal,—as we are!"

"As we are!" repeated Mr. Rochester—"so," he added, enclosing me in his arms, gathering me to his breast, pressing his lips on my lips: "so, Jane!"

"Yes, so, sir," I rejoined: "and yet not so; for you are a married man—or as good as a married man, and wed to one inferior to you—to one with whom you have no sympathy—whom I do not believe you truly love; for I have seen and heard you sneer at her. I would scorn such a union: therefore I am better than you—let me go!"

"Where, Jane? To Ireland?"

"Yes—to Ireland. I have spoken my mind, and can go anywhere now."

"Jane, be still; don't struggle so, like a wild, frantic bird that is rending its own plumage in its desperation."

"I am no bird; and no net ensnares me: I am a free human being with an independent will; which I now exert to leave you."

Another effort set me at liberty, and I stood erect before him.

"And your will shall decide your destiny," he said: "I offer you my hand, my heart, and a share of all my possessions."

"You play a farce, which I merely laugh at."

"I ask you to pass through life at my side—to be my second self, and best earthly companion."

"For that fate you have already made your choice, and must abide by it."

"Jane, be still a few moments; you are over-excited: I will be still too."

A waft of wind came sweeping down the laurel-walk, and trembled through the boughs of the chestnut: it wandered away—away—to an indefinite distance—it died. The nightingale's song was then the only voice of the hour: in listening to it, I again wept. Mr. Rochester sat quiet, looking at me gently and seriously. Some time passed before he spoke; he at last said:—

"Come to my side, Jane, and let us explain and understand one another."

"I will never again come to your side: I am torn away now, and cannot return."

"But, Jane, I summon you as my wife: it is you only I intend to marry."

I was silent: I thought he mocked me.

"Come, Jane—come hither."

"Your bride stands between us."

He rose, and with a stride reached me.

"My bride is here," he said, again drawing me to him, "because my equal is here, and my likeness. Jane, will you marry me?"

Still I did not answer, and still I writhed myself from his grasp: for I was still incredulous.

"Do you doubt me, Jane?"

"Entirely."

"You have no faith in me?"

"Not a whit."

"Am I a liar in your eyes?" he asked passionately. "Little sceptic, you *shall* be convinced. What love have I for Miss Ingram? None: and that you know. What love has she for me? None; as I have taken pains to prove: I caused a rumour to reach her that my fortune was not a third of what was supposed, and after that I presented myself to see the result; it was coldness both from her and her mother. I would not—I could not—marry Miss Ingram. You—you strange—you almost unearthly thing!—I love as my own flesh. You—poor and obscure, and small and plain as you are—I entreat to accept me as a husband."

"What, me!" I ejaculated: beginning in his earnestness—and especially in his incivility—to credit his sincerity: "me, who have not a friend in the world but you—if you are my friend: not a shilling but what you have given me?"

"You, Jane. I must have you for my own—entirely my own. Will you be mine? Say yes, quickly."

"Mr. Rochester, let me look at your face: turn to the moonlight."

"Why?"

"Because I want to read your countenance; turn!"

"There: you will find it scarcely more legible than a crumpled, scratched page. Read on: only make haste, for I suffer."

His face was very much agitated and very much flushed, and there were strong workings in the features, and strange gleams in the eyes.

"Oh, Jane, you torture me!" he exclaimed. "With that searching and yet faithful and generous look, you torture me!"

"How can I do that? If you are true, and your offer real, my only feelings to you must be gratitude and devotion—they cannot torture."

"Gratitude!" he ejaculated; and added wildly—"Jane, accept me quickly. Say, Edward—give me my name—Edward—I will marry you."

"Are you in earnest?—Do you truly love me?—Do you sincerely wish me to be your wife?"

"I do; and if an oath is necessary to satisfy you, I swear it."

"Then, sir, I will marry you."

"Edward—my little wife!"

"Dear Edward!"

"Come to me—come to me entirely now," said he: and added, in his deepest tone, speaking in my ear as his check was laid on mine, "Make my happiness—I will make yours."

"God pardon me!" he subjoined ere long; "and man meddle not with me: I have her, and will hold her."

"There is no one to meddle, sir. I have no kindred to interfere."

"No—that is the best of it," he said. And if I had loved him less I should have thought his accent and look of exultation savage: but, sitting by him, roused from the nightmare of parting—called to the paradise of union—I thought only of the bliss given me to drink in so abundant a flow. Again and again he said, "Are you happy, Jane?" And again and again I answered, "Yes." After which he murmured, "It will atone—it will atone. Have I not found her friendless, and cold, and comfortless? Will I not guard, and cherish, and solace her? Is there not love in my heart, and constancy in my resolves? It will expiate at God's tribunal. I know my Maker sanctions what I do. For the world's judgment—I wash my hands thereof. For man's opinion—I defy it."

But what had befallen the night? The moon was not yet set, and we were all in shadow: I could scarcely see my master's face near as I was. And what ailed the chestnut tree? It writhed and groaned; while wind roared in the laurel walk, and came sweeping over us.

"We must go in," said Mr. Rochester: "the weather changes. I could have sat with thee till morning, Jane."

"And so," thought I, "could I with you." I should have said so, perhaps, but a livid, vivid spark leapt out of a cloud at which I was looking, and there was a crack, a crash, and close rattling peal; and I thought only of hiding my dazzled eyes against Mr. Rochester's shoulder.

The rain rushed down. He hurried me up the walk, through the grounds, and into the house; but we were quite wet before we could pass the threshold. He was taking off my shawl in the hall, and shaking the water out of my loosened hair, when Mrs. Fairfax emerged from her room. I did not observe her at first, nor did Mr. Rochester. The lamp was lit. The clock was on the stroke of twelve.

"Hasten to take off your wet things," said he; "and before you go, good-night—good-night, my darling!"

He kissed me repeatedly. When I looked up, on leaving his arms, there stood the widow, pale, grave, and amazed. I only smiled at her, and ran up stairs. "Explanation will do for another time," thought I. Still, when I reached my chamber, I felt a pang at the idea she should even temporarily misconstrue what she had seen. But joy soon effaced every other feeling; and loud as the wind blew, near and deep as the thunder crashed, fierce and frequent as the lightning gleamed, cataract-like as the rain fell during a storm of two hours' duration, I experienced no fear, and little awe. Mr. Rochester came thrice to my door in the course of it, to ask if I was safe and tranquil: and that was comfort, that was strength for anything.

Before I left my bed in the morning, little Adèle came running in to tell me that the great horse-chestnut at the bottom of the orchard had been struck by lightning in the night, and half of it split away.

· · · · · · · ·

Chapter 24

As I rose and dressed, I thought over what had happened, and wondered if it were a dream. I could not be certain of the reality till I had seen Mr. Rochester again, and heard him renew his words of love and promise.

While arranging my hair, I looked at my face in the glass, and felt it was no longer plain: there was hope in its aspect, and life in its colour; and my eyes seemed as if they had beheld the fount of fruition, and borrowed beams from the lustrous ripple. I had often been unwilling to look at my master, because I feared he could not be pleased at my look; but I was sure I might lift my face to his now, and not cool his affection by its expression. I took a plain but clean and light summer dress from my drawer and put it on: it seemed no attire had ever so well become me; because none had I ever worn in so blissful a mood.

I was not surprised, when I ran down into the hall, to see that a brilliant June morning had succeeded to the tempest of the night; and to feel, through the open glass door, the breathing of a fresh and fragrant breeze. Nature must be gladsome when I was so happy. A beggar-woman and her little boy—pale, ragged objects both—were coming up the walk, and I ran down and gave them all the money I happened to have in my purse—some three or four shillings: good or bad, they must partake of my jubilee. The rooks cawed, and blither birds sang; but nothing was so merry or so musical as my own rejoicing heart.

Mrs. Fairfax surprised me by looking out of the window with a sad countenance, and saying gravely:—"Miss Eyre, will you come to breakfast?" During the meal she was quiet and cool: but I could not undeceive her then. I must wait for my master to give explanations; and so must she. I ate what I could, and then I hastened up stairs. I met Adèle leaving the school-room.

"Where are you going? It is time for lessons."

"Mr. Rochester has sent me away to the nursery."

"Where is he?"

"In there," pointing to the apartment she had left; and I went in, and there he stood.

"Come and bid me good-morning," said he. I gladly advanced; and it was not merely a cold word now, or even a shake of the hand that I received, but an embrace and a kiss. It seemed natural: it seemed genial to be so well-loved, so caressed by him.

"Jane, you look blooming, and smiling, and pretty," said he: "truly pretty this morning. Is this my pale, little elf? Is this my mustard-seed? This little sunny-faced girl with the dimpled cheek and rosy lips; the satin-smooth hazel hair, and the radiant hazel eyes?" (I had green eyes, reader; but you must excuse the mistake: for him they were new-dyed, I suppose.)

"It is Jane Eyre, sir."

"Soon to be Jane Rochester," he added: "in four weeks, Janet; not a day more. Do you hear that?"

I did, and I could not quite comprehend it: it made me giddy. The feeling, the announcement sent through me, was something stronger than was consistent with joy—something that smote and stunned: it was, I think, almost fear.

"You blushed, and now you are white, Jane: what is that for?"

"Because you gave me a new name—Jane Rochester; and it seems so strange."

"Yes; Mrs. Rochester," said he; "young Mrs. Rochester—Fairfax Rochester's girl-bride."

"It can never be, sir; it does not sound likely. Human beings never enjoy complete happiness in this world. I was not born for a different destiny to the rest of my species: to imagine such a lot befalling me is a fairy tale—a day-dream."

"Which I can and will realize. I shall begin to-day. This morning I wrote to my banker in London to send me certain jewels he has in his keeping,—heir-looms for the ladies of Thornfield. In a day or two I hope to pour them into your lap: for every privilege, every attention shall be yours, that I would accord a peer's daughter, if about to marry her."

"Oh, sir!—never mind jewels! I don't like to hear them spoken of. Jewels for Jane Eyre sounds unnatural and strange: I would rather not have them."

"I will myself put the diamond chain round your neck, and the circlet on your forehead,—which it will become: for nature, at least, has stamped her patent of nobility on this brow, Jane; and I will clasp the bracelets on these fine wrists, and load these fairy-like fingers with rings."

"No, no, sir! think of other subjects, and speak of other things, and in another strain. Don't address me as if I were a beauty; I am your plain, Quakerish governess."

"You are a beauty, in my eyes; and a beauty just after the desire of my heart,—delicate and aerial."

"Puny and insignificant, you mean. You are dreaming, sir—or you are sneering. For God's sake don't be ironical!"

"I will make the world acknowledge you a beauty, too," he went on, while I really become uneasy at the strain he had adopted; because I felt he was either deluding himself, or trying to delude me. "I will attire my Jane in satin and lace, and she shall have roses in her hair; and I will cover the head I love best with a priceless veil."

"And then you won't know me, sir; and I shall not be your Jane Eyre any longer, but an ape in a harlequin's jacket,—a jay in borrowed plumes. I would as soon see you, Mr. Rochester, tricked out in stage-trappings, as myself clad in a court-lady's robe; and I don't call you handsome, sir, though I love you most dearly: far too dearly to flatter you. Don't flatter me."

He pursued his theme, however, without noticing my deprecation. "This very day I shall take you in the carriage to Millcote, and you must choose some dresses for yourself. I told you we shall be married in four weeks. The wedding is to take place quietly, in the church down below yonder; and then I shall waft you away at once to town. After a brief stay there, I shall bear my treasure to regions nearer the sun: to French vineyards and Italian plains; and she shall see whatever is famous in old story and in modern record: she shall taste, too, of the life of cities; and she shall learn to value herself by just comparison with others."

"Shall I travel?—and with you, sir?"

"You shall sojourn at Paris, Rome, and Naples: at Florence, Venice, and Vienna: all the ground I have wandered over shall be re-trodden by you: wherever I stamped my hoof, your sylph's foot shall step also. Ten years since, I flew through Europe half mad; with disgust, hate, and rage, as my companions: now I shall revisit it healed and cleansed, with a very angel as my comforter."

I laughed at him as he said this. "I am not an angel," I asserted; "and I will not be one till I die: I will be myself. Mr. Rochester, you must neither expect nor exact anything celestial of me—for you will not get it, any more than I shall get it of you; which I do not at all anticipate."

"What do you anticipate of me?"

"For a little while you will perhaps be as you are now,—a very little while; and then you will turn cool; and then you will be capricious; and then you will be stern, and I shall have much ado to please you: but when you get well used to me, you will perhaps like me again,—*like* me, I say, not *love* me. I suppose your love will effervesce in six months, or less. I have observed in books written by men, that period assigned as the farthest to which a husband's ardour extends. Yet, after all, as a friend and companion, I hope never to become quite distasteful to my dear master."

"Distasteful! and like you again! I think I shall like you again and yet again: and I will make you confess I do not only *like*, but *love* you—with truth, fervour, constancy."

"Yet are you not capricious, sir?"

"To women who please me only by their faces, I am the very devil when I find out they have neither souls nor hearts—when they open to me a perspective of flatness, triviality, and perhaps imbecility, coarseness, and ill-temper: but to the clear eye and eloquent tongue, to the soul made of fire, and the character that bends but does not break—at once supple and stable, tractable and consistent—I am ever tender and true."

"Had you ever experience of such a character, sir? Did you ever love such an one?"

"I love it now."

"But before me: if I, indeed, in any respect come up to that difficult standard?"

"I never met your likeness. Jane: you please me, and you master me— you seem to submit, and I like the sense of pliancy you impart; and while I am twining the soft, silken skein round my finger, it sends a thrill up my arm to my heart. I am influenced—conquered; and the influence is sweeter than I can express; and the conquest I undergo has a witchery beyond any triumph *I* can win. Why do you smile, Jane? What does that inexplicable, that uncanny turn of countenance mean?"

"I was thinking, sir (you will excuse the idea; it was involuntary), I was thinking of Hercules and Samson with their charmers——"

"You were, you little elfish ——"

"Hush, sir! You don't talk very wisely just now; any more than those gentlemen acted very wisely. However, had they been married, they would no doubt by their severity as husbands have made up for their softness as suitors; and so will you, I fear. I wonder how you will answer me a year hence, should I ask a favour it does not suit your convenience or pleasure to grant."

"Ask me something now, Janet—the least thing: I desire to be entreated——"

"Indeed, I will, sir; I have my petition all ready."

"Speak! But if you look up and smile with that countenance, I shall swear concession before I know to what, and that will make a fool of me."

"Not at all, sir; I ask only this: don't send for the jewels, and don't crown me with roses: you might as well put a border of gold lace round that plain pocket handkerchief you have there."

"I might as well 'gild refined gold.' I know it: your request is granted then—for the time. I will remand the order I despatched to my banker. But you have not yet asked for anything; you have prayed a gift to be withdrawn: try again."

"Well, then, sir; have the goodness to gratify my curiosity, which is much piqued on one point."

He looked disturbed. "What? what?" he said hastily. "Curiosity is a dangerous petitioner: it is well I have not taken a vow to accord every request——"

"But there can be no danger in complying with this, sir."

"Utter it, Jane: but I wish that instead of a mere inquiry into, perhaps, a secret, it was a wish for half my estate."

"Now, king Ahasuerus! What do I want with half your estate? Do you think I am a Jew-usurer, seeking good investment in land? I would much rather have all your confidence. You will not exclude me from your confidence, if you admit me to your heart?"

"You are welcome to all of my confidence that is worth having, Jane: but for God's sake, don't desire a useless burden! Don't long for poison—don't turn out a downright Eve on my hands!"

"Why not, sir? You have just been telling me how much you like to be conquered, and how pleasant overpersuasion is to you. Don't you think I had better take advantage of the confession, and begin and coax, and entreat—even cry and be sulky if necessary—for the sake of a mere essay of my power?"

"I dare you to any such experiment. Encroach, presume, and the game is up."

"Is it, sir? You soon give in. How stern you look now! Your eyebrows have become as thick as my finger, and your forehead resembles, what, in some very astonishing poetry, I once saw styled, 'a blue-piled thunderloft.' That will be your married look, sir, I suppose?"

"If that will be *your* married look, I, as a Christian, will soon give up the notion of consorting with a mere sprite or salamander. But what had you to ask, thing?—out with it!"

"There, you are less than civil now; and I like rudeness a great deal better than flattery. I had rather be a *thing* than an angel. This is what I have to ask,—Why did you take such pains to make me believe you wished to marry Miss Ingram?"

"Is that all? Thank God, it is no worse!" And now he unknit his black brows; looked down, smiling at me, and stroked my hair, as if well pleased at seeing a danger averted. "I think I may confess," he continued, "even although I should make you a little indignant, Jane—and I have seen what a fire-spirit you can be when you are indignant. You glowed in the cool moonlight last night, when you mutinied against fate, and claimed your rank as my equal. Janet, by-the-by, it was you who made me the offer."

"Of course I did. But to the point if you please, sir—Miss Ingram?"

"Well, I feigned courtship of Miss Ingram, because I wished to render you as madly in love with me as I was with you; and I knew jealousy would be the best ally I could call in for the furtherance of that end."

"Excellent!—Now you are small—not one whit bigger than the end of my little finger. It was a burning shame, and a scandalous disgrace to act in that way. Did you think nothing of Miss Ingram's feelings, sir?"

"Her feelings are concentrated on one—pride; and that needs humbling. Were you jealous, Jane?"

"Never mind, Mr. Rochester: it is in no way interesting to you to know that. Answer me truly once more. Do you think Miss Ingram will not suffer from your dishonest coquetry? Won't she feel forsaken and deserted?"

"Impossible!—when I told you how she, on the contrary, deserted me: the idea of my insolvency cooled, or rather extinguished, her flame in a moment."

"You have a curious, designing mind, Mr. Rochester. I am afraid your principles on some points are eccentric."

"My principles were never trained, Jane: they may have grown a little awry for want of attention."

"Once again, seriously; may I enjoy the great good that has been vouchsafed to me, without fearing that any one else is suffering the bitter pain I myself felt a while ago?"

"That you may, my good little girl: there is not another being in the world has the same pure love for me as yourself—for I lay that pleasant unction to my soul, Jane, a belief in your affection."

I turned my lips to the hand that lay on my shoulder. I loved him very much—more than I could trust myself to say—more than words had power to express.

"Ask something more," he said presently; "it is my delight to be entreated, and to yield."

I was again ready with my request. "Communicate your intentions to Mrs. Fairfax, sir: she saw me with you last night in the hall, and she was shocked. Give her some explanation before I see her again. It pains me to be misjudged by so good a woman."

"Go to your room, and put on your bonnet," he replied. "I mean you to accompany me to Millcote this morning; and while you prepare for the drive, I will enlighten the old lady's understanding. Did she think, Janet, you had given the world for love, and considered it well lost?"

"I believe she thought I had forgotten my station; and yours, sir."

"Station! station!—your station is in my heart, and on the necks of those who would insult you, now or hereafter.—Go."

I was soon dressed; and when I heard Mr. Rochester quit Mrs. Fairfax's parlour, I hurried down to it. The old lady had been reading her morning portion of Scripture—the lesson for the day; her Bible lay open before her, and her spectacles were upon it. Her occupation, suspended by Mr. Rochester's announcement, seemed now forgotten: her eyes, fixed

on the blank wall opposite, expressed the surprise of a quiet mind, stirred
by unwonted tidings. Seeing me, she roused herself: she made a sort of
effort to smile, and framed a few words of congratulation; but the smile
expired, and the sentence was abandoned unfinished. She put up her spectacles, shut the Bible, and pushed her chair back from the table.

"I feel so astonished," she began, "I hardly know what to say to you,
Miss Eyre. I have surely not been dreaming, have I? Sometimes I half
fall asleep when I am sitting alone, and fancy things that have never happened. It has seemed to me more than once, when I have been in a doze,
that my dear husband, who died fifteen years since, has come in and sat
down beside me; and that I have even heard him call me by my name,
Alice, as he used to do. Now, can you tell me whether it is actually true
that Mr. Rochester has asked you to marry him? Don't laugh at me. But
I really thought he came in here five minutes ago, and said, that in a month
you would be his wife."

"He has said the same thing to me," I replied.

"He has! Do you believe him? Have you accepted him?"

"Yes."

She looked at me bewildered.

"I could never have thought it. He is a proud man: all the Rochesters
were proud: and his father, at least, liked money. He, too, has always been
called careful. He means to marry you?"

"He tells me so."

She surveyed my whole person: in her eyes I read that they had there
found no charm powerful enough to solve the enigma.

"It passes me!" she continued: "but no doubt it is true since you say
so. How it will answer, I cannot tell: I really don't know. Equality of position and fortune is often advisable in such cases; and there are twenty years
of difference in your ages. He might almost be your father."

"No, indeed, Mrs. Fairfax!" exclaimed I, nettled; "he is nothing like
my father! No one, who saw us together, would suppose it for an instant.
Mr. Rochester looks as young, and is as young as some men at five-and-
twenty."

"Is it really for love he is going to marry you?" she asked.

I was so hurt by her coldness and scepticism, that the tears rose to my eyes.

"I am sorry to grieve you," pursued the widow; "but you are so young,
and so little acquainted with men, I wished to put you on your guard. It
is an old saying that 'all is not gold that glitters;' and in this case I do
fear there will be something found to be different to what either you or
I expect."

"Why?—am I a monster?" I said: "is it impossible that Mr. Rochester
should have a sincere affection for me?"

"No: you are very well; and much improved of late; and Mr. Rochester,
I daresay, is fond of you. I have always noticed that you were a sort of
pet of his. There are times when, for your sake, I have been a little uneasy
at his marked preference, and have wished to put you on your guard: but
I did not like to suggest even the possibility of wrong. I knew such an
idea would shock, perhaps offend you; and you were so discreet, and so
thoroughly modest and sensible, I hoped you might be trusted to protect
yourself. Last night I cannot tell you what I suffered when I sought all
over the house, and could find you nowhere, nor the master either: and
then, at twelve o'clock, saw you come in with him."

"Well, never mind that now," I interrupted, impatiently: "It is enough that all was right."

"I hope all will be right in the end," she said: "but, believe me, you cannot be too careful. Try and keep Mr. Rochester at a distance: distrust yourself as well as him. Gentlemen in his station are not accustomed to marry their governesses."

I was growing truly irritated: happily, Adèle ran in.

"Let me go,—let me go to Millcote too!" she cried. "Mr. Rochester won't: though there is so much room in the new carriage. Beg him to let me go, mademoiselle."

"That I will, Adèle;" and I hastened away with her, glad to quit my gloomy monitress. The carriage was ready: they were bringing it round to the front, and my master was pacing the pavement, Pilot following him backwards and forwards.

"Adèle may accompany us, may she not, sir?"

"I told her no. I'll have no brats!—I'll have only you."

"Do let her go, Mr. Rochester, if you please: it would be better."

"Not it: she will be a restraint."

He was quite peremptory, both in look and voice. The chill of Mrs. Fairfax's warnings, and the damp of her doubts, were upon me: something of unsubstantiality and uncertainty had beset my hopes. I half lost the sense of power over him. I was about mechanically to obey him, without further remonstrance; but as he helped me into the carriage, he looked at my face.

"What is the matter?" he asked: "all the sunshine is gone. Do you really wish the bairn to go? Will it annoy you if she is left behind?"

"I would far rather she went, sir."

"Then off for your bonnet, and back, like a flash of lightning!" cried he to Adèle.

She obeyed him with what speed she might.

"After all, a single morning's interruption will not matter much," said he, "when I mean shortly to claim you—your thoughts, conversation, and company—for life."

Adèle, when lifted in, commenced kissing me, by way of expressing her gratitude for my intercession: she was instantly stowed away into a corner on the other side of him. She then peeped round to where I sat; so stern a neighbour was too restrictive: to him in his present fractious mood, she dared whisper no observations, nor ask of him any information.

"Let her come to me," I entreated; "she will, perhaps, trouble you, sir: there is plenty of room on this side."

He handed her over as if she had been a lap-dog; "I'll send her to school yet," he said, but now he was smiling.

Adèle heard him, and asked if she was to go to school *"sans mademoiselle?"*

"Yes," he replied, "absolutely sans mademoiselle; for I am to take mademoiselle to the moon, and there I shall seek a cave in one of the white valleys among the volcano-tops, and mademoiselle shall live with me there, and only me."

"She will have nothing to eat: you will starve her," observed Adèle.

"I shall gather manna for her morning and night: the plains and hillsides in the moon are bleached with manna, Adèle."

"She will want to warm herself: what will she do for a fire?"

"Fire rises out of the lunar mountains: when she is cold, I'll carry her up to a peak and lay her down on the edge of a crater."

"*Oh, qu'elle y sera mal—peu comfortable!* And her clothes, they will wear out: how can she get new ones?"

Mr. Rochester professed to be puzzled. "Hem!" said he. "What would you do, Adèle? Cudgel your brains for an expedient. How would a white or a pink cloud answer for a gown, do you think? And one could cut a pretty enough scarf out of a rainbow."

"She is far better as she is," concluded Adèle, after musing some time: "besides, she would get tired of living with only you in the moon. If I were *mademoiselle*, I would never consent to go with you."

"She has consented: she has pledged her word."

"But you can't get her there: there is no road to the moon: it is all air; and neither you nor she can fly."

"Adèle, look at that field." We were now outside Thornfield gates, and bowling lightly along the smooth road to Millcote, where the dust was well laid by the thunder-storm, and where the low hedges and lofty timber trees on each side glistening green, and rain-refreshed.

"In that field, Adele, I was walking late one evening about a fortnight since—the evening of the day you helped me to make hay in the orchard meadows; and as I was tired with raking swaths, I sat down to rest me on a stile; and there I took out a little book and a pencil, and began to write about a misfortune that befell me long ago, and a wish I had for happy days to come: I was writing away very fast, though daylight was fading from the leaf, when something came up the path and stopped two yards off me. I looked at it. It was a little thing with a veil of gossamer on its head. I beckoned it to come near me: it stood soon at my knee. I never spoke to it, and it never spoke to me, in words: but I read its eyes, and it read mine; and our speechless colloquy was to this effect:—

"It was a fairy, and come from Elf-land, it said; and its errand was to make me happy: I must go with it out of the common world to a lonely place—such as the moon, for instance—and it nodded its head towards her horn, rising over Hay-hill: it told me of the alabaster cave and silver vale where we might live. I said I should like to go; but reminded it, as you did me, that I had no wings to fly.

" 'Oh,' returned the fairy, 'that does not signify! Here is a talisman will remove all difficulties;' and she held out a pretty gold ring. 'Put it,' she said, 'on the fourth finger of my left hand, and I am yours, and you are mine; and we shall leave earth, and make our own heaven yonder.' She nodded again at the moon. The ring, Adèle, is in my breeches-pocket, under the disguise of a sovereign: but I mean soon to change it to a ring again."

"But what has *mademoiselle* to do with it? I don't care for the fairy: you said it was *mademoiselle* you would take to the moon ——?"

"*Mademoiselle* is a fairy," he said, whispering mysteriously. Whereupon I told her not to mind his badinage; and she, on her part, evinced a fund of genuine French scepticism: denominating Mr. Rochester "*un vrai menteur*," and assuring him that she made no account whatever of his "*Contes de fée*," and that "*du reste, il n'y avait pas de fées, et quand même il y en avait*," she was sure they would never appear to him, nor ever give him rings, or offer to live with him in the moon.

The hour spent at Millcote was a somewhat harassing one to me. Mr. Rochester obliged me to go to a certain silk warehouse: there I was ordered to choose half a dozen dresses. I hated the business, I begged leave to defer it: no—it should be gone through with now. By dint of entreaties expressed in energetic whispers, I reduced the half-dozen to two: these, however, he vowed he would select himself. With anxiety I watched his eye rove over the gay stores: he fixed on a rich silk of the most brilliant amethyst dye, and a superb pink satin. I told him in a new series of whispers, that he might as well buy me a gold gown and a silver bonnet at once: I should certainly never venture to wear his choice. With infinite difficulty, for he was stubborn as a stone, I persuaded him to make an exchange in favour of a sober black satin and pearl-grey silk. "It might pass for the present," he said; "but he would yet see me glittering like a parterre."

Glad was I to get him out of the silk warehouse, and then out of a jeweller's shop: the more he bought me, the more my cheek burned with a sense of annoyance and degradation. As we re-entered the carriage, and I sat back feverish and fagged, I remembered what in the hurry of events, dark and bright, I had wholly forgotten—the letter of my uncle, John Eyre, to Mrs. Reed: his intention to adopt me and make me his testatrix. "It would, indeed, be a relief," I thought, "if I had ever so small an independency; I never can bear being dressed like a doll by Mr. Rochester, or sitting like a second Danae with the golden shower falling daily round me. I will write to Madeira the moment I get home, and tell my uncle John I am going to be married, and to whom: if I had but a prospect of one day bringing Mr. Rochester an accession of fortune, I could better endure to be kept by him now." And somewhat relieved by this idea (which I failed not to execute that day), I ventured once more to meet my master's and lover's eye; which most pertinaciously sought mine, though I averted both face and gaze. He smiled; and I thought his smile was such as a sultan might, in a blissful and fond moment, bestow on a slave his gold and gems had enriched: I crushed his hand, which was ever hunting mine, vigorously, and thrust it back to him red with the passionate pressure—

"You need not look in that way," I said: "if you do, I'll wear nothing but my old Lowood frocks to the end of the chapter. I'll be married in this lilac gingham—you may make a dressing-gown for yourself out of the pearl-grey silk, and an infinite series of waistcoats out of the black satin."

He chuckled; he rubbed his hands: "Oh, it is rich to see and hear her!" he exclaimed. "Is she original? Is she piquant? I would not exchange this one little English girl for the grand Turk's whole seraglio; gazelle-eyes, houri forms and all!"

The eastern allusion bit me again: "I'll not stand you an inch in the stead of a seraglio," I said; "so don't consider me an equivalent for one; if you have a fancy for anything in that line, away with you, sir, to the bazaars of Stamboul without delay; and lay out in extensive slave-purchases some of that spare cash you seem at a loss to spend satisfactorily here."

"And what will you do, Janet, while I am bargaining for so many tons of flesh and such an assortment of black eyes?"

"I'll be preparing myself to go out as a missionary to preach liberty to them that are enslaved—your harem inmates amongst the rest. I'll get admitted there, and I'll stir up mutiny; and you, three-tailed bashaw as you are, sir, shall in a trice find yourself fettered amongst our hands: nor will I, for one, consent to cut your bonds till you have signed a charter, the most liberal that despot ever yet conferred."

"I would consent to be at your mercy, Jane."

"I would have no mercy, Mr. Rochester, if you supplicated for it with an eye like that. While you looked so, I should be certain that whatever charter you might grant under coercion, your first act, when released, would be to violate its conditions."

"Why, Jane, what would you have? I fear you will compel me to go through a private marriage ceremony, besides that performed at the altar. You will stipulate, I see, for peculiar terms—what will they be?"

"I only want an easy mind, sir; not crushed by crowded obligations. Do you remember what you said of Céline Varens?—of the diamonds, the cashmeres you gave her? I will not be your English Celine Varens. I shall continue to act as Adèle's governess: by that I shall earn my board and lodging, and thirty pounds a year besides. I'll furnish my own wardrobe out of that money, and you shall give me nothing but ——"

"Well, but what?"

"Your regard: and if I give you mine in return, that debt will be quit."

"Well, for cool native impudence, and pure innate pride, you haven't your equal," said he. We were now approaching Thornfield. "Will it please you to dine with me to-day?" he asked, as we re-entered the gates.

"No, thank you, sir."

"And what for, 'no, thank you'? if one may inquire."

"I never have dined with you, sir; and I see no reason why I should now: till ——"

"Till what? You delight in half phrases."

"Till I can't help it."

"Do you suppose I eat like an ogre, or a ghoul, that you dread being the companion of my repast?"

"I have formed no supposition on the subject, sir; but I want to go on as usual for another month."

"You will give up your governessing slavery at once."

"Indeed! begging your pardon, sir, I shall not. I shall just go on with it as usual, I shall keep out of your way all day, as I have been accustomed to do: you may send for me in the evening, when you feel disposed to see me, and I'll come then; but at no other time."

"I want a smoke, Jane, or a pinch of snuff, to comfort me under all this *'pour me donner une contenance,'* as Adèle would say; and unfortunately I have neither my cigar-case, nor my snuff-box, But listen—whisper—it is your time now, little tyrant, but it will be mine presently: and when once I have fairly seized you, to have and to hold, I'll just—figuratively speaking—attach you to a chain like this (touching his watch-guard). Yes, bonny wee thing, I'll wear you in my bosom, lest my jewel I should tyne."

He said this as he helped me to alight from the carriage; and while he afterwards lifted out Adèle, I entered the house, and made good my retreat up stairs.

He duly summoned me to his presence in the evening. I had prepared an occupation for him; for I was determined not to spend the whole time in a *tête-à-tête* conversation; I remembered his fine voice; I knew he liked to sing—good singers generally do. I was no vocalist myself, and in his fastidious judgment, no musician, either; but I delighted in listening when the performance was good. No sooner had twilight, that hour of romance, began to lower her blue and starry banner over the lattice, than I rose, opened the piano, and entreated him, for the love of heaven, to give me a song. He said I was a capricious witch, and that he would rather sing another time; but I averred that no time was like the present.

"Did I like his voice?" he asked.

"Very much," I was not fond of pampering that susceptible vanity of his; but for once, and from motives of expediency, I would e'en soothe and stimulate it.

"Then, Jane, you must play the accompaniment."

"Very well, sir, I will try."

I did try, but was presently swept off the stool and denominated, "a little bungler." Being pushed unceremoniously to one side—which was precisely what I wished—he usurped my place, and proceeded to accompany himself: for he could play as well as sing. I hied me to the window-recess; and while I sat there and looked out on the still trees and dim lawn, to a sweet air was sung in mellow tones, the following strain:—

> The truest love that ever heart
>   Felt as its kindled core
> Did through each vein, in quickened start,
>   The tide of being pour.
>
> Her coming was my hope each day,
>   Her parting was my pain;
> The chance that did her steps delay,
>   Was ice in every vein.
>
> I dreamed it would be nameless bliss,
>   As I loved, loved to be;
> And to this object did I press
>   As blind as eagerly.
>
> But wide as pathless was the space
>   That lay, our lives, between,
> And dangerous as the foamy race
>   Of ocean-surges green.
>
> And haunted as a robber-path
>   Through wilderness or wood;
> For Might and Right, and Woe and Wrath,
>   Between our spirits stood.
>
> I dangers dared; I hind'rance scorned;
>   I omens did defy:
> Whatever menaced, harassed, warned,
>   I passed impetuous by.
>
> On sped my rainbow, fast as light;
>   I flew as in a dream;
> For glorious rose upon my sight
>   That child of Shower and Gleam.
>
> Still bright on clouds of suffering dim
>   Shines that soft, solemn joy;
> Nor care I now, how dense and grim
>   Disasters gather nigh:

I care not in this moment sweet,
   Though all I have rushed o'er
Should come on pinion, strong and fleet,
   Proclaiming vengeance sore:

Though haughty Hate should strike me down,
   Right, bar approach to me,
And grinding Might, with furious frown,
   Swear endless enmity.

My love has placed her little hand
   With noble faith in mine,
And vowed that wedlock's sacred band
   Our natures shall entwine.

My love has sworn, with sealing kiss,
   With me to live—to die;
I have at last my nameless bliss:
   As I love—loved am I!

He rose and came towards me, and I saw his face all kindled, and his full falcon-eye flashing, and tenderness and passion in every lineament. I quailed momentarily—then I rallied. Soft scene, daring demonstration, I would not have; and I stood in peril of both: a weapon of defence must be prepared—I whetted my tongue: as he reached me, I asked with asperity, "whom he was going to marry now?"

"That was a strange question to be put by his darling Jane."

"Indeed! I considered it a very natural and necessary one: he had talked of his future wife dying with him. What did he mean by such a pagan idea? *I* had no intention of dying with him—he might depend on that."

"Oh, all he longed, all he prayed for, was that I might live with him! Death was not for such as I."

"Indeed it was: I had as good a right to die when my time came as he had: but I should bide that time, and not be hurried away in a suttee."

"Would I forgive him for the selfish idea, and prove my pardon by a reconciling kiss?"

"No: I would rather be excused."

Here I heard myself apostrophized as a "hard little thing;" and it was added, "any other woman would have been melted to marrow at hearing such stanzas crooned in her praise."

I assured him I was naturally hard—very flinty, and that he would often find me so; and that, moreover, I was determined to show him divers rugged points in my character before the ensuing four weeks elapsed: he should know fully what sort of a bargain he had made, while there was yet time to rescind it.

"Would I be quiet, and talk rationally?"

"I would be quiet if he liked; and as to talking rationally, I flattered myself I was doing that now."

He fretted, pished and pshawed. "Very good," I thought; "you may fume and fidget as you please: but this is the best plan to pursue with you, I am certain. I like you more than I can say; but I'll not sink into a bathos of sentiment: and with this needle of repartee I'll keep you from the edge of the gulph too; and, moreover, maintain by its pungent aid that distance between you and myself most conducive to our real mutual advantage."

From less to more, I worked him up to considerable irritation; then, after he had retired, in dudgeon, quite to the other end of the room, I got up, and saying, "I wish you good-night, sir," in my natural and wonted respectful manner, I slipped out by the side-door and got away.

The system thus entered on, I pursued during the whole season of probation; and with the best success. He was kept, to be sure, rather cross and crusty: but on the whole I could see he was excellently entertained; and that a lamb-like submission and turtle-dove sensibility, while fostering his despotism more, would have pleased his judgment, satisfied his common-sense, and even suited his taste, less.

In other people's presence I was, as formerly, deferential and quiet; any other line of conduct being uncalled-for: it was only in the evening conferences I thus thwarted and afflicted him. He continued to send for me punctually the moment the clock struck seven; though when I appeared before him now, he had no such honeyed terms as "love" and "darling" on his lips: the best words at my service were "provoking puppet," "malicious elf," "sprite," "changeling," etc. For caresses too, I now got grimaces; for a pressure of the hand, a pinch on the arm; for a kiss on the cheek, a severe tweak of the ear. It was all right: at present I decidedly preferred these fierce favours to anything more tender. Mrs. Fairfax, I saw approved me: her anxiety on my account vanished; therefore I was certain I did well. Meantime, Mr. Rochester affirmed I was wearing him to skin and bone, and threatened awful vengeance for my present conduct at some period fast coming. I laughed in my sleeve at his menaces: "I can keep you in reasonable check now," I reflected; "and I don't doubt to be able to do it hereafter: if one expedient loses its virtue, another must be devised."

Yet after all my task was not an easy one; often I would rather have pleased than teased him. My future husband was becoming to me my whole world; and more than the world: almost my hope of heaven. He stood between me and every thought of religion, as an eclipse intervenes between man and the broad sun. I could not, in those days, see God for his creature: of whom I had made an idol.

· · · · · · · ·

Chapter 25

The month of courtship had wasted: its very last hours were being numbered. There was no putting off the day that advanced—the bridal day; and all preparations for its arrival were complete. I, at least, had nothing more to do: there were my trunks, packed, locked, corded, ranged in a row along the wall of my little chamber; to-morrow, at this time, they would be far on their road to London: and so should I (D. V.),—or rather, not I, but one Jane Rochester, a person whom as yet I knew not. The cards of address alone remained to nail on: they lay, four little squares, on the drawer. Mr. Rochester had himself written the direction, "Mrs. Rochester,—Hotel, London," on each: I could not persuade myself to affix them, or to have them affixed. Mrs. Rochester! She did not exist: she would not be born till to-morrow, some time after eight o'clock A.M.; and I would wait to be assured she had come into the world alive, before I assigned to her all that property. It was enough that in yonder closet; opposite my

dressing-table, garments said to be hers had already displaced my black
stuff Lowood frock and straw bonnet: for not to me appertained that
suit of wedding raiment; the pearl-coloured robe, the vapoury veil, pendent from the usurped portmanteau. I shut the closet, to conceal the
strange, wraith-like apparel it contained; which, at this evening hour—
nine o'clock—gave out certainly a most ghostly shimmer through the
shadow of my apartment. "I will leave you by yourself, white dream,"
I said. "I am feverish: I hear the wind blowing; I will go out of doors
and feel it."

It was not only the hurry of preparation that made me feverish; not only
the anticipation of the great change—the new life which was to commence
to-morrow: both these circumstances had their share, doubtless, in producing that restless, excited mood which hurried me forth at this late hour
into the darkening grounds; but a third cause influenced my mind more
than they.

I had at heart a strange and anxious thought. Something had happened
which I could not comprehend; no one knew of or had seen the event but
myself: it had taken place the preceding night. Mr. Rochester that night
was absent from home; nor was he yet returned: business had called him
to a small estate of two or three farms he possessed thirty miles off—
business it was requisite he should settle in person, previously to his meditated departure from England. I waited now his return; eager to disbur-
then my mind, and to seek of him the solution of the enigma that perplexed me. Stay till he comes reader; and, when I disclose my secret to
him, you shall share the confidence.

I sought the orchard: driven to its shelter by the wind, which all day
had blown strong and full from the south; without, however, bringing a
speck of rain. Instead of subsiding as night drew on, it seemed to augment its rush and deepen its roar: the trees blew stedfastly one way, never
writhing round, and scarcely tossing back their boughs once in an hour;
so continuous was the strain bending their branchy heads northward—
the clouds drifted from pole to pole, fast following, mass on mass: no
glimpse of blue sky had been visible that July day.

It was not without a certain wild pleasure I ran before the wind delivering my trouble of mind to the measureless air-torrent thundering through
space. Descending the laurel-walk, I faced the wreck of the chestnut tree;
it stood up, black and riven: the trunk, split down the centre, gasped
ghastly. The cloven halves were not broken from each other, for the firm
base and strong roots kept them unsundered below; though community
of vitality was destroyed—the sap could flow no more: their great boughs
on each side were dead, and next winter's tempests would be sure to fell
one or both to earth: as yet, however, they might be said to form one
tree—a ruin, but an entire ruin.

"You did right to hold fast to each other," I said: as if the monster-
splinters were living things, and could hear me. "I think, scathed as you
look, and charred and scorched, there must be a little sense of life in you
yet; rising out of that adhesion at the faithful, honest roots: you will never
have green leaves more—never more see birds making nests and singing
idylls in your boughs; the time of pleasure and love is over with you; but
you are not desolate: each of you has a comrade to sympathize with him
in his decay." As I looked up at them, the moon appeared momentarily
in that part of the sky which filled their fissure; her disk was blood-red

and half overcast: she seemed to throw on me one bewildered, dreary glance, and buried herself again instantly in the deep drift of cloud. The wind fell, for a second, round Thornfield; but far away over wood and water, poured a wild, melancholy wail: it was sad to listen to, and I ran off again.

Here and there I strayed through the orchard, gathered up the apples with which the grass round the tree roots was thickly strewn: then I employed myself in dividing the ripe from the unripe; I carried them into the house and put them away in the store-room. Then I repaired to the library to ascertain whether the fire was lit; for, though summer, I knew on such a gloomy evening, Mr. Rochester would like to see a cheerful hearth when he came in: yes, the fire had been kindled some time, and burnt well. I placed his arm-chair by the chimney-corner: I wheeled the table near it: I let down the curtain, and had the candles brought in ready for lighting. More restless than ever, when I had completed these arrangements I could not sit still, nor even remain in the house: a little time-piece in the room and the old clock in the hall simultaneously struck ten.

"How late it grows!" I said: "I will run down to the gates: it is moonlight at intervals; I can see a good way on the road. He may be coming now, and to meet him will save some minutes of suspense."

The wind roared high in the great trees which embowered the gates; but the road as far as I could see, to the right hand and the left, was all still and solitary: save for the shadows of clouds crossing it at intervals, as the moon looked out, it was but a long pale line, unvaried by one moving speck.

A puerile tear dimmed my eye while I looked—a tear of disappointment and impatience: ashamed of it, I wiped it away. I lingered; the moon shut herself wholly within her chamber, and drew close her curtain of dense cloud: the night grew dark; rain came driving fast on the gale.

"I wish he would come! I wish he would come!" I exclaimed, seized with hypochondriac foreboding. I had expected his arrival before tea; now it was dark: what could keep him? Had an accident happened? The event of last night again recurred to me. I interpreted it as a warning of disaster. I feared my hopes were too bright to be realized; and I had enjoyed so much bliss lately that I imagined my fortune had passed its meridian, and must now decline.

"Well, I cannot return to the house," I thought; "I cannot sit by the fireside, while he is abroad in inclement weather: better tire my limbs than strain my heart; I will go forward and meet him."

I set out; I walked fast, but not far: ere I had measured a quarter of a mile, I heard the tramp of hoofs; a horseman came on, full gallop; a dog ran by his side. Away with evil presentiment! It was he: here he was, mounted on Mesrour, followed by Pilot. He saw me; for the moon had opened a blue field in the sky, and rode in it watery bright: he took his hat off, and waved it round his head. I now ran to meet him.

"There!" he exclaimed, as he stretched out his hand and bent from the saddle: "You can't do without me, that is evident. Step on my boot-toe; give me both hands: mount!"

I obeyed; joy made me agile: I sprang up before him. A hearty kissing I got for a welcome: and some boastful triumph; which I swallowed as well as I could. He checked himself in his exultation to demand, "But is there anything the matter, Jane, that you come to meet me at such an hour? Is there anything wrong?"

"No; but I thought you would never come. I could not bear to wait in the house for you, especially with this rain and wind."

"Rain and wind, indeed! Yes, you are dripping like a mermaid; pull my cloak round you: but I think you are feverish, Jane; both your cheek and hand are burning hot. I ask again, is there anything the matter?"

"Nothing, now: I am neither afraid nor unhappy."

"Then you have been both?"

"Rather: but I'll tell you all about it by-and-by, sir; and I dare say you will only laugh at me for my pains."

"I'll laugh at you heartily when to-morrow is past; till then I dare not: my prize is not certain. This is you; who have been as slippery as an eel this last month, and as thorny as a briar-rose? I could not lay a finger anywhere but I was pricked; and now I seem to have gathered up a stray lamb in my arms: you wandered out of the fold to seek your shepherd, did you, Jane?"

"I wanted you: but don't boast. Here we are at Thornfield: now let me get down."

He landed me on the pavement. As John took his horse, and he followed me into the hall, he told me to make haste and put something dry on, and then to return to him in the library; and he stopped me, as I made for the staircase, to extort a promise that I would not be long: nor was I long; in five minutes I rejoined him. I found him at supper.

"Take a seat, and bear me company, Jane: please God, it is the last meal but one you will eat at Thornfield Hall for a long time."

I sat down near him; but told him I could not eat.

"Is it because you have the prospect of a journey before you, Jane? Is it the thoughts of going to London that takes away your appetite?"

"I cannot see my prospects clearly to-night, sir; and I hardly know what thoughts I have in my head. Everything in life seems unreal."

"Except me: I am substantial enough:—touch me."

"You, sir, are the most phantom-like of all: you are a mere dream."

He held out his hand, laughing: "Is that a dream?" said he, placing it close to my eyes. He had a rounded, muscular, and vigorous hand, as well as a long, strong arm.

"Yes; though I touch it, it is a dream," said I, as I put it down from before my face. "Sir, have you finished supper?"

"Yes, Jane."

I rang the bell, and ordered away the tray. When we were again alone, I stirred the fire, and then took a low seat at my master's knee.

"It is near midnight," I said.

"Yes: but remember, Jane, you promised to wake with me the night before my wedding."

"I did; and I will keep my promise, for an hour or two at least: I have no wish to go to bed."

"Are all your arrangements complete?"

"All, sir."

"And on my part, likewise," he returned. "I have settled everything; and we shall leave Thornfield to-morrow, within half an hour after our return from church."

"Very well, sir."

"With what an extraordinary smile you uttered that word—'very well,' Jane! What a bright spot of colour you have on each cheek! and how strangely your eyes glitter! Are you well?"

"I believe I am."

"Believe! What is the matter?—Tell me what you feel."

"I could not, sir: no words could tell you what I feel. I wish this present hour would never end: who knows with what fate the next may come charged?"

"This is hypochondria, Jane. You have been over-excited, or over-fatigued."

"Do you, sir, feel calm and happy?"

"Calm?—no: but happy—to the heart's core."

I looked up at him to read the signs of bliss in his face: it was ardent and flushed.

"Give me your confidence, Jane," he said: "relieve your mind of any weight that oppresses it, by imparting it to me. What do you fear?—that I shall not prove a good husband?"

"It is the idea farthest from my thoughts."

"Are you apprehensive of the new sphere you are about to enter?—of the new life into which you are passing?"

"No."

"You puzzle me, Jane: your look and tone of sorrowful audacity perplex and pain me. I want an explanation."

"Then, sir,—listen. You were from home last night?"

"I was: I know that; and you hinted a while ago at something which had happened in my absence:—nothing, probably, of consequence; but, in short, it has disturbed you. Let me hear it. Mrs. Fairfax has said something, perhaps? or you have overheard the servants talk?—your sensitive self-respect has been wounded?"

"No, sir." It struck twelve—I waited till the time-piece had concluded its silver chime, and the clock its hoarse, vibrating stroke, and then I proceeded.

"All day, yesterday, I was very busy, and very happy in my ceaseless bustle; for I am not, as you seem to think, troubled by any haunting fears about the new sphere, et cetera: I think it a glorious thing to have the hope of living with you, because I love you. No, sir, don't caress me now—let me talk undisturbed. Yesterday I trusted well in Providence, and believed that events were working together for your good and mine: it was a fine day, if you recollect—the calmness of the air and sky forbade apprehensions respecting your safety or comfort on your journey. I walked a little while on the pavement after tea, thinking of you; and I beheld you in imagination so near me, I scarcely missed your actual presence. I thought of the life that lay before me—*your* life, sir—an existence more expansive and stirring than my own: as much more so as the depths of the sea to which the brook runs, are than the shallows of its own strait channel. I wondered why moralists call this world a dreary wilderness: for me it blossomed like a rose. Just at sunset, the air turned cold and the sky cloudy: I went in. Sophie called me up stairs to look at my wedding-dress, which they had just brought; and under it in the box I found your present—the veil which, in your princely extravagance, you sent for from London: resolved, I suppose, since I would not have jewels, to cheat me into accepting something as costly. I smiled as I unfolded it, and devised how I would tease you about your aristocratic tastes, and your efforts to masque your plebeian bride in the attributes of a peeress. I thought how I would carry down to you the square of unembroidered blonde I had myself prepared as a covering for my low-born head, and ask if that was not good enough for a woman who could bring her husband neither fortune, beauty, nor connections. I saw plainly how you would look; and heard your impetuous republican answers, and your haughty disavowal of any necessity on your part to augment your wealth, or elevate your standing, by marrying either a purse or a coronet."

"How well you read me, you witch!" interposed Mr. Rochester: "but what did you find in the veil besides its embroidery? Did you find poison, or a dagger, that you look so mournful now?"

"No, no, sir; besides the delicacy and richness of the fabric, I found nothing save Fairfax Rochester's pride; and that did not scare me, because I am used to the sight of the demon. But, sir, as it grew dark, the wind rose: it blew yesterday evening, not as it blows now—wild and high—but "with a sullen, moaning sound" far more eerie. I wished you were at home. I came into this room, and the sight of the empty chair and fireless hearth chilled me. For some time after I went to bed, I could not sleep—a sense of anxious excitement distressed me. The gale still rising, seemed to my ear to muffle a mournful under-sound; whether in the house or abroad I could not at first tell, but it recurred, doubtful yet doleful at every lull: at last I made out it must be some dog howling at a distance. I was glad when it ceased. On sleeping, I continued in dreams the idea of a dark and gusty night. I continued also the wish to be with you, and experienced a strange, regretful consciousness of some barrier dividing us. During all my first sleep, I was following the windings of an unknown road; total obscurity environed me; rain pelted me; I was burdened with the charge of a little child: a very small creature, too young and feeble to walk, and which shivered in my cold arms, and wailed piteously in my ear. I thought, sir, that you were on the road a long way before me; and I strained every nerve to overtake you, and made effort on effort to utter your name and entreat you to stop—but my movements were fettered; and my voice still died away inarticulate; while you, I felt, withdrew farther and farther every moment."

"And these dreams weigh on your spirits now, Jane, when I am close to you? Little nervous subject! Forget visionary woe, and think only of real happiness! You say you love me, Jane: yes—I will not forget that; and you cannot deny it. *Those* words did not die inarticulate on your lips. I heard them clear and soft: a thought too solemn perhaps, but sweet as music—'I think it is a glorious thing to have the hope of living with you, Edward, because I love you.'—Do you love me, Jane? repeat it."

"I do, sir,—I do, with my whole heart."

"Well," he said, after some minutes' silence, "it is strange: but that sentence has penetrated my breast painfully. Why? I think because you said it with such an earnest, religious energy; and because your upward gaze at me now is the very sublime of faith, truth, and devotion: it is too much as if some spirit were near me. Look wicked, Jane; as you know well how to look; coin one of your wild, shy, provoking smiles; tell me you hate me—tease me, vex me; do anything but move me: I would rather be incensed than saddened."

"I will tease you and vex you to your heart's content, when I have finished my tale: but hear me to the end."

"I thought, Jane, you had told me all. I thought I had found the source of your melancholy in a dream!"

I shook my head. "What! is there more? But I will not believe it to be anything important. I warn you of incredulity beforehand. Go on."

The disquietude of his air, the somewhat apprehensive impatience of his manner, surprised me: but I proceeded.

"I dreamt another dream, sir: that Thornfield Hall was a dreary ruin, the retreat of bats and owls. I thought that of all the stately front nothing remained but a shell-like wall, very high and very fragile-looking. I wandered, on a moonlight night, through the grass-grown enclosure within: here I stumbled over a marble hearth, and there over a fallen fragment of cornice. Wrapped up in a shawl, I still carried the unknown little child: I might not lay it down anywhere, however tired were my arms—however much its weight impeded my progress, I must retain it. I heard the gallop of a horse at a distance on the road: I was sure it was you; and you were departing for many years, and for a distant country. I climbed the thin wall with frantic perilous haste, eager to catch one glimpse of you from the top: the stones rolled from under my feet, the ivy branches I grasped gave way, the child clung round my neck in terror, and almost strangled me: at last I gained the summit. I saw you like a speck on a white track, lessening every moment. The blast blew so strong I could not stand. I sat down on the narrow ledge; I hushed the scared infant in my lap: you turned an angle of the road; I bent forward to take a last look; the wall crumbled; I was shaken; the child rolled from my knee; I lost my balance, fell, and woke."

"Now, Jane, that is all."

"All the preface, sir; the tale is yet to come. On waking, a gleam dazzled my eyes: I thought—oh, it is daylight! But I was mistaken: it was only candle-light. Sophie, I supposed, had come in. There was a light on the dressing-table, and the door of the closet, where, before going to bed, I had hung my wedding-dress and veil, stood open: I heard a rustling there. I asked, 'Sophie, what are you doing?' No one answered; but a form emerged from the closet: it took the light, held it aloft and surveyed the garments pendent from the portmanteau. 'Sophie! Sophie!' I again cried: and still it was silent. I had risen up in bed, I bent forward: first, surprise, then bewilderment, came over me; and then my blood crept cold through my veins. Mr. Rochester, this was not Sophie, it was not Leah, it was not Mrs. Fairfax: it was not—no, I was sure of it, and am still—it was not even that strange woman, Grace Poole."

"It must have been one of them," interrupted my master.

"No, sir, I solemnly assure you to the contrary. The shape standing before me had never crossed my eyes within the precincts of Thornfield Hall before; the height, the contour were new to me."

"Describe it, Jane."

"It seemed, sir, a woman, tall and large, with thick and dark hair hanging long down her back. I know not what dress she had on: it was white and straight; but whether gown, sheet, or shroud, I cannot tell."

"Did you see her face?"

"Not at first. But presently she took my veil from its place; she held it up, gazed at it long, and then she threw it over her own head, and turned to the mirror. At that moment I saw the reflection of the visage and features quite distinctly in the dark oblong glass."

"And how were they?"

"Fearful and ghastly to me—oh, sir, I never saw a face like it! It was a discoloured face—it was a savage face. I wish I could forget the roll of the red eyes and the fearful blackened inflation of the lineaments!"

"Ghosts are usually pale, Jane."

"This, sir, was purple: the lips were swelled and dark; the brow furrowed; the black eyebrows widely raised over the blood-shot eyes. Shall I tell you of what it reminded me?"

"You may."

"Of the foul German spectre—the Vampyre."

"Ah!—What did it do?"

"Sir, it removed my veil from its gaunt head, rent it in two parts, and flinging both on the floor, trampled on them."

"Afterwards?"

"It drew aside the window-curtain and looked out: perhaps it saw dawn approaching, for, taking the candle, it retreated to the door. Just at my bedside, the figure stopped: the fiery eye glared upon me—she thrust up her candle close to my face, and extinguished it under my eyes. I was aware her lurid visage flamed over mine, and I lost consciousness: for the second time in my life—only the second time—I became insensible from terror."

"Who was with you when you revived?"

"No one, sir; but the broad day. I rose, bathed my head and face in water, drank a long draught; felt that though enfeebled I was not ill, and determined that to none but you would I impart this vision. Now, sir, tell me who and what that woman was?"

"The creature of an over-stimulated brain; that is certain. I must be careful of you, my treasure: nerves like yours were not made for rough handling."

"Sir, depend on it, my nerves were not in fault; the thing was real: the transaction actually took place."

"And your previous dreams: were they real too? Is Thornfield Hall a ruin? Am I severed from you by insuperable obstacles? Am I leaving you without a tear—without a kiss—without a word?"

"Not yet."

"Am I about to do it?—Why the day is already commenced which is to bind us indissolubly; and when we are once united, there shall be no recurrence of these mental terrors: I guarantee that."

"Mental terrors, sir! I wish I could believe them to be only such: I wish it more now than ever; since even you cannot explain to me the mystery of that awful visitant."

"And since I cannot do it, Jane, it must have been unreal."

"But, sir, when I said so to myself on rising this morning, and when I looked round the room to gather courage and comfort from the cheerful aspect of each familiar object in full daylight, there—on the carpet—I saw what gave the distinct lie to my hypothesis,—the veil, torn from top to bottom in two halves!"

I felt Mr. Rochester start and shudder; he hastily flung his arms round me: "Thank God!" he exclaimed, "that if anything malignant did come near you last night, it was only the veil that was harmed.—Oh, to think what might have happened!"

He drew his breath short, and strained me so close to him, I could scarcely pant. After some minutes' silence, he continued, cheerily:—

"Now, Jane, I'll explain to you all about it. It was half dream, half reality: a woman did, I doubt not, enter your room: and that woman was—must have been—Grace Poole. You call her a strange being yourself: from all you know, you have reason so to call her—what did she do to me? what to Mason? In a state between sleeping and waking, you noticed her entrance and her actions; but feverish, almost delirious as you were, you ascribed to her a goblin appearance different from her own: the long dishevelled hair, the swelled black face, the exaggerated stature, were figments of imagination, results of nightmare: the spiteful tearing of the veil was real: and it is like her. I see you would ask why I keep such a woman in my house: when we have been married a year and a day, I will tell you; but not now. Are you satisfied, Jane? Do you accept my solution of the mystery?"

I reflected, and in truth it appeared to me the only possible one: satisfied I was not, but to please him I endeavoured to appear so—relieved, I certainly did feel; so I answered him with a contented smile. And now, as it was long past one, I prepared to leave him.

"Does not Sophie sleep with Adèle in the nursery?" he asked, as I lit my candle.

"Yes, sir."

"And there is room enough in Adèle's little bed for you. You must share it with her to-night, Jane: it is no wonder that the incident you have related should make you nervous, and I would rather you did not sleep alone:- promise me to go to the nursery."

"I shall be very glad to do so, sir."

"And fasten the door securely on the inside. Wake Sophie when you go up stairs, under pretence of requesting her to rouse you in good time to-morrow; for you must be dressed and have finished breakfast before eight. And now, no more sombre thoughts: chase dull care away, Jane. Don't you hear to what soft whispers the wind has fallen? and there is no more beating of rain against the window-panes: look here—(he lifted up the curtain) it is a lovely night!"

It was. Half heaven was pure and stainless: the clouds, now trooping before the wind, which had shifted to the west, were filing off eastward in long, silvered columns. The moon shone peacefully.

"Well," said Mr. Rochester, gazing inquiringly into my eyes, "how is my Jane now?"

"The night is serene, sir; and so am I."

"And you will not dream of separation and sorrow to-night; but of happy love and blissful union."

This prediction was but half fulfilled: I did not indeed dream of sorrow, but as little did I dream of joy; for I never slept at all. With little Adèle in my arms, I watched the slumber of childhood—so tranquil, so passionless, so innocent—and waited for the coming day: all my life was awake and astir in my frame: and as soon as the sun rose, I rose too. I remember Adèle clung to me as I left her: I remember I kissed her as I loosened her little hands from my neck; and I cried over her with strange emotion, and quitted her because I feared my sobs would break her still sound repose. She seemed the emblem of my past life; and he, I was now to array myself to meet, the dread, but adored, type of my unknown future day.

········

Chapter 26

Sophie came at seven to dress me; she was very long indeed in accomplishing her task; so long that Mr. Rochester, grown, I suppose, impatient of my delay, sent up to ask why I did not come. She was just fastening my veil (the plain square of blond after all) to my hair with a brooch; I hurried from under her hands as soon as I could.

"Stop!" she cried in French. "Look at yourself in the mirror: you have not taken one peep."

So I turned at the door: I saw a robed and veiled figure, so unlike my usual self that it seemed almost the image of a stranger. "Jane!" called a voice, and I hastened down. I was received at the foot of the stairs by Mr. Rochester.

"Lingerer," he said, "my brain is on fire with impatience; and you tarry so long!"

He took me into the dining-room, surveyed me keenly all over, pronounced me "fair as a lily, and not only the pride of his life, but the desire of his eyes," and then telling me he would give my but ten minutes to eat some breakfast, he rang the bell. One of his lately hired servants, a footman, answered it.

"Is John getting the carriage ready?"

"Yes, sir."

"Is the luggage brought down?"

"They are bringing it down, sir."

"Go you to the church: see if Mr. Wood (the clergyman) and the clerk are there: return and tell me."

The church, as the reader knows, was but just beyond the gates; the footman soon returned.

"Mr. Wood is in the vestry, sir, putting on his surplice."

"The horses are harnessing."

"We shall not want it to go to church; but it must be ready the moment we return: all the boxes and luggage arranged and strapped on, and the coachman in his seat."

"Yes, sir."

"Jane, are you ready?"

I rose. There were no groomsmen, no bridesmaids, no relatives to wait for or marshal: none but Mr. Rochester and I. Mrs. Fairfax stood in the hall as we passed. I would fain have spoken to her, but my hand was held by a grasp of iron: I was hurried along by a stride I could hardly follow; and to look at Mr. Rochester's face was to feel that not a second of delay would be tolerated for any purpose. I wonder what other bridegroom ever looked as he did—so bent up to a purpose, so grimly resolute: or who, under such steadfast brows, ever revealed such flaming and flashing eyes.

I know not whether the day was fair or foul; in descending the drive, I gazed neither on sky nor earth: my heart was with my eyes; and both seemed migrated into Mr. Rochester's frame. I wanted to see the invisible thing on which, as we went along, he appeared to fasten a glance fierce and fell. I wanted to feel the thoughts whose force he seemed breasting and resisting.

At the churchyard wicket he stopped: he discovered I was quite out of breath. "Am I cruel in my love?" he said. "Delay an instant: lean on me, Jane."

And now I can recall the picture of the gray old house of God rising calm before me, of a rook wheeling round the steeple, of a ruddy morning sky beyond. I remember something, too, of the green grave-mounds; and I have not forgotten, either, two figures of strangers, straying amongst the low hillocks, and reading the mementoes graven on the few mossy head-stones. I noticed them, because as they saw us, they passed round to the back of the church; and I doubted not they were going to enter by the side-aisle door, and witness the ceremony. By Mr. Rochester they were not observed; he was earnestly looking at my face, from which the blood had, I dare say, momentarily fled: for I felt my forehead dewy, and my cheeks and lips cold. When I rallied, which I soon did, he walked gently with me up the path to the porch.

We entered the quiet and humble temple; the priest waited in his white surplice at the lowly altar, the clerk beside him. All was still: two shadows only moved in a remote corner. My conjecture had been correct: the strangers had slipped in before us, and they now stood by the vault of the Rochesters, their backs towards us, viewing through the rails the old, time-stained marble tomb, where a kneeling angel guarded the remains of Damer de Rochester, slain at Marston Moor in the time of the civil wars; and of Elizabeth, his wife.

Our place was taken at the communion-rails. Hearing a cautious step behind me, I glanced over my shoulder: one of the strangers—a gentleman, evidently—was advancing up the chancel. The service began. The explanation of the intent of matrimony was gone through; and then the clergyman came a step further forward, and bending slightly towards Mr. Rochester, went on.

"I require and charge you both (as ye will answer at the dreadful day of judgment, when the secrets of all hearts shall be disclosed), that if either of you know any impediment why ye may not lawfully be joined together in matrimony, ye do now confess it; for be ye well assured that so many as are coupled together otherwise than God's word doth allow, are not joined together by God, neither is their matrimony lawful."

He paused, as the custom is. When is the pause after that sentence ever broken by a reply? Not, perhaps, once in a hundred years. And the clergyman, who had not lifted his eyes from his book, and had held his breath but for a moment, was proceeding: his hand was already stretched towards Mr. Rochester, as his lips unclosed to ask, "Wilt thou have this woman for thy wedded wife?"—when a distinct and near voice said:—

"The marriage cannot go on: I declare the existence of an impediment."

The clergyman looked up at the speaker, and stood mute; the clerk did the same; Mr. Rochester moved slightly, as if an earthquake had rolled under his feet: taking a firmer footing, and not turning his head or eyes, he said, "Proceed."

Profound silence fell when he had uttered that word, with deep but low intonation. Presently Mr. Wood said:—

"I cannot proceed without some investigation into what has been asserted, and evidence of its truth or falsehood."

"The ceremony is quite broken off," subjoined the voice behind us. "I am in a condition to prove my allegation: an insuperable impediment to this marriage exists."

Mr. Rochester heard, but heeded not: he stood stubborn and rigid: making no movement, but to possess himself of my hand. What a hot and strong grasp he had!—and how like quarried marble was his pale, firm, massive front at this moment! How his eye shone, still watchful, and yet wild beneath!

Mr. Wood seemed at a loss. "What is the nature of the impediment?" he asked. "Perhaps it may be got over—explained away?"

"Hardly," was the answer: "I have called it insuperable, and I speak advisedly."

The speaker came forwards, and leaned on the rails. He continued, uttering each word distinctly, calmly, steadily, but not loudly.

"It simply consists in the existence of a previous marriage: Mr. Rochester has a wife now living."

My nerves vibrated to those low-spoken words as they had never vibrated to thunder—my blood felt their subtle violence as it had never felt frost or fire: but I was collected, and in no danger of swooning. I looked at Mr. Rochester: I made him look at me. His whole face was colourless rock: his eye was both spark and flint. He disavowed nothing: he seemed as if he would defy all things. Without speaking; without smiling; without seeming to recognise in me a human being, he only twined my waist with his arm, and riveted me to his side.

"Who are you?" he asked of the intruder.

"My name is Briggs—a solicitor of —— Street, London."

"And you would thrust on me a wife?"

"I would remind you of your lady's existence, sir: which the law recognizes, if you do not."

"Favour me with an account of her—with her name, her parentage, her place of abode."

"Certainly." Mr. Briggs calmly took a paper from his pocket, and read out in a sort of official, nasal voice:—

" 'I affirm and can prove that on the 20th of October, A.D. ——, (a date of fifteen years back) Edward Fairfax Rochester of Thornfield Hall, in the county of ——, and of Ferndean Manor, in ——shire, England, was married to my sister, Bertha Antoinetta Mason, daughter of Jonas Mason, merchant, and of Antoinetta his wife, a Creole—at —— church, Spanish Town, Jamaica. The record of the marriage will be found in the register of that church—a copy of it is not in my possession. Signed, Richard Mason.' "

"That—if a genuine document—may prove I have been married, but it does not prove that the woman mentioned therein as my wife is still living."

"She was living three months ago," returned the lawyer.

"How do you know?"

"I have a witness to the fact; whose testimony even you, sir, will scarcely controvert."

"Produce him—or go to hell."

"I will produce him first—he is on the spot: Mr. Mason, have the goodness to step forward."

Mr. Rochester, on hearing the name, set his teeth; he experienced, too, a sort of strong convulsive quiver; near to him as I was, I felt the spasmodic movement of fury or despair run through his frame. The second stranger, who had hitherto lingered in the background, now drew near; a pale face looked over the solicitor's shoulder—yes, it was Mason himself. Mr. Rochester turned and glared at him. His eye, as I have often said, was a black eye: it had now a tawny, nay a bloody light in its gloom; and his face flushed—olive cheek, and hueless forehead received a glow, as from spreading, ascending heart-fire: and he stirred, lifted his strong arm—he could have struck Mason—dashed him on the church-floor—shocked by ruthless blow the breath from his body—but Mason shrank away, and cried faintly, "Good God!" Contempt fell cool on Mr. Rochester—his passion died as if a blight had shrivelled it up: he only asked, "What have *you* to say?"

An inaudible reply escaped Mason's white lips.

"The devil is in it if you cannot answer distinctly. I again demand, what have *you* to say?"

"Sir—sir—" interrupted the clergyman, "do not forget you are in a sacred place." Then addressing Mason, he inquired gently, "Are you aware, sir, whether or not his gentleman's wife is still living?"

"Courage," urged the lawyer,—"speak out."

"She is now living at Thornfield Hall;" said Mason, in more articulate tones: "I saw her there last April. I am her brother."

"At Thornfield Hall!" ejaculated the clergyman. "Impossible! I am on old resident in this neighbourhood, sir, and I never heard of a Mrs. Rochester at Thornfield Hall."

I saw a grim smile contort Mr. Rochester's lip and he muttered:—

"No—by God! I took care that none should hear of it—or of her under that name." He mused—for ten minutes he held counsel with himself: he formed his resolve, and announced it:—

"Enough—all shall bolt out at once, like the bullet from the barrel.—Wood, close your book and take off your surplice; John Green, (to the clerk) leave the church: there will be no wedding to-day:" the man obeyed.

Mr. Rochester continued, hardily and recklessly: "Bigamy is an ugly word!—I meant, however, to be a bigamist: but fate has out-manœuvred me; or Providence has checked me,—perhaps the last. I am little better than a devil at this moment; and, as my pastor there would tell me, deserve no doubt the sternest judgments of God,—even to the quenchless fire and deathless worm. Gentlemen, my plan is broken up!—what this lawyer and his client say is true: I have been married; and the woman to whom I was married lives! You say you never heard of a Mrs. Rochester at the house up yonder, Wood: but I daresay you have many a time inclined your ear to gossip about the mysterious lunatic kept there under watch and ward.

Some have whispered to you that she is my bastard half-sister: some, my cast-off mistress; I now inform you that she is my wife, whom I married fifteen years ago,—Bertha Mason by name; sister of this resolute personage, who is now, with his quivering limbs and white cheeks, showing you what a stout heart men may bear. Cheer up, Dick!—never fear me!—I'd almost strike a woman as you. Bertha Mason is mad; and she came of a mad family;—idiots and maniacs through three generations! Her mother, the Creole, was both a mad woman and a drunkard!—as I found out after I had wed the daughter: for they were silent on family secrets before. Bertha, like a dutiful child, copied her parent in both points. I had a charming partner—pure, wise, modest: you can fancy I was a happy man.—I went through rich scenes! Oh! my experience has been heavenly, if you only knew it! But I owe you no further explanation. Briggs, Wood, Mason,—I invite you all to come up to the house and visit Mrs. Poole's patient, and *my wife!*—You shall see what sort of a being I was cheated into espousing, and judge whether or not I had a right to break the compact, and seek sympathy with something at least human. This girl," he continued, looking at me, "knew no more than you, Wood, of the disgusting secret: she thought all was fair and legal; and never dreamt she was going to be entrapped into a feigned union with a defrauded wretch, already bound to a bad, mad, and embruted partner! Come, all of you, follow!"

Still holding me fast, he left the church: the three gentlemen came after. At the front door of the hall we found the carriage.

"Take it back to the coach-house, John," said Mr. Rochester, coolly; "it will not be wanted to-day."

At our entrance, Mrs. Fairfax, Adèle, Sophie, Leah, advanced to meet and greet us.

"To the right about—every soul!" cried the master: "away with your congratulations! Who wants them?—Not I!—they are fifteen years too late!"

He passed on and ascended the stairs, still holding my hand, and still beckoning the gentlemen to follow him; which they did. We mounted the first staircase, passed up the gallery, proceeded to the third story: the low, black door, opened by Mr. Rochester's master key, admitted us to the tapestried room, with its great bed, and its pictorial cabinet.

"You know this place, Mason," said our guide; "she bit and stabbed you here."

He lifted the hangings from the wall, uncovering the second door: this, too, he opened. In a room without a window, there burnt a fire, guarded by a high and strong fender, and a lamp suspended from the ceiling by a chain. Grace Poole bent over the fire, apparently cooking something in a saucepan. In the deep shade, at the further end of the room, a figure ran backwards and forwards. What it was, whether beast or human being, one could not, at first sight, tell: it grovelled, seemingly, on all fours; it snatched and growled like some strange wild animal: but it was covered with clothing; and a quanitity of dark, grizzled hair, wild as a mane, hid its head and face.

"Good-morrow, Mrs. Poole!" said Mr. Rochester. "How are you? and how is your charge to-day?"

"We're tolerable, sir, I thank you," replied Grace, lifting the boiling mess carefully on to the hob: "rather snappish, but not 'rageous."

A fierce cry seemed to give the lie to her favourable report: the clothed hyena rose up, and stood tall on its hind feet.

"Ah, sir, she sees you!" exclaimed Grace: "you'd better not stay."

"Only a few moments, Grace: you must allow me a few moments."

"Take care then, sir!—for God's sake, take care!"

The maniac bellowed: she parted her shaggy locks from her visage, and gazed wildly at her visitors. I recognized well that purple face,—those bloated features. Mrs. Poole advanced.

"Keep out of the way," said Mr. Rochester, thrusting her aside: "she has no knife now, I suppose? and I'm on my guard."

"One never knows what she has, sir: she is so cunning: it is not in mortal discretion to fathom her craft."

"We had better leave her," whispered Mason.

"Go to the devil!" was his brother-in-law's recommendation.

"'Ware!" cried Grace. The three gentlemen retreated simultaneously. Mr. Rochester flung me behind him: the lunatic sprang and grappled his throat viciously, and laid her teeth to his cheek: they struggled. She was a big woman, in stature almost equalling her husband, and corpulent besides: she showed virile force in the contest—more than once she almost throttled him, athletic as he was. He could have settled her with a well-planted blow; but he would not strike: he would only wrestle. At last he mastered her arms; Grace Poole gave him a cord, and he pinioned them behind her: with more rope, which was at hand, he bound her to a chair. The operation was performed amidst the fiercest yells, and the most convulsive plunges. Mr. Rochester then turned to the spectators: he looked at them with a smile both acrid and desolate.

"That is *my wife*," said he. "Such is the sole conjugal embrace I am ever to know—such are the endearments which are to solace my leisure hours! And *this* is what I wished to have (laying his hand on my shoulder): this young girl, who stands so grave and quiet at the mouth of hell, looking collectedly at the gambols of a demon. I wanted her just as a change after that fierce ragout. Wood and Briggs, look at the difference! Compare these clear eyes with the red balls yonder—this face with that mask—this form with that bulk; then judge me, priest of the Gospel and man of the law, and remember, with what judgment ye judge ye shall be judged! Off with you now. I must shut up my prize."

We all withdrew. Mr. Rochester stayed a moment behind us, to give some further order to Grace Poole. The solicitor addressed me as he descended the stair.

"You, madam," said he, "are cleared from all blame: your uncle will be glad to hear it—if, indeed, be should he still living—when Mr. Mason returns to Madeira."

"My uncle! What of him? Do you know him?"

"Mr. Mason does: Mr. Eyre has been the Funchal correspondent of his house for some years. When your uncle received your letter intimating the contemplated union between yourself and Mr. Rochester, Mr. Mason, who was staying at Madeira to recruit his health, on his way back to Jamaica, happened to be with him. Mr. Eyre mentioned the intelligence; for he knew that my client here was acquainted with a gentlemen of the name of Rochester. Mr. Mason, astonished and distressed as you may suppose, revealed the real state of matters. Your uncle, I am sorry to say, is now on a sick bed; from which, considering the nature of his disease—

decline—and the stage it has reached, it is unlikely he will ever rise. He could not then hasten to England himself, to extricate you from the snare into which you had fallen, but he implored Mr. Mason to lose no time in taking steps to prevent the false marriage. He referred him to me for assistance. I used all despatch, and am thankful I was not too late: as you, doubtless, must be also. Were I not morally certain that your uncle will be dead ere you reach Madeira, I would advise you to accompany Mr. Mason back: but as it is, I think you had better remain in England till you can hear further, either from or of Mr. Eyre. Have we anything else to stay for?" he inquired of Mr. Mason.

"No, no—let us be gone," was the anxious reply; and without waiting to take leave of Mr. Rochester, they made their exit at the hall door. The clergyman stayed to exchange a few sentences, either of admoition or reproof, with his haughty parishioner: this duty done, he too departed.

I heard him go as I stood at the half open door of my own room, to which I had now withdrawn. The house cleared, I shut myself in, fastened the bolt that none might intrude, and proceeded—not to week, not to mourn, I was yet too calm for that, but—mechanically to take off the wedding dress, and replace it by the stuff gown I had worn yesterday, as I thought, for the last time. I then sat down: I felt weak and tired. I leaned my arms on a table, and my head dropped on them. And now I thought: till now I had only heard, seen, moved—dollowed up and down where I was led or dragged—watched event rush on event, disclosure open beyond disclosure: but *now, I thought.*

The morning had been a quiet morning enough—all except the brief scene with the lunatic: the transaction in the church had not been noisy; there was no explosion of passion, no loud altercation, no dispute, no defiance or challenge, no tears, no sobs: a few words had been spoken, a calmly pronounced objection to the marriage made; some stern, short questions put by Mr. Rochester; answers, explanations given, evidence adduced; an open admission of the truth had been uttered by my master; then the living proof had been seen; the intruders were gone, and all was over.

I was in my own room as usual—just myself, without obvious change: nothing had smitten me, or scathed me, or maimed me. And yet, where was the Jane Eyre of yesterday?—where was her life?—where were her prospects?

Jane Eyre, who had been an ardent, expectant woman—almost a bride—was a cold, solitary girl again: her life was pale; her prospects were desolate. A Christmas frost had come at midsummer; a white December storm had whirled over June; ice glazed the ripe apples, drifts crushed the blowing roses; on hay-field and corn-field lay a frozen shroud: lanes which last night blushed full of flowers, to-day were pathless with untrodden snow; and the woods, which twelve hours since waved leafy and fragrant as groves between the tropics, now spread, waste, wild, and white as pine-forests in wintry Norway. My hopes were all dead—struck with a subtle doom, such as, in one night, fell on all the first-born in the land of Egypt. I looked on my cherished wishes, yesterday so blooming and glowing; they lay stark, chill, livid corpses that could never revive. I looked at my love: that feeling which was my master's—which he had created; it shivered in my heart, like a suffering child in a cold cradle; sickness and anguish had seized it; it could not seek Mr. Rochester's arms—it could not derive warmth from his breast. Oh, never more could it turn to him; for faith was blighted—confidence destroyed! Mr. Rochester was not to me what he had been; for he was not what I had thought him. I would not ascribe vice to him; I would not say he had betrayed me: but the attribute of stainless truth was gone from his idea; and from his presence I must go: *that* I perceived well. When—how—whither, I could not yet discern: but he himself I doubted not, would hurry me from Thornfield. Real affection, it seemed, he could not have for me; it had been only fitful passion: that was balked; he would want me no more. I should fear even to cross his path now: my view must be hateful to him. Oh, how blind had been my eyes! How weak my conduct!

My eyes were covered and closed; eddying darkness seemed to swim round me, and reflection came in as black and confused a flow. Self-abandoned, relaxed, and effortless, I seemed to have laid me down in the dried-up bed of a great river; I heard a flood loosened in remote mountains, and felt the torrent come: to rise I had no will, to flee I had no strength. I lay faint; longing to be dead. One idea only still throbbed life-like within me—a remembrance of God: it begot an un-uttered prayer: these words went wandering up and down in my rayless mind, as something that should be whispered; but no energy was found to express them:—

"Be not far from me, for trouble is near: there is none to help."

It was near: and as I had lifted no petition to Heaven to avert it—as I had neither joined my hands, nor bent my knees, nor moved my lips—it came: in full, heavy swing the torrent poured over me. The whole consciousness of my life lorn, my love lost, my hope quenched, my faith death-struck, swayed full and mighty above me in one sullen mass. That bitter hour cannot be described: in truth, "the waters came into my soul; I sank in deep mire: I felt no standing; I came into deep waters; the floods overflowed me."

·······

Chapter 27

Some time in the afternoon I raised my head, and looking round and seeing the western sun gilding the sign of its decline on the wall, I asked, "What am I to do?"

But the answer my mind gave—"Leave Thornfield at once"—was so prompt, so dread, that I stopped my ears: I said, I could not bear such words now. "That I am not Edward Rochester's bride, is the least part of my woe." I alleged: "that I have wakened out of most glorious dreams, and found them all void and vain, is a horror I could bear and master; but that I must leave him decidedly, instantly, entirely, is intolerable. I cannot do it."

But, then, a voice within me averred that I could do it; and foretold that I should do it. I wrestled with my own resolution: I wanted to be weak that I might avoid the awful passage of further suffering I saw laid out for me; and conscience, turned tyrant, held passion by the throat, told her, tauntingly, she had yet but dipped her dainty foot in the slough, and swore that with that arm of iron, he would thrust her down to unsounded depths of agony.

"Let me be torn away, then!" I cried, "Let another help me!"

"No; you shall tear yourself away, none shall help you: you shall, your-self, pluck out your right eye; yourself cut off your right hand: your heart shall be the victim; and you, the priest, to transfix it."

I rose up suddenly, terror-struck at the solitude which so ruthless a judge haunted,—at the silence which so awful a voice filled. My head swam as I stood erect: I perceived that I was sickening from excitement and inani-tion: neither meat nor drink had passed my lips that day, for I had taken no breakfast. And, with a strange pang, I now reflected that, long as I had been shut up here, no message had been sent to ask how I was, or to invite me to come down: not even little Adèle had tapped at the door; not even Mrs. Fairfax had sought me. "Friends always forget those whom fortune forsakes," I murmured, as I undrew the bolt and passed out. I stumbled over an obstacle: my head was still dizzy, my sight was dim, and my limbs were feeble. I could not soon recover myself. I fell, but not on to the ground: an out-stretched arm caught me; I looked up—I was supported by Mr. Rochester, who sat in a chair across my chamber threshold.

"You come out at last," he said. "Well, I have been waiting for you long, and listening: yet not one movement have I heard, nor one sob: five minutes more of that death-like hush, and I should have forced the lock like a burglar. So, you shun me?—you shut yourself up and grieve alone! I would rather you had come and upbraided me with vehemence. You are passionate: I expected a scene of some kind. I was prepared for the hot rain of tears; only I wanted them to be shed on my breast: now a senseless floor has received them, or your drenched handkerchief. But I err: you have not wept at all! I see a white cheek and a faded eye, but no trace of tears. I suppose, then, your heart has been weeping blood!

"Well, Jane; not a word of reproach? Nothing bitter—nothing poignant? Nothing to cut a feeling or sting a passion? You sit quietly where I have placed you, and regard me with a weary, passive look.

"Jane, I never meant to would you thus. If the man who had but one little ewe lamb that was dear to him as a daughter, that ate of his bread and drank of his cup, and lay in his bosom, had by some mistake slaugh-tered it at the shambles, he would not have rued his bloody blunder more than I now rue mine. Will you ever forgive me?"

Reader!—I forgave him at the moment, and on the spot. There was such deep remorse in his eye, such true pity in his tone, such manly energy in his manner; and, besides, there was such unchanged love in his whole look and mein—I forgave him all: yet not in words, not outwardly; only at my heart's core.

"You know I am a scoundrel, Jane?" ere long he inquired wistfully—wondering, I suppose, at my continued silence and tameness: the result rather of weakness than of will.

"Yes, sir."

"Then tell me so roundly and sharply—don't spare me."

"I cannot: I am tired and sick. I want some water." He heaved a sort of shuddering sigh and taking me in his arms, carried me down stairs. At first I did not know to what room he had borne me; all was cloudy to my glazed sight: presently I felt the reviving warmth of a fire; for, sum-mer as it was, I had become icy cold in my chamber. He put wine to my lips; I tasted it and revived; then I ate something he offered me, and was soon myself. I was in the library—sitting in his chair—he was quite near. "If I could go out of life now, without too sharp a pang, it would be well for me," I thought; "then I should not have to make the effort of cracking my heart-strings in rending them from among Mr. Rochester's. I must leave him, it appears. I do not want to leave him—I cannot leave him."

"How are you now, Jane?"

"Much better, sir: I shall be well soon."

"Taste the wine again, Jane."

I obeyed him; then he put the glass on the table, stood before me, and looked at me attentively. Suddenly he turned away, with an inarticulate exclamation, full of passionate emotion of some kind: he walked fast through the room and came back: he stooped towards me as if to kiss me; but I remembered caresses were now forbidden. I turned my face away, and put his aside.

"What!—How is this?" he exclaimed hastily, "Oh, I know! you won't kiss the husband of Bertha Mason? You consider my arms filled, and my embraces appropriated?"

"At any rate, there is neither room nor claim for me, sir."

"Why, Jane? I will spare you the trouble of much talking: I will answer for you—because I have a wife already, you would reply.—I guess rightly?"

"Yes."

"If you think so, you must have a strange opinion of me: you must regard me as a plotting profligate—a base and low rake who has been simulating disinterested love in order to draw you into a snare deliberately laid, and strip you of honour, and rob you of self-respect. What do you say to that? I see you can say nothing: in the first place, you are faint, still, and have enough to do to draw your breath; in the second place, you cannot yet accustom yourself to accuse and revile me; and, besides, the flood-gates of tears are opened, and they would rush out if you spoke much; and you have no desire to expostulate, to upbraid, to make a scene: you are thinking how *to act*—*talking*, you consider, is of no use. I know you—I am on my guard."

"Sir, I do not wish to act against you," I said; and my unsteady voice warned me to curtail my sentence.

"Not in *your* sense of the word but in *mine*, you are scheming to destroy me. You have as good as said that I am a married man—as a married man you will shun me, keep out of my way: just now you have refused to kiss me. You intend to make yourself a complete stranger to me; to live under this roof only as Adèle's governess: if ever I say a friendly word to you; if ever a friendly feeling inclines you again to me, you will say,—'That man had nearly made me his mistress: I must be ice and rock to him;' and ice and rock you will accordingly become."

I cleared and steadied my voice to reply: "All is changed about me, sir; I must change too—there is no doubt of that; and, to avoid fluctuations of feeling, and continual combats with recollections and associations, there is only one way—Adèle must have a new governess, sir."

"Oh, Adèle will go to school—I have settled that already: nor do I mean to torment you with the hideous associations and recollections of Thornfield Hall—this accursed place—this tent of Achan—this insolent vault, offering the ghastliness of living death to the light of the open sky—this narrow stone hell, with its one real fiend, worse than a legion of such as we imagine.—Jane, you shall not stay here, nor will I. I was wrong ever to bring you to Thornfield Hall, knowing as I did now it was haunted. I charged them to conceal from you, before I ever saw you, all knowledge of the curse of the place; merely because I feared Adèle never would have a governess to stay if she knew with what inmate she was housed, and my plans would not permit me to remove the maniac elsewhere—though I possess an old house, Ferndean Manor, even more retired and hidden than this, where I could have lodged her safely enough, had not a scruple about the unhealthiness of the situation, in the heart of a wood, made my conscience recoil from the arrangement. Probably those damp walls would soon have eased me of her charge: but to each villain his own vice; and mine is not a tendency to indirect assassination, even of what I most hate.

"Concealing the mad-woman's neighbourhood from you, however, was something like covering a child with a cloak, and laying it down near a upas-tree: that demon's vicinage is poisoned, and always was. But I'll shut up Thornfield Hall: I'll nail up the front door, and board the lower windows; I'll give Mrs. Poole two hundred a year to live here with *my wife*, as you term that fearful hag: Grace will do much for money, and she shall have her son, the keeper at Grimsby Retreat, to bear her company and be at hand to give her aid in the paroxysms, when *my wife* is prompted by her familiar to burn people in their beds at night, to stab them, to bite their flesh from their bones, and so on—"

"Sir," I interrupted him, "you are inexorable for that unfortunate lady: you speak of her with hate—with vindictive antipathy. It is cruel—she cannot help being mad."

"Jane, my little darling, (so I will call you, for so you are), you don't know what you are talking about; you misjudge me again: it is not because she is mad I hate her. If you were mad, do you think I should hate you?"

"I do indeed, sir."

"Then you are mistaken, and you know nothing about me, and nothing about the sort of love of which I am capable. Every atom of your flesh is as dear to me as my own; in pain and sickness it would still be dear. Your mind is my treasure, and if it were broken, it would be my treasure still: if you raved, my arms should confine you, and not a strait waist-coat—your grasp, even in fury, would have a charm for me: if you flew at me as wildly as that woman did this morning, I should receive you in an embrace, at least as fond as it would be restrictive. I should not shrink from you with disgust as I did from her: in your quiet moments you should have no watcher and no nurse but me; and I could hang over you with untiring tenderness, though you gave me no smile in return; and never weary of gazing into your eyes, though they had no longer a ray of recognition for me.—But why do I follow that train of ideas? I was talking of removing you from Thornfield. All, you know, is prepared for prompt departure: to-morrow you shall go. I only ask you to endure one more night under this roof, Jane; and then, farewell to its miseries and terrors for ever! I have a place to repair to, which will be a secure sanctuary from hateful reminiscences, from unwelcome intrusion—even from falsehood and slander."

"And take Adèle with you, sir," I interrupted; "she will be a companion for you."

"What do you mean, Jane? I told you I would send Adèle to school: and what do I want with a child for a companion? and not my own child,— a French dancer's bastard. Why do you importune me about her? I say, why do you assign Adèle to me for a companion?"

"You spoke of a retirement, sir; and retirement and solitude are dull: to dull for you."

"Solitude! solitude!" he reiterated, with irritation. "I see I must come to an explanation. I don't know what sphynx-like expression is forming in your countenance. *You* are to share my solitude. Do you understand?"

I shook my head: it required a degree of courage, excited as he was becoming, even to risk that mute sign of dissent. He had been walking fast about the room, and he stopped, as if suddenly rooted to one spot. He looked at me long and hard: I turned my eyes from him, fixed them on the fire, and tried to assume and maintain a quiet, collected aspect.

"Now for the hitch in Jane's character," he said at last, speaking more calmly than from his look I had expected him to speak. "The reel of silk has run smoothly enough so far; but I always knew there would come a knot and a puzzle: here it is. Now for vexation, and exasperation, and endless trouble! By God! I long to exert a fraction of Samson's strength, and break the entanglement like tow!"

He recommenced his walk: but soon again stopped, and this time just before me.

"Jane! will you hear reason?" (he stooped and approached his lips to my ear) "because, if you won't, I'll try violence." His voice was hoarse; his look that of a man who is just about to burst an insufferable bond and plunge headlong into wild licence. I saw that in another moment, and with one impetus of frenzy more, I should be able to do nothing with him. The present—the passing second of time—was all I had in which to control and restrain him: a movement of repulsion, flight, fear, would have sealed my doom,—and his. But I was not afraid: not in the least. I felt an inward power; a sense of influence, which supported me. The crisis was perilous; but not without its charm: such as the Indian, perhaps, feels when he slips over the rapid in his canoe. I took hold of his clenched hand; loosened the contorted fingers; and said to him, soothingly,—

"Sit down; I'll talk to you as long as you like, and hear all you have to say, whether reasonable or unreasonable."

He sat down: but he did not get leave to speak directly. I had been struggling with tears for some time: I had taken great pains to repress them, because I knew he would not like to see me weep. Now, however, I considered it well to let them flow as freely and as long as they liked. If the flood annoyed him, so much the better. So I gave way and cried heartily.

Soon I heard him earnestly entreating me to be composed. I said I could not while he was in such a passion.

"But I am not angry, Jane: I only love you too well; and you had steeled your little pale face with such a resolute, frozen look, I could not endure it. Hush, now, and wipe your eyes."

His softened voice announced that he was subdued; so I, in my turn, became calm. Now he made an effort to rest his head on my shoulder: but I would not permit it. Then he would draw me to him: no.

"Jane! Jane!" he said—in such an accent of bitter sadness, it thrilled along every nerve I had; "you don't love me, then? It was only my station, and the rank of my wife, that you valued? Now that you think me disqualified to become your husband, you recoil from my touch as if I were some toad or ape."

These words cut me: yet what could I do or say? I ought probably to have done or said nothing: but I was so tortured by a sense of remorse at thus hurting his feelings, I could not control the wish to drop balm where I had wounded.

"I *do* love you," I said, "more than ever: but I must not show or indulge the feeling; and this is the last time I must express it."

"The last time, Jane! What! do you think you can live with me, and see me daily, and yet, if you still love me, be always cold and distant?"

"No, sir; that I am certain I could not; and therefore I see there is but one way: but you will be furious if I mention it."

"Oh, mention it! If I storm, you have the art of weeping."

"Mr. Rochester, I must leave you."

"For how long, Jane? For a few minutes, while you smooth your hair—which is somewhat dishevelled; and bathe your face—which looks feverish?"

"I must leave Adèle and Thornfield. I must part with you for my whole life: I must begin a new existence amongst strange faces and strange scenes."

"Of course: I told you you should. I pass over the madness about parting from me. You mean you must become a part of me. As to the new existence, it is all right: you shall yet be my wife: I am not married. You shall be Mrs. Rochester—both virtually and nominally. I shall keep only to you so long as you and I live. You shall go to a place I have in the south of France: a white-walled villa on the shores of the Mediterranean. There you shall live a happy, and guarded, and most innocent life. Never fear that I wish to lure you into error—to make you my mistress. Why do you shake your head? Jane, you must be reasonable; or in truth I shall again become frantic."

His voice and hand quivered; his large nostrils dilated; his eye blazed: still, I dared to speak:—

"Sir, your wife is living: that is a fact acknowledged this morning by yourself. If I lived with you as you desire, I should then be your mistress: to say otherwise is sophistical—is false."

"Jane, I am not a gentle-tempered man—you forget that: I am not long-enduring; I am not cool and dispassionate. Out of pity to me and yourself, but your finger on my pulse, feel how it throbs, and—beware!"

He bared his wrist, and offered it to me: the blood was forsaking his cheek and lips, they were growing livid; I was distressed on all hands. To agitate him thus deeply, by a resistance he so abhorred, was cruel: to yield was out of the question. I did what human beings do instinctively when they are driven to utter extremity—looked for aid to one higher than man: the words "God help me!" burst involuntarily from my lips.

"I am a fool!" cried Mr. Rochester, suddenly. "I keep telling her I am not married, and do not explain to her why. I forget she knows nothing of the character of that woman, or of the circumstances attending my infernal union with her. Oh, I am certain Jane will agree with me in opinion, when she knows all that I know! Just put your hand in mine, Janet—that I may have the evidence of touch as well as sight, to prove you are near me—and I will in a few words show you the real state of the case. Can you listen to me?"

"Yes, sir; for hours if you will."

"I ask only minutes. Jane, did you ever hear, or know, that I was not the eldest son of my house: that I had once a brother older than I?"

"I remember Mrs. Fairfax told me so once."

"And did you ever hear that my father was an avaricious, grasping man?"

"I have understood something to that effect."

"Well, Jane, being so, it was his resolution to keep the property together; he could not bear the idea of dividing his estate and leaving me a fair portion: all, he resolved, should go to my brother, Russell. Yet as little could he endure that a son of his should be a poor man. I must be provided for by a wealthy marriage. He sought me a partner betimes. Mr. Mason, a West India planter and merchant, was his old acquaintance. He was certain his possessions were real and vast: he made inquiries. Mr. Mason, he found, had a son and daughter; and he learned from him that he could and would give the latter a fortune of thirty thousand pounds: that sufficed. When I left college, I was sent out to Jamaica, to espouse a bride already courted for me. My father said nothing about her money; but he told me Miss Mason was the boast of Spanish Town for her beauty: and this was no lie. I found her a fine woman, in the style of Blanche Ingram; tall, dark, and majestic. Her family wished to secure me, because I was of a good race; and so did she. They showed her to me in parties, splendidly dressed. I seldom saw her alone, and had very little private conversation with her. She flattered me, and lavishly displayed for my pleasure her charms and accomplishments. All the men in her circle seemed to admire her and envy me. I was dazzled, stimulated: my senses were excited; and being ignorant, raw, and inexperienced, I thought I loved her. There is no folly so besotted that the idiotic rivalries of society, the prurience, the rashness, the blindness of youth, will not hurry a man to its commission. Her relatives encouraged me; competitors piqued me; she allured me: a marriage was achieved almost before I knew where I was. Oh, I have no respect for myself when I think of that act!—an agony of inward contempt masters me. I never loved, I never esteemed, I did not even know her. I was not sure of the existence of one virtue in her nature: I had marked neither modesty, nor benevolence, nor candour, nor refinement in her mind or manners—and, I married her:—gross, grovelling, mole-eyed blockhead that I was! With less sin I might have—but let me remember to whom I am speaking.

"My bride's mother I had never seen: I understood she was dead. The honey-moon over, I learned my mistake; she was only mad, and shut up in a lunatic asylum. There was a younger brother, too; a complete dumb idiot. The elder one, whom you have seen (and whom I cannot hate, whilst I abhor all his kindred, because he has some grains of affection in his feeble mind; shown in the continued interest he takes in his wretched sister, and also in a dog-like attachment he once bore me), will probably be in the same state one day. My father, and my brother Russell, knew all this; but they thought only of the thirty thousand pounds, and joined in the plot against me.

"These were vile discoveries; but, except for the treachery of concealment, I should have made them no subject of reproach to my wife: even when I found her nature wholly alien to mine; her tastes obnoxious to me; her cast of mind common, low, narrow, and singularly incapable of being led to anything higher, expanded to anything larger—when I found that I could not pass a single evening, nor even a single hour of the day with her in comfort; that kindly conversation could not be sustained between us, because, whatever topic I started, immediately received from her a turn at once coarse and trite, perverse and imbecile—when I perceived that I should never have a quiet or settled household, because no servant would bear the continued outbreaks of her violent and unreasonable temper, or the vexations of her absurd, contradictory, exacting orders—even then I restrained myself: I eschewed upbraiding, I curtailed remonstrance; I tried to devour my repentance and disgust in secret; I repressed the deep antipathy I felt.

"Jane, I will not trouble you with abominable details: some strong words shall express what I have to say. I lived with that woman upstairs four years, and before that time she had tried me indeed: her character ripened and developed with frightful rapidity; her vices sprang up fast and rank: they were so strong, only cruelty could check them; and I would not use cruelty. What a pigmy intellect she had—and what giant propensities! How fearful were the curses those propensities entailed on me! Bertha Mason,—the true daughter of an infamous mother,—dragged me through all the hideous and degrading agonies which must attend a man bound to a wife at once intemperate and unchaste.

"My brother in the interval was dead; and at the end of the four years my father died too. I was rich enough now—yet poor to hideous indigence: a nature the most gross, impure, depraved I ever saw, was associated with mine, and called by the law and by society a part of me. And I could not rid myself of it by any legal proceedings: for the doctors now discovered that *my wife* was mad—her excesses had prematurely developed the germs of insanity:—Jane, you don't like my narrative; you look almost sick— shall I defer the rest to another day?"

"No sir, finish it now: I pity you—I do earnestly pity you."

"Pity, Jane, from some people is a noxious and insulting sort of tribute, which one is justified in hurling back in the teeth of those who offer it; but that is the sort of pity native to callous, selfish hearts: it is a hybrid, egotistical pain at hearing of woes, crossed with ignorant contempt for those who have endured them. But that is not your pity, Jane: it is not the feeling of which your whole face is full at this moment—with which your heart is heaving—with which your hand is trembling in mine. Your pity, my darling, is the suffering mother of love: its anguish is the very natal pang of the divine passion. I accept it, Jane; let the daughter have free advent—my arms wait to receive her."

"Now, sir, proceed: what did you do when you found she was mad?"

"Jane—I approached the verge of despair: a remnant of self-respect was all that intervened between me and the gulf. In the eyes of the world, I was doubtless covered with grimy dishonour: but I resolved to be clean in my own sight—and to the last I repudiated the contamination of her crimes, and wrenched myself from connection with her mental defects. Still, society associated my name and person with hers; I yet saw her and heard her daily: something of her breath (faugh!) mixed with the air I breathed; and, besides, I remembered I had once been her husband— that recollection was then, and is now, inexpressibly odious to me: moreover, I knew that while she lived I could never be the husband of another and better wife; and, though five years my senior, (her family and my father had lied to me even in the particular of her age), she was likely to live as long as I, being as robust in frame as she was infirm in mind. Thus, at the age of twenty-six, I was hopeless.

"One night I had been awakened by her yells—(since the medical men had pronounced her mad, she had of course been shut up)—it was a fiery West Indian night; one of the description that frequently precede the hurricanes of those climates; being unable to sleep in bed, I got up and opened the window. The air was like sulphur-steams—I could find no refreshment anywhere. Mosquitoes came buzzing in and hummed sullenly round the room; the sea, which I could hear from thence, rumbled dull like an earthquake—black clouds were casting up over it; the moon was setting in the waves, broad and red, like a hot connor-ball—she threw her last bloody glance over a world quivering with the ferment of tempest. I was physically influenced by the atmosphere and scene, and my ears were filled with the curses the maniac still shrieked out; wherein she momentarily mingled my name with such a tone of demon-hate, with such language!—no professed harlot ever had a fouler vocabulary than she: though two rooms off, I heard every word—the thin partitions of the West India house opposing but slight obstruction to her wolfish cries.

" 'This life,' said I at last, 'is hell! this is the air—those are the sounds of the bottomless pit! I have a right to deliver myself from it if I can. The sufferings of this mortal state will leave me with the heavy flesh that now cumbers my soul. Of the fanatic's burning eternity I have no fear: there is not a future state worse than this present one—let me break away, and go home to God!'

"I said this while I knelt down at, and unlocked a trunk which contained a brace of loaded pistols: I meant to shoot myself. I only entertained the intention for a moment; for, not being insane, the crisis of exquisite and unalloyed despair which had originated the wish and design of self-destruction, was past in a second.

"A wind fresh from Europe blew over the ocean and rushed through the open casement: the storm broke, streamed, thundered, blazed, and the air grew pure. I then framed and fixed a resolution. While I walked under the dripping orange-trees of my wet garden, and amongst its drenched pomegranates and pine-apples, and while the refulgent dawn of the tropics kindled round me—I reasoned thus, Jane:—and now listen; for it was true Wisdom that consoled me in that hour, and showed me the right path to follow.

"The sweet wind from Europe was still whispering in the refreshed leaves, and the Atlantic was thundering in glorious liberty; my heart, dried up and scorched for a long time, swelled to the tone, and filled with living blood—my being longed for renewal—my soul thirsted for a pure draught. I saw Hope revive—and felt Regeneration possible. From a flowery arch at the bottom of my garden I gazed over the sea—bluer than the sky: the old world was beyond; clear prospects opened thus:—

" 'Go,' said Hope, 'and live again in Europe: there it is not known what a sallied name you bear, nor what a filthy burden is bound to you. You may take the maniac with you to England; confine her with due attendance and precautions at Thornfield: then travel yourself to what clime you will, and form what new tie you like. That woman, who has so abused your name; so outraged your honour; so blighted your youth—is not your wife: nor are you her husband. See that she is cared for as her condition demands, and you have done all that God and humanity require of you.

Let her identity, her connection with yourself, be buried in oblivion: you are bound to impart them to no living being. Place her in safety and comfort: shelter her degradation with secrecy, and leave her.'

"I acted precisely on this suggestion. My father and brother had not made my marriage known to their acquaintance; because, in the very first letter I wrote to apprise them of the union—having already begun to experience extreme disgust of its consequences; and from the family character and constitution, seeing a hideous future opening to me—I added an urgent charge to keep it secret: and very soon, the infamous conduct of the wife my father had selected for me, was such as to make him blush to own her as his daughter-in-law. Far from desiring to publish the connection, he became as anxious to conceal it as myself.

"To England, then, I conveyed her; a fearful voyage I had with such a monster in the vessel. Glad was I when I at last got her to Thornfield, and saw her safely lodged in that third story room, of whose secret inner cabinet she has now for ten years made a wild beast's den—a goblin's cell. I had some trouble in finding an attendant for her; as it was necessary to select one on whose fidelity dependence could be placed; for her ravings would inevitably betray my secret: besides, she had lucid intervals of days—sometimes weeks—which she filled up with abuse of me. At last I hired Grace Poole, from the Grimsby Retreat. She and the surgeon, Carter (who dressed Mason's wounds that night he was stabbed and worried), are the only two I have ever admitted to my confidence. Mrs. Fairfax may indeed have suspected something; but she could have gained no precise knowledge as to facts. Grace has, on the whole, proved a good keeper: though, owing partly to a fault of her own, of which it appears nothing can cure her, and which is incident to her harassing profession, her vigilance has been more than once lulled and baffled. The lunatic is both cunning and malignant; she has never failed to take advantage of her guardian's temporary lapses; once to secret the knife with which she stabbed her brother, and twice to possess herself of the key of her cell, and issue therefrom in the night-time. On the first of these occasions, she perpetrated the attempt to burn me in my bed; on the second, she paid that ghastly visit to you. I thank Providence, who watched over you, that she then spent her fury on your wedding apparel; which perhaps brought back vague reminiscences of her own bridal days: but on what might have happened, I cannot endure to reflect. When I think of the thing which flew at my throat this morning, hanging its black and scarlet visage over the nest of my dove, my blood curdles——"

"And what, sir," I asked, while he paused, "did you do when you had settled her here? Where did you go?"

"What did I do, Jane? I transformed myself into a Will-o'-the-wisp. Where did I go? I pursued wanderings as wild as those of the March-spirit. I sought the Continent, and went devious through all its lands. My fixed desire was to seek and find a good and intelligent woman, whom I could love: a contrast to the fury I left at Thornfield——"

"But you could not marry, sir."

"I had determined, and was convinced, that, I could and ought. It was not my original intention to deceive, as I have deceived you. I meant to tell my tale plainly, and make my proposals openly: and it appeared to me so absolutely rational that I should be considered free to love and be loved, I never doubted some woman might be found willing and able to understand my case and acept me, in spite off the curse with which I was burdened."

"Well, sir?"

"When you are inquisitive, Jane, you always make me smile. You open your eyes like an eager bird, and make every now and then a restless movement; as if answers in speech did not flow fast enough for you, and you wanted to read the tablet of one's heart. But before I go on, tell me what you mean by your 'Well, sir?' It is a small phrase very frequent with you; and which many a time has drawn me on and on through interminable talk: I don't very well know why."

"I mean,—What next? How did you proceed? What came of such an event?"

"Precisely: and what do you wish to know now?"

"Whether you found any one you liked: whether you asked her to marry you; and what she said."

"I can tell you whether I found any one I liked, and whether I asked her to marry me: but what she said is yet to be recorded in the book of Fate. For ten long years I roved about, living first in one capital, then another: sometimes in St. Petersburgh; oftener in Paris; occasionally in Rome, Naples, and Florence. Provided with plenty of money, and the passport of an old name, I could choose my own society: no circles were closed against me. I sought my ideal of a woman amongst English ladies, French countesses, Italian signoras, and German gräfinnen. I could not find her. Sometimes, for a fleeting moment, I thought I caught a glance, heard a tone, beheld a form, which announced the realization of my dream: but I was presently undeceived. You are not to suppose that I desired perfection, either of mind or person. I longed only for what suited me—for the antipodes of the Creole: and I longed vainly. Amongst them all I found not one, whom, had I been ever so free, I—warned as I was of the risks, the horrors, the loathings of incongruous unions—would have asked to marry me. Disappointment made me reckless. I tried dissipation—never debauchery: that I hated, and hate. That was my Indian Messalina's attribute: rooted disgust at it and her restrained me much, even in pleasure. Any enjoyment that bordered on riot seemed to approach me to her and her vices, and I eschewed it.

"Yet I could not live alone: so I tried the companionship of mistresses. The first I chose was Céline Varens—another of those steps which make a man spurn himself when he recalls them. You already know what she was, and how my liaison with her terminated. She had two successors: an Italian, Giacinta, and a German, Clara; both considered singularly handsome. What was their beauty to me in a few weeks? Giacinta was unprincipled and violent: I tired of her in three months. Clara was honest and quiet; but heavy, mindless, unimpressible: not one whit to my taste. I was glad to give her a sufficient sum to set her up in a good line of business, and so get decently rid of her. But, Jane, I see by your face you are not forming a very favourable opinion of me just now. You think me an unfeeling, loose-principled rake: don't you?"

"I don't like you so well as I have done sometimes, indeed, sir. Did it not seem to you in the least wrong to live in that way: first with one mistress and then another? You talk of it as a mere matter of course."

"It was with me; and I did not like it. It was a grovelling fashion of existence: I should never like to return to it. Hiring a mistress is the next

worst thing to buying a slave: both are often by nature, and always by position, inferior: and to live familiarly with inferiors is degrading. I now hate
the recollection of the time I passed with Céline, Giacinta, and Clara."

I felt the truth of these words; and I drew from them the certain inference, that if I were so far to forget myself and all the teaching that had
ever been instilled into me, as—under any pretext—with any justification—through any temptation—to become the successor of these poor
girls, he would one day regard me with the same feeling which now in
his mind desecrated their memory. I did not give utterance to this conviction: it was enough to feel it. I impressed it on my heart, that it might
remain there to serve me as aid in the time of trial.

"Now, Jane, why don't you say 'Well, sir?' I have not done. You are
looking grave. You disapprove of me still, I see. But let me come to the
point. Last January, rid of all mistresses—in a harsh, bitter, frame of mind,
the result of a useless, roving, lonely life—corroded with disappointment,
sourly disposed against all men, and especially against all *woman*kind (for
I began to regard the notion of an intellectual, faithful, loving woman as
a mere dream), recalled by business, I came back to England.

"On a frosty winter afternoon, I rode in sight of Thornfield Hall.
Abhorred spot! I expected no peace—no pleasure there. On a style in Hay
Lane I saw a quiet little figure sitting by itself. I passed it as negligently
as I did the pollard willow opposite it: I had no presentiment of what it
would be to me; no inward warning that the arbitress of my life—my genius
for good or evil—waited there in humble guise. I did not know it, even
when, on the occasion of Mesrour's accident, it came up and gravely offered me help. Childish and slender creature! It seemed as if a linnet had
hopped to my foot and proposed to bear me on its tiny wing. I was surly;
but the thing would not go: it stood by me with strange perseverance, and
looked and spoke with a sort of authority. I must be aided, and by that
hand: and aided I was.

"When once I had pressed the frail shoulder, something new—a fresh
sap and sense—stole into my frame. It was well I had learnt that this elf
must return to me—that it belonged to my house down below—or I could
not have felt it pass away from under my hand, and seen it vanish behind
the dim hedge, without singular regret. I heard you come home that night,
Jane: though probably you were not aware that I thought of you, or
watched for you. The next day I observed you—myself unseen—for half
an hour, while you played with Adèle in the gallery. It was a snowy day,
I recollect, and you could not go out of doors. I was in my room; the door
was ajar: I could both listen and watch. Adèle claimed your outward attention for a while; yet I fancied your thoughts were elsewhere: but you were
very patient with her, my little Jane; you talked to her and amused her
a long time. When at last she left you, you lapsed at once into deep reverie:
you betook yourself slowly to pace the gallery. Now and then, in passing
a casement, you glanced out at the thick-falling snow; you listened to the
sobbing wind, and again you paced gently on, and dreamed. I think those
day-visions were not dark: there was a pleasurable illumination in your
eye occasionally, a soft excitement in your aspect, which told of no bitter, bilious, hypochondriac brooding: your look revealed rather the sweet
musings of youth, when its spirit follows on willing wings the flight of
Hope, up and on to an ideal heaven. The voice of Mrs. Fairfax, speaking
to a servant in the hall, wakened you: and how curiously you smiled to

and at yourself, Janet! There was much sense in your smile: it was very shrewd, and seemed to make light of your own abstraction. It seemed to say—'My fine visions are all very well, but I must not forget they are absolutely unreal. I have a rosy sky, and a green flowery Eden in my brain; but without, I am perfectly aware, lies at my feet a rough tract to travel, and around me gather black tempests to encounter.' You ran down stairs and demanded of Mrs. Fairfax some occupation: the weekly house-accounts to make up, or something of that sort, I think it was. I was vexed with you for getting out of my sight.

"Impatiently I waited for evening, when I might summon you to my presence. An unusual—to me—a perfectly new character I suspected was yours: I desired to search it deeper, and know it better. You entered the room with a look and air at once shy and independent; you were quaintly dressed—much as you are now. I made you talk: ere long I found you full of strange contrasts. Your garb and manner were restricted by rule; your air was often diffident, and altogether that of one refined by nature, but absolutely unused to society, and a good deal afraid of making herself disadvantageously conspicuous by some solecism or blunder; yet, when addressed, you lifted a keen, a daring, and a glowing eye to your interlocutor's face: there was penetration and power in each glance you gave; when plied by close questions, you found ready and round answers. Very soon, you seemed to get used to me—I believe you felt the existence of sympathy between you and your grim and cross master, Jane; for it was astonishing to see how quickly a certain pleasant ease tranquillized your manner: snarl as I would, you showed no surprise, fear, annoyance, or displeasure at my moroseness; you watched me, and now and then smiled at me with a simple yet sagacious grace I cannot describe. I was at once content and stimulated with what I saw: I liked what I had seen, and wished to see more. Yet, for a long time, I treated you distantly, and sought your company rarely. I was an intellectual epicure, and wished to prolong the gratification of making this novel and piquant acquaintance: besides, I was for a while troubled with a haunting fear that if I handled the flower freely its bloom would fade—the sweet charm of freshness would leave it. I did not then know that it was no transitory blossom; but rather the radiant resemblance of one, but in an indestructible gem. Moreover, I wished to see whether you would seek me if I shunned you—but you did not; you kept in the school-room as still as your own desk and easel: if by chance I met you, you passed me as soon, and with as little token of recognition, as was consistent with respect. Your habitual expression in those days, Jane, was a thoughtful look: not despondent, for you had little hope, and no actual pleasure. I wondered what you thought of me—or if you ever thought of me: to find this out, I resumed my notice of you. There was something glad in your glance, and genial in your manner, when you conversed: I saw you had a social heart; it was the silent school-room—it was the tedium of your life that made you mournful. I permitted myself the delight of being kind to you; kindness stirred emotion soon: your face became soft in expression, your tones gentle; I liked my name pronounced by your lips in a grateful, happy accent. I used to enjoy a chance meeting with you, Jane, at this time: there was a curious hesitation in your manner; you glanced at me with a slight trouble—a hovering doubt: you did not know that my caprice might be—whether I was going to play the master and be stern, or the friend and be benignant. I was now too fond of you often to simulate the first whim; and, when I stretched my hand out cordially, such bloom and light and bliss rose to your young, wistful features, I had much ado often to avoid straining you then and there to my heart."

"Don't talk any more of those days, sir," I interrupted, furtively dashing away some tears from my eyes; his language was torture to me; for I knew what I must do—and do soon—and all these reminiscences, and these revelations of his feelings only made my work more difficult.

"No, Jane," he returned: "what necessity is there to dwell on the Past, when the Present is so much surer—the Future so much brighter?"

I shuddered to hear the infatuated assertion.

"You see now how the case stands—do you not?" he continued. "After a youth and manhood passed half in unutterable misery and half in dreary solitude, I have for the first time found what I can truly love—I have found *you*. You are my sympathy—my better self—my good angel—I am bound to you with a strong attachment. I think you good, gifted, lovely: a fervent, a solemn passion is conceived in my heart; it leans to you, draws you to my centre and spring of life, wraps my existence about you—and, kindling in pure, powerful flame, fuses you and me in one.

"It was because I felt and knew this, that I resolved to marry you. To tell me that I had already a wife is empty mockery: you know now that I had but a hideous demon. I was wrong to attempt to deceive you; but I feared a stubbornness that exists in your character. I feared early instilled prejudice: I wanted to have you safe before hazarding confidences. This was cowardly: I should have appealed to your nobleness and magnanimity at first, as I do now—opened to you plainly my life of agony—described to you my hunger and thirst after a higher and worthier existence—shown to you, not my *resolution* (that word is weak) but my resistless *bent* to love faithfully and well, where I am faithfully and well loved in return. Then I should have asked you to accept my pledge of fidelity, and to give me yours: Jane—give it me now."

A pause.

"Why are you silent, Jane?"

I was experiencing an ordeal: a hand of fiery iron grasped my vitals. Terrible moment: full of struggle, blackness, burning! Not a human being that ever lived could wish to be loved better than I was loved; and him who thus loved me I absolutely worshipped: and I must renounce love and idol. One drear word comprised my intolerable duty—"Depart!"

"Jane, you understand what I want of you? Just this promise—'I will be yours, Mr. Rochester.' "

"Mr. Rochester, I will *not* be yours."

Another long silence.

"Jane!" recommenced he, with a gentleness that broke me down with grief, and turned me stone-cold with ominous terror—for this still voice was the pant of a lion rising—"Jane, do you mean to go one way in the world, and to let me go another?"

"I do."

"Jane," (bending towards and embracing me) "do you mean it now?"

"I do."

"And now?" softly kissing my forehead and cheek.

"I do—" extricating myself from restraint rapidly and completely.

"Oh, Jane, this is bitter! This—this is wicked. It would not be wicked to love me."

"It would to obey you."

A wild look raised his brows—crossed his features: he rose; but he for-bore yet. I laid my hand on the back of a chair for support: I shook, I feared—but I resolved.

"One instant, Jane. Give one glance to my horrible life when you are gone. All happiness will be torn away with you. What then is left? For a wife I have but the maniac up-stairs: as well might you refer me to some corpse in yonder church-yard. What shall I do, Jane? Where turn for a companion, and for some hope?"

"Do as I do: trust in God and yourself. Believe in Heaven. Hope to meet again there."

"Then you will not yield?"

"No."

"Then you condemn me to live wretched, and to die accursed?" His voice rose.

"I advise you to live sinless; and I wish you to die tranquil."

"Then you snatch love and innocence from me? You fling me back on lust for a passion—vice for an occupation?"

"Mr. Rochester, I no more assign this fate to you than I grasp at it for myself. We were born to strive and endure—you as well as I: do so. You will forget me before I forget you."

"You make me a liar by such language: you sully my honour. I declared I could not change: you tell me to my face I shall change soon. And what a distortion in your judgment, what a perversity in your ideas, is proved by your conduct! Is it better to drive a fellow-creature to despair than to transgress a mere human law—no man being injured by the breach? for you have neither relatives nor acquaintances whom you need fear to of-fend by living with me."

This was true: and while he spoke my very Conscience and Reason turned traitors against me, and charged me with crime in resisting him. They spoke almost as loud as Feeling: and that clamoured wildly. "Oh, comply!" it said. "Think of his misery; think of his danger—look at his state when left alone; remember his headlong nature; consider the reck-lessness following on despair—soothe him; save him; love him; tell him you love him and will be his. Who in the world cares for *you?* or who will be injured by what you do?"

Still indomitable was the reply—"*I* care for myself. The more solitary, the more friendless, the more unsustained I am, the more I will respect myself. I will keep the law given by God; sanctioned by man. I will hold to the principles received by me when I was sane, and not mad—as I am now. Laws and principles are not for the times when there is no tempta-tion: they are for such moments as this, when body and soul rise in mutiny against their rigour; stringent are they; inviolate they shall be. If at my individual convenience I might break them, what would be their worth? They have a worth—so I have always believed; and if I cannot believe it now, it is because I am insane—quite insane: with my veins running fire, and my heart beating faster than I can count its throbs. Preconceived opin-ions, foregone determinations, are all I have at this hour to stand by: there I plant my foot."

I did. Mr. Rochester, reading my countenance, saw I had done so. His fury was wrought to the highest: he must yield to it for a moment, what-ever followed; he crossed the floor and seized my arm, and grasped my waist. He seemed to devour me with his flaming glance: physically, I felt, at the moment, powerless as stubble exposed to the draught and glow of a furnace—mentally, I still possessed my soul, and with it the certainty of ultimate safety. The soul, fortunately, has an interpreter—often an unconscious, but still a truthful interpreter—in the eye. My eye rose to his; and while I looked in his fierce face, I gave an involuntary sigh: his gripe was painful, and my over-tasked strength almost exhausted.

"Never," said he, as he ground his teeth, "never was anything at once so frail and so indomitable. A mere reed she feels in my hand! (and he shook me with the force of his hold.) I could bend her with my finger and thumb: and what good would it do if I bent, if I uptore, if I crushed her? Consider that eye: consider the resolute, wild, free thing looking out of it, defying me, with more than courage—with a stern triumph. Whatever I do with its cage, I cannot get at it—the savage, beautiful creature! If I tear, if I rend the slight prison, my outrage will only let the captive loose. Conqueror I might be of the house; but the inmate would escape to heaven before I could call myself possessor of its clay dwelling-place. And it is you, spirit—with will and energy, and virtue and purity—that I want: not alone your brittle frame. Of yourself, you could come with soft flight and nestle against my heart, if you would: seized against your will, you will elude the grasp like an essence—you will vanish ere I inhale your fragrance. Oh! come, Jane, come!"

As he said this, he released me from his clutch, and only looked at me. The look was far worse to resist than the frantic strain: only an idiot, however, would have succumbed now. I had dared and baffled his fury; I must elude his sorrow: I retired to the door.

"You are going, Jane?"

"I am going, sir."

"You are leaving me?"

"Yes."

"You will not come?— you will not be my comforter, my rescuer?— My deep love, my wild woe, my frantic prayer, are all nothing to you?"

What unutterable pathos was in his voice! How hard it was to reiterate firmly, "I am going."

"Jane!"

"Mr. Rochester!"

"Withdraw, then—I consent—but remember, you leave me here in anguish. Go up to your own room; think over all I have said, and, Jane, cast a glance on my sufferings—think of me."

He turned away; he threw himself on his face on the sofa. "Oh, Jane! my hope—my love—my life!" broke in anguish from his lips. Then came a deep, strong sob.

I had already gained the door: but, reader, I walked back—walked back as determinedly as I had retreated. I knelt down by him; I turned his face from the cushion to me; I kissed his cheek; I smoothed his hair with my hand.

"God bless you, my dear master!" I said. "God keep you from harm and wrong—direct you, solace you—reward you well for your past kindness to me."

"Little Jane's love would have been my best reward," he answered: "without it, my heart is broken. But Jane will give me her love: yes—nobly, generously."

Up the blood rushed to his face; forth flashed the fire from his eyes; erect he sprang; he held his arms out; but I evaded the embrace, and at once quitted the room.

"Farewell!" was the cry of my heart, as I left him. Despair added, "Farewell, for ever!"

* * * * *

That night I never thought to sleep: but a slumber fell on me as soon as I lay down in bed. I was transported in thought to the scenes of child-hood: I dreamt I lay in the red-room at Gateshead; that the night was dark, and my mind impressed with strange fears. The light that long ago had struck me into syncope, recalled in this vision, seemed glidingly to mount the wall, and tremblingly to pause in the centre of the obscured ceiling. I lifted up my head to look: the roof resolved to clouds, high and dim; the gleam was such as the moon imparts to vapours, she is about to sever. I watched her come—watched with the strangest anticipation; as though some word of doom were to be written on her disk. She broke forth as never moon yet burst from cloud: a hand first penetrated the sable folds and waved them away; then, not a moon, but a white human form shone in the azure, inclining a glorious brow earthward. It gazed and gazed on me. It spoke to my spirit: immeasureably distant was the tone, yet so near, it whispered in my heart—

"My daughter, flee temptation!"

"Mother, I will."

So I answered after I had waked from the trance-like dream. It was yet night, but July nights are short: soon after midnight, dawn comes. "It can-not be too early to commence the task I have to fulfill," thought I. I rose: I was dressed; for I had taken off nothing but my shoes. I knew where to find in my drawers some linen, a locket, a ring. In seeking these ar-ticles, I encountered the beads of a pearl necklace Mr. Rochester had forced me to accept a few days ago. I left that; it was not mine: it was the visionary bride's, who had melted in air. The other articles I made up in a parcel; my purse, containing twenty shillings (it was all I had), I put in my pocket: I tied on my straw bonnet, pinned my shawl, took the parcel and my slippers, which I would not put on yet, and stole from my room.

"Farewell, kind Mrs. Fairfax!" I whispered, as I glided past her door. "Farewell, my darling Adèle!" I said, as I glanced towards the nursery. No thought could be admitted of entering to embrace her. I had to deceive a fine ear: for aught I knew, it might now be listening.

I would have got past Mr. Rochester's chamber without a pause; but my heart momentarily stopping its beat at that threshold, my foot was forced to stop also. No sleep was there: the inmate was walking restlessly from wall to wall; and again and again he sighed while I listened. There was a heaven—a temporary heaven—in this room for me, if I chose: I had but to go in and to say—

"Mr. Rochester, I will love you and live with you through life till death," and a fount of rapture would spring to my lips. I thought of this.

That kind master, who could not sleep now, was waiting with impa-tience for day. He would send for me in the morning; I should be gone. He would have me sought for: vainly. He would feel himself forsaken; his love rejected: he would suffer; perhaps grow desperate. I thought of this too. My hand moved towards the lock: I caught it back, and glided on.

Drearily I wound my way down stairs: I knew what I had to do, and I did it mechanically. I sought the key of the side-door in the kitchen: I sought, too, a phial of oil and a feather; I oiled the key and the lock. I got some water, I got some bread: for perhaps I should have to walk far; and my strength, sorely shaken of late, must not break down. All this I did without one sound. I opened the door, passed out, shut it softly. Dim dawn glimmered in the yard. The great gates were closed and locked; but a wicket in one of them was only latched. Through that I departed: it, too, I shut; and now I was out of Thornfield.

A mile off, beyond the fields, lay a road which stretched in the contrary direction to Millcote; a road I had never travelled, but often noticed, and wondered where it led: thither I bent my steps. No reflection was to be allowed now: not one glance was to be cast back; not even one forward. Not one thought was to be given either to the past or the future. The first was a page so heavenly sweet—so deadly sad—that to read one line of it would dissolve my courage and break down my energy. The last was an awful blank: something like the world when the deluge was gone by.

I skirted fields, and hedges, and lanes, till after sunrise. I believe it was a lovely summer morning: I know my shoes, which I had put on when I left the house, were soon wet with dew. But I looked neither to rising sun, nor smiling sky, nor wakening nature. He who is taken out to pass through a fair scene to the scaffold, thinks not of the flowers that smile on his road, but of the block and axe-edge; of the disseverment of bone and vein; of the grave gaping at the end: and I thought of drear flight and homeless wandering—and, oh! with agony I thought of what I left. I could not help it. I thought of him now—in his room—watching the sunrise; hoping I should soon come to say I should stay with him, and be his. I longed to be his; I panted to return: it was not too late; I could yet spare him the bitter pang of bereavement. As yet my flight, I was sure, was undiscovered. I could go back and be his comforter—his pride; his redeemer from misery; perhaps from ruin. Oh, that fear of his self-abandonment—far worse than my abandonment—how it goaded me! it was a barbed arrow-head in my breast; it tore me when I tried to extract it; it sickened me when remembrance thrust it further in. Birds began singing in brake and copse: birds were faithful to their mates; birds were emblems of love. What was I? In the midst off my pain of heart, and frantic effort of principle, I abhorred myself. I had no solace from self-approbation: none even from self-respect. I had injured—wounded—left my master. I was hateful in my own eyes. Still I could not turn, nor retrace one step. God must have led me on. As to my own will or conscience, impassioned grief had trampled one and stifled the other. I was weeping wildly as I walked along my solitary way: fast, fast I went like one delirious. A weakness, beginning inwardly, extending to the limbs, seized me, and I fell: I lay on the ground some minutes, pressing my face to the wet turf. I had some fear—or hope—that here I should die: but I was soon up; crawling forwards on my hands and knees, and then again raised to my feet—as eager and as determined as ever to reach the road.

When I got there I was forced to sit to rest me under the hedge; and while I sat, I heard wheels, and saw a coach come on. I stood up and lifted my hand; it stopped. I asked where it was going: the driver named a place a long way off, and where I was sure Mr. Rochester had no connections. I asked for what sum he would take me there; he said thirty shillings; I answered I had but twenty; well, he would try to make it do. He further gave me leave to get into the inside, as the vehicle was empty: I entered, was shut in, and it rolled on its way.

Gentle reader, may you never feel what I then felt! May your eyes never shed such stormy, scalding, heart-wrung tears as poured from mine. May you never appeal to heaven in prayers so hopeless and so agonized as in that hour left my lips: for never may you, like me, dread to be the instrument of evil to what you wholly love.

· · · · · · ·

Chapter 28

Two days are passed. It is a summer evening; the coachman has set me down at a place called Whitcross: he could take me no farther for the sum I had given, and I was not possessed of another shilling in the world. The coach is a mile off by this time; I am alone. At this moment I discover that I forgot to take my parcel out of the pocket of the coach, where I had placed it for safety; there it remains, there it must remain; and now I am absolutely destitute.

Whitcross is no town, nor even a hamlet; it is but a stone pillar set up where four roads meet: white-washed, I suppose, to be more obvious at a distance and in darkness. Four arms spring from its summit: the nearest town to which these point is, according to the inscription, distant ten miles; the farthest, above twenty. From the well-known names of these towns I learn in what county I have lighted; a north-midland shire, dusk with moorland, ridged with mountain: this I see. There are great moors behind and on each hand of me; there are waves of mountains far beyond that deep valley at my feet. The population here must be this, and I see no passengers on these roads: they stretch out east, west, north, and south—white, broad, lonely; they are all cut in the moor, and the heather grows deep and wild to their very verge. Yet a chance traveller might pass by; and I wish no eye to see me now: strangers would wonder what I am doing, lingering here at the sign-post, evidently objectless and lost. I might be questioned: I could give no answer but what would sound incredible, and excite suspicion. Not a tie holds me to human society at this moment—not a charm or hope calls me where my fellow-creatures are— none that saw me would have a kind thought or a good wish for me. I have no relative but the universal mother, Nature: I will seek her breast and ask repose.

I struck straight into the heath: I held on to a hollow I saw deeply furrowing the brown moor-side; I waded, knee-deep in its dark growth; I turned with its turnings, and finding a moss-blackened granite crag in a hidden angle, I sat down under it. High banks of moor were about me; the crag protected my head: the sky was over that.

Some time passed before I felt tranquil even here: I had a vague dread that wild cattle might be near, or that some sportsman or poacher might discover me. If a gust of wind swept the waste, I looked up, fearing it was the rush of a bull; if a plover whistled, I imagined it a man. Finding my apprehensions unfounded, however, and calmed by the deep silence that reigned as evening declined to night-fall, I took confidence. As yet I had not thought; I had only listened, watched, dreaded: now I regained the faculty of reflection.

What was I to do? Where to go? Oh, intolerable questions, when I could do nothing and go nowhere!—when a long way must yet be measured by my weary, trembling limbs, before I could reach human habitation—when cold charity must be entreated before I could get a lodging: reluctant sympathy importuned: almost certain repulse incurred: before my tale could be listened to, or one of my wants relieved!

I touched the heath: it was dry, and yet warm with the heat of the summer-day. I looked at the sky; it was pure: a kindly star twinkled just above the chasm ridge. The dew fell, but with propitious softness; no breeze whispered. Nature seemed to me benign and good: I thought she loved me, outcast as I was; and I, who from man could anticipate only mistrust, rejection, insult, clung to her with filial fondness. To-night, at least, I would be her guest—as I was her child: my mother would lodge me without money and without price. I had one morsel of bread yet: the remnant of a roll I had bought in a town we passed through at noon with a stray penny—my last coin. I saw ripe bilberries gleaming here and there, like jet beads in the heath: I gathered a handful and ate them with the bread. My hunger, sharp before, was, if not satisfied, appeased by this hermit's meal. I said my evening prayers at its conclusion, and then chose my couch.

Beside the crag, the heath was very deep: when I lay down my feet were buried in it; rising high on each side, it left only a narrow space for the night-air to invade. I folded my shawl double, and spread it over me for a coverlet; a low, mossy swell was my pillow. Thus lodged, I was not, at least at the commencement of the night, cold.

My rest might have been blissful enough, only a sad heart broke it. It pained of its gaping wounds, its inward bleeding, its riven chords. It trembled for Mr. Rochester and his doom: it bemoaned him with bitter pity; it demanded him with ceaseless longing: and, impotent as a bird with both wings broken, it still quivered its shattered pinions in vain attempts to seek him.

Worn out with this torture of thought, I rose to my knees. Night was come, and her planets were risen: a safe, still night; too serene for the companionship of fear. We know that God is everywhere; but certainly we feel His presence most when His works are on the grandest scale spread before us: and it is in the unclouded night-sky, where His worlds wheel their silent course, that we read clearest His infinitude, His omnipotence, His ominpresence. I had risen to my knees to pray for Mr. Rochester. Looking up, I, with tear-dimmed eyes, saw the mighty Milky Way. Remembering what it was—what countless systems there swept space like a soft trace of light—I felt the might and strength of God. Sure was I of His efficiency to save what He had made: convinced I grew that neither earth should perish, nor one of the souls it treasured. I turned my prayer to thanksgiving: the Source of Life was also the Saviour of spirits. Mr. Rochester was safe: he was God's, and by God would he be guarded. I again nestled to the breast of the hill; and ere long, in sleep, forgot sorrow.

But next day, Want came to me, pale and bare. Long after the little birds had left their nests: long after bees had come in the sweet prime of day to gather the heath honey before the dew was dried—when the long morning shadows were curtailed, and the sun filled earth and sky—I got up, and I looked round me.

What a still, hot, perfect day! What a golden desert this spreading moor! Everywhere sunshine. I wished I could live in it and on it. I saw a lizard run over the crag; I saw a bee busy among the sweet bilberries. I would fain at the moment have become bee or lizard, that I might have found fitting nutriment, permanent shelter here. But I was a human being, and had a human being's wants: I must not linger where there was nothing to supply them. I rose; I looked back at the bed I had left. Hopeless of the future, I wished but this—that my Maker had that night thought good to require my soul of me while I slept; and that this weary frame, absolved by death from further conflict with fate, had now but to decay quietly, and mingle in peace with the soil of this wilderness. Life, however, was yet in my possession; with all its requirements, and pains, and responsibilities. The burden must be carried; the want provided for; the suffering endured; the responsibility fulfilled. I set out.

Whitcross regained, I followed a road which led from the sun, how fervent and high. By no other circumstance had I will to decide my choice. I walked a long time, and when I thought I had nearly done enough, and might conscientiously yield to the fatigue that almost overpowered me—might relax this forced action, and sitting down on a stone I saw near, submit resistlessly to the apathy that clogged heart and limb—I heard a bell chime—a church bell.

I turned in the direction of the sound, and there, amongst the romantic hills, whose changes and aspect I had ceased to note an hour ago, I saw a hamlet and a spire. All the valley at my right hand was full of pasture-fields, and corn-fields, and wood: and a glittering stream ran zig-zag through the varied shades of green, the mellowing grain, the sombre woodland, the clear and sunny lea. Recalled by the rumbling of wheels to the road before me, I saw a heavily-laden waggon labouring up the hill; and not far beyond were two cows and their drover. Human life and human labour were near. I must struggle on: strive to live and bend to toil like the rest.

About two o'clock, P.M., I entered the village. At the bottom of its one street, there was a little shop with some cakes of bread in the window. I coveted a cake of bread. With that refreshment I could perhaps regain a degree of energy; without it, it would be difficult to proceed. The wish to have some strength and some vigor returned to me as soon as I was amongst my fellow-beings. I felt it would be degrading to faint with hunger on the causeway of a hamlet. Had I nothing about me I could offer in exchange for one of these rolls? I considered. I had a small silk handkerchief tied round my throat; I had my gloves. I could hardly tell how men and women in extremities of destitution proceeded. I did not know whether either of these articles would be accepted: probably they would not; but I must try.

I entered the shop: a woman was there. Seeing a respectably-dressed person, a lady as she supposed, she came forward with civility. How could she serve me? I was seized with shame: my tongue would not utter the request I had prepared. I dared not offer her the half-worn gloves, the creased handkerchief: besides, I felt it would be absurd. I only begged permission to sit down a moment, as I was tired. Disappointed in the

expectation of a customer, she coolly acceded to my request. She pointed
to a seat; I sank into it. I felt sorely urged to weep; but conscious how
unseasonable such a manifestation would be, I restrained it. Soon I asked
her, "if there were any dressmaker or plain-work-woman in the village?"

"Yes; two or three. Quite as many as there was employment for."

I reflected. I was driven to the point now. I was brought face to face
with Necessity. I stood in the position of one without a resource: without a friend; without a coin. I must do something. What? I must apply
somewhere. Where?

"Did she know of any place in the neighbourhood where a servant was
wanted?"

"Nay; she couldn't say."

"What was the chief trade in this place? What did most of the people
do?"

"Some were farm labourers; a good deal worked at Mr. Oliver's needle-
factory, and at the foundry."

"Did Mr. Oliver employ women?"

"Nay; it was men's work."

"And what do the women do?"

"I knawn't," was the answer. "Some does one thing, and some another.
Poor folk mun get on as they can."

She seemed to be tired of my questions: and, indeed, what claim had
I to importune her? A neighbour or two came in; my chair was evidently
wanted. I took leave.

I passed up the street, looking as I went at all the houses to the right
hand and to the left: but I could discover no pretext, nor see an inducement, to enter any. I rambled round the hamlet, going sometimes to a little distance and returning again, for an hour or more. Much exhausted,
and suffering greatly now for want of food, I turned aside into a lane and
sat down under the hedge. Ere many minutes had elapsed, I was again
on my feet, however, and again searching something—a resource, or at
least an informant. A pretty little house stood at the top of the lane, with
a garden before it; exquisitely neat, and brilliantly blooming. I stopped
at it. What business had I to approach the white door, or touch the glittering knocker? In what way could it possibly be the interest of the inhabitants of that dwelling to serve me? Yet I drew near and knocked. A
mild-looking, cleanly-attired young woman opened the door. In such a
voice as might be expected from a hopeless heart and fainting frame—a
voice wretchedly low and faltering—I asked if a servant was wanted here?

"No," said she; "we do not keep a servant."

"Can you tell me where I could get employment of any kind?" I continued. "I am a stranger, without acquaintance, in this place. I want some
work: no matter what."

But it was not her business to think for me, or to seek a place for me:
besides, in her eyes, how doubtful must have appeared my character, position, tale. She shook her head, she "was sorry she could give me no
information," and the white door closed, quite gently and civilly: but it
shut me out. If she had held it open a little longer, I believe I should have
begged a piece of bread; for I was now brought low.

I could not bear to return to the sordid village; where, besides, no prospect of aid was visible. I should have longed rather to deviate to a wood
I saw not far off, which appeared in its thick shade to offer inviting shel-

ter; but I was so sick, so weak, so gnawed with nature's cravings, instinct kept me roaming round abodes where there was a chance of food. Solitude would be no solitude—rest no rest—while the vulture, hunger, thus sunk beak and talons in my side.

I drew near houses; I left them, and came back again, and again I wandered away: always repelled by the consciousness of having no claim to ask—no right to expect interest in my isolated lot. Meantime, the afternoon advanced, while I thus wandered about like a lost and starving dog. In crossing a field, I saw the church-spire before me: I hastened towards it. Near the church-yard, and in the middle of a garden, stood a well-built though small house, which I had no doubt was the parsonage. I remembered that strangers who arrive at a place where they have no friends, and who want employment, sometimes apply to the clergyman for introduction and aid. It is the clergyman's function to help—at least with advice—those who wish to help themselves. I seemed to have something like a right to seek counsel here. Renewing then, my courage, and gathering my feeble remains of strength, I pushed on. I reached the house, and knocked at the kitchen-door. An old woman opened: I asked was this the parsonage?

"Yes."

"Was the clergyman in?"

"No."

"Would he be in soon?"

"No, he was gone from home."

"To a distance?"

"Not so far—happen three mile. He had been called away by the sudden death of his father: he was at Marsh End now, and would very likely stay there a fortnight longer."

"Was there any lady of the house?"

"Nay, there was naught but her, and she was housekeeper;" and of her, reader, I could not bear to ask the relief for want of which I was sinking; I could not yet beg; and again I crawled away.

Once more I took off my handkerchief—once more I thought of the cakes of bread in the little shop. Oh, for but a crust! for but one mouthful to allay the pang of famine! Instinctively I turned my face again to the village: I found the shop again, and I went in; and though others were there besides the woman, I ventured the request, "Would she give me a roll for this handkerchief?"

She looked at me with evident suspicion: "Nay, she never sold stuff i' that way."

Almost desperate, I asked for half a cake; she again refused. "How could she tell where I had got the handkerchief," she said.

"Would she take my gloves?"

"No? what could she do with them?"

Reader, it is not pleasant to dwell on these details. Some say there is enjoyment in looking back to painful experience past; but at this day I can scarcely bear to review the times to which I allude: the moral degradation, blent with the physical suffering, form too distressing a recollection ever to be willingly dwelt on. I blamed none of those who repulsed me. I felt it was what was to be expected, and what could not be helped: an ordinary beggar is frequently an object of suspicion; a well-dressed beggar inevitably so. To be sure, what I begged was employment: but whose business was it to provide me with employment? Not, certainly that of persons who saw me then for the first time, and who knew nothing about my character. And as to the woman who would not take my handkerchief in exchange for her bread, why, she was right; if the offer appeared to her sinister, or the exchange unprofitable. Let me condense now. I am sick of the subject.

A little before dark I passed a farm-house, at the open door of which the farmer was sitting, eating his supper of bread and cheese: I stopped and said:—

"Will you give me a piece of bread? for I am very hungry." He cast on me a glance of surprise; but without answering, he cut a thick slice from his loaf, and gave it to me. I imagine he did not think I was a beggar, but only an eccentric sort of lady, who had taken a fancy to his brown loaf. As soon as I was out of sight of his house, I sat down and ate it.

I could not hope to get a lodging under a roof, and sought it in the wood I have before alluded to. But my night was wretched, my rest broken: the ground was damp, the air cold: besides, intruders passed near me more than once, and I had again and again to change my quarters: no sense of safety or tranquillity befriended me. Towards morning it rained; the whole of the following day was wet. Do not ask me, reader, to give a minute account of that day; as before, I sought work; as before, I was repulsed; as before, starved; but once did food pass my lips. At the door of a cottage I saw a little girl about to throw a mess of cold porridge into a pig-trough. "Will you give me that?" I asked.

She stared at me. "Mother!" she exclaimed; "there is a woman wants me to give her this porridge."

"Well, lass," replied a voice within, "give it her if she's a beggar. T' pig doesn't want it."

The girl emptied the stiffened mould into my hand, and I devoured it ravenously.

As the wet twilight deepened, I stopped in a solitary bridle-path, which I had been pursuing an hour or more.

"My strength is quite failing me," I said, in soliloquy. "I feel I cannot go much further. Shall I be an outcast again this night? While the rain descends so, must I lay my head on the cold drenched ground! I fear I cannot do otherwise: for who will receive me? But it will be very dreadful: with this feeling of hunger, faintness, chill, and this sense of desolation—this total prostration of hope. In all likelihood, though, I should die before morning. And why cannot I reconcile myself to the prospect of death? Why do I struggle to retain a valueless life? Because I know, or believe, Mr. Rochester is still living: and then, to die of want and cold, is a fate to which nature cannot submit passively. Oh, Providence! sustain me a little longer! Aid—direct me!"

My glazed eye wandered over the dim and misty landscape. I saw I had strayed far from the village: it was quite out of sight. The very cultivation surrounding it had disappeared. I had, by cross-ways and by-paths, once more drawn near the tract of moorland; and now, only a few fields, almost as wild and unproductive as the heath from which they were scarcely reclaimed, lay between me and the dusky hill.

"Well, I would rather die yonder than in a street, or on a frequented road," I reflected. "And far better that crows and ravens—if any ravens there be in these regions—should pick my flesh from my bones, than that they should be prisoned in a workhouse coffin, and moulder in a pauper's grave."

To the hill, then, I turned. I reached it. It remained now only to find a hollow where I could lie down, and feel at least hidden, if not secure: but all the surface of the waste looked level. It showed no variation but of tint: green, where rush and moss overgrew the marshes; black, where the dry soil bore only heath. Dark as it was getting, I could still see these changes; though but as mere alternations of light and shade: for colour had faded with the daylight.

My eye still roved over the sullen swell, and along the moor-edge, vanishing amidst the wildest scenery; when, at one dim point, far in among the marshes and the ridges, a light sprang up. "That is an *ignis fatuus*," was my first thought; and I expected it would soon vanish, It burnt on, however, quite steadily; neither receding nor advancing. "Is it then a bonfire just kindled?" I questioned. I watched to see whether it would spread: but no; as it did not diminish, so it did not enlarge. "It may be a candle in a house," I then conjectured: "but if so, I can never reach it. It is much too far away: and were it within a yard of me, what would it avail? I should but knock at the door to have it shut in my face."

And I sank down where I stood, and hid my face against the ground. I lay still a while: the night-wind swept over the hill and over me, and died moaning in the distance; the rain fell fast, wetting me afresh to the skin. Could I but have stiffened to the still frost—the friendly numbness of death—it might have pelted on: I should not have felt it; but my yet living flesh shuddered to its chilling influence. I rose ere long.

The light was yet there; shining dim, but constant, through the rain. I tried to walk again: I dragged my exhausted limbs slowly towards it. It led me aslant over the hill, through a wide bog; which would have been impassable in winter, and was splashy and shaking even now, in the height of summer. Here I fell twice; but as often I rose and rallied my faculties. This light was my forlorn hope: I must gain it.

Having crossed the marsh, I saw a trace of white over the moor. I approached it; it was a road or a track: it led straight up to the light, which now beamed from a sort of knoll, amidst a clump of trees—firs, apparently, from what I could distinguish of the character of their forms and foliage through the gloom. My star vanished as I drew near: some obstacle had intervened between me and it. I put out my hand to feel the dark mass before me; I discriminated the rough stones of a low wall—above it, something like palisades, and within a high and prickly hedge. I groped on. Again a whitish object gleamed before me: it was a gate—a wicket; it moved on its hinges as I touched it. On each side stood a sable bush—holly or yew.

Entering the gate and passing the shrubs, the silhouette of a house rose to view; black, low, and rather long: but the guiding light shone nowhere. All was obscurity. Were the inmates retired to rest? I feared it must be so. In seeking the door, I turned an angle: there shot out the friendly gleam again, from the lozenged panes of a very small latticed window, within a foot of the ground; made still smaller by the growth of ivy or some other creeping plant, whose leaves clustered thick over the portion of the house wall in which it was set. The aperture was so screened and narrow, that curtain or shutter had been deemed unnecessary; and when I stooped down and put aside the spray of foliage shooting over it, I could see all within.

I could see clearly a room with a sanded floor, clean scoured; a dresser of walnut, with pewter plates ranged in rows, reflecting the redness and radiance of a glowing peat-fire. I could see a clock, a white deal table, some chairs. The candle, whose ray had been my beacon, burnt on the table; and by its light an elderly woman, somewhat rough-looking, but scrupulously clean, like all about her, was knitting a stocking.

I noticed these objects cursorily only—in them there was nothing extraordinary. A group of more interest appeared near the hearth, sitting still amidst the rosy peace and warmth suffusing it. Two young, graceful women—ladies in every point—sat, one in a low rocking-chair, the other on a lower stool; both wore deep mourning of crape and bombazeen, which sombre garb singularly set off very fair necks and faces: a large old pointer dog rested its massive head on the knee of one girl—in the lap of the other was cushioned a black cat.

A strange place was this humble kitchen for such occupants! Who were they? They could not be the daughters of the elderly person at the table; for she looked like a rustic, and they were all delicacy and cultivation. I had nowhere seen such faces as theirs: and yet, as I gazed on them, I seemed intimate with every lineament. I cannot call them handsome—they were too pale and grave for the word: as they each bent over a book, they looked thoughtful almost to severity. A stand between them supported a second candle and two great volumes, to which they frequently referred; comparing them seemingly with the smaller books they held in their hands, like people consulting a dictionary to aid them in the task of translation. This scene was as silent as if all the figures had been shadows, and the fire-lit apartment a picture: so hushed was it, I could hear the cinders fall from the grate, the clock tick in its obscure corner; and I even fancied I could distinguish the click-click of the woman's knitting-needles. When, therefore, a voice broke the strange stillness at last, it was audible enough to me.

"Listen, Diana," said one of the absorbed students; "Franz and old Daniel are together in the night-time, and Franz is telling a dream from which he has wakened in terror—listen!" And in a low voice she read something, of which not one word was intelligible to me; for it was in an unknown tongue—neither French nor Latin. Whether it were Greek or German I could not tell.

"That is strong," she said, when she had finished: "I relish it." The other girl, who had lifted her head to listen to her sister, repeated, while she gazed at the fire, a line of what had been read. At a later day, I knew the language and the book; therefore I will here quote the line: though, when I first heard it, it was only like a stroke on sounding brass to me—conveying no meaning:—

" 'Da trat hervor Einer, anzusehen wie die Sternen Nacht.' Good! good!" she exclaimed, while her dark and deep eye sparkled. "There you have a dim and mighty archangel fitly set before you! The line is worth a hundred pages of fustian. 'Ich wäge die Gedanken in der Schale meines Zornes und die Werke mit dem Gewichte meines Grimms.' I like it!"

Both were again silent.

"Is there any country where they talk i' that way?" asked the old woman, looking up from her knitting.

"Yes, Hannah—a far larger country than England; where they talk in no other way."

"Well, for sure case, I knawn't how they can understand t' one t' other: and if either o'ye went there, ye could tell what they said, I guess?"

"We could probably tell something of what they said, but not all—for we are not as clever as you think us, Hannah. We don't speak German, and we cannot read it without a dictionary to help us."

"And what good does it do you?"

"We mean to teach it sometime—or at least the elements, as they say; and then we shall get more money than we do now."

"Varry like: but give ower studying; ye've done enough for to-night."

"I think we have: at least, I'm tired. Mary, are you?"

"Mortally: after all, it's tough work fagging away at a language with no master but a lexicon."

"It is: especially such a language as this crabbed but glorious Deutsch. I wonder when St. John will come home."

"Surely he will not be long now: it is just ten" (looking at a little gold watch she drew from her girdle). "It rains fast. Hannah, will you have the goodness to look at the fire in the parlour?"

The woman rose; she opened a door, through which I dimly saw a passage: soon I heard her stir a fire in an inner room; she presently came back.

"Ah, childer!" said she, "it fair troubles me to go into yond' room now: it looks so lonesome wi' the chair empty and set back in a corner."

She wiped her eyes with her apron: the two girls, grave before, looked sad now.

"But he is in a better place," continued Hannah: "we shouldn't wish him here again. And then, nobody need to have a quieter death nor he had."

"You say he never mentioned us?" inquired one of the ladies.

"He hadn't time, bairn: he was gone in a minute—was your father. He had been a bit ailing like the day before, but naught to signify; and when Mr. St. John asked if he would like either o' ye to be sent for, he fair laughed at him. He began again with a bit of a heaviness in his head the next day—that is, a fortnight sin'—and he went to sleep and niver wakened: he wor a'most stark when your brother went into t'chamber and fand him. Ah, childer! that's t' last o' t' old stock—for ye and Mr. St. John is like of a different soart to them 'at's gone; for all your mother wor mich i' your way; and a'most as book-learned. She wor the pictur' o' ye, Mary: Diana is more like your father."

I thought them so similar I could not tell where the old servant (for such I now concluded her to be) saw the difference. Both were fair complexioned and slenderly made; both possessed faces full of distinction and intelligence. One, to be sure, had hair a shade darker than the other, and there was a difference in their style of wearing it: Mary's pale brown locks were parted and braided smooth; Diana's duskier tresses covered her neck with thick curls. The clock struck ten.

"Ye'll want your supper, I'm sure," observed Hannah; "and so will Mr. St. John when he comes in."

And she proceeded to prepare the meal. The ladies rose: they seemed about to withdraw to the parlour. Till this moment, I had been so intent on watching them, their appearance and conversation had excited in me so keen an interest, I had half-forgotten my own wretched position: now it recurred to me. More desolate, more desperate than ever, it seemed from contrast. And how impossible did it appear to touch the inmates of this house with concern on my behalf: to make them believe in the truth of my wants and woes—to induce them to vouchsafe a rest for my wanderings! As I groped out the door, and knocked at it hesitatingly, I felt that last idea to be indeed a mere chimera. Hannah opened.

"What do you want?" she inquired, in a voice of surprise, as she surveyed me by the light of the candle she held.

"May I speak to your mistresses?" I said.

"You had better tell me what you have to say to them. Where do you come from?"

"I am a stranger."

"What is your business here at this hour?"

"I want a night's shelter in an out-house or anywhere, and a morsel of bread to eat."

Distrust, the very feeling I dreaded, appeared in Hannah's face. "I'll give you a piece of bread," she said, after a pause; "but we can't take in a vagrant to lodge. It isn't likely."

"Do let me speak to your mistresses."

"No; not I. What can they do for you? You should not be roving about now: it looks very ill."

"But where shall I go if you drive me away? What shall I do?"

"Oh, I'll warrant you know where to go, and what to do. Mind you don't do wrong, that's all. Here is a penny; now go——"

"A penny cannot feed me, and I have no strength to go farther. Don't shut the door:—oh, don't, for God's sake!"

"I must; the rain is driving in——"

"Tell the young ladies.—Let me see them—"

"Indeed, I will not. You are not what you ought to be, or you wouldn't make such a noise. Move off!"

"But I must die if I am turned away."

"Not you. I'm fear'd you have some ill plans agate, that bring you about folk's houses at this time o' night. If you've any followers—housebreakers or such like—anywhere near, you may tell them we are not by ourselves in the house: we have a gentleman, and dogs, and guns." Here the honest but inflexible servant clapped the door to and bolted it within.

This was the climax. A pang of exquisite suffering—a throe of true despair—rent and heaved my heart. Worn out, indeed, I was; not another step could I stir. I sank on the wet door-step: I groaned—I wrung my hands—I wept in utter anguish. Oh, this spectre of death! Oh, this last hour, approaching in such horror! Alas, this isolation—this banishment from my kind! Not only the anchor of home, but the footing of fortitude was gone—at least for a moment: but the last I soon endeavoured to regain.

"I can but die," I said, "and I believe in God. Let me try to wait His will in silence."

These words I not only thought but uttered; and thrusting back all my misery into my heart, I made an effort to compel it to remain there—dumb and still.

"All men must die," said a voice quite close at hand; "but all are not comdemned to meet a lingering and premature doom, such as yours would be if you perished here of want."

"Who or what speaks?" I asked, terrified at the unexpected sound, and incapable now of deriving from any occurrence a hope of aid. A form was near—what form, the pitch-dark night and my enfeebled vision prevented me from distinguishing. With a loud, long knock, the new comer appealed to the door.

"Is it you, Mr. St. John?" cried Hannah.

"Yes—yes; open quickly."

"Well, how wet and cold you must be, such a wild night as it is! Come in—your sisters are quite uneasy about you, and I believe there are bad folks about. There has been a beggar-woman—I declare she is not gone yet!—laid down there. Get up! for shame! Move off, I say!"

"Hush, Hannah! I have a word to say to the woman. You have done your duty in excluding, now let me do mine in admitting her. I was near, and listened to both you and her. I think this is a peculiar case—I must at least examine into it. Young woman, rise, and pass before me into the house."

With difficulty I obeyed him. Presently I stood within that clean, bright kitchen—on the very hearth—trembling, sickening; conscious of an aspect in the last degree ghastly, wild, and weather-beaten. The two ladies, their brother, Mr. St. John, the old servant, were all gazing at me.

"St. John, who is it?" I heard one ask.

"I cannot tell: I found her at the door," was the reply.

"She does look white," said Hannah.

"As white as clay or death," was responded. "She will fall: let her sit."

And indeed my head swam: I dropped; but a chair received me. I still possessed my senses; though just now I could not speak.

"Perhaps a little water would restore her. Hannah, fetch some. But she is worn to nothing. How very thin, and how very bloodless!"

"A mere spectre!"

"Is she ill, or only famished?"

"Famished, I think. Hannah, is that milk? Give it me, and a piece of bread."

Diana (I knew her by the long curls which I saw drooping between me and the fire as she bent over me) broke some bread, dipped it in milk, and put it to my lips. Her face was near mine: I saw there was pity in it, and I felt sympathy in her hurried breathing. In her simple words, too, the same balm-like emotion spoke: "Try to eat."

"Yes—try," repeated Mary gently; and Mary's hand removed my sodden bonnet and lifted my head. I tasted what they offered me: feebly at first, eagerly soon.

"Not too much at first—restrain her," said the brother; "she has had enough." And he withdrew the cup of milk and the plate of bread.

"A little more, St. John—look at the avidity in her eyes."

"No more at present, sister. Try if she can speak now—ask her her name."

I felt I could speak, and I answered—"My name is Jane Elliott." Anxious as ever to avoid discovery, I had before resolved to assume an *alias*.

"And where do you live? Where are your friends?"

I was silent.

"Can we send for any one you know?"

I shook my head.

"What account can you give of yourself?"

Somehow, now that I had once crossed the threshold of this house, and once was brought face to face with its owners, I felt no longer outcast, vagrant, and disowned by the wide world. I dared to put off the mendi-

cant—to resume my natural manner and character. I began once more to
know myself; and when Mr. St. John demanded an account—which at
present I was far too weak to render—I said after a brief pause,—
    "Sir, I can give you no details to-night."
    "But what, then," said he, "do you expect me to do for you?"
    "Nothing," I replied. My strength sufficed for but short answers. Diana
took the word:—
    "Do you mean," she asked, "that we have now given you what aid you
require; and that we may dismiss you to the moor and the rainy night?"
    I looked at her. She had, I thought, a remarkable countenance; instinct
both with power and goodness. I took sudden courage. Answering her
with compassionate gaze with a smile, I said: "I will trust you. If I were
a masterless and stray dog, I know that you would not turn me from your
hearth to-night: as it is, I really have no fear. Do with me and for me as
you like; but excuse me from much discourse—my breath is short—I feel
a spasm when I speak." All three surveyed me, and all three were silent.
    "Hannah," said Mr. St. John, at last, "let her sit there at present, and
ask her no questions; in ten minutes more, give her the remainder of that
milk and bread. Mary and Diana, let us go into the parlour and talk the
matter over."
    They withdrew. Very soon one of the ladies returned—I could not tell
which. A kind of pleasant stupor was stealing over me as I sat by the genial
fire. In an undertone she gave some directions to Hannah. Ere long, with
the servant's aid, I contrived to mount a staircase: my dripping clothes
were removed; soon, a warm, dry bed received me. I thanked God—experienced amidst unutterable exhaustion a glow of grateful joy—and slept.

······

Chapter 29

The recollection of about three days and nights succeeding this is very
dim in my mind. I can recall some sensations felt in that interval; but few
thoughts framed, and no actions performed. I knew I was in a small room,
and in a narrow bed. To that bed I seemed to have grown: I lay on it
motionless as a stone; and to have torn me from it would have been almost
to kill me. I took no note of the lapse of time—of the change from morning to noon, from noon to evening. I observed when any one entered or
left the apartment; I could even tell who they were; I could understand
what was said when the speaker stood near to me; but I could not answer:
to open my lips or move my limbs was equally impossible. Hannah, the
servant, was my most frequent visitor. Her coming disturbed me. I had
a feeling that she wished me away; that she did not understand me or my
circumstances; that she was prejudiced against me. Diana and Mary appeared in the chamber once or twice a day. They would whisper sentences
of this sort at my bed-side:—
    "It is very well we took her in."
    "Yes; she would certainly have been found dead at the door in the morn-
ing, had she been left out all night. I wonder what she has gone through?"
    "Strange hardships, I imagine—poor, emaciated, pallid wanderer!"
    "She is not an uneducated person, I should think, by her manner of

speaking; her accent was quite pure; and the clothes she took off, though splashed and wet, were little worn and fine."

"She has a peculiar face; fleshless and haggard as it is, I rather like it; and when in good health and animated, I can fancy her physiognomy would be agreeable."

Never once in their dialogues did I hear a syllable of regret at the hospitality they had extended to me; or of suspicion of, or aversion to, myself. I was comforted.

Mr. St. John came but once: he looked at me, and said my state of lethargy was the result of reaction from excessive and protracted fatigue. He pronounced it needless to send for a doctor: nature, he was sure, would manage best, left to herself. He said every nerve had been over-strained in some way, and the whole system must sleep torpid awhile. He imagined my recovery would be rapid enough when once commenced. These opinions he delivered in a few words, in a quiet, low voice; and added, after a pause, in the tone of a man little accustomed to expansive comment, "rather an unusual physiognomy; certainly, not indicative of vulgarity or degradation."

"Far otherwise," responded Diana. "To speak truth, St. John, my heart rather warms to the poor little soul. I wish we may be able to benefit her permanently."

"That is hardly likely," was the reply. "You will find she is some young lady who has had a misunderstanding with her friends, and has probably injudiciously left them. We may, perhaps succeed in restoring her to them, if she is not obstinate: but I trace lines of force in her face which make me sceptical of her tractability." He stood considering me some minutes; then added, "She looks sensible, but not at all handsome."

"She is so ill, St. John."

"Ill or well, she would always be plain. The grace and harmony of beauty are quite wanting in those features."

On the third day, I was better; on the fourth, I could speak, move, rise in bed, and turn. Hannah had brought me some gruel and dry toast, about, as I supposed, the dinner hour. I had eaten with relish: the food was good—void of the feverish flavour which had hitherto poisoned what I had swallowed. When she left me, I felt comparatively strong and revived; ere long satiety of repose, and desire for action stirred me. I wished to rise; but what could I put on? Only my damp and bemired apparel; in which I had slept on the ground and fallen in the marsh. I felt ashamed to appear before my benefactors so clad. I was spared the humiliation.

On a chair by the bed-side were all my own things, clean and dry. My black silk frock hung against the wall. The traces of the bog were removed from it; the creases left by the wet smoothed out: it was quite decent. My very shoes and stockings were purified and rendered presentable. There were the means of washing in the room, and a comb and brush to smooth my hair. After a weary process, and resting every five minutes, I succeeded in dressing myself. My clothes hung loose on me; for I was much wasted, but I covered deficiencies with a shawl, and once more, clean and respectable-looking—no speck of the dirt, no trace of the disorder I so hated, and which seemed so to degrade me, left—I crept down a stone staircase, with the aid of the banisters, to a narrow, low passage, and found my way presently to the kitchen.

It was full of the fragrance of new bread, and the warmth of a gener-

ous fire. Hannah was baking. Prejudices, it is well known, are most difficult to eradicate from the heart whose soil has never been loosened or
fertilized by education: they grow there, firm as weeds among stones. Hannah had been cold and stiff, indeed, at the first: latterly, she had begun
to relent a little; and when she saw me come in tidy and well-dressed,
she even smiled.

"What, you have got up?" she said. "You are better, then. You may sit
you down in my chair on the hearthstone, if you will."

She pointed to the rocking chair: I took it. She bustled about, examining me every now and then with the corner of her eye. Turning to me,
as she took some loaves from the oven, she asked, bluntly—

"Did you ever go a-begging afore you came here?"

I was indignant for a moment: but remembering that anger was out of
the question, and that I had indeed appeared as a beggar to her, I answered
quietly; but still not without a certain marked firmness,—

"You are mistaken in supposing me a beggar. I am no beggar; any more
than yourself or your young ladies."

After a pause, she said, "I dunnut understand that: you've like no house,
nor no brass, I guess?"

"The want of house or brass (by which I suppose you mean money)
does not make a beggar in your sense of the word."

"Are you book-learned?" she inquired, presently.

"Yes, very."

"But you've never been to boarding-school?"

"I was at a boarding-school eight years."

She opened her eyes wide. "Whatever cannot ye keep yourself for, then?"

"I have kept myself; and, I trust, shall keep myself again. What are you
going to do with these gooseberries?" I inquired, as she brought out a
basket of the fruit.

"Mak'em into pies."

"Give them to me and I'll pick them."

"Nay; I dunnut want ye to do nought."

"But I must do something. Let me have them."

She consented; and she even brought me a clean towel to spread over
my dress, "lest," as she said, "I should mucky it."

"Ye've not been used to sarvant's wark, I see by your hands," she
remarked. "Happen ye've been a dressmaker?"

"No, you are wrong. And, now, never mind what I have been: don't
trouble your head further about me; but tell me the name of the house
where we are."

"Some calls it Marsh-End, and some calls it Moor House."

"And the gentleman who lives here is called Mr. St. John?"

"Nay; he doesn't live here: he is only staying awhile. When he is at
home, he is in his own parish at Morton."

"That village a few miles off?"

"Aye."

"And what is he?"

"He is a parson."

I remembered the answer of the old housekeeper at the parsonage, when
I had asked to see the clergyman. "This, then, was his father's residence?"

"Aye; old Mr. Rivers lived here, and his father, and grandfather, and
gurt (great) grandfather afore him."

"The name, then, of that gentleman, is Mr. St. John Rivers?"

"Aye; St. John is like his kirstened name."

"And his sisters are called Diana and Mary Rivers?"

"Yes."

"Their father is dead?"

"Dead three weeks sin' of a stroke."

"They have no mother?"

"The mistress has been dead this mony a year."

"Have you lived with the family long?"

"I've lived here thirty year. I nursed them all three."

"That proves you must have been an honest and faithful servant. I will say so much for you; though you have had the incivility to call me a beggar."

She again regarded me with a surprised stare. "I believe," she said, "I was quite mista'en in my thoughts of you: but there is so mony cheats goes about, you mun forgie me."

"And though," I continued, rather severely, "you wished to turn me from the door, on a night when you should not have shut out a dog."

"Well, it was hard: but what can a body do? I thought more o' th' childer nor of mysel: poor things! They've like nobody to tak' care on 'em but me. I'm like to look sharpish."

I maintained a grave silence for some minutes.

"You munnut think too hardly of me," she again remarked.

"But I do think hardly of you," I said; "and I'll tell you why—not so much because you refused to give me shelter, or regarded me as an impostor, as because you just now made it a species of reproach that I had no 'brass,' and no house. Some of the best people that ever lived have been as destitute as I am; and if you are a Christian, you ought not to consider poverty a crime."

"No more I ought," said she: "Mr. St. John tells me so too; and I see I wor wrang—but I've clear a different notion on you now to what I had. You look a raight dow dacent little crater."

"That will do—I forgive you now. Shake hands."

She put her floury and horny hand into mine; another and heartier smile illumined her rough face: and from that moment we were friends.

Hannah was evidently fond of talking. While I picked the fruit, and she made the paste for the pies, she proceeded to give me sundry details about her deceased master and mistress, and "the childer," as she called the young people.

Old Mr. Rivers, she said, was a plain man enough; but a gentleman, and of as ancient a family as could be found. Marsh-End had belonged to the Rivers' ever since it was a house: and it was, she affirmed, "aboon two hundred year old—for all it looked but a small, humble place, naught to compare wi' Mr. Oliver's grand hall down i' Morton Vale. But she could remember Bill Oliver's father a journeyman needle-maker; and th' Rivers' wor gentry i' th' owd days o' th' Henrys, as onybody might see by looking into th' registers i' Morton Church vestry." Still, she allowed, "the owd maister was like other folk—naught mich out o' t' common way: stark mad o' shooting, and farming, and sich like." The mistress was different. She was a great reader, and studied a deal; and the "bairns" had taken after her. There was nothing like them in these parts, nor ever had been: they had liked learning, all three, almost from the time they could speak; and they had always been "of a mak' of their own." Mr. St. John, when he grew up, would go to college and be a parson; and the girls, as soon as they left school, would seek places as governesses: for they had told her their father had some years ago lost a great deal of money, by a man he had trusted turning bankrupt; and as he was now not rich enough to give them fortunes, they must provide for themselves. They had lived very little at home for a long while, and were only come now to stay a few weeks on account of their father's death: but they did so like Marsh-End and Morton, and all these moors and hills about. They had been in London, and many other grand towns; but they always said there was no place like home: and then they were so agreeable with each other—never fell out nor "threaped." She did not know where there was such a family for being united.

Having finished my task of gooseberry picking, I asked where the two ladies and their brother were now.

"Gone over to Morton for a walk; but they would be back in half an hour to tea."

They returned within the time Hannah had allotted them: they entered by the kitchen door. Mr. St. John, when he saw me, merely bowed and passed through; the two ladies stopped: Mary in a few words, kindly and calmly expressed the pleasure she felt in seeing me well enough to be able to come down; Diana took my hand: she shook her head at me.

"You should have waited for my leave to descend," she said. "You still look very pale—and so thin! Poor child!—poor girl!"

Diana had a voice toned, to my ear, like the cooing of a dove. She possessed eyes whose gaze I delighted to encounter. Her whole face seemed to me full of charm. Mary's countenance was equally intelligent—her features equally pretty: but her expression was more reserved; and her manners, though gentle, more distant. Diana looked and spoke with a certain authority: she had a will evidently. It was my nature to feel pleasure in yielding to an authority supported like hers; and to bend, where my conscience and self-respect permitted, to an active will.

"And what business have you here?" she continued. "It is not your place. Mary and I sit in the kitchen sometimes, because at home we like to be free, even to license—but you are a visitor, and must go into the parlour."

"I am very well here."

"Not at all—with Hannah bustling about and covering you with flour."

"Besides, the fire is too hot for you," interposed Mary.

"To be sure," added her sister. "Come, you must be obedient." And still holding my hand, she made me rise, and led me into the inner room.

"Sit there," she said, placing me on the sofa, "while we take out things off and get the tea ready: it is another privilege we exercise in our little moorland home—to prepare our own meals when we are so inclined; or when Hannah is baking, brewing, washing, or ironing."

She closed the door, leaving me solus with Mr. St. John, who sat opposite; a book or newspaper in his hand. I examined, first, the parlour, and then its occupant.

The parlour was rather a small room, very plainly furnished; yet comfortable, because clean and neat. The old-fashioned chairs were very bright, and the walnut-wood table was like a looking-glass. A few strange, antique portraits of the men and women of other days decorated the stained walls; a cupboard with glass doors contained some books and an ancient set of china. There was no superfluous ornament in the room—not one modern piece of furniture, save a brace of work-boxed and a lady's desk in rosewood, which stood on a side-table: every thing—including the carpet and curtains—looked once well worn and well saved.

Mr. St. John—sitting as still as one of the dusky pictures on the walls; keeping his eyes fixed on the page he perused, and his lips mutely sealed—was easy enough to examine. Had he been a statue instead of a man, he could not have been easier. He was young—perhaps from twenty-eight to thirty—tall, slender; his face riveted the eye: it was like a Greek face, very pure in outline; quite a straight, classic nose; quite an Athenian mouth and chin. It is seldom, indeed, an English face comes so near the antique models as did his. He might well be a little shocked at the irregularity of my lineaments, his own being so harmonious. His eyes were large and blue, with brown lashes; his high forehead, colourless as ivory, was partially streaked over by careless locks of fair hair.

This is a gentle delineation, is it not, reader? Yet he whom it describes scarcely impressed one with the idea of a gentle, a yielding, an impressible, or even of a placid nature. Quiescent as he now sat, there was something about his nostril, his mouth, his brow, which, to my perceptions, indicated elements within either restless, or hard, or eager. He did not speak to me one word nor ever direct to me one glance, till his sisters returned. Diana, as she passed in and out, in the course of preparing tea, brought me a little cake, baked on the top of the oven.

"Eat that now," she said: "you must be hungry. Hannah says you have had nothing but some gruel since breakfast."

I did not refuse it, for my appetite was awakened and keen. Mr. Rivers now closed his book, approached the table, and, as he took a seat, fixed his blue, pictorial-looking eyes full on me. There was an unceremonious directness, a searching, decided steadfastness in his gaze now, which told that intention, and not diffidence, had hitherto kept it averted from the stranger.

"You are very hungry," he said.

"I am, sir. It is my way—it always was my way, by instinct—ever to meet the brief with brevity, the direct with plainness."

"It is well for you that a low fever has forced you to abstain for the last three days: there would have been danger in yielding to the cravings of your appetite at first. Now you may eat; though still not immoderately."

"I trust I shall not eat long at your expense, sir," was my very clumsily-contrived, unpolished answer.

"No," he said, coolly: "when you have indicated to us the residence of your friends, we can write to them, and you may be restored to home."

"That, I must plainly tell you, it is out of my power to do; being absolutely without home and friends."

The three looked at me: but not distrustfully. I felt there was no suspicion in their glances: there was more of curiosity. I speak particularly of the young ladies. St. John's eyes, though clear enough in a literal sense, in a figurative one were difficult to fathom. He seemed to use them rather as instruments to search other people's thoughts, than as agents to reveal his own: the which combination of keenness and reserve was considerably more calculated to embarrass than to encourage.

"Do you mean to say," he asked, "that you are completely isolated from every connection?"

"I do. Not a tie links me to any living thing: not a claim do I possess at admittance under any roof in England."

"A most singular position at your age!"

Here I saw his glance directed to my hands, which were folded on the table before me. I wondered what he sought there: his words soon explained the quest.

"You have never been married? You are a spinster?"

Diana laughed. "Why, she can't be above seventeen or eighteen years old, St. John," said she.

"I am near nineteen: but I am not married. No."

I felt a burning glow mount to my face; for bitter and agitating recollections were awakened by the allusion to marriage. They all saw the embarrassment, and the emotion. Diana and Mary relieved me by turning their eyes elsewhere than to my crimsoned visage; but the colder and sterner brother continued to gaze, till the trouble he had excited forced out tears as well as colour.

"Where did you last reside?" he now asked.

"You are too inquisitive, St. John," murmured Mary, in a low voice; but he leaned over the table and required an answer, by a second firm and piercing look.

"The name of the place where, and of the person with whom I lived, is my secret," I replied concisely.

"Which, if you like, you have, in my opinion, a right to keep, both from St. John and every other questioner," remarked Diana.

"Yet if I know nothing about you or your history, I cannot help you," he said. "And you need help: do you not?"

"I need it, and I seek it; so far, sir, that some true philanthropist will put me in the way of getting work which I can do, and the remuneration for which will keep me: if but in the barest necessaries of life."

"I know not whether I am a true philanthropist; yet I am willing to aid you to the utmost of my power, in a purpose so honest. First, then, tell me what you have been accustomed to do, and what you *can* do."

I had now swallowed my tea. I was mightily refreshed by the beverage; as much so as a giant with wine: it gave new tone to my unstrung nerves, and enabled me to address this penetrating young judge steadily.

"Mr. Rivers," I said, turning to him, and looking at him, as he looked at me, openly and without diffidence, "you and your sisters have done me a great service—the greatest man can do his fellow-being; you have rescued me, by your noble hospitality, from death. This benefit conferred gives you an unlimited claim on my gratitude; and a claim, to a certain extent, on my confidence. I will tell you as much of the history of the wanderer you have harboured, as I can tell without compromising my own peace of mind—my own security, moral and physical, and that of others.

"I am an orphan; the daughter of a clergyman. My parents died before I could know them. I was brought up a dependant; educated in a charitable institution. I will even tell you the name of the establishment, where I passed six years as a pupil, and two as a teacher—Lowood Orphan Asylum, ——shire: you will have heard of it, Mr. Rivers?—the Rev. Robert Brocklehurst is the treasurer."

"I have heard of Mr. Brocklehurst, and I have seen the school."

"I left Lowood nearly a year since to become a private governess. I obtained a good situation, and was happy. This place I was obliged to leave four days before I came here. The reason of my departure I cannot and ought not to explain: it would be useless—dangerous; and would sound incredible. No blame attached to me: I am as free from culpability as any one of you three. Miserable I am, and must be for a time; for the catastrophe which drove me from a house I had found a paradise was of a strange and direful nature. I observèd but two points in planning my departure—speed, secrecy: to secure these, I had to leave behind me everything I possessed, except a small parcel; which, in my hurry and trouble of mind, I forgot to take out of the coach that brought me to Whitcross. To this neighbourhood, then, I came, quite destitute. I slept two nights in the open air, and wandered about two days without crossing a threshold: but twice in that space of time did I taste food; and it was when brought by hunger, exhaustion, and despair, almost to the last gasp, that you, Mr. Rivers, forbade me to perish of want at your door, and took me under the shelter of your roof. I know all your sisters have done for me since—for I have not been insensible during my seeming torpor—and I owe to their spontaneous, genuine, genial compassion, as large a debt as to your evangelical charity."

"Don't make her talk any more now, St. John," said Diana, as I paused; "she is evidently not yet fit for excitement. Come to the sofa, and sit down now, Miss Elliott."

I gave an involuntary half-start at hearing the *alias:* I had forgotten my new name. Mr. Rivers, whom nothing seemed to escape, noticed it at once.

"You said your name was Jane Elliott?" he obseved.

"I did say so; and it is the name by which I think it expedient to be called at present but it is not my real name, and when I hear it, it sounds strange to me."

"Your real name you will not give?"

"No: I fear discovery above all things; and whatever disclosure would lead to it I avoid."

"You are quite right, I am sure," said Diana. "Now, do, brother, let her be at peace a while."

But when St. John had mused a few moments, he recommenced, and imperturbably, and with as much acumen as ever.

"You would not like to be long dependent on our hospitality—you would wish, I see, to dispense as soon as may be with my sisters' compassion; and, above all, with my *charity* (I am quite sensible of the distinction drawn, nor do I resent it—it is just): you desire to be independent of us?"

"I do: I have already said so. Show me how to work, or how to seek work: that is all I now ask; then let me go, if it be but to the meanest cottage—but *till then,* allow me to stay here: I dread another essay of the horrors of homeless destitution."

"Indeed, you *shall* stay here," said Diana, putting her white hand on my head. "You *shall,*" repeated Mary, in the tone of undemonstrative sincerity, which seemed natural to her.

"My sisters, you see, have a pleasure in keeping you," said Mr. St. John, "as they would have a pleasure in keeping and cherishing a half-frozen bird, some wintry wind might have driven through their casement. *I* feel more inclination to put you in the way of keeping yourself; and shall endeavour to do so: but observe, my sphere is narrow. I am but the in-

cumbent of a poor country parish: my aid must be of the humblest sort.
And if you are inclined to despise the day of small things, seek some more
efficient succor than such as I can offer."

"She has already said that she is willing to do anything honest she *can*
do," answered Diana, for me; "and you know, St. John, she has no choice
of helpers: she is forced to put up with such crusty people as you."

"I will be a dressmaker: I will be a plain work-woman; I will be a servant, a nurse-girl, if I can be no better," I answered.

"Right," said Mr. St. John, quite coolly. "If such is your spirit, I promise to aid you; in my own time and way."

He now resumed the book with which he had been occupied before tea.
I soon withdrew; for had talked as much, and sat up as long, as my present strength would permit.

＊＊＊＊＊＊＊

Chapter 30

The more I knew of the inmates of Moor House, the better I liked them.
In a few days I had so far recovered my health that I could sit up all day,
and walk out sometimes. I could join with Diana and Mary in all their
occupations; converse with them as much as they wished, and aid them
when and where they would allow me. There was a reviving pleasure in
this intercourse, of a kind now tasted by me for the first time—the pleasure arising from perfect congeniality of tastes, sentiments, and principles.

I liked to read what they liked to read: what they enjoyed, delighted
me; what they approved, I reverenced. They loved their sequestered home.
I, too, in the gray, small, antique structure, with its low roof, its latticed
casements, its mouldering walls, its avenue for aged firs—all grown aslant
under the stress of mountain winds; its garden, dark with yew and holly—
and where no flowers but of the hardiest species would bloom—found a
charm, both potent and permanent. They clung to the purple moors behind
and around their dwelling—to the hollow vale into which the pebbly bridle-
path leading from their gate descended; and which would between fern-
banks forest, and then amongst a few of the wildest little pasture-fields
that ever bordered a wilderness of heath, or gave sustenance to a flock
of gray moorland sheep, with their little mossy-faced lambs:—they clung
to this scene, I say, with a perfect enthusiasm of attachment. I could comprehend the feeling, and share both its strength and truth. I saw the fascination of the locality. I felt the consecration of its loneliness: my eye
feasted on the outline of swell and sweep—on the wild colouring communicated to ridge and dell, by moss, by heath-bell, by flower-sprinkled
turf, by brilliant bracken, and mellow granite crag. These details were
just to me what they were to them—so many pure and sweet sources of
pleasure. The strong blast and the soft breeze; the rough and halcyon day;
the hours of sunrise and sunset; the moonlight and the clouded night,
developed for me, in these regions, the same attraction as for them—
wound round my faculties the same spell that entranced theirs.

In-doors we agreed equally well. They were both more accomplished
and better read than I was: but with eagerness I followed in the path of
knowledge they had trodden before me. I devoured the books they lent

me: then it was full satisfaction to discuss with them in the evening what I had perused during the day. Thought fitted thought; opinion met opinion: we coincided, in short, perfectly.

It in our trio there was a superior and a leader, it was Diana. Physically, she far excelled me: she was handsome; she was vigorous. In her animal spirits, there was an affluence of life, and certainty of flow, such as excited my wonder, while it baffled my comprehension. I could talk a while when the evening commenced: but the first gush of vivacity and fluency gone, I was fain to sit on a stool at Diana's feet, to rest my head on her knee, and listen alternately to her and Mary; while they sounded thoroughly the topic on which I had but touched. Diana offered to teach me German. I liked to learn of her: I saw the part of instructress pleased and suited her; that of scholar pleased and suited me no less. Our natures dovetailed: mutual affection—of the strongest kind—was the result. They discovered I could draw: their pencils and colour-boxes were immediately at my service. My skill, greater in this one point than theirs, surprised and charmed them. Mary would sit and watch me by the hour together: then she would take lessons; and a docile, intelligent, assiduous pupil, she made. Thus occupied, and mutually entertained, days passed like hours, and weeks like days.

As to Mr. St. John, the intimacy which had arisen so naturally and rapidly between me and his sisters, did not extend to him. One reason of the distance yet observed between us was, that he was comparatively seldom at home: a large proportion of his time appeared devoted to visiting the sick and poor among the scattered population of his parish.

No weather seemed to hinder him in these pastoral excursions: rain or fair, he would, when his hours of morning study were over, take his hat, and, followed by his father's old pointer, Carlo, go out on his mission of love or duty—I scarcely know in which light he regarded it. Sometimes, when the day was very unfavourable, his sisters would expostulate. He would then say, with a peculiar smile, more solemn than cheerful,—

"And if I let a gust of wind or a sprinkling of rain turn me aside from these easy tasks, what preparation would such sloth be for the future I propose to myself?"

Diana and Mary's general answer to this question was a sigh, and some minutes of apparently mournful meditation.

But besides his frequent absences, there was another barrier to friendship with him: he seemed of a reserved, an abstracted, and even of a brooding nature. Zealous in his ministerial labours, blameless in his life and habits, he yet did not appear to enjoy that mental serenity, that inward content, which should be the reward of every sincere Christian and practical philanthropist. Often, of an evening, when he sat at the window, his desk and papers before him, he would cease reading or writing, rest his chin on his hand, and deliver himself up to I know not what course of thought: but that it was perturbed and exciting might be seen in the frequent flash and changeful dilation of his eye.

I think, moreover, that Nature was not to him that treasury of delight it was to his sisters. He expressed once, and but once in my hearing, a strong sense of the rugged charm of the hills, and an inborn affection for the dark roof and hoary walls he called his home: but there was more of gloom than pleasure in the tone and words in which the sentiment was manifested; and never did he seem to roam the moors for the sake of their soothing silence—never seek out or dwell upon the thousand peaceful delights they could yield.

Incommunicative as he was,some time elapsed before I had an opportunity of gauging his mind. I first got an idea of its calibre when I heard him preach in his own church at Morton. I wish I could describe that sermon: but it is past my power. I cannot even render faithfully the effect it produced on me.

It began calm—and indeed, as far as delivery and pitch of voice went, it was calm to the end: an earnestly felt, yet strictly restrained zeal breathed soon in the distinct accents, and prompted the nervous language. This grew to force—compressed, condensed, controlled. The heart was thrilled, the mind astonished, by the power of the preacher: neither were softened. Throughout there was a strange bitterness; an absence of consolatory gentleness: stern allusions to Calvinistic doctrines—election, predestination, reprobation—were frequent; and each reference to these points sounded like a sentence pronounced for doom. When he had done, instead of feeling better, calmer, more enlightened by his discourse, I experienced an inexpressible sadness; for it seemed to me—I know not whether equally so to others—that the eloquence to which I had been listening had sprung from a depth where lay turbid dregs of disappointment—where moved troubling impulses of insatiate yearnings and disquieting aspirations. I was sure St. John Rivers—pure-lived, conscientious, zealous as he was—had not yet found that peace of God which passeth all understanding: he had no more found it, I thought, than had I; with my concealed and racking regrets for my broken idol and lost elysium—regrets to which I have latterly avoided referring; but which possessed me and tyrannized over me ruthlessly.

Meanwhile a month was gone. Diana and Mary were soon to leave Moor House, and return to the different life, and scene which awaited them, as governesses in a large, fashionable, south-of-England city; where each held a situation in families, by whose wealthy and haughty members they were regarded only as humble dependants, and who neither knew nor sought one of their innate excellences, and appreciated only their acquired accomplishments as they appreciated the skill of their cook, or the taste of their waiting-woman. Mr. St. John had said nothing to me yet about the employment he had promised to obtain for me: yet it became urgent that I should have a vocation of some kind. One morning, being left alone with him a few minutes in the parlour, I ventured to approach the window-recess—which his table, chair, and desk consecrated as a kind of study—and I was going to speak; though not very well knowing in what words to frame my inquiry—for it is at all times difficult to break the ice of reserve glassing over such natures as his—when he saved me the trouble, by being the first to commence a dialogue.

Looking up as I drew near—"You have a question to ask of me?" he said.

"Yes; I wish to know whether you have heard of any service I can offer myself to undertake."

"I found or devised something for you three weeks ago; but as you seemed both useful and happy here—as my sisters had evidently become attached to you, and your society gave them unusual pleasure—I deemed it inexpedient to break in on your mutual comfort, till their approaching departure from Marsh-End should render yours necessary."

"And they will go in three days now?" I said.

"Yes; and when they go, I shall return to the parsonage at Morton: Hannah will accompany me; and this old house will be shut up."

I waited a few moments, expecting he would go on with the subject first broached; but he seemed to have entered another train of reflection; his look denoted abstraction from me and my business. I was obliged to recall him to a theme which was of necessity one of close and anxious interest to me.

"What is the employment you had in view, Mr. Rivers? I hope this delay will not have increased the difficulty of securing it."

"Oh, no; since it is an employment which depends only on me to give, and you to accept."

He again paused: there seemed a reluctance to continue. I grew impatient: a restless movement or two, and an eager and exacting glance fastened on his face, conveyed the feeling to him as effectually as words could have done, and with less trouble.

"You need be in no hurry to hear," he said: "let me frankly tell you, I have nothing eligible or profitable to suggest. Before I explain, recall, if you please, my notice, clearly given, that if I helped you, it must be as the blind man would help the lame. I am poor; for I find that, when I have paid my father's debts, all the patrimony remaining to me will be this crumbling grange, the row of scathed firs behind, and the patch of moorish soil, with the yew-trees and holly-bushes in front. I am obscure: Rivers is an old name; but of the three sole descendants of the race, two earn the dependant's crust among strangers, and the third considers himself an alien from his native country—not only for life, but in death. Yes, and deems, and is bound to deem, himself honoured by the lot; and aspires but after the day when the cross of separation from fleshly ties shall be laid on his shoulders, and when the Head of that church-militant of whose humblest members he is one, shall give the word, 'Rise, and follow me!' "

St. John said these words as he pronounced his sermons, with a quiet, deep voice; with an unflushed cheek, and a coruscating radiance of glance. He resumed:—

"And since I am myself poor and obscure, I can offer you but a service of poverty and obscurity. You may even think it degrading—for I see now your habits have been what the world calls refined: your tastes lean to the ideal; and your society has at least been amongst the educated—but I consider that no service degrades which can better our race. I hold that the more arid and unreclaimed the soil where the Christian labourer's task of tillage is appointed him—the scantier the meed his toil brings—the higher the honour. His, under such circumstances, is the destiny of the pioneer: and the first pioneers of the Gospel were the Apostles—their captain was Jesus, the Redeemer, himself."

"Well?" I said, as he again paused—"proceed."

He looked at me before he proceeded: indeed, he seemed leisurely to read my face, as if its features and lines were characters on a page. The conclusions drawn from this scrutiny he partially expressed in his succeeding observations.

"I believe you will accept the post I offer you," said he; "and hold it for a while: not permanently, though: any more than I could permanently keep the narrow and narrowing—the tranquil, hidden office of English country incumbent: for in your nature is an alloy as detrimental to repose as that in mine; though of a different kind."

"Do explain," I urged, when he halted once more.

"I will; and you shall hear how poor the proposal is—how trivial—how cramping. I shall not stay long at Morton, now that my father is dead, and that I am my own master. I shall leave the place probably in the course of a twelve-month: but while I *do* stay, I will exert myself to the utmost for its improvement. Morton, when I came to it two years ago, had no school: the children of the poor were excluded from every hope of progress. I established one for boys: I mean now to open a second school for girls. I have hired a building for the purpose, with a cottage of two rooms attached to it for the mistress's house. Her salary will be thirty pounds a year: her house is already furnished, very simply, but sufficiently, by the kindness of a lady, Miss Oliver; the only daughter of the sole rich man in my parish—Mr. Oliver, the proprietor of a needle-factory and iron-foundry in the valley. The same lady pays for the education and clothing of an orphan from the workhouse; on condition that she shall aid the mistress in such menial offices connected with her own house and the school, as her occupation of teaching will prevent her having time to discharge in person. Will you be this mistress?"

He put the question rather hurriedly; he seemed half to expect an indignant, or at least a disdainful rejection of the offer: not knowing all my thoughts and feelings, though guessing some, he could not tell in what light the lot would appear to me. In truth it was humble—but then is was sheltered, and I wanted a safe asylum: it was plodding—but then, compared with that of a governess in a rich house, it was independent; and the fear of servitude with strangers entered my soul like iron: it was not ignoble—not unworthy—not mentally degrading. I made my decision.

"I thank you for the proposal, Mr. Rivers; and I accept it with all my heart."

"But you comprehend me?" he said. "It is a village-school: your scholars will be only poor girls—cottagers' children—at best, farmers' daughters. Knitting, sewing, reading, writing, cyphering, will be all you will have to teach. What will you do with your accomplishments? What, with the largest portion of your mind—sentiments—tastes?"

"Save them till they are wanted. They will keep."

"You know what you undertake, then?"

"I do."

He now smiled: and not a bitter or a sad smile; but one well pleased and deeply gratified.

"And when will you commence the exercise of your function?"

"I will go to my house to-morrow; and open the school, if you like, next week."

"Very well: so be it."

He rose and walked through the room. Standing still, he again looked at me. He shook his head.

"What do you disapprove of, Mr. Rivers?" I asked.

"You will not stay at Morton long: no, no!"

"Why? What is your reason for saying so?"

"I read it in your eye: it is not of that description which promises the maintenance of an even tenor in life."

"I am not ambitious."

He started at the word "ambitious." He repeated, "No. What made you think of ambition? Who is ambitious? I know I am: but how did you find it out?"

"I was speaking of myself."

"Well, if you are not ambitious, you are——" He paused.

"What?"

"I was going to say, impassioned: but perhaps you would have misunderstood the word, and been displeased. I mean, that human affections and sympathies have a most powerful hold on you. I am sure you cannot long be content to pass your leisure in solitude, and to devote your working hours to a monotonous labour wholly void of stimulus; any more than I can be content," he added, with emphasis, "to live here buried in morass, pent in with mountain—my nature, that God gave me, contrived; my faculties, heaven-bestowed, paralyzed—made useless. You hear now how I contradict myself. I, who preached contentment with a humble lot, and justified the vocation even of hewers of wood, and drawers of water, in God's service—I, his ordained minister, almost rave in my restlessness. Well, propensities and principles must be reconciled by some means."

He left the room. I this brief hour I had learnt more of him than in the whole previous month: yet still he puzzled me.

Diana and Mary Rivers became more sad and silent as the day approached for leaving their brother, and their home. They both tried to appear as usual; but the sorrow they had to struggle against was one that could not be entirely conquered or concealed. Diana intimated that this would be a different parting from any they had ever yet known. It would probably, as far as St. John was concerned, be a parting for years: it might be a parting for life.

"He will sacrifice all to his long-framed resolves," she said: "natural affection and feelings more potent still. St. John looks quiet, Jane; but he hides a fever in his vitals. You would think him gentle, yet in some things he is inexorable as death; and the worst if it is, my conscience will hardly permit me to dissuade him from his severe decision: certainly, I cannot for a moment blame him for it. It is right, noble, Christian: yet it breaks my heart." And the tears gushed to her fine eyes. Mary bent her head low over her work.

"We are now without father: we shall soon be without home and brother," she murmured.

At that moment a little accident supervened, which seemed decreed by fate, purposely to prove the truth of the adage, that "misfortunes never come singly:" and to add to their distresses the vexing one of the slip between the cup and the lip. St. John passed the window reading a letter. He entered.

"Our uncle John is dead," said he.

Both the sisters seemed struck: not shocked or appalled: the tidings appeared in their eyes rather momentous than afflicting.

"Dead?" repeated Diana.

"Yes."

She riveted a searching gaze on her brother's face. "And what then?" she demanded, in a low voice.

"What then, Die?" he replied, maintaining a marble immobility of feature. "What then? Why—nothing. Read."

He threw the letter into her lap. She glanced over it, and handed it to Mary. Mary perused it in silence, and returned it to her brother. All three looked at each other, and all three smiled—a dreary, pensive smile enough.

"Amen! We can yet live," said Diana, at last.

"At any rate, it makes us no worse off than we were before," remarked Mary.

"Only it forces rather strongly on the mind the picture of what *might have been*," said Mr. Rivers; "and contrasts it somewhat too vividly with what *is*."

He folded the letter, locked it in his desk, and again went out.

For some minutes no one spoke. Diana then turned to me.

"Jane, you will wonder at us and our mysteries," she said; "and think us hard-hearted beings not to be more moved at the death of so near a relation as an uncle; but we have never seen him or known him. He was my mother's brother. My father and he quarrelled long ago. It was by his advice that my father risked most of his property in the speculation that ruined him. Mutual recriminations passed between them: they parted in anger, and were never reconciled. My uncle engaged afterwards in more prosperous undertakings: it appears he realized a fortune of twenty thousand pounds. He was never married, and had no near kindred but ourselves, and one other person, not more closely related than we. My father always cherished the idea that he would atone for his error, by leaving his possessions to us; that letter informs us that he has bequeathed every penny to the other relation; with the exception of thirty guineas, to be divided between St. John, Diana, and Mary Rivers, for the purchase of three mourning rings. He had a right, of course, to do as he pleased: and yet a momentary damp is cast on the spirits by the receipt of such news. Mary and I would have esteemed ourselves rich with a thousand pounds each; and to St. John such a sum would have been valuable, for the good it would have enabled him to do."

This explanation given, the subject was dropped, and no further reference made to it, by either Mr. Rivers or his sisters. The next day, I left Marsh-End for Morton. The day after, Diana and Mary quitted it for distant B——. In a week, Mr. Rivers and Hannah repaired to the parsonage: and so the old grange was abandoned.

． ． ． ． ． ． ．

Chapter 31

My home, then,—when I at last find a home,—is a cottage: a little room with white-washed walls, and a sanded floor; containing four painted chairs and a table, a clock, a cupboard, with two or three plates and dishes, and a set of tea-things in delf. Above, a chamber of the same dimensions as the kitchen, with a deal bedstead, and chest of drawers; small, yet too large to be filled with my scanty wardrobe: though the kindness of my gentle and generous friends has increased that, by a modest stock of such things as are necessary.

It is evening. I have dismissed, with the fee of an orange, the little orphan who serves me as a handmaid. I am sitting alone on the hearth. This morning, the village school opened. I had twenty scholars. But three of the number can read: none write or cypher. Several knit, and a few sew a little. They speak with the broadest accent of the district. At present, they and I have a difficulty in understanding each other's language. Some of them are unmannered, rough, intractable, as well as ignorant; but others are docile, have a wish to learn, and evince a disposition that pleases me. I must not forget that these coarsely-clad little peasants are of flesh and blood as good as the scions of gentlest genealogy; and that the germs of native excellence, refinement, intelligence, kind feeling, are as likely to exist in their hearts as in those of the best-born. My duty will be to develop these germs: surely I shall find some happiness in discharging that office. Much enjoyment I do not expect in the life opening before me: yet it will, doubtless, if I regulate my mind, and exert my powers as I ought, yield me enough to live on from day to day.

Was I very gleeful, settled, content, during the hours I passed in yonder bare, humble school-room this morning and afternoon? Not to deceive myself, I must reply—No: I felt desolate to a degree. I felt—yes, idiot that I am—I felt degraded. I doubted I had taken a step which sank instead of raising me in the scale of social existence. I was weakly dismayed at the ignorance, the poverty, the coarseness of all I heard and saw round me. But let me not hate and despise myself too much for these feelings: I know them to be wrong—that is a great step gained; I shall strive to overcome them. To-morrow, I trust, I shall get the better of them partially; and in a few weeks, perhaps, they will be quite subdued. In a few months, it is possible, the happiness of seeing progress, and a change for the better in my scholars, may substitute gratification for disgust.

Meantime, let me ask myself one question—Which is better?—To have surrendered to temptation; listened to passion; made no painful effort—no struggle;—but to have sunk down in the silken snare; fallen asleep on the flowers covering it; wakened in a southern clime, amongst the luxuries of a pleasure-villa: to have been now living in France, Mr. Rochester's mistress; delirious with his love half my time—for he would—oh, yes, he would have loved me well for a while. He *did* love me—no one will ever love me so again. I shall never more know the sweet homage given to beauty, youth, and grace—for never to any one else shall I seem to possess these charms. He was fond and proud of me—it is what no man besides will ever be.—But where am I wandering, and what am I saying; and, above all, feeling? Whether is it better, I ask, to be a slave in a fool's paradise at Marseilles—fevered with delusive bliss one hour—suffocating with the bitterest tears of remorse and shame the next—or to be a village-schoolmistress, free and honest, in a breezy mountain nook in the healthy heart of England?

Yes; I feel now that I was right when I adhered to principle and law, and scorned and crushed the insane promptings of a frenzied moment. God directed me to a correct choice: I thank His providence for the guidance!

Having brought my eventide musings to this point, I rose, went to my door, and looked at the sunset of the harvest-day, and at the quiet fields before my cottage; which, with the school, was distant half a mile from the village. The birds were singing their last strains—

"The air was mild; the dew was balm."

While I looked, I thought myself happy, and was surprised to find myself ere long weeping—and why? For the doom which had reft me from adhesion to my master: for him I was no more to see; for the desperate grief and fatal fury—consequences of my departure—which might now, per-haps, be dragging him from the path of right, too far to leave hope of ulti-mate restoration thither. At this thought, I turned my face aside from the lovely sky of eve and lonely vale of Morton—I say *lonely,* for in that bend of it visible to me, there was no building apparent save the church and the parsonage, half-hid in trees; and, quite at the extremity, the roof of Vale Hall, where the rich Mr. Oliver and his daughter lived. I hid my eyes, and leant my head against the stone frame of my door; but soon a slight noise near the wicket which shut in my tiny garden from the meadow beyond it, made me look up. A dog—old Carlo, Mr. Rivers' pointer, as I saw in a moment—was pushing the gate with his nose, and St. John him-self leant upon it with folded arms; his brow knit, his gaze, grave almost to displeasure, fixed on me. I asked him to come in.

"No, I cannot stay: I have only brought you a little parcel my sisters left for you. I think it contains a colour-box, pencils, and paper."

I approached to take it: a welcome gift it was. He examined my face, I thought, with austerity, as I came near: the traces of tears were doubt-less very visible upon it.

"Have you found your first day's work harder than you expected?" he asked.

"Oh, no! On the contrary, I think in time I shall get on with my schol-ars very well."

"But perhaps your accommodations—your cottage—your furniture—have disappointed your expectations? They are, in truth, scanty enough; but"——I interrupted:

"My cottage is clean and weather-proof; my furniture sufficient and commodious. All I see has made me thankful, not despondent. I am not absolutely such a fool and sensualist as to regret the absence of a carpet, a sofa, and silver-plate: besides, five weeks ago I had nothing—I was an outcast, a beggar, a vagrant; now I have acquaintance, a home, a busi-ness. I wonder at the goodness of God; the generosity of my friends; the bounty of my lot. I do not repine."

"But you feel solitude an oppression? The little house there behind you is dark and empty."

"I have hardly had time yet to enjoy a sense of tranquillity, much less to grow impatient under one of loneliness."

"Very well; I hope you feel the content you express: at any rate, your good sense will tell you that it is too soon yet to yield to the vacillating fears of Lot's wife. What you had left before I saw you, of course I do not know; but I counsel you to resist, firmly, every temptation which would incline you to look back: pursue your present career steadily for some months at least."

"It is what I mean to do," I answered. St. John continued:—

"It is hard work to control the workings of inclination, and turn the bent of nature: but that it may be done, I know from experience. God has given us, in a measure, the power to make our own fate; and when our ener-gies seem to demand a sustenance they cannot get—when our will strains after a path we may not follow—we need neither starve from inanition, nor stand still in despair: we have but to seek another nourishment for the mind, as strong as the forbidden food it longed to taste—and perhaps purer; and to hew out for the adventurous foot a road as direct and broad as the one Fortune has blocked up against us, if rougher than it.

"A year ago, I was myself intensely miserable, because I thought I had made a mistake in entering the ministry: its uniform duties wearied me to death. I burnt for the more active life of the world—for the more exciting toils of a literary career—for the destiny of an artist, author, orator; anything rather than that of a priest: yes, the heart of a politician, of a soldier, of a votary of glory, a lover of renown, a luster after power, beat under my curate's surplice. I considered; my life was so wretched, it must be changed, or I must die. After a season of darkness and struggling, light broke and relief fell: my cramped existence all at once spread out to a plain without bounds—my powers heard a call from heaven to rise, gather their full strength, spread their wings and mount beyond ken. God had an errand for me; to bear which afar, to deliver it well, skill and strength, courage and eloquence, the best qualifications of soldier, statesman, and orator, were all needed: for these all centre in the good missionary.

"A missionary I resolved to be. From that moment my state of mind changed: the fetters dissolved and dropped from every faculty, leaving nothing of bondage but its galling soreness—which time only can heal. My father, in deed, opposed the determination; but since his death, I have not a ligitimate obstacle to contend with: some affairs settled, a successor for Morton provided, an entanglement or two of the feelings broken through or cut assunder—a last conflict with human weakness, in which I know I shall overcome, because I have vowed that I *will* overcome—and I leave Europe for the East."

He said this in his peculiar, subdued, yet emphatic voice; looking, when he had ceased speaking, not at me, but at the setting sun: at which I looked too. Both he and I had our backs towards the path leading up the field to the wicket. We had heard no step on that grass-grown track; the water running in the vale was the one lulling sound of the hour and scene: we might well then start, when a gay voice, sweet as a silver bell, exclaimed:—

"Good evening, Mr. Rivers. And good evening, old Carlo. Your dog is quicker to recognize his friends that you are, sir: he pricked his ears and wagged his tail when I was at the bottom of the field, and you have your back towards me now."

It was true. Though Mr. Rivers had started at the first of those musical accents, as if a thunderbolt had split a cloud over his head, he stood yet, at the close of the sentence, in the same attitude in which the speaker had surprised him: his arm resting on the gate, his face directed towards the west. He turned at last, with measured deliberation. A vision, as it seemed to me, had risen at his side. There appeared, within three feet of him, a form clad in pure white—a youthful, graceful form: full, yet fine in contour; and when, after bending to caress Carlo, it lifted up its head, and threw back a long veil, there bloomed under his glance a face of perfect beauty. Perfect beauty is a strong expression; but I do not retrace or qualify it: as sweet features as ever the temperate clime of Albion moulded; as pure hues of rose and lily as ever her humid gales and vapoury skies generated and screened, justified, in this instance, the term. No charm was wanting, no defect was perceptible: the young girl had regular and delicate lineaments; eyes shaped and coloured as we see them in lovely pictures, large, and dark, and full; the long and shadowy eyelash which encircles a fine eye with so soft a fascination; the pencilled brow which gives such clearness; the white, smooth forehead, which adds such repose to the livelier beauties of tint and ray; the cheek, oval, fresh and smooth;

the lips, fresh too, ruddy, healthy, sweetly formed; the even and gleaming teeth without flaw; the small, dimpled chin; the ornament of rich,
plenteous tresses,—all advantages, in short, which combined, realize the
ideal of beauty, were fully hers. I wondered, as I looked at this fair creature: I admired her with my whole heart. Nature had surely formed her
in a partial mood; and, forgetting her usual stinted step-mother dole of
gifts, had endowed this, her darling, with a granddame's bounty.

What did St. John Rivers think of this earthly angel? I naturally asked
myself that question as I saw him turn to her and look at her; and, as naturally, I sought the answer to the inquiry in his countenance. He had
already withdrawn his eye from Peri, and was looking at a humble tuft
of daisies which grew by the wicket.

"A lovely evening; but late for you to be out alone," he said, and he
crushed the snowy heads of the closed flowers with his foot.

"Oh, I only came home from S—— (she mentioned the name of a large
town some twenty miles distant) this afternoon. Papa told me you had
opened your school, and that the new mistress was come; and so I put
on my bonnet after tea, and ran up the valley to see her: this is she?" pointing to me.

"It is," said St. John.

"Do you think you shall like Morton?" she asked of me, with a direct
and naive simplicity of tone and manner, pleasing, if child-like.

"I hope I shall. I have many inducements to do so."

"Did you find your scholars as attentive as you expected?"

"Quite."

"Do you like your house?"

"Very much."

"Have I furnished it nicely?"

"Very nicely, indeed."

"And made a good choice of an attendant for you in Alice Wood?"

"You have, indeed. She is teachable and handy." (This, then, I thought,
is Miss Oliver, the heiress: favoured, it seems, in the gifts of fortune, as
well as in those of nature! What a happy combination of planets presided
over her birth, I wonder?)

"I shall come up and help you teach sometimes," she added. "It will
be a change for me to visit you now and then; and I like a change. Mr.
Rivers, I have been so gay during my stay at S——. Last night, or rather
this morning, I was dancing till two o'clock. The ——th regiment are stationed there, since the riots; and the officers are the most agreeable men
in the world: they put all our young knife-grinders and scissor merchants
to shame."

It seemed to me that Mr. St. John's under lip protruded, and his upper
lip curled a moment. His mouth certainly looked a good deal compressed,
and the lower part of his face unusually stern and square, as the laughing
girl gave him this information. He lifted his gaze, too, from the daisies,
and turned it on her. An unsmiling, a searching, a meaning gaze it was.
She answered it with a second laugh: and laughter well became her youth,
her roses, her dimples, her bright eyes.

As he stood, mute and grave, she again fell to caressing Carlo. "Poor
Carlo loves me," said she. "He is not stern and distant to his friends; and
if he could speak, he would not be silent."

As she patted the dog's head, bending with native grace before his young and austere master, I saw a glow rise to that master's face. I saw his solemn eye melt with sudden fire, and flicker with resistless emotion. Flushed and kindled thus, he looked nearly as beautiful for a man as she for a woman. His chest heaved once, as if his large heart, weary of despotic constriction, had expanded, despite the will, and made a vigorous bound for the attainment of liberty. But he curbed it, I think, as a resolute rider would curb a rearing steed. He responded neither by word nor movement to the gentle advances made him.

"Papa says you never come to see us now," continued Miss Oliver, looking up. "You are quite a stranger at Vale Hall. He is alone this evening, and not very well: will you return with me and visit him?"

"It is not a seasonable hour to intrude on Mr. Oliver," answered St. John.

"Not a seasonable hour! But, I declare, it is. It is just the hour when papa most wants company: when the works are closed, and he has no business to occupy him. Now, Mr. Rivers, *do* come. Why are you so very shy, and so very sombre?" She filled up the hiatus his silence left by a reply of her own.

"I forgot!" she exclaimed, shaking her beautiful curled head, as if shocked at herself. "I am so giddy and thoughtless! *Do* excuse me. It had slipped my memory that you have good reasons to be indisposed for joining in my chatter. Diana and Mary have left you, and Moor House is shut up, and you are so lonely. I am sure I pity you. Do come and see papa."

"Not to-night, Miss Rosamond, not to-night."

Mr. St. John spoke almost like an automaton: himself only knew the effort it cost him thus to refuse.

"Well, if you are so obstinate, I will leave you; for I dare not stay any longer: the dew begins to fall. Good-evening!"

She held out her hand. He just touched it. "Good-evening!" he repeated, in a voice low and hollow as an echo. She turned; but in a moment returned.

"Are you well?" she asked. Well might she put the question: his face was blanched as her gown.

"Quite well," he enunciated; and, with a bow, he left the gate. She went one way; he another. She turned twice to gaze after him, as she tripped fairy-like down the field; he, as he strode firmly across, never turned at all.

This spectacle of another's suffering and sacrifice, rapt my thoughts from exclusive meditation on my own. Diana Rivers had designated her brother "inexorable as death." She had not exaggerated.

• • • • • • •

Chapter 32

I continued the labours of the village-school as actively and faithfully as I could. It was truly hard work at first. Some time elapsed before, with all my efforts, I could comprehend my scholars and their nature. Wholly untaught, with faculties quite torpid, they seemed to me hopelessly dull; and, at first sight, all dull alike: but I soon found I was mistaken. There was a difference amongst them as amongst the educated; and when I got to know them, and they me, this difference rapidly developed itself. Their

amazement at me, my language, my rules and ways, once subsided, I found
some of these heavy-looking, gaping rustics wake up into sharp-witted
girls enough. Many showed themselves obliging, and amiable too; and
I discovered amongst them not a few examples of natural politeness, and
innate self-respect, as well as of excellent capacity, that won both my good-
will and my admiration. These soon took a pleasure in doing their work
well; in keeping their persons neat; in learning their tasks regularly; in
acquiring quiet and orderly manners. The rapidity of their progress, in
some instances, was even surprising; and an honest and happy pride I took
in it: besides, I began personally to like some of the best girls; and they
liked me. I had amongst my scholars several farmers' daughters: young
women grown, almost. These could already read, write, and sew; and
to them I taught the elements of grammar, geography, history, and the finer
kinds of needlework. I found estimable characters amongst them—
characters desirous of information, and disposed for improvement—with
whom I passed many a pleasant evening hour in their own homes. Their
parents then (the farmer and his wife) loaded me with attentions. There
was an enjoyment in accepting their simple kindness, and in repaying it
by a consideration—a scrupulous regard to their feelings—to which they
were not, perhaps, at all times accustomed, and which both charmed and
benefited them; because, while it elevated them in their own eyes, it made
them emulous to merit the deferential treatment they received.

I felt I became a favourite in the neighbourhood. Whenever I went out,
I heard on all sides cordial salutations, and was welcomed with friendly
smiles. To live amidst general regard, though it be but the regard of
working-people, is like "sitting in sunshine, calm and sweet:" serene inward feelings bud and bloom under the ray. At this period of my life, my
heart far oftener swelled with thankfulness than sank with dejection: and
yet, reader, to tell you all, in the midst of this calm, this useful existence—
after a day passed in honourable exertion amongst my scholars, an evening spent in drawing or reading contentedly alone—I used to rush into
strange dreams at night: dreams many-coloured, agitated, full of the ideal,
the stirring, the stormy—dreams where, amidst unusual scenes, charged
with adventure, with agitating risk and romantic chance, I still again and
again met Mr. Rochester, always at some exciting crisis; and then the sense
of being in his arms, hearing his voice, meeting his eye, touching his hand
and cheek, loving him, being loved by him—the hope of passing a lifetime at his side, would be renewed, with all its first force and fire. Then
I awoke. Then I recalled where I was, and how situated. Then I rose up
on my curtainless bed, trembling and quivering; and then the still, dark
night witnessed the convulsion of despair, and heard the burst of passion.
By nine o'clock the next morning, I was punctually opening the school;
tranquil, settled, prepared for the steady duties of the day.

Rosamond Oliver kept her word in coming to visit me. Her call at the
school was generally made in the course of her morning ride. She would
canter up to the door on her pony, followed by a mounted livery servant.
Anything more exquisite than her appearance, in her purple habit, with
her Amazon's cap of black velvet placed gracefully above the long curls
that kissed her cheek and floated to her shoulders, can scarcely be imagined: and it was thus she would enter the rustic building, and glide through
the dazzled ranks of the village children. She generally came at the hour
when Mr. Rivers was engaged in giving his daily catechising lesson.

Keenly, I fear, did the eye of the visitress pierce the young pastor's heart. A sort of instinct seemed to warn him of her entrance, even when he did not see it; and when he was looking quite away from the door, if she appeared at it, his cheek would glow, and his marble-seeming features, though they refused to relax, changed indescribably; and in their very quiescence became expressive of a repressed fervour, stronger than working muscle or darting glance could indicate.

Of course, she knew her power: indeed, he did not, because he could not, conceal it from her. In spite of his Christian stoicism, when she went up and addressed him, and smiled gaily, encouragingly, even fondly in his face, his hand would tremble, and his eye burn. He seemed to say, with his sad and resolute look, if he did not say it with his lips, "I love you, and I know you prefer me. It is not despair of success that keeps me dumb. If I offered my heart, I believe you would accept it. But that heart is already laid on a sacred altar: the fire is arranged round it. It will soon be no more than a sacrifice consumed."

And then she would pout like a disappointed child; a pensive cloud would soften her radiant vivacity; she would withdraw her hand hastily from his, and turn in transient petulance from his aspect, at once so heroic and so martyr-like. St. John, no doubt, would have given the world to follow, recall, retain her, when she thus left him: but he would not give one chance of Heaven; nor relinquish, for the elysium of her love, one hope of the true, eternal Paradise. Besides, he could not bound all that he had in his nature—the rover, the aspirant, the poet, the priest—in the limits of a single passion. He could not—he would not—renounce his wild field of mission warfare for the parlours and the peace of Vale Hall. I learnt so much from himself, in an inroad I once, despite his reserve, had the daring to make on his confidence.

Miss Oliver already honoured me with frequent visits to my cottage. I had learnt her whole character; which was without mystery or disguise: she was coquettish, but not heartless; exacting, but not worthlessly selfish. She had been indulged from her birth, but was not absolutely spoilt. She was hasty, but good-humoured; vain (she could not help it, when every glance in the glass showed her such a flush of loveliness), but not affected; liberal-handed; innocent of the pride of wealth; ingenuous; sufficiently intelligent; gay, lively, and unthinking: she was very charming, in short, even to a cool observer of her own sex like me; but she was not profoundly interesting or thoroughly impressive. A very different sort of mind was hers from that, for instance, of the sisters of St. John. Still, I liked her almost as I liked my pupil Adèle: except that, for a child whom we have watched over and taught, a closer affection is engendered than we can give an equally attractive adult acquaintance.

She had taken an amiable caprice to me. She said I was like Mr. Rivers (only, certainly, she allowed, "not one-tenth so handsome; though I was a nice neat little soul enough, but he was an angel"). I was, however, good, clever, composed, and firm, like him. I was a *lusus naturæ*, she affirmed, as a village-schoolmistress: she was sure my previous history, if known, would make a delightful romance.

One evening, while, with her usual child-like activity, and thoughtless yet not offensive inquisitiveness, she was rummaging the cupboard and the table-drawer of my little kitchen, she discovered first two French books, a volume of Schiller, a German grammar and dictionary; and then

my drawing-materials and some sketches, including a pencil-head of a
pretty, little cherub-like girl, one of my scholars, and sundry views from
nature, taken in the Vale of Morton and on the surrounding moors. She
was first transfixed with surprise, and then electrified with delight.
"Had I done these pictures? Did I know French and German? What a
love—what a miracle I was! I drew better than her master in the first school
in S——. Would I sketch a portrait of her, to show to papa?"

"With pleasure," I replied; and I felt a thrill of artist-delight at the idea
of copying from so perfect and radiant a model. She had then on a dark-
blue silk dress; her arms and her neck were bare; her only ornament was
her chestnut tresses, which waved over her shoulders with all the wild
grace of natural curls. I took a sheet of fine cardboard, and drew a careful outline. I promised myself the pleasure of colouring it; and, as it was
getting late then, I told her she must come and sit another day.

She made such a report of me to her father, that Mr. Oliver himself
accompanied her next evening—a tall, massive-featured, middle-aged, and
gray-headed man, at whose side his lovely daughter looked like a bright
flower near a hoary turret. He appeared a taciturn, and perhaps a proud
personage; but he was very kind to me. The sketch of Rosamond's portrait pleased him highly: he said I must make a finished picture of it. He
insisted, too, on my coming the next day to spend the evening at Vale Hall.

I went. I found it a large, handsome residence, showing abundant
evidences of wealth in the proprietor. Rosamond was full of glee and pleasure all the time I stayed. Her father was affable; and when he entered
into conversation with me after tea, he expressed in strong terms his
approbation of what I had done in Morton school; and said he only feared,
from what he saw and heard, I was too good for the place, and would
soon quit it for one more suitable.

"Indeed!" cried Rosamond, "she is clever enough to be a governess
in a high family, papa."

I thought—I would far rather be where I am than in any high family
in the land. Mr. Oliver spoke of Mr. Rivers—of the Rivers family—with
great respect. He said it was a very old name in that neighbourhood; that
the ancestors of the house were wealthy; that all Morton had once belonged
to them; that even now he considered the representative of that house
might, if he liked, make an alliance with the best. He accounted it a pity
that so fine and talented a young man should have formed the design of
going out as a missionary; it was quite throwing a valuable life away. It
appeared, then, that her father would throw no obstacle in the way of Rosamond's union with St. John. Mr. Oliver evidently regarded the young
clergyman's good birth, old name, and sacred profession, as sufficient
compensation for the want of fortune.

It was the fifth of November, and a holiday. My little servant, after helping me to clean my house, was gone, well satisfied with the fee of a penny
for her aid. All about me was spotless and bright—scoured floor, polished grate, and well rubbed chairs. I had also made myself neat, and had
now the afternoon before me to spend as I would.

The translation of a few pages of German occupied an hour; then I got
my palette and pencils, and fell to the more soothing, because easier occupation, of completing Rosamond Oliver's miniature. The head was finished
already: there was but the background to tint, and the drapery to shade
off; a touch of carmine, too, to add to the ripe lips—a soft curl here and

there to the tresses—a deeper tinge to the shadow of the lash under the azured eyelid. I was absorbed in the execution of these nice details, when, after one rapid tap, my door unclosed, admitting St. John Rivers.

"I am come to see how you are spending your holiday," he said. "Not, I hope in thought? No, that is well: while you draw you will not feel lonely. You see, I mistrust you still: though you have borne up wonderfully so far. I have brought you a book for evening solace," and he laid on the table a new publication—a poem: one of those genuine productions so often vouchsafed to the fortunate public of those days—the golden age of modern literature. Alas! the readers of our era are less favoured. But, courage! I will not pause either to accuse or repine. I know poetry is not dead, nor genius lost; nor has Mammon gained power over either, to bind or slay: they will both assert their existence, their presence, their liberty, and strength again one day. Powerful angels, safe in heaven! they smile when sordid souls triumph, and feeble ones weep over their destruction. Poetry destroyed? Genius banished? No! Mediocrity, no: do not let envy prompt you to the thought. No; they not only live, but reign, and redeem: and without their divine influence spread everywhere, you would be in hell—the hell of your own meanness.

While I was eagerly glancing at the bright pages of Marmion (for Marmion it was), St. John stooped to examine my drawing. His tall figure sprang erect again with a start: he said nothing. I looked up at him: he shunned my eye. I knew his thoughts well, and could read his heart plainly; at the moment I felt calmer and cooler than he: and I conceived an inclination to do him some good, if I could.

"With all his firmness and self-control," thought I, "he tasks himself too far: locks every feeling and pang within—expresses, confesses, imparts nothing. I am sure it would benefit him to talk a little about this sweet Rosamond, whom he thinks he ought not to marry: I will make him talk."

I said first: "Take a chair, Mr. Rivers." But he answered, as he always did, that he could not stay. "Very well," I responded, mentally, "stand if you like; but you shall not go just yet, I am determined: solitude is at least as bad for you as it is for me. I'll try if I cannot discover the secret spring of your confidence, and find an aperture in that marble breast through which I can shed one drop of the balm of sympathy."

"Is this portrait like?" I asked, bluntly.

"Like! Like whom? I did not observe it closely."

"You did, Mr. River."

He almost started at my sudden and strange abruptness: he looked at me astonished. "Oh, that is nothing yet," I muttered within. "I don't mean to be baffled by a little stiffness on your part; I'm prepared to go to considerable lengths." I continued, "You observed it closely and distinctly: but I have no objection to your looking at it again," and I rose and placed it in his hand.

"A well-executed picture," he said; "very soft, clear colouring; very graceful and correct drawing."

"Yes, yes; I know all that. But what of the resemblance? Who is it like?"

Mastering some hesitation, he answered, "Miss Oliver, I presume."

"Of course. And now, sir, to reward you for the accurate guess, I will promise to paint you a careful duplicate of this very picture, provided you admit that the gift would be acceptable to you. I don't wish to throw away my time and trouble on an offering you would deem worthless."

He continued to gaze at the picture: the longer he looked, the firmer he held it, the more he seemed to covet it. "It is like!" he murmured; "The eye is well managed: the colour, light, expression, are perfect. It smiles!"

"Would it comfort, or would it wound you to have a similar painting? Tell me that. When you are at Madagascar, or at the Cape, or in India, would it be a consolation to have that mememto in your possession? or would the sight of it bring recollections calculated to enervate and distress?"

He now furtively raised his eyes: he glanced at me, irresolute, disturbed: he again surveyed the picture.

"That I should like to have it, is certain: whether it would be judicious or wise is another question."

Since I had ascertained that Rosamond really preferred him, and that her father was not likely to oppose the match, I—less exalted in my views than St. John—had been strongly disposed in my own heart to advocate their union. It seemed to me that, should he become the possessor of Mr. Oliver's large fortune, he might do as much good with it as if he went and laid his genius out to wither, and his strength to waste, under a tropical sun. With this persuasion I now answered:—

"As far as I can see, it would be wiser and more judicious if you were to take to yourself the original at once."

By this time he had sat down: he had laid the picture on the table before him, and, with his brow supported on both hands, hung fondly over it. I discerned he was now neither angry nor shocked at my audacity. I saw even that to be thus frankly addressed on a subject he had deemed unapproachable—to hear it thus freely handled—was beginning to be felt by him as a new pleasure—an unhoped-for relief. Reserved people often really need the frank discussion of their sentiments and griefs more than the expansive. The sternest-seeming stoic is human after all; and to "burst" with boldness and good will into "the silent sea" of their souls, is often to confer on them the first of obligations.

"She likes you, I am sure," said I, as I stood behind his chair, "and her father respects you. Moreover, she is a sweet girl—rather thoughtless; but you would have sufficient thought for both yourself and her. You ought to marry her."

"*Does* she like me?" he asked.

"Certainly; better than she likes any one else. She talks of you continually: there is no subject she enjoys so much, or touches upon so often."

"It is very pleasant to hear this," he said—"very: go on for another quarter of an hour." And he actually took out his watch and laid it upon the table to measure the time.

"But where is the use of going on," I asked, "when you are probably preparing some iron blow of contradiction, or forging a fresh chain to fetter your heart?"

"Don't imagine such hard things. Fancy me yielding and melting, as I am doing: human love rising like a freshly opened fountain in my mind, and overflowing with sweet inundation all the field I have so carefully, and with such labour prepared—so assiduously sown with the seeds of good intentions, of self-denying plans. And now it is deluged with a nectarous flood—the young germs swamped—delicious poison cankering them: now I see myself stretched on an ottoman in the drawing-room at

Vale Hall, at my bride Rosamond Oliver's feet: she is talking to me with her sweet voice—gazing down on me with those eyes your skilful hand has copied so well—smiling at me with these coral lips. She is mine—I am hers—this present life and passing world suffice to me. Hush! say nothing—my heart is full of delight—my senses are entranced—let the time I marked pass in peace."

I humoured him: the watch ticked on: he breathed fast and low: I stood silent. Amidst this hush the quarter sped: he replaced the watch, laid the picture down, rose, and stood on the hearth.

"Now," said he, "that little space was given to delirium and delusion. I rested my temples on the breast of temptation, and put my neck voluntarily under her yoke of flowers; I tasted her cup. The pillow was burning: there is an asp in the garland: the wine has a bitter taste: her promises are hollow—her offers false: I see and know all this."

I gazed at him in wonder.

"It is strange," pursued he, "that while I love Rosamond Oliver so wildly—with all the intensity, indeed, of a first passion, the object of which is exquisitely beautiful, graceful, and fascinating—I experience at the same time a calm, unwarped consciousness, that she would not make me a good wife; that she is not the partner suited to me; that I should discover this within a year after marriage; and that to twelve months' rapture would succeed a lifetime of regret. This I know."

"Strange, indeed!" I could not help ejaculating.

"While something in me," he went on, "is acutely sensible to her charms, something else is as deeply impressed with her defects: they are such that she could sympathize in nothing I aspired to—co-operate in nothing I undertook. Rosamond a sufferer, a labourer, a female apostle? Rosamond a missionary's wife? No!"

"But you need not be a missionary. You might relinquish that scheme."

"Relinquish! What! my vocation? My great work? My foundation laid on earth for a mansion in heaven? My hopes of being numbered in the band who have merged all ambitions in the glorious one of bettering their race—of carrying knowledge into the realms of ignorance—of substituting peace for war—freedom for bondage—religion for superstition—the hope of heaven for the fear of hell? Must I relinquish that? It is dearer than the blood in my veins. It is what I have to look forward to, and to live for."

"Miss Oliver is ever surrounded by suitors and flatterers: in less than a month, my image will be effaced from her heart. She will forget me; and will marry, probably, some one who will make her far happier than I should do."

"You speak coolly enough; but you suffer in the conflict. You are wasting away."

"No. If I get a little thin, it is with anxiety about my prospects, yet unsettled—my departure, continually procrastinated. Only this morning, I received intelligence that the successor, whose arrival I have been so long expecting, cannot be ready to replace me for three months to come yet: and perhaps the three months may extend to six."

"You tremble and become flushed whenever Miss Oliver enters the school-room."

Again the surprised expression crossed his face. He had not imagined that a woman would dare to speak so to a man. For me, I felt at home in this sort of discourse. I could never rest in communication with strong discreet, and refined minds, whether male or female, till I had passed the outworks of conventional reserve, and crossed the threshold of confidence, and won a place by their heart's very hearthstone.

"You *are* original," said he, "and not timid. Thee is something brave in your spirit, as well as penetrating in your eye: but allow me to assure you that you partially misinterpret my emotions. You think them more profound and potent than they are. You give me a larger allowance of sympathy than I have a just claim to. When I colour, and when I shake before Miss Oliver, I do not pity myself. I scorn the weakness. I know it is ignoble; a mere fever of the flesh: not, I declare, a convulsion of the soul. *That* is just as fixed as a rock, firm set in the depths of a restless sea. Know me to be what I am—a cold, hard 'man."

I smiled incredulously.

"You have taken my confidence by storm," he continued; "and now it is much at your service. I am simply, in my original state—stripped of that blood-bleached robe with which Christianity covers human deformity—a cold, hard, ambitious man. Natural affection only, of all the sentiments, has permanent power over me. Reason, and not Feeling, is my guide: my ambition is unlimited; my desire to rise higher, to do more than others, insatiable. I honour endurance, perseverance, industry, talent; because these are the means by which men achieve great ends, and mount to lofty eminence. I watch your career with interest, because I consider you a specimen of a diligent, orderly, energetic woman: not because I deeply compassionate what you have gone through, or what you still suffer."

"You would describe yourself as a mere pagan philosopher," I said.

"No. There is this difference between me and deistic philosophers: I believe; and I believe the Gospel. You missed your epithet. I am not a pagan, but a Christian philosopher—a follower of the sect of Jesus. As his disciple, I adopt his pure, his merciful, his benignant doctrines. I advocate them: I am sworn to spread them. Won in youth to religion, she has cultivated my original qualities thus:—From the minute germ, natural affection, she has developed the overshadowing tree, philanthropy. From the wild, stringy root of human uprightness, she has reared a due sense of the Divine justice. Of the ambition to win power and renown for my wretched self, she has formed the ambition to spread my Master's kingdom; to achieve victories for the standard of the cross. So much has religion done for me; turning the original materials to the best account; pruning and training nature. But she could not eradicate nature: nor will it be eradicated 'till this mortal shall be put on immortality.' "

Having said this, he took his hat, which lay on the table beside my palette. Once more he looked at the portrait.

"She *is* lovely," he murmured. "She is well named the Rose of the World, indeed!"

"And may I not paint one like it for you?"

"*Cui bono?* No."

He drew over the picture the sheet of thin paper on which I was accustomed to rest my hand in painting to prevent the card-board from being sullied. What he suddenly saw on this blank paper, it was impossible for me to tell: but something caught his eye. He took it up with a snatch; he looked at the edge; then shot a glance at me, inexpressibly peculiar, and quite imcomprehensible: a glance that seemed to take and make note of every point in my shape, face, and dress; for it traversed all, quick, keen as lightning. His lips parted, as if to speak: but he checked the coming sentence, whatever it was.

"What is the matter?" I asked.

"Nothing in the world," was the reply; and, replacing the paper, I saw him dexterously tear a narrow slip from the margin. It disappeared in his glove; and, with one hasty nod and "good afternoon," he vanished.

"Well!" I exclaimed, using an expression of the district; "that caps the glove, however!"

I, in my turn, scrutinized the paper; but saw nothing on it, save a few dingy stains of paint, where I had tried the tint in my pencil. I pondered the mystery a minute or two; but finding it insolvable, and being certain it could not be of much moment, I dismissed, and soon forgot it.

· · · · · · ·

Chapter 33

When Mr. St. John went, it was beginning to snow: the whirling storm continued all night. The next day a keen wind brought fresh and blinding falls: by twilight the valley was drifted up and almost impassable. I had closed my shutter, laid a mat to the door to prevent the snow from blowing in under it, trimmed my fire, and after sitting nearly an hour on the hearth listening to the muffled fury of the tempest, I lit a candle, took down Marmion, and beginning—

> "Day set on Norham's castled steep,
> And Tweed's fair river broad and deep,
>   And Cheviot mountains lone;
> The massive towers, the donjon keep,
> The flanking walls that round them sweet,
>   In yellow lustre shone."

I soon forgot storm in music.

I heard a noise: the wind, I thought, shook the door. No; it was St. John Rivers, who, lifting the latch, came in out of the frozen hurricane—the howling darkness—and stood before me; the cloak that covered his tall figure all white as a glacier. I was almost in consternation; so little had I expected any guest from the blocked-up vale that night.

"Any ill news?" I demanded. "Has anything happened?"

"No. How very easily alarmed you are!" he answered, removing his cloak and hanging it up against the door: towards which he again coolly pushed the mat which his entrance had deranged. He stamped the snow from his boots.

"I shall sully the purity of your floor," said he, "but you must excuse me for once." Then he approached the fire: "I have had hard work to get here, I assure you," he observed, as he warmed his hands over the flame. "One drift took me up to the waist: happily the snow is quite soft yet."

"But why are you come?" I could not forbear saying.

"Rather an inhospitable question to put to a visitor; but since you ask it, I answer, simply to have a little talk with you; I got tired of my mute books and empty rooms. Besides, since yesterday, I have experienced the excitement of a person to whom a tale has been half-told, and who is impatient to hear the sequel.

He sat down. I recalled his singular conduct of yesterday, and really I began to fear his wits were touched. If he were insane, however, his was a very cool and collected insanity: I had never seen that handsome-featured face of his look more like chiselled marble that it did just now; as he put aside his snow-wet hair from his forehead and let the fire-light shine free on his pale brow and cheek as pale: where it grieved me to discover the hollow trace of care or sorrow now so plainly graved. I waited, expecting he would say something I could at least comprehend; but his hand was now at his chin, his finger on his lip: he was thinking. It struck me that his hand looked wasted like his face. A perhaps uncalled-for gush of pity came over my heart: I was moved to say—

"I wish Diana or Mary would come and live with you: it is too bad that you should be quite alone; and you are recklessly rash about your own health."

"Not at all," said he: "I care for myself when necessary: I am well now. What do you see amiss in me?"

This was said with a careless, abstracted indifference, which showed that my solicitude was, at least in his opinion, wholly superfluous. I was silenced.

He still slowly moved his finger over his upper lip, and still his eye dwelt dreamily on the glowing grate: thinking it urgent to say something, I asked him presently if he felt any cold draught from the door, which was behind him.

"No, no;" he responded, shortly and somewhat testily.

"Well," I reflected, "if you won't talk, you may be still: I'll let you alone now, and return to my book."

So I snuffed the candle, and resumed the perusal of Marmion. He soon stirred; my eye was instantly drawn to his movements: he only took out a morocco pocket-book, thence produced a letter, which he read in silence, folded it, put it back, relapsed into meditation. It was vain to try to read with such an inscrutable fixture before me; nor could I, in my impatience, consent to be dumb: he might rebuff me if he liked, but talk I would.

"Have you heard from Diana and Mary lately?"

"Not since the letter I showed you a week ago."

"There has not been any change made about your own arrangements? You will not be summoned to leave England sooner than you expected?"

"I fear not, indeed: such chance is too good to befall me." Baffled so far, I changed my ground—I bethought myself to talk about the school and my scholars.

"Mary Garrett's mother is better, and Mary came back to the school this morning, and I shall have four new girls next week from the Foundry Close—they would have come to-day but for the snow."

"Indeed!"

"Mr. Oliver pays for two."

"Does he?"

"He means to give the whole school a treat at Christmas."

"I know."

"Was it your suggestion?"

"No."

"Whose then?"

"His daughter's, I think."

"It is like her: she is so good-natured."

"Yes."

Again came the blank of a pause: the clock struck eight strokes. It aroused him; he uncrossed his legs, sat erect, turned to me.

"Leave your book a moment, and come a little nearer the fire," he said. Wondering, and of my wonder finding no end, I complied.

"Half an hour ago," he pursued, "I spoke of my impatience to hear the sequel of a tale: on reflection, I find the matter will be better managed by assuming the narrator's part, and converting you into a listener. Before commencing, it is but fair to warn you that the story will sound somewhat hackneyed in your ears: but stale details often regain a degree of freshness when they pass through new lips. For the rest, whether trite or novel, it is short.

"Twenty years ago, a poor curate—never mind his name at this moment—fell in love with a rich man's daughter: she fell in love with him, and married him, against the advice of all her friends; who consequently disowned her immediately after the wedding. Before two years passed, the rash pair were both dead, and laid quietly side by side under one slab. (I have seen their grave; it formed part of the pavement of a huge churchyard surrounding the grim, soot-black old cathedral of an overgrown manufacturing town in ——shire.) They left a daughter, which, at its very birth, Charity received in her lap—cold as that of the snow-drift I almost stuck fast in to-night. Charity carried the friendless thing to the house of its rich, maternal relations; it was reared by an aunt-in-law, called (I come to names now) Mrs. Reed of Gateshead—you start—did you hear a noise? I daresay it is only a rat scrambling along the rafters of the adjoining schoolroom: it was a barn before I had it repaired and altered, and barns are generally haunted by rats. To proceed. Mrs. Reed kept the orphan ten years: whether it was happy or not with her, I cannot say, never having been told; but at the end of that time she transferred it to a place you know—being no other than Lowood school, where you so long resided yourself. It seems her career there was very honourable: from a pupil, she became a teacher, like yourself—really it strikes me there are parallel points in her history and yours—she left it to be a governess: there, again, your fates were analogous; she undertook the education of the ward of a certain Mr. Rochester."

"Mr. Rivers!" I interrupted.

"I can guess your feelings," he said, "but restrain them for a while: I have nearly finished; hear me to the end. Of Mr. Rochester's character I know nothing, but the one fact that he professed to offer honourable marriage to this young girl, and that at the very altar she discovered he had a wife yet alive, though a lunatic. What his subsequent conduct and proposals were is a matter of pure conjecture; but when an event transpired which rendered inquiry after the governess necessary, it was discovered she was gone—no one could tell when, where, or how. She had left Thornfield Hall in the night; every research after her course had been vain: the country had been scoured far and wide; no vestige of information could be gathered respecting her. Yet that she should be found is become a matter of serious urgency: advertisements have been put in all the papers; I myself have received a letter from one Mr. Briggs, a solicitor, communicating the details I have just imparted. Is it not an odd tale?"

"Just tell me this," said I, "and since you know so much, you surely *can* tell it me—what of Mr. Rochester? How and where is he? What is he doing? Is he well?"

"I am ignorant of all concerning Mr. Rochester: the letter never mentions him but to narrate the fraudulent and illegal attempt I have advertised to. You should rather ask the name of the governess—the nature of the event which requires her appearance."

"Did no one go to Thornfield Hall then? Did no one see Mr. Rochester?"

"I suppose not."

"But they wrote to him?"

"Of course."

"And what did he say? Who has his letters?"

"Mr. Briggs intimates that the answer to his application was not from Mr. Rochester but from a lady: it is signed 'Alice Fairfax.' "

I felt cold and dismayed: my worst fears then were probably true: he had in all probability left England and rushed in reckless desperation to some former haunt on the continent. And what opiate for his severe sufferings—what object for his strong passions—had he sought there? I dared not answer the question. Oh, my poor master—once almost my husband—whom I had often called "my dear Edward!"

"He must have been a bad man," observed Mr. Rivers.

"You don't know him—don't pronounce an opinion upon him," I said, with warmth.

"Very well," he answered, quietly: "and indeed my head is otherwise occupied than with him: I have my tale to finish. Since you won't ask the governess's name, I must tell it of my own accord—stay—I have it here—it is always more satisfactory to see important points written down, fairly committed to black and white."

And the pocket-book was again deliberately produced, opened, sought through; from one of its compartments was extracted a shabby slip of paper, hastily torn off: I recognised in its texture and its stains of ultramarine, and lake, and vermilion, the ravished margin of the portrait-cover. He got up, held it close to my eyes: and I read, traced in Indian ink, in my own handwriting, the words "JANE EYRE"—the work doubtless of some moment of abstraction.

"Briggs wrote to me of a Jane Eyre:" he said, "the advertisements demanded a Jane Eyre: I knew a Jane Elliot—I confess I had my suspicions, but it was only yesterday afternoon they were at once resolved into certainty. You own the name and renounce the *alias?*"

"Yes—yes—but where is Mr. Briggs? He perhaps knows more of Mr. Rochester than you do."

"Briggs is in London; I should doubt his knowing anything at all about Mr. Rochester; it is not in Mr. Rochester he is interested. Meantime, you forget essential points in pursuing trifles: you do not inquire why Mr. Briggs sought after you—what he wanted with you."

"Well, what did he want?"

"Merely to tell you that your uncle, Mr. Eyre of Madeira, is dead; that he has left you all his property, and that you are now rich—merely that—nothing more."

"I! rich?"

"Yes, you, rich—quite an heiress."

Silence succeeded.

"You must prove your identity of course," resumed St. John, presently: "a step which will offer no difficulties; you can then enter on immediate possession. Your fortune is vested in the English funds; Briggs has the will and the necessary documents."

Here was a new card turned up! It is a fine thing, reader, to be lifted in a moment from indigence to wealth—a very fine thing: but not a matter one can comprehend, or consequently enjoy, all at once. And then there are other chances in life far more thrilling and rapture-giving: *this* is solid, an affair of the actual world, nothing ideal about it: all its associations are solid and sober, and its manifestations are the same. One does not jump, and spring, and shout hurrah! at hearing one has got a fortune; one begins to consider responsibilities, and ponder business; on a base of steady satisfaction rise certain grave cares—and we contain ourselves, and brood over our bliss with a solemn brow.

Besides, the words Legacy, Bequest, go side by side with the words Death, Funeral. My uncle I had heard was dead—my only relative; ever since being made aware of his existence, I had cherished the hope of one day seeing him: now, I never should. And then this money came only to me: not to me and a rejoicing family, but to my isolated self. It was a grand boon doubtless; and independence would be glorious—yes, I felt that— *that* thought swelled my heart.

"You unbend your forehead at last," said Mr. Rivers: "I thought Medusa had looked at you, and that you were turning to stone—perhaps now you will ask now much you are worth?"

"How much am I worth?"

"Oh, a trifle! Nothing of course to speak of—twenty thousand pounds, I think they say—but what is that?"

"Twenty thousand pounds!"

Here was a new stunner—I had been calculating on four or five thousand. This news actually took my breath for a moment: Mr. St. John, whom I had never heard laugh before, laughed now.

"Well," said he, "if you had committed a murder, and I had told you your crime was discovered, you could scarcely look more aghast."

"It is a large sum—don't you think there is a mistake?"

"No mistake at all."

"Perhaps you have read the figures wrong—it may be 2000?"

"It is written in letters, not figures,—twenty thousand."

I again felt rather like an individual of but average gastronomical powers, sitting down to feast alone at a table spread with provisions for a hundred. Mr. Rivers rose now and put his cloak on.

"If it were not such a very wild night," he said, "I would send Hannah down to keep you company: you look too desperately miserable to be left alone. But Hannah, poor woman! could not stride the drifts so well as I: her legs are not quite so long: so I must e'en leave you to your sorrows. Good night."

He was lifting the latch: a sudden thought occurred to me.

"Stop one minute!" I cried.

"Well?"

"It puzzles me to know why Mr. Briggs wrote to you about me; or how he knew you, or could fancy that you, living in such an out-of-the-way place, had the power to aid in my discovery."

"Oh! I am a clergyman," he said; "and the clergy are often appealed to about odd matters." Again the latch rattled.

"No: that does not satisfy me!" I exclaimed: and, indeed there was something in the hasty and unexplanatory reply, which, instead of allaying, piqued my curiosity more than ever.

"It is a very strange piece of business," I added: "I must know more about it."

"Another time."

"No: to-night!—to-night!" and as he turned from the door, I placed myself between it and him. He looked rather embarrassed.

"You certainly shall not go till you have told me all!" I said.

"I would rather not, just now."

"You shall!—you must!"

"I would rather Diana or Mary informed you."

Of course these objections wrought my eagerness to a climax: gratified it must be, and that without delay; and I told him so.

"But I apprised you that I was a hard man," said he; "difficult to persuade."

"And I am a hard woman,—impossible to put off."

"And then," he pursued, "I am cold: no fervour infects me."

"Whereas I am hot, and fire dissolves ice. The blaze there has thawed all the snow from your cloak; but the same token, it has streamed on to my floor, and made it like a trampled street. As you hope ever to be forgiven, Mr. Rivers, the high crime and misdemeanor of spoiling a sanded kitchen, tell me what I wish to know."

"Well, then," he said, "I yield; if not to your earnestness, to your perseverance: as stone is worn by continual dropping. Besides, you must know some day,—as well now as later. Your name is Jane Eyre?"

"Of course: that was all settled before."

"You are not, perhaps, aware that I am your namesake?—that I was christened St. John Eyre Rivers?"

"No, indeed! I remember now seeing the letter E comprised in your initials written in books you have at different times lent me; but I never asked for what name it stood. But what then? Surely——"

I stopped: I could not trust myself to entertain, much less to express, the thought that rushed upon me—that embodied itself,—that, in a second, stood out a strong, solid probability. Circumstances knit themselves, fitted themselves, shot into order: the chain that had been lying hitherto a formless lump of links, was drawn out straight,—every ring was perfect, the connection complete. I knew, by instinct, how the matter stood, before St. John had said another word: but I cannot expect the reader to have the same intuitive perception, so I must repeat his explanation.

"My mother's name was Eyre: she had two brothers; one a clergyman, who married Miss Jane Reed, of Gateshead; the other, John Eyre, Esq., merchant, late of Funchal, Madeira. Mr. Briggs, being Mr. Eyre's solicitor, wrote to us last August to inform us of our uncle's death; and to say that he had left his property to his brother the clergyman's orphan daughter; overlooking us, in consequence of a quarrel, never forgiven, between him and my father. He wrote again a few weeks since, to intimate that the heiress was lost; and asking if we knew anything of her. A name casually written on a slip of paper has enabled me to find her out. You know the rest." Again he was going, but I set my back against the door.

"Do let me speak," I said; "let me have one moment to draw breath and reflect." I paused—he stood before me, hat in hand, looking composed enough. I resumed:—

"Your mother was my father's sister."

"Yes."

"My aunt, consequently?"

He bowed.

"My uncle John was your uncle John? You Diana and Mary, are his sister's children; as I am his brother's child?"

"Undeniably."

"You three, then, are my cousins: half our blood on each side flows from the same source?"

"We are cousins; yes."

I surveyed him. It seemed I had found a brother: one I could be proud of,—one I could love; and two sisters, whose qualities were such, that, when I knew them but as mere strangers, they had inspired me with genuine affection and admiration. The two girls, on whom, kneeling down on the wet ground, and looking through the low, latticed window of Moor House kitchen, I had gazed with so bitter a mixture of interest and despair, were my near kinswomen; and the young and stately gentleman who had found me almost dying at his threshold, was my blood relation. Glorious discovery to a lonely wretch! This was wealth indeed!—wealth to the heart!—a mine of pure, genial affections. This was a blessing, bright, vivid, and exhilarating!—not like the ponderous gift of gold: rich and welcome enough in its way, but sobering from its weight. I now clapped my hands in sudden joy—my pulse bounded, my veins thrilled.

"Oh, I am glad!—I am glad!" I exclaimed.

St. John smiled. "Did I not say you neglected essential points to pursue trifles?" he asked. "You were serious when I told you you had a fortune; and now, for a matter of no moment, you are excited."

"What *can* you mean? It may be of no moment to you: you have sisters, and don't care for a cousin; but I had nobody; and now three relations,—or two, if you don't choose to be counted,—are born into my world, full grown. I say again, I am glad!"

I walked fast through the room: I stopped, half suffocated with the thoughts that rose faster then I could receive, comprehend, settle them:—thoughts of what might, could, would, and should be, and that ere long. I looked at the blank wall: it seemed a sky, thick with ascending stars,—every one lit me to a purpose or delight. Those who had saved my life, whom, till this hour, I had loved barrenly, I could now benefit. They were under a yoke: I could free them: they were scattered,—I could reunite them—the independence, the affluence which was mine, might be theirs too. Were we not four? Twenty thousand pounds shared equally, would be five thousand each,—enough and to spare: justice would be done,—mutual happiness secured. Now the wealth did not weigh on me: now it was not a mere bequest of coin,—it was a legacy of life, hope, enjoyment.

How I looked while these ideas were taking my spirit by storm, I cannot tell; but I perceived soon that Mr. Rivers had placed a chair behind me, and was gently attempting to make me sit down on it. He also advised me to be composed. I scorned the insinuation of helplessness and distraction, shook off his hand, and began to walk about again.

"Write to Diana and Mary to-morrow," I said, "and tell them to come home directly; Diana said they would both consider themselves rich with a thousand pounds, so with five thousand, they will do very well."

"Tell me where I can get you a glass of water," said St. John; "you must really make an effort to tranquillize your feelings."

"Nonsense! and what sort of an effect will the bequest have on you? Will it keep you in England, induce you to marry Miss Oliver, and settle down like an ordinary mortal?"

"You wander: your head becomes confused. I have been too abrupt in communicating the news: it has excited you beyond your strength."

"Mr. Rivers! you quite put me out of patience; I am rational enough; it is you who misunderstand; or rather, who affect to misunderstand."

"Perhaps if you explained yourself a little more fully, I should comprehend better."

"Explain! What is there it explain? You cannot fail to see that twenty thousand pounds, the sum in question, divided equally between the nephew and three nieces of our uncle, will give five thousand to each? What I want is, that you should write to your sisters and tell them of the fortune that has accrued to them."

"To you, you mean."

"I have intimated my view of the case: I am incapable of taking any other. I am not brutally selfish, blindly unjust, or fiendishly ungrateful. Besides, I am resolved I will have a home and connections. I like Moor House, and I will live at Moor House; I like Diana, and Mary, and I will attach myself for life to Diana and Mary. It would please and benefit me to have five thousand pounds; it would torment and oppress me to have twenty thousand; which, moreover, could never be mine in justice, though it might in law. I abandon to you, then, what is absolutely superfluous to me. Let there be no opposition, and no discussion about it; let us agree amongst each other, and decide the point at once."

"This is acting on first impulses; you must take days to consider such a matter, ere your word can be regarded as valid."

"Oh! if all you doubt is my sincerity, I am easy: you see the justice of the case?"

"I *do* see a certain justice; but it is contrary to all custom. Besides, the entire fortune is your right: my uncle gained it by his own efforts; he was free to leave it to whom he would: he left it to you. After all, justice permits you to keep it: you may, with a clear conscience, consider it absolutely your own."

"With me," said I, "it is fully as much a matter of feeling as of conscience: I must indulge my feelings; I so seldom have had an opportunity of doing so. Were you to argue, object, and annoy me for a year, I could not forego the delicious pleasure of which I have caught a glimpse—that of repaying, in part, a mighty obligation, and winning to myself life-long friends."

"You think so now," rejoined St. John; "because you do not know what it is to possess, nor consequently to enjoy wealth: you cannot form a notion of the importance twenty thousand pounds would give you; of the place it would enable you to take in society; of the prospects it would open to you: you cannot——"

"And you," I interrupted, "cannot at all imagine the craving I have for fraternal and sisterly love. I never had a home, I never had brothers or sisters; I must and will have them now: you are not reluctant to admit me and own me, are you?"

"Jane: I will be your brother—my sisters will be your sisters—without stipulating for this sacrifice of your just rights."

"Brother? Yes; at the distance of a thousand leagues! Sisters? Yes; slaving amongst strangers! I, wealthy—gorged with gold I never earned and do not merit! You, pennyless! Famous equality and fraternization! Close union! Intimate attachment!"

"But, Jane, your aspirations after family ties and domestic happiness may be realized otherwise than by the means you contemplate: you may marry."

"Nonsense, again! Marry! I don't want to marry, and never shall marry."

"It is saying too much: I know what I feel, and how averse are my inclinations to the bare thought of marriage. No one would take me for love; and I well not be regarded in the light of a mere money-speculation. And I do not want a stranger—unsympathizing, alien, different from me; I want my kindred: those with whom I have full fellow-feeling. Say again you will be my brother: when you uttered the words I was satisfied, happy; repeat them if you can repeat them sincerely."

"I think I can. I know I have always loved my own sisters; and I know on what my affection for them is grounded,—respect for their worth, and admiration of their talents. You too have principle and mind: your tastes and habits resemble Diana's and Mary's; your presence is always agreeable to me; in your conversation I have already for some time found a salutary solace. I feel I can easily and naturally make room in my heart for you, as my third and youngest sister."

"Thank you: that contents me for to-night. Now you had better go; for if you stay longer, you will perhaps irritate me afresh by some mistrustful scruple."

"And the school, Miss Eyre? It must now be shut up, I suppose?"

"No. I will retain my post of mistress till you get a substitute."

He smiled approbation: we shook hands, and he took leave.

I need not narrate in detail the further struggles I had, and arguments I used, to get matters regarding the legacy settled as I wished. My task was a very hard one: but, as I was absolutely resolved—as my cousins saw at length that my mind was really and immutably fixed on making a just division of the property—as they must in their own hearts have felt the equity of the intention; and must, besides, have been innately conscious that in my place they would have done precisely what I wished to do—they yielded at length so far as to consent to put the affair to arbitration. The judges chosen were Mr. Oliver and an able lawyer: both coincided in my opinion: I carried my point. The instruments of transfer were drawn out: St. John, Diana, Mary, and I, each became possessed of a competency.

· · · · · · ·

Chapter 34

It was near Christmas by the time all was settled: the season of general holiday approached. I now closed Morton school; taking care that the parting should not be barren on my side. Good fortune opens the hand as well as the heart wonderfully; and to give somewhat when we have largely received, is but to afford a vent to the unusual ebullition of the sensations. I had long felt with pleasure that many of my rustic scholars liked me, and when we parted, that consciousness was confirmed: they manifested their affection plainly and strongly. Deep was my gratification to find I had really a place in their unsophisticated hearts: I promised them that never a week should pass in future that I did not visit them, and give them an hour's teaching in their school.

Mr. Rivers came up, as—having seen the classes, now numbering sixty girls, file out before me, and locked the door—I stood with the key in my hand, exchanging a few words of special farewell with some half-dozen of my best scholars: as decent, respectable, modest, and well-informed young women as could be found in the ranks of the British peasantry. And that is saying a great deal; for after all, the British peasantry are the best taught, best mannered, most self-respecting of any in Europe: since those days I have seen paysannes and Bäuerinnen; and the best of them seemed to me ignorant, coarse, and besotted, compared with my Morton girls.

"Do you consider you have got your reward for a season of exertion?" asked Mr. Rivers when they were gone. "Does not the consciousness of having done some real good in your day and generation give pleasure?"

"Doubtless."

"And you have only toiled a few months! Would not a life devoted to the task of regenerating your race be well spent?"

"Yes," I said; "but I could not go on for ever so: I want to enjoy my own faculties as well as to cultivate those of other people. I must enjoy them now: don't recall either my mind or body to the school; I am out of it and disposed for full holiday."

He looked grave. "What now? What sudden eagerness is this you evince? What are you going to do?"

"To be active: as active as I can. And first I must beg you to set Hannah at liberty, and get somebody else to wait on you."

"Do you want her?"

"Yes, to go with me to Moor House: Diana and Mary will be at home in a week, and I want to have everything in order against their arrival."

"I understand: I thought you were for flying off on some excursion. It is better so: Hannah shall go with you."

"Tell her to be ready by to-morrow then; and here is the school-room key: I will give you the key of my cottage in the morning."

He took it. "You give it up very gleefully," said he: "I don't quite understand your light-heartedness; because I cannot tell what employment you propose to yourself as a substitute for the one you are relinquishing. What aim, what purpose, what ambition in life have you now?"

"My first aim will be to *clean down* (do you comprehend the full force of the expression?) to *clean down* Moor House from chamber to cellar; my next to rub it up with beeswax, oil, and an indefinite number of cloths, till it glitters again; my third, to arrange every chair, table, bed, carpet, with mathematical precision; afterwards I shall go near to ruin you in coals and peat to keep up good fires in every room; and lastly, the two days preceding that on which your sisters are expected, will be devoted by Hannah and me to such a beating of eggs, sorting of currants, grating of spices, compounding of Christmas cakes, chopping up of materials for mince-pies, and solemnizing of other culinary rites, as words can convey but an inadequate notion of to the uninitiated like you. My purpose, in short, is to have all things in absolutely perfect state of readiness for Diana and Mary, before next Thursday; and my ambition is to give them a beau-ideal of a welcome when they come."

St. John smiled slightly: still he was dissatisfied.

"It is all very well for the present," said he: "but seriously, I trust that when the first flush of vivacity is over, you will look a little higher than domestic endearments and household joys."

"The best things the world has!" I interrupted.

"No, Jane, no: this world is not the scene of fruition; do not attempt to make it so: nor of rest; do not turn slothful."

"I mean, on the contrary, to be busy."

"Jane, I excuse you for the present: two months' grace I allow you for the full enjoyment of your new position, and for pleasing yourself with this late-found charm of relationship; but *then,* I hope you will begin to look beyond Moor House and Morton, and sisterly society, and the selfish calm and sensual comfort of civilized affluence. I hope your energies will then once more trouble you with their strength."

I looked at him with surprise. "St. John," I said, "I think you are almost wicked to talk so. I am disposed to be as content as a queen, and you try to stir me up to restlessness! To what end?"

"To the end of turning to profit the talents which God has committed to your keeping; and of which he will surely one day demand a strict account. Jane, I shall watch you closely and anxiously—I warn you of that. And try to restrain the disproportionate fervour with which you throw yourself into common-place home pleasures. Don't cling so tenaciously to ties of the flesh; save your constancy and ardour for an adequate cause; forbear to waste them on trite transient objects. Do you hear, Jane?"

"Yes; just as if you were speaking Greek. I feel I have adequate cause to be happy, and I *will* be happy. Good-bye!"

Happy at Moor House I was, and hard I worked; and so did Hannah: she was charmed to see how jovial I could be amidst the bustle of a house turned topsy-turvy—how I could brush, and dust, and clean, and cook. And really after a day or two of confusion worse confounded, it was delightful, by degrees, to invoke order from the chaos ourselves had made. I had previously taken a journey to S——, to purchase some new furniture: my cousins having given me carte blanche to effect what alterations I pleased, and a sum having been set aside for that purpose. The ordinary sitting-room and bed-rooms I left much as they were: for I knew Diana and Mary would derive more pleasure from seeing again the old homely tables, chairs, and beds, than from the spectacle of the smartest innovations. Still some novelty was necessary, to give to their return the piquancy with which I wished it to be invested. Dark handsome new carpets and curtains, an arrangement of some carefully selected antique ornaments in porcelain and bronze, new coverings, and mirrors, and dressing-cases for the toilet tables, answered the end: they looked fresh without being glaring. A spare parlour and bed-room I refurnished entirely, with old mahogany and crimson upholstery: I laid canvas on the passage, and carpets on the stairs. When all was finished, I thought Moor House as complete a model of bright modest snugness within, as it was, at this season, a specimen of wintry waste and desert dreariness without.

The eventful Thursday at length came. They were expected about dark,
and ere dusk, fires were lit up stairs and below; the kitchen was in perfect trim; Hannah and I were dressed and all was in readiness.

St. John arrived first. I had entreated him to keep quite clear of the house
till everything was arranged: and, indeed, the bare idea of the commotion, at once sordid and trivial, going on within its walls sufficed to scare
him to estrangement. He found me in the kitchen, watching the progress
of certain cakes for tea, then baking. Approaching the hearth, he asked,
"If I was at last satisfied with house-maid's work?" I answered by inviting him to accompany me on a general inspection of the result of my
labours. With some difficulty, I got him to make the tour of the house.
He just looked in at the doors I opened; and when he had wandered up
stairs and down stairs, he said I must have gone through a great deal of
fatigue and trouble to have effected such considerable changes in so short
a time: but not a syllable did he utter indicating pleasure in the improved
aspect of his abode.

This silence damped me. I thought perhaps the alterations had disturbed
some old associations he valued. I inquired whether this was the case:
no doubt in somewhat crest-fallen tone.

"Not at all; he had, on the contrary, remarked that I had scrupulously
respected every association: he feared, indeed, I must have bestowed more
thought on the matter than it was worth: How many minutes, for instance,
had I devoted to studying the arrangement of this very room?—By-the-
by, could I tell him where such a book was?"

I showed him the volume on the shelf: he took it down and withdrawing to his accustomed window recess, he began to read it.

Now, I did not like this, reader. St. John was a good man; but I began
to feel he had spoken truth of himself, when he said he was hard and cold.
The humanities and amenities of life had no attraction for him—its peaceful enjoyments no charm. Literally, he lived only to aspire—after what
was good and great, certainly: but still he would never rest; nor approve
of others resting round him. As I looked at his lofty forehead, still and
pale as a white stone—at his fine lineaments fixed in study—I comprehended all at once that he would hardly make a good husband: that it
would be a trying thing to be his wife. I understood, as by inspiration,
the nature of his love for Miss Oliver; I agreed with him that it was but
a love of the senses. I comprehended how he should despise himself for
the feverish influence it exercised over him; how he should wish to stifle
and destroy it; how he should mistrust its ever conducing permanently
to his happiness, or hers, I saw he was of the material from which nature
hews her heroes—Christian and Pagan—her lawgivers, her statesmen, her
conquerors: a steadfast bulwark for great interests to rest upon; but, at
the fireside, too often a cold cumbrous column, gloomy and out of place.

"This parlour is not his sphere," I reflected: "The Himalayan ridge,
or Caffre bush, even the plague-cursed Guinea coast swamp, would suit
him better. Well may he eschew the calm of domestic life; it is not his
element: there his faculties stagnate—they cannot develop or appear to
advantage. It is in scenes of strife and danger—where courage is proved,
and energy exercised, and fortitude tasked—that he will speak and move,
the leader and superior. A merry child would have the advantage of him
on this hearth. He is right to choose a missionary's career—I see it now."

"They are coming! they are coming! cried Hannah, throwing open the parlour door. At the same moment old Carlo barked joyfully. Out I ran. It was not dark; but a rumbling of wheels was audible. Hannah soon had a lantern lit. The vehicle stopped at the wicket; the driver opened the door: first one well-known form, then another, stepped. In a minute I had my face under their bonnets, in contact, first with Mary's soft cheek, then with Diana's flowing curls. They laughed—kissed me—then Hannah: patted Carlo, who was half wild with delight, asked eagerly if all was well; and being assured in the affirmative, hastened into the house.

They were stiff with their long and jolting drive from Whitcross, and chilled with the frosty night air; but their pleasant countenances expanded to the cheering fore light. While the driver and Hannah brought in the boxes, they demanded St. John. At this moment he advanced from the parlour. They both threw their arms round his neck at once. He gave each one quiet kiss, said in a low tone a few words of welcome, stood a while to be talked to, and then, intimating that he supposed they would soon rejoin him in the parlour, withdrew there as to a place of refuge.

I had lit their candles to go up stairs, but Diana had first to give hospitable orders respecting the driver; this done, both followed me. They were delighted with the renovation and decoration of their rooms; with the new drapery, and fresh carpets, and rich tinted china vases: they expressed their gratification ungrudgingly. I had the pleasure of feeling that my arrangements met their wishes exactly; and that what I had done added a vivid charm to their joyous return home.

Sweet was that evening. My cousins, full of exhilaration, were so eloquent in narrative and comment, that their fluency covered St. John's taciturnity: he was sincerely glad to see his sisters; but in their glow of fervour and flow of joy he could not sympathize. The event of the day—that is, the return of Diana and Mary—pleased him; but the accompaniments of that event, the glad tumult, the garrulous glee of reception, irked him: I saw he wished the calmer morrow was come. In the very meridian of the night's enjoyment, about an hour after tea, a rap was heard at the door. Hannah entered with the intimation that "a poor lad was come, at that unlikely time, to fetch Mr. Rivers to see his mother, who was drawing away."

"Where does she live, Hannah?"

"Clear up at Whitcross Brow, almost four miles off; and moor and moss all the way."

"Tell him I will go."

"I'm sure, sir, you had better not. It's the worst road to travel after dark that can be: there's no track at all over the bog. And then it is such a bitter night—the keenest wind you ever felt. You had better send word, sir, that you will be there in the morning."

But he was already in the passage, putting on his cloak; and without one objection, one murmur, he departed. It was then nine o'clock: he did not return till midnight. Starved and tired enough he was: but he looked happier than when he set out. He had performed an act of duty; made an exertion; felt his own strength to do and deny, and was on better terms with himself.

I am afraid the whole of the ensuing week tried his patience. It was Christmas week: we took to no settled employment, but spent it in a sort of merry domestic dissipation. The air of the moors, the freedom of home, the dawn of prosperity, acted on Diana and Mary's spirits like some life-giving elixir: they were gay from morning till noon, and from noon till night. They could always talk; and their discourse, witty, pithy, original, had such charms for me, that I preferred listening to, and sharing in it, to doing anything else. St. John did not rebuke our vivacity; but he escaped from it: he was seldom in the house: his parish was large, the population scattered, and he found daily business in visiting the sick and poor in its different districts.

One morning, at breakfast, Diana, after looking a little pensive for some minutes, asked him, "If his plans were yet unchanged?"

"Unchanged and unchangeable," was the reply. And he proceeded to inform us that his departure from England was now definitively fixed for the ensuing year.

"And Rosamond Oliver?" suggested Mary: the words seeming to escape her lips involuntarily; for no sooner had she uttered them, than she made a gesture as if wishing to recall them. St. John had a book in his hand—it was his unsocial custom to read at meals—he closed it, and looked up.

"Rosamond Oliver," said he, "is about to be married to Mr. Granby; one of the best connected and most estimable residents in S——, grandson and heir to Sir Frederic Granby: I had the intelligence from her father yesterday."

His sisters looked at each other, and at me; we all three looked at him: he was serene as glass.

"The match must have been got up hastily," said Diana: "they cannot have known each other long."

"But two months: they met in October at the county ball at S——. But where there are no obstacles to a union, as in the present case, where the connection is in every point desirable, delays are unnecessary: they will be married as soon as S—— Place, which Sir Frederic gives up to them, can be refitted for their reception."

The first time I found St. John alone after this communication, I felt tempted to inquire if the event distressed him: but he seemed so little to need sympathy, that, so far from venturing to offer him more, I experienced some shame at the recollection of what I had already hazarded. Besides, I was out of practice in talking to him: his reserve was again frozen over, and my frankness was congealed beneath it. He had not kept his promise of treating me like his sisters; he continually made little, chilling differences between us, which did not at all tend to the development of cordiality: in short, now that I was acknowledged his kinswoman, and lived under the same roof with him, I felt the distance between us to be far greater than when he had known me only as the village schoolmistress. When I remembered how far I had once been admitted to his confidence, I could hardly comprehend his present frigidity.

Such being the case, I felt not a little surprised when he raised his head suddenly from the desk over which he was stooping, and said:—

"You see, Jane, the battle is fought and the victory won."

Startled at being thus addressed, I did not immediately reply: after a moment's hesitation I answered:—

"But are you sure, you are not in the position of those conquerors whose triumphs have cost them too dear? Would not such another ruin you?"

"I think not; and if I were, it does not much signify: I shall never be called upon to contend for such another. The event of the conflict is decisive: my way is now clear; I thank God for it!" So saying, he returned to his papers and his silence.

As our mutual happiness (*i.e.* Diana's, Mary's and mine) settled into a quieter character, and we resumed our usual habits and regular studies, St. John stayed more at home: he sat with us in the same room, sometimes for hours together. While Mary drew, Diana pursued a course of encyclopædic reading she had (to my awe and amazement) undertaken, and I fagged away at German, he pondered a mystic lore of his own: that of some Eastern tongue, the acquisition of which he thought necessary to his plans.

Thus engaged, he appeared, sitting in his own recess, quiet and absorbed enough; but that blue eye of his had a habit of leaving the outlandish-looking grammar, and wandering over, and sometimes fixing upon us, his fellow-students, with a curious intensity of observation: if caught, it would be instantly withdrawn; yet ever and anon, it returned searchingly to our table. I wondered what it meant: I wondered, too, at the punctual satisfaction he never failed to exhibit on an occasion that seemed to me of small moment, namely,—my weekly visit to Morton school; and still more was I puzzled when, if the day was unfavourable, if there was snow, or rain, or high wind, and his sisters urged me not to go, he would invariably make light of their solicitude, and encourage me to accomplish the task without regard to the elements.

"Jane is not such a weakling as you would make her," he would say: "she can bear a mountain blast, or a shower, or a few flakes of snow, as well as any of us. Her constitution is both sound and elastic—better calculated to endure variations of climate than many more robust."

And when I returned, sometimes a good deal tired, and a little weather-beaten, I never dared complain, because I saw that to murmur would be to vex him: on all occasions fortitude pleased him; the reverse was a special annoyance.

One afternoon, however, I got leave to stay at home, because I really had a cold. His sisters were gone to Morton in my stead: I sat reading Schiller; he, deciphering his crabbed Oriental scrolls. As I exchanged a translation for an exercise, I happened to look his way: there I found myself under the influence of the ever-watchful blue eye. How long it had been searching me through and through, and over and over, I cannot tell: so keen was it, and yet so cold, I felt for the moment superstitious—as if I were sitting in the room with something uncanny.

"Jane, what are you doing?"

"Learning German."

"I want you to give up German, and learn Hindostanee."

"You are not in earnest?"

"In such earnest that I must have it so: and I will tell you why."

He then went on to explain that Hindostanee was the language he was himself at present studying: that, as he advanced, he was apt to forget the commencement; that it would assist him greatly to have a pupil with whom he might again and again go over the elements, and so fix them thoroughly in his mind; that his choice had hovered for some time between me and his sisters; but that he had fixed on me, because he saw I could sit at a task the longest of the three. Would I do him this favour? I should not, perhaps, have to make the sacrifice long; as it wanted now barely three months to his departure.

St. John was not a man to be lightly refused: you felt that every impression made on him, either for pain or pleasure, was deep-graved and permanent. I consented. When Diana and Mary returned, the former found her scholar transferred from her to her brother: she laughed; and both she and Mary agreed that St. John should never have persuaded them to such a step. He answered, quietly:—

"I knew it."

I found him a very patient, very forbearing, and yet an exacting master: he expected me to do a great deal; and when I fulfilled his expectations he, in his own way, fully testified his approbation. By degrees, he acquired a certain influence over me that took away my liberty of mind: his praise and notice were more restraining than his indifference. I could no longer talk or laugh freely when he was by; because a tiresomely importunate instinct reminded me that vivacity (at least in me) was distasteful to him. I was so fully aware that only serious moods and occupations were acceptable, that in his presence every effort to sustain or follow any other became vain: I fell under a freezing spell. When he said "go," I went; "come," I came; "do this," I did it. But I did not love my servitude: I wished, many a time, he had continued to neglect me.

One evening when, at bed-time, his sisters and I stood round him, bidding him good-night, he kissed each of them, as was his custom; and, as was equally his custom, he gave me his hand. Diana, who chanced to be in a frolicksome humour (*she* was not painfully controlled by his will; for hers, in another way, was as strong), exclaimed:—

"St. John! you used to call Jane your third sister, but you don't treat her as such: you should kiss her too."

She pushed me towards him. I thought Diana very provoking, and felt uncomfortably confused; and while I was thus thinking and feeling, St. John bent his head, his Greek face was brought to a level with mine, his eyes questioned my eyes piercingly—he kissed me. There are no such things as marble kisses, or ice kisses, or I should say, my ecclesiastical cousin's salute belonged to one of these classes; but there may be experiment kisses, and his was an experiment kiss. When given, he viewed me to learn the result; it was not striking: I am sure I did not blush; perhaps I might have turned a little pale, for I felt as if this kiss were a seal affixed to my fetters. He never omitted the ceremony afterwards, and the gravity and quiescence with which I underwent it, seemed to invest it for him with a certain charm.

As for me, I daily wished more to please him: but to do so, I felt daily more and more that I must disown half my nature, stifle half my faculties, wrest my tastes from their original bent, force myself to the adoption of pursuits for which I had not natural vocation. He wanted to train me to an elevation I could never reach; it racked me hourly to aspire to the standard he uplifted. The thing was as impossible as to mould my irregular features to his correct and classic pattern, to give to my changeable green eyes the sea-blue tint and solemn lustre of his own.

Not his ascendancy alone, however, held me in thrall at present. Of late it had been easy enough for me to look sad: a cankering evil sat at my heart and drained my happiness at its source—the evil of suspense.

Perhaps you think I had forgotten Mr. Rochester, reader, amidst these changes of place and fortune. Not for a moment. His idea was still with me; because it was not a vapour sunshine could disperse; nor a sand-traced effigy storms could wash away: it was a name graven on a tablet, fated to last as long as the marble it inscribed. The craving to know what had become of him followed me everywhere; when I was at Morton, I re-entered my cottage every evening to think of that; and now at Moor House, I sought my bed-room each night to brood over it.

In the course of my necessary correspondence with Mr. Briggs about the will, I had inquired if he knew anything of Mr. Rochester's present residence and state of health: but, as St. John had conjectured, he was quite ignorant of all concerning him. I then wrote to Mrs. Fairfax, entreating information on the subject. I had calculated with certainty on this step answering my end: I felt sure it would elicit an early answer. I was astonished when a fortnight passed without reply; but, when two months wore away, and day after day the post arrived and brought nothing for me, I fell a prey to the keenest anxiety.

I wrote again: there was a chance of my first letter having missed. Renewed hope followed renewed effort: it shone like the former for some weeks, then, like it, it faded, flickered: not a line, not a word reached me. When half a year wasted in vain expectancy, my hope died out; and then I felt dark indeed.

A fine spring shone round me, which I could not enjoy. Summer approached; Diana tried to cheer me: she said I looked ill, and wished to accompany me to the sea-side. This St. John opposed; he said I did not want dissipation, I wanted employment: my present life was too purposeless, I required an aim; and, I suppose, by way of supplying deficiencies, he prolonged still further my lessons in Hindostanee, and grew more urgent in requiring their accomplishment: and I, like a fool, never thought of resisting him—I could not resist him.

One day I had come to my studies in lower spirits than usual; the ebb was occasioned by a poignantly felt disappointment: Hannah had told me in the morning there was a letter for me, and when I went down to take it, almost certain that the long looked-for tidings were vouchsafed me at last, I found only an unimportant note from Mr. Briggs on business. The bitter check had wrung from me some tears; and now as I sat poring over the crabbed characters and flourishing tropes of an Indian scribe, my eyes filled again.

St. John called me to his side to read; in attempting to do this my voice failed me: words were lost in sobs. He and I were the only occupants of the parlour: Diana was practising her music in the drawing-room, Mary was gardening—it was a very fine May day, clear, sunny, and breezy. My companion expressed no surprise at this emotion, nor did he question me as to its cause; he only said:—

"We will wait a few minutes, Jane, till you are more composed." And while I smothered the paroxysm with all haste, he sat calm and patient, leaning on his desk and looking like a physician watching with the eye of science an expected and fully-understood crisis in a patient's malady. Having stifled my sobs, wiped my eyes, and muttered something about not being very well that morning, I resumed my task, and succeeded in completing it. St. John put away my books and his, locked his desk, and said:—

"Now, Jane, you shall take a walk; and with me."

"I will call Diana and Mary."

"No. I want only one companion this morning, and that must be you:

put on your things; go out by the kitchen door; take the road towards the head of Marsh Glen: I will join you in a moment."

I know no medium: I never in my life have known any medium in my dealings with positive, hard characters, antagonistic to my own, between absolute submission and determined revolt. I have always faithfully observed the one, up to the very moment of bursting, sometimes with volcanic vehemence, into the other; and as neither present circumstances warranted, nor my present mood inclined me to mutiny, I observed careful obedience to St. John's directions; and in ten minutes I was treading the wild track of the glen, side by side with him.

The breeze was from the west: it came over the hills, sweet with scents of heath and rush; the sky was of stainless blue; the stream descending the ravine, swelled with past spring rains, poured along plentiful and clear, catching golden gleams from the sun, and sapphire tints from the firmament. As we advanced and left the track, we trod a soft turf, mossy fine and emerald green, minutely enamelled with a tiny white flower, and spangled with a star-like yellow blossom: the hills, meantime, shut us quite in; for the glen, towards its head, wound to their very core.

"Let us rest here," said St. John, as we reached the first stragglers of a battalion of rocks, guarding a sort of pass, beyond which the beck rushed down a waterfall; and where, still a little further, the mountain shook off turf and flower, had only heath for raiment, and crag for gem—where it exaggerated the wild to the savage, and exchanged the fresh for the frowning—where it guarded the forlorn hope of solitude, and a last refuge for silence.

I took a seat: St. John stood near me. He looked up the pass and down the hollow; his glance wandered away with the stream, and returned to traverse the unclouded heaven which coloured it: he removed his hat, let the breeze stir his hair and kiss his brow. He seemed in communion with the genius of the haunt: with his eye he bade farewell to something.

"And I shall see it again," he said aloud, "in dreams, when I sleep by the Ganges: and again, in a more remote hour—when another slumber overcomes me—on the shore of a darker stream."

Strange words of a strange love! An austere patriot's passion for his fatherland! He sat down; for half an hour we never spoke; neither he to me nor I to him: that interval past, he recommenced:—

"Jane, I go in six weeks; I have taken my berth in an East Indiaman which sails on the twentieth of June."

"God will protect you; for you have undertaken His work," I answered.

"Yes," said he, "there is my glory and joy. I am the servant of an infallible master. I am not going out under human guidance, subject to the defective laws and erring control of my feeble fellow-worms: my king, my lawgiver, my captain, is the All-perfect. It seems strange to me that all round me do not burn to enlist under the same banner,—to join in the same enterprise."

"All have not your powers; and it would be folly for the feeble to wish to march with the strong."

"I do not speak to the feeble, or think of them: I address only such as are worthy of the work, and competent to accomplish it."

"Those are few in number, and difficult to discover."

"You say truly: but when found, it is right to stir them up—to urge and exhort them to the effort—to show them what their gifts are, and why they were given—to speak Heaven's message in their ear,—to offer them, direct from God, a place in the ranks of his chosen."

"If they are really qualified for the task, will not their own hearts be the first to inform them of it?"

I felt as if an awful charm was framing round and gathering over me: I trembled to hear some fatal word spoken which would at once declare and rivet the spell.

"And what does *your* heart say?" demanded St. John.

"My heart is mute,—my heart is mute," I answered, struck and thrilled.

"Then I must speak for it," continued the deep, relentless voice. "Jane, come with me to India: come as my helpmeet and fellow-labourer."

The glen and sky spun round: the hills heaved! It was as if I had heard a summons from Heaven—as if a visionary messenger, like him of Macedonia, had enounced, "Come over and help us!" But I was no apostle,—I could not behold the herald,—I could not receive his call.

"Oh, St. John!" I cried, "have some mercy!"

I appealed to one who, in the discharge of what he believed his duty, knew neither mercy nor remorse. He continued:—

"God and nature intended you for a missionary's wife. It is not personal, but mental endowments they have given you: you are formed for labour, not for love. A missionary's wife you must—shall be. You shall be mine: I claim you—not for my pleasure, but for my Sovereign's service."

"I am not fit for it: I have no vocation," I said.

He had calculated on these first objections: he was not irritated by them. Indeed, as he leaned back against the crag behind him, folded his arms on his chest, and fixed his countenance, I saw he was prepared for a long and trying opposition, and had taken in a stock of patience to last him to its close—resolved, however, that that close should be conquest for him.

"Humility, Jane," said he, "is the groundwork of Christian virtues: you say right that you are not fit for the work. Who is fit for it? Or who, that ever was truly called, believed himself worthy of the summons? I, for instance, am but dust and ashes. With St. Paul, I acknowledge myself the chiefest of sinners: but I do not suffer this sense of my personal vileness to daunt me. I know my Leader: that He is just as well as mighty; and while he has chosen a feeble instrument to perform a great task, He will, from the boundless stores of His providence, supply the inadequacy of the means to the end. Think like me, Jane—trust like me. It is the Rock of Ages I ask you to lean on: do not doubt but it will bear the weight of your human weakness."

"I do not understand a missionary life: I have never studied missionary labours."

"There, I, humble as I am, can give you the aid you want: I can set you your task from hour to hour; stand by you always; help you from moment to moment. This I could do in the beginning: soon (for I know your powers) you would be as strong and apt as myself, and would not require my help."

"But my powers—where are they for this undertaking? I do not feel them. Nothing speaks or stirs in me while you talk. I am sensible of no light kindling—no life quickening—no voice counselling or cheering. Oh, I wish I could make you see how much my mind is at this moment like a rayless dungeon, with one shrinking fear fettered in its depths—the fear of being persuaded by you to attempt what I cannot accomplish!"

"I have an answer for you—hear it. I have watched you ever since we first met: I have made you my study for ten months. I have proved you in that time by sundry tests: and what have I seen and elicited? In the village school I found you could perform well, punctually, uprightly, labour uncongenial to your habits and inclinations; I saw you could perform it with capacity and tact: you could win while you controlled. In the calm with which you learnt you had become suddenly rich, I read a mind clear of the vice of Demas:— lucre had no undue power over you. In the resolute readiness with which you cut your wealth into four shares, keeping but one to yourself, and relinquishing the three others to the claim of abstract justice, I recognised a soul that revelled in the flame and excitement of sacrifice. In the tractability with which, at my wish, you forsook a study in which you were interested, and adopted another, because it interested me; in the untiring assiduity with which you have since persevered in it—in the unflagging energy and unshaken temper with which you have met its difficulties—I acknowledge the complement of the qualities I seek. Jane, you are docile, diligent, disinterested, faithful, constant, and courageous; very gentle, and very heroic: cease to mistrust yourself—I can trust you unreservedly. As a conductress of Indian schools, and a helper amongst Indian women, your assistance will be to me invaluable."

My iron shroud contracted round me: persuasion advanced with slow sure step. Shut my eyes as I would, these last words of his succeeded in making the way, which had seemed blocked up comparatively clear. My work, which had appeared so vague, so hopelessly diffuse, condensed itself as he proceeded, and assumed a definite form under his shaping hand. He waited for an answer. I demanded a quarter of an hour to think before I again hazarded a reply.

"Very willingly," he rejoined: and rising, he strode a little distance up the pass, threw himself down on a swell of heath, and there lay still.

"I *can* do what he wants me to do: I am forced to see and acknowledge that," I meditated—"That is, if life be spared me. But I feel mine is not the existence to be long protracted under an Indian sun.—What then? He does not care for that: when my time came to die he would resign me, in all serenity and sanctity, to the God who gave me. The case is very plain before me. In leaving England, I should leave a loved but empty land—Mr. Rochester is not there: and if he were, what is, what can that ever be to me? My business is to live without him now: nothing so absurd, so weak as to drag on from day to day, as if I were waiting some impossible change in circumstances, which might reunite me to him. Of course (as St. John once said) I must seek another interest in life to replace the one lost: is not the occupation he now offers me truly the most glorious man can adopt or God assign? Is it not, by its noble cares and sublime results, the one best calculated to fill the void left by uptorn affections and demolished hopes? I believe I must say, yes—and yet I shudder. Alas! If I join St. John, I abandon half myself: if I go to India, I go to premature death. And how will the interval between leaving England for India, and India for the grave, be filled? Oh, I know well! That, too, is very clear to my vision. By straining to satisfy St. John till my sinews ache, I *shall* satisfy him—to the finest central point and farthest outward circle of his expectations. If I *do* go with him—if I *do* make the sacrifice he urges, I will make it absolutely: I will throw all on the altar—heart, vitals, the entire victim. He will never love me; but he shall approve me: I will show him energies he has not yet seen, resources he has never suspected. Yes: I can work as hard as he can; and with as little grudging.

"Consent, then, to his demand is possible: but for one item—one dreadful item. It is—that he asks me to be his wife, and has no more of a husband's heart for me than that frowning giant of a rock, down which the stream is foaming in yonder gorge. He prizes me as a soldier would a good weapon; and that is all. Unmarried to him, this would never grieve me; but can I let him complete his calculations—coolly put into practice his plans—go through the wedding ceremony? Can I receive from him the bridal ring, endure all the forms of love (which I doubt not he would scrupulously observe) and know that the spirit was quite absent? Can I bear the consciousness that every endearment he bestows is a sacrifice made on principle? No: such a martyrdom would be monstrous. I will never undergo it: As his sister, I might accompany him—not as his wife: I will tell him so."

I looked towards the knoll: there he lay, still as a prostrate column; his face turned to me: his eye beaming watchful, and keen. He started to his feet, and approached me.

"I am ready to go to India, if I may go free."

"Your answer requires a commentary," he said; "it is not clear."

"You have hitherto been my adopted brother: I, your adopted sister; let us continue as such: you and I had better not marry."

He shook his head. "Adopted fraternity will not do in this case. If you were my real sister it would be different: I should take you, and seek no wife. But, as it is, either our union must be consecrated and sealed by marriage, or it cannot exist: practical obstacles oppose themselves to any other plan. Do you not see it, Jane? Consider a moment—your strong sense will guide you."

I did consider: and still my sense, such as it was, directed me only to the fact that we did not love each other as man and wife should; and therefore it inferred we ought not marry. I said so. "St. John," I returned, "I regard you as a brother—you, me as a sister: so let us continue."

"We cannot—we cannot," he answered, with short, sharp determination: "it would not do. You have said you will go with me to India: remember—you have said that."

"Conditionally."

"Well—well. To the main point—the departure with me from England, the co-operation with me in my future labours—you do not object. You have already as good as put your hand to the plough: you are too consistent to withdraw it. You have but one end to keep in view—how the work you have undertaken can best be done. Simplify your complicated interests, feelings, thoughts, wishes, aims; merge all considerations in one purpose: that of fulfilling with effect—with power—the mission of your great Master. To do so, you must have a coadjutor—not a brother; that is a loose tie: but a husband. I, too, do not want a sister: a sister might any day be taken from me. I want a wife: the sole helpmeet I can influence efficiently in life, and retain absolutely till death."

I shuddered as he spoke: I felt his influence in my marrow—his hold on my limbs.

"Seek one elsewhere than in me, St. John: seek one fitted to you."

"One fitted to my purpose, you mean—fitted to my vocation. Again I tell you it is not the insignificant private individual—the mere man, with the man's selfish senses—I wish to mate: it is the missionary."

"And I will give the missionary my energies—it is all he wants—but not myself: that would be only adding the husk and shell to the kernel. For them he has no use: I retain them."

"You cannot—you ought not. Do you think God will be satisfied with half an obligation? Will He accept a mutilated sacrifice? It is the cause of God I advocate: it is under his standard I enlist you. I cannot accept on His behalf a divided allegiance: it must be entire."

"Oh! I will give my heart to God," I said, *"You* do not want it."

I will not swear, reader, that there was not something of repressed sarcasm both in the tone in which I uttered this sentence, and in the feeling that accompanied it. I had silently feared St. John till now, because I had not understood him. He had held me in awe, because he had held me in doubt. How much of him was saint, how much mortal, I could not heretofore tell; but revelations were being made in this conference: the analysis of his nature was proceeding before my eyes. I saw his fallibilities: I comprehended them. I understood that, sitting there where I did, on the bank of heath, and with that handsome form before me, I sat at the feet of a man, erring as I. The veil fell from his hardness and despotism. Having felt in him the presence of these qualities, I felt his imperfection, and took courage. I was with an equal—one whom I might argue—one whom, if I saw good, I might resist.

He was silent after I had uttered the last sentence, and I presently risked an upward glance at his countenance. His eye, bent on me, expressed at once stern surprise and keen inquiry. "Is she sarcastic, and sarcastic to *me!"* it seemed to say. "What does this signify?"

"Do not let us forget that this is a solemn matter," he said, ere long; "one of which we may neither think nor talk lightly without sin. I trust, Jane, you are in earnest when you say you will give your heart to God: it is all I want. Once wrench your heart from man, and fix it on your Maker, the advancement of that Maker's spiritual kingdom on earth will be your chief delight and endeavour: you will be ready to do at once whatever furthers that end. You will see what impetus would be given to your efforts and mine by our physical and mental union in marriage: the only union that gives a character of permanent conformity to the destinies and designs of human beings: and, passing over all minor caprices—all scruple about the degree, kind, strength, or tenderness of mere personal inclination—you will hasten to enter into that union at once."

"Shall I?" I said, briefly; and I looked at his features, beautiful in their harmony, but strangely formidable in their still severity; at his brow, commanding but not open; at his eyes, bright and deep, and searching, but never soft; at his tall, imposing figure; and fancied myself in idea *his wife.* Oh! it would never do! As his curate, his comrade, all would be right: I would cross oceans with him in that capacity; toil under eastern suns, in Asian deserts with him in that office; admire and emulate his courage, and devotion, and vigour; accommodate quietly to his masterhood; smile undisturbed at his ineradicable ambition; discriminate the Christian from the man: profoundly esteem the one, and freely forgive the other. I should suffer often, no doubt, attached to him only in this capacity: my body would be under rather a stringent yoke, but my heart and mind would be free. I should still have my unblighted self to turn to: my natural unenslaved feelings with which to communicate in moments of loneliness.

There would be recesses in my mind which would be only mine, to which he never came; and sentiments growing there fresh and sheltered, which his austerity could never blight, nor his measured warrior-march trample down: but as his wife—at his side always, and always restrained, and always checked—forced to keep the fire of my nature continually low, to compel it to burn inwardly and never utter a cry, though the imprisoned flame consumed vital after vital—*this* would be unendurable.

"St. John!" I exclaimed, when I had got so far in my meditation.

"Well?" he answered, icily.

"I repeat: I freely consent to go with you as your fellow-missionary; but not as your wife; I cannot marry you and become a part of you."

"A part of me you must become," he answered steadily; "otherwise the whole bargain is void. How can I, a man not yet thirty, take out with me to India a girl of nineteen, unless she be married to me? How can we be for ever together—sometimes in solitudes, sometimes amidst savage tribes—and unwed?"

"Very well," I said, shortly; "under the circumstances, quite as well as if I were either your real sister; or a man and a clergyman like yourself."

"It is known that you are not my sister; I cannot introduce you as such: to attempt it would be to fasten injurious suspicions on us both. And for the rest, though you have a man's vigorous brain, you have a woman's heart, and—it would not do."

"It would do," I affirmed with some disdain, "perfectly well. I have a woman's heart; but not where you are concerned: for you I have only a comrade's constancy; a fellow-soldier's frankness, fidelity, fraternity, if you like; a neophyte's respect and submission to his hierophant: nothing more—don't fear."

"It is what I want," he said, speaking to himself; "it is just what I want. And there are obstacles in the way: they must be hewn down. Jane, you would not repent marrying me; be certain of that; we *must* be married, I repeat it: there is no other way; and undoubtedly enough of love would follow upon marriage to render the union right even in your eyes."

"I scorn your idea of love," I could not help saying; as I rose up and stood before him, leaning my back against the rock. "I scorn the counterfeit sentiment you offer: yes, St. John, and I scorn you when you offer it."

He looked at me fixedly: compressing his well-cut lips while he did so. Whether he was incensed or surprised, or what, it was not easy to tell: he could command his countenance thoroughly.

"I scarcely expected to hear that expression from you," he said: "I think I have done and uttered nothing to deserve scorn."

I was touched by his gentle tone, and overawed by his high, calm mien.

"Forgive me the words, St. John: but it is your own fault that I have been roused to speak so unguardedly. You have introduced a topic on which our natures are at variance—a topic we should never discuss: the very name of love is an apple of discord between us—if the reality were required what should we do? How should we feel? My dear cousin, abandon your scheme of marriage—forget it."

"No," said he; "it is a long-cherished scheme, and the only one which can secure my great end: but I shall urge you no further at present. Tomorrow I leave home for Cambridge: I have many friends there to whom I should wish to say farewell. I shall be absent a fortnight—take that space of time to consider my offer: and do not forget that if you reject it, it is not me you deny, but God. Through my means, He opens to you a noble career: as my wife only can you enter upon it. Refuse to be my wife, and you limit yourself for ever to a track of selfish ease and barren obscurity. Tremble, lest in that case you should be numbered with those who have denied the faith and are worse than infidels!"

He had done. Turning from me, he once more—

"Looked to river, looked to the hill:"

But this time his feelings were all pent in his heart: I was not worthy to hear them uttered. As I walked by his side homeward, I read well in his iron silence all he felt towards me: the disappointment of an austere and despotic nature, which has met resistance where it expected submission— the disapprobation of a cool, inflexible judgment, which has detected in another feelings and views in which it has no power to sympathize: in short, as a man, he would have wished to coerce me into obedience: it was only as a sincere Christian he bore so patiently with my perversity, and allowed so long a space for reflection and repentance.

That night, after he had kissed his sisters, he thought proper to forget even to shake hands with me; but left the room in silence. I—who, though I had no love, had much friendship for him—was hurt by the marked omission: so much hurt that tears started to my eyes.

"I see you and St. John have been quarrelling, Jane," said Diana, "during your walk on the moor. But go after him; he is now lingering in the passage, expecting you—he will make it up."

I have not much pride under such circumstances: I would always rather be happy than dignified; and I ran after him—he stood at the foot of the stairs.

"Good-night, St. John," said I.

"Good-night, Jane," he replied, calmly.

"Then shake hands," I added.

What a cold, loose touch he impressed on my fingers! He was deeply displeased by what had occurred that day: cordiality would not warm, nor tears move him. No happy reconciliation was to be had with him—no cheering smile or generous word: but still the Christian was patient and placid; and when I asked him if he forgave me, he answered that he was not in the habit of cherishing the remembrance of vexation; that he had nothing to forgive; not having been offended.

And with that answer, he left me. I would much rather he had knocked me down.

. . . .

Chapter 35

He did not leave for Cambridge the next day, as he had said he would. He deferred his departure a whole week; and during that time he made me feel what severe punishment a good, yet stern, a conscientious, yet implacable man can inflict on one who has offended him. Without one overt act of hostility, one upbraiding word, he contrived to impress me momentarily with the conviction that I was put beyond the pale of his favour.

Not that St. John harboured a spirit of unchristian vindictiveness—not that he would have injured a hair of my head, if it had been fully in his power to do so. Both by nature and principle he was superior to the mean gratification of vengeance: he had forgiven me for saying I scorned him and his love, but he had not forgotten the words; and as long as he and I lived he never would forget them. I saw by his look, when he turned to me, that they were always written on the air between me and him; whenever I spoke, they sounded in my voice to his ear; and their echo toned every answer he gave me.

He did not abstain from conversing with me: he even called me as usual each morning to join him at his desk; and I fear the corrupt man within him had a pleasure unimparted to, and unshared by, the pure Christian, in evincing with what skill he could, while acting and speaking apparently just as usual, extract from every deed and every phrase the spirit of interest and approval which had formerly communicated a certain austere charm to his language and manner. To me, he was in reality become no longer flesh, but marble: his eye was a cold, bright, blue gem; his tongue, a speaking instrument—nothing more.

All this was torture to me—refined, lingering torture. It kept up a slow fire of indignation, and a trembling trouble of grief, which harassed and crushed me altogether. I felt how—if I were his wife—this good man, pure as the deep sunless source, could soon kill me: without drawing from my veins a single drop of blood, or receiving on his own crystal conscience the faintest stain of crime. Especially I felt this, when I made any attempt to propitiate him. No ruth met my ruth. *He* experienced no suffering from estrangement—no yearning after reconciliation; and though, more than once, my fast falling tears blistered the page over which we both bent, they produced no more effect on him than if his heart had been really a matter of stone or metal. To his sisters, meantime, he was somewhat kinder than usual: as if afraid that mere coldness would not sufficiently convince me how completely I was banished and banned, he added the force of contrast: and this I am sure he did, not by malace, but on principle.

The night before he left home, happening to see him walking in the garden about sunset, and remembering, as I looked at him, that this man, alienated as he now was, had once saved my life, and that we were near relations, I was moved to make a last attempt to regain his friendship. I went out and approached him, as he stood leaning over the little gate: I spoke to the point at once.

"St. John, I am unhappy, because you are still angry with me. Let us be friends."

"I hope we are friends," was the unmoved reply; while he still watched the rising of the moon, which he had been contemplating as I approached.

"No, St. John, we are not friends as we were. You know that."

"Are we not? That is wrong. For my part, I wish you no ill and all good."

"I believe you, St. John; for I am sure you are incapable of wishing any one ill: but, as I am your kinswoman, I should desire somewhat more of affection than that sort of general philanthropy you extend to mere strangers."

"Of course," he said. "Your wish is reasonable; and I am far from regarding you as a stranger."

This, spoken in a cool, tranquil tone, was mortifying and baffling enough. Had I attended to the suggestions of pride and ire, I should immediately have left him: but something worked within me more strongly than those feelings could. I deeply venerated my cousin's talent and principle. His friendship was of value to me: to lose it tried me severely. I would not so soon relinquish the attempt to reconquer it.

"Must we part in this way, St. John? And when you go to India, will you leave me so, without a kinder word than you have yet spoken?"

He turned quite from the moon, and faced me.

"When I go to India, Jane, will I leave you? What! do you not go to India?"

"You said I could not, unless I married you."

"And you will not marry me? You adhere to that resolution?"

Reader, do you know, as I do, what terror those cold people can put into the ice of their questions? How much of the fall of the avalanche is in their anger? of the breaking up of the frozen sea in their displeasure?

"No, St. John, I will not marry you. I adhere to my resolution."

The avalanche had shaken and slid a little forward; but it did not yet crash down.

"Once more, why this refusal?" he asked.

"Formerly," I answered, "because you did not love me; now, I reply, because you almost hate me. If I were to marry you, you would kill me. You are killing me now."

His lips and cheeks turned white—quite white.

"*I should kill you—I am killing you?* Your words are such as ought not to be used: violent, unfeminine, and untrue. They betray an unfortunate state of mind: they merit severe reproof: they would seem inexcusable; but that it is the duty of man to forgive his fellow, even until seventy-and-seven times."

I had finished the business now. While earnestly wishing to erase from his mind the trace of my former offence, I had stamped on that tenacious surface, another and far deeper impression: I had burnt it in.

"Now you will indeed hate me," I said. "It is useless to attempt to conciliate you: I see I have made an eternal enemy of you."

A fresh wrong did these words inflict: the worse, because they touched on the truth. That bloodless lip quivered to a temporary spasm. I knew the steely ire I had whetted. I was heart-wrung.

"You utterly misinterpret my words," I said, at once seizing his hand: "I have no intention to grieve or pain you—indeed, I have not."

Most bitterly he smiled—most decidedly he withdrew his hand from mine. "And now you recall your promise, and will not go to India at all, I presume?" said he, after a considerable pause.

"Yes, I will, as your assistant," I answered.

A very long silence succeeded. What struggle there was in him between Nature and Grace in this interval, I cannot tell: only singular gleams scintillated in his eyes, and strange shadows passed over his face. He spoke at last.

"I before proved to you the absurdity of a single woman of your age proposing to accompany abroad a single man of mine. I proved it to you in such terms as, I should have thought, would have prevented your ever again alluding to the plan. That you have done so, I regret—for your sake."

I interrupted him. Anything like a tangible reproach gave me courage at once. "Keep to common sense, St. John: you are verging on nonsense. You pretend to be shocked by what I have said. You are not really shocked; for, with your superior mind, you cannot be either so dull or so conceited as to misunderstand my meaning. I say again, I will be your curate, if you like, but never your wife."

Again he turned lividly pale; but, as before controlled his passion perfectly. He answered emphatically, but calmly:—

"A female curate, who is not my wife, would never suit me. With me, then, it seems, you cannot go: but if you are sincere in your offer, I will, while in town, speak to a married missionary, whose wife needs a co-adjutor. Your own fortune will make you independent of the Society's aid; and thus you may still be spared the dishonour of breaking your promise, and deserting the band you engaged to join."

Now I never had, as the reader knows, either given any formal promise, or entered into any engagement; and this language was all much too hard, and much too despotic for the occasion. I replied:—

"There is no dishonour; no breach of promise; no desertion in the case. I am not under the slightest obligation to go to India: especially with strangers. With you, I would have ventured much; because I admire, confide in, and, as a sister, I love you: but I am convinced that, go when and with whom I would, I should not live long in that climate."

"Ah! you are afraid of yourself," he said curling his lip.

"I am. God did not give me my life to throw away; and to do as you wish me, would, I begin to think, be almost equivalent to committing suicide. Moreover, before I definitively resolve on quitting England, I will know for certain, whether I cannot be of greater use by remaining in it than by leaving it."

"What do you mean?"

"It would be fruitless to attempt to explain: but there is a point on which I have long endured painful doubt; and I can go nowhere till by some means that doubt is removed."

"I know where your heart turns, and to what it clings. The interest you cherish is lawless and unconsecrated. Long since you ought to have crushed it: not you should blush to allude to it. You think of Mr. Rochester?"

It was true. I confessed it by silence.

"Are you going to seek Mr. Rochester?"

"I must find out what is become of him."

"It remains for me, then," he said, "to remember you in my prayers; and to entreat God for you, in all earnestness, that you may not indeed become a castaway. I had thought I recognized in you one of the chosen. But God sees not as man sees: *His* will be done."

He opened the gate, passed through it, and strayed away down the glen. He was soon out of sight.

On re-entering the parlour, I found Diana standing at the window, looking very thoughtful. Diana was a great deal taller than I: she put her hand on my shoulder, and stooping, examined my face.

"Jane," she said, "you are always agitated and pale now. I am sure there is something the matter. Tell me what business St. John and you have on hands. I have watched you this half hour from the window: you must forgive my being such a spy, but for a long time I have fancied I hardly know what. St. John is a strange being——"

She paused—I did not speak: soon she resumed:—

"That brother of mine cherishes peculiar views of some sort respecting you, I am sure: he has long distinguished you by a notice and interest he never showed to any one else—to what end? I wish he loved you—does he, Jane?"

I put her cool hand to my hot forehead: "No, Die, not one whit."

"Then why does he follow you so with his eyes—and get you so frequently alone with him, and keep you so continually at his side? Mary and I had both concluded he wished you to marry him."

"He does—he has asked me to be his wife."

Diana clapped her hands. "That is just what we hoped and thought! And you will marry him, Jane, won't you? And then he will stay in England."

"Far from that, Diana; his sole idea in proposing to me is to procure a fitting fellow-labourer in his Indian toils."

"What! He wishes you to go to India?"

"Yes."

"Madness!" she exclaimed. "You would not live three months there, I am certain. You never shall go: you have not consented—have you, Jane?"

"I have refused to marry him"——

"And have consequently displeased him?" she suggested.

"Deeply: he will never forgive me, I fear: yet I offered to accompany him as his sister."

"It was frantic folly to do so, Jane. Think of the task you undertook—one of incessant fatigue: where fatigue kills even the strong; and you are weak. St. John—you know him—would urge you to impossibilities: with him there would be no permission to rest during the hot hours; and unfortunately, I have noticed, whatever he exacts, you force yourself to perform. I am astonished you found courage to refuse his hand. You do not love him then, Jane?"

"Not as a husband."

"Yet he is a handsome fellow."

"And I am so plain you see, Die. We should never suit."

"Plain! You? Not at all. You are much too pretty, as well as too good, to be grilled alive in Calcutta." And again she earnestly conjured me to give up all thoughts of going out with her brother.

"I must, indeed," I said; "for when just now I repeated the offer of serving him for a deacon, he expressed himself shocked at my want of decency. He seemed to think I had committed an impropriety in proposing to accompany him unmarried: as if I had not from the first hoped to find in him a brother; and habitually regarded him as such."

"What makes you say he does not love you, Jane?"

"You should hear himself on the subject. He has again and again explained that it is not himself, but his office he wishes to mate. He has told me I am formed for labour—not for love: which is true, no doubt. But, in my opinion, if I am not formed for love, it follows that I am not formed for marriage. Would that not be strange, Die, to be chained for life to a man who regarded one but as a useful tool?"

"Insupportable—unnatural—out of the question!"

"And then," I continued, "though I have only sisterly affection for him now, yet, if forced to be his wife, I can imagine the possibility of conceiving an inevitable, strange, torturing kind of love for him: because he is so talented; and there is often a certain heroic grandeur in his look, manner, and conversation. In that case, my lot would become unspeakably wretched. He would not want me to love him; and if I showed the feeling, he would make me sensible that it was a superfluity, unrequired by him, unbecoming in me. I know he would."

"And yet, St. John is a good man," said Diana.

"He is a good and a great man: but he forgets, pitilessly, the feelings and claims of little people, in pursuing his own large views. It is better, therefore, for the insignificant to keep out of his way; lest, in his progress, he should trample them down. Here he comes! I will leave you, Diana."

And I hastened up stairs, as I saw him entering the garden.

But I was forced to meet him again at supper. During that meal he appeared just as composed as usual. I had thought he would hardly speak to me, and I was certain he had given up the pursuit of his matrimonial scheme: the sequel showed I was mistaken on both points. He addressed me precisely in his ordinary manner; or what had, of late, been his ordinary manner; one scrupulously polite. No doubt he had invoked the help of the Holy Spirit to subdue the anger I had roused in him, and now believed he had forgiven me once more.

For the evening reading before prayers, he selected the twenty-first chapter of Revelations. It was at all times pleasant to listen, while from his lips fell the words of the Bible: never did his fine voice sound at once so sweet and full—never did his manner become so impressive in its noble simplicity, as when he delivered the oracles of God; and to-night that voice took a more solemn tone—that manner a more thrilling meaning—as he sat in the midst of his household circle (the May moon shining in through the uncurtained window, and rendering almost unnecessary the light of the candle on the table): as he sat there, bending over the great old Bible, and described from its page the vision of the new heaven and the new earth—told how God would come to dwell with men, how he would wipe away all tears from their eyes, and promised that there should be no more death, neither sorrow nor crying, nor any more pain, because the former things were passed away.

The succeeding words thrilled me strangely as he spoke them: especially as I felt, but the slight, indescribable alteration is sound, that in uttering them, his eye had turned on me.

"He that overcometh shall inherit all things; and I will be his God, and he shall be my son. But," was slowly, distinctly read, the "fearful, the unbelieving, etc., shall have their part in the lake which burneth with fire and brimstone, which is the second death."

Henceforward, I knew what fate St. John feared for me.

A calm, subdued triumph, blent with a longing earnestness, marked his enunciation of the last glorious verses of that chapter. The reader believed his name was already written in the Lamb's book of life, and he yearned after the hour which should admit him to the city to which the kings of the earth bring their glory and honour; which has no need of sun or moon to shine in it, because the glory of God lightens it, and the Lamb is the light thereof.

In the prayer following the chapter, all his energy gathered—all his stern zeal woke: he was in deep earnest, wrestling with God, and resolved on a conquest. He supplicated strength for the weak-hearted; guidance for wanderers from the fold: a return, even at the eleventh hour, for those whom the temptations of the world and the flesh were luring from the narrow path. He asked, he urged, he claimed the boon of a brand snatched from the burning. Earnestness is ever deeply solemn: first, as I listened to that prayer, I wondered at his; then, when it continued and rose, I was touched by it, and at last awed. He felt the greatness and goodness of his purpose so sincerely: others who heard him plead for it, could not but feel it too.

The prayer over, we took leave of him: he was to go at a very early hour in the morning. Diana and Mary having kissed him, left the room—in compliance, I think, with a whispered hint from him: I tendered my hand, and wished him a pleasant journey.

"Thank you, Jane. As I said, I shall return from Cambridge in a fortnight: that space, then, is yet left you for reflection. If I listened to human pride, I should say no more to you of marriage with me; but I listen to my duty, and keep steadily in view my first aim—to do all things to the glory of God. My Master was long-suffering: so will I be. I cannot give you up to perdition as a vessel of wrath: repent—resolve; while there is yet time. Remember we are bid to work while it is day—warned that 'the night cometh when no man shall work.' Remember the fate of Dives, who had his good things in this life. God give you strength to choose that better part which shall not be taken from you!"

He laid his hand on my head as he uttered the last words. He had spoken earnestly, mildly: his look was not, indeed, that of a lover beholding his mistress; but it was that of a pastor recalling his wandering sheep—or better, of a guardian angel watching the soul for which he is responsible. All men of talent, whether they be men of feeling or not; whether they be zealots, or aspirants, or despots—provided only they be sincere—have their sublime moments: when they subdue and rule. I felt veneration for St. John—veneration so strong that its impetus thrust me at once to the point I had so long shunned. I was tempted to cease struggling with him—to rush down the torrent of his will into the gulf of his existence, and there lose my own. I was almost as hard beset by him now as I had been once before, in a different way, by another. I was a fool both times. To have yielded then would have been an error of principle; to have yielded now would have been an error or judgment. So I think at his hour, when I look back to the crisis through the quiet medium of time: I was unconscious of folly at the instant.

I stood motionless under my hierophant's touch. My refusals were forgotten—my fears overcome—my wrestlings paralyzed. The Impossible—*i.e.* my marriage with St. John—was fast becoming the Possible. All was changing utterly, with a sudden sweep. Religion called—Angels beckoned—God commanded—life rolled together like a scroll—death's gates opening, showed eternity beyond: it seemed, that for safety and bliss there, all here might be sacrificed in a second. The dim room was full of visions.

"Could you decide now?" asked the missionary. The inquiry was put in gentle tones: he drew me to him as gently. Oh, that gentleness! how far more potent is it than force! I could resist St. John's wrath: I grew pliant as a reed under his kindness. Yet I knew all the time, if I yielded now, I should not the less be made to repent, some day, of my former rebellion. His nature was not changed by one hour of solemn prayer: it was only elevated.

"I could decide if I were but certain," I answered: "were I but convinced that it is God's will I should marry you, I could vow to marry you here and now—come afterwards what would!"

"My prayers are heard!" ejaculated St. John. He pressed his hand firmer on my head, as if he claimed me: he surrounded me with his arm, *almost* as if he loved me (I say *almost*—I knew the difference—for I had felt what it was to be loved; but, like him, I had now put love out of the question, and thought only of duty): I contended with my inward dimness of vision, before which clouds yet rolled. I sincerely, deeply, fervently longed to do what was right; and only that. "Show me, show me the path!" I entreated of Heaven. I was excited more than I had ever been; and whether what followed was the effect of excitement, the reader shall judge.

All the house was still; for I believe all, except St. John and myself, were now retired to rest. The one candle was dying out: the room was full of moonlight. My heart beat fast and thick: I heard its throb. Suddenly it stood still to an inexpressible feeling that thrilled it through, and passed at once to my head and extremities. The feeling was not like an electric shock; but it was quite as sharp, as strange, as startling: it acted on my senses as if their utmost activity hitherto had been but torpor; from which they were now summoned, and forced to wake. They rose expectant: eye and ear waited, while the flesh quivered on my bones.

"What have you heard? What do you see?" asked St. John. I saw nothing: but I heard a voice somewhere cry—

"Jane! Jane! Jane!" nothing more.

"Oh, God! what is it?" I gasped.

I might have said, "Where is it?" for it did not seem in the room—nor in the house—nor in the garden: it did not come out of the air—nor from under the earth—nor from overhead. I had heard it—where, or whence, for ever impossible to know! And it was the voice of a human being—a known, loved, well-remembered voice—that of Edward Fairfax Rochester: and it spoke in pain and woe wildly, eerily, urgently.

"I am coming!" I cried. "Wait for me! Oh, I will come!" I flew to the door, and looked into the passage: it was dark. I ran out into the garden: it was void.

"Where are you?" I exclaimed.

The hills beyond Marsh Glen sent the answer faintly back—"Where are you?" I listened. the wind sighed low in the firs: all was moorland loneliness and midnight hush.

"Down superstition!" I commented, as that spectre rose up black by the black yew at the gate. "This is not thy deception, nor thy witchcraft: it is the work of nature. She was roused, and did—no miracle—but her best."

I broke from St. John; who had followed, and would have detained me. It was *my* turn to assume ascendancy. *My* powers were in play, and in force. I told him to forbear question or remark; I desired him to leave me: I must, and would be alone. He obeyed at once. Where there is energy to command well enough, obedience never fails. I mounted to my chamber; locked myself in; fell on my knees; and prayed in my way—a different way to St. John's, but effective in its own fashion. I seemed to penetrate very near a Mighty Spirit; and my soul rushed out in gratitude at His feet.

I rose from the thanksgiving—took a resolve—and lay down, unscared, enlightened—eager but for daylight.

·······

Chapter 36

The daylight came. I rose at dawn. I busied myself for an hour or two with arranging my things in my chamber, drawers and wardrobe, in the order wherein I should wish to leave them during a brief absence. Meantime, I heard St. John quit his room. He sfopped at my door: I feared he would knock—no, but a slip of paper was passed under the door. I took it up. It bore the words—

"You left me too suddenly last night. Had you stayed but a little longer, you would have laid your hand on the Christian's cross and the angel's crown. I shall expect your clear decision when I return this day fortnight. Meantime, the spirit, I trust, is willing, but the flesh, I see, is weak. I shall pray for you hourly,—Yours, St. John."

"My spirit," I answered, mentally, "is willing to do what is right; and my flesh, I hope is strong enough to accomplish the will of Heaven, when once that well is distinctly known to me. At any rate, it shall be strong enough to search—inquire—to grope an outlet from this cloud of doubt, and find the open day of certainty."

It was the first of June; yet the morning was overcast and chilly: rain beat fast on my casement. I heard the front door open, and St. John pass out. Looking through the window, I saw him traverse the garden. He took the way over the misty moors in the direction of Whitcross—there he would meet the coach.

"In a few more hours I shall succeed you in that track, cousin," thought I: "I too have a coach to meet at Whitcross. I too have some to see and ask after in England, before I depart for ever."

It wanted yet two hours of breakfast-time. I filled the interval in walking softly about my room, and pondering the visitation which had given my plans their present bent. I recalled that inward sensation I had experienced: for I could recall it, with all its unspeakable strangeness. I recalled the voice I had heard; again I questioned whence it came, as vainly as before: is seemed in *me*—not in the external world. I asked, was it a mere nervous impression—a delusion? I could not conceive or believe: it was more like an inspiration. The wondrous shock of feeling had come like the earthquake which shook the foundations of Paul and Silas's prison: it had opened the doors of the soul's cell, and loosed its bands—it had wakened it out of its sleep, whence it sprang trembling, listening, aghast; then vibrated thrice a cry on my startled ear, and in my quaking heart, and through my spirit; which neither feared nor shook, but exulted as if in joy over the success of one effort it had been privileged to make, independent of the combrous body.

"Ere many days," I said, as I terminated my musings, "I will know something of him whose voice seemed last night to summon me. Letters have proved of no avail—personal inquiry shall replace them."

At breakfast, I announced to Diana and Mary that I was going a journey, and should be absent at least four days.

"Alone, Jane?" they asked.

"Yes; it was to see, or hear news of, a friend about whom I had for some time been uneasy."

They might have said, as I have no doubt they thought, that they had believed me to be without any friends save for them: for, indeed, I had often said so; but with their true, natural delicacy, they abstained from comment: except that Diana asked me if I was sure I was well enough to travel. I looked very pale, she observed. I replied, that nothing ailed me save anxiety of mind, which I hoped soon to alleviate.

It was easy to make my further arrangements; for I was troubled with no inquiries—no surmises. Having once explained to them that I could not now be explicit about my plans, they kindly and wisely acquiesced in the silence with which I pursued them; according to me the privilege of free action I should, under similar circumstances, have accorded them.

I left Moor House at three o'clock P.M., and soon after four, I stood at the foot of the sign-post of Whitcross, waiting the arrival of the coach which was to take me to distant Thornfield. Amidst the silence of those solitary roads and desert hills, I heard it approach from a great distance. It was the same vehicle whence, a year ago, I had alighted one summer evening on this very spot—how desolate, and hopeless, and objectless! It stopped as I beckoned. I entered—not now obliged to part with my whole fortune as the price of its accommodation. Once more on the road to Thornfield, I felt like the messenger-pigeon flying home.

It was a journey of six-and-thirty hours. I had set out from Whitcross on a Tuesday afternoon, and early on the succeeding Thursday morning the coach stopped to water the horses at a wayside inn, situated in the midst of scenery whose green hedges and large fields, and low pastoral hills, (how mild of feature and verdant of hue compared with the stern north-midland moors of Morton!) met my eye like the lineaments of a once familiar face. Yes, I knew the character of this landscape: I was sure we were near my bourne.

"How far is Thornfield Hall from here?" I asked of the ostler.

"Just two miles, ma'am, across the fields."

"My journey is closed," I thought to myself. I got out of the coach, gave a box I had into the ostler's charge, to be kept till I called for it; paid my fare; satisfied the coachman, and was going: the brightening day gleamed on the sign of the inn, and I read in gilt letters, "The Rochester Arms." My heart leapt up: I was already on my master's very lands. It fell again: the thought struck it:—

"Your master himself may be beyond the British Channel, for aught you know: and then, if he is at Thornfield Hall, towards which you hasten, who besides him is there? His lunatic wife; and you have nothing to do with him: you dare not speak to him or seek his presence. You have lost your labour—you had better go no farther," urged the monitor. "Ask information of the people at the inn; they can give you all you seek: they can solve your doubts at once. Go up to that man, and inquire if Mr. Rochester be at home."

The suggestion was sensible; and yet I could not force myself to act on it. I so dreaded a reply that would crush me with despair. To prolong doubt was to prolong hope. I might yet once more see the Hall under the ray of her star. There was the stile before me—the very fields through which I had hurried, blind, deaf, distracted, with a revengeful fury tracking and scourging me, on the morning I fled from Thornfield: ere I well knew what course I had resolved to take, I was in the midst of them. How fast I walked! How I ran sometimes! How I looked forward to catch the first view of the well-known woods! With what feelings I welcomed single trees I knew, and familiar glimpses of meadow and hill between them!

At last the woods rose; the rookery clustered dark; a loud cawing broke the morning stillness. Strange delight inspired me: on I hastened. Another field crossed—a lane threaded—and there were the court-yard walls— the back-offices: the house itself, the rookery still hid. "My first view of it shall be in front," I determined, "where its bold battlements will strike the eye nobly at once, and where I can single out my master's very window: perhaps he will be standing at it—he rises early: perhaps he is now walking in the orchard, or on the pavement in front. Could I but see him!— but a moment! Surely, in that case, I should not be so mad as to run to him? I cannot tell—I am not certain. And if I did—what then? God bless him! What then? Who would be hurt by my once more tasting the life his glance can give me?—I rave: perhaps at this moment he is watching the sun rise over the Pyrenees, or on the tideless sea of the south."

I had coasted along the lower wall of the orchard—turned its angle: there was a gate just there, opening into the meadow, between two stone pillars, crowned by stone balls. From behind one pillar, I could peep round quietly at the full front of the mansion. I advanced my head with precaution, desirous to ascertain if any bedroom window-blinds were yet drawn up: battlements, windows, long front—all from this sheltered station were at my command.

The crows sailing over head perhaps watched me while I took this survey. I wonder what they thought: they must have considered I was very careful and timid at first, and that gradually I grew very bold and reckless. A peep, and then a long stare; and then a departure from my niche and a straying out into the meadow; and a sudden stop full in front of the great mansion, and a protracted, hardy gaze towards it. "What affectation of diffidence was this at first!" they might have demanded, "What stupid regardlessness now?"

Hear an illustration, reader.

A lover finds his mistress asleep in a mossy bank; he wishes to catch a glimpse of her fair face without waking her. He steals softly over the grass, careful to make no sound; he pauses—fancying she has stirred: he withdraws; not for worlds would he be seen. All is still: he again advances: he bends above her; a light veil rests on her features: he lifts it, bends lower; now his eyes anticipate the vision of beauty—warm, and blooming, and lovely, in rest. How hurried was their first glance! But how they fix! How he starts! How he suddenly and vehemently clasps in both arms the form he dared not, a moment since, touch with his finger! How he calls aloud a name, and drops his burden, and gazes on it wildly! He thus grasps and cries, and gazes, because he no longer fears to waken by any sound he can utter—by any movement he can make. He thought his love slept sweetly: he finds she is stone-dead.

I looked with timorous joy towards a stately house: I saw a blackened ruin.

No need to cower behind a gate-post, indeed!—to peep up at chamber lattices, fearing life was astir behind them! No need to listen for doors opening—to fancy steps on the pavement or the gravel-walk! The lawn, the grounds were trodden and waste: the portal yawned void. The front was, as I had once seen it in a dream, but a shell-like wall, very high and very fragile looking, perforated with paneless windows: no roof, no battlements, no chimneys—all had crashed in.

And there was the silence of death about it: the solitude of a lonesome wild. No wonder that letters addressed to people here had never received an answer: as well despatch epistles to a vault in a church aisle. The grim blackness of the stones told by what fate the Hall had fallen—by conflagration: but how kindled? What story belonged to this disaster? What loss, besides mortar, and marble, and wood-work, had followed upon it? Had life been wrecked, as well as property? If so, whose? Dreadful question: there was no one here to answer it—not even dumb sign, mute token.

In wondering round the shattered walls and through the devastated interior, I gathered evidence that the calamity was not of late occurrence. Winter snows, I thought, had drifted through that void arch, winter rains beaten in at those hollow casements; for, amidst the drenched piles of rubbish, spring had cherished vegetation: grass and weed grew here and there between the stones and fallen rafters. And oh! where, meantime, was the hapless owner of this wreck? In what land? Under what auspices? My eye involuntarily wandered to the gray church tower near the gates, and I asked, "Is he with Damer de Rochester, sharing the shelter of his narrow marble house?"

Some answer must be had to these questions. I could find it nowhere but at the inn, and thither, ere long, I returned. The host himself brought my breakfast into the parlour. I requested him to shut the door and sit down: I had some questions to ask him. But when he complied, I scarcely knew how to begin; such horror had I of the possible answers. And yet the spectacle of desolation I had just left, prepared me in a measure for a tale of misery. The host was a respectable-looking, middle-aged man.

"You know Thornfield Hall, of course?" I managed to say at last.

"Yes, ma'am; I lived there once."

"Did you?" Not in my time, I thought: you are a stranger to me.

"I was the late Mr. Rochester's butler," he added.

The late! I seemed to have received with full force the blow I had been trying to evade.

"The late!" I gasped. "Is he dead?"

"I mean the present gentleman, Mr. Edward's father," he explained. I breathed again: my blood resumed its flow. Fully assured by these words that Mr. Edward—my Mr. Rochester (God bless him, wherever he was!)—was at least alive: was, in short, "the present gentleman." Gladdening words! It seemed I could hear all that was to come—whatever the disclosures might be—with comparative tranquillity. Since he was not in the grave, I could bear, I thought, to learn that he was at the Antipodes.

"Is Mr. Rochester living at Thornfield Hall now?" I asked, knowing, of course, what the answer would be, but yet desirous of deferring the direct question as to where he really was.

"No, ma'am—oh, no! No one is living there. I suppose you are a stranger in these parts, or you would have heard what happened last autumn,—Thornfield Hall is quite a ruin: it was burnt down just about harvest time. A dreadful calamity! such an immense quantity of valuable property destroyed: hardly any of the furniture could be saved. The fire broke out at dead of night, and before the engines arrived from Millcote, the building was one mass of flame. It was a terrible spectacle: I witnessed it myself."

"At dead of night!" I muttered. Yes, that was ever the hour of fatality at Thornfield. "Was it known how it originated?" I demanded.

"They guessed, ma'am: they guessed. Indeed, I should say it was ascertained beyond a doubt. You are not perhaps aware," he continued, edging his chair a little nearer the table, and speaking low, "that there was a lady,—a—a lunatic, kept in the house?"

"I have heard something of it."

"She was kept in very close confinement, ma'am: people even for some years was not absolutely certain of her existence. No one saw her: they only knew by rumour that such a person was at the Hall; and who or what she was it was difficult to conjecture. They said Mr. Edward had brought her from abroad; and some believed she had been his mistress. But a queer thing happened a year since—a very queer thing."

I feared now to hear my own story. I endeavoured to recall him to the main fact.

"And this lady?"

"This lady, ma'am," he answered, "turned out to me Mr. Rochester's wife! The discovery was brought about in the strangest way. There was a young lady, a governess at the Hall, that Mr. Rochester fell in—"

"But the fire," I suggested.

"I'm coming to that, ma'am—that Mr. Edward fell in love with. The servants say they never saw anybody so much in love as he was: he was after her continually. They used to watch him—servants will, you know, ma'am—and he set store on her past everything: for all, nobody but him thought her so very handsome. She was a little small thing, they say, almost like a child. I never saw herself; but I've heard Leah, the housemaid, tell of her. Leah liked her well enough. Mr. Rochester was about forty, and this governess not twenty; and, you see, when gentlemen of his age fall in love with girls, they are often like as if they were bewitched: well, he would marry her."

"You shall tell me this part of the story another time," I said; "but now I have a particular reason for wishing to hear all about the fire. Was it suspected that this lunatic, Mrs. Rochester, had any hand in it?"

"You've hit it, ma'am: it's quite certain that it was her, and nobody but her, that set it going. She had a woman to take care of her called Mrs. Poole—an able woman in her line, and very trust-worthy, but for one fault—a fault common to a deal of them nurses and matrons—*she kept a private bottle of gin by her,* and now and then took a drop over much. It's excusable, for she had a hard life of it: but still it was dangerous; for, when Mrs. Poole was fast asleep, after the gin and water, the mad lady, who was as cunning as a witch, would take the keys out of her pocket, let herself out of her chamber, and go roaming about the house, doing any wild mischief that came into her head. They say she had nearly burnt her husband in his bed once: but I don't know about that. However, on this night, she set fire first to the hangings of the room next her own; and then she got down to a lower story, and made her way to the chamber that had been the governess's—(she was like as if she knew somehow how matters had gone on, and had a spite at her)—and she kindled the bed there: but there was nobody sleeping in it, fortunately. The governess had run away two months before; and for all Mr. Rochester sought her as if she had been the most precious thing he had in the world, he never could hear a word of her; and he grew savage—quite savage on his disappointment: he never was a wild man, but he got dangerous after he lost her. He would be alone, too. He sent Mrs. Fairfax, the housekeeper, away to her friends at a distance; but he did it handsomely, for he settled an annuity on her for life: and she deserved it—she was a very good woman. Miss Adèle, a ward he had, was put to school. He broke off acquaintance with all the gentry, and shut himself up, like a hermit, at the Hall."

"Then Mr. Rochester was at home when the fire broke out?"

"Yes, indeed was he; and he went up to the attics when all was burning above and below, and got the servants out of their beds and helped them down himself—and went back to get his mad wife out of her cell. And then they called out to him that she was on the roof; where she was standing waving her arms, above the battlements, and shouting out till they could hear her a mile off: I saw her and heard her with my own eyes. She was a big woman, and had long, black hair: we could see it streaming against the flames as she stood. I witnessed, and several more witnessed Mr. Rochester ascend through the skylight on to the roof: we heard him call "Bertha!" We saw him approach her; and then, ma'am, she yelled, and gave a spring, and the next minute she lay smashed on the pavement."

"Dead?"

"Dead? Ay, dead as the stones on which her brains and blood were scattered."

"Good God!"

"You may well say so, ma'am: it was frightful!"

He shuddered.

"And afterwards?" I urged.

"Well, ma'am, afterwards the house was burnt to the ground: there are only some bits of walls standing now."

"Were any other lives lost?"

"No—perhaps it would have been better if there had."

"What do you mean?"

"Poor Mr. Edward!" he ejaculated, "I little thought ever to have seen it! Some say it was a just judgment on him for keeping his first marriage secret, and wanting to take another wife while he had one living: but I pity him, for my part."

"You said he was alive?" I exclaimed.

"Yes, yes: he is alive; but many think he had better be dead."

"Why? How?" My blood was again running cold. "Where is he?" I demanded. "Is he in England?"

"Ay—ay—he's in England; he can't get out of England, I fancy—he's a fixture now."

What agony was this! And the man seemed resolved to protract it.

"He is stone-blind," he said at last. "Yes—he is stone-blind—is Mr. Edward."

I had dreaded worse. I had dreaded he was mad. I summoned strength to ask what caused this calamity.

"It was all his own courage, and a body may say, his kindness, in a way, ma'am: he wouldn't leave the house till every one else was out before him. As he came down the great staircase at last, after Mrs. Rochester had flung herself from the battlements, there was a great crash—all fell. He was

taken out from under the ruins, alive, but sadly hurt: a beam had fallen
in such a way as to protect him partly, but one eye was knocked out, and
one hand so crushed that Mr. Carter, the surgeon, had to amputate it
directly. The other eye inflamed: he lost the sight of that also. He is now
helpless, indeed—blind and a cripple."

"Where is he? Where does he now live?"

"At Ferndean, a manor-house on a farm he has about thirty miles off:
quite a desolate spot."

"Who is with him?"

"Old John and his wife: he would have none else. He is quite broken
down, they say."

"Have you any sort of conveyance?"

"We have a chaise, ma'am, a very handsome chaise."

"Let it be got ready instantly; and if your post-boy can drive me to Ferndean before dark this day, I'll pay both you and him twice the hire you
usually demand."

·······

Chapter 37

The manor-house of Ferndean was a building of considerable antiquity,
moderate size, and no architectural pretensions, deep buried in a wood.
I had heard of it before. Mr. Rochester often spoke of it, and sometimes
went there. His father had purchased the estate for the sake of the game
covers. He would have let the house; but could find no tenant, in consequence of its ineligible and insalubrious site. Ferndean then remained
uninhabited and unfurnished; with the exception of some two or three
rooms fitted up for the accommodation of the squire when he went there
in the season to shoot.

To this house I came, just ere dark, on an evening marked by the char-
acteristics of sad sky, cold gale, and continued small, penetrating rain.
The last mile I performed on foot, having dismissed the chaise and driver
with the double remuneration I had promised. Even when within a very
short distance of the manor-house, you could see nothing of it; so thick
and dark grew the timber of the gloomy wood about it. Iron gates between
granite pillars showed me where to enter, and passing through them, I
found myself at once in the twilight of close-ranked trees. There was a
grass-grown track descending the forest-aisle, between hoar and knotty
shafts and under branched arches. I followed it, expecting soon to reach
the dwelling; but it stretched on and on, it wound far and farther: no sign
of habitation or grounds was visible.

I thought I had taken a wrong direction and lost my way. The darkness
of natural as well as of sylvan dusk gathered over me: I looked round in
search of another road. There was none: all was interwoven stem, colum-
nar trunk, dense, summer foliage—no opening anywhere.

I proceeded: at last my way opened, the trees thinned a little; presently I beheld a railing, then the house—scarce, by this dim light,
distinguishable from the trees; so dank and green were its decaying walls.
Entering a portal, fastened only by a latch, I stood amidst a space of
enclosed ground, from which the wood swept away in a semicircle. There

were no flowers, no garden-beds; only a broad gravel-walk girdling a grass-plot, and this set in the heavy frame of the forest. The house presented two pointed gables in its front; the windows were latticed and narrow: the front-door was narrow too, one step led up to it. The whole looked, as the host of the Rochester Arms had said, "quite a desolate spot." It was as still as a church on a week-day: the pattering rain on the forest leaves was the only sound audible in its vicinage.

"Can there be life here?" I asked.

Yes: life of some kind there was; for I heard a movement—that narrow front-door was unclosing, and some shape was about to issue from the grange.

It opened slowly: a figure came out into the twilight and stood on the step; a man without a hat: he stretched forth his hand as if to feel whether it rained. Dusk as it was, I had recognised him—it was my master, Edward Fairfax Rochester, and no other.

I stayed my step, almost my breath, and stood to watch him—to examine him, myself unseen, and alas! to him invisible. It was a sudden meeting, and one in which rapture was kept well in check by pain. I had no difficulty in restraining my voice from exclamation, my step from hasty advance.

His form was of the same strong and stalwart contour as ever: his port was still erect, his hair was still raven-black; nor were his features altered or sunk: not in one year's space, by any sorrow, could his athletic strength be quelled, or his vigorous prime blighted. But in his countenance, I saw a change: that looked desperate and brooding—that reminded me of some wronged and fettered wild beast or bird, dangerous to approach in his sullen woe. The caged eagle, whose gold-ringed eyes cruelty has extinguished, might look as looked that sightless Samson.

And, reader, do you think I feared him in his blind ferocity?—if you do, you little know me. A soft hope blent with my sorrow that soon I should dare to drop a kiss on that brow of rock, and on those lips so sternly sealed beneath it: but not yet. I would not accost him yet.

He descended the one step, and advanced slowly and gropingly towards the grass-plat. Where was his daring stride now? Then he paused, as if he knew not which way to turn. He lifted his hand and opened his eyelids; gazed blank, and with a straining effort, on the sky, and towards the amphitheatre of trees: one saw that all to him was void darkness. He stretched his right hand (the left arm, the mutilated one, he kept hidden in his bosom); he seemed to wish by touch to gain an idea of what lay around him: he met but vacancy still; for the trees were some yards off where he stood. He relinquished the endeavour, folded his arms, and stood quiet and mute in the rain, now falling fast on his uncovered head. At this moment John approached him from some quarter.

"Will you take my arm, sir?" he said; "there is a heavy shower coming on: had you not better go in?"

"Let me alone," was the answer.

John withdrew, without having observed me. Mr. Rochester now tried to walk about: vainly,—all was too uncertain. He groped his way back to the house, and, re-entering it, closed the door.

I now drew near and knocked: John's wife opened for me. "Mary," I said, "how are you?"

She started as if she had seen a ghost: I calmed her. To her hurried "Is it really you, Miss, come at this late hour to this 'only place?" I answered by taking her hand; and then I followed her into the kitchen, where John now sat by a good fire. I explained to them, in few words, that I had heard all which had happened since I left Thornfield, and that I was come to see Mr. Rochester. I asked John to go down to the turnpike-house, where I had dismissed the chaise, and bring my trunk, which I had left there: and then, while I removed my bonnet and shawl, I questioned Mary as to whether I could be accommodated at the Manor House for the night; and finding that arrangements to that effect, though difficult, would not be impossible, I informed her I should stay. Just at this moment the parlour-bell rang.

"When you go in," said I, "tell your master that a person wishes to speak to him, but do not give my name."

"I don't think he will see you," she answered; "he refuses everybody."

When she returned, I inquired what he had said.

"You are to send in your name and your business," she replied. She then proceeded to fill a glass with water, and place it on a tray, together with candles.

"Is that what he rang for?" I asked.

"Yes: he always has candles brought in at dark, though he is blind."

"Give the tray to me, I will carry it in."

I took it from her hand: she pointed me out the parlour door. The tray shook as I held it; the water spilt from the glass; my heart struck my ribs loud and fast. Mary opened the door for me, and shut it behind me.

This parlour looked gloomy: a neglected handful of fire burnt low in the grate; and, leaning over it, with his head supported against the high, old-fashioned mantel-piece, appeared the blind tenant of the room. His old dog, Pilot, lay on one side, removed out of the way, and coiled up as if afraid of being inadvertently trodden upon. Pilot pricked up his ears when I came in; when he jumped up with a yelp and a whine, and bounded towards me: he almost knocked the tray from my hands. I set it on the table; then patted him, and said softly, "Lie down!" Mr. Rochester turned mechanically to *see* what the commotion was: but as he *saw* nothing, he returned and sighed.

I approached him with the now only half-filled glass: Pilot followed me, still excited.

"What is the matter?" he inquired.

"Down Pilot!" I again said. He checked the water on its way to his lips, and seemed to listen: he drank, and put the glass down. "This is you, Mary, is it not?"

"Mary is in the kitchen," I answered.

He put out his hand with a quick gesture, but not seeing where I stood, he did not touch me. "Who is this? Who is this?" he demanded, trying, as it seemed, to *see* with those sightless eyes—unavailing and distressing attempt! "Answer me—speak again!" he ordered, imperiously and aloud.

"Will you have a little more water, sir? I spilt half of what was in the glass," I said.

"*Who* is it? *What* is it? Who speaks?"

"Pilot knows me, and John and Mary know I am here. I came only this evening," I answered.

"Great God!—what delusion has come over me? What sweet madness has seized me?"

"No delusion—no madness: your mind, sir, is too strong for delusion, your health too sound for frenzy."

"And where is the speaker? Is it only a voice? Oh! I *cannot* see, but I must feel, or my heart will stop and my brain burst. Whatever—whoever you are—be perceptible to the touch or I cannot live!"

He groped: I arrested his wandering hand, and prisoned it in both mine.

"Her very fingers!" he cried; "her small slight fingers! If so, there must be more of her."

The muscular hand broke from my custody; my arm was seized, my shoulder—neck—waist—I was entwined and gathered to him.

"Is it Jane? *What* is it? This is her shape—this is her size——"

"And this her voice," I added. "She is here: her heart, too. God bless you, sir! I am glad to be so near you again."

"Jane Eyre!—Jane Eyre," was all he said.

"My dear master," I answered, "I am come back to you."

"In truth?—in the flesh? My living Jane"

"You touch me, sir,—you hold me, and fast enough: I am not cold like a corpse, nor vacant like air, am I?"

"My living darling! These are certainly her limbs, and these her features: but I cannot be so blest after all my misery. It is a dream: such dreams as I have had at night when I have clasped her once more to my heart, as I do now; and kissed her, as thus—and felt that she loved me, and trusted that she would not leave me."

"Which I never will, sir, from this day."

"Never will, says the vision? But I always woke and found it an empty mockery; and I was desolate and abandoned—my life dark, lonely, hopeless—my soul athirst and forbidden to drink—my heart famished and never to be fed. Gentle, soft dream, nestling in my arms now, you will fly, too; as your sisters have all fled before you: but kiss me before you go—embrace me, Jane."

"There, sir—and there!"

I pressed my lips to his once brilliant and now rayless eyes—I swept his hair from his brow, and kissed that too. He suddenly seemed to rouse himself: the conviction of the reality of all this seized him.

"It is you—is it Jane? You are come back to me then?"

"I am."

"And you do not lie dead in some ditch, under some stream? And you are not a pining outcast amongst strangers?"

"No, sir; I am an independent woman now."

"Independent! What do you mean, Jane?"

"My uncle in Madeira is dead, and he left me five thousand pounds."

"Ah, this is practical—this is real!" he cried: I should never dream that. Besides, there is that peculiar voice of hers, so animating and piquant, as well as soft: it cheers my withered heart; it puts life into it.—What Janet! Are you an independent woman? A rich woman?"

"Quite rich, sir. If you won't let me live with you, I can build a house of my own close up to your door, and you may come and sit in my parlour when you want company of an evening."

"But as you are rich, Jane, you have now, no doubt, friends who will look after you, and not suffer you to devote yourself to a blind lameter like me?"

"I told you I am independent, sir, as well as rich: I am my own mistress."

"And you will stay with me?"

"Certainly—unless you object. I will be your neighbour, your nurse, your housekeeper. I find you lonely: I will be your companion—to read to you, to walk with you, to sit with you, to wait on you, to be eyes and hands to you. Cease to look so melancholy, my dear master; you shall not be left desolate, so long as I live."

He replied not: he seemed serious—abstracted; he sighed; he half-opened his lips as if to speak: he closed them again. I felt a little embarrassed. Perhaps I had too rashly overleaped conventionalities; and he, like St. John, saw impropriety in my inconsiderateness. I had indeed made my proposal from the idea that he wished and would ask me to be his wife: an expectation, not the less certain because unexpressed, had buoyed me up, that he would claim me at once as his own. But no hint to that effect escaping him and his countenance becoming more overcast, I suddenly remembered that I might have been all wrong, and was perhaps playing the fool unwittingly; and I began gently to withdraw myself from his arms—but he eagerly snatched me closer.

"No—no—Jane; you must not go. No—I have touched you, heard you, felt the comfort of your presence—the sweetness of your consolation: I cannot give up these joys. I have little left in myself—I must have you. The world may laugh—may call me absurd, selfish—but it does not signify. My very soul demands you: it will be satisfied: or it will take deadly vengeance on its frame."

"Well, sir, I will stay with you: I have said so."

"Yes—but you understand one thing by staying with me; and I understand another. You, perhaps, could make up your mind to be about my hand and chair—to wait on me as a kind little nurse (for you have an affectionate heart and a generous spirit, which prompt you to make sacrifices for those you pity), and that ought to suffice for me no doubt. I suppose I should now entertain none but fatherly feelings for you: do you think so? Come—tell me."

"I will think what you like, sir: I am content to be only your nurse, if you think it better."

"But you cannot always be my nurse, Janet: you are young—you must marry one day."

"I don't care about being married."

"You should care, Janet: if I were what I once was, I would try to make you care—but—a sightless block!"

He relapsed again into gloom. I, on the contrary, became more cheerful, and took fresh courage: these last words gave me an insight as to where the difficulty lay; and as it was no difficulty with me, I felt quite relieved from my previous embarrassment. I resumed a livelier vein of conversation.

"It is time some one undertook to rehumanize you," said I, parting his thick and long uncut locks; "for I see you are being metamorphosed into a lion, or something of that sort. You have a 'faux air' of Nebuchadnezzar in the fields about you, that is certain: your hair reminds me of eagles' feathers; whether your nails are grown like birds' claws or not, I have not yet noticed."

"On this arm, I have neither hand nor nails," he said, drawing the mutilated limb from his breast, and showing it to me. "It is a mere stump—a ghastly sight! Don't you think so, Jane?"

"It is a pity to see it; and a pity to see your eyes—and the scar of fire on your forehead: and the worst of it is, one is in danger of loving you too well for all this; and making too much of you."

"I thought you would be revolted, Jane, when you saw my arm, and my cicatrized visage."

"Did you? Don't tell me so—lest I should say something disparaging to your judgment. Now, let me leave you an instant, to make a better fire, and have the hearth swept up. Can you tell when there is a good fire?"

"Yes; with the right eye I see a glow—a ruddy haze."

"And you see the candles?"

"Very dimly—each is a luminous cloud."

"Can you see me?"

"No, my fairy: but I am only too thankful to hear and feel you."

"When do you take supper?"

"I never take supper."

"But you shall have some to-night. I am hungry: so are you, I dare say, only you forget."

Summoning Mary, I soon had the room in more cheerful order: I prepared him, likewise, a comfortable repast. My spirits were excited, and with pleasure and ease I talked to him during supper, and for a long time after. There was no harassing restraint, no repressing of glee and vivacity with him; for with him I was at perfect ease, because I knew I suited him: all I said or did seemed either to console or revive him. Delightful consciousness! It brought to life and light my whole nature: in his presence I thoroughly lived; and he lived in mine. Blind as he was, smiles played over his face, joy dawned on his forehead: his lineaments softened and warmed.

After supper, he began to ask me many questions, of where I had been, what I had been doing, how I had found him out; but I gave him only very partial replies: it was too late to enter into particulars that night. Besides, I wished to touch no deep-thrilling chord—to open no fresh well of emotion in his heart: my sole present aim was to cheer him. Cheered, as I have said, he was: and yet but by fits. If a moment's silence broke the conversation, he would turn restless, touch me, then say, "Jane."

"You are altogether a human being, Jane, You are certain of that?"

"I conscientiously believe so, Mr. Rochester."

"Yet how, on this dark and doleful evening, could you so suddenly rise on my lone hearth? I stretched my hand to take a glass of water from a hireling, and it was given me by you: I asked a question, expecting John's wife to answer me, and your voice spoke at my ear."

"Because I had come in, in Mary's stead, with the tray."

"And there is enchantment in the very hour I am now spending with you. Who can tell what a dark, dreary, hopeless life I have dragged on for months past? Doing nothing, expecting nothing; merging night in day; feeling but the sensation of cold when I let the fire go out, of hunger when I forgot to eat: and then a ceaseless sorrow, and at times, a very delirium of desire to behold my Jane again. Yes: for her restoration I longed far more than for that of my lost sight. How can it be that Jane is with me, and says she loves me? Will she not depart as suddenly as she came? To-morrow I fear I shall find her no more."

A common-place, practical reply, out of the train of his own disturbed ideas, was, I was sure, the best and most re-assuring for him in this frame of mind. I passed my finger over his eyebrows, and remarked that they were scorched, and that I would apply something which should make them grow as broad and black as ever.

"Where is the use of doing me good in any way, beneficent spirit, when, at some fatal moment, you will again desert me—passing like a shadow, whither and how, to me unknown; and for me, remaining afterwards undiscoverable?"

"Have you a pocket-comb about you, sir?"

"What for, Jane?"

"Just to comb out this shaggy black mane. I find you rather alarming, when I examine you close at hand: you talk of my being a fairy; but I am sure, you are more like a brownie."

"Am I hideous, Jane?"

"Very, sir: you always were, you know."

"Humph! The wickedness has not been taken out of you, wherever you have sojourned."

"Yet I have been with good people; far better than you: a hundred times better people; possessed of ideas and views you never entertained in your life: quite more refined and exalted."

"Who the deuce have you been with?"

"If you twist in that way, you will make me pull the hair out of your head; and then I think you will cease to entertain doubts of my substantiality."

"Who have you been with, Jane?"

"You shall not get it out of me to-night, sir; you must wait till to-morrow: to leave my tale half-told, will, you know, be a sort of security that I shall appear at your breakfast-table to finish it. By-the-by, I must mind not to rise on your hearth with only a glass of water, then: I must bring an egg at the least, to say nothing of fried ham."

"You mocking changeling—fairy-born and human-bred! You make me feel as I have not felt these twelve months. If Saul could have had you for his David, the evil spirit would have been exorcised without the aid of the harp."

"There, sir, you are redd up and made decent. Now I'll leave you: I have been travelling these last three days, and I believe I am tired. Goodnight!"

"Just one word, Jane: were there only ladies in the house where you have been?"

I laughed and made my escape, still laughing as I ran up stairs. "A good idea!" I thought, with glee. "I see I have the means of fretting him out of his melancholy for some time to come."

Very early the next morning, I heard him up and astir, wandering from one room to another. As soon as Mary came down, I heard the question: "Is Miss Eyre here?" Then: "Which room did you put her into? Was it dry? Is she up? Go and ask if she wants anything; and when she will come down."

I came down as soon as I thought there was a prospect of breakfast. Entering the room very softly, I had a view of him before he discovered my presence. It was mournful, indeed, to witness the subjugation of that vigorous spirit to a corporeal infirmity. He sat in his chair,—still, but not at rest: expectant evidently; the lines of now habitual sadness marking his strong features. His countenance reminded one of a lamp quenched, waiting to be relit—and alas! it was not himself that could now kindle the lustre of animated expression: he was dependent on another for that office! I had meant to be gay and careless, but the powerlessness of the strong man touched my heart to the quick: still I accosted him with what vivacity I could:—

"It is a bright, sunny morning, sir," I said. "The rain is over and gone, and there is a tender shining after it: you shall have a walk soon."

I had wakened the glow: his features beamed.

"Oh, you are indeed there, my skylark! Come to me. You are not gone: not vanished? I heard one of your kind an hour ago, singing high over the wood: but its song had no music for me, any more than the rising sun had rays. All the melody of earth is concentrated in my Jane's tongue to my ear: (I am glad it is not naturally a silent one), all the sunshine I can feel is in her presence."

The water stood in my eyes to hear this avowal of his dependence: just as if a royal eagle, chained to a perch, should be forced to entreat a sparrow to become its purveyor. But I would not be lachrymose: I dashed off the salt-drops, and busied myself with preparing breakfast.

Most of the morning was spent in the open air. I led him out of the wet and wild wood into some cheerful fields: I described to him how brilliantly green they were; how the flowers and hedges looked refreshed; how sparklingly blue was the sky. I sought a seat for him in a hidden and lovely spot: a dry stump of a tree; nor did I refuse to let him, when seated, place me on his knee: why should I, when both he and I were happier near than apart? Pilot lay beside us: all was quiet. He broke out suddenly while clasping me in his arms:—

"Cruel, cruel deserter! Oh, Jane, what did I feel when I discovered you had fled from Thornfield, and when I could nowhere find you; and, after examining your apartment, ascertained that you had taken no money, nor anything which could serve as an equivalent! A pearl necklace I had given you lay untouched in its little casket; your trunks were left corded and locked as they had been prepared for the bridal tour. What could my darling do, I asked, left destitute and pennyless? And what did she do? Let me hear now."

Thus urged, I began the narrative of my experience for the last year. I softened considerably what related to the three days of wandering and starvation, because to have told him all would have been to inflict unnecessary pain: the little I did say lacerated his faithful heart deeper than I wished.

I should not have left him thus, he said, without any means of making my way: I should have told him my intention. I should have confided in him: he would never have forced me to be his mistress. Violent as he had seemed in his despair, he, in truth, loved me far too well and too tenderly to constitute himself my tyrant: he would have given me half his fortune, without demanding so much as a kiss in return, rather than I should have flung myself friendless on the wide world. I had endured, he was certain, more than I had confessed to him.

"Well, whatever my sufferings had been they were very short," I answered: and then I prodeeded to tell him how I had been received at Moor House; how I had obtained the office of schoolmistress, etc. The accession of fortune, the discovery of my relations, followed in due order.

Of course, St. John Rivers' name came in frequently in the progress of my tale. When I had done, that name was immediately taken up.

"This St. John, then, is your cousin?"

"Yes."

"You have spoken of him often: did you like him?"

"He was a very good man, sir; I could not help liking him."

"A good man? Does that men a respectable, well-conducted man of fifty? Or what does it mean?"

"St. John is only twenty-nine, sir."

" 'Jeune encore,' as the French say. Is he a person of low stature, phlegmatic, and plain? A person whose goodness consists rather in his guiltlessness of vice, than in his prowess in virtue?"

"He is untiringly active. Great and exalted deeds are what he lives to perform."

"But his brain? That is probably rather soft? He means well: but you shrug your shoulders to hear him talk?"

"He talks little, sir: what he does say is ever to the point. His brain is first rate, I should think: not impressible, but vigorous."

"Is he an able man, then?"

"Truly able."

"A thoroughly educated man?"

"St. John is an accomplished and profound scholar."

"His manners, I think, you said are not to your taste?—priggish and parsonic?"

"I never mentioned his manners; but, unless I had a very bad taste, they must suit it: they are polished, calm, and gentlemanlike."

"His appearance,—I forget what description you gave of his appearance;—a sort of raw curate, half strangled with his white neck-cloth, and stilted up on his thick-soled high-lows, eh?"

"St. John dresses well. He is a handsome man: tall, fair, with blue eyes, and a Grecian profile."

(Aside.) "Damn him!" (To me.) "Did you like him, Jane?"

"Yes, Mr. Rochester, I liked him: but you asked me that before."

I perceived, of course, the drift of my interlocutor. Jealousy had got hold of him: she stung him; but the sting was salutary: it gave him respite from the gnawing fang of melancholy. I would not, therefore, immediately charm the snake.

"Perhaps you would rather not sit any longer on my knee, Miss Eyre?" was the next somewhat unexpected observation.

"Why not, Mr. Rochester?"

"The picture you have just drawn is suggestive of a rather too overwhelming contrast. Your words have delineated very prettily a graceful Apollo: he is present to your imagination,—tall, fair, blue-eyed, and with a Grecian profile. Your eyes dwell on a Vulcan,—a real blacksmith, brown, broad-shouldered; and blind and lame into the bargain."

"I never thought of it, before; but you certainly are rather like Vulcan, sir."

"Well,—you can leave, ma'am: but before you go (and he retained me by a firmer grasp than ever), you will be pleased just to answer me a question or two." He paused.

"St. John made you schoolmistress of Morton before he knew you were his cousin?"

"Yes."

"You would often see him? He would visit the school sometimes?"

"Daily."

"He would approve of your plans, Jane? I know they would be clever, for you are a talented creature?"

"He approved of them—yes."

"He would discover many things in you he could not have expected to find? Some of your accomplishments are not ordinary."

"I don't know about that."

"You had a little cottage near the school, you say: did he ever come there to see you?"

"Now and then."

"Of an evening?"

"Once or twice."

A pause.

"How long did you reside with him and his sisters after the cousinship was discovered?"

"Five months."

"Did Rivers spend much time with the ladies of his family?"

"Yes; the back parlour was both his study and ours: he sat near the window, and we by the table."

"Did he study much?"

"A good deal."

"What?"

"Hindostanee."

"And what did you do meantime?"

"I learnt German, at first."

"Did he teach you?"

"He did not understand German."

"Did he teach you nothing?"

"A little Hindostanee."

"Rivers taught you Hindostanee?"

"Yes, sir."

"And his sisters also?"

"No."

"Only you?"

"Only me."

"Did you ask to learn?"

"No."

"He wished to teach you?"

"Yes."

A second pause.

"Why did he wish it? Of what use could Hindostanee be to you?"

"He intended me to go with him to India."

"Ah! here I reach the root of the matter. He wanted you to marry him?"

"He asked me to marry him."

"That is a fiction—an impudent invention to vex me."

"I beg your pardon, it is the literal truth: he asked me more than once, and was as stiff about urging his point as ever you could be."

"Miss Eyre, I repeat it, you can leave me. How often am I to say the same thing? Why do you remain pertinaciously perched on my knee, when I have given you notice to quit?"

"Because I am comfortable there."

"No, Jane, you are not comfortable there, because your heart is not with me: it is with this cousin—this St. John. Oh, till this moment, I thought my little Jane was all mine! I had a belief she loved me even when she left me: that was an atom of sweet in much bitter. Long as we have been parted, hot tears as I have wept over our separation, I never thought that while I was mourning her, she was loving another! But it is useless grieving. Jane, leave me: go and marry Rivers."

"Shake me off, then, sir—push me away, for I'll not leave you of my own accord."

"Jane, I ever like your tone of voice: it still renews hope, it sounds so truthful. When I hear it, it carries me back a year. I forget that you have formed a new tie. But I am not a fool—go——"

"Where must I go, sir?"

"Your own way—with the husband you have chosen."

"Who is that?"

"You know—this St. John Rivers."

"He is not my husband, nor ever will be. He does not love me: I do not love him. He loves (as he *can* love, and that is not as you love) a beautiful young lady called Rosamond. He wanted to marry me only because he thought I should make a suitable missionary's wife, which she would not have done. He is good and great, but severe; and, for me, cold as an iceberg. He is not like you, sir: I am not happy at his side, nor near him, nor with him. He has no indulgence for me—no fondness. He sees nothing attractive in me: not even youth—only a few useful mental points.— Then I must leave you, sir, to go to him?"

I shuddered involuntarily, and clung instinctively closer to my blind but beloved master. He smiled.

"What, Jane! Is this true? Is such really the state of matters between you and Rivers?"

"Absolutely, sir. Oh, you need not be jealous! I wanted to tease you a little to make you less sad: I thought anger would be better than grief. But if you wish me to love you, could you but see how much I *do* love you, you would be proud and content. All my heart is yours, sir: it belongs to you; and with you it would remain, were fate to exile the rest of me from your presence for ever."

Again, as he kissed me, painful thoughts darkened his aspect.

"My seared vision! My crippled strength!" he murmured regretfully.

I caressed, in order to soothe him. I knew of what he was thinking, and wanted to speak for him; but dared not. As he turned aside his face a minute, I saw a tear slide from under the sealed eyelid, and trickle down the manly cheek. My heart swelled.

"I am no better than the old lightning-struck chestnut tree in Thornfield orchard," he remarked, ere long. "And what right would that ruin have to bid a budding woodbine cover its decay with freshness?"

"You are no ruin, sir—no lightning-struck tree: you are green and vigorous. Plants will grow about your roots, whether you ask then or not, because they take delight in your bountiful shadow; and as they grow they will lean towards you, and wind round you, because your strength offers them so safe a prop."

Again he smiled: I gave him comfort.

"You speak of friends, Jane?" he asked.

"Yes; of friends," I answered rather hesitatingly: for I knew I meant more than friends, but could not tell what other word to employ. He helped me.

"Ah! Jane. But I want a wife."

"Do you, sir?"

"Yes: is it news to you?"

"Of course: you said nothing about it before."

"Is it unwelcome news?"

"That depends on circumstances, sir—on your choice."

"Which you shall make for me, Jane I will abide by your decision."

"Choose then, sir—*her who loves you best.*"

"I will at least choose—*her I love best.* Jane, will you marry me?"

"Yes, sir."

"A poor blind man, whom you will have to lead about by the hand?"

"Yes, sir."

"A crippled man, twenty years older than you, whom you will have to wait on?"

"Yes, sir."

"Truly, Jane?"

"Most truly, sir."

"Oh! my darling! God bless you and reward you!"

"Mr. Rochester, if ever I did a good deed in my life—if ever I thought a good thought—if ever I prayed a sincere and blameless prayer—if ever I wished a righteous wish,—I am rewarded not. To be your wife, is, for me, to be as happy as I can be on earth."

"Because you delight in sacrifice."

"Sacrifice! What do I sacrifice? Famine for food, expectation for content. To be privileged to put my arms round what I value—to press my lips to what I love—to repose on what I trust: is that to make a sacrifice? If so, then certainly I delight in sacrifice."

"And to bear with my infirmities, Jane: to overlook my deficiencies."

"Which are none, sir, to me. I love you better now, when I can really be useful to you, than I did in your state of proud independence, when you disdained every part but that of the giver and protector."

"Hitherto I have hated to be helped—to be led: henceforth, I feel, I shall hate it no more. I did not like to put my hand into a hireling's, but it is pleasant to feel it circled by Jane's little fingers. I preferred utter loneliness to the constant attendance of servants; but Jane's soft ministry will be a perpetual joy. Jane suits me: do I suit her?"

"To the finest fibre of my nature, sir."

"The case being so, we have nothing in the world to wait for: we must be married instantly." He looked and spoke with eagerness: his old impetuousity was rising.

"We must become one flesh without any delay, Jane: there is but the licence to get—then we marry."

"Mr. Rochester, I have just discovered the sun is far declined from its meridian, and Pilot is actually gone home to his dinner. Let me look at your watch."

"Fasten it into your girdle, Janet, and keep it henceforward: I have no use for it."

"It is nearly four o'clock in the afternoon, sir. Don't you feel hungry?"

"The third day from this must be our wedding-day, Jane. Never mind fine clothes and jewels, now: all that is not worth a fillip."

"The sun has dried up all the rain-drops, sir. The breeze is still: it is quite hot."

"Do you know, Jane, I have your little pearl necklace at this moment fastened round my bronze scrag under my cravat? I have worn it since the day I lost my only treasure: as a momento of her."

"We will go home through the wood: that will be the shadiest way."

He pursued his own thoughts without heeding me.

"Jane! you think me, I daresay, an irreligious dog: but my heart swells with gratitude to the beneficent God of this earth just now. He sees not as man sees, but far clearer: judges not as man judges, but far more wisely. I did wrong: I would have sullied my innocent flower—breathed guilt on its purity: the Ominpotent snatched it from me. I, in my stiff-necked rebellion, almost cursed the dispensation: instead of bending to the decree, I defied it. Divine justice pursued its course; disasters came thick on me: I was forced to pass through the valley of the shadow of death. *His* chastisements are mighty; and one smote me which has humbled me for ever. You know I was proud of my strength: but what is it now, when I must give it over to foreign guidance, as a child does its weakness? Of late, Jane—only—only of late—I began to see and acknowledge the hand of God in my doom. I began to experience remorse, repentance; the wish for reconcilement to my Maker. I began sometimes to pray: very brief prayers they were, but very sincere.

"Some days since: nay, I can number them—four; it was last Monday night, a singular mood came over me: one in which grief replaced frenzy—sorrow, sullenness. I had long the impression that since I could nowhere find you, you must be dead. Late that night—perhaps it might be between eleven and twelve o'clock—ere I retired to my dreary rest, I supplicated God, that, if it seemed good to Him, I might soon be taken from this life, and admitted to that world to come, where there was still hope of rejoining Jane.

"I was in my own room, and sitting by the window, which was open: it soothed me to feel the balmy night-air; though I could see no stars and only by a vague, luminous haze, knew the presence of a moon. I longed for thee, Janet! Oh, I longed for thee both with soul and flesh! I asked of God, at once in anguish and humility, if I had not been long enough desolate, afflicted, tormented; and might not soon taste bliss and peace once more. That I merited all I endured, I acknowledged—that I could scarcely endure more, I pleaded; and the alpha and omega of my heart's wishes broke involuntarily from my lips, in the words—'Jane! Jane! Jane!' "

"Did you speak these words aloud?"

"I did, Jane. If any listener had heard me, he would have thought me mad: I pronounced them with such frantic energy."

"And it was last Monday night: somewhere near midnight?"

"Yes; but the time is of no consequence: what followed is the strange point. You will think me superstitious—some superstition I have in my blood, and always had: nevertheless, this is true—true at least it is that I heard what I now relate.

"As I exclaimed 'Jane! Jane! Jane!' a voice—I cannot tell whence the voice came, but I know whose voice it was—replied, 'I am coming: wait for me;' and a moment after, went whispering on the wind, the words—'where are you?'

"I'll tell you, if I can, the idea, the picture these words opened to my mind: yet it is difficult to express what I want to express. Ferndean is buried, as you see, in a heavy wood, where sound falls dull, and dies unreverberating. 'Where are you?' seemed spoken amongst mountains; for I heard a hill-sent echo repeat the words. Cooler and fresher at the moment the gale seemed to visit my brow: I could have deemed that in some wild, lone scene, I and Jane were meeting. In spirit, I believe, we must have met. You no doubt were at that hour, in unconscious sleep, Jane: perhaps your soul wandered from its cell to comfort mine; for those were your accents—as certain as I live—they were yours!"

Reader, it was on Monday night—near midnight—that I too had received the mysterious summons: those were the very words by which I replied to it. I listened to Mr. Rochester's narrative; but made no disclosure in return. The coincidence struck me as too awful and inexplicable to be communicated or discussed. If I told anything, my tale would be such as must necessarily make a profound impression on the mind of my hearer; and that mind, yet from its sufferings too prone to gloom, needed not the deeper shade of the supernatural. I kept these things, then, and pondered them in my heart.

"You cannot now wonder," continued my master, "that when you rose upon me so unexpectedly last night, I had difficulty in believing you only other than a mere voice and vision: something that would melt to silence and annihilation, as the midnight whisper and mountain echo had melted before. Now, I thank God! I know it to be otherwise. Yes, I thank God!"

He put me off his knee, rose, and reverently lifting his hat from his brow, and bending his sight-less eyes to the earth, he stood in mute devotion. Only the last words of the worship were audible.

"I thank my Maker, that in the midst of judgment he has remembered mercy. I humbly entreat my Redeemer to give me strength to lead henceforth a purer life than I have done hitherto!"

Then he stretched his hand out to be led. I took that dear hand, held it a moment to my lips, then let it pass round my shoulder: being so much lower of stature than he, I served both for his prop and guide. We entered the wood, and wended homeward.

·······

Conclusion

Reader, I married him. A quiet wedding we had: he and I, the parson and clerk, were alone present. When we got back from church, I went into the kitchen of the manor-house, where Mary was cooking the dinner, and John cleaning the knives and I said:—

"Mary, I have been married to Mr. Rochester this morning." The housekeeper and her husband were both of that decent phlegmatic order of people, to whom one may at any time safely communicate a remarkable piece of news without incurring the danger of having one's ears pierced by some shrill ejaculation, and subsequently stunned by a torrent of wordy wonderment. Mary did look up, and she did stare at me: the ladle with which she was basting a pair of chickens roasting at the fire, did for some three minutes hang suspended in air; and for the same space of time John's

knives also had rest from the polishing process: but Mary, bending again
over the roast, said only—

"Have you, miss? Well, for sure!"

A short time after she pursued: "I seed you go out with the master,
but I didn't know you were gone to church to be wed;" and she basted
away. John, when I turned to him, was grinning from ear to ear.

"I told Mary how it would be," he said: "I knew what Mr. Edward"
(John was an old servant, and had known his master when he was the cadet
of the house, therefore, he often gave him his Christian name)—"I knew
what Mr. Edward would do; and I was certain he would not wait long neither: and he's done right, for aught I know. I wish you joy, miss!" and
he politely pulled his forelock.

"Thank you, John. Mr. Rochester told me to give you and Mary this."
I put into his hand a five-pound note. Without waiting to hear more, I left
the kitchen. In passing the door of that sanctum some time after, I caught
the words,—

"She'll happen do better for him nor ony o' t' grand ladies." And again,
"If she ben't one o' th' handsomest, she's noan faäl and varry good-
natured; and i' his een she's fair beautiful, onybody may see that."

I wrote to Moor House and to Cambridge immediately, to say what I
had done: fully explaining also why I had thus acted. Diana and Mary
approved the step unreservedly. Diana announced that she would just give
me time to get over the honey-moon, and then she would come and see me.

"She had better not wait till then, Jane," said Mr. Rochester, when I
red her letter to him; "if she does, she will be too late, for our honey-
moon will shine our life-long: its beams will only fade over your grave
or mine."

How St. John received the news, I don't know; he never answered the
letter in which I communicated it: yet six months after, he wrote to me;
without, however, mentioning Mr. Rochester's name, or alluding to my
marriage. His letter was calm; and, though very serious, kind. He has
maintained a regular, though not frequent correspondence ever since: he
hopes I am happy, and trusts I am not of those who live without God in
the world, and only mind earthly things.

You have not quite forgotten little Adèle, have you, reader? I had not;
I soon asked and obtained leave of Mr. Rochester, to go and see her at
the school where he placed her. Her frantic joy at beholding me again
moved me much. She looked pale and thin: she said she was not happy.
I found the rules of the establishment were too strict, its course of study
too severe, for a child of her age: I took her home with me. I meant to
become her governess once more; but I soon found this impracticable;
my time and cares were now required by another—my husband needed
them all. So I sought out a school conducted on a more indulgent system; and near enough to permit of my visiting her often, and bringing
her home sometimes. I took care she should never want for anything that
could contribute to her comfort: she soon settled in her new abode,
became very happy there, and made fair progress in her studies. As she
grew up, a sound English education corrected in a great measure her
French defects; and when she left school, I found in her a pleasing and
obliging companion: docile, good-tempered and well-principled. By her
grateful attention to me and mine, she has long since well repaid any little
kindness I ever had it in my power to offer her.

My tale draws to its close: one word respecting my experience of married life, and one brief glance at the fortunes of those whose names have most frequently recurred in this narrative, and I have done.

I have now been married ten years. I know what it is to live entirely for and with what I love best on earth. I hold myself supremely blest—blest beyond what language can express; because I am my husband's life as fully as he is mine. No woman was ever nearer to her mate than I am: ever more absolutely bone of his bone, and flesh of his flesh. I know no weariness of my Edward's society: he knows none of mine, any more than we do of the pulsation of the heart that beats in our separate bosoms; consequently, we are ever together. To be together is for us to be at once as free as in solitude, as gay as in company. We talk, I believe, all day long: to talk to each other is but a more animated and an audible thinking. All my confidence is bestowed on him, all his confidence is devoted to me; we are precisely suited in character—perfect concord is the result.

Mr. Rochester continued blind the first two years of our union: perhaps it was that circumstance that drew us so very near—that knit us so very close; for I was then his vision, as I am still his right hand. Literally, I was (what he often called me) the apple of his eye. He saw nature—he saw books through me; and never did I weary of gazing for his behalf, and of putting into words the effect of field, tree, town, river, cloud, sunbeam—of the landscape before us; of the weather round us—and impressing by sound on his ear what light could no longer stamp on his eye. Never did I weary of reading to him; never did I weary of conducting him where he wished to go: of doing for him what he wished to be done. And there was a pleasure in my services, most full, most exquisite, even though sad—because he claimed these services without painful shame or damping humiliation. He loved me so truly, that he knew no reluctance in profiting by my attendance: he felt I loved him so fondly, that to yield that attendance was to indulge my sweetest wishes.

One morning at the end of the two years, as I was writing a letter to his dictation, he came and bent over me, and said—

"Jane, have you a glittering ornament round your neck?"

I had a gold watch-chain: I answered "Yes."

"And have you a pale blue dress on?"

I had. He informed me then, that for some time he had fancied the obscurity clouding one eye was becoming less dense; and that now he was sure of it.

He and I went up to London. He had the advice of an eminent oculist; and he eventually recovered the sight of that one eye. He cannot now see very distinctly: he cannot read or write much; but he can find his way without being led by the hand: the sky is no longer a blank to him—the earth no longer a void. When his first-born was put into his arms, he could see that the boy had inherited his own eyes, as they once were—large, brilliant, and black. On that occasion, he again with a full heart, acknowledged that God had tempered judgment with mercy.

My Edward and I, then, are happy: and the more so, because those we most love are happy likewise. Diana and Mary Rivers are both married: alternately, once every year, they come to see us, and we go to see them. Diana's husband is a captain in the navy; a gallant officer, and a good man. Mary's is a clergyman: a college friend of her brother's; and, from his attainments and principles, worthy of the connection. Both Captain Fitzjames and Mr. Wharton love their wives, and are loved by them.

As to St. John Rivers, he left England: he went to India. He entered on the path he had marked for himself; he pursues it still. A more resolute, indefatigable pioneer never wrought amidst rocks and dangers. Firm, faithful, and devoted; full of energy, and zeal, and truth, he labours for his race: he clears their painful way to improvement; he hews down like a giant the prejudices of creed and caste that encumber it. He may be stern; he may be exacting; he may be ambitious yet; but his is the sterness of the warrior Greatheart, who guards his pilgrim convoy from the onslaught of Apollyon. His is the exaction of the apostle, who speaks but for Christ, when he says—"Whosoever will come after me, let him deny himself, and take up his cross and follow me." His is the ambition of the high master-spirit, which aims to fill a place in the first rank of those who are redeemed from the earth—who stand without fault before the throne of God; who share the last mighty victories of the Lamb; who are called, and chosen, and faithful.

St. John is unmarried: he never will marry now. Himself has hitherto sufficed to the toil; and the toil draws near its close: his glorious sun hastens to its setting. The last letter I received from him drew from my eyes human tears, and yet filled my heart with Divine joy: he anticipated his sure reward, his incorruptible crown. I know that a stranger's hand will write to me next, to say that the good and faithful servant has been called at length into the joy of his Lord. And why weep for this? No fear of death will darken St. John's last hour: his mind will be unclouded; his heart will be undaunted; his hope will be sure; his faith steadfast. His own words are a pledge of this:—

"My Master," he says, "has forewarned me. Daily he announces more distinctly,—'Surely I come quickly!' and hourly I more eagerly respond,— 'Amen; even so come, Lord Jesus!' "

Wuthering Heights

by
Emily Brontë

. . . .

Chapter 1

1801—I have just returned from a visit to my landlord—the solitary neighbor that I shall be troubled with. This is certainly a beautiful country! In all England I do not believe that I could have fixed on a situation so completely removed from the stir of society. A perfect misanthropist's Heaven—and Mr. Heathcliff and I are such a suitable pair to divide the desolation between us. A capital fellow! He little imagined how my heart warmed toward him when I beheld his black eyes withdraw so suspiciously under their brows as I rode up, and when his fingers sheltered themselves, with a jealous resolution, still further in his waistcoat, as I announced my name.

"Mr. Heathcliff?" I said.

A nod was the answer.

"Mr. Lockwood, your new tenant, sir—I do myself the honor of calling as soon as possible after my arrival, to express the hope that I have not inconvenienced you by my perseverance in soliciting the occupation of Thrushcross Grange: I heard yesterday you had had some thoughts—"

"Thrushcross Grange is my own, sir," he interrupted wincing, "I should not allow anyone to inconvenience me, if I could hinder it—walk in!"

The "walk in" was uttered with closed teeth, and expressed the sentiment, "Go to the Deuce!" Even the gate over which he leaned manifested no sympathizing movement to the words; and I think that circumstance determined me to accept the invitation: I felt interested in a man who seemed more exaggeratedly reserved than myself.

When he saw my horse's breast fairly pushing the barrier, he did pull out his hand to unchain it, and then sullenly preceded me up the causeway, calling as we entered the court:

"Joseph, take Mr. Lockwood's horse; and bring up some wine."

"Here we have the whole establishment of domestics, I suppose," was the reflection suggested by this compound order. "No wonder the grass grows up between the flags, and cattle are the only hedge-cutters."

Joseph was an elderly, nay, an old man, very old, perhaps, though hale and sinewy.

"The Lord help us!" he soliloquized in an undertone of peevish displeasure, while relieving me of my horse: looking, meantime, in my face so sourly, that I charitably conjectured he must have need of divine aid to digest his dinner, and his pious ejaculation had no reference to my unexpected advent.

Wuthering Heights is the name of Mr. Heathcliff's dwelling. "Wuthering" being a significant provincial adjective, descriptive of the atmospheric tumult to which its station is exposed in stormy weather. Pure, bracing ventilation they must have up there at all times, indeed: one may guess the power of the north wind blowing over the hedge, by the excessive slant of a few stunted firs at the end of the house; and by a range of gaunt thorns all stretching their limbs one way, as if craving alms of the sun. Happily, the architect had foresight to build it strong: the narrow windows are deeply set in the wall, and the corners defended with large jutting stones.

Before passing the threshold, I paused to admire a quantity of grotesque carving lavished over the front, and especially about the principal door, above which, among a wilderness of crumbling griffins and shameless little boys, I detected the date, "1500," and the name, "Hareton Earnshaw;" I would have made a few comments, and requested a short history of the place from the surly owner, but his attitude at the door appeared to demand my speedy entrance or complete departure, and I had no desire to aggravate his impatience previous to inspecting the penetralium.

One step brought us into the family sitting-room without any introductory lobby or passage: they call it here "the house" pre-eminently. It includes kitchen and parlor generally; but I believe at Wuthering Heights, the kitchen is forced to retreat altogether into another quarter; at least I distinguished a chatter of tongues and a clatter of culinary utensils deep within; and I observed no signs of roasting, boiling, or baking about the huge fire-place, nor any glitter of copper saucepans and tin cullenders on the walls. One end, indeed, reflected splendidly both light and heat from ranks of immense pewter dishes, interspersed with silver jugs and tankards, towering row after row in a vast oak dresser, to the very roof. The latter had never been underdrawn, its entire anatomy lay bare to an inquiring eye, except where a frame of wood laden with oatcakes, and clusters of legs of beef, mutton, and ham, concealed it. Above the chimney were sundry villainous old guns, and a couple of horse-pistols, and, by way of ornament, three gaudily painted canisters disposed along its ledge. The floor was of smooth, white stone; the chairs, high-backed, primitive structures, painted green; one or two heavy black ones lurking in the shade. In an arch, under the dresser, reposed a huge, liver-colored bitch pointer, surrounded by a swarm of squealing puppies; and other dogs haunted other recesses.

The apartment and furniture would have been nothing extraordinary as belonging to a homely northern farmer, with a stubborn countenance, and stalwart limbs, set out to advantage in knee-breeches and gaiters. Such an individual, seated in his arm-chair, his mug of ale frothing on the round table before him, is to be seen in any circuit of five or six miles among these hills, if you go at the right time after dinner. But Mr. Heathcliff forms a singular contrast to his abode and style of living. He is a dark-skinned gipsy in aspect, in dress and manners a gentleman; that is, as much a gentleman as many a country squire; rather slovenly, perhaps, yet not looking amiss with his negligence, because he has an erect and handsome figure; and rather morose; possibly some people might suspect him of a degree of under-bred pride. I have a sympathetic chord within that tells me it is nothing of the sort; I know, by instinct, his reserve springs from an aversion to showy displays of feeling, to manifestations of mutual kindliness. He'll love and hate, equally under cover, and esteem it a species of impertinence to be loved or hated again — No, I'm running on too fast. I bestow my own attributes over liberally on him. Mr. Heathcliff may have entirely dissimilar reasons for keeping his hand out of the way, when he meets a would-be acquaintance, to those which actuate me. Let me hope my constitution is almost peculiar; my dear mother used to say I should never have a comfortable home, and only last summer I proved myself perfectly unworthy of one.

While enjoying a month of fine weather at the sea-coast, I was thrown into the company of a most fascinating creature, a real goddess, in my eyes, as long as she took no notice of me. I "never told my love" vocally; still, if looks have language, the merest idiot might have guessed I was over head and ears; she understood me, at last, and looked a return—the sweetest of all imaginable looks—and what did I do? I confess it with shame—shrunk icily into myself, like a snail, at every glance retired colder and farther; till, finally, the poor innocent was led to doubt her own senses, and overwhelmed with confusion at her supposed mistake, persuaded her mamma to decamp.

By this curious turn of disposition, I have gained the reputation of deliberate heartlessness, how undeserved, I alone can appreciate.

I took a seat at the end of the hearthstone opposite that toward which my landlord advanced, and filled up an interval of silence by attempting to caress the canine mother, who had left her nursery, and was sneaking wolfishly to the back of my legs, her lip curled up, and her white teeth watering for a snatch.

My caress provoked a long, guttural snarl.

"You'd better let the dog alone," growled Mr. Heathcliff, in unison, checking fiercer demonstrations with a punch of his foot. "She's not accustomed to be spoiled—not kept for a pet."

Then, striding to a side-door, he shouted again, "Joseph."

Joseph mumbled indistinctly in the depths of the cellar; but gave no intimation of ascending; so his master dived down to him, leaving me *vis-à-vis* with the ruffianly bitch and a pair of grim, shaggy sheep-dogs, who shared with her a jealous guardianship over all my movements.

Not anxious to come in contact with their fangs, I sat still—but, imagining they would scarcely understand tacit insults, I unfortunately indulged in winking and making faces at the trio, and some turn of my physiognomy so irritated madam, that she suddenly broke into a fury, and leapt on my knees. I flung her back, and hastened to interpose the table between us. This proceeding roused the whole hive. Half-a-dozen four-footed fiends, of various sizes, and ages, issued from hidden dens to the common center. I felt my heels and coat laps peculiar subjects of assault; and, parrying off the larger combatants, as effectually as I could, with the poker, I was constrained to demand aloud assistance from some of the household, in re-establishing peace.

Mr. Heathcliff and his man climbed the cellar steps with vexatious phlegm. I don't think they moved one second faster than usual, though the hearth was an absolute tempest of worrying and yelping.

Happily, an inhabitant of the kitchen made more dispatch; a lusty dame, with tucked up gown, bare arms, and fire-flushed cheeks, rushed into the midst of us, flourishing a frying-pan and used that weapon, and her tongue, to such purpose, that the storm subsided magically, and she only remained, heaving like a sea after a high wind, when her master entered on the scene.

"What the devil is the matter?" he asked, eyeing me in a manner that I could ill endure after this inhospitable treatment.

"What the devil, indeed!" I muttered."The herd of possessed' swine could have had no worse spirits in them than those animals of yours, sir. You might as well leave a stranger with a brood of tigers!"

"They won't meddle with persons who touch nothing," he remarked putting the bottle before me, and restoring the displaced table. "The dogs do right to be vigilant. Take a glass of wine?"

"No, thank you."

"Not bitten, are you?"

"If I had been, I would have set my signet on the biter."

Heathcliff's countenance relaxed into a grin.

"Come, come," he said, "you are flurried, Mr. Lockwood. Here, take a little wine. Guests are so exceedingly rare in this house that I and my dogs, I am willing to own, hardly know how to receive them. Your health, sir!"

I bowed and returned the pledge; beginning to perceive that it would be foolish to sit sulking for the misbehavior of a pack of curs; besides, I felt loth to yield the fellow further amusement at my expense, since his humor took that turn.

He—probably swayed by prudential considerations of the folly of offending a good tenant—relaxed a little in the laconic style of chipping of his pronouns and auxiliary verbs; and introduced, what he supposed would be a subject of interest to me, a discourse on the advantages and disadvantages of my present place of retirement.

I found him very intelligent on the topics we touched; and, before I went home, I was encouraged so far as to volunteer another visit to-morrow.

He evidently wished no repetition of my intrusion. I shall go notwithstanding. It is astonishing how sociable I feel myself compared with him.

. . . .

Chapter 2

Yesterday afternoon set in misty and cold. I had half a mind to spend it by my study fire, instead of wading through heath and mud to Wuthering Heights.

On coming up from dinner, however, (N.B., I dine between twelve and one o'clock; the housekeeper, a matronly lady taken as a fixture along with the house, could not, or would not, comprehend my request that I might be served at five.) On mounting the stairs with this lazy intention, and stepping into the room, I saw a servant-girl on her knees, surrounded by brushes and coal-scuttles, and raising an infernal dust as she extinguished the flames with heaps of cinders. This spectacle drove me back immediately; I took my hat, and, after a four miles' walk, arrived at Heathcliff's garden gate, just in time to escape the first feathery flakes of a snow shower.

On that bleak hill-top the earth was hard with a black frost, and the air made me shiver through every limb. Being unable to remove the chain, I jumped over, and, running up the flagged causeway bordered with straggling gooseberry bushes knocked vainly for admittance till my knuckles tingled and the dogs howled.

"Wretched inmates!" I ejaculated, mentally, "you deserve perpetual isolation from your species for your churlish inhospitality. At least, I would not keep my doors barred in the daytime; I don't care—I will get in!"

So resolved, I grasped the latch and shook it vehemently. Vinegar-faced Joseph projected his head from a round window of the barn.

"Whet are ye for?" he shouted. "T' maister's dahn i' t'fowld. Goa rahnd by th'end ut'laith, if yah went tuh spake tull him."

"Is there nobody inside to open the door?" I hallooed, responsively.

"They's nobbut t' missis, and shoo'll nut oppen't an ye mak yer flaysome dins till neegth."

"Why, can not you tell her who I am, eh, Joseph?"

"Nor-ne me! Aw'll hae noa hend wi't," muttered the head, vanishing.

The snow began to drive thickly. I seized the handle to essay another trial, when a young man, without coat, and shouldering a pitchfork, appeared in the yard behind. He hailed me to follow him, and, after marching through a wash-house, and a paved area containing a coal-shed, pump, and pigeon-cote, we at length arrived in the large, warm, cheerful apartment, where I was formerly received.

It glowed delightfully in the radiance of an immense fire, compounded of coal, peat, and wood; and near the table, laid for a plentiful evening meal, I was pleased to observe the "missis," an individual whose existence I had never previously suspected.

I bowed and waited, thinking she would bid me take a seat. She looked at me, leaning back in her chair, and remained motionless and mute.

"Rough weather!" I remarked. "I'm afraid, Mrs. Heathcliff, the door must bear the consequence of your servants' leisure attendance; I had hard work to make them hear me."

She never opened her mouth. I stared—she stared also. At any rate, she kept her eyes on me in a cool, regardless manner, exceedingly embarrassing and disagreeable.

"Sit down," said the young man, gruffly. "He'll be in soon."

I obeyed, and hemmed, and called the villain Juno, who deigned, at this second interview, to move the extreme tip of her tail, in token of owning my acquaintance.

"A beautiful animal!" I commenced again. "Do you intend parting with the little ones, madam?"

"They are not mine," said the amiable hostess, more repellingly than Heathcliff himself could have replied.

"Ah, your favorites are among these!" I continued, turning to an obscure cushion full of something like cats.

"A strange choice of favorites," she observed, scornfully.

Unluckily, it was a heap of dead rabbits. I hemmed once more, and drew closer to the hearth, repeating my comment on the wildness of the evening.

"You should not have come out," she said, rising and reaching from the chimney piece two of the painted canisters.

Her position before was sheltered from the light: now, I had a distinct view of her whole figure and countenance. She was slender, and apparently scarcely past girlhood: an admirable form, and the most exquisite little face that I have ever had the pleasure of beholding: small features, very fair; flaxen ringlets, or rather golden, hanging loose on her delicate neck; and eyes—had they been agreeable in expression, they would have been irresistible—fortunately for my susceptible heart, the only sentiment they evinced hovered between scorn and a kind of desperation, singularly unnatural to be detected there.

The canisters were almost out of her reach; I made a motion to aid her; she turned upon me as a miser might turn, if any one attempted to assist him in counting his gold.

"I don't want your help," she snapped, "I can get them for myself."

"I beg your pardon," I hastened to reply.

"Were you asked to tea?" she demanded, tying an apron over her neat black frock, and standing with a spoonful of the leaf poised over the pot.

"I shall be glad to have a cup," I answered.

"Were you asked?" she repeated.

"No;" I said, half smiling. "You are the proper person to ask me."

She flung the tea back, spoon and all; and resumed her chair in a pet, her forehead corrugated, and her red under-lip pushed out like a child's ready to cry.

Meanwhile, the young man had slung on to his person a decidedly shabby upper garment, and, erecting himself before the blaze, looked down on me from the corner of his eyes, for all the world as if there were some mortal feud unavenged between us. I began to doubt whether he were a servant or not; his dress and speech were both rude, entirely devoid of the superiority observable in Mr. and Mrs. Heathcliff; his thick, brown curls were rough and uncultivated, his whiskers encroached bearishly over his cheeks, and his hands were embrowned like those of a common laborer; still his bearing was free, almost haughty; and he showed none of a domestic's assiduity in attending on the lady of the house.

In the absence of clear proofs of his condition, I deemed it best to abstain from noticing his curious conduct, and, five minutes afterward, the entrance of Heathcliff relieved me, in some measure, from my uncomfortable state.

"You see, sir, I am come, according to promise!" I exclaimed, assuming the cheerful, "and I fear I shall be weather-bound for half an hour, if you can afford me shelter during that space."

"Half an hour?" he said, shaking the white flakes from his clothes; "I wonder you should select the thick of a snow-storm to ramble about in. Do you know that you run a risk of being lost in the marshes? People familiar with these moors often miss their road on such evenings, and, I can tell you, there is no chance of a change at present."

"Perhaps I can get a guide among your lads, and he might stay at the Grange till morning—could you spare me one?"

"No, I could not."

"Oh, indeed! Well then, I must trust to my own sagacity."

"Umph."

"Are you going to mak th' tea?" demanded he of the shabby coat, shifting his ferocious gaze from me to the young lady.

"Is *he* to have any?" she asked, appealing to Heathcliff.

"Get it ready, will you?" was the answer, uttered so savagely that I started. The tone in which the words were said revealed a genuine bad nature. I no longer felt inclined to call Heathcliff a capital fellow.

When the preparations were finished, he invited me with—

"Now, sir, bring forward your chair." And we all, including the rustic youth, drew round the table, an austere silence prevailing while we discussed our meal.

I thought, if I had caused the cloud, it was my duty to make an effort to dispel it. They could not every day sit so grim and taciturn, and it was impossible, however ill-tempered they might be, that the universal scowl they wore was their every-day countenance.

"It is strange," I began, in the interval of swallowing one cup of tea and receiving another, "it is strange how custom can mold our tastes and ideas; many could not imagine the existence of happiness in a life of such complete exile from the world as you spend, Mr. Heathcliff; yet, I'll venture to say, that, surrounded by your family, and with your amiable lady as the presiding genius over your home and heart—"

"My amiable lady!" he interruped, with an almost diabolical sneer on his face. "Where is she—my amiable lady?"

"Mrs. Heathcliff, your wife, I mean."

"Well, yes—Oh! you would intimate that her spirit has taken the post of ministering angel, and guards the fortunes of Wuthering Heights, even when her body is gone. Is that it?"

Perceiving myself in a blunder, I attempted to correct it. I might have seen there was too great a disparity between the ages of the parties to make it likely that they were man and wife. One was about forty; a period of mental vigor at which men seldom cherish the delusion of being married for love, by girls: that dream is reserved for the solace of our declining years. The other did not look seventeen.

Then it flashed upon me; "the clown at my elbow, who is drinking his tea out of the basin, and eating his bread with unwashed hands, may be her husband. Heathcliff junior, of course. Here is the consequence of being buried alive: she has thrown herself away upon that boor, from sheer ignorance that better individuals existed! A sad pity—I must beware how I cause her to regret her choice."

The last reflection may seem conceited; it was not. My neighbor struck me as bordering on repulsive. I knew, through experience, that I was tolerably attractive.

"Mrs. Heathcliff is my daughter-in-law," said Heathcliff, corroborating my surmise. He turned, as he spoke, a peculiar look in her direction, a look of hatred, unless he has a most perverse set of facial muscles that will not, like those of other people, interpret the language of his soul.

"Ah, certainly—I see now; you are the favored possessor of the beneficent fairy," I remarked, turning to my neighbor.

This was worse than before; the youth grew crimson, and clenched his fist with every appearance of meditated assault. But he seemed to recollect himself, presently; and smothered the storm in a brutal curse, muttered on my behalf, which, however, I took care not to notice.

"Unhappy in your conjectures, sir!" observed my host; "we neither of us have the privilege of owning your good fairy; her mate is dead. I said she was my daughter-in-law, therefore she must have married my son."

"And this young man is—"

"Not my son, assuredly!"

Heathcliff smiled again, as if it were rather too bold a jest to attribute the paternity of that bear to him.

"My name is Hareton Earnshaw," growled the other; "and I'd counsel you to respect it!"

"I've shown no disrespect," was my reply, laughing internally at the dignity with which he announced himself.

He fixed his eye on me longer than I cared to return the stare, for fear I might be tempted either to box his ears, or render my hilarity audible. I began to feel unmistakably out of place in that pleasant family circle. The dismal spiritual atmosphere overcame, and more than neutralized, the glowing physical comforts round me; and I resolved to be cautious how I ventured under those rafters a third time.

The business of eating being concluded, and no one uttering a word of sociable conversation, I approached a window to examine the weather.

A sorrowful sight I saw; dark night coming down prematurely, and sky and hills mingled in one bitter whirl of wind and suffocating snow.

"I don't think it possible for me to get home now without a guide," I could not help exclaiming. "The roads will be buried already; and if they were bare I could scarcely distinguish a foot in advance."

"Hareton, drive those dozen sheep into the barn porch. They'll be covered if left in the fold all night; and put a plank before them," said Heathcliff.

"How must I do?" I continued, with rising irritation.

There was no reply to my question; and on looking round I saw only Joseph, bringing in a pail of porridge for the dogs, and Mrs. Heathcliff, leaning over the fire, diverting herself with burning a bundle of matches which had fallen from the chimney-piece as she restored the tea-canister to its place.

The former, when he had deposited his burden, took a critical survey of the room; and in cracked tones grated out:

"Aw woonder hagh yah can faishion tuh stand thear i'idleness un war, when all on 'ems goan aght! Bud yah're a nowt, and it's noa use talking—yah'll niver mend uh yer ill ways; bud goa raight tuh t' divil, like yer mother afore ye!"

I imagined, for a moment, that this piece of eloquence was addressed to me; and, sufficiently enraged, stepped toward the aged rascal with an intention of kicking him out of the door.

Mrs. Heathcliff, however, checked me by her answer.

"You scandalous old hypocrite!" she replied; "are you not afraid of being carried away bodily, whenever you mention the devil's name? I warn you to refrain from provoking me, or I'll ask your abduction as a special favor. Stop, look here, Joseph," she continued, taking a long, dark book from a shelf. "I'll show you how far I've progressed in the Black Art—I shall soon be competent to make a clear house of it. The red cow didn't die by chance; and your rheumatism can hardly be reckoned among providential visitations!"

"Oh, wicked, wicked!" gasped the elder, "may the Lord deliver us from evil!"

"No, reprobate! you are a castaway—be off, or I'll hurt you seriouly! I'll have you all modeled in wax and clay; and the first who passes the limits I fix, shall—I'll not say what he shall be done to—but, you'll see! Go, I'm looking at you!"

The little witch put a mock malignity into her beautiful eyes, and Joseph, trembling with sincere horror, hurried out praying and ejaculating "wicked" as he went.

I thought her conduct must be prompted by a species of dreary fun; and, now that we were alone, I endeavored to interest her in my distress.

"Mrs. Heathcliff," I said, earnestly, "you must excuse me for troubling you—I presume, because, with that face, I'm sure you cannot help being good-hearted. Do point our some landmarks by which I may know my way home—I have no more idea how to get there than you would have how to get to London!"

"Take the road you came," she answered, ensconcing herself in a chair, with a candle, and the long book open before her. "It is brief advice; but as sound as I can give."

"Then, if you hear of me being discovered dead in a bog, or a pit full of snow, your conscience won't whisper that it is partly your fault?"

"How so? I cannot escort you. They wouldn't let me go to the end of the garden-wall."

"*You*! I should be sorry to ask you to cross the threshold for my convenience on such a night," I cried. "I want you to *tell* me my way, not to *show* it; or else to persuade Mr. Heathcliff to give me a guide."

"Who? There is himself, Earnshaw, Zillah, Joseph, and I. Which would you have?"

"Are there no boys at the farm?"

"No, those are all."

"Then it follows that I am compelled to stay."

"That you may settle with your host. I have nothing to do with it."

"I hope it will be a lesson to you, to make no more rash journeys on these hills," cried Heathcliff's stern voice from the kitchen entrance. "As to staying here, I don't keep accommodations for visitors; you must share a bed with Hareton or Joseph, if you do."

"I can sleep on a chair in this room," I replied.

"No, no! A stranger is a stranger, be he rich or poor—it will not suit me to permit any one the range of the place while I am off guard!" said the unmannerly wretch.

With this insult my patience was at an end. I uttered an expression of disgust, and pushed past him into the yard, running against Earnshaw in my haste. It was so dark that I could not see the means of exit, and as I wandered round I heard another specimen of their civil behavior among each other.

At first the young man appeared about to befriend me.

"I'll go with him as far as the park," he said.

"You'll go with him to hell!" exclaimed his master, or whatever relation he bore. "And who is to look after the horses, eh?"

"A man's life is of more consequence than one evening's neglect of the horses; somebody must go," murmured Mrs. Heathcliff, more kindly than I expected.

"Not at your command!" retorted Hareton. "If you set store on him you'd better be quiet."

"Then I hope his ghost will haunt you; and I hope Mr. Heathcliff will never get another tenant, till the Grange is a ruin!" she answered, sharply.

"Hearken, hearken, shoo's cursing on em!" muttered Joseph, toward whom I had been steering.

He sat within earshot, milking the cows by the aid of a lantern, which I seized unceremoniously, and calling out that I would send it back on the morrow, rushed to the nearest postern.

"Maister, maister, he's staling t' lantern!" shouted the ancient, pursuing my retreat. "Hey, Gnasher! Hey, dog! Hey, wolf, holld him, holld him!"

On opening the little door two hairy monsters flew at my throat, bearing me down and extinguishing the light, while a mingled guffaw from Heathcliff and Hareton put the copestone on my rage and humiliation.

Fortunately the beasts seemed more bent on stretching their paws and yawning and flourishing their tails, than devouring me alive; but they would suffer no resurrection, and I was forced to lie till their malignant masters pleased to deliver me; then hatless, and trembling with wrath, I ordered the miscreants to let me out—on their peril to keep me one minute longer—with several incoherent threats of retaliation, that, in their indefinite depth of virulence, smacked of King Lear.

The vehemence of my agitation brought on a copious bleeding at the nose, and still Heathcliff laughed, and still I scolded. I don't know what would have concluded the scene, had there not been one person at hand rather more rational than myself, and more benevolent than my entertainer. This was Zillah, the stout house-wife; who at length issued forth to inquire into the nature of the uproar. She thought that some of them had been laying violent hands on me; and, not daring to attack her master, she turned her vocal artillery against the younger scoundrel.

"Well, Mr. Earnshaw," she cried, "I wonder what you'll have agait next! Are we going to murder folk on our very door-stones? I see this house will never do for me—look at t' poor lad, he's fair choking! Wisht, wisht! you mun'n't go on so—come in, and I'll cure that. There, now, hold ye still."

With these words she suddenly splashed a pint of icy water down my neck, and pulled me into the kitchen. Mr. Heathcliff followed, his accidental merriment expiring quickly in his habitual moroseness.

I was sick exceedingly, and dizzy and faint; and thus compelled, perforce, to accept lodgings under his roof. He told Zillah to give me a glass of brandy, and then passed on to the inner room, while she condoled with me on my sorry predicament, and having obeyed his orders, whereby I was somewhat revived, ushered me to bed.

. . . .

Chapter 3

While leading the way up-stairs, she recommended that I should hide the candle and not make a noise, for her master had an odd notion about the chamber she would put me in, and never let anybody lodge there willingly.

I asked the reason.

She did not know, she answered; she had lived there only a year or two, and they had so many queer goings on she could not begin to be curious.

Too stupefied to be curious myself, I fastened my door and glanced round for the bed. The whole furniture consisted of a chair, a clothes-press, and a large oak case, with squares cut out near the top, resembling coach windows.

Having approached this structure, I looked inside, and perceived it to be a singular sort of old-fashioned couch, very conveniently designed to obviate the necessity for every member of the family having a room to himself. In fact, it formed a little closet; and the ledge of a window, which it enclosed, served as a table.

I slid back the panelled sides, got in with my light, pulled them together again, and felt secure against the vigilance of Heathcliff and every one else.

The ledge, where I placed my candle, had a few mildewed books piled up in one corner, and it was covered with writing scratched on the paint. This writing, however, was nothing but a name repeated in all kinds of characters, large and small— *Catherine Earnshaw*, here and there varied to *Catherine Heathcliff*, and then again to *Catherine Linton*.

In vapid listlessness I leaned my head against the window, and continued spelling over, Catherine Earnshaw—Heathcliff—Linton, till my eyes closed; but they had not rested five minutes when a glare of white letters started from the dark, as vivid as specters— the air swarmed with Catherines; and, rousing myself to dispel the obtrusive name, I discovered my candlewick reclining on one of the antique volumes, and perfuming the place with an odor of roasted calf-skin.

I snuffed it off, and, very ill at ease under the influence of cold and lingering nausea, sat up and spread open the injured tome on my knee. It was a Testament, in lean type, and smelling dreadfully musty: a fly-leaf bore the inscription—"Catherine Earnshaw, her book," and a date some quarter of a century back.

I shut it, and took up another and another, till I had examined all. Catherine's library was select, and its state of dilapidation proved· it to have been well used, though not altogether for a legitimate purpose; scarcely one chapter had escaped a pen-and-ink commentary, at least the appearance of one, covering every morsel of blank that the printer had left.

Some were detached sentences, other parts took the form of a regular diary, scrawled in an unformed, childish hand. At the top of an extra page, quite a treasure probably when first lighted on, I was greatly amused to behold an excellent caricature of my friend Joseph, rudely yet powerfully sketched.

An immediate interest kindled within me for the unknown Catherine, and I began forthwith to decipher her faded hieroglyphics.

"An awful Sunday!" commenced the paragraph beneath. "I wish my father were back again. Hindley is a detestable substitute—his conduct to Heathcliff is atrocious—H. and I are going to rebel—we took our initiatory step this evening.

"All day had been flooding with rain; we could not go to church, so Joseph must needs get up a congregation in the garret; and, while Hindley and his wife basked down stairs before a comfortable fire, doing anything but reading their Bibles, I'll answer for it, Heathcliff, myself, and the unhappy plow-boy were commanded to take our prayer-books, and mount. We were ranged in a row on a sack of corn, groaning and shivering, and hoping that Joseph would shiver too, so that he might give us a short homily for his own sake. A vain idea! The service lasted precisely three hours, and yet my brother had the face to exclaim, when he saw us descending,

"'What, done already!'

"On Sunday evenings we used to be permitted to play, if we did not make much noise; now a mere titter is sufficient to send us into corners!

"'You forget you have a master here,' says the tyrant. 'I'll demolish the first who puts me out of temper! I insist on perfect sobriety and silence. Oh, boy! was that you? Frances, darling, pull his hair as you go by: I heard him snap his fingers.'

"Frances pulled his hair heartily, and then went and seated herself on her husband's knee; and there they were, like two babies, kissing and talking nonsense by the hour—foolish palaver that we should be ashamed of.

"We made ourselves as snug as our means allowed in the arch of the dresser. I had just fastened our pinafores together, and hung them up for a curtain, when in comes Joseph on an errand from the stables. He tears down my handiwork, boxes my ears, and croaks,

"'T' maister nobbut just buried and Sabbath nut oe'red, und t' sahnd, uh't gospel still i' yer lugs, and yah darr be laiking!— shame on ye! sit ye dahn, ill childer! they's good books eneugh if ye'll read 'em; sit ye dahn, and think uh yer sowls!'

"Saying this, he compelled us so to square our positions that we might receive, from the far-off fire, a dull ray to show us the text of the lumber he thrust upon us.

"I could not bear the employment. I took my dingy volume by the scroop and hurled it into the dog-kennel, vowing I hated a good book.

"Heathcliff kicked his to the same place.

"Then there was a hubbub!

'Maister Hindley!' shouted our chaplain. 'Maister, coom hither! Miss Cathy's riven th' back off Th' Helmet uh Salvation, un' Heathcliff's pawsed his fit untuh t' first part uh T' Brooad Way to Destruction! It's fair flaysome ut yah let 'em goa on this gait. Ech! th'owd man ud uh laced 'em properly—bud he's goan!'

"Hindley hurried up from his paradise on the hearth, and, seizing one of us by the collar and the other by the arm, hurled both into the back kitchen, where, Joseph asseverated, 'owd Nick' would fetch us as sure as we were living; and, so comforted, we each sought a separate nook to await his advent.

"I reached this book and a pot of ink from the shelf, and pushed the house-door ajar to give me light, and I have got the time on with writing for twenty minutes; but my companion is impatient, and proposes that we should appropriate the dairy-woman's cloak and have a scamper on the moors under its shelter. A pleasant suggestion—and then, if the surly old man come in, he may believe his prophecy verified—we can not be damper or colder in the rain than we are here."

. . . .

I suppose Catherine fulfilled her project, for the next sentence took up another subject; she waxed lachrymose.

"How little did I dream that Hindley would ever make me cry so!" she wrote. "My head aches till I can not keep it on the pillow; and still I can't give over. Poor Heathcliff! Hindley calls him a vagabond, and won't let him sit with us, nor eat with us any more; and he says he and I must not play together, and threatens to turn him out of the house if we break his orders.

"He has been blaming our father (how dared he?) for treating H. too liberally, and swears he will reduce him to his right place—"

. . . .

I begin to nod drowsily over the dim page; my eye wandered from manuscript to print. I saw a red ornamented title—"Seventy Times Seven, and the First of the Seventy-First. A Pious Discourse delivered by the Reverend Jabes Branderham, in the Chapel of Gimmerden Sough." And while I was, half consciously, worrying my brain to guess what Jabes Branderham, would make of his subject, I sank back in bed, and fell asleep.

Alas, for the effects of bad tea and bad temper! what else could it be that made me pass such a terrible night? I don't remember another that I can at all compare with it since I was capable of suffering.

I began to dream, almost before I ceased to be sensible of my locality. I thought it was morning; and I had set out on my way home with Joseph for a guide. The snow lay yards deep in our road; and, as we floundered on, my companion wearied me with constant reproaches that I had not brought a pilgrim's staff: telling me I could never get into the house without one, and boastfully flourishing a heavy-headed cudgel, which I understood to be so denominated.

For a moment I considered it absurd that I should need such a weapon to gain admittance into my own residence. Then a new idea flashed across me. I was not going there; we were journeying to hear the famous Jabes Branderham preach from the text— "Seventy Times Seven;" and either Joseph, the preacher, or I had committed the "First of the Seventy First," and were to be publicly exposed and excommunicated.

We came to the chapel—I have passed it really in my walks twice or thrice—it lies in a hollow between two hills—an elevated hollow near a swamp, whose peaty moisture is said to answer all the purposes of embalming on the few corpses deposited there. The roof has been kept whole hitherto, but as the clergyman's stipend is only twenty pounds per annum, and a house with two rooms, threatening speedily to determine into one, no clergyman will undertake the duties of pastor, especially as it is currently reported that his flock would rather let him starve than increase the living by one penny from their own pockets. However, in my dream, Jabes had a full and attentive congregation: and He preached—good God—what a sermon! Divided into *four hundred and ninety* parts—each fully equal to an ordinary address from the pulpit—and each discussing a separate sin! Where he searched for them, I cannot tell; he had his private manner of interpreting the phrase, and it seemed necessary the brother should sin different sins on every occasion.

They were of the most curious character—odd transgressions that I never imagined previously.

Oh, how weary I grew. How I writhed, and yawned, and nodded, and revived! How I pinched and pricked myself, and rubbed my eyes, and stood up, and sat down again, and nudged Joseph to inform me if he would *ever* have done!

I was condemned to hear all out—finally, he reached the "*First of the Seventy-First.*" At that crisis a sudden inspiration descended on me; I was moved to rise and denounce Jabes Branderham as the sinner of the sin that no Christian need pardon.

"Sir," I exclaimed, "sitting here within these four walls, at one stretch, I have endured and forgiven the four hundred and ninety heads of your discourse. Seventy times seven times have I plucked up my hat, and been about to depart — Seventy times seven times have you preposterously forced me to resume my seat. The four hundred and ninety-first is too much. Fellow martyrs, have at him! Drag him down, and crush him to atoms, that the place which knows him may know him no more!"

"*Thou art the Man!*" cried Jabes, after a solemn pause leaning over his cushion. "Seventy times seven times didst thou gapingly contort thy visage—seventy times seven did I take counsel with my soul. Lo, this is human weakness; this also may be absolved! The First of the Seventy-First is come. Brethren, execute upon him the judgment written! such honor have all His saints!"

With that concluding word, the whole assembly, exalting their pilgrim's staves , rushed round me in a body, and I, having no weapon to raise in self-defense commenced grappling with Joseph, my nearest and most ferocious assailant, for his. In the confluence of the multitude, several clubs crossed; blows aimed at me fell on other sconces. Presently the whole chapel resounded with rappings and counter-rappings. Every man's hand was against his neighbor; and Branderham, unwilling to remain idle, poured forth his zeal in a shower of loud taps on the boards of the pulpit, which responded so smartly, that, at last, to my unspeakable relief, they woke me.

And what was it that had suggested the tremendous tumult? What had played Jabes' part in the row? Merely the branch of a fir-tree that touched my lattice, as the blast wailed by, and rattled its dry cones against the panes!

I listened doubtingly an instant; detected the disturber, then turned and dozed, and dreamed again; if possible, still more disagreeably than before.

This time I remembered I was lying in the oak closet, and I heard distinctly the gusty wind, and the driving of the snow; I heard also the fir-bough repeat its teasing sound, and ascribed it to the right cause; but it annoyed me so much that I resolved to silence it, if possible; and I thought I rose and endeavored to unhasp the casement. The hook was soldered into the staple, a circumstance observed by me, when awake, but forgotten.

"I must stop it, nevertheless!" I muttered, knocking my knuckles through the glass, and stretching an arm out to seize the importunate branch: instead of which, my fingers closed on the fingers of a little, ice-cold hand!

The intense horror of nightmare came over me; I tried to draw back my arm, but the hand clung to it, and a most melancholy voice sobbed—

"Let me in—let me in!"

"Who are you?" I asked, struggling meanwhile to disengage myself.

"Catherine Linton," it replied, shiveringly (why did I think of *Linton?* I had read *Earnshaw*, twenty times for Linton), "I'm come home, I'd lost my way on the moor!"

As it spoke I discerned, obscurely, a child's face looking through the window—Terror made me cruel; and finding it useless to attempt shaking the creature off, I pulled its wrist on to the broken pane, and rubbed it to and fro till the blood ran down and soaked the bed-clothes: still it wailed, "Let me in!" and maintained its tenacious gripe, almost maddening me with fear.

"How can I?" I said at length. "Let *me* go, if you want me to let you in!"

The fingers relaxed, I snatched mine through the hole, hurriedly piled the books up in a pyramid against it, and stopped my ears to exclude the lamentable prayer.

I seemed to keep them closed above a quarter of an hour, yet the instant I listened again, there was the doleful cry moaning on.

"Begone!" I shouted, "I'll never let you in, not if you beg for twenty years!"

"It's twenty years," mourned the voice, "twenty years, I've been a waif for twenty years!"

Thereat began a feeble scratching outside, and the pile of books moved, as if thrust forward.

I tried to jump up; but could not stir a limb, and so yelled aloud, in a frenzy of fright.

To my confusion, I discovered the yell was not ideal. Hasty footsteps approached my chamber door: somebody pushed it open with a vigorous hand, and a light glimmered through the squares at the top of the bed. I sat shuddering yet, and wiping the perspiration from my forehead: the intruder appeared to hesitate, and muttered to himself.

At last he said in a half-whisper, plainly not expecting an answer,

"Is any one here?"

I considered it best to confess my presence, for I knew Heathcliff's accents, and feared he might search further if I kept quiet.

With this intention, I turned and opened the panels—I shall not soon forget the effect my action produced.

Heathcliff stood near the entrance in his shirt and trousers; with a candle dripping over his fingers, and his face as white as the wall behind him. The first creak of the oak startled him like an electric shock: the light leaped from his hold to a distance of some feet, and his agitation was so extreme that he could hardly pick it up.

"It is only your guest, sir," I called out, desirous to spare him the humiliation of exposing his cowardice further. "I had the misfortune to scream in my sleep, owing to a frightful nightmare. I'm sorry I disturbed you."

"Oh, God confound you, Mr. Lockwood! I wish you were at the——," commenced my host, setting the candle on a chair, because he found it impossible to hold it steady.

"And who showed you up to this room?" he continued, crushing his nails into his palms, and grinding his teeth to subdue the maxillary convulsions. "Who was it? I've a good mind to turn them out of the house this moment."

"It was your servant Zillah," I replied, flinging myself on the floor, and rapidly resuming my garments. "I should not care if you did, Mr. Heathcliff; she richly deserves it. I suppose that she wanted to get another proof that the place was haunted, at my expense. Well, it is—swarming with ghost and goblins. You have reason in shutting it up, I assure you. No one will thank you for a doze in such a den!"

"What do you mean?" asked Heathcliff, "and what are you doing? Lie down and finish out the night, since you *are* here; but, for Heaven's sake, don't repeat that horrid noise. Nothing could excuse it, unless you were having your throat cut."

"If the little fiend had got in at the window, she probably would have strangled me!" I returned. "I'm not going to endure the persecutions of your hospitable ancestors, again. Was not the Reverend Jabes Branderham akin to you on the mother's side? And that minx, Catherine Linton, or Earnshaw, or however she was called—she must have been a changeling—wicked little soul. She told me she had been walking the earth these twenty years: a just punishment for her mortal transgressions, I've no doubt."

Scarcely were these words uttered, when I recollected the association of Heathcliff's with Catherine's name in the book, which had completely slipped from my memory till thus awakened. I blushed at my inconsideration ; but, without showing further consciousness of the offense, I hastened to add,

"The truth is, sir, I passed the first part of the night in"—Here I stopped afresh—I was about to say "perusing those old volumes," then it would have revealed my knowledge of their written, as well as their printed contents; so correcting myself, I went on,

"In spelling over the name scratched on that window-ledge. A monotonous occupation, calculated to set me asleep, like counting, or—"

"What *can* you mean, by talking in this way to *me!*" thundered Heathcliff with savage vehemence. "How—how *dare* you, under my roof—God! he's mad to speak so!" and he struck his forehead with rage.

I did not know whether to resent this language, or pursue my explanation; but he seemed so powerfully affected that I took pity, and proceeded with my dreams; affirming I had never heard the appellation of "Catherine Linton" before, but reading it often over produced an impression which personified itself when I had no longer my imagination under control.

Heathcliff gradually fell back into the shelter of the bed, as I spoke, finally sitting down almost concealed behind it. I guessed, however, by his irregular and intercepted breathing, that he struggled to vanquish an excess of violent emotion.

Not liking to show him that I heard the conflict, I continued my toilet rather noisily, looked at my watch, and soliloquized on the length of the night:

"Not three o'clock, yet! I could have taken oath it had been six—time stagnates here—we must surely have retired to rest at eight!"

"Always at nine in winter, and always rise at four," said my host, suppressing a groan; and, as I fancied, by the motion of his shadow's arm, dashing a tear from his eyes.

"Mr. Lockwood," he added, "you may go into my room; you'll only be in the way, coming down stairs so early: and your childish outcry has sent sleep to the devil for me."

"And for me too," I replied. "I'll walk in the yard till daylight, and then I'll be off; and you need not dread a repetition of my intrusion. I am now quite cured of seeking pleasure in society, be it country or town. A sensible man ought to find sufficient company in himself."

"Delightful company!" muttered Heathcliff. "Take the candle, and go where you please—I shall join you directly. Keep out of the yard though—the dogs are unchained; and the house—Juno mounts sentinel there—and—nay, you can only ramble about the steps and passages—but away with you—I'll come in two minutes."

I obeyed, so far as to quit the chamber; when, ignorant where the narrow lobbies led, I stood still, and was witness, involuntarily, to a piece of superstition on the part of my landlord, which belied, oddly, his apparent sense.

He got upon the bed, and wrenched open the lattice, bursting, as he pulled at it, into an uncontrollable passion of tears.

"Come in! come in!" he sobbed. "Cathy, do come. Oh, do— *once* more! Oh! my heart's darling, hear me *this* time—Catherine, at last!"

The specter showed a specter's ordinary caprice; it gave no sign of being; but the snow and wind whirled wildly through, even reaching my station, and blowing out the light.

There was such anguish in the gush of grief that accompanied this raving, that my compassion made me overlook its folly, and I drew off, half angry to have listened at all, and vexed at having related my ridiculous nightmare, since it produced that agony; though *why*, was beyond my comprehension.

I descended cautiously to the lower regions; and landed in the back-kitchen, where a gleam of fire, raked compactly together enabled me to re-kindle my candle.

Nothing was stirring except a brindled gray cat, which crept from the ashes and saluted me with a querulous mew.

Two benches, shaped in sections of a circle, nearly enclosed the hearth; on one of these I stretched myself, and Grimalkin mounted the other. We were both of us nodding ere any one invaded our retreat, and then it was Joseph shuffling down a wooden ladder that vanished in the roof, through a trap, the ascent to his garret, I suppose.

He cast a sinister look at the little flame which I had enticed to play between the ribs, swept the cat from its elevation, and, bestowing himself in the vacancy, commenced the operation of stuffing a three-inch pipe with tobacco; my presence in his sanctum was evidently esteemed a piece of impudence too shameful for remark. He silently applied the tube to his lips, folded his arms, and puffed away.

I let him enjoy the luxury unannoyed; and, after sucking out the last wreath, and heaving a profound sigh, he got up and departed as solemnly as he came.

A more elastic footstep entered next, and now I opened my mouth for a "good-morning," but closed it again, the salutation unachieved; for Hareton Earnshaw was performing his orisons, *sotto voce*, in a series of curses directed against every object he touched, while he rummaged a corner for a spade or shovel to dig through the drifts. He glanced over the back of the bench, dilating his nostrils, and thought as little of exchanging civilities with me as with my companion, the cat.

I guessed by his preparations that egress was allowed, and, leaving my hard couch, made a movement to follow him. He noticed this, and thrust at an inner door with the end of his spade, intimating, by an inarticulate sound, that there was the place where I must go if I changed my locality.

It opened into the house, where the females were already astir, Zillah urging flakes of flame up the chimney with a colossal bellows, and Mrs. Heathcliff, kneeling on the hearth, reading a book by the aid of the blaze.

She held her hand interposed between the furnace-heat and her eyes, and seemed absorbed in her occupation, desisting from it only to chide the servant for covering her with sparks, or to push away a dog, now and then, that snoozled its nose over forwardly into her face.

I was surprised to see Heathcliff there also. He stood by the fire, his back toward me, just finishing a stormy scene to poor Zillah, who ever and anon interrupted her labor to pluck up the corner of her apron, and heave an indignant groan.

"And you, you worthless—" he broke out as I entered, turning to his daughter-in-law, and employing an epithet as harmless as duck, or sheep, but generally represented by a dash.

"There you are at your idle tricks again! The rest of them do earn their bread—you live on my charity! Put your trash away, and find something to do. You shall pay me for the plague of having you eternally in my sight—do you hear, damnable jade?"

"I'll put my trash away, because you can make me if I refuse," answered the young lady, closing her book, and throwing it on a chair. "But I'll not do anything , though you should swear your tongue out, except what I please!"

Heathcliff lifted his hand, and the speaker sprang to a safer distance, obviously acquainted with its weight.

Having no desire to be entertained by a cat and dog combat, I stepped forward briskly, as if eager to partake the warmth of the hearth, and innocent of any knowledge of the interrupted dispute. Each had enough decorum to suspend further hostilities; Heathcliff placed his fists out of temptation, in his pockets: Mrs. Heathcliff curled her lip, and walked to a seat far off, where she kept her word by playing the part of a statue during the remainder of my stay.

That was not long. I declined joining their breakfast, and, at the first gleam of dawn, took an opportunity of escaping into the free air, now clear, and still, and cold as impalpable ice.

My landlord hallooed for me to stop, ere I reached the bottom of the garden, and offered to accompany me across the moor. It was well he did, for the whole hill-back was one billowy, white ocean; the swells and falls not indicating corresponding rises and depressions in the ground—many pits, at least, were filled to a level, and entire ranges of mounds, the refuse of the quarries, blotted from the chart which my yesterday's walk left pictured in my mind.

I had remarked on one side of the road, at intervals of six or seven yards, a line of upright stones, continued through the whole length of the barren: these were erected and daubed with lime, on purpose to serve as guides in the dark, and also when a fall, like the present, confounded the deep swamps on either hand with the firmer path: but, excepting a dirty dot pointing up, here and there, all traces of their existence had vanished; and my companion found it necessary to warn me frequently to steer to the right, or left, when I imagined I was following correctly the windings of the road.

We exchanged little conversation, and he halted at the entrance of Thrushcross park, saying I could make no error there. Our adieus were limited to a hasty bow, and then I pushed forward, trusting to my own resources, for the porter's lodge is untenanted as yet.

The distance from the gate to the Grange is two miles: I believe I managed to make it four, what with losing myself among the trees, and sinking up to the neck in snow—a predicament which only those who have experienced it can appreciate. At any rate, whatever were my wanderings, the clock chimed twelve as I entered the house; and that gave exactly an hour for every mile of the usual way from Wuthering Heights.

My human fixture and her satellites rushed to welcome me,

exclaiming, tumultuously, they had completely given me up; everybody conjectured that I perished last night; and they were wondering how they must set about the search for my remains.

I bid them be quiet, now that they saw me returned; and, benumbed to my very heart, I dragged up-stairs, whence, after putting on dry clothes, and pacing a considerable time to and fro to restore the animal heat, I am adjourned to my study, feeble as a kitten—almost too much so to enjoy the cheerful fire and smoking coffee which the servant has prepared for my refreshment.

. . . .

Chapter 4

What vain weathercocks we are! I, who had determined to hold myself independent of all social intercourse, and thanked my stars that at length I had lighted on a spot where it was next to impracticable. I, weak wretch, after maintaining till dusk a struggle with low spirits and solitude, was finally compelled to strike my colors; and, under pretense of gaining information concerning the necessities of my establishment, I desired Mrs. Dean, when she brought in supper, to sit down while I ate it, hoping sincerely she would prove a regular gossip, and either rouse me to animation, or lull me to sleep by her talk.

"You have lived here a considerable time," I commenced; "did you not say sixteen years?"

"Eighteen, sir; I came when the mistress was married, to wait on her; after she died the master retained me for his housekeeper."

"Indeed."

There ensued a pause. She was not a gossip, I feared, unless about her own affairs, and these could hardly interest me.

However, having studied for an interval, with a fist on either knee, and a cloud of meditation over her ruddy countenance, she ejaculated,

"Ah, times are greatly changed since then!"

"Yes," I remarked, "you've seen a good many alterations, I suppose?"

"I have: and troubles too," she said.

"Oh, I'll turn the talk on my landlord's family!" I thought to myself. "A good subject to start—and that pretty girl-widow—I should like to know her history; whether she be a native of the country, or, as is more probable, an exotic that the surly indigenæ will not recognize for kin."

With this intention I asked Mrs. Dean why Heathcliff left Thrushcross Grange, and preferred living in a situation and residence so much inferior.

"Is he not rich enough to keep the estate in good order?" I inquired.

"Rich sir!" she returned. "He has nobody knows what money, and every year it increases. Yes, yes, he's rich enough to live in a finer house than this, but he's very near—close-handed; and if he had meant to flit to Thrushcross Grange, as soon as he heard of a good tenant, he could not have borne to miss the chance of getting a few hundreds more. It is strange people should be so greedy, when they are alone in the world!"

"He had a son, it seems?"

"Yes, he had one—he is dead."

"And that young lady, Mrs. Heathcliff, is his widow!"

"Yes."

"Where did she come from originally?"

"Why, sir, she is my late master's daughter; Catherine Linton was her maiden name. I nursed her, poor thing! I did wish Mr. Heathcliff would remove here, and then we might have been together again."

"What, Catherine Linton!" I exclaimed, astonished. But a minute's reflection convinced me it was not my ghostly Catherine. "Then," I continued, "my predecessor's name was Linton?"

"It was."

"And who is that Earnshaw, Hareton Earnshaw, who lives with Mr. Heathcliff? are they relations?"

"No; he is the late Mrs. Linton's nephew."

"The young lady's cousin then!"

"Yes; and her husband was her cousin also—one on the mother's—the other on the father's side—Heathcliff married Mr. Linton's sister."

"I see the house at Wuthering Heights has 'Earnshaw' carved over the front door. Are they an old family?"

"Very old, sir; and Hareton is the last of them, as our Miss Cathy is of us—I mean, of the Lintons. Have you been to Wuthering Heights?—I beg pardon for asking, but I should like to hear how she is!"

"Mrs. Heathcliff? she looked very well, and very handsome; yet, I think, not very happy."

"Oh dear, I don't wonder!" And how did you like the master?"

"A rough fellow, rather, Mrs. Dean. Is not that his character?"

"Rough as a saw-edge, and hard as whinstone! The less you meddle with him the better."

"He must have had some ups and downs in life to make his such a churl. Do you know anything of his history?"

"It's a cuckoo's, sir; I know all about it, except where he was born, and who were his parents, and how he got his money at first—and Hareton has been cast out like an unfledged dunnock—the unfortunate lad is the only one in all this parish that does not guess how he has been cheated!"

"Well, Mrs. Dean, it will be a charitable deed to tell me something of my neighbors—I feel I shall not rest, if I go to bed; so be good enough to sit down and chat an hour."

"Oh, certainly, sir! I'll just fetch a little sewing, and then I'll sit as long as you please but you've caught cold, I saw you shivering, and you must have some gruel to drive it out."

The worthy woman bustled off; and I crouched nearer the fire: my head felt hot, and the rest of me chill; moreover I was excited, almost to a pitch of foolishness, through my nerves and brain.

This caused me to feel, not uncomfortable, but rather fearful, as I am still, of serious effects from the incidents of today and yesterday.

She returned presently, bringing a smoking basin, and a basket of work, and having placed the former on the hob, drew in her seat, evidently pleased to find me so companionable.

Before I came to live here,—she commenced, waiting no further invitation to her story,—I was almost always at Wuthering Heights, because my mother had nursed Mr. Hindley Earnshaw, that was Hareton's father, and I got used to playing with the children, I ran errands too, and helped to make hay, and hung about the farm ready for anything that anybody would set me to.

One fine summer morning—it was the beginning of harvest I remember—Mr. Earnshaw, the old master, came down stairs dressed for a journey, and after he had told Joseph what was to be done during the day, he turned to Hindley, and Cathy, and me—for I sat eating my porridge with them, and he said, speaking to his son,

"Now my bonny man, I'm going to Liverpool to-day, What shall I bring you? You may choose what you like, only let it be little, for I shall walk there and back, sixty miles each way, that is a long spell!"

Hindley named a fiddle, and then he asked Miss Cathy; she was hardly six years old, but she could ride any horse in the stable, and she chose a whip.

He did not forget me, for he had a kind heart, though he was rather severe sometimes. He promised to bring me a pocketful of apples and pears, and then he kissed his children good bye, and set off.

It seemed a long while to us all, the three days of his absence, and often did little Cathy ask when he would be home; Mrs. Earnshaw expected him by supper-time on the third evening, and she put the meal off hour after hour; there were no signs of his coming, however, and at last the children got tired of running down to the gate to look; then it grew dark, she would have had them to bed, but they begged sadly to be allowed to stay up; and just about eleven o'clock, the door-latch was raised quietly, and in stept the master. He threw himself into a chair, laughing and groaning, and bid them all stand off, for he was nearly killed, he would not have such another walk for the three kingdoms.

"And at the end of it, to be flighted to death!" he said, opening his great coat, which he held bundled up in his arms, "See here, wife, I was never so beaten with anything in my life; but you must e'en take it as a gift of God, though it's as dark almost as if it came from the devil."

We crowded round, and over Miss Cathy's head I had a peep at a dirty, ragged, black-haired child, big enough both to walk and talk—indeed its face looked older than Catherine's—yet, when it was set on its feet, it only stared round, and repeated over and over again, some gibberish that nobody could understand. I was frightened, and Mrs. Earnshaw was ready to fling it out of doors; she did fly up, asked how he could fashion to bring that gipsy brat into the house, when they had their own bairns to feed and fend for? What he meant to do with it, and whether he were mad?

The master tried to explain the matter, but he was really half dead with fatigue, and all that I could make out, amongst her scolding, was a tale of his seeing it starving, and houseless, and as good as dumb, in the streets of Liverpool, where he picked it up, and inquired for its owner. Not a soul knew to whom it belonged, he said, and his money and time being both limited, he thought it better to take it home with him at once, than run into vain expenses there, because he was determined he would not leave it as he found it.

Well, the conclusion was that my mistress grumbled herself calm; and Mr. Earnshaw told me to wash it, and give it clean things, and let it sleep with the children.

Hindley and Cathy contented themselves with looking and listening till peace was restored, then both began searching their father's pockets for the presents he had promised them. The former was a boy of fourteen, but when he drew out what had been a fiddle, crushed to morsels in the great coat, he blubbered aloud; and Cathy, when she learned the master had lost her whip in attending on the stranger, showed her humor by grinning and spitting at the stupid little thing, earning for her pains a sound blow from her father, to teach her cleaner manners.

They entirely refused to have it in bed with them, or even in their room, and I had no more sense, so I put it on the landing of the stairs, hoping it might be gone on the morrow. By chance, or else attracted by hearing his voice, it crept to Mr. Earnshaw's door, and there he found it on quitting his chamber. Inquiries were made as to how it got there. I was obliged to confess, and in recompense for my cowardice and inhumanity was sent out of the house.

This was Heathcliff's first introduction to the family. On coming back a few days afterwards, for I did not consider my banishment perpetual, I found they had christened him "Heathcliff." It was the name of a son who died in childhood, and it has served him ever since both for Christian and surname.

Miss Cathy and he were now very thick; but Hindley hated him, and to say the truth I did the same, and we plagued and went on with him shamefully, for I wasn't reasonable enough to feel my injustice, and the mistress never put in a word on his behalf when she saw him wronged.

He seemed a sullen, patient child; hardened, perhaps, to ill-treatment; he would stand Hindley's blows without winking or shedding a tear, and my pinches moved him only to draw in a breath, and open his eyes as if he had hurt himself by accident, and nobody was to blame.

This endurance made old Earnshaw furious when he discoved his son persecuting the poor fatherless child, as he called him. He took to Heathcliff strangely, believing all he said (for that matter, he said precious little, and generally the truth), and petting him up far above Cathy, who was too mischievous and wayward for a favorite.

So, from the very beginning, he bred bad feeling in the house; and at Mrs. Earnshaw's death, which happened in less than two years after, the young master had learned to regard his father as an oppressor rather than a friend, and Heathcliff as a usurper of his parent's affections, and his privileges, and he grew bitter with brooding over these injuries.

I sympathized awhile, but when the children fell ill of the measles, and I had to tend to them, and take on me the cares of a woman at once, I changed my ideas. Heathcliff was dangerously sick, and while he lay at the worst he would have me constantly by his pillow; I suppose he felt I did a good deal for him, and he hadn't wit enough to guess that I was compelled to do it. However, I will say this, he was the quietest child that ever nurse watched over. The difference between him and the others forced me to be less partial; Cathy and her brother harassed me terribly, *he* was as uncomplaining as a lamb; though hardness, not gentleness, made him give little trouble.

He got through, and the doctor affirmed it was in a great measure owing to me, and praised me for my care. I was vain of his commendations, and softened toward the being by whose means I earned them, and thus Hindley lost his last ally; still I couldn't dote on Heathcliff, and I wondered often what my master saw to admire so much in the sullen boy, who never, to my recollection, repaid his indulgence by any sign of gratitude. He was not insolent to his benefactor, he was simply insensible, though knowing perfectly the hold he had on his heart, and conscious he had only to speak, and all the house would be obliged to bend to his wishes.

As an instance, I remember Mr. Earnshaw once bought a couple of colts at the parish fair, and gave the lads each one. Heathcliff took the handsomest, but it soon fell lame, and when he discovered it he said to Hindley.

"You must exchange horses with me; I don't like mine, and, if you won't, I shall tell your father of the three thrashings you've given me this week, and show him my arm, which is black to the shoulder."

Hindley put out his tongue, and cuffed him over the ears.

"You had better do it at once," he persisted, escaping to the porch (they were in the stable), "you will have to, and if I speak of these blows you'll get them again with interest."

"Off, dog!" cried Hindley, threatening him with an iron weight, used for weighing potatoes and hay.

"Throw it," he replied, standing still, "and then I'll tell how you boasted that you would turn me out of doors as soon as he died, and see whether he will not turn you out directly."

Hindley threw it hitting him on the breast and down he fell, but staggered up immediately, breathless and white, and had not I prevented it he would have gone just so to the master, and got full revenge by letting his condition plead for him, intimating who had caused it.

"Take my colt, gipsy, then!" said young Earnshaw, "and I pray that he may break your neck, take him, and be damned, you beggarly interloper! and wheedle my father out of all he has, only

afterward show him what you are, imp of Satan—and take that, I
hope he'll kick out your brains!"

Heathcliff had gone to loose the beast, and shift to his own
stall—he was passing behind it, when Hindley finished his speech
by knocking him under its feet, and without stopping to examine
whether his hopes were fulfilled, ran away as fast as he could.

I was surprised to witness how coolly the child gathered himself
up, and went on with his intention, exchanging saddles and all;
and then sitting down on a bundle of hay to overcome the qualm
which the violent blow occasioned, before he entered the house.

I persuaded him easily to let me lay the blame of his bruises on
the horse; he minded little what tale was told, since he had what
he wanted. He complained so seldom, indeed, of such stirs as
these, that I really thought him not vindictive—I was deceived,
completely, as you will hear.
       . . . .

Chapter 5

In the course of time Mr. Earnshaw began to fail. He had been
active and healthy, yet his strength left him suddenly; and when
he was confined to the chimney-corner he grew grievously irritable. A nothing vexed him, and suspected slights of his authority
nearly threw him into fits.

This was especially to be remarked if any one attempted to
impose upon, or domineer over his favorite; he was painfully
jealous lest a word should be spoken amiss to him, seeming to
have got into his head the notion that, because he liked Heathcliff,
all hated, and longed to do him a ill-turn.

It was a disadvantage to the lad, for the kinder among us did
not wish to fret the master, so we humored his partiality; and that
humoring was rich nourishment to the child's pride and black
temper. Still it became in a manner necessary; twice, or thrice,
Hindley's manifestations of scorn, while his father was near,
roused the old man to a fury. He seized his stick to strike him, and
shook with rage that he could not do it.

At last our curate (we had a curate then, who made the living
answer by teaching the little Lintons and Earnshaws, and farming
his bit of land himself), he advised that the young man should be
sent to college, and Mr. Earnshaw agreed, though with a heavy
spirit, for he said—

"Hindley was naught, and would never thrive as where he wandered."

I hoped heartily we should have peace now. It hurt me to think
the master should be made uncomfortable by his own good deed.
I fancied the discontent of age and disease arose from his family
disagreements, as he would have it that it did—really you know,
sir, it was in his sinking frame.

We might have got on tolerably, notwithstanding, but for two
people—Miss Cathy, and Joseph the servant; you saw him, I dare

say, up yonder. He was, and is yet, most likely, the wearisomest self-righteous Pharisee that ever ransacked a Bible to rake the promises to himself, and fling the curses on his neighbors. By his knack of sermonizing and pious discoursing, he contrived to make a great impression on Mr. Earnshaw, and the more feeble the master became, the more influence he gained.

He was relentless in worrying him about his soul's concerns, and about ruling his children rigidly. He encouraged him to re-gard Hindley as a reprobate; and, night after night, he regularly grumbled out a long string of tales against Heathcliff and Catherine; always minding to flatter Earnshaw's weakness by heaping the heaviest blame on the last.

Certainly, she had ways with her such as I never saw a child take up before; and she put all of us past our patience fifty times and oftener in a day: from the hour she came down stairs, till the hour she went to bed, we had not a minute's security that she wouldn't be in mischief. Her spirits were always at high-water mark, her tongue always going—singing, laughing, and plaguing everybody who would not do the same. A wild, wicked slip she was—but she had the bonniest eye, and sweetest smile, and lightest foot in the parish; and, after all, I believe she meant no harm; for, when once she made you cry in good earnest, it seldom happened that she would not keep you company; and oblige you to be quiet that you might comfort her.

She was much too fond of Heathcliff. The greatest punishment we could invent for her was to keep her separate from him; yet, she got chided more than any of us on his account.

In play, she liked exceedingly to act the little mistress; using her hands freely, and commanding her companions: she did so to me, but I would not bear slapping and ordering; and so I let her know.

Now Mr. Earnshaw did not understand jokes from his children: he had always been strict and grave with them; and Catherine, on her part, had no idea why her father should be crosser and less patient in his ailing condition, than he was in his prime.

His peevish reproofs wakened in her a naughty delight to provoke him; she was never so happy as when we were all scolding her at once, and she defying us with her bold, saucy look, and her ready words; turning Joseph's religious curses into ridicule, bait-ing me, and doing just what her father hated most; showing how her pretended insolence, which he thought real, had more power over Heathcliff than his kindness; how the boy would do *her* bidding in anything, and *his* only when it suited his own inclina-tion.

After behaving as badly as possible all day, she sometimes came fondling to make it up at night.

"Nay, Cathy," the old man would say, "I cannot love thee; thou'rt worse than thy brother. Go, say thy prayers, child, and ask God's pardon. I doubt thy mother and I must rue that we ever reared thee!"

That made her cry, at first; and then, being repulsed continually hardened her, and she laughed if I told her to say she was sorry for her faults, and beg to be forgiven.

But the hour came at last, that ended Mr. Earnshaw's troubles
on earth. He died quietly in his chair one October evening, seated
by the fire-side.

A high wind blustered round the house, and roared in the
chimney: it sounded wild and stormy, yet it was not cold, and we
were all together—I, a little removed from the hearth, busy at my
knitting, and Joseph reading his Bible near the table (for the
servants generally sat in the house then, after their work was
done). Miss Cathy had been sick, and that made her still; she
leaned against her father's knee, and Heathcliff was lying on the
floor with his head in her lap.

I remember the master, before he fell into a doze, stroking her
bonny hair—it pleased him rarely to see her gentle—and saying—

"Why canst thou not always be a good lass, Cathy?"

And she turned her face up to his, and laughed, and answered,
"Why cannot you always be a good man, father?"

But as soon as she saw him vexed again, she kissed his hand,
and said she would sing him to sleep. She began singing very low,
till his fingers dropped from hers, and his head sank on his breast.
Then I told her to hush, and not stir, for fear she should wake him.
We all kept as mute as mice a full half-hour, and should have done
longer, only Joseph, having finished his chapter, got up and said
that he must rouse the master for prayers and bed. He stepped
forward, and called him by name, and touched his shoulder, but
he would not move—so he took the candle and looked at him.

I thought there was something wrong as he set down the light;
and seizing the children each by an arm, whispered them to
"frame up-stairs, and make little din—they might pray alone that
evening—he had summut to do."

"I shall bid father good-night first," said Catherine, putting her
arms round his neck, before we could hinder her.

The poor thing discovered her loss directly—she screamed
out—

"Oh, he's dead, Heathcliff! he's dead!"

And they both set up a heart-breaking cry.

I joined my wail to theirs, loud and bitter; but Joseph asked
what we could be thinking of, to roar in that way over a saint in
Heaven.

He told me to put on my cloak and run to Gimmerton for the
doctor and the parson. I could not guess the use that either would
be of, then. However, I went, through wind and rain, and brought
one, the doctor, back with me; the other said he would come in
the morning.

Leaving Joseph to explain matters, I ran to the children's room:
their door was ajar; I saw they had never laid down, though it was
past midnight; but they were calmer, and did not need me to
console them. The little souls were comforting each other with
better thoughts than I could have hit on; no parson in the world
every pictured Heaven so beautifully as they did, in their innocent talk; and, while I sobbed and listened I could not help wishing we were all there safe together.

Chapter 6

Mr. Hindley came home to the funeral; and—a thing that amazed us, and set the neighbors gossiping right and left—he brought a wife with him

What she was, and where she was born, he never informed us; probably she had neither money nor name to recommend her, or he would scarcely have kept the union from his father.

She was not one that would have disturbed the house much on her own account. Every object she saw, the moment she crossed the threshold, appeared to delight her; and every circumstance that took place about her, except the preparing for the burial, and the presence of the mourners.

I thought she was half silly, from her behavior while that went on; she ran into her chamber, and made me come with her, though I should have been dressing the children; and there she sat shivering and clasping her hands, and asking repeatedly—

"Are they gone yet?"

Then she began describing with hysterical emotion the effect it produced on her to see black, and started, and trembled, and at last fell a weeping; and when I asked what was the matter, answered she didn't know, but she felt so afraid of dying!

I imagined her as little to die as myself. She was rather thin, but young, and fresh-complexioned, and her eyes sparkled as bright as diamonds. I did remark, to be sure, that mounting the stairs made her breathe very quick, that the least sudden noise set her all in a quiver, and that she coughed troublesomely sometimes; but I knew nothing of what these symptoms portended, and had no impulse to sympathize with her. We don't in general take to foreigners here, Mr. Lockwood, unless they take to us first.

Young Earnshaw was altered considerably in the three years of his absence. He had grown sparer, and lost his color, and spoke and dressed quite differently; and, on the very day of his return, he told Joseph and me we must thenceforth quarter ourselves in the back-kitchen, and leave the house for him. Indeed, he would have carpeted and papered a small spare room for a parlor; but his wife expressed such pleasure at the white floor and huge glowing fireplace, at the pewter dishes and delf-case, and dog kennel, and the wide space there was to move about in, where they usually sat, that he thought it unnecessary to her comfort, and so dropped the intention.

She expressed pleasure, too, at finding a sister among her new acquaintance, and she prattled to Catherine, and kissed her, and ran about with her, and gave her quantities of presents, at the beginning. Her affection tired very soon, however, and when she grew peevish, Hindley became tyrannical. A few words from her, evincing a dislike to Heathcliff, were enough to rouse in him all his old hatred of the boy. He drove him from their company to the servants, deprived him of the instructions of the curate, and insisted that he should labor out of doors instead, compelling him to do so, as hard as any other lad on the farm.

He bore his degradation pretty well at first, because Cathy taught him what she learned, and worked or played with him in the fields. They both promised fair to grow up as rude as savages, the young master being entirely negligent how they behaved, and what they did, so they kept clear of him. He would not even have seen after their going to church on Sundays, only Joseph and the curate reprimanded his carelessness when they absented themselves, and that reminded him to order Heathcliff a flogging, and Catherine a fast from dinner or supper.

But it was one of their chief amusements to run away to the moors in the morning and remain there all day, and the after-punishment grew a mere thing to laugh at. The curate might set as many chapters as he pleased for Catherine to get by heart, and Joseph might thrash Heathcliff till his arm ached; they forgot everything the minute they were together again, at least the minute they had contrived some naughty plan of revenge; and many a time I've cried to myself to watch them growing more reckless daily, and I not daring to speak a syllable, for fear of losing the small power I still retained over the unfriended creatures.

One Sunday evening, it chanced that they were banished from the sitting-room, for making a noise, or a light offense of the kind, and when I went to call them to supper, I could discover them nowhere.

We searched the house, above and below, and the yard, and stables—they were invisible; and at last, Hindley, in a passion, told us to bolt the doors, and swore nobody should let them in that night.

The household went to bed; and I, too anxious to lie down, opened my lattice, and put my head out to hearken, though it rained, determined to admit them, in spite of the prohibition, should they return.

In a while, I distinguished steps coming up the road, and the light of a lantern glimmered through the gate.

I threw a shawl over my head, and ran to prevent them from waking Mr. Earnshaw by knocking. There was Heathcliff by himself; it gave me a start to see him alone.

"Where is Miss Catherine?" I cried, hurriedly. "No accident, I hope?"

"At Thrushcross Grange," he answered; "and I would have been there too, but they had not the manners to ask me to stay."

"Well, you will catch it!" I said; "you'll never be content till you're sent about your business. What in the world led you wandering to Thrushcross Grange?"

"Let me get off my wet clothes, and I'll tell you all about it, Nelly," he replied.

I bid him beware of rousing the master, and while he undressed, and I waited to put out the candle, he continued—

"Cathy and I escaped from the wash-house to have a ramble at liberty, and, getting a glimpse of the Grange lights, we thought we would just go and see whether the Lintons passed their Sunday evenings standing shivering in corners, while their father, and mother sat eating and drinking, and singing and laughing, and burning their eyes out before the fire. Do you think they do? Or reading sermons, and being catechised by their man-servant, and set to learn a column of Scripture names, if they don't answer properly?"

"Probably not," I responded. "They are good children, no doubt, and don't deserve the treatment you receive for your bad conduct."

"Don't you cant, Nelly," he said, "nonsense! We ran from the top of the Heights to the park, without stopping—Catherine completely beaten in the race, because she was barefoot. You'll have to seek for her shoes in the bog tomorrow. We crept through a broken hedge, groped our way up the path, and planted ourselves on a flower-pot under the drawing-room window. The light came from thence; they had not put up the shutters, and the curtains were only half closed. Both of us were able to look in, by standing on the basement and clinging to the ledge, and we saw—ah! it was beautiful—a splendid place carpeted with crimson, and crimson-covered chairs and tables, and a pure white ceiling bordered by gold, a shower of glass-drops hanging in silver chains from the center, and shimmering with little soft tapers. Old Mr. and Mrs. Linton were not there. Edgar and his sister had it entirely to themselves; shouldn't they have been happy? We should have thought ourselves in heaven! And now, guess what your good children were doing? Isabella—I believe she is eleven, a year younger than Cathy—lay screaming at the farther end of the room, shrieking as if witches were running red-hot needles into her. Edgar stood on the hearth weeping silently, and in the middle of the table sat a little dog shaking its paw and yelping, which, from their mutual accusations, we understood they had nearly pulled in two between them. The idiots! That was their pleasure! to quarrel who should hold a heap of warm hair; and each begin to cry because both, after struggling to get it, refused to take it. We laughed outright at the petted things, we did despise them! When would you catch me wishing to have what Catherine wanted? or find us by ourselves, seeking entertainment in yelling, and sobbing, and rolling on the ground, divided by the whole room? I'd not exchange, for a thousand lives, my condition here, for Edgar Linton's at Thrushcross Grange—not if I might have the privilege of flinging Joseph off the highest gable, and painting the house-front with Hindley's blood!"

"Hush, hush!" I interrupted. "Still you have not told me, Heathcliff, how Catherine is left behind?"

"I told you we laughed," he answered. "The Lintons heard us; and with one accord they shot like arrows to the door. There was silence, and then a cry, "Oh, mamma, mamma! Oh, papa! Oh, mamma, come here. Oh, papa, Oh!" They really did howl out something in that way. We made frightful noises to terrify them still more, and then we dropped off the ledge, because somebody was drawing the bars, and we felt we had better flee. I had Cathy by the hand, and was urging her on, when all at once she fell down.

"'Run, Heathcliff, run!' she whispered; 'they have let the bull-dog loose, and he holds me!'

"The devil had seized her ankle, Nelly; I heard his abominable snorting. She did not yell out—no! She would have scorned to do it, if she had been spitted on the horns of a mad cow. I did, though; I vociferated curses enough to annihilate any fiend in Christendom; and I got a stone and thrust it between his jaws, and tried with all my might to cram it down his throat. A beast of a servant came up with a lantern, at last, shouting—

"'Keep fast, Skulker, keep fast!'

"He changed his note, however, when he saw Skulker's game. The dog was throttled off—his huge, purple tongue hanging half a foot out of his mouth, and his pendant lips streaming with bloody slaver.

"The man took Cathy up—she was sick; not from fear, I'm certain, but from pain. He carried her in; I followed, grumbling execrations and vengeance.

"'What prey, Robert?' hollooed Linton from the entrance.

"'Skulker has caught a little girl, sir,' he replied, 'and there's a lad here,' he added, making a clutch at me, 'who looks an out-and-outer! Very like, the robbers were for putting them through the window, to open the doors to the gang, after all were asleep, that they might murder us at their ease. Hold your tongue, you foul-mouthed thief, you! you shall go to the gallows for this. Mr. Linton, sir, don't lay by your gun!'

"'No, no, Robert!' said the old fool. 'The rascals knew that yesterday was my rent day; they thought to have me cleverly. Come in; I'll furnish them a reception. There, John, fasten the chain. Give Skulker some water, Jenny. To beard a magistrate in his stronghold, and on the Sabbath, too! where will their inso-lence stop? Oh, my dear Mary, look here! Don't be afraid, it is but a boy—yet, the villain scowls so plainly in his face, would it not be a kindness to the country to hang him at once, before he shows his nature in acts, as well as features?'

"He pulled me under the chandelier, and Mrs. Linton placed her spectacles on her nose and raised her hands in horror. The cow-ardly children crept nearer, also, Isabella lisping—

"'Frightful thing! Put him in the cellar, papa. He's exactly like the son of the fortune-teller, that stole my tame pheasant. Isn't he, Edgar?'

"While they examined me, Cathy came round; she heard the last speech, and laughed. Edgar Linton, after an inquisitive stare, collected sufficient wit to recognize her. They see us at church, you know, though we seldom meet them elsewhere."

"'That's Miss Earnshaw!' he whispered to his mother, 'and look how Skulker has bitten her—how her foot bleeds!'

"'Miss Earnshaw? Nonsense!' cried the dame, 'Miss Earnshaw scouring the country with a gipsy! And yet, my dear, the child is in mourning—surely it is—and she may be lamed for life!'

"'What culpable carelessness in her brother!' exclaimed Mr.

Linton, turning from me to Catherine. 'I've understood from
Shielders (that was the curate, sir) that he lets her grow up in
absolute heathenism. But who is this? Where did she pick up this
companion? Oho! I declare he is the strange acquisition my late
neighbor made in his journey to Liverpool—a little Lascar, or an
American or Spanish castaway.'

"'A wicked boy, at all events,' remarked the old lady, 'and quite
unfit for a decent house! Did you notice his language,Linton? I'm
shocked that my children should have heard it.'

"I recommenced cursing—don't be angry, Nelly—and so
Robert was ordered to take me off. I refused to go without Cathy;
he dragged me into the garden, pushed the lantern into my hand,
assured me that Mr. Earnshaw should be informed of my behavior, and bidding me march directly, secured the door again.

"The curtains were still looped up at one corner, and I resumed
my station as spy, because, if Catherine had wished to return, I
intended shattering their great glass panes to a million fragments,
unless they let her out.

"She sat on the sofa quietly, Mrs. Linton took off the gray cloak
of the dairy maid which we had borrowed for our excursion—
shaking her head, and expostulating with her, I suppose; she was a
young lady, and they made a distinction between her treatment
and mine. Then the woman servant brought a basin of warm
water, and washed her feet, and Mr. Linton mixed a tumbler of
negus, and Isabella emptied a plateful of cakes into her lap, and
Edgar stood gaping at a distance. Afterward, they dried and
combed her beautiful hair, and gave her a pair of enormous slippers, and wheeled her to the fire; and I left her, as merry as she
could be, dividing her food between the little dog and Skulker,
whose nose she pinched as he ate, and kindling a spark of spirit in
the vacant blue eyes of the Lintons—a dim reflection from her
own enchanting face—I saw they were full of stupid admiration;
she is so immeasurably superior to them—to every body on
earth; is she not, Nelly?"

"There will more come of this business than you reckon on," I
answered, covering him up and extinguishing the light; "You are
incurable Heathcliff, and Mr. Hindley will have to proceed to
extremities, see if he won't."

My words came truer than I desired. The luckless adventure
made Earnshaw furious; and then Mr. Linton, to mend matters,
paid us a visit himself on the morrow, and read the young master
such a lecture on the road he guided his family, that he was stirred
to look about him in earnest.

Heathcliff received no flogging, but he was told that the first
word he spoke to Miss Catherine should ensure a dismissal and
Mrs. Earnshaw undertook to keep her sister-in-law in due restraint when she returned home, employing art, not force—with
force she would have found it impossible.

....

Chapter 7

Cathy stayed at Thrushcross Grange five weeks, till Christmas.
By that time her ankle was thoroughly cured, and her manners
much improved. The mistress visited her often, in the interval,
and commenced her plan of reform, by trying to raise her self-
respect with fine clothes, and flattery, which she took readily; so
that, instead of a wild, hatless little savage jumping into the house,
and rushing to squeeze us all breathless, there lighted from a
handsome black pony a very dignified person with brown ringlets
falling from the cover of a feathered beaver, and a long cloth habit
which she was obliged to hold up with both hands that she might
sail in.

Hindley lifted her from her horse, exclaiming, delightedly,
"Why, Cathy, you are quite a beauty! I should scarcely have
known you—you look like a lady now—Isabella Linton is not to
be compared with her, is she, Frances?"

"Isabella has not her natural advantages," replied his wife, "but
she must mind and not grow wild again here. Ellen help Miss
Catherine off with her things—stay, dear, you will disarrange your
curls—let me untie your hat."

I removed the habit, and there shone forth beneath a grand
plaid silk frock white trousers and burnished shoes; and, while
her eyes sparkled joyfully when the dogs came bounding up to
welcome her, she dare hardly touch them lest they should fawn
upon her splendid garments.

She kissed me gently, I was all flour making and Christmas
cake, and it would not have done to give me a hug; and, then, she
looked round for Heathcliff. Mr. and Mrs. Earnshaw watched
anxiously their meeting, thinking it would enable them to judge,
in some measure, what grounds they had for hoping to succeed in
separating the two friends.

Heathcliff was hard to discover, at first. If he were careless and
uncared for, before Catherine's absence, he had been ten times
more so since.

Nobody but I even did him the kindness to call him a dirty boy,
and bid him wash himself, once a week; and children of his age
seldom have a natural pleasure in soap and water. Therefore, not
to mention his clothes, which had seen three months' service, in
mire and dust, and his thick uncombed hair, the surface of his
face and hands was dismally beclouded. He might well skulk
behind the settle, on beholding such a bright, graceful damsel
enter the house, instead of a rough-headed counterpart to himself,
as he expected.

"Is Heathcliff not here?" she demanded, pulling off her gloves,
and displaying fingers wonderfully whitened with doing nothing,
and staying in doors.

"Heathcliff, you may come forward," cried Mr. Hindley enjoying his discomfiture, and gratified to see what a forbidding young blackguard he would be compelled to present himself. "You may come and wish Miss Catherine welcome, like the other servants."

Cathy, catching a glimpse of her friend in his concealment, flew to embrace him, she bestowed seven or eight kisses on his cheek within the second, and then stopped and, drawing back, burst into a laugh, exclaiming,

"Why, how very black and cross you look! and how—how funny and grim! But that's because I'm used to Edgar and Isabella Linton. Well, Heathcliff, have you forgotten me?"

She had some reason to put the question, for shame and pride threw double gloom over his countenance, and kept him immovable.

"Shake hands, Heathcliff," said Mr. Earnshaw, condescendingly; "once in a way, that is permitted."

"I shall not!" replied the boy, finding his tongue at last, "I shall not stand to be laughed at, I shall not bear it!"

And he would have broken from the circle, but Miss Cathy seized him again.

"I did not mean to laugh at you," she said, " I could not hinder myself, Heathcliff; shake hands, at least! What are you sulky for? It was only that you looked odd. If you wash your face and brush your hair it will be all right. But you are so dirty!"

She gazed concernedly at the dusky fingers she held in her own, and also at her dress, which she feared had gained no embellishment from its contact with his.

"You needn't have touched me!" he answered, following her eye, and snatching away his hand. "I shall be as dirty as I please, and I like to be dirty, and I will be dirty."

With that he dashed head foremost out of the room, amid the merriment of the master and mistress, and to the serious disturbance of Catherine, who could not comprehend how her remarks should have produced such an exhibition of bad temper.

After playing lady's maid to the new comer, and putting my cakes in the oven, and making the house and kitchen cheerful with great fires befitting Christmas eve, I prepared to sit down and amuse myself by singing carols, all alone; regardless of Joseph's affirmations that he considered the merry tunes I chose as next door to songs.

He had retired to private prayer in his chamber, and Mr. and Mrs. Earnshaw were engaging Missy's attention by sundry gay trifles bought for her to present to the little Lintons, as an acknowledgment of their kindness.

They had invited them to spend the morrow at Wuthering Heights, and the invitation had been accepted on one condition: Mrs. Linton begged that her darlings might be kept carefully apart from that "naughty, swearing boy."

Under these circumstances I remained solitary. I smelled the rich scent of the heating spices, and admired the shining kitchen utensils, the polished clock decked in holly, the silver mugs ranged on a tray ready to be filled with mulled ale for supper, and, above all, the speckless purity of my particular care—the scoured and well-swept floor.

I gave due inward applause to every object, and then I remembered how old Earnshaw used to come in when all was tidied, and call me a cant lass, and slip a shilling into my hand as a Christmas-box; and from that I went on to think of his fondness for Heathcliff, and his dread lest he should suffer neglect after death had removed him; and that naturally led me to consider the poor lad's situation now, and from singing I changed my mind to crying. It struck me soon, however, there would be more sense in endeavoring to repair some of his wrongs than shedding tears over them. I got up and walked into the court to seek him.

He was not far. I found him smoothing the glossy coat of the new pony in the stable, and feeding the other beasts, according to custom.

"Make haste, Heathcliff," I said, "the kitchen is so comfortable, and Joseph is up-stairs. Make haste, and let me dress you smart before Miss Cathy comes out, and then you can sit together, with the whole hearth to yourselves, and have a long chatter till bedtime."

He proceeded with his task, and never turned his head toward me.

"Come—are you coming?" I continued. "There's a little cake for each of you, nearly enough; and you'll need half an hour's donning."

I waited five minutes; but getting no answer, then left him. Catherine supped with her brother and sister-in-law; Joseph and I joined at an unsociable meal, seasoned with reproofs on one side and sauciness on the other. His cake and cheese remained on the table all night for the fairies. He managed to continue work till nine o'clock, and then marched dumb and dour to his chamber.

Cathy sat up late, having a world of things to order for the reception of her new friends: she came into the kitchen once to speak to her old one, but he was gone, and she only staid to ask what was the matter with him, and then went back.

In the morning he rose early; and, as it was a holiday, carried his ill-humor into the moors, not reappearing till the family were departed for church. Fasting and reflection seemed to have brought him to a better spirit. He hung about me for a while, and having screwed up his courage, exclaimed abruptly,

"Nelly, make me decent: I'm going to be good."

"High time, Heathcliff," I said; "you *have* grieved Catherine; she's sorry she ever came home, I dare say. It looks as if you envied her because she is more thought of than you."

The notion of *envying* Catherine was incomprehensible to him; but the notion of grieving her he understood clearly enough.

"Did she say she was grieved?" he inquired, looking very serious.

"She cried when I told her you were off again this morning."

"Well *I* cried last night," he returned, "and I had more reason to cry than she."

"Yes, you had the reason of going to bed with a proud heart and an empty stomach," said I. "Proud people breed sad sorrows for themselves. But if you be ashamed of your touchiness, you must ask pardon, mind, when she comes in. You must go up and offer to kiss her, and say—you know best what to say, only do it heartily, and not as if you thought her converted into a stranger by her grand dress. And now, though I have dinner to get ready, I'll steal time to arrange you so that Edgar Linton shall look quite a doll beside you, and that he does. You are younger, and yet I'll be bound you are taller and twice as broad across the shoulders: you could knock him down in a twinkling—don't you feel that you could?"

Heathcliff's face brightened a moment, then it was overcast afresh, and he sighed.

"But, Nelly, if I knocked him down twenty times, that wouldn't make him less handsome or me more so. I wish I had light hair and a fair skin, and was dressed, and behaved as well, and had a chance of being as rich as he will be!"

"And cried for mamma at every turn," I added, "and trembled if a country lad heaved his fist against you, and sat at home all day for a shower of rain. O, Heathcliff, you are showing a poor spirit! Come to the glass, and I'll let you see what you should wish. Do you mark those two lines between your eyes, and those thick brows, that, instead of rising arched, sink in the middle; and that couple of black fiends, so deeply buried, who never open their windows boldly, but lurk glinted under them, like devil's spies? Wish and learn to smooth away the surly wrinkles, to raise your lids frankly, and change the fiends to confident, innocent angels, suspecting and doubting nothing, and always seeing friends where they are not sure of foes. Don't get the expression of a vicious cur that appears to know the kicks it gets are its desert, and yet hates all the world, as well as the kicker, for what it suffers."

"In other words, I must wish for Edgar Linton's great blue eyes and even forehead," he replied. "I do, and that won't help me to them."

"A good heart will help you to a bonny face, my lad," I continued, "if you were a regular black, and a bad one will turn the bonniest into something worse than ugly. And now that we've done washing, and combing, and sulking, tell me whether you don't think yourself rather handsome? I'll tell you, I do. You're fit for a prince in disguise. Who knows but your father was Emperor of China and your mother an Indian queen, each of them able to buy up, with one week's income, Wuthering Heights and Thrushcross Grange together? And you were kidnapped by wicked sailors, and brought to England. Were I in your place, I would frame high notions of my birth, and the thoughts of what I was should give me courage and dignity to support the oppressions of a little farmer!"

So I chatted on; and Heathcliff gradually lost his frown, and began to look quite pleasant, when, all at once, our conversation was interrupted by a rumbling sound moving up the road and entering the court. He ran to the window and I to the door, just in time to behold the two Lintons descend from the family carriage,

smothered in cloaks and furs, and the Earnshaws dismount from
their horses: they often rode to church in winter. Catherine took a
hand of each of the children, and brought them into the house
and set them before the fire, which quickly put color into their
white faces.

I urged my companion to hasten now, and show his amiable
humor, and he willingly obeyed; but ill luck would have it that, as
he opened the door leading from the kitchen on one side, Hindley
opened it on the other. They met; and the master, irritated at
seeing him clean and cheerful, or perhaps eager to keep his promise to Mrs. Linton, shoved him back with a sudden thrust, and
angrily bade Joseph "keep the fellow out of the room—send him
into the garret till dinner is over. He'll be cramming his fingers in
the tarts, and stealing the fruit, if left alone with them a minute."

"Nay, Sir," I could not avoid answering, "he'll touch nothing,
not he—and, I suppose, he must have his share of the dainties as
well as we."

"He shall have his share of my hand, if I catch him down stairs
again till dark," cried Hindley. "Begone, you vagabond! What!
you are attempting the coxcomb, are you? Wait till I get hold of
those elegant locks—see if I won't pull them a bit longer!"

"They are long enough already," observed Master Linton, peeping from the door-way, "I wonder they don't make his head ache.
It's like a colt's mane over his eyes!"

He ventured this remark without any intention to insult; but
Heathcliff's violent nature was not prepared to endure the appearance of impertinence from one whom he seemed to hate,
even then, as a rival. He seized a tureen of hot apple-sauce, the
first thing that came over his gripe, and dashed it full against the
speaker's face and neck—who instantly commenced a lament
that brought Isabella and Catherine to the place.

Mr. Earnshaw snatched up the culprit directly, and conveyed
him to his chamber, where, doubtless, he administered a rough
remedy to cool the fit of passion, for he reappeared red and
breathless. I got the dishcloth, and, rather spitefully, scrubbed
Edgar's nose and mouth, affirming it served him right for meddling. His sister began weeping to go home, and Cathy stood by
confounded, blushing for all.

"You should not have spoken to him!" she expostulated with
Master Linton. "He was in a bad temper, and now you've spoiled
your visit, and he'll be flogged—I hate him to be flogged! I can't
eat my dinner. Why did you speak to him, Edgar?"

"I didn't," sobbed the youth, escaping from my hands, and
finished the remainder of the purification with his cambric
pocket-handkerchief. "I promised mamma that I wouldn't say
one word to him, and I didn't!"

"Well, don't cry!" replied Catherine contemptuously. "You're
not killed—don't make more mischief—my brother is coming—
be quiet! Give over, Isabella! Has any body hurt *you*?"

"There, there, children—to your seats!" cried Hindley, bustling
in. "That brute of a lad has warmed me nicely. Next time, Master

Edgar, take the law into your own fists—it will give you an appetite!"

The little party recovered its equanimity at the sight of the fragrant feast. They were hungry, after their ride, and easily consoled, since no real harm had befallen them.

Mr. Earnshaw carved bountiful platefuls; and the mistress made them merry with lively talk. I waited behind her chair, and was pained to behold Catherine, with dry eyes and an indifferent air, commence cutting up the wing of a goose before her.

"An unfeeling child," I thought to myself, "how lightly she dismisses her old playmate's troubles. I could not have imagined her to be so selfish."

She lifted a mouthful to her lips; then, she set it down again; her cheeks flushed, and the tears gushed over them. She slipped her fork to the floor, and hastily dived under the cloth to conceal her emotion. I did not call her unfeeling long, for I perceived she was in purgatory throughout the day, and wearying to find an opportunity of getting by herself, or paying a visit to Heathcliff, who had been locked up by the master, as I discovered on endeavoring to introduce to him a private mess of victuals.

In the evening we had a dance. Cathy begged that he might be liberated then, as Isabella Linton had no partner: her entreaties were vain, and I was appointed to supply the deficiency.

We got rid of all gloom in the excitement of the exercise, and our pleasure was increased by the arrival of the Gimmerton band, mustering fifteen strong; a trumpet, a trombone, clarionets, bassoons, French horns, and a bass viol, besides singers. They go the rounds of all the respectable houses, and receive contributions every Christmas, and we esteemed it a first-rate treat to hear them.

After the usual carols had been sung, we set them to songs and glees. Mrs. Earnshaw loved the music, and so they gave us plenty.

Catherine loved it too; but she said it sounded sweetest at the top of the steps, and she went up in the dark: I followed. They shut the house door below, never noting our absence, it was so full of people. She made no stay at the stair's head, but mounted farther to the garret where Heathcliff was confined; and called him. He stubbornly declined answering for a while—she persevered, and finally persuaded him to hold communion with her through the boards.

I let the poor things converse unmolested, till I supposed the songs were going to cease, and the singers to get some refreshment: then I clambered up the ladder to warn her.

Instead of finding her outside, I heard her voice within. The little monkey had crept by the skylight of one garret, along the roof, into the skylight of the other, and it was with the utmost difficulty I could coax her out again.

When she did come, Heathcliff came with her; and she insisted that I should take him into the kitchen, as my fellow-servant had gone to a neighbor's to be removed from the sound of our "devil's psalmody," as it pleased him to call it.

I told them I intended by no means to encourage their tricks, but as the prisoner had never broken his fast since yesterday's dinner, I would wink at his cheating Mr. Hindley that once.

He went down; I set him a stool by the fire, and offered him a quantity of good things; but he was sick, and could eat little, and my attempts to entertain him were thrown away. He leaned his two elbows on his knees, and his chin on his hands, and remained wrapt in dumb meditation. On my inquiring the subject of his thoughts, he answered, gravely—

"I'm trying to settle how I shall pay Hindley back. I don't care how long I wait, if I can only do it at last. I hope he will not die before I do!"

"For shame, Heathcliff!" said I. "It is for God to punish wicked people; we should learn to forgive."

"No, God won't have the satisfaction that I shall," he returned. "I only wish I knew the best way! Let me alone, and I'll plan it out: while I'm thinking of that I don't feel pain."

But, Mr. Lockwood, I forget these tales cannot divert you. I'm annoyed how I should dream of chattering on at such a rate; and your gruel cold, and you nodding for bed! I could have told Heathcliff's history, all that you need hear, in half-a-dozen words.

Thus interrupting herself, the housekeeper rose, and proceeded to lay aside her sewing; but I felt incapable of moving from the hearth, and I was very far from nodding.

"Sit still, Mrs. Dean," I cried, "do sit still another half-hour! You've done just right to tell the story leisurely. That is the method I like; and you must finish in the same style. I am interested in every character you have mentioned, more or less."

"The clock is on the stroke of eleven, sir."

"No matter—I'm not accustomed to go to bed in the long hours. One or two is early enough for a person who lies till ten."

"You shouldn't lie till ten. There's the very prime of the morning gone long before that time. A person who has not done one half his day's work by ten o'clock, runs a chance of leaving the other half undone."

"Nevertheless, Mrs. Dean, resume your chair; because tomorrow I intend lengthening the night till afternoon. I prognosticate for myself an obstinate cold, at least."

"I hope not, sir. Well, you must allow me to leap over some three years. During that space, Mrs. Earnshaw—"

"No, no, I'll allow nothing of the sort. Are you acquainted with the mood of mind in which, if you were seated alone, and the cat licking its kitten on the rug before you, you would watch the operation so intently that puss's neglect of one ear would put you seriously out of temper?"

"A terrible lazy mood, I should say."

"On the contrary, a tiresomely active one. It is mine at present, and therefore continue minutely. I perceive that people in these regions acquire over people in towns the value that a spider in a dungeon does over a spider in a cottage, to their various occupants; and yet the deepened attraction is not entirely owing to the situation of the looker-on. They *do* live more in earnest, more in themselves, and less in surface change and frivolous external things. I could fancy a love for life here almost possible; and I was a fixed unbeliever in any love of a year's standing. One state resembles setting a hungry man down to a single dish, on which he may concentrate his entire appetite, and do it justice—the other, introducing him to a table laid out by French cooks; he can perhaps extract as much enjoyment from the whole; but each part is a mere atom in his regard and remembrance."

"Oh! here we are the same as anywhere else, when you get to know us," observed Mrs. Dean, somewhat puzzled at my speech.

"Excuse me," I responded; "you, my good friend, are a striking evidence against that assertion. Excepting a few provincialisms of slight consequence, you have no marks of the manners that I am habituated to consider as peculiar to your class. I am sure you have thought a great deal more than the generality of servants think. You have been compelled to cultivate your reflective faculties, for want of occasions for frittering your life away in silly trifles."

Mrs. Dean laughed.

"I certainly esteem myself a steady, reasonable kind of body," she said, "not exactly from living among the hills, and seeing one set of faces, and one series of actions, from year's end to year's end: but I have undergone sharp discipline, which has taught me wisdom; and then I have read more than you would fancy, Mr. Lockwood. You could not open a book in this library that I have not looked into, and got something out of also; unless it be that range of Greek and Latin, and that of French; and those I know one from another—it is as much as you can expect of a poor man's daughter.

"However, if I am to follow my story in true gossip's fashion, I had better go on; and instead of leaping three years, I will be content to pass to the next summer—the summer of 1778—that is nearly twenty-three years ago."

. . . .

Chapter 8

On the morning of a fine June day, my first bonny little nursling, and the last of the ancient Earnshaw stock, was born.

We were busy with the hay in a far away field, when the girl that usually brought our breakfasts came running, an hour too soon, across the meadow and up the lane, calling me as she ran.

"Oh, such a grand bairn!" she panted out. "The finest lad that ever breathed! but the doctor says missis must go; he says she's been in a consumption these many months. I heard him tell Mr. Hindley—and now she has nothing to keep her, an she'll be dead before winter. You must come home directly. You're to nurse it, Nelly—to feed it with sugar and milk, and take care of it, day and night—I wish I were you, because it will be all yours when there is no missis!"

"But is she very ill?" I asked, flinging down my rake, and tying my bonnet.

"I guess she is; yet she looks bravely," replied the girl, "and she talks as if she thought of living to see it grow a man. She's out of her head for joy, it's such a beauty. If I were her I'm certain I should not die. I should get better at the bare sight of it, in spite of Kenneth. I was fairly mad at him. Dame Archer brought the cherub down to master, in the house, and his face just began to light up, then the old croaker steps forward, and, says he, 'Earnshaw, it's a blessing your wife has been spared to leave you this son. When she came, I felt convinced we shouldn't keep her long; and now, I must tell you, the winter will probably finish her. Don't take on, and fret about it too much; it can't be helped. And besides, you should have known better than to choose such a rush of a lass.'"

"And what did the master answer?" I inquired.

"I think he swore—but I didn't mind him, I was straining to see the bairn," and she began again to describe it rapturously. I, as zealous as herself, hurried eagerly home to admire, on my part, though I was very sad for Hindley's sake; he had room in his heart only for two idols—his wife and himself—he doted on both, and adored one; and I couldn't conceive how he would bear the loss.

When we got to Wuthering Heights, there he stood at the front door; and, as I passed in, I asked how was the baby?

"Nearly ready to run about, Nell!" he replied, putting on a cheerful smile.

"And the mistress?" I ventured to inquire, "the doctor says she's—"

"Damn the doctor!" He interrupted reddening. "Frances is quite right—she'll be perfectly well by this time next week. Are you going upstairs? will you tell her that I'll come, if she'll promise not to talk. I left her because she would not hold her tongue; and she must—tell her Mr. Kenneth says she must be quiet."

I delivered this message to Mrs. Earnshaw; she seemed in flighty spirits, and replied merrily—

"I hardly spoke a word, Ellen, and there he has gone out twice, crying. Well, say I promise I won't speak; but that does not bind me not to laugh at him!"

Poor soul! Till within a week of her death that gay heart never failed her; and her husband persisted doggedly, nay, furiously, in affirming her health improved every day. When Kenneth warned him that his medicines were useless at that stage of the malady, and he needn't put him to further expense by attending her, he retorted—

"I know you need not—she's well—she does not want any more attendance from you! She never was in a consumption. It was a fever; and it is gone—her pulse is as slow as mine now, and her cheek as cool."

He told his wife the same story, and she seemed to believe him; but one night while leaning on his shoulder, in the act of saying she thought she should be able to get up to-morrow, a fit of coughing took her—a very slight one—he raised her in his arms; she put her two hands about his neck, her face changed, and she was dead.

As the girl had anticipated, the child Hareton fell wholly into my hands. Mr. Earnshaw, provided he saw him healthy, and never heard him cry, was contented, as far as regarded him. For himself he grew desperate; his sorrow was of that kind that will not lament; he neither wept nor prayed; he cursed and defiled; execrated God and man, and gave himself up to reckless dissipation.

The servants could not bear his tyrannical and evil conduct long. Joseph and I were the only two that would stay. I had not the heart to leave my charge; and besides, you know I had been his foster-sister, and excused his behavior more readily than a stranger would.

Joseph remained to hector over tenants and laborers; and because it was his vocation to be where he had plenty of wickedness to reprove.

The master's bad ways and bad companions formed a pretty example for Catherine and Heathcliff. His treatment of the latter was enough to make a fiend of a saint. And truly it appeared as if the lad *were* possessed of something diabolical at that period. He delighted to witness Hindley degrading himself past redemption; and became daily more notable for savage sullenness and ferocity.

I could not half tell what an infernal house we had. The curate dropped calling, and nobody decent came near us at last; unless Edgar Linton's visits to Miss Cathy might be an exception. At fifteen she was the queen of the country-side; she had no peer: and she did turn out a haughty, headstrong creature! I own I did not like her, after her infancy was past; and I vexed her frequently by trying to bring down her arrogance; she never took an aversion to me, though. She had a wondrous constancy to old attachments; even Heathcliff kept his hold on her affections unalterably; and young Linton, with all his superiority, found it difficult to make an equally deep impression.

He was my late master; that is his portrait over the fireplace. It used to hang on one side, and his wife's on the other; but hers has been removed, or else you might see something of what she was. Can you make that out?

Mrs. Dean raised the candle, and I discerned a soft-featured face, exceedingly resembling the young lady at the Heights, but more pensive and amiable in expression. It formed a sweet picture. The long light hair curled slightly on the temples; the eyes were large and serious; the figure almost too graceful. I did not marvel how Catherine Earnshaw could forget her first friend for such an individual. I marveled much how he, with a mind to correspond to his person, could fancy my idea of Catherine Earnshaw.

"A very agreeable portrait," I observed to the housekeeper. "Is it like?"

Yes, she answered; but he looked better when he was animated; that is his everyday countenance; he wanted spirit in general.

Catherine had kept up her acquaintance with the Lintons since her five weeks' residence, among them; and as she had no temptation to show her rough side in their company, and had the sense to be ashamed of being rude where she experienced such invariable courtesy; she imposed unwittingly on the old lady and gentleman by her ingenuous cordiality; gained the admiration of Isabella, and the heart and soul of her brother—acquisitions that flattered her from the first, for she was full of ambition, and led her to adopt a double character, without exactly intending to deceive any one.

In the place where she heard Heathcliff termed a "vulgar young ruffian," and "worse than a brute," she took care not to act like him; but at home she had small inclination to practice politeness that would only be laughed at, and restrain an unruly nature when it would bring her neither credit nor praise.

Mr. Edgar seldom mustered courage to visit Wuthering Heights openly. He had a terror of Earnshaw's reputation, and shrunk from encountering him; and yet he was always received with our best attempts at civility; the master himself avoided offending him, knowing why he came; and if he could not be gracious, kept out of the way. I rather think his appearance there was distasteful to Catherine; she was not artful—never played the coquette, and had evidently an objection to her two friends meeting at all; for when Heathcliff expressed contempt of Linton, in his presence, she could not half coincide, as she did in his absence; and when Linton evinced disgust and antipathy to Heathcliff, she dared not treat his sentiments with indifference, as if depreciation of her playmate were of scarcely any consequence to her.

I've had many a laugh at her perplexities and untold troubles, which she vainly strove to hide from my mockery. That sounds ill-natured—but she was so proud, it became really impossible to pity her distresses, till she should be chastened into more humility.

She did bring herself finally to confess, and confide in me. There was not a soul else that she might fashion into an adviser.

Mr. Hindley had gone from home one afternoon, and Heathcliff presumed to give himself a holiday on the strength of it. He had reached the age of sixteen then, I think, and without having bad features or being deficient in intellect, he contrived to convey an impression of inward and outward repulsiveness that his present aspect retains no traces of.

In the first place, he had, by that time, lost the benefit of his early education: continual hard work, begun soon and concluded late, had extinguished any curiosity he once possessed in pursuit of knowledge, and any love for books or learning. His childhood's sense of superiority, instilled into him by the favors of old Mr. Earnshaw, was faded away. He struggled long to keep up an equality with Catherine in her studies, and yielded with poignant though silent regret; but he yielded completely, and there was no prevailing on him to take a step in the way of moving upward, when he found he must necessarily sink beneath his former level. Then personal appearance sympathized with mental deterioration; he acquired a slouching gait and ignoble look; his naturally reserved disposition was exaggerated into an almost idiotic excess of unsociable moroseness; and he took a grim pleasure, apparently, in exciting the aversion, rather than the esteem, of his few acquaintance.

Catherine and he were constant companions still, at his seasons of respite from labor; but he had ceased to express his fondness for her in words, and recoiled with angry suspicion from her girlish caresses, as if conscious there could be no gratification in lavishing such marks of affection on him. On the before-named occasion he came into the house to announce his intention of doing nothing, while I was assisting Miss Cathy to arrange her dress. She had not reckoned on his taking it into his head to be idle; and, imagining she would have the whole place to herself, she managed, by some means, to inform Mr. Edgar of her brother's absence, and was then preparing to receive him.

"Cathy, are you busy this afternoon?" asked Heathcliff. "Are you going anywhere?"

"No—it is raining," she answered.

"Why have you that silk frock on, then?" he said. "Nobody coming here, I hope?"

"Not that I know of," stammered Miss; "but you should be in the field now, Heathcliff—it is an hour past dinner time; I thought you were gone."

"Hindley does not often free us from his accursed presence," observed the boy; "I'll not work any more to-day—I'll stay with you."

"O, but Joseph will tell," she suggested—"you'd better go!"

"Joseph is loading lime on the farther side of Pennistow Crag; it will take him till dark, and he'll never know."

So saying, he lounged to the fire, and sat down. Catherine reflected an instant with knitted brows. She found it needful to smooth the way for an intrusion.

"Isabella and Edgar Linton talked of calling this afternoon," she said, at the conclusion of a minute's silence. "As it rains, I hardly expect them; but they may come, and if they do, you run the risk of being scolded for no good."

"Order Ellen to say you are engaged, Cathy," he persisted; "don't turn me out for those pitiful silly friends of yours! I'm on the point, sometimes, of complaining that they—but I'll not—"

"That they what?" cried Catherine, gazing at him with a troubled countenance. "Oh, Nelly!" she added, petulantly jerking her head away from my hands; "you've combed my hair quite out of curl! That's enough—let me alone. What are you on the point of complaining about, Heathcliff?"

"Nothing—only look at the almanac, on that wall;" he pointed to a framed sheet hanging near the window, and continued:

"The crosses are for the evenings you have spent with the Lintons, the dots for those spent with me. Do you see, I've marked every day?"

"Yes—very foolish; as if I took notice!" replied Catherine in a peevish tone. "And where is the sense of that?"

"To show that I *do* take notice," said Heathcliff.

"And should I always be sitting with you?" she demanded,

growing more irritated. "What good do I get? what do you talk about? You might be dumb or a baby, for anything you say to amuse me, or for anything you do either?"

"You never told me before that I talked too little, or that you disliked my company, Cathy!" exclaimed Heathcliff, in much agitation.

"It is no company at all, when people know nothing and say nothing," she muttered.

Her companion rose up, but he had not time to express his feelings further; for a horse's feet were heard on the flags, and, having knocked gently, young Linton entered, his face brilliant with delight at the unexpected summons he had received.

Doubtless Catherine marked the difference between her friends as one came in and the other went out. The contrast resembled what you see in exchanging a bleak, hilly coal-country for a beautiful, fertile valley; and his voice and greeting were as opposite as his aspect. He had a sweet, low manner of speaking, and pronounced his words as you do, that is, less gruff than we talk here, and softer.

"I'm not come too soon, am I?" he said, casting a look at me. I had begun to wipe the plate, and tidy some drawers at the far end in the dresser.

"No" answered Catherine. "What are you doing there, Nelly?"

"My work, Miss," I replied. (Mr. Hindley had given me directions to make a third party in any private visits Linton chose to pay.)

She stepped behind me and whispered crossly, "Take yourself and your dusters off! When company are in the house, servants don't commence scouring and cleaning in the room where they are!"

"It's a good opportunity, now that master is away," I answered aloud, "he hates me to be fidgeting over these things in his presence. I'm sure Mr. Edgar will excuse me."

"I hate you to be fidgeting in *my* presence," exclaimed the young lady imperiously, not allowing her guest time to speak. She had failed to recover her equanimity since the little dispute with Heathcliff.

"I'm sorry for it, Miss Catherine!" was my response; and I proceeded assiduously with my occupation.

She, supposing Edgar could not see her, snatched the cloth from my hand, and pinched me, with a prolonged wrench, very spitefully, on the arm.

I have said I did not love her; and rather relished mortifying her vanity now and then; besides, she hurt me extremely, so I started up from my knees, and screamed out—

"O, Miss, that's a nasty trick! you have no right to nip me, and I'm not going to bear it!"

"I didn't touch you, you lying creature!" cried she, her fingers tingling to repeat the act, and her ears red with rage. She never had power to conceal her passion, it always set her whole complexion in a blaze.

"What's that then?" I retorted, showing a decided purple witness to refute her.

She stamped her foot, wavered a moment, and then, irresistibly impelled by the naughty spirit within her, slapped me on the cheek a stinging blow that filled both eyes with water.

"Catherine, love! Catherine!" interposed Linton, greatly shocked at the double fault of falsehood and violence which his idol had committed.

"Leave the room, Ellen!" she repeated, trembling all over.

Little Hareton, who followed me everywhere, and was sitting near me on the floor, at seeing my tears, commenced crying himself, and sobbed out complaints against "wicked aunt Cathy," which drew her fury upon his unlucky head; she seized his shoulders, and shook him till the poor child waxed livid, and Edgar thoughtlessly laid hold of her hands to deliver him. In an instant one was wrung free, and the astonished young man felt it applied over his own ear in a way that could not be mistaken for jest.

He drew back in consternation—I lifted Hareton in my arms, and walked off to the kitchen with him, leaving the door of communication open; for I was curious to watch how they would settle their disagreement.

The insulted visitor moved to the spot where he had laid his hat, pale and with a quivering lip.

"That's right!" I said to myself, "take warning, and be gone! It's a kindness to let you have a glimpse of her genuine disposition."

"Where are you going?" demanded Catherine, advancing to the door.

He swerved aside, and attempted to pass.

"You must not go!" she exclaimed energetically.

"I must and shall!" he replied in a subdued voice.

"No," she persisted, grasping the handle, "not yet, Edgar Linton—sit down, you shall not leave me in that temper. I should be miserable all night, and I won't be miserable for you!"

"Can I stay after you have struck me?" asked Linton.

Catherine was mute.

"You've made me afraid, and ashamed of you," he continued, "I'll not come here again!"

Her eyes began to glisten and her lids to twinkle.

"And you told a deliberate untruth!" he said.

"I didn't!" she cried, recovering her speech: "I did nothing deliberately. Well, go if you please—get away. And now I'll cry—I'll cry myself sick!"

She dropped down on her knees by a chair, and set to weeping in serious earnest.

Edgar persevered in his resolution as far as the court; there he lingered. I resolved to encourage him.

"Miss is dreadfully wayward, sir!" I called out. "As bad as any marred child. You'd better be riding home, or else she will be sick, only to grieve us."

The soft thing looked askance through the window—he pos-

sessed the power to depart, as much as a cat possesses the power to
leave a mouse half killed, or a bird half eaten.

Ah, I thought, there will by no saving him. He is doomed, and
flies to his fate!

And so it was; he turned abruptly, hastened into the house
again, shut the door behind him; and when I went in a while after
to inform them that Earnshaw had come home rabid drunk, ready
to pull the old place about our ears (his ordinary frame of mind in
that condition), I saw the quarrel had merely effected a closer
intimacy—had broken the outworks of youthful timidity, and
enabled them to forsake the disguise of friendship, and confess
themselves lovers.

Intelligence of Mr. Hindley's arrival drove Linton speedily to his
horse, and Catherine to her chamber. I went to hide little
Hareton, and to take the shot out of the master's fowling-piece,
which he was fond of playing with in his insane excitement, to the
hazard of the lives of any who provoked, or even attracted his
notice too much; and I had hit upon the plan of removing it, that
he might do less mischief, if he did go the length of firing the gun.

·······

Chapter 9

He entered, vociferating oaths dreadful to hear; and caught me
in the act of stowing his son away in the kitchen cupboard.
Hareton was impressed with a wholesome terror of encountering
either his wild-beast's fondness, or his madman's rage—for in one
he ran a chance of being squeezed and kissed to death, and in the
other of being flung into the fire, or dashed against the wall—and
the poor thing remained perfectly quiet wherever I chose to put
him.

"There I've found it out at last!" cried Hindley, pulling me back
by the skin of the neck, like a dog. "By Heaven and Hell, you've
sworn between you to murder that child! I know how it is, now,
that he is always out of my way. But, with the help of Satan, I shall
make you swallow the carving knife, Nelly! you needn't laugh; for
I've just crammed Kenneth head downmost, in the Blackhorse
marsh; and two is the same as one—and I want to kill some of
you; I shall have no rest till I do!"

"But I don't like the carving knife, Mr. Hindley," I answered; "it
has been cutting red herrings—I'd rather be shot if you please."

"You'd rather be damned!" he said, "and so you shall. No law
in England can hinder a man from keeping his house decent, and
mine's abominable! open your mouth."

He held the knife in his hand, and pushed its point between my
teeth: but, for my part, I was never much afraid of his vagaries. I
spat out, and affirmed it tasted detestably— I would not take it
on any account.

"Oh," said he, releasing me, "I see that hideous little villain is
not Hareton—I beg your pardon, Nell—if it be, he deserves flay-

ing alive for not running to welcome me, and for screaming as if I
were a goblin. Unnatural cub, come hither! I'll teach thee to
impose on a good-hearted, deluded father. Now don't you think
the lad would be handsomer cropped! It makes a dog fiercer, and I
love something fierce. Get me a pair of scissors—something fierce
and trim! Besides, it's infernal affectation—devilish conceit, it is
to cherish our ears—we're asses enough without them. Hush,
child, hush! well then, it is my darling! wisht, dry thy eyes—
there's a joy; kiss me! What! it won't? Kiss me, Hareton! Damn
thee, kiss me! By God, as if I would rear such a monster! As sure
as I'm living, I'll break the brat's neck."

Poor Hareton was squalling and kicking in his father's arms
with all his might; and redoubled his yells when he carried him
up-stairs and lifted him over the bannister. I cried out that he
would frighten the child into fits, and ran to rescue him.

As I reached them, Hindley leaned forward on the rails to listen
to a noise below; almost forgetting what he had in his hands.

"Who is that?" he asked, hearing some one approaching the
stair's foot.

I leaned forward, also, for the purpose of signing to Heathcliff,
whose step I recognized, not to come further; and, at the instant
when my eye quitted Hareton, he gave a sudden spring, delivered
himself from the careless grasp that held him, and fell.

There was scarcely time to experience a thrill of horror before
we saw that the little wretch was safe. Heathcliff arrived underneath just at the critical moment; by a natural impulse he arrested
his descent, and setting him on his feet, looked up to discover the
author of the accident.

A miser who has parted with a lucky lottery ticket for five
shillings, and finds next day he has lost in the bargain five thousand pounds, could not show a blanker countenance than he did
on beholding the figure of Mr. Earnshaw above. It expressed,
plainer than words could do, the intensest anguish at having made
himself the instrument of thwarting his own revenge. Had it been
dark I dare say he would have tried to remedy the mistake by
smashing Hareton's skull on the steps; but we witnessed his salvation; and I was presently below, with my precious charge pressed
to my heart.

Hindley descended more leisurely, sobered and abashed.

"It is your fault, Ellen," he said, "you should have kept him out
of sight; you should have taken him from me! Is he injured any
where?"

"Injured!" I cried, angrily, "If he's not killed he'll be an idiot!
Oh! I wonder his mother does not rise from her grave to see how
you use him. You're worse than a heathen—treating your own
flesh and blood in that manner!"

He attempted to touch the child, who on finding himself with
me, sobbed off his terror directly. At the first finger his father laid
on him, however, he shrieked again louder than before, and struggled as if he would go into convulsions.

"You shall not meddle with him!" I continued, "He hates

you—they all hate you—that's the truth! A happy family you have; and a pretty state you're come to!"

"I shall come to a prettier, yet! Nelly," laughed the misguided man, recovering his hardness. "At present, convey yourself and him away.—And hark you, Heathcliff! clear you too, quite from my reach and hearing...I wouldn't murder you to-night, unless, perhaps, I set the house on fire; but that's as my fancy goes—"

While saying this he took a pint bottle of brandy from the dresser, and poured some into a tumbler.

"Nay don't!" I entreated, "Mr. Hindley, do take warning. Have mercy on this unfortunate boy, if you care nothing for yourself!"

"Any one will do better for him than I shall," he answered.

"Have mercy on your own soul!" I said, endeavoring to snatch the glass from his hand.

"Not I! on the contrary, I shall have great pleasure in sending it to perdition, to punish its Maker," exclaimed the blasphemer, "Here's to its hearty damnation!"

He drank the spirits, and impatiently bade us go; terminating his command with a sequel of horrid imprecations, too bad to repeat or remember.

"It's a pity he cannot kill himself with drink," observed Heathcliff, muttering an echo of curses back, when the door was shut. "He's doing his very utmost; but his constitution defies him — Mr. Kenneth says he would wager his mare that he'll outlive any man on this side Gimmerton, and go to the grave a hoary sinner; unless some happy chance, out of the common course, befall him."

I went into the kitchen, and sat down to lull my little lamb to sleep. Heathcliff, as I thought, walked through to the barn. It turned out afterward that he only got as far as the other side of the settle, when he flung himself on a bench by the wall, removed from the fire, and remained silent.

I was rocking Hareton on my knee, and humming a song that began,

> "It was far in the night, and the bairnies grat,
> The mither beneath the mools heard that,"

when Miss Cathy, who had listened to the hubbub from her room, put her head in, and whispered,

"Are you alone, Nelly?"

"Yes, Miss," I replied.

She entered and approached the hearth. I, supposing she was going to say something, looked up. The expression of her face seemed disturbed and anxious. Her lips were half asunder, as if she meant to speak; and she drew a breath, but it escaped in a sigh instead of a sentence.

I resumed my song: not having forgotten her recent behavior.

"Where's Heathcliff?" she said, interrupting me.

"About his work in the stable," was my answer.

He did not contradict me; perhaps, he had fallen into a doze.

There followed another long pause, during which I perceived a drop or two trickle from Catherine's cheek to the flags.

"Is she sorry for her shameful conduct?" I asked myself. "That will be a novelty, but, she may come to the point as she will—I shan't help her!"

No, she felt small trouble regarding any subject save her own concerns.

"Oh, dear!" she cried at last. "I am very unhappy!"

"A pity," observed I, "you're hard to please—so many friends and so few cares, and can't make yourself content!"

"Nelly, will you keep a secret for me?" she pursued, kneeling down by me and lifting her winsome eyes to my face with that sort of look which turns off bad temper, even when one has all the right in the world to indulge it.

"Is it worth keeping?" I inquired less sulkily.

"Yes, and it worries me, and I must let it out! I want to know what I should do. To-day Edgar Linton has asked me to marry him, and I've given him an answer. Now, before I tell you whether it was a consent or denial, you tell me which it ought to have been."

"Really, Miss Catherine, how can I know?" I replied. "To be sure, considering the exhibition you performed in his presence this afternoon, I might say it would be wise to refuse him; since, if he asked you after that, he must either be hopelessly stupid, or a venturesome fool."

"If you talk so, I won't tell you any more," she returned peevishly, rising to her feet; "I accepted him, Nelly; be quick, and say whether I was wrong!"

"You accepted him? then what good is it discussing the matter? You have pledged your word, and cannot retract."

"But say whether I should have done so—do!" she exclaimed in an irritated tone; chafing her hands together and frowning.

"There are many things to be considered before that question can be answered properly," I said sententiously; "first and foremost, do you love Mr. Edgar?"

"Who can help it? of course I do," she answered.

Then I put her through the following catechism; for a girl of twenty-two it was not injudicious.

"Why do you love him, Miss Cathy?"

"Nonsense, I do—that's sufficient."

"By no means; you must say why?"

"Well, because he is handsome, and pleasant to be with."

"Bad," was my commentary.

"And because he is young and cheerful."

"Bad, still."

"And because he loves me."

"Indifferent; coming there."

"And he will be rich, and I shall like to be the greatest woman of the neighborhood, and I shall be proud of having such a husband."

"Worst of all. And, now, say how you love him?"

"As anybody loves. You're silly, Nelly."

"Not at all. Answer."

"I love the ground under his feet, and the air over his head, and everything he touches, and every word he says; I love all his looks, and all his actions, and him entirely, and altogether. There now!"

"And why?"

"Nay—you are making a jest of it; it is exceedingly ill natured! It's no jest to me!" said the young lady, scowling and turning her face to the fire.

"I'm very far from jesting, Miss Catherine," I replied. "You love Mr. Edgar because he is handsome, and young, and cheerful, and rich, and loves you. The last, however, goes for nothing — You would love him without that, probably, and with it you wouldn't, unless he possessed the four former attractions."

"No, to be sure not—I should only pity him—hate him, perhaps, if he were ugly and a clown."

"But there are several other handsome, rich young men in the world; handsomer, possibly, and richer than he is. What should hinder you from loving them?"

"If there be any, they are out of my way—I've seen none like Edgar."

"You may see some; and he won't always be handsome, and young, and may not always be rich."

"He is now; and I have only to do with the present. I wish you would speak rationally."

"Well, that settles it. If you have only to do with the present, marry Mr. Linton."

"I don't want your permission for that—I *shall* marry him; and yet, you have not told me whether I'm right."

"Perfectly right; if people be right to marry only for the present. And now let us hear what you are unhappy about. Your brother will be pleased; the old lady and gentleman will not object, I think; you will escape from a disorderly, comfortless home, into a wealthy, respectable one; and you love Edgar, and Edgar loves you. All seems smooth and easy—where is the obstacle?"

"*Here!* and *here!*" replied Catherine, striking one hand on her forehead and the other on her breast. "In whichever place the soul lives—in my soul and in my heart, I'm convinced I'm wrong!"

"That's very strange! I cannot make it out."

"It's my secret; but if you will not mock at me, I'll explain it; I can't do it distinctly—but I'll give you a feeling of how I feel."

She seated herself by me again: her countenance grew sadder and graver, and her clasped hands trembled.

"Nelly, do you never dream queer dreams?" she said suddenly, after some minutes' reflection.

"Yes, now and then," I answered.

"And so do I. I've dreamed in my life dreams that have staid with me ever after, and changed my ideas; they've gone through and through me, like wine through water, and altered the color of my mind. And this is one—I'm going to tell it—but take care not to smile at any part of it."

"Oh! don't, Miss Catherine!" I cried. "We're dismal enough without conjuring up ghosts and visions to perplex us. Come, come, be merry, and like yourself! Look at little Hareton—*he's* dreaming nothing dreary. How sweetly he smiles in his sleep!"

"Yes; and how sweetly his father curses in his solitude! You remember him, I dare say, when he was just such another as that chubby thing—nearly as young and innocent. However, Nelly, I shall oblige you to listen—it's not long; and I've no power to be merry to-night."

"I won't hear it, I won't hear it!" I repeated, hastily.

I was superstitious about dreams then, and am still; and Catherine had an unusual gloom in her aspect, that made me dread something from which I might shape a prophecy, and foresee a fearful catastrophe.

She was vexed, but she did not proceed. Apparently taking up another subject, she re-commenced in a short time.

"If I were in heaven, Nelly, I should be extremely miserable."

"Because you are not fit to go there," I answered. "All sinners would be miserable in heaven."

"But it is not for that. I dreamed, once, that I was there."

"I tell you I won't hearken to your dreams, Miss Catherine! I'll go to bed," I interrupted again.

She laughed, and held me down, for I made a motion to leave my chair.

"This is nothing," cried she; "I was only going to say that heaven did not seem to be my home; and I broke my heart with weeping to come back to earth; and the angels were so angry that they flung me out into the middle of the heath on the top of Wuthering Heights; where I woke sobbing for joy. That will do to explain my secret, as well as the other. I've no more business to marry Edgar Linton than I have to be in heaven; and if the wicked man in there had not brought Heathcliff so low I shouldn't have thought of it. It would degrade me to marry Heathcliff now; so he shall never know how I love him; and that not because he's handsome, Nelly, but because he's more myself than I am. Whatever our souls are made of, his and mine are the same; and Linton's is as different as a moonbeam from lightning, or frost from fire."

Ere this speech ended I became sensible of Heathcliff's presence. Having noticed a slight movement, I turned my head, and saw him rise from the bench, and steal out noiselessly. He had listened till he heard Catherine say it would degrade her to marry him, and then he staid to hear no farther.

My companion, sitting on the ground, was prevented by the back of the settle from remarking his presence or departure; but I started, and bade her hush.

"Why?" she asked, gazing nervously round.

"Joseph is here," I answered, catching opportunely the roll of his cartwheels up the road; "and Heathcliff will come in with him. I'm not sure whether he were not at the door this moment."

"Oh, he couldn't overhear me at the door!" said she. "Give me Hareton while you get the supper, and when it is ready ask me to sup with you. I want to cheat my uncomfortable conscience, and be convinced that Heathcliff has no notion of these things—he has not, has he? He does not know what being in love is?"

"I see no reason that he should not know as well as you," I returned; "and if *you* are his choice, he'll be the most unfortunate

creature that ever was born! As soon as you become Mrs. Linton,
he loses friend, and love, and all! Have you considered how you'll
bear the separation, and how he'll bear to be quite deserted in the
world! Because, Miss Catherine—"

"He quite deserted! we separated!" she exclaimed, with an accent of indignation. "Who is to separate us, pray! They'll meet the
fate of Milo! Not as long as I live, Ellen—for no mortal creature.
Every Linton on the face of the earth might melt into nothing,
before I could consent to forsake Heathcliff. Oh, that's not what I
intend—that's not what I mean! I shouldn't be Mrs. Linton were
such a price demanded! He'll be as much to me as he has been all
his lifetime. Edgar must shake off his antipathy, and tolerate him,
at least. He will, when he learns my true feelings toward him.
Nelly, I see now, you think me a selfish wretch, but did it never
strike you that if Heathcliff and I married we should be beggars?
whereas, if I marry Linton I can aid Heathcliff to rise, and place
him out of my brother's power."

"With your husband's money, Miss Catherine?" I asked. "You'll
find him not so pliable as you calculate upon; and, though I'm
hardly a judge, I think that's the worst motive you've given yet for
being the wife of young Linton."

"It is not," retorted she, "it is the best! The others were the
satisfaction of my whims; and for Edgar's sake, too, to satisfy him.
This is for the sake of one who comprehends in his person my
feelings to Edgar and myself. I cannot express it; but surely you
and everybody have a notion that there is, or should be, an
existence of yours beyond you. What were the use of my creation
if I were entirely contained here? My great miseries in this world
have been Heathcliff's miseries, and I watched and felt each from
the beginning; my great thought in living is himself. If all else
perished, and *he* remained, I should still continue to be; and, if all
else remained, and he were annihilated, the universe would turn
to a mighty stranger. I should not seem a part of it. My love for
Linton is like the foliage in the woods: time will change it, I'm
well aware, as winter changes the trees. My love for Heathcliff
resembles the eternal rocks beneath: a source of little visible delight, but necessary. Nelly, I *am* Heathcliff—he's always, always in
my mind—not as a pleasure, any more than I am always a pleasure to myself—but as my own being; so don't talk of our separation again—it is impracticable; and—"

She paused, and hid her face in the folds of my gown; but I
jerked if forcibly away. I was out of patience with her folly.

"If I can make any sense of your nonsense, miss," I said, "it
only goes to convince me that you are ignorant of the duties you
undertake in marrying, or else that you are a wicked, unprincipled girl. But trouble me with no more secrets; I'll not promise
to keep them."

"You'll keep that?" she asked, eagerly.

"No, I'll not promise," I repeated.

She was about to insist, when the entrance of Joseph finished
our conversation; and Catherine removed her seat to a corner,
and nursed Hareton, while I made the supper.

After it was cooked, my fellow-servant and I began to quarrel who should carry some to Mr. Hindley; and we didn't settle it till all was nearly cold. Then we came to the agreement that we would let him ask, if he wanted any, for we feared particularly to go into his presence when he had been some time alone.

"Und hah isn't that nowt comed in frough th' field, be this time? What is he abaht? girt eedle seeght?" demanded the old man, looking round for Heathcliff.

"I'll call him," I replied. "He's in the barn, I've no doubt."

I went and called, but got no answer. On returning, I whispered to Catherine that he had heard a good part of what she said, I was sure; and told how I saw him quit the kitchen just as she complained of her brother's conduct regarding him.

She jumped up in a fine fright—flung Hareton upon the settle, and ran to seek for her friend herself; not taking leisure to consider why she was so flurried, or how her talk would have affected him.

She was absent such a while that Joseph proposed we should wait no longer. He cunningly conjectured they were staying away in order to avoid hearing his protracted blessing. They were "ill eneuph for ony fahl manners," he affirmed. And, on their behalf, he added that night a special prayer to the usual quarter of an hour's supplication before meat; and would have tacked another to the end of the grace, had not his young mistress broken in upon him with a hurried command that he must run down the road, and wherever Heathcliff had rambled, find and make him re-enter directly!

"I want to speak to him, and I *must* before I go up-stairs," she said. "And the gate is open, he is somewhere out of hearing; for he would not reply, though I shouted at the top of the fold as loud as I could."

Joseph objected at first; she was too much in earnest, however, to suffer contradiction; and at last he placed his hat on his head, and walked grumbling forth.

Meantime Catherine paced up and down the floor, exclaiming—

"I wonder where his is—I wonder where he *can* be! What did I say, Nelly? I've forgotten. Was he vexed at my bad humor this afternoon? Dear! tell me what I've said to grieve him? I do wish he'd come. I do wish he would!"

"What a noise for nothing!" I cried, though rather uneasy myself. "What a trifle scares you! It's surely no great cause of alarm that Heathcliff should take a moonlight saunter on the moors, or even lie, too sulky to speak to us, in the hay-loft. I'll engage he's lurking there. See, if I don't ferret him out!"

I departed to renew my search; its result was disappointment, and Joseph's quest ended in the same.

"Yon lad gets war un war!" observed he on re-entering "He's left th' yate ut t' full swing, and Miss's pony has trodden dahn two rigs uh corn, un plottered through, raight o'er intuh t' meadow! Hahsomdiver, t' maister 'ull play t' divil to-morn, and he'll do weel. He's patience itsseln wi' sich careless, offald craters—patience itsseln he is! Bud he'll nut be soa allus—yah's see, all on ye! Yah mun'n't drive him aht uf his heead fur nowt!"

"Have you found Heathcliff, you ass?" interrupted Catherine. "Have you been looking for him, as I ordered?"

"Aw sud more likker look for th'horse," he replied. "It 'ud be tuh more sense. But, aw can look for norther horse, nur man uf a neeght loike this—as black as t' chimbley! und Heathcliff's noan t' chap tuh coom ut *maw* whistle—happen he'll be less hard uh hearing wi' *ye!*"

It *was* a very dark evening for summer; the clouds appeared inclined to thunder, and I said we had better all sit down; the approaching rain would be certain to bring him home without further trouble.

However, Catherine would not be persuaded into tranquility. She kept wandering to and fro, from the gate to the door, in a state of agitation which permitted no repose: and at length took up a permanent situation on one side of the wall, near the road; where, heedless of my expostulations, and the growling thunder, and the great drops that began to plash around her, she remained, calling at intervals, and then listening, and then crying outright. She beat Hareton, or any child, at a good passionate fit of crying.

About midnight, while we still sat up, the storm came rattling over the Heights in full fury. There was a violent wind as well as thunder, and either one or the other split a tree off at the corner of the building; a huge bough fell across the roof, and knocked down a portion of the east chimney-stack, sending a clatter of stones and soot into the kitchen fire.

We thought a bolt had fallen in the middle of us, and Joseph swung upon his knees, beseeching the Lord to remember the Patriarchs, Noah and Lot; and, as in former times, spare the righteous, though he smote the ungodly. I felt some sentiment that it must be a judgment on us also. The Jonah, in my mind, was Mr. Earnshaw, and I shook the handle of his den that I might ascertain if he were yet living. He replied audibly enough, in a fashion which made my companion vociferate more clamorously than before, that a wide distinction might be drawn between saints like himself and sinners like his master. But the uproar passed away in twenty minutes, leaving us all unharmed, excepting Cathy, who got thoroughly drenched for her obstinacy in refusing to take shelter, and standing bonnetless and shawlless to catch as much water as she could with her hair and clothes.

She came in, and lay down on the settle, all soaked as she was, turning her face to the back, and putting her hands before it.

"Well, Miss!" I exclaimed, touching her shoulder; "you are not bent on getting your death, are you? Do you know what o'clock it is? Half-past twelve. Come! come to bed; these's no use waiting longer for that foolish boy—he'll be gone to Gimmerton, and he'll stay there now. He guesses we shouldn't wake for him till this late hour; at least, he guesses that only Mr. Hindley would be up; and he'd rather avoid having the door opened by the master."

"Nay, nay, he's noan at Gimmerton!" said Joseph. "Aw's niver wonder, bud he's at t' bothom uf a bog-hoile. This visitation

worn't for nowt, und aw wod hev ye tuh look aht, Miss—yah muh
be t' next. Thank Hivin for all! All warks togither for gooid tuh
them as is chozzen, and piked aht froo' th' rubbidge! Yah knaw
whet t' Scripture ses—"

And he began quoting several texts—referring us to the chapters and verses where we might find them.

I, having vainly begged the wilful girl to rise and remove
her wet things, left him preaching, and her shivering, and betook
myself to bed with little Hareton; who slept as fast as if everyone
had been sleeping round him.

I heard Joseph read on a while afterward; then I distinguished
his slow step on the ladder, and then I dropped asleep.

Coming down somewhat later than usual, I saw, by the sun-
beams piercing the chinks of the shutters, Miss Catherine still
seated near the fireplace. The house door was ajar too; light entered from its unclosed windows; Hindley had come out, and
stood on the kitchen hearth, haggard and drowsy.

"What ails you, Cathy?" he was saying when I entered; "you
look as dismal as a drowned whelp. Why are you so damp and
pale, child?"

"I've been wet," she answered reluctantly; "and I'm cold, that's
all."

"Oh, she is naughty?" I cried, perceiving the master to be tolerably sober; "She got steeped in the shower of yesterday evening,
and there she has sat, the night through, and I couldn't prevail on
her to stir."

Mr. Earnshaw stared at us in surprise. "The night through," he
repeated. "What kept her up? not fear of the thunder, surely? That
was over, hours since."

Neither of us wished to mention Heathcliff's absence, as long as
we could conceal it; so, I replied, I didn't know how she took it
into her head to sit up; and she said nothing.

The morning was fresh and cool; I threw back the lattice, and
presently the room was filled with sweet scents from the garden:
but Catherine called peevishly to me.

"Ellen, shut the window. I'm starving!" And her teeth chattered
as she shrunk closer to the almost extinguished embers.

"She's ill," said Hindley, taking her wrist, "I suppose that's the
reason she would not go to bed. Damn it! I don't want to be
troubled with more sickness here. What took her into the rain?"

"Running after t'lads, as usuald!" croaked Joseph, catching an
opportunity, from our hesitation, to thrust in his evil tongue.

"If aw wur yah, maister, aw'd just slam t'boards i' their faces all
on 'em, gentle and simple! Never a day ut yah're off, but yon cat
uh Linton comes sneaking hither—and Miss Nelly shoo's a fine
lass! shoo sits watching for ye i' t'kitchen; and as yah're in at one
door, he's aht at t'other. Und, then, wer grand lady goes a coorting
uf hor side! Its bonny behavior, lurking amang t'fields, after
twelve ut' night, wi that fahl, flaysome divil uf a gipsy, Heathcliff!
They think *aw'm* blind; but aw'm noan, now't ut t'soart! Aw seed
young Linton, boath coming and going, and aw seed *yah* (directing his discourse to me). Yah gooid fur nowt, slattenly witch! nip

up and bolt intuh th' hahs, t' minute yah heard t'maister's horse
fit clatter up t'road."

"Silence, eavesdropper!" cried Catherine. "None of your insolence before me! Edgar Linton came yesterday by chance,
Hindley: and it was *I* who told him to be off: because I knew you
would not like to have met him as you were."

"You lie, Cathy, no doubt," answered her brother, "and you are
a confounded simpleton! But never mind Linton at present. Tell
me, were you not with Heathcliff last night? Speak the truth now.
You need not be afraid of harming him. Though I hate him as
much as ever, he did me a good turn, a short time ago that will
make my conscience tender of breaking his neck. To prevent it I
shall send him about his business this very morning; and after he's
gone I'd advise you all to look sharp. I shall only have the more
humor for you!"

"I never saw Heathcliff last night," answered Catherine, beginning to sob bitterly: "and if you do turn him out of doors I'll go
with him. But perhaps you'll never have an opportunity—perhaps he's gone." Here she burst into uncontrollable grief, and the
remainder of her words were inarticulate.

Hindley lavished on her a torrent of scornful abuse, and bid her
get to her room immediately, or she shouldn't cry for nothing! I
obliged her to obey; and I shall never forget what a scene she acted
when we reached her chamber. It terrified me. I thought she was
going mad, and I begged Joseph to run for the doctor.

It proved the commencement of delirium; Mr. Kenneth, as
soon as he saw her, pronounced her dangerously ill; she had a
fever.

He bled her, and he told me to let her live on whey and water-
gruel; and take care she did not throw herself down stairs or out of
the window; and then he left, for he had enough to do in the
parish, where two or three miles was the ordinary distance between cottage and cottage.

Though I cannot say I made a gentle nurse, and Joseph and the
master were no better; and though our patient was as wearisome
and as headstrong as a patient could be, she weathered it through.

Old Mrs. Linton paid us several visits, to be sure, and set things
to rights, and scolded and ordered us all; and when Catherine was
convalescent, she insisted on conveying her to Thrushcross
Grange; for which deliverance we were very grateful. But the poor
dame had reason to repent of her kindness; she and her husband
took the fever, and died within a few days of each other.

Our young lady returned to us saucier and more passionate and
haughtier than ever. Heathcliff had never been heard of since the
evening of the thunder-storm; and one day I had the misfortune,
when she had provoked me exceedingly, to lay the blame of his
disappearance on her (where indeed it belonged, as she well
knew). From that period, for several months, she ceased to hold
any communication with me, save in the relation of a mere servant. Joseph fell under a ban also; he *would* speak his mind, and
lecture her all the same as if she were a little girl; and she esteemed
herself a woman, and our mistress; and thought that her recent

illness gave her a claim to be treated with consideration. Then the
doctor had said that she would not bear crossing much; she ought
to have her own way; and it was nothing less than murder, in her
eyes, for any one to presume to stand up and contradict her.

From Mr. Earnshaw and his companions she kept aloof; and,
tutored by Kenneth and by serious threats of a fit that often
attended her rages, her brother allowed her whatever she pleased
to demand, and generally avoided aggravating her fiery temper.
He was rather *too* indulgent in humoring her caprices; not from
affection, but from pride; he wished earnestly to see her bring
honor to the family by an alliance with the Lintons; and as long as
she let him alone, she might trample us like slaves, for aught he
cared!

Edgar Linton, as multitudes have been before, and will be after
him, was infatuated; and believed himself the happiest man alive
on the day he led her to Gimmerton chapel, three years subsequent to his father's death.

Much against my inclination, I was persuaded to leave Wuthering Heights and accompany her here. Little Hareton was nearly
five years old, and I had just begun to teach him his letters. We
made a sad parting, but Catherine's tears were more powerful
than ours. When I refused to go, and when she found her entreaties did not move me, she went lamenting to her husband and
brother. The former offered me munificent wages; the latter ordered me to pack up—he wanted no women in the house, he said,
now that there was no mistress; and as to Hareton, the curate
should take him in hand, by and by. And so I had but one choice
left—to do as I was ordered. I told the master he got rid of all
decent people only to run to ruin a little faster; I kissed Hareton
good by; and, since then, he has been a stranger, and it's very
queer to think it, but I've no doubt, he has completely forgotten
all about Ellen Dean, and that he was ever more than all the world
to her, and she to him!

At this point of the housekeeper's story she chanced to glance
toward the time-piece over the chimney; and was in amazement,
on seeing the minute-hand measure half-past one. She would not
hear of staying a second longer. In truth, I felt rather disposed to
defer the sequel of her narrative, myself: and now, that she is
vanished to her rest, and I have meditated for another hour or
two, I shall summon courage to go also, in spite of aching laziness
of head and limbs.

. . . .

Chapter 10

A charming introduction to a hermit's life! Four weeks' torture,
tossing, and sickness! Oh, these bleak winds, and bitter, northern
skies, and impassable roads, and dilatory country surgeons! And,
oh, this dearth of the human physiognomy, and, worse than all,

the terrible intimation of Kenneth that I need not expect to be out of doors till spring!

Mr. Heathcliff has just honored me with a call. About seven days ago he sent me a brace of grouse—the last of the season. Scoundrel! He is not altogether guiltless in this illness of mine; and that I had a great mind to tell him. But, alas! how could I offend a man who was charitable enough to sit at my bedside a good hour, and talk on some other subject than pills and draughts, blisters and leeches?

This is quite an easy interval. I am too weak to read, yet I feel as if I could enjoy something interesting. Why not have up Mrs. Dean to finish her tale? I can recollect its chief incidents, as far as she had gone. Yes, I remember her hero had run off, and never been heard of for three years: and the heroine was married. I'll ring; she'll be delighted to find me capable of talking cheerfully.

Mrs. Dean came.

"It wants twenty minutes, sir, to taking the medicine," she commenced.

"Away, away with it!" I replied; "I desire to have—"

"The doctor says you must drop the powders."

"With all my heart! Don't interrupt me. Come and take your seat here. Keep your fingers from that bitter phalanx of phials. Draw your knitting out of your pocket—that will do—now continue the history of Mr. Heathcliff, from where you left off, to the present day. Did he finish his education on the Continent, and come back a gentleman? or did he get a sizer's place at college? or escape to America, and earn honors by drawing blood from his foster country? or make a fortune more promptly on the English highways?"

"He may have done a little in all these vocations, Mr. Lockwood; but I couldn't know how he gained his money; neither am I aware of the means he took to raise his mind from the savage ignorance into which it was sunk; but, with your leave, I'll proceed in my own fashion, if you think it will amuse, and not weary you. Are you feeling better this morning?"

"Much."—

That's good news. I got Miss Catherine and myself to Thrushcross Grange; and, to my agreeable disappointment, she behaved infinitely better than I dared to expect. She seemed almost over fond of Mr. Linton; and even to his sister she showed plenty of affection. They were both very attentive to her comfort, certainly. It was not the thorn bending to the honysuckles, but the honeysuckles embracing the thorn. There were no mutual concessions; one stood erect, and the others yielded; and who *can* be ill-natured and bad-tempered when they encounter neither opposition nor indifference?

I observed that Mr. Edgar had a deep-rooted fear of ruffling her humor. He concealed it from her; but if ever he heard me answer sharply, or saw any other servant grow cloudy at some imperious order of hers, he would show his trouble by a frown of displeasure that never darkened on his own account. He, many a time, spoke sternly to me about my pertness; and averred that the stab of a knife could not inflict a worse pang than he suffered at seeing his lady vexed.

Not to grieve a kind master, I learned to be less touchy; and, for the space of half a year, the gunpowder lay as harmless as sand, because no fire came near to explode it. Catherine had seasons of gloom and silence, now and then; they were respected with sympathizing silence by her husband, who ascribed them to an alteration in her constitution, produced by her perilous illness, as she was never subject to depression of spirits before. The return of sunshine was welcomed by answering sunshine from him. I believe I may assert that they were really in possession of deep and growing happiness.

It ended. Well, we *must* be for ourselves in the long run; the mild and generous are only more justly selfish than the domineering—and it ended when circumstances caused each to feel the one's interest was not the chief consideration in the other's thoughts.

On a mellow evening in September, I was coming from the garden with a heavy basket of apples which I had been gathering. It had got dusk, and the moon looked over the high wall of the court, causing undefined shadows to lurk in the corners of the numerous projecting portions of the building. I set my burden on the house steps by the kitchen door, and lingered to rest, and draw in a few more breaths of the soft, sweet air; my eyes were on the moon, and my back to the entrance, when I heard a voice behind me say —

"Nelly, is that you?"

It was a deep voice, and foreign in tone; yet there was something in the manner of pronouncing my name which made it sound familiar. I turned about to discover who spoke, fearfully, for the doors were shut, and I had seen nobody on approaching the steps.

Something stirred in the porch; and moving nearer, I distinguished a tall man, dressed in dark clothes, with dark face and hair. He leaned against the side, and held his fingers on the latch, as if intending to open for himself.

"Who can it be?" I thought. "Mr. Earnshaw? Oh, no! The voice has no resemblance to his."

"I have waited here an hour," he resumed, while I continued staring; "and the whole of that time all round has been as still as death, I dared not enter. You do not know me? Look, I'm not a stranger!"

A ray fell on his features; the cheeks were sallow, and half covered with black whiskers; the brows lowering, the eyes deep set and singular. I remembered the eyes.

"What!" I cried, uncertain whether to regard him as a worldly visitor, and I raised my hands in amazement. "What! you come back? Is it really you? Is it?"

"Yes, Heathcliff," he replied, glancing from me up to the windows which reflected a score of glittering moons, but showed no lights from within. "Are they at home—where is she? Nelly, you are not glad—you needn't be so disturbed. Is she here? Speak! I want to have one word with her—your mistress. Go, and say some person from Gimmerton desires to see her."

"How will she take it?" I exclaimed, "what will she do? The surprise bewilders me—it will put her out of her head! And you *are* Heathcliff? But altered! Nay, there's no comprehending it. Have you been for a soldier?"

"Go, and carry my message," he interrupted, impatiently; "I'm in hell till you do!"

He lifted the latch, and I entered; but when I got to the parlor where Mr. and Mrs. Linton were, I could not persuade myself to proceed.

At length, I resolved on making an excuse to ask if they would have the candles lighted, and I opened the door.

They sat together in a window whose lattice lay back against the wall, and displayed beyond the garden trees and the wild green park, the valley of Gimmerton, with a long line of mist winding nearly to its top (for very soon after you pass the chapel, as you may have noticed, the slough that runs from the marshes joins a beck which follows the bend of the glen); Wuthering Heights rose above this silent vapor, but our old house was invisible—it rather dips down on the other side.

Both the room, and its occupants, and the scene they gazed on, looked wondrously peaceful. I shrank reluctantly from performing my errand; and was actually going away, leaving it unsaid, after having put my question about the candles, when a sense of my folly compelled me to return, and mutter,

"A person from Gimmerton wishes to see you, ma'am."

"What does he want?" asked Mrs. Linton.

"I did not question him," I answered.

"Well, close the curtains, Nelly," she said, "and bring up tea. I'll be back again directly."

She quitted the apartment; Mr. Edgar inquired carelessly, who it was?

"Some one the mistress does not expect," I replied. "That Heathcliff, you recollect him, sir, who used to live at Mr. Earnshaw's."

"What, the gipsy—the plough-boy?" he cried. "Why did you not say so to Catherine?"

"Hush! you must not call him by those names, master," I said. "She'd be sadly grieved to hear you. She was nearly heart-broken when he ran off; I guess his return will make a jubilee to her."

Mr. Linton walked to a window on the other side of the room that overlooked the court. He unfastened it, and leaned out. I suppose they were below, for he exclaimed quickly,

"Don't stand there, love! Bring the person in, if it be any one particular."

Ere long, I heard the click of the latch, and Catherine flew upstairs, breathless and wild, too excited to show gladness; indeed by her face, you would rather have surmised an awful calamity.

"Oh, Edgar, Edgar!" she panted, flinging her arms around his neck. "Oh, Edgar, darling! Heathcliff's come back—he is!" And she tightened her embrace to a squeeze.

"Well, well," cried her husband, crossly, "don't strangle me for that! He never struck me as such a marvelous treasure. There is no need to be frantic!"

"I know you didn't like him," she answered, repressing a little the intensity of her delight. "Yet for my sake, you must be friends now. Shall I tell him to come up?"

"Here," he said, "into the parlor?"

"Where else?" she asked.

He looked vexed, and suggested the kitchen as a more suitable place for him.

Mrs. Linton eyed him with a droll expression—half angry, half laughing at his fastidiousness.

"No," she added, after a while, "I cannot sit in the kitchen. Set two tables here, Ellen, one for your master and Miss Isabella, being gentry; the other of Heathcliff and myself, being of the lower orders. Will that please you, dear? Or must I have a fire lighted elsewhere? If so, give directions. I'll run down and secure my guest. I'm afraid the joy is too great to be real!"

She was about to dart off again; but Edgar arrested her.

"*You* bid him step up," he said, addressing me, "and, Catherine, try to be glad, without being absurd! The whole household need not witness the sight of your welcoming a runaway servant as a brother."

I descended, and found Heathcliff waiting under the porch, evidently anticipating an invitation to enter. He followed my guidance, without waste of words; and I ushered him into the presence of the master and mistress, whose flushed cheeks betrayed signs of warm talking. But the lady's glowed with another feeling when her friend appeared at the door; she sprang forward, took both his hands, and led him to Linton: and then she seized Linton's reluctant fingers, and crushed them into his.

Now fully revealed by the fire and candlelight, I was amazed more than ever, to behold the transformation of Heathcliff. He had grown a tall, athletic, well-formed man; beside whom my master seemed quite slender and youthlike. His upright carriage suggested the idea of his having been in the army. His countenance was much older in expression and decision of feature than Mr. Linton's; it looked intelligent, and retained no marks of former degradation. A half-civilized ferocity lurked yet in the depressed brows, and eyes full of black fire, but it was subdued; and his manner was even dignified, quite divested of roughness though too stern for grace.

My master's surprise equaled or exceeded mine; he remained for a minute at a loss how to address the plough-boy, as he had called him; Heathcliff dropped his slight hand, and stood looking at him coolly till he chose to speak.

"Sit down, sir," he said, at length. "Mrs. Linton, recalling old times, would have me give you a cordial reception, and, of course, I am gratified when anything occurs to please her."

"And I also," answered Heathcliff, "especially if it be anything in which I have a part. I shall stay an hour or two willingly."

He took a seat opposite Catherine, who kept her gaze fixed on

him as if she feared he would vanish were she to remove it. He did
not often raise his to her; a quick glance now and then sufficed;
but it flashed back, each time more confidently, the undisguised
delight he drank from hers.

They were too much absorbed in their mutual joy to suffer
embarrassment; not so Mr. Edgar, he grew pale with pure annoyance, a feeling that reached its climax when his lady rose—
and stepping across the rug, seized Heathcliff's hands again, and
laughed like one beside herself.

"I shall think it a dream to-morrow!" she cried. "I shall not be
able to believe that I have seen, and touched, and spoken to you
once more—and yet, cruel Heathcliff! you don't deserve this welcome. To be absent and silent for three years, and never to think
of me!"

"A little more than you have thought of me!" he murmured. "I
heard of your marriage, Cathy, not long since; and, while waiting
in the yard below, I meditated this plan—just to have one glimpse
of your face—a stare of surprise, perhaps, and pretended pleasure; afterward settle my score with Hindley; and then prevent the
law by doing execution on myself. Your welcome has put these
ideas out of my mind; but beware of meeting me with another
aspect next time! Nay, you'll not drive me off again. You were
really sorry for me, were you? Well, there was a cause. I've fought
through a bitter life since I last heard your voice, and you must
forgive me, for I struggled only for you!"

"Catherine, unless we are to have cold tea, please to come to the
table," interrupted Linton, striving to preserve his ordinary tone,
and a due measure of politeness. "Mr. Heathcliff will have a long
walk, wherever he may lodge to-night; and I'm thirsty."

She took her post before the urn; and Miss Isabella came, summoned by the bell: then, having handed their chairs forward, I left
the room.

The meal hardly endured ten minutes. Catherine's cup was
never filled, she could neither eat, nor drink. Edgar had made a
slop in the saucer, and scarcely swallowed a mouthful.

Their guest did not protract his stay, that evening, above an
hour longer. I asked, as he departed, if he went to Gimmerton?

"No, to Wuthering Heights," he answered, "Mr. Earnshaw invited me when I called this morning."

Mr. Earnshaw invited *him*! and *he* called on Mr. Earnshaw! I
pondered this sentence painfully, after he was gone. Is he turning
out a bit of a hypocrite, and coming into the country to work
mischief under a cloak? I mused—I had a presentiment, in the
bottom of my heart, that he had better have remained away.

About the middle of the night, I was wakened from my first nap
by Mrs. Linton gliding into my chamber, taking a seat on my bed-
side, and pulling me by the hair to rouse me.

"I cannot rest, Ellen," she said by way of apology. "And I want
some living creature to keep me company in my happiness! Edgar
is sulky, because I'm glad of a thing that does not interest him. He
refuses to open his mouth, except to utter pettish, silly speeches;
and he affirmed I was cruel and selfish for wishing to talk when he

was so sick and sleepy. He always contrives to be sick at the least cross! I gave a few sentences of commendation to Heathcliff, and he, either for a headache or a pang of envy, began to cry; so I got up and left him."

"What use is it praising Heathcliff to him?" I answered, "As lads they had an aversion to each other, and Heathcliff would hate just as much to hear him praised—it's human nature. Let Mr. Linton alone about him, unless you would like an open quarrel between them."

"But does it not show great weakness?" pursued she. "I'm not envious—I never feel hurt at the brightness of Isabella's yellow hair, and the whiteness of her skin; at her dainty elegance, and the fondness all the family exhibit for her. Even you, Nelly, if we have a dispute sometimes, you back Isabella at once; and I yield, like a foolish mother. I call her a darling, and flatter her into a good temper. It pleases her brother to see us cordial, and that pleases me. But they are very much alike. They are spoiled children, and fancy the world was made for their accommodation; and, though I humor both, I think a smart chastisement might improve them, all the same."

"You're mistaken, Mrs. Linton," said I, "They humor you—I know what there would be to do if they did not! You can well afford to indulge their passing whims, as long as their business is to anticipate all your desires. You may, however, fall out, at last, over something of equal consequence to both sides; and then those you term weak are very capable of being as obstinate as you!"

"And then we shall fight to the death, shan't we, Nelly?" she returned, laughing. "No! I tell you, I have such faith in Linton's love that I believe I might kill him, and he wouldn't wish to retaliate."

I advised her to value him the more for his affection.

"I do," she answered, "but he needn't resort to whining for trifles. It is childish; and instead of melting into tears because I said that Heathcliff was now worthy of any one's regard, and it would honor the first gentleman in the country to be his friend, he ought to have said it for me, and been delighted from sympathy. He must get accustomed to him, and he may as well like him—considering how Heathcliff has reason to object to him, I'm sure he behaved excellently!"

"What do you think of his going to Wuthering Heights?" I inquired. "He is reformed in every respect, apparently—quite a Christian—offering the right hand of fellowship to his enemies all round!"

"He explained it," she replied. "I wondered as much as you. He said he called to gather information concerning me from you, supposing you resided there still; and Joseph told Hindley, who came out and fell to questioning him of what he had been doing, and how he had been living, and finally desired him to walk in. There were some persons sitting at cards—Heathcliff joined them; my brother lost some money to him; and, finding him plentifully supplied, he requested that he would come again in the evening, to which he consented. Hindley is too reckless to select his acquaintance prudently; he doesn't trouble himself to reflect on the causes he might have for mistrusting one whom he has basely injured. But Heathcliff affirms his principal reason for resuming a connection with his ancient persecutor is a wish to install himself in quarters at walking distance from the Grange, and an attachment to the house where we lived together; and, likewise, a hope that I shall have more opportunities of seeing him there than I could have if he settled in Gimmerton. He means to offer liberal payment for permission to lodge at the Heights; and doubtless my brother's covetousness will prompt him to accept the terms; he was always greedy, though what he grasps with one hand, he flings away with the other."

"It's a nice place for a young man to fix his dwelling in!" said I, "Have you no fear of the consequences, Mrs. Linton?"

"None for my friend," she replied, "his strong head will keep him from danger: a little for Hindley; but he can't be made morally worse than he is; and I stand between him and bodily harm. The event of this evening has reconciled me to God and humanity! I had risen in angry rebellion against providence. Oh, I've endured very, very bitter misery. Nelly, if that creature knew how bitter, he'd be ashamed to cloud its removal with idle petulance. It was kindness for him which induced me to bear it alone: had I expressed the agony I frequently felt, he would have been taught to long for its alleviation as ardently as I. However, it's over, and I'll take no revenge on his folly. I can afford to suffer anything hereafter! Should the meanest thing alive slap me on the cheek, I'd not only turn the other, but I'd ask pardon for provoking it; and, as a proof, I'll go make my peace with Edgar instantly. Good night—I'm an angel!"

In this self-complacent conviction she departed; and the success of her fulfilled resolution was obvious on the morrow. Mr. Linton had not only abjured his peevishness (though his spirits seemed still subdued by the exuberance of Catherine's vivacity), but he ventured no objection to her taking Isabella with her to Wuthering Heights in the afternoon; and she rewarded him with such a summer of sweetness and affection in return, as made the house a paradise for several days; both master and servants profiting from the perpetual sunshine.

Heathcliff—Mr. Heathcliff I should say in future—used the liberty of visiting at Thrushcross Grange cautiously at first: he seemed estimating how far its owner would bear his intrusion. Catherine also deemed it judicious to moderate her expressions of pleasure in receiving him; and he gradually established his right to be expected.

He retained a great deal of the reserve for which his boyhood was remarkable, and that served to repress all startling demonstrations of feeling. My master's uneasiness experienced a lull, and further circumstances diverted it into another channel for a space.

His new source of trouble sprang from the not anticipated misfortune of Isabella Linton evincing a sudden and irresistible attraction toward the tolerated guest. She was at that time a charming young lady of eighteen; infantile in manners, though possessed of keen wit, keen feelings, and a keen temper, too, if irritated. Her brother, who loved her tenderly, was appalled at this fantastic preference. Leaving aside the degradation of an alliance with a nameless man, and the possible fact that his property, in default of heirs male, might pass into such a one's power, he had sense to comprehend Heathcliff's disposition—to know that, though his exterior was altered, his mind was unchangeable and unchanged. And he dreaded that mind; it revolted him; he shrank forebodingly from the idea of committing Isabella to its keeping.

He would have recoiled still more had he been aware that her attachment rose unsolicited, and was bestowed where it awakened no reciprocation of sentiment; for the minute he discovered its existence, he laid the blame on Heathcliff's deliberate designing.

We had all remarked, during some time, that Miss Linton fretted and pined over something. She grew cross and wearisome, snapping at and teasing Catherine continually, at the imminent risk of exhausting her limited patience. We excused her, to a certain extent, on the plea of ill health; she was dwindling and fading before our eyes. But one day when she had been peculiarly wayward, rejecting her breakfast, complaining that the servants did not do what she told them; that the mistress would allow her to be nothing in the house, and Edgar neglected her; that she had caught a cold with the doors being left open, and we let the parlor fire go out on purpose to vex her; with a hundred yet more frivolous accusations, Mrs. Linton peremptorily insisted that she should get to bed; and, having scolded her heartily, threatened to send for the doctor.

Mention of Kenneth caused her to exclaim instantly that her health was perfect, and it was only Catherine's harshness which made her unhappy.

"How can you say I am harsh, you naughty fondling?" cried the mistress, amazed at the unreasonable assertion. "You are surely losing your reason. When have I been harsh, tell me?"

"Yesterday," sobbed Isabella, "and now!"

"Yesterday!" said her sister-in-law. "On what occasion?"

"In our walk along the moor; you told me to ramble where I pleased, while you sauntered on with Mr. Heathcliff."

"And that's your notion of harshness?" said Catherine, laughing. "It was no hint that your company was superfluous; we didn't care whether you kept with us or not; I merely thought Heathcliff's talk would have nothing entertaining for your ears."

"Oh no," wept the young lady, "you wished me away because you knew I liked to be there."

"Is she sane?" asked Mrs. Linton, appealing to me. "I'll repeat our conversation word for word, Isabella, and you point out any charm it could have had for you."

"I don't mind the conversation," she answered: "I wanted to be with—"

"Well!" said Catherine, perceiving her hesitate to complete the sentence.

"With him; and I won't be always sent off!" she continued, kindling up. "You are a dog in the manger, Cathy, and desire no one to be loved but yourself!"

"You are an impertinent little monkey!" exclaimed Mrs. Linton, in surprise. "But I'll not believe this idiocy! It is impossible that you can covet the admiration of Heathcliff—that you can consider him an agreeable person! I hope I have misunderstood you, Isabella?"

"No you have not," said the infatuated girl. "I love him more than ever you loved Edgar; and he might love me if you would let him!"

"I wouldn't be you for a kingdom, then!" Catherine declared, emphatically—and she seemed to speak sincerely. "Nelly, help me to convince her of her madness. Tell her what Heathcliff is—an unreclaimed creature, without refinement—without cultivation; an arid wilderness of furze and whinstone. I'd as soon put that little canary into the park on a winter's day as recommend you to bestow your heart on him! It is deplorable ignorance of his character, child, and nothing else, which makes that dream enter your head. Pray don't imagine that he conceals depths of benevolence and affection beneath a stern exterior! He's not a rough diamond—a pearl-containing oyster of a rustic; he's a fierce, pitiless, wolfish man. I never say to him, Let this or that enemy alone, because it would be ungenerous or cruel to harm them. I say, Let them alone, because *I* should hate them to be wronged: and he'd crush you, like a sparrow's egg, Isabella, if he found you a troublesome charge. I know he couldn't love a Linton; and yet, he'd be quite capable of marrying your fortune and expectations. Avarice is growing with him a besetting sin. There's my picture; and I'm his friend—so much so that had he thought seriously to catch you, I should, perhaps, have held my tongue and let you fall into this trap."

Miss Linton regarded her sister-in-law with indignation.

"For shame! for shame!" she repeated, angrily. "You are worse than twenty foes, you poisonous friend!"

"Ah! you won't believe me then?" said Catherine. "You think I speak from wicked selfishness?"

"I'm certain you do," retorted Isabella; "and I shudder at you!"

"Good!" cried the other. "Try for yourself, if that be your spirit; I have done, and yield the argument to your saucy insolence."

"And I must suffer for her egotism!" she sobbed, as Mrs. Linton left the room. "All, all is against me; she has blighted my single consolation. But she uttered falsehoods, didn't she? Mr. Heathcliff is not a fiend; he has an honorable soul, and a true one, or how could he remember her?"

"Banish him from your thoughts, Miss," I said. "He's a bird of bad omen; no mate for you. Mrs. Linton spoke strongly, and yet I can't contradict her. She is better acquainted with his heart than I, or any one besides; and she never would represent him as worse than he is. Honest people don't hide their deeds. How has he been living? how has he got rich? why is he staying at Wuthering Heights—the house of a man whom he abhors? They say Mr.

Earnshaw is worse and worse since he came. They sit up all night together continually: and Hindley has been borrowing money on his land; and does nothing but play and drink, I heard only a week ago; it was Joseph who told me—I met him at Gimmerton."

"'Nelly,' he said, 'we's hae a Crahnr's' quest enah, at ahr folks. One on e'm's a'most gettin his finger cut off wi' hauding t'other froo' sticking hisseln loike a cawlf. That's maister, yah knaw, ut's soa up uh going tuh t'grand 'sizes. He's noan feared uh t' Bench uh judges, norther Paul, nur Peter, nur John, nor Mathew, nor noan on 'em, nut he! He fair like's he langs tuh set his brazened face agean 'em! And you bonny lad Heathcliff, yah mind, he's a rare un! He can girn a laugh, as weel's onybody at a raight divil's jest. Does he niver say nowt of his fine living amang us, when he goes tuh t' Grange? This is t' way on't—up at sun-dahn; dice, brandy, cloised shutters, und can'le lught till next day, at nooin— then t' fooil gangs banning un raving tuh his cham'er, makking dacent fowks dig thur fingers i' thur lugs for varry shaume; un' th' knave, wah, he earn cahnt his brass, un' ate, un' sleep, un' off tuh his neighbor's tuh gossip wi' t' wife. I' course, he tells Dame Catherine hah hor father's goold runs intuh his pocket, and her father's son gallops dahn t' broad road, while he flees afore tuh oppen t' pikes?' Now, Miss Linton, Joseph is an old rascal, but no liar; and, if his account of Heathcliff's conduct be true, you would never think of desiring such a husband, would you?"

"You are leagued with the rest, Ellen!" she replied. "I'll not listen to your slanders. What malevolence you must have to wish to convince me that there is no happiness in the world!" Whether she would have got over this fancy if left to herself, or persevered in nursing it perpetually, I cannot say; she had little time to reflect. The day after there was a justice-meeting at the next town; my master was obliged to attend; and Mr. Heathcliff, aware of his absence, called rather earlier than usual.

Catherine and Isabella were sitting in the library, on hostile terms, but silent. The latter alarmed at her recent indiscretion, and the disclosure she had made of her secret feelings in a transient fit of passion; the former, on mature consideration, really offended with her companion; and, if she laughed again at her pertness, inclined to make it no laughing matter to *her*.

She did laugh as she saw Heathcliff pass the window. I was sweeping the hearth, and I noticed a mischievous smile on her lips. Isabella, absorbed in her meditations, or a book, remained till the door opened, and it was too late to attempt an escape, which she would gladly have done had it been practicable.

"Come in, that's right!" exclaimed the mistress, gayly, pulling a chair to the fire. "Here are two people sadly in need of a third to thaw the ice between them; and you are the very one we should both of us choose. Heathcliff, I'm proud to show you, at last, somebody that dotes on you more than myself. I expect you to feel flattered—nay, it's not Nelly; don't look at her! My poor little sister-in-law is breaking her heart by mere contemplation of your physical and moral beauty. It lies in your own power to be Edgar's brother! No, no, Isabella, you shan't run off," she continued, arresting, with feigned playfulness, the confounded girl who had risen indignantly. "We were quarreling like cats about you, Heathcliff; and I was fairly beaten in protestations of devotion and admiration; and, moreover, I was informed that if I would but have the manners to stand aside, my rival, as she will have herself to be, would shoot a shaft into your soul that would fix you for ever, and send my image into eternal oblivion!"

"Catherine," said Isabella, calling up her dignity, and disdaining to struggle from the tight grasp that held her. "I'd thank you to adhere to the truth, and not slander me, even in joke! Mr. Heathcliff, be kind enough to bid this friend of yours release me—she forgets that you and I are not intimate acquaintances, and what amuses her is painful to me beyond expression."

As the guest answered nothing, but took his seat, and looked thoroughly indifferent what sentiments she cherished concerning him, she turned, and whispered an earnest appeal for liberty to her tormentor.

"By no means!" cried Mrs. Linton in answer. "I won't be named a dog in the manger again. You *shall* stay, now then! Heathcliff, why don't you evince satisfaction at my pleasant news? Isabella swears that the love Edgar has for me, is nothing to that she entertains for you. I'm sure she made some speech of the kind, did she not, Ellen? And she has fasted ever since the day before yesterday's walk, from sorrow and rage that I dispatched her out of your society, under the idea of its being unacceptable."

"I think you belie her," said Heathcliff, twisting his chair to face them. "She wishes to be out of my society now, at any rate!"

And he stared hard at the object of discourse, as one might do at a strange repulsive animal, a centipede from the Indies, for instance, which curiosity leads one to examine in spite of the aversion it raises.

The poor thing couldn't bear that; she grew white and red in rapid succession, and, white tears beaded her lashes, bent the strength of her small fingers to loosen the firm clutch of Catherine, and perceiving that, as fast as she raised one finger off her arm, another closed down, and she could not remove the whole together, she began to make use of her nails, and their sharpness presently ornamented the detainer's with crescents of red.

"There's a tigress!" exclaimed Mrs. Linton, setting her free, and shaking her hand with pain. "Begone, for God's sake, and hide your vixen face! How foolish to reveal those talons to *him*. Can't you fancy the conclusions he'll draw? Look, Heathcliff! they are instruments that will do execution—you must beware of your eyes."

"I'd wrench them off her fingers, if they ever menaced me," he answered, brutally, when the door had closed after her. "But, what did you mean by teasing the creature in that manner, Cathy? You were not speaking the truth, were you?"

"I assure you I was," she returned. "She has been pining for your sake several weeks; and raving about you this morning, and pouring forth a deluge of abuse, because I represented your fail-ings in a plain light, for the purpose of mitigating her adoration. But don't notice it further. I wished to punish her sauciness, that's all. I like her too well, my dear Heathcliff, to let you absolutely seize and devour her up."

"And I like her too ill to attempt it," said he, "except in a very ghoulish fashion. You'd hear of odd things, if I lived alone with that mawkish, waxen face, the most ordinary would be painting on its white the colors of the rainbow, and turning the blue eyes black, every day or two; they detestably resemble Linton's."

"Delectably," observed Catherine. "They are dove's eyes—angel's!"

"She's her brother's heir, is she not?" he asked, after a brief silence.

"I should be sorry to think so," returned his companion. "Half-a-dozen nephews shall erase her title, please Heaven! Abstract your mind from the subject, at present—you are too prone to covet your neighbor's goods: remember *this* neighbor's goods are mine."

"If they were *mine*, they would be none the less that," said Heathcliff, "but though Isabella Linton may be silly, she is scarcely mad; and—in short we'll dismiss the matter as you advise."

From their tongues, they did dismiss it; and Catherine, probably, from her thoughts. The other, I felt certain, recalled it often in the course of the evening; I saw him smile to himself—grin rather—and lapse into ominous musing whenever Mrs. Linton had occasion to be absent from the apartment.

I determined to watch his movements. My heart invariably cleaved to the master's, in preference to Catherine's side; with reason, I imagined, for he was kind, and trustful, and honorable: and she—she could not be called the *opposite*, yet she seemed to allow herself such wide latitude that I had little faith in her principles, and still less sympathy for her feelings. I wanted something to happen which might have the effect of freeing both Wuthering Heights and the Grange of Mr. Heathcliff, quietly, leaving us as we had been prior to his advent. His visits were a continual nightmare to me; and, I suspected, to my master also. His abode at the Heights was an oppression past explaining. I felt that God had forsaken the stray sheep there to its own wicked wanderings, and an evil beast prowled between it and the fold, waiting his time to spring and destroy.

. . . .

Chapter 11

Sometimes, while meditating on these things in solitude, I have got up in a sudden terror, and put on my bonnet to go see how all was at the farm; I have persuaded my conscience that it was a duty to warn him how people talked regarding his ways; and then I have recollected his confirmed bad habits, and hopeless of benefiting him, have flinched from re-entering the dismal house, doubting if I could bear to be taken at my word.

One time I passed the old gate, going out of my way, on a journey to Gimmerton. It was about the period that my narrative has reached—a bright, frosty afternoon; the ground bare, and the road hard and dry.

I came to a stone where the highway branches off on to the moor at your left hand; a rough sand-pillar, with the letters W.H. cut on its north side, on the east G., and on the south west T.G. It serves as guide-post to the Grange, and Heights, and village.

The sun shone yellow on its gray head, reminding me of summer; and I can not say why, but all at once a gush of child's sensations flowed into my heart. Hindley and I held it a favorite spot twenty years before.

I gazed long at the weather-worn block; and, stooping down, perceived a hole near the bottom still full of snail-shells and pebbles, which we were fond of storing there with more perishable things—and, as fresh as reality, it appeared that I beheld my early playmate seated on the withered turf; his dark, square head bent forward, and his little hand scooping out the earth with a piece of slate.

"Poor Hindley!" I exclaimed involuntarily.

I started—my bodily eye was cheated into a momentary belief that the child lifted its face and stared straight into mine! It vanished in a twinkling; but immediately I felt an irresistible yearning to be at the Heights. Superstition urged me to comply with this impulse—supposing he should be dead! I thought—or should die soon!—supposing it were a sign of death!

The nearer I got to the house the more agitated I grew: and on catching sight of it I trembled in every limb. The apparition had outstripped me; it stood looking through the gate. That was my first idea on observing an elf-locked, brown-eyed boy setting his ruddy countenance against the bars. Further reflection suggested this must be Hareton, *my* Hareton, not altered greatly since I left him, ten months since.

"God bless thee, darling!" I cried, forgetting instantaneously my foolish fears. "Hareton, it's Nelly—Nelly, thy nurse."

He retreated out of arm's length, and picked up a large flint.

"I am come to see thy father, Hareton," I added, guessing from the action that Nelly, if she lived in his memory at all, was not recognized as one with me.

He raised his missile to hurl it; I commenced a soothing speech, but could not stay his hand. The stone struck my bonnet, and then ensued from the stammering lips of the little fellow a string of curses, which, whether he comprehended them or not, were delivered with practiced emphasis, and distorted his baby features into a shocking expression of malignity.

You may be certain this grieved more than angered me. Fit to cry, I took an orange from my pocket, and offered it to propitiate him.

He hesitated, and then snatched it from my hold, as if he fancied I only intended to tempt and disappoint him.

I showed another, keeping it out of his reach.

"Who has taught you those fine words, my bairn," I inquired. "The curate?"

"Damn the curate and thee! Gie me that," he replied.

"Tell us where you got your lessons, and you shall have it," said I. "Who's your master?"

"Devil daddy," was his answer.

"And what do you learn from daddy?" I continued.

He jumped at the fruit; I raised it higher. "What does he teach you?" I asked.

"Naught," said he, "but to keep out of his gait. Daddy cannot bide me, because I swear at him."

"Ah! and the devil teaches you to swear at daddy?" I observed.

"Ay—nay," he drawled.

"Who then?"

"Heathcliff."

I asked if he liked Mr. Heathcliff?

"Aye!" he answered again.

Desiring to have his reasons for liking him, I could only gather the sentences. "I known't—he pays dad back what he gies to me—he curses daddy for cursing me—he says I mun do as I will."

"And the curate does not teach you to read and write, then?" I pursued.

No; I was told the curate should have his—teeth dashed down his—throat, if he stepped over the threshold—Heathcliff had promised that.

I put the orange in his hand; and bade him tell his father that a woman called Nelly Dean was waiting to speak with him, by the garden gate.

He went up the walk, and entered the house; but instead of Hindley, Heathcliff appeared on the door stones, and I turned directly and ran down the road as hard as ever I could race, making no halt till I gained the guide-post, and feeling as scared as if I had raised a goblin.

This is not much connected with Miss Isabella's affair, except that it urged me to resolve, further, on mounting vigilant guard and doing my utmost to check the spread of such bad influence at the Grange, even though I should wake a domestic storm by thwarting Mrs. Linton's pleasure.

The next time Heathcliff came, my young lady chanced to be feeding some pigeons in the court. She had never spoken a word to her sister-in-law for three days; but she had likewise dropped her fretful complaining, and we found it a great comfort.

Heathcliff had not the habit of bestowing a single unnecessary civility on Miss Linton, I knew. Now, as soon as he beheld her, his first precaution was to take a sweeping survey of the house-front. I was standing by the kitchen window, but I drew out of sight. He then stepped across the pavement to her, and said something; she seemed embarrassed, and desirous of getting away; to prevent it, he laid his hand on her arm: she averted her face; he apparently put some question which she had no mind to answer. There was another rapid glance at the house, and supposing himself unseen, the scoundrel had the impudence to embrace her.

"Judas! Traitor!" I ejaculated; "you are a hypocrite, too, are you? A deliberate deceiver."

"Who is, Nelly?" said Catherine's voice at my elbow—I had been over-intent on watching the pair outside to mark her entrance.

"Your worthless friend!" I answered warmly, "the sneaking rascal yonder—ah, he has caught a glimpse of us—he is coming in! In wonder will he have the art to find a plausible excuse, for making love to Miss, when he told you he hated her!"

Mrs. Linton saw Isabella tear herself free, and run into the garden; and a minute after, Heathcliff opened the door.

I couldn't withhold giving some loose to my indignation; but Catherine angrily insisted on silence, and threatened to order me out of the kitchen, if I dared be so presumptuous as to put in my insolent tongue.

"To hear you, people might think *you* were the mistress!" she cried. "You want setting down in your right place! Heathcliff, what are you about, raising this stir? I said you must let Isabella alone! I beg you will, unless you are tired of being received here, and wish Linton to draw the bolts against you!"

"God fordid that he should try!" answered the black villain—I detested him just then. "God keep him meek and patient! Every day I grow madder after sending him to heaven!"

"Hush!" said Catherine shutting the inner door. "Don't vex me. Why have you disregarded my request? Did she come across you on purpose?"

"What is it to you?" he growled. "I have a right to kiss her, if she chooses, and you have no right to object—I'm not *your* husband; *you* needn't be jealous of me!"

"I'm not jealous of you;" replied the mistress; "I'm jealous for you. Clear your face, you shan't scowl at me! If you like Isabella, you shall marry her. But, do you like her? Tell the truth, Heathcliff. There, you won't answer. I'm certain you don't."

"And would Mr. Linton approve of his sister marrying that man?" I inquired.

"Mr. Linton should approve," returned my lady decisively.

"He might spare himself the trouble," said Heathcliff, "I could do as well without his approbation; and, as to you, Catherine, I have a mind to speak a few words now, while we are at it—I want you to be aware that I *know* you have treated me infernally—infernally! Do you hear? And, if you flatter yourself that I don't perceive it you are a fool—and if you think I can be consoled by sweet words you are an idiot—and if you fancy I'll suffer unrevenged, I'll convince you of the contrary in a very little while! Meantime, thank you for telling me your sister-in-law's secret. I swear I'll make the most of it, and stand you aside!"

"What new phase of his character is this?" exclaimed Mrs. Linton, in amazement. "I've treated you infernally—and you'll take revenge! How will you take it, ungrateful brute? How have I treated you infernally?"

"I seek no revenge on you," replied Heathcliff less vehemently. "That's not the plan. The tyrant grinds down his slaves and they don't turn against him, they crush those beneath them. You are welcome to torture me to death for your amusement; only allow me to amuse myself a little in the same style. And refrain from insult as much as you are able. Having leveled my palace, don't erect a hovel and complacently admire your own charity in giving me that for a home. If I imagined you really wished me to marry Isabella, I'd cut my throat."

"Oh the evil is that I am *not* jealous, is it?" cried Catherine. "Well, I won't repeat my offer of a wife. It is as bad as offering Satan a lost soul Your bliss lies, like his, in inflicting misery. You prove it. Edgar is restored from the ill-temper he gave way to at your coming; I begin to be secure and tranquil; and you, restless to know us at peace, appear resolved on exciting a quarrel. Quarrel with Edgar if you please, Heathcliff, and deceive his sister; you'll hit on exactly the most efficient method of revenging yourself on me."

The conversation ceased; Mrs. Linton sat down by the fire, flushed and gloomy. The spirit which served her was growing intractable: she could neither lay nor control it. He stood on the hearth, with folded arms, brooding on his evil thoughts; and in this position I left them, to seek the master who was wondering what kept Catherine below so long.

"Ellen," said he, when I entered, "have you seen your mistress?"

"Yes, she's in the kitchen, sir," I answered. "She's sadly put out by Mr. Heathcliff's behavior: and, indeed, I do think it's time to arrange his visits on another footing. There's harm in being too soft, and now it's come to this—." And I related the scene in the court, and, as near as I dared, the whole subsequent dispute. I fancied it could not be very prejudicial to Mrs. Linton, unless she made it so afterward, by assuming the defensive for her guest.

Edgar Linton had difficulty in hearing me to the close. His first words revealed that he did not clear his wife of blame.

"This is insufferable!" he exclaimed. "It is disgraceful that she should own him for a friend, and force his company on me! Call me two men out of the hall, Ellen. Catherine shall linger no longer to argue with the low ruffian—I have humored her enough."

He descended, and, bidding the servants wait in the passage, went, followed by me, to the kitchen. Its occupants had recommenced their angry discussion; Mrs. Linton, at least, was scolding with renewed vigor; Heathcliff had moved to the window, and hung his head, apparently somewhat cowed by her violent rating.

He saw the master first, and made a hasty motion that she should be silent; which she obeyed abruptly, on discovering the reason of his intimation.

"How is this?" said Linton, addressing her; "what notion of propriety must you have to remain here, after the language which has been held to you by that blackguard? I suppose because it is his ordinary talk you think nothing of it; you are habituated to his baseness, and, perhaps, imagine I can get used to it too!"

"Have you been listening at the door, Edgar?" asked the mistress, in a tone particularly calculated to provoke her husband, implying both carelessness and contempt of his irritation.

Heathcliff, who had raised his eyes at the former speech, gave a sneering laugh at the latter, on purpose, it seemed, to draw Mr. Linton's attention to him.

He succeeded; but Edgar did not mean to entertain him with any high flights of passion.

"I have been so far forbearing with you, sir," he said, quietly; "not that I was ignorant of your miserable, degraded character, but I felt you were only partly responsible for that; and Catherine, wishing to keep up your acquaintance, I acquiesced—foolishly. Your presence is a moral poison that would contaminate the most virtuous; for that cause, and to prevent worse consequences, I shall deny you hereafter admission into this house, and give notice now that I require your instant departure. Three minutes' delay will render it involuntary and ignominious."

Heathcliff measured the height and breadth of the speaker with an eye full of derision.

"Cathy, this lamb of yours threatens like a bull!" he said. "It is in danger of splitting its skull against my knuckles. By God, Mr. Linton, I'm mortally sorry that you are not worth knocking down!"

My master glanced toward the passage, and signed me to fetch the men—he had no intention of hazarding a personal encounter.

I obeyed the hint; but Mrs. Linton suspecting something, followed, and when I attempted to call them, she pulled me back, slammed the door to, and locked it.

"Fair means!" she said, in answer to her husband's look of angry surprise. "If you have not the courage to attack him, make an apology, or allow yourself to be beaten. It will correct you of feigning more valor than you possess. No, I'll swallow the key before you shall get it! I'm delightfully rewarded for my kindness to each! After constant indulgence of one's weak nature, and the other's bad one, I earn, for thanks, two samples of blind ingratitude, stupid to absurdity! Edgar, I was defending you and yours; and I wish Heathcliff may flog you sick, for daring to think an evil thought of me!"

It did not need the medium of a flogging to produce that effect on the master. He tried to wrest the key from Catherine's grasp; and for safety she flung it into the hottest part of the fire; whereupon Mr. Edgar was taken with a nervous trembling, and his countenance grew deadly pale. For his life he could not avert that access of emotion; mingled anguish and humiliation overcame him completely. He leaned on the back of a chair, and covered his face.

"Oh! Heavens! In old days this would win you knighthood!" exclaimed Mrs. Linton. "We are vanquished! Heathcliff would as soon lift a finger at you as the king would march his army against a colony of mice. Cheer up, you shan't be hurt! Your type is not a lamb, it's a sucking leveret."

I wish you joy of the milk-blooded coward, Cathy!" said her

friend. "I compliment you on your taste: and that is the slavering, shivering thing you preferred to me! I would not strike him with my fist, but I'd kick him with my foot, and experience considerable satisfaction. Is he weeping, or is he going to faint for fear?"

The fellow approached and gave the chair on which Linton rested a push. He'd better have kept his distance: my master quickly sprang erect, and struck him full on the throat a blow that would have leveled a slighter man.

It took his breath for a minute; and, while he choked, Mr. Linton walked out by the back door into the yard, and from thence to the front entrance.

"There! you've done with coming here," cried Catherine. "Get away, now—he'll return with a brace of pistols, and half-a-dozen assistants. If he did overhear us, of course, he'd never forgive you. You've played me an ill turn, Heathcliff! But go—make haste! I'd rather see Edgar at bay than you."

"Do you suppose I'm going with that blow burning in my gullet?" he thundered. "By Hell, no! I'll crush his ribs in like a rotten hazel-nut before I cross the threshold! If I don't floor him now, I shall murder him sometime; so, as you value his existence, let me get at him!"

"He is not coming," I interposed, framing a bit of a lie. "There's the coachman, and the two gardeners; you'll surely not wait to be thrust into the road by them! Each has a bludgeon, and master will, very likely, be watching from the parlor windows to see that they fulfil his orders."

The gardeners and coachman *were* there, but Linton was with them. They had already entered the court. Heathcliff, on second thoughts, resolved to avoid a struggle against three underlings; he seized the poker, smashed the lock from the inner door, and made his escape as they tramped in.

Mrs. Linton, who was very much excited, bid me accompany her upstairs. She did not know my share in contributing to the disturbance, and I was anxious to keep her in ignorance.

"I'm nearly distracted, Nelly!" she exclaimed, throwing herself on the sofa. "A thousand smiths' hammers are beating in my head! Tell Isabella to shun me—this uproar is owing to her; and should she or any one else aggravate my anger at present, I shall get wild. And, Nelly, say to Edgar, if you see him again to-night, that I'm in danger of being seriously ill—I wish it may prove true. He has startled and distressed me shockingly! I want to frighten him. Besides, he might come and begin a string of abuse or complainings; I'm certain I should recriminate, and God knows where we should end! Will you do so, my good Nelly? You are aware that I am no way blamable in this matter. What possessed him to turn listener? Heathcliff's talk was outrageous after you left us; but I could soon have diverted him from Isabella, and the rest meant nothing. Now, all is dashed wrong by the fool's craving to hear evil of self, that haunts some people like a demon! Had Edgar never gathered our conversation, he would never have been the worse for it. Really, when he opened on me in that unreasonable tone of displeasure, after I had scolded Heathcliff till I was hoarse for *him*, I did not care, hardly, what they did to each other, especially as I felt that, however the scene closed, we should all be driven asunder, for nobody knows how long! Well, if I cannot keep Heathcliff for my friend, if Edgar will be mean and jealous, I'll try to break their hearts by breaking my own. That will be a prompt way of finishing all, when I am pushed to extremity! But it's a deed to be reserved for a forlorn hope—I'd not take Linton by surprise with it. To this point he has been discreet in dreading to provoke me; you must represent the peril of quitting that policy; and remind him of my passionate temper, verging, when kindled, on frenzy. I wish you could dismiss that apathy out of your countenance, and look rather more anxious about me!"

The stolidity with which I received these instructions was, no doubt, rather exasperating; for they were delivered in perfect sincerity; but I believed a person who could plan the turning of her fits of passion to account beforehand, might, by exerting her will, manage to control herself tolerably, even while under their influence; and I did not wish to "frighten" her husband, as she said, and multiply his annoyance for the purpose of serving her selfishness.

Therefore I said nothing when I met the master coming toward the parlor; but I took the liberty of turning back to listen whether they would resume their quarrel together.

He began to speak first.

"Remain where you are, Catherine," he said, without any anger in his voice, but with much sorrowful despondency, "I shall not stay. I am neither come to wrangle, nor be reconciled: but I wish just to learn whether, after this evening's events, you intend to continue your intimacy with—"

"Oh, for mercy's sake," interrupted the mistress, stamping her foot, "for mercy's sake, let us hear no more of it now! Your cold blood cannot be worked into a fever—your veins are full of ice-water—but mine are boiling; and the sight of such chillness makes them dance."

"To get rid of me—answer my question," persevered Mr. Linton. "You *must* answer it; and that violence does not alarm me. I have found that you can be as stoical as any one when you please. Will you give up Heathcliff hereafter, or will you give up me? It is impossible for you to be *my* friend and *his* at the same time, and I absolutely *require* to know which you choose."

"I require to be let alone!" exclaimed Catherine, furiously. "I demand it! Don't you see I can scarcely stand? Edgar, you—you leave me!"

She rung the bell till it broke with a twang: I entered leisurely. It was enough to try the temper of a saint, such senseless, wicked rages! There she lay, dashing her head against the arm of the sofa and grinding her teeth, so that you might fancy she would crush them to splinters!

Mr. Linton stood looking at her in sudden compunction and fear. He told me to fetch some water. She had no breath for speaking.

I brought a glassful, and, as she would not drink, I sprinkled it on her face. In a few seconds she stretched herself out stiff, and turned up her eyes, while her cheeks, at once blanched and livid, assumed the aspect of death.

Linton looked terrified.

"There is nothing in the world the matter," I whispered. I did not want him to yield, though I could not help being afraid in my heart.

"She has blood on her lips!" he said, shuddering.

"Never mind!" I answered, tartly; and I told him how she had resolved, previous to his coming, on exhibiting a fit of frenzy.

I incautiously gave the account aloud, and she heard me, for she started up—her hair flying over her shoulders, her eyes flashing, the muscles of her neck and arms standing out preternaturally. I made up my mind for broken bones at least; but she only glared about her for an instant, and then rushed from the room.

The master directed me to follow; I did, to her chamber door; she hindered me from going farther by securing it against me.

As she never offered to descend to breakfast next morning I went to ask whether she would have some carried up.

"No!" she replied, peremptorily.

The same question was repeated at dinner and tea, and again on the morrow after, and received the same answer.

Mr. Linton, on his part, spent his time in the library, and did not inquire concerning his wife's occupations. Isabella and he had had an hour's interview, during which he tried to elicit from her some sentiment of proper horror for Heathcliff's advances; but he could make nothing of her evasive replies, and was obliged to close the examination unsatisfactorily, adding, however, a solemn warning, that if she were so insane as to encourage that worthless suitor, it would dissolve all bonds of relationship between herself and him.

. . . .

Chapter 12

While Miss Linton moped about the park and garden, always silent, and almost always in tears, and her brother shut himself up among books that he never opened, wearying, I guessed, with a continual vague expectation that Catherine, repenting her conduct, would come of her own accord to ask pardon and seek a reconciliation—and *she* fasted pertinaciously, under the idea, probably, that at every meal Edgar was ready to choke for her absence, and pride alone held him from running to cast himself at her feet—I went about my household duties, convinced that the Grange had but one sensible soul in its walls, and that lodged in my body.

I wasted no condolences on Miss, nor any expostulations on my mistress, nor did I pay attention to the sighs of my master, who yearned to hear his lady's name, since he might not hear her voice.

I determined they should come about as they pleased for me; and though it was a tiresomely slow process, I began to rejoice at length in a faint dawn of its progress, as I thought at first.

Mrs. Linton on the third day unbarred her door, and having finished the water in her pitcher and decanter, desired a renewed supply and a basin of gruel, for she believed she was dying. That I set down as a speech meant for Edgar's ears. I believed no such thing; so I kept it to myself, and brought her some tea and dry toast.

She ate and drank eagerly; and sank back on her pillow, again clenching her hands and groaning.

"Oh, I will die," she exclaimed, "since no one cares anything about me. I wish I had not taken that."

Then a good while after I heard her murmur,

"No, I'll not die—he'd be glad—he does not love me at all—he would never miss me!"

"Did you want anything, ma'am?" I enquired, still preserving my external composure, in spite of her ghastly countenance, and strange, exaggerated manner.

"What is that apathetic being doing?" she demanded, pushing the thick entangled locks from her wasted face. "Has he fallen into a lethargy, or is he dead?"

"Neither," replied I; "if you mean Mr. Linton. He's tolerably well, I think, though his studies occupy him rather more than they ought; he is continually among his books, since he has no other society."

I should not have spoken so, if I had known her true condition, but I could not get rid of the notion that she acted a part of her disorder.

"Among his books!" she cried, confounded. "And I dying! I on the brink of the grave! My God! does he know how I'm altered?" continued she, staring at her reflection in a mirror, hanging against the opposite wall. "Is that Catherine Linton? He imagines me in a pet—in play, perhaps. Cannot you inform him that it is frightful earnest? Nelly, if it be not too late, as soon as I learn how he feels, I'll choose between these two: either to starve, at once—that would be no punishment unless he had a heart—or to recover and leave the country. Are you speaking the truth about him now? Take care. Is he actually so utterly indifferent for my life?"

"Why, ma'am," I answered, "the master has no ideas of your being deranged; and, of course, he does not fear that you will let yourself die of hunger."

"You think not? Cannot you tell him I will?" she returned; "persuade him—speak of your own mind—say you are certain I will!"

"No, you forget, Mrs. Linton," I suggested, "that you have eaten some food with a relish this evening, and to-morrow you will perceive its good effects."

"If I were only sure it would kill him," she interrupted, "I'd kill myself directly! These three awful nights, I've never closed my lids—and oh, I've been tormented! I've been haunted, Nelly! But I begin to fancy you don't like me. How strange! I thought, though everybody hated and despised each other, they could not avoid loving me—and they have all turned to enemies in a few hours. *They* have, I'm positive the people *here*. How dreary to meet death, surrounded by their cold faces! Isabella, terrified and repelled, afraid to enter the room, it would be so dreadful to watch Catherine go. And Edgar standing solemnly by to see it over; then offering prayers of thanks to God for restoring peace to his house, and going back to his *books!* What, in the name of all that feels, has he to do with *books*, when I am dying?"

She could not bear the notion which I had put into her head of Mr. Linton's philosophical resignation. Tossing about, she increased her feverish bewilderment to madness, and tore the pillow with her teeth; then, raising herself up all burning, desired that I would open the window. We were in the middle of winter, the wind blew strong from the northeast, and I objected.

Both the expressions flitting over her face, and the changes of her moods, began to alarm me terribly; and brought to my recollection her former illness, and the doctor's injunction that she should not be crossed.

A minute previously she was violent; now, supported on one arm, and not noticing my refusal to obey her, she seemed to find childish diversion in pulling the feathers from the rents she had just made, and ranging them on the sheet according to their different species: her mind had strayed to other associations.

"That's a turkey's," she murmured to herself; "and this is a wild-duck's; and this is a pigeon's. Ah, they put pigeons' feathers in the pillows—no wonder I couldn't die! Let me take care to throw it on the floor when I lie down. And here is a moor-cock's; and this—I should know it among a thousand—it's a lapwing's. Bonny bird! wheeling over our heads in the middle of the moor. It wanted to get to its nest, for the clouds touched the swells, and it felt rain coming. This feather was picked up from the heath, the bird was not shot—we saw its nest in the winter, full of little skeletons. Heathcliff set a trap over it, and the old ones dare not come. I made him promise he'd never shoot a lapwing after that, and he didn't. Yes, here are more! Did he shoot my lapwings, Nelly? Are they red, any of them? Let me look."

"Give over with that baby-work!" I interrupted, dragging the pillow away, and turning the holes toward the mattress, for she was removing its contents by handfuls. "Lie down and shut your eyes, you're wandering. There's a mess! The down is flying about like snow!"

I went here and there collecting it.

"I see in you, Nelly," she continued, dreamily, "an aged woman—you have gray hair and bent shoulders. This bed is the fairy cave under Penistone Crag, and you are gathering elfbolts to hurt our heifers; pretending, while I am near, that they are only locks of wool. That's what you'll come to fifty years hence; I know you are not so now. I'm not wandering, you're mistaken, or else I should believe you really *were* that withered hag, and I should think I *was* under Penistone Crag; and I'm conscious it's night, and there are two candles on the table, making the black press shine like jet."

"The black press? where is that?" I asked. "You are talking in your sleep!"

"It's against the wall, as it always is," she replied. "It *does* appear odd—I see a face in it!"

"There is no press in the room, and never was," said I, resuming my seat, and looping up the curtain that I might watch her.

"Don't *you* see that face?" she inquired, gazing earnestly at the mirror.

And say what I could, I was incapable of making her comprehend it to be her own; so I rose and covered it with a shawl.

"It's behind there still!" she pursued, anxiously. "And it stirred. Who is it? I hope it will not come out when you are gone! Oh, Nelly, the room is haunted! I'm afraid of being alone!"

I took her hand in mine, and bid her be composed, for a succession of shudders convulsed her frame, and she *would* keep straining her gaze toward the glass.

"There's nobody here," I insisted, "It was *yourself*, Mrs. Linton; you knew it a while since."

"Myself!" she gasped, "and the clock is striking twelve! It's true, then; that's dreadful!"

Her fingers clutched the clothes, and gathered them over her eyes. I attempted to steal to the door with an intention of calling her husband, but I was summoned back by a piercing shriek. The shawl had dropped from the frame.

"Why, what *is* the matter?" cried I. "Who is coward now? Wake up! That is the glass—the mirror, Mrs. Linton; and you see yourself in it, and there am I, too, by your side."

Trembling and bewildered, she held me fast, but the horror gradually passed from her countenance; its paleness gave place to a glow of shame.

"Oh, dear! I thought I was at home," she sighed. "I thought I was lying in my chamber at Wuthering Heights. Because I'm weak, my brain got confused, and I screamed unconsciously. Don't say anything, but stay with me. I dread sleeping; my dreams appall me."

"A sound sleep would do you good, ma'am," I answered; "and I hope this suffering will prevent your trying starving again."

"Oh, if I were but in my own bed in the old house!" she went on bitterly, wringing her hands. "And that wind sounding in the firs by the lattice. Do let me feel it—it comes straight down the moor—do let me have one breath!"

To pacify her, I held the casement ajar a few seconds. A cold blast rushed through; I closed it, and returned to my post.

She lay still now, her face bathed in tears. Exhaustion of body had entirely subdued her spirit; our fiery Catherine was no better than a wailing child!

"How long is it since I shut myself in here?" she asked, suddenly reviving.

"It was Monday evening," I replied, "and this is Thursday night, or rather Friday morning, at present."

"What! of the same week?" she exclaimed. "Only that brief time?"

"Long enough to live on nothing but cold water and ill-temper," observed I.

"Well, it seems a weary number of hours," she muttered, doubtfully; "it must be more—I remember being in the parlor after they had quarreled; and Edgar being cruelly provoking, and me running into this room desperate. As soon as ever I had barred the door, utter blackness overwhelmed me, and I fell on the floor. I couldn't explain to Edgar how certain I felt of having a fit, or going raging mad, if he persisted in teasing me! I had no command of tongue or brain, and he did not guess my agony, perhaps; it barely left me sense to try to escape from him and his voice. Before I recovered sufficiently to see and hear, it began to be dawn; and, Nelly, I'll tell you what I thought, and what has kept recurring and recurring till I feared for my reason: I thought, as I lay there with my head against that table leg, and my eyes dimly discerning the gray square of the window, that I was enclosed in the oak-panelled bed at home; and my heart ached with some great grief which, just waking, I could not recollect. I pondered and worried myself to discover what it could be; and, most strangely, the whole last seven years of my life grew a blank! I did not recall that they had been at all. I was a child; my father was just buried, and my misery arose from the separation that Hindley had ordered between me and Heathcliff. I was laid alone, for the first time, and rousing from a dismal doze after a night of weeping, I lifted my hand to push the panels aside; it struck the table-top! I swept it along the carpet, and then memory burst in—my late anguish was swallowed in a paroxysm of despair. I cannot say why I felt so wildly wretched; it must have been temporary derangement, for there is scarcely cause. But, supposing, at twelve years old, I had been wrenched from the Heights, and every early association, and my all in all, as Heathcliff was at that time, and been converted at a stroke into Mrs. Linton, the lady of Thrushcross Grange, and the wife of a stranger, an exile and outcast thenceforth from what had been my world—you may fancy a glimpse of the abyss where I grovelled! Shake your head as you will, Nelly, *you* have helped to unsettle me! You should have spoken to Edgar, indeed you should, and compelled him to leave me quiet. Oh, I'm burning! I wish I were out of doors. I wish I were a girl again, half savage, and hardy, and free, and laughing at injuries, not maddening under them! Why am I so changed? why does my blood rush into a hell of tumult at a few words? I'm sure I should be myself were I once among the heather on those hills. Open the window again wide, fasten it open! Quick! why don't you move?"

"Because I won't give you your death of cold," I answered.

"You won't give me a chance of life, you mean," she said sullenly. "However, I'm not helpless yet, I'll open it myself."

And sliding from the bed before I could hinder her, she crossed the room, walking very uncertainly, threw it back, and bent out, careless of the frosty air, that cut about her shoulders as keen as a knife.

I entreated, and finally attempted to force her to retire. But I soon found her delirious strength much surpassed mine (she *was* delirious I became convinced by her subsequent actions and ravings).

There was no moon, and everything beneath lay in misty darkness; not a light gleamed from any house, far or near; all had been extinguished long ago; and those at Wuthering Heights were never visible—still she asserted she caught their shining.

"Look!" she cried eagerly, "that's my room, with the candle in it, and the trees swaying before it—and the other candle is in Joseph's garret—Joseph sits up late, doesn't he? He's waiting till I come home that he may lock the gate: well, he'll wait a while yet. It's a rough journey, and a sad heart to travel it; and we must pass by Gimmerton Kirk, to go that journey! We've braved its ghosts often together, and dared each other to stand among the graves, and ask them to come. But Heathcliff, if I dare you now, will you venture? If you do, I'll keep you. I'll not lie there by myself; they may bury me twelve feet deep, and throw the church down over me; but I won't rest till you are with me—I never will!"

She paused, and resumed with a strange smile, "He's considering—he'd rather I'd come to him! Find a way, then! not through that kirkyard. You are slow! Be content, you always followed me!"

Perceiving it vain to argue against her insanity, I was planning how I could reach something to wrap about her, without quitting my hold of herself, for I could not trust her alone by the gaping lattice; when to my consternation, I heard the rattle of the doorhandle, and Mr. Linton entered. He had only then come from the library; and, in passing through the lobby, had noticed our talking, and been attracted by curiosity or fear to examine what it signified, at that late hour.

"Oh, sir!" I cried, checking the exclamation risen to his lips at the sight which met him, and the bleak atmosphere of the chamber, "my poor mistress is ill, and she quite masters me; I cannot manage her at all; pray, come and persuade her to go to bed. Forget your anger, for she's hard to guide any way but her own."

"Catherine ill?" he said, hastening to us. "Shut the window, Ellen! Catherine! Why—"

He was silent; the haggardness of Mrs. Linton's appearance smote him speechless, and he could only glance from her to me in horrified astonishment.

"She's been fretting here," I continued, "and eating scarcely anything, and never complaining; she would admit none of us till this evening, and so we couldn't inform you of her state, as we were not aware of it ourselves—but it is nothing."

I felt I uttered my explanations awkwardly; the master frowned. "It is nothing, is it, Ellen Dean?" he said sternly. "You shall account more clearly for keeping me ignorant of this!" And he took his wife in his arms, and looked at her with anguish.

At first she gave him no glance of recognition—he was invisible to her abstracted gaze. The delirium was not fixed, however; having weaned her eyes from contemplating the outer darkness, by degrees she centered her attention on him, and discovered who it was that held her.

"Ah! you are come, are you, Edgar Linton?" she said, with angry animation. "You are one of those things that are ever found when least wanted, and when you are wanted, never! I suppose we shall have plenty of lamentations, now—I see we shall—but they can't keep me from my narrow home out yonder—my resting place where I'm bound before spring is over! There it is, not among the Lintons, mind, under the chapel-roof; but in the open air with a headstone, and you may please yourself, whether you go to them or come to me!"

"Catherine, what have you done?" commenced the master. "Am I nothing to you, any more? Do you love that wretch, Heath—"

"Hush!" cried Mrs. Linton. "Hush, this moment! You mention that name, and I end the matter instantly by a spring from the window! What you touch at present, you may have; but my soul will be on that hill-top before you lay hands on me again. I don't want you, Edgar; I'm past wanting you. Return to your books; I'm glad you possess a consolation, for all you had in me is gone."

"Her mind wanders, sir," I interposed. "She has been talking nonsense the whole evening; but let her have quiet and proper attendance, and she'll rally. Hereafter, we must be cautious how we vex her."

"I desire no further advice from you," answered Mr. Linton. "You knew your mistress's nature, and you encouraged me to harass her. And not to give me one hint of how she has been these three days! It was heartless! months of sickness could not cause such a change!"

I began to defend myself, thinking it too bad to be blamed for another's wicked waywardness!

"I knew Mrs. Linton's nature to be headstrong and domineering," cried I, "but I didn't know that you wished to foster her fierce temper! I did not know that, to humor her, I should wink at Mr. Heathcliff. I performed the duty of a faithful servant in telling you, and I have got a faithful servant's wages! Well it will teach me to be careful next time. Next time you may gather intelligence for yourself!"

"The next time you bring a tale to me, you shall quit my service, Ellen Dean," he replied.

"You'd rather hear nothing about it, I suppose, then, Mr. Linton? said I. "Heathcliff has your permission to come a courting to Miss, and to drop in at every opportunity your absence offers, on purpose to poison the mistress against you?"

Confused as Catherine was, her wits were alert at applying our conversation.

"Ah! Nelly has played traitor," she exclaimed, passionately, "Nelly is my hidden enemy—you witch! So you do seek elf-bolts to hurt us! Let me go, and I'll make her rue! I'll make her howl a recantation!"

A maniac's fury kindled under her brows; she struggled desperately to disengage herself from Linton's arms. I felt no inclination to tarry the event; and resolving to seek medical aid on my own responsibility, I quitted the chamber.

In passing the garden to reach the road, at a place where a bridle hook is driven into the wall, I saw something white moved irregularly, evidently by another agent than the wind. Notwithstanding my hurry, I staid to examine it, lest ever after I should have the conviction impressed on my imagination that it was a creature of the other world.

My surprise and perplexity were great to discover, by touch more than vision, Miss Isabella's springer, Fanny, suspended to a handkerchief, and nearly at its last gasp.

I quickly released the animal, and lifted it into the garden. I had seen it follow its mistress up-stairs, when she went to bed, and wondered much how it could have got out there, and what mischievous person had treated it so.

While untying the knot round the hook, it seemed to me that I repeatedly caught the beat of horses' feet galloping at some distance; but there were such a number of things to occupy my reflections that I hardly gave the circumstance a thought, though it was a strange sound, in that place, at two o'clock in the morning.

Mr. Kenneth was fortunately just issuing from his house to see a patient in the village as I came up the street; and my account of Catherine Linton's malady induced him to accompany me back immediately.

He was a plain, rough man; and he made no scruple to speak his doubts of her surviving this second attack; unless she were more submissive to his directions than she had shown herself before.

"Nelly Dean," said he, "I can't help fancying there's an extra cause for this. What has there been to do at the Grange? We've odd reports up here. A stout, hearty lass like Catherine does not fall ill for a trifle; and that sort of people should not either. It's hard work bringing them through fevers, and such things. How did it begin?"

"The master will inform you," I answered; "but you are acquainted with the Earnshaws' violent dispositions, and Mrs. Linton caps them all. I may say this; it commenced in a quarrel. She was struck during a tempest of passion with a kind of fit. That's her account, at least; for she flew off in the height of it, and locked herself up. Afterward, she refused to eat, and now she alternately raves, and remains in a half dream, knowing those about her, but having her mind filled with all sorts of strange ideas and illusions."

"Mr. Linton will be sorry?" observed Kenneth, interrogatively.

"Sorry? he'll break his heart should anything happen!" I replied. "Don't alarm him more than necessary."

"Well, I told him to beware," said my companion, "and he must bide the consequences of neglecting my warning! Hasn't he been thick with Mr. Heathcliff lately?"

"Heathcliff frequently visits at the Grange," replied I, "though more on the strength of the mistress having known him when a boy, than because the master likes his company. At present, he's discharged from the trouble of calling; owing to some presumptuous aspirations after Miss Linton which he manifested. I hardly think he'll be taken in again."

"And does Miss Linton turn a cold shoulder on him?" was the doctor's next question.

"I'm not in her confidence," returned I, reluctant to continue the subject.

"No, she's a sly one," he remarked, shaking his head. "She keeps her own counsel! But she's a real little fool, I have it from good authority, that last night, and a pretty night it was! she and Heathcliff were walking in the plantation at the back of your house above two hours; and he pressed her not to go in again, but just mount his horse and away with him! My informant said she could only put him off by pledging her word of honor to be prepared on their first meeting after that; when it was to be, he didn't hear, but you urge Mr. Linton to look sharp!"

This news filled me with fresh fears; I outstripped Kenneth, and ran most of the way back. The little dog was yelping in the garden yet. I spared a minute to open the gate for it, but instead of going to the house door, it coursed up and down, snuffing the grass, and would have escaped to the road, had I not seized and conveyed it in with me.

On ascending to Isabella's room, my suspicions were confirmed; it was empty. Had I been a few hours sooner, Mrs. Linton's illness might have arrested her rash step. But what could be done now? There was a bare possibility of overtaking them if pursued instantly. *I* could not pursue them, however; and I dare not rouse the family, and fill the place with confusion; still less unfold the business to my master, absorbed as he was in his present calamity, and having no heart to spare for a second grief!

I saw nothing for it, but to hold my tongue, and suffer matters to take their course; and Kenneth being arrived, I went with a badly composed countenance to announce him.

Catherine lay in a troubled sleep; her husband had succeeded in soothing the access of frenzy; he now hung over her pillow, watching every shade, and every change of her painfully expressive features.

The doctor, on examining the case for himself, spoke hopefully to him of its having a favorable termination, if we could only preserve around her perfect and constant tranquillity. To me, he signified the threatening danger was, not so much death as permanent alienation of intellect.

I did not close my eyes that night, nor did Mr. Linton; indeed, we never went to bed; and the servants were all up long before the usual hour, moving through the house with stealthy tread, and exchanging whispers as they encountered each other in their vocations. Every one was active but Miss Isabella; and they began to remark how sound she slept. Her brother too asked if she had risen, and seemed impatient for her presence, and hurt that she showed so little anxiety for her sister-in-law.

I trembled lest he should send me to call her; but I was spared the pain of being the first proclaimant of her flight. One of the maids, a thoughtless girl, who had been on an early errand to Gimmerton, came panting up-stairs, open-mouthed, and dashed into the chamber, crying.

"Oh, dear, dear! What mun we have next? Master, master, our young lady—"

"Hold your noise!" cried I hastily, enraged at her clamorous manner.

"Speak lower, Mary. What is the matter?" said Mr. Linton. "What ails your young lady?"

"She's gone, she's gone! Yon' Heathcliff's run off wi' her!" gasped the girl.

"That is not true!" exclaimed Linton, rising in agitation. "It cannot be. How has the idea entered your head? Ellen Dean, go and seek her—it is incredible—it cannot be."

As he spoke, he took the servant to the door, and then repeated his demand to know her reasons for such an assertion.

"Why, I met on the road a lad that fetches milk here," she stammered, "and he asked whether we weren't in trouble at the Grange. I thought he meant for Missis's sickness, so I answered, yes. Then says he, 'They's somebody gone after 'em, I guess.' I stared. He saw I knew naught about it, and he told how a gentleman and lady had stopped to have a horse's shoe fastened at a blacksmith's shop, two miles out of Gimmerton, not very long after midnight! and how the blacksmith's lass had got up to spy who they were; she knew them both directly. And she noticed the man. Heathcliff it was, she felt certain, nob'dy could mistake him; besides he put a sovereign in her father's hand for payment. The lady had a cloak about her face; but having desired a sup of water, while she drank it fell back, and she saw her very plain. Heathcliff held both bridles as they rode on, and they set their faces from the village, and went as fast as the rough roads would let them. The lass said nothing to her father, but she told it all over Gimmerton this morning."

I ran and peeped, for form's sake, into Isabella's room: confirming, when I returned, the servant's statement. Mr. Linton had resumed his seat by the bed; on my re-entrance, he raised his eyes, read the meaning of my blank aspect, and dropped them without giving an order, or uttering a word.

"Are we to try any measures for overtaking and bringing her back," I inquired. "How should we do?"

"She went of her own accord," answered the master; "she had a right to go if she pleased. Trouble me no more about her. Hereafter she is only my sister in name; not because I disown her, but because she has disowned me."

And that was all he said on the subject; he did not make a single inquiry further, or mention her in any way, except directing me to send what property she had in the house to her fresh home, wherever it was, when I knew it.

·······

Chapter 13

For two months the fugitives remained absent; in those two months Mrs. Linton encountered and conquered the worst shock of what was denominated a brain fever. No mother could have nursed an only child more devotedly than Edgar tended her. Day and night he was watching, and patiently enduring all the annoyances that irritable nerves and a shaken reason could inflict: and, though Kenneth remarked that what he saved from the grave would only recompense his care by forming the source of constant future anxiety; in fact, that his health and strength were being sacrificed to preserve a mere ruin of humanity, he knew no limits in gratitude and joy when Catherine's life was declared out of danger; and hour after hour he would sit beside her, tracing the gradual return to bodily health, and flattering his too sanguine hopes with the illusion that her mind would settle back to its right balance also, and she would soon be entirely her former self.

The first time she left her chamber, was at the commencement of the following March. Mr. Linton had put on her pillow, in the morning, a handful of golden crocuses; her eye, long stranger to any gleam of pleasure, caught them in waking, and shone delighted as she gathered them eagerly together.

"Those are the earliest flowers at the Heights!" she exclaimed. "They remind me of soft thaw winds, and warm sunshine, and nearly melted snow. Edgar, is there not a south wind, and is not the snow almost gone?"

"The snow is quite gone; down here, darling!" replied her husband, "and I only see two white spots on the whole range of moors. The sky is blue, and the larks are singing, and the becks and brooks are all brim full. Catherine, last spring at this time, I was longing to have you under this roof—now, I wish you were a mile or two up those hills, the air blows so sweetly, I feel that it would cure you."

"I shall never be there, but once more!" said the invalid; "and then you'll leave me, and I shall remain, for ever. Next spring you'll long again to have me under this roof, and you'll look back, and think you were happy to-day."

Linton lavished on her the kindest caresses, and tried to cheer her by the fondest words; but, vaguely regarding the flowers, she let the tears collect on her lashes, and stream down her cheeks unheeded.

We knew she was really better and therefore decided that long confinement to a single place produced much of this despondency, and it might be partially removed by a change of scene.

The master told me to light a fire in the many weeks' deserted parlor, and to set an easy chair in the sunshine by the window; and then he brought her down, and she sat a long while, enjoying the genial heat, and, as we expected, revived by the objects round

her, which, though familiar, were free from the dreary associations investing her hated sick-chamber. By evening she seemed
greatly exhausted; yet no arguments could persuade her to return
to that apartment, and I had to arrange the parlor sofa for her
bed, till another room could be prepared.

To obviate the fatigue of mounting and descending the stairs,
we fitted up this, where you lie at present, on the same floor with
the parlor: and she was soon strong enough to move from one to
the other, leaning on Edgar's arm.

Ah, I thought myself she might recover, so waited on as she was.
And there was double cause to desire it, for on her existence
depended that of another; we cherished the hope that in a little
while Mr. Linton's heart would be gladdened, and his lands secured from a stranger's gripe, by the birth of an heir.

I should mention that Isabella sent to her brother, some six
weeks from her departure, a short note, announcing her marriage
with Heathcliff. It appeared dry and cold; but at the bottom was
dotted in with pencil an obscure apology, and an entreaty for kind
remembrance and reconciliation, if her proceeding had offended
him, asserting that she could not help it then, and, being done,
she had now no power to repeal it.

Linton did not reply to this, I believe; and in a fortnight more I
got a long letter which I considered odd, coming from the pen of a
bride just out of the honeymoon. I'll read it, for I keep it yet. Any
relic of the dead is precious, if they were valued living. It begins—

"DEAR ELLEN,
"I came last night to Wuthering Heights, and heard, for the first
time, that Catherine has been, and is yet, very ill. I must not write
to her, I suppose, and my brother is either too angry or too distressed to answer what I sent him. Still, I must write to somebody,
and the only choice left me is you.

"Inform Edgar that I'd give the world to see his face again—
that my heart returned to Thrushcross Grange in twenty-four
hours after I left it, and is there at this moment, full of warm
feelings for him and Catherine! I *can't follow it though*—(those
words are underlined)—they need not expect me, and they may
draw what conclusions they please, taking care, however, to lay
nothing at the door of my weak will or deficient affection.

"The remainder of the letter is for yourself alone. I want to ask
you two questions: the first is—

"How did you contrive to preserve the common sympathies of
human nature when you resided here? I cannot recognize any
sentiment which those around share with me.

"The second question I have great interest in: it is this—

"Is Mr. Heathcliff a man? If so, is he mad? And if not, is he a
devil? I shan't tell my reasons for making this inquiry; but I
beseech you to explain, if you can, what I have married—that is,
when you call to see me; and you must call, Ellen, very soon.
Don't write, but come, and bring me something from Edgar.

"Now you shall hear how I have been received in my new home,
as I am led to imagine the Heights will be. It is to amuse myself

that I dwell on such subjects as the lack of external comforts; they never occupy my thoughts except at the moment when I miss them. I should laugh and dance for joy if I found their absence was the total of my miseries, and the rest was an unnatural dream!

"The sun set behind the Grange, as we turned upon the moors; by that I judged it to be six o'clock; and my companion halted half-an-hour to inspect the park and the gardens, and, probably, the place itself, as well as he could; so it was dark when we dismounted in the paved yard of the farmhouse, and your old fellow-servant, Joseph, issued out to receive us by the light of a dip candle. He did it with a courtesy that redounded to his credit. His first act was to elevate his torch to a level with my face, squint malignantly, project his under lip, and turn away.

"Then he took the two horses and led them into the stables, reappearing for the purpose of locking the outer gate, as if we lived in an ancient castle.

"Heathcliff staid to speak to him, and I entered the kitchen—a dingy, untidy hole; I dare say you would not know it, it is so changed since it was in your charge.

"By the fire stood a ruffianly child, strong in limb and dirty in garb with a look of Catherine in his eyes and about his mouth.

"'This is Edgar's legal nephew,' I reflected— 'mine in a manner; I must shake hands, and—yes—I must kiss him. It is right to establish a good understanding at the beginning.'

"I approached, and, attempting to take his chubby fist, said, "'How do you do, my dear?'

"He replied in a jargon I did not comprehend.

"'Shall you and I be friends, Hareton?' was my next essay at conversation.

"An oath, and a threat to set Throttler on me if I did not 'frame off,' rewarded my perseverance.

"'Hey, Throttler, lad!' whispered the little wretch, rousing a half-bred bull-dog from its lair in a corner. 'Now, wilt tuh be ganging?' he asked, authoritatively.

"Love for my life urged a compliance; I stepped over the threshold to wait till the others should enter. Mr. Heathcliff was nowhere visible; and Joseph, whom I followed to the stables, and requested to accompany me in, after staring and muttering to himself, screwed up his nose and replied—

"'Mim! mim! mim! Did iver Christian body hear owt like it? Minching un' munching! Hah can aw tell whet ye say?'

"'I say, I wish you to come with me into the house!' I cried, thinking him deaf, yet highly disgusted at his rudeness.

"'Nor nuh me! Aw getten summut else to do,' he answered, and continued his work, moving his lantern jaws meanwhile, and surveying my dress and countenance (the former a great deal too fine, but the latter, I'm sure, as sad as he could desire) with sovereign contempt.

"I walked round the yard, and through a wicket, to another door, at which I took the liberty of knocking, in hopes some more civil servant might show himself.

"After a short suspense it was opened by a tall, gaunt man,

without neckerchief, and otherwise extremely slovenly; his features were lost in masses of shaggy hair that hung on his shoulders; and *his* eyes, too, were like a ghostly Catherine's, with all
their beauty annihilated.

"'What's your business here?' he demanded, grimly. 'Who are
you?'

"'My name *was* Isabella Linton,' I replied. 'You've seen me
before, sir. I'm lately married to Mr. Heathcliff; and he has
brought me here—I suppose by your permission.'

"'Is he come back, then?' asked the hermit, glaring like a hungry wolf.

"'Yes—we came just now,' I said; 'but he left me by the kitchen
door; and when I would have gone in, your little boy played sentinel over the place, and frightened me off by the help of a bull-
dog.'

"'It's well the hellish villain has kept his word!' growled my
future host, searching the darkness beyond me in expectation of
discovering Heathcliff, and then he indulged in a soliloquy of
execrations, and threats of what he would have done had the
'fiend' deceived him.

"I repented having tried this second entrance; and was almost
inclined to slip away before he finished cursing, but ere I could
execute that intention, he ordered me in, and shut and re-fas-
tened the door.

"There was a great fire, and that was all the light in the huge
apartment, whose floor had grown a uniform gray; and the once
brilliant pewter dishes, which used to attract my gaze when I was
a girl, partook of a similar obscurity, created by tarnish and dust.

"I inquired whether I might call the maid, and be conducted to
a bed-room? Mr. Earnshaw vouchsafed no answer. He walked up
and down, with his hands in his pockets, apparently quite forgetting my presence; and his abstraction was evidently so deep, and
his whole aspect so misanthropical, that I shrank from disturbing
him again.

"You'll not be surprised, Ellen, at my feeling particularly
cheerless, seated in worse than solitude, on that inhospitable
hearth, and remembering that four miles distant lay my delightful
home, containing the only people I loved on earth: and there
might as well be the Atlantic to part us, instead of those four
miles. I could not overpass them.

"I questioned with myself—Where must I turn for comfort?
and—mind you don't tell Edgar, or Catherine—above every sorrow beside, this rose pre-eminent—despair at finding nobody
who could or would be my ally against Heathcliff!

"I had sought shelter at Wuthering Heights, almost gladly, because I was secured by that arrangement from living alone with
him; but he knew the people we were coming among, and he did
not fear their intermeddling.

"I sat and thought a doleful time; the clock struck eight, and
nine, and still my companion paced to and fro, his head bend on
his breast, and perfectly silent, unless a groan, or a bitter ejaculation forced itself out at intervals.

"I listened to detect a woman's voice in the house, and filled the interim with wild regrets, and dismal anticipations, which, at last, spoke audibly in irrepressible sighing, and weeping.

"I was not aware how openly I grieved, till Earnshaw halted opposite, in his measured walk, and gave me a stare of newly awakened surprise. Taking advantage of his recovered attention, I exclaimed—

"'I'm tired with my journey, and I want to go to bed! Where is the maid-servant? Direct me to her, as she won't come to me!'

"'We have none,' he answered; 'you must wait on yourself!'

"'Where must I sleep, then?' I sobbed. I was beyond regarding self-respect, weighed down by fatigue and wretchedness.

"'Joseph will show you Heathcliff's chamber,' said he; 'open that door—he's in there.'

"I was going to obey, but he suddenly arrested me, and added in the strangest tone—

"'Be so good as to turn your lock, and draw your bolt —don't omit it!'

"'Well!' I said. 'But why, Mr. Earnshaw?' I did not relish the notion of deliberately fastening myself in with Heathcliff.

"'Look here!' he replied, pulling from his waistcoat a curiously constructed pistol, having a double edged spring knife attached to the barrel. 'That's a great tempter to a desperate man, is it not? I cannot resist going up with this, every night, and trying his door: if once I find it open, he's done for! I do it invariably, even though the minute before I have been recalling a hundred reasons that should make me refrain—it is some devil that urges me to thwart my own schemes by killing him. You fight against the devil, for love, as long as you may; when the time comes, not all the angels in heaven shall save him!'

"I surveyed the weapon inquisitively; a hideous notion struck me. How powerful I should be possessing such an instrument! I took it from his hand, and touched the blade. He looked astonished at the expression my face assumed during a brief second. It was not horror, it was covetousness. He snatched the pistol back, jealously; shut the knife, and returned it to its concealment.

"'I don't care if you tell him,' said he. 'Put him on his guard, and watch for him. You know the terms we are on, I see; his danger does not shock you.'

"'What has Heathcliff done to you?' I asked. 'In what has he wronged you, to warrant this appalling hatred? Wouldn't it be wiser to bid him quit the house?'

"'No,' thundered Earnshaw, 'should he offer to leave me, he's a dead man; persuade him to attempt it, and you are a murderess! Am I to lose *all*, without a chance of retrieval? Is Hareton to be a beggar? Oh, damnation! I *will* have it back; and I'll have *his* gold too; and then his blood; and hell shall have his soul! It will be ten times blacker with that guest than ever it was before!'

"You've acquainted me, Ellen, with your old master's habits. He is clearly on the verge of madness—he was so, last night, at least. I shuddered to be near him, and thought on the servant's ill-bred moroseness as comparatively agreeable.

"He now recommenced his moody walk, and I raised the latch, and escaped into the kitchen.

"Joseph was bending over the fire, peering into a large pan that swung above it; and a wooden bowl of oatmeal stood on the settle close by. The contents of the pan began to boil, and he turned to plunge his hand into the bowl; I conjectured that this preparation was probably for our supper, and, being hungry, I resolved it should be eatable—so crying out, sharply—'I'll make the porridge!' I removed the vessel out of his reach, and proceeded to take off my hat and riding habit. 'Mr. Earnshaw,' I continued, 'directs me to wait on myself—I will. I'm not going to act the lady among you, for fear I should starve.'

"'Good Lord!' he muttered, sitting down, and stroking his ribbed stockings from the knee to the ankle. 'If they's tuh be fresh ortherings—just when aw getten used tuh two maisters, if aw mun hev a *mistress* set o'er my heead, it's loike time tuh be flitting. Aw niver *did* think tuh say t'day ut aw mud have the owld place—but aw daht it's night at hend!'

"This lamentation drew no notice from me; I went briskly to work; sighing to remember a period when it would have been all merry fun; but compelled speedily to drive off the remembrance. It racked me to recall past happiness, and the greater peril there was of conjuring up its apparition, the quicker the thible ran round, and the faster the handfuls of meal fell into the water.

"Joseph beheld my style of cookery with growing indignation.

"'Thear!' he ejaculated. 'Hareton, thah will'nt sup thy porridge tuh neeght; they'll be nowt bud lumps as big as maw have. Thear, agean! Aw'd fling in bowl un all, if aw were yah! Thear, pale t' guilp off, un' then yah'll hae done wi't. Bang, bang. It's a marcy t' bothom isn't deaved aht!'

"It *was* rather a rough mess, I own, when poured into the basins; four had been provided, and a gallon pitcher of new milk was brought from the dairy, which Hareton seized, and commenced drinking and spilling from the expansive lip.

"I expostulated, and desired that he should have his in a mug; affirming that I could not taste the liquid treated so dirtily. The old cynic chose to be vastly offended at this nicety; assuring me, repeatedly, that 'the bairn was every bit as gooid' as I, 'and every bit as wollsome,' and wondering how I could fashion to be so conceited; meanwhile, the infant ruffian continued sucking; and glowered up at me defyingly, as he slavered into the jug.

"'I shall have my supper in another room,' I said. 'Have you no place you call a parlor?'

"'*Parlor!*' he echoed, sneeringly, '*parlor!* Nay, we've noa *parlors*. If yah dunnut loike wer company, they's maister's; un' if yah dunnut loike maister, they's us.'

"'Then I shall go up-stairs,' I answered; 'show me a chamber!'

"I put my basin on a tray, and went myself to fetch some more milk.

"With great grumblings, the fellow rose, and preceded me in my ascent: we mounted to the garrets; he opening a door, now and then, to look into the apartments we passed.

"'Here's a rahm,' he said, at last, flinging back a cranky board on hinges. 'It's weel eneugh tuh ate a few porridge in. They's a pack uh corn i' t' corner, thear, meeterly clane; if yah're feared uh muckying yer grand silk cloes, spread yer hankerchir ut t'top on't.'

"The 'rahm' was a kind of lumber-hole smelling strong of malt and grain; various sacks of which articles were piled around, leaving a wide, bare space in the middle.

"'Why, man!' I exclaimed, facing him angrily, 'this is not a place to sleep in. I wish to see my bed-room.'

"'*Bed-rume!*' he repeated, in a tone of mockery. 'Yah's see all t' *bed-rumes* thear is—yon's mine.'

"He pointed into the second garret, only differing from the first in being more naked about the walls, and having a large, low, curtainless bed, with an indigo-colored quilt, at one end.

"'What do I want with yours?' I retorted. 'I suppose Mr. Heathcliff does not lodge at the top of the house, does he?'

"'Oh! it's Maister *Heathcliff's* yah're wenting?' cried he, as if making a new discovery. 'Couldn't ye uh said soa, at onst? un then, aw mud uh telled ye, baht all this wark, ut that's just one yah cannut sea—he allas keeps it locked, un'nob'dy iver mells on't but hisseln.'

"'You've a nice house, Joseph,' I could not refrain from observing, 'and pleasant inmates; and I think the concentrated essence of all the madness in the world took up its abode in my brain the day I linked my fate with theirs! However, that is not to the present purpose—there are other rooms. For heaven's sake, be quick, and let me settle somewhere!'

"He made no reply to this adjuration; only plodding doggedly down the wooden steps, and halting before an apartment which, from that halt, and the superior quality of its furniture, I conjectured to be the best one.

"There was a carpet, a good one; but the pattern was obliterated by dust; a fireplace hung with cut paper, dropping to pieces; a handsome oak bedstead with ample crimson curtains of rather expensive material, and modern make. But they had evidently experienced rough usage, the valances hung in festoons, wrenched from their rings; and the iron rod supporting them was bent in an arc, on one side, causing the drapery to trail upon the floor. The chairs were also damaged, many of them severely; and deep indentations deformed the panels of the walls.

"I was endeavoring to gather resolution for entering, and taking possession, when my fool of a guide announced—

"'This here is t' maister's.'

"My supper by this time was cold, my appetite gone, and my patience exhausted. I insisted on being provided instantly with a place of refuge, and means of repose.

"'Whear the divil,' began the religious elder. 'The Lord bless us! The Lord forgie us! Whear the *hell*, wold ye gang? ye marred, wearisome nowt! Yah seen all bud Hareton't bit uf a cham'er. They's nut another hoile tuh lig dahn in i' th' hahse!'

"I was so vexed, I flung my tray, and its contents on the ground;

and then seated myself at the stair's head, hid my face in my hands, and cried.

"'Ech! ech!' exclaimed Joseph. "Weel done, Miss Cathy! Hahsiver, t' maister sall just tum'le o'er them brocken pots; un' then we's hear summut; we's hear hah it's tuh be. Gooid—fur—nowt madling! yah desarve pining froo this tuh Churstmas, flinging-t' precious gifts uh God under fooit i' yer flaysome rages! But, aw'm mista'en if yah shew yer sperrit lang. Will Heathcliff bide sich bonny ways, think ye? Aw nobbut wish he muh cotch ye i' that plisky. Aw nobbut wish he may.'

"And so he went scolding to his den beneath, taking the candle with him, and I remained in the dark.

"The period of reflection succeeding this silly action, compelled me to admit the necessity of smothering my pride, and choking my wrath, and bestirring myself to remove its effects.

"An unexpected aid presently appeared in the shape of Throttler, whom I now recognized as a son of our old Skulker; it had spent its whelphood at the Grange, and was given by my father to Mr. Hindley. I fancy it knew me—it pushed its nose against mine by way of salute, and then hastened to devour the porridge, while I groped from step to step, collecting the shattered earthenware, and drying the spatters of milk from the bannister with my pocket-handkerchief.

"Our labors were scarcely over when I heard Earnshaw's tread in the passage; my assistant tucked in his tail, and pressed to the wall; I stole into the nearest doorway. The dog's endeavor to avoid him was unsuccessful, as I guessed by a scutter down stairs, and a prolonged, piteous yelping. I had better luck. He passed on, entered his chamber, and shut the door.

"Directly after, Joseph came up with Hareton, to put him to bed. I had found shelter in Hareton's room, and the old man on seeing me, said—

"'They's rahm fur boath yah, un yer pride, nah, aw sud think i' th' hahse. It's empty; yah muh hev it all tuh yerseln, un Him as allas maks a third, i' sich ill company!'

"Gladly did I take advantage of this intimation; and the minute I flung myself into a chair, by the fire, I nodded, and slept.

"My slumber was deep and sweet; though over far too soon. Mr. Heathcliff awoke me; he had just come in, and demanded, in his loving manner, what I was doing there?

"I told him the cause of my staying up so late—that he had the key of our room in his pocket.

"The adjective *our* gave mortal offence. He swore it was not, nor never should be mine; and he'd—but I'll not repeat his language, nor describe his habitual conduct; he is ingenious and unresting in seeking to gain my abhorrence! I sometimes wonder at him, with an intensity that deadens my fear: yet, I assure you, a tiger, or a venomous serpent could not rouse terror in me equal to that which he wakens. He told me of Catherine's illness, and accused my brother of causing it; promising that I should be Edgar's proxy in suffering, till he could get a hold of him.

"I do hate him—I am wretched—I have been a fool! Beware of

uttering one breath of this to any one at the Grange. I shall expect you every day—don't disappoint me!

"ISABELLA."

. . . .

Chapter 14

As soon as I had perused this epistle, I went to the master, and informed him that his sister had arrived at the Heights, and sent me a letter expressing her sorrow for Mrs. Linton's situation, and her ardent desire to see him; with a wish that he would transmit to her, as early as possible, some token of forgiveness by me.

"Forgiveness?" said Linton. "I have nothing to forgive her, Ellen—you may call at Wuthering Heights this afternoon, if you like, and say that I am not *angry*, but I'm *sorry* to have lost her: especially as I can never think she'll be happy. It is out of the question my going to see her, however; we are eternally divided; and should she really wish to oblige me, let her persuade the villain she has married to leave the country."

"And you won't write her a little note, sir?" I asked, imploringly.

"No," he answered; "it is needless. My communication with Heathcliff's family shall be as sparing as his with mine. It shall not exist!"

Mr. Edgar's coldness depressed me exceedingly; and all the way from the Grange, I puzzled my brains how to put more heart into what he said, when I repeated it; and how to soften his refusal of even a few lines to console Isabella.

I dare say she had been on the watch for me since morning: I saw her looking through the lattice, as I came up to the garden causeway, and I nodded to her; but she drew back, as if afraid of being observed.

I entered without knocking. There never was such a dreary, dismal scene as the formerly cheerful house presented! I must confess that, if I had been in the young lady's place, I would at least have swept the hearth, and wiped the tables with a duster. But she already partook of the pervading spirit of neglect which encompassed her. Her pretty face was wan and listless; her hair uncurled; some locks hanging lankly down, and some carelessly twisted around her head. Probably she had not touched her dress since yester-evening.

Hindley was not there. Mr. Heathcliff sat at a table, turning over some papers in his pocket-book; but he rose when I appeared, asked me how I did, quite friendly, and offered me a chair.

He was the only thing there that seemed decent, and I thought he never looked better. So much had circumstances altered their positions, that he would certainly have struck a stranger as a born and bred gentleman, and his wife as a thorough little slattern!

She came forward eagerly to greet me; and held out one hand to take the expected letter.

I shook my head. She wouldn't understand the hint, but followed me to a sideboard, where I went to lay my bonnet, and importuned me, in a whisper, to give her directly what I had brought.

Heathcliff guessed the meaning of her manœuvres, and said, "If you have got anything for Isabella, as no doubt you have, Nelly, give it to her. You needn't make a secret of it; we have no secrets between us."

"Oh, I have nothing," I replied, thinking it best to speak the truth at once. "My master bid me tell his sister that she must not expect either a letter or a visit from him at present. He sends his love, ma'am, and his wishes for your happiness, and his pardon for the grief you have occasioned; but he thinks that after this time his household and the household here should drop intercommunication; as nothing good could come of keeping it up."

Mrs. Heathcliff's lip quivered slightly, and she returned to her seat in the window. Her husband took his stand on the hearthstone, near me, and began to put questions concerning Catherine.

I told him as much as I thought proper of her illness, and he extorted from me, by cross-examination, most of the facts connected with its origin.

I blamed her, as she deserved, for bringing it all on herself; and ended by hoping that he would follow Mr. Linton's example, and avoid future interference with his family, for good or evil.

"Mrs. Linton is now just recovering," I said; "she'll never be like she was, but her life is spared, and if you really have a regard for her, you'll shun crossing her way again. Nay, you'll move out of this country entirely; and that you may not regret it, I'll inform you Catherine Linton is as different now from your old friend Catherine Earnshaw as that young lady is different from me! Her appearance is changed greatly, her character much more so; and the person who is compelled of necessity to be her companion, will only sustain his affection hereafter by the remembrance of what she once was, by common humanity, and a sense of duty!"

"That is quite possible," remarked Heathcliff, forcing himself to seem calm, "quite possible that your master should have nothing but common humanity, and a sense of duty to fall back upon. But do you imagine that I shall leave Catherine to his *duty* and *humanity?* and can you compare my feelings respecting Catherine to his? Before you leave this house, I must exact a promise from you, that you'll get me an interview with her—consent or refuse, I *will* see her! What do you say?"

"I say, Mr. Heathcliff," I replied, "you must not—you never shall through my means. Another encounter between you and the master would kill her altogether!"

"With your aid that may be avoided," he continued; "and should there be danger of such an event—should he be the cause of adding a single trouble more to her existence—why, I think I shall be justified in going to extremes! I wish you had sincerity enough to tell me whether Catherine would suffer greatly from his loss. The fear that she would restrains me, and there you see the distinction between our feelings. Had he been in my place, and I in his, though I hated him with a hatred that turned my life to gall, I never would have raised a hand against him. You may look incredulous if you please! I never would have banished him from her society as long as she desired his. The moment her regard ceased, I would have torn his heart out and drank his blood! But till then, if you don't believe me, you don't know me—till then, I would have died by inches before I touched a single hair of his head!"

"And yet," I interrupted, "you have no scruples in completely ruining all hopes of her perfect restoration, by thrusting yourself into her remembrance, now when she has nearly forgotten you, and involving her in a new tumult of discord and distress."

"You suppose she has nearly forgotten me?" he said. "Oh, Nelly! you know she has not! You know as well as I do, that for every thought she spends on Linton, she spends a thousand on me! At a most miserable period of my life, I had a notion of the kind; it haunted me on my return to the neighborhood, last summer; but only her own assurance could make me admit the horrible idea again. And then, Linton would be nothing, nor Hindley, nor all the dreams that ever I dreamed. Two words would comprehend my future—*death* and *hell*—existence, after losing her, would be hell.

"Yet I was a fool to fancy for a moment that she valued Edgar Linton's attachment more than mine; if he loved with all the powers of his puny being, he couldn't love as much in eighty years as I could in a day. And Catherine has a heart as deep as I have; the sea could be as readily contained in the horse-trough as her whole affection be monopolized by him. Tush! He is scarcely a degree dearer to her than her dog, or her horse. It is not in him to be loved like me; how can she love in him what he has not?"

"Catherine and Edgar are as fond of each other as any two people can be!" cried Isabella, with sudden vivacity. "No one has a right to talk in that manner, and I won't hear my brother depreciated in silence!"

"Your brother is wondrous fond of you, too, isn't he?" observed Heathcliff, scornfully. "He turns you adrift on the world with surprising alacrity."

"He is not aware of what I suffer," she replied. "I didn't tell him that."

"You have been telling him something, then—you have written, have you?"

"To say that I was married, I did write—you saw the note."

"And nothing since?"

"No."

"My young lady is looking sadly the worse for her change of condition," I remarked. "Somebody's love comes short in her case, obviously—whose, I may guess; but perhaps I shouldn't say."

"I should guess it was her own," said Heathcliff. "She degenerates into a mere slut! She is tired of trying to please me, uncommonly early. You'd hardly credit it, but the very morrow of our wedding, she was weeping to go home. However, she'll suit this

house so much the better for not being over nice and I'll take care
she does not disgrace me by rambling abroad."

"Well, sir," returned I, "I hope you'll consider that Mrs. Heathcliff is accustomed to be looked after, and waited on; and that she
has been brought up like an only daughter whom every one was
ready to serve. You must let her have a maid to keep things tidy
about her, and you must treat her kindly. Whatever be your notion of Mr. Edgar, you cannot doubt that she has a capacity for
strong attachments, or she wouldn't have abandoned the elegan-
cies, and comforts, and friends of her former home, to fix contentedly in such a wilderness as this with you."

"She abandoned them under a delusion," he answered, "picturing in me a hero of romance, and expecting unlimited indul-
gences from my chivalrous devotion. I can hardly regard her in
the light of a rational creature, so obstinately has she persisted in
forming a fabulous notion of my character, and acting on the false
impressions she cherished. But at last, I think she begins to know
me—I don't perceive the silly smiles and grimaces that provoked
me at first; and the senseless incapability of discerning that I was
in earnest when I gave her my opinion of her infatuation, and
herself. It was a remarkable effort of perspicacity to discover that I
did not love her. I believed, at one time, no lessons could teach her
that! and yet it is poorly learned; for this morning she announced,
as a piece of appalling intelligence, that I had actually succeeded
in making her hate me! A positive labor of Hercules, I assure you!
If it be achieved, I have cause to return thanks; can I trust your
assertion, Isabella—are you sure you hate me? If I let you alone
for half a day, won't you come sighing and wheedling to me again?
I dare say she would rather I had seemed all tenderness before
you; it wounds her vanity to have the truth exposed. But I don't
care who knows that the passion was wholly on one side, and I
never told her a lie about it. She cannot accuse me of showing a
bit of deceitful softness. The first thing she saw me do, on coming
out of the Grange, was to hang up her little dog; and when she
pleaded for it, the first words I uttered were a wish that I had the
hanging of every being belonging to her, except one: possibly, she
took that exception for herself. But no brutality disgusted her—I
suppose she has an innate admiration of it, if only her precious
person were secure from injury! Now, was it not the depth of
absurdity—of genuine idiocy—for the pitiful, slavish, mean-
minded brach to dream that I could love her? Tell your master,
Nelly, that I never, in all my life, met with such an abject thing as
she is; she even disgraces the name of Linton; and I've relented,
from pure lack of invention, in my experiments on what she could
endure, and still creep shamefully cringing back! But tell him also
to set his fraternal and magisterial heart at ease—that I keep
strictly within the limits of the law—I have avoided, up to this
period, giving her the slightest right to claim a separation; and
what's more, she'd thank nobody for dividing us—if she desired
to go she might—the nuisance of her presence outweighs the
gratification to be derived from tormenting her!"

"Mr. Heathcliff," said I, "this is the talk of a madman, and your wife, most likely, is convinced you are mad; and, for that reason, she has borne with you hitherto: but now that you say she may go, she'll doubtless avail herself of the permission. You are not so bewitched, ma'am, are you, as to remain with him of your own accord?"

"Take care, Ellen!" answered Isabella, her eyes sparkling irefully; there was no misdoubting, by their expression, the full success of her partner's endeavors to make himself detested. "Don't put faith in a single word he speaks. He's a lying fiend, a monster, and not a human being! I've been told I might leave him before; and I've made the attempt, but I dare not repeat it! Only, Ellen, promise you'll not mention a syllable of his infamous conversation to my brother or Catherine. Whatever he may pretend, he wishes to provoke Edgar to desperation. He says he has married me on purpose to obtain power over him; and he shan't obtain it—I'll die first! I just hope, I pray, that he may forget his diabolical prudence, and kill me! The single pleasure I can imagine, is to die, or to see him dead!"

"There—that will do for the present!" said Heathcliff. If you are called upon in a court of law, you'll remember her language, Nelly! And take a good look at that countenance—she's near the point which would suit me. No, you're not fit to be your own guardian, Isabella, now; and I, being your legal protector, must retain you in my custody, however distasteful the obligation may be. Go up-stairs; I have something to say to Ellen Dean, in private. That's not the way—up-stairs, I tell you! Why this is the road up-stairs, child!"

He seized, and thrust her from the room; and returned muttering,

"I have no pity! I have no pity! The worms writhe, the more I yearn to crush out their entrails! It is a moral teething, and I grind with greater energy, in proportion to the increase of pain."

"Do you understand what the word pity means?" I said, hastening to resume my bonnet. "Did you ever feel a touch of it in your life?"

"Put that down!" he interrupted, perceiving my intention to depart. "You are not going yet. Come here now, Nelly; I must either persuade or compel you to aid me in fulfilling my determination to see Catherine, and that without delay. I swear that I meditate no harm; I don't desire to cause any disturbance, or to exasperate or insult Mr. Linton; I only wish to hear from herself how she is, and why she has been ill; and to ask if anything that I could do would be of use to her. Last night I was in the Grange garden six hours, and I'll return there tonight ; and every night I'll haunt the place, and every day, till I find an opportunity of entering. If Edgar Linton meets me, I shall not hesitate to knock him down, and give him enough to ensure his quiescence while I stay. If his servants oppose me, I shall threaten them off with these pistols. But wouldn't it be better to prevent my coming in contact with them, or their master? And you could do it so easily! I'd warn you when I came, and then you might let me in unobserved,

as soon as she was alone, and watch till I departed—your conscience quite calm, you would be hindering mischief."

I protested against playing that treacherous part in my employer's house; and besides, I urged the cruelty and selfishness of
his destroying Mrs. Linton's tranquillity, for his satifaction.

"The commonest occurrence startles her painfully," I said.
"She's all nerves, and she couldn't bear the surprise, I'm positive.
Don't persist, sir! or else, I shall be obliged to inform my master
of your designs, and he'll take measures to secure his house and
its inmates from any such unwarrantable intrusions!"

"In that case, I'll take measures to secure you, woman!" exclaimed Heathcliff; "you shall not leave Wuthering Heights till to-
morrow morning. It is a foolish story to assert that Catherine
could not bear to see me; and as to surprising her, I don't desire it,
you must prepare her—ask her if I may come. You say she never
mentions my name, and that I am never mentioned to her. To
whom should she mention me, if I am a forbidden topic in the
house? She thinks you are all spies for her husband. Oh, I've no
doubt she's in hell among you! I guess, by her silence, as much as
anything, what she feels. You say she is often restless, and anx-
ious-looking—is that a proof of tranquillity! You talk of her mind
being unsettled—how the devil could it be otherwise, in her
frightful isolation? And that insipid, paltry creature attending her
from *duty* and *humanity!* From *pity* and *charity*. He might as well
plant an oak in a flower-pot, and expect it to thrive, as imagine he
can restore her to vigor in the soil of his shallow cares! Let us
settle it at once; will you stay here, and am I to fight my way to
Catherine over Linton and his footmen? Or will you be my friend,
as you have been hitherto, and do what I request? Decide! because
there is no reason for my lingering another minute, if you persist
in your stubborn ill-nature."

Well, Mr. Lockwood, I argued, and complained, and flatly refused him fifty times; but, in the long run, he forced me to an
agreement. I engaged to carry a letter from him to my mistress;
and should she consent, I promised to let him have intelligence of
Linton's next absence from home, when he might come, and get
in as he was able—I wouldn't be there, and my fellow servants
should be equally out of the way.

Was it right or wrong? I fear it was wrong, though expedient. I
thought I prevented another explosion by my compliance: and I
thought too, it might create a favorable crisis in Catherine's mental illness: and then I remembered Mr. Edgar's stern rebuke of my
carrying tales; and I tried to smooth away all disquietude on the
subject, by affirming with frequent iteration, that this betrayal of
trust, if it merited so harsh an appellation, should be the last.

Notwithstanding, my journey homeward was sadder than my
journey thither; and many misgivings I had ere I could prevail on
myself to put the missive into Mrs. Linton's hand.

But here is Kenneth—I'll go down and tell him how much
better you are. My history is *dree*, as we say, and will serve to while
away another morning.

Dree, and dreary! I reflected as the good woman descended to receive the doctor; and not exactly of the kind which I should have chosen to amuse me; but never mind! I'll extract wholesome medicines from Mrs. Dean's bitter herbs; and firstly, let me beware of the fascination that lurks in Catherine Heathcliff's brilliant eyes. I should be in a curious taking, if I surrendered my heart to that young person, and the daughter turned out a second edition of the mother!

. . . .

Chapter 15

Another week over—and I am so many days nearer health and spring! I have now heard all my neighbor's history at different sittings, as the housekeeper could spare time from more important occupations. I'll continue it in her own words, only a little condensed. She is, on the whole, a very fair narrator, and I don't think I could improve her style.

In the evening, she said, the evening of my visit to the Heights, I knew as well as if I saw him, that Mr. Heathcliff was about the place; and I shunned going out, because I still carried his letter in my pocket, and didn't want to be threatened, or teased any more.

I had made up my mind not to give it till my master went somewhere; as I could not guess how its receipt would affect Catherine. The consequence was, that it did not reach her before the lapse of three days. The fourth was Sunday, and I brought it into her room, after the family were gone to church.

There was a man servant left to keep the house with me, and we generally made a practice of locking the doors during the hours of service; but on that occasion the weather was so warm and pleasant that I set them wide open; and to fulfill my engagement, as I knew who would be coming, I told my companion that the mistress wished very much for some oranges, and he must run over to the village and get a few, to be paid for on the morrow. He departed, and I went up-stairs.

Mrs. Linton sat in a loose, white dress, with a light shawl over her shoulder, in the recess of the open window, as usual. Her thick, long hair had been partly removed at the beginning of her illness; and now she wore it simply combed over her temples and neck. Her appearance was altered, as I had told Heathcliff, but when she was calm, there seemed unearthly beauty in the change.

The flash of her eyes had been succeeded by a dreamy and melancholy softness: they no longer gave the impression of looking at the objects around her; they appeared always to gaze beyond, and far beyond—you would have said out of this world—then the paleness of her face its haggard aspect having vanished as she recovered flesh, and the peculiar expression arising from her mental state, though painfully suggestive of their causes, added to the touching interest, which she wakened, and invariably to me, I know, and to any person who saw her, I should think, refuted

more tangible proofs of convalescence, and stamped her as one
doomed to decay.

A book lay spread on the sill before her, and the scarcely perceptible wind fluttered its leaves at intervals. I believe Linton had
laid it there, for she never endeavored to divert herself with reading, or occupation of any kind; and he would spend many an hour
in trying to entice her attention to some subject which had formerly been her amusement.

She was conscious of his aim, and in her better moods endured
his efforts placidly; only showing their uselessness by now and
then suppressing a wearied sigh, and checking him at least with
the saddest of smiles and kisses. At other times she would turn
petulantly away, and hide her face in her hands, or even push him
off angrily; and then he took care to let her alone, for he was
certain of doing no good.

Gimmerton chapel bells were still ringing; and the full, mellow
flow of the beck in the valley, came soothingly on the ear. It was a
sweet substitute for the yet absent murmur of the summer foliage,
which drowned that music about the Grange when the trees were
in leaf. At Wuthering Heights it always sounded on quiet days,
following a great thaw, or a season of steady rain—and of Wuthering Heights Catherine was thinking, as she listened; that is, if she
thought or listened at all; but she had the vague, distant look I
mentioned before, which expressed no recognition of material
things either by ear or eye.

"There's a letter for you, Mrs. Linton," I said, gently inserting it
in one hand that rested on her knee. "You must read it immediately, because it wants an answer. Shall I break the seal?"

"Yes," she answered, without altering the direction of her eyes.
I opened it—it was very short.

"Now," I continued, "read it."

She drew away her hand, and let it fall. I replaced it in her lap,
and stood waiting till it should please her to glance down; but that
movement was so long delayed that at last I resumed—

"Must I read it, ma'am? It is from Mr. Heathcliff."

There was a start, and a troubled gleam of recollection, and a
struggle to arrange her ideas. She lifted the letter, and seemed to
peruse it; and when she came to the signature she sighed; yet still I
found she had not gathered its import; for upon my desiring to
hear her reply, she merely pointed to the name, and gazed at me
with mournful and questioning eagerness.

"Well, he wishes to see you," said I, guessing her need of an
interpreter. "He's in the garden by this time, and impatient to
know what answer I shall bring."

As I spoke, I observed a large dog, lying on the sunny grass
beneath, raise its ears, as if about to bark; and then smoothing
them back, announce by a wag of the tail that some one approached whom it did not consider a stranger.

Mrs. Linton bent forward, and listened breathlessly. The minute after a step traversed the hall; the open house was too tempting for Heathcliff to resist walking in: most likely he supposed

that I was inclined to shirk my promise, and so resolved to trust to his own audacity.

With straining eagerness Catherine gazed toward the entrance of her chamber. He did not hit the right room directly; she motioned me to admit him; but he found it out ere I could reach the door, and in a stride or two was at her side, and had her grasped in his arms.

He neither spoke nor loosed his hold for some five minutes, during which period he bestowed more kisses than ever he gave in his life before, I dare say; but then my mistress had kissed him first, and I plainly saw that he could hardly bear, for downright agony, to look into her face! The same conviction had stricken him as me, from the instant he beheld her, that there was no prospect of ultimate recovery there—she was fated, sure to die.

"Oh, Cathy! Oh, my life! how can I bear it?" was the first sentence he uttered, in a tone that did not seek to disguise his despair.

And now he stared at her so earnestly that I thought the very intensity of his gaze would bring tears into his eyes; but they burned with anguish, they did not melt.

"What now?" said Catherine, leaning back, and returning his look with a suddenly clouded brow—her humor was a mere vane for constantly varying caprices. "You and Edgar have broken my heart, Heathcliff! And you both come to bewail the deed to me, as if you were the people to be pitied! I shall not pity you, not I. You have killed me—and thriven on it, I think. How strong you are! How many years do you mean to live after I am gone?"

Heathcliff had knelt on one knee to embrace her; he attempted to rise, but she seized his hair, and kept him down.

"I wish I could hold you," she continued, bitterly, "till we were both dead! I shouldn't care what you suffered. I care nothing for your sufferings. Why shouldn't you suffer? I do! Will you forget me—will you be happy when I am in the earth? Will you say, twenty years hence, 'That's the grave of Catherine Earnshaw. I loved her long ago, and was wretched to lose her; but it is past. I've loved many others since—my children are dearer to me than she was; and, at death, I shall not rejoice that I am going to her, I shall be sorry that I must leave them!' Will you say so, Heathcliff?"

"Don't torture me till I'm as mad as yourself," cried he, wrenching his head free, and grinding his teeth.

The two, to a cool spectator, made a strange and fearful picture. Well might Catherine deem that Heaven would be a land of exile to her, unless, with her mortal body, she cast away her mortal character also. Her present countenance had a wild vindictiveness in its white cheek, and bloodless lip and scintillating eye; and she retained in her closed fingers a portion of the locks she had been grasping. As to her companion, while raising himself with one hand, he had taken her arm with the other; and so inadequate was his stock of gentleness to the requirements of her condition, that on his letting go, I saw four distinct impressions left blue in the colorless skin.

"Are you possessed with a devil," he pursued, savagely, "to talk in that manner to me, when you are dying? Do you reflect that all those words will be branded in my memory, and eating deeper eternally, after you have left me? You know you lie to say I have killed you; and, Catherine, you know that I could as soon forget you as my existence! Is it not sufficient for your infernal selfishness that while you are at peace I shall writhe in the torments of hell?"

"I shall not be at peace," moaned Catherine, recalled to a sense of physical weakness by the violent, unequal throbbing of her heart, which beat, visibly and audibly, under the excess of agitation.

She said nothing further till the paroxysm was over; then she continued, more kindly—

"I'm not wishing you greater torment than I have, Heathcliff! I only wish us never to be parted—and should a word of mine distress you hereafter, think I feel the same distress underground, and for my own sake, forgive me! Come here and kneel down again! You never harmed me in your life. Nay, if you nurse anger, that will be worse to remember than my harsh words! Won't you come here again? Do!"

Heathcliff went to the back of her chair, and leaned over, but not so far as to let her see his face, which was livid with emotion. She bent round to look at him; he would not permit it; turning abruptly, he walked to the fireplace, where he stood silent, with his back toward us.

Mrs. Linton's glance followed him suspiciously; every movement woke a new sentiment in her. After a pause, and a prolonged gaze, she resumed, addressing me in accents of indignant disappointment.

"Oh, you see, Nelly! he would not relent a moment, to keep me out of the grave! *That* is how I'm loved! Well, never mind! That is not *my* Heathcliff. I shall love mine yet; and take him with me— he's in my soul. And," added she, musingly, "the thing that irks me most is this shattered prison, after all. I'm tired, tired of being enclosed here. I'm wearying to escape into that glorious world, and to be always there; not seeing it dimly through tears, and yearning for it through the walls of an aching heart: but really with it, and in it. Nelly, you think you are better and more fortunate than I; in full health and strength—you are sorry for me— very soon that will be altered. I shall be sorry for *you*. I shall be incomparably beyond and above you all. I *wonder* he won't be near me!" She went on to herself. "I thought he wished it. Heathcliff dear! you should not be sullen now. Do come to me, Heathcliff."

In the eagerness, she rose and supported herself on the arm of the chair. At that earnest appeal, he turned to her, looking absolutely desperate. His eyes wide, and wet at last, flashed fiercely on her; his breath heaved convulsively. An instant they held asunder; and then how they met I hardly saw, but Catherine made a spring, and he caught her, and they were locked in an embrace from which I thought my mistress would never be released alive. In fact, to my eyes, she seemed directly insensible. He flung himself into the nearest seat, and on my approaching hurriedly to ascertain if she had fainted, he gnashed at me, and foamed like a mad dog, and gathered her to him with greedy jealousy. I did not feel as if I were in the company of a creature of my own species; it appeared that he would not understand, though I spoke to him; so I stood off and held my tongue, in great perplexity.

A movement of Catherine's relieved me a little presently; she put up her hand to clasp his neck, and bring her cheek to his, as he held her; while he, in return, covering her with frantic caresses, said, wildly—

"You teach me now how cruel you've been—cruel and false. *Why* did you despise me? *Why* did you betray your own heart, Cathy? I have not one word of comfort—you deserve this. You have killed yourself. Yes, you may kiss me, and cry; and wring out my kisses and tears. They'll blight you—they'll damn you. You loved me—then what *right* had you to leave me? What right—answer me—for the poor fancy you felt for Linton? Because misery, and degradation, and death, and nothing that God or Satan could inflict would have parted us, *you*, of your own will, did it. I have not broken your heart—*you*, have broken it—and in breaking it, you have broken mine. So much the worse for me, that I am strong. Do I want to live? What kind of living will it be when you—Oh, God! would *you* live with your soul in the grave?"

"Let me alone. Let me alone," sobbed Catherine. "If I've done wrong, I'm dying for it. It is enough! You left me too; but I won't upbraid you! I forgive you. Forgive me!"

"It is hard to forgive, and to look at those eyes, and feel those wasted hands," he answered. "Kiss me again; and don't let me see your eyes! I forgive what you have done to me. I love *my* murderer—but *yours*! How can I?"

They were silent—their faces hid against each other, and washed by each other's tears. At least, I suppose the weeping was on both sides; as it seemed Heathcliff *could* weep on a great occasion like this.

I grew very uncomfortable, meanwhile; for the afternoon wore fast away, the man whom I had sent off returned from his errand; and I could distinguish, by the shine of the westering sun up the valley, a concourse thickening outside Gimmerton chapel porch.

"Service is over. My master will be here in half an hour."

Heathcliff groaned a curse, and strained Catherine closer—she never moved.

Ere long I perceived a group of the servants passing up the road toward the kitchen wing. Mr. Linton was not far behind; he opened the gate himself, and sauntered slowly up, probably enjoying the lovely afternoon that breathed as soft as summer.

"Now he is here," I exclaimed. "For Heaven's sake, hurry down! You'll not meet any one on the front stairs. Do be quick; and stay among the trees till he is fairly in."

"I must go, Cathy," said Heathcliff, seeking to extricate himself from his companion's arms. "But, if I live, I'll see you again before you are asleep. I won't stray five yards from your window."

"You must not go!" she answered, holding him as firmly as her strength allowed. "You shall not, I tell you."

"For one hour," he pleaded, earnestly.

"Not for one minute," she replied.

"I *must*—Linton will be up immediately," persisted the alarmed intruder.

He would have risen, and unfixed her finger by the act—she clung fast, gasping; there was mad resolution in her face.

"No!" she shrieked. "Oh, don't, don't go. It is the last time! Edgar will not hurt us. Heathcliff, I shall die! I shall die!"

"Damn the fool. There he is," cried Heathcliff sinking back into his seat. "Hush, my darling! Hush, hush, Catherine! I'll stay. If he shot me so, I'd expire with a blessing on my lips."

And there they were fast again. I heard my master mounting the stairs—the cold sweat ran from by forehead; I was horrified.

"Are you going to listen to her ravings?" I said passionately. "She does not know what she says. Will you ruin her, because she has not wit to help herself? Get up! you could be free instantly. That is the most diabolical deed that ever you did. We are all done for—master, mistress, and servant."

I wrung my hands, and cried out; and Mr. Linton hastened his step at the noise. In the midst of my agitation, I was sincerely glad to observe that Catherine's arms had fallen relaxed, and her head hung down.

"She's fainted or dead," I thought, "so much the better. Far better that she should be dead, than lingering a burden and a misery-maker to all around her."

Edgar sprang to his unbidden guest, blanched with astonishment and rage. What he meant to do, I cannot tell; however the other stopped all demonstrations at once, by placing the lifeless looking form in his arms.

"Look there," he said, "unless you be a fiend, help her first, then you shall speak to me!"

He walked into the parlor, and sat down. Mr. Linton summoned me, and with great difficulty, and after resorting to many means, we managed to restore her to sensation; but she was all bewildered; she sighed and moaned and knew nobody. Edgar, in his anxiety for her forgot her hated friend. I did not. I went, at the earliest opportunity, and besought him to depart, affirming that Catherine was better, and he should hear from me in the morning, how she passed the night.

"I shall not refuse to go out of doors," he answered, "but I shall stay in the garden; and, Nelly, mind you keep your word to-morrow. I shall be under those larch trees, mind! or I pay another visit, whether Linton be in or not."

He sent a rapid glance through the half-open door of the chamber, and ascertaining that what I stated was apparently true, delivered the house of his luckless presence.

. . . .

Chapter 16

About twelve o'clock that night, was born the Catherine you saw at Wuthering Heights, a puny, seven months' child; and two hours after, the mother died, having never recovered sufficient consciousness to miss Heathcliff, or know Edgar.

The latter's distraction at his bereavement is a subject too painful to be dwelt on; its after effects showed how deep the sorrow sunk.

A great addition, in my eyes, was his being left without an heir. I bemoaned that, as I gazed on the feeble orphan; and I mentally abused old Linton for—what was only natural partiality—the securing his estate to his own daughter, instead of his son's.

An unwelcomed infant it was, poor thing! It might have wailed out of life, and nobody cared a morsel during those first hours of existence. We redeemed the neglect afterward; but its beginning was as friendless as its end is likely to be.

Next morning—bright and cheerful out of doors–stole softened in through the blinds of the silent room, and suffused the couch and its occupant with a mellow, tender glow.

Edgar Linton had his head laid on the pillow, and his eyes shut. His young and fair features were almost as deathlike as those of the form beside him, and almost as fixed; but *his* was the hush of exhausted, and *hers* of perfect peace. Her brow smooth, her lids closed, her lips wearing the expression of a smile. No angel in heaven could be more beautiful than she appeared; and I partook of the infinite calm in which she lay. My mind was never in a holier frame than while I gazed on that untroubled image of divine rest. I instinctively echoed the words she had uttered a few hours before. "Incomparably beyond and above us all! Whether still on earth or now in Heaven, her spirit is at home with God!"

I didn't know if it be a peculiarity in me, but I am seldom otherwise than happy while watching in the chamber of death, should no frenzied or despairing mourner share the duty with me. I see a repose that neither earth nor hell can break; and I feel an assurance of the endless and shadowless hereafter—the eternity they have entered—where life is boundless in its duration, and love in its sympathy, and joy in its fullness. I noticed on that occasion how much selfishness there is even in a love like Mr. Linton's, when he so regretted Catherine's blessed release.

To be sure, one might have doubted, after the wayward and impatient existence she had led, whether she merited a heaven of peace at last. One might doubt, in seasons of cold reflection, but not then, in the presence of her corpse. It asserted its own tranquillity, which seemed a pledge of equal quiet to its former inhabitant.

Do you believe such people *are* happy in the other world, sir? I'd give a great deal to know.

I declined answering Mrs. Dean's question, which struck me as
something heterodox. She proceeded:

Retracing the course of Catherine Linton, I fear we have no
right to think she is; but we'll leave her with her Maker.

The master looked asleep, and I ventured soon after sunrise to
quit the room, and steal out to the pure, refreshing air. The servants thought me gone to shake off the drowsiness of my protracted watch; in reality my chief motive was seeing Mr. Heathcliff. If he had remained among the larches all night he would
have heard nothing of the stir at the Grange, unless, perhaps, he
might catch the gallop of the messenger going to Gimmerton. If
he had come nearer he would probably be aware, from the lights
flitting to and fro, and the opening and shutting of the outer
doors, that all was not right within.

I wished, yet feared, to find him. I felt the terrible news must be
told, and I longed to get it over; but *how* to do it I did not know.

He was there—at least a few yards further in the park, leaning
against an old ash-tree, his hat off, and his hair soaked with the
dew that had gathered on the budded branches, and fell pattering
round him. He had been standing a long time in that position, for
I saw a pair of ousels passing and repassing, scarcely three feet
from him, busy in building their nest, and regarding his proximity
no more than that of a piece of timber. They flew off at my
approach, and he raised his eyes and spoke:

"She's dead!" he said; "I've not waited for you to learn that. Put
your handkerchief away—don't snivel before me. Damn you all!
She wants none of *your* tears!"

I was weeping as much for him as her: we do sometimes pity
creatures that have none of the feeling either for themselves or
others; and when I first looked into his face I perceived that he
had got intelligence of the catastrophe; and a foolish notion
struck me that his heart was quelled, and he prayed, because his
lips moved, and his gaze was bent on the ground.

"Yes, she's dead!" I answered, checking my sobs, and drying my
cheeks. "Gone to heaven, I hope, where we may every one join
her if we take due warning, and leave our evil ways to follow
good."

"Did *she* take due warning, then?" asked Heathcliff, attempting
a sneer. "Did she die like a saint? Come, give me a true history of
the event. How did——" He endeavored to pronounce the name,
but could not manage it; and, compressing his mouth, he held a
silent combat with his inward agony, defying, meanwhile, my
sympathy with an unflinching, ferocious stare.

"How did she die?" he resumed, at last, fain, notwithstanding
his hardihood, to have a support behind him, for after the struggle, he trembled, in spite of himself, to his very fingerends.

"Poor wretch!" I thought, "you have a heart and nerves, the
same as your brother men! Why should you be so anxious to
conceal them? Your pride cannot blind God! You tempt Him to
wring them, till He forces a cry of humiliation!"

"Quietly as a lamb!" I answered, aloud. "She drew a sigh, and
stretched herself, like a child reviving, and sinking again to sleep;

and five minutes after I felt one little pulse at her heart, and nothing more."

"And—and did she ever mention me?" he asked, hesitating, as if he dreaded the answer to his question would introduce details that he could not bear to hear.

"Her senses never returned—she recognized nobody from the time you left her," I said. "She lies with a sweet smile on her face, and her latest ideas wandered back to pleasant early days. Her life closed in a gentle dream—may she wake as kindly in the other world!"

"May she wake in torment!" he cried, with frightful vehemence, stamping his foot, and groaning, in a sudden paroxysm of ungovernable passion. "Why, she's a liar to the end! Where is she? Not *there*—not in heaven—not perished—where? Oh, you said you cared nothing for my sufferings! And I pray one prayer—I repeat it till my tongue stiffens—Catherine Earnshaw, may you not rest as long as I am living! You said I killed you—haunt me then! The murdered *do* haunt their murderers, I believe; I know that ghosts *have* wandered on earth. Be with me always—take any form—drive me mad! only *do* not leave me in this abyss where I cannot find you! Oh, God! it is unutterable! I *cannot* live without my life! I *cannot* live without my soul!"

He dashed his head against the knotted trunk; and, lifting up his eyes, howled, not like a man, but like a savage beast getting goaded to death with knives and spears.

I observed several splashes of blood about the bark of the tree, and his hand and forehead were both stained; probably the scene I witnessed was repetition of others acted during the night. It hardly moved my compassion—it appalled me; still I felt reluctant to quit him so. But the moment he recollected himself enough to notice me watching, he thundered a command for me to go, and I obeyed. He was beyond my skill to quiet or console!

Mrs. Linton's funeral was appointed to take place on the Friday following her decease; and till then her coffin remained uncovered, and strewn with flowers and scented leaves, in the great drawing-room. Linton spent his days and nights there, a sleepless guardian; and—a circumstance concealed from all but me—Heathcliff spent his nights, at least, outside, equally a stranger to repose.

I held no communication with him; still I was conscious of his design to enter, if he could; and on the Tuesday, a little after dark, when my master, from sheer fatigue, had been compelled to retire a couple of hours, I went and opened one of the windows, moved by his perseverance to give him a chance of bestowing on the fading image of his idol one final adieu.

He did not omit to avail himself of the opportunity, cautiously and briefly; too cautiously to betray his presence by the slightest noise; indeed, I shouldn't have discovered that he had been there, except for the disarrangement of the drapery about the corpse's face, and for observing on the floor a curl of light hair, fastened with a silver thread, which, on examination, I ascertained to have been taken from a locket hung round Catherine's neck. Heathcliff had opened the trinket, and cast out its contents, replacing them by a black lock of his own. I twisted the two, and enclosed them together.

Mr. Earnshaw was, of course, invited to attend the remains of his sister to the grave, and he sent no excuse, but he never came; so that besides her husband, the mourners were wholly composed of tenants and servants. Isabella was not asked.

The place of Catherine's interment, to the surprise of the villagers, was neither in the chapel under the carved monument of the Lintons, nor yet by the tombs of her own relations, outside. It was dug on a green slope, in a corner of the kirkyard, where the wall is so low that heath and bilberry plants have climbed over it from the moor; and peat mold almost buries it. Her husband lies in the same spot, now; and they have each a simple headstone above, and a plain gray block at their feet, to mark the graves.

·······

Chapter 17

That Friday made the last of our fine days, for a month. In the evening the weather broke; the wind shifted from south to northeast, and brought rain first, and then sleet and snow.

On the morrow one could hardly imagine that there had been three weeks of summer: the primroses and crocuses were hidden under wintry drifts: the larks were silent, the young leaves of the early trees smitten and blackened. And dreary, and chill, and dismal that morrow did creep over! My master kept his room—I took possession of the lonely parlor, converting it into a nursery; and there I was sitting, with the moaning doll of a child laid on my knee, rocking it to and fro; and watching, meanwhile, the still driving flakes build up the uncurtained window, when the door opened, and some person entered, out of breath and laughing!

My anger was greater than my astonishment for a minute; I supposed it one of the maids, and I cried,

"Have done! How dare you show your giddiness here? What would Mr. Linton say if he heard you?"

"Excuse me!" answered a familiar voice, "but I know Edgar is in bed, and I cannot stop myself."

With that, the speaker came forward to the fire, panting and holding her hand to her side.

"I have run the whole way from Wuthering Heights!" she continued, after a pause. "Except where I've flown. I couldn't count the number of falls I've had. Oh, I'm aching all over! Don't be alarmed—there shall be an explanation as soon as I can give it— only just have the goodness to step out, and order the carriage to take me on to Gimmerton, and tell a servant to seek up a few clothes in my wardrobe."

The intruder was Mrs. Heathcliff—she certainly seemed in no laughing predicament: her hair streamed on her shoulders, dripping with snow and water; she was dressed in the girlish dress she commonly wore, befitting her age more than her position; a low frock, with short sleeves, and nothing on either head or neck. The frock was of light silk, and clung to her with wet; and her feet were protected merely by thin slippers; add to this a deep cut under one ear, which only the cold prevented from bleeding profusely, a white face scratched and bruised, and a frame hardly able to support itself, through fatigue, and you may fancy my first fright was not much allayed when I had leisure to examine her.

"My dear young lady," I exclaimed; "I'll stir nowhere, and hear nothing, till you have removed every article of your clothes, and put on dry things; and certainly you shall not go to Gimmerton to-night; so it is needless to order the carriage."

"Certainly I shall," she said; "walking or riding—yet I've no objection to dress myself decently; and—ah, see how it flows down my neck now! the fire does make it smart."

She insisted on my fulfilling her directions, before she would let me touch her; and not till after the coachman had been instructed to get ready, and a maid sent to pack up some necessary attire, did I obtain her consent for binding the wound, and helping to change her garments.

"Now Ellen," she said when my task was finished, and she was seated in an easy chair on the hearth, with a cup of tea before her, "You sit down opposite me, and put poor Catherine's baby away—I don't like to see it! You mustn't think I care little for Catherine, because I behaved so foolishly on entering—I've cried, too, bitterly—yes, more than any one else has reason to cry—we parted unreconciled, you remember, and I shan't forgive myself. But for all that I was not going to sympathize with him—the brute beast! O give me the poker! this is the last thing of his I have about me," she slipped the gold ring from her third finger, and threw it on the floor. "I'll smash it!" she continued, striking with childish spite. "And then I'll burn it!" and she took and dropped the misused article among the coals. "There! he shall buy another if he gets me back again. He'd be capable of coming to seek me, to tease Edgar. I dare not stay, lest the notion should possess his wicked head! And besides, Edgar has not been kind, has he? And I won't come suing for his assistance; nor will I bring him into more trouble. Necessity compelled me to seek shelter here; though if I had not learned he was out of the way, I'd have halted at the kitchen, washed my face, warmed myself, got you to bring what I wanted, and departed again to anywhere out of the reach of my accursed—of that incarnate goblin! Ah, he was in such a fury—if he had caught me! It's a pity Earnshaw is not his match in strength—I wouldn't have run till I'd seen him all but demol-ished, had Hindley been able to do it!"

"Well, don't talk so fast, Miss," I interrupted, "you'll disorder the handkerchief I have tied round your face, and make the cut bleed again. Drink your tea, and take breath, and give over laugh-ing. Laughter is sadly out of place under this roof, and in your condition!"

"An undeniable truth," she replied, "Listen to that child! it maintains a constant wail—send it out of my hearing, for an hour; I shan't stay any longer."

I rang the bell, and committed it to a servant's care; and then I inquired what had urged her to escape from Wuthering Heights in such an unlikely plight—and where she meant to go, as she refused remaining with us.

"I ought, and I wish to remain," answered she; "to cheer Edgar, and take care of the baby, for two things, and because the Grange is my right home—but I tell you, he wouldn't let me! Do you think he could bear to see me grow fat, and merry; and could bear to think that we were tranquil, and not resolve on poisoning our comfort? Now I have the satisfaction of being sure that he detests me to the point of its annoying him seriously to have me within ear-shot or eye-sight. I notice when I enter his presence, the muscles of his countenance are involuntarily distorted into an expression of hatred; partly arising from his knowledge of the good causes I have to feel that sentiment for him, and partly from original aversion. It is strong enough to make me feel pretty certain that he would not chase me over England, supposing I contrived a clear escape; and therefore I must get quite away. I've recovered from my first desire to be killed by him: I'd rather he'd kill himself! He has extinguished my love effectually, and so I'm at my ease. I can recollect yet how I loved him; and can dimly imagine that I could still be loving him, if—no, no! Even, if he had doted on me, the devilish nature would have revealed its existence somehow. Catherine had an awfully perverted taste to esteem him so dearly, knowing him so well. Monster! would that he could be blotted out of creation, and out of my memory!"

"Hush, Hush! he's a human being," I said. "Be more charitable; there are worse men than he is, yet!"

"He's not a human being," she retorted; "and he has no claim on my charity. I gave him my heart, and he took and pinched it to death; and flung it back to me—people feel with their hearts, Ellen—and since he has destroyed mine, I have not power to feel for him; and I would not, though he groaned from this to his dying day; and wept tears of blood for Catherine! No, indeed, indeed, I wouldn't!" And here Isabella began to cry; but, immediately dashing the water from her lashes, she recommenced.

"You asked what has driven me to flight at last? I was compelled to attempt it, because I had succeeded in rousing his rage a pitch above his malignity. Pulling out the nerves with red hot pincers requires more coolness than knocking on the head. He was worked up to forget the fiendish prudence he boasted of, and proceeded to murderous violence. I experienced pleasure in being able to exasperate him: the sense of pleasure woke my instinct of self-preservation; so I fairly broke free, and if ever I come into his hands again he is welcome to a signal revenge.

"Yesterday, you know, Mr. Earnshaw should have been at the funeral. He kept himself sober for the purpose—tolerably sober; not going to bed mad at six o'clock, and getting up drunk at twelve. Consequently he rose, in suicidal low spirits; as fit for the church as for a dance; and instead, he sat down by the fire and swallowed gin or brandy by tumblerfuls.

"Heathcliff—I shudder to name him! has been a stranger in the house from last Sunday till to-day. Whether the angels have fed him, or his kin beneath, I cannot tell; but he has not eaten a meal with us for nearly a week. He had just come home at dawn, and gone up-stairs to his chamber; locking himself in—as if anybody dreamed of coveting his company! There he continued, praying like a Methodist; only the deity he implored is senseless dust and ashes; and God, when addressed, was curiously confounded with his own black father! After concluding these precious orisons— and they lasted generally till he grew hoarse, and his voice was strangled in his throat—he would be off again; always straight down to the Grange! I wonder Edgar did not send for a constable, and give him into custody! For me, grieved as I was about Catherine, it was impossible to avoid regarding this season of deliverance from degrading oppression as a holiday.

"I recovered spirits sufficient to hear Joseph's eternal lectures without weeping; and to move up and down the house less with the foot of a frightened thief than formerly. You wouldn't think that I should cry at anything Joseph could say, but he and Hareton are detestable companions. I'd rather sit with Hindley, and hear his awful talk, than with 't' little maister,' and his staunch supporter, that odious old man!

"When Heathcliff is in, I'm often obliged to seek the kitchen and their society, or starve among the damp, uninhabited chambers, when he is not, as was the case this week, I establish a table and chair, at one corner of the house-fire, and never mind how Mr. Earnshaw may occupy himself; and he does not interfere with my arrangements: he is quieter now than he used to be, if no one provokes him; more sullen and depressed, and less furious. Joseph affirms he's sure he's an altered man; that the Lord has touched his heart, and he is saved ' so as by fire.' I'm puzzled to detect signs of the favorable change, but it is not my business.

"Yester-evening, I sat in my nook, reading some old books, till late on toward twelve. It seemed so dismal to go up-stairs, with the wild snow blowing outside, and my thoughts continually reverting to the kirkyard, and the new made grave! I dared hardly lift my eyes from the page before me, that melancholy scene so instantly usurped its place.

"Hindley sat opposite, his head leaned on his hand, perhaps meditating on the same subject. He had ceased drinking at a point below irrationality, and had neither stirred nor spoken during two or three hours. There was no sound through the house, but the moaning wind which shook the windows every now and then; the faint crackling of the coals; and the click of my snuffers as I removed at intervals the long wick of the candle. Hareton and Joseph were probably fast asleep in bed. It was very, very sad, and while I read I sighed, for it seemed as if all joy had vanished from the world, never to be restored.

The doleful silence was broken, at length, by the sound of the kitchen latch. Heathcliff had returned from his watch earlier than usual, owing, I suppose, to the sudden storm.

"That entrance was fastened; and we heard him coming round to get in by the other. I rose with an irrepressible expression of what I felt on my lips, which induced my companion, who had been staring toward the door, to turn and look at me.

'I'll keep him out five minutes,' he exclaimed; 'you won't object?'

'No, you may keep him out the whole night, for me,' I answered. 'Do! put the key in the lock, and draw the bolts.'

"Earnshaw accomplished this ere his guest reached the front; he then came and brought his chair to the other side of my table; leaning over it, and searching in my eyes a sympathy with the burning hate that gleamed from his: as he both looked and felt like an assassin, he couldn't exactly find that; but he discovered enough to encourage him to speak.

"'You, and I,' he said, 'have each a great debt to settle with the man out yonder! If we were neither of us cowards we might combine to discharge it. Are you as soft as your brother? Are you willing to endure to the last, and not once attempt a repayment?'

"'I'm weary of enduring now,' I replied, 'and I'd be glad of a retaliation that wouldn't recoil on myself; but treachery and violence are spears pointed at both ends—they wound those who resort to them worse than their enemies.'

"'Treachery and violence are a just return for treachery and violence!' cried Hindley. 'Mrs. Heathcliff, I'll ask you to do nothing but sit still and be dumb. Tell me now, can you? I'm sure you would have as much pleasure as I in witnessing the conclusion of the fiend's existence. He'll be *your* death unless you overreach him—and he'll be *my* ruin. Damn the hellish villain! He knocks at the door as if he were master here already! Promise to hold your tongue, and before that clock strikes—it wants three minutes of one—you're a free woman!'

"He took the implements which I described to you in my letter from his breast, and would have turned down the candle. I snatched it away, however, and seized his arm.

"'I'll not hold my tongue!' I said. 'You mustn't touch him. Let the door remain shut, and be quiet!'

"'No! I've formed my resolution, and by God I'll execute it!' cried the desperate being; 'I'll do you a kindness, in spite of yourself, and Hareton justice! And you needn't trouble your head to screen me. Catherine is gone—nobody alive would regret me, or be ashamed though I cut my throat this minute—and it's time to make an end!'

"I might as well have struggled with a bear, or reasoned with a lunatic. The only resource left me was to run to a lattice, and warn his intended victim of the fate which awaited him.

"'You'd better seek shelter somewhere else to-night!' I exclaimed in a rather triumphant tone. 'Mr. Earnshaw has a mind to shoot you, if you persist in endeavoring to enter.'

"'You'd better open the door, you——,' he answered, addressing me by some elegant term that I don't care to repeat.

"'I shall not meddle in the matter,' I retorted again. 'Come in and get shot, if you please. I've done my duty.'

"With that I shut the window, and returned to my place by the fire, having too small a stock of hypocrisy at my command to pretend any anxiety for the danger that menaced him.

"Earnshaw swore passionately at me, affirming that I loved the villain yet, and calling me all sorts of names for the base spirit I evinced. And I, in my secret heart (and conscience never reproached me), thought what a blessing it would be for *him* should Heathcliff put him out of misery, and what a blessing for *me* should he send Heathcliff to his right abode! As I sat nursing these reflections, the casement behind me was banged upon the floor by a blow from the latter individual, and his black countenance looked blightingly through. The stanchions stood too close to suffer his shoulders to follow, and I smiled, exulting in my fancied security. His hair and clothes were whitened with snow, and his sharp cannibal teeth, revealed by cold and wrath, gleamed through the dark.

"'Isabella, let me in, or I'll make you repent!' he 'girned,' as Joseph calls it.

"'I cannot commit murder!' I replied. 'Mr. Hindley stands sentinel, with a knife and loaded pistol.'

"'Let me in by the kitchen door,' he said.

"'Hindley will be there before me,' I answered. 'And that's a poor love of yours, that cannot bear a shower of snow! We were left at peace in our beds as long as the summer moon shone, but the moment a blast of winter returns you must run for shelter! Heathcliff, if I were you I'd go stretch myself over her grave, and die like a faithful dog. The world is surely not worth living in now, is it? You had distinctly impressed on me the idea that Catherine was the whole joy of your life. I can't imagine how you think of surviving her loss.'

"'He's there, is he?' exclaimed my companion, rushing to the gap. 'If I can get my arm out I can hit him.'

"I'm afraid, Ellen, you'll set me down as really wicked; but you don't know all, so don't judge. I wouldn't have aided or abetted an attempt on even *his* life, for anything. Wish that he were dead I must; and therefore I was fearfully disappointed, and unnerved by terror for the consequences of my taunting speech, when he flung himself on Earnshaw's weapon and wrenched it from his grasp. The charge exploded, and the knife, in springing back, closed into its owner's wrist. Heathcliff pulled it away by main force, slitting up the flesh as it passed on, and thrust it dripping into his pocket. He then took a stone, struck down the division between two windows, and sprung in. His adversary had fallen senseless with excessive pain, and the flow of blood that gushed from an artery or a large vein.

"The ruffian kicked and trampled on him, and dashed his head repeatedly against the flags, holding me with one hand, meantime, to prevent me summoning Joseph. He exerted preterhuman self-denial in abstaining from finishing him completely; but, getting out of breath, he finally desisted, and dragged the apparently

inanimate body to the settle. There he tore off the sleeve of Earnshaw's coat, and bound up the wound with brutal roughness,
spitting and cursing during the operation as energetically as he
had kicked before. Being at liberty, I lost no time in seeking the
old servant, who, having gathered by degrees the purport of my
hasty tale, hurried below, gasping, as he descended the steps, two
at once.

"'Whet is thur tuh do, nah? whet is thur tuh do, nah?'

"'There's this to do,' thundered Heathcliff, 'that your master's
mad, and, should he last another month, I'll have him to an
asylum. And how the devil did you come to fasten me out, you
toothless hound? Don't stand muttering and mumbling there.
Come, I'm not going to nurse him. Wash that stuff away—and
mind the sparks of your candle—it is more than half brandy!'

"'Und soa, yah been murthering on him?' exclaimed Joseph,
lifting his hands and eyes in horror. 'If iver aw seed a seeght loike
this! May the Lord—'

"Heathcliff gave him a push upon his knees, in the middle of
the blood; and flung a towel to him; but instead of proceeding to
dry it up, he joined his hands, and began a prayer which excited
my laughter from its odd phraseology. I was in the condition of
mind to be shocked at nothing; in fact, I was as reckless as some
malefactors show themselves at the foot of the gallows.

"'Oh, I forgot you,' said that tyrant, 'you shall do that. Down
with you. And you conspire with him against me, do you, viper?
There, that is work fit for you!'

"He shook me till my teeth rattled, and pitched me beside
Joseph, who steadily concluded his supplications, and then rose,
vowing he would set off for the Grange directly. Mr. Linton was a
magistrate, and though he had fifty wives dead, he should inquire
into this. He was so obstinate in his resolution that Heathcliff
deemed it expedient to compel from my lips a recapitulation of
what had taken place; standing over me, heaving with malevolence, as I reluctantly delivered the account in answer to his
questions. It required a great deal of labor to satisfy the old man
that he was not the aggressor; especially with my hardly-wrung
replies. However, Mr. Earnshaw soon convinced him that he was
alive still; he hastened to administer a dose of spirits, and by their
succor his master presently regained motion and consciousness.
Heathcliff, aware that he was ignorant of the treatment received
while insensible, called him deliriously intoxicated; and said he
should not notice his atrocious conduct further; but advised him
to get to bed. To my joy, he left us after giving this judicious
counsel, and Hindley stretched himself on the hearth-stone. I
departed to my own room marveling that I had escaped so easily.

"This morning, when I came down, about half an hour before
noon, Mr. Earnshaw was sitting by the fire, deadly sick; his evil
genius, almost as gaunt and ghastly, leaned against the chimney.
Neither appeared inclined to dine; and having waited till all was
cold on the table, I commenced alone. Nothing hindered me from
eating heartily; and I experienced a certain sense of satisfaction
and superiority, as, at intervals, I cast a look toward my silent

companions, and felt the comfort of a quiet conscience within me.

"After I had done, I ventured on the unusual liberty of drawing near the fire; going round Earnshaw's seat, and kneeling in the corner beside him. Heathcliff did not glance my way, and I gazed up, and contemplated his features, almost as confidently as if they had been turned to stone. His forehead, that I once thought so manly, and that I now think so diabolical, was shaded with a heavy cloud; his basilisk eyes were nearly quenched by sleeplessness—and weeping, perhaps, for the lashes were wet then; his lips devoid of their ferocious sneer, and sealed in an expression of unspeakable sadness. Had it been another, I would have covered my face, in the presence of such grief. In *his* case, I was gratified: and ignoble as it seems to insult a fallen enemy, I couldn't miss this chance of sticking in a dart; his weakness was the only time when I could taste the delight of paying wrong for wrong."

"Fie, fie, Miss!" I interrupted. "One might suppose you had never opened a Bible in your life. If God afflict your enemies, surely that ought to suffice you. It is both mean and presumptuous to add your torture to his!"

"In general, I'll allow that it would be, Ellen," she continued. "But what misery laid on Heathcliff could content me, unless I have a hand in it? I'd rather he suffered *less*, if I might cause his sufferings, and he might *know* that I was the cause. Oh, I owe him so much. On only one condition can I hope to forgive him. It is, if I may take an eye for an eye, a tooth for a tooth, for every wrench of agony, return a wrench, reduce him to my level. As he was the first to injure, make him the first to implore pardon; and then—why then, Ellen, I might show you some generosity. But it is utterly impossible I can ever be revenged, and therefore I cannot forgive him. Hindley wanted some water, and I handed him a glass, and asked him how he was."

"'Not as ill as I wish,' he replied. 'But leaving out my arm, every inch of me is as sore as if I had been fighting with a legion of imps!'

"'Yes, no wonder,' was my next remark. 'Catherine used to boast that she stood between you and bodily harm—she meant that certain persons would not hurt you, for fear of offending her. It's well people don't *really* rise from the grave, or, last night, she might have witnessed a repulsive scene! Are not you bruised and cut over your chest and shoulders?'

"'I can't say,' he answered; 'but what do you mean? Did he dare to strike me when I was down?'

"'He trampled on, and kicked you, and dashed you on the ground,' I whispered. 'And his mouth watered to tear you with his teeth; because, he's only half a man—not so much.'

"Mr. Earnshaw looked up, like me, to the countenance of our mutual foe; who, absorbed in his anguish, seemed insensible to anything around him; the longer he stood, the plainer his reflections revealed their blackness through his features.

"'Oh, if God, would but give me strength to strangle him in my last agony, I'd go to hell with joy,' groaned the impatient man, writhing to rise, and sinking back in despair, convinced of his inadequacy for the struggle.

"'Nay, it's enough that he has murdered one of you,' I observed aloud. 'At the Grange, every one knows your sister would have been living now had it not been for Mr. Heathcliff. After all, it is preferable to be hated than loved by him. When I recollect how happy we were—how happy Catherine was before he came—I'm fit to curse the day!'

"Most likely, Heathcliff noticed more the truth of what was said, than the spirit of the person who said it. His attention was roused, I saw, for his eyes rained down tears among the ashes, and he drew his breath in suffocating sighs. I stared full at him, and laughed scornfully. The clouded windows of hell flashed a moment toward me; the fiend which usually looked out, however, was so dimmed and drowned that I did not fear to hazard another sound of derision.

"'Get up, and begone out of my sight,' said the mourner.

"I guessed he uttered those words, at least, though his voice was hardly intelligible.

"'I beg your pardon,' I replied. 'But I loved Catherine too; and her brother requires attendance which, for her sake, I shall supply. Now that she's dead, I see her in Hindley. Hindley has exactly her eyes, if you had not tried to gouge them out, and make them black and red, and her—'

"'Get up, wretched idiot, before I stamp you to death!' he cried, making a movement that caused me to make one also.

"'But then,' I continued, holding myself ready to flee; 'if poor Catherine had trusted you, and assumed the ridiculous, contemptible, degrading title of Mrs. Heathcliff, she would soon have presented a similar picture! *She* wouldn't have borne your abominable behavior quietly; her detestation and disgust must have found voice.'

"The back of the settle, and Earnshaw's person interposed between me and him; so, instead of endeavoring to reach me, he snatched a dinner knife from the table, and flung it at my head. It struck beneath my ear, and stopped the sentence I was uttering; but pulling it out, I sprang to the door, and delivered another which I hope went a little deeper than his missile.

"The last glimpse I caught of him was a furious rush, on his part, checked by the embrace of his host; and both fell locked together on the hearth. In my flight through the kitchen I bid Joseph speed to his master; I knocked over Hareton, who was hanging a litter of puppies from a chair-back in the doorway; and, blest as a soul escaped from purgatory, I bounded, leaped, and flew down the steep road: then, quitting its windings, shot direct across the moor, rolling over banks, and wading through marshes; precipitating myself, in fact, toward the beacon light of the Grange. And far rather would I be condemned to a perpetual dwelling in the infernal regions, then even for one night abide beneath the roof of Wuthering Heights again."

Isabella ceased speaking, and took a drink of tea; then she rose, and bidding me put on her bonnet, and a great shawl I had brought, and turning a deaf ear to my entreaties for her to remain another hour, she stepped upon a chair, kissed Edgar's and Catherine's portraits, bestowed a similar salute on me, and descended to the carriage accompanied by Fanny, who yelped wild with joy at recovering her mistress. She was driven away, never to revisit this neighborhood; but a regular correspondence was established between her and my master, when things were more settled.

I believe her new abode was in the south, near London; there she had a son born, a few months subsequent to her escape. He was christened Linton, and, from the first, she reported him to be an ailing, peevish creature. Mr. Heathcliff, meeting me one day in the village, inquired where she lived. I refused to tell. He remarked that it was not of any moment, only she must beware of coming to her brother; she should not be with him, if he had to keep her himself.

Though I would give no information, he discovered, through some of the other servants, both her place of residence, and the existence of the child. Still he didn't molest her; for which forbearance she might thank his aversion, I suppose. He often asked about the infant when he saw me; and on hearing its name, smiled grimly, and observed:

"They wish me to hate it too, do they?"

"I don't think they wish you to know any thing about it," I answered.

"But I'll have it," he said, "when I want it. They may reckon on that!"

Fortunately; its mother died before the time arrived, some thirteen years after the decease of Catherine, when Linton was twelve, or a little more.

On the day succeeding Isabella's unexpected visit, I had no opportunity of speaking to my master: he shunned conversation, and was fit for discussing nothing. When I could get him to listen, I saw it pleased him that his sister had left her husband, whom he abhorred with an intensity which the mildness of his nature would scarcely seem to allow. So deep and sensitive was his aversion, that he refrained from going anywhere where he was likely to see or hear of Heathcliff. Grief, and that together, transformed him into a complete hermit: he threw up his office of magistrate, ceased even to attend church, avoided the village on all occasions, and spent a life of entire seclusion within the limits of his park and grounds: only varied by solitary rambles on the moors, and visits to the grave of his wife, mostly at evening, or early morning, before other wanderers were abroad.

But he was too good to be thoroughly unhappy long. *He* didn't pray for Catherine's soul to haunt him. Time brought resignation, and a melancholy sweeter than common joy. He recalled her memory with ardent, tender love, and hopeful aspiring to the better world, where, he doubted not she was gone.

And he had earthly consolation and affections also. For a few days, I said, he seemed regardless of the puny successor to the departed: the coldness melted as fast as snow in April, and ere the tiny thing could stammer a word or totter a step, it wielded a despot's scepter in his heart. It was named Catherine, but he never called it the name in full, as he had never called the first Catherine short, probably because Heathcliff had a habit of doing so. The little one was always Cathy, it formed to him a distinction from the mother, and yet, a connection with her; and his attachment sprang from its relation to her, far more than from its being his own.

I used to draw a comparison between him and Hindley Earnshaw, and perplex myself to explain satisfactorily why their conduct was so opposite in similar circumstances. They had both been found husbands, and were both attached to their children; and I could not see how they shouldn't both have taken the same road, for good or evil. But, I thought in my mind, Hindley with apparently the stronger head, has shown himself sadly the worse and the weaker man. When his ship struck, the captain abandoned his post; and the crew, instead of trying to save her, rushed into riot and confusion, leaving no hope for their luckless vessel. Linton, on the contrary, displayed the true courage of a loyal and faithful soul: he trusted God—and God comforted him. One hoped, and the other despaired: they chose their own lots, and were righteously doomed to endure them.

But you'll not want to hear my moralizing, Mr. Lockwood: you'll judge as well as I can, all these things; at least, you'll think you will, and that's the same.

The end of Earnshaw was what might have been expected; it followed fast on his sister's; there was scarcely six months between them. We, at the Grange, never got a very succinct account of his state preceding it; all that I did learn, was on occasion of going to aid in the preparations for the funeral. Mr. Kenneth came to announce the event to my master.

"Well, Nelly," said he, riding into the yard one morning, too early not to alarm me with an instant presentiment of bad news. "It's your and my turn to go into mourning at present. Who's given us the slip now, do you think?"

"Who?" I asked in a flurry.

"Why, guess!" he returned, dismounting, and slinging his bridle on a hook by the door. "And nip up the corner of your apron; I'm certain you'll need it."

"Not Mr. Heathcliff, surely?" I exclaimed.

"What! would you have tears for him?" said the doctor. "No, Heathcliff's a tough young fellow; he looks blooming today—I've just seen him. He's rapidly regaining flesh since he lost his better half."

"Who is it then, Mr. Kenneth?" I repeated impatiently.

"Hindley Earnshaw! Your old friend Hindley," he replied. "And my wicked gossip; though he's been too wild for me this long while. There! I said we should draw water. But cheer up! He died true to his character, drunk as a lord. Poor lad! I'm sorry too. One can't help missing an old companion; though he had the worst tricks with him that ever man imagined; and has done me many a rascally turn. He's barely twenty-seven, it seems; that's your own age; who would have thought you were born in one year!"

I confess this blow was greater to me than the shock of Mrs. Linton's death; ancient associations lingered round my heart; I sat down in the porch, and wept as for a blood relation, desiring Kenneth to get another servant to introduce him to the master. I could not hinder myself from pondering on the question—"Had he had fair play?" Whatever I did, that idea would bother me: it was so tiresomely pertinacious that I resolved on requesting leave to go to Wuthering Heights, and assist in the last duties to the dead. Mr. Linton was extremely reluctant to consent, but I pleaded eloquently for the friendless condition in which he lay; and I said my old master and foster brother had a claim on my services as strong as his own. Besides, I reminded him that the child, Hareton, was his wife's nephew; and, in the absence of nearer kin, he ought to act as its guardian; and he ought to and must inquire how the property was left, and look over the concerns of his brother-in-law.

He was unfit for attending to such matters then, but he bid me speak to his lawyer; and at length permitted me to go. His lawyer had been Earnshaw's also: I called at the village, and asked him to accompany me. He shook his head, and advised that Heathcliff should be let alone; affirming, if the truth were known, Hareton would be found little else than a beggar.

"His father died in debt," he said, "the whole property is mortgaged, and the sole chance for the natural heir is to allow him an opportunity of creating some interest in the creditor's heart, that he may be inclined to deal leniently toward him."

When I reached the Heights, I explained that I had come to see everything carried on decently, and Joseph, who appeared in sufficient distress, expressed satisfaction at my presence. Mr. Heathcliff said he did not perceive that I was wanted, but I might stay and order the arrangements for the funeral, if I chose.

"Correctly," he remarked, "that fool's body should be buried at the cross-roads, without ceremony of any kind. I happened to leave him ten minutes, yesterday afternoon, and, in that interval, he fastened the two doors of the house against me, and he has spent the night in drinking himself to death deliberately! We broke in this morning, for we heard him snorting like a horse; and there he was, laid over the settle—flaying and scalping would not have wakened him. I sent for Kenneth, and he came; but not till the beast had changed into carrion—he was both dead, and cold, and stark; and so you'll allow, it was useless making more stir about him!"

The old servant confirmed this statement, but muttered, "Awd rather he'd goan hisseln fur t'doctor! Aw sud uh taen tent uh t'maister better nur him—un he warn't deead when aw left, nowt uh t'soart!"

I insisted on the funeral being respectable. Mr. Heathcliff said I might have my own way there, too; only, he desired me to remember, that the money for the whole affair came out of his pocket.

He maintained a hard, careless deportment, indicative of neither joy nor sorrow; if anything, it expressed flinty gratification at a piece of difficult work, successfully executed. I observed once, indeed, something like exultation in his aspect. It was just when the people were bearing the coffin from the house; he had the hypocrisy to represent a mourner; and previous to following with Hareton he lifted the unfortunate child upon the table, and muttered with peculiar gusto,

"Now, my bonny lad, you are *mine!* And we'll see if one tree won't grow as crooked as another, with the same wind to twist it!"

The unsuspecting thing was pleased at this speech; he played with Heathcliff's whiskers, and stroked his cheek, but I divined its meaning, and observed tartly,

"That boy must go back with me to Thrushcross Grange, sir. There is nothing in the world less yours than he is!"

"Does Linton say so?" he demanded.

"Of course—he has ordered me to take him," I replied.

"Well," said the scoundrel, "we'll not argue the subject now; but I have a fancy to try my hand at rearing a young one; so intimate to your master, that I must supply the place of this with my own, if he attempt to remove it; I don't engage to let Hareton go, undisputed; but I'll be pretty sure to make the other come! remember to tell him."

This hint was enough to bind our hands. I repeated its substance, on my return, and Edgar Linton, little interested at the commencement, spoke no more of interfering. I'm not aware that he could have done it to any purpose had he been ever so willing.

The guest was now the master of Wuthering Heights: he held firm possession, and proved to the attorney, who, in his turn, proved it to Mr. Linton, that Earnshaw had mortgaged every yard of land he owned for cash to supply his mania for gaming: and he, Heathcliff, was the mortgagee.

In that manner, Hareton, who should now be the first gentleman in the neighborhood, was reduced to a state of complete dependence on his father's inveterate enemy; and lives in his own house as a servant, deprived of the advantage of wages, and quite unable to right himself, because of his friendlessness, and his ignorance that he has been wronged.

. . . .

Chapter 18

The twelve years, continued Mrs. Dean, following that dismal period, were the happiest of my life: my greatest troubles, in their passage, rose from our little lady's trifling illnesses, which she had to experience in common with all children, rich and poor.

For the rest, after the first six months, she grew like a larch: and could walk and talk too, in her own way, before the heath blossomed a second time over Mrs. Linton's dust. She was the most winning thing that ever brought sunshine into a desolate house—a real beauty in face—with the Earnshaws' handsome dark eyes, but the Lintons' fair skin, and small features, and yellow curling hair. Her spirit was high, though not rough, and qualified by a heart sensitive and lively to excess in its affections. That capacity for intense attachments reminded me of her mother; still she did not resemble her; for she could be soft and mild as a dove, and she had a gentle voice, and pensive expression: her anger was never furious; her love never fierce; it was deep and tender.

However, it must be acknowledged, she had faults to foil her gifts. A propensity to be saucy was one; and a perverse will that indulged children invariably acquire, whether they be good tempered or cross. If a servant chanced to vex her, it was always, "I shall tell papa!" And if he reproved her, even by a look, you would have thought it a heart-breaking business; I don't believe he ever did speak a harsh word to her.

He took her education entirely on himself, and made it an amusement; fortunately, curiosity and a quick intellect urged her into an apt scholar; she learned rapidly and eagerly, and did honor to his teaching. Till she reached the age of thirteen, she had not once been beyond the range of the park by herself. Mr. Linton would take her with him, a mile or so outside, on rare occasions; but he trusted her to no one else. Gimmerton was an unsubstantial name in her ears; the chapel the only building she had approached or entered, except her own home; Wuthering Heights and Mr. Heathcliff did not exist for her; she was a perfect recluse, and, apparently, perfectly contented. Sometimes, indeed, while surveying the country from her nursery window, she would observe—

"Ellen, how long will it be before I can walk to the top of those hills? I wonder what lies on the other side—is it the sea?"

"No, Miss Cathy," I would answer, "it is hills again, just like these."

"And what are those golden rocks like, when you stand under them?" she once asked.

The abrupt descent of Penistone Crags particularly attracted her notice, especially when the setting sun shone on it, and the topmost heights; and the whole extent of landscape besides lay in shadow. I explained that they were bare masses of stone, with hardly enough earth in their clefts to nourish a stunted tree.

"And why are they bright so long after it is evening here?" she pursued.

"Because they are a great deal higher up than we are," replied I; "you could not climb them—they are too high and steep. In winter the frost is always there before it comes to us; and, deep into summer, I have found snow under that black hollow on the northeast side."

"Oh, you have been on them!" she cried, gleefully. "Then I can go, too, when I am a woman. Has papa been, Ellen?"

"Papa would tell you, miss," I answered, hastily, "that they are not worth the trouble of visiting. The moors, where you ramble with him, are much nicer; and Thrushcross park is the finest place in the world."

"But I know the park, and I don't know those," she murmured to herself. "And I should delight to look round me, from the brow of that tallest point. My little pony, Minny, shall take me some time."

One of the maids mentioning the fairy cave, quite turned her head with a desire to fulfill this project; she teased Mr. Linton about it, and he promised she should have the journey when she got older; but Miss Catherine measured her age by months, and—

"Now, am I old enough to go to Penistone Crags?" was the constant question in her mouth.

The road thither wound close by Wuthering Heights. Edgar had not the heart to pass it; so she received as constantly the answer—

"Not yet, love, not yet."

I said Mrs. Heathcliff lived about a dozen years after quitting her husband. Her family were of a delicate constitution; she and Edgar both lacked the ruddy health that you will generally meet in these parts. What her last illness was, I am not certain; I conjecture they died of the same thing, a kind of fever, slow at its commencement, but incurable, and rapidly consuming life toward the close.

She wrote to inform her brother of the probable conclusion of a four months' indisposition under which she had suffered; and entreated him to come to her, if possible, for she had much to settle, and she wished to bid him adieu, and deliver Linton safely into his hands. Her hope was, that Linton might be left with him, as he had been with her; his father, she would fain convince herself, had no desire to assume the burden of his maintenance or education.

My master hesitated not a moment in complying with her request; reluctant as he was to leave home at ordinary calls, he flew to answer this, commending Catherine to my peculiar vigilance in his absence, with reiterated orders that she must not wander out of the park, even under my escort; he did not calculate on her going unaccompanied.

He was away three weeks. The first day or two my charge sat in a corner of the library, too sad for either reading or playing; in that quiet state she caused me little trouble; but it was succeeded by an interval of impatient, fretful weariness: and, being too busy and too old then to run up and down amusing her, I hit on a method by which she might entertain herself.

I used to send her on her travels round the grounds—now on foot, and now on a pony; indulging her with a patient audience of all her real and imaginary adventures, when she returned.

The summer shone in full prime, and she took such a taste for this solitary rambling that she often contrived to remain out from breakfast till tea; and then the evenings were spent in recounting her fanciful tales. I did not fear her breaking bounds, because the gates were generally locked, and I thought she would scarcely venture forth alone, if they had stood wide open. Unluckily, my

confidence proved misplaced. Catherine came to me, one morning at eight o'clock, and said she was that day an Arabian merchant, going to cross the desert with his caravan; and I must give
her plenty of provisions for herself and beasts, a horse, and three
camels, personated by a large hound and a couple of pointers.

I got together a good store of dainties, and slung then in a basket
on one side of the saddle; and she sprang up as gay as a fairy,
sheltered by her wide-brimmed hat and gauze veil from the July
sun, and trotted off with a merry laugh, mocking my cautious
counsel to avoid galloping, and come back early. The naughty
thing never made her appearance at tea. One traveller, the hound,
being an old dog, and fond of its ease, returned; but neither Cathy,
nor the pony, nor the two pointers were visible in any direction;
and I dispatched emissaries down this path, and that path, and, at
last, went wandering in search of her myself.

There was a laborer working at a fence round a plantation, on
the borders of the grounds. I inquired of him if he had seen our
young lady?

"I saw her at morn," he replied, "she would have me to cut her a
hazel switch; and then she leaped her galloway over the hedge
yonder, where it is lowest, and galloped out of sight."

You may guess how I felt at hearing this news. It struck me
directly she must have started for Penistone Crags.

"What will become of her?" I ejaculated, pushing through a gap
which the man was repairing, and making straight to the high
road. I walked as if for a wager, mile after mile, till a turn brought
me in view of the Heights, but no Catherine could I detect, far or
near.

The Crags lie about a mile and a half beyond Mr. Heathcliff's
place, and that is four from the Grange, so I began to fear night
would fall ere I could reach them.

"And what if she should have slipped in clambering among
them," I reflected, "and been killed, or broken some of her
bones?"

My suspense was truly painful; and, at first, it gave me delightful relief to observe , in hurrying by the farm-house, Charlie,
the fiercest of the pointers, lying under a window, with swelled
head and bleeding ear. I opened the wicket, and ran to the door,
knocking vehemently for admittance. A woman whom I knew,
and who formerly lived at Gimmerton, answered—she had been
servant there since the death of Mr. Earnshaw.

"Ah," said she, "you are come a seeking your little mistress!
don't be frightened. She's here safe—but I'm glad it isn't the
master."

"He is not at home then, is he?" I panted, quite breathless with
quick walking and alarm.

"No, no," she replied, "both he and Joseph are off, and I think
they won't return this hour or more. Step in and rest you a bit."

I entered, and beheld my stray lamb, seated on the hearth,
rocking herself in a little chair that had been her mother's when a
child. Her hat was hung against the wall, and she seemed perfectly
at home, laughing and chattering, in the best spirits imaginable,

to Hareton, now a great, strong lad of eighteen, who stared at her with considerable curiosity and astonishment; comprehending precious little of the fluent succession of remarks and questions which her tongue never ceased pouring forth.

"Very well, Miss," I exclaimed, concealing my joy under an angry countenance. "This is your last ride till papa comes back. I'll not trust you over the threshold again, you naughty, naughty girl."

"Aha, Ellen!" she cried, gayly, jumping up and running to my side. "I shall have a pretty story to tell to-night—and so you've found me out. Have you ever been here in your life before?"

"Put that hat on, and home at once," said I. "I'm dreadfully grieved at you, Miss Cathy—you've done extremely wrong! It's no use pouting and crying; that won't repay the trouble I've had, scouring the country after you. To think how Mr. Linton charged me to keep you in, and you stealing off so; it shows you are a cunning little fox, and nobody will put faith in you any more."

"What have I done?" sobbed she, instantly checked. "Papa charged me nothing—he'll not scold me, Ellen—he's never cross, like you!"

"Come, come!" I repeated. "I'll tie the ribbon. Now let us have no petulance. Oh, for shame. You thirteen years old, and such a baby!"

This exclamation was caused by her pushing the hat from her head, and retreating to the chimney, out of my reach.

"Nay," said the servant, "don't be hard on the bonny lass, Mrs. Dean. We made her stop; she'd fain have ridden forward, afeard you should be uneasy. But Hareton offered to go with her, and I thought he should. It's a wild road over the hills."

Hareton, during the discussion, stood with his hands in his pockets, too awkward to speak, though he looked as if he did not relish my intrusion.

"How long am I to wait?" I continued, disregarding the woman's interference. "It will be dark in ten minutes. Where is the pony, Miss Cathy? And where is Phoenix? I shall leave you, unless you be quick—so please yourself."

"The pony is in the yard," she replied, "and Phoenix is shut in there. He's bitten, and so is Charlie. I was going to tell you all about it, but you are in a bad temper, and don't deserve to hear."

I picked up her hat, and approached to reinstate it; but perceiving that the people of the house took her part, she commenced capering round the room; and, on my giving chase, ran like a mouse, over and under and behind the furniture, rendering it ridiculous for me to pursue. Hareton and the woman laughed, and she joined them, and waxed more impertinent still, till I cried, in great irritation,

"Well, Miss Cathy, if you were aware whose house this is, you'd be glad enough to get out."

"It's *your* father's isn't it?" said she, turing to Hareton.

"Nay," he replied, looking down, and blushing bashfully.

He could not stand a steady gaze from her eyes, though they were just his own.

"Whose then—your master's?" she asked.

He colored deeper, with a different feeling, muttered an oath, and turned away.

"Who is his master?" continued the tiresome girl, appealing to me. "He talked about 'our house,' and 'our folk'—I thought he had been the owner's son. And he never said Miss; he should have done, shouldn't he, if he's a servant?"

Hareton grew black as a thunder-cloud, at this childish speech. I silently shook my questioner, and at last succeeded in equipping her for departure.

"Now get my horse," she said, addressing her unknown kinsman as she would one of the stable-boys at the Grange. "And you may come with me. I want to see where the goblin hunter rises in the marsh, and to hear about the *fairishes*, as you call them—but make haste! What's the matter? Get my horse, I say."

"I'll see thee damned, before I be *thy* servant!" growled the lad.

"You'll see me *what*?" asked Catherine in surprise.

"Damned, thou saucy witch!" he replied.

"There, Miss Cathy! you see you have got into pretty company," I interposed. "Nice words to be used to a young lady! Pray don't begin to dispute with him. Come, let us seek for Minny ourselves, and be gone."

"But, Ellen," cried she, staring, fixed in astonishment. "How dare he speak so to me? Mustn't he be made to do as I ask him? You wicked creature, I shall tell papa what you said, Now then!"

Hareton did not appear to feel this threat; so the tears sprung into her eyes with indignation. "You bring the pony," she exclaimed, turning to the woman, "and let my dog free this moment!"

"Softly, Miss," answered the addressed. "You'll lose nothing by being civil. Though Mr. Hareton, there, be not the master's son, he's your cousin; and I was never hired to serve you."

"*He* my cousin!" cried Cathy, with a scornful laugh.

"Yes, indeed," responded her reprover.

"Oh, Ellen! don't let them say much things," she pursued in great trouble. "Papa is gone to fetch my cousin from London—my cousin is a gentleman's son. That my—" she stopped and wept outright, upset at the bare notion of relationship with such a clown.

"Hush, hush!" I whispered, "people can have many cousins, and of all sorts, Miss Cathy, without being any the worse for it; only they needn't keep their company, if they be disagreeable and bad."

"He's not, he's not my cousin, Ellen!" she went on, gathering fresh grief from reflection, and flinging herself into my arms for refuge from the idea. I was much vexed at her and the servant for their mutual revelations; having no doubt of Linton's approaching arrival, communicated by the former, being reported to Mr. Heathcliff; and feeling that Catherine's first thought on her father's return, would be to seek an explanation of the latter's assertion concerning her rude-bred kindred.

Hareton, recovering from his disgust at being taken for a servant, seemed moved by her distress; and, having fetched the pony round to the door, he took, to propitiate her, a fine crooked-legged terrier whelp from the kennel; and, putting it into her hand, bid her wisht, for he meant naught. Pausing in her lamentations, she surveyed him with a glance of awe and horror, then burst forth anew.

I could scarcely refrain from smiling at this antipathy to the poor fellow, who was a well made, athletic youth, good-looking in features, and stout and healthy, but attired in garments befitting his daily occupations of working on a farm, and lounging among the moors after rabbits and game. Still, I thought I could detect in his physiognomy a mind owning better qualities than his father ever possessed. Good things lost amid a wilderness of weeds, to be sure, whose rankness far overtopped their neglected growth; yet, notwithstanding, evidence of a wealthy soil that might yield luxuriant crops, under other and favorable circumstances. Mr. Heathcliff, I believe, had not treated him physically ill, thanks to his fearless nature which offered no temptation to that course of oppression; it had none of the timid susceptibility that would have given zest to ill- treatment in Heathcliff's judgment. He appeared to have bent his malevolence on making him a brute; he was never taught to read or write; never rebuked for any bad habit which did not annoy his keeper; never led a single step toward virtue, or guarded by a single precept against vice. And from what I heard, Joseph contributed much to his deterioration by a narrow-minded partiality, which prompted him to flatter and pet him as a boy, because he was the head of the old family. And as he had been in the habit of accusing Catherine Earnshaw and Heathcliff, when children, of putting the master past his patience, and compelling him to seek solace in drink, by what he termed, their "offalld ways," so at present, he laid the whole burden of Hareton's faults on the shoulders of the usurper of his property.

If the lad swore, he wouldn't correct him, nor however culpably he behaved. It gave Joseph satisfaction, apparently, to watch him go the worst lengths. He allowed that he was ruined, that his soul was abandoned to perdition; but then he reflected that Heathcliff must answer for it. Hareton's blood would be required at his hands; and there lay immense consolation in that thought. Joseph had instilled into him a pride of name, and of his lineage; he would, had he dared, have fostered hate between him and the present owner of the Heights, but his dread of that owner amounted to superstition: and he confined his feelings, regarding him to muttered inuendoes and private comminations.

I don't pretend to be intimately acquainted with the mode of living customary in those days at Wuthering Heights. I only speak from hearsay; for I saw little, The villagers affirmed Mr. Heathcliff was *near*, and a cruel, hard landlord to his tenants; but the house inside had regained its ancient aspect of comfort under female management; and the scenes of riot common in Hindley's time, were not now enacted within its walls. The master was too gloomy to seek companionship with any people, good or bad; and he is yet.

This, however, is not making progress with my story.—Miss Cathy rejected the peace-offering of the terrier, and demanded her own dogs, Charlie and Phœnix. They came, limping and hanging their heads; and we set out for home, sadly out of sorts, every one of us.

I could not wring from my little lady how she had spent the day; except that, as I supposed, the goal of her pilgrimage was Penistone Crags; and she arrived without adventure to the gate of the farmhouse, when Hareton happened to issue forth, attended by some canine followers who attacked her train. They had a smart battle before their owners could separate them; that formed an introducton. Catherine told Hareton who she was, and where she was going; and asked him to show her the way; finally beguiling him to accompany her.

He opened the mysteries of the fairy cave, and twenty other queer places; but being in disgrace, I was not favored with a description of the interesting objects she saw. I could gather, however, that her guide had been a favorite, till she hurt his feelngs by addressing him as a servant, and Heathcliff's housekeeper hurt hers, by calling him her cousin. Then the language he had held to her rankled in her heart; she who was always "love," and "darling," and "queen," and "angel," with everybody at the Grange, to be insulted so shockingly by a stranger! She did not comprehend it, and hard work I had to obtain a promise that she would not lay the grievance before her father.

I explained how he objected to the whole household at the Heights, and how sorry he would be to find she had been there; but I insisted most on the fact, that if she revealed my negligence of his orders, he would, perhaps, be so angry that I should have to leave; and Cathy couldn't bear that prospect; she pledged her word, and kept it, for my sake. After all, she was a sweet little girl.

. . . .

Chapter 19

A letter edged with black announced the day of my Master's return. Isabella was dead; and he wrote to bid me get mourning for his daughter, and arrange a room, and other accommodations, for his youthful nephew. Catherine ran wild with joy at the idea of welcoming her father back; and indulged most sanguine anticipations of the innumerable excellencies of her "real" cousin.

The evening of their expected arrival came. Since early morning she had been busy, ordering her own small affairs; and now, attired in her new black frock—poor thing! her aunt's death impressed her with no definite sorrow—she obliged me, by constant worrying, to walk with her down through the grounds to meet them.

"Linton is just six months younger than I am," she chattered, as we strolled leisurely over the swells and hollows of mossy turf, under shadow of the trees. "How delightful it will be to have him for a playfellow! Aunt Isabella sent papa a beautiful lock of his hair; it was lighter than mine—more flaxen, and quite as fine. I have it carefully preserved in a little glass box; and I've often thought what pleasure it would be to see its owner. Oh! I am happy—and papa, dear, dear papa! come Ellen, let us run! come run!"

She ran, and returned and ran again many times, before my sober footsteps reached the gate, and then she seated herself on the grassy bank beside the path, and tried to wait patiently; but that was impossible; she couldn't be still a minute.

"How long they are!" she exclaimed. "Ah, I see some dust on the road—they are coming! No! When will they be here? May we not go a little way—half a mile, Ellen, only just half a mile? Do say yes—to that clump of birches at the turn!"

I refused staunchly: and, at length, her suspense was ended; the travelling carriage rolled in sight. Miss Cathy shrieked, and stretched out her arms, as soon as she caught her father's face looking from the window. He descended, nearly as eager as herself; and a considerable interval elapsed, ere they had a thought to spare for any but themselves.

While they exchanged caresses, I took a peep in to see after Linton. He was asleep in a corner, wrapped in a warm, fur lined cloak, as if it had been winter. A pale, delicate, effeminate boy, who might have been taken for my master's younger brother, so strong was the resemblance; but there was a sickly peevishness in his aspect, that Edgar Linton never had.

The latter saw me looking; and having shaken hands, advised me to close the door and leave him undisturbed; for the journey had fatigued him. Cathy would fain have taken one glance; but her father told her to come on, and they walked together up the park, while I hastened before to prepare the servants.

"Now, darling," said Mr. Linton, addressing his daughter, as they halted at the bottom of the front steps. "Your cousin is not so strong, or so merry as you are, and he has lost his mother, remember, a very short time since; therefore, don't expect him to play; and run about with you directly. And don't harass him much by talking—let him be quiet this evening, at least, will you?"

"Yes, yes, papa," answered Catherine; "but I do want to see him; and he hasn't once looked out."

The carriage stopped; and the sleeper, being roused, was lifted to the ground by his uncle.

"This is your cousin Cathy, Linton," he said, putting their little hands together. "She's fond of you already; and mind you don't grieve her by crying to-night. Try to be cheerful now; the travelling is at an end, and you have nothing to do but rest and amuse yourself as you please."

"Let me go to bed then," answered the boy, shrinking from Catherine's salute; and he put his fingers to his eyes to remove incipient tears.

"Come, come, there's a good child," I whispered, leading him in. "You'll make her weep too—see how sorry she is for you!"

I do not know whether it were sorrow for him, but his cousin put on as sad a countenance as himself, and returned to her father. All three entered, and mounted to the library, where tea was laid ready. I proceeded to remove Linton's cap and mantle, and placed him on a chair by the table; but he was no sooner seated than he began to cry afresh. My master inquired what was the matter.

"I can't sit on a chair," sobbed the boy.

"Go to the sofa then; and Ellen shall bring you some tea," answered his uncle, patiently.

He had been greatly tried during the journey, I felt convinced, by his fretful, ailing charge.

Linton slowly trailed himself off, and lay down. Cathy carried a footstool and her cup to his side. At first he sat silent; but that could not last; she had resolved to make a pet of her little cousin, as she would have him to be; and she commenced stroking his curls, and kissing his cheek, and offering him tea in her saucer, like a baby. This pleased him, for he was not much better; he dried his eyes, and lightened into a faint smile.

"Oh, he'll do very well," said the master to me, after watching them a minute. "Very well, if we can keep him, Ellen. The company of a child of his own age will instill new spirit into him soon; and by wishing for strength he'll gain it."

Aye, if we can keep him! I mused to myself; and sore misgivings came over me that there was slight hope of that. And then, I thought, how will that weakling ever live at Wuthering Heights, between his father and Hareton? what playmates and instructors they'll be.

Our doubts were presently decided; even earlier than I expected. I had just taken the children up-stairs, after tea was finished; and seen Linton asleep—he would not suffer me to leave him, till that was the case. I had come down, and was standing by the table in the hall, lighting a bedroom candle for Mr. Edgar, when a maid stepped out of the kitchen, and informed me that Mr. Heathcliff's servant, Joseph, was at the door, and wished to speak with the master.

"I shall ask him what he wants first," I said, in considerable trepidation. "A very unlikely hour to be troubling people, and the instant they have returned from a long journey. I don't think the master can see him."

Joseph had advanced through the kitchen, as I uttered these words, and now presented himself in the hall. He was donned in his Sunday garments, with his most sanctimonious and sourest face; and holding his hat in one hand, and his stick in the other, he proceeded to clean his shoes on the mat.

"Good evening, Joseph," I said, coldly. "What business brings you here to-night?"

"It's Maister Linton aw mun spake tull," he answered waving me disdainfully aside.

"Mr. Linton is going to bed; unless you have something particular to say, I'm sure he won't hear it now," I continued. "You had better sit down there and entrust your message to me."

"Which is his rahm?" pursued the fellow, surveying the range of closed doors.

I perceived he was bent on refusing my mediation; so, very reluctantly, I went up to the library, and announced the unseasonable visitor; advising that he should be dismissed till next day. Mr. Linton had no time to empower me to do so, for he mounted close at my heels, and pushing into the apartment, planted himself at the far side of the table, with his two fists clapped on the head of his stick, and began, in an elevated tone, as if he anticipated opposition,

"Heathcliff has sent me for his lad, un aw mun'n't goa back 'baht him."

Edgar Linton was silent a minute; an expression of exceeding sorrow overcast his features; he would have pitied the child on his own account; but, recalling Isabella's hopes and fears and anxious wishes for her son, and her commendations of him to his care, he grieved bitterly at the prospect of yielding him up, and searched in his heart how it might be avoided. No plan offered itself; the very exhibition of any desire to keep him would have rendered the claimant more peremptory; there was nothing left but to resign him. However, he was not going to rouse him from his sleep.

"Tell Mr. Heathcliff," he answered, calmly, "that his son shall come to Wuthering Heights to-morrow. He is in bed, and too tired to go the distance now. You may also tell him that the mother of Linton desired him to remain under my guardianship; and, at present, his health is very precarious."

"Noa!" said Joseph, giving a thud with his prop on the floor, and assuming an authoritative air. "Noa! that manes nowt—Heathcliff maks noa 'cahnt uh t' mother, nur yah norther—bud he'll hev his lad; und aw mun tak him—soa nah yah knaw!"

"You shall not to-night!" answered Linton, decisively. "Walk down stairs at once, and repeat to your master what I have said. Ellen, show him down. Go—"

And, aiding the indignant elder with a lift by the arm, he rid the room of him and closed the door.

"Varrah weel!" shouted Joseph, as he slowly drew off "Tuh morn, he's come hisseln, un' thrust *him* aht, if yah darr!"

. . . .

Chapter 20

To obviate the danger of this threat being fulfilled, Mr. Linton commissioned me to take the boy home early, on Catherine's pony, and, said he—

"As we shall have no influence over his destiny, good or bad, you must say nothing of where he is gone to my daughter; she can not associate with him hereafter; and it is better for her to remain in ignorance of his proximity, lest she should be restless, and anxious to visit the Heights—merely tell her, his father sent for him suddenly, and he has been obliged to leave us."

Linton was very reluctant to be roused from his bed at five o'clock, and astonished to be informed that he must prepare for further travelling: but I softened off the matter by stating that he was going to spend some time with his father, Mr. Heathcliff, who wished to see him so much, he did not like to defer the pleasure till he should recover from his late journey.

"My father?" he cried, in strange perplexity. "Mamma never told me I had a father. Where does he live? I'd rather stay with uncle."

"He lives a little distance from the Grange," I replied, "just beyond those hills—not so far but you may walk over here, when you get hearty. And you should be glad to go home and to see him. You must try to love him, as you did your mother, and then he will love you."

"But why have I not heard of him before?" asked Linton; "why didn't mamma and he live together as other people do?"

"He had business to keep him in the north," I answered; "and you mother's health required her to reside in the south."

"And why didn't mamma speak to me about him?" persevered the child. "She often talked of uncle, and I learned to love him long ago. How am I to love papa? I don't know him."

"Oh, all children love their parents," I said. "Your mother, perhaps, thought you would want to be with him, if she mentioned him often to you. Let us make haste. An early ride on such a beautiful morning is much preferable to an hour's more sleep."

"Is *she* to go with us?" he demanded. "The little girl I saw yesterday?"

"Not now," replied I.

"Is uncle?" he continued.

"No, I shall be your companion there," I said. Linton sank back on his pillow, and fell into a brown study.

"I won't go without uncle;" he cried at length: "I can't tell where you mean to take me."

I attempted to persuade him of the naughtiness of showing reluctance to meet his father: still he obstinately resisted any progress toward dressing; and I had to call for my master's assistance in coaxing him out of bed. The poor thing was finally got off with several delusive assurances that his absence should be short; that Mr. Edgar and Cathy would visit him; and other promises, equally ill-founded, which I invented and reiterated, at intervals, throughout the way.

The pure heather-scented air, the bright sunshine, and the gentle canter of Minny, relieved his despondency after a while. He began to put questions concerning his new home, and its inhabitants, with greater interest and liveliness.

"Is Wuthering Heights as pleasant a place as Thrushcross Grange?" he inquired, turning to take a last glance into the valley, whence a light mist mounted, and formed fleecy clouds, on the skirts of the blue.

"It is not so buried in trees," I replied, "and it is not quite so large, but you can see the country beautifully, all round; and the air is healthier for you—fresher and dryer. You will, perhaps, think the building old and dark, at first—though it is a respectable house, the next best in the neighborhood. And you will have such nice rambles on the moors! Hareton Earnshaw—that is Miss Cathy's other cousin, and so yours in a manner—will show you all the sweetest spots; and you can bring a book in fine weather, and make a green hollow your study; and, now and then, your uncle may join you in a walk; he does frequently walk out on the hills."

"And what is my father like?" he asked. "Is he as young and handsome as uncle?"

"He's as young" said I, "but he has black hair and eyes, and looks sterner; and he is taller and bigger altogether. He'll not seem to you so gentle and kind at first, perhaps, because it is not his way; still, mind you be frank and cordial with him, and, naturally, he'll be fonder of you than any uncle, for you are his own."

"Black hair and eyes!" mused Linton. "I can't fancy him. Then I am not like him, am I?"

"Not much," I answered. "Not a morsel," I thought; surveying with regret the white complexion and slim frame of my companion, and his large languid eyes—his mother's eyes, save that, unless a morbid touchiness kindled them a moment, they had not a vestige of her sparkling spirit.

"How strange that he should never come to see mamma and me," he murmured. "Has he ever seen me? If he have, I must have been a baby—I remember not a single thing about him!"

"Why, Master Linton," said I, "three hundred miles is a great distance; and ten years seem very different in length to a grown up person, compared with what they do to you. It is probable Mr. Heathcliff proposed going, from summer to summer, but never found a convenient opportunity; and now it is too late. Don't trouble him with questions on the subject; it will disturb him for no good."

The boy was fully occupied with his own cogitations for the remainder of the ride, till we halted before the farmhouse garden gate. I watched to catch his impressions in his countenance. He surveyed the carved front, and low-browed lattices, the straggling gooseberry bushes, and crooked firs, with solemn intentness, and then shook his head; his private feelings entirely disapproved of the exterior of his new abode; but he had sense to postpone complaining—there might be compensation within.

Before he dismounted, I went and opened the door. It was half-past six; the family had just finished breakfast; the servant was clearing and wiping down the table; Joseph stood by his master's chair telling some tale concerning a lame horse; and Hareton was preparing for the hay-field.

"Hallo, Nelly!" cried Mr. Heathcliff, when he saw me. "I feared I should have to come down and fetch my property myself. You've brought it, have you? Let us see what we can make of it."

He got up and strode to the door: Hareton and Joseph followed in gaping curiosity. Poor Linton ran a frightened eye over the face of the three.

"Sure-ly," said Joseph, after a grave inspection, "he's swopped wi' ye, maister, an' yon's his lass!"

Heathcliff having stared his son into an ague of confusion, uttered a scornful laugh.

"God! what a beauty! what a lovely, charming thing!" he exclaimed. "Haven't they reared it on snails and sour milk, Nelly? Oh, damn my soul! but that's worse than I expected—and the devil knows I was not sanguine!"

I bid the trembling and bewildered child get down and enter. He did not thoroughly comprehend the meaning of his father's speech, or whether it were intended for him: indeed, he was not yet certain that the grim, sneering stranger was his father; but he clung to me with growing trepidation; and on Mr. Heathcliff's taking a seat, and bidding him "come hither," he hid his face on my shoulder, and wept.

"Tut, tut!" said Heathcliff, stretching out a hand and dragging him roughly between his knees, and then holding up his head by the chin. "None of that nonsense! we're not going to hurt thee, *Linton*—isn't that thy name? Thou art thy mother's child, entirely! Where is *my* share in thee, puling chicken?"

He took off the boy's cap and brushed back his thick flaxen curls, felt his slender arms, and his small fingers; during which examination, Linton ceased crying, and lifted his great blue eyes to inspect the inspector.

"Do you know me?" asked Heathcliff, having satisfied himself that the limbs were equally frail and feeble.

"No!" said Linton, with a gaze of vacant fear.

"You've heard of me, I dare say?"

"No," he replied again.

"No? What a shame of your mother, never to waken your filial regard for me! You are my son, then, I'll tell you; and your mother was a wicked slut to leave you in ignorance of the sort of father you possessed. Now, don't wince and color up! though it *is* something to see you have not white blood. Be a good lad; and I'll do for you. Nelly, if you be tired you may sit down, if not, get home again. I guess you'll report what you hear and see, to the cipher at the Grange; and this thing won't be settled while you linger about it."

"Well," replied I, "I hope you'll be kind to the boy, Mr. Heathcliff, or you'll not keep him long, and he's all you have akin in the wide world that you will ever know—remember."

"I'll be *very* kind to him; you needn't fear!" he said, laughing. "Only nobody else must be kind to him. I'm jealous of monopolizing his affection. And, to begin my kindness, Joseph, bring the lad some breakfast. Hareton, you infernal calf, begone to your work. Yes, Nell," he added when they were departed, "my son is prospective owner of your place, and I should not wish him to die till I was certain of being his successor. Besides, he's *mine*, and I want the triumph of seeing *my* descendant fairly lord of their estates—my child hiring their children to till their fathers' lands for wages. That is the sole consideration which can make me endure the whelp—I despise him for himself, and hate him for the memories he revives! But that consideration is sufficient; he's as safe with me, and shall be tended as carefully as your master tends

his own. I have a room up-stairs, furnished for him in handsome
style; I've engaged a tutor, also, to come three times a week from
twenty miles distance, to teach him what he pleases to learn. I've
ordered Hareton to obey him; and, in fact, I've arranged every
thing with a view to preserve the superior and the gentleman in
him above his associates. I do regret, however, that he so little
deserves the trouble. If I wished any blessing in the world, it was
to find him a worthy object of pride, and I'm bitterly disappointed with the whey-faced whining wretch!"

While he was speaking, Joseph returned, bearing a basin of
milk-porridge, and placed it before Linton. He stirred round the
homely mess with a look of aversion, and affirmed he could not
eat it. I saw the old man-servant shared largely in his master's
scorn of the child, though he was compelled to retain the sentiment in his heart, because Heathcliff plainly meant his underlings
to hold him in honor.

"Cannut ate it?" repeated he, peering in Linton's face, and
subduing his voice to a whisper, for fear of being overheard. "But
Master Hareton nivir ate nowt else when he wer a little un; und
what wer gooid enough fur him's gooid enough fur yah, aw's
rayther think!"

"I *shan't* eat it!" answered Linton, snappishly. "Take it away."

Joseph snatched up the food indignantly, and brought it to us.

"Is there owt ails th'victuals?" he asked, thrusting the tray under Heathcliff's nose.

"What should ail them?" he said.

"Wah!" answered Joseph, "you dainty chap says he cannut ate
'em. Bud aw guess it's raight. His mother wer just soa—we wer
a'most too mucky tuh sow th' corn fur makking her breead."

"Don't mention his mother to me," said the master angrily.
"Get him something that he can eat, that's all. What is his usual
food, Nelly?"

I suggested boiling milk or tea, and the housekeeper received
instructions to prepare some.

"Come," I reflected, "his father's selfishness may contribute to
his comfort. He perceives his delicate constitution, and the necessity of treating him tolerably. I'll console Mr. Edgar by acquainting him with the turn Heathcliff's humor has taken."

Having no excuse for lingering longer, I slipped out, while Linton was engaged in timidly rebuffing the advances of a friendly
sheep-dog. But he was too much on the alert to be cheated: as I
closed the door I heard a cry, and a frantic repetition of the
words—

"Don't leave me! I'll not stay here! I'll not stay here!"

Then the latch was raised and fell—they did not suffer him to
come forth. I mounted Minny, and urged her to a trot, and so my
brief guardianship ended.

. . . .

Chapter 21

We had sad work with little Cathy that day: she rose in high glee, eager to join her cousin; and such passionate tears and lamentations followed the news of his departure, that Edgar himself was obliged to soothe her by affirming he should come back soon; he added, however, "if I can get him," and there were no hopes of that. This promise poorly pacified her; but time was more potent; and though still at intervals she inquired of her father when Linton would return, before she did see him again his features had waxed so dim in her memory that she did not recognize him.

When I chanced to encounter the housekeeper of Wuthering Heights, in paying business visits to Gimmerton, I used to ask how the young master got on; for he lived almost as secluded as Catherine herself, and was never to be seen. I could gather from her that he continued in weak health, and was a tiresome inmate. She said Mr. Heathcliff seemed to dislike him ever longer and worse, though he took some trouble to conceal it. He had an antipathy to the sound of his voice, and could not do at all with his sitting in the same room with him many minutes together. There seldom passed much talk between them; Linton learned his lessons, and spent his evenings in a small apartment they called the parlor; or else lay in bed all day; for he was constantly getting coughs, and colds, and aches, and pains of some sort.

"And I never knew such a faint-hearted creature," added the woman; "nor one so careful of hisseln. He *will* go on, if I leave the window open a bit late in the evening. Oh! it's killing, a breath of night air! And he must have a fire in the middle of summer; and Joseph's 'bacca pipe is poison; and he must always have sweets and dainties, and always milk, milk for ever—heeding naught how the rest of us are pinched in winter—and there he'll sit, wrapped in his furred cloak, in his chair by the fire, and some toast and water, or other slop, on the hob to sip at; and if Hareton, for pity, comes to amuse him—Hareton is not bad-natured, though he's rough—they're sure to part, one swearing, and the other crying. I believe the master would relish Earnshaw's thrashing him to a mummy, if he were not his son: and, I'm certain, he would be fit to turn him out of doors, if he knew half the nursing he gives hisseln. But then, he won't go into danger of temptation; he never enters the parlor, and should Linton show those ways in the house where he is, he sends him up stairs directly."

I divined, from this account, that utter lack of sympathy had rendered young Heathcliff selfish and disagreeable, if he were not so originally; and my interest in him, consequently, decayed; though still I was moved with a sense of grief at his lot, and a wish that he had been left with us.

Mr. Edgar encouraged me to gain information; he thought a great deal about him, I fancy, and would have run some risk to see him; and he told me once to ask the housekeeper whether he ever came into the village? She said he had only been twice, on horseback, accompanying his father: and both times he pretended to be quite knocked up for three or four days afterward. The housekeeper left, if I recollect rightly, two years after he came; and another, whom I did not know, was her successor: she lives there still.

Time wore on at the Grange in its former pleasant way, till Miss Cathy reached sixteen. On the anniversary of her birth we never manifested any signs of rejoicing, because it was also the anniversary of my late mistress's death. Her father invariably spent that day alone in the library; and walked, at dusk, as far as Gimmerton kirkyard, where he would frequently prolong his stay beyond midnight. Therefore Catherine was thrown on her own resources for amusement.

This twentieth of March was a beautiful spring day, and when her father had retired, my young lady came down, dressed for going out, and said she had asked to have a ramble on the edge of the moors with me; and Mr. Linton had given her leave, if we went only a short distance, and were back within the hour.

"So make haste, Ellen!" she cried. "I know where I wish to go; where a colony of moor game are settled; I want to see whether they have a made their nests yet."

"That must be a good distance up," I answered; "they don't breed on the edge of the moor."

"No, it's not," she said. "I've gone very near with papa."

I put on my bonnet, and sallied out; thinking nothing more of the matter. She bounded before me, and returned to my side, and was off again like a young greyhound; and, at first, I found plenty of entertainment in listening to the larks singing far and near; and enjoying the sweet, warm sunshine; and watching her, my pet and my delight, with her golden ringlets flying loose behind, and her bright cheek, as soft and pure in its bloom as a wild rose, and her eyes radiant with cloudless pleasure. She was a happy creature, and an angel, in those days. It's a pity she could not be content.

"Well, said I, "where are your moor game, Miss Cathy? We should be at them—the Grange park-fence is a great way off now."

"Oh, a little further—only a little further, Ellen," was her answer, continually. "Climb to that hillock, pass that bank, and by the time you reach the other side, I shall have raised the birds."

But there were so many hillocks and banks to climb and pass, that, at length, I began to be weary, and told her we must halt, and retrace our steps. I shouted to her, as she had outstripped me a long way; she either did not hear, or did not regard, for she still sprang on, and I was compelled to follow. Finally, she dived into a hollow; and before I came in sight of her again, she was two miles nearer Wuthering Heights than her own home; and I beheld a couple of persons arrest her, one of whom I felt convinced was Mr. Heathcliff himself.

Cathy had been caught in the fact of plundering, or, at least, hunting out the nests of the grouse. The Heights were Heathcliff's land, and he was reproving the poacher.

"I've neither taken any nor found any," she said, as I toiled to them, expanding her hands in corroboration of the statement. "I didn't mean to take them; but papa told me there were quantities up here, and I wished to see the eggs."

Heathcliff glanced at me with an ill-meaning smile, expressing his acquaintance with the party, and, consequently, his malevolence toward it, and demanded who "papa" was?

"Mr. Linton of Thrushcross Grange," she replied. "I thought you did not know me, or you wouldn't have spoken in that way."

"You suppose papa is highly esteemed and respected then?" he said, sarcastically.

"And what are you?" inquired Catherine, gazing curiously on the speaker. "That man I've seen before. Is he your son?"

She pointed to Hareton, the other individual; who had gained nothing but increased bulk and strength by the addition of two years to his age: he seemed as awkward and rough as ever.

"Miss Cathy," I interrupted, "it will be three hours instead of one, that we are out, presently. We really must go back."

"No, that man is not my son," answered Heathcliff, pushing me aside. "But I have one, and you have seen him before too; and, though your nurse is in a hurry, I think both you and she would be the better for a little rest. Will you just turn this nab of heath, and walk into my house? You'll get home earlier for the ease; and you shall receive a kind welcome."

I whispered to Catherine that she mustn't, on any account, accede to the proposal; it was entirely out of the question.

"Why?" she asked aloud. "I'm tired of running, and the ground is dewy—I can't sit here. Let us go, Ellen! Besides, he says I have seen his son. He's mistaken, I think; but I guess where he lives—at the farmhouse I visited in coming from Penistone Crags. Don't you?"

"I do. Come, Nelly, hold you tongue—it will be a treat for her to look in on us. Hareton, get forward with the lass. You shall walk with me, Nelly."

"No, she's not going to any such place," I cried, struggling to release my arm which he had seized; but she was almost at the door-stones already, scampering round the brow at full speed. Her appointed companion did not pretend to escort her; he shyed off by the roadside, and vanished.

"Mr. Heathcliff, it's very wrong," I continued, "you know you mean no good; and there she'll see Linton, and all will be told as soon as ever we return, and I shall have the blame."

"I want her to see Linton," he answered: "he's looking better these few days; it's not often he's fit to be seen. And we'll soon persuade her to keep the visit secret—where is the harm of it?"

"The harm of it is, that her father would hate me, if he found I suffered her to enter your house; and I am convinced you have a bad design in encouraging her to do so," I replied.

"My design is as honest as possible. I'll inform you of its whole scope," he said. "That the two cousins may fall in love and get married. I'm acting generously to your master; his young chit has no expectations; and should she second my wishes, she'll be provided for at once as joint successor with Linton."

"If Linton died," I answered, "and his life is quite uncertain, Catherine would be the heir."

"No she would not," he said; "there is no clause in the will to secure it so; his property would go to me; but, to prevent disputes, I desire their union, and am resolved to bring it about."

"And I'm resolved she shall never approach your house with me again," I returned, as we reached the gate, where Miss Cathy waited our coming,

Heathcliff bid me be quiet; and, preceding us up the path, hastened to open the door. My young lady gave him several looks, as if she could not exactly make up her mind what to think of him; but now he smiled when he met her eye, and softened his voice in addressing her, and I was foolish enough to imagine the memory of her mother might disarm him from desiring her injury.

Linton stood on the hearth. He had been out walking in the fields, for his cap was on, and he was calling to Joseph to bring him dry shoes. He had grown tall of his age, still wanting some months of sixteen. His features were pretty yet, and his eye and complexion brighter than I remembered them, though with merely temporary lustre borrowed from the salubrious air and genial sun.

"Now, who is that?" asked Mr. Heathcliff, turning to Cathy. "Can you tell?"

"Your son?" she said, having doubtfully surveyed first one and then the other.

"Yes, yes," answered he; "but is this the only time you have beheld him? Think! Ah! you have a short memory. Linton don't you recall your cousin, that you used to tease us so with wishing to see?"

"What, Linton!" cried Cathy, kindling into joyful surprise at the name. "Is that little Linton? He's taller than I am! Are you Linton?"

The youth stepped forward and acknowledged himself: she kissed him fervently, and they gazed with wonder at the change time had wrought in the appearance of each.

Catherine had reached her full height; her figure was both plump and slender, elastic as steel, and her whole aspect sparkling with health and spirits. Linton's looks and movements were very languid, and his form extremely slight; but there was a grace in his manner that mitigated these defects, and rendered him not unpleasing.

After exchanging numerous marks of fondness with him, his cousin went to Mr. Heathcliff, who lingered by the door, dividing his attention between the objects inside, and those that lay without, pretending, that is, to observe the latter, and really noting the former alone.

"And you are my uncle, then!" she cried, reaching up to salute him. "I thought I liked you, though you were cross at first. Why don't you visit at the Grange with Linton? To live all these years such close neighbors, and never see us, is odd; what have you done so for?"

"I visited it once or twice too often before you were born," he answered. "There—damn it! If you have any kisses to spare, give them to Linton—they are thrown away on me."

"Naughty Ellen!" exclaimed Catherine, flying to attack me next with her lavish caresses. "Wicked Ellen! to try to hinder me from entering. But I'll take this walk every morning in future—may I, uncle—and sometimes bring papa? Won't you be glad to see us?"

"Of course!" replied the uncle, with a hardly suppressed grimace, resulting from his deep aversion to both the proposed visitors. "But stay," he continued, turning toward the young lady. "Now I think of it, I'd better tell you. Mr. Linton has a prejudice against me; we quarreled at one time of our lives with unchristian ferocity; and, if you mention coming here to him, he'll put a veto on your visits altogether. Therefore, you must not mention it, unless you be careless of seeing your cousin hereafter—you may come, if you will, but you must not mention it."

"Why did you quarrel?" asked Catherine, considerably crestfallen.

"He thought me too poor to wed his sister," answered Heathcliff, "and was grieved that I got her—his pride was hurt, and he'll never forgive it."

"That's wrong!" said the young lady: "sometime I'll tell him so; but Linton and I have no share in your quarrel. I'll not come here, then, he shall come to the Grange."

"It will be too far for me," murmured her cousin, "to walk four miles would kill me. No, come here, Miss Catherine, now and then, not every morning, but once or twice a week."

The father launched toward his son a glance of bitter contempt.

"I am afraid, Nelly, I shall lose my labor," he muttered to me. "Miss Catherine, as the ninny calls her, will discover his value, and send him to the devil. Now, if it had been Hareton—do you know that, twenty times a day, I covet Hareton, with all his degradation? I'd have loved the lad had he been some one else. But I think he's safe from *her* love. I'll pit him against that paltry creature, unless it bestir itself briskly. We calculate it will scarcely last till it is eighteen. Oh, confound the vapid thing. He's absorbed in drying his feet, and never looks at her—Linton!"

"Yes, father," answered the boy.

"Have you nothing to show your cousin, anywhere about; not even a rabbit, or a weasel's nest? Take her into the garden, before you change your shoes; and into the stable to see your horse."

"Wouldn't you rather sit here?" asked Linton, addressing Cathy in a tone which expressed reluctance to move again.

"I don't know," she replied, casting a longing look to the door, and evidently eager to be active.

He kept his seat, and shrank closer to the fire. Heathcliff rose, and went into the kitchen, and from thence to the yard, calling out for Hareton. Hareton responded, and presently the two reentered. The young man had been washing himself, as was visible by the glow on his cheeks, and his wetted hair.

"Oh, I'll ask *you*, uncle;" cried Miss Cathy, recollecting the housekeeper's assertion. "That's not my cousin, is he?"

"Yes," he replied, "your mother's nephew. Don't you like him?"

Catherine looked queer.

"Is he not a handsome lad?" he continued.

The uncivil little thing stood on tiptoe, and whispered a sentence in Heathcliff's ear.

He laughed; Hareton darkened; I perceived he was very sensitive to suspected slights, and had obviously a dim notion of his inferiority. But his master or guardian chased the frown by exclaiming—

"You'll be the favorite among us, Hareton! She says you are a— what was it? Well, something very flattering. Here! you go with her round the farm. And behave like a gentleman, mind! Don't use any bad words; and don't stare when the young lady is not looking at you, and be ready to hide your face when she is, and, when you speak, say your words slowly, and keep your hands out of your pockets. Be off, and entertain her as nicely as you can."

He watched the couple walking past the window. Earnshaw had his countenance completely averted from his companion. He seemed studying the familiar landscape with a stranger's, and an artist's interest. Catherine took a sly look at him, expressing small admiration. She then turned her attention to seeking out objects of amusement for herself, and tripped merrily on, lilting a tune to supply the lack of conversation.

"I've tied his tongue," observed Heathcliff. "He'll not venture a single syllable all the time! Nelly, you recollect me at his age—nay, some years younger. Did I ever look so stupid, so 'gaumless', as Joseph calls it?"

"Worse," I replied, "because more sullen with it."

"I've a pleasure in him!" he continued, reflecting aloud.

"He has satisfied my expectations. If he were a born fool I should not enjoy it half so much. But he's no fool; and I can sympathize with all his feelings, having felt them myself. I know what he suffers now, for instance, exactly—it is merely a beginning of what he shall suffer, though. And he'll never be able to emerge from his bathos of coarseness and ignorance. I've got him faster than his scoundrel of a father secured me, and lower; for he takes a pride in his brutishness. I've taught him to scorn every thing extra-animal, as silly and weak. Don't you think Hindley would be proud of his son, if he could see him? almost as proud as I am of mine. But there's this difference, one is gold put to the use of paving stones; and the other is tin polished to ape a service of silver. *Mine* has nothing valuable about it; yet I shall have the merit of making it go as far as such poor stuff can go. *His* had first-rate qualities, and they are lost—rendered worse than unavailing. I have nothing to regret; he would have more than any but I are aware of. And the best of it is, Hareton is damnably fond of me! You'll own that I've out-matched Hindley there. If the dead villain could rise from his grave to abuse me for his offspring's wrongs, I should have the fun of seeing the said offspring fight him back again, indignant that he should dare to rail at the one friend he has in the world!"

Heathcliff chuckled a fiendish laugh at the idea; I made no reply, because I saw that he expected none.

Meantime, our young companion, who sat too removed from us to hear what was said, began to evince symptoms of uneasiness: probably repenting that he had denied himself the treat of Catherine's society, for fear of a little fatigue. His father remarked the restless glances wandering to the window, and the hand irresolutely extended toward his cap.

"Get up, you idle boy!" he exclaimed with assumed heartiness. "Away after them—they are just at the corner, by the stand of hives."

Linton gathered his energies, and left the hearth. The lattice was open, and, as he stepped out, I heard Cathy inquiring of her unsociable attendant, what was that inscription over the door?

Hareton stared up, and scratched his head like a true clown.

"It's some damnable writing," he answered. "I cannot read it."

"Can't read it?" cried Catherine, "I can read it—it's English— but I want to know why it is there."

Linton giggled—the first appearance of mirth he had exhibited.

"He does not know his letters," he said to his cousin. "Could you believe in the existence of such a colossal dunce?"

"Is he all as he should be?" asked Miss Cathy seriously, "or is he simple—not right? I've questioned him twice now, and each time he looked so stupid, I think he does not understand me; I can hardly understand *him* I'm sure."

Linton repeated his laugh, and glanced at Hareton tauntingly, who certainly did not seem quite clear of comprehension at that moment.

"There's nothing the matter but laziness, is there, Earnshaw?" he said. "My cousin fancies you are an idiot. There you experience the consequence of scorning 'book larning,' as you would say. Have you noticed, Catherine, his frightful Yorkshire pronunciation?"

"Why, where the devil is the use on't?" growled Hareton, more ready in answering his daily companion. He was about to enlarge further, but the two youngsters broke into a noisy fit of merriment; my giddy Miss being delighted to discover that she might turn his strange talk to matter of amusement.

"Where is the use of 'the devil' in that sentence?" tittered Linton. "Papa told you not to say any bad words, and you can't open your mouth without one. Do try to behave like a gentleman, now do!"

"If thou wern't more a lass than a lad, I'd fell thee this minute, I would; pitiful lath of a crater!" retorted the angry boor retreating, while his face burned with mingled rage and mortification; for he was conscious of being insulted, and embarrassed how to resent it.

Mr. Heathcliff, having overheard the conversation, as well as I, smiled when he saw him go, but immediately afterward cast a look of singular aversion on the flippant pair, who remained chattering in the door-way. The boy finding animation enough while discussing Hareton's faults and deficiencies, and relating anecdotes of his goings on; and the girl relishing his pert and spiteful sayings, without considering the ill-nature they evinced: but I began to dislike, more than to compassionate, Linton, and to excuse his father, in some measure, for holding him cheap.

We stayed till afternoon; I could not tear Miss Cathy away before; but, happily, my master had not quitted his apartment and remained ignorant of our prolonged absence.

As we walked home, I would fain have enlightened my charge on the characters of the people we had quitted; but she got it into her head that I was prejudiced against them.

"Aha!" she cried, "you take papa's side, Ellen—you are partial, I know, or else you wouldn't have cheated me so many years, into the notion that Linton lived a long way from here, I'm really extremely angry, only, I'm so pleased, I can't show it! But you must hold your tongue about my uncle—he's *my* uncle, remember, and I'll scold papa for quarreling with him."

And so she ran on, till I dropped endeavoring to convince her of his mistake. She did not mention the visit that night, because she did not see Mr. Linton. Next day it all came out, sadly to my chagrin; and still, I was not altogether sorry: I thought the burden of directing and warning would be more efficiently borne by him than me, but he was too timid in giving satisfactory reasons for his wish that she would shun connection with the household of the Heights, and Catherine liked good reasons for every restraint that harassed her petted will.

"Papa!" she exclaimed after the morning's salutations, "guess whom I saw yesterday, in my walk on the moors. Ah, papa, you started! you've not done right, have you, now? I saw. But listen, and you shall hear how I found you out, and Ellen, who is in league with you, and yet pretended to pity me so, when I kept hoping, and was always disappointed about Linton's coming back!"

She gave a faithful account of her excursion and its consequences; and my master, though he cast more than one reproachful look at me, said nothing, till she had concluded. Then he drew her to him, and asked if she knew why he had concealed Linton's near neighborhood from her? Could she think it was to deny her a pleasure that she might harmlessly enjoy?

"It was because you disliked Mr. Heathcliff," she answered.

"Then you believe I care more for my own feelings than yours, Cathy?" he said. "No, it was not because I disliked Mr. Heathcliff; but because Mr. Heathcliff dislikes me; and is a most diabolical man, delighting to wrong and ruin those he hates, if they give him the slightest opportunity. I knew that you could not keep up an acquaintance with your cousin, without being brought into contact with him; and I knew he would detest you, on my account; so, for your own good, and nothing else, I took precautions that you should not see Linton again. I meant to explain this, some time, as you grew older, and I'm sorry I delayed it!"

"But Heathcliff was quite cordial, papa," observed Catherine, not at all convinced; "and *he* didn't object to our seeing each other: he said I might come to his house when I pleased, only I must not tell you, because you had quarrelled with him, and would not forgive him for marrying Aunt Isabella. And you won't—*you* are the one to be blamed—he is willing to let *us* be friends, at least; Linton and I—and you are not."

My master, perceiving that she would not take his word for her uncle-in-law's evil disposition, gave a hasty sketch of his conduct to Isabella, and the manner in which Wuthering Heights became his property. He could not bear to discourse long upon the topic, for though he spoke little of it, he still felt the same horror, and detestation of his ancient enemy that had occupied his heart ever since Mrs. Linton's death. "She might have been living yet, if it had not been for him!" was his constant, bitter reflection; and, in his eyes, Heathcliff seemed a murderer.

Miss Cathy, conversant with no bad deeds except her own slight acts of disobedience, injustice, and passion, rising from hot temper, and thoughtlessness, and repented of on the day they were committed, was amazed at the blackness of spirit that could brood on, and cover revenge for years; and deliberately prosecute its plans, without a visitation of remorse. She appeared so deeply impressed and shocked at this new view of human nature—excluded from all her studies and all her ideas till now—that Mr. Edgar deemed it unnecessary to pursue the subject. He merely added,

"You will know hereafter, darling, why I wish you to avoid his house and family—now, return to your old employments and amusements, and think no more about them!"

Catherine kissed her father, and sat down quietly to her lessons for a couple of hours, according to custom: then she accompanied him into the grounds, and the whole day passed as usual: but in the evening, when she had retired to her room, and I went to help her to undress, I found her crying, on her knees by the bedside.

"Oh, fie, silly child!" I exclaimed. "If you had any real griefs, you'd be ashamed to waste a tear on this little contrariety. You never had one shadow of substantial sorrow, Miss Catherine. Suppose, for a minute, that master and I were dead, and you were by yourself in the world—how would you feel then? Compare the present occasion with such an affliction as that, and be thankful for the friends you have, instead of coveting more."

"I'm not crying for myself, Ellen," she answered, "it's for him. He expected to see me again to-morrow, and then he'll be so disappointed—and he'll wait for me, and I shan't come!"

"Nonsense!" said I, "do you imagine he has thought as much of you as you have of him? Hasn't he Hareton for a companion? Not one in a hundred would weep at losing a relation they had just seen twice, for two afternoons. Linton will conjecture how it is, and trouble himself no further about you."

"But may I not write a note to tell him why I cannot come?" she asked rising to her feet. "And just send those books I promised to lend him. His books are not as nice as mine, and he wanted to have them extremely, when I told him how interesting they were. May I not, Ellen?"

"No, indeed, no indeed!" replied I with decision. "Then he would write to you, and there'd never be an end of it. No, Miss Catherine, the acquaintance must be dropped entirely—so your papa expects, and I shall see that it is done!"

"But how can one little note—" she recommenced, putting on an imploring countenance.

"Silence!" I interrupted. "We'll not begin with your little notes. Get into bed!"

She threw at me a very naughty look, so naughty that I would not kiss her good-night at first: I covered her up, and shut her door, in great displeasure—but, repenting half-way, I returned softly, and lo! there was Miss, standing at the table with a bit of blank paper before her, and a pencil in her hand, which she guilt-ily slipped out of sight, on my re-entrance.

"You'll get nobody to take that, Catherine," I said, "if you write it; and at present I shall put out your candle."

I set the extinguisher on the flame, receiving as I did so, a slap on the hand, and a petulant "cross thing!" I then quitted her again, and she drew the bolt in one of her worst, most peevish humors.

The letter was finished, and forwarded to its destination by a milk-fetcher who came from the village, but that I didn't learn till some time afterwards. Weeks passed on, and Cathy recovered her temper, though she grew wondrous fond of stealing off to corners by herself, and often, if I came near her suddenly while reading, she would start, and bend over the book, evidently desirous to hide it; and I detected edges of loose paper sticking out beyond the leaves.

She also got a trick of coming down early in the morning, and lingering about the kitchen, as if she were expecting the arrival of something; and she had a small drawer in a cabinet in the library which she would trifle over for hours, and whose key she took special care to remove when she left it.

One day, as she inspected this drawer, I observed that the play-things and trinkets which recently formed its contents, were transmuted into bits of folded paper.

My curiosity and suspicions were roused; I determined to take a peep at her mysterious treasures; so, at night, as soon as she and my master were safe up-stairs, I searched and readily found among my house keys, one that would fit the lock. Having opened, I emptied the whole contents into my apron, and took them with me to examine at leisure in my own chamber.

Though I could not but suspect, I was still surprised to discover that they were a mass of correspondence, daily almost, it must have been, from Linton Heathcliff, answers to documents for-warded by her. The earlier dated were embarrassed and short; gradually, however, they expanded into copious love letters, foolish as the age of the writer rendered natural, yet with touches, here and there, which I thought were borrowed from a more experienced source.

Some of them struck me as singularly odd compounds of ardor and flatness; commencing in strong feeling, and concluding in the affected, wordy way that a school-boy might use to a fancied, incorporeal sweetheart. Whether they satisfied Cathy, I don't know, but they appeared very worthless trash to me. After turning over as many as I thought proper, I tied them in a handkerchief, and set them aside, re-locking the vacant drawer.

Following her habit, my young lady descended early, and visited the kitchen: I watched her go to the door, on the arrival of a certain little boy; and, while the dairy maid filled his can, she tucked something into his jacket-pocket, and plucked something out. I went round by the garden, and laid wait for the messenger; who fought valorously to defend his trust, and we spilled the milk between us; but I succeeded in abstracting the epistle; and threatening serious consequences if he did not look sharp home, I remained under the wall, and perused Miss Cathy's affectionate composition. It was more simple and more eloquent than her cousin's, very pretty and very silly. I shook my head, and went meditating into the house.

The day being wet, she could not divert herself with rambling about the park; so, at the conclusion of her morning studies, she resorted to the solace of the drawer. Her father sat reading at the table; and I, on purpose, had sought a bit of work in some un-ripped fringes of the window curtain, keeping my eye steadily fixed on her proceedings.

Never did any bird flying back to a plundered nest which it had left brimful of chirping young ones, express more complete despair in its anguished cries and flutterings, than she by her single "Oh!" and the change that transfigured her late happy countenance. Mr. Linton looked up.

"What is the matter, love? Have you hurt yourself?" he said.

His tone and look assured her *he* had not been the discoverer of the hoard.

"No papa—" she gasped. "Ellen! Ellen! come up-stairs—I'm sick!"

I obeyed her summons, and accompanied her out.

"Oh, Ellen! you have got them," she commenced immediately, dropping on her knees, when we were enclosed alone. "Oh, give them to me, and I'll never never do so again! Don't tell papa. You have not told papa, Ellen, say you have not! I've been exceedingly naughty, but I won't do it any more!"

With a grave severity in my manner, I bid her stand up.

"So," I exclaimed, "Miss Catherine, you are tolerably far on, it seems—you may well be ashamed of them! A fine bundle of trash you study in your leisure hours, to be sure. Why it's good enough to be printed! And what do you suppose the master will think, when I display it before him? I haven't shown it yet, but you needn't imagine I shall keep your ridiculous secrets. For shame! And you must have led the way in writing such absurdities; he would not have thought of beginning, I'm certain."

"I didn't! I didn't!" sobbed Cathy, fit to break her heart. "I didn't once think of loving him till—"

"*Loving!*" cried I, as scornfully as I could utter the word. "*Loving!* Did anybody ever hear the like! I might just as well talk of loving the miller who comes once a year to buy our corn. Pretty loving indeed, and both times together you have seen Linton hardly four hours, in your life! Now here is the babyish trash. I'm going with it to the library; and we'll see what your father says to such *loving*."

She sprang at her precious epistles, but I held them above my head; and then she poured out further frantic entreaties that I would burn them—do anything rather than show them. And being really fully as inclined to laugh as scold, for I esteemed it all girlish vanity, I at length, relented in a measure, and asked,

"If I consent to burn them, will you promise faithfully, neither to send, nor receive a letter again, nor a book—for I perceive you have sent him books—nor locks of hair, nor rings, nor playthings!"

"We don't send playthings!" cried Catherine, her pride overcoming her shame.

"Nor anything at all, then, my lady!" I said. "Unless you will, here I go."

"I promise, Ellen!" she cried, catching my dress. "Oh, put them in the fire, do, do!"

But when I proceeded to open the place with the poker, the sacrifice was too painful to be borne. She earnestly supplicated that I would spare her one or two.

"One or two, Ellen, to keep for Linton's sake!"

I unknotted the handkerchief, and commenced dropping them in from an angle, and the flame curled up the chimney.

"I will have one, you cruel wretch!" she screamed, darting her hand into the fire, and drawing forth some half-consumed fragments, at the expense of her fingers.

"Very well—and I will have some to exhibit to papa!" I answered, shaking back the rest into the bundle, and turning anew to the door.

She emptied her blackened pieces into the flames, and motioned me to finish the immolation. It was done; I stirred up the ashes, and interred them under a shovelful of coals; and she mutely, and with a sense of intense injury, retired to her private apartment. I descended to tell my master that the young lady's qualm of sickness was almost gone, but I judged it best for her to lie down a while.

She wouldn't dine; but she re-appeared at tea, pale and red about the eyes, and marvelously subdued in outward aspect.

Next morning I answered the letter by a slip of paper inscribed, "Master Heathcliff is requested to send no more notes to Miss Linton, as she will not receive them." And, thenceforth the little boy came with vacant pockets.

. . . .

Chapter 22

Summer drew to an end, and early autumn; it was past Michaelmas, but the harvest was late that year, and a few of our fields were still uncleared. Mr. Linton and his daughter would frequently walk out among the reapers; at the carrying of the last sheaves, they stayed till dusk, and the evening happening to be chill and damp, my master caught a bad cold, that, settling obstinately on his lungs, confined him indoors throughout the whole of the winter, nearly without intermission.

Poor Cathy, frightened from her little romance, had been considerably sadder and duller since its abandonment; and her father insisted on her reading less, and taking more exercise. She had his companionship no longer; I esteemed it a duty to supply its lack, as much as possible, with mine—an efficient substitute, for I could only spare two or three hours, from my numerous diurnal occupations, to follow her footsteps, and then my society was obviously less desirable than his.

On an afternoon in October, or the beginning of November, a fresh watery afternoon, when the turf and paths were rustling with moist, withered leaves, and the cold, blue sky was half hidden by clouds, dark gray streamers, rapidly mounting from the west, and boding abundant rain, I requested my young lady to forego her ramble, because I was certain of showers. She refused, and I unwillingly donned a cloak, and took my umbrella to accompany her on a stroll to the bottom of the park—a formal walk which she generally affected if low-spirited; and that she invariably was when Mr. Edgar had been worse than ordinary—a thing never known from his confession, but guessed both by her and me from his increased silence, and the melancholy of his countenance.

She went sadly on; there was no running or bounding now, though the chill wind might well have tempted her to a race. And often, from the side of my eye, I could detect her raising a hand, and brushing something off her cheek. I gazed round for a means of diverting her thoughts. On one side of the road rose a high, rough bank, where hazels and stunted oaks, with their roots half exposed, held uncertain tenure; the soil was too loose for the latter, and strong winds had blown some nearly horizontal. In summer, Miss Catherine delighted to climb along these trunks, and sit in the branches, swinging twenty feet above the ground; and I, pleased with her agility, and her light, childish heart, still considering it proper to scold every time I caught her at such an elevation, but so that she knew there was no neccessity for descending. From dinner to tea she would lie in her breeze-rocked cradle, doing nothing except singing old songs—my nursery lore—to herself, or watching the birds, joint tenants, feed and entice their young ones to fly, or nestling with closed lids, half thinking, half dreaming, happier than words can express.

"Look, miss!" I exclaimed, pointing to a nook under the roots of one twisted tree; "winter is not here yet. There's a little flower up yonder, the last bud from the multitude of bluebells that clouded those turf steps in July with a lilac mist. Will you clamber up, and pluck it to show papa?"

Cathy stared a long time at the lonely blossom trembling in its earthy shelter, and replied at length—

"No, I'll not touch it; but it looks melancholy, does it not, Ellen?"

"Yes," I observed, "about as starved and sackless as you—your cheeks are bloodless; let us take hold of hands and run. You're so slow, I dare say I shall keep up with you."

"No," she repeated, and continued sauntering on, pausing at intervals to muse over a bit of moss, or a tuft of blanched grass, or a fungus spreading its bright orange among the heaps of brown foliage; and, ever and anon, her hand was lifted to her averted face.

"Catherine why are you crying, love?" I asked, approaching and putting my arm over her shoulder. "You mustn't cry because papa has a cold; be thankful that it is nothing worse."

She now put no further restraint on her tears; her breath was stifled by sobs.

"Oh, it *will* be something worse," she said. "And what shall I do when papa and you leave me, and I am by myself? I can't forget your words, Ellen, they are always in my ear. How life will be changed, how dreary the world will be, when papa and you are dead!"

"None can tell whether you won't die before us," I replied. "It's wrong to anticipate evil—we'll hope there are years and years to come before any of us go; master is young, and I am strong, and hardly forty-five. My mother lived till eighty, a canty dame to the last. And suppose Mr. Linton were spared till he saw sixty, that would be more years than you have counted, miss. And would it not be foolish to mourn a calamity above twenty years beforehand?"

"But Aunt Isabella was younger than papa," she remarked, gazing up with timid hope to seek further consolation.

"Aunt Isabella had not you and me to nurse her," I replied. "She wasn't as happy as master; she hadn't as much to live for. All you need do is to wait well on your father, and cheer him by letting him see you cheerful; and avoid giving him anxiety on any subject—mind that, Cathy! I'll not disguise but you might kill him, if you were wild and reckless, and cherished a foolish, fanciful affection for the son of a person who would be glad to have him in his grave, and allowed him to discover that you fretted over the separation he has judged it expedient to make."

"I fret about nothing on earth except papa's illness," answered my companion. "I care for nothing in comparison with papa. And I'll never—never—Oh, never, while I have my senses, do an act, or say a word to vex him. I love him better than myself, Ellen;

and I know it by this—I pray every night that I may live after him; because I would rather be miserable than that he should be—that proves I love him better than myself."

"Good words," I replied. "But deeds, must prove it also; and after he is well, remember you don't forget resolutions formed in the hour of fear."

As we talked, we neared a door that opened on the road; and my young lady, lightening into sunshine again, climbed up, and seated herself on the top of the wall, reaching over to gather some hips that bloomed scarlet on the summit branches of the wild rose trees, shadowing the highway side; the lower fruit had disappeared, but only birds could touch the upper, except from Cathy's present station.

In stretching to pull them, her hat fell off; and as the door was locked, she proposed scrambling down to recover it. I bid her be cautious lest she got a fall, and she nimbly disappeared.

But the return was no such easy matter; the stones were smooth and neatly cemented, and the rosebushes and blackberry stragglers could yield no assistance in re-ascending. I, like a fool, didn't recollect that till I heard her laughing, and exclaiming—

"Ellen! you'll have to fetch the key, or else I must run round to the porter's lodge. I can't scale the ramparts on this side!"

"Stay where you are," I answered; "I have my bundle of keys in my pocket; perhaps I may manage to open it; if not, I'll go."

Catherine amused herself with dancing to and fro before the door, while I tried all the large keys in succession. I had applied the last, and found that none would do; so, repeating my desire that she would remain there, I was about to hurry home as fast as I could, when an approaching sound arrested me. It was the trot of a horse; Cathy's dance stopped, and in a minute the horse stopped also.

"Who is that?" I whispered.

"Ellen, I wish you could open the door," whispered back my companion, anxiously.

"Ho, Miss Linton?" cried a deep voice (the rider's). "I'm glad to meet you. Don't be in haste to enter, for I have an explanation to ask and obtain."

"I shan't speak to you, Mr. Heathcliff!" answered Catherine. "Papa says you are a wicked man, and you hate both him and me; and Ellen says the same."

"That is nothing to the purpose," said Heathcliff. (He it was.) "I don't hate my son, I suppose, and it is concerning him that I demand your attention. Yes! you have cause to blush. Two or three months since, were you not in the habit of writing to Linton?—making love in play, eh? You deserved, both of you, flogging for that! You especially, the elder, and less sensitive, as it turns out. I've got your letters, and if you give me any pertness, I'll send them to your father. I presume you grew weary of the amusement, and dropped it, didn't you? Well, you dropped Linton with it, into a Slough of Despond. He was in earnest—in love—really. As true as I live, he's dying for you—breaking his heart at your fickleness, not figuratively, but actually. Though

Hareton has made him a standing jest for six weeks, and I have used more serious measures, and attempted to frighten him out of his idiocy, he gets worse daily, and he'll be under the sod before summer, unless you restore him!"

"How can you lie so glaringly to the poor child!" I called from the inside. "Pray ride on! How can you deliberately get up such paltry falsehoods? Miss Cathy, I'll knock the lock off with a stone. You won't believe that vile nonsense. You can feel in yourself, it is impossible that a person should die for love of a stranger."

"I was not aware there were eaves-droppers," muttered the detected villain. "Worthy Mrs. Dean, I like you, but I don't like your double dealing," he added, aloud. "How could *you* lie so glaringly as to affirm I hated the 'poor child?' And invent bugbear stories to terrify her from my door-stones? Catherine Linton (the very name warms me), my bonny lass, I shall be from home all this week—go and see if I have not spoken truth; do—there's a darling! Just imagine your father in my place, and Linton in yours; then think how you would value your careless lover, if he refused to stir a step to comfort you, when your father himself entreated him; and don't, from pure stupidity, fall into the same error. I swear, on my salvation, he's going to his grave, and none but you can save him!"

The lock gave way, and I issued out.

"I swear Linton is dying," repeated Heathcliff, looking hard at me. "And grief and disappointment are hastening his death. Nelly, if you won't let her go, you can walk over yourself. But I shall not return till this time next week; and I think your master himself would scarcely object to her visiting her cousin!"

"Come in," said I taking Cathy by the arm, and half forcing her to re-enter, for she lingered, viewing, with troubled eyes, the features of the speaker, too stern to express his inward deceit.

He pushed his horse close, and, bending down, observed—

"Miss Catherine, I'll own to you that I have little patience with Linton, and Hareton and Joseph have less. I'll own that he's with a harsh set. He pines for kindness as well as love, and a kind word from you would be his best medicine. Don't mind Mrs. Dean's cruel cautions, but be generous, and contrive to see him. He dreams of you day and night, and cannot be persuaded that you don't hate him, since you neither write nor call."

I closed the door, and rolled a stone to assist the loosened lock in holding it; and spreading my umbrella, I drew my charge underneath, for the rain began to drive through the moaning branches of the trees, and warned us to avoid delay.

Our hurry prevented any comment on the encounter with Heathcliff, as we stretched toward home; but I divined instinctively that Catherine's heart was clouded now in double darkness. Her features were so sad, they did not seem hers: she evidently regarded what she had heard as every syllable true.

The master had retired to rest before we came in. Cathy stole to his room to inquire how he was; he had fallen asleep. She returned, and asked me to sit with her in the library. We took our tea together; and afterward she lay down on the rug, and told me not to talk, for she was weary.

I got a book, and pretended to read. As soon as she supposed me absorbed in my occupation, she recommenced her silent weeping: it appeared, at present, her favorite diversion. I suffered her to enjoy it a while; then I expostulated, deriding and ridiculing all Mr. Heathcliff's assertions about his son, as if I were certain she would coincide. Alas! I hadn't skill to counteract the effect his account had produced—it was just what he intended.

"You may be right, Ellen," she answered; "but I shall never feel at ease till I know—and I must tell Linton it is not my fault that I don't write, and convince him that I shall not change."

What use were anger and protestations against her silly credulity? We parted that night hostile; but next day beheld me on the road to Wuthering Heights, by the side of my willful young mistress's pony, I couldn't bear to witness her sorrow—to see her pale, dejected countenance and heavy eyes—and I yielded in the faint hope that Linton himself might prove, by his reception of us, how little of the tale was founded on fact.

. . . .

Chapter 23

The rainy night had ushered in a misty morning—half frost, half drizzle—and temporary brooks crossed our path, gurgling from the uplands. My feet were thoroughly wetted; I was cross and low, exactly the humor suited for making the most of these disagreeable things. We entered the farmhouse by the kitchen way, to ascertain whether Mr. Heathcliff were really absent, because I put slight faith in his own affirmation.

Joseph seemed sitting alone, in a sort of elysium, beside a roaring fire, a quart of ale on the table near him, bristling with large pieces of toasted oat cake, and his black, short pipe in his mouth. Catherine ran to the hearth to warm herself. I asked if the master were in? My question remained so long unanswered, that I thought the old man had grown deaf, and I repeated it louder.

"Na—ay!" he snarled, or rather screamed through his nose. "Na—ay! yah muh goa back whear yah coom frough."

"Joseph," cried a peevish voice, simultaneously with me, from the inner room, "how often am I to call you? There are only a few red ashes now. Joseph! come this moment."

Vigorous puffs, and a resolute stare into the grate declared he had no ear for this appeal. The housekeeper and Hareton were invisible—one gone on an errand, and the other at his work, probably. We knew Linton's tones, and entered.

"Oh, I hope you'll die in a garret, starved to death!" said the boy, mistaking our approach for that of his negligent attendant.

He stopped on observing his error; his cousin flew to him.

"Is that you, Miss Linton?" he said, raising his head from the arm of the great chair in which he reclined. "No—don't kiss me. It takes my breath—dear me! Papa said you would call," continued he, after recovering a little from Catherine's embrace, while she stood by, looking very contrite. "Will you shut the door, if you please?—you left it open, and those—those *detestable* creatures won't bring coals to the fire. It's so cold!"

I stirred up the cinders, and fetched a scuttleful myself. The invalid complained of being covered with ashes; but he had a tiresome cough, and looked feverish and ill, so I did not rebuke his temper.

"Well, Linton," murmured Catherine, when his corrugated brow relaxed. "Are you glad to see me? Can I do you any good?"

"Why didn't you come before?" he said. "You should have come, instead of writing. It tired me dreadfully writing those long letters. I'd far rather have talked to you. Now, I can neither bear to talk, nor anything else. I wonder where Zillah is! Will you (looking at me) step into the kitchen and see?"

I had received no thanks for my other service; and being unwilling to run to and fro at his behest, I replied—

"Nobody is out there but Joseph."

"I want to drink," he exclaimed, fretfully turning away. "Zillah is constantly gadding off to Gimmerton since papa went. It's miserable! And I'm obliged to come down here—they resolved never to hear me up stairs."

"Is your father attentive to you, Master Heathcliff?" I asked, perceiving Catherine to be checked in her friendly advances.

"Attentive? He makes *them* a little more attentive, at least," he cried. "The wretches! Do you know, Miss Linton, that brute Hareton laughs at me? I hate him—indeed, I hate them all—they are odious beings."

Cathy began searching for some water; she lighted on a pitcher in the dresser, filled a tumbler, and brought it. He bid her add a spoonful of wine from a bottle on the table; and, having swallowed a small portion, appeared more tranquil, and said she was very kind.

"And are you glad to see me?" asked she reiterating her former question, and pleased to detect the faint dawn of a smile.

"Yes, I am. It's something new to hear a voice like yours!" he replied, "but I *have* been vexed, because you wouldn't come. And papa swore it was owing to me; he called me a pitiful, shuffling, worthless thing, and said you despised me; and if he had been in my place he would be more the master of the Grange than your father by this time. But you don't despise me, do you Miss—"

"I wish you would say Catherine, or Cathy!" interrupted my young lady. "Despise you? No! Next to papa, and Ellen, I love you better than anybody living. I don't love Mr. Heathcliff, though; and I dare not come when he returns; will he stay away many days?"

"Not many:" answered Linton, but he goes to the moors frequently, since the shooting season commenced, and you might spend an hour or two with me in his absence. Do say you will! I think I should not be peevish with you; you'd not provoke me, and you'd always be ready to help me, wouldn't you?"

"Yes," said Catherine, stroking his long, soft hair; "if I could only get papa's consent, I'd spend half my time with you. Pretty Linton! I wish you were my brother!"

"And then you would like me as well as your father?" observed he more cheerfully. "But papa says you would love me better than him and all the world, if you were my wife—so I'd rather you were that!"

"No! I should never love anybody better than papa," she returned gravely. "And people hate their wives, sometimes; but not their sisters and brothers, and if you were the latter, you would live with us, and papa would be as fond of you, as he is of me."

Linton denied that people ever hated their wives; but Cathy affirmed they did, and in her wisdom, instanced his own father's aversion to her aunt. I endeavored to stop her thoughtless tongue. I couldn't succeed, till everything she knew was out. Master Heathcliff, much irritated, asserted her relation was false.

"Papa told me; and papa does not tell falsehoods!" she answered, pertly.

"*My* papa scorns yours!" cried Linton. "He calls him a sneaking fool!"

"Yours is a wicked man," retorted Catherine, "and you are very naughty to dare to repeat what he says. He must be wicked, to have made Aunt Isabella leave him as she did!"

"She didn't leave him," said the boy. "You shan't contradict me!"

"She did!" cried my young lady.

"Well I'll tell *you* something!" said Linton. "Your mother hated your father; now then."

"Oh!" exclaimed Catherine, too enraged to continue.

"And she loved mine!" added he.

"You little liar! I hate you now," she panted, and her face grew red with passion.

"She did! she did!" sang Linton, sinking into the recess of his chair, and leaning back his head to enjoy the agitation of the other disputant, who stood behind.

"Hush, Master Heathcliff!" I said, "that's your father's tale too, I suppose."

"It isn't—you hold your tongue!" he answered, "she did, she did, Catherine, she did, she did!"

Cathy, beside herself, gave the chair a violent push, and caused him to fall against one arm. He was immediately seized by a suffocating cough, that soon ended his triumph. It lasted so long that it frightened even me. As to his cousin, she wept with all her might, aghast at the mischief she had done, though she said nothing. I held him till the fit exhausted itself. Then he thrust me away, and leaned his head down, silently. Catherine quelled her lamentations also, took a seat opposite, and looked solemnly into the fire.

"How do you feel now, Master Heathcliff," I inquired, after waiting ten minutes.

"I wish *she* felt as I do," he replied, "spiteful, cruel thing! Hareton never touches me, he never struck me in his life. And I was better to-day—and there"—his voice died in a whimper.

"*I* didn't strike you!" muttered Cathy, chewing her lip to prevent another burst of emotion.

He sighed and moaned like one under great suffering, and kept it up for a quarter of an hour, on purpose to distress his cousin, apparently, for whenever he caught a stifled sob from her, he put renewed pain and pathos into the inflections of his voice.

"I'm sorry I hurt you, Linton!" she said at length, racked beyond endurance. "But *I* couldn't have been hurt by that little push; and I had no idea that you could, either—you're not much, are you, Linton? Don't let me go home, thinking I've done you harm! answer, speak to me."

"I can't speak to you," he murmured, "you've hurt me so that I shall lie awake all night, choking with this cough. If you had it you'd know what it was—but *you'll* be comfortably asleep, while I'm in agony—and nobody near me! I wonder how you would like to pass those fearful nights!" And he began to wail aloud for very pity of himself.

"Since you are in the habit of passing dreadful nights," I said, "it won't be Miss who spoils your ease; you'd be the same had she never come. However, she shall not disturb you again—and perhaps you'll get quieter when we leave you."

"Must I go?" asked Catherine dolefully, bending over him. "Do you want me to go, Linton?"

"You can't alter what you've done," he replied pettishly, shrinking from her, "unless you alter it for the worse, by teasing me into a fever!"

"Well, then I must go?" she repeated.

"Let me alone, at least," said he; "I can't bear your talking!"

She lingered, and resisted my persuasions to departure, a tiresome while, but as he neither looked up nor spoke, she finally made a movement to the door, and I followed. We were recalled by a scream. Linton had slid from his seat upon the hearthstone, and lay writhing in the mere perverseness of an indulged plague of a child, determined to be as grievous and harassing as it can. I thoroughly gauged his disposition from his behavior, and saw at once it would be folly to attempt humoring him. Not so my companion, she ran back in terror, knelt down, and cried, and soothed, and entreated, till he grew quiet from lack of breath, by no means from compunction at distressing her.

"I shall lift him upon the settle," I said, "and he may roll about as he pleases; we can't stop to watch him. I hope you are satisfied, Miss Cathy, that *you* are not the person to benefit him, and that his condition of health is not occasioned by attachment to you. Now, then, there he is! Come away; as soon as he knows there is nobody by to care for his nonsense, he'll be glad to lie still!"

She placed a cushion under his head, and offered him some water, he rejected the latter, and tossed uneasily on the former, as

if it were a stone, or a block of wood. She tried to put it more
comfortably.

"I can't do with that," he said, "it's not high enough!"

Catherine brought another to lay above it.

"That's *too* high!" murmured the provoking thing.

"How must I arrange it, then?" she asked, despairingly.

He twined himself up to her, as she half knelt by the settle, and
converted her shoulder into a support.

"No, that won't do!" I said. "You'll be content with the
cushion, Master Heathcliff! Miss has wasted too much time on
you already; we can not remain five minutes longer."

"Yes, yes, we can!" replied Cathy. "He's good and patient, now.
He's beginning to think I shall have far greater misery than he
will, to-night, if I believe he is the worse for my visit; and then I
dare not come again. Tell the truth about it, Linton—for I
mustn't come if I have hurt you."

"You must come to cure me," he answered. "You ought to
come because you have hurt me. You know you have, extremely! I
was not as ill when you entered as I am at present—was I?"

"But you've made yourself ill by crying, and being in a passion."

"I didn't do it all," said his cousin. "However, we'll be friends
now. And you want me—you would wish to see me sometimes,
really?"

"I told you I did!" he replied impatiently. "Sit on the settle, and
let me lean on your knee. That's as mamma used to do, whole
afternoons together. Sit quite still, and don't talk, but you may
sing a song if you can sing, or you may say a nice long interesting
ballad—one of those you promised to teach me, or a story—I'd
rather have a ballad though; begin."

Catherine repeated the longest she could remember. The employment pleased both mightily. Linton would have another, and
after that another, notwithstanding my strenuous objections; and
so they went on until the clock struck twelve, and we heard
Hareton in the court, returning for his dinner.

"And to-morrow, Catherine; will you be here to-morrow?"
asked young Heathcliff, holding her frock, as she rose reluctantly.

"No!" I answered, "nor next day neither." She, however, gave a
different response, evidently, for his forehead cleared, as she
stooped, and whispered in his ear.

"You won't go to-morrow, recollect, Miss!" I commenced,
when we were out of the house. "You are not dreaming of it, are
you?"

She smiled.

"Oh, I'll take good care!" I continued, "I'll have that lock mended, and you can escape by no way else."

"I can get over the wall," she said, laughing. "The Grange is not
a prison, Ellen, and you are not my jailer. And besides, I'm almost
seventeen. I'm a woman—and I'm certain Linton would recover
quickly if he had me to look after him. I'm older than he is, you
know, and wiser, less childish, am I not? And he'll soon do as I
direct him, with some slight coaxing. He's a pretty lttle darling

when he's good. I'd make such a pet of him, if he were mine. We should never quarrel, should we, after we were used to each other? Don't you like him, Ellen?"

"Like him?" I exclaimed. "The worst tempered bit of a sickly slip that ever struggled into its teens! Happily, as Mr. Heathcliff conjectured, he'll not win twenty! I doubt whether he'll see spring indeed—and small loss to his family, whenever he drops off; and lucky it is for us that his father took him. The kinder he was treated, the more tedious and selfish he'd be! I'm glad you have no chance of having him for a husband, Miss Catherine!"

My companion waxed serious at hearing this speech. To speak of his death so regardlessly wounded her feelings.

"He's younger than I," she answered, after a protracted pause of meditation, "and he ought to live the longest, he will—he must live as long as I do. He's as now strong as when he first came into the north, I'm positive of that! It's only a cold that ails him, the same as papa has. You say papa will get better, and why shouldn't he?"

"Well, well," I cried, "after all, we needn't trouble ourselves; for listen, Miss, and mind, I'll keep my word. If you attempt going to Wuthering Heights again, with, or without me, I shall inform Mr. Linton, and unless he allow it, the intimacy with your cousin must not be revived."

"It has been revived!" muttered Cathy, sulkily.

"Must not be continued, then?" I said.

"We'll see!" was her reply, and she set off at a gallop, leaving me to toil in the rear.

We both reached home before our dinner-time; my master supposed we had been wandering through the park, and therefore he demanded no explanation of our absence. As soon as I entered, I hastened to change my soaked shoes and stockings; but sitting such a while at the Heights, had done the mischief. On the succeeding morning I was laid up; and during three weeks I remained incapacitated for attending to my duties—a calamity never experienced prior to that period, and never, I am thankful to say since.

My little mistress behaved like an angel in coming to wait on me, and cheer my solitude; the confinement brought me exceedingly low. It is wearisome to a stirring active body—but few have slighter reasons for complaint than I had. The moment Catherine left Mr. Linton's room, she appeared at my bedside. Her day was divided between us; no amusement usurped a minute; she neglected her meals, her studies, and her play; and she was the fondest nurse that ever watched; she must have had a warm heart, when she loved her father so, to give so much to me! I said her days were divided between us; but the master retired early, and I generally needed nothing after six o'clock, thus her evening was her own.

Poor thing, I never considered what she did with herself after tea. And though frequently, when she looked in to bid me good night I remarked a fresh color in her cheeks, and a pinkness over her slender fingers; instead of fancying the hue borrowed from a cold ride across the moors, I laid it to the charge of a hot fire in the library.

. . . .

Chapter 24

At the close of three weeks, I was able to quit my chamber, and move about the house. And on the first occasion of my sitting up in the evening, I asked Catherine to read to me, because my eyes were weak. We were in the library, the master having gone to bed; she consented, rather unwillingly, I fancied; and imagining my sort of books did not suit her, I bid her please herself in the choice of what she perused.

She selected one of her own favorites, and got forward steadily about an hour; then came frequent questions.

"Ellen, are you not tired? Hadn't you better lie down now? You'll be sick, keeping up so long, Ellen."

"No, no, dear, I'm not tired," I returned, continually.

Perceiving me immovable, she essayed another method of showing her disrelish for her occupation. It changed to yawning, and stretching, and—

"Ellen, I'm tired."

"Give over then, and talk," I answered.

That was worse; she fretted and sighed, and looked at her watch till eight; and finally went to her room, completely overdone with sleep, judging by her peevish, heavy look, and the constant rubbing she inflicted on her eyes.

The following night she seemed more impatient still; and on the third she complained of a head-ache, and left me. I thought her conduct odd; and having remained alone a long while, I resolved on going and inquiring whether she were better, and asking her to come and lie on the sofa, instead of up-stairs, in the dark.

No Catherine could I discover up-stairs, and none below. The servants affirmed they had not seen her. I listened at Mr. Edgar's door—all was silence. I returned to her apartment, extinguished my candle, and seated myself in the window.

The moon shone bright; a sprinkling of snow covered the ground, and I reflected that she might, possibly, have taken it into her head to walk about the garden, for refreshment. I did detect a figure creeping along the inner fence of the park; but it was not my young mistress; on its emerging into the light, I recognized one of the grooms. He stood a considerable period viewing the carriage road through the grounds; then started off at a brisk pace, as if he had detected something, and reappeared, presently, leading Miss's pony; and there she was, just dismounted, and walking by its side.

The man took his charge stealthily across the grass toward the stable. Cathy entered by the casement window of the drawing-room, and glided noiselessly up to where I awaited her. She put the door gently to, slipped off her snowy shoes, untied her hat, and was proceeding, unconscious of my espionage, to lay aside her mantle, when I suddenly rose, and revealed myself. The surprise petrified her an instant; she uttered an inarticulate exclamation, and stood fixed.

"My dear Miss Catherine," I began, too vividly impressed by her recent kindness to break into a scold, "where have you been riding at this hour? And now why should you try to deceive me, by telling a tale. Where have you been? Speak!"

"To the bottom of the park," she stammered. "I didn't tell a tale."

"And nowhere else?" I demanded.

"No," was the muttered reply.

"Oh, Catherine," I cried sorrowfully. "you know you have been doing wrong, or you wouldn't be driven to uttering an untruth to me. That does grieve me. I'd rather be three months ill, than hear you frame a deliberate lie."

She sprang forward, and bursting into tears, threw her arms round my neck.

"Well, Ellen, I'm so afraid of your being angry," she said. "Promise not to be angry, and you shall know the very truth. I hate to hide."

We sat down in the window-seat; I assured her I would not scold, whatever her secret might be, and I guessed it, of course; so she commenced—

"I've been to Wuthering Heights, Ellen, and I've never missed going a day since you fell ill, except thrice before, and twice after you left your room. I gave Michael books and pictures to prepare Minny every evening, and to put her back in the stable; you mustn't scold *him* either, mind. I was at the Heights by half-past six, and generally stayed till half-past eight, and then galloped home. It was not to amuse myself that I went; I was often wretched all the time. Now and then, I was happy, once in a week perhaps. At first, I expected there would be sad work persuading you to let me keep my word to Linton, for I had engaged to call again next day, when we quitted him; but, as you staid up-stairs on the morrow, I escaped that trouble; and while Michael was refastening the lock of the park door in the afternoon, I got possession of the key, and told him how my cousin wished me to visit him, because he was sick, and couldn't come to the Grange; and how papa would object to my going. And then I negotiated with him about the pony. He is fond of reading, and he thinks of leaving soon to get married, so he offered, if I would lend him books out of the library, to do what I wished; but I preferred giving him my own, and that satisfied him better.

"On my second visit, Linton seemed in lively spirits; and Zillah, that is their housekeeper, made us a clean room, and a good fire, and told us that as Joseph was out at a prayer-meeting, and Hareton was off with his dogs, robbing our woods of pheasants, as I heard afterward, we might do what we liked.

"She brought me some warm wine and gingerbread; and appeared exceedingly good-natured; and Linton sat in the armchair, and I in the little rocking chair, on the hearthstone, and we laughed and talked so merrily, and found so much to say; we planned where we would go, and what we would do in summer. I needn't repeat that, because you would call it silly.

"One time, however, we were near quarrelling. He said the pleasantest manner of spending a hot July day was lying from morning till evening on a bank of heath in the middle of the moors, with the bees humming dreamily about among the bloom, and the larks singing high up over head, and the blue sky, and bright sun shining steadily and cloudlessly. That was his most perfect idea of heaven's happiness—mine was rocking in a rustling green tree, with a west wind blowing, and bright, white clouds flitting rapidly above; and not only larks, but throstles, and blackbirds, and linnets, and cuckoos pouring out music on every side, and the moors seen at a distance, broken into cool dusky dells; but close by great swells of long grass undulating in waves to the breeze; and woods and sounding water, and the whole world awake and wild with joy. He wanted all to lie in an ecstacy of peace; I wanted all to sparkle, and dance in a glorious jubilee.

"I said his heaven would be only half alive, and he said mine would be drunk; I said I should fall asleep in his, and he said he could not breathe in mine, and began to grow very snappish. At last, we agreed to try both, as soon as the right weather came; and then we kissed each other and were friends. After sitting still an hour, I looked at the great room with its smooth, uncarpeted floor; and thought how nice it would be to play in, if we removed the table; and I asked Linton to call Zillah in to help us—and we'd have a game of blind-man's buff—she should try to catch us—you used to, you know, Ellen. He wouldn't; there was no pleasure in it, he said; but he consented to play at ball with me. We found two, in a cupboard, among a heap of old toys; tops, and hoops, and battledoors, and shuttlecocks. One was marked C., and the other H., I wished to have the C., because that stood for Catherine, and the H. might be for Heathcliff, his name; but the bran came out of H., and Linton didn't like it.

"I beat him constantly; and he got cross again, and coughed, and returned to his chair: that night, though, he easily recovered his good humor; he was charmed with two or three pretty songs—*your* songs, Ellen; and when I was obliged to go, he begged and entreated me to come the following evening, and I promised.

"Minny and I went flying home, as light as air: and I dreamed of Wuthering Heights, and my sweet, darling cousin, till morning.

"On the morrow I was sad; partly because you were poorly, and partly that I wished my father knew and approved of my excursions: but it was beautiful moonlight after tea; and, as I rode on, the gloom cleared.

"I shall have another happy evening, I thought to myself, and what delights me more, my pretty Linton will.

"I trotted up their garden, and was turning round to the back, when that fellow Earnshaw met me, took my bridle, and bid me go in by the front entrance. He patted Minny's neck, and said she was a bonny beast, and appeared as if he wanted me to speak to him. I only told him to leave my horse alone, or else it would kick him. He answered in his vulgar accent.

"'It wouldn't do mitch hurt if it did;' and surveyed its legs with a smile.

"I was half inclined to make it try; however, he moved off to open the door, and, as he raised the latch, he looked up to the inscription above, and said, with a stupid mixture of awkwardness and elation:

"'Miss Catherine! I can read yon, nah.'

" 'Wonderful,' I exclaimed. 'Pray let us hear you—you *are* grown clever!'

"He spelled, and drawled over by syllables, the name—

"'Hareton Earnshaw.'

" 'And the figures?' I cried, encouragingly, perceiving that he came to a dead halt.

"'I cannot tell them yet,' he answered.

"'Oh, you dunce!'" I said, laughing heartily at his failure.

"The fool stared, with a grin hovering about his lips, and a scowl gathering over his eyes, as if uncertain whether he might not join in my mirth; whether it were not pleasant familiarity, or what it really was, contempt. I settled his doubts by suddenly retrieving my gravity, and desiring him to walk away, for I came to see Linton, not him.

"He reddened—I saw that by the moonlight—dropped his hand from the latch, and skulked off, a picture of mortified vanity. He imagined himself to be as accomplished as Linton, I suppose, because he could spell his own name; and was marvelously discomfited that I didn't think the same.

"Stop, Miss Catherine, dear!" I interrupted. "I shall not scold, but I don't like your conduct there. If you had remembered that Hareton was your cousin, as much as Master Heathcliff, you would have felt how improper it was to behave in that way. At least, it was praiseworthy ambition for him to desire to be as accomplished as Linton: and probably he did not learn merely to show off; you had made him ashamed of his ignorance before—I have no doubt; and he wished to remedy it and please you. To sneer at his imperfect attempt was very bad breeding—had *you* been brought up in his circumstances, would you be less rude? he was as quick and as intelligent a child as ever you were, and I'm hurt that he should be despised now, because that base Heathcliff has treated him so unjustly."

"Well, Ellen, you won't cry about it, will you?" she exclaimed, surprised at my earnestness. "But wait, and you shall hear if he conned his *a b c*, to please me; and if it were worth while being civil to the brute. I entered, Linton was lying on the settle and half got up to welcome me.

"'I'm ill to-night, Catherine, love,' he said, 'and you must have all the talk, and let me listen. Come, and sit by me; I was sure you wouldn't break your word, and I'll make you promise again, before you go.'

"I knew now that I mustn't tease him, as he was ill; and I spoke softly and put no questions, and avoided irritating him in any way. I had brought some of my nicest books for him; he asked me to read a little of one, and I was about to comply when Earnshaw burst the door open having gathered venom with reflection. He advanced direct to us; seized Linton by the arm, and swung him off the seat.

"'Get to thy own room!' he said, in a voice almost inarticulate with passion, and his face looked swelled and furious. 'Take her there if she comes to see thee—thou shalln't keep me out of this. Begone wi' ye both!'

"He swore at us, and left Linton no time to answer, nearly throwing him into the kitchen; and he clenched his fist, as I followed, seemingly longing to knock me down. I was afraid, for a moment, and I let one volume fall; he kicked it after me, and shut us out.

"I heard a malignant, crackly laugh by the fire, and, turning, beheld that odious Joseph, standing rubbing his bony hands, and quivering.

"'Aw wer sure he'd sarve ye eht! He's a grand lad! He's getten t'raight sperrit in him! *He* knaws—aye, he knaws as weel as aw do, who sud be t'maister yonder. Ech, ech, ech! He mad ye skift properly! Ech, ech, ech!'

"'Where must we go?' I said to my cousin, disregarding the old wretch's mockery.

"Linton was white and trembling. He was not pretty then, Ellen. Oh, no; he looked frightful, for his thin face and large eyes were wrought into an expression of frantic, powerless fury. He grasped the handle of the door, and shook it. It was fastened inside.

"'If you don't let me in I'll kill you—if you don't let me in I'll kill you!' he rather shrieked than said. 'Devil! devil! I'll kill you, I'll kill you!'

"Joseph uttered his croaking laugh again.

"'Thear, that's t'father!' he cried. 'That's father! We've allas summut uh orther side in us. Niver heed, Hareton, lad—dunnut be 'feard—he cannot get at thee!'

"I took hold of Linton's hands, and tried to pull him away; but he shrieked so shockingly that I dared not proceed. At last, his cries were choked by a dreadful fit of coughing; blood gushed from his mouth, and he fell on the ground.

"I ran into the yard, sick with terror, and called for Zillah as loud as I could. She soon heard me; she was milking the cows in a shed behind the barn, and, hurrying from her work, she inquired what there was to do?

"I hadn't breath to explain; dragging her in, I looked about for Linton. Earnshaw had come out to examine the mischief he had caused, and he was then conveying the poor thing up stairs. Zillah and I ascended after him; but he stopped me at the top of the steps, and said I shouldn't go in, I must go home. I exclaimed that he had killed Linton, and I *would* enter.

"Joseph locked the door, and declared I should do 'no sich stuff,' and asked me whether I were 'bahn to be as mad as him?'

"I stood crying, till the housekeeper re-appeared; she affirmed he would be better in a bit; but he couldn't do with that shrieking and din, and she took me, and nearly carried me into the house.

"Ellen, I was ready to tear my hair off my head! I sobbed and wept, so that my eyes were almost blind; and the ruffian you have such sympathy with stood opposite, presuming every now and then to bid me 'wisht,' and denying that it was his fault; and, finally, frightened by my assertions that I would tell papa, and he should be put in prison and hanged, he commenced blubbering himself, and hurried out to hide his cowardly agitation. Still I was not rid of him. When at length they compelled me to depart, and I had got some hundred yards off the premises, he suddenly issued from the shadow of the road-side, and checked Minny and took hold of me.

"'Miss Catherine, I'm ill grieved,' he began, 'but it's rayther too bad—'

"I gave him a cut with my whip, thinking, perhaps he would murder me. He let go, thundering one of his horrid curses, and I galloped home, more than half out of my senses.

"I didn't bid you good-night that evening; and I didn't go to Wuthering Heights the next. I wished to exceedingly; but I was strangely excited, and dreaded to hear that Linton was dead, sometimes, and sometimes shuddered at the thought of encountering Hareton.

"On the third day I took courage—at least I couldn't bear longer suspense—and stole off once more. I went at five o'clock, and walked, fancying I might manage to creep into the house, and up to Linton's room, unobserved. However, the dogs gave notice of my approach; Zillah received me, and saying, 'the lad was mending nicely,' showed me into a small, tidy, carpeted apartment, where, to my inexpressible joy, I beheld Linton laid on a little sofa, reading one of my books. But he would neither speak to me nor look at me through a whole hour, Ellen. He has such an unhappy temper; and what quite confounded me, when he did open his mouth, it was to utter the falsehood, that I had occasioned the uproar, and Hareton was not to blame!

"Unable to reply, except passionately, I got up, and walked from the room. He sent after me a faint 'Catherine!' he did not reckon on being answered so—but I wouldn't turn back; and the morrow was the second day on which I stayed at home, nearly determined to visit him no more.

"But it was so miserable going to bed, and getting up, and never hearing anything about him, that my resolution melted into air, before it was properly formed. It *had* appeared wrong to take the journey once; now it seemed wrong to refrain. Michael came to ask if he must saddle Minny; I said 'Yes,' and considered myself doing a duty as she bore me over the hills. I was forced to pass the front windows to get to the court; it was no use trying to conceal my presence.

"'Young master is in the house,' said Zillah, as she saw me making for the parlor.

"I went in; Earnshaw was there also, but he quitted the room directly. Linton sat in the great arm-chair half asleep; walking up to the fire, I began in a serious tone, partly meaning it to be true.

"'As you don't like me, Linton, and as you think I come on purpose to hurt you, and pretend that I do so every time, this is our last meeting—let us say good bye; and tell Mr. Heathcliff that you have no wish to see me, and that he mustn't invent any more falsehoods on the subject.'

"'Sit down and take your hat off, Catherine,' he answered. 'You are so much happier than I am, you ought to be better. Papa talks enough of my defects, and shows enough scorn of me, to make it natural I should doubt myself. I doubt whether I am not altogether as worthless as he calls me, frequently; and then I feel so cross and bitter, I hate everybody! I *am* worthless, and bad in temper, and bad in spirit, almost always—and if you choose, you *may* say good bye—you'll get rid of an annoyance. Only, Catherine, do me this justice; believe that if I might be as sweet, and as kind, and as good as you are, I would be, as willingly, and more so, than as happy and as healthy. And, believe that your kindness has made me love you deeper than if I deserved your love, and though I couldn't, and cannot help showing my nature to you, I regret it, and repent it, and shall regret, and repent it, till I die!'

"I felt he spoke the truth; and I felt I must forgive him; and, though he should quarrel the next moment, I must forgive him again. We were reconciled, but we cried, both of us, the whole time I stayed. Not entirely for sorrow, yet I *was* sorry Linton had that distorted nature. He'll never let his friends be at ease, and he'll never be at ease himself!

"I have always gone to his little parlor, since that night; because his father returned the day after. About three times, I think, we have been merry and hopeful, as we were the first evening; the rest of my visits were dreary and troubled—now with his selfishness and spite; and now with his sufferings: but I've learned to endure the former with nearly as little resentment as the latter.

"Mr. Heathcliff purposely avoids me. I have hardly seen him at all. Last Sunday, indeed, coming earlier than usual, I heard him abusing poor Linton, cruelly, for his conduct of the night before. I can't tell how he knew of it, unless he listened. Linton had certainly behaved provokingly; however, it was the business of nobody but me; and I interrupted Mr. Heathcliff's lecture, by entering, and telling him so. He burst into a laugh, and went away, saying he was glad I took that view of the matter. Since then, I've told Linton he must whisper his bitter things.

"Now, Ellen, you have heard all; and I can't be prevented from going to Wuthering Heights, except by inflicting misery on two people—whereas, if you'll only not tell papa, my going need disturb the tranquillity of none. You'll not tell, will you? It will be very heartless if you do."

"I'll make up my mind on that point by to-morrow, Miss Catherine," I replied. "It requires some study; and so I'll leave you to your rest, and go think it over."

I thought it over aloud in my master's presence; walking straight from her room to his, and relating the whole story with the exception of her conversations with her cousin, and any mention of Hareton.

Mr. Linton was alarmed and distressed more than he would acknowledge to me. In the morning, Catherine learned my betrayal of her confidence, and she learned also that her secret visits were to end.

In vain she wept and writhed against the interdict; and implored her father to have pity on Linton: all she got to comfort her was a promise that he would write, and give him leave to come to the Grange when he pleased; but explaining that he must no longer expect to see Catherine at Wuthering Heights. Perhaps, had he been aware of his nephew's disposition and state of health, he would have seen fit to withhold even that slight consolation.

. . . .

Chapter 25

These things happened last winter, sir, said Mrs. Dean; hardly more than a year ago. Last winter, I did not think, at another twelve months' end, I should be amusing a stranger to the family with relating them! Yet, who knows how long you'll be a stranger? You're too young to rest always contented, living by yourself; and I some way fancy no one could see Catherine Linton, and not love her. You smile; but why do you look so lively and interested, when I talk about her—and why have you asked me to hang her picture over your fireplace? and why—

"Stop, my good friend!" I cried. "It may be very possible that *I* should love her; but would she love me? I doubt it too much to venture my tranquillity, by running into temptation; and then my home is not here. I'm of the busy world, and to its arms I must return. Go on. Was Catherine obedient to her father's commands?"

She was, continued the housekeeper.—Her affection for him was still the chief sentiment in her heart; and he spoke without anger; he spoke in the deep tenderness of one about to leave his treasure amid perils and foes, where his remembered words would be the only aid that he could bequeath to guide her.

He said to me, a few days afterward,

"I wish my nephew would write, Ellen, or call. Tell me, sincerely, what do you think of him; is he changed for the better, or is there a prospect of improvement, as he grows a man?"

"He's very delicate, sir," I replied; "and scarcely likely to reach manhood; but this I can say, he does not resemble his father; and if Miss Catherine had the misfortune to marry him, he would not be beyond her control, unless she were extremely and foolishly indulgent. However, master, you'll have plenty of time to get acquainted with him, and see whether he would suit her; he wants four years and more to his being of age."

Edgar sighed; and, walking to the window, looked out toward
Gimmerton Kirk. It was a misty afternoon, but the February sun
shone dimly, and we could just distinguish the two fir-trees in the
yard, and the sparely scattered gravestones.

"I've prayed often," he half soliloquized, "for the approach of
what is coming; and now I begin to shrink and fear it. I thought
the memory of the hour I came down that glen a bridegroom,
would be less sweet than the anticipation that I was soon, in a few
months, or, possibly weeks, to be carried up and laid in its lonely
hollow! Ellen, I've been very happy with my little Cathy. Through
winter nights and summer days she was a living hope at my side—
but I've been as happy musing by myself among those stones,
under that old church—lying, through the long June evenings, on
the green mound of her mother's grave, and wishing, yearning for
the time when I might lie beneath it. What can I do for Cathy?
How must I quit her? I'd not care one moment for Linton being
Heathcliff's son; nor for his taking her from me, if he could console her for my loss. I'd not care that Heathcliff gained his ends,
and triumphed in robbing me of my last blessing! But should
Linton be unworthy—only a feeble tool to his father—I cannot
abandon her to him! And, hard though it be to crush her buoyant
spirit, I must persevere in making her sad while I live, and leaving
her solitary when I die. Darling! I'd rather resign her to God, and
lay her in the earth before me."

"Resign her to God, as it is, sir," I answered, "and if we should
lose you—which may He forbid—under His providence I'll stand
her friend and counsellor to the last. Miss Catherine is a good girl;
I don't fear that she will go willfully wrong, and people who do
their duty are always finally rewarded."

Spring advanced; yet my master gathered no real strength,
though he resumed his walks in the grounds with his daughter. To
her inexperienced notions, this itself was a sign of convalescence;
and then his cheek was often flushed, and his eyes were bright; she
felt sure of his recovering.

On her seventeenth birthday he did not visit the churchyard; it
was raining, and I observed—

"You'll surely not go out to-night, sir?"

"No, I'll defer it, this year, a little longer," he answered.

He wrote again to Linton, expressing his great desire to see him;
and, had the invalid been presentable, I've no doubt his father
would have permitted him to come. As it was, being instructed, he
returned an answer, intimating that Mr. Heathcliff objected to his
calling at the Grange; but his uncle's kind remembrance delighted
him, and he hoped to meet him sometimes in his rambles, and
personally to petition that his cousin and he might not remain
long so utterly divided.

That part of his letter was simple, and, probably, his own.
Heathcliff knew he could plead eloquently enough for Catherine's
company. Then—

"I do not ask," he said, "that she may visit here; but am I never
to see her, because my father forbids me to go to her home, and
you forbid her to come to mine? Do, now and then, ride with her

toward the Heights; and let us exchange a few words in your presence! we have done nothing to deserve this separation; and you are not angry with me—you have no reason to dislike me— you allow yourself. Dear uncle! send me a kind note to-morrow; and leave to join you anywhere you please, except at Thrushcross Grange. I believe an interview would convince you that my father's character is not mine; he affirms I am more your nephew than his son; and though I have faults which render me unworthy of Catherine, she has excused them, and, for her sake, you should also. You inquire after my health—it is better; but while I remain cut off from all hope, and doomed to solitude, or to the society of those who never did, and never will like me, how can I be cheerful and well?"

Edgar, though he felt for the boy, could not consent to grant his request; because he could not accompany Catherine.

He said, in summer, perhaps, they might meet; meantime, he wished him to continue writing at intervals, and engaged to give him what advice and comfort he was able by letter; being well aware of his hard position in his family.

Linton complied; and had he been unrestrained, would probably have spoiled all by filling his epistles with complaints and lamentations; but his father kept a sharp watch over him; and, of course, insisted on every line that my master sent being shown; so instead of penning his peculiar personal sufferings and distresses, the themes constantly uppermost in his thoughts, he harped on the cruel obligation of being held asunder from his friend and love; and gently intimated that Mr. Linton must allow an interview soon, or he should fear he was purposely deceiving him with empty promises.

Cathy was a powerful ally at home: and, between them, they, at length, persuaded my master to acquiesce in their having a ride or a walk together, about once a week, under my guardianship, and on the moors nearest the Grange; for June found him still declining; and, though he had set aside yearly a portion of his income for my young lady's fortune, he had a natural desire that she might retain, or, at least, return in a short time to the house of her ancestors; and he considered her only prospect of doing that was by a union with his heir: he had no idea that the latter was failing almost as fast as himself; nor had any one, I believe; no doctor visited the Heights, and no one saw Master Heathcliff, to make report of his condition among us.

I, for my part, began to fancy my forebodings were false and that he must be actually rallying, when he mentioned riding and walking on the moors, and seemed so earnest in pursuing his object. I could not picture a father treating a dying child as tyrannically and wickedly as I afterward learned Heathcliff had treated him, to compel this apparent eagerness; his efforts redoubling the more imminently his avaricious and unfeeling plans were threatened with defeat by death.

. . . .

Chapter 26

Summer was already past its prime, when Edgar reluctantly yielded his assent to their entreaties, and Catherine and I set out on our first ride to join her cousin.

It was a close, sultry day, devoid of sunshine, but with a sky too dappled and hazy to threaten rain; and our place of meeting had been fixed at the guide-stone, by the cross-roads. On arriving there, however, a little herd-boy, dispatched as a messenger, told us that—

"Maister Linton wer just ut this side th' Heights, and he'd be mitch obleeged to us to gang on a bit further."

"Then Master Linton has forgot the first injunction of his uncle," I observed: "he bid us keep on the Grange land, and here we are, off at once."

"Well, we'll turn our horses' heads round when we reach him," answered my companion; "our excursion shall lie toward home."

But when we reached him, and that was scarcely a quarter of a mile from his own door, we found he had no horse, and we were forced to dismount, and leave ours to graze.

He lay on the heath, awaiting our approach, and did not rise till we came within a few yards. Then he walked so feebly, and looked so pale, that I immediately exclaimed—

"Why, Master Heathcliff, you are not fit for enjoying a ramble this morning. How ill you do look!"

Catherine surveyed him with grief and astonishment, and changed the ejaculation of joy on her lips to one of alarm, and the congratulation on their long-postponed meeting to an anxious inquiry whether he were worse than usual?

"No—better—better!" he panted, trembling, and retaining her hand as if he needed its support, while his large blue eyes wandered timidly over her, the hollowness round them transforming to haggard wildness the languid expression they once possessed.

"But you have been worse," persisted his cousin, "worse than when I saw you last—you are thinner, and—"

"I'm tired," he interrupted, hurriedly. "It is too hot for walking: let us rest here. And in the morning I often feel sick—papa says I grow so fast."

Badly satisfied, Cathy sat down, and he reclined beside her.

"This is something like your paradise," said she, making an effort at cheerfulness. "You recollect the two days we agreed to spend in the place and way each thought pleasantest? This is nearly yours, only there are clouds; but then, they are so soft and mellow, it is nicer than sunshine. Next week, if you can, we'll ride down to the Grange Park, and try mine."

Linton did not appear to remember what she talked of, and he had evidently great difficulty in sustaining any kind of conversation. His lack of interest in the subjects she started, and his equal incapacity to contribute to her entertainment, were so obvious that she could not conceal her disappointment. An indefinite alteration had come over his whole person and manner. The pettishness that might be caressed into fondness had yielded to a listless apathy; there was less of the peevish temper of a child which frets and teases on purpose to be soothed, and more of the self-absorbed moroseness of a confirmed invalid, repelling consolation, and ready to regard the good-humored mirth of others as an insult.

Catherine perceived, as well as I did, that he held it rather a punishment than a gratification to endure our company; and she made no scruple of proposing, presently, to depart. That proposal, unexpectedly, roused Linton from his lethargy, and threw him into a strange state of agitation. He glanced fearfully toward the Heights, begging she would remain another half-hour at least.

"But, I think," said Cathy, "you'd be more comfortable at home than sitting here; and I can not amuse you to-day, I see, by my tales, and songs, and chatter. You have grown wiser than I, in these six months; you have little taste for my diversions now; or else, if I could amuse you, I'd willingly stay."

"Stay to rest yourself," he replied. "And, Catherine, don't think or say that I'm *very* unwell—it is the heavy weather and heat that make me dull; and I walked about, before you came, a great deal, for me. Tell uncle, I'm in tolerable health, will you?"

"I'll tell him that *you* say so, Linton. I couldn't affirm that you are," observed my young lady, wondering at his pertinacious assertion of what was evidently an untruth.

"And be here again next Thursday," continued he, shunning her puzzled gaze. "And give him my thanks for permitting you to come—my best thanks, Catherine. And—and, if you *did* meet my father, and he asked you about me, don't lead him to suppose that I've been extremely silent and stupid—don't look sad and downcast, as you *are* doing—he'll be angry."

"I care nothing for his anger," exclaimed Cathy, imagining she would be its object.

"But I do," said her cousin, shuddering. "*Don't* provoke him against me, Catherine, for he is very hard."

"Is he severe to you, Master Heathcliff?" I inquired." Has he grown weary of indulgence, and passed from passive to active hatred?"

Linton looked at me, but did not answer; and after keeping her seat by his side another ten minutes, during which his head fell drowsily on his breast, and he uttered nothing except suppressed moans of exhaustion, or pain, Cathy began to seek solace in looking for bilberries, and sharing the produce of her researches with me: she did not offer them to him, for she saw further notice would only weary and annoy.

"Is it half an hour now, Ellen!" she whispered in my ear at last. "I can't tell why we should stay. He's asleep, and papa will be wanting us back."

"Well, we must not leave him asleep," I answered; "wait till he wakes, and be patient. You were mighty eager to set off, but your longing to see poor Linton has soon evaporated."

"Why did *he* wish to see me?" returned Catherine. "In his crossest humors, formerly, I liked him better than I do in his present curious mood. It's just as if it were a task he was compelled to perform—this interview—for fear his father should scold him. But I'm hardly going to come to give Mr. Heathcliff pleasure; whatever reason he may have for ordering Linton to undergo this penance. And, though I'm glad he's better in health, I'm sorry he's so much less pleasant, and so much less affectionate to me."

"You think *he is* better in health, then?" I said.

"Yes," she answered; "because he always made such a great deal of his sufferings, you know. He is not tolerably well, as he told me to tell papa, but he's better, very likely."

"There you differ with me, Miss Cathy," I remarked; "I should conjecture him to be far worse."

Linton here started from his slumber, in bewildered terror and asked if any one had called his name.

"No," said Catherine; "unless in dreams. I cannot conceive how you manage to doze, out of doors, in the morning."

"I thought I heard my father," he gasped, glancing up to the frowning nab above us. "You are sure nobody spoke?"

"Quite sure," replied his cousin. "Only Ellen and I were disputing concerning your health. Are you truly stronger, Linton, than when we separated in winter? If you be, I'm certain one thing is not stronger—your regard for me—speak, are you?"

Tears gushed from Linton's eyes as he answered—

"Yes, yes, I am!"

And, still under the spell of the imaginary voice, his gaze wandered up and down to detect its owner. Cathy rose.

"For to-day we must part," she said. "And I won't conceal that I have been sadly disappointed with our meeting, though I'll mention it to nobody but you—not that I stand in awe of Mr. Heathcliff!"

"Hush," murmured Linton; "for God's sake, hush! He's coming." And he clung to Catherine's arm, striving to detain her; but, at that announcement, she hastily disengaged herself, and whistled to Minny, who obeyed her like a dog.

"I'll be here next Thursday," she cried, springing to the saddle. "Good bye. Quick, Ellen!"

And so we left him, scarcely conscious of our departure, so absorbed was he in anticipating his father's approach.

Before we reached home, Catherine's displeasure softened into a perplexed sensation of pity and regret, largely blended with vague, uneasy doubts about Linton's actual circumstances, physical and social; in which I partook, though I counselled her not to say much, for a second journey would make us better judges.

My master requested an account of our ongoings: his nephew's offering of thanks was duly delivered, Miss Cathy gently touching on the rest: I also threw little light on his inquiries, for I hardly knew what to hide and what to reveal.

·······

Chapter 27

Seven days glided away, every one marking its course by the henceforth rapid alteration of Edgar Linton's state. The havoc that months had previously wrought was now emulated by the inroads of hours. Catherine we would fain have deluded, yet but her own quick spirit refused to delude her. It divined in secret, and brooded on the dreadful probability, gradually ripening into certainty.

She had not the heart to mention her ride, when Thursday came round; I mentioned it for her, and obtained permission to order her out of doors; for the library, where her father stopped a short time daily, the brief period he could bear to sit up, and the chamber, had become her whole world. She grudged each moment that did not find her bending over his pillow, or seated by his side. Her countenance grew wan with watching and sorrow, and my master gladly dismissed her to what he flattered himself would be a happy change of scene and society, drawing comfort from the hope that she would not now be left entirely alone after his death.

He had a fixed idea, I guessed by several observations he let fall, that as his nephew resembled him in person, he would resemble him in mind; for Linton's letters bore few, or no indications of his defective character. And I, through pardonable weakness, refrained from correcting the error; asking myself what good there would be in disturbing his last moments with information that he had neither power nor opportunity to turn to account.

We deferred our excursion till the afternoon; a golden afternoon of August—every breath from the hills so full of life, that it seemed whoever respired it, though dying, might revive. Catherine's face was just like the landscape—shadows and sunshine flitting over it in rapid succession; but the shadows rested longer and the sunshine was more transient, and her poor little heart reproached itself for even that passing forgetfulness of its cares.

We discerned Linton watching at the same spot he had selected before. My young mistress alighted, and told me that as she was resolved to stay a very little while, I had better hold the pony and remain on horseback; but I dissented, I wouldn't risk losing sight of the charge committed to me a minute; so we climbed the slope of heath together.

Master Heathcliff received us with greater animation on this occasion; not the animation of high spirits, though, nor yet of joy; it looked more like fear.

"It is late!" he said, speaking short, and with difficulty. "Is not your father very ill? I thought you wouldn't come."

"*Why* won't you be candid?" cried Catherine, swallowing her greeting. "Why cannot you say at once, you don't want me? It is strange, Linton, that for the second time you have brought me here on purpose, apparently, to distress us both, and for no reason besides!"

Linton shivered, and glanced at her, half supplicating, half ashamed, but his cousin's patience was not sufficient to endure this enigmatical behavior.

"My father *is* very ill," she said, "and why am I called from his bedside—why didn't you send to absolve me from my promise when you wished I wouldn't keep it? Come! I desire an explanation—playing and trifling are completely banished out of my mind; and I can't dance attendance on your affectations now!"

"My affectations!" he murmured, "what are they? For heaven's sake, Catherine, don't look so angry! Despise me as much as you please; I am a worthless, cowardly wretch—I can't be scorned enough! but I'm too mean for your anger—hate my father, and spare me—for contempt!"

"Nonsense!" cried Catherine, in a passion. "Foolish, silly boy! And there! he trembles, as if I were really going to touch him! You needn't bespeak contempt, Linton; anybody will have it spontaneously at your service. Get off! I shall return home—it is folly dragging you from the hearth stone, and pretending—what do we pretend? Let go my frock—if I pitied you for crying and looking so very frightened, you should spurn such pity! Ellen, tell him how disgraceful this conduct is. Rise, and don't degrade yourself into an abject reptile—*don't*."

With streaming face and an expression of agony, Linton had thrown his nerveless frame along the ground; he seemed convulsed with exquisite terror.

"Oh!" he sobbed, "I cannot bear it! Catherine, Catherine, I'm a traitor, too, and I dare not tell you! But leave me and I shall be killed! *Dear* Catherine, my life is in your hands; and you have said you loved me—and if you did it wouldn't harm you. You'll not go, then? kind, sweet, good Catherine! And perhaps you *will* consent—and he'll let me die with you!"

My young lady, on witnessing his intense anguish, stooped to raise him. The old feeling of indulgent tenderness overcame her vexation, and she grew thoroughly moved and alarmed.

"Consent to what?" she asked. "To stay? Tell me the meaning of this strange talk, and I will. You contradict your own words, and distract me! Be calm and frank, and confess at once all that weighs on your heart. You wouldn't injure me, Linton, would you? You wouldn't let any enemy hurt me, if you could prevent it? I'll believe you are a coward, for yourself, but not a cowardly betrayer of your best friend."

"But my father threatened me," gasped the boy, clasping his attenuated fingers, "and I dread him—I dread him! I *dare* not tell!"

"Oh, well!" said Catherine, with scornful compassion, "keep your secret, *I'm* no coward—save yourself, I'm not afraid!"

Her magnanimity provoked his tears; he wept wildly; kissing

her supporting hands, and yet could not summon courage to speak out.

I was cogitating what the mystery might be, and determined Catherine should never suffer, to benefit him or anyone else, by my good will. When, hearing a rustle among the ling, I looked up, and saw Mr. Heathcliff almost close upon us, descending the Heights. He didn't cast a glance toward my companions, though they were sufficiently near for Linton's sobs to be audible; but hailing me, in the almost hearty tone he assumed to none besides, and the sincerity of which I couldn't avoid doubting, he said,

"It is something to see you so near to my house, Nelly! How are you at the Grange? Let us hear! The rumor goes," he added in a lower tone, "that Edgar Linton is on his deathbed—perhaps they exaggerate his illness?"

"No; my master is dying," I replied, "it is true enough. A sad thing it will be for us all, but a blessing for him!"

"How long will he last, do you think?" he asked.

"I don't know," I said.

"Because," he continued, looking at the two young people, who were fixed under his eye—Linton appeared as if he could not venture to stir, or raise his head, and Catherine could not move, on his account—"because that lad yonder, seems determined to beat me—and I'd thank his uncle to be quick and go before him. Hallo! Has the whelp been playing that game long? I *did* give him some lessons about snivelling. Is he pretty lively with Miss Linton generally?"

"Lively? no—he has shown the greatest distress;" I answered. "To see him, I should say that, instead of rambling with his sweetheart on the hills, he ought to be in bed, under the hands of a doctor."

"He shall be, in a day or two," muttered Heathcliff. "But first—get up, Linton! Get up!" he shouted. "Don't grovel on the ground there—up this moment!"

Linton had sunk prostrate again in another paroxysm of helpless fear, caused by his father's glance toward him, I suppose; there was nothing else to produce such humiliation. He made several efforts to obey, but his little strength was annihilated, for the time, and he fell back again with a moan. Mr. Heathcliff advanced, and lifted him to lean against a ridge of turf.

"Now," said he with curbed ferocity, "I'm getting angry—and if you don't command that paltry spirit of yours—*Damn* you! Get up, directly!"

"I will, father!" he panted. "Only, let me alone, or I shall faint! I've done as you wished, I'm sure. Catherine will tell you that I—that I—have been cheerful. Ah! keep by me, Catherine; give me your hand."

"Take mine," said his father; "stand on your feet! There now—she'll lend you her arm—that's right—look at *her*. You would imagine I was the devil himself, Miss Linton, to excite such horror. Be so kind as to walk home with him, will you? He shudders if I touch him."

"Linton, dear," whispered Catherine, "I can't go to Wuthering

Heights—papa has forbidden me. He'll not harm you, why are you so afraid?"

"I can never re-enter that house," he answered. "I am *not* to re-enter it without you."

"Stop—" cried his father. "We'll respect Catherine's filial scruples. Nelly, take him in, and I'll follow your advice concerning the doctor, without delay."

"You'll do well," replied I, "but I must remain with my mistress. To mind your son is not my business."

"You are very stiff!" said Heathcliff, "I know that—but you'll force me to pinch the baby, and make it scream, before it moves your charity. Come, then, my hero, are you willing to return, escorted by me?"

He approached once more, and made as if he would seize the fragile being; but shrinking back, Linton clung to his cousin, and implored her to accompany him, with a frantic importunity that admitted no denial.

However I disapproved, I couldn't hinder her; indeed how could she have refused him herself? What was filling him with dread we had no means of discerning; but there he was, powerless under its gripe, and any addition seemed capable of shocking him into idiocy. We reached the threshold; Catherine walked in; and I stood waiting till she had conducted the invalid to a chair, expecting her out immediately, when Mr. Heathcliff, pushing me forward, exclaimed,—

"My house is not stricken with the plague, Nelly; and I have a mind to be hospitable to-day; sit down, and allow me to shut the door."

He shut and locked it also. I started.

"You shall have tea before you go home," he added. "I am by myself. Hareton is gone with some cattle to the Lees—and Zillah and Joseph are off on a journey of pleasure. And, though I'm used to being alone, I'd rather have some interesting company if I can get it. Miss Linton, take your seat by *him*. I give you what I have; the present is hardly worth accepting; but I have nothing else to offer—it is Linton I mean. How she does stare! It's odd what a savage feeling I have to anything that seems afraid of me! Had I been born where laws are less strict, and tastes less dainty, I should treat myself to a slow vivifisection of those two, as an evening's amusement."

He drew in his breath, struck the table, and swore to himself, "By hell! I hate them."

"I'm not afraid of you!" exclaimed Catherine, who could not hear the latter part of his speech.

She stepped close up; her black eyes flashing with passion and resolution.

"Give me that key—I will have it!" she said. "I wouldn't eat or drink here if I were starving."

Heathcliff had the key in his hand that remained on the table. He looked up, seized with a sort of surprise at her boldness, or, possibly, reminded, by her voice and glance, of the person from whom she inherited it.

She snatched at the instrument, and half succeeded in getting it out of his loosened fingers; but her action recalled him to the present; he recovered it speedily.

"Now, Catherine Linton," he said, "stand off, or I shall knock you down; and that will make Mrs. Dean mad."

Regardless of this warning, she captured his closed hand, and its contents again.

"We *will* go!" she repeated, exerting her utmost efforts to cause the iron muscles to relax; and finding that her nails made no impression, she applied her teeth pretty sharply.

Heathcliff glanced at me a glance that kept me from interfering a moment. Catherine was too intent on his fingers to notice his face. He opened them, suddenly, and resigned the object of dispute; but, ere she had well secured it, he seized her with the liberated hand, and, pulling her on his knee, administered, with the other, a shower of terrific slaps on both sides of the head, each sufficient to have fulfilled his threat, had she been able to fall.

At this diabolical violence, I rushed on him furiously,

"You villain!" I began to cry, "you villain!"

A touch on the chest silenced me; I am stout, and soon put out of breath; and, what with that and the rage, I staggered dizzily back, and felt ready to suffocate, or to burst a bloodvessel.

The scene was over in two minutes; Catherine, released, put her two hands to her temples, and looked just as if she were not sure whether her ears were off or on. She trembled like a reed, poor thing, and leaned against the table perfectly bewildered.

"I know how to chastise children, you see," said the scoundrel, grimly, as he stooped to repossess himself of the key, which had dropped to the floor. "Go to Linton now, as I told you; and cry at your ease! I shall be your father to-morrow—all the father you'll have in a few days—and you shall have plenty of that—you can bear plenty—you're no weakling—you shall have a daily taste, if I catch such a devil of a temper in your eyes again!"

Cathy ran to me instead of Linton, and knelt down, and put her burning cheek on my lap, weeping aloud. Her cousin had shrunk into a corner of the settle, as quiet as a mouse, congratulating himself, I dare say, that the correction had lighted on another than him.

Mr. Heathcliff, perceiving us all confounded, rose, and expeditiously made the tea himself. The cups and saucers were laid ready. He poured it out, and handed me a cup.

"Wash away your spleen," he said. "And help your own naughty pet and mine. It is not poisoned, though I prepared it. I'm going out to seek your horses."

Our first thought, on his departure, was to force an exit somewhere. We tried the kitchen door, but that was fastened outside; we looked at the windows—they were too narrow for even Cathy's little figure.

"Master Linton," I cried, seeing we were regularly imprisoned, "you know what your diabolical father is after, and you shall tell us, or I'll box your ears, as he has done your cousin's."

"Yes, Linton; you must tell," said Catherine. "It was for your sake I came; and it will be wickedly ungrateful if you refuse."

"Give me some, tea. I'm thirsty, and then I'll tell you," he answered. "Mrs. Dean, go away. I don't like you standing over me. Now, Catherine, you are letting your tears fall into my cup! I won't drink that. Give me another."

Catherine pushed another to him, and wiped her face. I felt disgusted at the little wretch's composure, since he was no longer in terror for himself. The anguish he had exhibited on the moor subsided as soon as ever he entered Wuthering Heights; so I guessed he had been menaced with an awful visitation of wrath, if he failed in decoying us there; and, that accomplished, he had no further immediate fears.

"Papa wants us to be married," he continued, after sipping some of the liquid. "And he knows your papa wouldn't let us marry now; and he's afraid of my dying if we wait; so we are to be married in the morning, and you are to stay here all night; and if you do as he wishes you shall return home next day, and take me with you."

"Take you with her, pitiful changeling?" I exclaimed. "*You* marry? Why, the man is mad, or he thinks us fools, every one. And do you imagine that beautiful young lady, that healthy, hearty girl, will tie herself to a little perishing monkey like you? Are you cherishing the notion that *anybody*, let alone Miss Catherine Linton, would have you for a husband? You want whipping for bringing us in here at all, with your dastardly, puling tricks; and—don't look so silly now! I've a very good mind to shake you severely, for your contemptible treachery, and your imbecile conceit."

I did give him a slight shaking, but it brought on the cough, and he took to his ordinary resource of moaning and weeping, and Catherine rebuked me.

"Stay all night? No!" she said, looking slowly round. "Ellen, I'll burn that door down, but I'll get out."

And she would have commenced the execution of her threat directly, but Linton was up in alarm, for his dear self, again. He clasped her in his two feeble arms, sobbing—

"Won't you have me, and save me—not let me come to the Grange? Oh! darling Catherine! you mustn't go, and leave me, after all. You *must* obey my father, you *must!*"

"I must obey my own," she replied, "and relieve him from this cruel suspense. The whole night! What would he think? He'll be distressed already. I'll either break or burn a way out of the house. Be quiet! You're in no danger—but if you hinder me, Linton—I love papa better than you!"

The mortal terror he felt of Mr. Heathcliff's anger, restored to the boy his coward's eloquence. Catherine was near distraught—still she persisted that she must go home, and tried entreaty, in her turn, persuading him to subdue his selfish agony.

While they were thus occupied, our jailer re-entered.

"Your beasts have trotted off," he said; "and—now, Linton!

sniveling again? What has she been doing to you? Come, come, have done, and get to bed. In a month or two, my lad, you'll be able to pay her back her present tyrannies, with a vigorous hand—you're pining for pure love, are you not? nothing else in the world—and she shall have you! There, to bed! Zillah won't be here tonight—you must undress yourself. Hush! hold your noise! Once in your own room, I'll not come near you, you needn't fear. By chance, you've managed tolerably. I'll look to the rest."

He spoke these words, holding the door open for his son to pass; and the latter achieved his exit exactly as a spaniel might which suspected the person who attended on it of designing a spiteful squeeze.

The lock was re-secured. Heathcliff approached the fire, where my mistress and I stood silent. Catherine looked up, and instinctively raised her hand to her cheek—his neighborhood revived a painful sensation. Anybody else would have been incapable of regarding the childish act with sternness, but he scowled on her, and muttered—

"Oh, you are not afraid of me? Your courage is well disguised—you *seem* damnably afraid!"

"I *am* afraid now," she replied; "because if I stay, papa will be miserable; and how can I endure making him miserable—when he—when he—Mr. Heathcliff, *let* me go home! I promise to marry Linton—papa would like me to, and I love him—and why should you wish to force me to do what I'll willingly do of myself?"

"Let him dare to force you!" I cried. "There's law in the land, thank God, there is! though we *be* in an out-of-the-way place. I'd inform, if he were my own son, and it's felony without benefit of clergy!"

"Silence!" said the ruffian. "To the devil with your clamor! I don't want *you* to speak. Miss Linton, I shall enjoy myself remarkably in thinking your father will be miserable; I shall not sleep for satisfaction. You could have hit on no surer way of fixing your residence under my roof, for the next twenty-four hours, than informing me that such an event would follow. As to your promise to marry Linton, I'll take care you shall keep it, for you shall not quit the place till it is fulfilled."

"Send Ellen then, to let papa know I'm safe!" exclaimed Catherine, weeping bitterly. "Or marry me now. Poor papa! Ellen, he'll think we're lost. What shall we do?"

"Not he! He'll think you are tired of waiting on him, and run off for a little amusement," answered Heathcliff. "You cannot deny that you entered my house of your own accord, in contempt of his injunctions to the contrary. And it is quite natural that you should desire amusement at your age; and that you should weary of nursing a sick man, and that man *only* your father. Catherine, his happiest days were over when your days began. He cursed you, I dare say, for coming into the world—I did, at least. And it would just do if he cursed you as *he* went out of it. I'd join him. I don't love you! How should I? Weep away. As far as I can see, it will be your chief diversion hereafter, unless Linton make amends for other losses, and your provident parent appears to fancy he may. His letters of advice and consolation entertained me vastly. In his last, he recommended my jewel to be careful of his; and kind to her when he got her. Careful and kind—that's paternal! But Linton requires his whole stock of care and kindness for himself. Linton can play the little tyrant well. He'll undertake to torture any number of cats, if their teeth be drawn and their claws pared. You'll be able to tell his uncle fine tales of his *kindness*, when you get home again, I assure you."

"You're right there!" I said, "explain your son's character. Show his resemblance to yourself; and then, I hope, Miss Cathy will think twice, before she takes the cockatrice!"

"I don't much mind speaking of his amiable qualities now," he answered, "because she must either accept him, or remain a prisoner, and you along with her, till your master dies. I can detain you both, quite concealed, here. If you doubt, encourage her to retract her word, and you'll have an opportunity of judging!"

"I'll not retract my word," said Catherine. "I'll marry him, within this hour, if I may go to Thrushcross Grange afterward. Mr. Heathcliff, you're a cruel man, but you're not a fiend; and you won't, from *mere* malice, destroy, irrevocably, all my happiness. If papa thought I had left him on purpose; and if he died before I returned, could I bear to live? I've given over crying; but I'm going to kneel here, at your knee, and I'll not get up, and I'll not take my eyes from your face, till you look back at me! No, don't turn away! *do* look! You'll see nothing to provoke you. I don't hate you. I'm not angry that you struck me. Have you never loved *anybody*, in all your life, uncle? *never*? Ah! you must look once—I'm so wretched—you can't help being sorry and pitying me."

"Keep your eft's fingers off; and move, or I'll kick you!" cried Heathcliff, brutally repulsing her. "I'd rather be hugged by a snake. How the devil can you dream of fawning on me? I *detest* you!"

He shrugged his shoulders—shook himself, indeed, as if his flesh crept with aversion—and thrust back his chair: while I got up, and opened my mouth to commence a downright torrent of abuse; but I was rendered dumb in the middle of the first sentence, by a threat that I should be shown into a room by myself, the very next syllable I uttered.

It was growing dark—we heard a sound of voices at the garden gate. Our host hurried out, instantly; *he* had his wits about him; *we* had not. There was a talk of two or three minutes, and he returned alone.

"I thought it had been your cousin Hareton," I observed to Catherine. "I wish he would arrive! Who knows but he might take our part?"

"It was three servants sent to seek you from the Grange," said Heathcliff, overhearing me. "You should have opened a lattice and called out; but I could swear that chit is glad you didn't. She's glad to be obliged to stay, I'm certain."

At learning the chance we had missed, we both gave vent to our grief without control; and he allowed us to wail on till nine o'clock; then he bid us to up-stairs, through the kitchen, to Zillah's chamber; and I whispered my companion to obey; perhaps we might contrive to get through the window there, or into a garret, and out by its skylight.

The window, however, was narrow like those below, and the garret trap was safe from our attempts; for we were fastened in as before. We neither of us lay down: Catherine took her station by the lattice, and watched anxiously for morning—a deep sigh being the only answer I could obtain to my frequent entreaties that she would try to rest.

I seated myself in a chair, and rocked to and fro, passing harsh judgment on my many derelictions of duty; from which, it struck me then, all the misfortunes of all my employers sprang. It was not the case, in reality, I am aware; but it was, in my imagination, that dismal night, and I thought Heathcliff himself less guilty than I.

At seven o'clock he came, and inquired if Miss Linton had risen. She ran to the door immediately, and answered—

"Yes."

"Here, then," he said, opening it, and pulling her out.

I rose to follow, but he turned the lock again. I demanded my release.

"Be patient," he replied; "I'll send up your breakfast in a while."

I thumped on the panels, and rattled the latch angrily; and Catherine asked why I was still shut up? He answered, I must try to endure it another hour, and they went away. I endured it two or three hours; at length, I heard a footstep, not Heathcliff's.

"I've brought you something to eat," said a voice; "oppen t' door!"

Complying eagerly, I beheld Hareton, laden with food enough to last me all day.

"Tak it!" he added, thrusting the tray into my hand.

"Stay one minute," I began.

"Nay!" cried he, and retired, regardless of any prayers I could pour forth to detain him.

"And there I remained enclosed the whole day, and the whole of the next night; and another and another. Five nights and four days I remained, altogether, seeing nobody but Hareton, once every morning; and he was a model of a jailer—surly, and dumb, and deaf to every attempt at moving his sense of justice or compassion.

. . . .

Chapter 28

On the fifth morning, or rather afternoon, a different step approached—lighter and shorter—and, this time, the person entered the room. It was Zillah; donned in her scarlet shawl, with a black silk bonnet on her head, and a willow basket swung to her arm.

"Eh, dear! Mrs. Dean," she exclaimed. "Well! there is a talk about you at Gimmerton. I never thought but you were sunk in the Blackhorse marsh, and Missy with you, till master told me you'd been found, and he'd lodged you here! What, and you must have got on an island, sure? And how long were you in the hole? Did master save you, Mrs. Dean? But you're not so thin—you've not been so poorly, have you?"

"Your master is a true scoundrel!" I replied. "But he shall answer for it. He needn't have raised that tale—it shall all be laid bare!"

"What do you mean?" asked Zillah. "It's not his tale—they tell that in the village—about your being lost in the marsh; and I calls to Earnshaw, when I come in—

"Eh, they's queer things, Mr. Hareton, happened since I went off. It's a sad pity of that likely young lass, and cant Nelly Dean.'

"He stared. I thought he had not heard aught, so I told him the rumor.

"The master listened, and he just smiled to himself, and said—

'If they have been in the marsh, they are out now, Zillah. Nelly Dean is lodged, at this minute, in your room. You can tell her to flit, when you go up; here is the key. The bogwater got into her head, and she would have run home, quite flighty, but I fixed her, till she came round to her senses. You can bid her go to the Grange at once, if she be able, and carry a message from me, that her young lady will follow in time to attend the squire's funeral.'"

"Mr. Edgar is not dead?" I gasped. "Oh! Zillah, Zillah!"

"No, no—sit you down, my good mistress," she replied, "You're right sickly yet. He's not dead: Doctor Kenneth thinks he may last another day—I met him on the road and asked."

Instead of sitting down, I snatched my outdoor things, and hastened below, for the way was free.

On entering the house, I looked about for someone to give information of Catherine.

The place was filled with sunshine, and the door stood wide open, but nobody seemed at hand.

As I hesitated whether to go off at once, or return and seek my mistress, a slight cough drew my attention to the hearth.

Linton lay on the settle, sole tenant, sucking a stick of sugar candy, and pursuing my movements with apathetic eyes.

"Where is Miss Catherine?" I demanded sternly, supposing I could frighten him into giving intelligence, by catching him thus alone.

He sucked like an innocent.

"Is she gone?" I said.

"No," he replied; "she's up-stairs—she's not to go; we won't let her."

"You won't let her, little idiot!" I exclaimed. "Direct me to her room immediately, or I'll make you sing out sharply."

"Papa would make you sing out, if you attempted to get there," he answered. "He says I'm not to be soft with Catherine—she's my wife, and it's shameful that she should wish to leave me! He says, she hates me, and wants me to die, that she may have my money, but she shan't have it; and she shan't go home! she never shall! she may cry, and be sick as much as she pleases!"

He resumed his former occupation, closing his lids, as if he meant to drop asleep.

"Master Heathcliff," I resumed, "have you forgotten all Catherine's kindness to you, last winter, when you affirmed you loved her, and when she brought you books, and sung you songs, and came many a time through wind and snow to see you? She wept to miss one evening, because you would be disappointed; and you felt then that she was a hundred times too good to you; and now you believe the lies your father tells, though you know he detests you both! And you join him against her. That's fine gratitude, is it not?"

The corner of Linton's mouth fell, and he took the sugar candy from his lips.

"Did she come to Wuthering Heights, because she hated you?" I continued. "Think for yourself! As to your money, she does not even know that you will have any. And you say she's sick; and yet, you leave her alone, up there in a strange house! *You*, who have felt what it is to be so neglected! You could pity your own sufferings, and she pitied them, too, but you won't pity hers! I shed tears Master Heathcliff, you see—an elderly woman, and a servant merely—and you, after pretending such affection, and having reason to worship her, almost, store every tear you have for yourself, and lie there quite at ease. Ah! you're a heartless, selfish boy!"

"I can't stay with her," he answered crossly. "I'll not stay, by myself. She cries so I can't bear it. And she won't give over, though I say I'll call my father. I did call him once; and he threatened to strangle her, if she was not quiet; but she began again the instant, he left the room; moaning and grieving all night long, though I screamed for vexation that I couldn't sleep."

"Is Mr. Heathcliff out," I inquired, perceiving that the wretched creature had no power to sympathize with his cousin's mental tortures.

"He's in the court," he replied, "talking to Doctor Kenneth who says uncle is dying, truly, at last. I'm glad, for I shall be master of the Grange after him—Catherine always spoke of it as *her house*. It isn't hers! It's mine— papa says everything she has is mine. All her nice books are mine—she offered to give me them, and her pretty birds, and her pony Minny, if I would get the key of our room, and let her out: but I told her she had nothing to give, they were all, all mine. And then she cried, and took a little picture from her neck, and said I should have that—two pictures in a gold case—on one side her mother, and on the other, uncle, when they were young. That was yesterday. I said *they* were mine, too; and tried to get them from her. The spiteful thing wouldn't let me; she pushed me off, and hurt me. I shrieked out—that frightened her—she heard papa coming, and she broke the hinges and divided the case, and gave me her mother's portrait; the other she attempted to hide; but papa asked what was the matter, and I explained it. He took the one I had away; and ordered her to resign hers to me; she refused, and he—he struck her down and wrenched it off the chain, and crushed it with his foot."

"And were you pleased to see her struck?" I asked: having my designs in encouraging his talk.

"I winked," he answered. "I wink to see my father strike a dog, or a horse, he does it so hard—yet I was glad at first—she deserved punishing for pushing me: but when papa was gone she made me come to the window and showed me her cheek cut on the inside against her teeth, and her mouth filling with blood: and then she gathered up the bits of the picture, and went and sat down with her face to the wall, and she has never spoken to me since; and I sometimes think she can't speak for pain. I don't like to think so! but she's a naughty thing for crying continually; and she looks so pale and wild, I'm afraid of her!"

"And you can get the key if you choose!" I said

"Yes, when I am up-stairs," he answered, "but I can't walk up-stairs now."

"In what apartment is it?" I asked.

"Oh," he cried, "I shan't tell *you* where it is! It is our secret. Nobody, neither Hareton nor Zillah, are to know. There! you've tired me—go away, go away!" And he turned his face upon his arm, and shut his eyes again.

I considered it best to depart without seeing Mr. Heathcliff; and bring a rescue for my young lady from the Grange.

On reaching it, the astonishment of my fellow servants to see me, and their joy also, was intense; and when they heard that their little mistress was safe, two or three were about to hurry up, and shout the news at Mr. Edgar's door: but I bespoke the announcement of it myself.

How changed I found him, even in those few days! He lay an image of sadness and resignation, waiting his death. Very young he looked: though his actual age was thirty-nine; one would have called him ten years younger, at least. He thought of Catherine, for he murmured her name. I touched his hand and spoke.

"Catherine is coming, dear master!" I whispered; "she is alive and well, and will be here I hope to-night."

I trembled at the first effects of this intelligence: he half rose up, looked eagerly round the apartment, and then sunk back in a swoon.

As soon as he recovered I related our compulsory visit and detention at the Heights: I said Heathcliff forced me to go in, which was not quite true; I uttered as little as possible against Linton; nor did I describe all his father's brutal conduct—my intentions being to add no bitterness, if I could help it, to his already overflowing cup.

He divined that one of his enemy's purposes was to secure the personal property as well as the estate to his son, or rather himself; yet why he did not wait till his decease was a puzzle to my master; because ignorant how nearly he and his nephew would quit the world together.

However, he felt his will had better be altered; instead of leaving

Catherine's fortune at her own disposal, he determined to put it in the hands of trustees, for her use during life; and for her children, if she had any, after her. By that means it could not fall to Mr. Heathcliff, should Linton die.

Having received his orders I dispatched a man to fetch the attorney, and four more, provided with serviceable weapons, to demand my young lady of her jailer. Both parties were delayed very late. The single servant returned first.

He said Mr. Green, the lawyer, was out when he arrived at his house, and he had to wait two hours for his re-entrance; and then Mr. Green told him he had a little business in the village that must be done, but he would be at Thrushcross Grange before morning.

The four men came back unaccompanied also. They brought word that Catherine was ill; too ill to quit her room: and Heathcliff could not suffer them to see her.

I scolded the stupid fellows well for listening to that tale, which I would not carry to my master, resolving to take a whole bevy up to the Heights, at daylight, and storm it literally, unless the prisoner were quietly surrendered to us.

Her father *shall* see her, I vowed, and vowed again, if that devil be killed on his own door-stones in trying to prevent it!

Happily I was spared the journey and the trouble.

I had gone down stairs at three o'clock to fetch a jug of water; and was passing through the hall with it in my hand, when a sharp knock at the front door made me jump.

"Oh! it is Green," I said, recollecting myself, "only Green"— and I went on, intending to send somebody else to open it: but the knock was repeated, not loud, and still importunately.

I put the jug on the bannister, and hastened to admit him myself.

The harvest moon shone clear outside. It was not the attorney. My sweet little mistress sprung on my neck, sobbing,

"Ellen! Ellen! is papa alive?"

"Yes," I cried, "yes , my angel , he is. God be thanked, you are safe with us again!"

She wanted to run, breathless as she was, up-stairs to Mr. Linton's room; but I compelled her to sit down on a chair, and made her drink, and washed her pale face, chafing it into a faint color with my apron. Then I said I must go first, and tell of her arrival; imploring her to say she would be happy with young Heathcliff. She stared, but soon comprehending why I counselled her to utter the falsehood, she assured me she would not complain.

I couldn't abide to be present at their meeting. I stood outside the chamber-door a quarter of an hour, and hardly ventured near the bed them.

All was composed, however; Catherine's despair was as silent as her father's joy. She supported him calmly, in appearance; and he fixed on her features his raised eyes, that seemed dilating with ecstasy.

He died blissfully, Mr. Lockwood; he died so; kissing her cheek, he murmured,

"I am going to her, and you, darling child, shall come to us;"

and never stirred or spoke again, but continued that rapt, radiant gaze, till his pulse impercptibly stopped, and his soul departed. None could have noticed the exact minute of his death, it was so entirely without a struggle.

Whether Catherine had spent her tears, or whether the grief were too weighty to let them flow, she sat there dry-eyed till the sun rose—she sat till noon, and would still have remained, brooding over that death-bed, but I insisted on her coming away and taking some repose.

It was well I succeeded in removing her, for at dinner-time appeared the lawyer, having called at Wuthering Heights to get his instructions how to behave. He had sold himself to Mr. Heathcliff, and that was the cause of his delay in obeying my master's summons. Fortunately, no thought of worldly affairs crossed the latter's mind, to disturb him after his daughter's arrival.

Mr. Green took upon himself to order everything and everybody about the place. He gave all the servants but me notice to quit. He would have carried his delegated authority to the point of insisting that Edgar Linton should not be buried beside his wife, but in the chapel with his family. There was the will, however, to hinder that, and my loud protestations against any infringement of its direction.

The funeral was hurried over; Catherine, Mrs. Linton Heathcliff now, was suffered to stay at the Grange, till her father's corpse had quitted it.

She told me that her anguish had at last spurred Linton to incur the risk of liberating her. She heard the men I sent disputing at the door, and she gathered the sense of Heathcliff's answer. It drove her desperate. Linton, who had been conveyed up to the little parlor soon after I left, was terrified into fetching the key before his father re-ascended.

He had the cunning to unlock and re-lock the door, without shutting it; and when he should have gone to bed, he begged to sleep with Hareton, and his petition was granted, for once.

Catherine stole out before break of day. She dare not try the doors, lest the dogs should raise an alarm; she visited the empty chambers, and examined their windows; and, luckily, lighting on her mother's, she got easily out of its lattice and to the ground, by means of the fir-tree close by. Her accomplice suffered for his share in the escape, notwithstanding his timid contrivances.
. . . .

Chapter 29

The evening after the funeral, my young lady and I were seated in the library; now musing mournfully, one of us despairingly, on our loss; now venturing conjectures as to the gloomy future.

We had just agreed the best destiny which could await Catherine would be a permission to continue resident at the Grange, at least during Linton's life; he being allowed to join her there, and I to remain as housekeeper. That seemed rather too favorable an arrangement to be hoped for; and yet I did hope, and began to cheer up under the prospect of retaining my home and my employment, and, above all, my beloved young mistress, when a servant—one of the discarded ones, not yet departed—rushed hastily in, and said, "that devil Heathcliff" was coming through the court—should he fasten the door in his face?

If we had been mad enough to order that proceeding, we had not time. He made no ceremony of knocking, or announcing his name; he was master, and availed himself of the master's privilege to walk straight in, without saying a word.

The sound of our informant's voice directed him to the library; he entered, and, motioning him out, shut the door.

It was the same room into which he had been ushered, as a guest, eighteen years before; the same moon shone through the window, and the same autumn landscape lay outside. We had not yet lighted a candle, but all the apartment was visible, even to the portraits on the wall—the splendid head of Mrs. Linton, and the graceful one of her husband.

Heathcliff advanced to the hearth. Time had little altered his person either. There was the same man—his dark face rather sallower and more composed, his frame a stone or two heavier, perhaps, and no other difference.

Catherine had risen, with an impulse to dash out, when she saw him.

"Stop!" he said, arresting her by the arm. "No more runnings away! Where would you go? I'm come to fetch you home; and I hope you'll be a dutiful daughter, and not encourage my son to further disobedience. I was embarrassed how to punish him, when I discovered his part in the business—he's such a cobweb, a pinch would annihilate him—but you'll see by his look that he has received his due. I brought him down one evening, the day before yesterday, and just set him in a chair, and never touched him afterward. I sent Hareton out, and we had the room to ourselves. In two hours I called Joseph to carry him up again, and since then my presence is as potent on his nerves as a ghost; and I fancy he sees me often, though I am not near. Hareton says he wakes and shrieks in the night by the hour together, and calls you to protect him from me; and, whether you like your precious mate or not, you must come—he's your concern now; I yield all my interest in him to you."

"Why not let Catherine continue here?" I pleaded, "and send Master Linton to her. As you hate them both, you'd not miss them—they *can* only be daily plague to your unnatural heart."

"I'm seeking a tenant for the Grange," he answered; "and I want my children about me, to be sure. Besides, that lass owes me her services for her bread: I'm not gong to nurture her in luxury and idleness after Linton is gone. Make haste and get ready now, and don't oblige me to compel you."

"I shall," said Catherine. "Linton is all I have to love in the world; and, though you have done what you could to make him hateful to me, and me to him, you *cannot* make us hate each other; and I defy you to hurt him when I am by, and I defy you to frighten me."

"You are a boastful champion," replied Heathcliff; "but I don't like you well enough to hurt him—you shall get the full benefit of the torment, as long as it lasts. It is not I who will make him hateful to you—it is his own sweet spirit. He's as bitter as gall at your desertion and its consequences: don't expect thanks for this noble devotion. I heard him draw a pleasant picture to Zillah of what he would do if he were as strong as I. The inclination is there, and his very weakness will sharpen his wits to find a substitute for strength."

"I know he had a bad nature," said Catherine: "he's your son. But I'm glad I've a better, to forgive it; and I know he loves me, and for that reason I love him. Mr. Heathcliff, *you* have *nobody* to love you; and, however miserable you make us, we shall still have the revenge of thinking that your cruelty rises from your greater misery! You *are* miserable, are you not? Lonely, like the devil, and envious like him? *Nobody* loves you—*nobody* will cry for you when you die! I wouldn't be you."

Catherine spoke with a kind of dreary triumph: she seemed to have made up her mind to enter into the spirit of her future family, and draw pleasure from the griefs of her enemies.

"You shall be sorry to be yourself presently," said her father-in-law, "if you stand there another minute. Begone, witch, and get your things."

She scornfully withdrew.

In her absence, I began to beg for Zillah's place at the Heights, offering to resign her mine; but he would suffer it on no account. He bid me be silent, and then, for the first time, allowed himself a glance round the room and a look at the pictures. Having studied Mrs. Linton, he said—

"I shall have that at home. Not because I need it, but—"

He turned abruptly to the fire, and continued, with what, for lack of a better word, I must call a smile—

"I'll tell you what I did yesterday! I got the sexton, who was digging Linton's grave, to remove the earth off her coffin lid, and I opened it. I thought, once, I would have stayed there, when I saw her face again—it is hers yet—he had hard work to stir me; but he said it would change if the air blew on it, and so I struck one side of the coffin loose—and covered it up—not Linton's side, damn him! I wish he'd been soldered in lead—and I bribed the sexton to pull it away, when I'm laid there, and slide mine out too, I'll have it made so, and then, by the time Linton gets to us, he'll not know which is which!"

"You were very wicked. Mr. Heathcliff!" I exclaimed "were you not ashamed to disturb the dead?"

"I disturbed nobody, Nelly," he replied; "and I gave some ease to myself. I shall be a great deal more comfortable now; and you'll have a better chance of keeping me underground, when I get there. Disturbed her? No! she has disturbed me, night and day, through eighteen years—incessantly—remorselessly—till yesternight—and yesternight, I was tranquil. I dreamed I was sleeping the last sleep by that sleeper, with my heart stopped and my cheek frozen against hers."

"And if she had been dissolved into earth, or worse, what would you have dreamed of then?" I said.

"Of dissolving with her, and being more happy still!" he answered. "Do you suppose I dread any change of that sort? I expected such a transformation on raising the lid, but I'm better pleased that it should not commence till I share it. Besides, unless I had received a distinct impression of her passionless features, that strange feeling would hardly have been removed. It began oddly. You know I was wild after she died, and eternally, from dawn to dawn, praying her to return to me—her spirit—I have a strong faith in ghosts; I have a conviction that they can and do exist among us!

"The day she was buried there came a fall of snow. In the evening I went to the churchyard. It blew bleak as winter—all around was solitary: I didn't fear that her fool of a husband would wander up the den so late—and no one else had business to bring them there.

"Being alone, and conscious two yards of loose earth was the sole barrier between us, said to myself—

" 'I'll have her in my arms again! If she be cold, I'll think it is this north wind that chills *me*; and if she be motionless, it is sleep.'

"I got a spade from the tool-house, and began to delve with all my might—it scraped the coffin: I fell to work with my hands; the wood commenced cracking about the screws, I was on the point of attaining my object, when it seemed that I heard a sigh from some one above, close at the edge of the grave, and bending down. 'If I can only get this off,' I muttered, 'I wish they may shovel in the earth over us both!' and I wrenched at it more desperately still. There was another sigh close at my ear. I appeared to feel the warm breath of it, displacing the sleet-laden wind. I knew no living thing in flesh and blood was by—but as certainly as you perceive the approach to some substantial body in the dark, though it cannotl be discerned, so certainly I felt that Cathy was there, not under me, but on the earth.

"A sudden sense of relief flowed from my heart, through every limb. I relinquished my labor of agony, and turned consoled at once, unspeakably consoled. Her presence was with me; it remained while I refilled the grave, and led me home. You may laugh, if you will, but I was sure I should see her there. I was sure she was with me, and could not help talking to her.

"Having reached the Heights, I rushed eagerly to the door. It was fastened; and I remember that accursed Earnshaw and my wife opposed my entrance. I remember stopping to kick the breath out of him, and then hurrying up-stairs to my room, and hers—I looked round impatiently—I felt her by me—I could *almost* see her, and yet I *could not!* I ought to have sweat blood then, from the anguish of my yearning, from the fervor of my supplications to have but one glimpse! I had not one. She showed herself, as she often was in life, a devil to me! And since then, sometimes more, and sometimes less, I've been the sport of that intolerable torture! Infernal—keeping my nerves at such a stretch, that, if they had not resembled catgut, they would, long ago, have relaxed to the feebleness of Linton's.

"When I sat in the house with Hareton, it seemed that on going out, I should meet her; when I walked on the moors, I should meet her coming in. When I went from home, I hastened to return, she *must* be somewhere at the Heights, I was certain! And when I slept in her chamber—I was beaten out of that—I couldn't lie there; for the moment I closed my eyes, she was either outside the window, or sliding back the panels, or entering the room, or even resting her darling head on the same pillow as she did when a child. And I must open my lids to see. And so I opened and closed them a hundred times a night—to be always disappointed! It racked me! I've often groaned aloud, till that old rascal Joseph, no doubt believed that my conscience was playing the fiend inside of me.

"Now since I've seen her, I'm pacified—a little. It was a strange way of killing, not by inches, but by fractions of hairbreadths, to beguile me with the specter of a hope through eighteen years!"

Mr. Heathcliff paused, and wiped his forehead—his hair clung to it, wet with perspiration; his eyes were fixed on the red embers of the fire; the brows not contracted, but raised next the temples, diminishing the grim aspect of his countenance, but imparting a peculiar look of trouble, and a painful appearance of mental tension toward one absorbing subject. He only half addressed me, and I maintained silence—I did not like to hear him talk.

After a short period, he resumed his meditation on the picture, took it down, and leaned it against the sofa to contemplate it at better advantage; and while so occupied Catherine entered, announcing that she was ready, when her pony should be saddled.

"Send that over to-morrow," said Heathcliff to me; then turning to her, he added, "You may do without your pony—it is a fine evening, and you'll need no ponies at Wuthering Heights, for what journeys you take your own feet will serve you. Come along."

"Good-bye, Ellen!" whispered my dear little mistress. As she kissed me, her lips felt like ice. "Come and see me, Ellen, don't forget."

"Take care you do no such thing, Mrs. Dean!" said her new father. "When I wish to speak to you, I'll come here. I want none of your prying at my house!"

He signed her to precede him; and casting back a look that cut my heart, she obeyed.

I watched them, from the window, walk down the garden. Heathcliff fixed Catherine's arm under his, though she disputed the act at first, evidently, and with rapid strides he hurried her into the alley, whose trees concealed them.

. . . .

Chapter 30

I have paid a visit to the Heights, but I have not seen her since she left; Joseph held the door in his hand, when I called to ask after her, and wouldn't let me pass. He said Mrs. Linton was "thrang," and the master was not in. Zillah has told me something of the way they go on, otherwise I should hardly know who was dead, and who living.

She thinks Catherine haughty, and does not like her, I can guess by her talk. My young lady asked some aid of her, when she first came, but Mr. Heathcliff told her to follow her own business, and let his daughter-in-law look after herself, and Zillah willingly acquiesced, being a narrow-minded, selfish woman. Catherine evinced a child's annoyance at this neglect; repaid it with contempt, and thus enlisted my informant among her enemies, as securely as if she had done her a great wrong.

I had a long talk with Zillah, about six weeks ago, a little before you came, one day when we foregathered on the moor; and this is what she told me.

"The first thing Mrs. Linton did," she said, "on her arrival at the Heights, was to run up-stairs without even wishing good-evening to me and Joseph; she shut herself into Linton's room, and remained till morning—then, while the master and Earnshaw were at breakfast, she entered the house and asked, all in a quiver, if the doctor might be sent for? her cousin was very ill.

"'We know that!' answered Heathcliff, 'but his life is not worth a farthing, and I won't spend a farthing on him.'

"'But I cannot tell how to do,' she said. 'If nobody will help me, he'll die!'

"'Walk out of the room!' cried the master, 'and let me never hear a word more about him! None here care what becomes of him; if you do, act the nurse; if you do not, lock him up and leave him.'

"Then she began to bother me, and I said I'd had enough plague with the tiresome thing; we each had our tasks, and hers was to wait on Linton. Mr. Heathcliff bid me leave that labor to her.

"How they managed together, I can't tell. I fancy he fretted a great deal, and moaned hisseln, night and day; and she had precious little rest, one could guess by her white face and heavy eye— she sometimes came into the kitchen all wildered like, and looked as if she would fain beg assistance; but I was not going to disobey the master—I never dare disobey him, Mrs. Dean; and though I thought it wrong that Kenneth should not be sent for, it was no concern of mine, either to advise or complain; and I always refused to meddle.

"Once or twice, after we had gone to bed, I've happened to open my door again, and seen her sitting crying on the stairs' top;

and then I've shut myself in quick, for fear of being moved to interfere. I did pity her then, I'm sure; still I didn't wish to lose my place, you know!

"At last, one night she came boldly into my chamber, and frightened me out of my wits by saying,

" 'Tell Mr. Heathcliff that his son is dying—I'm sure he is this time. Get up instantly, and tell him!'

"Having uttered this speech, she vanished again. I lay a quarter of an hour, listening and trembling. Nothing stirred—the house was quiet.

" 'She's mistaken,' I said to myself. 'He's got over it. I needn't disturb them.' And I began to doze. But my sleep was marred a second time, by a sharp ringing of the bell—the only bell we have, put up on purpose for Linton; and the master called to me to see what was the matter, and inform them that he wouldn't have that noise repeated.

"I delivered Catherine's message. He cursed to himself, and in a few minutes came out with a lighted candle, and proceeded to their room; I followed. Mrs. Heathcliff was seated by the bedside, with her hands folded on her knees. Her father-in-law went up, held the light to Linton's face, looked at him, and touched him: afterward he turned to her.

" 'Now—Catherine,' he said, 'how do you feel?'

"She was dumb.

" 'How do you feel, Catherine?' he repeated.

" 'He's safe, and I'm free,' she answered; 'I should feel well—but,' she continued, with a bitterness she couldn't conceal. 'You have left me so long to struggle against death, alone, that I feel and see only death! I feel like death!'

"And she looked like it, too! I gave her a little wine. Hareton and Joseph, who had been wakened by the ringing, and the sound of feet, and heard our talk from outside, now entered. Joseph was fain, I believe, of the lad's removal: Hareton seemed a thought bothered, though he was more taken up with staring at Catherine than thinking of Linton. But the master bid him get off to bed again—we didn't want his help. He afterward made Joseph remove the body to his chamber, and told me to return to mine, and Mrs. Heathcliff remained by herself.

"In the morning he sent me to tell her she must come down to breakfast. She had undressed, and appeared going to sleep; and said she was ill—at which I hardly wondered. I informed Mr. Heathcliff, and he replied,

" 'Well, let her be till after the funeral, and go up now and then to get her what is needful; and as soon as she seems better, tell me.' "

Cathy stayed up stairs a fortnight, according to Zillah, who visited her twice a day, and would have been rather more friendly, but her attempts at increasing kindness were proudly and promptly repelled. Heathcliff went up once, to show her Linton's will. He had bequeathed the whole of his and what had been her movable property to his father. The poor creature was threatened or coaxed into that act, during her week's absence, when his uncle died. The lands, being a minor, he could not meddle with. However, Mr. Heathcliff has claimed, and kept them in his wife's right, and his also—I suppose legally, at any rate Catherine, destitute of cash and friends, cannot disturb his possession.

"Nobody," said Zillah, "ever approached her door, except that once, but I; and nobody asked anything about her. The first occasion of her coming down into the house was on a Sunday afternoon.

"She had cried out, when I carried up her dinner, that she couldn't bear any longer being in the cold; and I told her the master was going to Thrushcross Grange; and Earnshaw and I needn't hinder her from descending; so, as soon as she heard Heathcliff's horse trot off, she made her appearance, donned in black, and her yellow curls combed back behind her ears—as plain as a Quaker she couldn't comb them out. Joseph and I generally go to chapel on Sundays." (The kirk, you know, has no minister, now, explained Mrs. Dean, and they call the Methodists' or Baptists' place, I can't say which it is, at Gimmerton, a chapel.) "Joseph had gone," she continued, "but I thought proper to bide at home. Young folks are always the better for an elder's overlooking, and Hareton, with all his bashfulness, isn't a model of nice behavior. I let him know that his cousin would very likely sit with us, and she had been always used to see the Sabbath respected, so he had as good leave his guns and bits of in-door work alone, while she staid.

"He colored up at the news; and cast his eyes over his hands and clothes. The train-oil and gunpowder were shoved out of sight in a minute. I saw he meant to give her his company; and I guessed, by his way, he wanted to be presentable; so, laughing as I durst not laugh when the master is by, I offered to help him, if he would, and joked at his confusion. He grew sullen, and began to swear.

"Now, Mrs. Dean," she went on, seeing me not pleased by her manner, "you happen think your young lady too fine for Mr. Hareton, and happen you're right—I own, I should love well to bring her pride a peg lower. And what will all her learning and all her daintiness do for her, now? She's as poor as you, or I—poorer. I'll be bound, you're saving—and I'm doing my little all that road."

Hareton allowed Zillah to give him her aid; and she flattered him into a good humor; so, when Catherine came, half forgetting her former insults, he tried to make himself agreeable, by the housekeeper's account.

"Missis walked in," she said, "as chill as an icicle, and as high as a princess. I got up and offered her my seat in the arm-chair. No, she turned up her nose at my civility. Earnshaw rose too, and bid her come to the settle, and sit close by the fire; he was sure she was starved.

"'I've been starved a month and more,' she answered, resting on the word, as scornful as she could.

"And she got a chair for herself, and placed it at a distance from both of us. Having sat till she was warm, she began to look round, and discovered a number of books in the dresser; she was instantly upon her feet again, stretching to reach them, but they were too high up. Her cousin, after watching her endeavors a while, at last summoned courage to help her; she held her frock, and he filled it with the first that came to hand.

"That was a great advance for the lad—she didn't thank him; still he felt gratified that she had accepted his assistance, and ventured to stand behind, as she examined them, and even to stoop and point out what struck his fancy in certain old pictures which they contained—nor was he daunted by the saucy style in which she jerked the page from his finger; he contented himself with going a bit farther back, and looking at her, instead of the book.

"She continued reading, or seeking for something to read. His attention became, by degrees, quite centered in the study of her thick, silky curls—her face he couldn't see, and she couldn't see him. And, perhaps, not quite awake to what he did, but attracted like a child to a candle, at last he proceeded from staring to touching; he put out his hand and stroked one curl, as gently as if it were a bird. He might have stuck a knife into her neck, she started round in such a taking.

"'Get away, this moment! How dare you touch me? Why are you stopping there?' she cried, in a tone of disgust. 'I can't endure you! I'll go up-stairs again, if you come near me.'

"Mr. Hareton recoiled, looking as foolish as he could do; he sat down in the settle, very quiet, and she continued turning over her volumes another half-hour——finally, Earnshaw crossed over and whispered to me.

"'Will you ask her to read to us, Zillah? I'm stalled of doing naught—and I do like—I could like to hear her! dunnot say I wanted it, but ask of yourseln.'

"'Mr. Hareton wishes you would read to us, ma'am,' I said, immediately. 'He'd take it very kind—he'd be much obliged.'

"She frowned; and, looking up, answered—

"'Mr. Hareton, and the whole set of you, will be good enough to understand that I reject any pretense at kindness you have the hypocrisy to offer! I despise you, and will have nothing to say to any of you! When I would have given my life for one kind word, even to see one of your faces, you all kept off. But I won't complain to you! I'm driven down here by the cold, not either to amuse you, or enjoy your society.'

"'What could I ha' done?' began Earnshaw. 'How was I to blame?'

"'Oh! you are an exception,' answered Mrs. Heathcliff. 'I never missed such a concern as you.'

"'But I offered more than once, and asked,' he said, kindling up at her pertness—'I asked Mr. Heathcliff to let me wake for you—'

"'Be silent! I'll go out of doors, or anywhere, rather than have your disagreeable voice in my ear!' said my lady.

"Hareton muttered, she might go to hell, for him! and unslinging his gun, restrained himself from his Sunday occupations no longer. He talked now, freely enough; and she presently saw fit to retreat to her solitude: but the frost had set in, and, in spite of her pride, she was forced to condescend to our company more and more. However, I took care there should be no further scorning at my good nature. Ever since, I've been as stiff as herself; and she has no lover or liker among us, and she does not deserve one—for, let them say the least word to her, and she'll curl back without respect of any one! She'll snap at the master himself, and as good as dares him to thrash her; and the more hurt she gets, the more venomous she grows."

At first, on hearing this account from Zillah, I determined to leave my situation, take a cottage, and get Catherine to come and live with me; but Mr. Heathcliff would as soon permit that as he would set up Hareton in an independent house: and I can see no remedy at present, unless she could marry again; and that scheme, it does not come within my province to arrange.

Thus ended Mrs. Dean's story. Notwithstanding the doctor's prophecy, I am rapidly recovering strength, and though it be only the second week in January, I propose getting out on horseback in a day or two, and riding over to Wuthering Heights, to inform my landlord that I shall spend the next six months in London; and, if he likes, he may look out for another tenant to take the place after October. I would not pass another winter here for much.

. . . .

Chapter 31

Yesterday was bright, calm, and frosty. I went to the Heights, as I proposed; my housekeeper entreated me to bear a little note from her to her young lady, and I did not refuse, for the worthy woman was not conscious of anything odd in her request.

The front door stood open, but the jealous gate was fastened, as at my last visit; I knocked and invoked Earnshaw from among the garden beds; he unchained it and I entered. The fellow is as handsome a rustic as need be seen. I took particular notice of him this time; but then he does his best, apparently, to make the least of his advantages.

I asked if Mr. Heathcliff were at home? He answered, no; but he would be in at dinner-time. It was eleven o'clock, and I announced my intention of going in and waiting for him, at which he immediately flung down his tools and accompanied me, in the office of watch-dog, not as a substitute for the host.

We entered together; Catherine was there, making herself useful in preparing some vegetables for the approaching meal; she looked more sulky and less spirited than when I had seen her first. She hardly raised her eyes to notice me, and continued her employment with the same disregard to common forms of politeness as before, never returning my bow and good-morning by the slightest acknowledgment.

"She does not seem so amiable," I thought, "as Mrs. Dean

would persuade me to believe. She's a beauty, it is true, but not an angel."

Earnshaw surlily bid her remove her things to the kitchen.

"Remove them yourself," she said, pushing them from her, as soon as she had done; and retiring to a stool by the window, where she began to carve figures of birds and beasts, out of the turnip-parings in her lap. I approached her, pretending to desire a view of the garden, and, as I fancied, adroitly dropped Mrs. Dean's note upon her knee, unnoticed by Hareton, but she asked aloud—

"What is that?" and chucked it off.

"A letter from your old acquaintance, the housekeeper at the Grange," I answered, annoyed at her exposing my kind deed, and fearful lest it should be imagined a missive of my own. She would gladly have gathered it up at this information, but Hareton beat her; he seized and put it in his waistcoat, saying Mr. Heathcliff should look at it first.

Thereat, Catherine silently turned her face from us, and, very stealthily, drew out her pocket-handkerchief and applied it to her eyes; and her cousin, after struggling a while to keep down his softer feelings, pulled out the letter and flung it on the floor beside her, as ungraciously as he could. Catherine caught and perused it eagerly; then she put a few questions to me concerning the inmates, rational and irrational, of her former home, and, gazing toward the hills, murmured in soliloquy—

"I should like to be riding Minny down there! I should like to be climbing up there! Oh, I'm tired!—I'm *stalled*, Hareton!"

And she leaned her pretty head back against the sill, with half a yawn and half a sigh, and lapsed into an aspect of abstracted sadness, neither caring nor knowing whether we remarked her.

"Mrs. Heathcliff," I said, after sitting some time mute, "you are not aware that I am an acquaintance of yours; so intimate, that I think it strange you won't come and speak to me. My housekeeper never wearies of talking about and praising you; and she'll be greatly disappointed if I return with no news of, or from you, except that you received her letter, and said nothing!"

She appeared to wonder at this speech and asked,

"Does Ellen like you?"

"Yes, very well," I replied unhesitatingly.

"You must tell her," she continued, "that I would answer her letter, but I have no materials for writing, not even a book from which I might tear a leaf."

"No books!" I exclaimed. "How do you contrive to live here without them? if I may take the liberty to inquire. Though provided with a large library, I'm frequently very dull at the Grange—take my books away, and I should be desperate!"

"I was always reading, when I had them;" said Catherine, "and Mr. Heathcliff never reads; so he took it into his head to destroy my books. I have not had a glimpse of one for weeks. Only once, I searched through Joseph's store of theology, to his great irritation: and once, Hareton, I came upon a secret stock in your room—some Latin and Greek, and some tales and poetry; all old friends.

I brought the last here—and you gathered them, as a magpie gathers silver spoons, for the mere love of stealing! They are of no use to you—or else you concealed them in the bad spirit that as you cannot enjoy them, nobody else shall. Perhaps *your* envy counseled Mr. Heathcliff to rob me of my treasures? But, I've most of them written on my brain and printed in my heart, and you cannot deprive me of those!"

Earnshaw blushed crimson, when his cousin made this revelation of his private literary accumulations, and stammered an indignant denial of her accusations.

"Mr. Hareton is desirous of increasing his amount of knowledge," I said, coming to his rescue. "He is not *envious* but *emulous* of your attainments. He'll be a clever scholar in a few years!"

"And he wants *me* to sink into a dunce, meantime," answered Catherine. "Yes, I hear him trying to spell and read to himself, and pretty blunders he makes! I wish you would repeat Chevy Chase, as you did yesterday. It was extremely funny! I heard you; and I heard you turning over the dictionary, to seek out the hard words, and then cursing because you couldn't read their explanations!"

The young man evidently thought it too bad that he should be laughed at for his ignorance, and then laughed at for trying to remove it. I had a similar notion, and, remembering Mrs. Dean's anecdote of his first attempt at enlightening the darkness in which he had been reared, I observed,

"But, Mrs. Heathcliff, we have each had a commencement, and each stumbled and tottered on the threshold, and had our teachers scorned, instead of aiding us, we should stumble and totter yet."

"Oh!" she replied, "I don't wish to limit his acquirements—still, he has no right to appropriate what is mine, and make it ridiculous to me with his vile mistakes and mispronunciations! Those books, both prose and verse, were consecrated to me by other associations, and I hate to have them debased and profaned in his mouth! Besides, of all, he has selected my favorite pieces that I love the most to repeat, as if out of deliberate malice!"

Hareton's chest heaved in silence a minute; he labored under a severe sense of mortification and wrath, which it was no easy task to suppress.

I rose, and from a gentlemanly idea of relieving his embarrassment, took up my station in the door-way, surveying the external prospect, as I stood. He followed my example, and left the room, but presently reappeared, bearing half-a-dozen volumes in his hands, which he threw into Catherine's lap exclaiming,

"Take them! I never want to hear, or read, or think of them again!"

"I won't have them, now!" she answered. "I shall connect them with you, and hate them!"

She opened one that had obviously been often turned over, and read a portion in the drawling tone of a beginner; then laughed, and threw it from her.

"And listen!" she continued provokingly, commencing a verse of an old ballad in the same fashion.

But his self-love would endure no further torment—I heard, and not altogether disapprovingly, a manual check given to her saucy tongue. The little wretch had done her utmost to hurt her cousin's sensitive though uncultivated feelings, and a physical argument was the only mode he had of balancing the account, and repaying its effects on the inflicter.

He afterwards gathered the books and hurled them on the fire. I read in his countenance what anguish it was to offer that sacrifice to spleen. I fancied that as they consumed, he recalled the pleasure they had already imparted; and the triumph and ever increasing pleasure he had anticipated from them—and I fancied I guessed the incitement to his secret studies, also. He had been content with daily labor and rough animal enjoyments, till Catherine crossed his path. Shame at her scorn and hope of her approval were his first prompters to higher pursuits; and instead of guarding him from one, and winning him the other, his endeavors to raise himself had produced just the contrary result.

"Yes, that's all the good that such a brute as you can get from them!" cried Catherine, sucking her damaged lip, and watching the conflagration with indignant eyes.

"You'd *better* hold your tongue now!" he answered fiercely. And his agitation precluding further speech, he advanced hastily to the entrance, where I made way for him to pass. But, ere he had crossed the door-stones, Mr. Heathcliff, coming up the causeway, encountered him, and laying hold of his shoulder, asked,

"What's to do now, my lad?"

"Naught, naught!" he said, and broke away, to enjoy his grief and anger in solitude. Heathcliff gazed after him, and sighed.

"It will be odd, if I thwart myself!" he muttered, unconscious that I was behind him. "But when I look for his father in his face I find *her* every day more! How the devil is he so like? I can hardly bear to see him."

He bent his eyes to the ground, and walked moodily in. There was a restless, anxious expression in his countenance I had never remarked there before, and he looked sparer in person. His daughter-in-law on perceiving him through the window, immediately escaped to the kitchen, so that I remained alone.

"I'm glad to see you out of doors again, Mr. Lockwood," he said in reply to my greeting, "from selfish motives partly, I don't think I could readily supply your loss in this desolation. I've wondered, more than once, what brought you here."

"An idle whim, I fear, sir," was my answer, "or else an idle whim is going to spirit me away. I shall set out for London, next week, and I must give you warning, that I feel no disposition to retain Thrushcross Grange beyond the twelve-month I agreed to rent it. I believe I shall not live there any more.

"Oh, indeed! you're tired of being banished from the world, are you?" he said. "But if you be coming to plead off paying for a place you won't occupy, your journey is useless—I never relent in exacting my due from any one."

"I'm coming to plead off nothing about it!" I exclaimed, considerably irritated. "Should you wish it, I'll settle with you now," and I drew my notebook from my pocket.

"No, no," he replied, coolly, "you'll leave sufficient behind to cover your debts, if you fail to return. I'm not in such a hurry—sit down and take your dinner with us—a guest that is safe from repeating his visit, can generally be made welcome. Catherine! bring the things in—where are you?"

Catherine reappeared, bearing a tray of knives and forks.

"You may get your dinner with Joseph," muttered Heathcliff aside, "and remain in the kitchen till he is gone."

She obeyed his directions very punctually—perhaps she had no temptation to transgress. Living among clowns and misanthropists, she probably cannot appreciate a better class of people, when she meets them.

With Mr. Heathcliff, grim and saturnine, on one hand, and Hareton absolutely dumb, on the other, I made a somewhat cheerless meal, and bid adieu early. I would have departed by the back way, to get a last glimpse of Catherine and annoy old Joseph; but Hareton received orders to lead up my horse, and my host himself escorted me to the door, so I could not fulfill my wish.

"How dreary life gets over in that house!" I reflected, while riding down the road. "What a realization of something more romantic than a fairy tale it would have been for Mrs. Linton Heathcliff, had she and I struck up an attachment, as her good nurse desired, and migrated together into the stirring atmosphere of the town!"

. . . .

Chapter 32

1802—This September, I was invited to devastate the moors of a friend, in the north; and, on my journey to his abode, I unexpectedly came within fifteen miles of Gimmerton. The hostler, at a roadside public-house, was holding a pail of water to refresh my horses, when a cart of very green oats, newly reaped, passed by, and he remarked—

"Yon's frough Gimmerton, nah! They're allas three wick' after other folk wi' ther harvest."

"Gimmerton?" I repeated, my residence in that locality had already grown dim and dreamy. "Ah! I know! How far is it from this?"

"Happen fourteen mile' o'er th' hills, and a rough road," he answered.

A sudden impulse seized me to visit Thrushcross Grange. It was scarcely noon, and I conceived that I might as well pass the night under my own roof as in an inn. Besides, I could spare a day easily, to arrange matters with my landlord, and thus save myself the trouble of invading the neighborhood again.

Having rested a while, I directed my servant to inquire the way to the village; and, with great fatigue to our beasts, we managed the distance in some three hours. I left him there, and proceeded down the valley alone. The gray church looked grayer, and the lonely churchyard lonelier. I distinguished a moor sheep cropping the short turf on the graves. It was sweet, warm weather—too warm for travelling; but the heat did not hinder me from enjoying the delightful scenery above and below; had I seen it nearer August, I am sure it would have tempted me to waste a month among its solitudes. In winter nothing more dreary, in summer nothing more divine, than those glens shut in by hills, and those bluff, bold swells of heath.

I reached the Grange before sunset, and knocked for admittance; but the family had retreated into the back premises, I judged by one thin, blue wreath curling from the kitchen chimney, and they did not hear. I rode into the court. Under the porch a girl of nine or ten sat knitting, and an old woman reclined on the horse-steps, smoking a meditative pipe.

"Is Mrs. Dean within?" I demanded of the dame.

"Mistress Dean? Nay!" she answered, "shoo doesn't bide here; shoo's up at th' Heights."

"Are you the housekeeper, then?" I continued.

"Eea, aw keep th' hause," she replied.

"Well, I'm Mr. Lockwood, the master. Are there any rooms to lodge me in? I wish to stay here all night."

"T' maister!" she cried in astonishment, "Whet, whoiver knew yah wur coming? Yah sud ha' send word! They's nowt norther dry nor mensful abaht t' place—nowt ther isn't!"

She threw down her pipe and bustled in, the girl followed and I entered too; soon perceiving that her report was true and, moreover, that I had almost upset her wits by my unwelcome apparition.

I bid her be composed—I would go out for a walk; and, meantime, she must try to prepare a corner of a sitting-room for me to sup in, and a bed-room to sleep in. No sweeping and dusting, only good fires and dry sheets were necessary. She seemed willing to do her best; though she thrust the hearth-brush into the grate in mistake for the poker; and mal-appropriated several other articles of her craft: but I retired, confiding in her energy for a resting-place against my return.

Wuthering Heights was the goal of my proposed excursion. An after-thought brought me back, when I had left the court.

"All well at the Heights?" I inquired of the woman.

"Eea, f'r owt aw knaw!" she answered, skurrying away with a pan of hot cinders.

I would have asked why Mrs. Dean had deserted the Grange; but it was impossible to delay her at such a crisis, so I turned away and made my exit rambling leisurely along with the glow of a sinking sun behind, and the mild glory of a rising moon in front; one fading and the other brightening, as I quitted the park and climbed the stony by-road branching off to Mr. Heathcliff's dwelling. Before I arrived in sight of it, all that remained of day was a beamless, amber light along the west; but I could see every pebble on the path, and every blade of grass, by that splendid moon.

I had neither to climb the gate, nor to knock—it yielded to my hand. That is an improvement, I thought. And I noticed another, by the aid of my nostrils; a fragrance of stocks and wall flowers, wafted on the air from among the fruit trees.

Both doors and lattices were open; and yet, as is usually the case in a coal district, a fine, red fire illuminated the chimney; the comfort which the eye derives from it renders the extra heat endurable. But the house of Wuthering Heights is so large, that the inmates have plenty of space for withdrawing out of its influence; and, accordingly, what inmates there were had stationed themselves not far from one of the windows. I could both see them and hear them talk before I entered; and looked and listened in consequence, being moved thereto by a mingled sense of curiosity and envy, that grew as I lingered.

"Con-*trary*!" said a voice, as sweet as a silver bell. "That for the third time, you dunce! I'm not going to tell you again. Recollect, or I pull your hair!"

"Contrary, then," answered another, in deep, but softened tones. "And now, kiss me, for minding so well."

"No, read it over first correctly, without a single mistake."

The male speaker began to read—he was a young man, respectably dressed, and seated at a table, having a book before him. His handsome features glowed with pleasure, and his eyes kept impatiently wandering from the page to a small white hand over his shoulder, which recalled him by a smart slap on the cheek, whenever its owner detected such signs of inattention.

Its owner stood behind; her light shining ringlets blending at intervals with his brown locks, as she bent to superintend his studies; and her face—it was lucky he could not see her face, or he would never have been so steady—I could, and I bit my lip in spite, at having thrown away the chance I might have had, of doing something besides staring at its smiling beauty.

The task was done, not free from further blunders, but the pupil claimed a reward, and received at least five kisses, which, however, he generously returned. Then they came to the door, and from their conversation I judged they were about to issue out and have a walk on the moors. I supposed I should be condemned in Hareton Earnshaw's heart, if not by his mouth, to the lowest pit in the infernal regions if I showed my unfortunate person in his neighborhood then: and feeling very mean and malignant, I skulked round to seek refuge in the kitchen. There was unobstructed admittance on that side also; and at the door sat my old friend Nelly Dean, sewing, and singing a song, which was often interrupted from within, by harsh words of scorn and intolerance, uttered in far from musical accents.

"Aw'd rayther, by th' haulf, hev 'em swearing i' my lugs frough morn tuh neeght, nur hearken yah, hahsiver!" said the tenant of the kitchen, in answer to an unheard speech of Nelly's. "It's a blazing shaime, ut aw cannut oppen t' Blessed Book, bud yah set up them glories tuh Sattan, un' all t' flaysome wickednesses ut iver wer born intuh t' warld! Oh! yah're a raight nowt; un' shoo's another; un' that poor lad 'ull be lost, atween ye. Poor lad!" he added, with a groan, "he's witched, aw'm sartin on't! Oh, Lord, judge 'em, fur they's norther law nur justice amang wer rullers!"

"No! or we should be sitting in flaming fagots, I suppose," retorted the singer. "But wisht, old man, and read your Bible, like a Christian, and never mind me. This is 'Fairy Annie's Wedding'—a bonny tune—it goes to a dance."

Mrs. Dean was about to recommence when I advanced; and, recognizing me directly, she jumped to her feet, crying—

"Why, bless you, Mr. Lockwood, how could you think of returning in this way? All's shut up at Thrushcross Grange. You should have given us notice."

I've arranged to be accommodated there for as long as I shall stay," I answered. "I depart again to-morrow. And how are you transplanted here, Mrs. Dean? tell me that."

"Zillah left, and Mr. Heathcliff wished me to come, soon after you went to London, and stay till you returned. But step in, pray. Have you walked from Gimmerton this evening?"

"From the Grange," I replied; "and, while they make me lodging room there, I want to finish my business with your master—I don't think of having another opportunity in a hurry."

"What business, sir?" said Nelly, conducting me into the house. "He's gone out at present, and won't return soon."

"About the rent," I answered.

"Oh! then it is with Mrs. Heathcliff you must settle," she observed, "or rather with me. She has not learned to manage her affairs yet, and I act for her—there's nobody else."

I looked surprised.

"Ah! you have not heard of Heathcliff's death, I see," she continued.

"Heathcliff dead!" I exclaimed, astonished. "How long ago?"

"Three months since. But sit down, and let me take your hat, and I'll tell you all about it. Stop, you have had nothing to eat, have you?"

"I want nothing. I have ordered supper at home. You sit down too. I never dreamed of his dying. Let me hear how it came to pass. You say you don't expect them back for some time—the young people?"

"No. I have to scold them every evening for their late rambles; but they don't care for me. At least, have a drink of our old ale: it will do you good—you seem weary."

She hastened to fetch it before I could refuse; and I heard Joseph asking whether "it warn't a crying scandal that she should have fellies at her time of life? And then, to get them jocks out uh t' maister's cellar! He fair shaamed to 'bide still and see it."

She did not stay to retaliate, but re-entered in a minute, bearing a creaming silver pint, whose contents I lauded with becoming earnestness; and afterward she furnished me with the sequel of Heathcliff's history. He had a "queer" end, as she expressed it.

I was summoned to Wuthering Heights within a fortnight of your leaving, she said, and I obeyed joyfully for Catherine's sake.

My first interview with her grieved and shocked me, she had altered so much since our separation. Mr. Heathcliff did not explain his reasons for taking a new mind about my coming here; he only told me he wanted me, and he was tired of seeing Catherine; I must make the little parlor my sitting room, and keep her with me. It was enough if he were obliged to see her once or twice a day.

She seemed pleased at this arrangement; and, by degrees, I smuggled over a great number of books and other articles that had formed her amusement at the Grange, and flattered myself we should get on in tolerable comfort.

The delusion did not last long. Catherine, contented at first, in a brief space grew irritable and restless. For one thing, she was forbidden to move out of the garden, and it fretted her sadly to be confined to its narrow bounds as spring drew on; for another, in following the house, I was forced to quit her frequently, and she complained of loneliness; she preferred quarrelling with Joseph in the kitchen to sitting at peace in her solitude.

"I did not mind their skirmishes; but Hareton was often obliged to seek the kitchen also, when the master wanted to have the house to himself; and though, in the beginning, she either left it at his approach, or quietly joined in my occupations, and shunned remarking or addressing him—and though he was always sullen and silent as possible—after a while she changed her behavior, and became incapable of letting him alone. Talking at him; commenting on his stupidity and idleness; expressing her wonder how he could endure the life he lived—how he could sit a whole evening, staring into the fire and dozing.

"He's just like a dog, is he not, Ellen?" she once observed, "or a cart-horse? He does his work, eats his food, and sleeps, eternally! What a blank, dreary mind he must have! Do you ever dream, Hareton? And, if you do, what is it about? But, you can't speak to me!"

Then she looked at him; but he would neither open his mouth, nor look again.

"He's perhaps, dreaming now," she continued. "He twitched his shoulder as Juno twitches hers. Ask him, Ellen."

"Mr. Hareton will ask the master to send you up stairs, if you don't behave!" I said. He had not only twitched his shoulder, but clenched his fist, as if tempted to use it.

"I know why Hareton never speaks when I am in the kitchen," she exclaimed, on another occasion. "He is afraid I shall laugh at him. Ellen, what do you think? He began to teach himself to read once; and, because I laughed, he burned his books, and dropped it—was he not a fool?"

"Were not you naughty?" I said; "answer me that."

"Perhaps I was," she went on, "but I did not expect him to be so silly. Hareton, if I gave you a book, would you take it now? I'll try!"

She placed one she had been perusing on his hand; he flung it off, and muttered if she did not give over he'd break her neck.

"Well, I shall put it here," she said, "in the table drawer, and am going to bed."

Then she whispered me to watch whether he touched it , and departed. But he would not come near it, and so I informed her in the morning, to her great disappointment. I saw she was sorry for his persevering sulkiness and indolence—her conscience reproved her for frightening him off improving himself. She had done it effectually.

But her ingenuity was at work to remedy the injury; while I ironed, or pursued other stationary employments I could not well do in the parlor—she would bring some pleasant volume, and read it aloud to me. When Hareton was there, she generally paused in an interesting part, and left the book lying about—that she did repeatedly; but he was as obstinate as a mule, and, instead of snatching at her bait, in wet weather he took to smoking with Joseph, and they sat like automata, one on each side of the fire, the elder happily too deaf to understand her wicked nonsense, as he would have called it; the younger doing his best to seem to disregard it. On fine evenings the latter followed his shooting expeditions, and Catherine yawned and sighed, and teased me to talk to her, and ran off into the court or garden, the moment I began; and, as a last resource, cried, and said she was tired of living, her life was useless.

Mr. Heathcliff, who grew more and more disinclined to society, had almost banished Earnshaw out of his apartment. Owing to an accident, at the commencement of March, he became for some days a fixture in the kitchen. His gun burst while out on the hills by himself; a splinter cut his arm, and he lost a good deal of blood before he could reach home. The consequence was, that, perforce, he was condemned to the fireside and tranquillity till he made it up again.

It suited Catherine to have him there; at any rate, it made her hate her room up stairs more than ever; and she would compel me to find out business below, that she might accompany me.

On Easter Monday, Joseph went to Gimmerton fair with some cattle; and in the afternoon I was busy getting up linen in the kitchen. Earnshaw sat, morose as usual, at the chimney corner, and my little mistress was beguiling an idle hour with drawing pictures on the window panes, varying her amusement by smothered bursts of songs, and whispering ejaculations, and quick glances of annoyance and impatience in the direction of her cousin, who steadfastly smoked, and looked into the grate.

At a notice that I could do with her no longer, intercepting my light, she removed to the hearth-stone. I bestowed little attention on her proceedings, but, presently, I heard her begin—

"I've found out, Hareton, that I want—that I'm glad—that I should like you to be my cousin, now, if you had not grown so cross to me, and so rough." Hareton returned no answer.

"Hareton, Hareton, Hareton! do you hear?" she continued.

"Get off wi' ye!" he growled, with uncompromising gruffness.

"Let me take that pipe," she said, cautiously advancing her hand, and abstracting it from his mouth.

Before he could attempt to recover it, it was broken and behind the fire. He swore at her and seized another.

"Stop," she cried, "you must listen to me, first; and I can't speak while those clouds are floating in my face."

"Will you go to the devil!" he exclaimed, "and let me be!"

"No," she persisted, "I won't. I can't tell what to do to make you talk to me, and you are determined not to understand. When I call you stupid, I don't mean anything —I don't mean that I despise you. Come, you shall take notice of me, Hareton—you are my cousin and you shall own me."

"I shall have naught to do wi' you, and your mucky pride, and your damned, mocking tricks!" he answered. "I'll go to hell, body and soul, before I look sideways after you again! side out of t' gait, now; this minute!"

Catherine frowned, and retreated to the window-seat, chewing her lip, and endeavoring, by humming an eccentric tune, to conceal a growing tendency to sob.

"You should be friends with you cousin, Mr. Hareton," I interrupted, "since she repents of her sauciness! it would do you a great deal of good—it would make you another man, to have her for a companion."

"A companion?" he cried; "when she hates me, and does not think me fit to wipe her shoon! Nay, if it made me a king, I'd not be scorned for seeking her good will any more."

"It is not I who hate you, it is you who hate me!" wept Cathy, no longer disguising her trouble. "You hate me as much as Mr. Heathcliff does, and more."

"You're a damned liar," began Earnshaw; "why have I made him angry by taking your part, then, a hundred times? and that, when you sneered at, and despised me, and—. Go on plaguing me, and I'll step in yonder, and say you worried me out of the kitchen!"

"I didn't know you took my part," she answered, drying her eyes; "and I was miserable and bitter at everybody; but, now I thank you, and beg you to forgive me; what can I do besides?"

She returned to the hearth, and frankly extended her hand.

He blackened, and scowled like a thunder-cloud, and kept his fists resolutely clenched, and his gaze fixed on the ground.

Catherine, by instinct, must have divined it was obdurate perversity, and not dislike, that prompted this dogged conduct; for, after remaining an instant, undecided, she stooped, and impressed on his cheek a gentle kiss. The little rogue thought I had not seen her, and, drawing back, she took her former station by the window, quite demurely. I shook my head reprovingly; and then she blushed, and whispered.

"Well, what should I have done, Ellen? He wouldn't shake hands, and he wouldn't look. I must show him some way that I like him—that I want to be frineds."

Whether the kiss convinced Hareton, I cannot tell; he was very careful, for some minutes, that his face should not be seen; and when he did raise it, he was sadly puzzled where to turn his eyes.

Catherine employed herself in wrapping a handsome book

neatly in white paper; and having tied it with a bit of ribbon, and addressed it to "Mr. Hareton Earnshaw," she desired me to be her ambassadress, and convey the present to its destined recipient.

"And tell him, if he'll take it, I'll come and teach him to read it right," she said, "and, if he refuse it, I'll go up stairs, and never tease him again."

I carried it, and repeated the message, anxiously watched by my employer. Hareton would not open his fingers, so I laid it on his knee. He did not strike it off, either, I returned to my work: Catherine leaned her head and arms on the table, till she heard the slight rustle of the covering being removed; then she stole away, and quietly seated herself beside her cousin. He trembled, and his face glowed—all his rudeness and all his surly harshness had deserted him—he could not summon courage, at first, to utter a syllable, in reply to her questioning look and her murmured petition,

"Say you forgive me, Hareton, do! You can make me so happy, by speaking that little word." He muttered something. "And you'll be my friend?" added Catherine, interrogatively.

"Nay! you'll be ashamed of me every day of your life; and the more, the more you know me, and I cannot abide it."

"So you won't be my friend?" she said, smiling as sweet as honey, and creeping close up.

I overheard no further distinguishable talk; but on looking round again, I perceived two such radiant countenances bent over the page of the accepted book, that I did not doubt the treaty had been ratified on both sides, and the enemies were thenceforth sworn allies.

The work they studied was full of costly pictures; and those and their position had charm enough to keep them unmoved, till Joseph came home. He, poor man, was perfectly aghast at the spectacle of Catherine seated on the same bench with Hareton Earnshaw, leaning her hand on his shoulder; and confounded at his favorite's endurance of her proximity. It affected him too deeply to allow an observation on the subject that night. His emotion was only revealed by the immense sighs he drew, as he solemnly spread his large Bible on the table, and overlaid it with dirty bank-notes from his pocket-book, the produce of the day's transactions. At length he summoned Hareton.

"Tak' these in tuh t' maister, lad," he said, "un bide theare, aw's gang up tuh my awn rahm. This hoile's norther mensful nor seemly fur us—we mun side aht, and seearch another!"

"Come, Catherine," I said, "we must 'side out,' too—I've done my ironing, are you ready to go?"

"It is not eight o'clock!" she answered, rising unwillingly. "Hareton, I'll leave this book upon the chimney-piece, and I'll bring you some more to-morrow."

"Ony books ut yah leave, aw shall tak' intuh th' hahse," said Joseph, "un' it 'ull be mitch if yah find 'em agean; soa, yah muh plase yourseln!"

Cathy threatened that his library should pay for hers; and, smiling as she passed Hareton, went singing up-stairs, lighter of heart,

I venture to say, than ever she had been under that roof; except, perhaps, during her earliest visits to Linton.

The intimacy, thus commenced, grew rapidly; though it encountered temporary interruptions. Earnshaw was not to be civilized with a wish; and my young lady was no philosopher, and no paragon of patience; but both their minds tending to the same point—one loving and desiring to esteem; and the other loving and desiring to be esteemed—they contrived, in the end, to reach it.

You see, Mr. Lockwood, it was easy enough to win Mrs. Heathcliff's heart; but now, I'm glad you did not try—the crown of all my wishes will be the union of those two; I shall envy no one on their wedding-day—there won't be a happier woman than myself in England!

. . . .

Chapter 33

On the morrow of that Monday, Earnshaw being still unable to follow his ordinary employments, and, therefore, remaining about the house, I speedily found it would be impracticable to retain my charge beside me, as heretofore.

She got down stairs before me, and out into the garden; where she had seen her cousin performing some easy work; and when I went to bid them come to breakfast, I saw she had persuaded him to clear a large space of ground from currant and gooseberry bushes, and they were busy planning together an importation of plants from the Grange.

I was terrified at the devastation which had been accomplished in a brief-half hour; the black currant trees were the apple of Joseph's eye, and she had just fixed her choice of a flower bed in the midst of them!

"There! That will be all shown to the master," I exclaimed, "the minute it is discovered. And what excuse have you to offer for taking such liberties with the garden? We shall have a fine explosion on the head of it: see if we don't! Mr. Hareton, I wonder you should have no more wit than to go and make that mess at her bidding!"

"I'd forgotten they were Joseph's," answered Earnshaw, rather puzzled, "but I'll tell him I did it."

We always ate our meals with Mr. Heathcliff. I held the mistress's post in making tea and carving; so I was indispensable at table. Catherine usually sat by me; but to-day she stole nearer to Hareton, and I presently saw she would have no more discretion in her friendship than she had in her hostility.

"Now, mind you don't talk with and notice your cousin too much," were my whispered instructions as we entered the room; "It will certainly annoy Mr. Heathcliff, and he'll be mad at you both."

"I'm not going to," she answered.

The minute after, she had sidled to him, and was sticking primroses in his plate of porridge. He dared not speak to her, there; he
dared hardly look; and yet she went on teasing, till he twice was
on the point of being provoked to laugh; and I frowned, and then
she glanced toward the master, whose mind was occupied on
other subjects than his company, as his countenance evinced, and
she grew serious for an instant, scrutinizing him with deep gravity.
Afterward she turned, and recommenced her nonsense; at last
Hareton uttered a smothered laugh.

Mr. Heathcliff started; his eyes rapidly surveyed our faces.
Catherine met it with her accustomed look of nervousness, and yet
defiance, which he abhorred.

"It is well you are out of my reach;" he exclaimed. "What fiend
possesses you to stare back at me, continually, with those infernal
eyes? Down with them! and don't remind me of your existence
again. I thought I had cured you of laughing!"

"It was me," muttered Hareton.

"What do you say?" demanded the master.

Hareton looked at his plate, and did not repeat the confession.
Mr. Heathcliff looked at him a bit, and then silently resumed his
breakfast, and his interrupted musing.

We had nearly finished, and the two young people prudently
shifted wider asunder, so I anticipated no further disturbance
during that sitting; when Joseph appeared at the door, revealing
by his quivering lip and furious eyes, that the outrage committed
on his precious shrubs was detected.

He must have seen Cathy and her cousin about the spot, before
he examined it, for while his jaws worked like those of a cow
chewing its cud, and rendered his speech difficult to understand,
he began:

"Aw mun hev my wage, and aw mun goa! Aw *hed* aimed tuh
dee, wheare aw'd sarved fur sixty year; un' aw thowt aw'd lug my
books up intuh t' garret, un' all my bits uh stuff, un' they sud hev
t' kitchen tuh theirseln; fur t' sake uh quietness. It wur hard tuh
gie up my awn heartshun, but aw thowt aw *could* do that! But,
nah, shoo's taan my garden frough me, un' by th' heart! Maister,
aw cannot stand it! Yah muh bend tuh th' yoak, an ye will. *Aw*
noan used to't and an ow'd man doesn't sooin get used tuh new
barthens—aw'd rayther arn my bite an' my sup wi' a hammer in
th' road!"

"Now, now, idiot!" interrupted Heathcliff, "cut it short! What's
your grievance? I'll interfere in no quarrels between you and Nelly.
She may thrust you into the coal-hole for anything I care."

"It's noan Nelly!" answered Joseph. "Aw sudn't shift fur Nelly.
Nasty, ill-nowt as shoo is. Thank God! *shoo* can not stale t'sowl uh
nob'dy! Shoo wer niver soa handsome, bud whet a body mud look
at her 'baht winking. It's yon flaysome, graceless quean, ut's
witched ahr lad, wi' her bold een, un her forrard ways—till! Nay! I
fair brusts my heart! He's forgetten all aw done for him, un made
on him, un' goan un' riven up a whole row ut t' grandest currant
trees, i' t' garden!" and here he lamented outright, unmanned by

a sense of his bitter injuries, and Earnshaw's ingratitude and dangerous condition.

"Is the fool drunk?" asked Mr. Heathcliff. "Hareton is it you he's finding fault with?"

"I've pulled up two or three bushes," replied the young man, "but I'm going to set 'em again."

"And why have you pulled them up?" said the master.

Catherine wisely put in her tongue.

"We wanted to plant some flowers there," she cried. "I'm the only person to blame, for I wished him to do it."

"And who the devil gave *you* leave to touch a stick about the place?" demanded her father-in-law, much surprised. "And who ordered *you* to obey her?" he added, turning to Hareton. The latter was speechless, his cousin replied—

"You shouldn't grudge a few yards of earth for me to ornament, when you have taken all my land!"

"Your land, insolent slut? you never had any!" said Heathcliff.

"And my money," she continued, returning his angry glare, and, meantime, biting a piece of crust, the remnant of her breakfast.

"Silence!" he exclaimed. "Get done, and begone!"

"And Hareton's land and his money," pursued the reckless thing. "Hareton and I are friends now; and I shall tell him all about you!"

The master seemed confounded a moment, he grew pale, and rose up, eyeing her all the while with an expression of mortal hate.

"If you strike me, Hareton will strike you!" she said, "so you may as well sit down."

"If Hareton does not turn you out of the room I'll strike him to hell," thundered Heathcliff. "Damnable witch! dare you pretend to rouse him against me? Off with her! Do you hear? Fling her into the kitchen! I'll kill her, Ellen Dean, if you let her come into my sight again!"

Hareton tried, under his breath, to persuade her to go.

"Drag her away!" he cried savagely. "Are you staying to talk?" And he approached to execute his own command.

"He'll not obey you, wicked man, any more!" said Catherine, "and he'll soon detest you as much as I do!"

"Wisht! wisht!" muttered the young man reproachfully. "I will not hear you speak so to him. Have done!"

"But you won't let him strike me?" she cried.

"Come then!" he whispered earnestly.

It was too late—Heathcliff had caught hold of her.

"Now *you* go!" he said to Earnshaw. "Accursed witch! this time she has provoked me when I could not bear it; and I'll make her repent it for ever!"

He had his hand in her hair; Hareton attempted to release the locks, entreating him not to hurt her, that once. His black eyes flashed, he seemed ready to tear Catherine in pieces, and I was just worked up to risk going to the rescue, when, of a sudden, his fingers relaxed, he shifted his grasp from her head, to her arm, and gazed intently in her face. Then he drew his hand over his eyes, stood a moment to collect himself, apparently, and turning to Catherine, said, with assumed calmness,

"You must learn to avoid putting me in a passion, or I shall really murder you some time! go with Mrs. Dean, and keep wth her, and confine your insolence to her ears. As to Hareton Earnshaw, if I see him listen to you, I'll send him seeking his bread where he can get it! your love will make him an outcast and a beggar. Nelly, take her; and leave me, all of you! Leave me!"

I led my young lady out; she was too glad of her escape to resist; the other followed, and Mr. Heathcliff had the room to himself till dinner.

I had counseled Catherine to get hers up-stairs; but as soon as he perceived her vacant seat, he sent me to call her. He spoke to none of us, ate very little, and went out directly afterward, intimating that he should not return before evening.

The two new friends established themselves in the house during his absence, where I heard Hareton sternly check his cousin, on her offering a revelation of her father-in-law's conduct to his father. He said he would not suffer a word to be uttered to him in his disparagement; if he were the devil, it did not signify, he would stand by him; and he had rather she would abuse himself, as she used to, than begin on Mr. Heathcliff.

Catherine was waxing cross at this; but he found means to make her hold her tongue, by asking how she would like *him* to speak ill of her father? and then she comprehended that Earnshaw took the master's reputation home to himself: and was attached by ties stronger than reason could break—chains, forged by habit, which it would be cruel to attempt to loosen.

She showed a good heart, thenceforth, in avoiding both complaints and expressions of antipathy concerning Heathcliff; and confessed to me her sorrow that she had endeavored to raise a bad spirit between him and Hareton—indeed, I do not believe she has ever breathed a syllable, in the latter's hearing, against her oppressor since.

When this slight disagreement was over, they were thick again, and as busy as possible in their several occupations of pupil and teacher. I came in to sit with them, after I had done my work, and I felt so soothed and comforted to watch them, that I did not notice how time got on. You know they both appeared, in a measure, my children: I had long been proud of one, and now I was sure the other would be a source of equal satisfaction. His honest, warm, and intelligent nature shook off rapidly the clouds of ignorance and degradation in which it had been bred; and Catherine's sincere commendations acted as a spur to his industry. His brightening mind brightened his features, and added spirit and nobility to their aspect. I could hardly fancy it the same individual I had beheld on the day I discovered my little lady at Wuthering Heights, after her expedition to the Crags.

While I admired, and they labored, dusk drew on, and with it returned the master. He came upon us quite unexpectedly, entering by the front way, and had a full view of the whole three, ere we could raise our heads to glance at him.

"Well," I reflected, "there was never a pleasanter, or more harmless sight; and it will be a burning shame to scold them." The red firelight glowed on their two bonny heads, and revealed their faces, animated with the eager interest of children; for though he was twenty-three, and she eighteen, each had so much of novelty to feel and learn, that neither experienced nor evinced the sentiments of sober disenchanted maturity.

They lifted their eyes together to encounter Mr. Heathcliff—perhaps you have never remarked that their eyes are precisely similiar, and they are those of Catherine Earnshaw. The present Catherine has no other likeness to her except a breadth of forehead and a certain arch of the nostril, that makes her appear rather haughty, whether she will or not. With Hareton the resemblance is carried farther, it is singular at all times—then it was particularly striking; because his senses were alert and his mental faculties wakened to unwonted activity.

I suppose this resemblance disarmed Mr. Heathcliff: he walked to the hearth in evident agitation, but it quickly subsided as he looked at the young man; or, I should stay, altered its character, for it was there yet.

He took the book from his hand, and glanced at the open page, then returned it without any observation; merely signing Catherine away. Her companion lingered very little behind her, and I was about to depart also, but he bid me sit still.

"It is a poor conclusion, is it not?" he observed, having brooded a while on the scene he had just witnessed. "An absurd termination to my violent exertions? I get levers and mattocks to demolish the two houses, and train myself to be capable of working like Hercules, and when every thing is ready and in my power, I find the will to lift a slate off either roof has vanished! My old enemies have not beaten me—now would be the precise time to revenge myself on their representatives. I could do it, and none could hinder me; but where is the use? I don't care for striking—I can't take the trouble to raise my hand! That sounds as if I had been laboring the whole time only to exhibit a fine trait of magnanimity. It is far from being the case. I have lost the faculty of enjoying their destruction, and I am too idle to destroy for nothing.

"Nelly, there is a strange change approaching; I'm in its shadow at present. I take so little interest in my daily life, that I hardly remember to eat and drink. Those two, who have left the room, are the only objects which retain a distinct material appearance to me; and that appearance causes me pain, amounting to agony. About *her* I won't speak, and I don't desire to think; but I earnestly wish she were invisible—her presence invokes only maddening sensations. *He* moves me differently; and yet if I could do it without seeming insane, I'd never see him again! You'll perhaps think me rather inclined to become so," he added, making an effort to smile, "if I try to describe the thousand forms of past associations and ideas he awakens or embodies. But you'll not talk of what I tell you, and my mind is so eternally secluded in itself it is tempting at last to turn it out to another.

"Five minutes ago Hareton seemed a personification of my youth, not a human being. I felt to him in such a variety of ways, that it would have been impossible to have accosted him rationally.

"In the first place, his startling likeness to Catherine connected him fearfully with her. That, however, which you may suppose the most potent to arrest my imagination is actually the least; for what is not connected with her to me? and what does not recall her? I cannot look down to this floor but her features are shaped on the flags! In every cloud, in every tree—filling the air at night, and caught by glimpses in every object by day—I am surrounded with her image! The most ordinary faces of men and women— my own features mock me with a resemblance. The entire world is a dreadful collection of memoranda that she did exist, and that I have lost her!

"Well, Hareton's aspect was the ghost of my immortal love, of my wild endeavors to hold my right; my degradation, my pride, my happiness, and my anguish. But it is frenzy to repeat these thoughts to you; only it will let you know why, with a reluctance to be always alone, his society is no benefit, rather an aggravation of the constant torment I suffer—and it partly contributes to render me regardless how he and his cousin go on together. I can give them no attention any more."

"But what do you mean by a *change*, Mr. Heathcliff?" I said, alarmed at his manner, though he was neither in danger of losing his senses nor dying; according to my judgment, he was quite strong and healthy; and as to his reason, from childhood he had a delight in dwelling on dark things, and entertaining odd fancies: he might have had a monomania on the subject of his departed idol; but on every other point his wits were as sound as mine.

"I shall not know that till it comes," he said, "I'm only half conscious of it now."

"You have no feeling of illness, have you?" I asked.

"No, Nelly, I have not," he answered.

"Then, you are not afraid of death?" I pursued.

"Afraid? No!" he replied. "I have neither a fear, nor a presentiment, nor a hope of death. Why should I? With my hard constitution, and temperate mode of living, and unperilous occupations, I ought to, and probably *shall* remain above ground, till there is scarcely a black hair on my head. And yet I cannot continue in this condition! I have to remind myself to breathe—almost to remind my heart to beat! And it is like bending back a stiff spring—it is by compulsion that I do the slightest act, not prompted by one thought; and by compulsion that I notice anything alive or dead, which is not associated with one universal idea. I have a single wish, and my whole being and faculties are yearning to attain it. They have yearned toward it so long and so unwaveringly, that I'm convinced it *will* be reached—and *soon*— because it has devoured my existence. I am swallowed in the anticipation of its fulfillment. My confessions have not relieved me—but, they may account for some otherwise unaccountable

phases of humor which I show. Oh, God! It's a long fight, I wish it
were over!"

He began to pace the room, muttering terrible things to himself, till I was inclined to believe, as he said Joseph did, that
conscience had turned his heart to an earthly hell. I wondered
greatly how it would end.

Though he seldom before had revealed this state of mind, even
by looks, it was his habitual mood, I had no doubt: he asserted it
himself—but not a soul, from his general bearing would have
conjectured the fact. You did not, when you saw him, Mr. Lockwood—and at the point of which I speak he was just the same as
then, only fonder of continued solitude and perhaps still more
laconic in company.

. . . .

Chapter 34

For some days after that evening Mr. Heathcliff shunned meeting us at meals; yet he would not consent formally to exclude
Hareton and Cathy. He had an aversion to yielding so completely
to his feelings, choosing, rather, to absent himself; and eating
once in twenty-four hours seemed sufficient sustenance for him.

One night, after the family were in bed, I heard him go down
stairs, and out at the front door: I did not hear him re-enter, and
in the morning I found he was still away. We were in April then,
the weather was sweet and warm, the grass as green as showers
and sun could make it, and the two dwarf apple trees near the
southern wall in full bloom.

After breakfast, Catherine insisted on my bringing a chair, and
sitting, with my work, under the fir-trees at the end of the house;
and she beguiled Hareton, who had recovered from his accident,
to dig and arrange her little garden, which was shifted to that
corner by the influence of Joseph's complaints.

I was comfortably revelling in the spring fragrance around, and
the beautiful soft blue overhead, when my young lady, who had
run down near the gate, to procure some primrose roots for a
border, returned only half laden, and informed us that Mr. Heathcliff was coming in.

"And he spoke to me," she added with a perplexed look.

"What did he say?" asked Hareton.

"He told me to begone as fast as I could," she answered. "But
he looked so different from his usual look that I stopped a moment to stare at him."

"How?" he inquired.

"Why, almost bright and cheerful—no, almost nothing—*very
much* excited, and wild and glad!" she replied.

"Night-walking amuses him, then," I remarked, affecting a
careless manner; in reality as surprised as she was, and anxious to
ascertain the truth of her statement, for to see the master looking

glad would not be an every-day spectacle, I framed an excuse to go in.

Heathcliff stood at the open door; he was pale, and he trembled; yet, certainly, he had a strange joyful glitter in his eyes, that altered the aspect of his whole face.

"Will you have some breakfast?" I said. "You must be hungry, rambling about all night!"

I wanted to discover where he had been; but I did not like to ask directly.

"No, I'm not hungry," he answered, averting his head, and speaking rather contemptuously, as if he guessed I was trying to divine the occasion of his good humor.

I felt perplexed—I didn't know whether it were not a proper opportunity to offer a bit of admonition.

"I don't think it right to wander out of doors," I observed, "instead of being in bed: it is not wise, at any rate, this moist season. I dare say you'll catch a bad cold, or a fever—you have something the matter with you now!"

"Nothing but what I can bear," he replied, "and with the greatest pleasure, provided you'll leave me alone—get in, and don't annoy me."

I obeyed; and, in passing, I saw he breathed as fast as a cat.

"Yes!" I reflected to myself, "we shall have a fit of illness. I can not conceive what he has been doing!"

That noon, he sat down to dinner with us, and received a heaped-up plate from my hands, as if he intended to make amends for previous fasting.

"I've neither cold nor fever, Nelly," he remarked, in allusion to my morning's speech. "And I'm ready to do justice to the food you give me."

He took his knife and fork, and was going to commence eating, when the inclination appeared to become suddenly extinct. He laid them on the table, looked eagerly toward the window, then rose and went out. We saw him walking, to and fro, in the garden, while we concluded our meal; and Earnshaw said he'd go and ask why he would not dine; he thought we had grieved him some way.

"Well, is he coming?" cried Catherine, when he returned.

"Nay," he answered, "but he's not angry; he seemed rare and pleased indeed; only I made him impatient by speaking to him twice; and then he bid me be off to you; he wondered how I could want the company of anybody else."

I set his plate to keep warm on the fender; and after an hour or two he re-entered, when the room was clear; in no degree calmer—the same unnatural—it was unnatural—appearance of joy under his black brows; the same bloodless hue; and his teeth visible now and then in a kind of smile; his frame shivering, not as one shivers with chill or weakness, but as a tight-stretched cord vibrates—a strong thrilling rather than trembling.

"I will ask what is the matter," I thought, "or who should?" And I exclaimed—"Have you heard any good news, Mr. Heathcliff? You look uncommonly animated."

"Where should good news come from to me?" he said. "I'm animated with hunger; and seemingly, I must not eat."

"Your dinner is here," I returned; "why won't you get it?"

"I don't want it now," he muttered hastily. "I'll wait till supper. And, Nelly, once for all, let me beg you to warn Hareton and the other away from me. I wish to be troubled by nobody—I wish to have this place to myself."

"Is there some new reason for this banishment?" I inquired. "Tell me why you are so queer, Mr. Heathcliff? Where were you last night? I'm not putting the question through idle curiosity, but—"

"You are putting the question through very idle curiosity," he interrupted, with a laugh. "Yet I'll answer it. Last night I was on the threshold of hell. To-day I am within sight of my heaven—I have my eyes on it—hardly three feet to sever me. And now you'd better go. You'll neither see nor hear anything to frighten you, if you refrain from prying."

Having swept the hearth and wiped the table, I departed, more perplexed than ever. He did not quit the house again that after- noon, and no one intruded on his solitude till, at eight o'clock, I deemed it proper, though unsummoned, to carry a candle, and his supper to him.

He was leaning against the ledge of an open lattice, but not looking out; his face was turned to the interior gloom. The fire had smoldered to ashes; the room was filled with the damp, mild air of the cloudy evening; and so still, that not only the murmur of the beck down Gimmerton was distinguishable, but its ripples, and its gurgling over the pebbles, or through the large stones which it could not cover.

I uttered an ejaculation of discontent at seeing the dismal grate, and commenced shutting the casements, one after another, till I came to his.

"Must I close this?" I asked, in order to rouse him, for he would not stir.

The light flashed on his features, as I spoke. Oh, Mr. Lockwood, I can not express what a terrible start I got, by the momentary view! Those deep black eyes! That smile, and ghastly paleness! It appeared to me, not Mr. Heathcliff, but a goblin; and, in my terror, I let the candle bend toward the wall, and it left me in darkness.

"Yes, close it," he replied, in his familiar voice. "There, that is pure awkwardness! Why did you hold the candle horizontally? Be quick, and bring another."

I hurried out in a foolish state of dread, and said to Joseph— "The master wishes you to take him a light, and rekindle the fire." For I dare not go in myself again just then.

Joseph rattled some fire into the shovel, and went; but he brought it back immediately, with the supper tray in his other hand, explaining that Mr. Heathcliff was going to bed, and he wanted nothing to eat till morning.

We heard him mount the stairs directly; he did not proceed to his ordinary chamber, but turned into that with the panelled bed—its window, as I mentioned before, is wide enough for any body to get through, and it struck me that he plotted another midnight excursion, which he had rather we had no suspicion of.

"Is he a ghoul, or a vampire?" I mused. I had read of such hideous, incarnate demons. And then, I set myself to reflect how I had tended him in infancy; and watched him grow to youth; and followed him almost through his whole course; and what nonsense it was to yield to that sense of horror.

"But, where did he come from, the little dark thing, harbored by a good man to his bane?" muttered superstition, as I dozed into unconsciousness. And I began, half dreaming, to weary myself with imagining some fit parentage for him; and repeating my waking meditations, I tracked his existence over again, with grim variations; at last, picturing his death and funeral; of which, all I can remember is, being exceedingly vexed at having the task of dictating an inscription for his monument, and consulting the sexton about it; and, as he had no surname, and we could not tell his age, we were obliged to content ourselves with the single word, "Heathcliff." That came true—we were. If you enter the kirkyard, you'll read on his headstone only that, and the date of his death. Dawn restored me to common sense. I rose, and went into the garden, as soon as I could see, to ascertain if there were any footmarks under his window. There were none.

"He has staid at home," I thought, "and he'll be all right to-day!"

I prepared breakfast for the household, as was my usual custom, but told Hareton and Catherine to get theirs ere the master came down, for he lay late. They preferred taking it out of doors, under the trees, and I set a little table to accommodate them.

On my re-entrance, I found Mr. Heathcliff below. He and Joseph were conversing about some farming business; he gave clear, minute directions concerning the matter discussed, but he spoke rapidly, and turned his head continually aside, and had the same excited expression, even more exaggerated.

When Joseph quitted the room, he took his seat in the place he generally chose, and I put a basin of coffee before him. He drew it nearer, and then rested his arms on the table, and looked at the opposite wall, as I supposed, surveying one particular portion, up and down, with glittering, restless eyes, and with such eager interest, that he stopped breathing, during half a minute together.

"Come, now," I exclaimed, pushing some bread against his hand. "Eat and drink that while it is hot. It has been waiting near an hour."

He didn't notice me, and yet he smiled. I'd rather have seen him gnash his teeth than smile so.

"Mr. Heathcliff! master!" I cried. "Don't, for God's sake, stare as if you saw an unearthly vision."

"Don't, for God's sake, shout so loud," he replied. "Turn round, and tell me, are we by ourselves?"

"Of course," was my answer, "of course we are!"

Still I involuntarily obeyed him, as if I were not quite sure.

With a sweep of his hand, he cleared a vacant space in front among the breakfast things, and leaned forward to gaze more at his ease.

Now I perceived he was not looking at the wall, for when I regarded him alone, it seemed, exactly, that he gazed at something within two yards distance. And, whatever it was, it communicated, apparently, both pleasure and pain, in exquisite extremes; at least the anguished yet raptured expression of his countenance suggested that idea.

The fancied object was not fixed either; his eyes pursued it with unwearied vigilance, and, even in speaking to me, were never weaned away.

I vainly reminded him of his protracted abstinence from food. If he stirred to touch anything in compliance with my entreaties—if he stretched his hand out to get a piece of bread—his fingers clenched before they reached it, and remained on the table, forgetful of their aim.

I sat, a model of patience, trying to attract his absorbed attention from its engrossing speculation, till he grew irritable and got up, asking why I would not allow him to have his own time in taking his meals? and saying that on the next occasion I needn't wait—I might set the things down and go. Having uttered these words, he left the house, slowly sauntered down the garden path, and disappeared through the gate.

The hours crept anxiously by: another evening came. I did not retire to rest till late, and when I did I could not sleep. He returned after midnight, and, instead of going to bed, shut himself into the room beneath. I listened and tossed about, and finally dressed and descended. It was too irksome to lie up there, harassing my brain with a hundred idle misgivings.

I distinguished Mr. Heathcliff's step, restlessly measuring the floor; and he frequently broke the silence by a deep inspiration, resembling a groan. He muttered detached words also; the only one I could catch was the name of Catherine, coupled with some wild term of endearment or suffering, and spoken as one would speak to a person present—low and earnest, and wrung from the depth of his soul.

I had not courage to walk straight into the apartment; but I desired to divert him from his revery, and therefore fell foul of the kitchen fire; stirred it and began to scrape the cinders. It drew him forth sooner than I expected. He opened the door immediately, and said—

"Nelly, come here—is it morning? Come in with your light."

"It is striking four." I answered; "you want a candle to take upstairs—you might have lighted one at this fire."

"No, I don't wish to go up-stairs," he said. "Come in, and kindle *me* a fire, and do anything there is to do about the room."

"I must blow the coals red first, before I can carry any," I replied, getting a chair and the bellows.

He roamed to and fro, meantime, in a state approaching distraction, his heavy sighs succeeding each other so thick as to leave no space for common breathing between.

"When day breaks, I'll send for Green," he said; "I wish to make some legal inquiries of him, while I can bestow a thought on those matters, and while I can act calmly. I have not written my will yet, and how to leave my property I cannot determine! I wish I could annihilate it from the face of the earth."

"I would not talk so, Mr. Heathcliff," I interposed. "Let your will be a while—you'll be spared to repent of your many injustices yet! I never expected that your nerves would be disordered—they are, at present, marvelously so, however; and almost entirely through your own fault. The way you've passed these three last days might knock up a Titan. Do take some food and some repose. You need only look at yourself in a glass to see how you require both. Your cheeks are hollow and your eyes bloodshot, like a person starving with hunger and going blind with loss of sleep."

"It is not my fault, that I cannot eat or rest," he replied. "I assure you it is through no settled designs. I'll do both as soon as I possibly can. But you might as well bid a man struggling in the water, rest within arms-length of the shore! I must reach it first, and then I'll rest. Well, never mind Mr. Green; as to repenting of my injustices, I've done no injustice, and I repent of nothing. I'm too happy, and yet I'm not happy enough. My soul's bliss kills my body, but does not satisfy itself."

"Happy, master?" I cried. "Strange happiness! If you would hear me without being angry, I might offer some advice that would make you happier."

"What is that?" he asked. "Give it."

"You are aware, Mr. Heathcliff," I said, "that from the time you were thirteen years old, you have lived a selfish, unchristian life: and probably hardly had a Bible in your hands, during all that period. You must have forgotten the contents to the book, and you may not have space to search it now. Could it be hurtful to send for some one—some minister of any denomination, it does not matter which, to explain it, and show you how very far you have erred from its precepts, and how unfit you will be for its heaven, unless a change takes place before you die?"

"I'm rather obliged than angry, Nelly," he said, "for you remind me of the manner that I desire to be buried in. It is to be carried to the churchyard in the evening. You and Hareton may, if you please, accompany me—and mind, particularly, to notice that the sexton obeys my directions concerning the two coffins! No minister need come; nor need anything be said over me. I tell you, I have nearly attained *my* heaven; and that of others is altogether unvalued and uncoveted by me!"

"And supposing you persevered in your obstinate fast, and died by that means, and they refused to bury you in the precincts of the kirk?" I said, shocked at his godless indifference. "How would you like it?"

"They won't do that," he replied, "if they did, you must have me removed secretly; and if you neglect it, you shall prove, practically, that the dead are not annihilated!"

As soon as he heard the other members of the family stirring, he retired to his den, and I breathed freer. But in the afternoon, while Joseph and Hareton were at their work, he came into the kitchen again, and, with a wild look, bid me come and sit in the house—he wanted somebody with him.

I declined, telling him plainly that his strange talk and manner frightened me, and I had neither the nerve or the will to be his companion alone.

"I believe you think me a fiend!" he said, with his dismal laugh, "something too horrible to live under a decent roof!"

Then turning to Catherine, who was there, and who drew behind me at his approach, he added, half sneeringly.

"Will *you* come, chuck? I'll not hurt you. No! to you, I've made myself worse than the devil. Well, there is *one* who won't shrink from my company! By God! she's relentless. Oh, damn it! It's unutterably too much for flesh and blood to bear, even mine."

He solicited the society of no one more. At dusk he went into his chamber. Through the whole night, and far into the morning, we heard him groaning and murmuring to himself. Hareton was anxious to enter, but I bid him fetch Mr. Kenneth, and he should go in and see him.

When he came, and I requested admittance and tried to open the door, I found it locked; and Heathcliff bid us be damned. He was better, and would be left alone; so the doctor went away.

The following evening was very wet, indeed it poured down till day-dawn; and, as I took my morning walk round the house, I observed the master's window swinging open, and the rain driving straight in.

"He cannot be in bed," I thought, "those showers would drench him through! He must be either up or out. But I'll make no more ado, I'll go boldly, and look!"

Having succeeded in obtaining entrance with another key, I ran to unclose the panels, for the chamber was vacant—quickly pushing them aside, I peeped in. Mr. Heathcliff was there—laid on his back. His eyes met mine, so keen and fierce that I started; and then he seemed to smile.

I could not think him dead—but his face and throat were washed with rain; the bed-clothes dripped, and he was perfectly still. The lattice, flapping to and fro, had grazed one hand that rested on the sill—no blood trickled from the broken skin, and when I put my fingers to it I could doubt no more—he was dead and stark!

I hasped the window; I combed his long, black hair from his forehead; I tried to close his eyes—to extinguish, if possible, that frightful, life-like exultation, before any one else beheld it. They would not shut—they seemed to sneer at my attempts, and his parted lips and sharp, white teeth sneered too! Taken with another fit of cowardice, I cried out for Joseph. Joseph shuffled up, and made a noise, but resolutely refused to meddle with him.

"Th' divil's harried off his soul," he cried, "and he muh hev his carcass intuh t' bargin, for ow't aw care! Ech! what a wicked un he looks, grinning at death!" and the old sinner grinned in mockery.

I thought he intended to cut a caper round the bed; but suddenly composing himself, he fell on his knees, and raised his hands, and returned thanks that the lawful master and the ancient stock were restored to their rights.

I felt stunned by the awful event; and my memory unavoidably recurred to former times with a sort of oppressive sadness. But poor Hareton, the most wronged, was the only one that really suffered much. He sat by the corpse all night, weeping in bitter earnest. He pressed its hand, and kissed the sarcastic, savage face that every one else shrank from contemplating; and bemoaned him with that strong grief which springs naturally from a generous heart, though it be tough as tempered steel.

Kenneth was perplexed to pronounce of what disorder the master died. I concealed the fact of his having swallowed nothing for four days, fearing it might lead to trouble; and then, I am persuaded, he did not not abstain on purpose: it was the consequence of his strange illness, not the cause.

We buried him, to the scandal of the whole neighborhood, as he had wished. Earnshaw and I, the sexton, and six men to carry the coffin, comprehended the whole attendance.

The six men departed when they had let it down into the grave: we stayed to see it covered. Hareton, with a streaming face, dug green sods, and laid them over the brown mold himself. At present it is as smooth and verdant as its companion mounds—and I hope its tenant sleeps as soundly. But the country folks, if you asked them, would swear on their Bibles that he *walks*. There are those who speak to having met him near the church, and on the moor, and even within this house. Idle tales, you'll say, and so say I. Yet that old man by the kitchen fire affirms he has seen "two on 'em" looking out of his chamber window, on every rainy night, since his death—and an odd thing happened to me about a month ago.

I was going to the Grange one evening—a dark evening threatening thunder—and, just at the turn of the Heights, I encountered a little boy with a sheep and two lambs before him. He was crying terribly, and I supposed the lambs were skittish, and would not be guided.

"What is the matter, my little man?" I asked.

"They's Heathcliff and a woman yonder, under t'nab," he blubbered, "un' aw darnut pass 'em."

I saw nothing; but neither the sheep nor he would go on, so I bid him take the road lower down. He probably raised the phantoms from thinking, as he traversed the moors alone, on the nonsense he had heard his parents and companions repeat; yet, still, I don't like being out in the dark now, and I don't like being left by myself in this grim house. I cannot help it; I shall be glad when they leave it, and shift to the Grange!

"They are going to the Grange, then?" I said.

"Yes," answered Mrs. Dean, "as soon as they are married; and that will be on New Year's day."

"And who will live here then?"

"Why, Joseph will take care of the house, and, perhaps, a lad to

keep him company. They will live in the kitchen, and the rest will
be shut up."

"For the use of such ghosts as choose to inhabit it," I observed.

"No, Mr. Lockwood," said Nelly, shaking her head. "I believe
the dead are at peace, but it is not right to speak of them with
levity."

At that moment the garden gate swung to; the ramblers were
returning.

"*They* are afraid of nothing," I grumbled, watching their approach through the window. "Together they would brave Satan
and all his legions."

As they stepped upon the door-stones, and halted to take a last
look at the moon, or, more correctly, at each other, by her light, I
felt irresistibly impelled to escape them again; and, pressing a
remembrance into the hands of Mrs. Dean, and disregarding her
expostulations at my rudeness, I vanished through the kitchen, as
they opened the house-door; and so should have confirmed
Joseph in his opinion of his fellow-servant's gay indiscretions, had
he not, fortunately, recognized me for a respectable character, by
the sweet ring of a sovereign at his feet.

My walk home was lengthened by a diversion in the direction
of the kirk. When beneath its walls, I perceived decay had made
progress, even in seven months—many a window showed black
gaps deprived of glass; and slates jutted off, here and there,
beyond the right line of the roof, to be gradually worked off in
coming autumn storms.

I sought, and soon discovered, the three head-stones on the
slope next the moor—the middle one, gray, and half buried in the
heath—Edgar Linton's only harmonized by the turf and moss
creeping up its foot—Heathcliff's still bare.

I lingered round them, under that benign sky; watched the
moths fluttering among the heath and harebells; listened to the
soft wind breathing through the grass; and wondered how any one
could ever imagine unquiet slumbers for the sleepers in that quiet
earth.

Collected Poems

of
Emily Dickinson

· · ·

PREFACE

THE verses of Emily Dickinson belong emphatically to what Emerson long since called "the Poetry of the Portfolio" – something produced absolutely without the thought of publication, and solely by way of expression of the writer's own mind. Such verse must inevitably forfeit whatever advantage lies in the discipline of public criticism and the enforced conformity to accepted ways. On the other hand, it may often gain something through the habit of freedom and the unconventional utterance of daring thoughts. In the case of the present author, there was absolutely no choice in the matter; she must write thus, or not at all. A recluse by temperament and habit, literally spending years without setting her foot beyond the doorstep, and many more years during which her walks were strictly limited to her father's grounds, she habitually concealed her mind, like her person, from all but a very few friends; and it was with great difficulty that she was persuaded to print, during her lifetime, three or four poems. Yet she wrote verses in great abundance; and though curiously indifferent to all conventional rules, had yet a rigorous literary standard of her own, and often altered a word many times to suit an ear which had its own tenacious fastidiousness.

Miss Dickinson was born in Amherst, Mass., Dec. 10, 1830, and died there May 15, 1886. Her father, Hon. Edward Dickinson, was the leading lawyer of Amherst, and was treasurer of the well-known college there situated. It was his custom once a year to hold a large reception at his house, attended by all the families connected with the institution and by the leading people of the town. On these occasions his

daughter Emily emerged from her wonted retirement and did
her part as gracious hostess; nor would any one have known
from her manner, I have been told, that this was not a daily
occurrence. The annual occasion once past, she withdrew again
into her seclusion, and except for a very few friends was as
invisible to the world as if she had dwelt in a nunnery. For
myself, although I had corresponded with her for many years, I
saw her but twice face to face, and brought away the impression
of something as unique and remote as Undine or Mignon or
Thekla.

This selection from her poems is published to meet the
desire of her personal friends, and especially of her surviving
sister. It is believed that the thoughtful reader will find in these
pages a quality more suggestive of the poetry of William Blake
than of anything to be elsewhere found,—flashes of wholly
original and profound insight into nature and life; words and
phrases exhibiting an extraordinary vividness of descriptive and
imaginative power, yet often set in a seemingly whimsical or
even rugged frame. They are here published as they were
written, with very few and superficial changes. In many cases
these verses will seem to the reader like poetry torn up by the
roots, with rain and dew and earth still clinging to them, giving
a freshness and a fragrance not otherwise to be conveyed. In
other cases, as in the few poems of shipwreck or of mental
conflict, we can only wonder at the gift of vivid imagination by
which this recluse woman can delineate, by a few touches, the
very crises of physical or mental struggle. And sometimes again
we catch glimpses of a lyric strain, sustained perhaps but for a
line or two at a time, and making the reader regret its sudden
cessation. But the main quality of these poems is that of
extraordinary grasp and insight, uttered with an uneven vigor
sometimes exasperating, seemingly wayward, but really
unsought and inevitable. After all, when a thought takes one's
breath away, a lesson on grammar seems an impertinence. As

Ruskin wrote in his earlier and better days, "No weight nor mass nor beauty of execution can outweigh one grain or fragment of thought."

THOMAS WENTWORTH HIGGINSON

I. LIFE

I.

SUCCESS is counted sweetest
　　　By those who ne'er succeed.
To comprehend a nectar
Requires sorest need.

Not one of all the purple host
Who took the flag to-day
Can tell the definition,
So clear, of victory,

As he, defeated, dying,
On whose forbidden ear
The distant strains of triumph
Break, agonized and clear.

II.

OUR share of night to bear,
　　　Our share of morning,
Our blank in bliss to fill,
Our blank in scorning.

Here a star, and there a star,
Some lose their way.
Here a mist, and there a mist,
Afterwards—day!

III.

SOUL, wilt thou toss again?
      By just such a hazard
Hundreds have lost, indeed,
But tens have won an all.

Angels' breathless ballot
Lingers to record thee;
Imps in eager caucus
Raffle for my soul

IV.

'TIS so much joy! 'T is so much joy!
      If I should fail, what poverty!
And yet, as poor as I
Have ventured all upon a throw;
Have gained! Yes! Hesitated so
This side the victory!

Life is but life, and death but death!
Bliss is but bliss, and breath but breath!
And if, indeed, I fail,
At least to know the worst is sweet.
Defeat means nothing but defeat,
No drearier can prevail!

And if I gain,—oh, gun at sea,
Oh, bells that in the steeples be,
At first repeat it slow!
For heaven is a different thing
Conjectured, and waked sudden in,
And might o'erwhelm me so!

V.

GLEE! the great storm is over!
    Four have recovered the land;
Forty gone down together
Into the boiling sand.

Ring, for the scant salvation!
Toll, for the bonnie souls,—
Neighbor and friend and bridegroom,
Spinning upon the shoals!

How they will tell the shipwreck
When winter shakes the door,
Till the children ask, "But the forty?
Did they come back no more?"

Then a silence suffuses the story,
And a softness the teller's eye;
And the children no further question,
And only the waves reply.

VI.

IF I can stop one heart from breaking,
    I shall not live in vain;
If I can ease one life the aching,
Or cool one pain,
Or help one fainting robin
Unto his nest again,
I shall not live in vain.

VII.

WITHIN my reach!
        I could have touched!
I might have chanced that way!
Soft sauntered through the village,
Sauntered as soft away!
So unsuspected violets
Within the fields lie low,
Too late for striving fingers
That passed, an hour ago.

VIII.

A WOUNDED deer leaps highest,
        I've heard the hunter tell;
'Tis but the ecstasy of death,
And then the brake is still.

The smitten rock that gushes,
The trampled steel that springs:
A cheek is always redder
Just where the hectic stings!

Mirth is the mail of anguish,
In which it cautious arm,
Lest anybody spy the blood
And "You're hurt" exclaim!

IX.

THE heart asks pleasure first,
        And then, excuse from pain;
And then, those little anodynes
That deaden suffering;

And then, to go to sleep;
And then, if it should be
The will of its Inquisitor,
The liberty to die.

X.

A PRECIOUS, mouldering pleasure 't is
        To meet an antique book,
In just the dress his century wore;
A privilege, I think,

His venerable hand to take,
And warming in our own,
A passage back, or two, to make
To times when he was young.

His quaint opinions to inspect,
His knowledge to unfold
On what concerns our mutual mind,
The literature of old;

What interested scholars most,
What competitions ran
When Plato was a certainty,
And Sophocles a man;

When Sappho was a living girl,
And Beatrice wore
The gown that Dante deified.
Facts, centuries before,

He traverses familiar,
As one should come to town
And tell you all your dreams were true:
He lived where dreams were sown.

His presence is enchantment,
You beg him not to go;
Old volumes shake their vellum heads
And tantalize, just so.

XI.

MUCH madness is divinest sense
        To a discerning eye;
Much sense the starkest madness.
'T is the majority
In this, as all, prevails.
Assent, and you are sane;
Demur,—you're straightway dangerous,
And handled with a chain.

XII.

I ASKED no other thing,
    No other was denied.
I offered Being for it;
The mighty merchant smiled.

Brazil? He twirled a button,
Without a glance my way:
"But madam, is there nothing else
That we can show to-day?"

XIII.

THE soul selects her own society,
    Then shuts the door;
On her divine majority
Obtrude no more.

Unmoved, she notes the chariot's pausing
At her low gate;
Unmoved, an emperor is kneeling
Upon her mat.

I've known her from an ample nation
Choose one;
Then close the valves of her attention
Like stone.

XIV.

SOME things that fly there be,–
      Birds, hours, the bumble-bee:
Of these no elegy.

Some things that stay there be,–
Grief, hills, eternity:
Nor this behooveth me.

There are, that resting, rise.
Can I expound the skies?
How still the riddle lies!

XV.

I KNOW some lonely houses off the road
      A robber'd like the look of,–
Wooden barred,
And windows hanging low,
Inviting to
A portico,
Where two could creep:
One hand the tools,
The other peep
To make sure all's asleep.
Old-fashioned eyes,
Not easy to surprise!

How orderly the kitchen'd look by night,
With just a clock,–
But they could gag the tick,
And mice won't bark;
And so the walls don't tell, None will.
A pair of spectacles ajar just stir–
An almanac's aware.
Was it the mat winked,
Or a nervous star?
The moon slides down the stair
To see who's there.

There's plunder,–where?
Tankard, or spoon,
Earring, or stone,
A watch, some ancient brooch
To match the grandmamma,
Staid sleeping there.

Day-rattles, too,
Stealth's slow;
The sun has got as far
As the third sycamore.
Screams chanticleer,
"Who's there?"
Sneer–"Where?"
While the old couple, just astir,
Fancy the sunrise left the door ajar!

XVI.

TO fight aloud is very brave,
        But gallanter, I know,
Who charge within the bosom,
The cavalry of woe.

Who win, and nations do not see,
Who fall, and none observe,
Whose dying eyes no country
Regards with patriot love.

We trust, in plumed procession,
For such the angels go,
Rank after rank, with even feet
And uniforms of snow.

XVII.

WHEN night is almost done,
        And sunrise grows so near
That we can touch the spaces,
It's time to smooth the hair.

And get the dimples ready,
And wonder we could care
For that old faded midnight
That frightened but an hour.

XVIII.

READ, sweet, how others strove,
    Till we are stouter;
What they renounced,
Till we are less afraid;
How many times they bore
The faithful witness,
Till we are helped,
As if a kingdom cared!

Read then of faith
That shone above the fagot;
Clear strains of hymn
The river could not drown;
Brave names of men
And celestial women,
Passed out of record
Into renown!

XIX.

PAIN has an element of blank;
    It cannot recollect
When it began, or if there were
A day when it was not.

It has no future but itself,
Its infinite realms contain
Its past, enlightened to perceive
New periods of pain.

XX.

I TASTE a liquor never brewed,
        From tankards scooped in pearl;
Not all the vats upon the Rhine
Yield such an alcohol!

Inebriate of air am I,
And debauchee of dew,
Reeling, through endless summer days,
From inns of molten blue.

When landlords turn the drunken bee
Out of the foxglove's door,
When butterflies renounce their drams,
I shall but drink the more!

Till seraphs swing their snowy hats,
And saints to windows run,
To see the little tippler
Leaning against the sun!

XXI.

HE ate and drank the precious words,
        His spirit grew robust;
He knew no more that he was poor,
Nor that his frame was dust.
He danced along the dingy days,
And this bequest of wings
Was but a book. What liberty
A loosened spirit brings!

XXII.

I HAD no time to hate, because
        The grave would hinder me,
And life was not so ample I
Could finish enmity.

Nor had I time to love; but since
Some industry must be,
The little toil of love, I thought,
Was large enough for me.

XXIII.

'T WAS such a little, little boat
        That toddled down the bay!
'T was such a gallant, gallant sea
That beckoned it away!

'T was such a greedy, greedy wave
That licked it from the coast;
Nor ever guessed the stately sails
My little craft was lost!

XXIV.

WHETHER my bark went down at sea,
        Whether she met with gales,
Whether to isles enchanted
She bent her docile sails;

By what mystic mooring
She is held to-day,—
This is the errand of the eye
Out upon the bay.

XXV.

BELSHAZZAR had a letter,—
        He never had but one;
Belshazzar's correspondent
Concluded and begun
In that immortal copy
The conscience of us all
Can read without its glasses
On revelation's wall.

XXVI.

THE brain within its groove
      Runs evenly and true;
But let a splinter swerve,
'T were easier for you
To put the water back
When floods have slit the hills,
And scooped a turnpike for themselves,
And blotted out the mills!

II. LOVE

I.

MINE by the right of the white election!
        Mine by the royal seal!
Mine by the sign in the scarlet prison
Bars cannot conceal!

Mine, here in vision and in veto!
Mine, by the grave's repeal
Titled, confirmed,–delirious charter!
Mine, while the ages steal!

II.

YOU left me, sweet, two legacies,–
        A legacy of love
A Heavenly Father would content,
Had He the offer of;

You left me boundaries of pain
Capacious as the sea,
Between eternity and time,
Your consciousness and me.

III.

ALTER? When the hills do.
         Falter? When the sun
Question if his glory
Be the perfect one.

Surfeit? When the daffodil
Doth of the dew:
Even as herself, O friend!
I will of you!

IV.

ELYSIUM is as far as to
         The very nearest room,
If in that room a friend await
Felicity or doom.

What fortitude the soul contains,
That it can so endure
The accent of a coming foot,
The opening of a door!

V.

DOUBT me, my dim companion!
        Why, God would be content
With but a fraction of the love
Poured thee without a stint.
The whole of me, forever,
What more the woman can,–
Say quick, that I may dower thee
With last delight I own!

It cannot be my spirit,
For that was thine before;
I ceded all of dust I knew,–
What opulence the more
Had I, a humble maiden,
Whose farthest of degree
Was that she might,
Some distant heaven,
Dwell timidly with thee!

VI.

IF you were coming in the fall,
        I'd brush the summer by
With half a smile and half a spurn,
As housewives do a fly.

If I could see you in a year,
I'd wind the months in balls,
And put them each in separate drawers,
Until their time befalls.

If only centuries delayed,
I'd count them on my hand,
Subtracting till my fingers dropped
Into Van Diemen's land.

If certain, when this life was out,
That yours and mine should be,
I'd toss it yonder like a rind,
And taste eternity.

But now, all ignorant of the length
Of time's uncertain wing,
It goads me, like the goblin bee,
That will not state its sting.

VII.

I HIDE myself within my flower,
        That wearing on your breast,
You, unsuspecting, wear me too—
And angels know the rest.

I hide myself within my flower,
That, fading from your vase,
You, unsuspecting, feel for me
Almost a loneliness.

VIII.

THAT I did always love,
      I bring thee proof:
That till I loved
I did not love enough.

That I shall love alway,
I offer thee
That love is life,
And life hath immorality.

This, dost thou doubt, sweet?
Then have I
Nothing to show
But Calvary.

IX.

HAVE you got a brook in your little heart,
      Where bashful flowers blow,
And blushing birds go down to drink,
And shadows tremble so?

And nobody knows, so still it flows,
That any brook is there;
And yet your little draught of life
Is daily drunken there.

Then look out for the little brook in March,
When the rivers overflow,
And the snows come hurrying from the hills,
And the bridges often go.

And later, in August it may be,
When the meadows parching lie,
Beware, lest this little brook of life
Some burning noon go dry!

X.

As if some little Arctic flower,
      Upon the polar hem,
Went wandering down the latitudes,
Until it puzzled came
To continents of summer,
To firmaments of sun,
To strange, bright crowds of flowers,
And birds of foreign tongue!
I say, as if this little flower
To Eden wandered in —
What then? Why, nothing, only
Your inference therefrom!

XI.

MY river runs to thee:
    Blue sea, wilt
welcome me?

My river waits reply.
Oh, sea, look graciously!

I'll fetch thee brooks
From spotted nooks,–

Say, sea,
Take me!

XII.

I CANNOT live with you,
        It would be life,
And life is over there
Behind the shelf

The sexton keeps the key to,
Putting up
Our life, his porcelain,
Like a cup

Discarded of the housewife,
Quaint or broken;
A newer Sèvres pleases,
Old ones crack.

I could not die with you,
For one must wait
To shut the other's gaze down,–
You could not.

And I, could I stand by
And see you freeze,
Without my right of frost,
Death's privilege?

Nor could I rise with you,
Because your face
Would put out Jesus',
That new grace

Glow-plain and foreign
On my homesick eye,
Except that you, than he
Shone closer by.

They'd judge us—how?
For you served Heaven, you know,
Or sought to;
I could not,

Because you saturated sight,
And I had no more eyes
For sordid excellence
As Paradise.

And were you lost, I would be,
Though my name
Rang loudest
On the heavenly fame.

And were you saved,
And I condemned to be
Where you were not,
That self were hell to me.

So we must keep apart,
You there, I here,
With just the door ajar
That oceans are,
And prayer,
And that pale sustenance,
Despair!

XIII.

THERE came a day at summer's full
      Entirely for me;
I thought that such were for the saints,
Where revelations be.

The sun, as common, went abroad,
The flowers, accustomed, blew,
As if no soul the solstice passed
That maketh all things new.

The time was scarce profaned by speech;
The symbol of a word
Was needless, as at sacrament
The wardrobe of our Lord.

Each was to each the sealed church,
Permitted to commune this time,
Lest we too awkward show
At supper of the Lamb.

The hours slid fast, as hours will,
Clutched tight by greedy hands;
So faces on two decks look back,
Bound to opposing lands.

And so, when all the time had failed,
Without external sound,
Each bound the other's crucifix,
We gave no other bond.

Sufficient troth that we shall rise—
Deposed, at length, the grave—
To that new marriage, justified
Through Calvaries of Love!

XIV.

I'M ceded, I've stopped being theirs;
        The name they dropped upon my face
With water, in the country church,
Is finished using now,
And they can put it with my dolls,
My childhood, and the string of spools
I've finished threading too.

Baptized before without the choice,
But this time consciously, of grace
Unto supremest name,
Called to my full, the crescent dropped,
Existence's whole arc filled up
With one small diadem.

My second rank, too small the first,
Crowned, crowing on my father's breast,
A half unconscious queen;
But this time, adequate, erect,
With will to choose or to reject,
And I choose—just a throne.

XV.

'TWAS a long parting, but the time
  For interview had come;
Before the judgment-seat of God,
The last and second time

These fleshless lovers met,
A heaven in a gaze,
A heaven of heavens, the privilege
On one another's eyes.

No lifetime set on them,
Apparelled as the new
Unborn, except they had beheld,
Born everlasting now.

Was bridal e'er like this?
A paradise, the host,
A cherubim and seraphim
The most familiar guest.

XVI.

I'M wife; I've finished that,
    That other state;
I'm Czar, I'm woman now:
It's safer so.

How odd the girl's life looks
Behind this soft eclipse!
I think that earth seems so
To those in heaven now.

This being comfort, then
That other kind was pain;
But why compare?
I'm wife! stop there!

XVII.

SHE rose to his requirement, dropped
        The playthings of her life
To take the honorable work
Of woman and of wife.

If aught she missed in her new day
Of amplitude, or awe,
Or first prospective, or the gold
In using wore away,

It lay unmentioned, as the sea
Develops pearl and weed,
But only to himself is known
The fathoms they abide.

XVIII.

COME slowly, Eden!
        Lips unused to thee,
Bashful, sip thy jasmines,
As the fainting bee,

Reaching late his flower,
Round her chamber hums,
Counts his nectars—enters,
And is lost in balms!

III. NATURE

I.

NEW feet within my garden go,
    New fingers stir the sod;
A troubadour upon the elm
Betrays the solitude.

New children play upon the green,
New weary sleep below;
And still the pensive spring returns,
And still the punctual snow!

II.

PINK, small, and punctual,
    Aromatic, low,
Covert in April,
Candid in May,

Dear to the moss,
Known by the knoll,
Next to the robin
In every human soul.

Bold little beauty,
Bedecked with thee,
Nature forswears
Antiquity.

III.

THE murmur of a bee
       A witchcraft yieldeth me.
If any ask me why,
'T were easier to die
Than tell.

The red upon the hill
Taketh away my will;
If anybody sneer,
Take care, for God is here,
That's all.

The breaking of the day
Addeth to my degree;
If any ask me how,
Artist, who drew me so,
Must tell!

IV.

PERHAPS you'd like to buy a flower?
       But I could never sell.
If you would like to borrow
Until the daffodil

Unties her yellow bonnet
Beneath the village door,
Until the bees, from clover rows
Their hock and sherry draw,

Why, I will lend until just then,
But not an hour more!

V.

THE pedigree of honey
      Does not concern the bee;
A clover, any time, to him
Is aristocracy.

VI.

SOME keep the Sabbath going to church;
      I keep it staying at home,
With bobolink for a chorister,
And an orchard for a dome.

Some keep the Sabbath in surplice;
I just wear my wings,
And instead of tolling the bell for church,
Our little sexton sings.

God preaches,—a noted clergyman,—
And the sermon is never long;
So instead of getting to heaven at last,
I'm going all along!

VII.

THE bee is not afraid of me,
    I know the butterfly;
The pretty people in the woods
Receive me cordially.

The brooks laugh louder when I come,
The breezes madder play.
Wherefore, mine eyes, they silver mists?
Wherefore, O summer's day?

VIII.

SOME rainbow coming from the fair!
      Some vision of the world Cashmere
I confidently see!
Or else a peacock's purple train,
Feather by feather, on the plain
Fritters itself away!

The dreamy butterflies bestir,
Lethargic pools resume the whir
Of last year's sundered tune.
From some old fortress on the sun
Baronial bees march, one by one,
In murmuring platoon!

The robins stand as thick today
As flakes of snow stood yesterday,
On fence and roof and twig.
The orchis binds her feather on
For her old lover, Don the Sun,
Revisiting the bog!

Without commander, countless, still,
The regiment of wood and hill
In bright detachment stand.
Behold! Whose multitudes are these?
The children of whose turbaned seas,
Or what Circassian land?

IX.

THE grass so little has to do,–
      A sphere of simple green,
With only butterflies to brood,
And bees to entertain,

And stir all day to pretty tunes
The breezes fetch along,
And hold the sunshine in its lap
And bow to everything;

And thread the dews all night, like pearls,
And make itself so fine,–
A duchess were too common
For such a noticing.

And even when it dies, to pass
In odors so divine,
As lowly spices gone to sleep,
Or amulets of pine.

And then to dwell in sovereign barns,
And dream the days away,–
The grass so little has to do,
I wish I were the hay!

X.

A LITTLE road not made of man,
     Enabled of the eye,
Accessible to thill of bee,
Or cart of butterfly.

If town it have, beyond itself,
'T is that I cannot say;
I only sigh,—no vehicle
Bears me along that way.

XI.

A DROP fell on the apple tree,
     Another on the roof;
A half a dozen kissed the eaves,
And made the gables laugh.

A few went out to help the brook,
That went to help the sea.
Myself conjectured, Were they pearls,
What necklaces could be!

The dust replaced in hoisted roads,
The birds jocoser sung;
The sunshine threw his hat away,
The orchards spangles hung.

The breezes brought dejected lutes,
And bathed them in the glee;
The East put out a single flag,
And signed the fête away.

XII.

A SOMETHING in a summer's day,
      As slow her flambeaux burn away,
Which solemnizes me.

A something in a summer's noon,–
An azure depth, a wordless tune,
Transcending ecstasy.

And still within a summer's night
A something so transporting bright,
I clap my hands to see;

The veil my too inspecting face,
Lest such a subtle, shimmering grace
Flutter too far for me.

The wizard-fingers never rest,
The purple brook within the breast
Still chafes its narrow bed;

Still rears the East her amber flag,
Guides still the sun along the crag
His caravan of red,

Like flowers that heard the tale of dews,
But never deemed the dripping prize
Awaited their low brows;

Or bees, that thought the summer's name
Some rumor of delirium
No summer could for them;

Or Arctic creature, dimly stirred
By tropic hint,—some travelled bird
Imported to the wood;

Or wind's bright signal to the ear,
Making that homely and severe,
Contented, known, before

The heaven unexpected came,
To lives that thought their worshiping
A too presumptuous psalm.

XIII.

THIS is the land the sunset washes,
    These are the banks of the Yellow Sea;
Where it rose, or whither it rushes,
These are the western mystery!

Night after night her purple traffic
Strews the landing with opal bales;
Merchantmen poise upon horizons,
Dip, and vanish with fairy sails.

XIV.

THERE is a flower that bees prefer,
    And butterflies desire;
To gain the purple democrat
The hummingbirds aspire.

And whatsoever insect pass,
A honey bears away
Proportioned to his several dearth
And her capacity.

Her face is rounder than the moon,
And ruddier than the gown
Of orchis in the pasture,
Or rhododendron worn.

She doth not wait for June;
Before the world is green
Her sturdy little countenance
Against the wind is seen,

Contending with the grass,
Near kinsman to herself,
For privilege of sod and sun,
Sweet litigants for life.

And when the hills are full, and newer fashions blow,
Doth not retract a single spice
For pang of jealousy.

Her public is the noon,
Her providence the sun,
Her progress by the bee proclaimed
In sovereign, swerveless tune.

The bravest of the host,
Surrendering the last,
Nor even of defeat aware
When cancelled by the frost.

XV.

LIKE trains of cars on tracks of plush
        I hear the level bee:
A jar across the flowers goes,
Their velvet masonry

Withstands until the sweet assault
Their chivalry consumes,
While he, victorious, tilts away
To vanquish other blooms.

His feet are shod with gauze,
His helmet is of gold;
His breast, a single onyx
With chrysoprase, inlaid.

His labor is a chant,
His idleness a tune;
Oh, for a bee's experience
Of clovers and of noon!

XVI.

PRESENTIMENT is that long shadow on the lawn
       Indicative that suns go down;
The notice to the startled grass
That darkness is about to pass.

XVII.

AS children bid the guest good-night,
       And then reluctant turn,
My flowers raise their pretty lips,
Then put their nightgowns on.

As children caper when they wake,
Merry that it is morn,
My flowers from a hundred cribs
Will peep, and prance again.

XVIII.

ANGELS in the early morning
       May be seen the dews among,
Stooping, plucking, smiling, flying:
Do the buds to them belong?

Angels when the sun is hottest
May be seen the sands among,
Stooping, plucking, sighing, flying;
Parched the flowers they bear along.

XIX.

SO bashful when I spied her,
       So pretty, so ashamed!
So hidden in her leaflets,
Lest anybody find;

So breathless till I passed her,
So helpless when I turned
And bore her, struggling, blushing,
Her simple haunts beyond!

For whom I robbed the dingle,
For whom betrayed the dell,
Many will doubtless ask me,
But I shall never tell!

XX.

IT makes no difference abroad,
       The seasons fit the same,
The mornings blossom into noons,
And split their pods of flame.

Wild-flowers kindle in the woods,
The brooks brag all the day;
No blackbird bates his jargoning
For passing Calvary.

Auto-da-fé and judgment
Are nothing to the bee;
His separation from the rose
To him seems misery.

XXI.

THE mountain sat upon the plain
        In his eternal chair,
His observation omnifold,
His inquest everywhere.

The seasons prayed around his knees,
Like children round a sire:
Grandfather of the days is he,
Of dawn the ancestor.

XXII.

I'LL tell you how the sun rose,—
        A ribbon at a time.
The steeples swam in amethyst,
The news like squirrels ran.

The hills untied their bonnets,
The bobolinks begun.
Then I said softly to myself,
"That must have been the sun!"

  .   .   .   .   .   .

But how he set, I know not.
There seemed a purple stile
Which little yellow boys and girls
Were climbing all the while

Till when they reached the other side,
A dominie in gray
Put gently up the evening bars,
And led the flock away.

XXIII.

THE butterfly's assumption-gown,
        In chrysoprase apartments hung,
    This afternoon put on.

How condescending to descend,
And be of buttercups the friend
    In a New England town!

XXIV.

OF all the sounds despatched abroad,
        There's not a charge to me
Like that old measure in the boughs,
That phraseless melody

The wind does, working like a hand
Whose fingers brush the sky,
Then quiver down, with tufts of tune
Permitted gods and me.

When winds go round and round in bands,
And thrum upon the door,
And birds take places overhead,
To bear them orchestra,

I crave him grace, of summer boughs,
If such an outcast be,
He never heard that fleshless chant
Rise solemn in the tree,

As if some caravan of sound
On deserts, in the sky,
Had broken rank,
Then knit, and passed
In seamless company.

XXV.

APPARENTLY with no surprise
        To any happy flower,
The frost beheads it at its play
In accidental power.
The blond assassin passes on,
The sun proceeds unmoved
To measure off another day
For an approving God.

XXVI.

'T WAS later when the summer went
        Than when the cricket came,
And yet we knew that gentle clock
Meant nought but going home.

'T was sooner when the cricket went
Than when the winter came,
Yet that pathetic pendulum
Keeps esoteric time.

XXVII.

THESE are the days when birds come back,
    A very few, a bird or two,
To take a backward look.

These are the days when skies put on
The old, old sophistries of June,–
A blue and gold mistake.

Oh, fraud that cannot cheat the bee,
Almost thy plausibility
Induces my belief,

Till ranks of seeds their witness bear,
And softly through the altered air
Hurries a timid leaf!

Oh, sacrament of summer days,
Oh, last communion in the haze,
Permit a child to join,

Thy sacred emblems to partake,
Thy consecrated bread to break,
Taste thine immortal wine!

XXVIII.

THE morns are meeker than they were,
    The nuts are getting brown;
The berry's cheek is plumper,
The rose is out of town.

The maple wears a gayer scarf,
The field a scarlet gown.
Lest I should be old-fashioned,
I'll put a trinket on.

XXIX.

THE sky is low, the clouds are mean,
    A travelling flake of snow
Across a barn or through a rut
Debates if it will go.

A narrow wind complains all day
How some one treated him;
Nature, like us, is sometimes caught
Without her diadem.

XXX.

I THINK the hemlock likes to stand
      Upon a marge of snow;
It suits his own austerity,
And satisfies an awe

That men must slake in wilderness,
Or in the desert cloy,–
An instinct for the hoar, the bald,
Lapland's necessity.

The hemlock's nature thrives on cold;
The gnash of northern winds
Is sweetest nutriment to him,
His best Norwegian wines.

To satin races he is nought;
But children on the Don
Beneath his tabernacles play,
And Dnieper wrestlers run.

XXXI.

THERE'S a certain slant of light,
On winter afternoons,
That oppresses, like the weight
Of cathedral tunes.

Heavenly hurt it gives us;
We can find no scar,
But internal difference
Where the meanings are.

None may teach it anything,
'T is the seal, despair,—
An imperial affliction
Sent us of the air.

When it comes, the landscape listens,
Shadows hold their breath;
When it goes, 't is like the distance
On the look of death.

IV. TIME AND ETERNITY

I.

ONE dignity delays for all,
　　One mitred afternoon.
None can avoid this purple,
None evade this crown.

Coach it insures, and footmen,
Chamber and state and throng;
Bells, also, in the village,
As we ride grand along.

What dignified attendants,
What service when we pause!
How loyally at parting
Their hundred hats they raise!

How pomp surpassing ermine,
When simple you and I
Present our meek escutcheon,
And claim the rank to die!

II.

DELAYED till she had ceased to know,
  Delayed till in its vest of snow
 Her loving bosom lay.
An hour behind the fleeting breath,
Later by just an hour than death,–
 Oh, lagging yesterday!

Could she have guessed that it would be;
Could but a crier of the glee
 Have climbed the distant hill;
Had not the bliss so slow a pace,–
Who knows but this surrendered face
 Were undefeated still?

Oh, if there may departing be
Any forgot by victory
 In her imperial round,
Show them this meek apparelled thing,
That could not stop to be a king,
 Doubtful if it be crowned!

III.

DEPARTED to the judgment,
    A mighty afternoon;
Great clouds like ushers leaning,
Creation looking on.

The flesh surrendered, cancelled,
The bodiless begun;
Two worlds, like audiences, disperse
And leave the soul alone.

IV.

SAFE in their alabaster chambers,
    Untouched by morning and untouched by noon,
Sleep the meek members of the resurrection,
Rafter of satin, and roof of stone.

Light laughs the breeze in her castle of sunshine;
Babbles the bee in a stolid ear;
Pipe the sweet birds in ignorant cadence,–
Ah, what sagacity perished here!

Grand go the years in the crescent above them;
Worlds scoop their arcs, and firmaments row,
Diadems drop and Doges surrender,
Soundless as dots on a disk of snow.

V.

ON this long storm the rainbow rose,
    On this late morn the sun;
The clouds, like listless elephants,
Horizons straggled down.

The birds rose smiling in their nests,
The gales indeed were done;
Alas! how heedless were the eyes
On whom the summer shone!

The quiet nonchalance of death
No daybreak can bestir;
The slow archangel's syllables
Must awaken her.

VI.

MY cocoon tightens, colors tease,
    I'm feeling for the air;
A dim capacity for wings
Degrades the dress I wear.

A power of butterfly must be
The aptitude to fly,
Meadows of majesty concedes
And easy sweeps of sky.

So I must baffle at the hint
And cipher at the sign,
And make much blunder, if at last
I take the clew divine.

VII.

EXULTATION is the going
        Of an inland soul to sea,–
Past the houses, past the headlands,
Into deep eternity!

Bred as we, among the mountains,
Can the sailor understand
The divine intoxication
Of the first league out from land?

VIII.

LOOK back on time with kindly eyes,
        He doubtless did his best;
How softly sinks his trembling sun
In human nature's west!

IX.

A TRAIN went through a burial gate,
    A bird broke forth and sang,
And trilled, and quivered, and shook his throat
Till all the churchyard rang;

And then adjusted his little notes,
And bowed and sang again.
Doubtless, he thought it meet of him
To say good-by to men.

X.

I DIED for beauty, but was scarce
    Adjusted in the tomb,
When one who died for truth was lain
In an adjoining room.

He questioned softly why I failed?
"For beauty," I replied.
"And I for truth,—the two are one;
We brethren are," he said.

And so, as kinsmen met a night,
We talked between the rooms,
Until the moss had reached our lips,
And covered up our names.

XI.

HOW many times these low feet staggered,
    Only the soldered mouth can tell;
Try! can you stir the awful rivet?
Try! can you lift the hasps of steel?

Stroke the cool forehead, hot so often,
Lift, if you can, the listless hair;
Handle the adamantine fingers
Never a thimble more shall wear.

Buzz the dull flies on the chamber window;
Brave shines the sun through the freckled pane;
Fearless the cobweb swings from the ceiling—
Indolent housewife, in daisies lain!

XII.

I LIKE a look of agony,
    Because I know it's true;
Men do not sham convulsion,
Nor stimulate a throe.

The eyes glaze once, and that is death.
Impossible to feign
The beads upon the forehead
By homely anguish strung.

XIII.

THAT short, potential stir
    That each can make but once,
That bustle so illustrious
'T is almost consequence,

Is the *éclat* of death.
Oh, thou unknown renown
That not a beggar would accept,
Had he the power to spurn!

XIV.

I WENT to thank her,
    But she slept;
Her bed a funnelled stone,
With nosegays at the head and foot,
That travellers had thrown,

Who went to thank her;
But she slept.
'T was short to cross the sea
To look upon her like, alive,
But turning back 't was slow.

XV.

I'VE seen a dying eye
      Run round and round a room
In search of something, as it seemed,
Then cloudier become;
And then, obscure with fog,
And then be soldered down,
Without disclosing what it be,
'T were blessed to have seen.

XVI.

THE clouds their backs together laid,
      The north begun to push,
The forests galloped till they fell,
The lightning skipped like mice;
The thunder crumbled like a stuff—
How good to be safe in tombs,
Where nature's temper cannot reach,
Nor vengeance ever comes!

XVII.

I NEVER saw a moor,
　　　I never saw the sea;
Yet know I how the heather looks,
And what a wave must be.

I never spoke with God,
Nor visited in heaven;
Yet certain am I of the spot
As if the chart were given.

XVIII.

GOD permits industrious angels
　　　Afternoons to play.
I met one,—forgot my school-mates,
All, for him, straightway.

God calls home the angels promptly
At the setting sun;
I missed mine. How dreary marbles,
After playing Crown!

XIX.

TO know just how he suffered would be dear;
    To know if any human eyes were near
To whom he could intrust his wavering gaze,
Until it settled firm on Paradise.

To know if he was patient, part content,
Was dying as he thought, or different;
Was it a pleasant day to die,
And did the sunshine face his way?

What was his furthest mind, of home, or God,
Or what the distant say
At news that he ceased human nature
On such a day?

And wishes, had he any?
Just his sigh, accented,
Had been legible to me.
And was he confident until
Ill fluttered out in everlasting well?

And if he spoke, what name was best,
What first,
What one broke off with
At the drowsiest?

Was he afraid, or tranquil?
Might he know
How conscious consciousness could grow,
Till love that was, and love too blest to be,
Meet—and the junction be Eternity?

XX.

THE last night that she lived,
     It was a common night,
Except the dying; this to us
Made nature different.

We noticed smallest things,—
Things overlooked before,
By this great light upon our minds
Italicized, as 't were.

That others could exist
While she must finish quite,
A jealousy for her arose
So nearly infinite.

We waited while she passed;
It was a narrow time,
Too jostled were our souls to speak,
At length the notice came.

She mentioned, and forgot;
Then lightly as a reed
Bent to the water, shivered scarce,
Consented, and was dead.

And we, we placed the hair,
And drew the head erect;
And then an awful leisure was,
Our faith to regulate.

XXI.

NOT in this world to see his face
      Sounds long, until I read the place
Where this is said to be
But just the primer to a life
Unopened, rare, upon the shelf,
Clasped yet to him and me.

And yet, my primer suits me so
I would not choose a book to know
Than that, be sweeter wise;
Might some one else so learned be
And leave me just my A B C,
Himself could have the skies.

XXII.

THE bustle in a house
      The morning after death
Is solemnest of industries
Enacted upon earth,—

The sweeping up the heart,
And putting love away
We shall not want to use again
Until eternity.

XXIII.

I REASON, earth is short,
    And anguish absolute.
And many hurt;
But what of that?

I reason, we could die:
The best vitality
Cannot excel decay;
But what of that?

I reason that in heaven
Somehow, it will be even,
Some new equation given;
But what of that?

XXIV.

AFRAID? Of whom am I afraid?
    Not death; for who is he?
The porter of my father's lodge
As much abasheth me.

Of life? 'T were odd I fear a thing
That comprehendeth me
In one or more existences
At Deity's decree.

Of resurrection? Is the east
Afraid to trust the morn
With her fastidious forehead?
As soon impeach my crown!

XXV.

THE sun kept setting, setting still;
      No hue of afternoon
Upon the village I perceived,–
From house to house 't was noon.

The dusk kept dropping, dropping still;
No dew upon the grass,
But only on my forehead stopped,
And wandered in my face.

My feet kept drowsing, drowsing still,
My fingers were awake;
Yet why so little sound myself
Unto my seeming make?

How well I knew the light before!
I could not see it now.
'T is dying, I am doing; but
I'm not afraid to know.

XXVI.

TWO swimmers wrestled on the spar
      Until the morning sun,
When one turned smiling to the land.
O God, the other one!

The stray ships passing spied a face
Upon the waters borne,
With eyes in death still begging raised,
And hands beseeching thrown.

XXVII.

BECAUSE I could not stop for Death,
  He kindly stopped for me;
The carriage held but just ourselves
And Immortality.

We slowly drove, he knew no haste,
And I had put away
My labor, and my leisure too,
For his civility.

We passed the school where children played,
Their lessons scarcely done;
We passed the fields of gazing grain,
We passed the setting sun.

We paused before a house that seemed
A swelling of the ground;
The roof was scarcely visible,
The cornice but a mound.

Since then 't is centuries; but each
Feels shorter than the day
I first surmised the horses' heads
Were toward eternity.

XXVIII.

SHE went as quiet as the dew
     From a familiar flower.
Not like the dew did she return
At the accustomed hour!

She dropt as softly as a star
From out my summer's eve;
Less skilful than Leverrier
It's sorer to believe!

XXIX.

AT last to be identified!
     At last, the lamps upon thy side,
The rest of life to see!
Past midnight, past the morning star!
Past sunrise! Ah! what leagues there are
Between our feet and day!

XXX.

EXCEPT to heaven, she is nought;
         Except for angels, lone;
Except to some wide-wandering bee,
A flower superfluous blown;

Except for winds, provincial;
Except by butterflies,
Unnoticed as a single dew
That on the acre lies.

The smallest housewife in the grass,
Yet take her from the lawn,
And somebody has lost the face
That made existence home!

XXXI.

DEATH is a dialogue between
         The spirit and the dust.
"Dissolve," says Death. The Spirit, "Sir,
I have another trust."

Death doubts it, argues from the ground.
The Spirit turns away,
Just laying off, for evidence,
An overcoat of clay.

XXXII.

IT was too late for man,
        But early yet for God;
Creation impotent to help,
But prayer remained our side.

How excellent the heaven,
When earth cannot be had;
How hospitable, then, the face
Of our old neighbor, God!

XXXIII.

WHEN I was small, a woman
        died.
        To-day her only boy
Went up from the Potomac,
His face all victory,

To look at her; how slowly
The seasons must have turned
Till bullets clipt an angle,
And he passed quickly round!

If pride shall be in Paradise
I never can decide;
Of their imperial conduct,
No person testified.

But proud in apparition,
That woman and her boy
Pass back and forth before my brain,
As ever in the sky.

XXXIV.

THE daisy follows soft the sun,
   And when his golden walk is done,
   Sits shyly at his feet.
He, waking, finds the flower near.
"Wherefore, marauder, art thou here?
   "Because, sir, love is sweet!"

We are the flower, Thou the sun!
Forgive us, if as days decline,
   We nearer steal to Thee,—
Enamoured of the parting west,
The peace, the flight, the amethyst,
   Night's possibility!

XXXV.

NO rack can torture me,
      My soul's at liberty.
Behind this mortal bone
There knits a bolder one

You cannot prick with saw,
Nor rend with scymitar.
Two bodies therefore be;
Bind one, and one will flee.

The eagle of his nest
No easier divest
And gain the sky,
Than mayest thou,

Except thyself may be
Thine enemy;
Captivity is consciousness,
So's liberty.

XXXVI.

I LOST a world the other day.
　　　Has anybody found?
You'll know it by the row of stars
Around its forehead bound.

A rich man might not notice it;
Yet to my frugal eye
Of more esteem than ducats.
Oh, find it, sir, for me!

XXXVII.

IF I should n't be alive
　　　When the robins come,
Give the one in red cravat
A memorial crumb.

If I could n't thank you,
Being just asleep,
You will know I'm trying
With my granite lip!

XXXVIII.

SLEEP is supposed to be,
        By souls of sanity,
The shutting of the eye.

Sleep is the station grand
Down which on either hand
The hosts of witness stand!

Morn is supposed to be,
By people of degree,
The breaking of the day.

Morning has not occurred!
That shall aurora be
East of eternity;

One with the banner gay,
One in the red array,–
That is the break of day.

XXXIX.

I SHALL know why, when time is over,
        And I have ceased to wonder why;
Christ will explain each separate anguish
In the fair schoolroom of the sky.

He will tell me what Peter promised,
And I, for wonder at his woe,
I shall forget the drop of anguish
That scalds me now, that scalds me now.

XL.

I NEVER lost as much but twice,
        And that was in the sod;
Twice have I stood a beggar
Before the door of God!

Angels, twice descending,
Reimbursed my store.
Burglar, banker, father,
I am poor once more!

...

POEMS

BY

EMILY DICKINSON

· *SECOND SERIES* ·

. . .

PREFACE

THE eagerness with which the first volume of Emily
Dickinson's poems has been read shows very clearly
that all our alleged modern artificiality does not prevent a
prompt appreciation of the qualities of directness and
simplicity in approaching the greatest themes,—life and love
and death. That "irresistible needle-touch," as one of her best
critics has called it, piercing at once the very core of a thought,
has found a response as wide and sympathetic as it has been
unexpected even to those who knew best her compelling power.
This second volume, while open to the same criticism as to
form with its predecessor, shows also the same shining beauties.

Although Emily Dickinson had been in the habit of sending
occasional poems to friends and correspondents, the full extent
of her writing was by no means imagined by them. Her friend
"H.H." must at least have suspected it, for in a letter dated 5th
September, 1884, she wrote:—

MY DEAR FRIEND,—What portfolios full of verses you must
have! It is a cruel wrong to your "day and generation" that you
will not give them light.

If such a thing should happen as that I should outlive you, I
wish you would make me your literary legatee and executor.
Surely after you are what is called "dead" you will be willing
that the poor ghosts you have left behind should be cheered
and pleased by your verses, will you not? You ought to be. I do
not think we have a right to withhold from the world a word or
a thought any more than a *deed* which might help a single
soul....

Truly yours,

HELEN JACKSON.

The "portfolios" were found, shortly after Emily Dickinson's death, by her sister and only surviving housemate. Most of the poems had been carefully copied on sheets of note-paper, and tied in little fascicules, each of six or eight sheets. While many of them bear evidence of having been thrown off at white heat, still more had received thoughtful revision. There is the frequent addition of rather perplexing foot-notes, affording large choice of words and phrases. And in the copies which she sent to friends, sometimes one form, sometimes another, is found to have been used. Without important exception, her friends have generously placed at the disposal of the Editors any poems they had received from her; and these have given the obvious advantage of comparison among several renderings of the same verse.

To what further rigorous pruning her verses would have been subjected had she published them herself, we cannot know. They should be regarded in many cases as merely the first strong and suggestive sketches of an artist, intended to be embodied at some time in the finished picture.

Emily Dickinson appears to have written her first poems in the winter of 1862. In a letter to one of the present Editors the April following, she says, "I made no verse, but one or two, until this winter."

The handwriting was at first somewhat like the delicate, running Italian hand of our elder gentlewomen; but as she advanced in breadth of thought, it grew bolder and more abrupt, until in her latest years each letter stood distinct and separate from its fellows. In most of her poems, particularly the later ones, everything by way of punctuation was discarded, except numerous dashes; and all important words began with capitals. The effect of a page of her more recent manuscript is exceedingly quaint and strong. Although there is nowhere a date, the handwriting makes it possible to arrange the poems with general chronologic accuracy. . . .

The variation of readings, with the fact that she often wrote in pencil and not always clearly, have at times thrown a good deal of responsibility upon her Editors. But all interference not absolutely inevitable has been avoided. The very roughness of her own rendering is part of herself, and not lightly to be touched; for it seems in many cases that she intentionally avoided the smoother and more usual rhymes.

Like impressionist pictures or Wagner's rugged music, the very absence of conventional form challenges attention. In Emily Dickinson's exacting hands the especial, intrinsic fitness of a particular order of words might not be sacrificed to anything virtually extrinsic; and her verses all show a strange cadence of inner rhythmical music. Lines are always daringly constructed, and the "thought-rhyme" appears frequently,— appealing, indeed, to an unrecognized sense more elusive than hearing.

Emily Dickinson scrutinized everything with clear-eyed frankness. Every subject was proper ground for legitimate study, even the sombre facts of death and burial, and the unknown life beyond. She touches these themes sometimes lightly, sometimes almost humorously, more often with weird and peculiar power; but she is never by any chance frivolous or trivial. And while, as one critic has said, she may exhibit toward God "an Emersonian self-possession," it was because she looked upon all life with a candor as unprejudiced as it is rare.

She had tried society and the world, and found them lacking. She was not an invalid, and she lived in seclusion from no love-disappointment. Her life was the normal blossoming of a nature introspective to a high degree, whose best thought could not exist in pretence.

Storm, wind, the wild March sky, sunsets and dawns; the birds and bees, butterflies and flowers of her garden, with a few trusted human friends, were sufficient companionship. The coming of the first robin was a jubilee beyond drowning of monarch or birthday of pope; the first red leaf hurrying through "the altered air," an epoch. Immortality was close about her; and while never morbid or melancholy, she lived in its presence.

MABEL LOOMIS TODD.

AMHERST, MASSACHUSETTS,
    August 1891.

. . .

Prelude

My nosegays are for captives;
    Dim, long-expectant eyes,
Fingers denied the plucking,
    Patient till paradise.

To such, if they should whisper
    Of morning and the moor,
They bear no other errand,
    And I, no other prayer.

I. Life

I.

I'M nobody! Who are you?
     Are you nobody, too?
Then there's a pair of us—don't tell!
They'd banish us, you know.

How dreary to be somebody!
How public, like a frog
To tell your name the livelong day
To an admiring bog!

II.

I BRING an unaccustomed wine
     To lips long parching, next to mine,
And summon them to drink.

Crackling with fever, they essay;
I turn my brimming eyes away,
And come next hour to look.

The hands still hug the tardy glass;
The lips I would have cooled, alas!
Are so superfluous cold,

I would as soon attempt to warm
The bosoms where the frost has lain
Ages beneath the mould.

Some other thirsty there may be
To whom this would have pointed me
Had it remained to speak.

And so I always bear the cup
If haply, mine may be the drop
Some pilgrim thirst to slake,—

If, haply, any say to me,
"Unto the little, unto me,"
When I at last awake.

III.

THE nearest dream recedes, unrealized.
  The heaven we chase
  Like the June bee
  Before the school-boy
  Invites the race;
  Stoops to an easy clover—
Dips—evades—teases—deploys;
  Then to the royal clouds
  Lifts his light pinnace
  Heedless of the boy
Staring, bewildered, at the mocking sky.

  Homesick for steadfast honey,
  Ah! the bee flies not
That brews that rare variety.

IV.

WE play at paste,
    Till qualified for pearl,
Then drop the paste,
And deem ourself a fool.
The shapes, though, were similar,
And our new hands
Learned gem-tactics
Practising sands.

V.

I FOUND the phrase to every thought
    I ever had, but one;
And that defies me,—as a hand
Did try to chalk the sun

To races nurtured in the dark;—
How would your own begin?
Can blaze be done in cochineal,
Or noon in mazarin?

VI.

HOPE is the thing with feathers
    That perches in the soul,
And sings the tune without the words,
And never stops at all,

And sweetest in the gale is heard;
And sore must be the storm
That could abash the little bird
That kept so many warm.

I've heard it in the chillest land,
And on the strangest sea;
Yet, never, in extremity,
It asked a crumb of me.

VII.

DARE you see a soul at the white heat?
    Then crouch within the door.
Red is the fire's common tint;
    But when the vivid ore

Has sated flame's conditions,
    Its quivering substance plays
Without a color but the light
    Of unanointed blaze.

Least village boasts its blacksmith,
    Whose anvil's even din
Stands symbol for the finer forge
That soundless tugs within,

Refining these impatient ores
    With hammer and with blaze,
Until the designated light
    Repudiate the forge.

VIII.

WHO never lost, are unprepared
    A coronet to find;
Who never thirsted, flagons
And cooling tamarind.

Who never climbed the weary league —
Can such a foot explore
The purple territories
On Pizarro's shore?

How many legions overcome?
The emperor will say.
How many colors taken
On Revolution Day?

How many bullets bearest?
The royal scar hast thou?
Angels, write "Promoted"
On this soldier's brow!

IX.

I CAN wade grief,
   Whole pools of it,–
I'm used to that.
But the least push of joy
Breaks up my feet,
And I tip–drunken.
Let no pebble smile,
'T was the new liquor,–
That was all!

Power is only pain,
Stranded, through discipline,
Till weights will hang.
Give balm to giants,
And they'll wilt, like men.
Give Himmaleh,–
They'll carry him!

X.

I NEVER hear the word "escape"
   Without a quicker blood,
A sudden expectation,
A flying attitude.

I never hear of prisons broad
By soldiers battered down,
But I tug childish at my bars,–
Only to fail again!

XI.

FOR each ecstatic instant
        We must an anguish pay
In keen and quivering ratio
To the ecstasy.

For each beloved hour
Sharp pittances of years,
Bitter contested farthings
And coffers heaped with tears.

XII.

THROUGH the straight pass of suffering
        The martyrs even trod,
Their feet upon temptation,
Their faces upon God.

A stately, shriven company;
Convulsion playing round,
Harmless as streaks of meteor
Upon a planet's bound.

Their faith the everlasting troth;
Their expectation fair;
The needle to the north degree
Wades so, through polar air.

XIII.

I MEANT to have but modest needs,
    Such as content, and heaven;
Within my income these could lie,
And life and I keep even.

But since the last included both,
It would suffice my prayer
But just for one to stipulate,
And grace would grant the pair.

And so, upon this wise I prayed,—
Great Spirit, give to me
A heaven not so large as yours,
But large enough for me.

A smile suffused Jehovah's face;
The cherubim withdrew;
Grave saints stole out to look at me,
And showed their dimples, too.

I left the place with all my might,—
My prayer away I threw;
The quiet ages picked it up,
And Judgment twinkled, too,

That one so honest be extant
As take the tale for true
That "Whatsoever you shall ask,
Itself be given you."

But I, grown shrewder, scan the skies
With a suspicious air,—
As children, swindled for the first,
All swindlers be, infer.

XIV.

THE thought beneath so slight a film
        Is more distinctly seen,–
As laces just reveal the surge,
Or mists the Apennine.

XV.

THE soul unto itself
        Is an imperial friend,–
Or the most agonizing spy
An enemy could send.

Secure against its own,
No treason it can fear;
Itself its sovereign, of itself
The soul should stand in awe.

XVI.

SURGEONS must be very careful
    When they take the knife!
Underneath their fine incisions
Stirs the culprit,—Life!

XVII.

I LIKE to see it lap the miles,
    And lick the valleys up,
And stop to feed itself at tanks;
Ant then, prodigious, step

Around a pile of mountains,
And, supercilious, peer
In shanties by the sides of roads;
And then a quarry pare

To fit its sides, and crawl between,
Complaining all the while
In horrid, hooting stanza;
Then chase itself down hill

And neigh like Boanerges;
Then, punctual as a star,
Stop—docile and omnipotent—
At its own stable door.

XVIII.

THE show is not the show,
        But they that go.
Menagerie to me
My neighbor be.
Fair play—
Both went to see.

XIX.

DELIGHT becomes pictorial
        When viewed through pain,—
More fair, because impossible
That any gain.

The mountain at a given distance
In amber lies;
Approached, the amber flits a little,—
And that's the skies!

XX.

A THOUGHT went up my mind to-day
     That I have had before,
But did not finish,—some way back,
I could not fix the year,

Nor where it went, nor why it came
The second time to me,
Nor definitely what it was,
Have I the art to say.

But somewhere in my soul, I know
I've met the thing before;
It just reminded me—'t was all—
And came my way no more.

XXI.

IS Heaven a physician?
     They say that He can heal;
But medicine posthumous
   Is unavailable.

Is Heaven an exchequer?
   They speak of what we owe;
But that negotiation
   I'm not a party to.

XXII.

THOUGH I get home how late, how late!
    So I get home, 't will compensate.
Better will be the ecstasy
That they have done expecting me,
When, night descending, dumb and dark,
They hear my unexpected knock.
Transporting must the moment be
Brewed from decades of agony!

To think just how the fire will burn,
Just how long-cheated eyes will turn
To wonder what myself will say,
And what itself will say to me,
Beguiles the centuries of way!

XXIII.

A POOR torn heart, a tattered heart,
    That sat it down to rest,
Nor noticed that the ebbing day
Flowed silver to the west,
Nor noticed night did soft descend
Nor constellation burn,
Intent upon the vision
Of latitudes unknown.

The angels, happening that way,
This dusty heart espied;
Tenderly took it up from toil
And carried it to God.
There,—sandals for the barefoot;
There,—gathered from the gales,
Do the blue havens by the hand
Lead the wandering sails.

XXIV.

I SHOULD have been too glad, I see,
    Too lifted for the scant degree
  Of life's penurious round;
My little circuit would have shamed
This new circumference, have blamed
  The homelier time behind.

I should have been too saved, I see,
Too rescued; fear too dim to me
  That I could spell the prayer
I knew so perfect yesterday,–
That scalding one, "Sabachthani,"
  Recited fluent here.

Earth would have been too much, I see,
And heaven not enough for me;
  I should have had the joy
Without the fear to justify,–
The palm without the Calvary;
  So, Saviour, crucify.

Defeat whets victory, they say;
The reefs in old Gethsemane
  Endear the shore beyond.
'T is beggars banquets best define;
'T is thirsting vitalizes wine,–
  Faith faints to understand.

XXV.

IT tossed and tossed,–
    A little brig I knew,–
O'ertook by blast,
It spun and spun,
And groped delirious, for morn.

It slipped and slipped,
As one that drunken stepped;
Its white foot tripped,
Then dropped from sight.

Ah, brig, good-night
To crew and you;
The ocean's heart too smooth, too blue,
To break for you.

XXVI.

VICTORY comes late,
    And is held low to freezing lips
Too rapt with frost
To take it.
How sweet it would have tasted,
Just a drop!
Was God so economical?
His table's spread too high for us
Unless we dine on tip-toe.
Crumbs fit such little mouths,
Cherries suit robins;
The eagle's golden breakfast
Strangles them.
God keeps his oath to sparrows,
Who of little love
Know how to starve!

XXXVII.

GOD gave a loaf to every bird,
　　But just a crumb to me;
I dare not eat it, though I starve,–
My poignant luxury
To own it, touch it, prove the feat
That made the pellet mine,–
Too happy in my sparrow chance
For ampler coveting.

It might be famine all around,
I could not miss an ear,
Such plenty smiles upon my board,
My garner shows so fair.
I wonder how the rich may feel,–
An Indiaman – an Earl?
I deem that I with but a crumb
Am sovereign of them all.

XXVIII.

EXPERIMENT to me
　　Is every one I meet
If it contain a kernel?
The figure of a nut

Presents upon a tree,
Equally plausibly;
But meat within is requisite,
To squirrels and to me.

XXIX.

MY country need not change her gown,
        Her triple suit as sweet
As when 't was cut at Lexington,
And first pronounced "a fit."

Great Britain disapproves "the stars;"
Disparagement discreet,–
There's something in their attitude
That taunts her bayonet.

XXX.

FAITH is a fine invention
        For gentlemen who see;
But microscopes are prudent
In an emergency!

XXXI.

EXCEPT the heaven had come so near,
        So seemed to choose my door,
The distance would not haunt me so;
I had not hoped before.

But just to hear the grace depart
I never thought to see,
Afflicts me with a double loss;
'T is lost, and lost to me.

XXXII.

PORTRAITS are to daily faces
        As an evening west
To a fine, pedantic sunshine
In a satin vest.

XXXIII.

I TOOK my power in my hand
        And went against the world;
'T was not so much as David had,
But I was twice as bold.

I aimed my pebble, but myself
Was all the one that fell.
Was it Goliath was too large,
Or only I too small?

XXXIV.

A SHADY friend for torrid days
        Is easier to find
Than one of higher temperature
For frigid hour of mind.

The vane a little to the east
Scares muslin souls away;
If broadcloth breasts are firmer
Than those of organdy,

Who is to blame? The weaver?
Ah! the bewildering thread!
The tapestries of paradise
So notelessly are made!

XXXV.

EACH life converges to some centre
       Expressed or still;
Exists in every human nature
A goal,

Admitted scarcely to itself, it may be,
Too fair
For credibility's temerity
To dare.

Adored with caution, as a brittle heaven,
To reach
Were hopeless as the rainbow's raiment
To touch,

Yet persevered toward, surer for the distance;
How high
Unto the saints' slow diligence
The sky!

Ungained, it may be, by a life's low venture,
But then,
Eternity enables the endeavoring
Again.

XXXVI.

BEFORE I got my eye put out,
        I liked as well to see
As other creatures that have eyes,
And know no other way.

But were it told to me, to-day,
That I might have the sky
For mine, I tell you that my heart
Would split, for size of me.

The meadows mine, the mountains mine,—
All forests, stintless stars,
As much of noon as I could take
Between my finite eyes.

The motions of the dipping birds,
The lightning's jointed road,
For mine to look at when I liked,—
The news would strike me dead!

So, safer, guess, with just my soul
Upon the window-pane
Where other creatures put their eyes,
Incautious of the sun.

XXXVII.

TALK with prudence to a beggar
      Of 'Potosi' and the mines!
Reverently to the hungry
Of your viands and your wines!

Cautious, hint to any captive
You have passed enfranchised feet!
Anecdotes of air in dungeons
Have sometimes proved deadly sweet!

XXXVIII.

HE preached upon "breadth" till it argued
      him narrow,—
The broad are too broad to define;
And of "truth" until it proclaimed him a liar,—
The truth never flaunted a sign.

Simplicity fled from his counterfeit presence
As gold the pyrites would shun.
What confusion would cover the innocent Jesus
To meet so enabled a man!

XXXIX.

GOOD night! which put the candle out?
  A jealous zephyr, not a doubt.
 Ah! friend, you little knew
How long at that celestial wick
The angels labored diligent;
 Extinguished, now, for you!

It might have been the lighthouse spark
Some sailor, rowing in the dark,
 Had importuned to see!
It might have been the waning lamp
That lit the drummer from the camp
 To purer reveille!

XL.

WHEN I hoped I feared,
  Since I hoped I dared;
Everywhere alone
As a church remain;
Spectre cannot harm,
Serpent cannot charm;
He deposes doom,
Who hath suffered him.

XLI.

A DEED knocks first at thought,
    And then it knocks at will.
That is the manufacturing spot,
And will at home and well.

It then goes out an act,
Or is entombed so still
That only to the ear of God
Its doom is audible.

XLII.

MINE enemy is growing old,–
    I have at last revenge.
The palate of the hate departs;
If any would avenge,–

Let him be quick, the viand flits,
It is a faded meat.
Anger as soon as fed is dead;
'T is starving makes it fat.

XLIII.

REMORSE is memory awake,
    Her companies astir,—
A presence of departed acts
At window and at door.

It's past set down before the soul,
And lighted with a match,
Perusal to facilitate
Of its condensed despatch.

Remorse is cureless,— the disease
Not even God can heal;
For 't is his institution,—
The complement of hell.

XLIV.

THE body grows outside,—
    The more convenient way,—
That if the spirit like to hide,
Its temple stands alway

Ajar, secure, inviting;
It never did betray
The soul that asked its shelter
In timid honesty.

XLV.

UNDUE significance a starving man attaches
   To food
Far off; he sighs, and therefore hopeless,
And therefore good.

Partaken, it relieves indeed, but proves us
That spices fly
In the receipt. It was the distance
Was savory.

XLVI.

HEART not so heavy as mine,
   Wending late home,
As it passed my window
Whistled itself a tune,—

A careless snatch, a ballad,
A ditty of the street;
Yet to my irritated ear
An anodyne so sweet,

It was as if a bobolink,
Sauntering this way,
Carolled and mused and carolled,
Then bubbled slow away.

It was as if a chirping brook
Upon a toilsome way
Set bleeding feet to minuets
Without the knowing why.

To-morrow, night will come again,
Weary, perhaps, and sore.
Ah, bugle, by my window,
I pray you stroll once more!

XLVII.

I MANY times thought peace had come,
        When peace was far away;
As wrecked men deem they sight the land
At centre of the sea,

And struggle slacker, but to prove,
As hopelessly as I,
How many the fictitious shores
Before the harbor lie.

XLVIII.

UNTO my books so good to turn
      Far ends of tired days;
It half endears the abstinence,
And pain is missed in praise.

As flavors cheer retarded guests
With banquetings to be,
So spices stimulate the time
Till my small library.

It may be wilderness without,
Far feet of failing men,
But holiday excludes the night,
And it is bells within.

I thank these kinsmen of the shelf;
Their countenances bland
Enamour in prospective,
And satisfy, obtained.

XLIX.

THIS merit hath the worst,—
      It cannot be again.
When Fate hath taunted last
And thrown her furthest stone,

The maimed may pause and breathe,
And glance securely round.
The deer invites no longer
Than it eludes the hound.

L.

I HAD been hungry all the years;
　　My noon had come, to dine;
I trembling, drew the table near,
And touched the curious wine.

'T was this on tables I had seen,
When turning, hungry, lone,
I looked in windows, for the wealth
I could not hope to own.

I did not know the ample bread,
'T was so unlike the crumb
The birds and I had often shared
In Nature's dining-room.

The plenty hurt me, 't was so new,—
Myself felt ill and odd,
As berry of a mountain bush
Transplanted to the road.

Nor was I hungry; so I found
That hunger was a way
Of persons outside windows,
The entering takes away.

LI.

I GAINED it so,
By climbing slow,
By catching at the twigs that grow
Between the bliss and me.
It hung so high,
As well the sky
Attempt by strategy.

I said I gained it,—
This was all.
Look, how I clutch it,
Lest it fall,
And I a pauper go;
Unfitted by an instant's grace
For the contented beggar's face
I wore an hour ago.

LII.

TO learn the transport by the pain,
        As blind men learn the sun;
To die of thirst, suspecting
That brooks in meadows run;

To stay the homesick, homesick feet
Upon a foreign shore
Haunted by native lands, the while,
And blue, beloved air—

This is the sovereign anguish,
This, the signal woe!
These are the patient laureates
Whose voices, trained below,

Ascend in ceaseless carol,
Inaudible, indeed,
To us, the duller scholars
Of the mysterious bard!

LIII.

I YEARS had been from home,
        And now, before the door,
I dared not open, lest a face
I never saw before

Stare vacant into mine
And ask my business there.
My business,—just a life I left,
Was such still dwelling there?

I fumbled at my nerve,
I scanned the windows near;
The silence like an ocean rolled,
And broke against my ear.

I laughed a wooden laugh
That I could fear a door,
Who danger and the dead had faced,
But never quaked before.

I fitted to the latch
My hand, with trembling care,
Lest back the awful door should spring,
And leave me standing there.

I moved my fingers off
As cautiously as glass,
And held my ears, and like a thief
Fled gasping from the house.

LIV.

PRAYER is the little implement
        Through which men reach
Where presence is denied them.
They fling their speech

By means of it in God's ear;
If then He hear,
This sums the apparatus
Comprised in prayer.

LV.

I KNOW that he exists
        Somewhere, in silence.
He has hid his rare life
From our gross eyes.

'T is an instant's play,
'T is a fond ambush,
Just to make bliss
Earn her own surprise!

But should the play
Prove piercing earnest,
Should the glee glaze
In death's stiff stare,

Would not the fun
Look too expensive?
Would not the jest
Have crawled too far?

LVI.

MUSICIANS wrestle everywhere:
    All day, among the crowded air,
  I hear the silver strife;
And—waking long before the dawn—
Such transport breaks upon the town
  I think it that "new life!"

It is not bird, it has no nest;
Nor band, in brass and scarlet dressed,
  Nor tambourine, nor man;
It is not hymn from pulpit read,—
The morning stars the treble led
  On time's first afternoon!

Some say it is the spheres at play!
Some say that bright majority
  Of vanished dames and men!
Some think it service in the place
Where we, with late, celestial face,
  Please God, shall ascertain!

LVII.

JUST lost when I was saved!
        Just felt the world go by!
Just girt me for the onset with eternity,
When breath blew back,
And on the other side
I heard recede the disappointed tide!

Therefore, as one returned, I feel,
Odd secrets of the line to tell!
Some sailor, skirting foreign shores,
Some pale reporter from the awful doors
Before the seal!

Next time, to Stay!
Next time, the things to see
By ear unheard,
Unscrutinized by eye.

Next time, to tarry,
While the ages steal,—
Slow tramp the centuries,
And the cycles wheel.

II. LOVE

I.

OF all the souls that stand create
        I have elected one.
When sense from spirit files away,
And subterfuge is done;

When that which is and that which was
Apart, intrinsic, stand,
And this brief tragedy of flesh
Is shifted like a sand;

When figures show their royal front
And mists are carved away,—
Behold the atom I preferred
To all the lists of clay!

II.

I HAVE no life but this,
        To lead it here;
Nor any death, but lest
Dispelled from there;

Nor tie to earths to come,
Nor action new,
Except through this extent,
The realm of you.

III.

YOUR riches taught me poverty.
        Myself a millionnaire
In little wealths—as girls could boast,—
Till broad as Buenos Ayre,

You drifted your dominions
A different Peru;
And I esteemed all poverty,
For life's estate with you.

Of mines I little know, myself,
But just the names of gems,—
The colors of the commonest;
And scarce of diadems

So much that, did I meet the queen,
Her glory I should know:
But this must be a different wealth,
To miss it beggars so.

I'm sure 't is India all day
To those who look on you
Without a stint, without a blame,–
Might I but be the Jew!

I'm sure it is Golconda,
Beyond my power to deem,–
To have a smile for mine each day,
How better than a gem!

At least, it solaces to know
That there exists a gold,
Although I prove it just in time
Its distance to behold!

It's far, far treasure to surmise,
And estimate the pearl
That slipped my simple fingers through
While just a girl at school!

IV.

I GAVE myself to him,
    And took himself for pay.
The solemn contract of a life
Was ratified this way.

The wealth might disappoint,
Myself a poorer prove
Than this great purchaser suspect,
The daily own of Love

Depreciate the vision;
But, till the merchant buy,
Still fable, in the isles of spice,
The subtle cargoes lie.

At least, 't is mutual risk,—
Some found it mutual gain;
Sweet debt of Life — each night to owe,
Insolvent, every noon.

V.

"GOING to him! Happy letter! Tell him—
  Tell him the page I did n't write;
Tell him I only said the syntax,
And left the verb and the pronoun out.
Tell him just how the fingers hurried,
Then how they waded, slow, slow, slow;
And then you wished you had eyes in your pages,
So you could see what moved them so.

"Tell him it was n't a practised writer,
You guessed, from the way the sentence toiled;
You could hear the bodice tug, behind you,
As if it held but the might of a child;
You almost pitied it, you, it worked so.
Tell him—No, you may quibble there,
For it would split his heart to know it,
And then you and I were silenter.

"Tell him night finished before we finished,
And the old clock kept neighing 'day!'
And you got sleepy and begged to be ended—
What could it hinder so, to say?
Tell him just how she sealed you, cautious,
But if he ask where you are hid
Until to-morrow,—happy letter!
Gesture, coquette, and shake your head!"

VI.

THE way I read a letter's this:
　　'T is first I lock the door,
And push it with my fingers next,
For transport it be sure.

And then I go the furthest off
To counteract a knock;
Then draw my little letter forth
And softly pick its lock.

Then, glancing narrow at the wall,
And narrow at the floor,
For firm conviction of a mouse
Not exorcised before,

Peruse how infinite I am
To—no one that you know!
And sigh for lack of heaven,—but not
The heaven the creeds bestow.

VII.

WILD nights! Wild nights!
    Were I with thee,
Wild nights should be
Our luxury!

Futile the winds
To a heart in port,—
Done with the compass,
Done with the chart.

Rowing in Eden!
Ah! the sea!
Might I but moor
To-night in thee!

VIII.

THE night was wide, and furnished scant
        With but a single star,
That often as a cloud it met
Blew out itself for fear.

The wind pursued the little bush,
And drove away the leaves
November left; then clambered up
And fretted in the eaves.

No squirrel went abroad;
A dog's belated feet
Like intermittent plush were heard
Adown the empty street.

To feel if blinds be fast,
And closer to the fire
Her little rocking-chair to draw,
And shiver for the poor,

The housewife's gentle task.
"How pleasanter," said she
Unto the sofa opposite,
"The sleet than May—no thee!"

IX.

DID the harebell loose her girdle
    To the lover bee,
Would the bee the harebell hallow
Much as formerly?

Did the paradise, persuaded,
Yield her moat of pearl,
Would the Eden be an Eden,
Or the earl an earl?

X.

A CHARM invests a face
    Imperfectly beheld,–
The lady dare not lift her veil
For fear it be dispelled.

But peers beyond her mesh,
And wishes, and denies,–
Lest interview annul a want
That image satisfies.

XI.

THE rose did caper on her cheek,
    Her bodice rose and fell,
Her pretty speech, like drunken men,
Did stagger pitiful.

Her fingers fumbled at her work,–
Her needle would not go;
What ailed so smart a little maid
It puzzled me to know,

Till opposite I spied a cheek
That bore another rose;
Just opposite, another speech
That like the drunkard goes;

A vest that, like the bodice, danced
To the immortal tune,–
Till those two troubled little clocks
Ticked softly into one.

XII.

IN lands I never saw, they say,
        Immortal Alps look down,
Whose bonnets touch the firmament,
Whose sandals touch the town,–

Meek at whose everlasting feet
A myriad daisies play.
Which, sir, are you, and which am I,
Upon an August day?

XIII.

THE moon is distant from the sea,
        And yet with amber hands
She leads him, docile as a boy,
Along appointed sands.

He never misses a degree;
Obedient to her eye,
He comes just so far toward the town,
Just so far goes away.

Oh, Signor, thine the amber hand,
And mine the distant sea,–
Obedient to the least command
Thine eyes impose on me.

XIV.

HE put the belt around my life,—
    I heard the buckle snap,
And turned away, imperial,
My lifetime folding up
Deliberate, as a duke would do
A kingdom's title-deed,—
Henceforth a dedicated sort,
A member of the cloud.

Yet not too far to come at call,
And do the little toils
That make the circuit of the rest,
And deal occasional smiles
To lives that stoop to notice mine
And kindly ask it in,—
Whose invitation, knew you not
For whom I must decline?

XV.

I HELD a jewel in my fingers
    And went to sleep.
The day was warm, and winds were prosy;
I said: "'T will keep."

I woke and chid my honest fingers,—
The gem was gone;
And now an amethyst remembrance
Is all I own.

XVI.

WHAT if I say I shall not wait?
        What if I burst the fleshly gate
And pass, escaped, to thee?
What if I file this mortal off,
See where it hurt me,–that's enough,–
And wade in liberty?

They cannot take us any more,–
Dungeons may call, and guns implore;
Unmeaning now, to me,
As laughter was an hour ago,
Or laces, or a travelling show,
Or who died yesterday!

III. Nature

I.

NATURE, the gentlest mother,
  Impatient of no child,
The feeblest or the waywardest,–
Her admonition mild

In forest and the hill
By traveller is heard,
Restraining rampant squirrel
Or too impetuous bird.

How fair her conversation,
A summer afternoon,–
Her household, her assembly;
And when the sun goes down

Her voice among the aisles
Incites the timid prayer
Of the minutest cricket,
The most unworthy flower.

When all the children sleep
She turns as long away
As will suffice to light her lamps;
Then, bending from the sky

With infinite affection
And infiniter care,
Her golden finger on her lip,
Wills silence everywhere.

II.

WILL there really be a morning?
        Is there such a thing as day?
Could I see it from the mountains
If I were as tall as they?

Has it feet like water-lilies?
Has it feathers like a bird?
Is it brought from famous countries
Of which I have never heard?

Oh, some scholar! Oh, some sailor!
Oh, some wise man from the skies!
Please to tell a little pilgrim
Where the place called morning lies!

III.

AT half-past three a single bird
        Unto a silent sky
Propounded but a single term
Of cautious melody.

At half-past four, experiment
Had subjugated test,
And lo! her silver principle
Supplanted all the rest.

At half-past seven, element
Nor implement was seen,
And place was where the presence was,
Circumference between.

IV.

THE day came slow, till five o'clock,
    Then sprang before the hills
Like hindered rubies, or the light
A sudden musket spills.

The purple could not keep the east,
The sunrise shook from fold,
Like breadths of topaz, packed a night,
The lady just unrolled.

The happy winds their timbrels took;
The birds, in docile rows,
Arranged themselves around their prince
(The wind is prince of those).

The orchard sparkled like a Jew,—
How mighty 't was, to stay
A guest in this stupendous place,
The parlor of the day!

V.

THE sun just touched the morning;
        The morning, happy thing,
Supposed that he had come to dwell,
And life would be all spring.

She felt herself supremer,–
    raised, ethereal thing;
Henceforth for her what holiday!
Meanwhile, her wheeling king

Trailed slow along the orchards
His haughty, spangled hems.
Leaving a new necessity,–
The want of diadems!

The morning fluttered, staggered,
Felt feebly for her crown,–
Her unanointed forehead
Henceforth her only one.

VI.

THE robin is the one
　　　That interrupts the morn
With hurried, few, express reports
When March is scarcely on.

The robin is the one
That overflows the noon
With her cherubic quantity,
An April but begun.

The robin is the one
That speechless from her nest
Submits that home and certainty
And sanctity are best.

VII.

FROM cocoon forth a butterfly
        As lady from her door
Emerged—a summer afternoon—
Repairing everywhere,

Without design, that I could trace,
Except to stray abroad
On miscellaneous enterprise
The clovers understood.

Her pretty parasol was seen
Contracting in a field
Where men made hay, then struggling hard
With an opposing cloud,

Where parties, phantom as herself,
To Nowhere seemed to go
In purposeless circumference,
As 't were a tropic show.

And notwithstanding bee that worked,
And flower that zealous blew,
This audience of idleness
Disdained them, from the sky,

Till sundown crept, a steady tide,
And men that made the hay,
And afternoon, and butterfly,
Extinguished in its sea.

VIII.

BEFORE you thought of spring,
      Except as a surmise,
You see, God bless his sud-
denness,
A fellow in the skies
Of independent hues,
A little weather-worn,
Inspiriting habiliments
Of indigo and brown.

With specimens of song,
As if for you to choose,
Discretion in the interval,
With gay delays he goes
To some superior tree
Without a single leaf,
And shouts for joy to nobody
But his seraphic self!

IX.

AN altered look about the hills;
      A Tyrian light the village fills;
A wider sunrise in the dawn;
A deeper twilight on the lawn;
A print of a vermilion foot;
A purple finger on the slope;
A flippant fly upon the pane;
A spider at his trade again;
An added strut in chanticleer;
A flower expected everywhere;
An axe shrill singing in the woods;
Fern-odors on untravelled roads,—
All this, and more I cannot tell,
A furtive look you know as well,
And Nicodemus' mystery
Receives its annual reply.

X.

"WHOSE are the little beds," I asked,
    "Which in the valleys lie?"
Some shook their heads, and others smiled,
And no one made reply.

"Perhaps they did not hear," I said;
"I will inquire again.
Whose are the beds, the tiny beds
So thick upon the plain?"

"'T is daisy in the shortest;
A little farther on,
Nearest the door to wake the first,
Little leontodon.

"'T is iris, sir, and aster,
Anemone and bell,
Batschia in the blanket red,
And chubby daffodil."

Meanwhile at many cradles
Her busy foot she plied,
Humming the quaintest lullaby
That ever rocked a child.

"Hush! Epigea wakens!
The crocus stirs her lids,
Rhodora's cheek is crimson,–
She's dreaming of the woods."

Then, turning from them, reverent,
"Their bed-time 't is," she said;
"The bumble-bees will waken them
When April woods are red."

XI.

PIGMY seraphs gone astray,
     Velvet people from Vevay,
Belles from some lost summer day,
Bees' exclusive coterie.
Paris could not lay the fold
Belted down with emerald;
Venice could not show a cheek
Of a tint so lustrous meek.
Never such an ambuscade
As of brier and leaf displayed
For my little damask maid.
I had rather wear her grace
Than an earl's distinguished face;
I had rather dwell like her
Than be Duke of Exeter
Royalty enough for me
To subdue the bumble-bee!

XII.

TO hear an oriole sing
      May be a common thing,
Or only a divine.

It is not of the bird
Who sings the same, unheard,
As unto crowd.

The fashion of the ear
Attireth that it hear
In dun or fair.

So whether it be rune,
Or whether it be none,
Is of within;

The "tune is in the tree,"
The sceptic showeth me;
"No, sir! In thee!"

XIII.

ONE of the ones that Midas touched,
    Who failed to touch us all,
Was that confiding prodigal,
The blissful oriole.

So drunk, he disavows it
With badinage divine;
So dazzling, we mistake him
For an alighting mine.

A pleader, a dissembler,
An epicure, a thief,—
Betimes an oratorio,
An ecstasy in chief;

The Jesuit of orchards,
He cheats as he enchants
Of an entire attar
For his decamping wants.

The splendor of a Burmah,
The meteor of birds,
Departing like a pageant
Of ballads and of bards.

I never thought that Jason sought
For any golden fleece;
But then I am a rural man,
With thoughts that make for peace.

But if there were a Jason,
Tradition suffer me
Behold his lost emolument
Upon the apple-tree.

XIV.

I DREADED that first robin so,
    But he is mastered now,
And I'm accustomed to him grown,–
He hurts a little, though.

I thought if I could only live
Till that first shout got by,
Not all pianos in the woods
Had power to mangle me.

I dared not meet the daffodils,
For fear their yellow gown
Would pierce me with a fashion
So foreign to my own.

I wished the grass would hurry,
So when 't was time to see,
He'd be too tall, the tallest one
Could stretch to look at me.

I could not bear the bees should come,
I wished they'd stay away
In those dim countries where they go:
What word had they for me?

They're here, though; not a creature failed,
No blossom stayed away
In gentle deference to me,
The Queen of Calvary.

Each one salutes me as he goes,
And I my childish plumes
Lift, in bereaved acknowledgment
Of their unthinking drums.

XV.

A ROUTE of evanescence
                With a revolving wheel;
A resonance of emerald,
A rush of cochineal;
And every blossom on the bush
Adjusts its tumbled head,–
The mail from Tunis, probably,
As easy morning's ride.

XVI.

THE skies can't keep their secret!
                They tell it to the hills–
The hills just tell the orchards–
And they the daffodils!

A bird, by chance, that goes that way
Soft overhead the whole.
If I should bribe the little bird,
Who knows but she would tell?

I think I won't, however,
It's finer not to know;
If summer were an axiom,
What sorcery had snow?

So keep your secret, Father!
I would not, if I could,
Know what the sapphire fellows do,
In your new-fashioned world!

XVII.

WHO robbed the woods,
        The trusting woods?
The unsuspecting trees
Brought out their burrs and mosses
His fantasy to please.
He scanned their trinkets, curious,
He grasped, he bore away.
What will the solemn hemlock,
What will the fir-tree say?

XVIII.

TWO butterflies went out at noon
        And waltzed above a stream,
Then stepped straight through the firmament
And rested on a beam;

And then together bore away
Upon a shining sea,–
Though never yet, in any port,
Their coming mentioned be.

If spoken by the distant bird,
If met in ether sea
By frigate or by merchantman,
Report was not to me.

XIX.

I STARTED early, took my dog,
    And visited the sea;
The mermaids in the basement
Came out to look at me,

And frigates in the upper floor
Extended hempen hands,
Presuming me to be a mouse
Aground, upon the sands.

But no man moved me till the tide
Went past my simple shoe,
And past my apron and my belt,
And past my bodice too,

And made as he would eat me up
As wholly as a dew
Upon a dandelion's sleeve —
And then I started too.

And he — he followed close behind;
I felt his silver heel
Upon my ankle, — then my shoes
Would overflow with pearl.

Until we met the solid town,
No man he seemed to know;
And bowing with a mighty look
At me, the sea withdrew.

XX.

ARCTURUS is his other name,—
    I'd rather call him star!
It's so unkind of science
To go and interfere!

I pull a flower from the woods,—
A monster with a glass
Computes the stamens in a breath,
And has her in a class.

Whereas I took the butterfly
Aforetime in my hat,
He sits erect in cabinets,
The clover-bells forgot.

What once was heaven, is zenith now.
Where I proposed to go
When time's brief masquerade was done,
Is mapped, and charted too!

What if the poles should frisk about
And stand upon their heads!
I hope I'm ready for the worst,
Whatever prank betides!

Perhaps the kingdom of Heaven's changed!
I hope the children there
Won't be new-fashioned when I come,
And laugh at me, and stare!

I hope the father in the skies
Will lift his little girl,—
Old-fashioned, naughty, everything,—
Over the stile of pearl!

XXI.

AN awful tempest mashed the air,
        The clouds were gaunt and few;
A black, as of a spectre's cloak,
Hid heaven and earth from view.

The creatures chuckled on the roofs
And whistled in the air,
And shook their fists and gnashed their teeth,
And swung their frenzied hair.

The morning lit, the birds arose;
The monster's faded eyes
Turned slowly to his native coast,
And peace was Paradise!

XXII.

AN everywhere of silver,
        With ropes of sand
To keep it from effacing
The track called land.

XXIII.

A BIRD came down the walk:
      He did not know I saw;
He bit an angle-worm in halves
And ate the fellow, raw.

And then he drank a dew
From a convenient grass,
And then hopped sidewise to the wall
To let a beetle pass.

He glanced with rapid eyes
That hurried all abroad,–
They looked like frightened beads, I thought;
He stirred his velvet head

Like one in danger; cautious,
I offered him a crumb,
And he unrolled his feathers
And rowed him softer home

Than oars divide the ocean,
Too silver for a seam,
Or butterflies, off banks of noon,
Leap, plashless, as they swim.

XXIV.

A NARROW fellow in the grass
    Occasionally rides;
You may have met him,—did you not,
His notice sudden is.

The grass divides as with a comb,
A spotted shaft is seen;
And then it closes at your feet
And opens further on.

He likes a boggy acre,
A floor too cool for corn.
Yet when a child, and barefoot,
I more than once, at morn,

Have passed, I thought, a whip-lash
Unbraiding in the sun,—
When, stooping to secure it,
It wrinkled, and was gone.

Several of nature's people
I know, and they know me;
I feel for them a transport
Of cordiality;

But never met this fellow,
Attended or alone,
Without a tighter breathing,
And zero at the bone.

XXV.

THE mushroom is the elf of plants,
    At evening it is not;
At morning in a truffled hut
It stops upon a spot

As if it tarried always;
And yet its whole career
Is shorter than a snake's delay,
And fleeter than a tare.

'T is vegetation's juggler,
The germ of alibi;
Doth like a bubble antedate,
And like a bubble hie.

I feel as if the grass were pleased
To have it intermit;
The surreptitious scion
Of summer's circumspect.

Had nature any outcast face,
Could she a son contemn,
Had nature an Iscariot,
That mushroom,—it is him.

XXVI.

THERE came a wind like a bugle;
    It quivered through the grass,
And a green chill upon the heat
So ominous did pass
We barred the windows and the doors
As from an emerald ghost;
The doom's electric moccason
That very instant passed.
On a strange mob of panting trees,
And fences fled away,
And rivers where the houses ran
The living looked that day.
The bell within the steeple wild
The flying tidings whirled.
How much can come
And much can go,
And yet abide the world!

XXVII.

A SPIDER sewed at night
    Without a light
Upon an arc of white.
If ruff it was of dame
Or shroud of gnome,
Himself, himself inform.
Of immortality
His strategy
Was physiognomy.

XXVIII.

I KNOW a place where summer strives
                With such a practised frost,
She each year leads her daisies back,
Recording briefly, "Lost."

But when the south wind stirs the pools
And struggles in the lanes,
Her heart misgives her for her vow,
And she pours soft refrains

Into the lap of adamant,
And spices, and the dew,
That stiffens quietly to quartz,
Upon her amber shoe.

XXIX.

THE one that could repeat the summer day
                Were greater than itself, though he
Minutest of mankind might be.
And who could reproduce the sun,
At period of going down —
The lingering and the stain, I mean —
When Orient has been outgrown,
And Occident becomes unknown,
His name remain.

XXX.

THE wind tapped like a tired man,
        And like a host, "Come in,"
I boldly answered; entered then
My residence within

A rapid, footless guest,
To offer whom a chair
Were as impossible as hand
A sofa to the air.

No bone had he to bind him,
His speech was like the push
Of numerous humming-birds at once.
From a superior bush.

His countenance a billow,
His fingers, if he pass,
Let go a music, as of tunes
Blown tremulous in glass.

He visited, still flitting;
Then, like a timid man,
Again he tapped–'t was flurriedly–
And I became alone.

XXXI.

NATURE rarer uses yellow
        Than another hue;
Saves she all of that for sunsets,–
    Prodigal of blue,

Spending scarlet like a woman,
    Yellow she affords
Only scantly and selectly,
    Like a lover's words.

XXXII.

THE leaves, like women, interchange
        Sagacious confidence;
Somewhat of nods, and somewhat of
    Portentous inference,

The parties in both cases
    Enjoining secrecy,–
Inviolable compact
    To notoriety.

XXXIII.

HOW happy is the little stone
              That rambles in the road alone,
And does n't care about careers,
And exigencies never fears;
Whose coat of elemental brown
A passing universe put on;
And independent as the sun,
Associates or glows alone,
Fulfilling absolute decree
In casual simplicity.

XXXIV.

IT sounded as if the streets were running,
              And then the streets stood still.
Eclipse was all we could see at the window,
And awe was all we could feel.

By and by the boldest stole out of his covert,
To see if time was there.
Nature was in her beryl apron,
Mixing fresher air.

XXXV.

THE rat is the concisest tenant.
    He pays no rent,–
Repudiates the obligation,
On schemes intent.

Balking our wit
To sound or circumvent,
Hate cannot harm
A foe so reticent.

Neither decree
Prohibits him,
Lawful as
Equilibrium.

XXXVI.

FREQUENTLY the woods are pink,
    Frequently are brown;
Frequently the hills undress
Behind my native town.

Oft a head is crested
I was wont to see,
And as oft a cranny
Where it used to be.

And the earth, they tell me,
On its axis turned,–
Wonderful rotation
By but twelve performed!

XXXVII.

THE wind begun to rock the grass
     With threatening tunes and low,–
He flung a menace at the earth,
A menace at the sky.

The leaves unhooked themselves from trees
And started all abroad;
The dust did scoop itself like hands
And throw away the road.

The wagons quickened on the streets,
The thunder hurried slow;
The lightning showed a yellow beak,
And then a livid claw.

The birds put up the bars to nests,
The cattle fled to barns;
There came one drop of giant rain,
And then, as if the hands

That held the dams had parted hold,
The waters wrecked the sky,
But overlooked my father's house,
Just quartering a tree.

XXXVIII.

SOUTH winds jostle them,
        Bumblebees come,
Hover, hesitate,
Drink, and are gone.

Butterflies pause
On their passage Cashmere;
I, softly plucking,
Present them here!

XXXIX.

WHERE ships of purple gently toss
        On seas of daffodil,
Fantastic sailors mingle,
And then – the wharf is still.

XL.

SHE sweeps with many-colored brooms,
        And leaves the shreds behind;
Oh, housewife in the evening west,
Come back, and dust the pond!

You dropped a purple ravelling in,
You dropped an amber thread;
And now you've littered all the East
With duds of emerald!

And still she plies her spotted brooms,
And still the aprons fly,
Till brooms fade softly into stars—
And then I come away.

XLI.

LIKE mighty footlights burned the red
        At bases of the trees,—
The far theatricals of day
Exhibiting to these.

'T was universe that did applaud
While, chiefest of the crowd,
Enabled by his royal dress,
Myself distinguished God.

XLII.

BRING me the sunset in a cup,
  Reckon the morning's flagons up,
 And say how many dew;
Tell me how far the morning leaps,
Tell me what time the weaver sleeps
  Who spun the breadths of blue!

Write me how many notes there be
In the new robin's ecstasy
  Among astonished boughs;
How many trips the tortoise makes,
How many cups the bee partakes,—
  The debauchee of dews!

Also, who laid the rainbow's piers,
Also, who leads the docile spheres
  By withes of supple blue?
Whose fingers string the stalactite,
Who counts the wampum of the night,
  To see that none is due?

Who built this little Alban house
And shut the windows down so close
  My spirit cannot see?
Who 'll let me out some gala day,
Wit implements to fly away,
  Passing pomposity?

XLIII.

Blazing in gold and quenching in purple,
    Leaping like leopards to the sky,
Then at the feet of the old horizon
Laying her spotted face, to die;

Stooping as low as the otter's window,
Touching the roof and tinting the barn,
Kissing her bonnet to the meadow,–
And the juggler of day is gone!

XLIV.

Farther in summer than the birds,
    Pathetic from the grass,
A minor nation celebrates
Its unobtrusive mass.

No ordinance is seen,
So gradual the grace,
A pensive custom it becomes,
Enlarging loneliness.

Antiquest felt at noon
When August, burning low,
Calls forth this spectral canticle,
Repose to typify.

Remit as yet no grace,
No furrow on the glow,
Yet a druidic difference
Enhances nature now.

XLV.

AS imperceptibly as grief
          The summer lapsed away,–
Too imperceptible, at last,
To seem like perfidy.

A quietness distilled,
As twilight long begun,
Or Nature, spending with herself
Sequestered afternoon.

The dusk drew earlier in,
The morning foreign shone,–
A courteous, yet harrowing grace,
As guest who would be gone.

And thus, without a wing,
Or service of a keel,
Our summer made her light escape
Into the beautiful.

XLVI.

IT can't be summer,–that got through;
          It's early yet for spring;
There's that long town of white to cross
Before the blackbirds sing.

It can't be dying,–it's too rouge,–
The dead shall go in white.
So sunset shuts my question down
With clasps of chrysolite.

XLVII.

THE gentian weaves her fringes,
    The maple's loom is red.
My departing blossoms
Obviate parade.

A brief, but patient illness,
An hour to prepare;
And one, below this morning,
Is where the angels are.

It was a short procession,—
The bobolink was there,
An aged bee addressed us,
And then we knelt in prayer.

We trust that she was willing,—
We ask that we may be.
Summer, sister, seraph,
Let us go with thee!

In the name of the bee
And of the butterfly
And of the breeze, amen!

XLVIII.

GOD made a little gentian;
        It tried to be a rose
And failed, and all the summer laughed.
But just before the snows
There came a purple creature
That ravished all the hill;
And summer hid her forehead,
And mockery was still.
The frosts were her condition;
The Tyrian would not come
Until the North evoked it.
"Creator! shall I bloom?"

XLIX.

BESIDES the autumn poets sing,
        A few prosaic days
A little this side of the snow
And that side of the haze.

A few incisive mornings,
A few ascetic eves,—
Gone Mr. Bryant's golden-rod,
And Mr. Thomson's sheaves.

Still is the bustle in the brook,
Sealed are the spicy valves;
Mesmeric fingers softly touch
The eyes of many elves.

Perhaps a squirrel may remain,
My sentiments to share.
Grant me, O Lord, a sunny mind,
Thy windy will to bear!

L.

IT sifts from leaden sieves,
    It powders all the wood,
It fills with alabaster wool
The wrinkles of the road.

It makes an even face
Of mountain and of plain,—
Unbroken forehead from the east
Unto the east again.

It reaches to the fence,
It wraps it, rail by rail,
Till it is lost in fleeces;
It flings a crystal veil

On stump and stack and stem,—
The summer's empty room,
Acres of seams where harvests were,
Recordless, but for them.

It ruffles wrists of posts,
As ankles of a queen,—
Then stills its artisans like ghosts,
Denying they have been.

LI.

NO brigadier throughout the year
So civic as the jay.
A neighbor and a warrior too,
With shrill felicity

Pursuing winds that censure us
A February day,
The brother of the universe
Was never blown away.

The snow and he are intimate;
I've often seen them play
When heaven looked upon us all
With such severity,

I felt apology were due
To an insulted sky,
Whose pompous frown was nutriment
To their temerity.

The pillow of this daring head
Is pungent evergreens;
His larder – terse and militant –
Unknown, refreshing things;

His character a tonic,
His future a dispute;
Unfair an immortality
That leaves this neighbor out.

IV. Time and Eternity

I.

LET down the bars, O Death!
        The tired flocks come in
Whose bleating ceases to repeat,
Whose wandering is done.

Thine is the stillest night,
Thine the securest fold;
Too near thou art for seeking thee,
Too tender to be told.

II.

GOING to heaven!
      I don't know when,
Pray do not ask me how,–
Indeed, I'm too astonished
To think of answering you!
Going to heaven!–
How dim it sounds!
And yet it will be done
As sure as flocks go home at night
Unto the shepherd's arm!

Perhaps you're going too!
Who knows?
If you should get there first,
Save just a little place for me
Close to the two I lost!
The smallest "robe" will fit me,
And just a bit of "crown;"
For you know we do not mind our dress
When we are going home.

I'm glad I don't believe it,
For it would stop my breath,
And I'd like to look a little more
At such a curious earth!
I am glad they did believe it
Whom I have never found
Since the mighty autumn afternoon
I left them in the ground.

III.

AT least to pray is left, is left.
        O Jesus! in the air
I know not which thy chamber is,—
I'm knocking everywhere.

Thou stirrest earthquake in the South,
And maelstrom in the sea;
Say, Jesus Christ of Nazareth,
Hast thou no arm for me?

IV.

STEP lightly on this narrow spot!
        The broadest land that grows
Is not so ample as the breast
These emerald seams enclose.

Step lofty; for this name is told
As far as cannon dwell,
Or flag subsist, or fame export
Her deathless syllable.

V.

MORNS like these we parted;
          Noons like these she rose,
Fluttering first, then firmer,
To her fair repose.

Never did she lisp it,
And 't was not for me;
She was mute from transport,
I, from agony!

Till the evening, nearing,
One the shutters drew—
Quick! a sharper rustling!
And this linnet flew!

VI.

A DEATH-BLOW is a life-blow to some
          Who, till they died, did not alive become;
Who, had they lived, and died, but when
They died, vitality begun.

VII.

I READ my sentence steadily,
        Reviewed it with my eyes,
To see that I made no mistake
In its extremest clause,—

The date, and manner of the shame;
And then the pious form
That "God have mercy" on the soul
The jury voted him.

I made my soul familiar
With her extremity,
That at the last it should not be
A novel agony,

But she and Death, acquainted,
Meet tranquilly as friends,
Salute and pass without a hint,—
And there the matter ends.

VIII.

I HAVE not told my garden yet,
    Lest that should conquer me;
I have not quite the strength now
To break it to the bee.

I will not name it in the street,
For shops would stare, that I,
So shy, so very ignorant,
Should have the face to die.

The hillsides must not know it,
Where I have rambled so,
Nor tell the loving forests
The day that I shall go,

Nor lisp it at the table,
Nor heedless by the way
Hint that within the riddle
One will walk to-day!

IX.

They dropped like flakes, they dropped like stars,
    Like petals from a rose,
When suddenly across the June
    A wind with fingers goes.

They perished in the seamless grass,—
    No eye could find the place;
But God on his repealless list
    Can summon every face.

X.

THE only ghost I ever saw
    Was dressed in mechlin,—so;
He wore no sandal on his foot,
And stepped like flakes of snow.
His gait was soundless, like the bird,
But rapid, like the roe;
His fashions quaint, mosaic,
Or, haply, mistletoe.

His conversation seldom,
His laughter like the breeze
That dies away in dimples
Among the pensive trees.
Our interview was transient,—
Of me, himself was shy;
And God forbid I look behind
Since that appalling day!

XI.

SOME, too fragile for winter winds,
        The thoughtful grave encloses,–
Tenderly tucking them in from frost
Before their feet are cold.

Never the treasures in her nest
The cautious grave exposes,
Building where schoolboy dare not look
And sportsman is not bold.

This covert have all the children
Early aged, and often cold,–
Sparrows unnoticed by the Father;
Lambs for whom time had not a fold.

XII.

AS by the dead we love to sit,
        Become so wondrous dear,
As for the lost we grapple,
Though all the rest are here,–

In broken mathematics
We estimate our prize,
Vast, in its fading ratio,
To our penurious eyes!

XIII.

DEATH sets a thing significant
        The eye had hurried by,
Except a perished creature
Entreat us tenderly

To ponder little workmanships
In crayon or in wool,
With "This was last her fingers did,"
Industrious until

The thimble weighed too heavy,
The stitches stopped themselves,
And then 't was put among the dust
Upon the closet shelves.

A book I have, a friend gave,
Whose pencil, here and there,
Had notched the place that pleased him,—
At rest his fingers are.

Now, when I read, I read not,
For interrupting tears
Obliterate the etchings
Too costly for repairs.

XIV.

I WENT to heaven,—
    'T was a small town,
Lit with a ruby,
Lathed with down.
Stiller than the fields
At the full dew,
Beautiful as pictures
No man drew.
People like the moth,
Of mechlin, frames,
Duties of gossamer,
And eider names.
Almost contented
I could be
'Mong such unique
Society.

XV.

THEIR height in heaven comforts not,
          Their glory nought to me;
'Twas best imperfect, as it was;
I'm finite, I can't see.

The house of supposition,
The glimmering frontier
The skirts the acres of perhaps,
To me shows insecure.

The wealth I had contented me;
If't was a meaner size,
Then I had counted it until
It pleased my narrow eyes

Better than larger values,
However true their show;
This timid life of evidence
Keeps pleading, "I don't know."

XVI.

THERE is a shame of nobleness
          Confronting sudden pelf,–
A finer shame of ecstasy
Convicted of itself.

A best disgrace a brave man feels,
Acknowledged of the brave,–
One more "Ye Blessed" to be told;
But this involves the grave.

XVII.

TRIUMPH may be of several kinds.
        There's triumph in the room
When that old imperator, Death,
By faith is overcome.

There's triumph of the finer mind
When truth, affronted long,
Advances calm to her supreme,
Her God her only throng.

A triumph when temptation's bribe
Is slowly handed back,
One eye upon the heaven renounced
And one upon the rack.

Severer triumph, by himself
Experienced, who can pass
Acquitted from that naked bar,
Jehovah's countenance!

XVIII.

POMPLESS no life can pass away;
        The lowliest career
To the same pageant wends its way
        As that exalted here.
How cordial is the mystery!
        The hospitable pall
A "this way" beckons spaciously,–
        A miracle for all!

XIX.

I NOTICED people disappeared,
        When but a little child,–
Supposed they visited remote,
Or settled regions wild.

Now know I they both visited
And settled regions wild,
But did because they died,–a fact
Withheld the little child!

XX.

I HAD no cause to be awake,
   My best was gone to sleep,
And morn a new politeness took,
And failed to wake them up,

But called the others clear,
And passed their curtains by.
Sweet morning, when I over-sleep,
Knock, recollect, for me!

I looked at sunrise once,
And then I looked at them,
At wishfulness in me arose
For circumstance the same.

'T was such an ample peace,
It could not hold a sigh,–
'T was Sabbath with the bells divorced,
'T was sunset all the day.

So choosing but a gown
And taking but a prayer,
The only raiment I should need,
I struggled, and was there.

XXI.

IF anybody's friend be dead,
    It's sharpest of the theme
The thinking how they walked alive,
At such and such a time.

Their costume, of a Sunday,
Some manner of the hair,—
A prank nobody knew but them,
Lost, in the sepulchre.

How warm they were on such a day:
You almost feel the date,
So short way off it seems; and now,
They're centuries from that.

How pleased they were at what you said;
You try to touch the smile,
And dip your fingers in the frost:
When was it, can you tell,

You asked the company to tea,
Acquaintance, just a few,
And chatted close with this grand thing
That don't remember you?

Past bows and invitations,
Past interview, and vow,
Past what ourselves can estimate,—
That makes the quick of woe!

XXII.

OUR journey had advanced;
　　　Our feet were almost come
To that odd fork in Being's road,
Eternity by term.

Our pace took sudden awe,
Our feet reluctant led.
Before were cities, but between,
The forest of the dead.

Retreat was out of hope,—
Behind, a sealed route,
Eternity's white flag before,
And God at every gate.

XXIII.

AMPLE make this bed.
　　　Make this bed with awe;
In it wait till judgment break
Excellent and fair.

Be its mattress straight,
Be its pillow round;
Let no sunrise's yellow noise
Interrupt this ground.

XXIV.

ON such a night, or such a night,
      Would anybody care
Of such a little figure
Slipped quiet from its chair,

So quiet, oh, how quiet!
That nobody might know
But that the little figure
Rocked softer, to and fro?

On such a dawn, or such a dawn,
Would anybody sigh
That such a little figure
Too sound asleep did lie

For chanticleer to wake it,—
Or stirring house below,
Or giddy bird in orchard,
Or early task to do?

There was a little figure plump
For every little knoll,
Busy needles, and spools of thread,
And trudging feet from school.

Playmates, and holidays, and nuts,
And visions vast and small.
Strange that the feet so precious charged
Should reach so small a goal!

XXV.

ESSENTIAL oils are wrung:
    The attar from the rose
Is not expressed by suns alone,
It is the gift of screws.

The general rose decays;
But this, in lady's drawer,
Makes summer when the lady lies
In ceaseless rosemary.

XXVI.

I LIVED on dread; to those who know
    The stimulus there is
In danger, other impetus
Is numb and vital-less.

As 't were a spur upon the soul,
A fear will urge it where
To go without the spectre's aid
Were challenging despair.

XXVII.

IF I should die,
        And you should live,
And time should gurgle on,
And morn should beam,
And noon should burn,
As it has usual done;
If birds should build as early,
And bees as bustling go,—
One might depart at option
From enterprise below!
'T is sweet to know that stocks will stand
When we with daisies lie,
That commerce will continue,
And trades as briskly fly.
It makes the parting tranquil
And keeps the soul serene,
That gentlemen so sprightly
Conduct the pleasing scene!

XXVIII.

HER final summer was it,
  And yet we guessed it not;
If tenderer industriousness
Pervaded her, we thought

A further force of life
Developed from within,—
When Death lit all the shortness up,
And made the hurry plain.

We wondered at our blindness,—
When nothing was to see
But her Carrara guide-post,—
At our stupidity,

When, duller than our dulness,
The busy darling lay,
So busy was she, finishing,
So leisurely were we!

XXIX.

ONE need not be a chamber to be haunted,
        One need not be a house;
The brain has corridors surpassing
Material place.

Far safer, of a midnight meeting
External ghost,
Than an interior confronting
That whiter host.

Far safer through an Abbey gallop,
The stones achase,
Than, moonless, one's own self encounter
In lonesome place.

Ourself, behind ourself concealed,
Should startle most;
Assassin, hid in our apartment,
Be horror's least.

The prudent carries a revolver,
He bolts the door,
O'erlooking a superior spectre
More near.

XXX.

SHE died,—this was the way she died;
        And when her breath was done,
Took up her simple wardrobe
And started for the sun.

Her little figure at the gate
The angels must have spied,
Since I could never find her
Upon the mortal side.

XXXI.

WAIT till the majesty of Death
        Invests so mean a brow!
Almost a powdered footman
Might dare to touch it now!

Wait till in everlasting robes
This democrat is dressed,
Then prate about "preferment"
And "station" and the rest!

Around this quiet courtier
Obsequious angels wait!
Full royal is his retinue,
Full purple is his state!

A lord might dare to lift the hat
To such a modest clay,
Since that my Lord, "the Lord of lords"
Receives unblushingly!

XXXII.

WENT up a year this evening!
        I recollect it well!
Amid no bells nor bravos
The bystanders will tell!
Cheerful, as to the village,
Tranquil, as to repose,
Chastened, as to the chapel,
This humble tourist rose.
Did not talk of returning,
Alluded to no time
When, were the gales propitious,
We might look for him;
Was grateful for the roses
In life's diverse bouquet,
Talked softly of new species
To pick another day.
Beguiling thus the wonder,
The wondrous nearer drew;
Hands bustled at the moorings—
The crowd respectful grew.
Ascended from our vision
To countenances new!
A difference, a daisy,
Is all the rest I knew!

XXXIII.

TAKEN from men this morning,
      Carried by men to-day,
Met by the gods with banners
Who marshalled her away.

One little maid from playmates,
One little mind from school,–
There must be guests in Eden;
All the rooms are full.

Far as the east from even,
Dim as the border star,–
Courtiers quaint, in kingdoms,
Our departed are.

XXXIV.

WHAT inn is this
      Where for the night
Peculiar traveller comes?
Who is the landlord?
Where the maids?
Behold, what curious rooms!
No ruddy fires on the hearth,
No brimming tankards flow.
Necromancer, landlord,
Who are these below?

XXXV.

IT was not death, for I stood up,
        And all the dead lie down;
It was not night, for all the bells
Put out their tongues, for noon.

It was not frost, for on my flesh
I felt siroccos crawl,—
Nor fire, for just my marble feet
Could keep a chancel cool.

And yet it tasted like them all;
The figures I have seen
Set orderly, for burial,
Reminded me of mine,

As if my life were shaven
And fitted to a frame,
And could not breathe without a key;
And 't was like midnight, some,

When everything that ticked has stopped,
And space stares, all around,
Or grisly frosts, first autumn morns,
Repeal the beating ground.

But most like chaos,—stopless, cool,—
Without a chance or spar,
Or even a report of land
To justify despair.

XXXVI.

I SHOULD not dare to leave my friend,
    Because—because if he should die
While I was gone, and I—too late—
Should reach the heart that wanted me;

If I should disappoint the eyes
That hunted, hunted so, to see,
And could not bear to shut until
They "noticed" me—they noticed me;

If I should stab the patient faith
So sure I'd come—so sure I'd come,
It listening, listening, went to sleep
Telling my tardy name,—

My heart would wish it broke before,
Since breaking then, since breaking then,
Were useless as next morning's sun,
Where midnight frosts had lain!

XXXVII.

GREAT streets of silence led away
        To neighborhoods of pause;
Here was no notice, no dissent,
No universe, no laws.

By clocks 't was morning, and for night
The bells at distance called;
But epoch had no basis here,
For period exhaled.

XXXVIII.

A THROE upon the features
        A hurry in the breath,
An ecstasy of parting
Denominated "Death,"–

An anguish at the mention,
Which, when to patience grown,
I've known permission given
To rejoin its own.

XXXIX.

OF tribulation these are they
        Denoted by the white;
The spangled gowns, a lesser rand
Of victors designate.

All these did conquer; but the ones
Who overcame most times
Wear nothing commoner than snow,
No ornament but palms.

Surrender is a sort unknown
On this superior soil;
Defeat, an outgrown anguish,
Remembered as the mile

Our panting ankle barely gained
When night devoured the road;
But we stood whispering in the house,
And all we said was "Saved"!

XL.

I THINK just how my shape will rise
    When I shall be forgiven,
Till hair and eyes and timid head
Are out of sight, in heaven.

I think just how my lips will weigh
With shapeless, quivering prayer
That you, so late, consider me,
The sparrow of your care.

I mind me that of anguish sent,
Some drifts were moved away
Before my simple bosom broke,–
And why not this, if they?

And so, until delirious borne
I con that thing,–"forgiven,"–
Till with long fright and longer trust
I drop my heart, unshriven!

XLI.

AFTER a hundred years
        Nobody knows the place,—
Agony, that enacted there,
Motionless as peace.

Weeds triumphant ranged.
Strangers strolled and spelled
At the lone orthography
Of the elder dead.

Winds of summer fields
Recollect the way,—
Instinct picking up the key
Dropped by memory.

XLII.

LAY this laurel on the one
        Too intrinsic for renown.
Laurel! veil your deathless tree,—
Him you chasten, that is he!

· · ·

POEMS

BY

EMILY DICKINSON

·*THIRD SERIES*·

. . .

PRELUDE

It's all I have to bring to-day
This, and my heart beside,
This and my heart, and all the fields,
And all the meadows wide.
Be sure you count, should I forget,—
Some one the sum could tell,—
This, and my heart, and all the bees
Which in the clover dwell.

. . .

PREFACE

THE intellectual activity of Emily Dickinson was so great that a large and characteristic choice is still possible among her literary material, and this third volume of her verses is put forth in response to the repeated wish of the admirers of her peculiar genius.

Much of Emily Dickinson's prose was rhythmic,—even rhymed, though frequently not set apart in lines. Also many verses, written as such, were sent to friends in letters; these were published in 1894, in the volumes of her *Letters*. It has not been necessary, however, to include them in this Series, and all have been omitted, except three or four exceptionally strong ones, as ["There is no frigate like a book"] and ["If recollecting were forgetting. . ."].

There is internal evidence that many of the poems were simply spontaneous flashes of insight, apparently unrelated to outward circumstance. Others, however, had an obvious personal origin; for example, the verses "I had a Guinea golden," which seem to have been sent to some friend travelling in Europe, as a dainty reminder of letter-writing delinquencies. The surroundings in which any of Emily Dickinson's verses are known to have been written usually serve to explain them clearly; but in general the present volume is full of thoughts needing no interpretation to those who apprehend this scintillating spirit.

M.L.T.

AMHERST, *October,* 1896

I. LIFE

I.

'T IS little I could care for pearls
    Who own the ample sea;
Or brooches, when the Emperor
    With rubies pelteth me;

Or gold, who am the Prince of Mines;
    Or diamonds, when I see
A diadem to fit a dome
Continual crowning me.

II.

SUPERIORITY to fate
    Is difficult to learn.
'T is not conferred by any,
    But possible to earn

A pittance at a time,
    Until, to her surprise,
The soul with strict economy
    Subsists till Paradise.

III.

HOPE is a subtle glutton;
    He feeds upon the fair;
And yet, inspected closely,
    What abstinence is there!

His is the halcyon table
    That never seats but one,
And whatsoever is consumed
    The same amounts remain.

IV.

FORBIDDEN fruit a flavor has
    That lawful orchards mocks;
How luscious lies the pea within
    The pod that Duty locks!

V.

HEAVEN is what I cannot reach!
　　The apple on the tree,
Provided it do hopeless hang,
　　That "heaven" is, to me.

The color on the cruising cloud,
　　The interdicted ground
Behind the hill, the house
behind,–
　　There Paradise is found!

VI.

A WORD is dead
　　　When it is said,
　　Some say.
I say it just
Begins to live
　　That day.

VII.

TO venerate the simple days
        Which lead the seasons by,
Needs but to remember
    That from you or me
They take the trifle
    Termed mortality!

To invest existence with a stately air,
Needs but to remember
    That the acorn there
Is the egg of forests
    For the upper air!

VIII.

IT'S such a little thing to weep,
        So short a thing to sigh;
And yet by trades the size of these
    We men and women die!

IX.

DROWNING is not so pitiful
    As the attempt to rise.
Three times, 't is said, a sinking man
    Comes up to face the skies,
And then declines forever
    To that abhorred abode
Where hope and he part company,—
    For he is grasped of God.
The Maker's cordial visage,
    However good to see,
Is shunned, we must admit it,
    Like an adversity.

X.

HOW still the bells in steeples stand,
    Till, swollen with the sky,
They leap upon their silver feet
    In frantic melody!

XI.

IF the foolish call them "flowers,"
    Need the wiser tell?
If the savans "classify" them,
    It is just as well!

Those who read the *Revelations*
    Must not criticise
Those who read the same edition
    With beclouded eyes!

Could we stand with that old Moses
    Canaan denied,–
Scan, like him, the stately landscape
    On the other side,–

Doubtless we should deem superfluous
    Many sciences
Not pursued by learned angels
    In scholastic skies!

Low amid that glad *Belles lettres*
    Grant that we may stand,
Stars, amid profound Galaxies,
    At that grand "Right hand"!

XII.

COULD mortal lip divine
    The undeveloped freight
Of a delivered syllable,
    'T would crumble with the weight.

XIII.

MY life closed twice before its close;
    It yet remains to see
If Immortality unveil
    A third event to me,

So huge, so hopeless to conceive,
    As these that twice befell.
Parting is all we know of heaven,
    And all we need of hell.

XIV.

WE never know how high we are
    Till we are called to rise;
And then, if we are true to plan,
    Our statures touch the skies.

The heroism we recite
    Would be a daily thing,
Did not ourselves the cubits warp
    For fear to be a king.

XV.

WHILE I was fearing it, it came,
　　But came with less of fear,
Because that fearing it so long
　　Had almost made it dear.
There is a fitting a dismay,
　　A fitting a despair.
'T is harder knowing it is due,
　　Than knowing it is here.
The trying on the utmost,
　　The morning it is new,
Is terribler than wearing it
　　A whole existence through.

XVI.

THERE is no frigate like a book
　　To take us lands away,
Nor any coursers like a page
　　Of prancing poetry.
This traverse may the poorest take
　　Without oppress of toll:
How frugal is the chariot
　　That bears a human soul!

XVII.

WHO has not found the heaven below
    Will fail of it above.
God's residence is next to mine,
    His furniture is love.

XVIII.

A FACE devoid of love or grace,
    A hateful, hard, successful face,
    A face with which a stone
Would feel as thoroughly at ease
As were they old acquaintances,—
    First time together thrown.

XIX.

I HAD a guinea golden;
 I lost it in the sand,
And though the sum was simple,
 And pounds were in the land,
Still had it such a value
 Unto my frugal eye,
That when I could not find it
 I sat me down to sigh.

I had a crimson robin
 Who sang full many a day,
But when the woods were painted
 He, too, did fly away.
Time brought me other robins,–
 Their ballads were the same,–
Still for my missing troubadour
 I kept the "house at hame."

I had a star in heaven;
 One Pleiad was its name,
And when I was not heeding
 It wandered from the same.
And though the skies are crowded,
 And all the night ashine,
I do not care about it,
 Since none of them are mine.

My story has a moral;
 I have a missing friend,–
Pleiad its name, and robin,
 And guinea in the sand,–
And when this mournful ditty,
 Accompanied with tear,

Shall meet the eye of traitor
   In country far from here,
Grant that repentance solemn
   May seize upon his mind,
And he no consolation
   Beneath the sun may find.

XX.

FROM all the jails the boys and girls
   Ecstatically leap,–
Beloved, only afternoon
   That prison doesn't keep.

They storm the earth and stun the
air,
   A mob of solid bliss.
Alas! that frowns could lie in wait
   For such a foe as this!

XXI.

FEW get enough,—enough is one;
　　To that ethereal throng
Have not each one of us the right
　　To stealthily belong?

XXII.

UPON the gallows hung a wretch,
　　Too sullied for the hell
To which the law entitled him.
　　As nature's curtain fell
The one who bore him tottered in,
　　For this was woman's son.
"'T was all I had," she stricken gasped;
　　Oh, what a livid boon!

XXIII.

I FELT a clearing in my mind
    As if my brain had split;
I tried to match it, seam by seam,
    But could not make them fit.

The thought behind I strove to join
    Unto the thought before,
But sequence ravelled out of reach
    Like balls upon a floor.

XXIV.

THE reticent volcano keeps
    His never slumbering plan;
Confided are his projects pink
    To no precarious man.

If nature will not tell the tale
    Jehovah told to her,
Can human nature not survive
    Without a listener?

Admonished by her buckled lips
    Let every babbler be.
The only secret people keep
    Is Immortality.

XXV.

IF recollecting were forgetting,
 Then I remember not;
And if forgetting, recollecting,
 How near I had forgot!
And if to miss were merry,
 And if to mourn were gay,
How very blithe the fingers
 That gathered these to-day!

XXVI.

THE farthest thunder that I heard
 Was nearer than the sky,
And rumbles still, though torrid noons
 Have lain their missiles by.
The lightning that preceded it
 Struck no one but myself,
But I would not exchange the bolt
 For all the rest of life.
Indebtedness to oxygen
 The chemist may repay,
But not the obligation
 To electricity.
It founds the homes and decks the days,
 And every clamor bright
Is but the gleam concomitant
 Of that waylaying light.
The thought is quiet as a flake,—
 A crash without a sound;
How life's reverberation
 Its explanation found!

XXVII.

ON the bleakness of my lot
        Bloom I strove to raise.
Late, my acre of a rock
    Yielded grape and maize.

Soil of flint if steadfast tilled
    Will reward the hand;
Seed of palm by Lybian sun
    Fructified in sand.

XXVIII.

A DOOR just opened on a street—
        I, lost, was passing by—
An instant's width of warmth
disclosed,
    And wealth, and company.

The door as sudden shut, and I,
    I, lost, was passing by,—
Lost doubly, but by contrast most,
    Enlightening misery.

XXIX.

ARE friends delight or pain?
    Could bounty but remain
Riches were good.

But if they only stay
Bolder to fly away,
    Riches are sad.

XXX.

ASHES denote that fire was;
    Respect the grayest pile
For the departed creature's sake
    That hovered there awhile.

Fire exists the first in light,
    And then consolidates,–
Only the chemist can disclose
    Into what carbonates.

XXXI.

FATE slew him, but he did not drop;
    She felled—he did not fall—
Impaled him on her fiercest stakes—
    He neutralized them all.

She stung him, sapped his firm advance,
    But, when her worst was done,
And he, unmoved, regarded her,
    Acknowledged him a man.

XXXII.

FINITE to fail, but infinite to venture.
    For the one ship that struts the shore
Many's the gallant, overwhelmed creature
    Nodding in navies nevermore.

XXXIII.

I MEASURE every grief I meet
  With analytic eyes;
I wonder if it weighs like mine,
  Or has an easier size.

I wonder if they bore it long,
  Or did it just begin?
I could not tell the date of mine,
  It feels so old a pain.

I wonder if it hurts to live,
  And if they have to try,
And whether, could they choose between,
  They would not rather die.

I wonder if when years have piled –
  Some thousands – on the cause
Of early hurt, if such a lapse
  Could give them any pause;

Or would they go on aching still
  Through centuries above,
Enlightened to a larger pain
  By contrast with the love.

The grieved are many, I am told;
  The reason deeper lies, –
Death is but one and comes but once,
  And only nails the eyes.

There's grief of want, and grief of cold,—
    A sort they call "despair";
There's banishment from native eyes,
    In sight of native air.

And though I may not guess the kind
    Correctly, yet to me
A piercing comfort it affords
    In passing Calvary,

To note the fashions of the cross,
    Of those that stand alone,
Still fascinated to presume
    That some are like my own.

XXXIV.

I HAVE a king who does not speak;
    So, wondering, thro' the hours meek
    I trudge the day away,—
Half glad when it is night and sleep,
If, haply, thro' a dream to peep
    In parlors shut by day.

And if I do, when morning comes,
It is as if a hundred drums
    Did round my pillow roll,
And shouts fill all my childish sky,
And bells keep saying "victory"
    From steeples in my soul!

And if I don't, the little Bird
Within the Orchard is not heard,
   And I omit to pray,
"Father, thy will be done" to-day,
For my will goes the other way,
   And it were perjury!

XXXV.

IT dropped so low in my regard
     I heard it hit the ground,
And go to pieces on the stones
   At bottom of my mind;

Yet blamed the fate that fractured, less
   Than I reviled myself
For entertaining plated wares
   Upon my silver shelf.

XXXVI.

TO lose one's faith surpasses
        The loss of an estate,
Because estates can be
        Replenished,—faith cannot.

Inherited with life,
        Belief but once can be;
Annihilate a single clause,
        And Being's beggary.

XXXVII.

I HAD a daily bliss
        I half indifferent viewed,
Till sudden I perceived it stir,—
        It grew as I pursued,

Till when, around a crag,
        It wasted from my sight,
Enlarged beyond my utmost scope,
        I learned its sweetness right.

XXXVIII.

I WORKED for chaff, and earning wheat
     Was haughty and betrayed.
What right had fields to arbitrate
  In matters ratified?

I tasted wheat,—and hated chaff,
  And thanked the ample friend;
Wisdom is more becoming viewed
  At distance than at hand.

XXXIX.

LIFE, and Death, and Giants
     Such as these, are still.
Minor apparatus, hopper of the mill,
Beetle at the candle,
  Or a fife's small fame,
Maintain by accident
  That they proclaim.

XL.

OUR lives are Swiss,—
      So still, so cool,
Till, some odd afternoon,
The Alps neglect their curtains,
      And we look farther on.

Italy stands the other side,
      While, like a guard between,
The solemn Alps,
The siren Alps,
      Forever intervene!

XLI.

REMEMBRANCE has a rear and front,—
      'T is something like a house;
It has a garret also
      For refuse and the mouse.

Besides, the deepest cellar
      That ever mason hewed;
Look to it, by its fathoms
      Ourselves be not pursued.

XLII.

TO hand our head ostensibly,
        And subsequent to find
That such was not the posture
    Of our immortal mind,

Affords the sly presumption
    That, in so dense a fuzz,
You, too, take cobweb attitudes
    Upon a plane of gauze!

XLIII.

THE brain is wider than the sky,
        For, put them side by side,
The one the other will include
    With ease, and you beside.

The brain is deeper than the sea,
    For, hold them, blue to blue,
The one the other will absorb,
    As sponges, buckets do.

The brain is just the weight of God,
    For, lift them, pound for pound,
And they will differ, if they do,
    As syllable from sound.

XLIV.

THE bone that has no marrow;
    What ultimate for that?
It is not fit for table,
    For beggar, or for cat.

A bone has obligations,
    A being has the same;
A marrowless assembly
    Is culpabler than shame.

But how shall finished creatures
    A function fresh obtain? –
Old Nicodemus' phantom
    Confronting us again!

XLV.

THE past is such a curious creature,
    To look her in the face
A transport may reward us,
    Or a disgrace.

Unarmed if any meet her,
    I charge him, fly!
Her rusty ammunition
    Might yet reply!

XLVI.

TO help our bleaker parts
     Salubrious hours are given,
Which if they do not fit for earth
    Drill silently for heaven.

XLVII.

WHAT soft, cherubic creatures
    These gentlewomen are!
One would as soon assault a plush
    Or violate a star.

Such dimity convictions,
    A horror so refined
Of freckled human nature,
    Of Deity ashamed,—

It's such a common glory,
    A fisherman's degree!
Redemption, brittle lady,
    Be so, ashamed of thee.

XLVIII.

WHO never wanted,—maddest joy
    Remains to him unknown:
The banquet of abstemiousness
    Surpasses that of wine.

Within its hope, though yet ungrasped
    Desire's perfect goal,
No nearer, lest reality
    Should disenthrall thy soul.

XLIX.

IT might be easier
    To fail with land in sight,
Than gain by blue peninsula
    To perish of delight.

L.

YOU cannot put a fire out;
    A thing that can ignite
Can go, itself, without a fan
    Upon the slowest night.

You cannot fold a flood
    And put it in a drawer,—
Because the winds would find it out,
    And tell your cedar floor.

LI.

A MODEST lot, a fame *petite,*
　　　A brief campaign of sting and sweet
Is plenty! Is enough!
A sailor's business is the shore,
　　A soldier's—balls. Who asketh more
Must seek the neighboring life!

LII.

IS bliss, then, such abyss
　　　I must not put my foot amiss
For fear I spoil my shoe?

I'd rather suit my foot
Than save my boot,
For yet to buy another pair
Is possible
At any fair.

But bliss is sold just once;
The patent lost
None buy it any more.

LIII.

I STEPPED from plank to plank
        So slow and cautiously;
The stars about my head I felt,
        About my feet the sea.

I knew not but the next
        Would be my final inch,—
This gave me that precarious gait
        Some call experience.

LIV.

ONE day is there of the series
        Termed Thanksgiving day,
Celebrated part at table,
        Part in memory.

Neither patriarch nor pussy,
        I dissect the play;
Seems it, to my hooded thinking,
        Reflex holiday.

Had there been no sharp subtraction
        From the early sum,
Not an acre or a caption
        Where was once a room,

Not a mention, whose small pebble
        Wrinkled any bay,—
Unto such, were such assembly,
        'T were Thanksgiving day.

LV.

SOFTENED by Time's consummate plush,
　　How sleek the woe appears
That threatened childhood's citadel
　　And undermined the years!

Bisected now by bleaker griefs,
　　We envy the despair
That devastated childhood's realm,
　　So easy to repair.

II. LOVE

I.

PROUD of my broken heart since thou didst break it,
    Proud of the pain I did not feel till thee,
Proud of my night since thou with moons dost slake it,
    Not to partake thy passion, my humility.

II.

MY worthiness is all my doubt,
    His merit all my fear,
Contrasting which, my qualities
    Do lowlier appear;

Lest I should insufficient prove
    For his beloved need,
The chiefest apprehension
    Within my loving creed.

So I, the undivine abode
    Of his elect content,
Conform my soul as 't were a church
    Unto her sacrament.

III.

LOVE is anterior to life,
    Posterior to death,
Initial of creation, and
    The exponent of breath.

IV.

ONE blessing had I, than the rest
    So larger to my eyes
That I stopped gauging, satisfied,
    For this enchanted size.

It was the limit of my dream,
    The focus of my prayer,–
A perfect, paralyzing bliss
    Contented as despair.

I knew no more of want or cold,
    Phantasms both become,
For this new value in the soul,
    Supremest earthly sum.

The heaven below the heaven above
    Obscured with ruddier hue.
Life's latitude leant over-full;
    The judgment perished, too.

Why joys so scantily disburse,
    Why Paradise defer,
Why floods are served to us in bowls,–
    I speculate no more.

V.

WHEN roses cease to bloom, dear,
　　And violets are done,
When bumble-bees in solemn flight
　　Have passed beyond the sun,

The hand that paused to gather
　　Upon this summer's day
Will idle lie, in Auburn,–
　　Then take my flower, pray!

VI.

SUMMER for thee grant I may be
　　When summer days are flown!
Thy music still when whippoorwill
　　And oriole are done!

For thee to bloom, I'll skip the tomb
　　And sow my blossoms o'er!
Pray gather me, Anemone,
　　Thy flower forevermore!

VII.

SPLIT the lark and you'll find the music,
     Bulb after bulb, in silver rolled,
Scantily dealt to the summer morning,
     Saved for your ear when lutes be old.

Loose the flood, you shall find it patent,
     Gush after gush, reserved for you;
Scarlet experiment! sceptic Thomas,
     Now, do you doubt that your bird was true?

VIII.

TO lose thee, sweeter than to gain
     All other hearts I knew.
'T is true the drought is destitute,
But then I had the dew!

The Caspian has its realms of sand,
     Its other realm of sea;
Without the sterile perquisite
     No Caspian could be.

IX.

POOR little heart!
       Did they forget thee?
Then dinna care! Then dinna care!

       Proud little heart!
Did they forsake thee?
Be debonair! Be debonair!

       Frail little heart!
I would not break thee:
Could'st credit me? Could'st credit me?

       Gay little heart!
Like morning glory
Thou'll wilted be; thou'll wilted be!

X.

THERE is a word
　　Which bears a sword
　Can pierce an armed man.
It hurls its barbed syllables,–
　At once is mute again.
But where it fell
The saved will tell
　On patriotic day,
Some epauletted brother
　Gave his breath away.

Wherever runs the breathless sun,
　Wherever roams the day,
There is its noiseless onset,
　There is its victory!
Behold the keenest marksman!
　The most accomplished shot!
Time's sublimest target
Is a soul "forgot"!

XI.

I'VE got an arrow here;
　　Loving the hand that sent it,
I the dart revere.

Fell, they will say in "skirmish"!
　Vanquished, my soul will know,
By but a simple arrow
　Sped by an archer's bow.

XII.

HE fumbles at your spirit
    As players at the keys
Before they drop full music on;
    He stuns you by degrees,

Prepares your brittle substance
    For the ethereal blow,
By fainter hammers, further heard,
    Then nearer, then so slow

Your breath has time to straighten,
    Your brain to bubble cool,–
Deals one imperial thunderbolt
    That scalps your naked soul.

XIII.

HEART, we will forget him!
    You and I, to-night!
You may forget the warmth he gave,
    I will forget the light.

When you have done, pray tell me,
    That I my thoughts may dim;
Haste! lest while you're lagging,
    I may remember him!

XIV.

FATHER, I bring thee not myself,—
    That were the little load;
I bring thee the imperial heart
    I had not strength to hold.

The heart I cherished in my own
    Till mine too heavy grew,
Yet strangest, heavier since it went,
    Is it too large for you?

XV.

WE outgrow love like other things
    And put it in the drawer,
Till it an antique fashion shows
    Like costumes grandsires wore.

XVI.

NOT with a club the heart is broken,
       Nor with a stone;
A whip, so small you could not see it.
       I've known

To lash the magic creature
       Till it fell,
Yet that whip's name too noble
       Then to tell.

Magnanimous of bird
       By boy descried,
To sing unto the stone
       Of which it died.

XVII.

MY friend must be a bird,
       Because it flies!
Mortal my friend must be,
       Because it dies!
Barbs has it, like a bee.
Ah, curious friend,
       Thou puzzlest me!

XVIII.

HE touched me, so I live to know
  That such a day, permitted so,
 I groped upon his breast.
It was a boundless place to me,
And silenced, as the awful sea
 Puts minor streams to rest.

And now, I'm different from before,
As if I breathed superior air,
 Or brushed a royal gown;
My feet, too, that had wandered so,
My gypsy face transfigured now
 To tenderer renown.

XIX.

LET me not mar that perfect dream
  By an auroral stain,
But so adjust my daily night
 That it will come again.

XX.

I LIVE with him, I see his face;
　　I go no more away
For visitor, or sundown;
　　Death's single privacy,

The only one forestalling mine,
　　And that by right that he
Presents a claim invisible,
　　No wedlock granted me.

I live with him, I hear his voice,
　　I stand alive to-day
To witness to the certainty
　　Of immortality

Taught me by Time,—the lower way,
　　Conviction every day,—
That life like this is endless,
　　Be judgment what it may.

XXI.

I ENVY seas whereon he rides,
　　I envy spokes of wheels
Of chariots that him convey,
　　I envy speechless hills

That gaze upon his journey;
　　How easy all can see
What is forbidden utterly
　　As heaven, unto me!

I envy nests of sparrows
    That dot his distant eaves,
The wealthy fly upon his pane,
    The happy, happy leaves

That just abroad his window
    Have summer's leave to be,
The earrings of Pizarro
    Could not obtain for me.

I envy light that wakes him,
    And bells that boldly ring
To tell him it is noon abroad,–
    Myself his noon could bring,

Yet interdict my blossom
    And abrogate my bee,
Lest noon in everlasting night
    Drop Gabriel and me.

XXII.

A SOLEMN thing it was, I said,
    A woman white to be,
And wear, if God should count me fit,
    Her hallowed mystery.

A timid thing to drop a life
    Into the purple well,
Too plummetless that it come back
    Eternity until.

III. NATURE

I.

THE springtime's pallid landscape
    Will glow like bright bouquet,
Through drifted deep in parian
    The village lies to-day.

The lilacs, bending many a year,
    With purple load will hang;
The bees will not forget the tune
    Their old forefathers sang.

The rose will redden in the bog,
    The aster on the hill
Her everlasting fashion set,
    And covenant gentians frill,

Till summer folds her miracle
    As women do their gown,
Or priests adjust the symbols
    When sacrament is done.

II.

SHE slept beneath a tree
      Remembered but by me.
I touched her cradle mute;
She recognized the foot,
Put on her carmine suit,–
      And see!

III.

A LIGHT exists in spring
      Not present on the year
At any other period.
    When March is scarcely here

A color stands abroad
    On solitary hills
That science cannot overtake,
    But human nature *feels*.

It waits upon the lawn;
    It shows the furthest tree
Upon the furthest slope we know;
    It almost speaks to me.

Then, as horizons step,
    Or noons report away,
Without the formula of sound.
It passes, and we stay:

A quality of loss
    Affecting our content,
As trade had suddenly encroached
    Upon a sacrament.

IV.

A LADY red upon the hill
  Her annual secret keeps;
A lady white within the field
 In placid lily sleeps!

The tidy breezes with their brooms
  Sweep vale, and hill, and tree!
Prithee, my pretty housewives!
  Who may expected by?

The neighbors do not yet suspect!
  The woods exchange a smile—
Orchard, and buttercup, and bird—
  In such a little while!

And yet how still the landscape stands,
  How nonchalant the wood,
As if the resurrection
  Were nothing very odd!

V.

DEAR March, come in!
    How glad I am!
I looked for you before.
Put down your hat—
You must have walked—
How out of breath you are!
Dear March, how are you?
And the rest?
Did you leave Nature well?
Oh, March, come right upstairs with me,
I have so much to tell!

I got the letter, and the birds';
The maples never knew
That you were coming,—I declare,
How red their faces grew!
But, March, forgive me—
And all those hills
You left for me to hue;
There was no purple suitable,
You took it all with you.

Who knocks? That April!
Lock the door!
I will not be pursued!
He stayed away a year, to call
When I am occupied.
But trifles look so trivial
As soon as you have come,
That blame is just as dear as praise
And praise as mere as blame.

VI.

WE like March, his shoes are purple,
    He is new and high;
Makes he mud for dog and peddler,
    Makes he forest dry;
Knows the adder's tongue his coming,
    And begets her spot.
Stands the sun so close and mighty
    That our minds are hot.
News is he of all the others;
    Bold it were to die
With the blue-birds buccaneering
    On his British sky.

VII.

NOT knowing when the dawn will come
    I open every door;
Or has it feathers like a bird,
    Or billows like a shore?

VIII.

A MURMUR in the trees to note,
    Not loud enough for wind;
A star not far enough to seek,
    Nor near enough to find;

A long, long yellow on the lawn,
    A hubbub as of feet;
Not audible, as ours to us,
    But dapperer, more sweet;

A hurrying home of·little men
    To houses unperceived,–
All this, and more, if I should tell,
    Would never be believed.

Of robins in the trundle bed
    How many I espy
Whose nightgowns could not hide the wings,
    Although I heard them try!

But then I promised ne'er to tell;
    How could I break my word?
So go your way and I'll go mine,–
    No fear you'll miss the road.

IX.

MORNING is the place for dew,
    Corn is made at noon,
After dinner light for flowers,
    Dukes for setting sun!

X.

TO my quick ear the leaves conferred;
    The bushes they were bells;
I could not find a privacy
    From Nature's sentinels.

In cave if I presumed to hide,
    The walls began to tell;
Creation seemed a mighty crack
    To make me visible.

XI.

A SEPAL, petal, and a thorn
    Upon a common summer's morn,
A flash of dew, a bee or two,
A breeze
A caper in the trees,—
    And I'm a rose!

XII.

HIGH from the earth I heard a bird;
        He trod upon the trees
As he esteemed them trifles,
        And then he spied a breeze,
And situated softly
        Upon a pile of wind
Which in a perturbation
        Nature had left behind.
A joyous-going fellow
        I gathered from his talk,
Which both of benediction
        And badinage partook,
Without apparent burden,
        I learned, in leafy wood
He was the faithful father
        Of a dependent brood;
And this untoward transport
        His remedy of care,—
A contrast to our respites.
        How different we are!

XIII.

THE spider as an artist
        Has never been employed
Though his surpassing merit
        Is freely certified

By every broom and Bridget
        Throughout a Christian land.
Neglected son of genius,
        I take thee by the hand.

XIV.

WHAT mystery pervades a well!
    The water lives so far,
Like neighbor from another world
    Residing in a jar.

The grass does not appear afraid;
    I often wonder he
Can stand so close and look so bold
    At what is dread to me.

Related somehow they may be,–
    The sedge stands next the sea,
Where he is floorless, yet of fear
    No evidence gives he.

But nature is stranger yet;
    The ones that cite her most
Have never passed her haunted house,
    Nor simplified her ghost.

To pity those that know her not
    Is helped by the regret
That those who know her, know her less
    The nearer her they get.

XV.

TO make a prairie it takes a clover
        and one bee,–
One clover, and a bee,
And revery.
The revery alone will do
If bees are few.

XVI.

IT'S like the light,–
        A fashionless delight
It's like the bee,–
    A dateless melody.

It's like the woods,
    Private like breeze,
Phraseless, yet it stirs
    The proudest trees.

It's like the morning,–
    Best when it's done,–
The everlasting clocks
    Chime noon.

XVII.

A DEW sufficed itself
        And satisfied a leaf,
And felt, "how vast a destiny!
    How trivial is life!"

The sun went out to work,
    The day went out to play,
But not again that dew was seen
    By physiognomy.

Whether by day abducted,
    Or emptied by the sun
Into the sea, in passing,
    Eternally unknown.

XVIII.

HIS bill an auger is,
       His head, a cap and frill.
He laboreth at every tree,–
    A worm his utmost goal.

XIX.

SWEET is the swamp with its secrets,
       Until we meet a snake;
'T is then we sigh for houses,
    And our departure take
At that enthralling gallop
    That only childhood knows.
A snake is summer's treason,
    And guile is where it goes.

XX.

COULD I but ride indefinite,
    As doth the meadow-bee,
And visit only where I liked,
    And no man visit me,

And flirt all day with buttercups,
    And marry whom I may,
And dwell a little everywhere,
    Or better, run away

With no police to follow,
    Or chase me if I do,
Till I should jump peninsulas
    To get away from you,–

I said, but just to be a bee
    Upon a raft of air,
And row in nowhere all day
long,
    And anchor off the bar,–
What liberty! So captives deem
    Who tight in dungeons are.

XXI.

THE moon was but a chin of gold
        A night or two ago,
And now she turns her perfect face
    Upon the world below.

Her forehead is of amplest blond;
    Her cheek like beryl stone;
Her eye unto the summer dew
    The likest I have known.

Her lips of amber never part;
    But what must be the smile
Upon her friend she could bestow
    Were such her silver will!

And what a privilege to be
    But the remotest star!
For certainly her way might pass
    Beside your twinkling door.

Her bonnet is the firmament,
    The universe her shoe,
The stars the trinkets at her belt,
    Her dimities of blue.

XXII.

THE bat is dun with wrinkled wings
    Like fallow article,
And not a song pervades his lips,
    Or none perceptible.

His small umbrella, quaintly halved,
    Describing in the air
An arc alike inscrutable,—
    Elate philosopher!

Deputed from what firmament
    Of what astute abode,
Empowered with what malevolence
    Auspiciously withheld.

To his adroit Creator
    Ascribe no less the praise;
Beneficent, believe me,
    His eccentricities.

XXIII.

YOU'VE seen balloons set, have n't you?
    So stately they ascend
It is as swans discarded you
    For duties diamond.

Their liquid feet go softly out
    Upon a sea of blond;
They spurn the air as 't were too mean
    For creatures so renowned.

Their ribbons just beyond the eye,
    They struggle some for breath,
And yet the crowd applauds below;
    They would not encore death.

The gilded creature strains and spins,
    Trips frantic in a tree,
Tears open her imperial veins
    And tumbles in the sea.

The crowd retire with an oath
    The dust in streets goes down,
And clerks in counting-rooms observe,
    "'T was only a balloon."

XXIV.

THE cricket sang,
    And set the sun,
And workmen finished, one by one,
    Their seam the day upon.

The low grass loaded with the dew,
The twilight stood as strangers do
With hat in hand, polite and new,
    To stay as if, or go.

A vastness, as a neighbor, came,–
A wisdom without face or name,
A peace, as hemispheres at home,–
    And so the night became.

XXV.

DRAB habitation of whom?
    Tabernacle or tomb,
Or dome of worm,
Or porch of gnome,
Or some elf's catacomb?

XXVI.

A SLOOP of amber slips away
    Upon an ether sea,
And wrecks in peace a purple tar,
    The son of ecstasy.

XXVII.

OF bronze and blaze
    The north, to-night!
So adequate its forms,
So preconcerted with itself,
    So distant to alarms,—
An unconcern so sovereign
    To universe, or me,
It paints my simple spirit
    With tints of majesty,
Till I take vaster attitudes,
    And strut upon my stem,
Disdaining men and oxygen,
    For arrogance of them.

My splendors are menagerie;
    But their competeless show
Will entertain the centuries
    When I am, long ago,
An island in dishonored grass,
    Whom none but daisies know.

XXVIII.

HOW the old mountains drip with sunset,
    And the brake of dun!
How the hemlocks are tipped in tinsel
    By the wizard sun!

How the old steeples hand the scarlet,
    Till the ball is full,—
Have I the lip of the flamingo
    That I dare to tell?

Then, how the fire ebbs like billows,
    Touching all the grass
With a departing, sapphire feature,
    As if a duchess pass!

How a small dusk crawls on the village
    Till the houses blot;
And the odd flambeaux no men carry
    Glimmer on the spot!
Now it is night in nest and kennel,
    And where was the wood,
Just a dome of abyss is nodding
    Into solitude! –

These are the visions baffled Guido;
    Titian never told;
Domenichino dropped the pencil,
    Powerless to unfold.

XXIX.

THE murmuring of bees has ceased;
    But murmuring of some
Posterior, prophetic,
    Has simultaneous come, –

The lower metres of the year,
    When nature's laugh is done, –
The Revelations of the book
    Whose Genesis is June.

IV. Time and Eternity

I.

THIS world is not conclusion;
    A sequel stands beyond,
Invisible, as music,
    But positive, as sound.
It beckons and it baffles;
    Philosophies don't know,
And through a riddle, at the last,
    Sagacity must go.
To guess it puzzles scholars;
To gain it, men have shown
Contempt of generations,
    And crucifixion known.

II.

WE learn in the retreating
    How vast an one
Was recently among us.
    A perished sun

Endears in the departure
    How doubly more
Than all the golden presence
    It was before!

III.

THEY say that "time assuages,"–
　　Time never did assuage;
An actual suffering strengthens,
　　As sinews do, with age.

Time is a test of trouble,
　　But not a remedy.
If such it prove, it prove too
　　There was no malady.

IV.

WE cover thee, sweet face.
　　Not that we tire of thee,
But that thyself fatigue of us;
　　Remember, as thou flee,
We follow thee until
　　Thou notice us no more,
And then, reluctant, turn away
　　To con thee o'er and o'er,
Ad blame the scanty love
　　We were content to show,
Augmented, sweet, a hundred fold
　　If thou would'st take it now.

V.

THAT is solemn we have ended,–
    Be it but a play,
Or a glee among the garrets,
    Or a holiday,

Or a leaving home; or later,
    Parting with a world
We have understood, for better
    Still it be unfurled.

VI.

THE stimulus, beyond the grave
    His countenance to see,
Supports me like imperial drams
    Afforded royally.

VII.

GIVEN in marriage unto thee,
    Oh, thou celestial host!
Bride of the Father and the Son,
    Bride of the Holy Ghost!

Other betrothal shall dissolve,
    Wedlock of will decay;
Only the keeper of this seal
    Conquers mortality.

VIII.

THAT such have died enables us
        The tranquiller to die;
That such have lived, certificate
    For immortality.

IX.

THEY won't frown always,—some sweet day
        When I forget to tease,
They'll recollect how cold I looked,
    And how I just said "please."

Then they will hasten to the door
    To call the little child,
Who cannot thank them, for the ice
    That on her lisping piled.

X.

IT is an honorable thought,
        And makes one lift one's hat,
As one encountered gentlefolk
    Upon a daily street,

That we've immortal place,
    Though pyramids decay,
And kingdoms, like the orchard,
    Flit russetly away.

XI.

THE distance that the dead have gone
        Does not at first appear;
Their coming back seems possible
        For many an ardent year.

And then, that we have followed them
        We more than half suspect,
So intimate have we become
        With their dear retrospect.

XII.

HOW dare the robins sing,
        When men and women hear
Who since they went to their account
        Have settled with the year!—
Paid all that life had earned
        In one consummate bill,
And now, what life or death can do
        Is immaterial.
Insulting is the sun
        To him whose mortal light,
Beguiled of immortality,
        Bequeaths him to the night.
In deference to him
        Extinct be every hum,
Whose garden wrestles with the dew,
        At daybreak overcome!

XIII.

DEATH is like the insect
        Menacing the tree,
Competent to kill it,
        But decoyed may be.

Bait it with the balsam,
        Seek it with the knife,
Baffle, if it cost you
        Everything in life.

Then, if it have burrowed
        Out of reach of skill,
Ring the tree and leave it, —
        'T is the vermin's will.

XIV.

'T IS sunrise, little maid, hast thou
    No station in the day?
'T was not thy wont to hinder so,–
    Retrieve thine industry.

'T is noon, my little maid, alas!
    And art thou sleeping yet?
The lily waiting to be wed,
    The bee, dost thou forget?

My little maid, 't is night; alas,
    That night should be to thee
Instead of morning! Hadst thou broached
    Thy little plan to me,
Dissuade thee if I could not, sweet,
    I might have aided thee.

XV.

EACH that we lose takes part of us;
    A crescent still abides,
Which like the moon, some turbid night,
    Is summoned by the tides.

XVI.

NOT any higher stands the grave
    For heroes than for men;
Not any nearer for the child
    Than numb three-score and ten.

This latest leisure equal lulls
    The beggar and his queen;
Propitiate this democrat
    By summer's gracious mien.

XVII.

AS far from pity as complaint,
        As cool to speech as stone,
As numb to revelation
    As if my trade were bone.

As far from time as history,
    As near yourself to-day
As children to the rainbow's scarf,
    Or sunset's yellow play

To eyelids in the sepulchre.
    How still the dancer lies,
While color's revelations break,
    And blaze the butterflies!

XVIII.

'T IS whiter than an Indian pipe;
        'T is dimmer than a lace;
No stature has it, like a fog,
    When you approach the place.

Not any voice denotes it here,
    Or intimates it there;
A spirit, how doth it accost?
    What customs hath the air?

This limitless hyperbole
    Each one of us shall be;
'T is drama, if (hypothesis)
    It be not tragedy!

XIX.

SHE laid her docile crescent down,
 And this mechanic stone
Still states, to dates that have forgot,
 The news that she is gone.

So constant to its stolid trust,
 The shaft that never knew,
It shames the constancy that fled
 Before its emblem flew.

XX.

BLESS God, he went as soldiers,
 His musket on his breast;
Grant, God, he charge the bravest
 Of all the martial blest.

Please God, might I behold him
 In ipauletted white,
I should not fear the foe then,
 I should not fear the fight.

XXI.

IMMORTAL is an ample word
        When what we need is by,
But when it leaves us for a time,
    'T is a necessity.

Of heaven above the firmest proof
    We fundamental know,
Except for its marauding hand,
    It had been heaven below.

XXII.

WHERE every bird is bold to go,
        And bees abashless play,
The foreigner before he knocks
    Must thrust the tears away.

XXIII.

THE grave my little cottage is,
        Where, keeping house for thee,
I make my parlor orderly,
    And lay the marble tea,

For two divided, briefly,
    A cycle, it may be,
Till everlasting life unite
    In strong society.

XXIV.

THIS was in the white of the year,
    That was in the green,
Drifts were as difficult then to think
    As daisies now to be seen.

Looking back is best that is left,
    Or if it be before,
Retrospection is prospect's half,
    Sometimes almost more.

XXV.

SWEET hours have perished here;
    This is a mighty room;
Within its precincts hopes have played, —
    Now shadows in the tomb.

XXVI.

ME! Come! My dazzled face
    In such a shining place!

Me! Hear! My foreign ear
The sounds of welcome near!

The saints shall meet
Our bashful feet.

My holiday shall be
That they remember me;

My paradise, the fame
That they pronounce my name.

XXVII.

FROM us she wandered now a year,
    Her tarrying unknown;
If wilderness prevent her feet,
  Or that ethereal zone

No eye hath seen and lived,
  We ignorant must be.
We only know what time of year
  We took the mystery.

XXVIII.

I WISH I knew that woman's name,
    So, when she comes this way,
To hold my life, and hold my ears,
    For fear I hear her say

She's "sorry I am dead," again,
    Just when the grave and I
Have sobbed ourselves almost to sleep,—
    Our only lullaby.

XXIX.

BEREAVED of all, I went abroad,
    No less bereaved to be
Upon a new peninsula,—
    The grave preceded me,

Obtained my lodgings ere myself,
    And when I sought my bed,
The grave it was, reposed upon
    The pillow for my head.

I waked, to find it first awake,
    I rose,—it followed me;
I tried to drop it in the crowd,
    To lose it in the sea,

In cups of artificial drowse
    To sleep its shape away,—
The grave finished, but the spade
    Remained in memory.

XXX.

I FELT a funeral in my brain,
    And mourners, to and fro,
Kept treading, treading, till it seemed
    That sense was breaking through.

And when they all were seated,
    A service like a drum
Kept beating, beating, till I thought
    My mind was going numb.

And then I heard them lift a box,
    And creak across my soul
With those same boots of lead, again.
    Then space began to toll

As all the heavens were a bell,
    And Being but an ear,
And I and silence some strange race,
    Wrecked, solitary, here.

XXXI.

I MEANT to find her when I came;
    Death had the same design;
But the success was his, it seems,
    And the discomfit mine.

I meant to tell her how I longed
    For just this single time;
But Death had told her so the first,
    And she had harkened him.

To wander now is my abode;
   To rest,—to rest would be
A privilege of hurricane
   To memory and me.

XXXII.

I SING to use the waiting,
   My bonnet but to tie,
And shut the door unto my house;
   No more to do have I,

Till, his best step approaching,
   We journey to the day,
And tell each other how we sang
   To keep the dark away.

XXXIII.

A SICKNESS of this world it most occasions
   When best men die;
A wishfulness their far condition
   To occupy.

A chief indifference, as foreign
   A world must be
Themselves forsake contented,
   For Deity.

XXXIV.

SUPERFLUOUS were the sun
    When excellence is dead;
He were superfluous every day,
    For every day is said

That syllable whose faith
    Just saves it from despair,
And whose "I'll meet you" hesitates
    If love inquire, "Where?"

Upon his dateless fame
    Our periods may lie,
As stars that drop anonymous
    From an abundant sky.

XXXV.

SO proud she was to die
    It made us all ashamed
That what we cherished, so unknown
    To her desire seemed.

So satisfied to go
    Where none of us should be,
Immediately, that anguish stooped
    Almost to jealousy.

XXXVI.

TIE the strings to my life, my Lord,
  Then I am ready to go!
Just a look at the horses—
 Rapid! That will do!

Put me in on the firmest side,
 So I shall never fall;
For we must ride to the Judgment,
 And it's partly down hill.

But never I mind the bridges,
 And never I mind the sea;
Held fast in everlasting race
 By my own choice and thee.

Good-by to the life I used to live,
 And the world I used to know;
And kiss the hills for me, just once;
 Now I am ready to go!

XXXVII.

THE dying need but little, dear,—
  A glass of water's all,
A flower's unobtrusive face
 To punctuate the wall,

A fan, perhaps, a friend's regret,
 And certainly that one
No color in the rainbow
 Perceives when you are gone.

XXXVIII.

THERE'S something quieter than sleep
        Within this inner room!
It wears a sprig upon its breast,
        And will not tell its name.

Some touch it and some kiss it,
        Some chafe its idle hand;
It has a simple gravity
        I do not understand!

While simple-hearted neighbors
        Chat of the "early dead,"
We, prone to periphrasis,
        Remark that birds have fled!

XXXIX.

THE soul should always stand ajar,
        That if the heaven inquire,
He will not be obliged to wait,
        Or shy of troubling her.

Depart, before the host has slid
        The bolt upon the door,
To seek for the accomplished guest,—
        Her visitor no more.

XL.

THREE weeks passed since I had seen her, –
      Some disease had vexed;
'T was with text and village singing
      I beheld her next,
And a company – our pleasure
      To discourse alone;
Gracious now to me as any,
      Gracious unto none.

Borne, without dissent of either,
      To the parish night;
Of the separated people
      Which are out of sight?

XLI.

I BREATHED enough to learn the trick,
      And now, removed from air,
I simulate the breath so well,
      That one, to be quite sure

The lungs are stirless, must descend
      Among the cunning cells,
And touch the pantomine himself.
      How cool the bellows feels!

XLII.

I WONDER if the sepulchre
　　Is not a lonesome way,
When men and boys, and larks and June
　　Go down the fields to hay!

XLIII.

IF tolling bell I ask the cause.
　　"A soul has gone to God,"
I'm answered in a lonesome tone;
　　Is heaven then so sad?

That bells should joyful ring to tell
　　A soul had gone to heaven,
Would seem to me the proper way
　　A good news should be given.

XLIV.

IF I may have it when it's dead
    I will contented be;
If just as soon as breath is out
It shall belong to me,

Until they lock it in the grave,
    'T is bliss I cannot weigh,
For though they lock thee in the grave,
    Myself can hold the key.

Think of it, lover! I and thee
    Permitted face to face to be;
After a life, a death we'll say,—
    For death was that, and this is thee.

XLV.

BEFORE the ice is in the pools,
    Before the skaters go,
Or any cheek at nightfall
    Is tarnished by the snow,

Before the fields have finished,
    Before the Christmas tree,
Wonder upon wonder
    Will arrive to me!

What we touch the hems of
    On a summer's day;
What is only walking
    Just a bridge away;

That which sings so, speaks so,
    When there's no one here,—
Will the frock I wept in
    Answer me to wear?

XLVI.

I HEARD a fly buzz when I died;
        The stillness round my form
Was like the stillness in the air
    Between the heaves of storm.

The eyes beside had wrung them dry,
    And breaths were gathering sure
For that last onset, when the king
    Be witnessed in his power.

I willed my keepsakes, signed away
    What portion of me I
Could make assignable,—and then
    There interposed a fly,

With blue, uncertain, stumbling buzz,
    Between the light and me;
And then the windows failed, and then
    I could not see to see.

XLVII.

ADRIFT! A little boat adrift!
    And night is coming down!
Will no one guide a little boat
    Unto the nearest town?

So sailors say, on yesterday,
    Just as the dusk was brown,
One little boat gave up its strife,
    And gurgled down and down.

But angels say, on yesterday,
    Just as the dawn was red,
One little boat gave up its strife,
    And gurgled down and down.

But angels say, on yesterday,
    Just as the dawn was red,
One little boat o'erspent with gales
Retrimmed its masts, redecked its sails
    Exultant, onward sped!

XLVIII.

THERE'S been a death in the opposite house
        As lately as to-day.
I know it by the numb look
        Such houses have alway.

The neighbors rustle in and out,
        The doctor drives away.
A window opens like a pod,
        Abrupt, mechanically;

Somebody flings a mattress out,–
        The children hurry by;
They wonder if It died on that,–
        I used to when a boy.

The minister goes stiffly in
        As if the house were his,
And he owned all the mourners now,
        And little boys besides;

And then the milliner, and the man
        Of the appalling trade,
To take the measure of the house.
        There'll be that dark parade

Of tassels and of coaches soon;
        It's easy as a sign,–
The intuition of the news
        In just a country town.

XLIX.

WE never know we go,—when we are going
        We jest and shut the door;
Fate following behind us bolts it,
    · And we accost no more.

L.

IT struck me every day
        The lightning was as new
As if the cloud that instant slit
    And let the fire through.

It burned me in the night,
    It blistered in my dream;
It sickened fresh upon my sight
    With every morning's beam.

I thought that storm was brief,—
    The maddest, quickest by;
But Nature lost the date of this,
    And left it in the sky.

LI.

WATER is taught by thirst;
        Land, by the oceans passed;
    Transport, by throe;
Peace, by its battles told;
Love, by memorial mould;
        Birds, by the snow.

LII.

WE thirst at first,—'t is Nature's act;
        And later, when we die,
A little water supplicate
        Of fingers going by.

It intimates the finer want,
        Whose adequate supply
Is that great water in the west
        Termed immortality.

LIII.

A CLOCK stopped—not the mantel's;
    Geneva's farthest skill
Can't put the puppet bowing
    That just now dangled still.

An awe came on the trinket!
    The figures hunched with pain,
Then quivered out of decimals
    Into degreeless noon.

It will not stir for doctors,
    This pendulum of snow;
The shopman importunes it,
    While cool, concernless No

Nods from the gilded pointers,
    Nods from the seconds slim,
Decades of arrogance between
    The dial life and him.

LIV.

ALL overgrown by cunning moss,
    All interspersed with weed,
The little cage of "Currer Bell,"
    In quiet Haworth laid.

This bird, observing others,
    When frosts too sharp became,
Retire to other latitudes,
    Quietly did the same,

But differed in returning;
    Since Yorkshire hills are green,
Yet not in all the nests I meet
    Can nightingale be seen.

Gathered from many wanderings,
    Gethsemane can tell
Through what transporting anguish
    She reached the asphodel!

Soft fall the sounds of Eden
    Upon her puzzled ear;
Oh, what an afternoon for heaven,
    When "Brontë" entered there!

LV.

A TOAD can die of light!
        Death is the common right
    Of toads and men,–
Of earl and midge
The privilege.
        Why swagger then?
The gnat's supremacy
Is large as thine.

LVI.

FAR from love the Heavenly Father
        Leads the chosen child;
Oftener through realm of briar
    Than the meadow mild,

Oftener by the claw of dragon
    Than the hand of friend,
Guides the little one predestined
    To the native land.

LVII.

A LONG, long sleep, a famous sleep
    That makes no show for dawn
By stretch of limb or stir of lid,–
    An independent one.

Was ever idleness like this?
    Within a hut of stone
To bask the centuries away
    Nor once look up for noon?

LVIII.

'T WAS just this time last year I died.
    I know I heard the corn,
When I was carried by the farms,–
    It had tassels on.

I thought how yellow it would look
    When Richard went to mill;
And then I wanted to get out,
    But something held my will.

I thought just how red apples wedged
    The stubble's joints between;
And carts went stooping round the fields
    To take the pumpkins in.

I wondered which would miss me least,
    And then Thanksgiving came
As father'd multiply the plates
    To make an even sum.

And if my stocking hung too high,
    Would it blur the Christmas glee,
That not a Santa Claus could reach
    The altitude of me?

But this sort grieved myself, and so
    I thought how it would be
When just this time, some perfect year,
    Themselves should come to me.

LIX.

ON this wondrous sea,
    Sailing silently,
  Ho! pilot, ho!
Knowest thou the shore
Where no breakers roar,
  Where the storm is o'er?

In the silent west
Many sails at rest,
  Their anchors fast;
Thither I pilot thee,—
Land, ho! Eternity!
  Ashore at last!